THE DRAGON SONGS SAGA

A LEGENDS OF TIVARA STORY

JC KANG

To: The Secret Order. You know who you are.

This is a work of fiction. Names, places, characters, and events are either fictitious or are used fictitiously. Any resemblance to actual events, locations, organizations, or persons, alive or dead, is entirely coincidental and unintended.

Copyright © 2018 by Dragonstone Press, LLC
http://www.jckang.info
DragonstonePressRVA@gmail.com

All rights reserved, including the right to reproduce this work or portions thereof in any way whatsoever, as provided by law. For permission, questions, or contact information, see www.jckang.info.

Cover Layout and Maps by Laura Kang

Logos by Emily Jose Burlingame

Cover Art by Chacha Wang:
http://www.bobkehl.com

November 2018

CONTENTS

MAP

Of Tivaralan

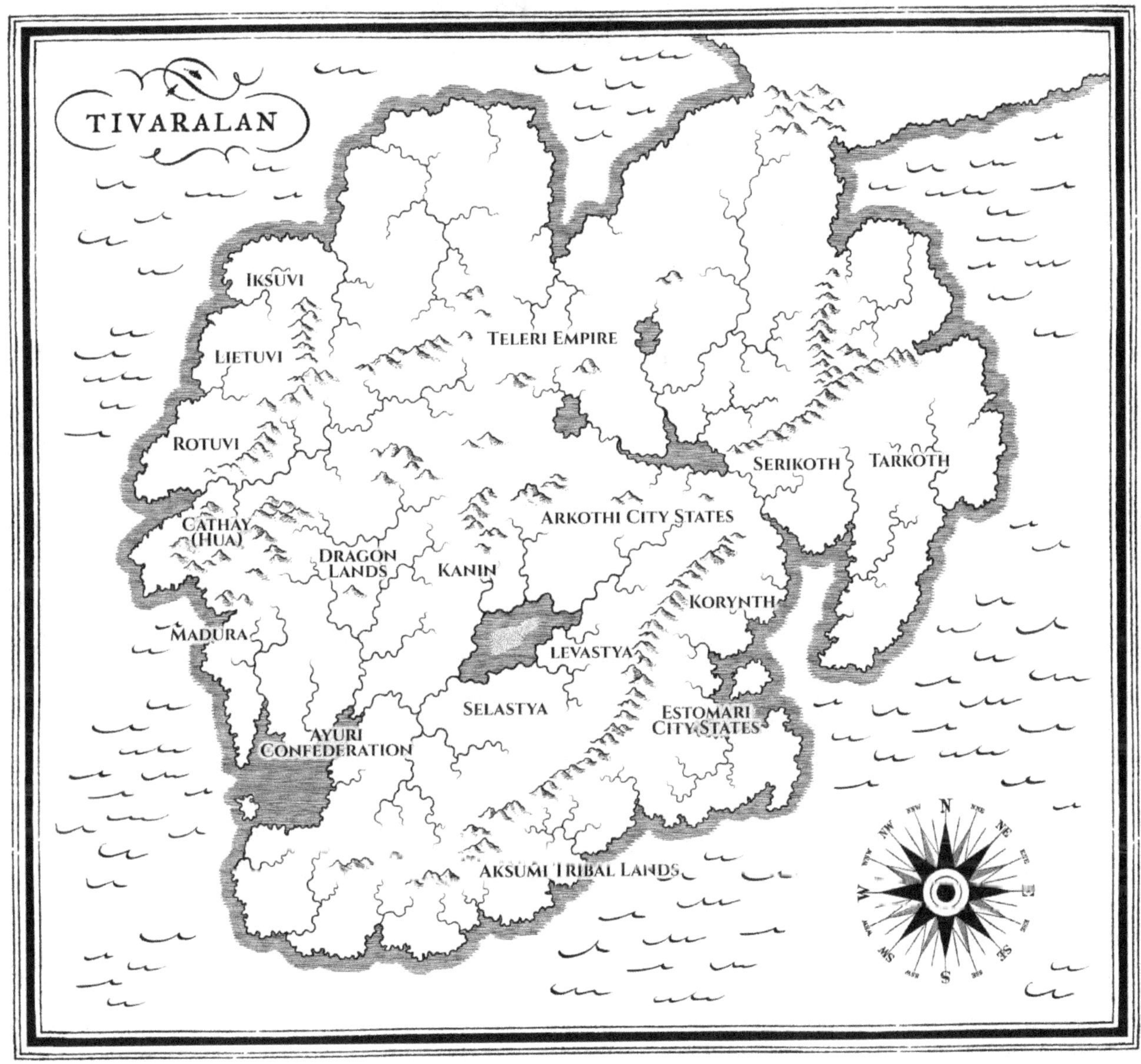

More maps in the appendices

SONGS OF INSURRECTION

A LEGENDS OF TIVARA STORY

JC KANG

SONGS OF INSURRECTION

PROLOGUE

The Dragon Scale Lute

With the echo of the Dragon Scale Lute fading around him, Avarax coiled his hind legs and vaulted skyward. He stretched out his wings to catch an updraft. Cool wind caressed his scales as he climbed higher. After three hundred years imprisoned in the pathetic body of a human, it felt good to be a dragon again.

Down below in the sparkling city of domes and spires and canals, thousands of bronze-skinned humans pointed at him and screamed. The world thought he had slumbered for a millennium, telling stories about how a honey-toned slave girl sang him to sleep with a Dragon Song. He had let them believe that tale, to prevent enemies from tracking him down.

He belched sparks with his laugh. Now, it was time to announce his return with a blast of his fiery breath. It would immolate a million people, and the city. More importantly, it would destroy the artifact that could again force his unwilling transformation. He filled his lungs with a deep breath and exhaled in an ear-splitting roar.

Nothing.

Not even sparks. Avarax's breath remained locked away. He wrapped his consciousness around the gemstone in his gullet, a dragon's source of almost infinite energy. Its pulsations pounded like an angry river against a dam.

Below, the Dragon Scale Lute's strings moaned again, vibrating in answer to his roar. Its wail swelled, scattering the pitiful humans like a disturbed rats' nest. Then, with a disjointed pop, the sound ceased.

CHAPTER 1

Not-So-Chance Meetings

If marriage were a woman's grave, as the proverb claimed, sixteen-year-old Kaiya suspected the emperor was arranging her funeral. Entourage in tow, she shuffled through the castle halls toward the garden where General Lu waited. Given his notorious dislike of the arts, the self-proclaimed *Guardian Dragon of Hua* had undoubtedly envisioned a different kind of audition when he requested to hear her sing.

After all, she was dressed like a potential bride.

She buried a snort. The Guardian Dragon—such a pretentious nickname. The only real dragon, Avarax, who lorded over some faraway land, might make for a more appealing audience. A quick trip down his gullet would spare her a slow death in a marriage with neither love nor music.

And she wouldn't have to wear this gaudy dress. It compensated for her numerous physical imperfections, but stifled the only thing that made her special. How was she supposed to sing with the inner robe and gold sash squeezing her chest, in a futile attempt to misrepresent her woefully underdeveloped curves? The tight fold of the skirts concealed her lanky legs, but forced a deliberate pace. At least the short stride delayed the inevitable, while preventing her unsightly feet from tripping on the hanging sleeves of the vermilion outer gown.

At her side, Crown Princess Xiulan glided across the chirping floorboards. Kaiya suppressed a sigh. If only she could move with the nonchalant grace of her sister-in-law, or even the six handmaidens trailing them. She dug her nails into clammy palms. Through this choreographed farce, appearances had to be maintained, lest she embarrass her father, the *Tianzi*.

Chin up, back straight. A racing heart threatened to ruin her already meager semblance of imperial grace. Eyes forward. Servants knelt on either side of the looming double doors, ready to slide them open. She forced a smile, with her best approximation of feminine charm. If only she'd lived before Dragon Songs had faded into legend, she could've sent the realm's victorious hero fleeing with the song he supposedly wanted to hear.

An aging palace official stepped into her line of sight.

Singular focus on the doors broken, she blinked. Her fluttering pulse lurched to a stop as she blew out a breath.

His blue robes ruffled as he tottered forward with averted eyes and a bobbing head. He creaked down into a bow. "Emergency, *Dian-xia*," he said, using the formal address for her rank. "The *Tianzi* commands you to greet a foreign delegation in the Hall of Bountiful Harvests."

Her heart remembered to beat again, and she looked first toward the doors and then down at the man, whose insignias marked him as a secretary for the Ministry of Appointments. Outlandish excuses had mercifully cut short each of her previous meetings with eligible young lords: six times in all.

But a foreign delegation? Before even meeting the suitor? *That* was a first. Her expression slipped as much as it could beneath the layers of pearl powder caked to her face. Mouth dry, her voice came out hoarse. "There must be a mistake. Surely the honor would fall to the Crown Prince."

He bowed his head again. "No, *Dian-xia*. With your linguistic talents, the *Tianzi* thought you better suited to meet with them."

Apparently, small talk with some foreign lord's wife constituted an emergency these days. Still, the unspoken message needed little interpretation: the foreigners were beneath a prince.

At least it meant delaying the matchmaking. Kaiya cast a glance at Xiulan. "Then shall the Crown Prince take my place and sing to General Lu?"

Her supposed chaperone covered a giggle with slender fingers. The wide sleeves of her aquamarine gown slid and bunched in her elbow, revealing the porcelain-like skin of her arm. It was as perfect as her complexion.

The man's eyes darted back and forth, his lips quivering. "I...I..."

Xiulan stepped forward and brushed a gentle hand across Kaiya's arm. "Go on, meet with the foreigners. I will explain things to the general."

Kaiya bowed her head. "As you command, Eldest Sister." She turned to the official, gesturing with an open hand for him to take the lead.

As she wobbled after him, two of her handmaidens fell in behind. They were more beautiful than her, even after her hours of preening to smother meddlesome acne and subdue unruly hair.

Which now meant she'd look ridiculous receiving dignitaries. Like an opera singer, maybe. "Who are our guests?"

The official coughed. "Prince Hardeep Vaswani of Ankira."

A man? Kaiya's stomach leapt into her throat. With limited court training, she *might* be able to entertain a lady. But a prince... Without any experience in diplomacy, that was an international incident waiting to happen. Given the choice between greeting foreign royalty and the prospect of marriage, that trip into Avarax's jaws sounded tempting. "What does he want?" she asked.

"He has been in the capital for a week now, incessantly requesting an audience."

And now they were sending her, an awkward sixteen-year-old, undoubtedly as a message. Prince Hardeep wouldn't see the *Tianzi* until her complexion cleared or the orc gods returned on their flaming chariots, whichever came first. A betting princess would put her money on the orc gods.

She sighed. After preparing to play the role of demure and dainty maiden before a potential husband, this new situation required a confident demeanor...and neither came easily.

There was no time to tone down the make-up or change the extravagant gown. Unpinning the outer robe's constraining fold, she squared her shoulders and lengthened her gait.

No, this wasn't bad. A reprieve from meeting a dour general. She could do this. How hard could it be? With each step, she concentrated on composing a dignified expression. By the time they arrived at the moat separating the castle from the rest of the sprawling palace grounds, she'd mentally transformed herself from prospective bride into imperial representative.

Right. She still looked like the former, and felt like neither.

At the head of the bridge waited eight imperial guards dressed in blue court robes. The magic etched into their breastplates' five-clawed dragon evoked awe, though she'd grown used to it over the years.

"*Dian-xia*," the guards shouted in unison. They each dropped to one knee, fist to the ground. The most talented swordsmen in the realm submitted to a pimply girl, for nothing more than the circumstances of her birth.

If only she could live up to the accompanying expectations. Kaiya acknowledged them with a nod. Bowing, the handmaidens shuffled back. The imperial guards deployed behind her. She crossed the stone bridge, leaving behind the relative comfort of private life to enter the formal world of the imperial court.

They wound through stone-paved alleys. White buildings with blue-tiled eaves rose up beyond spotless courtyard walls with circular windows. At the Hall of Bountiful Harvests, Kaiya walked up the veranda and stepped over the ghost-tripping threshold.

Inside, three chattering men gestured at the green ceiling panels and gold latticework. Their burgundy *kurta* shirts hung to their knees, collars riding high on their necks. On their left breasts sparkled an embroidered nine-pointed lotus, the crest of the embattled nation of Ankira.

The visitors' discussion came to an abrupt halt as they turned to greet her, heads bowed and palms pressed together. Dark bronze skin and rounded features marked them as ethnic Ayuri. Meticulously coifed black hair fell to their shoulders. The centermost man looked no older than twenty. Taller and more handsome than his companions, he met her gaze.

With blue irises. Luminous like the Blue Moon, Guanyin's Eye. They captured her image in their liquid depths and reflected it back, more beautiful than make-up could ever accomplish. Maybe even as beautiful as Xiulan.

He tilted his head and flashed...a smoldering smile.

Kaiya cast her eyes down, only to peek up through her lashes. Her lips twitched, struggling against all discipline in their urge to return the smile. Ridiculous! Where had the carefully crafted mask of an imperial diplomat fled to? She tightened her mouth, squared her chin, and looked up.

When he spoke, his deep, baritone voice flowed out of his mouth like honeysuckle vines, entangling her. "I am Prince Hardeep. You must be the Princess of Cathay. The stories of your beauty do you no justice."

What? Nobody could say her plain looks warranted praise, at least not sincerely. Yet his earnest words sounded nothing like the hollow compliments of court sycophants and suitors.

Heat rose to her cheeks, threatening to melt away her make-up, and her nominally dignified expression with it. His language tumbled off her tongue, accent lilting in her ears. "Welcome to Sun-Moon Palace, Prince Hardeep. I act as the ears of my father, the emperor."

Cringe-worthy. She could speak Ayuri better than that. Almost perfectly, but—

"And your voice! Saraswati, our people's Goddess of the Arts, would be jealous. Perhaps you would sing for me?"

Kaiya's head swam. Her mouth opened to beg off the unexpected request, but no words came out.

He waved a hand, and his manner stiffened. "I forget myself. Your song would certainly invigorate me, and I confess I hoped to catch a glimpse of you during my visit. However, my country's needs are more pressing. I have a request of your emperor."

Whatever spell his previous tone had woven through her mind loosened enough for her to find her voice. "I am afraid you misinterpret his intentions. By sending me, he has already denied you."

No. Did she just say that out loud? Kaiya covered her mouth. If only Avarax would swoop in and devour her now.

The Ankiran prince's lips melted into a frown and his attention shifted to her slippers. "Please hear our entreaty. The Kingdom of Madura occupies almost all of Ankira, in part because of their twice-renewed trade agreement with Cathay. For almost thirty years, you have sold them firepowder. Now, our soldiers are weary and our coffers depleted. The agreement expires soon. We ask—no, beg—that you not renew it."

Released from his gaze, her mind began to clear. "How were you able to make it through the Maduran lines?"

Prince Hardeep raised his head. Kaiya avoided those mesmerizing eyes, and instead focused on his chin as he spoke. "One of your lords, Peng Kai-Long, has long supported us. I came with him on a Cathayi trade ship."

It made sense. Cousin Kai-Long served as a trade negotiator in Ayuri lands and knew many influential people in Tivaralan's South. He had recently returned to the capital to attend the upcoming wedding of Second Brother.

"He is my father's favorite nephew," she said. "I am sure he could present a more convincing argument to the Son of Heaven than I."

Prince Hardeep shook his head. "Search inside yourself and speak with your heart. A father cannot deny the compassionate voice of his beloved daughter. Please. Our riches have been plundered, our people enslaved." His voice beckoned her head up. "Widows must sell their bodies, while orphans starve in the streets."

His dejected gaze twisted into her. Her heart, suddenly hot, sank into her belly. All those unfortunate people, suffering because of Hua's firepowder, while she enjoyed the comfort of the palace. Father must not have known the consequences of the trade agreement, since he ruled with the moral authority of Heaven. Someone had to speak for these downtrodden people.

"I will convey your message. Please make yourself comfortable until my return." She paused for a moment to search his expression. All signs of his earlier frivolity were gone. He'd just been toying with her to get what he wanted.

It didn't matter. It was the right thing to do. All the heroes from her favorite songs would've done the same. With an inward sigh, she turned and swept out of the hall, her guards marching behind her.

Outside, Kaiya took a deep breath of cool spring air to calm her thoughts and ease the hot constriction in her chest. Never before had a man made her pulse race like that. Then again, she had nothing but six fawning suitors with which to compare him.

No, this had nothing to do with Prince Hardeep's charm. An entire nation suffered, with Hua's complicity. Father had always preached morality, demanded her to always do the right thing.

In her mind, she hummed a ballad recounting heroic Dragon Singers and the perils they willingly faced. Her heart swelled, and she turned to the official. "Where is the *Tianzi* now?"

The old man gawked. "I do not think—"

She cast a silencing glare.

He bowed his head. "In the Hall of Supreme Harmony."

As the palace's central audience chamber, the Hall of Supreme Harmony was just a few minutes away, up one hundred sixty-eight arduous steps. Father rode an ornate golden palanquin to the top, but Kaiya, like anyone else who wasn't the *Tianzi*, had to climb.

Each step planted a seed of doubt in her head. A princess had no business in politics, besides solidifying loyalties through marriage. Remonstrating the *Tianzi* in front of all the lords and ministers would embarrass Father, so much that he would have no choice but to punish her.

CHAPTER 2
Treacherous Intents

Eighteen-year-old Zheng Tian knelt by the blockwood door, cursing under his breath. In his former life as Princess Kaiya's childhood confidante, he would've never broken into a warehouse. Now a *Moquan* spy, whose clan served the *Tianzi*, he should've already picked the lock.

"Hurry up." Cell leader Yan Jie's whisper tickled his ear. "The guards are halfway to the corner."

Tian glanced up to the south, where the alley between the warehouses provided a view of the smallest of the three moons, Caiyue.

Swirling with colors like a soap bubble, it waned to fourth gibbous—two hours before dawn. The guards were running ahead of schedule. He hadn't heard them coming, but Jie's half-elf blood gave her adorable pointed ears with exceptional hearing.

He motioned to the lock. "Shine the light there."

The roll of her eyes carried in her hushed tone. "A blindfolded orc with three fingers missing would have broken in by now."

Now, even his ears picked up the guards' laughter. He twisted the pick in the narrow hole for the third time. With a soft click, the lock yielded. A little pressure on the door confirmed the hinges were well-oiled, and he pushed it open. Without a sound, he pulled Jie in and closed the door behind them.

In the silent darkness, Jie tapped her fingers on his forearm in their clan code. *Two guards, now turning corner... Now passing door... All clear.*

He blew out a breath. As risky as the work was, he fit in better among spies and assassins than with the realm's ruling elite. Not like he could ever go back to that life. Not after what he'd done to Princess Kaiya.

A dim light from Jie's magic bauble spilled from between her fingers, casting her childlike features in a shadowed hue. Though ten years, three months and two days his senior, she looked no older than twelve, thanks to her elf heritage.

He rotated the lock back into place with another quiet *snick*. "It's a new device. Dwarf-made. Very expensive. I noticed it during the last harbormaster inspection."

Jie's large almond eyes narrowed to normal Hua size as she squinted at the door. That look...she was more interested than she let on, if only about the dwarven lock. "A nice lock doesn't mean they are hiding anything."

How could he even begin to explain the incremental increase in value on deliveries using specific ships in specific months, to this specific warehouse, when specific customs officials were on duty? The patterns, so clear to him, never made sense to anyone else. "Their manifests were suspicious. Come on." He beckoned her toward the dozens of wooden crates.

Yawning, she padded after him. It was doubtless feigned boredom—if anyone ever supported him, it was Jie, the clan master's adopted daughter.

He stopped at a crate with the word *fragile* painted around the lid. Its markings listed an origin of Wailian County in the unsettled North, with a destination of Yutou Province in the South.

He slid a finger over the rough edge of a crate and held it up. "Ground rice powder."

"So, they want to keep something dry. That could be just about anything. Beef jerky and pearl powder aren't going to lead to the realm's downfall." Shrugging, she produced a nail extractor from one of the twenty-seven hidden pockets in her utility suit.

"Wait." Tian stayed her hand. If only he could explain things as quickly as the thoughts came to him. Customs forms declared the box's contents to be sesame seeds, whose oils would be ruined by rice powder. Not to mention that Yutou Province was the largest supplier of sesame seeds in the realm. So unless Yutou's *Tai-Ming* Lord Liang planned on cornering a low-margin market by buying up every seed in the nation and labelling them fragile, it wasn't sesame seeds in that crate.

He picked up a nearby crowbar and gingerly wedged it under the lid, far from any of the nails. Wailian County's chief resource was saltpeter, shipments of which were restricted to the capital. It wouldn't do to send any sparks flying. Opening the lid sent a cloud of rice dust into the air.

Jie waved a hand in front of her eyes and peeled open the cloth lining inside, revealing... "Imagine that, a box marked *sesame seeds* having...sesame seeds."

With a frown, Tian knifed his hand into the seeds. Half a *chi* in, his fingers, rough from ironpalm training, thunked against wood.

Her ears twitched. "How deep?"

"Seven *cun*." He indicated a handlength, then eased a large box out with a rustling of sesame. This was why he was meant for spying. Even if it meant never seeing Princess Kaiya again.

He cast a triumphant glance at Jie. "There's more in there. Several."

"I could've told you that." She blinked innocently as she ran a hand across the lid.

Of course. He swatted her hands away. Opening the box revealed a fine black powder. Tian had expected coarse white saltpeter. He exchanged glances with Jie. "What is it?"

She sucked on the right side of her bottom lip. "I don't know."

"Take a sample—"

Jie's ears perked up and her head jerked toward the door. She stashed the light bauble, drowning the room in darkness.

The door whispered open with a breeze, and light crept in from a light bauble lamp. Three cloaked men pushed their way in and closed the door behind them. None of them looked familiar; they were certainly none of the sixteen guards who rotated shifts around this building. Their clothes bore no identifying sigils.

Pulse racing, Tian eased the lid back on top of the incriminating crate as quietly as he could. His fingers worked the nails back into their holes. If the conspirators discovered the tampering, they would cover their tracks.

"There are twenty crates marked fragile," said the smallest of the men, his enunciation thick with the North. He held up the lamp and opened its shutters. It illuminated the front third of the building, leaving Tian and Jie in the dark. "I'll show you where they are spread throughout the warehouse."

The largest man crossed his arms. "You could have put them all together, close to the front. The porters' guild would charge you an extra ten percent."

"Then it's a good thing you aren't with the guild." Lamp Man's lips drew into a tight frown.

The porter crossed his arms. "I'm sure the porters' guild, harbormaster, and other authorities might take issue with, how shall I say..."

The third man, a fellow with a fat nose and the telltale bump of a short sword concealed beneath his cloak, exchanged glances with Lamp Man, then waved a hand. "My lord is more than willing to pay five percent."

Tian's ears perked up. Fat Nose's lord was someone from the South, if he shared the same rough features and accent.

The porter grinned. "Plus a silver *jiao* for dragging me over here at this hour."

"Two silver *jiao* for the inconvenience and discretion," Fat Nose said.

The porter licked his lips. "The porter guild is scheduled to unload the *Wild Orchid* at first light. My other men will come to collect your shipment tonight."

Tian tapped his chin. The *Wild Orchid*, belonging to *Tai-Ming* Lord Peng in Nanling Province, had been sighted at sea late this night. *Yu-Ming* Lord Tong of Wailian County had never before used it to transport the questionable shipments.

"Then we are agreed." Fat Nose gestured toward the crates, inviting the men to follow him.

Tian's muscles tensed. If the conspirators discovered them, someone would likely die. He backed deeper into the warehouse, with Jie pressing her back into his stomach as if he needed the prompting. Her fingers tapped on his forearm. *Left two mine. If necessary. On my signal.*

Of course she would leave the one with the sword to him. Hopefully, it wouldn't come to that. What was the old proverb Princess Kaiya had first told him, four thousand, twenty-one days ago? *Hold the dragonfly with care, for even their fleeting lives have value.*

What was the value of a man's life? Tian looked from face to face. As long as these new arrivals didn't find evidence of tampering, they would live to see the morning.

There had to be a way to ensure that, if only because the porter had a family to go home to. At least, the carp marriage charm around his neck implied as much. He tapped on Jie's forearm. *I distract, you seal crate.*

"That one." Lamp Man led the way, pointing to several of the boxes marked fragile.

Treading quietly just outside the edge of the lamp's light, Tian worked his way toward the entrance. If they moved the light over too much, they'd see him.

As the three men continued, the light shifted deeper into the warehouse. Once the darkness enveloped the front door, he eased it open and slipped out. On the other side, he closed the door and looked past the setting full Blue Moon to the Iridescent Moon. Never moving from its seat in the heavens, it now waned halfway between its fourth and fifth crescents. An hour and a half to dawn. He rapped on the door. "Harbormaster's office here," he yelled.

A brief commotion broke out, followed by silence. A set of footsteps approached the door. It opened, and Lamp Man peered out and scrutinized Tian up and down.

"Harbormaster's office." Tian flashed an apologetic grin. With a black utility suit instead of the blue robes marking him as a government official... "Two ships coming in. Before dawn. Anything to declare?"

Lamp Man's forehead crinkled. "Who are you?"

"I'm from the Harbormaster's office. On my way to work. I saw you three enter." Tian memorized Lamp Man's fine features and light complexion as he stalled...with the light at the door, Jie could work those nails back into place with her iron palms.

Lamp Man looked Tian over again. "You don't look like an official."

"Just a scribe, sir." Tian wiped his hands over his clothes. Almost all people in Hua believed the *Moquan* to be nothing more than boogeymen who kidnapped unruly children. At least, that's what mothers told children to keep them in line. "My robes are at work."

Lamp Man reached into his cloak, sending Tian's hand for his hidden knife. Then, Lamp Man proffered a copper *fen*. "What's your name, boy?"

"Zheng." Tian peered at the coin for a few seconds, then plucked it up and bobbed his head. Let Lamp Man believe a bribe went a long way, as it certainly did with many government officials, and it might be a means of finding out more information.

"Well, Little Zheng, I may need you in the future."

Tian bobbed his head a few more times. "Happy to help. But soon. I will be transferred in a few weeks."

Lamp Man nodded. "I will be visiting the harbormaster's office this afternoon. I will need some help filing some documents." A silver *jiao* appeared in his hand.

Filing, or perhaps forging. Tian feigned an avaricious grin and swiped it. There was a conspiracy of some sort, and he would soon find out its nature.

CHAPTER 3
Incendiary Rumors

As a half-elf raised among humans, Jie hated being treated like someone half her age. Especially by Tian. Now that they were safe in a nearby alley, she swatted his hand away as he tousled her hair. His impertinence would be annoying if he weren't so handsome.

"You left me!" she said. And not for the first time in their lives as partners.

"My improvisation worked, right?" Tian's grin begged to be slapped.

Jie snorted. When he improvised, it usually led to disaster. His plans, on the other hand, had a high rate of success, as long as she was the one executing them.

He tapped his chin. "Did you push the nails back in place?"

Jie made a show of examining her fingernails. "Yes, but with such calloused fingers, I won't be sent to the Floating World to trawl for information anytime soon."

"You wouldn't belong there, anyway. The Night Blossoms of Floating World are beautiful beyond compare." Tian reached for her hair again.

His tone carried no hint of malice, and it would be expected with his lack of social graces, but still. What a boor! With a swipe of her hand, she seized his and pushed up on his elbow to put him in a chicken-wing lock. Before she could finish the motion, he grasped her wrist and twisted. Not to be outdone, she snaked her arm out of his grasp. "Are you quite done?"

"Yes." Tian pointed to the warehouse entrance, a block away. "I'll keep an eye on Fat Nose until I report to work. You check out the *Wild Orchid*'s cargo."

Jie sucked on her lower lip. Not only did he treat her like a little girl, he also gave orders—even though she was his senior, the clan master's adopted daughter, and the cell leader. The things she tolerated, if only from Tian. "Fine."

He didn't even notice, so intent was he on crouching by a stack of kegs and peering at the warehouse. Harrumphing, Jie turned toward the docks.

Night still hung over Jiangkou. Even if her no-good father had abandoned her as a baby, at least he had left her with exceptional elven senses. Now that the crescent White Moon Renyue and the Blue Moon Guanyin's Eye had set, human eyes would strain in the darkness. However, the world appeared clearly in shades of green to her elven vision.

Pausing in an alley between warehouses, she uncovered the plain breeches and shirt she'd stashed just for this purpose. After slipping into them, Jie adjusted a thick headband to cover her ears. When the clan needed someone disguised as a kid, she was the one who invariably got stuck playing the part.

She peered out onto the long stretch of wharfs along the harbor front. An enormous sablewood vessel towered over the already large Hua trading ships. A handful of likely non-guild longshoremen milled about, scrounging for a piece of Hua's wealth. With its ships and trade routes dominating the western seas, the nation was like a golden pig, fattened to the point that the lords swam in riches and even the poor wanted for little. If only the citizens knew what the Black Lotus Clan did: that a rebellion brewed in the North. Fueled by greed, it was kept in check only by the delicate systems of interdependence set up by the dynasty's founder.

Out in the water, the *Wild Orchid* made its way toward a pier. Sails lowered, its oarsmen rowed to the beat of a drum. Jie headed in the same direction, slipping between the growing crowds of workers. With dawn stretching tendrils of red and pink through the morning clouds, her vision shifted to color. Her attention was drawn from the *Wild Orchid* to a huge black ship, already docked. Its green flag, emblazoned with a silver sun with nine points, marked it as Tarkothi. With treaties demarcating trade spheres between the world's great naval powers, it was strange to see them this far west.

By the time she reached the *Wild Orchid*, dockworkers were already tying down the moorings. Jie sighed as she mixed in with the queue of child laborers. With the possibility of insurrection, there were a dozen more interesting places to be than here. All on Tian's hunch. The sailors' banter, laced with language that could make a Night Blossom fake a blush, provided the only entertainment during the wait.

At last, the gangplank lowered. Twenty-one black-haired, bronze-skinned people wobbled down. The men wore threadbare *kurta* shirts, while faded *sari* hung from the women's shoulders. Ayuri folk, but from which nation, and why would they come to Hua?

"Finally!" Speaking in the Ayuri language, a middle-aged man with a scar on his cheek dropped to his knees on the dock.

A woman patted him on his shoulder. She had a large birthmark on her neck, and a toe ring marked her as married, per Ayuri custom. "We can start a new life here."

A younger woman, face partially obscured by a scarf, found Jie's gaze. Unlike her comrades, this one had a lighter, cinnamon complexion and more slanted eyes. Half-Hua, perhaps, and beautiful in an exotic way. She ducked her head and hid her face beneath the scarf. In that flash of her hand, a black birthmark, or perhaps a tattoo, peeked out from the brown henna patterns on her wrist.

As curious as she was about these people, Jie couldn't ask in their language lest she reveal herself as anything other than a boy looking for a job. Still, it wasn't hard to deduce their story: refugees from Ankira, which was steadily losing a thirty-year war to Madura.

At the head of the dock, a group of Hua men dressed in the red-and-black livery of Nanling Province approached. Their leader pressed his palms together and bowed his head in Ayuri fashion to the refugees. In perfect Ayuri he said, "On behalf of Young Lord Peng Kai-Long, I welcome you to Cathay."

All the refugees returned his salute.

"You must be tired after your long journey. Young Lord Peng has made arrangements for you to join your countrymen. Please come with me."

"I need ten boys," yelled a voice in Hua from the gangplank. "Two copper *fen* for a day's work."

Just what she had been waiting for. Forgetting the Ankirans, Jie deftly slipped between the reaching, shouting boys. At the front, a man with a leathery complexion chewed on what appeared to be salted meat, pointing at recruits. Jie hip-butted a kid and placed herself in the line of his finger.

He started to shake his head, but paused. His focus locked on her. "No, you'll do. It takes small, nimble hands for the job I have in mind." He beckoned the boys up the gangplank, but smacked an unchosen one who tried to board. He led the group across the deck, pointing out work.

When they passed the hatch to the lower decks, Jie waited for him to turn his back, then dashed through and took the steps down two at a time. Dimly lit by banks of oar holes, the open space was full of benches and oars, small chests and hammocks. It reeked of sweat and seawater. Crew berths, in all likelihood, with plenty of places to hide. With their backs to her, six men worked winches, bringing a platform of crates up from yet another hatch near the middle of the ship.

Using the creaking of pulleys and yawning of ropes to mask her footsteps, Jie crept closer, and then dropped behind a nearby bench. They unloaded the crates and lowered the platform.

"Load up!" a man shouted down.

When they carried the crates to the upper deck, Jie slunk forward and inspected the hatch. Ropes attached to pulleys and winches led down into the very bowels of the ship; below the waterline, by her best estimate. Below, a man set a keg on the platform and spun around.

She leapt down, catching one winch line and swinging to another before landing in a forward roll. It stank of sweat and curry powder. Even her elven vision wouldn't penetrate the darkness here; luckily light bauble lamps provided illumination as well as shadows in which to hide. If any of the porters had seen her before she ducked behind a crate, they were hopefully too concerned with their own work to care about a trespasser.

Jie picked her way among the cargo, glancing back at every voice and footstep. Red paint marked contents and destinations. The bulk of the crates were labelled as Ayuri gooseweed and Levanthi spices, imported by Golden Fu Trading Company, bound for Nanling Province's villa in the capital. Tian's suspicions, though rarely wrong, were wrong now. Hardly worth the risk of mingling among boisterous sailors. If they discovered her, found out she was a girl...

The smell of rotten eggs, unmistakable but likely undetectable to a human nose, caught her attention. She sniffed, following the scent to several kegs. The writing marked the contents as turmeric, a ubiquitous ingredient of Ayuri cooking, originating from Pelastya and bound for Wailian County.

Jie examined one of the kegs. Well-sealed, no residue. There was no way of telling the contents without opening it. However, turmeric didn't smell like rotting eggs, and Pelastya didn't grow turmeric. It *did* have volcanoes and sulfur mines.

Sulfur, bound for Wailian County, the world's only major source of saltpeter. As clan master's daughter, she was privy to the closely guarded recipe for firepowder. The only major ingredient left would be charcoal.

Against the laws of interdependence that kept the nation at peace, someone was making firepowder in the rebellious North. If that was the mysterious substance they'd found in the warehouse, it was being sent south to Yutou Province. An alliance of North and South, ready to fall on the capital.

Jie needed to alert the clan. She started back toward the hatch.

"You!" a male voice called.

CHAPTER 4
Intents and Purposes

The shuffling of court robes and the cloying scent of incense greeted Kaiya as she stepped over the high threshold and into the cavernous hall. Dozens of golden columns vaulted toward the ceiling, where a tiled mosaic depicted a dragon and phoenix circling each other. Chest so tight that each breath hurt, she considered their symbolic significance. The male dragon and female phoenix represented balance, even though men and women's roles were far from equal.

All the more reason not to be here, presenting a case Father had no intention of hearing. Palms clammy, Kaiya ventured down an aisle formed by dozens of kneeling ministers and hereditary lords. Save for Eldest Brother Kai-Guo, all pressed their heads to the marble floor as she made her way toward the white marble dais. Carved into its sides were dozens of bat and lotus symbols, which she counted to calm her nerves.

Father slouched on the Jade Throne, which was chiseled in the form of a coiled dragon. Yellow robes embroidered with auspicious symbols on the chest and elbows hung over his gaunt frame. Gone was the robust optimism she remembered from her childhood. Mother's recent passing had left the gold phoenix throne at his side as empty as his heart. As always, General Zheng, bearing the Broken Sword, stood a step behind him.

A lump formed in Kaiya's throat. She sank to both knees. Stretching her arms out to straighten her sleeves, she placed her hands in front of her as she pressed her forehead to the floor.

The *Tianzi*'s voice wobbled. "Rise, my daughter."

Kaiya straightened and met his piercing regard, one that warned not to mention the foreign prince. Her clenching chest squeezed out all her resolve.

No, Father would never condone the suffering of Prince Hardeep and his people for mere profit. The assembled lords must be hiding the truth. Someone had to tell him, lest Heaven punish the realm for its immorality. She lifted her chin. "Please hear the request of Prince Hardeep Vaswani of Ankira."

Behind her, the lords and ministers stifled gasps.

Yet Father's expression softened. "What does Prince Hardeep ask of Hua?"

"*Huang-Shang*," she said, using the formal address for the *Tianzi*. "He asks that we cease sales of firepowder to the Madurans."

The ministers broke into a low murmur until Chief Minister Tan rose to one knee, head bowed. "*Huang-Shang*, I negotiated our original agreement with Madura. It has been mutually beneficial."

Beneficial. Riches for Hua, conquest for Madura. Misery for Hardeep's Ankira. The Dragon Singers from the old songs would've never tolerated such injustice. Breaking all decorum, Kaiya spun and scowled at Chief Minister Tan. Fine lines of age framed his triangular face, giving him a foxlike appearance. When she released him from her glare, he averted his eyes as protocol demanded.

She turned back to Father. "*Huang-Shang*, do the Five Classics not say that a ruler must act morally? Our actions have led to an unenviable situation in Ankira that we should seek to rectify."

Cousin Kai-Long rose up to one knee. "*Huang-Shang*, I agree with the princess. Not only that, but once the Madurans pacify Ankira, and the trade agreement *does* expire, they will turn their ambitions toward us."

Chief Minister Tan shook his head. "We are their source of firepowder. They will make war with someone else."

And spread despair, with Hua's complicity. Kaiya formulated a dignified response in her head. What kind of country put profit over people? Not only should they not renew the trade agreement... "A moral nation would terminate the treaty now."

More murmurs, undoubtedly from greedy lords who cared more about gold than morality.

"Unfortunately, that is not an option," the Chief Minister said. "In the original negotiations, I bore an imperial plaque. To go against our word, sealed with a plaque, is tantamount to the *Tianzi* forsaking the Mandate of Heaven. It would invite another Hellstorm."

Kaiya sucked in her breath at the implication. Three centuries before, the last emperor of the Yu Dynasty had reneged on his plaque-bound obligations. The gods rained divine fire from the sky as punishment, blasting open a new sea in the fertile plains of the Ayuri South and plunging the world into the Long Winter.

It was unusual for an imperial plaque to be used in simple trade negotiations, since it represented the honor of the *Tianzi*. However, as a girl—even as a princess—she couldn't challenge the Chief Minister's word directly. She raised an eyebrow at him. "How much longer does the agreement last?"

Tan's brows furrowed as he looked to the ceiling. "A year, maybe? I do not recall."

Prince Hardeep didn't have a year. Kaiya turned back to Father. "Should we delay a decision until we find the original contract in the Trade Ministry's archives?"

The *Tianzi* straightened on the throne. He waved toward the lords and officials. "Everyone but Crown Prince Kai-Guo, Young Lord Peng, and Princess Kaiya will withdraw for tea."

All present bowed their foreheads to the floor before rising. Whether they drank tea or not, the *Tianzi's* suggestion left no doubt, they would drink something, somewhere else. They filed out in precise order.

Pulse skittering, Kaiya folded her hands into her lap. Father's stare might as well have been a dwarven anvil on her shoulders.

Once the room cleared, servants closed the doors. The hall seemed more cavernous with only Eldest Brother, Cousin Kai-Long, and a dozen imperial guards remaining, and was made even more so by the *Tianzi's* echoing voice.

"Kai-Long," he said. "It seems the foreign prince ignored the unspoken denial and deigned to pressure the princess into acting as his mouthpiece."

Cousin Kai-Long pressed his head to the floor. "*Huang-Shang*, forgive me for suggesting it."

Kaiya found him in the corner of her eye. Her stomach felt hollow. She'd failed all their expectations, even when doing the right thing by helping Ankira.

"I warned you, Cousin." Eldest Brother Kai-Guo's lips drew into a tight line. "Kaiya isn't trained. She should have just occupied him with idle banter. She is more musician than diplomat."

Heat pulsated in Kaiya's cheeks. Apparently, they'd forgotten she was kneeling right there beside them. Then Eldest Brother's attention fell on her hand, which was subconsciously twirling a lock of her hair, proving his point. She jerked the hand back to her lap.

Kai-Guo looked to the throne. "Father, may I speak freely?"

"I would not have sequestered the family if not to allow you the latitude."

Kai-Guo bowed his head. "Then if I may, you dote on Kaiya to the detriment of the realm. She wastes her time on music when she should be learning how to be a proper princess. You could have ordered her to marry any six of the previous young lords she met. Instead, you not only allowed her to choose, you pulled her out of matchmaking meetings."

Father's brows clashed together for a split second. "She is not ready to be married, not to one of those men."

Kaiya's head spun. So the interruptions had been Father's doing, but why? What was wrong with those suitors, besides their lack of wit and self-absorbed attitudes?

"She *needs* to marry one of *those* men," Kai-Guo said. "A princess' duty—"

The *Tianzi*'s lip quirked just a fraction into a frown. Kai-Guo fell silent and bowed.

Father's expression softened as he turned to her. "My daughter, it was unfair of me to assign you this task after shielding you from court intrigue all this time. I indulged your love of music when I should have prepared you to become my eyes and ears in your future husband's fief."

Suppressing a sigh, Kaiya bowed her head. To the realm, her worth as a musician would never surpass her value as a bride. "Why one of those six men?"

Father's eyes searched hers. "What do they have in common?"

Besides having less personality than a rock and egos larger than the three moons combined? Kaiya cocked her head. "They are all sons of *Yu-Ming* lords."

"Yes. Second-rank prefectural and county nobles." Father's stare bored into her. "From where?"

Why was it important? Especially compared to Ankira's plight? She caught herself before twirling the stubborn lock of hair again. "The North. Regions near the Wall."

"What can you tell me about the area?"

Had she known a geography test would follow matchmaking and greeting foreign dignitaries, maybe she would have stolen a few minutes out of her rigid schedule to study a map. Her brows furrowed. On her last trip, she'd seen... "Rolling hills rise into mountains. Bloodwood trees

dot the mountainsides. The land is poor for farming, but the counties thrive from mining."

He looked to Eldest Brother and Cousin Kai-Long. "See? She understands more than it appears." He turned back to her. "My daughter, while the realm may seem prosperous and stable, not all under Heaven is well. My spies say several of the lords of the North harbor rebellious intent. They are as hard as the mountains they defend. To keep them content and docile, we buy saltpeter from their mines and process it in the capital to make firepowder."

Kaiya stifled a gasp. For Prince Hardeep and his Ankira, that meant... "We need foreign markets to sell the firepowder to."

The *Tianzi* tilted his head a fraction. "We reserve the freshest for ourselves and sell older stocks."

She sucked in a breath. "What about Ankira? We profit from their misery."

"Sometimes, practicality shades moral precepts."

At her side, Brother nodded. Cousin Kai-Long's lips pursed.

Kaiya lowered her hand from where she was again twisting that lock of hair. Her own father was rationalizing actions which caused another people's suffering. Wasn't this the paragon of nobility who had taught her songs of past heroes and ingrained a sense of morality in her? "But—"

His eyes narrowed, their warmth replaced by authority. "Convey my regret to Prince Hardeep."

Cowed by his stern tone, she bowed. Kai-Guo and Kai-Long followed suit.

When she raised her head, Father's regard softened. "You are so beautiful, my daughter. I will announce your betrothal at the reception tonight. After you send the foreign prince away, go meet with General Lu."

The bottom dropped out of her belly. Betrothal! To the commander of the armies in the North. Their planned meeting had been more than a choreographed farce, and with a possible rebellion brewing, perhaps the self-proclaimed

Guardian Dragon of Hua had not been the one to request it after all.

She started to speak, but Father's genuine smile stifled her protest. Her heart sank into her stomach. Betrothal appeared as immutable as Hua's agreement with Madura. She'd be married, probably as soon as she flowered with Heaven's Dew, perhaps even forbidden by a dour new husband from singing. Forget her stomach; her heart lay shattered on the marble tiles.

Rising, she trudged out of the hall, back into bright sunlight. This had to be a dream. Marriage. Like Xiulan, night after night of trying to make babies with Eldest Brother Kai-Guo. Monotonous routines all day. But at least Xiulan could practice the magic of her Dragon Script with friends and family.

Not Kaiya. She'd be shipped away to barren hills. Devoid of music. Alone. No, it couldn't be real. She took a deep breath to slow her stuttering pulse. A smooth river pebble found its way from her sash into her hand. Cool and soothing, it was a token from her childhood friend Zheng Tian, the boy she'd once laughingly promised to marry. How simple and carefree those days were! When there was no grey area between Right and Wrong, just like in the songs. If only she could marry him instead of some pompous soldier. But no; even though he might be the son of a first-rank *Tai-Ming* lord, he'd been banished years ago for a stupid mistake.

She glanced back at her senior-most imperial guard, Chen Xin. He was looking at her hand, frowning. Even on the worst day of her life, it would not do to let anyone see weakness. With a wistful sigh, she straightened her spine and squirrelled the pebble back into its place in her sash. Before meeting her future husband, there was first the equally onerous task of walking back and denying a desperate plea. Thoughts of her own dismal future would have to wait.

Outside the Hall of Bountiful Harvests, she paused and composed herself. Prince Hardeep was just a man. A handsome one, for sure, but she'd met many other good-looking men without wilting into a starry-eyed fool. Steeling herself against whatever magic Prince Hardeep had used to beguile her, she stepped over the threshold.

The prince pressed his hands together and bent his head as she entered. He looked up expectantly.

His irises. They again entranced her.

Her straight posture softened as her insides somersaulted. She bowed low. It broke formal court etiquette, and indeed, the ministry secretary clucked his disapproval. At least it would conceal her spine melting to jelly. She held the position and focused on the prince's red-and-gold-threaded shoes. "I am afraid that Cathay must honor its agreements, lest the *Tianzi* lose the Mandate of Heaven and the realm descend into chaos."

"Do not apologize." His voice was sweet again, with a touch of melancholy. General Lu would probably never speak to her with such affection. "Please, raise your head."

His last words filled her like a warm breath into a soap bubble. She straightened.

Shoulders slumping, the prince tilted his eyes downward. He was handsome, even in sadness. "Will you sing for me? As a memory of our meeting?"

A song. Kaiya's heart flitted. She would do this for him, appropriate or not. At least someone today would appreciate her voice. She looked over her shoulder toward the official, who scowled and shook his head. No? Who was he to defy her wishes?

The prince's lips trembled into a brittle smile.

Her first foray into diplomacy might have ended in disaster, but with music, very few in Hua could rival her. Perhaps if the fabled magic of Dragon Songs still existed, she could sing the rebellious lords into submission. Then, Father would value her ability over her marriage prospects. She lifted her voice in song, her soul soaring with each breath. The *Broken Sword* recounted how the Founder had transformed weakness into strength. Perhaps it would give Hardeep hope.

Exultation surged through her spine, into her limbs. All uncertainties and self-doubts melted away. With each note, she shed her poor imitation of imperial grace, replacing it with the sincerity of her soul. Not even the tight dress could contain her. Verse upon verse rose to a crescendo, her spirit floating with it.

Prince Hardeep's blue eyes sparkled. "Even Yanyan would envy your voice."

Heat rose to her cheeks. How could he compare her to the girl from a thousand years before, who had summoned storms with her music and sung the dragon Avarax to sleep? "Yanyan charmed an orc army into surrender with her song. I could not even convince my father to change his mind."

"You spoke from your heart, and the emperor listened." His forlorn smile sent a chill up her spine. "With an indomitable spirit, you can move your people to do the right thing."

Could she? Besides Cousin Kai-Long, none of the men in the Hall of Supreme Harmony had shown any concern for morality. She sighed. "If I had the voice of Yanyan, he would have listened."

Those blue eyes searched hers. "Channeling magic through artistic endeavor is the gift of your people, just as the fighting arts are ours. Come with me, and scatter the Maduran armies with the power of your music."

Was he suggesting running away? With him? Escaping marriage with General Lu? She glanced back at the official. If he told anyone, the prince might lose his head. And if only shirking duty were so easy. They wouldn't make it to the front gates, even if she could bring herself to take up his offer.

And who knew? Maybe he was trying to kidnap her, and hold her hostage to get what he really wanted: an end to Hua's trade agreement with Madura.

Tearing her gaze away, she shook her head. "Even though master performers from Hua's past could accomplish amazing feats with Dragon Songs, those skills have since faded into legend. You would need an elf." Like Father's councilor, Lord Xu. Too bad nobody could predict when the enigmatic elf would make an appearance.

Prince Hardeep took her hands in his. Excitement rose in his tone. "With your voice and musical talent, you have the potential. We will research. I can help you scour your records. Together, we could learn how the masters of old did it."

His touch sent heat up her arms and into her core. Behind her, the official sucked in a sharp breath and the imperial guards stepped forward. Kaiya withdrew, for his safety, and raised an open hand to assuage the guards. Was Hardeep's idea even possible? "How can I learn from books what the elf angel taught Yanyan?"

"I would hazard to guess that singing a dragon to sleep is just a little more difficult than convincing a doting father to do the right thing." He put a finger to his chin. "And if—no, *when*—you succeed, you will save my nation."

Yes! No. Even if it were possible to learn from dusty old books, using magic to change a *Tianzi's* mind flirted with treason even more than running away. She met his gaze again. Those eyes implored her, making her belly flutter. No, helping Ankira was the moral thing to do. Here was a chance to show that music was still worth something. That she was worth something, beyond her value as a bride to some lord. "I will try."

A grin bloomed on his face. "Ankira owes you a debt of gratitude. *I* owe you."

Kaiya twirled an errant lock of hair. "We will need to retrace Yanyan's steps. To find out exactly where she met the elf angel." Which meant a trip to the imperial archives. After the mandated matchmaking with General Lu.

She looked into the prince's eyes. No. He was here, close, and marriage to the general seemed so far away. Hardeep's people needed her help, because everyone else would just let them suffer. Again, her hand found Tian's pebble, firm and resolute beneath her sash. He'd support her decision.

They'd go now, even though it meant disobeying Father.

CHAPTER 5
Crooked Detours

Clothes swished and footsteps shuffled across the marble floors as Kaiya gawked at the rows and rows of books bound in silk cords. When Father ordered her to send Prince Hardeep away, he likely didn't expect the route out of the palace to include a stop at the imperial archives.

Maybe it was a bad idea. *Her* bad idea, on the preposterous assumption she could learn the dead art of Dragon Songs.

A battalion of grey-robed scholars hovered nearby, their annoyance at the unannounced visit clear in their tight frowns. Though they hadn't dared oppose an imperial princess, they'd dispatched an apprentice clerk to lodge a complaint with the Ministry of Appointments.

All trouble waiting to happen, if the old secretary's wringing hands were any indication. She'd abused her position and strong-armed him into delaying the matchmaking meeting with General Lu. No doubt both the Ministries of Appointments and Household Affairs scoured the grounds for her.

Her imperial guards Chen Xin and Zhao Yue stood nearby, their usually stoic expressions now shadowed by uncertainty. Nothing good would come of this visit, no matter how noble the intentions. She'd tarnished her already-poor façade of Perfect Princess, and disobeyed the *Tianzi's* command to meet General Lu.

Was it worth it? She looked over at Prince Hardeep, a book in each hand, his face brightly illuminated by the magic baubles suspended from the ceiling. So handsome in his need! And unlike everyone else, he believed she could become more than an awkward political bride. Her stomach fluttered like a swarm of butterflies. She didn't need to be beautiful or graceful to revive Dragon Songs and save a downtrodden people.

If she could do it.

If they even had enough time.

She scanned the labels. "According to legend, Yanyan's magic awoke in the place where the elf angel Aralas revealed himself. Before the War of Ancient Gods."

Shrugging, Hardeep held up one book, entitled *The Fall of the Yu Dynasty*. "It's in your language, but the illustrations tell me we are in the wrong era." His sheepish smile was too adorable.

She covered a laugh with her hand. "That is about seven hundred years too late."

One scholar's face flushed red, while others glared at Hardeep's hands on their precious books.

His perfect lips formed a perfect circle. "The Hellstorm and Long Winter, then."

She stifled her giggle. There was nothing amusing about fire raining from the heavens, nor the three years of starvation in its aftermath.

Prince Hardeep returned the *Fall of the Yu Dynasty* to the shelf. With the other book cradled in his hand, he tapped his chin, just like her childhood playmate Tian. So cute, even more so with the pointed beard. "Where do we find the right era?"

Not like she knew where those historical accounts might be stored. She'd only visited the archives a few times in the past, always on a tightly regulated schedule. Kaiya turned to the irritated scholars. "Take us to the documents on the War of Ancient Gods."

A bearded middle-aged man bowed low and extended an open hand. "This way, *Dian-xia*." His begrudging tone left no doubt as to his opinion of an unauthorized visit by a girl, princess or not, and a foreign prince who might be trying to smuggle out a book.

She followed as he shuffled down the rows, Prince Hardeep at her side and the two imperial guards a sword's reach away. The Foreign Ministry secretary and the gaggle of scholars trailed an almost-respectful distance behind, though most kept staring at the book the prince swung about in his hand. If the archives had windows, they would have been eyeing the Iridescent Moon with a dwarven timepiece, counting the minutes until some bureaucrat, and maybe a few imperial guards, arrived to usher her out. The low-level archive clerk they'd sent must've reported to the Ministry of Appointments by now.

Which gave them ten, maybe fifteen minutes at best to find out where Aralas had met Yanyan a millennia ago. Over the next several twists and turns, the air became more stale and musty, the books more dusty and faded. They also dwindled in number, replaced by sheaves of unbound scrolls: Historical accounts. Interpretations of those histories. Financial implications of the interpretations. Somewhere in the mass of information, they could probably uncover how many demon hearts the Sun God Yang-Di paid the dwarf Da-Jin to forge the world for the Goddess of Mercy, Guanyin.

The head scholar came to a stop and bowed again. "Here, *Dian-xia*." His tone carried an unspoken warning to be extremely careful with the brittle-looking scrolls. As if she wasn't in enough trouble already, without damaging a priceless book or three.

Kaiya scanned the shelves. Labels protruded from each roll, inviting a browser to learn the title of the work without actually having to touch it. A few steps ahead, Prince Hardeep had all but forgotten her, his attention locked on some scroll. She shrugged the outer gown off her shoulders to expose her collarbones, the most feminine of her otherwise uninspiring features.

No response. He seemed fixated on that scroll. Maybe he saw her as a mere tool, a means of getting into the archives. She dug her nails into her clammy palms. He apparently didn't care about the risk she was taking for him.

No, not for him. He was just a man she'd just met, and good looks and charm had never swayed her before. Like the Dragon Singers of old, she took these risks for Ankira and the people suffering for Hua's profit.

And, of course, for the chance to learn Dragon Songs. Fists loosening, she turned back to the rows of shelves. A newer-looking book, bound in leather like those of the fair-skinned people in the East, stood out among the scrolls. Gold Arkothi lettering emblazoned on the spine screamed for her to read it.

She tilted her head to decipher the foreign words. *The Nine Loves of Aralas*. Countless Hua accounts told how the elf angel Aralas taught different types of magic to his human lovers so that they could help overthrow the orcs who enslaved them during the War of Ancient Gods. Invariably these stories emphasized Yanyan's role as the most important. Perhaps a foreign version might have a different opinion. Gesturing toward it with an open hand, she beckoned the head scholar. "What is an Arkothi book doing here?"

Without even looking at it, the scholar harrumphed. "The imperial archives have the largest collection of information in the world. Works come from all over the continent. If you wish to know this particular book's provenance, I would be happy to delve through piles of records to find out." His pursed lips and flippant tone suggested otherwise.

Curiously, two of his underlings stared at the book with narrowed eyes and leaned toward each other. Her sensitive ears made out their furtive whispers.

"Where did that come from?"

"I've never seen it before."

Exchanging a glance with Prince Hardeep, she thumbed through the pages to Yanyan's story. The handwritten foreign words came slowly.

He reached in and turned the page. The heat from his closeness sent her arms tingling. She looked up at him to find his eyes darting back and forth.

"Here," he said, pointing to a paragraph. "Yanyan labored in the rice paddies near Sun-Moon Lake. She stumbled upon the elf angel Aralas when he was investigating the remains of the dragon Pyarax."

Sun-Moon Lake! It was here in the capital. But... "I've never heard of dragon remains here."

He flipped another page, revealing a map.

Kaiya stared at the confusing lines. She might be talented at music and nominally good at pretending to be perfect; maps and directions were another story. "Dragon remains could be anywhere."

The head scholar's scoff transformed into a cough. Accentless Ayuri slid off his tongue. "If I may, *Dian-xia*, the book the prince holds might be of use." He extended an impertinent finger at the tome Hardeep had carried from the previous section.

Prince Hardeep gawped at the book as if it had magically appeared in his hand. With a sheepish grin, he offered *Geomancy Studies of Huajing* to the scholar.

The scholar blew out a sigh that managed to mix exasperation with relief, and gingerly plucked the volume from the prince's hands. "As Queen Regent, the Founder's consort commissioned several *Feng Shui* masters to lay out Huajing's precisely gridded network of roads to ensure national prosperity."

With fanatical reverence, he turned one page. Then another. In the time it took him to flip a page, empires could rise and fall. Maybe he was just biding time until a high official came to remove them from the archives.

And drag her to meet General Lu. Studying Hardeep's jawline, she twirled a lock of hair. They couldn't have much more than five minutes now.

At last, he held it open, beyond anyone's reach, revealing an illustration. The fearsome dragon looked nothing like the graceful, serpentine spirit dragons that controlled the weather and acted as Heaven's messengers. Not like any of the latter had appeared in three hundred years.

"Such a horrible beast." Hardeep recoiled. "Thank the gods that only Avarax remains."

She nodded. "And that he is content with controlling the Dragonlands."

"Content..." He looked up at her. "What do the words say?"

Kaiya read the passage aloud. "When the orcs thought they had finally exterminated the elves, they turned on their dragon allies in the Dragonpurge. Their gods descended in flaming chariots and slew the great wyrms until only Avarax remained."

Hardeep sucked in a sharp breath. "Avarax was too powerful, even for the Tivari gods."

With a nod, she skimmed into the next paragraph. "With the establishment of the Wang Dynasty, the Queen Regent ordered the construction of the Temple of Heaven over Pyarax's bones, and placed the chunk of a fallen star from the Founder's homeland there."

Reaching past her toward the book in the scholar's grasp, Hardeep's trembling hand flipped the page. He pointed. "Look."

A diagram showed the dragon bones as columns, protruding from the ground and forming the outline of the temple's elliptical walls. She shook her head. "Even the Emperor himself requires a special blessing from the temple priests to enter the tower, and he only goes on New Year's Day."

"Which is in four days." He held up four fingers.

She fiddled with a lock of hair. There was little hope of convincing Father to break three hundred years of tradition by allowing a foreigner to join in a trip to a set of dragon bones. And in four days' time, she'd already be betrothed to a different kind of reptile.

Muffled by distance and the labyrinth of bookshelves, boots clopped and slippered feet shuffled somewhere near the entrance. It was the Ministry of Appointments coming for her, no doubt, along with imperial guards to help Hardeep find the palace exit.

The head scholar cleared his throat and closed the book. "I am pleased to have been of service to the princess."

Though his tone implied otherwise, Kaiya nodded. "Thank you."

The scholar's shoulders relaxed as he returned the leather-bound book to the shelf. From somewhere closer to the entrance, voices spoke and footsteps approached.

"One more thing," she said.

The head scholar tensed up again, and his colleagues all muttered. "How may we serve the princess?"

"Would you happen to have any books of Yanyan's songs?"

"No." A tentative smile formed on the scholar's face. "If any survived, they would be in the Hall of Pure Melody."

Hardeep turned to her. "Where is that?"

"The music hall. Just across the central plaza." Kaiya pointed, toward what she hoped was the right area.

Tapping his chin, Hardeep looked the other way. He didn't seem to notice her poor sense of direction. No, he was in deep thought, perhaps thinking…

The same thing as her. She said, "Maybe if we saw what Yanyan sang, we could figure out how she did it."

"Yes," the head scholar said. "I think that is a wonderful idea."

Or was it? Kaiya fiddled with the long sleeves of her formal gown. She couldn't traipse all around the palace grounds while General Lu waited. Especially into the Hall of Pure Melody, which housed priceless musical instruments from antiquity.

As the old proverb said, there was opportunity in danger. Here was a chance to revive the lost magic of Dragon Songs and save a conquered nation. General Lu could wait.

Now if only they could get there before the Ministry of Appointments came and dragged her off to the self-proclaimed Guardian Dragon of Hua. It would be much more interesting to charm a real dragon.

Dozens of footsteps and voices grew louder.

CHAPTER 6:
Misdirection

In the three thousand, one hundred and forty-seven days since his banishment from the capital, Tian rarely had time to ponder how he, the fourth son of a *Tai-Ming* lord, had ended up as a *Moquan* adept. All he knew was that the clan was the only place he fit in, the only place where his talents outweighed his lack of social graces.

None of his colleagues in the harbormaster's office knew of either his noble birth, his childhood friendship with Princess Kaiya, or his identity as a spy; only that he could scribble notes quickly and accurately. Nobody seemed to notice how often he visited the records room today, nor that he lingered there an extra twenty-six seconds longer than average as he surreptitiously reviewed copies of the *Wild Orchid's* manifests and logs. Owned by Nanling Province, it had followed an unspectacular trade route over the last two years.

From here in Jiangkou, it would sail south to Yutou, then to its homeport in Nanling Province, then into the foreign waters of Ankiras and Ayudra Island. In addition to transporting Ankirans out of Ayuri lands, it leased cargo space to several trading companies. The only company that had ever stood out to Tian before was Golden Fu Trading, a newer corporation that imported addicting but legal gooseweed from the Ayuri South. So why had Yutou Province decided to use the ship for smuggling?

"Little Tian," his supervisor yelled from the main office.

Tian poked his head out of the records room. "Yes sir?"

"A trading company representative wants your help with a shipping declaration."

Lamp Man, no doubt, perhaps with unspoken answers. Tian walked out into the rows of knee-high desks, making a show of bumping into one of them. His twenty-seven kneeling colleagues all startled and shook their heads.

Old Chu, an honest licensing official, snorted. "You've been here a year and you still careen into desks. Once the Ministry of Trade ships you off to the barbarian lands, I can't say I will miss the shock to my old heart every time you crash into mine. I will miss your thoroughness, though."

A compliment, perhaps? They were rare. Tian bobbed his head, all the while keeping a surreptitious eye on his own desk.

Lamp Man stood there, his gaze roving over the clutter of brushes, inkstones, and papers. He bowed his head as Tian approached. "Scribe Zheng, thank you."

"How may I help you?" Tian dropped into a cross-legged sit on the floor.

Lamp Man sat down across the table, then withdrew two sheets of folded rice paper. "My company is new, and I want to make sure this customs declaration is correct." He proffered the sheets.

New, of course—likely a shell company creating another layer to protect whoever was behind the smuggling. Tian examined the neat handwriting. *Victorious Trading Corporation. Bloodwood furniture out of Wailian County.*

Victorious...the written character was rarely used, usually only in names like Princess Kaiya's. As for furniture, it provided an easy way to smuggle, as long as the right customs officials were bribed to ignore secret or not so secret compartments. Tian looked sidelong at a few of the most egregious offenders at their desks. "Everything seems to be in order on the first page." He started to flip the page.

Lamp Man's hand shot out and he shook his head. *Not now*, he mouthed. "Thank you for your help, Scribe Zheng." Bowing his head, he stood up and left.

Waiting for all eyes to return to their own work, Tian peeled away the top page, revealing a paper treasury note worth ten silver *yuan*. That was a substantial bribe, three and a third times more than the largest bribe he'd ever seen taken in this office. Lamp Man wanted something big, and the second page...

Beautiful script meandered over the sheet, seemingly moving of its own accord. He blinked several times and shook his head. Victorious Trading Company apparently employed a master of written magic, someone who had hoped to put the reader into some sort of charm. Thankfully, Black Lotus training involved exposure to many forms of Artistic Magic, conferring a mild resistance.

His head might be spinning now, but the uninitiated would likely feel drunk, and open to the command written in the words: *Bring all original manifests for the* Steadfast Mariner *to the warehouse at the third waxing gibbous.*

Stuffing the page and cash into the fold of his robes, Tian glanced at the dwarf-made water clock. The third waxing gibbous was just past sunset, several hours from now. The *Steadfast Mariner*, registered to Yutou Province, was the suspicious ship that had first led him to the warehouse that morning. If Lamp Man wanted the originals, it was probably to destroy the evidence and tie up loose ends.

Did he see Tian as a loose end? Or as a resource for future smuggling?

Tian scribbled two coded messages. Waiting for the instant all heads focused on their work, he slipped out of the building. In the mid-morning sun, longshoremen, dockworkers, and sailors all bustled about, too busy with their own affairs to care about him. He beckoned his usual runner out of a crowd of boys looking for odd jobs.

Up to now, Little Ju had proven reliable and discreet. The tween grinned and hustled up. "What do you need, Mister Zheng?"

With a street performer's sleight of hand, Tian retrieved the missive for his Black Lotus superiors. Creased into a twenty-fold shape that would tear apart if opened by untrained hands, it instructed them to track down Victorious Trading's incorporation papers. He pressed it, and the silver coin Lamp Man had given him that morning, into Little Ju's hand. "Run this to Sweet Lotus Shrine. Drop it in the donation box."

The boy dipped his head and dashed off. Making sure no one was looking, Tian stashed his note for Jie into the light bauble lamp sconce on the right side of the door. It might be out of her short reach, but she'd never failed to retrieve his messages before. Hopefully, she would do so before he reached the warehouse, just in case Lamp Man saw him as a loose end in need of tying up...at the neck.

CHAPTER 7

Resonance

Pages ruffled as Kaiya flipped through ancient musical texts with Prince Hardeep under the bright illumination of unshuttered light bauble lamps. She'd performed in the Hall of Pure Melody's acoustically perfect main chamber for large audiences of hereditary lords several times before, but it had been years since she visited its library.

Her two imperial guards stood at the doorway, expressions marked by tight-drawn lips and narrowed eyes. The Ministry of Appointments secretary clasped and unclasped his hands, turning his head out into the hall over and over again. He resembled a dwarf-made mechanical doll. Unlike those silent automatons, he had reminded her several times on the jaunt across the central plaza that General Lu awaited her, and that perhaps she should preen a little first. When it came time for him to file a daily log with his ministry, there was no telling what he would say about her.

Perhaps he would mention how she'd dallied with a foreign prince instead of meeting her future husband. The rumors would swirl through the palace for days, humiliating her—and worse, embarrassing Father.

Shifting her gaze from Prince Hardeep, she stifled a sigh. Helping him had sounded just and righteous earlier. Now though, rummaging through the music library, without permission no less, for the sake of a foreign country... Father might very well order her married immediately, before she even flowered with Heaven's Dew.

And for what? The possibility of unearthing lost Dragon Songs seemed bleak so far. None of the hundred song transcriptions looked out of the ordinary, beyond the beautiful sound they each sang in her head. Gritting her teeth, she replaced yet another bundle of brittle rice-paper scrolls.

With the enthusiasm of a puppy, Prince Hardeep pointed to a wall of books bound in faded silk cord. "Perhaps we should search the oldest ones."

A smile came unbidden to her lips. General Lu would never look at her like that, never think of her as more than a stepping stone. Never care about what was important to her. Yes, this was the right thing to do. Her hand left Tian's pebble and reached for one of the books—

"What are you doing?" a male voice barked from the door.

Kaiya's heart leapt into her throat. She swung around.

The Hall of Pure Melody's steward marched in, his blue robes swishing. His glower fell on her, widened, and then shifted downward as protocol demanded. "*Dian-xia*, I was not informed you would visit today."

She nodded. "I am..." She looked to Prince Hardeep, then back. "I am looking for a song to play for my brother's wedding." A cringe-worthy lie.

The steward shuffled on his feet. "It is uh, highly irregular for people to visit the musical archives, particularly the rare, and uh, especially delicate volumes. Perhaps I can help?"

"Yanyan," she said. "Do you have any of her music here?"

Frown returning to his face, the steward favored the prince with a furrowed brow. "Who is this?"

Kaiya straightened and channeled her most authoritative voice. "A guest of honor."

"And a fellow lover of music." Prince Hardeep pressed his palms together. "I have researched your peoples' music for years." He hummed a familiar tune.

Da-Xiong's Lullaby? The famous flautist Da-Xiong, one of the last to master Dragon Songs, had calmed a furious Yu Dynasty emperor with that song, sparing hundreds of innocents from his wrath. Prince Hardeep knew the song, while the only songs General Lu probably knew of were war chants.

He wasn't even using a flute to achieve the deep notes. His hum hung in the air, each note heavier than the next. Kaiya's shoulders relaxed as the melody settled her skittering pulse.

The steward's ridiculous grin spread from the edge of each eye, while he blinked as if he had dwarven anvils for eyelids. His Ayuri came out with a halting accent. "Simply amazing! Few have heard of that song, let alone can hum it. I am duly impressed."

"You are too kind." Nodding at the steward, Prince Hardeep winked at her. "I would love to see Yanyan's songs. Even if none of my people could invoke the magic in her tunes, legend has it the melodies are beautiful."

"Alas." The steward sighed. "Her songs were transcribed in one single book, lost in the chaos after the Hellstorm."

Prince Hardeep's lips quirked upward. "A shame. In any case, though I appreciate the offer, we do not need your help. You may all leave us."

"Let me know if you do." The steward bowed. He turned and left, the secretary and imperial guards escorting him out.

Leaving her alone. With Hardeep. Whose command both the steward *and* the secretary *and* guards had obeyed. Kaiya's heart buzzed like a dragonfly's wings. Maybe the secretary would report back to Father that she was alone with a man.

Hardeep brushed a finger across her thumb, and then clasped her hand. Excitement jolted from her palm to her chest. Smiling conspiratorially, he tilted his head toward the older books. "Come."

She cast her gaze down. Heat flared from her toes to her head. To think that an hour before, marriage seemed so onerous. With him, however... He understood her. Maybe he even liked her. She let him guide her toward the books.

He pulled a few off the shelves, handing her some while flipping through the pages of others. She peeked up through her lashes a few times to catch his singular focus on the task. From the bounce of his head, he could clearly read the musical transcription.

He passed another book to her. "What does the script say?"

The song itself was innocuous enough, a piece for the four-stringed, fretted *pipa* from the preceding Yu Dynasty. In that era, when the *Tianzi* had kept a large harem, a court musician had cheered a depressed concubine with it. "*Once you have seized the song's emotion and made it your own,*" she read, "*you must project it. Rooted to the ground, your spine aligned, let your heart impel your voice.*" Rooted to the ground, spine aligned...it sounded like her doctor's breathing exercises.

"As if people were trees." He laughed, clear and jubilant. Still, his eyes darted over the page before searching hers. "I wonder what it sounds like."

Her lips quirked upward as she contemplated his hand. Her own shot out to take his and she gave him a tug toward the exit. "Come."

"Where are we going?"

"The main hall," she said before she could change her mind. It was one thing to go to the library, but the main hall was off-limits except on rare occasions. If the *Tianzi* found out, he might never let her perform here again. Maybe it wasn't worth the risk.

Yes, it was. Here was a chance to evoke a Dragon Song, something no Hua artist had accomplished in centuries. She could be special, something more than just a chess piece in the game of national politics. And Prince Hardeep wanted—no, needed—her to succeed. She squared her shoulders and shuffled ahead of him.

Though steeply pitched eaves of blue tile capped the Hall of Pure Melody on the outside, the main hall vaulted in an elliptical dome. Prince Hardeep looked upward, his irises tracing the coffering that partitioned the porcelain tiles.

"We need an instrument." Kaiya beckoned him toward the front of the chamber, where she knelt and slid aside a wall panel to reveal a storage room. If he loved music as much as she, wait until he went inside. She invited him in with an open hand.

His hands barely brushed over her shoulder as he passed, sending a shiver through her. She stood and followed him in, almost running into his back when he skidded to a halt.

Arms outstretched, blue eyes round with wonder, he spun in a circle, pausing on some of the finest instruments: An antique *guzheng* zither, said to be worth more than a ship. An array of knobbed bronze bells, played only on New Year's Day.

And finally, a pipa, believed to have been given to Yanyan by her lover, the elf angel Aralas, resting on a cloth-covered pedestal. Its sound plate glittered in gold, while the strings caught the light like a spider web at dawn. The smooth resonator, supposedly made of a dragon's eggshell, swirled with color.

"What a beautiful lute!" Hardeep strode over and reverently picked Yanyan's pipa up in two hands. If only her potential suitors had even a fraction of his interest in music! No, they were more interested in talking about themselves. He presented the instrument with an encouraging nod.

She hesitated. Only designated people were allowed to touch any of the artifacts. Then again,

she hadn't stopped him, either. Bowing her head, she received the pipa in two hands.

And almost dropped it. It seemed alive in her hands, pulsing ever so subtly, as if it had a heart, beating in harmony with hers. As if it belonged to her. She started to return it to its stand.

It felt like leaving behind a long-lost friend. She looked up to see Hardeep disappearing into the performance hall. Pulse racing, she cradled the pipa against her chest and followed.

When she reached the door, he was scooting a bloodwood chair, carved with nightingale patterns, to the most ideal spot in the chamber for playing. He set the music book on it and gestured for her to sit, then walked across the chamber. Though the location wasn't marked on the white marble floors, he stopped where her father might relax—the most ideal spot for listening. Pressing his hands together, he bowed his head. "Please play."

Kaiya looked at the instrument in her hands, then up at him. Of all the pipas, he had chosen this one. "Do you know the significance of this lute?"

He shrugged. "It drew my eye. It was the most beautiful in the storeroom."

"Yanyan used it during the War of Ancient Gods."

His mouth formed a perfect circle. "Then you *must* play it."

She studied the pipa. She might be a talented musician, but... "No human in living memory has coaxed a sound out of it." Hushed rumors spoke of the elf lord Xu playing it for Father twenty-nine years ago; other than that, the last masters to play it lived almost three centuries before, and had all died under bizarre circumstances.

Tapping his chin, he regarded her. "You won't know unless you try."

Kaiya's head spun. If she succeeded where even the best musicians in the realm had failed, it would prove the worth of music. *Her* worth. Then again, if the pipa didn't respond, it would only confirm what Eldest Brother Kai-Guo and the other lords believed: her only value was that as a bride to General Lu. Even worse, Prince Hardeep would think he'd wasted his time trying to help her.

She took a deep breath. She could do this. Had to do it, even if it was just to prove to herself she could. She scanned the music book, memorizing the complex changes. Settling on the edge of the chair, she took a deep breath and plucked out the first note. A beautiful sound emanated from the resonator.

Kaiya's heart jolted and she nearly dropped the pipa in surprise. It couldn't be. It had to be her imagination. She looked up to Hardeep.

Eyes closed, smile broad, he looked enraptured by the sound.

Could it be? She strummed a chord, emitting a wondrous melody. There was no mistake. Heavens, she had done it! Something no one else had accomplished in over two centuries!

Plucking each string, pressing each fret, the music came out inspired. The joyous soul of the song bounded off the page, swirling in seemingly tangible currents.

"Each note raises my spirit higher," he said, yet his own tone was flat. "Maybe do what the book suggested. Adjust yourself in the chair? I think if you straightened your spine, feet more flat on the ground, it would sound even better. "

Such strange advice, sounding more like her doctor's counsel than anything her music teachers would ever say. Still, it couldn't hurt. She shifted in her chair and plucked out the tune. Its vibration echoed in her arms.

"One shoulder is higher than the other," he offered.

Adjusting her posture, she continued, and the pulsations merged into her core. With a slight tilt of her waist, they sank to her pelvis, awakening a flare of warmth there. After tucking her tailbone forward, the vibrations reached her legs as well. She looked up again.

Prince Hardeep's expression brightened from his luminous blue irises. He placed a hand over his breast. "Yes! More emotion!"

She closed her eyes and strummed. Her spirit soared to a place only music could take her. Even though she was plain-looking, music made her feel beautiful. And now, playing for this audience of one...her beauty might rival Guanyin, Goddess of Fertility, in her glorious splendor.

Her entire body tingled, from fingertips to toes. Her pulse quickened, roaring loud and torrential in her ears. Her insides writhed like ten thousand fish squirming over each other in a shallow pool. An immense source of energy lay just beyond her reach, like an ocean of power trickling through a pinprick in a wall. There, ready to tap into.

Then her fingers went slack on the pipa and the blood rushed from her head. A dark tunnel in her field of vision narrowed. All went black.

CHAPTER 8
Conspirators

Trapped like a rat. Avoiding the sailor's gaze, Jie ducked back down among the kegs of sulfur bound for Wailian County. It might be used to cure scabies and ringworm, but there was enough here to put every herb store and acupuncture clinic in the North out of business. No, against the *Tianzi's* law, someone in Wailian was making firepowder and shipping it south.

Getting the message to the clan would be difficult now that someone had spotted her. Near the only exit, seven different voices and hurried footsteps of varying lengths and weights echoed in the cargo hold.

"Are you sure it wasn't just rats?"

"It would have been a huge rat. No, it's an intruder."

"Inform the quartermaster."

Jie sucked her bottom lip. They knew she was here, and there was only one way out.

Winches and gears creaked. The platform to the main deck clunked up, and the door clanked shut.

"Fan out," a male voice called from near the hatch.

Jie leaned forward from between two kegs and peeked out. Three men congregated near the now-raised platform. Four others searched among the crates and kegs. Shadows danced as they raised and waved their light bauble lamps.

Until the hatch opened, there was no escape. At least the patches of darkness allowed her to work her way in that direction. As one man turned his head away, Jie scooted over one crate. When another swept his lamp in her direction, she used the arcing shadow to move to the next.

Child's play. She could keep this up all morning, if need be. Though if information won wars, the time wasted down here could mean the difference between quelling a rebellion in its infancy, and taking years rooting out a well-established insurgency.

A large man near the hatch crossed his arms. "We know you are down here. Just save us the trouble and show yourself."

Oh, she'd give them plenty of trouble. Unless they suddenly figured out a systematic search method, they'd never find her. Still, precious time slipped away.

"Damn stowaway," another muttered.

So they thought her a stowaway. Better that than a spy. It would get her above deck sooner, which would make escape all the easier, as long as the boatswain didn't recognize her as one of the boys he'd recruited. Just better not to let these ruffians know she was a girl. Jie ran her hand through dust and grime and smeared her face.

She then stood and stepped into the light. Lowering her voice, she said, "I'm sorry. I'll give you all my money. A silver *yuan*. Just let me out."

The large man guarding the hatch favored her with a sneer, exposing a long incisor. "Normally we'd take it, brat. Unfortunately, all the gold in Sun-Moon Palace won't buy you out of this situation."

Since when did a sailor not take a bribe? And what did they have in mind? Jie's pulse might have ticked up a beat. Or not. Seven men with more brawn than brains shouldn't be too hard to escape.

A sailor with a scar on his cheek came up and cuffed her on the side of the head, sending flashes through her field of vision. The stubby fingers of another clamped her shoulder.

Jie froze, feigning fear.

"We got 'im." Snaggletooth rapped on the door above with a belaying pin.

The hatch above opened. Standing on the platform as it lowered were two men, one a sailor from the look of his clothes, and a man in robes.

Fat Nose.

Or at least that's what Tian called him. The short sword, which he'd kept hidden in the warehouse, now flashed in his hand. He pointed it at her. "You, boy, what are you doing here?"

Jie threw her hands up. "I ran away from home." Hopefully he wouldn't ask where home was, since Tian, in his usual laconic manner, hadn't bothered to say where the *Wild Orchid* had sailed from.

"What did you see?"

Jie stared at the floor, pretending to be ashamed. "I ain't see nothin'. Just some curry-lovin' brown folk." Right, she could always tell them she'd travelled with the Ankirans, though it wouldn't exactly explain why she'd stayed behind when they disembarked.

With a dismissive wave of his hand, Fat Nose sheathed the sword and turned back to the platform. "Just a stowaway. Not my problem."

"One with a high-pitched voice," Snaggletooth said. "You didn't even bother to check for weapons." He nodded toward a thick-necked sailor.

No Neck patted her down, pausing where no gentleman would. "A girl." His leer left a stain on her clothes. He continued down, stopping again when his hand found one of her three knives. "What is this?"

"A knife?" Jie flashed a guilty grin.

Scarface smacked her on the side of the head again. "You're in no position to make jokes."

Looking at Fat Nose, Snaggletooth harrumphed. "She's been in the hold for Heaven knows how long. A runaway, who might have seen too much. Nobody will miss her. Save yourself the risk. We'll gut her."

"Afterwards." Grinning, No Neck slapped Snaggletooth on the back. "Just like that brownie refugee girl whose little body we threw overboard."

Rapists and murderers! Jie's muscles clenched, ready to break free of Stubby Fingers' grip. Nine men to avoid on her way to the ropes leading out of the cargo hold, though perhaps Snaggletooth and No Neck deserved a knife between their ribs first.

"She's just a girl," Fat Nose said. "Let her go."

"Wait." Scarface held the lamp closer to her face and yanked off her headband.

Jie shot her hands up to cover her ears.

"An elf?" Fat Nose cocked his head.

"Half-elf," Scarface said. "The one we saw on Ayudra."

Stubby Fingers nodded. "Yep. That's her, all right."

"It wasn't me!" Jie shook her head. She'd never left Hua before. Though trying to convince them might prove difficult, since elves hardly ever left their secluded valley kingdom, nor mated with humans like a certain dastard of a father.

"Hah! You want us to believe you have an evil twin?" Snaggletooth looked at his companions, who took up his chorus of laughter.

Jie's fists squeezed tight. They had to be making this up.

"It makes sense now." Stubby Fingers nodded. "She must've stowed away when we docked at Ayudra."

Snaggletooth turned to Fat Nose. "Mister Jiang, no need to waste your time. We'll take care of her."

Jiang held up a finger. "I don't think—"

With a jerk of his hand, Snaggletooth pointed the belaying pin at Jiang. "Our ship, our rules. Now, you can watch if you want…"

Jie lowered her chin, loosening his grip. With one hand, she seized his wrist and twisted it;

with the other, she whipped her third knife out in an arc, slicing Stubby Finger's wrist tendons. His fingers went limp on her shoulder. Twirling toward the platform, she continued with a backslash through Snaggletooth's wrist.

He stood, staring at his lifeless fingers, his belaying pin forgotten in his other hand. Jie swept under that arm, dislocated the elbow over her shoulder, and caught the weapon as he dropped it. Finishing her spin, she stepped on the platform with the knife pointed at Fat Nose Jiang's flank.

Thank the Heavens. Without the element of surprise, she wouldn't have stood a chance. But now, gaffer hooks, belaying pins, and knives swept out from boots and belts. While Stubby Fingers and Snaggletooth held their wounds moaning, the six remaining sailors encircled the platform.

And exposing her weapon skills would now alert the conspirators that someone might be on to their plans. Time to find out as much as possible. Keeping eyes and ears on the sailors, Jie pressed the tip of the knife into Jiang's ribs. "Tell me, what are you trying to hide here?"

"Silly girl, nothing."

"By now, you've surmised I'm more than a stowaway. Talk." Jie pushed the point through his clothes and ran it over bare flesh.

Jiang yelped. "Okay. I am an inventor." He nodded toward some crates. "I have the prototype for a new repeating crossbow. I didn't want any of my competitors to know."

And Jie's father was a pig. Well, he probably was, but... "Why bother when we have muskets?"

"Muskets have limitations. If it rains. If you need to arc projectiles over your own men."

It was almost believable. Might as well play along; make them think this was all about industrial sabotage. "Then the rumors are true. Open one up and show me."

Jiang nodded toward Scarface. "Go show her one."

Holding his injured wrist, Snaggletooth jerked his head back and forth. "No, that bitch is going to pay!"

"What's going on here?" a voice called from above.

Jie dared a glance. A burly longshoreman stood at the hatch's opening, hands on his hips.

"Nothing," Jiang said. "We will load up soon."

"No!" Scarface leaned into the column of light from above. "We have an intruder!"

Apparently, the two men's agendas had just reached an impasse, and soon her escape route would be compromised. Stowing her knife, she took one step back and leapt toward Jiang. Pop-vaulting off his back, she snared one of the ropes and climbed hand over hand to the tween deck.

The longshoreman's eyes widened.

Jie flashed a grin and bolted through the other workers toward the steps to the upper deck.

"Stop her!" the longshoreman yelled.

One man spun around, too late, and Jie avoided his grasp. Yet two more now blocked her exit. Four came clopping down the steps, broadswords in hand. No easy way out.

Unless... The oar ports provided several not-so-easy way outs. Even if she could squeeze through, it was a long drop into cold water. The winches groaned behind her, likely meaning Jiang, Snaggletooth, and Stubby Fingers were on their way. Right; freezing sounded more appealing than being gang-raped and murdered. She took a sharp turn toward the closest row of benches and then dove toward the oar port.

For once, her flat boy's body proved useful, as she swished through—only to have the hem of her pants catch on the oarlock. She dangled upside down, the drawstring of her pants biting into her waist and hips. Perhaps it was for better, given the narrow rocking space between the hull and the stone dock. The wrong timing would mean being crushed like a cherry. As the gap started to widen, she took a deep breath, drew her knife, and slashed the drawstring.

Into the water she went, wearing nothing more than undergarments. The frigid water sent a chill to her core, almost stopping her heart. Still, she dove deeper, kicking off the dockside and swimming over toward the next berth. The ship's crew would be scouring the waterfront for her, and the longer she remained underwater, the more she could confuse them.

Her lungs burned. At last, she came to stone steps leading from the harbor floor to the top of a dock. She poked her head out and gasped for air, looking back in the direction she'd come. Sure enough, two berths down, the *Wild Orchid* was at full alert, with sailors running along its dock. It was time to lay low, lest the information about Wailian's illegal firepowder die with her.

She looked at the ship docked here, its dark shadow swallowing up the sun's warmth. The Tarkothi blackship. On deck, a fair-haired man with fine features eyed her. Her chattering teeth rattled her brain. The foreigners may or may not turn her in, but staying in the water meant death by hypothermia. Waving both arms, she floundered.

CHAPTER 9

Honor in Question

Metal tinkled and chimed as Kaiya's head bobbled in the darkness. Cold seeped into her back, yet warmth cradled her head. The uncomfortable twisting in her stomach seemed to climb higher, almost into her chest. The black in her field of vision faded to a dark orange.

Heat surged through her. Her eyes fluttered open. Above her, the blurry coffered tile ceiling came into focus as she blinked.

Luminous blue irises encroached into her field of vision. Prince Hardeep's tight lips softened into a smile, the air gushing out in a long sigh. "Thank the gods."

The warmth around her head...the way his face hovered above hers...she must be lying in his lap. Her belly twisted into tangles worse than her hair on a bad morning. Heavens, how embarrassing. And if someone saw them like this, Prince Hardeep might be executed on the spot. She brought her elbows up under her, trying to sit up.

"Slowly now." He placed a hot hand on her forehead.

She looked around. Still in the main chamber of the concert hall. Alone. With him. Her heart fluttered. "What happened?"

"You fainted."

Heat flared in her cheeks. Her body *would* choose such an inopportune moment to faint for the first time ever. How mortifying. "For how long?"

"Only a minute."

Thank the Heavens, there—

He pointed to Yanyan's pipa, lying on the marble floor just out of arm's reach.

"Oh no." Kaiya covered her gaping mouth. She'd dropped it. Dropped a priceless antique, a treasure of her people. She scuttled across the floor and picked it up. Fingers trembling, she ran her hand across the smooth surface of the back. Thank the Heavens, it seemed undamaged.

Hardeep shuffled over on his knees and eased it from her stiff fingers. "Don't worry. The legends claim it survived mighty Avarax's wrath. I doubt such a short drop would do anything to it."

Hopefully. Then again, she should've never touched it in the first place. Never been in this room in the first place. Never been alone with a man, a foreign man. If anyone found out, Father might marry her off to the most domineering lout of a lord in the realm, one who would make General Lu seem chivalric. No telling what he'd do to Hardeep. Perspiration threatened to seep through the make-up on her forehead.

Setting the pipa on the chair, he clasped her hand. "It's fine. Trust me." His other hand reached behind her neck, and he leaned in.

Heat surged through her. Heavens, he was close. And it felt so right. His eyes were so kind. And he knew music. Of course he was right. The pipa was fine, and as long as nobody walked in—

"Unhand the princess!" Chen Xin shouted from the door.

Heavens, no! The compromising position would give rise to rumors faster than weeds sprouting after a spring rain. Kaiya glanced over Hardeep's shoulder. Outside the door, the Appointments Ministry secretary looked as if he would faint. Chen Xin and Zhao Yue pushed past him and charged in, blue robes swishing and curved *dao* swords rasping from their scabbards in deadly arcs. The dragons etched into their burnished breastplates appeared to move with a life of their own—their magic, imbued by master craftsmen, would strike poor Prince Hardeep with shock and awe. Even if he had a weapon, he wouldn't stand a chance against that magic, let alone against two of the best swordsmen in the realm.

She had to save him. Pulling his hands for leverage, she staggered to her feet and moved to interpose herself between the deadly blades and her prince.

He resisted her pull. His single footstep blocked her path and spun her around. So clumsy on his part; the guards would certainly slay him on the spot. With her feet crossed and legs still wobbly, it took all her balance to keep from falling.

The imperial guards closed the gap in the blink of an eye, weapons flashing in a synchronous dance of death. Hardeep released her hand and leaped forward into the storm of blades. Kaiya could only stare in horror.

Or amazement.

If he were a poet, his graceful movement would have been his poetry. He dodged Chen Xin's thrust and ducked Zhao Yue's hack, twirling and spinning like a ribbon dancer. In a split second, he had positioned himself so that Chen Xin stood between him and Zhao Yue.

At that moment, he turned his head and winked at her. His blue eyes glittered. Could he be possibly enjoying himself? When one misstep would mean decapitation? Her chest constricted, seizing her breath.

Chen Xin attacked with a horizontal slash, shredding through Hardeep's sleeve and cutting across his arm. No! Kaiya covered her mouth. Chen Xin followed with a downward chop, but Hardeep stepped inside and caught Chen Xin's hands. With a deft twist, he wrenched the *dao* away. Undaunted,

Chen Xin drew a dagger while Zhao Yue slipped between them.

"Stop!" Kaiya shook off the dread fascination. If she didn't do something, someone would get seriously hurt. And unbelievably, from the look of it, it wouldn't be Prince Hardeep. He had taken on not one, but two imperial guards and suffered only a cut. His shorn sleeve didn't even show sign of blood. She spoke again, invoking a tone of authority practiced since childhood. "Chen Xin, Zhao Yue, disengage. That is my command."

Zhao Yue held his sword in a defensive position as he took two steps back.

Lowering his dagger, Chen Xin cast a sidelong glance at her. "*Dian-xia*, are you all right? This man did not try anything inappropriate?"

Heat rose to Kaiya's cheeks. They had done many inappropriate things that afternoon, though probably not along the lines of Chen Xin's question. She shook her head. "No, Prince Hardeep has been a perfect gentleman. He just asked me to play a piece of music for him." Straightening her carriage, she strode over to the prince and held up his wounded arm. "Are you all right?"

Lines formed across his forehead as he looked first at it, then at her. "Yes. It looks like my shirt is the only casualty."

Kaiya parted the tear. No blood at all on the smooth skin over his toned muscle. She dropped his arm and covered her gawp with a hand. "How?"

Prince Hardeep smiled at her, sending her stomach into somersaults, then turned to her guards. With a bow of his head, he presented Chen Xin's *dao* in two hands.

Lips pursed, Chen Xin retrieved his weapon, his eyes locked on the alterations he'd made to Hardeep's sleeve. He sank to his knee and bowed his head. "*Dian-xia*, we have failed you. If it is your command, we will take our lives."

Zhao Yue followed suit, raising his sword above his head.

Such resolve and undeserved dedication! Kaiya shook her head. "This is just a misunderstanding. Wait at the door."

Bowing their heads, they said in unison, "As the princess commands."

Legs shaking, Kaiya scooped up the pipa and traipsed across the floor with Hardeep just a step behind. Hopefully, the guards would not object to her being alone in the storage room with him.

She returned the pipa to its honored place and turned to face him. "I have watched the imperial guards spar, and never before has anyone else come close to defeating even one of them. You fight faster than anyone I have ever seen. How did you do that?"

"Princess Kaiya, your imperial guards might be the most skilled swordsmen in Cathay, but—" He stared out the door into space "—there is a whole world beyond your Great Wall. Wonders beyond your imagination."

And the promise of a world beyond marriage to a suitable lord. And such an elusive answer. "Are you saying there are others who can fight like you?"

"I am embarrassed to say..." He shifted his gaze to the floor.

"Please."

Eyes still cast downward, he sucked in a voluminous breath. "Well... I started training as a Paladin."

Prince Hardeep was full of surprises. Kaiya fought to keep her jaw from freefalling to the ground. The Order of Paladins, defenders of the Ayuri South, sought out children who showed potential to manifest magic through their fighting arts. Their martial skill bordered on legendary, but to hear about it secondhand paled compared to witnessing it just now. It was like living in the song which recounted the First Paladin, Vanya, dueling with the Orc King.

And supposedly, Paladins could plant suggestions into people's minds. Had he done that to her guards?

Had he done that to her?

Maybe all these feelings were the result of his powers. A pit threatened to form in her gut. No, he had only... "Started?"

He sighed. "Yes. Unfortunately, Madura's aggression cut my studies short. I had to return to Ankira, to lead the defense of my homeland." His eyes searched hers. "I failed Ankira then, just like now, when I could not convince your people to end their trade agreement with Madura."

It couldn't end this way. Kaiya shook her head. Such a selfless, noble man couldn't go home unsuccessful. Not if she had means of rectifying Hua's misdeeds and helping his suffering people It seemed all the more possible now that she had tapped into the magic of music.

Her hand strayed to Tian's pebble. If a Dragon Song was the only way to convince Father and the lords to do the right thing, so be it. "I will do my best to help you. I will practice more."

A sad smile formed on his face. He pressed his palms together and bowed. "I thank you. Ankira thanks you." He raised his head and his expression brightened. "I have an idea, one that your father might approve of. I want to show you something."

"What?" Kaiya squeezed her sweaty palms together.

"The fabled Dragon Scale Lute. It can supposedly rout an army."

She gasped. A handful of musical instruments appeared in ancient tales, and Yanyan's pipa was the only one known to have survived. She'd never even heard of the Dragon Scale Lute. "How did you—"

"Can you meet me outside the palace tonight? At the first waxing gibbous."

Her heart lurched. She would need a good excuse to convince the Minister of Household Affairs to let her leave at night. Especially with the reception, and the announcement of her betrothal. And once the scholars, steward, secretary, or imperial guards reported her day's highly irregular activities, perhaps General Lu would reject her. Not a bad prospect in itself, but then she might not be let out of the palace until her hair faded to grey.

With a grin, he brought his fingers to her chin and closed her gaping mouth. "Young Lord Peng has Ankira's best interests at heart. I will ask him to arrange something."

She could only nod in a slow bob of her head. Cousin Kai-Long might be Father's favorite nephew, but even he couldn't convince the *Tianzi* to leave her unpunished...let alone to allow her out of the palace to meet a man. A foreign man. Not with her virtue at stake before an important marriage.

He pointed to the book, forgotten near the chair back in the room. "Please keep practicing your music. I hope to hear you again. Maybe as soon as tonight."

Back in the main hall, several booted feet clickety-clacked across the marble floors in rhythmic clops. Kaiya peeked out from behind the corner. At the entrance, the steward, secretary, and her own imperial guards bowed as two dozen imperial guards marched past them in formation. The Minister of Appointments himself shuffled at their head. A small man in both stature and attitude, Minister Hu was arrogant if nothing else. If his smirk was any indication, the consequences of the day's adventures would not be pleasant. Her stomach churned.

A warm hand grasped her shoulder and pulled her around. Prince Hardeep grinned. "Wait here while I talk to them."

She shook her head. They might not care what a sixteen-year-old girl, princess or not, would say, but she could influence them far better than a foreigner could.

The minister pushed past and walked into the hall. He jabbed a finger at the prince. "There he is!"

The imperial guards surged past the minster and surrounded him.

Prince Hardeep held his hands up, still smiling. "This is my fault. I took advantage of your princess' naïveté."

Naïveté! Kaiya's stomach twisted into a knot. Had all his charm just been an act?

He turned back and winked at her, sending her pulse into a flutter.

Then, the imperial guards grabbed him and thrust him to the ground. If they suspected he'd done anything inappropriate, they'd take his head.

CHAPTER 10
Interventions

Kaiya's silk shoes scuffed on the Hall of Pure Melody's marble steps as she hurried down. The imperial guards' and Household Ministry secretary's robes swished behind her. In the vast central plaza formed by the Hall of Supreme Harmony, the imperial archives, and the Hall of Pure Melody, a contingent of imperial guards surrounded Prince Hardeep.

All weapons remained sheathed, thank the Heavens. The prince might have survived two of the realm's best swordsmen with only a shorn sleeve, but two dozen was another matter. For now, his hands rested on his head in surrender.

Her insides squeezed like a grape in an Arkothi wine press. All her fault. She should've never taken him into the music hall or archives, or at least gone through the proper channels. Really, she should've just seen him off and then gone to meet General Lu, but Prince Hardeep was so, so...confusing.

General Lu was still waiting now, probably wondering if the orc gods would return to Tivara on their flaming chariots before she deigned to greet him. If it were up to her...

Appointments Minister Hu furiously scribbled on a scroll. When he looked up, he spoke in Hua. "Prince Hardeep, the *Tianzi* generously allowed you to visit the castle and even dispatched a member of his family to meet with you. You repay his magnanimity by kidnapping his young daughter and spiriting her from building to building."

Kidnapping! How did he come to that conclusion? Kaiya's heart pounded. Expulsion from the palace, perhaps deportation might be more appropriate for what actually happened, but the minister's charges warranted a slow death. Just what had all the scholars and other officials said?

The minister scrutinized her and her entourage before settling on the Household Ministry secretary. "And, Secretary Hong overheard you. You wanted the princess to meet you outside the palace? What did you plan to do? Defile her? Use her as a hostage to secure Hua's support against Madura?"

Hardeep only smiled. He probably didn't understand the Hua tongue, let alone the serious accusations and grave consequences. He turned and winked at her again.

Her chest tightened. This ill-advised escapade would never have happened if she hadn't allowed it. She was just as much at fault as he, perhaps even more so for her lack of judgment. Kaiya pushed through the imperial guards, who stepped to the side and dropped to a knee, fist to the ground, as she passed.

"Minister," she said.

He bowed at the waist. "*Dian-xia*. I am glad to see you unharmed. Please tell us what else this rogue did."

She scowled at the minister. "Prince Hardeep did nothing wrong. *I* chose to take him to the imperial archives and Hall of Pure Melody."

The minister sidled in and whispered, "*Dian-xia*, you do not understand. If rumor gets out that you were with the prince alone, it will besmirch your honor and affect your marriage prospects."

"If only it were so easy." Heavens, did she just think that, or say it aloud? Face flushing, she swept her gaze around all the assembled men, making sure all witnesses to her misadventures were now there: the imperial guards, Secretary Hong, Minister Hu, the scholars, and the steward. She raised her voice so all could hear. "Prince Hardeep only wished to save his homeland. I wanted to help him. He did nothing wrong. Any breeches of protocol were *my* choice."

"If I may, *Dian-xia*," called a male voice from beyond the cordon of men. The guards stepped aside to reveal Cousin Kai-Long. He folded a piece of paper as he approached.

Kaiya blew out a breath. If he and Prince Hardeep were good friends, he would surely use his considerable influence to prevent any possible misunderstanding. Kai-Long might only be a second son with little hope of inheriting his father's title of *Tai-Ming* provincial ruler, but all knew the *Tianzi* treated him like his own son.

Minister Hu bowed low, though not as low as he had to her. "Young Lord Peng Kai-Long, this matter does not concern you."

"But it does," Cousin Kai-Long said with an amiable smile. "I am ultimately responsible for Prince Hardeep's presence. It was I who brought him to Huajing, housed him in my family villa, and arranged for his visit to the castle. I even suggested to the *Tianzi* that Princess Kaiya meet him, as a test of her budding diplomatic skills."

Kaiya gaped at him. It had seemed strange that she was the one to greet the Ankirans, and now it was clear. Still, he deflected blame from both her and the prince.

The minister's slit eyes fell first on Hardeep, then on Cousin Kai-Long, and finally on her. "The evidence—"

"Wait." Prince Hardeep stomped a foot on the pavestones as he raised a hand.

Something fluttered in her belly. All heads turned to him. He rotated in a full circle as he spoke, his voice calm. "This is all a misunderstanding. I certainly did not do anything inappropriate with the princess. This is really just a trivial matter."

And he was right. So what if they had visited the archives and music hall? They hadn't damaged anything. Kaiya looked at the men, many who likely didn't speak Ayuri. They might not be convinced, but Minister Hu's expression softened.

He must have realized that with Cousin Kai-Long and her both vouching for the prince, very little would come of it. With a sigh, he said, "Young Lord Peng, I place Prince Hardeep in your care. Please see him out of the palace."

That was it? If Kaiya's mouth could hang any lower, her chin would touch the ground. Surely, somebody would be punished somehow. But Prince Hardeep allowed to just leave? A great resolution, for sure, but a complete surprise.

Something felt off. A resonance hung in the air, an echo from when Hardeep had stomped on the pavestones. Paladins could supposedly persuade others with their righteous magic.

Was Hardeep more than a trainee? It might explain how he'd calmed all those aggressive guards and unreasonable ministers. She, herself, had gone from worried to relaxed.

Her jaw tightened as the guards dispersed. Maybe he'd used magic on her. And not only then, but from the time they'd first met. Had he influenced her decisions?

No, he hadn't finished his Paladin training. He'd asked her to consider the plight of his people, but had not ordered her to do anything. The decision to help the Ankirans was her own. If anything, he'd shown that her unspoken, impossible dreams of rediscovering Dragon Songs were within reach.

"Follow me, Your Excellency." Ayuri rolled off Kai-Long's tongue.

Prince Hardeep flashed a smile at her.

Her heart sank into her stomach. She bowed her head a fraction, as protocol demanded. Maybe the resolution wasn't so great, after all.

After the day's debacle, she wouldn't be allowed to see him ever again. Ankira would fall without her ever having a chance to help it. She was nothing more than a plain, gangly girl, to be strategically married off. Never allowed to explore the power of Dragon Songs, even after her breakthrough.

She studied his back, hair, and gait as he and Kai-Long started toward the main gates. Her last memory of him.

Then he turned his head, his luminescent blue eyes fixed her. Her pulse pounded again, just like when she first met him.

Tonight, he mouthed. *At the first waxing gibbous.*

Tonight?

Secretary Hong, that was his name, cleared his throat. "*Dian-xia*, General Lu is waiting."

Kaiya looked back at Hardeep's diminishing form. Tonight... There would be no tonight, at least not with him. He wouldn't be let back in the palace, and there was no way for her to get out. Even if she could grow in her knowledge of Dragon Songs, Father would never let her go to Ankira. Not to mention, there was her own country's stability to consider.

Whatever Hardeep had done to addle her good judgment...well, it had been a fleeting diversion. A three-hour diversion, gauging from the Iridescent Moon's waning toward new. Her future husband, Hua's savior, waited. Her lip jutted out, unbidden. If only it could be Hardeep.

Hiking her gown up and holding her hair in place, Kaiya strode back toward the inner castle. Secretary Hong and her two guards rushed to keep up with her. The faster she could put distance between herself and Hardeep, the sooner she could forget him and accept her fate.

If only it were so simple.

Though abated, the squirming sensation in her belly was a constant reminder of the power and bliss she'd felt while playing Yanyan's pipa. With each step away from Hardeep, the chasm widened between her and *possibility*.

The possibility of being more than just a skinny, pimply political tool. Of being something special. She blinked and found herself at the inner moat. Behind her, Secretary Hong hunched over, hands on his knees, panting. Unlike him, her imperial guards Chen Xin and Zhao Yue managed to maintain a dignified demeanor and appearance.

In the middle of the arching stone bridge, she stopped and found her reflection in the dark water. Heavens, her hair appeared as if a family of songbirds had nested there, and perhaps rearranged her clips and pins as well. The gown, originally folded at an exact angle, now hung awkwardly over her shoulder. She must have looked ridiculous to Hardeep, who inexplicably thought there was even a remote chance she could escape the palace tonight.

"Hurry, Kaiya." With the slightest hint of a frown, Sister-In-Law Xiulan beckoned from the other side of the bridge. "General Lu has been waiting."

Kaiya's paternal cousin Wang Kai-Hua nodded from where she stood beside Xiulan. Several handmaidens bowed in a flash of colorful robes. One of them, Han Meiling, gawked, with wide eyes focused on Kaiya's head.

Kaiya's hand shot up to her disheveled hair. With a sigh, she descended the bridge. Her imperial guards stopped and dropped to a knee, fist to the ground.

"*Dian-xia*, you cannot meet General Lu looking like this." Meiling shuffled over and adjusted Kaiya's hair.

With a deft hand, Xiulan rewrapped Kaiya's sash. "You look like you wrestled a dragon."

"I hope you won." Kai-Hua tugged on Kaiya's sleeves. Though only a year older, she had already flowered with Heaven's Dew and filled out. She now glowed with radiance since her own betrothal to Liu Dezhen, heir to Jiangzhou Province.

Kaiya clenched her clammy hands. Neither Kai-Hua nor Xiulan were malicious, yet neither understood the stress of being sixteen and not yet flowered into womanhood, nor her lack of interest in marriage.

Xiulan stepped back. "General Lu has been waiting anxiously to hear you sing."

Given the general's reputation, he probably cared more about the sound of his own voice. At least today she had been able to sing for someone who *did* care.

"You are so fortunate," Kai-Hua said. "General Lu would make a wonderful husband. So dashing and handsome! With his experience and intelligence, he might rise to head of the Ministry of War."

A path to glory blazed with the dying heart of an imperial princess. Kaiya suppressed a snort. "I am not ready to marry."

Both Xiulan and Kai-Hua stared at her with round eyes. Xiulan said, "You will have to, sooner than later."

Kai-Hua nodded. "Yes, all the girls we grew up with are reaching that age. You know what they say: a woman unwed by sixteen is like a New Year's feast on the third day of the year."

As if a woman were meant to be devoured. Kaiya shuddered. In any case, being all skin and bones, she was more like a nun's rice porridge and tofu than a New Year's feast.

Leaning in, Xiulan said, "I met Kai-Wu's betrothed, Wu Yanli. She is quite...strict and reserved."

Kaiya cocked her head. That didn't seem to fit all the rumors. Second Brother's upcoming wedding hadn't been arranged, at least not in the formal sense. It had been a supposedly chance meeting, followed by a torrid love affair. The handmaidens whispered that the second prince had already partaken of *that* New Year's Feast.

And yet, in affairs of the heart, the *Tianzi* wouldn't extend any leeway to his only daughter. Kaiya stifled a sigh. Prince Hardeep, learning the magic of Dragon Songs: they might as well have been a storyteller's fanciful tale.

"Come along," Xiulan said. "You have made General Lu wait long enough."

Kaiya lifted her chin and squared her shoulders, only for her posture to slump. All the energy she'd put into projecting an imperial image this morning now flagged. Instability in the North had turned a match she'd planned to reject into a *fait accompli*. What she really wanted, Hardeep—no,

reviving Dragon Songs—now lay beyond reach. Each step through the inner castle grounds felt like slogging through knee-high mud toward a funeral.

So unlike Kai-Hua, whose graceful stride might have been skipping for all the effervescence she exuded. So different from Xiulan, the personification of dignity and elegance. Even the handmaidens would make better princesses.

A hand grasped her sleeve, pulling her to a stop. Xiulan nodded toward a gatehouse at the side. "General Lu is in Murder Gap."

How appropriate. A hypothetical invader would believe this the most direct route to the inner castle's gates, only to find themselves trapped in a dead-end courtyard surrounded by high walls. Now, it would be the site of her own proverbial death. But, "Why is General Lu here? I thought we were to meet in the *Danhua* Garden."

Xiulan covered a giggle. "While you were gallivanting about the palace, he took to wandering the castle grounds."

With all her willpower, Kaiya straightened her carriage. She strode through the gatehouse and then down the wide alley. At the hairpin turn, she paused and peeked into the courtyard.

A handsome man in formal court robes sat on a porcelain garden stool next to a bloodwood table. He appeared older than Hardeep, maybe in his early thirties. Long, glossy black hair framed an oval face with the chiseled jaw and high nose of North Hua. He reached for a teacup on the table, the very motion refined, almost effeminate. An unarmed soldier standing a respectful distance behind him wore blue robes, marking him as an officer in the imperial army.

Xiulan gave Kaiya a firm prod. With no time to prepare herself, she stumbled into the courtyard.

The officer knelt, fist to the ground. General Lu barely rose before sinking to his knee. "*Dian-xia*, thank you for honoring me." His voice echoed off the high courtyard walls.

"Rise," Xiulan said, her voice resonating.

He stood...and barely met Kaiya's eye level.

So short! She bowed her head. "I am sorry to have kept you waiting." Her own words resounded off the walls.

When his mouth opened, he spoke in a high pitch reminiscent of bird chirps. "Your grace and beauty made the wait worthwhile." His contrived smile and rote intonation suggested otherwise. If his insincerity didn't give her a headache, the persistent echo would. He motioned to the garden stool across from him, inviting her to sit.

With as much grace as she could muster under the circumstances, Kaiya shuffled over and settled on the edge of the stool. General Lu sat across from her, and Xiulan and Kai-Hua sat to the side. The handmaidens and imperial guards deployed in positions around them.

Meiling took up the kettle and poured tea.

"Thank you, General," Xiulan said, "for leaving the unsettled North just to meet Princess Kaiya."

He chuckled. "We inflicted heavy casualties on the pale-faced barbarians the last time. I do not think they will be returning soon."

"Pale-faced?" Kaiya ventured. "Don't they stay on their own side of the Great Wall?"

The officer harrumphed, but General Lu silenced him with a wave of his hand. "I am posted in Wailian County, outside of the wall."

That wasn't possible. Surely, Father wouldn't approve of establishing colonies in foreign lands. Kaiya turned to Xiulan, who nodded, then back to General Lu. "What can you tell me of Wailian?"

He laughed. "Had I known we would be discussing the North, I would have come better prepared."

"My apologies for Princess Kaiya." Xiulan bowed her head a fraction.

General Lu waved a hand, the same motion he had used to silence his own underling. "No need to apologize. The Five Classics say a ruler should know the land, and I would be happy to explain."

Heat flared in Kaiya's cheeks. Not like she would be anything more than a political tool, let alone a ruler. No doubt he was thinking of himself.

"We annexed Wailian County nearly a year ago," General Lu continued, "when we discovered abundant reserves of an essential firepowder ingredient. We could not let it fall into barbarian hands. Lord Tong has been building a castle overlooking the mines. A ravine surrounds the castle on three sides, and a sheer cliff drops away on the other side. It is impregnable."

Kaiya's head spun. Hua had invaded a neighbor, just as the Madurans had attacked Prince Hardeep's Ankira. Though, given the circumstances, it seemed this Lord Tong would be a more appropriate husband than General Lu. She bowed her head. "Thank you for your report."

He laughed again, living up to his reputation for arrogance. "Do not worry, *Dian-xia*. With our guns, Wailian is well-defended."

Kaiya's insides twisted. A lifetime with such a conceited little man, in occupied territory, might be worse than death. If only Avarax could swoop in from the Dragonlands and immolate the courtyard now.

"That's enough politics for the day," Xiulan said. "Princess Kaiya wished to sing for you."

Wished, indeed. As if General Lu even cared; he just played along. Kaiya's face must have flushed redder than Yanluo's Star, if her hot cheeks were any indication. Yet what choice did she have? She turned to Meiling. "My pipa, please."

Bowing, Meiling presented the instrument in two hands.

"Thank you." Kaiya extended both arms to receive it. How lifeless it felt compared to Yanyan's. She tilted her head toward General Lu. "If I may?"

"Please." He bowed his head, but not before revealing the tight lips and glassy eyes of boredom.

Sadness clamped her chest. He would never appreciate her beyond the prestige of her lineage. She took a deep breath and plucked.

The sound resonated off the high courtyard walls, sending subtle vibrations into her core. Her stomach coiled again, just like it had in the Hall of Pure Melody when she had played for Hardeep. How had she never noticed the sensation before?

Back straight, shoulders level, feet rooted to the ground, just as Prince Hardeep had suggested. Ah, Prince Hardeep. He was handsome and charming, for sure, but pining over him seemed silly. It must have been those beautiful, hypnotic eyes, convincing her of a happier future than the one for which she was destined. It must have been how the cobra felt when sung to by an Ayuri snake-charmer. How preposterous to consider such an impossibility.

Closing her eyes, Kaiya plucked out more notes. The book from the Hall of Pure Melody suggested that a skilled performer could project the emotion of a song. Yet for all the happiness this piece embodied, only melancholy trudged in the verses she played. *Align your spine*, the book implored. *Let your heart impel your voice.* Kaiya adjusted her posture, and the vibrations spread throughout her.

There it was, the ocean of power from before, dripping in small drops, the rhythm setting the beat of her music. The song seemed to change of its own accord, and Kaiya's brain somersaulted in her skull. Her vision darkened.

Gasps sheared the air. Robes shuffled. Porcelain shattered on the flagstones.

Lifting her hand from the strings, Kaiya opened her eyes. Though she'd stopped playing, the music trailed off in the echoes.

Tears streaked Xiulan's cheeks, while Kai-Hua and some of the handmaidens freely wept. General Lu...

He gawked at her. With sadness or anger, it was impossible to tell. Bolting up, he spun on his heel and stumbled out of the courtyard. His officer trailed after him, while Chen Xin and Zhao Yue looked on with what could only be described as bewilderment.

A cloaked figure materialized out of nothingness, just on the other side of her guards. The pipa slipped from Kaiya's startled hands and hit the pavestones with a discordant groan. Shaking their heads, Chen Xin and Zhao Yue both swept *dao* swords from their scabbards and backed into a defensive position.

Chen Xin pointed the tip of his weapon at the stranger. "Identify yourself."

The man strode forward. His hands made no move toward the thin longsword hanging at his side.

The guards sprang into action, attacking in a synchronized flash of blades that would have eviscerated even a highly skilled warrior. Yet the intruder blurred through the deadly barrage and arrived on the other side unscathed. Without looking back, he waved a hand at the guards, sending both tumbling to the flagstones.

Interposing herself between Xiulan and the intruder, Kaiya fumbled for the curved dagger tucked in her sash. Not that she stood a chance against someone who could effortlessly defeat two of the realm's best swordsmen. Her chest squeezed around her pounding heart.

CHAPTER 11
Ships and Sailors

Hua's magnificent sailing ships might have been dinghies compared to the enormous Tarkothi ship Jie found herself on. She huddled under the rough-spun blankets, shivering after her inadvertent swim in Jiangkou's frigid harbor. Even the midday sun on the black wood deck couldn't provide enough heat. No telling how hard Tian would be laughing if he could see her quivering like a maiden on her wedding night.

The only ones looking at her now were the curious faces of light-skinned sailors, likely Arkothi and Estomari from Tivaralan's east. Some had a darker complexion than the majority, with shorter heights and slimmer builds. Eldaeri humans, the first she'd ever seen. They had traces of elf blood coursing through their veins from millennia before, and perhaps that's why they'd helped her.

Even now, her pointed ears picked up the commotion along the docks. Fat Nose Jiang's henchmen were searching for her, unless the chorus of shouts about a half-naked half-elf girl referred to someone else. Sure, she was safe from them, but minutes slipped by without the clan knowing about the illegal firepowder production and shipments.

A fair-haired man strode over. His broad shoulders and robust frame nearly split the seams of his green uniform coat. She might have been a bug, the way he scowled at her with those snake eyes. With a sneer, he knelt down and thrust forth a mug of a steaming, aromatic tea, which looked and smelled nothing like tea.

"Thank you," Jie said in her best Arkothi. She jutted a hand from underneath the blanket and took it. The cup felt warm, yet did little to chase away the chill from her bones. She took a sip, and nearly spit it out.

Snake Eyes chortled. "First time drinking coffee? You Cathayi don't know what you're missing." He leaned forward, his face taking in her features. "But you're not all Cathayi. A curious girl, really. I would wager you are the reason for all the excitement down there?"

Apparently, no one onboard could speak the Hua language, or perhaps they were testing her. She tightened the blanket around her. Sometimes, half-truths worked better than outright lies. "I was hired to clean up their ship, but then the sailors tried to...tried to..." Blinking away crocodile tears, she cast her eyes at the ground, but peeked up through her lashes to see if her best imitation of a traumatized girl had worked.

"A ship is no place for a girl, save for the Pirate Queen herself," a male voice said, the perfect Arkothi enunciated with a tone that bordered on singing.

Jie turned to find the speaker. A slim man with large dark eyes and a high-bridged nose approached, with a marine to either side. The high collar of his own green coat was embroidered in gold. A captain, perhaps, from the way the men bowed, though no sailor spoke so properly. Not only that, a gold circlet adorned his dark hair.

She bowed her head. "An orphan takes what job she can."

"Ah, poor girl." Kneeling down, he lifted her chin and studied her. "A half-elf. There are so few of you in this world, always the result of sad circumstances."

Sad, for sure, but perhaps not what this man thought. At least, not according to the note pinned to her swaddling blanket when she was left at the gates of the Black Lotus Temple. Still, let him believe what he would, if it would help her cause. She nodded.

"What's your name, girl?"

"Jie."

"Jyeh." The man chewed on the sound. His Arkothi might be impeccable, but apparently, his tongue couldn't process Hua. "Well, your Arkothi is not bad. Perhaps I can offer you work during our stay?"

Snake Eyes cleared his throat. "Your Highness, we shouldn't be harboring strangers. For all we know, she's a wanted criminal. Let's hand her over to the men looking for her."

Highness. He must be a prince of Tarkoth. The prince held up a hand, silencing Snake Eyes. "So what do you say about that job?"

She cocked her head. "What kind of job?"

"I need guidance, and I assume you know the waterfront."

More than he could imagine. She nodded.

"The emperor of Cathay will assign me guides and a translator." He grinned. "Since these officials aren't always reliable, I would prefer to have one of my own. We'll pay you a silver crown a day."

With a furrowed forehead, Jie calculated the exchange rate. A silver *jiao* and two copper *fen*. Tian would have known automatically, probably to a fraction of a *fen*.

The prince's lips curved into a crooked grin. "What? No shouts of joy?"

Jie shook her head. "No, it's just that...well... I need to confer with my friends."

"The same ones who got you a job swabbing the deck of a Cathayi trade ship?" The prince stared at the sky.

Jie cast him a sheepish smile. She had to report to the relay station, but it wouldn't take much to slip away if this new job description interfered with her real work. "You are right. I accept."

Snake Eyes cleared his throat. "Your Highness, we know nothing about her. There are men searching for her."

Jie's breath stilled. She looked from the officer to the leader. As long as they turned her over to the authorities, and not the traitors from the ship...

He laughed. "It's not like she could be a spy. Now, tell the quartermaster to check if we have any dresses in our cargo." He spun on his heel and headed toward the forecastle.

Jie turned to Snake Eyes. "Who was that?"

"Prince Aryn of Tarkoth." The rude officer's incredulous tone almost made her feel stupid.

"Why would a prince come all the way to Cathay?"

Snake Eyes snorted. "He will be attending the wedding of your emperor's second son."

The same reason Master Yan himself was three hours away in the capital. It would also explain why a Tarkothi ship had come all the way to the west coast. Now if only she could get off it and share information about the firepowder with Tian.

CHAPTER 12
Challenges

With the reverberation of the pipa and the clattering of metal on the flagstones still echoing, Kaiya pointed her dagger at the intruder. As if that would deter someone who had just dispatched two imperial guards with even more ease than Prince Hardeep had.

Her pulse pattered like spring rain on the tiled roofs of Sun-Moon Palace. She swallowed the fear and found her tone of command. "Stand back."

The stranger lowered his dark hood, revealing the pointed ears of an elf. Relief washed over her. Lord Xu, her father's aloof councilor.

Though he shared his rarely seen brethren's slight build and delicate features, he stood as tall as a human did. He let his long golden hair flow freely, caring little about fashion trends that might come and go; he'd undoubtedly seen many in his centuries of life. His violet eyes sparkled with mischief. That, and his youthful appearance belied unknown years of wisdom. Now, as he scrutinized her, he looked just as startled as everyone else.

Behind her, Xiulan and Kai-Hua blew out long sighs.

Kaiya crossed her arms, frowning. "Lord Xu. You have a flair for the dramatic. Was that necessary?"

The elf didn't bother to bow. Her ancestor had decreed that Lord Xu need pay obeisance to no one, not even the *Tianzi* himself. His surprised expression disappeared. "I need to keep my skills sharp. Little around here is more challenging than approaching a princess protected by imperial guards." He looked back and grinned at Chen Xin and Zhao Yue, who staggered to their feet. "Though I guess they hardly constitute a challenge."

Both soldiers dropped to one knee, head bowed. Chen Xin held his sword up in two hands. "*Dian-xia*, forgive our incompetence. If you command it, we will take our own lives as punishment."

Xiulan waved them off. "There is no shame in being bested by the councilor. As you were." She turned back to the elf. "To what do we owe this unexpected visit, Lord Xu?"

He pointed to the pipa, lying forgotten on the ground. "Twice today, the energy of the world has rippled out from Sun-Moon Palace."

Kaiya searched the elf's unreadable eyes. Twice? The first was with Yanyan's pipa, which meant the second was just now. With General Lu. Perhaps that was why he had left so abruptly. Excitement tingled in every nerve.

His stare fixed on Kaiya. "You have finally made a breakthrough in your music."

Kaiya's eyebrows rose. Finally? And where had he been hiding? "You heard it?"

The elf's gaze bore into her, ripping away any mental armor she might have. "*Felt* it. We taught the Hua people to manifest magic through artistic endeavor, but the ability to do so with music—Dragon Songs—was lost. Great masters disappeared one by one, after your great-great-grandfather bade them to play Yanyan's pipa. Yet without a teacher, you have intuitively figured out the basics."

Maybe not so intuitively, but Xu didn't have to know about Hardeep. Heat rose to her cheeks.

He placed a hand over his chest. "You have learned to project emotions through your music, though you require an acoustically ideal location like the Hall of Pure Melody. Or this courtyard. However, before you learn to project energy through music, you should learn to listen. Close your eyes. What do you hear?"

Kaiya exchanged confused glances with Xiulan and Kai-Hua, and then listened. The sounds of spring mixed with the rippling of Sun-Moon Lake in the distance. "Waves, wind, and birds."

Xu snorted. "How about your guards' breaths? The beating of your handmaidens' hearts?"

Kaiya gawked. That was impossible, even for her exceptional hearing. Maybe the elf could, with his big ears, but it was too much to expect from a human.

To a collective gasp, the pipa materialized in his hands, looking none worse for the wear after its fall to the pavestones. He proffered it. "Close your eyes and listen."

She received it in two hands and closed her eyes. As if holding a pipa would make difference… But wait, there was Zhao Yue's inhale, barely a whisper over the other sounds. She straightened her spine. Chen Xin's exhale, vibrated in one of the strings. The handmaidens' heartbeats were soft puffs in her ear, yet they, too resonated almost inaudibly in the pipa strings. She looked up at Xu.

"You understand. You hear. Listening is your greatest asset." Ears twitching, he lifted a finger. "What do you hear now?"

Around her, Xiulan and the handmaidens quieted. Kaiya closed her eyes again. There. In the distance. The twang of a plucked instrument and whine of a bow on strings danced with one another.

She opened her eyes. "A pipa and erhu."

"Follow it to its source."

Xiulan nodded. "You go ahead. Kai-Hua and I will look for General Lu."

Kaiya favored Lord Xu with a tentative smile. Even with permission from Xiulan, it seemed inappropriate to wander the castle grounds with an elf. But why not? She'd done worse this day, and nobody would suspect Lord Xu of having any attraction to humans. General Lu had cut their matchmaking meeting short, leaving plenty of time before tonight's reception, where Father would likely *not* announce her betrothal. It wasn't as if she could get in that much more trouble.

It was worth the risk, for the improbable chance to grow in the power of Dragon Songs. With a bow, Kaiya left the courtyard and ambled through the paved alley until it came to a white rock path. She listened as it wound through a garden in the inner castle. Somewhere beyond the budding plum trees, master musicians sparred in an improvised duel between pipa and the two-stringed erhu.

Her imperial guards marched behind her, crunching the stones beneath their boots, synchronizing with the beat of the song in the background. The handmaidens followed with the shuffle of robes. Though the Spring Festival was just a few days away, winter maintained a tenuous grip on the breeze. She tightened the outer gown around her shoulders.

And discovered Lord Xu had not followed.

Her footsteps fell short at the edge of the *Danhua* Garden. Before her, the mottled trunk of a weeping *Danhua* tree curved upward, its willowy limbs cascading downward in strands of red buds. On the ground at the edge of the canopy, almond shrubs formed a circle, their still-grey buds clinging to bare branches. Inside the circle, two of her music teachers sat with perfect posture, playing ornate instruments.

Master Yong Shu ran his bow across the erhu in furious strokes, the whine of its two strings urgent. Master Ding Meihui plucked at her pipa, calm and resolute, waiting. Middle-aged now, rumor had it the two had been involved in a torrid relationship almost three decades before, culminating in their epic performance before her newly enthroned father.

That was then, and age and cynicism had since set in, evident from their strict lessons. Yet at this moment, their performance captured passion and youth, making them seem fresh and vibrant again. Buzzing like a hummingbird's wings, his notes pranced like a fire blazing, while hers churned like the swell of a tidal wave.

Kaiya's spirit soared and her belly fluttered. This was love, made tangible by sound.

Too soon, the duet ended. Master Yong turned to her and bowed low, and Master Ding followed suit.

Finding her breath, Kaiya returned their salute with a low bow. Princess or not, she might as well have been a beggar before her teachers. She straightened and walked into the ring of shrubs. "I have never heard such a passionate performance."

Master Yong nodded. "We will play tonight at a reception in honor of your brother's wedding."

Right, the reception. The one she would have to escape if she had any chance of leaving the castle and meeting Hardeep. Yet with a new world opened to her ears, and General Lu fleeing their matchmaking appointment, the opportunities seemed boundless. Everything fell into place as if Heaven had willed it.

"What made their song so distinctive?" Lord Xu whispered in her ear.

Kaiya's heart might have jumped into her throat. Where had he come from?

"Well?" Xu raised an eyebrow.

There were too many details to mention! Kaiya could barely contain her smile. "The harmony and balance. Two opposite styles coming together to form a whole."

"Very good," Xu said.

Master Ding clapped her hands. "You will soon outshine us."

"Never." Kaiya bowed her head.

Master Ding laughed. "The greatest honor for a teacher is for the student to surpass her."

Wiping sweat from his brow, Master Yong grunted. "Our piece reflects the interaction between Yin and Yang, the push and pull, the mutual creation of harmony."

Xu harrumphed. "Call it what you will, the key is that you listened and understood. Now, try it yourself."

Bowing, Master Ding stood and gestured to her seat. "Please, *Dian-xia*."

Try? Someone who was just learning about love could not imitate that music. To do so would be an insult to what they had just played. She begged them off with a wave of her hand.

With a scowl, Lord Xu nudged her toward the seat with a hand. "Please, *Dian-xia*."

It might as well have been an order, audacious for a lord, but perhaps not for Xu. Kaiya nodded. In any case, Hardeep had asked her to practice. What better way to practice, than with two of her best teachers and an elf wizard?

Master Ding bowed. "Remember what I played, but do not let that constrain you. Let Master Yong guide you, and you will find you are guiding him."

Such curious advice, especially given the rigidity with which both usually taught. Kaiya sat, rooting her feet to the ground and straightening her spine as Hardeep had suggested. Satisfied her posture met his standards, she nestled the pipa in her arms. Like before, it felt lifeless compared to Yanyan's.

"You have to give it life," Lord Xu said.

Kaiya's pulse skipped a beat. It was as if the elf could read minds.

Master Yong laughed and swept his bow across the *erhu*. A jubilant sound burst forth.

The melody would work so well with what Master Ding had just played. Kaiya plucked the strings, copying the beautiful music note for note. The sound resonated inside of her, coiling in her belly again as it had done in the Hall of Pure Melody. Kaiya adjusted her posture, and the vibrations percolated from her arms into her core, and then into the ground. Capture this, and she was one step closer to helping Prince Hardeep.

Seize the song's emotion and make it your own, the book had implored. This song was more difficult than the one in that ancient tome, mixing jubilance with resolve. Opposites. Impossible to grasp both at the same time. What had Master Ding thought of when she was playing?

Love, perhaps? What she might have felt for Master Yong so many years ago? Not like Kaiya could even understand, given her own limited experience. Zheng Tian? They'd talked about marriage at a time when they thought it just meant always being able to play with one another. Hardeep? She barely knew him, even if his eyes twisted her stomach into knots. General Lu? She'd never learn what love was with him.

On the periphery of her vision, Master Ding's tight lips sank into a frown. Master Yong's playing fell out of beat with Kaiya's own. No, she was losing it. Blowing out the breath she held, she lowered her hands.

"*Dian-xia*, if I may." Master Ding held up a hand. "Your playing is technically perfect. It would make a wonderful solo..."

But.

Master Yong lowered his bow. "If I may, *Dian-xia*. We are not playing off each other, as a duet should. Ideally, as my song pushes, yours receives. When you expand, I contract."

Lord Xu nodded. "You are playing what you want, and you are doing it very well. However, you are not listening. That is the key to playing a song like this."

No denying it. So focused had she been on replicating Master Ding's piece, Kaiya had missed the changes Master Yong had improvised. She bowed her head in contrition.

"Keep practicing, keep listening," Lord Xu said. "I will seek you out when you have made another breakthrough." He disappeared, the air popping where he had stood.

Kaiya covered her gasp with a hand. It was surprising to see him disappear just like that, but not nearly so shocking as his certainty that she would make another breakthrough.

CHAPTER 13
Dilemmas

Kaiya listened to the chirping of birds as a cold breeze whispered through new tree buds. Perhaps a garden wasn't the best place to practice the pipa; not when the chill brought goosebumps to her exposed arms. However, Lord Xu had implored her to listen, and it was near impossible to distinguish sounds with the preparations for tonight's reception stirring a ruckus inside the castle.

Never moving from its reliable spot in the halls of heaven, Caiyue waxed to mid-crescent. Prince Hardeep wanted to meet past sundown at the first waxing gibbous, four hours hence. That left plenty of time to practice. Maybe she could show how far she'd progressed just from the morning. The thought sent prickles dancing through her core.

Focus. She shook the excitement out of her head. The book instructed the musician to *seize the song's emotion* and make it her own. She'd read the lines over and over again since leaving her teachers, and tried to play the song with the happiness it embodied. If she could affect General Lu, certainly she could influence the mood of her handmaidens.

One more try. Adjusting her posture, she lowered her hands to the strings and plucked out perfect notes. Her rendition of the song was so precise, it had to work. She cast a glance at Han Meiling and the imperial guards Chen Xin and Ma Jun. They stood like statues on the veranda, almost blending into the background. Despite her best efforts with the music, they remained stoic as always; the exact opposite of the song's intended effect.

Her lower lip jutted out. Learning from a book was getting her nowhere. The sensation of power she'd felt, first in the Hall of Pure Melody with Yanyan's pipa, then later when playing for General Lu, seemed so distant. Like a dream.

Listen, Lord Xu's voice echoed in her mind, almost too real and with too much of an exasperated tone to be the memory from just an hour before.

She closed her eyes and opened her ears: the battle between spring and winter, played out in the birdsongs, wind, and waves. Spring sang an uncertain song as winter held a tenuous grip. The irregularity of weather seemed just like Prince Hardeep's influence. She had broken more rules this day than she had her entire life, even angered the man Father wanted her to marry.

The uncertainty found its way into her music as she strummed a random tune on her pipa, the hesitant notes reflecting the weather and her emotions. Duty dictated marriage to the general. Her soul wanted to sing with the song of the world. An impossible dream before today, but now her spirit soared. Between Prince Hardeep's promise of the Dragon Scale Lute, and Lord Xu's certainty of a future breakthrough, it now seemed possible.

It also meant leaving the palace tonight, during a formal reception no less, using some lie to meet Hardeep. His Ankira needed her help, but it shouldn't require sneaking behind Father's back. It shouldn't require imposing her will through magic. Even if it were the right thing to do. Surely, there had to be other avenues. Her notes wobbled.

She steadied her breath, and the music with it. Right. It was best to obey the rules. Stay in the castle tonight.

Not that it was even possible to escape. A thousand eyes would be on her, because either the Household Ministry secretary or the Hall of Pure Melody's steward had undoubtedly reported to Father about her unapproved adventures in the palace. Minister Hu had probably spread the lie that Hardeep wanted to take her hostage. Maybe he did.

Father might be too busy preparing for the reception now, but when it did come time to mete out punishment, he would probably forbid any more contact with Prince Hardeep—in addition to any other reprimand she might face.

In the corner of her eye, blue robes twitched in a short blur of motion. Chen Xin and Ma Jun had shuffled, perhaps from the uncertainties in her music.

Another flash of blue and black robes swirled from beyond the veranda. Maybe they were just reacting to that.

No. It was her music. It had to be. It was a sign. All uncertainties melted. She was destined to liberate Ankira.

"Young Lord Peng Kai-Long requests an audience with Princess Kaiya," a male voice cracked from the edge of the garden. Household Affairs Secretary Hong's. He'd been following her around quite a bit today. A spy perhaps, there at his ministry's bidding—or even Father's—to make sure she didn't break any more rules.

Her hands froze over the strings. She set the pipa down and searched for the voice's source. The old man bowed, his lips tight like he had just sucked on sour plums. Cousin Kai-Long stood at his side, folding a sheet of paper.

A letter from Prince Hardeep? Her heart pattered. Another sign.

Kai-Long took the steps down the veranda. "*Dian-xia*," he started, addressing her formally. Even though he was an elder cousin, her position as a princess from the direct ruling line ranked her above him.

Eyes on the letter, she smiled. "Cousin, you do not need to stand on formality."

"As you command, Kaiya." He flashed a devilish grin, his eyes searching hers.

His sarcasm was infectious. She covered a giggle with her fingers, then pointed at the paper in his hand. "Is that...?"

He looked down at the paper and then held it up. *Elephant left three.* "I am playing a game of blind chess. This is my latest move."

Her heart sunk. Instead of a letter from Hardeep, it was just part of a confusing game. Chess made little sense, but Father and Kai-Long bonded over it. "Are you winning?"

"Yes, though it wouldn't be evident." His lips twitched. He cast a glance at the imperial guards, then leaned in and whispered—practically mouthed: "I have a plan to get you out of the palace."

Kaiya stole a glance back at Chen Xin and Ma Jun, who showed no sign of having heard him. Thank the Heavens for her good ears. She held up a hand to stay her guards, and then shuffled a little farther down the path.

At a safe distance away, she turned to face him. "You can get me out during a reception in honor of my brother's wedding? What about General Lu and the betrothal announcement?"

Kai-Long's grin stretched from ear to ear, and he suppressed a chuckle. "When I got back to the palace, General Lu was storming out. His eyes were red-rimmed, like he'd been crying. The servants and officials all say he did not even report to the Ministry of Appointments."

The betrothal remained up in the air. Maybe the general had given up on marriage. Hopefully, someone would tell her something before tonight. "Still, I'm supposed to be sitting at the head of the room, next to Kai-Wu and his bride. Someone will notice my absence."

If Kai-Long shook his head any more, it might wobble off. "Trust me. Old Hong there—" he tilted his head toward the palace official still on the veranda, who ogled them and wrung his hands "—has agreed to help. It took a little convincing. I also called in several favors among the young lords and palace staff."

Kaiya searched his eyes. Nothing but sincerity. Before coming of age and being assigned as a diplomat, Kai-Long had virtually grown up in the palace, had always been close to her and Tian. More than once, he had kept them from getting into trouble. Of course he would have her best interests at heart. Still.... She shook her head. "It risks too many people. It will betray Father's trust in you."

Kai-Long cast his gaze down. In shame, no doubt, considering Father's fondness for him. Before Kai-Long had been sent to Ayuri lands, the two used to share tea on a regular basis, and play Hua chess. He raised his head. "That's too bad. Prince Hardeep told me only someone of your talent could use his magical instrument."

Like the Dragon Singers of old. It was her destiny. Was it worth breaking yet more rules? Exposing collaborators to potential punishment? The memory of Yanyan's pipa sent a tingling through Kaiya's hands and into her core. It had caused her to pass out. No telling what a similar instrument could do, with her out in the city without guards.

But oh, the possibilities! And Prince Hardeep would be there with his Paladin skills, to protect her. Her chest swelled. "What would *you* do?"

"Kaiya," Kai-Long said, taking her hand in his. "You must make that decision for yourself. Just know that Prince Hardeep told me you have a gift. He wholeheartedly believes it is like none other since Yanyan herself."

Heat flared, and her hands went sweaty. The exuberant bubble in her chest threatened to choke off her air. Prince Hardeep's kind blue eyes *saw* her. Her potential to do good in this world. He

didn't care about how plain she looked. To him, she was more than a stepping-stone to power.

Still, Father also loved her unconditionally. The excitement withered, and the swell of her chest deflated. "Whatever I choose, I will betray someone."

"Not necessarily." Kai-Long squeezed her hand. "I have friends in Vyara City who remember when the Dragon Scale Lute repelled Avarax. If you learn to use it, you can help Hua. Remember what the *Tianzi* said about the lords of the North. Remember that if Ankira falls, aggressive Madura will be on our border, and I am sure they have stockpiles of firepowder."

It did make sense, and provided a means of getting official permission. She nodded. "I am sure the *Tianzi* will see the logic. I will go to him—"

He released her hand and raised his own. "If you decide to leave the castle—and I will support whatever you choose—the *Tianzi* must not know. Because if he denies your request, all eyes will be on you during the reception, making my plan impossible. It will also be direct disobedience to his order, punishable by death."

Kaiya twirled a lock of hair. If it was just herself to consider, the chance to find her potential, beyond a political marriage, was worth the risk of death. After all, the proverb of marriage being a woman's grave rang even more true from what she'd seen of the short and pompous General Lu.

But what about collaborators? Anyone who helped her escape the castle—from servants, to Hardeep, and even Kai-Long—would face certain torture and execution. No, asking for permission was out of the question. She searched Kai-Long's eyes again, finding nothing but devotion and support. "Tell me your plan. If it endangers anyone besides myself, I cannot go through with it."

"There is magic in the world beyond Paladin fighting skills and our master craftsmen." Grinning, Kai-Long pulled her behind a large tree, out of the guards' line of sight. He withdrew a red silk pouch and emptied what appeared to be a light bauble into his bare palm.

Kaiya gasped. Kai-Long's face was gone, replaced by her own—or at least, a flattering rendition based off an official court painting. His broad shoulders and muscled frame now withered to her slim, flat build, and his court robes seemed to shrink to size.

Her mouth open and closed in an unladylike manner until one word could escape. "H-How?"

When he spoke, it was with his own voice, making the situation all the more disconcerting. "An Aksumi illusionist I knew in Vyara City made it."

An illusionist, no wonder. The dark-skinned Aksumi practiced all kinds of sorcery, including the mass production of the ubiquitous light baubles. But, "Whatever for?"

"An emergency. If you ever needed a decoy. Just like tonight, though I don't imagine the *Tianzi* had this sort of circumstance in mind." She—he—stared at the sky.

It definitely wasn't her body language...was it? "This will never work. It doesn't look like me and it certainly doesn't sound like me."

Kai-Long slipped the marble into its pouch and his form snapped back to normal. "My plan takes all that into account. Here's what we will do..."

CHAPTER 14

Cloaks and Daggers

Arriving two hours before his appointed meeting with Lamp Man, Tian checked the door's threshold for light and listened for any telltale signs of activity. Unlike the previous times he'd scouted the place out, no guards circled the building. Satisfied no one was there, he picked the lock, which yielded much more easily without imperious half-elves breathing down his neck, and padded in.

At first glance, the warehouse seemed little changed from the morning, but the crates Lamp Man had pointed out to the porter were now gone. They must've already loaded them onto the *Wild Orchid* by now. Jie, unaccounted for since dawn, would probably know, if she were still alive. It was so uncharacteristic of her not to check in with him for such a long time. His gut clenched. If Lamp Man had ill intentions, Tian shouldn't have sent her there alone.

He now climbed a stack of crates, and then shimmied over the dusty rafters to the lone skylight. High-quality glass, likely imported from the Estomari city states in the east. Unlatching the frame, he pushed up on it. The rusty hinges creaked as it opened. Gaining the flat roof, satisfied there was no breeze, he left the skylight open. People never looked up unless they had a reason.

He now stood two stories above the ground, a good vantage point to see if Lamp Man came early to prepare a nasty surprise. The sun had set, and the blue light from Guanyin's Eye mingled with the crescent White Moon to cast the gridded streets and alleys below in an aquamarine hue.

Light bauble lamps crawled along in the hands of drunken sailors as they boisterously made their way around the waterfront. If Jie had received his message, she would stay in the shifting dark spaces between lamps. Her approach would be so quiet, he would never know until she played some childish trick on him.

After an hour surveying the area, he had yet to fall victim to her games. She should've made contact by now. Instead, low voices emanated from the approaching glow of a partially shuttered light bauble. Tian dropped so that he could just see over the half-wall balustrade and crept to the warehouse's southeast corner. Four men strode in unison, their weapons protruding from cloaks. Broadswords. Curved daggers. One cradled a repeating crossbow. The conversation became clearer as they came closer.

"Mister Sha said to meet him here by the second waxing gibbous," Crossbow Man said.

Tian glanced up to the south at Caiyue. Unless this Mister Sha—Lamp Man, perhaps—made it a point of coming late, he'd be there soon.

"How much is that bastard paying?" the largest asked. "I have some gambling debts."

The one holding the lantern harrumphed. "I told you not to play mahjong with the triads when you're drunk." Monk would make a fitting nickname, given his ascetic guidance.

Gambler stopped midstride, breaking their tight formation. "Mind your own business."

"Both of you, shut up," Crossbow Man said. "We'll make enough to visit to the Floating World afterwards."

"Speak for yourself," muttered the fourth. A short, slim man, his only obvious weapon was a knife.

Their hardened features and confident postures suggested military training. Hua had too many soldiers past their prime, in need of work. Most hung around the harbor city and capital, employed as guards for rich merchants. Master Yan had identified them as a potential source of instability, if they ever organized.

Footsteps from the other side of the alley drew Tian's attention. The length of the stride matched Lamp Man, and indeed, it was his northern Hua features illuminated by a dim light bauble approaching. He hung the same lamp from earlier on a hook above the door and opened the shutters.

The four newcomers turned into the alley and walked to the door. They nodded in greeting.

"Mister Sha," Crossbow Man said. "I hope we have not kept you waiting."

"You did, Mister Gu," Sha lied. He nodded first at Crossbow Man, then the others. "But it is my job to be early."

Gu bowed. "Our apologies."

"You are on time, and you have done good work for my master in the past." Little chance Sha would reveal that master without persuasion or trickery.

Crossbow Gu bowed again. "What's the job?"

Sha looked up and down the alley, and then lowered his voice. "In an hour, I will be meeting with a harbormaster scribe. When we are done, I need him dead and his body disposed of."

Tian's stomach tightened. So Sha planned to kill him.

Gu harrumphed. "A scribe, eh? Easy enough. It will cost you."

"A gold *yuan* each."

Tian's eyes widened as much as the mercenaries' did. Four *yuan* could feed a large family for a month. His life wasn't worth much more than Princess Kaiya's proverbial butterfly, let alone four *yuan*. Sha clearly valued whatever conspiracy he was involved in.

"The terms are acceptable." Gu placed a fist in his hand. "You asked for four of us, so you obviously have a plan?"

"Of course." Sha pointed at the door. "I will maneuver the scribe so his back is to the open door. Slim Kan can slash his throat from behind. A man will block both ends of the alley just in case he escapes." He pointed up. "You stand on the roof with your crossbow."

Tian stepped back from the balustrade just as Gu looked up.

"How am I supposed to get up there?"

"There's a ladder inside," Sha said, "and a skylight."

Damn! Tian bolted back to the skylight as quietly as he could. He had to close it before they opened the door, lest the creaky hinges draw their attention. In the seventeen and a half long strides, he considered the possibilities. Stay on the roof and Gu would find the closed skylight unlatched...but might not give a second thought to either that or the disturbed dust. Hide in the warehouse, and Tian would have to get back out again to meet Sha at the front door, and worry about Gu's crossbow.

Stay on the roof it was. Tian lowered the skylight, cringing at the hinges' whine. Then he backed to the southwest corner, far from the door below and outside the thirty-two-*chi* glow of Gu's lamp. He pressed his back to the half-wall.

The skylight groaned open. Lantern raised, Gu set the crossbow to the side and climbed up. Now without his cloak, it was clear he was armed with a broadsword and dagger. After giving a cough and brushing dust off his pants, he retrieved his crossbow and clunked over to the edge just above the door. He shuttered his lamp, leaving only glowing cracks.

Tian glanced south. The Iridescent Moon had waxed past its second crescent. Below, Gambler's silhouette pressed against the wall near the corner. If Monk had followed Sha's instructions, he would be waiting at the other end, while Slim Kan hid just inside the door.

Five against one, but since they were all separated, Tian could neutralize some of them one at a time. It would be child's play with Jie's help. If only she were here. Closing his eyes, he pressed his hand to the roof to feel for vibrations. Ears perked, he listened for any sign of his irrepressible friend.

Nothing. Time to put his own plan into action. Drawing a knife, he padded back across the rooftop. Gu stood at the edge, looking up and down the alley. As long as he didn't turn around…

Hold the dragonfly with care, for even their fleeting lives have value. Since their parting three thousand, one hundred and forty-seven days before, Princess Kaiya had rarely invaded his thoughts—only at times like this, as a reminder of what his hands could do. Had to do, even if his younger self would have been horrified.

Gu looked back.

Palming a *biao* throwing spike, Tian ducked behind the open skylight.

With a yawn, Gu returned to his post. At his distance from the open skylight, he likely saw only a reflection of Guanyin's Eye, whereas Tian could see right through it.

Tian closed his eyes for a split second to erect his mental armor. To banish thoughts of a gentle princess, the best friend he'd promised to marry. Memories led to indecisiveness, and that got people killed. Opening his eyes, he slunk right up behind Gu, covered his mouth, and slashed his neck.

Gu struggled for a second before going limp. The crossbow slipped from lifeless fingers, but Tian intercepted it with his foot and slowed its descent to the floor. A life snuffed out, as easily as crushing a dragonfly. He lowered the body and peeked over the balustrade.

Down below, Sha tapped his foot. Soon, he might join Gu in the netherworld. Tian worked his way back to the skylight. Jie might use a *Ghost Echo*, imitating and throwing Gu's voice to lure Slim Kan into an ambush, but Tian didn't trust his own

technique. No, as long as he kept Sha's back to the doorway, Slim wouldn't be able to attack.

Tian continued to the far side of the roof, then lowered himself over the edge. Fingers and toes finding purchase in the cracks between the stones, he descended about a story and then dropped lightly to the street. He dusted himself off and held his knife in an underhand grip to conceal it. Rounding the southwest corner, he walked down the middle of the street. Gambler, leaning back against the building, would see Tian's silhouette, but would likely wait until he turned into the alley before making a move.

Gambler's shadowed form spun, but made no move for the broadsword at his side. Maybe he could be spared, even if Tian would not afford the same courtesy back.

"Good evening." Tian nodded his head.

Gambler lifted his chin and grunted.

Tian leaped forward. With one hand, he pinned Gambler's right wrist; with the other, he drove the knife butt into Gambler's temple, and then set the blade at his throat. "Hands up, turn around," Tian whispered. "Slowly."

Wobbling, Gambler complied. Tian smashed the knife handle into the base of Gambler's skull, and then eased him down as he crumpled. The two successive shots would leave him unconscious for at least six minutes, and he would wake with an excruciating headache.

Stashing his knife in a wrist sheath, Tian turned the corner. Lamp Man Sha had not moved from his spot in front of the door, under the lamp. Their eyes met. He had no obvious weapons.

With a bow of his head, Tian withdrew the copied manifests. "Here, sir."

"Good." Sha beckoned him forward, edging back in an obvious move—at least to a trained eye—to put Tian's back at the open door and Slim Kan's waiting knife.

Tian stood fast. He repeated his lines in his head several times. "All these goods bound for Wailian County. For the new castle?"

Sha's eyes narrowed to slits as he received the papers, then opened and shifted from one end of the alley to the other.

Alas, the disconnect between Tian's thoughts and mouth had ruined subtle interrogation, and perhaps even blown his cover. On to the contingency plan, which had to be executed before Gambler came to. Muscles twitching, ready to fire, Tian stepped right where Sha wanted him.

A dagger flashed in Sha's hand. "Now!"

Before it could wrap around his throat, Tian intercepted Slim Kan's arm and twisted the wrist up. Using his shoulders as a fulcrum, Tian dislocated Kan's elbow with a wet pop. In the same motion, he spun and drove Kan into Sha's incoming stab.

Slim Kan screamed. Monk rounded the corner, his broadsword rasping from its sheath. Tian released Kan and seized Sha's knife arm. With a jump back and a yank, he drew Sha into the warehouse, and then twisted his wrist.

Sha went hurtling into the door, slamming it shut, drowning the space in darkness.

Before the image faded from his head, Tian swept the dagger from Sha's hand and pressed the tip to his throat. "Who do you work for?"

"Lord Zu."

Of course, these forms of interrogation were far less effective than subtle ones. "There's no Lord Zu in the North." Tian swept the dagger upward, nicking Sha's chin, before he returned the point to the throat. The door buckled, and Tian pulled the weapon back before the force drove Sha into it. Monk wouldn't be able to push it open, but the threat made for a good incentive. "Tell me."

"Lord Peng."

The *Tai-Ming* Lord? Impossible. "Married to the *Tianzi's* sister."

"No." Sha shook his head. "Not—"

The door slammed open, driving Sha into the dagger faster than Tian could withdraw it. Gambler stumbled into the warehouse, broadsword in hand. Monk stood behind him, holding a lamp and sword. Sha knelt, hands clawing his neck, choking on blood.

Tian glanced at the dagger. It had gone deep enough to puncture Sha's voice box, though whether it had or not would take further examination. For now, it was the dagger and a knife in his other hand against two men armed with broadswords. "Sha won't be paying. Don't risk your life."

Gambler glared back, though his eyes crossed. Two hits to the head and a jolt on a heavy door had taken their toll. He pointed the broadsword at Tian. "I'm going to gut you anyway." He raised the sword and charged.

Backing away, Tian flung the knife. It bit into the upper part of Gambler's chest. Two throwing stars followed, lodging in Gambler's gut. The brute continued undaunted, broadsword swinging in circles. Tian feigned fear—though perhaps it wasn't all an act—retreating deeper into the warehouse.

Gambler's mistake was the regularity of his swinging pattern. As his weapon swept up for the fourth time, Tian vaulted forward and sliced behind Gambler's elbow. Spinning to the side, Tian continued the downward slash to sever Gambler's knee ligaments. A shoulder-butt created distance for Tian's side kick to his shin. He spun to find Monk's sword starting a swing.

Decapitation was unavoidable.

The hack came up short, and the blade clattered on the floor as Monk sank to his knees and gripped his side. Behind him, a lantern on the ground lit a short silhouette in a one-piece dress with a frilly border. With a knife. His savior—but who? Tian slammed his heel into Monk's head, knocking him to the ground. A quick glance at Gambler found the man lying on the floor, holding his knee.

Tian circled around to get the light out of his eyes. Which immediately rounded so wide, his eyeballs might've fallen out of the sockets.

The strapless pink dress clinging to Jie's lithe body was far more suited for one of the fair-skinned merchant princesses out of the East. She actually looked like a girl, despite the color mismatch. She pointed a bloody knife at him. "Don't laugh."

He opened his mouth—

"Not. A. Word." Her tone left no room for negotiation, even as her scowl dared him to speak.

"Right." He leaned over Monk, whose unconscious wheezing rattled the air. Jie's knife had caught him in his flank, puncturing his lung. He would not be saying much, if he ever woke at all. Gritting his teeth, Tian slashed his throat. A quick, merciful death.

Jie's eyes roved from Slim Kan to Gambler to Monk to Sha. "Who are these people?"

"Mercenaries." Tian pointed to Sha, likely dead, since blood no longer squirted from his throat. "Hired by him. From Wailian County."

Jie nodded. "The *Wild Orchid* held several kegs of sulfur, bound for Wailian. They are making firepowder."

"Sha might work for Lord Tong himself." Squatting by the corpse, Tian examined the body. Sometimes, forensic clues yielded more information than interrogation. A grey crust lined the sole of Sha's shoe, while traces of what looked to be sawdust flecked his coifed hair. Tian lifted Sha's still-warm hand. Traitor or not, Tian had passed his death sentence.

Sha's smooth hand did not speak of a life of hard labor or frequency in wielding weapons. The index finger bore a gold ring shaped in the form of a coiled dragon, perhaps a replica of the Guardian Dragon of Hua itself. More curious was the pink grit under his fingernail.

Tian held up the hand for Jie to see. "What do you make of this?"

She leaned over and sniffed, no doubt her keen elven senses picking up more than his nose could. "It has a fishy smell."

He withdrew a fine lockpick and scooped out the pasty substance. "Fish paste? He seemed too cultured to eat with his hands." He held up the pick to her for confirmation.

"I'm *not* going to taste it." Jie sucked on her lower lip. "Perhaps he was a sloppy eater."

He glared at her, prompting her for her real answer.

She released her bottom lip with a smack. "Yutou Province is famous for preserved pink fish paste. Fat Nose Jiang has a Southern accent, and the *Wild Orchid* stops in Yutou on a regular basis."

And fish paste could keep for a year, or more. Tian tapped his chin with a finger. The problem was that Yutou Province exported a lot of fish paste, to all over the country. Now if only it were possible to find out how much fish paste Lord Tong in Wailian was buying. And rice. Five thousand *shi* of rice and five hundred *jin* of pink fish paste could feed his army of five thousand for a year. Then there was the firepowder.

He looked up at Jie. "You—"

"I have already sent word about the illegal firepowder. I would imagine Master Yan will be interrupting the imperial reception to brief the *Tianzi*."

Tian tapped his chin. What had appeared to be a brewing insurgency now threatened to boil into a full-blown rebellion, destabilizing Hua for the first time in three centuries.

CHAPTER 15

Not the Brightest Moment

Kneeling at the far end of the dais in the Golden Dragon Room, Kaiya listened to the music ensemble that played in the background. *Guzheng*, pipa, *erhu*, *ruan* guitar, recorder; all mingled in choreographed harmony, all technically perfect.

Though the sound didn't carry the same emotions as her masters' playing, it resonated through rice wine-fueled conversation among the hereditary lords and ladies. Dressed in their finest gowns and robes, they all sat on the imported sablewood floors around low tables, enjoying delicacies prepared by the finest chefs in the realm.

Each place was set with some of her favorite dishes, though Cousin Kai-Long's embarrassing plan had killed her appetite: a bowl of royal red rice, a low-rimmed bowl with jade asparagus and immortal mushrooms sautéed with royal-ox butter, a small saucer of soy sauce-braised golden pork belly cubes, a small plate of fried finger-length whitefish, a medium-sized plate of chopped crispy quail, and a lacquer bowl of shark fin soup. A small cup for rice wine sat on the right side, next to a pair of chopsticks. The Imperial Family's symbol of a blue five-clawed dragon decorated each white porcelain dish.

Insides twisting, Kaiya looked through the sliding doors. Painted with dark golden dragons flying among the clouds, they stood open to the garden beyond, thankfully allowing cool air off Sun-Moon Lake to percolate in and alleviate the stifling air. Facing north, they did not provide a view of the Iridescent Moon, so she would have to rely on Kai-Long to keep time. Going along with his potentially humiliating plan might tarnish the hard-to-maintain façade of Perfect Princess.

And she had been far from perfect today. Surprisingly enough, the Minister of Household Affairs hadn't approached her about her transgressions, nor had Father summoned her regarding the betrothal to General Lu. She shifted in her seat. Certainly, one of the witnesses would have reported everything by now.

Or perhaps they'd been too busy preparing for this reception to deal with a naughty sixteen-year-old. Tomorrow might be another story, but for now, Second Brother Kai-Wu and his soon-to-be bride took center stage.

Everyone took turns approaching the dais where the Imperial Family ate from small individual tables. Second Brother, never one for ceremony, slouched beside his bride-to-be. Wu Yanli, the daughter of *Tai-Ming* Lord Wu of Zhenjing Province, might have been a porcelain doll with her cold elegance. She almost rivaled Xiulan in beauty, and rumor had it she had enchanted Kai-Wu with the magic of her tea ceremony.

Young Lord Chen Qing, a *Yu-Ming* heir to a county in Jiangzhou Province, approached with a dumb smile on his face and a wine saucer in hand. He dropped to his knee. "*Dian-xia*, congratulations on your new sister-in-law. Let us toast." His eyes swept to the porcelain decanter at her side.

The one filled with water, part of Cousin Kai-Long's plan. She nodded. She filled Young Lord Chen's saucer and set the decanter down. He then took it and filled her saucer.

She took a dainty sip and her eyes widened. Hot and spicy, it stung her throat. She covered her cough. That was not water! There must have been a mistake. And now, an unprecedented line of young lords had formed up behind Chen Qing, all with feral grins.

Oh no. She craned her neck. Hopefully, Kai-Long was out there somewhere. Or a servant, who could swap out the decanter...but for what? Nobody knew it was supposed to be water. The next young man, Young Lord Fen of Fenggu Province, already knelt before her, filling her saucer with rice wine.

The alcohol burned her mouth, and showed no signs of abating even after several more young lords toasted her. She was to have feigned drunkenness and retired early, but now, it looked like her poor acting skills might not be needed.

Her stomach heaved. Head spinning, she covered her mouth, and luckily, nothing came up. Eyes rounding like the wine saucer, Young Lord Zi, the seventh to serve her, scuttled back several steps. Humiliating for sure, made worse by actually being drunk.

Still, no one could blame her. It would appear just as Kai-Long had planned: a bunch of potential young suitors trying to make an impression on her, but gone too far. At a reception like this, even a prince or princess was fair game, and Father could forgive a sixteen-year-old for not holding her wine.

Kai-Long appeared at her side, hand on her elbow. "Easy, *Dian-xia*. Come, let me help you." Releasing her, he walked through the crowd gathering in front of Eldest Brother Kai-Guo and Xiulan and bowed before Father at the center of the dais.

Father was engaged in discussion with a middle-aged minister, his brow furrowed in an uncommon show of public emotion. The minister shook his head and held up two fingers. Father

actually frowned, but then stayed the minister with an innocuous hand, and turned to Kai-Long. Kai-Long leaned in and whispered into Father's ear.

Turning and meeting her gaze, Father nodded. Permission to leave, with Cousin Kai-Long, his favorite nephew. Subtle enough to save face. With a bow of apology to the waiting young men, she rose.

And wobbled. Her head spun. Again, a firm hand grasped her arm.

Kai-Long leaned in and whispered, "You are doing great."

Great? If only he knew it was no act. Placing each foot in front of the other felt like a toddler's first steps. "Who is that speaking with the *Tianzi*?"

"Deputy Yan. One of his most trusted advisors."

She looked back to where Father still conferred with this Deputy Yan. "What were they talking about?"

Kai-Long shrugged. "I'm not sure. They quieted as soon as I came over. Now come along."

With his support, they made it to the garden, all under the watchful eye of imperial guards. Guanyin's Eye hung low in the night sky. At its largest this year, it seemed to scrutinize her foolishness.

Cold air filled her lungs, clearing her head, if only a little. "That wasn't water!" She spun and shoved him with two hands, and would have knocked herself over if he hadn't caught her.

"No!" He shook his head. "The servant must have made a mistake. It's okay though, the plan will still work."

Plan? Right. To see gorgeous Prince Hardeep and try the Dragon Scale Lute. It would certainly improve what had become a mortifying evening.

He draped a silken shawl over her shoulders, and then beckoned a servant. "Bring us some hot tea." He then guided her along the courtyard paths, their feet crunching in the white pebbles. Where were they? No matter how familiar the inner castle was, everything appeared the same through her bleary vision and spinning head. Up ahead, a small octagonal pagoda overlooked the moat between the inner castle and the main palace.

Holding her hand, he helped her up the steps. Inside she plopped into a seat, the marble cold on her behind. She scanned the far end of the path, where two imperial guards kept a respectful distance.

"Are you all right?" Kai-Long asked.

"I think so." No. With heat flaring in her cheeks, Kaiya fanned her face with a hand.

He leaned back and stretched his arms over the pagoda's half-wall. "I want you to bend over, so the guards can't see you, take off the shawl, and pretend to dry heave. Loudly. Stay down, then give the shawl and your outer robe to her." His head tilted down, to the side.

Kaiya jerked her head in the direction he indicated, the sudden motion making her brain twist and flip.

A palace maid was hunched over there, below the line of sight of anyone outside the pagoda. The dark partially shrouded her face, but she bore an uncanny resemblance to Kaiya. Probably from the illusion bauble.

Taking off her outer robe in front of a man, cousin or not, wasn't part of the plan. Dry heaves weren't either, and the way Kaiya's stomach twisted, things might not be particularly dry. "Who is she?"

"Someone who owes me a favor." Kai-Long chuckled. "I know a lot about many of the handmaidens and palace servants."

Curse the buzzing in her head. Why did this feel wrong?

"Hurry," Kai-Long said. "When the servant comes with the tea, you will swap places."

"How did you come up with this plan?"

Kai-Long grinned. "I've snuck a few ladies out this way in the past. More than a few. And it will work even better than ever this time with the magic." He held out his palm. Cradled in a silk kerchief was a marble, similar to the magical light baubles that lit the palace and probably every other house in the world. "Don't touch it directly. Not yet."

It must be another illusion bauble. Kaiya took up the kerchief, nearly knocking it out of his hand. "What will this one make me look like?"

"Just a plain girl. Trust me, everything will be all right. Nobody is going to get in trouble."

There'd been a little too much magic for one day already. Kaiya took a deep breath. The cool air did little to clear the alcohol-induced haze. She glanced toward the imperial guards, just shadows in the distance. The servant approached, holding a tray with a teacup and kettle in trembling hands. No, it would be okay. Kai-Long had done this many times.

"All right." She motioned for Kai-Long to turn his back. When he did, she gritted her teeth, leaned over, and did her best approximation of dry heaves. She ripped off the shawl and shrugged out of the robe, then passed them to the girl, who stood up, hand over her mouth, coughing.

"Good," Kai-Long whispered, patting the girl on the back. "Cough a little."

As the girl complied, the other servant, now cloaked against the chill, stepped into the pagoda with tea. She poured it into a cup and set the cup and kettle on the table. How wonderful tea would be right now! Kai-Long placed himself in the guards' line of sight and motioned Kaiya to her feet.

When she stood, the second servant dropped to all fours. Kai-Long pulled the cloak off and draped it over Kaiya's shoulders. The girl who now resembled her reached for the tea and took a sip. It happened so fast, a blur to Kaiya's addled head.

"Now," Kai-Long whispered to her, "Thank me and tell me to take my leave while you rest here."

Kaiya fought the urge to bow her head, lest the guards see the switch. "Thank you, Cousin Kai-Long. I am feeling a little better now. I am just going to sit for a while. You may take your leave."

"It has been my honor." Kai-Long bowed, then pulled the hood over her head and placed a hand on her shoulder. He whispered again, "I am going to report to your imperial guards. In about ten minutes, meet me on the other side of the bridge. Remember, the bauble must touch your bare skin at all times. Try to walk in a straight line, with the body language of a servant."

Whatever that meant. She watched as he left and walked up the path to where her guards waited.

"Princess Kaiya is feeling better," he told them. "The cool air is doing her well, and I think after sitting for a while with several cups of tea, she will be fine." With a nod of his head, he disappeared around a hedge.

Kaiya looked down at the girl pretending to be her. Who was she beneath the illusion? And had they crossed paths in the palace before? She must be new. Not to mention, her posture appeared much too stiff, the motions too jerky as she reached for the teacup. The tea smelled good, and it probably would help allay the throbbing in her head. Still, a servant would never dare drink after a princess. With the guards watching, thinking Kaiya to be the servant, it would ruin the illusion to drink the tea.

"Now, *Dian-xia*," the girl whispered, lips trembling.

Kaiya stood. With deliberate care, she took one step after another. As she approached the bridge over the moat, she glanced in the direction of the guards. Their dark shapes didn't move. Heavens, this plan was actually working.

On the other side, Kai-Long waited.

They hurried through the palace grounds, his pull on her hand forcing a quick pace. The twists and turns along the corridors between the buildings would have all been familiar with a clear head, but they might as well have been a maze tonight. Light from the three moons made it even more disorienting.

At last, they came to the central plaza formed by the Hall of Supreme Harmony, the Hall of Pure Melody, and the imperial archives. Aksumi light baubles hung in strings from the dozens of espaliered fruit trees, casting hypnotic shadows in all directions. Despite the particularly large crowd of palanquin bearers, palace guards, and provincial soldiers and staff, the courtyard still seemed vast. Hundreds of eyes fell on them as they neared Kai-

Long's Nanling provincial contingent, congregated near the main gates.

"Young Lord Peng," someone cried out. Soldiers snapped to attention.

Stopping in place, Kaiya peered back at Kai-Long. Even through her muddled head, everything was now clear: this wasn't right. If it was just her escaping the palace with no help, the risks barely outweighed the rewards. Now, it involved several people, many likely blackmailed. If this plan failed, any accessory to this ill-advised adventure would face severe punishment. She gripped Kai-Long's sleeve. "No, we can't do this."

"It's too late. If we head back now, it will draw too much attention. Don't worry."

She looked at his entourage. The porters prepared the two-person palanquin.

A palanquin, no...the narrow confines, the stuffiness... She skidded to a halt and nearly tripped over her gown. Her head spun and chest tightened. She squeezed Kai-Long's elbow. "We can walk."

He faced her, the light baubles casting webby shadows over his grinning face. "You won't be spotted this way."

She fixated on the palanquin...just one. Come to think of it, "Where is your family? I didn't see them at the reception."

"The horse-relay messengers said their ship was delayed. They are expected in Jiangkou harbor tomorrow morning."

His villa chamberlain shuffled over and bowed. "Leaving so soon, Young Lord? With a...friend, I see."

Kai-Long nodded. "Yes. I already paid my respects to Prince Kai-Wu, and my...friend...wished to depart early."

"To the Floating World, then?"

Kaiya's heart jumped into her throat. The Floating World, where men's dreams took flight, was so far away, it would take half the night to get there. And though it boasted a variety of entertainments from exotic music to theater, the most common diversion was...*that*. It certainly wasn't a place for a woman of high standing. She clutched Kai-Long's arm and shook her head.

He leaned over. "Don't worry. We are headed in that direction, but we won't go in. Come, lower your head." He stood by the palanquin door, blocking the chamberlain's sight of her.

With a sigh, she ducked in. The walls closed in. Head in a fog, her pulse raced. This was such a bad idea. Cousin Kai-Long dipped in to the palanquin and settled across from her. She sucked in a last breath of the outside air and the coolness filled her lungs. The door snapped shut.

She pressed Tian's pebble, firm and resolute beneath her sash. It would be all right. Handsome Hardeep's guidance would help her revive a long-lost art, and with it, she could save a beleaguered people. It would benefit Hua as well. Father would understand. Someday. Maybe.

The palanquin pitched upward, threatening to send her stomach into rebellion. She wouldn't be saving anyone tonight. As the men fell into a rhythm, the ride smoothed. From the sounds, the palace's front gates opened and a throng of guards marched out. For the first time in her life, she was outside of the palace, unscripted, with no imperial guard protection.

Kai-Long smiled at her. "Is everything okay now?"

She gulped. "I think so."

"We will have you back before anyone knows you are gone." He reached across and clasped her hand.

And when would that be? It wasn't like the decoy could sit and drink tea until dawn. She squirmed. "Heavens, this is a horrible idea. What do the girls who wait in the pagodas usually do?"

"Not to worry. Eventually, when no one is watching, they just head back to their own quarters."

"Someone is *always* watching me!" Everything was so clear now, even if alcohol burned in her veins. "She might look like me, but the poor girl doesn't know the secret imperial language or the codes that will get her into the Imperial Family's sleeping quarters." How hadn't she seen it before?

His expression did not look the least bit concerned. "Don't worry. All she has to do is drop the bauble and no one will be the wiser. I—"

The palanquin lurched to a stop, sending Kaiya's stomach into a flop. Only with supreme effort did she keep everything down. Still, any hope of meeting Hardeep was now dashed. Her shoulders slumped.

Outside, swords rasped from sheaths.

"Identify yourself," someone said.

CHAPTER 16
Conspiracy Theories

Jie slipped out of the ridiculous pink dress in a side room of the clan safehouse in Jiangkou. It had been tempting to intentionally stain the satin in one or five places during the hasty clean-up, but maybe she'd return it to the Tarkothi instead of burning it.

First, the possible rebellion in the North took precedence, and in their rush to organize information, they hadn't been able to completely scour the warehouse. If a conspirator with a trained eye came looking for the now-deceased Sha, they'd know their treachery had been compromised. Maybe they'd move their plans for rebellion up, before the *Tianzi* could preempt it. Tugging on her utility suit, Jie slid the door open and went into the main room.

As always, Tian was working on his convoluted mess of strings and paper notes and evidence, crisscrossing the room like a web spun by a spider addicted to gooseweed. He'd probably devised this visual method for organizing information not so much for himself, but for the sake of others: a glimpse into all the disjointed goings-on in his head.

His lips drew a tight line as he furiously scribbled more notes. Knowing him, the deaths of five men weighed heavily on his gentle soul. So smart, so skilled, yet so hesitant to use those skills. It's what made him so attract—endearing.

He looked up from his scraps of paper and presented Sha's shoe. "The dry mud on the sole is greyish."

Jie nodded. The only place around here with that color mud was along the Jade River, which emptied into Jiangkou Harbor. "Unless he was fishing in the Jade River shallows with those, I would bet he recently visited the quays near the river."

He held up a folded packet labelled *sawdust*. "Near the lumber mills."

"And the river barges," she said. "And then, there was the pink fish paste under his nails. Assuming he wasn't a sloppy eater, he must have been checking out barrels of it."

"It will keep for a year. Or more. Perfect for surviving a long siege."

The door whispered open and Huang Zhen, a boy of ten, slunk in. The initiate's stealth skills were improving, though not enough to assign him dangerous missions. "Eldest Sister Jie, Elder Brother Tian. We investigated Victorious Trading. It's a stock corporation, owned in part by Lord Chu, Lord Xi, Lord Qin, Lord Tong, and Evergreen Trading. And guess what?" His face brightened.

In contrast, Tian's face might have been the dark side of the White Moon. He jotted the names down on a sheet of paper. "None of those lords have arrived in the capital. For Prince Kai-Wu's wedding."

Jie followed his gaze into the web of notes. "What's the connection?"

"Lord Tong claims the barbarians are threatening the saltpeter mines." Tian pinned up the name list to one of the strings. "The others are all *Yu-Ming* lords of the North. A combined twenty-one thousand, three hundred provincial soldiers under them."

Jie outlined a map of the realm with her finger in the air. A quite accurate one, in all modesty. "And those counties are the major saltpeter producers. Working together, it would cut off fresh firepowder supply from the rest of the country."

"Aren't imperial stocks large enough to overwhelm those counties?" Huang Zhen asked.

"Maybe," Tian said, oblivious to the smudge of ink on his nose. "But Wailian Castle is impregnable. The *Tianzi* would have to commit ninety-two percent of the national army and seventy-three percent of the loyal provincial armies to a long siege."

Ninety-two and seventy-three? Exactly? Jie stifled a chuckle at his precision. "And that is assuming the rest of the *Yu-Ming* are loyal. What do we know of Lord Tong?"

Tian shrugged. "He is fifty-four. His wife died in childbirth three years ago. He hasn't remarried."

"Strange he hasn't," Jie thought aloud.

Huang Zhen's face flushed a red bright enough to light a dark room. "Little Sister Feng Mi says he likes young girls, and is very rough."

Jie shuddered. Feng Mi was only nine, a *Moquan* adept planted as a Night Blossom trainee in the Floating World. If Lord Tong had harmed her, Jie would make sure he paid for more than rebellious intent. She shook the idea out of her head. "No, a hereditary lord marries not to sate his appetite, but rather to build alliances."

"Suspicious." Tian set down the list of potentially rebellious lords. "What about Evergreen Trading?"

"I researched it." Huang Zhen flashed an impish grin. "It's a stock corporation, held by other companies, all in the South."

"The South," Tian repeated, pointing to the bottom of her imaginary map. "Where Lord Tong is illegally shipping firepowder."

On her air map, Jie traced the highway up the central valley. "If the *Tianzi* sent the bulk of the army to pacify the North, it would leave the capital vulnerable to a surprise attack from the South."

Huang Zhen looked from one to the other with rapt attention. "How do we uncover Lord Tong's allies in the South?"

"Well, to start," Jie said, "which lords from the South have not yet arrived in the capital for the imperial wedding?"

"*Yu-Ming* Lords Chi, Shen, and Bai from Yutou Province." Huang Zhen counted his fingers. "From Nanling Province, *Tai-Ming* Lord Peng—"

"That's it," Tian said. "Sha mentioned Lord Peng."

Jie shook her head. "He's married to the *Tianzi's* sister, and Nanling Province didn't get firepowder from Wailian."

"Not that we know of. And the *Wild Orchid* is registered to Nanling. So just in case..." Tian wrote Lord Peng's name on his list. "Let's scout the trade offices and warehouses near the river docks. Zhen: send every available adept in the area to meet us there."

"But first," Jie added, "Use the horse relays to send our suspicions to Master Yan. And I'll send a cleaner to that warehouse. The *Tianzi* will need time to formulate a response before Lord Tong can act."

CHAPTER 17

Blades of the Night

Head buzzing with rice wine, Kaiya listened as boots clopped and weapons rasped outside the suffocating confines of the palanquin. She squeezed her fists tight. Despite Kai-Long's reassurances, the servants who helped her risked torture and execution. Now, there might be a more immediate threat. This debacle couldn't get much worse. She didn't even have a dagger to defend herself.

Neither did Kai-Long. Still, he snapped open the door and jumped out. "Stay here."

No, that wasn't an option. Someone had to take responsibility for this mess. She crawled on all fours out of the palanquin, without any semblance of imperial grace. At least the hooded cloak and illusionist's bauble hid her identity. Legs quavering from alcohol and sitting, she staggered to her feet.

The surroundings didn't look familiar. Lined by two-story wood buildings, with storefronts on the first floor and residences on top, it could be virtually any side street in Huajing. Kai-Long's provincial soldiers all stood with broadswords drawn. He, himself, took a sword from a guard and strode toward the newcomer.

A lone figure with a curved blade in hand blocked the procession's way. He stepped forward into the light, both hands raised.

Prince Hardeep! His chin was now bare, the pointed beard gone in the hours since they met. His beautiful blue eyes found hers in the crowd. Though the hooded cloak hid her face, recognition dawned in his expression.

Trying to stand straight, Kaiya lowered the hood and smoothed out her dress.

"Prince Hardeep." Speaking perfectly in the Ayuri tongue, Kai-Long locked his gaze on Hardeep's backpack. "This is not where we had planned to meet."

Adjusting a pack, the prince shifted his intense gaze from her to her cousin. "Yes. I fear the Madurans have learned of my visit to the palace." He glanced back in the direction he'd come. "I was followed. I've lost them for now, with the help of my men. I thought you were bringing the princess. Who is that?"

Oh, the magic bead. Kaiya started to stuff it in her sash when Kai-Long placed a hand on her wrist.

Pulling her along, he sidled up to the prince and whispered in his ear. "This is her. Aksumi magic."

Hardeep's mouth gaped...though he had seemed to recognize her before. If only she had a mirror to see what the magic made her look like. He nodded in a slow bob.

"Are you unharmed?" Kaiya asked.

Shoulders squared, Hardeep made a single, resolute nod. "I came to warn you. You should return to the safety of the palace walls." Though his body language suggested confidence, his beautiful eyes fixed on the ground in defeat.

Kai-Long's brow furrowed. "What about the Dragon Scale Lute? What about her potential to save your country and protect ours?"

What about her accomplices back at the palace? Kaiya clenched and unclenched her fists. Her alcohol-addled mind made the dilemma even more confounding.

"I can't risk her life." Hardeep looked up at her. "Not even for my beloved homeland."

The trembling in his voice struck a chord, making Kaiya's legs wobble even more than her weak tolerance for rice wine. Even through the drunken haze, all indecision faded. Like the Dragon Singers in the epic songs of old, she would save a beleaguered nation. It was her choice, not his. "I—" She stumbled forward a few steps.

Arms outstretched, he caught her. Warm and enveloping, his embrace felt safer than a full complement of imperial guards. His luminous eyes gazed into hers. "No. You don't know the Madurans. They don't care about your noble intentions or your gentle soul. They don't care if you are just sixteen. If they think you are meddling in their affairs, they won't hesitate to kill you."

A moment of unadulterated clarity pierced through the mental fog. In the brevity of that moment, it all made sense. She pushed herself out of his arms. "No. My country's sale of guns and firepowder brought on your country's misery. Our classic texts on governance teach that we must rectify wrongs we have caused."

His eyes widened as he leaned back. "But..."

Her voice flowed more steadily than expected, reflecting the certainty in her heart. Maintaining defiant eye contact, she gave a decisive nod. "I *will* help."

Kai-Long shuffled on his feet. "This is wonderful, but how long will it take?"

Her moment ruined, she tried to glare at him, but wasn't sure which of the two Kai-Longs was the real one.

Hardeep looked up at the Iridescent Moon, now waxing to its third gibbous. "I can have Kaiya back at the palace in two hours."

More than enough time to swap out with the servants. Maybe even to return to the reception, since that would last until all hours of the morning.

Kai-Long clasped her hand. "Please be safe."

"I'll be all right." She leaned into the prince. "Prince Hardeep has Paladin training."

Kai-Long searched her eyes. With a sighing nod, he took a sheathed dagger from his guard and passed it to her. "Very well." He bowed to Prince Hardeep. "I entrust you with the princess' life. My uncle would be devastated if anything happened to her."

"As would I." Hardeep pressed his palms together and bowed his head.

Kaiya squared her shoulders. "I will be fine."

He then took her hand in his. The heat coursed through her. "Let's go."

Walking down the street, Kaiya glanced back at Kai-Long. His lips drew into a tight line. She would owe him quite a favor. He'd done so much already, helping to get her out of trouble. Unless...

She turned to Hardeep. "May I ask you a question?"

"Of course. Anything."

"When you were surrounded by all the angry guards, you stomped on the ground and told them everything was all right." She stopped, so her drunken legs wouldn't send her tumbling into an embarrassing heap, and met his gaze. "Was that Paladin magic? I felt the echo."

Smile broadening, he nodded. "You noticed! The stories from the War of Ancient Gods claim Yanyan could sense when Vanya used her Paladin skills. You have already grown more in a day than most Paladin trainees."

Her face flushed hot. Still, she had to ask the next question, the one that ate her. "You...you didn't use it on me, to convince me to help Ankira?"

His jovial expression turned serious. He took her hands in his. "Paladin magic doesn't work that way. Even if it could, I wouldn't use it to make you do something against your will."

Studying his face, she found nothing but sincerity. She hung her head. "I'm sorry. I should have never asked."

He lifted her chin. "Don't apologize. You are right to question magic. As I told you before, there is a world beyond your Great Wall."

She swallowed hard, even as relief mixed in with her embarrassment. It was time to change the subject. Her hand ventured toward his jaw. "What happened to your beard?"

Maybe it was the rice wine, but when he guided her fingers along his smooth chin, it sent her belly erupting in a swarm of butterflies.

"I shaved it, so that my enemies would have a harder time recognizing me."

She smiled. It made him look even younger, more handsome, though his unique blue irises were a dead giveaway. "Where is the Dragon Scale Lute?"

Hardeep looked around the street, and then leaned in. He spoke Ayuri in a low voice. "I don't have it. But I carry with me an old journal from my uncle's visit to Vyara City, twenty-nine years ago. He was there representing my country when your emperor dispatched a mission to negotiate the sale of muskets and firepowder with both Ankira and Madura."

Her alcohol-muddled mind took a few seconds to grasp the significance. Kaiya sucked in a sharp breath. Hua had played both sides of the conflict and profited. Anger churned inside her.

"I don't blame you for your nation's past sins." He squeezed her hand fondly. "I am just glad you recognize them."

"How does the journal relate to the Lute?"

"Twenty-nine years ago, the dragon Avarax awoke from a millennium of sleep. He descended on Vyara City and threatened to immolate it with his fiery breath."

Kaiya shuddered. A peninsular city of spires, domes, canals, and fruit trees, Vyara City was home to hundreds of thousands of people. They would have all perished in dragonfire. "What happened?"

"An elf prince played a song on a lute which repelled Avarax."

Repelled a dragon with just a lute, the Arkothi equivalent of a pipa! Kaiya gasped, and then cocked her head. "The Dragon Scale Lute?"

Prince Hardeep's grin spread from ear to ear. "Its resonance plate was made from one of Avarax's scales. Its strings were made from his whiskers. If it could scare away the mighty Avarax, it could certainly rout a human army. I have tracked it back here, to your capital."

Kaiya's brain swam in circles. All this time, she thought he had it. Even without rice wine, the revelation would have confused her. "How did it get here?"

Prince Hardeep's grin faded. "My uncle noted in his journal that it fell into the hands of Rumiya, the Grand Vizier of Madura. He gifted it to one of your trade officials after he helped negotiate the firepowder deal. We're going to his house now."

"Whose?" she asked. Chief Minister Tan, probably, given his defense of the agreement. He'd benefitted personally. Anger boiled in her chest.

"Wait. Something feels wrong." Hardeep fell silent and beckoned her along.

At this hour, they encountered only a handful of people, mostly laborers on their way home. Prince Hardeep held her right elbow and hand, supporting her shaky steps. On occasion, he took a furtive glance around. After a few minutes, they headed into a side street.

"Do you feel it?" he asked. "Someone is watching us."

She hadn't felt anything. There was no one around. Kaiya started to turn her head.

"No," he whispered. "Keep your attention forward."

At the intersection up ahead, a large man dressed in a black shirt and pants stepped into the street. He pointed a broadsword at Hardeep. "Give me the backpack."

Hand on his curved *talwar* sword, Prince Hardeep stopped in place, jerking her closer to him. The magical bead slipped from her fingers and tinkled to the ground.

Click, swoosh, click, swoosh. The rhythmic clicks came from behind.

Prince Hardeep pushed her to the side. Something—no, two things—zipped through the space where they had just stood and thunked into a house. He whipped out his sword, his backpack not seeming to affect the fluidity of his motion.

If only her head were a little clearer! Fumbling for her dagger, Kaiya searched for the source of the clicks. Another large man leveled a repeating crossbow at them. He pressed the trigger and cocked.

"Come on!" Kaiya pulled Prince Hardeep out of the line of fire and ran toward the swordsman. If they lined up with the other assailant, the crossbowman would likely think twice about shooting.

A pair of enormous men in black hoods turned the corner, joining the first. They all sank into attacking stances. Behind her, two more charged in. Six against two. Or one, considering she was just a drunk girl with a dagger.

"Help!" Kaiya yelled. It might be all she was good for. With lights shining behind sliding windows, many of the citizens had to be awake.

Though she had pulled Hardeep, now he hauled her forward, moving so fast her drunken feet nearly entangled each other. What was he doing?

Above, windows opened and heads poked out. In a city famed for its safety, the fighting must have come as a surprise.

The three in front leaped in with curved swords, cutting in deadly coordination. Prince Hardeep edged to one side while deflecting one of the blades and prodding her past the attacks. Cloth sheared open and one of the would-be-assassins buckled to the ground. Hardeep yanked his hooded mask off.

A boy about her age, perhaps younger despite his huge size, stared back at her.

"Come on!" Hardeep said, pulling her through the opening. On the other side, they broke into a run.

Eyes glinting, Hardeep mumbled something unintelligible, though the foul tone suggested some sort of curse. The sudden rush of blood to her head, combined with the alcohol, sent her vision blacking at the edges. A cold wind blasted through her hair. Her legs gave out and she staggered, nearly falling to the ground.

Hardeep propped her up and slowed to a stop. Stopping? It wasn't as if she ran that fast, and those men—boys—had long legs. She blinked a few times and searched for the assailants.

There was no sign of them.

Panting, she looked up at Hardeep. "How did we escape them so fast?"

"I'm not sure, but listen."

There were no sounds of pursuit, just the sound of several muted conversations behind second-floor windows. They couldn't have run that far, but maybe her muddled brain had warped her perception of time and space. Where were they now?

"I think we are safe now." He ran a hand through her hair. "You did well. I owe you my life."

"How so?" She tilted her head. He'd saved both of them, when her stumbling had slowed them down.

"The crossbow bolt would have hit me had you not pulled me out of the way." The sincerity in his tone and intensity of his gaze her pulse flutter.

"I've never heard of anything like this happening in the capital." She frowned. The gravity of what had just happened felt like a ship anchor on her shoulders. Something was wrong, but she couldn't pinpoint what.

He harrumphed. "I would expect nothing less from the Madurans."

She shook her head. "I don't think they were Madurans. They didn't look Ayuri." No, with the brown eyes and black hair... "They were definitely Cathayi."

"The Maduran trade office probably hired some mercenaries. They sure picked some large ones."

Very big, probably among the largest humans she'd ever seen. "And young, too."

"Well, we are safe for now. And we're here." He pointed.

She followed his gesture to the sparkling granite walls surrounding a good-sized villa. A fountain bubbled behind the walls, pouring into what was likely a pond. As a whole, the house looked too large and elegant to belong to even a high-level official. Not even a secretary or minister could afford such opulence.

Though maybe Chief Minister Tan could, with his ill-gotten wealth. It was corrupt men like him who undermined Father's moral authority. She might not be a Dragon Singer yet, but she could live by their principles. She squared her shoulders and started toward the gate.

"Wait." Hardeep seized her hand.

She turned and looked at him.

"We need a plan."

Oh, she had a plan. No one would dare deny an imperial princess. "Whose residence is this?"

"Lord Tong Baxian. He was one of the architects of the trade deal with Madura."

The name sounded familiar. A rich and powerful hereditary lord, given the size of the villa. If he'd sold Madura out, he'd sooner turn her over to Father for a reward than surrender the Lute. Liquid courage drying up, she paused and listened.

CHAPTER 18

The Dragon Scale Lute

The gurgle of water churning in the pond beyond Lord Tong's villa walls might have just as easily come from Kaiya's stomach. And not because of the rice wine.

She and Hardeep would have to trespass and steal, like common thieves. This plan was a far cry from the lofty ideals of the Dragon Singers. Her hand strayed to Tian's pebble. He'd never condone this.

Or maybe he would, considering how Lord Tong had acquired the Lute by selling out a small nation and its people. Swallowing down her mortification and replacing it with righteous indignation, she looked.

Two guards flanked the ornate iron gates. To think she'd almost marched right up to them and demanded entrance.

"There has to be a servant's entrance." She pulled Hardeep to the alley formed by the stone walls of this and the adjacent compound. As suspected, there was a plain wooden side door.

Unguarded.

Exchanging glances with her, Hardeep gave it a pull, and found it locked. He turned back to her. "I could break it down."

"His guards would hear it. I have another idea." A drunken one, but one which might actually work. She knocked.

His eyes widened. "What are you doing? You're letting them know we're here."

"Trust me." She flashed a confident smile that she wasn't really feeling.

The eye slot snapped open, revealing dark eyes framed by crinkles. "What do you want?"

She held up a jade bracelet, her favorite. It was worth a small house, but it was a small sacrifice to make if this bribe could benefit the Ankirans. "Let us in, and this is yours."

The eyes locked on the bangle, evaluating.

Kaiya held her breath. Maybe this wasn't such a good idea, if this lord inspired loyalty among his soldiers and servants. If whoever was on the other side alerted the rest of the villa, it would slam the door on any chance to get in.

Shaking his head, Hardeep frowned at her and reached for his blade.

The door opened. A middle-aged man in green livery stepped through, and snatched the bracelet. After a visual once-over of them, he started down the alley.

"Wait," she said, alcohol haze fading a fraction. She held out a gold ring, a treasured gift from Mother. "Tell me where I can find the Lute."

Licking his lips, he looked at the ring, then pointed to Hardeep's ornate *talwar*. "Give me the sword, too, and I'll answer your question."

Without a moment's hesitation, Hardeep unhooked his scabbard.

Kaiya placed a hand on his wrist. "Wait. What if we are attacked again?"

"No sword, no information." Crossing his arms, the servant jutted his chin out.

"It's all right," Hardeep said in Ayuri. "I can disarm anyone who doesn't have Paladin magic."

This was a bad idea. Still, Hardeep had been unarmed against the imperial guards and escaped with only a shredded sleeve. She retracted her hand.

With a smile, Hardeep presented his weapon in one hand.

The servant took it with greedy eyes. "What about the ring?"

"After you tell us what you know." Kaiya tried to glare, but the alcohol probably made her appear cross-eyed.

His brow creased for a moment. "The chamberlain plays the lute. Strange, foreign instrument."

Kaiya shook her head. "Impossible. Only a Dragon Singer could play it. It is made from a dragon scale."

"Oh, *that* lute." The servant's mouth rounded. "The lord shows it off sometimes. He keeps it in the vault in the northeast corner of the compound."

Hopefully, Hardeep had a better sense of direction than her. Kaiya frowned, but offered the ring.

The man snatched it up and scampered down the alley.

Kaiya swallowed hard, partially regretting the loss of her jewelry.

"How did you know that would work?" Hardeep beamed.

"The lord must be at the reception, with most of his guards. Without good reason to deny us, a servant wouldn't turn down the equivalent of a lifetime of pay."

The appreciation and admiration in his nod sent flutters into her belly.

She fanned her hot face. "Let's find the vault."

With Prince Hardeep one step behind her, Kaiya squared her shoulders and walked through the servants' door with as much grace as the alcohol allowed. Which was to say, she almost tripped on her borrowed cloak.

Cream paper lanterns with light baubles hung from a central string across the courtyard. Sharply pitched eaves of green tile capped a spacious two-story residence and several side buildings. Red latticework framed windows in the white walls. At the center of the manicured courtyard, a carp pond bubbled. The compound seemed devoid of activity, though the pluck of some stringed instrument echoed from within the main residence. The musical scale sounded foreign. Could it be?

It wasn't in the direction the servant had said. Her gaze locked on a small one-story building with a wooden door on the near side of the villa. After a quick visual sweep of the yard, she started toward it.

Hardeep grabbed her arm. "That's the servants' privy. The vault is that one." He pointed toward the far end.

Kaiya swallowed hard. They'd have to cross the entire compound without being seen. Unless... She pulled him along the shadowed wall, toward the privy, with the stealth of a legendary *Moquan*.

"Do you have to..." he gritted his teeth. "...relieve yourself?"

Heat flared in her cheeks. "No. We can hide behind the privy, and use the shadows between the other buildings to get there."

The silence between them was punctuated only by the plucks of the foreign-sounding instrument.

He grinned. "You're good at this sneaking around."

Her face flushed hotter, and she chuckled nervously. "I'm secretly a Black Fist."

"A what?"

Of course he wouldn't understand. "They're the boogeymen, stealing naughty children at night."

His brow furrowed.

"I'm joking; they're just a myth."

With a shrug, he followed her through the shadows.

Even on the outside, the privy stank worse than anything she'd ever smelled. How pampered her life was, to have servants taking care of every inconvenience. She held her breath as she peered around its corner.

A servant in green livery hurried down a path between the residence's two wings, but he wasn't facing them. She dashed toward the next building.

And tripped.

She fell face-first onto the light-colored gravel. Curse the rice wine. Biting her lip, she suppressed a squeak and looked toward the servant.

His eyes swept back and forth. His gaze paused right where Hardeep was.

Kaiya's chest tightened.

Then the man's head turned, and he continued on his way.

She let out her breath as quietly as she could, and allowed Hardeep to help her up. Her stumble now proved more humiliating than painful or frightening.

With only the instrument's sound and the occasional voice in the distance, they reached the vault without further incident. It was almost too easy. Surely, the Heavens must be smiling upon their task. Like the Dragon Singers, they were correcting a historical mistake.

Hardeep studied the heavy door and lock. He grinned. "I don't suppose a Black Fist could pick that?"

"Maybe if they really existed." She snorted and peered at the lock.

"Then we will need to hurry." Closing his eyes and taking a deep breath, he lowered his shoulder and slammed into the door.

The timbers shuddered with an ear-splitting crack.

The musical instrument in the distance went silent, then voices erupted in chatter.

Kaiya threw up her hands. Even in her drunken state, she knew... "The door opens outward!"

He gave the door a hard tug, and it opened.

"How?" She gawked.

With a grin, he pointed at the mangled locking mechanism. "Paladin training. I focused my power into that spot. Now let's hurry!"

They raced in. When he closed the door behind them, the room fell into darkness.

"Keep quiet," he whispered. "They won't notice the lock unless they look carefully. We just need to hide here until they pass. Now..."

They were about to lay eyes on the Dragon Scale Lute. Kaiya blinked as Hardeep opened his palm to expose a light bauble. Pulse racing with a mix of apprehension and excitement, she looked around.

The vault was empty.

How could that be? Had the servant lied? Then again, it didn't make sense for there to be nothing in here at all. She turned to Hardeep.

His eyes took in the vault without seeing.

Had this all been for naught? Her jewelry, gone. And now they'd have to hole up in this stuffy, narrow room until Heavens knew when. How long before the court realized she wasn't in the palace? This night couldn't possibly get worse. Panic rose in her voice. "Where...where could it be?"

"Wait." He took her hand and placed it on his chest. "Let me think." He felt hot, even through the smooth, thick cloth of his *kurta*. His heart thumped. Slow. Resolute. It seemed almost audible.

Like her guards and handmaidens earlier today.

Listen. Lord Xu had implored her to listen. She closed her eyes.

The heavy door and thick walls partially muffled voices and footsteps outside, but Hardeep's heartbeat now sounded clear.

And there was something odd—foreign and ominous—among the multitude of sounds outside. One hand on his chest, she placed the other on the door.

A symphony of vibrations echoed through the wood.

Then, the door opened.

Kaiya's heart leaped into her throat. Though the break in contact with the door had severed her link to the vibrations, sound now poured in. Boots crunching on gravel. Shouts. And that nearly inaudible, ominous pulse. Three guards burst in, weapons bared. If Heaven had smiled on them before, it now pointed and laughed. Behind them followed a young man with beautifully coifed hair and swishing green robes. He cradled a stringed instrument, like a pipa, in one arm. The light bauble lantern in his hand shined on the white powder on his face, which gave him an ivory complexion. He might be wearing more foundation than she had been this morning.

About her age, he was handsome, bordering on beautiful, with dignified features that might belong on a member of the imperial family. And of course, there was the lute in his arm.

Made of wood, not dragon scale. Its strings resonated, but it wasn't the source of the foreboding thrum.

"Who are you?" His voice came out high-pitched, tremulous, and effeminate, eliminating any resemblance to her brothers. Holding the lantern higher, the young man's eyes roved over them, then to a spot in the vault, when they widened. Panic made his voice crack. "What did you do with the Dragon Scale Lute?"

What? The servant hadn't misled them, then—the Lute was supposed to be here. She exchanged glances with Hardeep, who shrugged. She looked at the lute in the man's hands.

Gaze following hers, he snorted. "No, not this lute. *The* Lute."

She shook her head. How did this happen? And how were they going to get out of this predicament? The room was so stuffy, and one of the guards stank of rice wine, exacerbating her drunken haze. "We don't have it."

The leader beckoned to the soldiers. "Take them."

The men surged forward.

Hardeep's hand reached toward his sword hilt.

Which wasn't there, after their trade for information.

Kaiya stared, wide-eyed.

Undaunted, Hardeep twisted and weaved through their attacks. They pursued him deeper into the vault.

Leaving her near the entrance, with the leader. He wasn't that much larger than her.

She stepped to help Hardeep, but he waved her off. "Go! Find the Lute!"

Surely he'd be all right. These were two soldiers, certainly not the equal of imperial guards. Head still buzzing, she pushed past the leader.

His thin fingers clamped down around her left wrist.

Though she'd never taken it seriously, the contact reflexes from her Praise Spring Fist training kicked in. She rotated her left palm up, exposing the soft inside of his forearm. She dragged her fingernails across the flesh.

Crying out, he yanked his hand back.

She hiked up her skirts, turned, and ran. Her heart pumped, and for that moment her head felt nominally clear.

Not daring to look back, she dashed across the courtyard and rounded a red column on the residence's veranda.

Breaths heaving, she peered around the column toward the vault.

The three soldiers and their leader emerged, heads looking left and right.

There was no sign of Hardeep. Had they slain him? Kaiya covered her mouth.

"She can't have gotten far," the young man said. "They must have had an accomplice who took the Dragon Scale Lute. You, go get the captain. He's at the imperial reception."

She ducked back, closed her eyes, and took several deep breaths to fight down the rising panic and despair.

That haunting resonance pulsed between the thumps of her heart in her ears. Though nearly imperceptible, it sounded louder than before, and seemed to be taunting her. The source was close. Inside the residence.

Through her slippers, she gripped the stone veranda with her toes and straightened her spine.

The soldiers' footsteps spread throughout the courtyard, though none approached. She opened her eyes and scanned the area.

The armed men were marching along the wall. Their little leader, lute still cradled in his arms, swept his gaze over the compound.

He was still by the vault, making it impossible to check on Hardeep without getting caught.

Could he be bleeding to death?

Think, think. There had to be a way to create a diversion and double back. Drawing deeper onto the veranda, Kaiya edged toward a door. She pressed her ear to it, and heard nothing save for the eerie thrum that answered her heart. She slid the door open and slipped in.

Heat washed over her as she left the cool night air. Bloodwood stands, porcelain vases, and hanging scrolls all decorated the central hall. The quiet moan came from somewhere nearby.

It had to be the Lute. Find it, and she'd threaten to smash it unless they let her help Hardeep. She closed her eyes and, with one hand in front of her, followed the sound.

A dozen paces down the hall, the thrum's intensity blared from the left. The sound of her heartbeat echoed off of...she turned her head and looked through the circular archway into a side room.

Like an insect drawn to a light bauble, she ventured in. A red, blue, and white wool carpet from the Ayuri South felt soft beneath her feet, and covered much of the marble tiles. Calligraphy and paintings by famous artists evoked a sense of calm and welcome.

Bloodwood chairs surrounded a low table with a marble top, and on one of them rested a lute. Similar in appearance to a pipa, its fretted neck tilted at a sharp angle. It had at least a dozen strings compared to a pipa's four. Its soundboard was the color of cinnabar, and had a texture similar to leather.

Avarax's scale. Why would the chamberlain have expected it to be in the vault, if it was here?

Kaiya's eyes widened as she picked it up. It had a vibration, a life of its own, like Yanyan's pipa and so unlike her own. So ancient it must be; it smelled like rust. The several pairs of twisted strings shimmered like wet lines of spider silk in the morning sun. She ran her hand over the resonance plate. With its countless ridges, it resembled the cross-section of a tree stump.

"She's in here!" a high-pitched voice yelled from the doorway.

Kaiya's heart jumped into her throat. She turned to find the leader. So entranced had she been by the Lute, he'd come upon her unawares.

He stared at the instrument, mouth agape. "You! So you had it all along. Where did you get the strings? Do they work?"

Strings? Work? Kaiya looked down at them. They certainly looked new... She faced the man and studied him.

He didn't have a weapon. With his thin build and the way he wrung his delicate hands, he couldn't possibly be a soldier. Still his eyes looked at her, calculating.

Standing only half a head taller, he was still more than a match for any princess, save for little Lin Ziqiu, who took the Praise Spring fighting more seriously. He apparently came to the same conclusion, and took a step closer.

Her pulse raced. She raised the instrument above her head, though the very act sent her muddled head spinning. "Stay away, or I'll smash it."

He froze for a few seconds, then took a step closer. "Go ahead. I'd hoped the strings would remain forever lost, anyway."

Why? She lowered the Lute and took a step back.

Boots hurried across the wood floors in the hall, and a guard appeared at the doorway.

"We didn't find anyone else, Chamberlain Li," he said, his eyes on her.

A chamberlain? At such a young age? Kaiya studied his made-up features again. It would be a surprise if he were a day older than her.

The guard favored her with a curious expression. "Isn't that Princess Kaiya?"

"How do you know?" Chamberlain Li asked, now looking at her with renewed curiosity. "Have you seen her?"

"I had the impression she was prettier, but this is undoubtedly her."

Kaiya gritted her teeth.

"You're right." Li gave a slow nod, then narrowed his eyes. "*Dian-xia*, why did they send *you* to steal Lord Tong's lute? Now that I think about it, *who* sent you?"

Pulse skittering, hands shaking, Kaiya lifted the Lute again. "I'll smash it."

"Go ahead." Li waved a dismissive hand.

"No!" The guard stretched out a staying hand. "Chamberlin Li, it is you who is supposed to…"

Kaiya looked from one to the other. With Li's expression scrunched up into apprehension, he didn't appear to be bluffing. Or maybe the rice wine was still muddling her judgement.

"Bring her friend over. She'll be more inclined to negotiate."

Friend… Hardeep! He was alive! Hope rose in Kaiya's chest.

The guard turned on his heel and clacked down the hallway, leaving her with Li.

"There's no need for us to be uncivil." He gestured to a side table, where a porcelain decanter sat with several small matching cups. His fingers quivered. "Have some rice wine."

Tea, an inner voice implored.

Even as she kept the Lute cocked like a club in her own trembling hands, Kaiya gave a polite nod. She wouldn't drink another drop of alcohol for the rest of her life, but for now the request would get the chamberlain a few steps away.

He poured the rice wine into a cup, his grace in every motion that of a musician.

"Where did you learn to play a foreign instrument?" she asked with genuine curiosity.

He looked up from his work, eyes narrowed, searching hers. His expression softened. "My mother was a famous pipa player and singer in Yanhu, and she taught me. When Lord Tong hired me, he bade me learn. I taught myself."

What a strange demand of a chamberlain. "I would like to speak with Lord Tong."

The chamberlain wet his lips as he offered the cup. "He…he, uh… Barbarian uprisings have kept him busy in the North. He was unable to visit the capital for the prince's wedding."

Kaiya stayed back, ignoring the wine.

Two sets of bootsteps bracketed staggering footfalls in the hall outside. A pair of guards turned into the room, Hardeep draped between them.

Kaiya's heart leaped as they thrust him to the floor. He showed no outward sign of injury, and his breathing was light.

"The turtle egg is heavier than he looks," the one guard from before said.

Kaiya bristled at the insult, and fought the urge to run to Hardeep's side.

"Now, *Dian-xia*, turn over the Lute and I'll let you and your friend leave." Despite his offer, he still eyed the Dragon Scale Lute as if he'd just sucked a lemon and a bitter melon at the same time.

Could he be trusted? Probably not. Kaiya looked at the dwarf-made water clock, now indicating that Caiyue waxed to its third gibbous. One hour had already passed since she left the palace. They needed to get back before anyone realized she was gone. Her gaze shifted to Hardeep.

Chamberlain Li followed her eyes. "If you don't hand it over now, I'll have my men kill him."

CHAPTER 19
Treachery Afoot

A cool sea breeze blew through Tian's hair as he reached the top of the lighthouse, at the head of the seawall that separated the harbor from the mouth of the Jade River. Jie was briefing the four *Moquan* adepts gathered there.

Looking up, he found Caiyue in its usual spot, now waxing past its third gibbous, indicating less than two hours before midnight. Only a little more than an hour had passed since he'd killed Lamp Man Sha, and they'd already found Fat Nose Jiang. With the evidence on Sha leaving a trail here, it had been almost too easy.

Below, light bauble lamps hung from posts on the seventeen riverside docks, mingling with the soft blue light of Guanyin's Eye. Twenty-two men armed with broadswords stood guard as thirty-seven longshoremen and boatmen worked to load eleven privately owned river barges.

Fat Nose Jiang oversaw the operation at the head of one of the quays, personally inspecting a hundred and forty-two bales of rice, twelve barrels of fish paste, and eight kegs of sulfur. They were nearly done, and no doubt the barges would push off at first light, bound upstream for Lord Tong and his allies. Whatever else could be said about the conspirators, they were efficient.

Tian unfurled his official robes and passed them to Chong Xiang, a forty-two-year-old adept with a crook nose. "Put these on. You know the plan."

Chong beamed. "Brilliant. Just like the Architect."

Tian snorted. Chong must've just been a green recruit when the legendary Black Lotus strategist died on a secret mission thirty years before. He'd have no basis for comparison. Still, if Chong wanted to wax nostalgic... "That makes you the Surgeon," Tian said.

"Then that leaves me as the Beauty?" Jie peered at Guanyin's Eye, the Blue Moon.

Her reference to the last of the ill-fated trio would have made sense, except there would be no baiting gullible men. "No, you're the lookout and runner."

She sucked on her lower lip and released it with a pop.

He studied Chong, who shrugged into the official robes. "Have Jiang at the dock overseer's office in ten minutes."

With that, he started his mental countdown. He and the adepts descended the lighthouse. Jie motioned them to assigned lookout points as they snuck along the south end of the docks toward the overseer's office.

Its weathered plank siding afforded plenty of handholds, and in seconds he had gained the rooftop. The terrace provided a commanding view of the wharfs, just a *biao*'s throw away from where Jiang was now unfurling a scroll and reading. Stairs descended to the office below. Tian tested the door. Unlocked and well-oiled.

Slipping in, he padded down the steps. The overseer's office was only a twelfth the size of the harbormaster's, probably because the overseer was busy overseeing his own finances. Tian worked his way between several desks, taking note of the shuttered lamps, and came to the door. He unlocked it. Five minutes to spare, assuming Chong kept to the timeline. Cracking the wooden window shutters, he squinted out.

Jiang pressed the scroll to his chest while Chong crossed his arms. A guard flanked Jiang, hand on sword hilt.

"I don't recognize you from the harbormaster's office," Jiang said.

Chong's booming voice carried the chill air. "Look, I don't want to be out here at this hour any more than the harbormaster, but since I'm just the new deputy, he sent me. There's a minor clerical error we need to resolve."

Jiang leaned in toward Chong and whispered something beyond Tian's hearing. Something shiny glinted in his hand.

"A bribe," Jie whispered, her breath hot on his ear.

Tian whipped around. She'd snuck up on him, yet again. "Is everyone in place?"

She yawned. "Very soon."

He turned back to the crack between the shutters.

"I see everything is in order." Chong gestured toward the overseer's office. "You'll have to sign an affidavit."

Jiang threw up an arm. "Can't it wait?"

"My sleep is worth more than a gold *yuan*."

The guard's sword hand twitched. Chong settled ever so slightly in his stance, his hands reaching across into either sleeve. Jie placed one hand on the shutters while the other palmed a throwing spike.

"Very well." With a sigh, Jiang motioned for his guard to follow.

Tian blew out a long breath. It had worked just as he expected from what Jie'd told him about Jiang not wanting to hurt her on the *Wild Orchid*.

She tapped on his arm. *Guard is mine.*

Non-lethal, he tapped back.

Of course.

The men's footsteps came closer. Light feet pattered on the roof. Tian's grip tightened on his knife. The door pushed open.

"I'll get the light." Chong stepped in.

Jiang and the guard followed.

Pushing the door closed with his foot, Tian yanked Jiang's hair back and pressed a knife to his throat. "Not a word."

Across from him, a large body crumpled to the floor.

"You!" Jiang said. "I recognize your voice. You're the boy from this morning. I guess you didn't take Sha's bribes. Where is he?"

Dead, but Jiang didn't have to join him as long as he cooperated. In all likelihood, he wouldn't divulge much, not without time they didn't have. Tian spoke in Jie's direction. "Prepare the intoxicant. Chong, dim light."

A light bauble spilled a brittle light from between Chong's fingers, revealing Bu and Li's silent arrival. A cork popped off a snuff bottle. The sweet fragrance of *yinghua* flowers filled the air. The contact toxin affected only men, making them even more malleable to a woman's suggestion. It would also leave them with a splitting headache and little memory.

"Put him in a chair and take one step back," Jie whispered.

Tian dragged a chair over with his foot and then shoved Jiang into it. Keeping the knife at Jiang's throat, he backed off.

"What are you doing?" Jiang's voice quivered.

"Making you more comfortable." Casting a broad smile, Jie straddled Jiang and pressed her lips to the divot below his nose. In two seconds, the tension in his body melted. With a hand, she pushed Tian's knife hand away. "That isn't necessary. Mister Jiang will be cooperative, right?"

"No..." Jiang mumbled. "Yes..."

"Good boy." She ground into his lap and pressed her chest against him.

Disgusting. Tian's jaw twitched as he focused on Jiang's back, which would look better with a knife in it. The things the Black Lotus sisters did in the line of duty, even at such a young age, were unenviable.

Jie shifted back. "So Mister Jiang, who do you work for?"

"I really shouldn't say…"

"No, you shouldn't, but you will." Her voice was so…sultry. So wrong.

"Evergreen Trading." No surprise there.

"What do you do?"

His voice began to slur. "I have a budget to make sure things get to where they need to go."

"What things?"

"Turmeric." His hand reached to Jie's buttocks.

The son of a turtle egg deserved to have his manhood decapitated for lusting after…well, Jie might be twenty-nine, but she was still a girl, maybe not yet flowered for all that she let on. Knife flipped to an underhanded grip, Tian took a step forward.

She waved him off with one hand and moved Jiang's hand off her butt with the other. "Eight kegs of turmeric? Is Lord Tong opening up a chain of curry shops throughout the North?"

Jiang chuckled nervously. "Firepowder to Yutou, sulfur and food stores to Wailian."

"How much food so far?" Jie ran fingers through his hair.

"Twelve thousand *shi* of rice and twelve hundred *jin* of pink fish paste." Enough to feed Lord Tong's five thousand men for two years, four months and eight days, if the fish paste kept that long. Or less, if there were more soldiers.

She kissed his ear. "Why so much?"

"I don't ask questions, I just do what I'm told." Try as he might, Jiang's hand couldn't get past Jie's as he tried to grope her.

Tian sighed. Jiang was nothing more than an accessory. Not even a bad person, save for salacious proclivities and putting money ahead of nation. "What about Lord Peng? Is he involved in Evergreen Trading?"

Jiang's hands paused in their futile efforts and he snaked his head around. His words came out more and more slowly. "The *Tai-Ming* lord? No,

he's the *Tianzi's* lapdog. He wouldn't dream of skirting the laws of interdependence."

Tian looked at Jie. She'd defended Lord Peng and now had a smug look to prove it. Peng was clearly innocent, unlike the conspirators who paid little heed to the three-hundred-year-old rules set up by the Founder himself, which ensured everyone prospered but stayed dependent through specialization. Maybe Lord Tong and his allies were jealous that only the capital province was allowed economic diversification. Or, they were planning on outright rebellion.

Jiang's head jerked and his eyes blinked.

Jie slapped him lightly. "Stay awake. I don't want you falling asleep before the fun begins."

"I…won't." The last word came out as a mumble, and his eyes rolled up into his head. They'd get no more out of him for another ten hours.

Two sets of footsteps, an adult's and juvenile's, brushed across the roof and down the stairs. Bu and Li turned around, hands on their concealed weapons, but eased when Qu and Little Huang appeared.

Despite the chill air, sweat glistened on Little Huang's forehead. "We have an emergency! Princess Kaiya has gone missing."

Tian's stomach flipped. Princess Kaiya…as children, they'd been best friends. They'd promised to marry each other. Silly, for sure, and three thousand, one hundred and forty-seven days had passed since their last meeting, but still. Now she was missing while a rebellion brewed. "Who knows about it?"

"Two servants came forward," Little Huang said. "That's all I know. Master Yan ordered all available agents back to Huajing to search for her."

Tian exchanged glances with Jie. If the rebellious lords found out, they'd spare no effort to take the princess hostage. "If we ran, it would take us three hours to reach the West Gates."

"*You* can't go back." Jie picked herself off Jiang.

He frowned. If anyone could find clues to Kaiya's whereabouts, it would be him.

Jie seized his arm and searched his eyes. "They'll execute you."

Banishment or not, he had to help. Kaiya was his oldest, dearest friend. His last connection to a more innocent, idealistic time. "It doesn't matter."

"It does. And you need to make sure the river barges stay docked. And what if Jiang's men coming looking for him?" What was that look? Pleading?

Tian sighed. She was right. There was still a mission here, and anything could happen in three hours. Still, "We can't just let the rebels capture her."

"We don't even know if the traitors know. I will go back by horse relay, tell Master Yan what we've found out. You take care of things here."

Fists clenched, Tian nodded. She was right, of course. He still needed to complete the last part of his plan: go to the harbormaster, tell him about the contraband, and have him come to the docks with soldiers to impound the cargo. He looked up at Jie, his own eyes undoubtedly begging, *Please make sure she is safe.*

CHAPTER 20
Uncommitted Resolve

Standing in Lord Tong Baxian's receiving room with the Dragon Scale Lute in hand, Kaiya's heart roared in her ears. Give up the instrument, and maybe Chamberlain Li and his henchmen would let them go.

Maybe not.

And if she gave it up, she couldn't use it to help Ankira. Not only that, who might Lord Tong use it on? Could Li even play it? That would mean he was also becoming a Dragon Singer. Maybe he already was one.

A mix of jealousy, indecision, and fear stirred inside her. The lute buzzed of its own accord. With a trembling finger, she made a tentative pluck on a bass string.

The barely audible sound came out low and desolate, like the lament of an exiled ruler over the fall of his kingdom.

Despite the lack of resonance, a tremor coursed down Kaiya's spine. The chamberlain's eyes widened. The two soldiers took hesitant steps back.

At their feet, Hardeep stirred.

Fighting the urge to still the string and quell all the misgivings building in her heart, she picked at a treble string.

The wail keened like a small child, alone and hunted.

The chamberlain turned and ran, his footsteps fading down the hall. One of the guards dropped his blade and covered his ears. The other froze in place, mouth open in a silent scream.

Hardeep swept up the fallen broadsword and jumped to his feet. In a fluid motion, he whacked both men with the flat of the blade.

Both collapsed.

Shuddering from the Lute's horrific notes, Kaiya placed a hand over the strings to silence them, then ran over and wrapped Hardeep in an embrace. She'd never been so close to a man before, and after the eeriness of the Lute's sound, it felt comforting. Its ominous echo still resonated in her mind.

He pushed out of her arms and held her shoulders, beaming. "You did it. With practice, you'll be able to project its sound."

Not like she ever wanted to hear it, ever again. She studied the sound plate. "How did they acquire one of his scales?"

He scratched the back of his neck, brow furrowed and eyes looking up at his own lashes. "A legend from before the War of Ancient Gods has it that Aralas himself dislodged that scale from Avarax's neck."

"How? I have never heard such a legend."

"Perhaps the stories in the South differ from Cathay's." Hardeep tapped his bare chin. "An arrow made of pure light."

Paintings of that era did depict the elf angel's bow, shooting lightning.

"We need to get out of here before more men arrive. Come." He opened the bag he was carrying and gestured for her to put the Lute into it.

She did so, happy to be relieved of the instrument and its fell music. Cinching the drawstrings, he bent over and retrieved a scabbard for the sword he'd taken. Then he took her hand and guided her toward the front door.

Despite the horror and misgivings, her heart swelled. She'd coaxed a sound first out of Yanyan's Pipa, now out of the Dragon Scale Lute. It hadn't seemed possible this morning, but now, she might really be able to help Hardeep. Then again, just those two plucks gave birth to more misgivings than any of the day's other misadventures. Was it worth hearing the Lute's moan again? She shivered.

Outside, Prince Hardeep turned and took both her hands. "Thank you so much. I could never have done this by myself. You found the Dragon Scale Lute, and even plucked out a sound. I have more hope now than I have in a very long time."

His hands, on hers, drew her closer. The warmth was reassuring, mingling with the rice wine dancing in her head. Maybe she'd abused her position, but it was for the right reasons. The liberation of an occupied people. The revival of a lost art. The chance of being more than just a political bride. All possible because this one man saw true potential in her.

He placed one hand on the small of her back and cradled her nape with the other.

Fire erupted all through her. Never had a man embraced her like this. Her stomach buzzed like a hummingbird's wings. All three moons seemed to shine on only them. She closed her eyes and tilted her chin up to him, parting her lips to offer him her first kiss.

Nothing.

Then, a finger touched her lips. She opened her eyes to meet his sigh.

"We must stay focused," he said. "For now. I can't lose myself in you." His arms released her.

The warmth fled her body as the cool night air rushed in. The alcohol haze still fogged her mind, but at least now, things were a little clearer. She'd been about to kiss a man! How could she even consider something so inappropriate?

That, on top of breaking several rules, risking servants so she could escape the palace, and intimidating a chamberlain.

Now, the rejection. Of course he would. She was plain and lanky, and all he really needed was a gullible princess to find and steal a magical artifact.

"Please, Kaiya, come with me." The manipulator took her hand and tugged her along.

Pulling back, she held her ground. "No, this is wrong. I understand your need to help your country, but maybe there are better channels. Let me present the case to my father again."

He let out a long sigh. "You are right. I am so sorry. I was so excited at your breakthrough earlier today, and again, that we so easily retrieved the Dragon Scale Lute. I will take you home now, before anyone gets in trouble."

His beautiful eyes seemed so defeated. He was placing her concerns over the welfare of his own people. Guilt clawed at her chest. She stared down at the pavestones until he tugged her into a walk.

Kaiya kept her head down as they plodded in somber silence. At her side, Hardeep mumbled something unintelligible. She looked up and found the profile of his sharp chin. The sudden motion sent her head spinning again, a black tunnel narrowing her field of vision. She stumbled.

His arm shot out and caught her. "Let me support you. We are fairly close to the palace."

Blinking away the blurriness, she leaned into him. Oh, if only she could help him without having to break so many rules.

Up ahead, low voices muttered in Ayuri. Hardeep jerked to a stop, pulling her closer. If they had returned the way they had come, it might mean more Madurans, ready to ambush them again. Her hand strayed to Cousin Kai-Long's dagger as she scanned the surroundings.

Hardeep's hand patted her on the shoulder. "It's all right. They are my people."

"How can you tell?"

They turned a corner and he pointed. Dozens of men, women, and children huddled around tables in the middle of a street between two rows of dilapidated buildings.

Guilt knotted in her throat. So much poverty, while she never wanted for luxury.

"Your father, in his generosity, allowed refugees from Ankira to stay on this block."

This block, out of sight. She'd never heard of such a decision, nor had she ever seen such a run-down place so close to the noble's district. Then again, her processions always stuck to main roads, and the distance between the houses here suggested tertiary streets. No lord would come this way. They'd pretend it didn't even exist.

If everyone else would sweep these people under the rug, Kaiya would see them. Validate their suffering.

Lit by the plump Blue Moon and the half-White Moon, barefooted children wearing threadbare *kurta* shirts chased each other in raucous circles. At the tables, where light baubles cast domes of light, women in faded *saris* gossiped among each other as they ate a meager meal. The few men were all middle-aged, dressed in tattered clothes, sitting on rickety chairs as they chatted.

Guilt squeezed Kaiya's belly. They all had to be hungry and freezing, while her people feasted in the warmth of the palace.

At her side, Prince Hardeep sighed. "Lord Peng understands our plight. He suggested bringing you here to meet me, but the Madurans' hired knives were waiting. That's why I met you closer to the palace. Come."

His hand, so large and reassuring, released hers. The lingering warmth in her fingers tingled away, leaving a hollow sensation in her chest. He beckoned her to follow. Up close, the pungent scent of turmeric hung in the air, mixing in with a cinnamon aroma, which swirled from steaming cups. Children stopped running and the men and women all looked up.

Hardeep leaned in. "Most of these people had ties to the Hua trade office in Akira. Your officials there helped many escape. Now, they work as laborers and servants for wages so low, they can

barely feed themselves. Some of the prettier girls end up in the Floating World for rich men with exotic tastes."

Kaiya's chest constricted. How horrible. She'd compared marriage to death, but what these girls suffered... She studied their expressions. All bore lines of worry on their proud faces. One young woman in particular looked striking. Her features were less round, her complexion lighter, speaking of some Hua blood. She lowered her head.

"Prince...Hardeep?" The oldest man pressed his hands together. "Thank you for your assistance. Please, bring your guest to join us." He scooted over and gestured to a pair of seats.

Hardeep extended an open hand, inviting her to go first. "Please, Kaiya. You must be hungry."

Her tummy rumbled its assent. Heat flared in her cheeks. She'd had at least six or seven cups of rice wine, and never had a chance to actually eat anything solid. With a nod of her head, she settled in the indicated chair.

And nearly fell, again.

Hardeep grabbed her arm, sparing her yet more embarrassment.

"Poor girl." One of the middle-aged women clucked, placing a cup of dark liquid in front of her. "Here, drink some chai. It will warm you up on this chill night."

Kaiya accepted it, savoring the warmth the cup radiated into her hands. Certainly not as intense as Hardeep's warmth, but comforting nonetheless. She took a sip. The smooth tea slid down her throat, dancing in a burst of spices. Heat percolated through her.

"Eat, eat!" Another woman slid a cracked porcelain plate in front of her. Another ladled what appeared to be shredded chicken in a yellow sauce on top of a round disk of flatbread.

Kaiya looked at the center dishes from which the refugees served. Her own plate must have accounted for half of what remained. She shook her head. "No, I can't possibly..."

Hardeep laughed. "In my homeland, even beggars will treat their guests as royalty."

How ironic. Kaiya forced a polite smile.

He leaned in and whispered, "Eat. Otherwise, you will offend them."

Kaiya swept her gaze around the table. Expectant eyes met hers. Very well, she would eat. Her stomach certainly demanded it, and it would be bad manners to decline. However, there didn't seem to be any chopsticks or any other kind of utensils. She fiddled with a lock of hair.

"Use your hands," Hardeep said. "Tear the flatbread, eat it with the chicken."

Hands. Kaiya studied hers, which had touched ancient musical instruments, dirty shirts, furniture, and princes' hands. Gulping air, she reached out and ripped off a piece of sauce-covered bread. It smelled wonderful. Bad manners or not, she pushed the whole thing in her mouth and chewed. Turmeric, sugar, and other spices swirled over her tongue. Piece after piece disappeared as her stomach urged her on.

Around her, the Ankiran refugees broke out into laughter.

One woman clapped her hands. "She is hungry!"

"Your Excellency, you can't afford to feed her," one of the men said.

Prince Hardeep laughed. "Not with what is left in the national treasury, no."

Kaiya paused on a bite. Ankira was bankrupted because of Hua's avarice, which she put on full display now. Perhaps her dress, possibly worth more than everything on this block combined, was paid for on the backs of the Ankirans. The guilt felt like a dwarf anvil in her gut.

He placed a hand between her shoulder blades. "The way you are eating, you might deplete your own country's treasury."

Blood burned in Kaiya's cheeks.

"A song!" Hardeep rose from his seat and beckoned one of the middle-aged men. "Bring me a sitar."

The man disappeared into one of the houses and brought out what resembled a long lute with a bulbous resonator. It had so many strings, including several that did not seem reachable by the player. Hardeep received it in two hands.

Beaming, he started picking at the strings. The sitar whined in high-pitched shifts, with the lower strings echoing the main refrain with harmonic resonance. Some of the other men began beating on the table with their hands as the pace picked up, bobbing their heads to the rhythm.

Upbeat, the song spoke to Kaiya's soul, and it was all she could do to keep from standing and dancing.

"The drumming refrain is called a *tala*," one woman told her.

Blue eyes locked on hers, Hardeep began to sing. His low voice, rich like the chai, sent Kaiya's belly fluttering in a storm of butterflies.

Ankira, my home.
Land of rich soil and verdant valleys,
Home of the gods on earth.
Warmth of the heart
My heart yearns for my homeland.

The others joined in, their voices rising as one. The resonance surged inside of her, coiling just as it had in the Hall of Pure Melody. Prince Hardeep flashed a smile, beckoning her to join in.

She dropped her gaze to the street, shaking her head. The sentiment, she understood, and yet, it was her country that helped oppress his. How could she let her voice meld with theirs?

Their song came to a slow, melancholy end, and the sitar trailed off into a somber hum. These people missed their homeland, wanted to return, wanted to be free.

Hardeep sighed. "It is getting late. We must get you back before anyone realizes you are gone."

The power of music, flourishing in her as the Ankirans had sung, still spiraled throughout her core. It tingled in her fingers and toes, and she aligned her body. "No. Let's test the Lute."

"No," Hardeep said. "No, I have already caused you too much trouble."

"I want to. For you. For your people." She studied her feet. "For myself."

He lifted her chin. His eyes searched hers, rocking back and forth in mesmerizing sweeps. "Are you sure? Please, don't feel obligated just because a bunch of old men sang for you."

She nodded with heartfelt passion. "Yes. Yes. It is in my power to do so, and I shall."

Prince Hardeep looked from her to his people. "Her voice holds the key to our salvation!"

The men and women broke into a cheer, a genuine appreciation that no one in the court had ever shown her.

Beaming, Hardeep took her hand. "Let's go. Somewhere acoustically perfect, to magnify your voice."

Heat mingling into the echo of the song, she rose. Thanks to the trip to the archives, she knew just the place. "The Temple of Heaven."

He raised an eyebrow. "Are you sure?"

Was she? To enter the sacred tower without a blessing from its priests invited a death sentence. She searched his eyes again.

Her heart swelled. Yes. Better to die than to give up on the magic of Dragon Songs when she was so close. She nodded.

The Ankirans all pressed their hands together and bowed their heads as Hardeep led her down a street. Headed south, according to Caiyue's position.

After a few blocks, he stopped. His head swept from left to right and back, pausing at an empty wooden produce stand outside a shuttered green grocer.

"What is it?" Hand on her dagger, she peered through the dark at the stand.

He pulled her closer. "Our friends from before. They must have tracked us back here." IIe stomped a foot on the street, sending vibrations rippling out. After a second, he said, "Only two this time, one behind the stand, and one there." He twisted behind her and swept a sword out of its scabbard. Wood shattered with a loud crack.

He spun around to her front. Metal clinked against sword, and then clattered on the ground. The dark outline was shaped like a star. She squatted down to pick it up. Pain bit into her fingers as a sharp edge cut her.

"Stay down," Hardeep said. His blade whizzed, again cutting projectiles out of the air with clanks and thuds. As he moved, the silk bag containing the Dragon Scale Lute slipped from his shoulders. It hit the ground with a discordant groan, like the keen of a murderous beast in its death throes.

The villains stared at the bag, wide-eyed.

Fear crawled up Kaiya's spine. She shuddered at the sound. It was just like at Lord Tong's villa. If it evoked fear in those men, and now her, maybe... She reached for the bag and fumbled with the drawstrings. Pain bit where the star had cut her thumb. Still, she managed to fish the Lute out.

She rose from her low squat to a level horse stance, similar to the one Doctor Wu taught for breathing exercises. Spine straight, thighs parallel to the ground, she cradled the Lute and plucked one of the treble strings.

A sound like a widow mourning her dead husband wailed from the Lute, twisting in her core and then resonating into her limbs. Unlike her first attempt, it was louder. The barrage of attacks stopped and the two large men in the shadows lowered their weapons.

Kaiya strummed across all the strings. The dissonance of high and low pitches must have sounded like the chorus of souls tormented by Yanluo in the pits of hell. The would-be assassins dropped their weapons. One's crossbow crashed onto the pavestones, sending a loaded bolt soaring toward them.

With a low mutter, Hardeep jerked back, his hip jarring into her head and knocking her back.

Pain flared in her temples and white flashed in her field of vision. Just when the alcohol had begun to clear. She blinked away the cobwebs.

Hardeep knelt beside her, his brows furrowed. "Are you all right?"

Was she? Her head ached, her thumb stung. Her chest hurt from the Lute's echo in her heart. She gawked at the thin line of blood on her thumb.

Tearing a strip of cloth from his shirt, he wrapped the wound. Tight and firm. He helped her to her feet with a chuckle. "You must be lucky, to survive two attacks with just a small cut on your thumb."

It didn't seem lucky, nor a laughing matter. She pouted.

His smile flattened. He turned to the side and pointed. "We are here."

Already? And where had their attackers gone? She looked at him, and then followed his gesture. An eight-tiered stupa, its colors indistinct in the night, towered above white stone walls. Two soldiers in ceremonial robes and breastplates flanked the metal gates.

There was only one place in Huajing like this: the Temple of Heaven, which housed a chunk from a fallen star, brought to Hua by the Wang Dynasty Founder at the bidding of the gods. And if the story from the geomancy book was true, it was built over the spot where the elf angel Aralas revealed himself to Yanyan, the mother of musical magic.

Her pulse quickened. There was one last chance to leave before risking a capital offense.

CHAPTER 21
Gone Rogue

Jie had never ridden a horse before, and would hopefully never have to again. How the ruddy-skinned Kanin plainspeople spent all day in the saddle was beyond her. Their purebred swifthorses were part of the relay system that she used now.

It dated back to before the Hellstorm, during the Hundred Years of War between the Arkothi and Ayuri Empires. Though horses and messengers were meant to change at waystations every sixty *li*, she only changed horses. A trip that normally took the better part of a day on foot lasted only an hour, but left her butt and thighs so sore, she'd almost welcome Fat Nose Jiang's groping.

Or maybe Tian's. Not as if he'd even shown the least amount of jealousy when she used her feminine wiles on Jiang. Dismounting in the broad, moonlit plaza outside Sun-Moon Palace, outside a perimeter of imperial guards, she wobbled over to where several officials gathered. Every joint and muscle ached with each step.

Blue robes swished as a familiar imperial guard officer blocked her way. Either the horse had given her away, or perhaps sore muscles compromised her stealth. The five-clawed dragon on his breastplate sent a shiver through her spine. "You!" he said. "Who are you to commandeer an imperial swifthorse?"

Disguised as a court official, Master Yan shuffled over, bowing. "General Zheng, this is my daughter Jie. She has hurried all the way from Jiangkou to join in our task." He spoke in a loud whisper as his eyes roved past the perimeter.

Jie followed his gaze, her elven vision locking in on the armed men across the moat, their robes showing no symbol of allegiance. She turned back and bowed, looking up through her lashes at the commander of the imperial guard; Zheng, Tian's cousin, which explained the familiarity. Only a handful of the senior-most imperial guards knew of the *Moquan* and Master Yan's identity.

General Zheng favored her with furrowed eyebrows. Lowering his voice, he beckoned her past the cordon, across the plaza and into the ring of officials. "Thank you for coming. Master Yan has told me about your particular abilities."

Pretending to pay attention to the general's pleasantries, Jie leaned in to her adoptive father and whispered, "Tian thinks Lord Tong has gone beyond the illegal production of firepowder. He might also be plotting a rebellion with Northern Lords Chu, Xi, and Qin. All own part of a suspicious trading company, and none have arrived for the imperial wedding. He has also been stockpiling food. Also absent are Lords Chi, Shen, and Bai from Nanling Province, and much of the illegal firepowder has ended up there."

Without breaking stride, Master Yan bowed toward General Zheng. "I must brief the *Tianzi* on an urgent matter. I entrust Jie to you."

"What have we learned so far?" Jie asked.

General Zheng grunted. "The princess left the reception four and a half hours ago at the first waxing gibbous with Young Lord Peng Kai-Long of Nanling Province."

Jie sucked on her lower lip. Tian had adored Peng as a child, though a mistake by Kai-Long had led to Tian's banishment. As confirmed by Fat Nose Jiang, the Peng family was unquestioningly loyal to the *Tianzi*. "Do we know where they headed from there?"

"Young Lord Peng left her near a pagoda in the inner castle. She disappeared right after that, and nobody has seen her since."

Leave it to imperial guards to lose a princess. Jie swept a hand toward the palace walls. "Sun-Moon Palace is vast. Are you sure she is not here?"

General Zheng gave a perfunctory nod. "Everyone, including members of your clan, has swept the grounds thrice over."

The girl wasn't trained in stealth, so... "How did she get past the imperial guards?" Besides the fact they were witless strong-arms. "Surely someone would have seen her?"

"Magic." General Zheng spoke the word with a tone that suggested he had just eaten a bitter melon. He held a glass bauble, like an Aksumi magic light, cradled in a silk kerchief. "When it touches bare flesh, it makes someone look like her. The servants found it in the pagoda."

Jie took the bauble in hand.

General Zheng nearly choked. "That is disconcerting. Please, don't touch it. It makes you look a little like her."

If only she had a mirror. Jie had never seen the princess up close, but had heard she was a plain-looking girl. Whatever Tian had seen in her... She wrapped the bauble up as she thought. Tian's recollections of Princess Kaiya suggested a sweet and obedient girl, who would never dream of breaking any rules. Where had she acquired Aksumi magic baubles and what prompted her to run away? "Was there anything out of the ordinary in her schedule today?"

General Zheng harrumphed. "She met a suitor, but only after an interruption from a foreign supplicant to the *Tianzi*. She was quite smitten by him."

"The suitor?"

"No, the foreigner. General Lu broke off the matchmaking meeting halfway through."

Jie stifled a sigh. Oh, to be able to make connections like Tian. General Lu commanded the national armies in the North. Posted in Lord Tong's Wailian County, no less. Another conspirator? "What do we know of the foreigner?"

"Prince Hardeep Vaswani of Ankira. Nineteen years old according to the archives, and apparently trained in Ayuri Paladin arts."

Paladins could supposedly plant suggestions in the gullible, and if the Founder's Dictionary of the Hua Language were illustrated, it would probably show a picture of a sixteen-year-old girl in the entry for gullible. "Where would we find Prince Hardeep?"

"He was staying with Young Lord Peng Kai-Long."

Young Lord Peng again. Also something of a vainglorious narcissist if Tian's childhood recollections served him well. Perhaps Prince Hardeep had duped him, too. "Where is Young Lord Peng right now?"

"He is at the *Tianzi's* side, taking blame for this debacle. He said Prince Hardeep was visiting the Ankiran ghetto."

"I've never heard of such a thing." And Jie heard a *lot*.

"It's fairly new. Young Lord Peng petitioned the *Tianzi* to allow the Ankiran refugees to stay there."

With no other clues... "Then that's where I'll start. Where is it?"

"I will send Princess Kaiya's most senior imperial guards with you." He gestured toward a gaggle of blue-robed men who would stand out anywhere in Huajing.

Jie pursed her lips. It would far easier if he just told her. "Do you think they're reliable after they let the princess slip through their fingers?"

General Zheng's frown mirrored her own. "I charged them with watching the reception tonight, not the princess."

"They will only slow me down." Though as sore as her muscles burned, she might not be moving that fast.

Five imperial guards, all in their mid-to-late twenties, marched over. The dragons etched into their burnished breastplates scowled, sending the little human hairs on her arms prickling. In unison, they saluted General Zheng with a right fist in a left palm.

He gestured toward her. "This is...what is your name again?"

"Jie." She hopefully contained the roll of her eyes.

"Right. She will be searching for clues. You will accompany her. Jie, this is Captain Chen Xin, Zhao Yue, Ma Jun, Xu Zhan, and Li Wei."

Jie examined each. Even with her elven vision and *Moquan* training, little differentiated the five dour men. They might as well have been moving statues, bowing their heads and barking in unison, "Yes, General."

With an affable smile, Li Wei—or maybe it was Ma Jun—beckoned her, with his left hand. Unlike the others, he wore his sword on his right. "I know a fast way to get there."

Nodding, Jie followed him. The other four pushed past her, through the perimeter and east into the city's northeast quadrant. For all the interest they showed, she might as well not have been there.

"I thought he'd never let us go," said Chen Xin. Definitely Chen Xin, clearly the oldest with his rough skin and salt-and-pepper hair. The three gold stripes on his cuffs marked him as the leader. Tian had said something about a run-in with him years ago, before his banishment.

"Too bad we're stuck with *her*." Xu Zhan—or was it Zhao Yue—jerked a thumb at her.

Now away from the general, there was little need to hide the rolling of her eyes. "I'm right here."

"May I speak freely?" said Xu Zhan...yes, it was Xu Zhan. His knuckles were flat and worn, the mark of a brawler. "You might be an elf, but we'd be better off with scent hounds."

Jie's pulse roared in her ears. "I'm not an elf, and while a dog might have a good nose, it lacks my brains to connect all the clues. I doubt the five of you combined could compensate for that."

Xu Zhan's flat-knuckled hands closed into tight balls.

Laughing, Ma Jun, the one with the boyish face, clapped Flat-Knuckle Xu Zhan on the back. At least one of them *did* have a personality. "Never mind him, he's just worried."

"We'll never find her." Lefty Li Wei shook his head, sending the scar on his chin zigzagging. "Not before ruffians do, and do horrible things to her."

Zhao Yue, the one with a triangular head like a fox, held up a hand. "Everyone in the capital knows what she looks like. They wouldn't dare touch her."

Ruffians didn't fear the law, and rebels would do worse. Jie would never underestimate an imperial guard's idiocy again. Any more of their banter and she'd tear her hair out. "Is it much farther? Wait." She paused at an alley, where something sparkling in the three moons' light caught her eye.

The men all came to a stop and followed her gaze down the alley.

"What is it?" Salt-and-pepper-haired Chen Xin crowded over her shoulder like a monster from a horror novel.

Jie took in the alley. With the bright moons, her night vision hadn't taken over, but her visual acuity still picked up on details these five buffoons would miss. She pointed at the splintered wood of a two-story house. "Two holes, from crossbow bolts. The size is too big for standard-issue Hua bolts."

One eye closed, fox-faced Zhao Yue leaned toward the wall while Xu Zhan pushed past him and tested each hole with his finger, like a bear pawing for honey.

"Bring a lamp over here." Jie knelt down and picked up the cracked glass bauble that had originally drawn her attention. She withdrew the one General Zheng had given her. In boy-faced Ma Jun's lamplight, the texture, color, and size were close to identical. "Maybe the princess came this way."

Grinning and making himself look more like a fox, Zhao Yue elbowed Xu Zhan. "She's definitely better than a dog."

"Blood." The coppery smell drew Jie to a line of blood droplets. She leaned over and touched it. "Fairly fresh, two or three hours old. The spray pattern suggests blades—" she moved to the place where the wielder had likely stood and swung her arm as if holding a sword "—cut through an artery."

Lefty Li Wei fisted his hair with both hands. "This is horrible."

Chen Xin cleared his throat. "Citizens! Come out in the name of the *Tianzi*."

Perhaps they weren't that dumb after all. In the second stories, windows opened and faces peeked out.

"What happened here?" Chen Xin yelled.

Voices erupted all at once.

"An assault!"

"A girl and a man."

"A foreign man."

"Attacked by six masked men."

"Big men."

"Very big men."

Jie blew out a whistle shrill enough to wake ghosts. "One at a time. Were the man and girl harmed?"

"No."

Thank the Heavens. "How long ago? Which way did they go?"

Fingers pointed out the north end of the alley. "Two hours. They turned the corner, and that was that."

"That's the general direction of the Ankiran ghetto," Ma Jun whispered.

"Did the attackers give chase?" Chen Xin said.

"Yes."

Flat-Knuckled Xu Zhan took off in the direction they pointed, with Lefty Li Wei close on his heels. Not like it would make much difference given the two hours that had passed.

Jie started to join the rest of the imperial guards following them, but paused and grabbed Ma Jun's elbow and Chen Xin's wrist. "Wait. Captain, go retrieve your men. I have an idea." If someone was trying to capture the princess... She looked up at all the people. "I need a dress, large enough for him—" she thumbed at Ma Jun "—and four sets of male clothes. I'll pay a gold *yuan*, and we'll even return the dress when we're done if he doesn't like it."

Ma Jun snorted as commotion buzzed. "What are you trying to do?"

"You will be bait for anyone who is trying to harm the princess."

His forehead scrunched up. "I don't look anything like her."

Jie withdrew the magic bauble and pressed it to her skin. She didn't feel any different, but...

Ma Jun gasped. "It's just like Princess Kaiya, only pretty."

"Now *you* look like her." She pressed the bauble into his hand.

His appearance changed in a blink. He no longer towered above her, but now stood just a head taller. Gone were the broad shoulders and boyish face, replaced by a thin, pretty girl on the edge of womanhood. Perhaps prettier than what Tian remembered; and even in the imperial guard uniform, which had shrunk to size, it was clear how he could find her attractive.

Insides twisting, she plucked the bauble from his grasp. "But first, we need to size you."

"Why can't *you* do it?" A tight-lipped frown replaced his usually jovial expression.

"Because it will look strange for Princess Kaiya to sniff blood stains and examine weapons." Not to mention she'd already worn enough dresses today to last a lifetime.

A crowd of commoners gathered, pushing gowns into her face.

Jie shook her head. "Too coarse. Too small. Too plain. Too conservative. Yes!" She snatched up a light blue gown of silk, which must have belonged to a large woman, and held it up to Ma Jun.

His wide eyes protested. "I'll look fat in that."

"The magic will bring out all the right parts and hide the many wrong ones." She coughed. "Many, many wrong ones."

When the other guards returned, they occupied a citizen's foyer and changed into the disguises. The guards all poked fun at Ma Jun, even the curmudgeon Xu Zhan. Yet when Ma Jun pressed the bauble to his bare skin and transformed into Princess Kaiya, they all dropped to a knee, fist to the ground.

Reflex, no doubt, just like the temple dogs responding to a treat. Jie gave herself a mental pat on the back. The disguise might work better than expected. "Now, we are going to continue to the Ankiran ghetto. Princess Ma Jun and I will walk ahead, and the rest of you hang back. If the attackers are still out there, and they don't already have your princess, maybe we will draw them out."

After some grumbling, they set off again. Ma Jun's muttering about the dress leaving him cold and constrained made Jie grateful that her own duties never involved wearing formal gowns. In any case, his body language appeared too stiff, too...male. The Northern lords' agents would never take the bait.

After several blocks, Jie called for a halt in front of a greengrocer's empty cart. She knelt down and picked up a crossbow bolt's black fletching and round point. At first glance, it seemed to match the hole in the wall from before. And there, under the wheel of the cart...no, it couldn't be. She reached over and retrieved a *biao* throwing star, lacquered black. A *Moquan* weapon. Beneath it was a thin line of blood, fresher than the last.

"What is it?" Chen Xin knelt down next to her.

He couldn't know about the *biao*, not until she found out more. Jie stashed the weapon in her sleeve with a flick of her wrist, then wiped her finger across the blood and held it up. "Fresher blood here. I think we are getting close." Closer to a potential betrayal on Master Yan's part? No, never. A renegade, perhaps? Or an adept who tried to help the princess, but had not reported back?

Princess Ma Jun sashayed over. She—*he*—pointed north as he spoke with a deep voice mismatched for a young woman. "The Ankiran ghetto is a few blocks that way."

A scream pierced the night, right where he pointed.

Jie broke into a run. Even without Ma Jun's guidance, the disjointed chorus of screams, yells, and shouts might as well have been a beacon. That, and as she neared, the coppery scent of blood mingling with curry. She turned a corner into a side street lined by poorly maintained row houses.

From the far end of the block, three dark-clothed men with repeating crossbows pelted bolts into a mess of overturned tables and chairs. Bodies of men, women, and children sprawled in the jumble, blood slickening the pavestones. A few still lived, cowering behind splintered furniture.

Two more large men stood with their backs to her, swords in hand. Their form-fitting clothes resembled those *Moquan* wore on missions. From the bodies at their feet, which bled from ugly gashes, it appeared they had cut down anyone who tried to escape.

With each hand, Jie reached across and pulled three *biao* from either sleeve. In the same motion, she flung them at the nearest two. One dropped to his knees with a grunt as three stars lodged in his back.

The other man took one *biao* to the left shoulder—she'd need to practice more with her off hand—and spun around. Snarling, he loped over with his broadsword raised.

Better not to test her knife against that. She spun around to run...and slipped on a stray crossbow bolt. How had she not seen it earlier? She landed on her butt, already sore from the horseback ride. The huge man's blade came down.

It clanged against a curved *dao* sword just a fingerbreadth from her head. In the same motion with which Xu Zhan brushed away the incoming broadsword, he countered with a two-handed slash. The *dao* sliced through the murderer's neck and sent his head rolling to the ground in a swirling blood trail.

Jie popped up to her feet. The crossbowmen ran and the other imperial guards, save for Ma Jun in his dress, gave chase. Her short legs would never keep up. She turned to Xu Zhan and pointed to the headless body. "We needed to keep him alive for questioning!"

"You're welcome." With a smug smile, Xu Zhan examined his weapon.

Perhaps thanks were in order, but he didn't need to know that. Jie harrumphed. "I had everything under control."

Lip curled, he sheathed his blade. "Instead of risking yourself, you should've let soldiers take care of them."

"I did take care of one, and wounded the other enough to make him easy to apprehend. Not kill."

Xu Zhan cocked his head. "Was that you? I thought the other one got hit by friendly fire."

Right, the *Moquan* and their weapons were secrets that not even the imperial guard knew of. For all he knew, she was just some kind of investigator. It had to stay that way, even at the cost of a bruised ego. She bent over the corpse, technically not face-down given his decapitation, and retrieved the *biao* with a deft swipe. "Since this one won't talk, I'll see if the other one is beyond interrogation."

Ignoring Xu Zhan's smug face, she hurried over to the one she'd hit. Blond—blond?—locks of hair spilled out from his hooded mask. He lay on his side, chest heaving with labored breaths. Two of her *biao* had dug deep, likely puncturing both lungs. He wouldn't be answering any questions either.

She retrieved her throwing stars and went over to help survivors. They were all bronze-skinned Ayuri, likely Ankirans since this was their domicile. No, definitely Ankiran. The husband and wife she'd seen disembarking from the *Wild Orchid* that morning lay among the dozens of dead and mortally wounded. Jie's gut twisted. The cold-blooded murderers hadn't even spared women or children. And why? Nothing like this had ever happened in Huajing.

She followed the sound of whimpering and the stench of voided bowels. Three boys, maybe ten to twelve years of age, huddled under a table, tears in their eyes. At first glance, they appeared to be the only survivors. They must've had enough sense to hide just as the massacre began.

Poor boys, to have witnessed something so horrible. Still, they might have valuable information. She knelt down and pointed over at Ma Jun, still magically disguised as the princess. Using her halting Ayuri, she asked, "Was she here earlier?"

One of the boys nodded. "But she wore a different dress."

An observant one...perhaps worthy of training. "How long ago?"

He looked up at Caiyue, now waxing past its fourth crescent. "Maybe an hour?"

The trail would be getting colder. "Was she with someone?"

His voice trembled. "The noble."

"Where did they go?"

The boy pointed south, back in the direction she'd come.

"Look at this." Ma Jun held up the murderer's straight broadsword. "I've never seen a weapon like this."

Jie had. It was *Moquan*. Just like the throwing star she'd retrieved. And the men wore close-fitting but mobile utility suits. If the clan were helping enemies of the *Tianzi*... Certainly, Master Yan would have said something.

She swiped it from his hands before he could share the evidence with others. "You'll ruin the disguise."

Something was afoot, but now wasn't the time to think it through. The watch needed to be called, and a princess needed to be found.

A keening wail filled the night. The dreadful sound sent a spear of ice down Jie's spine.

CHAPTER 22
Foreboding Melodies

Whether the low buzz was in her head, echoed in the Dragon Scale Lute's strings, or emanated from the Temple of Heaven, Kaiya couldn't tell. Her spatial relations and sense of direction must have sunk to the bottom of Sun-Moon Lake. They couldn't have possibly reached the Temple of Heaven, in Huajing's south.

Maybe she and Kai-Long had ridden the palanquin farther than she thought; or she and Hardeep had just run a lot faster and longer than her drunken, jarred brain could register. She shook her head in hopes a clear thought would surface. No such luck, and no point in sounding like a fool.

Still, an inner voice that sounded suspiciously like her brother's soon-to-be bride reminded her: entry into the sacred grounds without a blessing was far worse than wandering the palace without permission or gallivanting through the city.

Another voice, which sounded like Crown Princess Xiulan's, rose above the warning. The Dragon Singers of old would risk death to do the right thing.

She closed her eyes and thought back to the Ankiran refugees. Impoverished. Downtrodden. A result of her country's profiteering. A wrong she had to rectify. Heart swelling, she edged back a step and studied Prince Hardeep.

Staring at the Temple of Heaven's eight-tiered stupa tower, his head bobbed in a rhythmic beat, as if listening to a song in his head.

He was so courageous, like the Dragon Singers in her favorite songs. Like she could be.

With one hand on Tian's pebble, she pointed at the walls. "How do we get past the guards?"

Prince Hardeep flashed a conspiratorial smile. "We'll climb over the walls."

She covered her mouth. He'd probably never worn a dress. Not to mention, "Patrols walk around the perimeter at regular intervals. It will be impossible to get over the walls without being seen."

His eyes strayed to the Lute, still in her hands.

How could he even suggest it? Using it on thugs was one thing, but on loyal soldiers... Shaking her head, she thrust the instrument into its bag and offered it to him.

A hint of a frown formed on his lips. "All right, I have an idea."

"What?"

"Trust me." He grinned. "Everything has worked so far."

Getting ambushed twice didn't seem to be part of any successful endeavor. Still, they had gotten out of it with little more than a cut on her thumb. Not to mention they had escaped the palace, itself a difficult proposition. "All right."

With his always-charming smile, he squeezed her hand and crept toward the Temple of Heaven's walls. As she had told him, guards in ceremonial breastplates and armed with broadswords circled the perimeter, always within line of sight of each other.

Again, he mumbled under his breath in sounds so foul, it could only be a curse. Not like she hadn't warned him. Serendipitously, both guards stopped in place and turned away from them. Had they heard something?

Hardeep tugged her forward to the wall. At the base, he cupped his hands together. "Your foot," he mouthed.

Kaiya stared at his hands, forming a makeshift stirrup. How unladylike. An unexpected grin tugged at her lips. It was like being a child with Tian again, far more fun than having tea with a dumpy general who only wanted her for a trophy.

She stepped into his hands, and he lifted her up, all the way to his shoulders. At that height, her hands just barely reached the top. Head spinning, she hopped and pushed her weight up to the top. Skirts and propriety be damned, she swung a leg over.

Below, the stone wall circled in an ellipse, with the stupa sitting on a three-tiered white marble base at one focus. An identical base stood at the other focus, with walls partially formed by dragon bones. Brittle leaves scattered across the empty grounds, unswept since Father's visit during the last Spring Festival.

"Your hand!" Hardeep hissed from the outside.

Right, Hardeep. Shaking her foggy head, she leaned back and extended a hand.

Hardeep backed up, and then bolted into a quick run and jump. He caught her hand, his weight nearly dragging her back down to the ground. Luckily, his other hand slapped up on top of the wall. Leaning back, she pulled him to the top. The yanking burned her arm and shoulder muscles. Heavens, he was heavier than he appeared. Down below, the guard was just then looking forward again.

Safe! Hopefully, their run of luck tonight would continue. She swung her other leg over and shimmied down to the marble ground. Hardeep leaped down after her, landing with nary a sound.

"Now what?" She scanned the compound, which she'd never seen from the inside. In just a few days, on the New Year, Father would come here for his annual prayers to the gods. How beautiful his voice always sounded, audible from almost anywhere in the city.

Hardeep pressed up against the wall. "Any guards? Priests?"

"No, the temple remains empty until just a day or so before the New Year, when priests from the Jianguo Shrine sweep it and prepare for the emperor's visit."

"Well, then." Walking toward the marble base at the near focus, he unshouldered the silk brocade bag and opened it. "According to your archives, this is where Aralas revealed himself to Yanyan."

Kaiya nodded, but, in retrospect, coming here just because of a chance meeting a thousand years before didn't make as much sense now as it had earlier in the day. So the elf angel had met the mother of Dragon Songs here. It wasn't as if he'd taught her here...unless he had? "Now what?"

Up a few steps, they arrived at the top of the base's three tiers. Hardeep stepped in the direct center and closed his eyes. "Our legends say Aralas met his Ayuri lover Shivani on Shakti's Hill in what is now Palimur City. It was there that martial magic flared in her." He offered the Lute.

Kaiya received it in two hands. "Our magic calligraphers, painters, and other artisans do not have to visit holy sites to gain their power. It just takes dedicated practice over many years."

"I see." He scanned the surroundings, his gaze pausing briefly at the top of the stupa. "There is something special about this place. Perhaps if you played, we might discover something?"

She shrugged. They had nothing to lose, except maybe some sleep from the haunting melody of the Lute.

He scooted off the center spot and gestured to it with an open hand. "A beautiful performer like you will need a stage."

Beaming at his compliment, she stepped onto it. The ever-present hum echoed louder in her ears.

"Don't let any other sound distract you," he said. "Concentrate only on the Lute. Maybe try that posture from before."

She lowered herself into a horse stance and gripped the marble with her toes, then looked up at him expectantly. "I don't know the sounds this instrument makes."

"You are so talented, I'm sure you will figure it out quickly." He tapped his chin with a finger, again invoking the image of her childhood friend, Tian. So cute. And reassuring. "Now, where in this compound does the emperor go to say his annual prayers?"

With an open hand, Kaiya gestured toward the stupa.

"I am going to take a look. From the shape of the ellipse, I would wager the sound is strongest there."

Inside the stupa was sacred territory, where the fallen star was kept. Only a select few were ever allowed to visit. If a foreigner entered, no telling what would happen. Perhaps another Hellstorm. She shook her head. "You mustn't."

He searched her eyes. His gaze was mesmerizing in the way it seemed to explore her soul.

But no, they had done too many things she shouldn't have today, culminating in the chance at a death sentence, and this would be a monumental mistake. The consequences would be borne not by her, but perhaps the entire nation. She broke eye contact and stared at the ground.

"Very well," he said. "I do want to get closer and admire the architecture. I promise I won't enter." His smile was reassuring. Of course he wouldn't do something against her wishes; he had yielded to her will time and time again.

Or would he? They'd already committed capital crimes. As he walked across the compound, she tentatively tried a string while pressing a fret. Though she kept the pluck light, its eerie moan came out loud. Even Hardeep turned his head, his irises reflecting the blue Eye of Guanyin in the heavens above.

Several more plucks reverberated louder than they should, given the amount of force she used. The descending heptatonic scales all made logical sense, and even if each note seemed to evoke the feeling of an emperor's betrayal, a queen's execution, or the outbreak of a plague, the sound was tonally perfect and frighteningly beautiful. No wonder that in the hands of an elf, it could compel a dragon to flee.

She experimented with chords and descending scales. Confident she could play, she increased the force of her plucks and strums, improvising an Arkothi marching song she'd once heard. The vibrations fluttered and twirled in her core, spreading through her arms and legs.

Outside the walls, dogs howled and birds cawed. She picked up the tempo, weaving bass and treble notes into a web of harmony. Her entire body tingled, her insides wriggling like the Guardian Dragon of Hua chasing after his Flaming Pearl. The power from earlier in the day, which had felt like an ocean dripping from a hole in a wall when she played Yanyan's pipa, now trickled through her.

If Yanyan's pipa made her beautiful, the Dragon Scale Lute transformed her into the embodiment of might and power. What would Hardeep think? She looked up.

He stood, pressing his back against the doors to the stupa, his expression one of awe...or perhaps, like her, exultation? They were here, together. He'd brought her and the Lute. Without him, this feeling wouldn't now be resonating in her chest, urging her to sing.

Behind her, the gates to the temple grounds rattled. From her music? Or maybe someone trying to get in? She started to turn her head.

Don't look back! Hardeep mouthed, or maybe spoke. No matter how, his message rang clear. *The power is within you! Sing!*

Yes, sing! No, someone was there, ready to expose this latest, worst transgression. Some of her fingers sped up while others slowed. The lute's song wobbled into a staccato, along with the vibrations inside her. Her heart thumped at irregular beats. The crushing pain felt as if a phoenix from the imperial aviary sat on her chest.

Everything blurred, bleeding into greys and blacks until darkness and silence overtook her senses.

CHAPTER 23

Aftermath

Metal tinkled and chimed as Kaiya's head bobbled on a cold, hard floor. Her body lurched. Something dug into the back of her head, over and over again. Her hairpins.

"*Dian-xia*," a female voice called. "Wake up."

A jolt of pain flared in the divot under Kaiya's nose. Her eyes fluttered open. Above her, the star-studded night sky came into focus as she blinked.

Luminous blue eyes encroached into her field of vision. Hardeep…no, a woman. Barely-visible lines of wisdom framed a familiar, matronly face. Pulled up into a tight, austere coil, her long silver hair seemed to have a faint bluish tinge to it, perhaps reflected from her eyes.

Those eyes. Pale blue like the moon Guanyin's Eye itself, unique in a Hua woman. Their depth and serenity evoked a soothing calm rivaling Sun-Moon Lake on the clearest of days. Kaiya loved those eyes as she adored the *Daoist* master to whom they belonged.

Struggling to sit up, Kaiya coughed a few times before finding words. "Doctor Wu. What are you doing here?"

"An awe-inspiring song pulsated through the city, coming from the Temple of Heaven," said the ancient woman—nobody knew her actual age, though some speculated her longevity rivaled that of a dwarf or even an elf. As a master of an art that sought the secret to immortality, she didn't look particularly old. That, despite the fact she eschewed the pearl creams and other make-up that most Hua women used as the passing years magnified the effect of gravity. "The question is what are *you* doing here?"

What *was* she doing here? Playing enchanted musical instruments in the middle of a forbidden area, with a foreign prince.

Foreign prince!

Hardeep must've been nearby. Kaiya scanned the surroundings. They were outside the gates of the temple compound. There was no sign of him or the Dragon Scale Lute, only a man whose blue-and-gold robes marked him as the Jianguo Shrine's high priest. He craned over her while several other priests huddled beyond, whispering among themselves as their judgmental stares fell on her. How mortifying.

One of the priests ran past, probably headed for the palace to report to Father. Once he learned about her sneaking out and entering the Temple of Heaven, on top of disobeying his initial order to send Prince Hardeep away…

She looked around again. "Where is Prince Hardeep?"

"Who?" Doctor Wu raised a perfectly sculpted eyebrow. She turned to the growing crowd of murmuring men. "Who is Prince Hardeep?"

The most charming and handsome man she'd ever seen. The only one who ever truly knew her. "A foreign supplicant to the *Tianzi*."

"Where is he now?" General Zheng, Commander of the Imperial Guard, shouldered his way to the front, several imperial guards in tow. The other men bowed and made way. He beckoned the hall steward and her guards. "Was he alone with the princess? Here?"

Kaiya's stomach churned. When the truth came out, Prince Hardeep would lose his head, foreign dignitary or not.

The priests all exchanged glances. Apparently, Hardeep had escaped without anyone seeing him. Which meant she had fainted, and he had just left her there.

To get help. He must have risked his life to get help. And he was safe.

General Zheng turned back to the priests. "Where is Prince Hardeep now?"

The men all looked among themselves, shrugging.

"I...I am not sure." The high priest squinted and blinked like a child testing new spectacles.

The general pointed to three imperial guards. "Go find the foreigner."

Kaiya twirled a loose lock of her hair. Maybe Prince Hardeep had just abandoned her to save his own skin. And like some silly daydream, she'd believed music made her beautiful in his eyes. How gullible she'd been. Breaking rules, acting like a love-struck fool. And now, possibly getting servants and Cousin Kai-Long executed. Her, too. Cold seeped into her hands, and her vision faded at the edges.

"Steady, *Dian-xia*." Doctor Wu placed one hand on Kaiya's back, the other on her wrist, feeling her pulse. Her eyebrows clashed together like charging goats. "Show me your tongue."

Kaiya glanced up at a different kind of audience than she was accustomed to. How embarrassing. Heat flared in her cheeks.

Doctor Wu swept an imperious gaze over the assembled men. "Turn around."

Like a temple's revolving storm door shutters, the men spun and snapped into place. Jaw tight, General Zheng nodded and turned around as well.

Thank the Heavens. Kaiya nodded to the doctor in thanks and stuck out her tongue.

"I see." Doctor Wu's lips pursed. She spent the next several minutes poking and prodding at her, while soldiers jogged around the temple walls and nervous priests shuffled at a respectful distance. How mortifying, to have so much attention for all the wrong reasons.

Just when Kaiya's heart was about to stop, a middle-aged man slunk through the wall of imperial guards. The white-and-red symbols stitched into his blue robes marked him as a member of the Ministry of Household Affairs. "*Dian-xia*, the *Tianzi* commands you to present yourself before him."

Heavens, no. Kaiya resigned to humiliating herself in front of all the hereditary lords. The *Tianzi*—Father—had no choice but to pass harsh judgment.

Doctor Wu's hand squeezed hers, sending a reassuring warmth coursing through her body. "Don't worry, *Dian-xia*. I will accompany you."

For whatever good that would do. No matter Father's respect for the doctor, he couldn't afford to appear weak and overlook a capital offense. Not when the North was unsettled. Not when she couldn't prove her budding skill at Dragon Songs. Hopefully, when meting out punishment, he would take into account that she had never done anything wrong in the past.

Doctor Wu helped her to her shaky feet. The men around her all bowed. Imperial guards formed up behind her. The Minister of Household Affairs led her from the Temple of Heaven's front gates to where a palanquin and a several dozen imperial guards awaited.

Kaiya peered at the palanquin, all vibrations of power from the Lute melting away from her core. She gritted her teeth and ducked into its narrow confines. It rose off the ground and lurched into a steady pace. Outside, the imperial guards marched in tight formation.

How foolish she'd been, believing Prince Hardeep wanted to help her. An accomplished musician himself, he'd probably taken the Lute. He might have already chartered a ship back to Ankiras, where he would scatter the Maduran armies with the instrument's fell magic.

Leaving her here, on her way to a possible death sentence. The palanquin walls seemed to close in around her. Memories of being locked in an armoire sent her pulse skittering. Kaiya took a deep breath of the hot, stuffy air in hopes it would calm her. She should be grateful for the privacy. Now hidden from prying eyes, salty-hot tears trickled unchecked down her cheeks.

An eternity in the bobbing coffin dragged on until the procession finally ground to a halt. Kaiya dried the tears with her sleeve. Her eyelids felt heavy and swollen. Herald calls and the swoosh of opening gates indicated their arrival at Sun-Moon Palace.

"*Dian-xia*," Chen Xin said from outside, reassuring her with a familiar voice. "We have passed the front gates of Sun-Moon Palace. Would you like to alight?"

The guards and servants knew her habits well, predicting she would want to walk the rest of the way to the castle. Not tonight. The Iridescent Moon neared full, ready to shine light on her shame. Her voice caught and she cleared her throat. "Take me to the Jade Gate. Take your time."

Kaiya shuddered, worried her cracking voice had revealed weakness. Nonetheless, the ride from the palace's main gate to the Imperial Family's residence would afford her just enough time to regain her composure. If she were to present herself before Father, she would hold her head high when accepting his judgment.

To calm herself, she envisioned her ride as a walk. Past the Hall of Supreme Harmony. To the Dragon Bridge between the palace grounds and the castle. Through the winding alleys of the inner castle compound.

The palanquin came to a gentle stop, and the porters lowered it to the ground. The doors slid open and a hand, smooth as phoenix feathers, took hers to help her out.

Her legs quavered. The imperial guards by the gatehouse dropped to one knee, fist to the ground.

Doctor Wu released her hand.

The palace chamberlain shuffled forward and bowed. "*Dian-xia.* The *Tianzi* summons you to his quarters immediately."

Kaiya nodded. She forced herself to achieve a semblance of grace as she crossed the covered stone bridge from the keep to the Imperial Family's walled-off, hilltop residence. Moonlight sparkled off the gold leaf of the one-story pavilion's tiled eaves. Surrounded by moats, the building was further protected from magical intrusion by an ancient ward.

Her personal retinue of handmaidens and guards stopped and knelt as she approached the gatehouse connecting the family's restricted bedrooms to the rest of the residence. There, eight imperial guard sentries stepped aside while the gatekeeper—an old nun from Praise Spring Temple—held up a light bauble lamp to Kaiya's face.

The woman spoke in the Imperial Family's secret language, her voice hoarse as she asked one of the hundreds of questions needed to validate Kaiya's identity. "What land did the Founder and his consort come from?"

"Great Peace Island," Kaiya answered, using the secret language's name for Jade Island.

"How many patron saints watch over Hua from Jade Island?"

"Eight," Kaiya said, "though some include The Dwarf as the Ninth."

"What are their names?"

"The Water Saint, The Metal Saint, The World Saint, The Fire Saint, The Wood Saint, The Earth Saint, The Heavenly King, and The Sea King. The Dwarf is King of the Underworld."

Without looking back, the gatekeeper rapped a code—changed hourly—on the heavy ironwood doors. They slid open, revealing the shaved pates of nine bowing nuns, armed only with the empty-handed *Yongchun* fighting style.

The Founder had established these security protocols, after having barely survived his most trusted vassal's surprise attack, just before he came to post-Hellstorm Hua. In his time, the nuns had used daggers. Later, his consort taught them her own unarmed combat skills.

Kaiya walked to the *Tianzi*'s quarters, surrounded by an escort of nuns and with Doctor Wu one step behind.

Her brothers and Xiulan, all kneeling on cushions, turned their heads toward her as she stepped into the bedroom antechamber. From where he sat on a cushioned bloodwood chair, Father fixed her with a severe gaze.

Belly tight, Kaiya dropped to her knees and pressed her forehead to the ground.

"Rise," Father said.

Straightening, she looked up to focus on something else. The ceiling was coffered, with jade insets carved to depict scenes from the Wang Dynasty's glorious history. Lacquered wooden panels with mother-of-pearl inlay adorned the red walls. Lanterns with bloodwood frames around paper-thin white jade and dangling red silk tassels hung from the ceiling, providing a soft light from the Aksumi baubles.

His dignified tone remained the same as if addressing dinner plans or a devastating flood. "I am told that you left the palace without permission, unprotected, and entered the Temple of Heaven."

Kaiya bowed her head. There was no point in denying what everyone knew. However, beyond that, she had to protect Hardeep, Kai-Long, and all the servants, even if it meant bending the truth. "Yes. Please, I acted on my own accord. I tricked the servants and imperial guards. I was selfish and foolish."

His eyes narrowed for a split second. "Did you enter the stupa? Did you behold the fallen star?"

She shook her head.

"Then we have some leeway in meting out punishment." He let out a long breath, so uncharacteristic of him, and then looked from Eldest Brother to Second Brother. "It seemed everyone in the city was drawn to the unique song emanating from the Temple of Heaven, like moths to a light bauble. With your ear for music and perceptive hearing, you must have gone first. Yes, you are undoubtedly the victim of evil magic. Luckily, you did not enter the stupa."

Kaiya tilted her head a fraction. He was fabricating an excuse to protect her, glossing over the fact that she did enter the compound. But apparently, no one considered that *she* could have created that music. And as much as she should have told the whole truth, including the attacks on her and Hardeep, it would risk too many people.

"Doctor," Father said, "perhaps with your broad understanding of the world, you could tell us what kind of instrument makes that sound?"

"I am not entirely sure." The doctor shifted on her feet, lips pursed. "Magic and music are Lord Xu's expertise."

Father turned back to Kaiya. "Now, I have heard some disturbing news about your actions from earlier in the day."

From earlier in the day? Was the issue with the Temple of Heaven resolved so easily? Something was wrong. "Yes." Kaiya pressed her forehead to the dark wood tiles. "I—"

Doctor Wu held up a silencing hand. "If I may, *Huang-Shang*, I have more pressing news. Good news."

More pressing than her directly disobeying his order and nearly damaging a priceless artifact? More important than the capital offense of breaking into the Temple of Heaven, even if Father glossed over it? Kaiya fidgeted on her knees.

Father's eyes shifted from Kaiya to the doctor. "Speak."

"I have felt the princess' pulse and studied her tongue. She is about to blossom with Heaven's Dew. I would guess in a few days, on the new White Moon."

Heat rose to Kaiya's head as she sucked in a breath. Such a private consideration, at least for most girls, was now dragged out for her brothers to hear Not like they wouldn't know soon, anyway. They'd likely been privy to this particular topic of speculation among the servants—and through their loose lips, among the hereditary lords and ministers as well. Curse her good ears for overhearing the furtive whispers.

Xiulan leaned past Eldest Brother Kai-Guo and winked. As usual, Kai-Wu showed little interest in state affairs, which apparently included her soon-to-start monthly rhythms.

At least it was finally coming. Most of the palace girls her age had already taken that step into womanhood. Even her spunky cousin Lin Ziqiu, two years younger, had already started. Kaiya dared a quick glance up.

A rare smile flitted across Father's face before his expressionless demeanor returned. "This is most welcome news. A marriage might help pacify the rebellion in the North."

Kaiya twirled a lock of hair. Just this morning, the North had been merely unsettled. Now it was a rebellion? And if what Doctor Wu said was true—and she was never wrong in matters of health—Kaiya would be eligible to marry in less than a week. "What rebellion?" she ventured.

"Yes, this is fortuitous," Father continued, seeming not to have heard her. "Especially with Kai-Wu's wedding so close. I hope to see grandchildren before I join your mother, and the realm will certainly be reassured by the birth of heirs to the Mandate of Heaven." He looked to Kai-Guo and Xiulan.

Xiulan averted her gaze while Kai-Guo fidgeted. A year into the marriage and the Crown Princess' private considerations were under even more public scrutiny than Kaiya's. And with their quarters right next door, she knew their lack of success had little to do with a lack of trying.

Kaiya bit her bottom lip. She might be jealous of Xiulan's peerless handwriting, perfect posture, impeccable manners, pearly complexion, doe eyes, and hair where no strand ever fell out of place; but Kaiya didn't envy the pressure to conceive an heir. Her own future sons would be far down the line, after her brothers' sons, after Father's younger brother and his sons. Poor Xiulan withered under Father's stare.

It wasn't fair. Clearing her throat, Kaiya set aside all questions about the rebellion and pressed her forehead to the floor. "Father, I apologize for the trouble and embarrassment I have caused. I should not have accompanied Prince Hardeep to the Hall of Pure Melody and nearly ruined Yanyan's pipa." Or violated the sanctity of the Temple of Heaven, but if he had forgotten about it, there was no need to provide a reminder.

Doctor Wu clucked. Yes, her earlier deflection had gone to waste, but someone had to rescue Xiulan from her awkward position. At least nobody's monthly cycles were under scrutiny for the moment.

The weight of Father's stare pressed her into a deeper bow. "Rise," he said.

Kaiya sat up. In the corner of her eye, Xiulan mouthed, *Thank you.*

The *Tianzi* said, "My daughter, it is good you recognize your mistakes and have made yourself accountable. However, as I rule by the Mandate of Heaven, if I were to show leniency, it would be perceived by the palace staff, officials, and hereditary lords as preferential treatment. Do you understand?"

"Yes, *Huang-Shang.*" Kaiya bowed her head.

Jawline set, he nodded. "In four days' time, the day after Kai-Wu's wedding, you shall present yourself before me with the hereditary lords in attendance. Until then, you shall be confined to the castle with limited visitation. I am assigning Secretary Hong to vet all who call on you."

Bowing again in acknowledgement, Kaiya suppressed a sigh. That list of visitors would certainly *not* include Prince Hardeep, if he even turned up. He probably wouldn't, since she was of no use to him anymore.

Kai-Guo said, "Father, perhaps you should assign a *Moquan* adept to follow Kaiya."

As if at sixteen years old, she still believed in the boogeymen that stole unruly children from their beds and forced them into a life of thievery. Kaiya would have rolled her eyes if Father weren't there to see it.

Father waved off Kai-Guo's empty threat. A smile formed on his face. "People in and around the Hall of Pure Melody report that your music this morning bordered on the divine."

What would they say about her song in the Temple of Heaven, if they knew?

Doctor Wu snorted. "If I may, *Huang-Shang*, she played with forces she did not understand or know how to control. It has thrown her energy out of balance, perhaps beyond the ability of the palace physicians to treat. She is fortunate that I came from Haikou to deliver herbal medicines to your family."

Father tilted his head a fraction, the appropriate recognition for a *Tianzi* to show someone as respected as Doctor Wu. "You shall be her first visitor then." He turned to Kaiya. "Now, off to bed."

Jie watched from the shadows as Princess Kaiya rose. Without a doubt, the magic bauble image was much prettier than the real deal, which cast Tian's taste further into question. Crown Princess Xiulan stood as well, and both ladies and the mysterious old woman bowed and shuffled out of the *Tianzi's* room. At the last second, Doctor Wu made direct eye contact.

Holding her breath, Jie froze in place. The old woman, with undoubtedly equally old eyes had picked her out of the shadows. Or had she? Without any sign of acknowledgement, Doctor Wu followed the princesses out.

The *Tianzi* cleared his throat. "Continue."

Master Yan melted out of the shadows and beckoned Jie to join him behind Prince Kai-Guo and Prince Kai-Wu. "Tell the *Tianzi* what you have seen."

The whole story? She'd already briefed Master Yan on the attackers' *Moquan* weapons, and he insisted the Black Lotus only served the Son of Heaven. Now, he nodded, answering her unasked question.

She turned to the *Tianzi* and pressed her forehead to the ground. Was that the right protocol? She'd never reported directly to the throne before. "*Huang-Shang*, the attackers were all large young men. They used *Moquan* tools but were not Black Lotus adepts. One was Hua, but another had blond hair and fair skin."

"The answer appears clear to me," the *Tianzi* said. "One of your own has trained others in your ways."

Master Yan shook his head. "Impossible. All masters, past and present, living and dead, are accounted for." Such audacity to be so direct!

The *Tianzi* just chuckled. "My old friend, perhaps it wasn't a master. In any case, I am more concerned about who they work for."

An enigma, to be sure. Jie let her lower lip smack as she released it. "With the rebellion in the North, I thought they might be hired by Lord Tong. But—"

Crown Prince Kai-Guo raised a hand. "But why would Lord Tong have the Ankiran refugees slaughtered?"

Jie said, "Guests of Young Lord Peng Kai-Long."

The *Tianzi* sighed. "Maybe they are sending a message to Young Kai-Long."

"Perhaps Cousin Kai-Long made enemies when he worked as a diplomat," Crown Prince Kai-Guo said. "Madurans?"

Master Yan raised a hand. "Remember, they targeted the princess, too. Until we gather more evidence, we cannot rule out anyone."

The Crown Prince nodded. "In the meantime, we must address Lord Tong's rebellion. Kaiya will flower soon. If she marries General Lu, that would send a message."

Master Yan shook his head. "General Lu was offended by the princess. He has already departed for the North."

"Lord Tong himself, then," the Crown Prince said. "Offer her as a bride, and in return, have his son brought to court as a hostage. That should secure his loyalty."

Jie searched the prince's expression. Marriages were preemptive, and Lord Tong looked to have already made his move. "*Huang-Shang*, if I may, Lord Tong plays, shall I say, both side of the chessboard. With females, his tastes have a sharp edge. I am not sure you would want to expose your own daughter to such humiliation."

The *Tianzi's* face might have been chiseled out of stone for all the emotion he showed. Though there it was, the vein in his temple bulging. "We will consider other options first. In any case, the hereditary lords will see her value as a bride as a good reason not to execute her."

Perhaps death would be better than marriage to Lord Tong. Jie sucked on her lower lip. No telling how Tian would react if the princess married such a degenerate. She composed her expression when the *Tianzi* settled his gaze on her.

"You will shadow her," he said.

If Jie's stomach could sink any more, she'd have to pick it off the floor. Babysitting would be such a waste of her skills. There had to be a way out... Right. "*Huang-Shang*, today I was hired as a guide and translator for the Tarkothi prince, Aryn. I must return to his ship in Jiangkou by dawn." Her butt ached at the thought of the horse ride back, and then having to wear that outrageous dress, though even that would be better than having to keep an eye on a stubborn girl.

The *Tianzi's* eyes shifted to Master Yan, who nodded. He turned back to Jie. "I find it quite the coincidence that a blond *Moquan* appears the same day a Tarkothi ship arrives. Look into it."

Crown Prince Kai-Guo nodded. "Also, a prince from Tarkoth's rival, Serikoth, will be arriving to negotiate trade. He will be attending Kai-Wu's wedding, as well."

Prince Kai-Wu's eyelids fluttered open. Apparently he had been dozing.

"Perhaps," the Crown Prince continued, "you could find ways to fan the hostilities. It would tempt them to order more cannons and firepowder."

Master Yan might have a point, but fanning hostilities didn't seem relevant to the impending rebellion. Still, it was certainly better than shadowing Princess Kaiya, even if it meant wearing that ridiculous dress again. Now if only her rear end could survive the night.

CHAPTER 24

All Paths Lead to Music

Eyes closed, Kaiya listened as spring sang its song through bird chirps and the wind rustling in fruit tree buds outside the Chrysanthemum Chamber. One of the many multipurpose rooms in Sun-Moon Castle, it had been appropriated by Doctor Wu for an acupuncture treatment.

Kaiya lay absolutely still, for Heavens knew how long. Gold needles protruded from points all over her body, throbbing and buzzing and blossoming as if her body hosted a fireworks display. It might as well have been one, given all the palace physicians who came and went, all bobbing their heads at Doctor Wu's wisdom. At least a dozen hands felt her pulses, and she had to stick her tongue out each time for their examination.

Had they been treating her themselves, they would have had to insert the needles blindfolded; but today, they held hand mirrors up to politely and indirectly see the points Doctor Wu had chosen. Not that it mattered; her lanky body might have just as easily belonged to a boy.

Not for long, though, if what Doctor Wu had said was right. And she was never wrong. Thank the Heavens. Maybe the news of her blossoming would stifle the rumors and jokes behind her back. Of course, it also meant her wedding to General Lu, or perhaps some rebellious Northern lord, might happen in less than a month. That future did not include Prince Hardeep or Dragon Songs. She let out a long sigh.

"Breathe more deeply!" Doctor Wu said. "No sighing. It constrains your *Qi*, just like when you tried learning to play magic from a book. You were too excited, weren't you?"

Yes. Although the needles didn't allow her to move or speak at the moment, the omniscient doctor didn't need to hear the answer to know it.

Doctor Wu harrumphed. "I have taught you about energy flow since you were a child. You should know better. And using *that* instrument."

Yanyan's pipa, nearly ruined by her own hand. If the doctor knew about the Dragon Scale Lute, she might be even more horrified. The needle in her belly sent a jolt radiating out in a wave.

"You might be as stubborn as Yanyan, herself."

Doctor Wu was old, but couldn't possibly be old enough to have known the first master of Dragon Songs. Could she?

"You can get up now."

Get up? Kaiya shuddered. Even the smallest motion caused her muscles to twist around the needles, sending surges along her body's energy paths.

From right above her, Doctor Wu's voice bordered on exasperation. "Quickly now. I already took all the needles out."

Kaiya opened her eyes. Stretching out her arms and legs, she wiggled her fingers and toes. Though she could move again, her body still sang from the symphony of Doctor Wu's treatment.

The doctor hovered above her, twisting a dozen needles between her fingers. "Now, get dressed. I will be back." She pointed toward a folded robe and left the room.

Groaning up to her knees, Kaiya retrieved the gown and held it up. The coarse brown cloth looked nothing like her usual embroidered silks, let alone the extravagant robe she'd worn to meet General Lu. Prince Hardeep had seen her in that, along with the thick layer of foundation, drawn-on eyebrows, and extended lashes. If he saw her now…

Blotches of pimples or not, her face certainly felt better without the cosmetic mask. If only she could be naturally beautiful like Xiulan. Catching her sigh, lest Doctor Wu hear it in the other room, Kaiya slipped the plain robe on. It could only mean one thing: one of the doctor's tortuous lessons.

No sooner had she tied the sash than Doctor Wu slid open the door and marched back in. Her eyes darted from up to down in a cursory evaluation before she nodded. "Good. You may not be particularly pretty, but you have a strong spirit."

Kaiya's chest tightened. The doctor's words probably hadn't been meant to hurt, but still…at least Tian had always adored her, no matter how plain she was. And Prince Hardeep…

"Straighten your spine," Doctor Wu said. "Good. Now listen: when you played *that* song with *that* instrument, you opened connections inside your body like the great musicians from the past. However, you were too excited and lost control of it."

Kaiya's mouth gaped of its own accord. Doctor Wu hadn't even heard her play, yet somehow knew.

"Close your mouth. I might not know Dragon Songs, but for your health, you have two paths: either master it, or give it up altogether."

The doctor could have just said to give it up and get married. Maybe the fact she mentioned mastering it first offered a hint as to what she thought was best. And to think it was even a possibility! Kaiya shuffled on her feet.

The doctor pointed to one of the east-facing windows. "No decision should be considered without meditation. Stand there, face Jade Mountain."

What did she want? What was best for Hua? Kaiya took short strides to the designated spot. Snow-capped Jade Mountain, dark green in the mist, rose over Sun-Moon Lake.

"Now, focus on your breathing, anchor yourself with the energies of Mother Earth."

Kaiya suppressed a shudder. It was one of the first exercises Doctor Wu had taught her eight years before, at the *Tianzi's* bidding, to treat childhood anxiety. The calm had helped her get over Tian's banishment. It also left her legs shaking in pain. She sank into a deep horse stance, her thighs parallel to the ground, spine straight, and attention locked on the mountain. The pose was thoroughly unladylike. Nonetheless, it had helped develop the strength and balance she needed for the most graceful dances.

Doctor Wu regarded her with a furrowed brow. With a nudge of a hand, she lifted Kaiya's chin to further straighten her back. "Now breathe, tongue on the roof of your mouth, in through the nose letting your belly expand; out through your mouth, pushing your belly in."

Gripping the floor with her bare toes, Kaiya did as told. Cool air settled into her lungs, and the tingling from the acupuncture spread and dispersed.

Doctor Wu afforded Kaiya a cursory glance. "Good. Your inherent Fire energies rage, fueling your creativity, but you must contain them with nourishing Water. Visualize your weight sinking deeper and deeper into Mother Earth as you exhale. Draw her life-giving energy through your *Yongquan* points in your soles as you inhale and bring them to your *Dantian* below your navel."

Kaiya obeyed, imagining the energy of the world as tangible. A deep breath in, a slow breath out. Thoughts of Prince Hardeep settled, replaced by a calm drawn from the resolute vibration of the earth. The cool sensation seemed almost like the tranquility she felt when lost in her own music.

Which, in turn, felt nothing like playing Yanyan's pipa or the Dragon Scale Lute.

The doctor clucked. "You practice too much of that *Praise Moon Fist* fighting. Its nature is Wood. It easily transforms into Fire and rises to your head. If you do not nurture your Water energies, your inherent Fire will burn out your *Sea of Marrow*. No wonder you lost control of the song's power."

Kaiya's knees burned from the strain, yet she almost forgot about them as she mulled over the doctor's perplexing words. The power of Dragon Songs didn't seem at all related to medicine.

Then again, Prince Hardeep, a non-Hua who shouldn't be able to channel magic through artistic endeavor, had told her to straighten her body and put her feet on the ground. If it came from just his love of music, then maybe her music teachers had left something out of their instruction. With no sign of the prince, she might never find out. He was probably on the first ship bound for his besieged Ankira, Dragon Scale Lute in hand.

"Focus." Doctor Wu pressed Kaiya's back, straightening her spine. "Remember to root yourself next time you decide to play with things you don't understand."

Kaiya might have cowered had she not been concentrating on the stance.

The doctor harrumphed. "In fact, maybe you shouldn't play these songs of power at all. That music last night...a frightening energy coursed through it, one that did not belong to Mother Earth. Lose control of such power in such a place, and it might have dire consequences. For you. For the world."

For the world? One song having dire consequences for the entire world...the very idea of it was overwhelming.

Doctor Wu came around and shot her an imperious look. "If you ask me, you should find a real instructor."

"There are none," Kaiya said. Her voice came out as a squeak, probably from not having spoken for the last few hours. She straightened out of her stance. "At least not for music."

Doctor Wu shrugged. "I don't know much about magic, but at its core, artistic endeavor is all the same: the expression of intention."

"I don't know..." Not that she had any reason to learn anymore. The whole idea of using a Dragon Song to change the minds of the lords and Father, which felt so right last night, was clearly treason. And Hardeep's other hope, expelling an invading army with fear, apparently involved powers that might be too terrible to invoke.

"You have always had the potential. I have long felt it in your pulse. You must make a choice."

Such revelations; why now? And if it was always there, maybe this was a chance to rediscover her people's lost art.

"You are prettier when you smile," Doctor Wu said.

Kaiya covered her mouth. "If I wanted to learn, what would you recommend?"

Doctor Wu tilted her head like a cobra. "Observe others who can evoke magic through their art."

"I can't go out into the palace grounds for two days." Kaiya sighed.

"There is always the Crown Princess."

Right. Xiulan could manifest magic through her calligraphy, and appeared even more radiant when doing it. After rescuing her from the uncomfortable discussion of unconceived heirs, she owed Kaiya a favor.

"Start there. Small steps," Doctor Wu said.

Kaiya caught herself before she sighed and earned another rebuke. "If only Lord Xu would teach me more."

"More?" Doctor Wu's lips twitched. "I would be wary of that rascal. Wherever he is in the world right now, I would wager that Lord Xu heard the song last night. It would not surprise me if he makes an appearance soon."

***

Kaiya knelt on a silk cushion on the veranda in the Gardenia Courtyard, listening to the smooth swoosh of Xiulan's brush across rice paper.

Her sister-in-law sat at the bloodwood table with her back straight, soles flat on the ground. She held her hanging sleeve with her left hand as the brush danced across the page. The posture looked similar to the way Hardeep had suggested Kaiya sit when playing the pipa.

The slow, graceful motions and steadfast whirr of the brush were lulling, hypnotic. Kaiya almost forgot how her legs still ached from the low stance hours before.

Several handmaidens stood at the edge of the veranda, all craning their necks to see the Crown Princess write. Four imperial guards flanked the doors, including her own Chen Xin and Xu Zhan, so still they might have been statues themselves.

Xiulan set the brush down and held up her paper. The handmaidens clapped.

Kai. Victorious, just like the first character in Kaiya's name, shared by her brothers, as well as cousins Kai-Long and Kai-Hua.

Kaiya's chest swelled with pride, and a smile tugged at her lips. For all her mistakes, she'd already accomplished more with music than any human had in two hundred years. "I feel it," Kaiya said. "How did you do it?"

"My master emphasizes getting in the right mood by sitting straight and grinding the inkstone. I held a sense of pride and satisfaction in my heart and wrote."

Once you have seized the song's emotion and made it your own, the music book from the Hall of Pure Melody had said, *you must project it. Rooted to the ground, your spine aligned, let your heart impel your voice.* Kaiya glanced back at the beaming handmaidens and stoic guards. None seemed as affected as her. "Why did it affect only me?"

Xiulan bowed her head. "I remembered the gratitude I felt when you saved me from embarrassment yesterday."

Kaiya nodded. While not exactly a lesson from a master, at least it was a small step in understanding. If only Prince Hardeep were there. When she was near him, it felt like she could do anything.

Appearing at the door, Secretary Hong creaked into a low bow. "Young Lord Peng Kai-Long has come to meet with Princess Kaiya."

Cousin Kai-Long stepped past the secretary and sank to his knee, fist to the ground. A large embroidered silk bag slipped from his shoulder. Could it be? He looked up to the Crown Princess. "If you would excuse me, *Dian-xia,* I would like to walk with Princess Kaiya."

"As you wish, Young Lord Peng." Xiulan gestured toward the garden.

"Thank you, Eldest Sister." Peering at his silk bag, Kaiya rose and nodded toward Kai-Long to take the lead.

White pebbles crunched beneath their feet as they wound along a path lined with glossy green gardenias. She lowered her voice. "Thank you for your help last night."

Kai-Long nodded. "I took full responsibility, even offered to cut my own throat. The *Tianzi* will withhold judgment for two days, and until then, I am confined to either the palace or my family villa."

"I am sorry." Kaiya bowed her head.

"It's all right. My role has been kept secret so as not to influence the opinions of the hereditary lords. I will prove my loyalty and worth to the *Tianzi* by leading the vanguard in an assault of Wailian Castle if we need to put down the rebellion."

Kaiya gasped. The impregnable fortress, if what General Lu said was true. And Kai-Long was confirming that the insurgency had indeed intensified.

He took her hand and patted it. Casting a glance back at the two imperial guards following several steps behind, he leaned in and whispered, "I managed to get Prince Hardeep to safety."

Hardeep! Alive and safe. Kaiya's pulse skipped a beat, and she almost stopped in her tracks. She turned away from Cousin Kai-Long and looked forward. "Where is he now?"

"Hiding at my pavilion. He apologizes for disappearing so quickly, but his life is in danger."

Kaiya sucked in a sharp breath. "The *Tianzi* must already know the entire story; not just about the morning, but the night, too. He would have Hardeep killed, wouldn't he?"

This time, it was Kai-Long's turn to stop and face her. "No—or at least, I do not think so. I have already spoken on Prince Hardeep's behalf."

"Then why is his life in danger?"

Cousin Kai-Long resumed his walk. "The Madurans received word that he is meddling with their trade agreement. My father's province shares a border with Ankira, and we have witnessed the refugees from Madura's brutal occupation. Madura is a warlike nation, and when they act, they rarely do so in moderation."

Kaiya's chest constricted. No doubt they were behind the massacre last night. And to think Hua sold these violent people firepowder. "Wouldn't Hardeep be safer in the palace?"

"I am working with palace officials to allow it. In the meantime, he asked me to give you this." He unslung the bag and presented it to her in two hands.

The Dragon Scale Lute? Kaiya stared at it for a few seconds before receiving it. She loosened the drawstrings and peeked inside. A lute. Though not the one made from dragon scale. Who would've imagined there would be three of these foreign instruments in the capital? She cinched the drawstrings and bowed. "Thank you."

He flashed a conspiratorial grin. "I would be happy to pass messages for you."

A smile came unbidden to Kaiya's lips. "Thank you, Cousin. Please tell him that I want to help him."

"Be wary," Kai-Long said. "If the Madurans think you are meddling in their affairs, they won't hesitate to snuff out your young life."

Prince Hardeep had said as much. And they had already snuffed out so many. Kaiya's breath hitched. How awful, to be murdered for doing the right thing. And to think the Madurans acted with impunity on Hua soil. She straightened her carriage, not wanting to show fear. "The prince and I were ambushed last night, twice."

Kai-Long stopped, spun, and faced her. His eyes could not open any wider. "Did you tell the *Tianzi*?"

She shook her head. "Everyone believes I was lured out of the palace by the music."

Kai-Long blew out a long exhalation. "At least you won't get Hardeep in trouble for *that*. Still, the *Tianzi* must know, so he can increase your guard."

"Don't worry. He assigned a *Moquan* to watch me." Kaiya rolled her eyes.

"A what?" Kai-Long's gawk, combined with his wide eyes, made him look like a caricature she'd once seen. His hand strayed to a folded piece of paper in his sash.

"Silly, right?" As though an imaginary boogeyman could do anything against Madura's very real hired knives.

Kai-Long offered a nervous laugh. "If I didn't know how much the *Tianzi* treasured you, I would say he is being lax with your protection."

"I always have at least two imperial guards whenever I am out of the residence."

Kai-Long glanced back at the two men, and then leaned in again. "Have you heard of the Golden Scorpions?"

Of course she'd heard of the evil warriors with expressionless masks, though mostly as scary bedtime stories. Cast-offs and deserters from the Order of Ayuri Paladins, the Golden Scorpions used their martial magic in the service of Madura's aggression—including assassinations. Fear crawled up her spine like a spider.

She tried to keep her voice confident. "The *Tianzi* forbids them from entering Hua. It's grounds for terminating the trade agreement."

"They don't always wear masks. Just be careful."

Her chest squeezed around her heart. What if Hardeep, trained in Paladin ways...

CHAPTER 25
Eldaeri Princes

Between the lack of sleep, her aching thighs and butt, and the ridiculous pink dress, Jie hoped she would have little need for her physical *Moquan* skills today. Just like the day before, she picked her way north among the longshoremen, sailors, and boys crowding the docks at dawn—the difference being that today, she wasn't disguised as a boy, and she waddled like a duck.

And these types were not known for their chivalry. If she castrated every man who catcalled her in the first two blocks, Hua's next generation of foul-mouthed, flea-ridden sailors might never be born. Instead, she ignored them, walking toward the five-mast Tarkothi ship moored at the twenty-sixth berth.

Or was it the twenty-third berth? That's what the sign at the head of the dock indicated. Had they taken the time and effort to move it three berths up overnight? The enormous black ship filled her visual field, and would have needlessly clogged up the harbor.

She walked up the dock to the gangplank. Two marines stood guard, cutlasses dangling at their sides. They looked too small to be soldiers, and their features were almost effeminate. Eldaeri, in all likelihood. The nine-pointed silver sun emblazoned on their crimson surcoats...

Crimson?

The Tarkothi livery had been forest green. Unless they'd moved the ship and dyed their wardrobes, this was the Serikothi ship bearing their Prince Koryn all the way from Tivara's far east.

Fan hostilities, Crown Prince Kai-Guo had said. As if she knew enough about these northerners' customs to do so.

"We have no need for whores," one of the marines called in Arkothi.

The other elbowed him. "The way she walks, I'd bet my mama's teats she serviced the entire Tarkothi ship last night."

The first laughed. "You'd lose that bet, since Tarkothi peckers are so small from crossbreeding."

Both men chortled.

Jie rolled her eyes and spun on her heel, but not before looking up at the deck. Unlike the Tarkothi, who employed the larger ethnic Arkothi and Estomari, all the Serikothi appeared to be the elf-blooded Eldaeri. If the two countries' rivalry were limited to trading insults about manhood sizes, Hua wouldn't sell many cannons.

Ignoring their continued jeers, she went back to the harbor front and continued north. Past the Serikothi giant, the Tarkothi behemoth loomed over the three-mast Hua ships. Jie paused and scanned from north to south and back, comparing. The two foreign vessels, with their black wood hulls and sheer size, might have been twins. Perhaps the size of their ships compensated for...

She blew out a sigh. Serikoth and Tarkoth—along with a third kingdom, Korynth—had once been a single Eldaeri empire, divided over a century ago by a greed-driven civil war. That made it a lesson for Hua to learn from, given present circumstances.

"Hurry up, girl," a male voice called.

She turned to find the large, belligerent Tarkothi officer from the day before. Snake Eyes, the one who had begrudgingly found her the dress that she begrudgingly wore now. Her attempt at an Arkothi-style curtsey met with a chuckle. "I am sorry, sir."

"We will be departing for the capital when the Iridescent Moon wanes to its second crescent."

Jie looked south to the moon. Just three hours before subjecting her poor body to yet more travel. Hopefully, it didn't involve horses. "I will be—"

"In the meantime, His Highness would like to see how the Cathayi river-barge system works." Snake Eyes' gaze paused on the *Saint Gong*, now completing docking procedures at the twenty-eighth berth, before he pointed past it. "I understand they start on the other side of the lighthouse? Go to the harbormaster's office to arrange a guide."

Jie nodded. What a coincidence that Prince Aryn wanted to visit the scene of last night's escapades. If Tian had done his job, there wouldn't be anything out of the ordinary to see. "My friend works for the harbormaster."

Snake Eyes stroked his bare chin. "Very well. Bring him here, but make it quick. I will inform the prince. And you—get yourself together and stop walking like a maid the morning after her wedding."

Heat rose to the tip of Jie's ears. No more boats, no more sailors after this. If only there were somewhere clean to sit that wouldn't wrinkle the dress. Right, no more dresses either.

She turned back toward the harbormaster's office, which might have been abandoned for all the activity going on outside. Usually, merchants and ship quartermasters crowded near the doors at this hour.

From the entrance, she poked her head into the huge room. The rows of low tables, each covered with papers, brushes, and inkstones, suggested two dozen people worked there, but today only a handful of clerks and officials were on duty. Tian included. He looked up, eyes meeting hers, a smile blooming on his face. She beckoned him out.

He reached her side almost before she could blink. "Was the princess all right?"

Not *good morning* or *I'm glad to see you're safe*. For show, Jie squeezed her mouth into a tight frown. Make him squirm a little. "Come, walk with me."

He glanced back into the building, and then nodded. "What happened?"

Jie started back toward the Tarkothi ship. "She was attacked by large men, using *Moquan* weapons."

He sucked in a breath. "So is she unharmed?"

For someone so smart, so able to draw connections, he missed the obvious. "The port would be on high alert if she were hurt. Yes, she is fine."

He blew out a sigh. "They had *Moquan* tools?"

"Throwing stars, *Moquan* swords, cat claws, and smoke packets. They also used repeating crossbows, though with a larger magazine and bolt head."

"Our weapons and tools are secrets." Tian tapped his chin. "There must be a traitor to the clan."

Yet everyone was accounted for. "Master Yan is devoting significant resources to uncovering the mystery. In the meantime, what did you do with Fat Nose Jiang and his henchman?"

"We drugged them. They won't remember a thing. I presume they are at the river docks arguing with the harbormaster."

Right, the docks. She pulled his sleeve. "I need your help."

"All right. Let me tell the manager on duty." He disappeared into the office.

Jie glanced at all the ships, each representing Hua's dominance in international trade. Its lifeblood. So much wealth, and so many people vying to control it.

"Lead the way," Tian said.

Had he snuck up on her? That would be a first! She nodded and headed north with Tian at her side.

"You are waddling. Like a duck. You shouldn't have grinded up against Fat Nose Jiang."

Concern? Even if the tone was matter-of-fact? She grinned. "Consider yourself lucky you're not a Black Lotus sister." The chorus of longshoreman and sailor whistles punctuated her point.

Tian glared at them, only to meet with laughs.

"Come on little girl, you can do better than a skinny clerk. I can show you what it's like with a real man."

Jie reached over and took Tian's hand in her own. He started to yank it away, but then stiffened up. The sailors laughed.

At the twenty-third dock, three Serikothi men in polished steel cuirasses and scarlet capes assessed a herd of some thirty horses led by three merchants. No doubt the stodgy harbormaster would have taken issue with the beasts blocking the way and leaving stinking piles in the roads, had he not been busy at the river docks.

One of the Eldaeri men shook his head. "Is this the best you have?"

"The best in Cathay," a merchant said in Arkothi with a thick Hua accent. "The Dongmen Provincial cavalry buys from me."

Jie glanced at Tian. His father ruled Dongmen, and his eldest brother was an officer in their cavalry. If he thought anything about the horse trader's comments, his expression revealed nothing.

"The *national* cavalry buys from me," said the second trader.

Another Serikothi harrumphed. "Then they are getting ripped off."

A third Serikothi laughed. "We make better ships, breed better horses."

"But no firepowder," Jie muttered.

"What is the commotion, lieutenant?" A Serikothi man in a crimson uniform approached from the docks. He walked with a confident gait and bore a strong resemblance to Tarkoth's Prince Aryn. Two other officers flanked him.

The second Serikothi crossed his arms against his chest and bowed his head. "Your Highness, none of these horses meets our standards. We would look foolish riding them into the capital."

Yet another Eldaeri prince. With the rebellion in the North, maybe having all the foreigners around was a bad idea. Not just for their own safety, but... Jie leaned in to Tian. "You don't think any of these foreign governments are helping Lord Tong? Perhaps in return for firepowder, funneled through Yutou Province?"

Tian tilted his head toward the Serikothi black ship. "According to the *Intimidator's* manifests, it stopped in Yutou. We'd have to sneak on board to find out more, but I don't know the first thing about Eldaeri ship layouts."

She didn't either. "Maybe—"

"You." The Serikothi prince beckoned Tian.

Bowing, Tian shuffled over. "Prince Koryn Vardamcar, welcome to Cathay. How may I be of service?"

"You look like an official. When did the Tarkothi dock?"

Why so curious? Jie studied the prince's fine features.

"Yesterday, Your Highness," Tian said.

"Be a good man and see to it that when your emperor sends our guide, we ride ahead of the Tarkothi. Pay the man, Captain." He bent his head toward his aide, even more handsome then the rest.

And blond. Eldaeri supposedly didn't come fair-haired. With his thin eyebrows and full lips, he might even be considered beautiful. Looking at the prince with fervent devotion, the captain crossed his arms in front of his chest and bowed. He withdrew two foreign gold coins and presented them to Tian.

Shaking his head, Tian held up a dismissing hand. "I am just a scribe. For the harbormaster. The Imperial Foreign Ministry will be in charge of assigning a guide."

Prince Koryn stroked his beardless chin. "Perhaps we shall take it up with the Tarkothi, then. Scribe, who leads them?"

"It is not my place to know." Tian said.

In all likelihood, he did know, even if his official position didn't require it. Still, Crown Prince Kai-Guo had given the order to spit in rice bowls, and if there was any chance either of these rival nations were in league with Lord Tong's rebellion, this might be a way to find out. Jie bowed. "If I may, Your Highness, that would be Prince Aryn."

Prince Koryn turned and scrutinized her. "What a pretty girl. Thank you."

Even if his words carried no emotion, heat flared in Jie's cheeks. Tian had undoubtedly heard the compliment. Still, his face remained blank. She said, "Prince Aryn hired me to translate for him. We are headed there now, where Scribe Zheng will give him a tour of the river docks. Perhaps I can facilitate an introduction." And instigate trouble.

Tian's brows clashed together. "What—?"

Apparently, Prince Koryn had a similar idea. "What is Prince Aryn paying you?"

"A silver crown a day, Your Highness." She curtseyed, or at least tried to.

"I'll pay you two silver crowns a day to be our guide."

To be a guide, and not a spy? This seemed more a battle of one-upmanship than a serious conflict. In any case, it might be a way to get aboard the ship. "I...I... Let me think about it."

Tian's brows furrowed, his lips drawn into a rigid line.

Prince Koryn peered at her. "Don't take too long. In the meantime, I'll take you up on your offer to introduce us." He turned to the first three men. "Choose the twelve best horses for your cavaliers. Captain, bring eight marines with us."

"What are you doing?" Tian hissed.

"Finding a way onto his ship." And seeding trouble, per the prince's orders, but Tian didn't have to know it.

His eyes widened for a split second, his beautiful brown irises darting toward the approaching Serikothi marines.

They all carried repeating crossbows. With a larger magazine, just like the *Moquan* last night.

"Lead on." Prince Koryn gestured toward the Tarkothi ship.

Jie exchanged glances with Tian, then bowed her head. There had to be some way to get ahold of one of the crossbows.

When they reached the Tarkothi ship, Prince Aryn was waiting with Snake Eyes and several marines dressed in green and silver livery. Hands crept toward weapons, though Prince Aryn himself yawned.

Snake Eyes growled. "Look what flotsam the tide brought in."

"Now, now, Peris," Prince Aryn said. "No need for hostilities to ruin a joyous occasion."

"It could hardly be joyous with *that* filth," Snake Eyes Peris growled.

Prince Koryn straightened, drawing himself to his full height, not even as tall as Tian. "Had I known the Cathayi had invited Tarkothi mutts, I wouldn't have considered our own invitation such an honor."

Peris pulled his sword a quarter of the way out of his scabbard. Marines on both sides all shouldered forward, cutlasses flashing and crossbows leveled. Jie would have rolled her eyes at men and their toys, but Jiangkou harbor was about to become the scene of an international incident.

"At ease, General." The Tarkothi prince stayed Peris' hand. "We are guests here."

Prince Koryn snapped his own longsword back, though not before revealing its strange grey metal. "Prince Aryn is right. Maybe when we leave, we can settle this outside of the harbor, ship to ship."

"You'll need firepowder," Jie offered. "Maybe extra cannon fitted to your deck. You know what they say about a ship and its number of cannons."

Tian nudged her. *What are you doing?* his eyes asked.

Neither of the princes appeared to have heard her. Prince Aryn's lighthearted demeanor melted away, replaced by eyes fixated on his counterpart's sword. "I am afraid you have me at a disadvantage. You are?"

Maybe the Serikothi Crown Prince paused for dramatic effect, or maybe he didn't plan to answer at all.

"Crown Prince Koryn," Jie supplied, ignoring a glare sharp enough to cut through steel.

A grin forming on his lips, Prince Aryn crossed his arms and bowed his arms. "Well met, Cousin. Distant cousin." He turned to the blond aide. "And you must be Captain Damaryn. Your reputation precedes you. Even in Tarkoth, it is said you have bedded half the noblewomen in Serikoth."

With his nonchalant expression, Prince Aryn sounded like the drunken uncle at a New Year's feast; not that Jie had any uncles to compare. His lip twitched for a split second. Had his words been premeditated?

Coughing, Captain Damaryn exchanged glances with Prince Koryn, then crossed his arms and bowed his head. "It is my honor to meet you, Your Highness."

"I'm sure." Prince Aryn yawned at his Serikothi counterpart. "You seem to have found my guide. Feel free to join us on our tour of their river docks."

The Serikothi prince held a finger up. "I came to discuss the order in which our parties will enter Cathay's capital."

"If it matters that much to you, the Serikothi may go first." Prince Aryn shrugged. With his unflappable nonchalance, it would be hard to instigate troubles between the two.

Whatever else, the enmity between the two nations likely discounted *both* the Eldaeri kingdoms conspiring with Lord Tong. Jie waved northward. "Didn't you want to see the docks? This is my friend, Scribe Zheng, who works for the harbormaster."

"Pleased to meet you." Tian placed his right fist into his left hand and bowed.

"Lead the way," Prince Aryn said. He looked over his shoulder at the Serikothi prince. "By all means, join us."

Prince Koryn's eyes shifted from Prince Aryn to Tian and back. "We have other matters to attend to." He turned to Jie. "Remember my offer."

Crossing his arms, he bowed his head. The captain and Serikothi marines saluted as well, and then followed their prince back to the *Intimidator*.

Harrumphing, Prince Aryn resumed his walk toward the river docks. "I thought we'd never be rid of them. Now, Jyeh, what is this offer he mentions?"

She feigned a shy smile. "He offered to pay me two silver crowns a day to act as his translator and guide."

He laughed. "Prince Koryn may be a capable field general, but in matters of state, he only cares about appearances. If it matters that much to him, then by all means, take up his offer. Just know that if you do your work well, I have a long-term job in mind."

Tian raised an eyebrow. Whatever Jie was up to with these Eldaeri princes, it had little to do with rooting out traitors or uncovering a conspiracy. It was also wasting his time. *The Saint Gong*, which had just docked when he joined Jie, was almost tied down to the moorings at berth twenty-eight, right beside them. According to the manifests, *Tai-Ming* Lord Peng and his first son were aboard, and deceased Lamp Man Sha had named him as one of the conspirators.

"Scribe Jung." Mispronouncing Tian's name, stout Peris' voice grated like a knife dragged across a whetstone. "The prince asked you a question."

Tian looked up. "I'm sorry. Question?"

Prince Aryn pointed toward the mouth of the Jade River, emptying into the harbor. "Why put the lighthouse so far inland?"

"To ensure oceangoing vessels don't run aground."

"I bet that seawall helps with that, too." Was that sarcasm in the prince's voice? It was hard to tell in Arkothi.

Tian nodded. "Jiangkou was established as close to the capital as possible. The Jade River gets shallow fast. There's a lot of silt from its tributary, the Iron River." Which flowed from the hotbed of rebellion. And the seawall ensured the shallowness, to prevent larger ships from getting *too* close to the capital. It was curious that the Tarkothi would be interested in the river barges. "This is as far as a ship can travel inland. That's why goods have to be transferred to river barges here."

Prince Aryn pointed. "So what is going on there? I'd wager the commotion is what kept me awake last night."

Tian looked past the lighthouse, where officials, the local watch, and imperial soldiers swarmed over the river docks like ants. His own doing, in an effort to impound the supplies bound for Wailian County and its allies. There, arguing with the harbormaster, was Fat Nose Jiang, looking much worse for the wear. Jie's intoxicant would have left him with an awful hangover and only vague recollections based on the suggestions Tian planted in his addled head.

He cast a sidelong glance at Jie. She'd gone beyond the call of duty, grinding her nether regions up against Jiang's lap when a simple kiss on the neck would have sufficed. Surely she hadn't needed to debase herself like that.

Grasping the prince's sleeve, she pointed at the chaos. "It looks like they are seizing rice and whatever is in those kegs."

Now she was blathering on. He'd said he wanted to see the river docks, not get a blow-by-blow account of cargo impoundment procedures. The lack of sleep must have really dulled her edge. Thankfully, Prince Aryn showed little interest. Tian interposed himself. "It might be dangerous to go down there. I advise waiting here."

Prince Aryn yawned at Peris. "Satisfied?"

So it was the large aide who actually wanted to see the docks. He crossed his arms over his chest. "Yes, Your Highness."

The prince waved a dismissive hand. "Your emperor's representatives should be arriving soon to escort us to the capital. Let's head back."

Tian studied Peris. What was this man's interest in the docks? Tapping his chin, he followed the Tarkothi entourage back toward their ship, the *Indomitable*.

Jie's ears twitched. She pulled him down. "Get down, get down!"

Prince Aryn's guards formed up around him, cutlasses drawn and crossbows leveled. Screams and crashes erupted nearby.

Tian followed her eyes to the source: the wharf to their side, berth twenty-eight, where the *Saint Gong* was docked. *Tai-Ming* Lord Peng Xian's honor guard of sixty-two men broke ranks. Two palanquins lay on their sides, a man clutching his neck in front of one. From behind the second, a set of legs sprawled out. Soldiers drew weapons while dockworkers and longshoremen cowered or fled.

"Repeater crossbows." Her eyes roved over the surroundings. "Same sound frequency as the ones used last night. Fired twice from two different locations."

On the dock, soldiers formed up around the palanquins.

"Lord Peng Xian is dead!" someone yelled.

"Young Lord Kai-Zhi is hit!"

"Call a doctor!"

Tian's gut knotted as he scanned all elevated points. The attackers would need to have sightlines high enough to shoot above the guards. Not only that, but they would have needed to know Lord Peng and his firstborn had arrived on the *Saint Gong* today.

"There." Jie pointed toward the Tarkothi *Indomitable*.

Tian squinted. A large man strolled down the gangplank, no visible weapons. "He's unarmed. Why him?"

"He's big. He's calm. Get him. I can't run in this stupid dress."

Tian hiked up his own robes and sprinted, undoubtedly blowing his cover in the process. Dockworkers, sailors, and longshoremen ran about yelling. Jie was right; whoever it was, now on the dock, he didn't seem to be in any hurry. Until their eyes met. He was a Hua boy, perhaps only fourteen despite his larger size.

Just ten *chi* away to start, the suspect's long stride gained distance faster than Tian could take it away. For someone so large, he effortlessly weaved through all the panicked people. And now he'd disappeared.

A fist caught Tian in the side of the head, but he ducked under the second and swept his leg out. The boy jumped over the leg and shot out a side-kick which Tian had to lie back to avoid. Popping back to his feet, he exchanged several strikes with his opponent, none of the blows landing. It was as if they each knew what the other was planning. The boy leapt away, grabbed a dockworker, and shoved him into Tian.

Tian spun away, but his quarry broke into the open and ran south. With his long legs, there was no hope of catching up. He looked back at Tian, grinning. But maybe...up ahead, ten Serikothi cavaliers were already mounted. Three imperial officials bowed before Prince Koryn, who stood with Captain Damaryn at his side.

"Assassin!" Tian yelled.

Prince Koryn swung up into a saddle and drew his sword. In what could only be described as poetry, the Serikothi men unslung their bows, notched arrows and maneuvered their horses in a precise curve around the officials and their liege. They loosed three volleys in quick succession, even as their horses advanced and circled the assassin.

All thirty arrows found their mark. There would be no questioning the boy.

Jie sidled up to Tian, a repeating crossbow looking huge in her hands. "Next time, maybe use the word *pickpocket* instead of *assassin*."

Not like he knew that Arkothi word until just then. Hua words were hard enough. Because of that, the assassin was dead, and the audacious plot of murdering a *Tai-Ming* lord in broad daylight became that much harder to unravel. There was yet another crime scene to process, on the eve of Prince Kai-Wu's wedding, with a rebellion brewing in the North.

CHAPTER 26
Father Figures

Kaiya sat atop the castle parapet, dangling her stick legs over the edge despite the silent protests of her imperial guards. Long shadows cast by the setting sun yawned out over Sun-Moon Lake, whose gentle waves lapped up against the base of the stone walls. The lake stretched to the horizon, its placid surface broken only by a few small islands.

If only her thoughts could be so calm.

A day remained until Kai-Wu's wedding, two until her judgment for wandering the palace with Hardeep. What if he was really one of Madura's Golden Scorpions, and he'd used her to steal the Dragon Scale Lute for his evil country? Niggling doubts remained.

No, it couldn't be. She'd sent Secretary Hong to the Foreign Ministry, and he'd confirmed Ankira indeed had a nineteen-year-old Prince Hardeep. Kai-Long had reassured her that he'd met Hardeep at the Ankiran palace. He'd taken her to the Ankiran refugees, who welcomed him as their ruler. And, of course, he was fighting to liberate Ankira *from* Madura.

She turned Tian's pebble over in her fingers, its smooth coolness comforting. She knew every imperfection by touch; cherished it as a talisman of a more carefree time. Eight years had passed since she last saw her childhood playmate, the one with whom she could always share her deepest secrets.

If only she could share the secret of Hardeep! And her dreams of reviving lost magic. Tian would understand. But no. Although he might be the son of a first rank *Tai-Ming* lord, Father had banished him long ago for a stupid prank. Who knew where he was now?

"*Dian-xia*," her handmaiden Han Meiling said from behind her. "Here is the lute you requested."

Kaiya closed her hand around the pebble and turned.

Her handmaiden knelt, with Hardeep's lute nestled in her arms.

Stowing the pebble into her sash, Kaiya received the instrument with both hands. She flipped it around and straightened her back. Her toes gripped the stone ground. Taking a deep breath, she strummed. The vibration of the strings flitted through her arms. Each note came together in technical perfection, yet her uncertainties and doubts wavered through the melody.

Xiulan had thought of her when writing calligraphy, which apparently guided the magic in the character to her; Kaiya looked to Han Meiling.

The handmaiden averted her gaze, then soon shuffled and tugged at her gown. Her fidgeting increased as uncertainty clouded her expression.

Could it be the effect of the song? An excited shiver coursed through her.

The lute disappeared into thin air, taking its song with it. Kaiya's heart leaped into her throat. Meiling gasped. Her guards all drew their *dao*.

"An interesting choice of instrument." Lord Xu stood there, her lute in his hand. The slight rise of an eyebrow and the tone of his voice asked for an explanation.

"I was told to practice."

He lifted a hand in a swift motion. All sound around them silenced, leaving only his voice. "I told you to practice your listening."

Mouths agape, her guards charged forward, only to hit an unseen barrier. Their palms circled against it, looking much like the Estomari mime who once entertained the court.

They might not have even been there for all the mind Lord Xu paid them. "You were responsible for the song at the Temple of Heaven. Even there, this lute could not make that music."

He knew! Kaiya shook her head. "I...no, it wasn't this instrument, but rather one made from a dragon scale."

Xu's eyes narrowed. "How did you acquire it?"

"It was in Lord Tong Baxian's possession. My understanding is that he received it during a trade mission to Vyara City."

The elf lord's face betrayed nothing. "Where is it now?"

As if she knew. Maybe Hardeep had stolen it, but there was only risk in telling Xu about the foreign prince at all. She shook her head. "I don't know. When I awoke, it was gone."

"I see." His gaze bored into her. "I am glad you revealed this to me. In any case, listen first. In order to project your sound farther, you need to hear and borrow the energy around you. To have the greatest effect, you must listen for the most opportune moment."

She shook her head. "I can't learn that by myself, I—"

He placed his index finger over her heart. "Most importantly, you must trust what you hear, to know if using the skill warrants the dangers of using it."

She stared at his finger for a few seconds, and then looked up. "Dangers?"

"Magic ripples out from its source, its strength greatest at the time and place of invocation. However, its echo spreads throughout the world and diminishes through the ages. Even the song Yanyan sang to Avarax a thousand years ago persists, hidden among all the other sounds of the world. In any case, magic serves as a beacon to those who know what it is. Not all of those people—and I use that term loosely—are as benign as I."

A shiver went down her spine. "Avarax."

He nodded. "Yes. He now knows there is again someone with the potential to affect him with her song."

"Will he seek me out?"

The elf shrugged. "Who understands the heart of a dragon? Perhaps he will entice you to seek him out, instead. I could not tell you whether he would kill you or twist your skill to his own benefit."

Kaiya shuddered. Perhaps the revival of lost skills was no longer worth the cost. "I will forget about music."

"You might forget about it, but he won't. If he has not already felt last night's song, he will soon." He tossed the lute back.

Maybe letting it smash against the pavestones would be better. Kaiya caught it nonetheless. "What can I do?" To think she had considered being devoured by a dragon favorable to marriage.

"Listen." He swept his hand down; the sounds of spring resumed and her guards tumbled forward. Without even looking, Lord Xu caught Chen Xin with one hand and supported Zhao Yue with the other. Letting go, he then pointed far out into the lake.

The two guards dropped to their knees and started to raise their swords above their heads.

Waving them off before they offered their lives in penance yet again, Kaiya followed the elf's gesture. In the distance, lumber herders guided felled trunks of eldarwood trees through Sun-Moon Lake's placid waters. Laboring during the early spring melt, they had already begun their annual transport from the forests of the empire's inner valley to the shipyards on the coast. Since commoners were prohibited from coming too close to the palace, the workers kept their distance. They seemed like children's balls bobbing on the waters.

"Can you play loudly enough for them to hear?"

Forgetting all sense of propriety, Kaiya gaped at the preposterous challenge. The castle parapet wasn't the Hall of Pure Melody, let alone the Temple of Heaven. "That's...that's impossible."

The elf shrugged. "Not for Yanyan."

Kaiya shook her head. As though her paltry skill could compare to the legendary slave girl. Nonetheless, she plucked a string as hard as she could, emitting a loud, disjointed note.

Lord Xu burst out laughing.

Chagrin and anger washed over her. No telling what shade of red her face was.

After stifling a chuckle, Lord Xu deftly swiped the lute from her hands and strummed.

The series of notes sang in jubilation, tangible in its clarity. It was as if all the heroes of Hua's past had marched into the present, urging her forward with their battle cries. Kaiya's uncertainties and embarrassment melted away. Her spirits rose, and even Chen Xin and Zhao Yue squared their shoulders and smiled. Out in the lake, the herders looked in their direction.

The elf turned back, face inscrutable. He returned the lute to her. "It is not the strength of the pluck that matters, but the intensity of your emotion. Only the power of your intent can compel the sound beyond its physical limitations. Hear the waves of Sun-Moon Lake and allow them to lend you their strength. Now try again."

Kaiya's focus shifted from Lord Xu to the lute. Her musical talents were renowned throughout Hua. Yet neither her own performances, nor any other she'd heard from famous musicians, could compare to the elf lord's improvisation.

She took a deep breath, aligned her posture, and listened. Waves sloshing against the walls below seemed to set a rhythm for the wind

rustling through the ripening buds on tree branches. Birds joined in, their melody harmonizing with the song of spring.

Without conscious thought, her fingers danced over the lute strings, melding with the symphony of natural sounds. Perhaps her hands created the music, or maybe the music moved her hands. Clear and resonant, the melody filled the garden and blossomed out across the lake and palace grounds. The lumber herders looked back at her.

A hollow pop startled her, bringing her song to an abrupt halt. The elf was gone. Only her guards and handmaidens remained, all shaking their heads and blinking as if waking from a trance.

"Keep listening," Xu's voice whispered on the wind.

Still staring at the lute in her hands, Kaiya turned as footsteps approached along the parapet. She looked up.

Flanked by two men from his native Nanling province, Peng Kai-Long dropped to a knee, fist to the ground. "*Dian-xia.*"

"Kaiya," she corrected.

He nodded. "Yes, Kaiya." His voice...did it wobble? It sounded abnormally somber, maybe something she wouldn't have picked up just a day before.

"What's wrong?" She motioned the handmaidens and guards to step back.

His lips tightened into a tight line. "How did you know something was amiss? I thought I hid it well."

She shrugged. "Something in your voice." Or was it his short breaths? They sounded loud in her ears, even if he showed no sign of labored breathing.

His shoulders slumped, so unlike his usual dashing demeanor, his pulse pattering like a tentative rabbit. "I have come to the palace to swear my loyalty to the *Tianzi.*"

For harboring Prince Hardeep? Kaiya's palms felt cold and clammy. "I am sure my father trusts you implicitly." Kai-Long was his favorite nephew, after all.

He shook his head. "No, formal vows. I have been elevated to *Tai-Ming* lord of Nanling Province."

"I don't understand." Kaiya's brow furrowed. Kai-Long's father was the ruler of Nanling. Something must have happened to him. But Kai-Long's brother would have inherited. And Kai-Long was supposed to lead an army to take Wailian Castle.

"My father and brother were on their way here to attend your brother's wedding." Kai-Long's voice cracked, his shoulders slumped. "They had just docked at Jiangkou when they were...were murdered."

Kaiya sucked in a sharp breath. How was that even possible? A *Tai-Ming* lord, undoubtedly travelling with a full entourage of unquestioningly loyal armed guards, would make for an intimidating sight. Poor Kai-Long, he must be in shock. He'd never been groomed to lead a province, never wanted to be anything more than a trade official, and now... She took his hand in hers. "I...I am so sorry."

A tear formed in his eye, which he wiped away. "It's so sudden."

"What happened?"

"We don't know yet. The *Tianzi's* agents are sorting through conflicting eyewitness accounts and uncovering evidence. They think rebels in the North are behind it. But I know." His fist tightened. "The Madurans knew of my friendship with Prince Hardeep. I am sure they have a spy in our villa in the capital, and knew he was staying with me. They are behind this, even if they don't dare to get their own hands dirty."

More evidence that Hardeep wasn't a Golden Scorpion. Of course he wasn't; and now, Kai-Long's family had suffered. She placed a hand on his shoulder. "I am so sorry."

His eyes met mine. "Be careful. They slaughtered a dozen Ankiran refugees in a ghetto last night. They must surely know about your meeting with the prince."

Blood drained from her head. Her legs wobbled. Kaiya reached out to keep from falling, and he caught her. All those poor people, killed.

Maybe because of her. To think that just two days ago, her main concern was having to meet potential suitors. Now, it looked like she'd made enemies in Madura. And maybe even a dragon.

Kai-Long had turned to leave when Secretary Hong appeared at the entrance to the garden. He bowed low. "*Dian-xia*, the *Tianzi* has requested your presence in the Hall of Supreme Harmony."

She was technically confined to the inner castle, but the *Tianzi* did not make requests. Of course, the unprecedented assassination of a *Tai-Ming* lord and the massacre of foreigners in the capital changed the circumstances.

Bowing her head, she passed the lute to Han Meiling. With a nod to her imperial guards, she stumbled over to Secretary Hong. He guided them through the castle bailey, past the courtyard where she'd embarrassed General Lu.

She walked in a haze as they continued across the moat and into the central palace grounds. The alleys between the buildings and walls had seemed like a maze to her rice-wine-induced haze the night before, and it was no easier to keep track of the directions today. The faces of all the innocent Ankirans haunted her. They'd been living, breathing, laughing. Treated her like an honored guest. Now, they were gone.

At last, they arrived in the central plaza, the scene of too many misadventures yesterday morning. Up the one hundred and sixty-eight steps to the Hall of Supreme Harmony. She fought to breathe evenly.

Inside, the rows of kneeling officials and hereditary lords nearly filled the floor. It was so rare to see the hall so full. As she walked down the central aisle, toward where her father sat on the Jade Throne, many murmured among themselves. Behind her, Kai-Long's booted footsteps clopped across the marble floors.

At the front, she turned and walked to a space on the other side of her brothers. Kai-Guo's fists clenched tight, while Kai-Wu barely kept his posture straight. Kai-Long's footsteps stopped in place just behind her.

Father looked somber, even more so than usual. How could he not be, with the murders of his brother-in-law and nephew on Hua soil? And then in two days, he'd have to dispense punishment on her. He seemed to have aged since yesterday. If his health were failing, she might be to blame.

From his place a step behind the *Tianzi*, Chief Minister Tan cleared his throat. "*Tai-Ming* Lord Peng Kai-Long, step forward."

She tilted her head a fraction to find Kai-Long in the corner of her eye. He cast a somber smile toward her and rose. Striding to the place just before the dais, he sank to his knees and pressed his forehead to the ground.

"Rise." Father's voice shook with fatigue. When Kai-Long straightened, he continued. "Nephew, as pleased as I am to see you elevated to *Tai-Ming*, I convey my regrets for the loss of your father and brother."

"Thank you, *Huang-Shang*." Kai-Long bowed his head again.

"Swear your loyalty to the *Tianzi*," the Chief Minister said. He placed the jade seal of state in Father's left hand.

General Zheng strode forward. With both hands, he placed the Broken Sword into Father's right.

Kai-Long's swordbearer shuffled down the central aisle and presented a ceremonial *dao* to his lord. Imperial guards stepped in closer to Father, their hands resting on their own swords. There was little need: by custom, only imperial guards were allowed to carry weapons in the hall, and the ceremonial *dao* was only a hilt and scabbard.

Bowing his head, Kai-Long held the blade up in two hands. "Under Heaven, I swear eternal loyalty to the Jade Throne. I serve at your pleasure. My sword is your sword."

He set the sword down on the floor before him, while another page came forth, bearing a seal on a silken cushion. Usually, the jade provincial seal would be used, though the immediacy had required a replica.

Again, Kai-Long bowed his head and lifted the seal in two hands. "Your command is my command."

Father beckoned him out of the bow. "You have trained as a diplomat and served magnificently in that capacity for the last few years. However, ruling a province will prove challenging. I will send advisors with you on your return to Nanling."

"Thank you, *Huang-Shang*." Kai-Long pressed his forehead to the floor. He straightened. "*Huang-Shang*, if I may, I am certain that agents of Madura perpetrated this act."

The assembled men broke into a chorus of murmurs. Kaiya's belly clenched. Kai-Long would undoubtedly bring Prince Hardeep into the conversation, which would in turn remind Father of her own transgressions from the previous day.

Father silenced them all with a twitch of his mustaches. "After you informed me of your suspicions, I sent my own agents to investigate." He faced the Chief Minister.

Tan cleared his throat again. "The Maduran trade mission vehemently denies involvement. They convey their regrets."

"Lies." Kai-Long's voice carried an edge of anger.

The Chief Minister gestured to an old man in the first row, on the other side of the central aisle. "Deputy Yan, please report."

Kaiya tried to find Deputy Yan in the corner of her eye. He only very rarely appeared at the palace, the last time being when her childhood friend Tian had been banished. Then, as now, his face moved whenever she tried to study his features. All she could say was that his face was plain. If foreigners had paintings of Hua faces in their encyclopedias, surely his would be the one.

The official bowed his head and stood. "*Huang-Shang*, my agents scoured the scene and followed up with eyewitnesses and the Jiangkou city watch. We recovered two of these." He held up two bloodstained crossbow bolts.

Kaiya looked at Kai-Long's fists, so tight the knuckles blanched. He must have known the Madurans had not used crossbows in nearly thirty years. They had Hua muskets, after all.

Deputy Yan continued, "The first penetrated Lord Peng through the throat. The second punctured his son's lung. Also, several eyewitnesses claim seeing five large Hua men fleeing the scene."

Just like the large men who had attacked her with crossbows. They might be the ones responsible for murdering the Ankirans, as well. Kaiya fiddled with one of her sleeves. All Kai-Long had to do was mention Prince Hardeep to give the Madurans a motive.

He glanced back at her, his eyes begging like the small court dogs. He then looked back to Father. "Thank you for devoting resources to the investigation, *Huang-Shang*."

Kaiya let out her breath. Kai-Long had spared her the embarrassment, at least for now. Still, that expression of his...

Father nodded a fraction. "We will keep you apprised, Little Peng. Now..." He turned to the Chief Minister.

No, poor Kai-Long had lost his father and brother. He could have exposed her secret to give the potential killers a motive. He'd protected her, to his own detriment. Summoning resolve from the firmness of Tian's pebble beneath her sash, Kaiya rose. "*Huang-Shang*." Her voice came out as a mouse's squeak.

The collective sucking in of breaths might have rid the room of half its air. The lords and ministers, already surprised by a girl even being present in this meeting, must have been shocked that she dare speak.

Chief Minister Tan gaped at her, his lips moving but no sound coming out.

Father's face showed no surprise. "Speak, Princess."

Kaiya glanced back at all the hostile scowls. Swallowing her nervousness, she straightened. "*Huang-Shang*, I believe Lord Peng's suspicions—"

"*Believe?*" The anger in Chief Minister Tan's voice almost silenced her.

"—because I was attacked last night, too."

A second collective gasp would certainly rob the room of air, or maybe it was just her head spinning with apprehension. The ensuing jumble of sudden conversations was disorienting.

The *Tianzi* showed not even the least amount of surprise at her revelation. Did he already know? He raised his hand and the room once again fell into silence.

She peeked over her shoulder. Behind her, the lords all gawped. Kai-Long, sitting at her side, nodded with a smile.

"On my way to the Temple of Heaven—"

Murmurs rumbled again. *Tai-Ming* Lord Liang of Yutou's voice sputtered above the rest. "The Temple of Heaven? Did she enter the stupa without a blessing from the priests? If not, to view the fallen star is punishable by death."

Apparently, her visit to the Temple of Heaven had been kept secret, and she'd just revealed it. Her belly tightened.

Kai-Guo jumped to his feet. "It was that eerie music, drawing her like a moth to a flame. It was not her fault."

Kaiya shifted on her knees. This lie, too, would one day be exposed. Probably today. Right now.

Eyes raking over the assembled men, silencing them again, Father fixed his gaze on her. "Continue."

She bowed her head. "Several large Hua men attacked me. Six the first time, two the second."

Father showed no sign of surprise, though he rarely revealed any emotion.

Lord Liang of Yutou scoffed. "Are you saying you were able to defend yourself against six armed men?"

The *Yu-Ming* lords from his province nodded, followed by several others.

Kaiya lowered her finger, which had unconsciously twirled a loose lock of her hair, and took a deep breath. "I was with Prince Hardeep of Ankira, who was trained by the Ayuri Paladins. He fended them off."

More murmurs. No telling what they thought about a young princess, alone with a man, wandering the city streets at a late hour.

She swallowed hard. "I went to Lord Tong Baxian's villa—"

Father raised a hand to halt her. "Lord Tong's?" He looked to his advisors.

Why the interest in Lord Tong? She gave a tentative nod. "I st...I retrieved an artifact there. An Arkothi lute, made from a dragon's scale. When I played it, two of the assailants fled. The song the city heard last night, I played it myself. I am sorry to say that I lost the Lute when I passed out."

"It concerns me," Father said, "that Lord Tong had such an instrument."

Foreign Minister Song, kneeling among the other high officials, cocked his head, a look of confusion on his face. He turned to Father and pressed his forehead to the ground. "*Huang-Shang*, I do recall Lord Tong Baxian receiving the Dragon Scale Lute directly from Madura's Grand Vizier."

Chief Minister Tan nodded. "There were many things which we received as gifts from Madura after a successful trade agreement. We all did." He nodded to Minister Song. "I do seem to recall the musical instrument from Grand Vizier Rumiya did not have strings."

"But it does now?" Father asked.

Kaiya nodded. "Even his chamberlain was surprised that it did."

"If the Lute does what you say, it could be a dangerous weapon. Where is it now?" Father's lips pressed tight in rare show of public emotion.

Kaiya cast her eyes down. "I think Prince Hardeep took it."

Chatter broke out among the assembled men, stayed by Father's hand. He turned to his ministers. "Deputy Yan, investigate the princess' claims. It may not be the Madurans, but I find it suspicious that large men would target the Ankiran refugees, the late Lord Peng, and the princess."

"As you command, *Huang-Shang*." Deputy Yan bowed.

"General Tang." Father gestured toward one of the armored men. "Report on your men's seizure of Lord Tong's villa."

Seizure? What had Lord Tong done to forfeit his land?

Sinking to a knee, General Tang placed a fist to the ground. "Dian-xia, we found it abandoned."

"Mobilize your men. Coordinate with the city watch to scour the streets for Prince Hardeep and the Dragon Scale Lute. I want it found, and him brought before me."

General Tang bowed his head. "As the *Tianzi* commands."

Kaiya's heart rattled in her chest. She might've just sacrificed Prince Hardeep and herself to help Cousin Kai-Long. Still, it was the right thing to do. A princess shouldn't hide behind others' lies.

"Lord Peng," Father said. "You may return to your place among your peers."

Kai-Long bowed his head, rose, and strode back to his place among the *Tai-Ming*. Kaiya started to sit.

"Wait." Father's gaze locked on her. "Since Lord Peng has been elevated to *Tai-Ming*, all the first-rank hereditary lords, and many of the second rank, are now here. With their advice, I will pass judgment on your transgressions yesterday, as it has bearing on how we deal with the rebellion in the North."

CHAPTER 27
Unenviable Choices

A hundred disparate breaths rustled behind Kaiya as she knelt in the front row of the Hall of Supreme Harmony. Apparently, her public humiliation would not wait until after her brother's wedding after all.

Chief Minister Tan cleared his throat again. "Princess Kaiya, step forward."

Rising, Kaiya kept her shoulders straight and chin high as she walked over to the place Cousin Kai-Long had just vacated. She focused on that spot, lest the curious faces of all the lords and ministers reduce her to a quivering mass of nerves. More than a few murmured, mostly showing appreciation for her poise. If only they knew how contrived it was.

She stretched her arms out to straighten her long-hanging sleeves and brushed her gown to her shins. Sinking to her knees, she placed her forehead to the floor.

"Rise." Father's voice quivered. If anything, the tone sounded like the one he'd used at Mother's funeral.

"*Huang-Shang*," she said, acknowledging his command and straightening.

"Yesterday, you entered the Hall of Pure Melody without permission and handled Yanyan's pipa. Last night, you left the palace without permission and entered the holy grounds of the Temple of Heaven."

There was no honor in denying what everyone in the room knew. "I did." She bowed low.

"What do you have to say in your defense?" His voice sounded imperious, as if he were addressing one of the rebellious lords of the North and not his own daughter.

So much for the rare smile he had afforded her the day before. Keeping her head down, she took a deep breath to settle herself. "I wanted to help the beleaguered people of Ankira."

"In the Hall of Pure Melody? In the Temple of Heaven?" Though he was undoubtedly expressionless, his voice hinted at a rise in his eyebrow.

It'd made so much sense yesterday, but sounded so stupid now. She'd let Hardeep's enthusiasm get the better of her. "I thought by learning the magic of Dragon Songs, I could use the Dragon Scale Lute to liberate Ankira." Her own voice squeaked in her ears.

Chuckling broke out among the assembled men. No doubt they thought her naïve to believe she could revive a long-lost art.

Then the hall fell silent.

She dared a glance up. Her father's lip hinted upward just a hair to one side, his tacit message ordering the men to silence. His voice swept from left to right, something she'd never noticed before. "We are a nation governed by the Mandate of Heaven, and everyone, including myself, must follow the laws set forth. Princess Kaiya has courageously confessed to her transgressions. For her punishment, I will hear counsel."

Someone—from the weight and motion, Kai-Long—rose to a knee. "*Huang-Shang*, if I may. The princess' intentions were good and selfless, even if her methods were misplaced. I would recommend lenience."

"Lord Peng," the *Tianzi* said, using Cousin Kai-Long's new title. "As the newest member of the *Tai-Ming*, you show bravery and initiative to speak first. We must remember, however, that horrible crimes have been committed in history with the best intentions. The Teleri Empire justifies the gang rape of every woman in its realm to breed an army of so-called peacekeepers."

Kaiya's heart lurched. Since when did rape become the moral equivalent of trespassing?

"*Huang-Shang*." Another man, Xiulan's father Lord Zhao from his voice, rose to a knee in a shuffle of robes. "The Five Classics state that a subject may learn more from forgiveness than punishment."

Father responded, "The classics also state that a ruler who is too gentle with his people invites rebellion. Just think if the Sultanate of Levastya had censured the priests who abandoned their patron god. Perhaps their king would not be living in exile and his people subjects of a foreign conqueror. With a rebellion now bubbling over in the North, wouldn't it be better for a ruler to make an example of those who disobey him?"

Kaiya's heart went from lurching to racing. Father really was going to make an example of her. If she was lucky, the penalty would be banishment. Then, she could follow Hardeep to Ankira. Maybe free the people from the yoke of Maduran oppression, if he still had the Dragon Scale Lute. However, if any of them mentioned the Temple of Heaven again, a death sentence could be warranted.

Just behind her, Eldest Brother Kai-Guo shuffled. He probably wanted to speak on her behalf, but he never went against Father. Second Brother Kai-Wu would certainly say something in her defense, but the light sound of his breath suggested he was dozing. Not surprising, given his lack of interest in these functions of state.

"*Huang-Shang*." The voice of Tian's father, Lord Zheng of Dongmen Province, echoed in the hall. "The princess has never shown any sign of defiance before today."

"As the classics say," the *Tianzi* said, "without correction from a parent for a first offense, no matter how mundane, a good son might one day become a rebel, a good daughter a whore. Such impertinence—"

Kaiya bristled inside, a roaring in her ears drowning out the rest of Father's words. All she had done was try to help a persecuted people. Apparently, that was the first step to selling her body and then instigating a rebellion. It wasn't like she had offered herself to the prince.

Impertinence, was it? Let them all see impertinence.

Gasps erupted as she rose from her bow. "If I may, *Huang-Shang*. The Five Classics also say that when no one acts to correct a moral wrong, a minister should remonstrate those who would turn a blind eye."

The *Tianzi* stared at her, expressionless. "I am glad you have studied the Five Classics. Are you now a minister in addition to being a priest and a grand musician?"

The words might as well have been a slap. Even though every fiber of her upbringing urged her to bow in contrition, Kaiya squared her shoulders. "*Huang-Shang*, I may not be a minister, but none have spoken on behalf of a people downtrodden by our open trade policies."

The hall fell utterly silent. She looked around. The Chief Minister had dismissed her plea to terminate the trade agreement just a few days ago. Now, he gawked.

Her mind raced through memories of the past few days. Each image felt like a fresh burn, fueling both her anger and courage. Her voice grew bolder and firmer. "I may not be a priest, but even the eyes of a girl can see the immorality of our ways."

The faces of the Ankiran refugees refused to fade from her vision. The smiles that welcomed her into their humble home, fed her when they had little to spare, and performed songs for her when they had little to celebrate. The faces of the innocent. "In the hands of an aggressive foreign army, our guns have widowed women. Our firepowder has orphaned children." Her voice broke toward the end.

The deafening silence of the hall carried the broken notes all the way to the far ends of the room. In the corner of her eye, the lords and officials gawked. A grim satisfaction grew inside her.

For the first time in her entire life, she held every person's attention. Heart swelling, she delivered her final words as gently as a prayer. "We profit from others' suffering. And last night, their people were murdered on our soil. Surely Heaven would not condone it."

The lords and ministers erupted in whispers. Father's withering stare fell on her.

Courage waning, Kaiya added the honorific address to the end of her tirade: "*Huang-Shang.*"

She pressed her forehead back down to the floor. What had possessed her to speak, to embarrass Father in front of all the lords and ministers like that? Maybe before her rant, she would have been confined to quarters until marriage. Now, she'd left the *Tianzi* no choice but to administer a more serious punishment. The Founder of the dynasty had stripped titles, cut out tongues, even executed families to five generations for such outbursts. Her palms clammed up.

"Chief Minister Tan," the *Tianzi* said.

"*Huang-Shang.*" The Chief Minister's voice sank, suggesting his bow.

Her insides twisted, comforted only by the cool marble against her forehead.

"Let it be noted that we shall not extend the trade agreement with Madura."

Another collective gasp might have finally sucked the last bit of air out of the room. It had, if her spinning head were any indication. She ventured a glance up.

"As the *Tianzi* commands, so shall it be noted." Chief Minister Tan beckoned toward a scribe.

"For her many crimes, I sentence Princess Kaiya to a quick, merciful death." Father held up a hand, silencing the hall before any protests started.

Of course this would be the punishment. Insides turning to jelly, she pressed her head to the floor again. At least her blood would pay for a respite for Ankira.

"Let it be further noted that Princess Kaiya's death sentence shall be suspended as long as she remains obedient, and shall be entirely revoked if she proves worthy to the realm."

Barely in control of her body, Kaiya looked up. Father was smiling. A real smile. Even more than when Mother had still been alive. "Very good, Kaiya," he said. "I knew you could do it. You acted out of compassion, and you defended your decision even at risk to yourself."

Her cheeks flushed. Praise from Father was rare, and in public was unheard of. There must have been a reason.

He continued, "Even if you one day learn to sing Dragon Songs, do not use it as a crutch when a moral argument, spoken from conviction in your heart, will suffice."

Especially if magic was a beacon for a dragon, as the elf Xu suggested. She bowed again. "Yes, *Huang-Shang.*"

"Remember this lesson well, for even though a woman will never sit on the Jade Throne, she may one day rule as regent."

Regent? Such a strange thing for Father to suggest. There had been no regent since the Founder's Consort, who ruled for eighty years in that capacity before dying at the unprecedented age of one hundred and twenty-four.

Kaiya would never assume such a title, but still, Father had offered her rare praise, in front of all the ministers and hereditary lords. Emboldened, she straightened. "What about the remaining year on the trade agreement?"

The *Tianzi's* smile faded. "As Chief Minister Tan said, the treaty was negotiated under the imperial plaque. To renege outside of the proscribed stipulations would be tantamount to me forsaking the Mandate of Heaven. Perhaps it would invite another Hellstorm. Do not fear. Less than a year remains."

Kaiya sighed. Ankira did not have a year. "And if Lord Peng's suspicions are confirmed, that the Madurans assassinated his father?"

"Of course, such an action would void the agreement." Father's gaze lifted from her and settled over the room. "However, my agents believe it is Lord Tong of Wailian County."

Kaiya sucked in a sharp breath. Lord Tong was the leader of the rebels. That's why the army had seized the villa. Not only that, he had expected it, emptying his vault and holing up in the impregnable Wailian Castle.

Father scrutinized her before addressing the assembly. "The rumors many of you have heard are true. Chief Minister."

Chief Minister Tan stepped forward, prompting Kaiya to kneel. He unfurled a scroll, cleared his throat, and read:

"To Wang Zhishen, Emperor of Hua. The four counties of Wailian, Tieshan, Jinjing, and Hongzhou have long been exploited by the rest of the realm. Our pleas for fairness have fallen on your deaf ears. Therefore, we hereby declare ourselves the independent Kingdom of Fengshan. Withdraw imperial troops from our sovereign land. Not only will any incursion on your part be faced with fierce resistance, we will cut off your firepowder supplies and share the secret formula with your enemies. From Tong Baxian, King of Fengshan."

A cacophony of angry protests echoed throughout the hall. Kaiya covered her ears to dull the roar.

After a moment, Father silenced them with a single glance. "I will hear your counsel."

Uncle Han, *Tai-Ming* lord of Fenggu Province, slammed his hand down on the marble floor. "*Huang-Shang*, we must crush them immediately."

Several of the *Yu-Ming* nodded in agreement, but *Tai-Ming* Lord Liang of Yutou Province shook his head. "Wailian Castle is impregnable, and those counties monopolize firepowder ingredients. If they sell to potential enemies…"

Kaiya twirled a lock of her hair. This must have been how Ankira felt so many years before.

Tai-Ming Lord Zheng of Dongmen Province cleared his throat. "*Huang-Shang*, we can blockade the Iron River and cut off their access to ports."

Lord Liang shook his head again. "*Huang-Shang*, if Wailian establishes direct trade with Rotuvi, they could access the deep-water port in Iskuvius and use the ships of Serikoth, with whom we do not have a sphere of trade agreement. It would tempt Tarkoth to end its own treaty with us. I advise we normalize relations with this Fengshan and levy tariffs so they can use Jiangkou."

"Appeasement!" Lord Han tugged his beard. "*Huang-Shang*, if you let those four counties go, you will only encourage others."

Xiulan's father, Lord Zhao, turned back to the lesser nobles. "Almost all the hereditary lords are here. I trust none of them would rise in arms against the Mandate of Heaven?"

All the assembled lords bowed like ripples gliding across Sun-Moon Lake.

"Good," Lord Han said. "Our combined provincial and imperial soldiers outnumber those four paltry countries thirty to one. Let us crush this rebellion."

The chamber shook with the confident roars of approval. Kaiya looked up at Father. His face betrayed nothing, which meant there was a possibility of civil war. Thousands would perish. Others would end up in poverty like the Ankiran refugees. Certainly there was another way. She peeked back at Lord Liang, the lone dissenter up to now, and Kai-Long. Their expressions might have been mirror images, staring off into the distance, jaws relaxed. Pensiveness, perhaps, and neither appeared ready to intervene.

And who would? Their voices would fall unheard, drowned out by the roar of bloodlust. Those robust chants, a symphony of voices speaking as…one? She closed her eyes and listened. Yes, there it was, a rhythm in the disparate voices. The pulse of fervent men.

Only the power of your intent can compel the sound beyond its physical limitations, Lord Xu had said not an hour before. *Hear the waves of Sun-Moon Lake and allow them to lend you their strength.* Holding the rhythm of the men in her heart, she stood. "*Huang-Shang.*"

The shouts swallowed up her voice. Even standing, she went ignored. No, she could not fail, not now. Toes gripped to the floor, she straightened her spine. Beneath the shaking marble dwelt a resolve, that of the earth, preventing the excitement from descending into cacophonic disorder. Seizing that resolve in her soul, she spoke again. "*Huang-Shang.*"

The din of men subsided. Father looked at her, eyes wide for the first time she could remember. Yet now that she had everyone's attention, what had she planned to say? She surveyed all those men, the ones who surely resented a woman—no, a girl not yet blossomed— in their midst. A few started to mutter.

Now was the time to speak, lest her single voice get lost. *Speak with the conviction of your heart*, Father had said. Tian's pebble squeezed tightly in her fist, she bowed her head. "*Huang-Shang*, allow me to marry Lord Tong on the condition that he submit to the Mandate of Heaven."

Silence.

Enough to consider the weight of her words. She knew nothing of Lord Tong. He was a stodgy Northerner, like General Lu. What if he were even worse? If he were the domineering type, all she'd learned about sound and music these past two days would go to waste. And no matter what, she would never see Hardeep again.

Lord Liang broke the silence. "*Huang-Shang*, the princess' suggestion is sound. It will allow us to bring the four counties back into the realm without conflict."

"Appeasement!" Lord Han said.

Locking eyes on her, Kai-Long—Lord Peng—nodded. "*Huang-Shang*, I agree with Lord Han. If another lord decides to rebel, there are no more imperial daughters left to marry out."

Kaiya stared at him. As a diplomat, he'd never advocated war.

"*Huang-Shang*," said *Tai-Ming* Lord Wu of Zhenjing Province, father of Kai-Wu's bride-to-be. "This is a special case. While no other place in Hua can repel your armies, we could never take Wailian Castle by force."

Father's lips curved downward for a split second. "Chief Minister Tan, send a messenger bearing an imperial plaque to Lord Tong. If he agrees to submit to the Mandate of Heaven, the four counties in rebellion will be incorporated into a new Fengshan Province with him promoted to *Tai-Ming* lord." He turned and held her gaze, his eyes drooping in defeat. "He will also wed my daughter, placing their future sons sixth in line to the Jade Throne."

Kaiya stopped herself from twirling a lock of her hair. With an imperial plaque, representing the honor of the *Tianzi* himself, there was no escaping this marriage. The one she'd volunteered for.

CHAPTER 28
Bodies of Evidence

Tian paced in the shadow of the Tarkothi ship *Indomitable*, reconsidering all the evidence they had uncovered over the course of a day. As a mere scribe in the local authorities' eyes, he'd remained at the periphery of an investigation that both the city watch and the imperial commander quickly deemed the act of a lone assassin.

A boy. His face didn't look much older than twelve, but he was easily taller and broader than a grown man. Ignoring the snickers and snide comments of passersby, Tian repeated his side of the martial exchange in the air while picturing the boy's responses in his head. Without a doubt, they were *Moquan* fighting skills.

Which didn't explain the murder weapons. Tian held the image of the two crossbow bolts in his mind. The heads were too large to shoot from a Hua repeater, and Jie had heard two crossbows loosed from different positions. Unfortunately, the echo off the water had prevented her from pinpointing the second assassin's hiding spot. The crossbows used in the attack had yet to be uncovered, and could have belonged to any of the Serikothi or Tarkothi marines. Little Huang Zhen had taken the Eldaeri crossbow Jie'd stolen back to the safehouse. If only they still had one of the bolts extracted from *Tai-Ming* Lord Peng's body to test if it fit.

Hua boy. Eldaeri weapon. Two precise shots. Had either Serikoth or Tarkoth hired the assassin and provided the weapon? And for what purpose? Perhaps to frame the other, so Hua would demand changes to the navigation treaties. In this, the Serikothi seemed the more suspicious. Claiming danger, Prince Koryn had refused to cooperate with the investigation and instead returned to his ship and anchored at the mouth of the harbor, guns pointed toward shore. But how could either of those two parties, both arrived the day before, have known when Lord Peng's ship would dock?

Tian looked toward the *Saint Gong*, still cordoned off by the city watch. The palanquins remained where they'd fallen, even though the bodies of Lord Peng and his son had already been honorably taken to the capital. Lord Peng had always been kind, before and after Tian's banishment. The other lords admired him. Maybe his murder had been a message to the *Tianzi*, and Peng had only been a target of opportunity.

Now, a few men gathered at the head of the dock where the *Saint Gong* was moored. From the jerky gestures, it appeared to be a merchant arguing with the guards. No closer to making connections than before, Tian went to intervene. At least he could fulfill some of his harbormaster office duties, and get a second, better look at the crime scene.

Up close, the merchant might have been one of the plainest-looking Hua men ever. Middle-aged, brown silk robes, not too short, not too tall... He wouldn't stand out in a group of plain men. He pounded his walking staff onto the road. "Please, it is just one box."

"For the tenth time, no." A lieutenant of the city watch waved a dismissive hand. "No one except city watch or a government official can board this ship until the lead investigator approves. Now move along."

Tian bowed. "Perhaps I can help?"

The merchant studied Tian's robes. "Ah, a harbormaster official. Yes, thank you. My company shipped some wares on the *Saint Gong*. One item is needed for Prince Kai-Wu's wedding tomorrow."

"What is your company's name? And your position?"

"Golden Fu Trading. I am Fu Jinxian, the owner." He bowed.

Right, the *Saint Gong's* manifest had indicated Golden Fu Trading's three crates and a box. "The Levanthi spice or Ayuri gooseweed?"

The merchant gawked. "All of it. Heavens, you have a good memory. Maybe I could entice you into leaving the harbormaster's office and entering the private sector."

"No, no." Tian waved both hands. "My family sacrificed a lot to get me this job. Let me see what I can do for you."

"Thank you." Nodding, Fu kept his eyes on Tian.

Tian turned to the guards, yet peered beyond them at the overturned palanquins. "May I?"

"You can go onto the dock, but not the ship." The lieutenant pointed at Tian's sleeve, where the embroidered badge showed his low rank.

Tian frowned. "When will they open this dock?"

The lieutenant shrugged.

Another young man pulled up in a rickshaw. His fine silk robes and jade rings suggested a life of luxury, and his smooth skin and soft-looking hands belonged to a boy who had spent too much time studying, not enough time in the sun. The silk pack slung over his shoulder suggested a traveler, yet flaunting so much wealth with no bodyguards was just asking for trouble. A Prodigal Son, wasting his father's wealth on adventure, in all likelihood. He looked from a piece of paper to the three-masted trading ship. "Is this the *Saint Gong*?"

Merchant Fu sighed. "You won't be boarding anytime soon."

The Prodigal Son alighted, paid the rickshaw driver, and sent him on his way. He straightened out his robes. "I'll be working as the quartermaster's assistant. I'll just wait until—" His eyes locked in on the fallen palanquins. He pointed at the bloodstains. "What happened here?"

Tian studied him. He didn't look like the type to survive a day at sea, and must have travelled all day to not hear the news. "*Tai-Ming* Lord Peng and his son were murdered."

The Prodigal Son covered his mouth with a hand. "Heavens. Have they caught the killers?"

The lieutenant nodded. "Kill*er*. There was just one. Of course we caught him."

Of course *not*. Not both of them at least, and the city watch had arrived well after the Serikothi had slain the one. Tian evaluated the deck of the *Indomitable*. At that distance, the boy must've been an expert with the specific murder weapon. Perhaps he'd been a Hua child raised among the Tarkothi, trained to use an Eldaeri repeater. Yet why would the Tarkothi want Lord Peng dead?

The Prodigal Son motioned to the palanquins. "There had to be at least two assassins, shooting from opposite directions."

Tian's eyes darted left to right. How could this newcomer of course. Why had no one seen it earlier? Lord Peng had fallen on the south side of his palanquin while his son fell on the north. Tian nodded toward the lieutenant. "You said I could go onto the dock?"

Scoffing at the Prodigal Son, the lieutenant motioned Tian by, but stopped Golden Fu and the young man from following.

"Come on, let me through," Prodigal Son said. "I am Foreign Minister Song's son."

The lieutenant snorted. "If you aren't Foreign Minister Song himself, you're going to stay off the dock."

Tian knelt by Young Lord Peng's blood, now dried into the dock's stone. He'd been shot in the chest, the bolt lodged deep. The assassin would have had to fire from the north...the deck of the *Saint Gong*? No, much too close, too sharp of a downward angle, and the bolt had entered...at a rising angle. Tian cursed himself. He'd seen the body from the head of the dock, but hadn't processed that until now. Neither had the lead investigator or anyone else. It had taken an observation from some wealthy brat, who saw the aftermath and drew conclusions. If the Black Lotus had discovered this kid years before, he might have been recruited.

Walking toward the *Saint Gong*, Tian estimated the space between the hull and the dock. Certainly wide enough for someone to fit, but how could they hold on to the side and shoot? Without being seen, no less. He would have had to levitate.

Or...if the slain assassin had used *Moquan* skills, perhaps the second one had similar training. Tian peered over the side of the dock again. If any of the mortar between the stones had been disturbed, it would be a sign of cat claws. Evidence of foot spikes would be down on the side of the dock, some five to six *chi*. Hard to tell from here—

A glint of sunlight flashed in Tian's eye from just beneath the waterline, fourteen and a half *chi* below the top of the dock. He looked back toward the head of the quay, where the guards didn't seem to care but both Fu and Song were watching with rapt attention.

Tian took off his shoes, robes, and pants, leaving him only in his undergarments and some concealed tools. Hands gripped to the side of the dock, he lowered himself down and probed the stones with his toes. There it was: dust from scraped mortar, and above it, deep indentations in the mortar itself. Evidence of cat claws. Taking a deep breath, he let go and plunged into the icy water, below the spot where whatever it was glinted.

He reached out and caught ahold of a fine cord in the water. With rapid kicks, he dove deeper, grasping the line and counting twenty-one *chi* to the seafloor, where it wrapped around a stone. Lungs burning, he returned to the surface and gulped air. There, right beside him just beneath the

water, floated a repeating crossbow, tied to the cord.

Now, at low tide, the metal cocking mechanism caught the setting sun's light. At the time of the attack, the tide had been close to high. The planner had been no legendary Architect, hadn't taken into account the tides or the fact that the cord fibers would expand in the water. In all likelihood, the crossbow that'd fired the bolt that killed Lord Peng also floated between dock twenty-three and the hull of the *Indomitable*. It was now a matter of retrieving both weapons before the city watch investigators ruined the evidence.

It would be much easier if Jie were around to help.

CHAPTER 29
Party Crashers

The horse-drawn carriage's cushions softened the jostling to Jie's poor aching butt as she accompanied Prince Aryn and his aide Peris from Jiangkou to Huajing. Snake Eyes Peris had protested her place of honor in the prince's covered carriage, but Prince Aryn just waived off the complaints. The more Jie talked to him, the more likable he became, and the less likely it seemed the Tarkothi were involved in *Tai-Ming* Lord Peng's murder.

Even before their departure, he'd opened up the ship to investigators, shown inventory logs of crossbows and bolts. Certainly, those could be misrepresented. However, as Tian had said, the Tarkothi had no way of knowing Lord Peng would arrive at that time, nor did they have any clear motive to kill him.

The Serikothi, on the other hand, had been far less accommodating to the imperial officials. Instead of joining this procession from the harbor, they sat safely aboard their ship at the mouth of the harbor. It looked a lot like a blockade. Jie sighed. If only she could be investigating in Jiangkou with Tian instead of stuck with a foreign prince.

By the time they arrived at Sun-Moon Palace, the sun's last rays illuminated the sloping blue roofs and high white walls. Jie stared out at it, admiring the beauty.

Prince Aryn leaned over. "I'd wager you never imagined getting so close to your imperial palace, let alone entering it."

At least not in the last twenty hours. Still, appearances had to be maintained. She nodded with her best approximation of enthusiasm.

Peris yawned. "Be sure she doesn't steal anything."

Prince Aryn fixed him with a severe gaze, and Peris returned to staring at his own feet.

The carriage slowed to a stop near the palace's front gates. Up ahead, an open carriage bore the bodies of *Tai-Ming* Lord Peng and his son, draped in black war banners emblazoned with Nanling Province's red wolf. Imperial officials reverently transferred them to biers, and an honor guard of imperial soldiers came out to escort them into the palace.

Prince Aryn blew out a sigh. "The assassin shot from our ship. I feel as if we bear responsibility for the lord's death. I am still trying to figure out how he got past our guards and boarded."

Jie had a good idea: with *Moquan* skills. The boy had been large and skilled, like the men who slaughtered the Ankirans the night before. Perhaps Peng Kai-Long's suspicions about the Madurans were well-founded. At war with Ankira, perhaps they'd tracked Prince Hardeep and stumbled on the refugees. The Peng family helped Ankira, making Lord Peng a target.

Still, Lord Tong couldn't be ruled out, and perhaps Serikoth's suspicious actions hinted at collusion. Jie found herself sucking on her lower lip.

"Come on, Miss Jyeh," Prince Aryn said.

She turned to find the carriage door already open, and the prince extending his hand to help her. Peris frowned.

Ignoring his glare, Jie accepted the help. With her other hand on the annoying skirts, she jumped down. Their official guide—a secretary from the Ministry of Appointments—took the lead, and six Tarkothi marines fell in behind them. They passed over the arching bridge. Imperial guards lined the sides, their *dao* drawn and held in salute. At the gatehouse, imperial officials bowed. Black Lotus brothers snickered at her from the shadows.

"Prince Aryn of Tarkoth," announced the Minister of Appointments.

Their guide took them to the central plaza, now being prepared for the wedding ceremony. He pointed out the buildings in better Arkothi than Jie could muster. Around them, other parties of foreign dignitaries looked around, mouths agape.

They arrived in the tree-lined Nine Courtyard on the east side of the palace, named for its nine guest pavilions. A veranda wrapped around the tree-filled yard, connecting three buildings on each side. Light illuminated their paper windows.

Jie took note of the imperial guards on either side of each door, as well as the half-banners hanging above. Several countries were represented. The Foreign Ministry apparently had the good sense of placing rivals Serikoth and Tarkoth as far away from each other as possible, though Madura's gold scorpion banner hung just two buildings down from the twenty-one-pointed sun of the Ayuri Confederation. Curiously, one banner depicted the red star of Tivar, symbol of the turquoise-skinned Tivari who had enslaved humankind until their loss in the War of Ancient Gods.

The guide bowed low and held a hand toward the door. It opened into a central room with an Ayuri wool rug and bloodwood furniture. Several sliding doors stood open to bedchambers. "Please make yourself comfortable, Prince Aryn," the guide said. "We shall bring you dinner soon. Afterwards, the *Tianzi* has arranged for Night Blossoms of the Floating World to entertain you."

The Eldaeri's blank expressions betrayed their obliviousness. Jie tiptoed and whispered into Prince Aryn's ear. "Ladies of the night."

A slight grin formed on the prince's face, and he leaned over and whispered to Peris, whose eyes rounded before he frowned.

The guide bowed again. "If you have any other needs, please let me know."

Prince Aryn plopped onto a plush cushion at the head of the central table. Stretching his legs out, he gestured at his entourage to relax. He patted the cushion next to him, inviting Jie to sit. She knelt and dutifully poured some rice wine. The sooner he passed out in a drunken haze, the sooner she could investigate the Madurans to see if they were involved in Lord Peng's murder.

Little did she expect him to pour her wine and insist she drink. It burned her throat and warmed her to the core.

Maids delivered a feast of roasted meats, quick-fried vegetables, and cold noodles, as well as Arkothi-style forks, knives, and spoons instead of chopsticks. Though the prince might be too dignified, his marines wouldn't be above pilfering silver cutlery. Sitting cross-legged around the table, the men attacked the food as only men could, with plenty of noise and mess.

"I bet you never ate so well," Prince Aryn said. Gazing at her through heavy lids, he rested a calloused hand on her thigh. So much for his charm. Perhaps his interest had little to do with her ability to translate. Never mind that by human standards, she didn't look much older than twelve.

She brushed his hand away. "Your Highness, I'm sure you'll find your dessert much more filling."

Pouting, he held out his cup. "I doubt dessert will taste as sweet."

"Then you have never seen a Night Blossom." She filled his cup to the brim.

He drained it with a single gulp and pointed at a mirror on the desk. "Look at yourself. Once you washed your face and put on a pretty dress, you took on a beauty no human could hope to emulate."

Even *in* that dress, Tian had laughed at her. Jie brushed her hair behind her tapered ear. Though the way the prince now gazed at her, perhaps the problem wasn't her immature body as much as Tian's cluelessness. That, despite his uncanny ability to make connections.

She studied Prince Aryn's face. Tian might be handsome, but he couldn't compare to the prince's fine features. And charisma...well, Prince Aryn had more in his pinkie than Tian could accumulate in two lifetimes.

Jie leaned into the prince and placed his hand on the small of her back. She tilted her head and closed her eyes, inviting his lips to take hers. Why not? In her twenty-eight years, she'd never given herself to a man for her own pleasure, always in the line of duty.

His other hand nestled her nape, and he brought his mouth to hers. He tasted of rice wine and need, and she parted her lips, welcoming him in. Her insides fluttered with either nerves or alcohol, and heat flared in her, from desire and maybe a little too much wine. Ignoring the marines' whoops and hoots, and Peris' frown, she swung a leg over and straddled him. His hardness pressed against her.

The doors slid open. In the corner of her eye, Jie saw two gorgeous Night Blossoms in provocative silk robes. Their maid carried several folded blankets in her arms. That maid! Feng Mi, a Black Lotus initiate.

One of the Night Blossoms covered her giggle. "It looks like the prince has little need of our services."

Jie's cheeks burned. Had Prince Aryn understood? Yes or no, his attention never left her. The Night Blossoms might as well have not been there for all the attention he paid her.

Feng Mi flashed subtle *Moquan* hand signals. *Master needs you. Castle. Half hour.*

Half an hour! The walk to the castle would take half that time, which left barely any time to enjoy Prince Aryn, or spy on the Madurans. Sighing, Jie pushed back. "Your Highness, your entertainment has arrived."

Only then did his eyes stray to the Night Blossoms before returning to her. His voice was breathy in her ear. "I want *you*."

The feeling was mutual, but she shook her head. "I mustn't interfere with the emperor's arrangements." A half-truth.

His shoulders slumped, and for the first time, he seemed more a man than a prince. "Understood. Well, get some rest. If it pleases you, you shall sit next to me at the wedding tomorrow."

Peris let out a sigh that could only be relief. The man either had a stodgy adherence to appearances, or adoration for the prince that went beyond that of a devoted retainer.

"Don't you have somewhere to be?" Aryn glared at him before turning to her. "How about tomorrow?"

Jie stood and curtseyed. "You honor me, Your Highness. I'm going to stroll around the courtyard and clear my head." And eavesdrop on the Madurans. She looked back at the prince, whose attention never left her. She turned around to find a bundle of black cloth in her hands.

Feng Mi winked.

Her utility suit. Jie tapped a code on the girl's arm as she passed. *I watch Madurans.*

Outside, the cool spring air filled her lungs and helped unscramble Jie's head. Heavens, to think she'd almost slept with a prince. Though it could've been explained off as duty; yet another half-truth in a life full of half-truths.

Striding down the veranda as quickly as her dress would allow, she headed toward the Madurans' villa. She paused midstride as three altivorcs emerged from their guesthouse. The Maduran's invitation to an imperial wedding made sense, but the Tivari...it wasn't as if Hua had trade routes with their subterranean cities, nor a need for their only product: mercenaries. Shorter, stockier than humans, their booted feet clopped on the wood terrace like horse hooves. Though the centermost altivorc might have been as beautiful as an elf, with coifed black hair and a black surcoat, his two guards were prototypically hideous.

One froze in place, grabbed the leader, and pointed at her. Three sets of Tivari eyes met hers and they broke into an animated series of grunts that vaguely resembled a language. While the leader and the right guard headed into the Maduran pavilion, the third came lumbering in her direction.

Not to share a recipe for post-dinner sweets, from the snarl on his face. Unless the main ingredient was half-elf ears and tongues. Jie ducked into an alley between pavilions, clenched her utility suit between her teeth, and then spider-climbed her way up. The dress got in her way, undoubtedly making her stand out like a prince among *Moquan*. Now where did that thought come from?

Before she reached the top, the altivorc turned the corner.

And rumbled through, without looking up. Predictable, like humans. Once he went around back of the pavilions, Jie continued to the roof. Keeping close to the steeply pitched tiles, she shrugged out of the dress and into her stealth suit.

Now properly dressed for the tasks at hand, Jie worked her way along the rooftops, jumping from pavilion to pavilion until she came to the Madurans'. She peeked into a second-floor window, and finding the room unoccupied, slipped in.

Angry voices argued in the central room. Jie crept across the sleeping chambers and slid the door open a crack. Light shone from below, leaving the mezzanine shrouded in shadow. She eased the door open wide enough to squeeze out and then parked herself near the guardrail.

Down in the central room, the third altivorc had joined the others. The handsome leader crossed his arms, addressing someone out of her line of sight. He spoke in heavily accented Ayuri. "So Prince Dhananad didn't respond to our request to negotiate? His invitation to the imperial wedding would have provided the perfect cover. Instead, I find *you*."

Dhananad...that name... Jie scrunched her forehead, trying to remember why it sounded so familiar.

The unseen Maduran, a male, answered, "Prince Dhananad does not have fond memories of the Cathayi."

The altivorc rumbled off a soliloquy of garbled sounds, with *Dhananad* the only intelligible word. The raw anger in the tone suggested nothing flattering, though it could have been Tivari romantic poetry for all Jie knew.

However, Dhananad's dislike of Hua sparked a memory. Twenty-eight years before, a young Prince Dhananad had been a collateral target of a *Moquan* operation—carried out by the famed Architect, Surgeon, and Beauty—to retrieve a secret artifact. The ill-fated mission had led to the deaths of those three, and Master Yan had used the *Tiger's Eye* technique to block the memories of all clan members, ensuring that only he knew their real names or the nature of the artifact.

Below, the altivorc switched back to Ayuri. "I assume you, in your capacity as Master of the Golden Scorpions, will act on behalf of Madura?"

Jie suppressed a gasp. A Golden Scorpion, a cast-off of the Paladin Order, here in Huajing. A master, no less. She edged forward, but no angle provided a good line of sight on the man.

"I will consider it."

"You have a reputation for sowing chaos and bringing down empires. I assumed you enjoyed it."

The Golden Scorpion laughed. "You know me too well."

"We are brokering a deal between Lord Tong and the Teleri. It depends on Madura's involvement."

Jie's head spun. The faraway Teleri Empire was busy gobbling up Arkothi city-states in Tivaralan's northeast. Their next target was likely to be Serikoth. However, an alliance with Lord Tong would allow them a way through the Wall in the North.

The man yawned. "You should know better than to rely on Madura. The Grand Vizier kept the royal family stupid for a century, leaving them ill-prepared for life after his sudden departure."

"Indeed." The altivorc scoffed. "Left them inept for nearly three decades. I am sure he is gloating as we speak."

"Indeed."

"So, you will take part in the attack?"

"You will know when I have decided."

Jie pictured a map in her head. In order for Madura to even consider invading the Hua's South through the Wall, they'd need to divert considerable resources from the siege of Ankiras and the occupation of Ankira.

Unless the attack referred to something else. A target of opportunity. A soft target. Like the imperial wedding, where Lord Tong and his allies could wipe out any number of hereditary lords. Did they have the numbers and weapons to do it? A Maduran Scorpion could even the odds against hundreds of imperial guards and the *Moquan*.

Jie snuck back into the room and took a deep breath. Master Yan needed to hear this, and the Madurans and altivorcs needed to be monitored.

CHAPTER 30
Ulterior Motives

The silence in the Hall of Supreme Harmony allowed Kaiya to hear the collective breaths and heartbeats of the assembled lords and ministers. None breathed more rapidly than she, and her pulse pattered faster than anyone else's.

After all, none of those men would be marrying a traitorous lord in the coming weeks. Perhaps days. And she'd resigned herself to this fate. Hopefully, Lord Tong was not like other Northerners in their dislike of the arts. He'd made his chamberlain learn the lute, after all.

Father gave the slightest of nods, and all the men pressed their foreheads to the ground.

Chief Minister Tan cleared his throat. "Distinguished lords, you may retire."

Around her, the lords stood, many of them discussing the implications of her impending marriage. Several approached and bowed their heads, offering their congratulations.

As she rose, she looked to Father. Cousin Kai-Long—Lord Peng—stood before him, whispering, his voice too low for even her keen ears to pick out from the surrounding conversations. He turned toward her, and Father's gaze followed. Father nodded.

They were discussing her. Kai-Long opposed her wedding; maybe it had to do with that. She'd know soon enough, with the way Cousin Kai-Long approached her wearing a broad grin. He bowed his head. "Congratulations, *Dian-xia*."

"Thank you, Lord Peng."

He started to laugh, a breach of protocol in the Hall of Supreme Harmony, but contorted his face into a smile. "Come with me. I would like to introduce you to the wife of Ambassador Vikram of the Ayuri Confederation. She is in the guest pavilions. The *Tianzi* has already approved."

Why bother with extending pleasantries, when now she was nothing more than a bride-to-be? She looked to the Jade Throne. Father, now barely sitting straight, nodded.

Cousin Kai-Long gestured toward Secretary Hong, who hovered nearby. "Go find the princess' handmaiden Meiling, and have her meet us in the central plaza with the princess' lute."

Prince Hardeep's lute, not hers. It was a cruel reminder of how much she was sacrificing. Her belly felt hollow. But why would an ambassador's wife care about a foreign instrument Kaiya couldn't even play?

Secretary Hong wetted his lips. "I am supposed to—"

"Hurry." Kai-Long leaned his head toward the doors. "I will take responsibility for the princess until you return."

The hapless secretary bowed his head. "As you command, Young Lord... I mean, *Jue-ye*."

Kai-Long beckoned two imperial guards, ones she recognized but who were never assigned to her. "Come."

They had started out of the hall when Appointments Minister Hu ventured into her path. His eyes narrowed like a snake. Perhaps he still bore resentment for her contradicting him the day before. "The princess has a dinner with the Crown Princess in two hours."

Kaiya suppressed a shudder. This sudden dinner, on the eve of her wedding announcement, could only mean one thing. *That* discussion. It was typically a mother's responsibility to discuss the arrival of *Heaven's Dew* with a daughter who was soon to blossom, but Mother's passing meant that duty had fallen to the elder sister-in-law.

Undoubtedly, a pillow book would be involved. Her younger friend Lin Ziqiu had already shown her the collection of graphic woodblock prints before, and it had made her blush hotter and brighter than Tivar's star during the Year of the Second Sun. Soon, Kaiya would be acting out those pictures, with a lord she'd only recently heard of. Now instead of blushing, her insides squeezed into a painful knot.

Cousin Kai-Long stepped forward, at an angle which interposed himself between her and Minister Hu like an imperial guard would do. "The *Tianzi* has approved Princess Kaiya's meeting. Two hours is more than enough time."

Eyes shifting from Father to her to Kai-Long, Minister Hu smiled with about as much warmth as a burnt-out hearth at midwinter. He spun on his heel and went fawning over to another *Tai-Ming* Lord.

Cousin Kai-Long grinned. "I think I could get used to this new position."

Kaiya would have at least faked a laugh if not for the reality of her situation. She was getting married to a stern man who might not even let her play music. She would never see Hardeep again. Not only that, it had been her own choice. Her lips tightened into a straight line. Thankfully, Cousin Kai-Long spared her embarrassment by turning around and leading her out of the hall.

Secretary Hong and Han Meiling met them on the far end of the central plaza, the handmaiden bowing with the lute in her hands, then joining the retinue two steps behind. Kaiya's belly writhed, like the twists and turns they took through the alleys between buildings. Somewhere up ahead, musical notes danced on the winds, plucked from…a lute?

The sound grew louder, taunting her as a reminder of what she would be losing. They rounded a corner into the Nine Courtyard. Carefully manicured by imperial gardeners, the open space featured a central pond bordered by soon-to-blossom flowers. Plum trees already bloomed, their white and pink petals drifting on a light breeze like snow. It might have been a metaphor for her own impending blossoming and deflowering.

She froze in place. One of the banners above the pavilion door was emblazoned with a golden scorpion, the symbol of Madura. The ones Prince Hardeep suspected of trying to kill them last night. Heart seizing, she clutched Kai-Long's sleeve. "How could the Foreign Ministry house the Madurans here?"

"It was my doing."

"Yours?" Her heartbeat resumed, only to roar in her ears. If the lute still played, she couldn't hear it through her shock.

Kai-Long squeezed her hand. "As the Founder wrote, keep your friends close, your enemies closer. In any case, their crown prince refused to come, so the pavilion is empty. Come along." He gestured toward a banner with a twenty-one-point star.

Thoughts clearing, she listened. The lute's melody came from inside the Ayuri Confederation's guest pavilion. The Ayuri South had many musical instruments, though the lute belonged to the Arkothi north. What a coincidence that Meiling now carried one as well.

No, it couldn't be just a coincidence, but rather a sign from the Heavens. Maybe her dreams weren't dead. Kaiya resumed her walk, stride lengthening.

The sound intensified when the bowing servants slid open the doors. Kaiya stepped over the high threshold and into a central room that vaulted two stories high. Standing along the walls, six Ayuri men in white *kurta* shirts with gold embroidered collars all turned and met her gaze, then pressed their hands together and bowed their heads.

A man lounged on the wool carpet in a copper-colored *kurta*, and a woman in an orange sari knelt beside him. Both rose and pressed their palms together. White wisps streaked through his black hair, which framed a deep brown face so dignified, he could only be Ambassador Vikram. His lighter-skinned wife looked old enough to be Kaiya's mother, yet maintained a lustrous beauty all the same.

However, neither drew her eye more than the blindfolded man sitting cross-legged at the head of the room. Several musical instruments, both from the Ayuri South and Arkothi North, surrounded him. He paused with his hands above a lute and bowed his head.

"Good evening, Lord Peng," Ambassador Vikram said.

Cousin Kai-Long bowed his head. "Good evening, Ambassador. Princess Kaiya, may I introduce you to Ashook Vikram and his wife Shariya."

Pressing her palms together, Kaiya bowed her head in Ayuri fashion. "I am pleased to meet you."

With a smile, Lady Shariya gestured to a cushion. "Please, Your Highness, sit."

"Thank you." After Kaiya's adventure with Prince Hardeep, the Ayuri words came out smoothly, almost as perfect as Kai-Long's. She brushed her skirts to her shins and knelt on the cushion, and the ambassador and his wife followed.

Head bobbling, reminiscent of Hardeep, Ambassador Vikram bowed toward Kai-Long. "Lord Peng, I cannot thank you enough for introducing us to the Blind Musician."

Kaiya studied the lute player, who wore Hua-style robes, yet whose dark skin tone marked him as Ayuri or Levanthi. The wide blindfold covered most of his forehead and nose.

Still standing, Kai-Long grinned. "Did you test him?"

Lady Shariya placed a hand over her chest. "Yes. I felt cruel at first, but then amazed. Your Highness, you must see this. Musician, please play."

With a bow of his head, the Blind Musician plucked out a forlorn melody on the lute: a low thrum, descending so low it might have been to the depths of hell.

Kaiya sighed. It was as if he could feel her sadness.

Removing some of their rings, both the ambassador and his wife flung the jewelry at the poor man. Kaiya covered her mouth. How could they do such a thing to a blind person?

Yet even as he played, he shifted in place, deftly avoiding each ring. The music not only remained steady, his movement seemed to shift with the ebb and flow of the notes.

Kaiya sucked in a breath. With practice, she had finally learned to hear heartbeats. That skill paled in comparison to the Blind Magician, who seemed to *see* with his ears.

Secretary Hong and Han Meiling also gasped. Kaiya found the imperial guards in the corner of her eyes. Even if they did not audibly express their shock, their gawking mouths betrayed rapt attention.

"This is the real reason I brought you here." Kai-Long's breath tickled her ear. "To meet the Blind Musician."

Kaiya's mind somersaulted. First Prince Hardeep, then Lord Xu, Doctor Wu, and Xiulan. In the last two days, they had all taught her abilities applicable to Dragon Songs. If she could learn the Blind Musician's skill...but alas, there was no time. Not with an impending marriage.

"My song resonates with your heart and comes back to me. It tells me your desires." The Blind Musician's low-pitched voice crackled like logs in a fire. "I will teach you what I can tonight. Bring your lute." He pointed to the instrument in Han Meiling's hands.

Kaiya could only stare. Perhaps Hua's Dragon Songs were not dead after all. Yet the Blind Musician's bronze skin tone could not belong to a Hua person. She dipped her head in slow nods.

Kai-Long chuckled. "We do not have much time before your dinner, *Dian-xia*. Let us take our leave of the ambassador and his wife."

Dinner...and the talk, the one that Kaiya's mother would have given had she not died already.

Yet that appointment seemed insignificant in this moment, save for the time constraints it presented.

She bowed her head. "Ambassador Vikram, it was an honor to meet you. I thank you for your hospitality. Please allow me to steal away the Blind Musician and leave you to the entertainment my father has arranged."

Both the ambassador and his wife rose, pressed their hands together, and bowed their heads. The Blind Musician stood as well. Playing his lute in smooth plucks, he navigated around the cushions and rings and came to the door.

Was this the right thing to do? After all the rules she'd broken the day before? Kaiya glanced at the imperial guards, who showed no sign of protest. Han Meiling chewed on her lower lip, but said nothing. Kai-Long only smiled.

Pressing her palms together, Kaiya bowed to the ambassador and his wife. Her pulse raced as she turned and stepped over the ghost-tripping threshold. Behind her, the Blind Musician seemed to have no issue negotiating it, either. "Where to?" she asked.

Kai-Long pointed to the guest pavilion designated for the Madurans.

Kaiya's pattering heart almost stopped even as her feet shuffled toward the entrance. It seemed so...wrong. Even if the Madurans weren't there. The imperial court allowed her dear Prince Hardeep's enemies a place of honor, while his own nation suffered. And there was nothing she could do. Not anymore. Not when her own homeland faced fragmentation. She was just as selfish as the advocates for unlimited firepowder trade.

"You'll be fine," Kai-Long said with a smile. "No Golden Scorpions will ambush you tonight. And you have two imperial guards to protect you."

"What about you?"

Kai-Long looked up to the Iridescent Moon, now waxing to its first gibbous. "I have another matter to attend to, but Secretary Hong will make sure you are on time for dinner with Crown Princess Xiulan." The last line was delivered with enough emphasis that poor old Hong cringed. Kai-Long leaned in and switched to Ayuri. "I

handpicked guards who can't speak Ayuri, and Hong will do anything you say."

Why would that matter? Unless the Blind Musician intended to tell her something not meant for prying ears? Maybe news of Hardeep, since Kai-Long had apparently arranged this. Pulse skipping again, Kaiya stepped over the threshold and into the guesthouse. Meiling hurried ahead to unshutter the light bauble lamps. The Blind Musician and the guards followed.

Striding across the carpet faster than even someone who could see, the Blind Musician sat cross-legged at the head of the vaulted central chamber. Then he removed the blindfold.

Blue eyes danced in front of her. Prince Hardeep.

CHAPTER 31
Hot and Bothered

Secretary Hong's breath wheezed in the background as Kaiya gawked at Prince Hardeep. The guards showed no signs of surprise; Kai-Long had probably chosen them not only for their lack of fluency in Ayuri, but also because they had not seen Prince Hardeep the day before.

Now, his eyes danced with mirth, sending Kaiya's mind spinning. Despite her best efforts to control them, her own lips quirked into a grin. When he spread his arms, inviting an embrace, she ran towards him as quickly as her gown would allow.

Dao rasped out of scabbards as the imperial guards closed in.

"Stand down." Kaiya stopped midstride and held out a halting hand. She locked an imperious gaze on them. Hopefully, as long as she did not fall into his arms, they would hold back.

One of the guards bowed his head. "*Dian-xia*. The *Tianzi* commands that no man touch you until your marriage."

Chest tightening, Kaiya offered Prince Hardeep a conciliatory smile. Even if he might not understand the Hua language, the swords and body language needed no translation. Still, to be absolutely sure, she said, "I am sorry, Prince Hardeep. For everyone's safety, you must not touch me."

Hands raised, Prince Hardeep looked from the imperial guards' blades and back to her. "I will do my best to obey the order, but my style of teaching is very...hands-on. I might not survive our lesson." A flirtatious smile formed on his lips.

Kaiya's belly fluttered like a dragonfly's wings. "Lesson? Do you really know how to see with your ears?"

He shook his head. "If such a feat of sound perception existed, it would have belonged to your people's Dragon Singers."

"Then how did you avoid the rings?"

"Paladin skills. I felt their trajectories."

All excitement drained away as Kaiya's heart sank into her belly. His was a different type of magic, one that a budding Dragon Singer could never learn. Not only that, if a Paladin could accomplish such an act, so could one of Madura's Golden Scorpions. It was time to end all doubts, once and for all. Subtly, so he wouldn't see through her questions. "Why the ruse with the Ayuri Confederation ambassador?"

His lips formed a tight line. "I didn't want them to recognize me. I have no love for them."

Not helping. "Why not?"

He shook his head, shoulders slumping in defeat. "In Ankira's time of need, when faced with Cathayi guns and the sting of the Golden Scorpions, the Confederation refused to send aid."

Neither the anguish when he spoke of Ankira's plight, nor the venom with which he named the Golden Scorpions could've been contrived. The defeat in his posture was real, unless it was the inspired performance of an unparalleled stage actor with thousands of years of experience. And, of course, Kai-Long had vouched for him. How could she have ever doubted?

If not for the watchful eyes of the guards, she would've taken his hand. "Maybe there was a reason they couldn't help?"

"The Confederation's Paladin protectors claimed to be too busy containing the ravages of the great Avarax." The awe in the prince's voice when he mentioned the dragon could only come from deep-rooted fear. "Speaking of which, I was serious about the lute. You should learn, so that when the time comes, you can play the Dragon Scale Lute."

"Do you have it?" Not that she ever wanted to play it again.

"One of our pursuers took it while I fought the others."

She sighed. "There won't be a chance for me to help you, anyway. I am betrothed. I will marry Lord Tong in a few weeks."

"The same Lord Tong?" Hardeep cocked his head. "It doesn't matter. We don't know what fate holds for us, only that it has brought us together."

Fate. The closest word in Hua, *yuan*, suggested that mountains and deserts and oceans could not stand between those fated to be together, while those without *yuan* could pass each other every day and never meet.

"Let us begin." As he approached, one slow step in front of another, his blue eyes seemed to look straight into her soul.

Kaiya's breath hitched. Every muscle froze in place, like a doe facing a hunter's arrow.

He stopped as the imperial guards strode forward with hands on their swords. "Sit." He motioned to the floor beyond.

"On the floor?" Her voice came out as a squeak.

He nodded. "Have you seen a painting of the Goddess Saraswati?"

She'd seen so many paintings of the many Ayuri deities: Surya, Lord of the Sun, riding his flaming chariot drawn by white horses. Beautiful Shakti, Goddess of Fertility, holding auspicious symbols in her many hands. Black-skinned Yama,

dragging sinners down to Hell. And of course, Saraswati, sitting cross-legged with an Ayuri-style lute cradled in her arms.

The pose might be appropriate for an Ayuri goddess, but a Hua woman of noble standing would never sit with her legs so...open. The constricting inner dress might not even allow it. Her blush must've now been illuminating the room better than the light baubles.

He smiled again, this time less flirtatious, more understanding. "Correct posture is important for everything in life."

Just like Doctor Wu had said. Kaiya glanced at the imperial guards, and then, with a deep breath, held the folds of her outer gown together while hitching up her inner dress. With the amount of heat her face put off, she might be able to warm the entire palace on this chilly evening. She met Hardeep's gaze again.

He gave her a perfunctory nod.

Reassured, she settled into a cross-legged seat on the floor. She arranged the outer gown, as much for modesty as to conceal her stick legs and enormous feet. No telling what the guards and handmaiden were thinking at this moment. Better not to even look in their direction. She kept her eyes focused on the prince as Han Meiling presented the lute, the one he'd given her through Kai-Long yesterday.

"Do you like it?" he asked.

"Yes." Mundane conversation. It was good. It would keep her mind off the unladylike pose. Maybe.

"I would have rather given you a lute that has been in my family for decades. Unfortunately, I had to borrow this one from the refugees."

Kaiya ran a hand over the wood. The varnish had faded in some places, and several scuffs scarred its belly. She shook her head. "You gave this one with the best of intentions. I will treasure it for that alone." Even if she might never be allowed to play it in her new husband's home.

He pressed his hands together. "You are too kind. Now—"

Secretary Hong cleared his throat. "If I may, Your Excellency, why did you abandon the princess at the Temple of Heaven?"

Prince Hardeep shook his head. "I had to draw away the assassins who wanted to harm us."

So that's why he had abandoned her. No, not abandoned her, but protected her. Again.

"Now, Princess," he said, "straighten your back, let your shoulders relax. Rest the resonator on the floor."

She looked at the foreign instrument in her hands. He had not been nearly as meticulous at the Temple of Heaven two nights before.

"In the Ayuri South, just as a warrior must become one with his weapon, we believe the performer must become one with her instrument."

Kaiya nodded. Her teachers had said pretty much the same thing.

"Cradle it as if it were your own baby."

She nearly dropped the lute. As if she had ever held a baby before; and to think she might very well be cradling her own in less than a year. Truth be told, the bawling babies brought to court by the great hereditary lords provided plenty of disincentive in that regard. Even when they had grown a little older, the snot-nosed brats lacked manners.

Hardeep cleared his throat, drawing her attention to him. He wore an amused smile. "Your arms are too rigid, and if that is holding a baby...you are choking its neck. Relax."

He drew in behind her. His body heat radiated into her back as he adjusted the instrument's position. She closed her eyes and listened for his heartbeat. Slow, powerful, like a spring-fed river sloshing against a dam. Fireworks burst in multiple explosions all through her core. So much for relaxation. It would be easier holding the low horse stance under Doctor Wu's glare than to concentrate with him so close.

Around her, the imperial guards' tension wound tighter than a dwarven coil. Hands gripped sword hilts. His head craned over her shoulder, his chin just a hair's breadth away from her neck. "Here," he said, breath warm on her ear. His hand covered hers as he loosened her fingers around the lute's neck. The jolt from her hand went up her arm and into her heart. It might have skipped a beat or three.

Blades swept out as the imperial guards closed in as fast as a viper strike.

Prince Hardeep jumped back, hands in the air. "I am sorry."

"He was just helping me hold the lute correctly." Kaiya waved the guards off.

They froze in aggressive stances, a sword's distance away from the prince. A low growl emitted from deep in one of their throats.

Secretary Hong's voice wobbled, whether from nervousness or his halting Ayuri or a combination of both. "Your Excellency, you may instruct, but do not touch."

Prince Hardeep pressed his palms together. "I apologize. I will do my best, but I must say that it is very hard to teach if I cannot help the princess feel the instrument."

Yes, feel the instrument... Kaiya banished thoughts of Hardeep caressing her like his lute.

"You will have to make do." The rigid line of Secretary Hong's lips, along with the lack of apology in his tone, left no doubt as to what he really thought.

The residual heat from Prince Hardeep's closeness clung to her back, tingling and percolating through her with the same slow, resolute pulsation. Maybe distance was for the better. If the prince remained so close, there would be no way she could concentrate on learning how to play.

The next hour dragged on like sweet torture. Hardeep would come tantalizingly close, making her pulse race and palms sweat. It took all her effort to keep her fingers from slipping on the lute's neck. Never before had she felt such a connection with a man, and to have him so close. Oh, for him envelop her in those strong arms, to brush his lips across her neck! A primal heat erupted deep inside her, making her squirm.

Each time he got too close, the imperial guards reacted within a split second, assuming offensive stances. He would ultimately raise his hands and back away with a bow. The constant tease left every one of her nerves on edge. It was nothing short of a miracle she learned anything.

If her nerves were on edge, the guards' must be even more so. Instead of the near-motionlessness and stoic expressions, their fierce scowls could have rivaled the dragon etched into each of their breastplates. Poor old Secretary Hong hunched over, and Meiling shuffled on her feet.

Still, in the short time, she managed to learn a few simple folk songs, as well as parts of a far more complicated piece. When he played it himself, the complex chords, rapid changes in pitch, and extreme key ranges left her head spinning.

Limbs languid, her bony bottom aching from sitting for so long, and her entire body still hot with desire, she looked up at him. "Your Excellency, it is almost time for me to go."

He offered an encouraging smile. "Maybe try it one more time. Do as the book you read says. Let your heart project your emotions into the song."

She held back a sigh. The only emotion she could project right now would be embarrassingly wanton lust. Or maybe irritability and exhaustion. She looked around. From their slouching, Secretary Hong, Meiling, and the imperial guards felt equally irritable and fatigued.

"I would wager since they already feel tired, it would make them more so." He grinned.

Perhaps. Kaiya closed her eyes and listened for their hearts. There…a cacophonous chorus of erratic thumps. She had never noticed before, at least not until Lord Xu had pointed them out on the castle walls earlier in the day. Among them, Hardeep's heart remained steady and powerful.

"Don't tax yourself," he said. "Relax. Listen to nothing except your own music."

Opening her eyes, she nodded. Still, though he might enjoy music, and might have read that single passage from the book, he certainly would know nothing of projecting power through borrowing other sound as Lord Xu had taught.

She closed her eyes and listened again. The collective heartbeats rung in her ears, all waves for her exhaustion to ride on. Loosening her stiff, tired

fingers, she played the first frame of Hardeep's song. The chords came out crisp. The changes in pitch resonated clearly. Aligning her spine and joints, feeling the ground through her behind, she continued. The sound filled the hall.

Behind her, Secretary Hong yawned.

She continued strumming and plucking, her own fatigue percolating through her core. The minister's robes ruffled as he dropped to a knee. The imperial guards wobbled in place. Heavens, it was working!

And there, among her own music and the beating of all the men's hearts, Hardeep's own heart throbbed with strength. Borrow that, as she had the sounds in the garden earlier, and it might be possible to magnify the effect.

"Sing!" Hardeep said. "Let me hear your beautiful voice."

Sing! Yes, the lute begged for an accompaniment, like the interplay between her masters' pipa and erhu. She raised her voice in song, letting the lute's melody guide her. Energy welled inside her, climbing toward the crescendo. Her spirit soared with it.

Hardeep smiled, his blue irises twinkling.

No! Breath hitching on the notes, her voice cracked. It was like trudging up the snowy slopes of Jade Mountain on an empty stomach. Her own heart refused to maintain the power. All energy drained from her arms. Her spine, held erect for so long, finally gave out. Gasping, she slumped over the lute.

Her gasp echoed the others around the room. She turned to see many of them crumpling over as well. The imperial guards knelt on one knee, their fists on the ground not in salute, but rather to prop themselves up.

She'd done it! This time without the use of a musical instrument imbued with an innate power, no longer in a place with perfect acoustics. A cool wave washed over her, and she filled her lungs as if it would help keep her sitting straight.

Hardeep crawled over to her side, panting. His words came out in gasps. "Very good, princess. Perhaps with more practice and the Dragon Scale Lute, you could repel even Avarax." He slumped over, the side of his head plopping on her lap and his hair splaying out in a blossom of silky tendrils. The warmth—no, the blazing heat—burned through the silk of both gowns and into her legs. A fever?

Behind her, the imperial guards stirred, but made no move to intervene.

She pushed the lute over and rested it on the floor. Running a hand through Hardeep's glossy black hair, she brushed it aside to reveal the bronze tone of his neck, smooth, save for a dark oval scar in one spot. So smooth, and...kissable. His eyes were closed, partially concealed by yet more of his voluminous hair.

She swept it over, pausing on his forehead. It was hot, for sure. Too hot. She beckoned Secretary Hong, now just regaining his feet. "Call a palace physician. No, Doctor Wu, if she is in the palace."

Secretary Hong said, "*Dian-xia*, she is searching for the Dragon Scale Lute."

That didn't make sense. Why would a doctor look for a musical instrument? She fixed him with an imperious stare. "It doesn't matter, any doctor then. Prince Hardeep needs help. He has a fever from the fatigue. He needs acupuncture."

Hardeep's eyelids flapped open. "No. No acupuncture."

With a giggle, Kaiya brushed a hand over his cheek. To think an almost-Paladin, who had dared face two imperial guards unarmed, would be scared of thin little needles. "It's okay, Prince Hardeep. They don't hurt. Your fever will break with just a few needles."

Behind her, the guards muttered. They were finding their feet.

"I will be all right." Prince Hardeep pushed himself off her lap and scuttled back. "I just need some rest. You, too. It has been a long day of hard practice. Rest and don't practice again tonight. I will find a way to meet you tomorrow."

Secretary Hong looked at them. The wrinkles around his eyes and jowls stood out in lines of black against his wan complexion. He turned, shuffled back toward the entrance, and beckoned someone in.

A palace official, a Foreign Ministry secretary from the markings on his robes, entered and bowed low. "Lord Peng petitioned the *Tianzi*. He has graciously allowed the Blind Musician to stay in these guest quarters."

Outside the doors, other officials were taking down Madura's banners. Such an honor! Guest quarters were usually reserved for visiting dignitaries from Hua's largest trading partners, and certainly not for a musician with no name. If Hardeep were on the palace grounds, there might be some way to meet again tonight. Even if this pavilion was a good walk from the inner castle and imperial residence.

Gaining his feet, Hardeep pressed his palms together. "I thank you for your hospitality, but my effects are in Lord Peng's villa. I will retire there for the night."

The secretary clucked his tongue. "To refuse The *Tianzi's* hospitality would be in very poor form. We have a fine meal prepared for you, as well as several Night Blossoms from the Floating World."

Kaiya's stomach twisted into a tight knot. Renowned for their beauty and grace, the Night Blossoms would make Hardeep forget all about her. Not to mention they would freely offer what she could not.

Or could she?

CHAPTER 32
Women's Secrets

Approaching the Phoenix Garden with the two imperial guards and Secretary Hong, Kaiya listened to the stream rustling toward the courtyard's central pond. Still, all she could hear were her inner insecurities. The beautiful and elegant Night Blossoms would make her Hardeep forget all about her flat body and plain face. Maybe he was already wrapped in their arms, preparing to personally hand her to Lord Tong.

She blinked away the tears blurring her vision. Another beauty came into focus, rubbing salt into her self-confidence's open wound. Wearing an elegant floral gown, Crown Princess Xiulan sat in an open pagoda overlooking the pond. Several handmaidens, including Meiling, stood at a respectful distance. Two of her imperial guards at the edge of the garden melded with the background. The scent of roasted pork and garlic-steamed vegetables wafted on a breeze.

Gently illuminated by a shuttered light bauble in the pagoda ceiling, Xiulan stood with a smile. "You're late," she called.

Because of Hardeep's lessons. If only there had been more time. While Secretary Hong and the two guards came to a stop at the garden's edge, Kaiya lowered her head as she walked up the path to the pagoda. "Forgive me, Eldest Sister."

"Your handmaiden informed me of your...visit. Come, sit." With a graceful wave of her hand, Xiulan indicated a porcelain garden seat by a stone table built into the center of the pagoda.

How much had Meiling said? How many ears had heard? How many people knew that a just-betrothed princess had allowed a foreign man so close? Almost close enough to touch. The memory of his lips within a hairbreadth from her neck sent her heart fluttering.

Kaiya shook the image out of her head and looked at the meal. Artfully arranged food graced porcelain dishes. Her stomach rumbled in the most unladylike fashion. Playing music much of the day, and then the audience with Father in front of all the lords, had left her hungry and drained. With no semblance of grace, she plopped down.

In contrast, nonchalantly graceful as a weeping willow, Xiulan settled on her own seat. She lifted a teakettle and filled Kaiya's cup. When she set the kettle down, Kaiya picked it up and poured tea into Xiulan's cup. Some of it splashed.

How embarrassing! Kaiya bowed her head in apology.

"It's okay." Xiulan placed a hand on hers. "You have had a long day."

And the last hour had felt like a full day of sweet torture. Kaiya's face flushed at the thought of Hardeep. Thank the Heavens her head was down to hide it.

"You are thinking about him, aren't you?" Xiulan's voice carried concern, but no accusation. How did she know?

Kaiya let out a long sigh. "I have never met any man like him. Beyond his handsomeness, his voice is so sweet. He might be a foreigner, but his eyes hypnotize me." Making her feel beautiful. She looked up.

Xiulan gawked, all her usual poise scattered to the four winds. It was if they were holding two different conversations. Oh, Heavens, Xiulan must not have been referring to Hardeep.

Covering her mouth, Kaiya turned to the handmaidens and guards. If they had heard... Well, Xiulan already had, Meiling already knew, and Kaiya's confession had left no ambiguity.

"Oh, Heavens," Xiulan said with a stuttered whisper. She placed a hand on her chest. "You are enamored with the foreigner."

Enamored? It sounded so shallow. It had to be love. Yes, she admitted it. If Kaiya could lower her head any more, her face would be in the food. And her appetite had just fled with her last vestige of dignity.

Xiulan squeezed her hand. "I was mistaken." Surprisingly, there was no rebuke in her tone.

Kaiya hazarded a glance up.

Xiulan smiled. "Let me tell you a secret. Before I was betrothed to your brother, my father's most trusted *Yu-Ming* wanted me to marry his first son. He was a handsome young man, and our parents had arranged a chance meeting so no one would lose face if things didn't work out." She took a deep breath and let it out. "They did."

Kaiya's pulse quickened. Kai-Guo and Xiulan made such a beautiful couple, even more so considering the imperial nature of their marriage. If any relationship provided even a semblance of hope, it was theirs. To think there had been someone before. Kaiya edged forward on her seat. "What happened?"

Xiulan sighed. "The *Tianzi* asked to strengthen the ties between our families. How could my father refuse?"

"And the *Yu-Ming* heir?" Kaiya tried to keep her voice low through her excitement.

"My father forbade him from contacting me." Xiulan leaned in with a conspiratorial smile. "But we maintained correspondence through one of my handmaidens and his page. It was a passionate exchange."

Was that a suggestion to defy the *Tianzi's* orders and maintain an illicit communication with Prince Hardeep? Kaiya cocked her head. "And now?"

Xiulan laughed. "As soon as Kai-Guo and I were married, the lord's son broke contact. Not for fear of punishment, but because of his integrity. He would have ended things whether my husband was Crown Prince or a beggar."

"Why are you telling me this?" The mixed signals made frustrating knot puzzles look simple in comparison.

"No reason, except to share a secret with my little sister." Xiulan covered her giggle. "The decision is yours. Though realistically, as an imperial princess, you would not be allowed to marry a foreigner, even if you weren't already betrothed."

Kaiya let a sigh escape. Of course that was the case, no matter how much she might want to believe otherwise. She and Hardeep would never be together.

"Kaiya, I used to think about that young lord in the first months of my marriage. However, I soon grew to adore your brother."

After meeting someone as charming as Hardeep, Kaiya didn't think she could ever love another. She peered into her teacup. "What do you know of Lord Tong?"

Breath hitching, Xiulan shifted in her seat. Kaiya looked up. Dear Sister-In-Law's lips pursed. Her expression darkened.

"Tell me." Kaiya's voice cracked. Rebel or not, he might still be a kind man.

"His late wife was a friend of my mother. She was spirited in her youth, but marriage broke her."

"Marriage is a woman's grave." Kaiya's sweaty hands tightened into fists.

Xiulan shook her head. "It doesn't have to be. No, Lord Tong is well-known for his depravity. Several of the houses in the Floating World have banned him for fear of what he might do to their Night Blossoms."

Kaiya's chest tightened. What had she gotten herself into? She summoned the memory of

Hardeep, so close, nearly pressed against her back as he taught her the lute. Run away. There was still time to run away.

"Which brings me to the reason the *Tianzi* asked me to meet privately with you tonight." Xiulan reached back to the seats built into the pagoda's sides and retrieved a silk-wrapped package. "Doctor Wu said Heaven's Dew will arrive soon. I think that might explain your sudden interest in foreign princes."

Yes, better to think of Hardeep. Kaiya eyed the vermillion silk bundle as Xiulan placed it on the table with two hands. No doubt a pillow book. With a shy tilt of her head, Xiulan gestured toward it with an appropriately delicate wave of her hand, inviting Kaiya to pick it up.

Feigning the disinterest she would have had just a few days before, Kaiya bowed her head and lifted it with the formality of a minister accepting an imperial decree. Hidden beneath her silk gown, her heart pounded. She unwound the red cord bindings, then the silk wrapping. The light green cover was innocuous enough, save for the title *Cloud Rain*, emblazoned in gold characters.

"It's fairly new," Xiulan said. "By imperial palace woodblock artist Gao Liang. It was presented to your mother thirty years ago, when she married the *Tianzi*. Open it."

Cheeks hot, Kaiya opened it somewhere in the middle. She sucked in a sharp breath. The imperial archives might boast the largest collection of books in the world, but no doubt, this particular book wasn't kept there.

Glimmering in vibrant colors, a man and woman were locked in an embrace with lifelike radiance. Not only that, their mutual affection spilled off the page. Just looking at it brought labored breaths. Heat surged inside of her. It seemed remotely similar to the emotions Hardeep stirred in her. If it were the two of them, acting out the image in the book...his weight on top of her... Biting her lip, Kaiya tried not to squirm.

Pulling her gaze away from the page, Xiulan wiped her brow. "Palace artist Gao Liang could infuse his art with emotion-evoking magic.

When I say how I grew close to the Crown Prince so quickly, I would credit this book for part of it."

How dangerous was that? Both dangerous and helpful, depending on the circumstance of a marriage. Thoughts of Hardeep's closeness earlier in the day mingled with the book's magical impact on her. Him, behind her, chest nearly pressed to her back. Kaiya shut the book and fanned herself with it. "Thank you for your gift."

Xiulan bowed her head. "Perhaps this will make your marriage to Lord Tong more palatable."

Him again. Faceless up to now, her inevitable destiny loomed in the recesses of her mind like the mythical *Moquan*. Kaiya set the book down as if it were a hot plate. If it couldn't be with Hardeep, perhaps it would be better to take the tonsure and live life out as a nun. Though it was unlikely anyone would let her do it, since her value as a princess was determined by whom she could marry.

Unless she could revive a long-dead art. Something she had already started, with Hardeep's help. On the table, the pillow book's gold lettering beckoned her. Heat and desire cascaded through her. Tonight, she'd give herself to Hardeep, just once before marrying Lord Tong, and no one would have to know. She just had to get to him before the Night Blossoms did.

CHAPTER 33
Spies Like Us

As Jie slipped into the solarium of Sun-Moon Castle's residential wing, Master Yan turned his head a fraction. Somehow, even at his old age, he still sensed her arrival when no other clan member could. With a subtle hand signal, he ordered her to stay in the shadows, out of sight of the nine *Tai-Ming* lords, the Chief Minister, and War Minister Shan.

Oblivious to the existence of the Black Lotus, they all knelt on silken cushions on the stone floor. They faced the two princes and the *Tianzi*, who sat in a cushioned bloodwood chair with his back to the night sky.

"When Lord Tong arrives," the *Tianzi* was saying, "take him into custody. It doesn't matter how many guards he has."

"*Huang-Shang*." Lord Peng rose to a knee. "So offering Princess Kaiya as a bride was just a ruse?"

Crown Prince Kai-Guo nodded. "Yes. She is our bait, to lure him into the capital."

The poor girl. Jie sucked on her lower lip. Perhaps it was far better to be an orphaned half-elf than a princess.

Lord Liang of Yutou rose to a knee. "*Huang-Shang*. Your messenger bore an imperial plaque. To renege on your offer is tantamount to forsaking the Mandate of Heaven. Another Hellstorm..."

"Lord Liang," the *Tianzi* said. "Our messenger bears a piece of jade artwork and the missive was written with a magic that will distract

Lord Tong from questioning its authenticity. I will not allow my daughter to marry a traitor, and I would sooner take his head than elevate him to *Tai-Ming*."

Jie suppressed a snort. Why bother to ever use a real plaque if it risked the wrath of Heaven?

Boots clopped in the hallway and heads craned to the solarium entrance. A messenger ran in and dropped to a knee, first to the ground. Head bowed, he proffered an envelope. "*Huang-Shang*, a message from Lord Tong."

The rebel certainly hadn't wasted any time in responding; the horse relays would've taken two hours to reach Wailian and return.

General Shan strode forward and swept the message away. He marched back to the *Tianzi*, where the Crown Prince received it. He unwrapped the cover and snapped it open. A messy script, reminiscent of Tian's careless hand.

The Crown Prince's eyes darted back and forth, his face darkening before finding the *Tianzi*. "*Huang-Shang*, Lord Tong agrees to the marriage, but insists that the matchmaking meeting occur in Wailian Castle. The wedding will take place before Prince Kai-Wu's so that Lord Tong may attend as brother-in-law."

The room rose in uproar. Jie slipped through the shadows to the side to better gauge the lords' body language.

"Impertinent!" Lord Han of Fenggu slammed a hand on the floor.

"The audacity!" shouted Lord Wu, whose daughter's marriage to the second prince might be affected.

Lord Liu's forehead furrowed, his look one of confusion. A slight smile formed on Lord Liang's face. Lord Zhao of Ximen, father of the Crown Princess, tightened his fists.

"It comes as no surprise," said Lord Peng. "We are dealing with a traitor, after all; an ambitious man with no honor."

Perhaps even more ambitious than they all suspected. Jie closed her eyes and thought of the voice in the Maduran guesthouse. If Lord Tong, in league with the altivorcs, Madurans, and other untold allies, attacked the imperial wedding, his marriage to Princess Kaiya would give him substantial standing in the aftermath.

The *Tianzi* swept his gaze over the men, silencing them. "I will hear your counsel."

Lord Liang rose to a knee. "*Huang-Shang*, unless we want a costly civil war where we could potentially run out of firepowder, we must acquiesce to Lord Tong's dem—requests."

Jie studied his expression. So much of Wailian's firepowder ended up in Lord Liang's province. Perhaps he, too, was in league with Lord Tong, a mole in the *Tianzi's* inner circle.

Lord Peng Kai-Long rose to a knee again. "*Huang-Shang*, I think Lord Liang is correct. However, maybe we can bend this to our advantage. Send Princess Kaiya to Wailian County with an appropriate honor guard of a thousand men. As her cousin, and now *Tai-Ming* myself, I will lead. Once inside Wailian Castle, the honor guard will weaken its defenses from the inside while General Lu leads the imperial armies in the North to assault it from the outside."

The room fell silent as the lords nodded. Jie shook her head. Leave it to military men to suggest cutting off an arm to remove a wart when a surgeon's knife would do. Only warlords could fathom this hare-brained plan actually working.

Master Yan shared her opinion. "*Huang-Shang*, what if Lord Tong does not allow so many in the entourage to approach the castle?"

General Shan's white mustaches quivered. "All we need to do is capture the gatehouse and hold it open long enough for reinforcements."

"General Shan," the *Tianzi* said, "were the plans for Wailian Castle submitted to the War Ministry?"

The general's jaw set at a hard angle. "No, but we can rely on General Lu."

Jie sucked on her lower lip. Maybe it was no a coincidence that the princess had met General Lu for a matchmaking meeting.

"We will keep the pretense by adhering to Lord Tong's demanded schedule." The *Tianzi* sighed. Actually sighed. "General Shan, how long will it take to reach Wailian Castle?"

"By forced march, nine hours to the Great Wall, another two to reach Wailian Castle."

"Then Princess Kaiya's procession must depart tonight. Mobilize a thousand of your best soldiers and send word to General Lu. Chief Minister, provide logistical support so we can depart in four hours. Deputy Yan, have your people ride ahead and learn of Wailian's defenses."

Jie rubbed her butt. It looked like another horse ride lay ahead.

Master Yan bowed his head. "Might I suggest instead you send an imperial phoenix rider? It will arrive sooner and get a better view."

"So it shall be done." The *Tianzi* peered around the room. "The rest of you withdraw and mobilize your vassals, in case Lord Peng's idea does not work."

The men pressed their heads to the floor. When the *Tianzi* released them from their bows, they rose and filed out of the room. Jie waited and watched. Once they left, the *Tianzi* would need to hear of the exchange in the Maduran guesthouse.

The Tianzi raised a hand. "Lord Peng, Deputy Yan, wait."

Both men knelt. The room cleared, save for them and the two princes.

Shoulders slumping, the *Tianzi* seemed to age. "I cannot have Kaiya marry Lord Tong. His late wife was always happy in her youth, but looked terrified after just a month of marriage. We know how he treats women. If the plan should fail, and there is no means of escape…" His voice choked. "She will have led a happy life."

Lord Peng bowed his head. "I shall take care of it myself. Quickly, mercifully."

"There is another way." To avoid revealing her identity Peng Kai-Long, Jie reached into a pouch and touched the magic bauble. Appearing as Princess Kaiya's idealized image, she stepped out of the shadow and bowed.

The *Tianzi's* eyes widened, while the princes gawked. Lord Peng covered a gasp.

Master Yan offered her a rare smile. "With this disguise, *my* daughter will be able to get close enough to the traitor to kill him. The princess needn't even go to Wailian."

"But the…" Lord Peng coughed. "She looks similar, but not exactly alike. And Lord Tong will have her checked for weapons."

Jie grinned. Not like she needed a weapon to kill a man. "That is not our biggest problem. I overheard our altivorc guests say Lord Tong is coordinating some attack with the Teleri Empire and Madura. At first, I suspected it was an invasion of Hua, but I wonder now if they plan to attack Prince Kai-Wu's wedding. They have smuggled a Golden Scorpion master in. I overheard him, but could not get a good look at his face."

"I will assign assets to every Ayuri in the palace," Master Yan said. "What about…"

The *Tianzi* turned to Lord Peng. "The Ankiran prince. Hardeep. Do you trust him?"

Face blanking, Lord Peng's head bobbled in slow bobs. "Yes, *Huang-Shang.* I've known him a long time, and trust him implicitly."

"Any other collaborators?" Master Yan asked.

"When I meet Lord Tong, I will find out how many traitors conspire with him."

Face blanking, Lord Peng's head bobbed in slow nods.

The *Tianzi* tilted his head a fraction. "Master Yan, your people are resourceful."

"Daughter," Master Yan said, "go trail the princess and learn her voice so you can imitate it with the *Mockingbird's Deception.*"

Crown Prince Kai-Guo raised a halting hand. "This must all be kept secret from the princess. She must not know the procession leaving tonight is meant for her. She might think to interfere."

Tian dumped the two crossbows used to assassinate the late Lord Peng and his eldest son onto a table next to the Eldaeri crossbow Jie had stolen and a standard Hua repeater. The authorities considered the case solved, making it easy to retrieve the murder weapons and bring them back to the safehouse. It had also been easy for his comrades to ambush the large boy who trailed him back.

Side by side, the Hua repeater was clearly smaller than the other three, which all appeared exactly the same. He popped open the magazines of the murder weapons. The one used to kill the *Tai-Ming* lord still held two bolts, while the one used to murder his son had one. Their heads were too large to fit the Hua repeater, while the shafts were as short as the Eldaeri ones. Either the Serikothi or Tarkothi must have provided the weapons.

Except…the Eldaeri used sablewood, whereas the bolts used in the assassination were made of ironwood, a tree that didn't grow in Eldaeri nations thanks to their forestry programs. And the bolt heads, the same width, were cast instead of wrought—a Hua technique. These crossbows posed more questions than they answered.

Back in the safehouse's main room, Chong and Huang discussed their prisoner. They'd have to wait for Little Wen to return. Her male-targeted contact toxins and feminine wiles should have no problem drawing information out of a strapping young man. That left some time to see if the crossbows themselves were as different as the bolts they fired.

With deft hands, Tian first disassembled the Serikothi crossbow. The articulating wood joints used wax to help with the cocking motion—an old technology, from when the Eldaeri first conquered the eastern coast nearly three centuries before, and which they apparently still used today.

In a side room, it sounded as if Little Wen had returned and had already started working her magic. Let her use her special skillset; Tian would use his. He took apart one of the murder weapons to look for any internal differences.

He sucked in a breath. Though it might look like an Eldaeri repeater on the outside, its internal mechanisms were Hua improvements. Oiled steel ball bearings for a smoother motion. Cogged gears to minimize the jerking of the cocking lever. An exact channel for the bolt. That, combined with the longer barrel, would improve its accuracy. Just as the Hua had reverse-engineered the Eldaeri repeater and designed a superior weapon, whoever made these crossbows had taken the guts of Hua innovations and made an even better weapon.

Turning away from this new piece of the puzzle, Tian went to the main room, where Chong and Huang combed through the boy's effects—all *Moquan* tools. From the side room, the boy's deep panting suggested a large lung capacity.

Tian lifted his chin to the boy's items. "Find anything interesting?"

"If I didn't know any better, I would swear he was *Moquan*."

So would Tian. Sliding the door into the interrogation room open a crack, he peeked in. The scent of *yinghua* flowers percolated out. Bare back to him, Little Wen tilted her head a fraction, enough so that she could probably see him in the corner of her eye, and then returned her attention to the sweating boy she straddled. With a stupid grin, he sat bound to a chair, naked save for undergarments, which strained against his excitement.

Clad in only her underpants herself, Wen rubbed against him while pressing her ample bosom into his face. She pulled back, just out of the reach of his craning neck. Her voice came out pouty, breathy. "Why did Lord Tong want Lord Peng dead?"

"I swear I don't know. He just gave the order."

"You're sure?" Her sultry tone stirred Tian's pulse.

The boy nodded like the seals that wintered in Jiangkou. "I swear."

"I will be back." Covering herself with crossed arms, she lifted herself off him and turned around.

Averting his eyes more out of politeness than because any of the Black Lotus cared, Tian found a cloak hanging next to the door. He draped it over her shoulders before making way for her into the main room. "What did you find out?"

"He claims they belong to a *Moquan* clan known as the Water Snake, trained by a Black Lotus defector."

A new clan didn't seem possible. Tian searched her eyes. *Moquan* interrogation methods could be painful or pleasurable, but none were completely reliable. "All Black Lotus members, past and present, are accounted for."

She shrugged. "They work for Lord Tong. He ordered the assassination of Lord Peng and his son. There were three in Jiangkou for the operation, and they know about *us*."

Now one was dead, another captured. A third remained at large. "How much do they know?"

"This one saw you retrieving the crossbows, and tracked you back to our base of operations."

"And their own base of operations?"

"Wailian Castle."

Tian tapped his chin. "Try to find out how many there are and if they had anything to do with the attacks in the capital last night."

Bu slipped in, panting. "Word from Master Yan, on the last horse of the night. Jie is disguised as Princess Kaiya and heading to Wailian Castle tonight."

"What?" Tian's heat jolted. It might keep Princess Kaiya out of danger; but if Water Snake *Moquan* defended Wailian Castle, it would be hard for Jie to infiltrate and even more difficult to attack. But how could he get word to the capital without use of the horse relays?

CHAPTER 34

Changes in Mind and Fortune

From where she stood just outside the double doors to the Hall of Pure Melody, Kaiya listened to the arrhythmic clops of boots across the central courtyard. There marched a contingent of imperial guards, casting long shadows from the Blue and White moons.

Every nerve tingling with desire for Hardeep, she couldn't return to the imperial residence. Not tonight, or at least not now. Once behind those walls, there would be no getting out until morning, and he'd forget all about her.

Her stomach twisted into a knot again, as her better sense warred with the primal urges brought on by the pillow book's magic. She'd strong-armed Secretary Hong into allowing her to come here, ostensibly to retrieve a book from the music library. From his wringing hands, no doubt he thought her insane given the trouble caused by visiting the day before. The poor old man seemed tired all the time, but ever since she played the lute for Hardeep, he looked as if he might keel over and die.

The two guards, as well, lacked their usual composure. Shoulders slumped and heads hanging, they resembled the crude illustrations of the laborers who built the Great Wall six hundred years before. She closed her eyes and listened. Yes, their hearts were beating slowly and sluggishly. If they were all so tired, perhaps it wouldn't take much more to put them into a sleep. There had been a song like that in the music book...

Light, slippered feet pattered up the Hall of Pure Melody's marble steps. Kaiya opened her eyes to find Han Meiling, cloak in hand. Bowing, she presented it.

"Come." Legs trembling, Kaiya stepped over the ghost-tripping threshold and into the main corridor.

Secretary Hong and her two guards followed. She shuffled down the hall to the performance hall's open double doors. If she entered without permission, it would be the second time breaking the same rule in as many days.

Was this worth the risk? Father had only suspended her death sentence as long as she remained obedient.

No, she was protected. They needed her to marry Lord Tong. Kaiya hummed the musical notes, considering. The Night Blossoms were the epitome of Hua beauty and grace, the exact opposite of her. Prince Hardeep wouldn't be able to resist their charms.

Then again, that's what men did. The Floating World wouldn't exist without men's urges. No, she couldn't let it happen. With a deep breath, she entered and swept across the performance hall's floor.

Near the center, Kaiya stopped and listened for the heartbeats of her small entourage. In this acoustically perfect chamber, they all pulsed loudly in her ears, the rhythm slow and tired.

Drawing in a quick breath, Kaiya gripped her toes to the floor and straightened her posture.

She hummed the tune more loudly. Like a lullaby, it dipped and rose in gentle waves, slowing with each refrain. Her men wavered in their spots.

Her own stamina guttered. Maybe it wouldn't hold out. Maybe she would pass out before they did. She forged ahead with her hum, despite her wobbling legs and heavy head. Just a little more. Like a flame burning the last of its wax, she spit out one last stanza.

Secretary Hong, the imperial guards, and Meiling all slumped to the ground. Kaiya, too.

She propped herself up on her elbows to find their eyes closed, breaths shallow. Asleep? Summoning her last drop of energy, she picked herself off the ground and trudged over. Her feet might be disproportionally large, but now, they also seemed to be encased in Estomari concrete.

She started to bend over to confirm they were asleep, but thought the better of it. She might very well fall over and not stand again until morning. If this were the cost of magic, it didn't seem possible for the legendary Yanyan to sing Avarax to sleep.

Several more paces and she reached the door. She rested against the doorframe, letting her flagging strength grow little by little. She took a few minutes to consider this foolishness. In the courtyard, she'd stick out like a cloud on a sunny day.

But past the courtyard, it was all alleys between the buildings, and the guest pavilions weren't that far away. Her heart pumped faster, replacing her fatigue with nervous energy. A few more deep breaths, and she was ready to try. For Hardeep.

Vitality returning by the moment, Kaiya tiptoed down the corridor to the hall's entrance. She paused at the threshold and peeked out. A few officials walked through the courtyard, but there were no imperial guards.

Donning the cloak Meiling had brought, Kaiya pulled the hood over her head and peeked out of the hall again. The officials from before had walked even farther away, and still, no imperial guards appeared to be around. She started to step out.

Across the plaza, motion flashed near the entrance of the Imperial Archives.

Freezing, Kaiya peered in that direction.

Nothing.

Just her imagination. Unless there really were such a thing as *Moquan*. She hurried down the steps, nearly tripping on her gown along the way.

Running would certainly draw the attention of any eyes she had missed in her initial scan, so Kaiya walked at a moderate pace. South and east towards the closest alley off the courtyard. When she turned the corner, she let out a sigh of relief. It didn't seem as if anyone had seen her, or at least noted it was her.

She would be reunited with Prince Hardeep soon. The fatigue from before seemed to melt away, replaced by a renewed vigor and excitement. And need. She shuffled quickly through the alleys, pausing to look around each corner for any stray official or guard.

After several minutes, she came within two turns of Nine Courtyard. Soon, very soon! Hugging the pillow book to her chest, Kaiya took a step into an alley. She caught an imperial guard in her peripheral vision and quickly ducked back the way she'd come. How stupid of her! In her excitement, she'd forgotten to check, even forgotten to use her ears. The guard would surely challenge a cloaked and hooded stranger, carrying a mysterious bundle to the chest.

Holding her breath, she pressed back against the wall and listened. The booted footsteps...headed in the opposite direction. Not daring to let out a breath, Kaiya loosened her sweaty fists. In the future, if she were to make a habit of sneaking around, it would be worthwhile to learn the patrol patterns.

When the footsteps turned a corner, she edged forward...and paused again. Another sound lurked in the symphony of the night, somewhere behind her. She spun around to find its source.

Nothing. She surveyed the space for a few more seconds. Shaking the doubts out of her head, Kaiya continued into the alley, stopping again at the edge of the courtyard and looking at the pavilion where she'd left Prince Hardeep.

No! Girls giggled from within, mingling with a deep male laugh. Kaiya's shoulders slumped. Perhaps he'd already started drinking, already started acting out pictures from the pillow book with the Night Blossoms.

Hollow in her belly, she crept from tree to tree, deeper into the garden, and then tiptoed up to the veranda that connected all the pavilions. Curiously, no guards stood watch outside. Perhaps they were posted inside.

At Hardeep's pavilion, she pressed her ear up against the closest window's latticework.

"Yes, lower," Prince Hardeep said, to the giggles of at least two Night Blossoms.

One of the ladies let out a primal moan. Voice panting, she said, "Your Excellency is so well-endowed."

If Kaiya's stomach could twist any more, it could be used as a New Year's knot decoration. She meant nothing to him beyond her ability to save his own homeland. She held a hand over her mouth.

"I didn't know the foreigner could speak Hua," a high-pitched girl's voice said from behind.

Kaiya's heart leapt into her throat. She whipped around. There was no one there. The courtyard was empty. "Show yourself."

"Is that even the prince's voice?" The voice changed, now sounding suspiciously similar to her own, and came from...the stone dragon overlooking the pond?

A ghost, perhaps? A chill crawled up Kaiya's spine. But no, it couldn't be. Sun-Moon Palace's layout confused ghosts, herding them out through the alleys' twists and turns.

"Who are you?" she hissed. Closing her eyes, she listened for a telltale breath.

There, in the eaves. Hidden in the trickling of the palace stream, quieter than the Night Blossoms making the clouds and rain with Hardeep, breathed a slow, light breath. Kaiya looked up, just in time to see a shadow flutter away. The breath disappeared.

Moquan? Kaiya shook the silly idea out of her head. Regardless who the mysterious girl was, she was right: that wasn't Prince Hardeep's voice in the pavilion, and up to now, all his words had been spoken in Hua. Steeling herself against what she would inevitably see, she burst through the doors.

There, a Night Blossom mounted the Minister of Appointments himself. Her gown hung loosely at her elbows. Another almost-naked Night Blossom lay on her side, head propped on an elbow, a hand hidden somewhere beneath the first's gowns.

Kaiya cast her eyes at the floor. "Where is Prince...the Blind Musician?"

"*Dian-xia!*" The minister pushed the woman off. Covering himself, he rose and bowed.

Wide-eyed, the Night Blossoms exchanged glances. *The princess?* one mouthed. The other nodded. They both gathered their gowns up around themselves. Kneeling, they pressed their foreheads to the ground.

Utter silence. Kaiya opened and closed her mouth. Had she gone deaf? Her cheeks burned hot. Minister Hu barely covered himself with a woman's silk gown, exposing his rotund belly. Not like Kaiya had a clear view, since she kept her gaze averted. The smell...

"Where is Prin—the Blind Musician?" she said, this time louder and with all the righteous indignation she could muster. Never mind all the rules she was breaking.

"*Dian-xia.*" Minister Hu's voice, usually harsh, wobbled with what could only be worry. "The musician...the musician wanted to see the moonlight over the gardens."

Kaiya stared at his forehead. "Where are the guards? There were explicit orders that the Blind Musician stay here."

"Yes, well..." the minister licked his lips as sweat gathered on his brow. Then, his eyebrows clashed together. "You are supposed to be dining with the Crown Princess. Why are you here?"

Both of them were in compromising positions, and now it was a battle of wills. One Kaiya refused to lose. She turned to the Night Blossoms. "Where is the Blind Musician?"

One looked up at the minister, then back. Her lips trembled. "*Dian-xia*, the musician bribed the minister."

Lips trembling, Minister Hu plopped to his knees and slammed his forehead to the Ayuri wool rug. "Forgive me, *Dian-xia*. Please, please, do not tell the *Tianzi*."

Kaiya's jaw clenched. The ever-uptight Minister Hu, literally caught with his pants down, partaking of prostitutes meant for someone else *and* taking a bribe. "When will the Blind Musician return?"

"He said by dawn," the second Night Blossom said.

Kaiya twirled a lock of her hair, so unruly compared to the Night Blossoms' perfection. Where would Prince Hardeep have gone? Someplace with something more important than the realm's best food and a pair of beautiful women. To think she'd almost shirked all sense of duty and given herself to him. "What are your names? What house do you come from?"

"Jasmine and Peony from the Jade Teahouse," one said.

"Be sure to tell your proprietress what happened tonight." Kaiya locked her glare on Minister Hu, whose head dropped again. "We will never speak of this again. And if I hear of any misfortune coming to the Jade Teahouse or its Night Blossoms, I will ensure that you are held responsible. Do you understand?"

"Yes, *Dian-xia*!" He knocked his head against the floor three more times.

"Now get back to what the *Tianzi* pays you for." Kaiya spun on her heel and left. She might have earned a life-long enemy in Minister Hu, but as long as she ensured Jasmine and Peony shared their story among their sisters, it would be leverage to use against him. She would send a handmaiden to the Jade Teahouse in the Floating World tomorrow to confirm everyone's wellbeing.

In the meantime, Prince Hardeep was gone, along with her impulse to escape marriage to Lord Tong. Her hand strayed to Tian's pebble. What had she been thinking? The nation's stability depended on her sacrifice. She squeezed the pillow book, angry at herself for succumbing to its magic.

That's all this feeling was. Artistic magic printed in the lines and colors of illustrations. Not the true love described in old ballads.

Now, she had to protect the guards and secretary from punishment. With extra spring in her step, she hurried back through the alleys with much less care than on her way.

Until the same sound as before whispered on the night's breeze. Footsteps? Breathing? It was almost a mingling of the two. The interloper who'd spoken, perhaps. She tracked it to its source, but saw nothing. Shrugging off her suspicions, she continued to the central plaza.

Dozens of soldiers, all armed for battle, marched toward the palace entrance in exacting ranks. It was strange, for this late hour, but thankfully nobody looked in her direction. The steps to the Hall of Supreme Harmony and imperial archives stood empty. There was no activity at the Hall of Pure Melody, at least not on the outside. Had her sleeping retinue been discovered, surely there would be quite the commotion there.

What a mistake. Father had said never to use magic as a crutch. She frowned at the pillow book, which she'd planned to give Prince Hardeep in hopes that it would spark his affection for her. That wasn't true love. No, if someone were to love her, it shouldn't be because of some magic cut into the lines of a woodblock print. Guilt wrenched her insides.

She ran as quietly as she could. Up the steps. Through the double doors. On the other side, she blew out a breath and listened. In the central chamber, at least one of the three men snored. Other than that, no other human sounds carried through the halls. For now, at least, her most recent ill-advised escapade had gone unnoticed.

Kaiya returned to the central chamber, where Secretary Hong, Meiling, and the two imperial guards slept. She walked across the floor and bent down over one of the guards. "Wake up."

He stretched his arms out and yawned, but then rolled over back into sleep. At his side, the other snored. Reaching out to both of them, she shook their shoulders. The second just grunted.

Sighing, she thought back to the book of musical magic. Had it told how to reverse a magically induced sleep? Kaiya mentally listed what she remembered: Inducing sleep. Evoking rage. Arousing lust. Stirring fear. But nothing on how to rouse someone from sleep. Walking back to the guards, she pondered the problem. In order to put them to sleep in the first place, they had to already be tired. Her, too. The song, like a child's lullaby, had gone from a moderate pace to quieter and slow.

At least now her energy had returned. Meanwhile, these four had already benefited from half an hour of sleep. Maybe reversing the song would work, by starting slow and soft and increasing the tempo. Like her masters' duet, where each part interacted with the other. It was worth a try.

First, she shook them some more, in hopes that it would bring them to the edge of consciousness. She squatted low, feet flat and toes gripping the floor. The men's breaths, though light, rose and fell in near synchronicity. She hummed, setting the beat to one's inhalations. Slow at first; then she increased the tempo.

The first guard responded, his chest rising in faster clips. The second and Meiling soon joined him. Secretary Hong, however, remained the same, like a bass beat; stubborn, fighting against her own song. She hummed louder, switching her focus to Hong's heart.

He squirmed a little, but still showed no other sign of waking. It wasn't working. Perhaps...she considered the storage room. A musical instrument should help magnify the effect. She started to the door.

Out in the corridor, boots clopped. Someone must have heard her song. This would not end well for her trusted servants. She dashed out of the performance hall and slid the door shut behind her. Turning, she searched for the source of the footsteps.

Cousin Kai-Long—Lord Peng. He held a light bauble lamp in one hand, while a helmet was tucked under the other arm. Instead of court robes, he wore lamellar armor. "*Dian-xia*, I thought I would find you here. Or at Prince Hardeep's pavilion."

Her cheeks flushed hot. She fixated on the floor. How predictable she'd become. If he knew what she'd planned to do with Hardeep...

"Come with me." He placed his hands on the sides of her shoulders and looked her up and down, very much like a tailor measuring her for a new dress. He pulled the hood of her cloak over her head.

She shook her head. The guards, Secretary Hong, and Meiling would all face punishment.

"There's no time to spare."

She searched his eyes. "What's happening?"

"I'm not supposed to tell you."

They were keeping secrets from her? "Tell me," she said. "That is my command."

He lowered his voice, as if the walls had ears. "Your wedding procession."

"What?" How was that even possible?

"I am leading it. We are headed to Wailian Castle tonight. Lord Tong wants to marry you tomorrow, before Prince Kai-Wu's wedding."

So her marriage was going to happen, sooner than later. Much sooner. And they weren't even going to tell her. Maybe this was Minister Hu's revenge. Kaiya's heart sank. "I...I will get ready."

He shook his head. "You're not going. They are risking a decoy instead. Now, let's get you back to your room before anyone else starts looking for you."

"What? A decoy?"

"It is a trick, to get us into Wailian Castle and capture Lord Tong."

Kaiya's head spun. "He won't let that many armed men in, if any."

"Prince Hardeep asked to join us. His Paladin fighting skills make him better than twenty men. "

So that's where Hardeep had gone. But why? Had he made a deal with Father? Still, one man, worth twenty or even a hundred, could not fight against a garrison of thousands. Loyal men might all die and the realm would fall into turmoil.

"Take me with you. If your plan does not work, I will offer myself in exchange for your lives."

Or use the budding power of her voice to sing Lord Tong to surrender. Some things were better left unsaid, especially if they might not be reliable.

Kai-Long shook his head. "I can't endanger you. Now, hurry back to the residence. I have to go now, my staff is assembling." He turned and headed back toward the entrance before she could stop him.

Kaiya looked from the doors leading out, then to the doors leading into the performance hall. Two paths lay ahead: one kept her safe but threatened the realm; the other could end the rebellion, perhaps at the cost of her dreams.

There was no choice, really. She'd made her decision earlier in the day, when she sacrificed her hopes before all the hereditary lords. The difference was that now, another option lay ahead. She'd sung men to sleep. Maybe that's all it would take to subdue Lord Tong.

CHAPTER 35

Easier to be a Soldier than a General

Kaiya's heart beat with a resolute calm, drowning out all other sounds in her ears. Squaring her shoulders, she strode toward the doors out of the Hall of Pure Melody. Surely, Yang-Di, smiling upon her in Heaven, would provide a means of mingling with the procession. *Her* wedding procession, to which she wasn't even invited.

She peeked out. Right in front of her on the Hall's steps, Cousin Kai-Long's command staff assembled. He, himself, stood at the bottom of the stairs, addressing them from left to right. She pulled back before his gaze swept over her, but he paused. Had he seen her?

Apparently not. He continued with his speech. She let out the breath she held and peeked out again. Surplus equipment was stacked right by the door. Weapons, armor. A set of lamellar armor and a T-slot helm, likely for a messenger boy, appeared to be her size and lay just within reach. And how strange it was for a leader to stand at the bottom of the steps, instead of the top, leaving his men with their backs to her.

It couldn't be a coincidence. Heaven had sent her a sign. This was the right thing to do.

When the men cheered at Kai-Long's words, she grabbed the armor and dragged it in. It was lighter than it appeared; she'd have no problem lifting it over her head and shrugging it on. First, though, she had to consider her own clothes. The inner gown hung lower than the armor, and the silk was too strong to tear.

Slinking back to the performance hall, she bent over and relieved one of the guards of his dagger. His *dao* would complete the disguise, but she thought the better of it. Like the silver ring that marked his station as an imperial guard, the sword represented his honor.

After gauging the length of the armor on her, she cut the bottom of her inner gown. The long sleeves of her outer gown became her leggings, bound with strips shorn from its hem. She shrugged on the armored tunic, and everything more or less looked right.

Removing her hairpins, she let her hair drop to the middle of her back. Much too long. She started to cut it, as well, but paused. Untamable as it was, her hair was the only feminine thing about her. Instead, she tied it back in a pony tail, like a man. For once, it obeyed. How easy men had it.

She glanced out again. The command staff marched toward the front of the plaza, where a hundred soldiers stood in orderly ranks. A contingent of imperial guards joined in, flanking her decoy and an unfamiliar handmaiden as they marched to her palanquin.

Up on the steps in front of her, young soldiers collected the gear and supplies. One of them, a boy who might have been her twin in his armor, reached for the helm she'd planned to take. She stepped out and grabbed it.

His eyes widened. "You're not allowed in there!" The simple marks on his armor, so different from the elaborate symbols on the imperial guards, did not suggest a high rank.

She donned the helmet, which strained her poor neck muscles. "I thought…" Too high-pitched! She cleared her throat and lowered her voice, as if singing a bass song. "I thought I heard someone in there."

"Well, hurry up." He pointed at a bundle of short spears.

Hugging them in her arms, she followed the boy to a line of horse-drawn carts, laden with weapons and bandages. Several grooms held the reins of messenger swifthorses. One of her palace physicians, Fang Weiyong, gave instructions to medics.

Keeping her head low to avoid his eyes, she dared a glance at the palanquin, some hundred paces away. The decoy resembled her, or at least an idealized version of her…of course! It was undoubtedly the work of the magic bauble Kai-Long had used the night before to help her escape. In all likelihood, the best warrior held it now, and would use it to get close to Lord Tong.

Who could it be? An imperial guard, perhaps. Not one of hers, since Chen Xin, Ma Jun, Zhao Yue, Li Wei, and Xu Zhan were all gathered around the palanquin. Maybe it was Prince Hardeep, with his Paladin skills? It made sense, given what Kai-Long had said about Hardeep offering to help. And for what reason? Why would he risk himself when his own country needed him? Kaiya's chest squeezed.

Then she shuddered as the decoy ducked into the palanquin. Better him than her! Even as heavy and languid as her limbs felt, it was far better to march all night than to ride in the suffocating confines of a glorified coffin.

"Soldiers of Hua!" Cousin Kai-Long's voice carried across the courtyard. He made for a dashing figure, sitting astride a white imperial stallion. The low murmurs guttered. "Tonight, we will march along the north highway. All night, double time."

Kaiya's legs buckled at the thought, and the lightweight armor and helm now might have been a dwarven anvil. Maybe the palanquin wasn't such a bad thing. Using a Dragon Song to vanquish Lord Tong required energy; energy she wouldn't have after a long night marching.

Kai-Long pointed north. "Our goal is to reach the Great Wall gate by dawn, then the outside of Wailian Castle by breakfast. We will rest for a short while to eat while we coordinate with General Lu's Army of the North, and gather information about the traitor's defenses. That might be your only rest before you are called on to storm an impregnable fortress."

Mutters broke out, sharing Kaiya's sentiment. This was a fool's errand, an engagement that would only work if the decoy succeeded. Even more reason to try *her* way.

Holding up a hand, Kai-Long's voice rose to a crescendo. "This may very well be the most difficult operation you will ever take part in. However, I know you. The best soldiers Hua has seen in centuries are up to the task. Let us teach the rebel Tong Baxian the punishment for violating the Mandate of Heaven!"

The soldiers erupted into cheers, but Kaiya cringed. If pretty words were enough to convince a man to throw his life away, there didn't need to be many orators to instigate wars. For now, she'd keep her head low, lest someone recognize her and end her first, and in all likelihood last, military campaign.

Horns blared, and the gatehouse opened. Kai-Long took the lead, followed by mounted senior staff, then the imperial guards surrounding her palanquin. The ranks of soldiers narrowed to six men abreast and filed out, their broadswords clanging and spears pounding. A light breeze caught the blue imperial banners.

The unit she'd joined, with the supply wagons and medics, followed on the order of a mounted officer. Luckily, years of dancing allowed her to imitate their body language and marching. As long as she made it past the gatehouse and all the familiar palace staff and guards, there would be little chance of anyone recognizing her.

"You!" a familiar male voice barked.

Kaiya turned, only to have the helmet slip and block her vision. She adjusted it and looked.

Just a dozen paces away, Minister Hu jabbed a finger at a clearly drowsy Secretary Hong, flanked by the two guards she'd sung to sleep. "It is your fault she is missing. If any harm comes to her, the *Tianzi* will have your head."

Heavens, this was a mistake. Perhaps she could force Minister Hu's silence by threatening to reveal his indiscretions with the Night Blossoms. However, it would have to wait until a successful return from Wailian Castle. And success wasn't guaranteed.

What a dilemma. Four people might face severe punishment if she didn't intervene; but then, her singing Lord Tong into submission might be the only way to keep the realm from sundering.

Shaking the uncertainties out of her head, she lifted her chin and marched. Through the plaza, into the gatehouse. On the other side, yet more soldiers assembled, joining the procession. By the time they reached the capital's north gates, they'd grown to nearly a thousand strong.

Thank the heavens Kaiya had gotten her second wind. What made her think it was enough to make it to the Great Wall, let alone Wailian County? She set her eyes forward, concentrating on the rapid rhythm of boots.

Boots! In her haste, she hadn't thought of that. She wore silk slippers. Perhaps no one had noticed in the dark, but at dawn...and that was assuming she didn't wear the soles through or give her poor feet blisters.

"What's your name?" she asked the young man.

"Su. Yours?"

"Wang." The truth was easy enough to remember.

The column of soldiers turned north to the gatehouse and the bridge beyond, but her supply unit continued west. She leaned over to Su. "Won't we travel with them?"

He laughed. "Where did they find you? They are marching too fast for the wagons to keep up for long. We'll take river barges to Honggang and meet up with the army. That Lord Peng is a genius."

Kaiya's chest swelled with pride. Cousin Kai-Long was already proving resourceful on a military operation. And they'd take a boat. At least that would save her feet; maybe even give her a chance to rest. Unless the river barges foundered and capsized in the dark...

Her unit arrived at Songyuan Quays, where the Jade River emerged from Sun-Moon Lake. At this late hour, light bauble lamps posted along the warehouses illuminated the wooden docks. Several river barges had already disembarked, while soldiers worked at loading others. With Little Su's prodding, Kaiya joined in the effort, hoping not to embarrass herself as she moved the heaviest loads she could.

Which were about half the size of the others. With a shake of his head, Little Su helped her. Within half an hour, her unit boarded a barge. A drummer set the rhythm for the rowers, and, combined with the spring melt current, they set off at a brisk pace.

For the first time in what seemed like forever, Kaiya had a chance to rest her feet. Back against a crate, she sat cross-legged. It was thoroughly unladylike, but it kept her slippered feet out of sight. Before long, they passed her wedding procession. At the head, she ducked, just in case Kai-Long or the imperial guards recognized her through the helm's T-slot.

After a while, the Iridescent Moon reached full. She sucked in a breath at its beauty. Usually in bed before midnight, she rarely saw Caiyue in its full glory. Depending on the outcome of this battle, she might never see it again. Never see Hardeep again, if he didn't survive. Her chest squeezed, foreboding thoughts bouncing in her head.

"Wake up!"

Kaiya's eyes fluttered open. Little Su came into focus as he shook her shoulder. The boats were docking and unloading at a town. An officer on horseback bearing the red wolf emblem of Cousin Kai-Long's Nanling Province oversaw the loading of twelve new horse-drawn carts. It was amazing to think Kai-Long had devised such a complex plan and coordinated the logistics in such a short time.

"Where are we?" She asked.

"Honggang." Su passed her half a pork bun. "Two-thirds of the way to the Great Wall."

And right on the border of Hongzhou, one of the rebellious counties. She'd visited it last year, and there appeared to be more docks now. Hills rose up not far past the town, and beyond, the dark outline of the mountains demarked the starry sky.

Once they'd loaded the supplies, they resumed their march. She gripped her spear haft so tightly, her knuckles turned white. Without the bulk of the expeditionary force, it was up to her unit of thirty exceedingly young men to defend against rebels and bandits. And the weapon in her hands...she could reasonably not kill herself using a straight sword and dagger, but a spear was another story.

Two hours, marching uphill at night. At least the paved highway made it a little easier. Windows lit up in the villages and towns along the road, but they didn't encounter any resistance. Only at Chengfu Township, in a dale next to the Great Wall's gate, did she feel safer. Home to the gatehouse's imperial garrison, they would gain some reinforcements as they crossed into Wailian County.

Or would they? Their unit's commander refused an armed escort. "This is all part of Lord Peng's plan," he said. "The garrison needs to defend this town, since it effectively cuts the rebellion in two. In any case, the rest of the procession is just an hour behind."

It meant travelling through the hotbed of rebellion for an hour, though Kaiya didn't want to draw undue attention to herself by speaking up about the danger. Instead, they continued through the gatehouse to the other side of the wall.

She scanned the darkened land below. To think that not long ago, this region had belonged to the Nothori Kingdom of Rotuvi. The march down the mountain took less effort than the march up. Still, Kaiya's entire body ached from the most continuous strain ever. Thankfully, she would never have to walk such a long distance again in her life.

As they descended, the Great Wall and mountains blocked the view of the Iridescent Moon behind them. Without it, she lost sense of how much time passed. Up ahead, the black of night began giving way to the inky blue before dawn.

The commanding officer called a halt at a bluff overlooking the next town. He pointed at it. "Wailian Township supports Wailian Castle, with barracks for many of Lord Tong's soldiers. We will wait here until the rest of the army arrives."

Kaiya squinted. In the low light, it was hard to make out the size of the town, but beyond it, the green-tiled roofs of Wailian Castle's central tower sparkled in the first rays of morning. A single bridge traversed the ravine, which yawned between the town and castle battlements.

What had General Lu said? *A ravine surrounds the castle on three sides, and a sheer cliff drops away on the other side.* The rustling of water indicated a river running through the ravine. It was impossible to take by force, which meant Kai-Long's plan hinged on her decoy eliminating Lord Tong.

And somewhere, hidden in the roar of the river, was the clopping of horse hooves. Hundreds, rumbling like thunder in the distance, but getting closer.

Tugging on Su's sleeve, Kaiya pointed in the direction of the approaching horses. "Do you hear that?"

He stared at her, brows furrowed. "Hear what?"

"Horses!" she called out to the commander. "Horses!"

The commander met her gaze and scoffed. "I don't hear anything. It's..."

Some of the other boys' ears picked up. Others shuffled uncomfortably. Now, even the commander looked.

Cresting the path were dozens of mounted soldiers, all bearing the green banners of Lord Tong. The boys around her started backing away from the carts. Kaiya's heart pounded faster than the horses' hooves.

The commander lowered his hand. "Steady, boys. Don't flee. We are still flying Wailian's banners. Let me talk to them."

The Wailian cavalry surged up and surrounded them, training bows on the outnumbered boys. Their leader pointed a broadsword toward the supplies. "Surrender. Put your weapons and armor in the wagons."

How did the enemy know they were with the imperial army? Kai-Long's logistics had failed. They should have just waited for him instead of going ahead alone. Kaiya joined her trembling unit members in looking up to the commander. Surely, he would order surrender.

"Do as he says," the commander said.

Kaiya let out her breath. At least for now, they would live. Except that beneath her armor was the silk inner gown she'd butchered. One by one, the boys placed their swords and spears inside the nearest carts and started removing their armor.

Her hands trembled as she surrendered her own weapons. She was a prisoner of war, and that fate sent a chill up her spine. They'd find out she was a girl, and no one would recognize her as the princess. Revealing her true identity would spare her gang rape, and get her an audience with Lord Tong, where she could try the magic of her voice. No, she was too exhausted for that, and even if they believed her, it would end all chances of her decoy getting close to Lord Tong.

"You, too." One of the Wailian soldiers prodded her in the back with the butt of a spear.

She stumbled forward, with Su grabbing her arm for support. Brushing him away, she removed the helm. She shook out her hair, lifted her chin, and faced the leader. "Sir, I am the daughter of *Tai-Ming* Lord Zheng Han." Never mind that Tian didn't have a sister, these rank and file soldiers wouldn't know that. She lifted the armor to expose the fine silk underneath. "He will pay handsomely for my return."

"I knew something was off," Su said, eyes wide.

The leader's expression hardened. "Take off your armor and put it in the cart."

She crossed her arms and shook her head. With the gown shredded and the mismatched leggings, she'd look ridiculous.

"Or shall I have my men confirm your identity the hard way?"

Several of the soldiers closed in. Little Su backed closer, arms outstretched in protection. Her limbs froze and refused to obey. With fingers stiff, she worked the armor off. Around her, the men laughed. Heat flared in her cheeks, even as the cold bit her exposed, armor-chaffed shoulders.

The leader unpinned his cloak and tossed it to her. "Now march. Not a word."

Their own commander looked over the defenseless boys and nodded. "March." His voice sounded wrong.

Something heavy settled in Kaiya's gut. His tone didn't gutter in defeat. And Heavens, they were providing supplies for the rebellion! Still, her comrades obeyed without question. What choice did they have?

At the point of rebel spears, they trudged through Wailian Town, which now roused with dawn. Men with picks and shovels walked in queues, humming in unison. Kaiya listened for the marching song's spirit, in hopes it would invigorate her.

It didn't work. She was a lone girl surrounded by many men, none who knew her true identity.

CHAPTER 36

Failing to Plan, Planning to Fail

The sound of defeated boys trudging over the highway pavestones rang in Kaiya's ears, so different from their confident march just earlier in the morning. Their supplies seized, taken prisoner by a rebel lord, exhausted from the long night...and who knew if they'd survive the day?

She shuddered as she walked through the town. Who knew how long her maidenhood would survive?

Right before the bridge, the enemy leader called for a halt. "Leave the equipment here. Follow me." He rode ahead. The bridge was wide enough for five of them to walk abreast.

Their own officer raised an eyebrow at the leader. Kaiya's stomach knotted. Her instincts were right; he'd betrayed them. He dismounted and beckoned. "Come."

Something sounded wrong, a tension in his voice. The rigidity of the rebels. Kaiya looked among her fellow young soldiers. Eyes down, shoulders slumped, it didn't appear that any of them shared her suspicions as they plodded across the bridge. Up ahead, the castle gates opened, and a several armed men marched out.

Halfway onto the bridge, their commander turned around. "Sorry, boys."

From his saddle, the enemy leader twisted around, unslung his bow, notched an arrow, and shot. It lodged deep into their commander's back.

The commander choked on blood, his voice coming out in wheezes. "What about the deal?"

"The lord said to kill the entire unit, including you." He raised a hand and made a fist.

From the town side of the bridge, bowstrings twanged. Kaiya glanced back. The cavalry were loosing arrows. Screaming, several of the boys scrambled forward and trampled over each other. Maybe in their panic, they didn't see that up ahead, soldiers were advancing with spears.

Her heart rapped hard in her chest. This was it. An ignoble ending to her noble intentions. All these poor boys, most no older than her, slaughtered on Lord Tong's command. The bridge vibrated with their frantic steps.

Hear the waves and allow them to lend you their strength. The memory of Lord Xu's lesson sounded in her mind, almost as if he spoke to her now. Tired as she was, she could borrow the sounds of chaos and the vibration of the bridge.

She gripped the stone with her toes through the tattered slippers. Her blisters protested, lending an edge to her voice. "Stop!"

The boys froze in place. The ambushers ahead halted in the charge. The rain of arrows stopped.

Kaiya gaped. It had worked—on the first try, no less. Still, her energy guttered, buckling her knees and sending her panting for breath. Once they came to their senses, the murder would resume, and she didn't have the energy to reprise the feat.

Shaking the fatigue out, she reached up and grasped the side of the bridge for support. Once she gained her feet, she squared her shoulders and strode toward the leader. Her hand found Tian's pebble.

She summoned a tone of command, speaking as she would to a palace servant. "I am Princess Wang Kaiya, here to meet my betrothed, Lord Tong Baxian." She gestured to the cowering boys. "These are my honor guard. An attack on them is an attack on me."

The leader favored her through slitted eyes. She'd just betrayed Kai-Long and the decoy, and there was no guarantee Lord Tong would spare any of them, let alone believe her in the first place.

The sound of drums in the distance drew Kaiya's attention from the enemy leader on the bridge to the road behind her.

A man on horseback, flying Lord Tong's green, cantered through the city. "Princess Kaiya's procession is coming, maybe half an hour away."

The enemy leader turned back and frowned at her, then beckoned the prisoners. "Hands on your head. Come on, hurry. Help your wounded comrades if they need it."

Kaiya evaluated her unit. A few lay unmoving on the bridge or sprawled over the edge, and those at the back of the line appeared to have suffered varying degrees of arrow wounds. Still, most seemed uninjured. Many bowed their heads to her as they passed.

She searched for Su, the boy who'd travelled with her, helped her pick up the slack when her energy flagged. There he was, his arm hanging from another young man who helped him limp along. An arrow protruded from his back. Kaiya pushed her way through the others and took his other arm.

He looked up at her through drooping eyes. "Are you really Princess Kaiya?"

Despite his labored breaths, his tone sounded...hopeful. She nodded.

"Then it is my honor to die for you." He started to drop to a knee in salute.

She clasped his hand. "You aren't going to die." Not like she could tell, and blood flecked his lips.

The boy on the other side of him met her eyes and shook his head. "You saved us all."

Not all. Now that many of her adopted unit had been taken to the castle, she could see arrows protruding from some of the bodies. Doctor Wu had taught enough about anatomy for Kaiya to recognize at least two of the boys would not draw another breath. Her stomach churned, and it was all she could do to force down the vomit. Even now, Lord Tong's men were throwing their remains off the bridge. Others, like Su, might not survive.

With much of his weight on her shoulders, she trudged over the bridge. At the gatehouse, she risked a glance back. No sign of the imperial banners, even though the drumbeats grew louder.

On the other side of the gatehouse, she walked out into another bare yard, surrounded by high, crenelated walls. If an invading army somehow made it over the bridge, they would be trapped at low ground, easy targets from all sides. Just like she and her comrades were now. The men atop the walls trained repeating crossbows on them.

The gates ahead were open as soldiers escorted the prisoners and pulled the stolen supply wagons through. If they were to be slaughtered here, the gates would be closed to bar escape. Passing through the second gatehouse, the commander led them not to the next part of the castle, but down into rough-hewn tunnels.

The air grew chill and stale, and Kaiya's skin crawled as the walls pressed in around her. "What is this place?"

One of the boys ran a hand over a column. "I would guess these were mines."

Kaiya shuddered. If Wailian had that much firepowder, and if it were stored down here, one accident could cause the supposedly impregnable castle to implode. And she'd be buried under it all, unable to breathe...

Sweat gathered on her neck as her hands trembled. She turned to their nearest captor. "I am Princess Kaiya. These men need medical attention. And I demand to speak with Lord Tong."

He shoved her in the back. "Keep moving. Someone will confirm your identity soon enough."

Thankfully, after a few more steps, the corridor opened into a large chamber. Kaiya took a deep breath and wiped the sweat from her brow.

The injured lay on blankets while healers tended to their wounds. One of the boys screamed as they pulled an arrow out of him. Kaiya's chest ached at the pitiful moans. Still, she knelt by Su and held his hand.

Someone grabbed her shoulder in a heavy grip and spun her around. A larger boy from the regiment glared at her. "If I'm going to die, I'm not going to die a virgin."

Kaiya's mind blanked.

Several other hands seized the boy and pulled him back as he struggled.

"You ingrate," said another one of the boys. "She saved our lives."

A spear butt crashed into the offender's head, sending him to the ground. One of the enemies raised the spear again. "Stay quiet. Nobody touch her until we learn her identity. If she's no one important, you can have her. After we're done, that is."

Kaiya clenched and unclenched her sweaty hands. Surely, someone would be able to identify her. Some of the boys, led by Su's friend, formed up around her.

"Don't worry," he said. "We won't let them do anything to you."

The reassurance wasn't enough to slow Kaiya's thumping heart, though the sentiment was kind enough. If she were in a position of real importance, beyond just a political tool, she'd reward him and the others who defended her.

For now, though, she'd have to wait. If her captors had bothered to tell Lord Tong, the decoy might fare worse than she.

Tian hadn't ridden a horse since childhood, and would never tease Jie again about how she looked after riding. Not the way his buttocks felt. Unable to enter the capital because of his banishment, he'd stolen an imperial stallion and followed the old dirt road along the Jade River at a trot. When his mount tired, he swapped it out for a farmer's draft horse who was none too keen about being ridden.

Eventually, he'd broken into an estate, appropriated a lady's riding horse, and made his way to Honggang. However, the beast refused to cross the river, so Tian had to leave it behind and swim himself.

The river town had been particularly busy at night, and he found out Princess Kaiya's wedding procession, thankfully minus Princess Kaiya, had passed through hours before. He'd followed, jogging uphill, sneaking through the town of Chengfu, and finally scaling the Great Wall with cat claws and coming down on the other side by dawn.

Now he was bent over, hands on his knees, heaving for breath, on a bluff overlooking Wailian Castle. Along the outskirts of the town, four thousand twenty-three enemy soldiers formed up in lines. The imperial procession of a thousand and seven crowded the highway through the town, all the way up to the bridge. From their vantage point, they had no way of knowing that an army just under four times their size was ready to envelop them.

The castle gates opened and soldiers flying green flags emerged. At the head of the imperial procession, the leader dismounted from his white stallion, his body language looking familiar. Eight porters lowered the palanquin. Jie was supposedly inside, unaware a new rival *Moquan* clan was defending the castle.

He had to warn them, even if it meant fighting through both the enemy and an imperial procession that had no idea who he was. He thought back to the poor horse he'd left behind, the one he'd promised himself to track down and return if he survived.

Survival didn't seem likely. Not without a plan, not without knowledge of the castle's layout or defenses. Certainly not with enemy *Moquan* agents who knew Black Lotus tactics.

If Jie had known how relaxing a palanquin ride was, she'd have signed up to be a princess sooner. The fast pace and mild bouncing had rocked her to into a deep slumber, the most relaxing sleep she'd enjoyed in quite a while.

Now, though, someone rapped on the palanquin's sliding window, jarring her awake. "*Dian-xia*." Chen Xin used the honorific, even though the real princess' five imperial guards had probably guessed she was a decoy. "We have arrived."

Jie propped herself up and opened the window. Indeed, Chen Xin's mug blocked her view. She gestured him out of the way and leaned close to get a better view.

Cannons pointed from Wailian Castle's battlements, trained on this very spot before a bridge. In all likelihood, a bombardment would exact heavy causalities on troops waiting to cross through the bottleneck.

She turned to Chen Xin and used the *Mockingbird's Deception* to imitate the princess' voice. "What is the status of General Lu's armies?"

His eyes rounded for a split second before he shook his head. "They are on the other side of the castle, held in place by an army from Rotuvi camped near our fortifications. General Lu is sending reserves, but the best they can do is attack the castle's rear, up the cliffs."

Jie sucked on her lower lip, but switched to the princess' hair twirling. Without General Lu's armies in support, this battle hinged entirely on her getting close to Lord Tong and forcing him to surrender. The window glided shut from the outside.

"I think it is the real princess," Chen Xin whispered, incredulous. "It was her voice."

"It was that magic marble." The roll of Zhao Yue's eyes carried in his tone.

"Jie, then?" Li Wei said.

Apparently, not everyone was apprised of the plan, though the imperial guards were smart enough to figure it out. Or maybe that was giving them too much credit. They were, after all, swordsmen and not alchemists.

She took stock of her weapons. In addition to several sharp hairpins, a garrote wound into her hair and pressed the magic bauble to her scalp. A knife was hidden in her sleeve; a vial of male-targeted toxin in her sash. And under the cushion, she'd stashed a *Moquan* sword and several *biao*, in the unlikely event they allowed the palanquin into the castle.

Outside, someone in robes approached and dropped to a knee. When he spoke, it sounded like cloth dragging across a washboard. "Lord Peng, greetings. I am Steward Qiu. We are honored to receive Princess Kaiya to Wailian Castle. Will she alight and come in?"

Sliding the window open, Jie cleared her throat and copied the princess' voice. "It is not for the common folk to lay eyes on the princess."

The open window provided the view of a middle-aged man with a porcine nose in green robes. His irises shifted back and forth, and his voice cracked like dried mud. "Very well. Lord Tong would be honored. Allow me to receive the swords of Lord Peng and the imperial guard for safekeeping."

Safekeeping, indeed. She put a hand out of the window and beckoned Pig Nose Qiu. "The laws of the empire require an imperial princess be protected by five imperial guards at all times." Pig Nose might not know for sure, but it would keep the princess' personal guards happy.

Qiu chewed on the inside of his cheek, looking more like a cow than a pig. "Even still, courtesy demands I protect their swords for them."

Lord Peng's voice cut through the debate. "Very well, five guards, as well as me and my aide. You may protect our weapons."

Aide? Jie contorted to see whom Lord Peng indicated, but Pig Nose Qiu's flat, round face blocked her view. "And my handmaiden," she added. Feng Mi, while young, could easily handle a few men as long as they didn't fight like *Moquan*.

"Men," Lord Peng said, his voice carrying back to the soldiers. "I leave you in the capable hands of General Feng until I send word."

"Yes, *Dajiang!*" the men shouted in unison.

The palanquin lifted and started forward onto the bridge. Jie closed her eyes and listened for the number of distinct footsteps. Lord Peng, his inordinately heavy aide, the five imperial guards, Feng Mi, Pig Nose, and two enemy soldiers.

And hundreds, if not thousands of soldiers in the castle itself. Maybe, just maybe they could take the gatehouse with the eight of them, or sixteen if the palanquin bearers were of any use. But then the rest of their procession would have to charge across the narrow bridge under a hail of arrows, musket fire, and cannon balls.

Hopefully, Lord Peng would have enough sense not to try. No, the fate of this mission rested on her ability to neutralize Lord Tong himself. As the Founder said, cut off the head, and surely, the demon would die.

The sunlight dimmed as they passed into the gatehouse.

Doors slammed shut in the front and back. All went dark, so dark even Jie's elven vision did not take over. Lord Peng cursed, while daggers rasped from sheathes. Hidden among the commotion, several men with large lung capacities high in the rafters whispered in barely intelligible Arkothi. One word stood out though.

Moquan.

Jie reached for her sword.

Glass shattered inside of the palanquin and outside. A musky scent percolated in the tight confines. Deer antler velvet, used in Black Lotus toxins to target females. Jie covered her nose.

Still, too late. With that one whiff, her head would begin to spin any second now.

The shouts of men, echoing so loudly just seconds before, subsided.

All went black.

CHAPTER 37
Unmistaken Identities

Jie's head and shoulders ached as slippered feet brushing across wood floors nudged her out of sleep.

That muted musk smell lingered on her...someone must have used a *Moquan* contact toxin, and of course, it would blot out some of her memories. What had she been doing? Right, going to Wailian Castle to capture Lord Tong. They'd been ambushed, but beyond that...

Feigning unconsciousness, she took stock of her situation. A rope made from smooth fibers bound her wrists above her head. She was completely naked, her hair askew. Her captors must've suspended her from something above, but in their foolishness, they let her toes touch the hardwood floors. A fountain rustled somewhere behind her; she would have never heard the footsteps over the gurgling water if they hadn't been so close.

She opened one eye a fraction. Torture devices of all types lay neatly arranged on a bloodwood table in front of her. Chains and ropes hung from the ceiling. A sturdy blockwood saltire cross with manacles rested against a wall in front of her. Whoever her captors were, they'd soon learn that no amount of pain would get her to reveal sensitive information.

Wait. She studied the table. The flaying blade and hot poker made sense, but since when did torturers use feathered whips and paddles? This was no torture chamber. It was some deviant's playroom. What Feng Mi had said about Lord Tong's Floating World habits left little doubt as to the identity of said deviant.

How had she gotten here? She searched her scrambled memory. They'd crossed the bridge, entered the gatehouse, and then...

Nothing. Curses! Whatever had happened, they must have failed. And now...

A whip cracked into her back, sending a wave of pain through her. She bit her lip and tensed up. The sick turtle egg wouldn't hear her scream— wait, she was supposed to be Princess Kaiya. She faked a whimper. Maybe it wasn't entirely fake.

A man came around to her front, whip slapping in his palm. Black hair streaked with white framed a mask that covered his entire face. A paunch poked out from his green robes. "Welcome to Wailian Castle, Princess Kaiya. Since this is how you will spend most of your time here, I felt you should get acquainted with your matrimonial duties."

Blinking away sham tears, Jie looked up at him. At least for now, he believed the ruse. "As you command, Lord Tong."

"Good girl. Now tell me, why did the *Tianzi* send a bride with an escort of a thousand men? If I didn't know any better, I would think my father-in-law-to-be planned to attack."

"Please, My Lord, we aren't married yet. Please cover me." She teetered back, exposing only her side. Baiting him. Once he came close...

"Answer me first." He drew the whip across her belly.

Yelping at the searing pain, she shook her head. "I don't know much of military matters, *Jue-ye*, but my father said I would need protection as I travelled through Fengshan Province." Tell him what he wanted to hear, address him with a title reserved for *Tai-Ming*, and maybe he'd believe the *Tianzi* had incorporated the new province and promoted Tong. If he let his guard down, he might come within leg's reach. Her muscles tensed, not from the pain, but in anticipation.

"And why did we find so many weapons on you and in your palanquin?" He stepped forward and ran a finger up the inside of her thigh.

Grabbing the rope, Jie jumped and pulled herself skyward, then twisted behind Lord Tong. She wrapped her right leg around his neck and hooked the left knee around her right ankle. Arching back, she took advantage of the new slack in the rope and pushed his head forward in the modified leg choke. He clawed at her shins, gasping for air.

Four, three, two, one. He went limp. When he crumpled to the ground, Jie lowered herself, feet firmly on his unconscious form. Reaching with a leg, she seized a flaying blade between her toes. Thank the Heavens—or rather, *Moquan* training—for flexibility.

A rope dart zipped in from behind her. It wrapped around her ankle and yanked the blade loose before she could cut through her bindings. She contorted to find a large Hua boy holding the other end of the line.

Behind her, clapping carried over the fountain's bubbling. "Very good," said a gravelly voice...

That voice, where had she heard it before? The palanquin stopping in front of the bridge and Pig Nose Qiu flashed in her memory. She twisted again to see the man from the bridge with the round, flat face. "The real Lord Tong, I presume?"

He grinned and nodded with a haughty bow. "*Not* Princess Kaiya, I presume?" He gestured to the unconscious man. "I was not about to risk myself, not when my informants told me about a decoy."

So he knew about the decoy. And he had an informant. Still, maybe the pretense might work. Chin down, she shook her head.

"Don't insult my intelligence. Look." In his hand, the magic bauble dangled from her garrote. "I wouldn't imagine Princess Kaiya to have so many scars. Really, it looks like you belong in this room, and you are much more exotic than any girl I have ever seen."

To be appreciated by a handsome Tarkothi prince was one thing; a hideous traitor another. She sucked on her lower lip.

"Kill her, Your Lordship," said the boy in heavily accented Hua. "She is too dangerous to leave alive."

Lord Tong waved him off. "I will hold my own counsel on this, Bovyan."

Bovyan? The brutish ruling race of the Teleri Empire? It would make sense, given what the altivorc in the palace had said about an agreement between Lord Tong and the Teleri.

Still, this boy looked too small, and his features were undeniably Hua. The Bovyan race, the cursed descendants of the Arkothi Sun God's mortal son, usually grew even larger, easily a head above the average human male, with fair skin. Tong must be mistaken.

"So, let me guess the *Tianzi's* plan." Lord Tong steeped his hands beneath his chin. "After I refused to go to Huajing, he sent you here to kill me. He'd then send his armies into this castle. No, you don't have to answer."

Jie sucked on her lower lip. What could she say? At each turn, Lord Tong was a step ahead of the *Tianzi's* plans.

He twirled the magic bauble on the cord. "Thanks to this, I know the girl we captured earlier really is Princess Kaiya."

It couldn't be true. She'd last seen Princess Kaiya in the alleys of Sun-Moon Palace, while learning to imitate her voice. Far away, in the capital. "You lie."

"Not as much as you. She's not as pretty as this makes her look. I'm quite disappointed."

So it was true. Jie hung her head. In everything, she had failed. She'd almost be happy for Tian to see her failure, if that meant being able to see him again.

He gestured to the Bovyan. "Keep an eye on her. Make sure nothing is in reach." He pointed to the wood cross. "I want her to have a good view of the real princess when I take her. Then, I'll brand her to show her father—if he survives the attack on the prince's wedding"

Cradling Su's head in her lap, Kaiya hummed a lullaby while trying to ignore his labored, dying breaths. Time dragged between each shorter inhalation. Tears welled in her eyes. She should have never come with the wedding procession, should have just stayed in the safe confines of Sun-Moon Palace. Dear Kai-Wu would be getting married tonight, and she'd miss it.

And for what? She was stuck in an old mine, with at least one boy who wanted to take her virginity, and apparently no chance of singing Lord Tong into surrender. How foolish she'd been, to think she would ever be more than a political tool.

She reached down and clasped Su's hand. His cold fingers stung hers, and she almost pulled back. His lips were pallid. She shook him. "Wake up, Su. Wake up."

His friend shook his head. A tear slid down his cheek and plopped onto the rough-hewn floors.

Kaiya's chest tightened, and her shoulders heaved. No, she couldn't cry. Not when all these boys saw her as an imperial princess. Sniffling, she straightened her spine and squared her shoulders.

The metal door swung open. She turned to see. To berate whatever guard came in, for letting a boy die. Her heart leapt into her throat.

Chen Xin, Zhao Yue, Li Wei, Ma Jun, and Xu Zhan spilled in, their faces bruised and their blue robes torn in places, their magic breastplates taken. Oh Heavens, if they were prisoners, it meant that the decoy—Hardeep—had failed.

She gently laid Su's head on the ground and stood. "Guards."

Their eyes widened in unison. It would have been funny if not for the grave circumstances. Immediately, they sank to their knee, fist to the ground. "*Dian-xia*," they shouted.

"It's true!" one boy said.

"She *is* the princess." Another could barely speak.

"She saved us."

The boys dropped to their knees and pressed their foreheads to the ground.

She certainly didn't feel like a princess. Wearing just a ripped-up inner gown, her shins exposed when she took off the shorn sleeves of her outer gown. "Rise. You knew me as Wang, and so it shall be now." She turned to Chen Xin. "What happened?"

"*Dian-xia*," he said. "Why are you here?"

Why indeed. The truth would make her look even more stupid than she felt. She shook her head. "It doesn't matter. Tell me, what happened?"

He sighed. "Lord Tong knew our plan. He separated us from the rest of the procession, and then ambushed us in the gatehouse."

"And Hardeep?"

Chen Xin cocked his head. "The foreign prince?"

She nodded. "Wasn't he my decoy?"

"No," he said, shaking his head. "It was...it was...Deputy Yan's daughter."

Now it was *her* turn to stare at *him* incredulously. "That strange minister?"

Chen Xin nodded. "She helped us track you down the night you went missing."

A reminder of yet another stupid choice. She swept her gaze over the guards. "And Kai-Long—I mean, Lord Peng?"

They exchanged glances and shrugged.

Ma Jun said, "We were fighting with our knives, in the dark. It was almost as if our opponents could see, even when we couldn't. When they subdued us and opened the doors, Lord Peng, his aide, and—"

The door creaked open again.

Two enemy soldiers thrust a man dressed in the colors of Kai-Long's Nanling Province in. He stumbled face-first into the ground. The imperial guards flipped him over.

"The aide." Xu Zhan pointed to the markings on the man's collar and then looked up at her.

Kaiya nudged the guards to the side and studied the unmoving man's face. Bronze, not honey-toned like the Hua; a high-bridged nose.

No, it couldn't be.

Heavens...Prince Hardeep. She patted her hands over him, checking for injuries. He had no visible wounds, but he didn't look to be breathing. She leaned over and pressed her ear to his heart.

Nothing. Her own heart might have stopped. No, they wouldn't have brought him here if he were dead. She closed her eyes.

Something pulsated. Slow, resolute, like waves pounding against a sea wall.

She let out a long sigh and looked up at her men. "How did you not recognize him as the Ankiran Prince?"

The guards exchanged shrugs. Li Wei said, "He wore a helmet the whole time, and never left Lord Peng's side."

And now, not even his Paladin skills could save him from the trap. This was her fault, too. Doubting her progress in musical magic, Hardeep had likely made a deal with Father. Join in the attack on Wailian Castle in return for Hua helping to repel the Madurans. Despondent, she hummed again, imitating the lute song he'd taught her.

He blinked several times and focused on her. "Princess Kaiya! What are you doing here?"

Heat flushed in her cheeks. Looking around, hoping no one spoke Ayuri, she said, "I had hoped to use the lessons you taught me. I wanted to sing Lord Tong into submission. I don't think he'll see me. I'm so sorry."

His hair swept through the dirt as he shook his head. "There is nothing to apologize for. When Lord Peng told me of his plan, I volunteered to help, to vanquish Lord Tong so that you would not have to marry him. I came for you."

She'd been wrong. He hadn't made a deal. Tears threatened to blur her vision. Oh, to be able to thank him with the only thing she could give. Cradling his head, she leaned in, eyes closed, lips parted. Who cared if her men saw? Her first kiss, maybe her only kiss, would belong to him. None of the guards moved to intervene.

The door groaned open again. His head snapped in the direction of the sound, just before their lips met.

No! Kaiya looked up to see who'd interrupted them now.

Eight soldiers, including the leader who'd captured them, stood by the doors.

"Princess Kaiya," the leader said. "Lord Tong will see you now."

One of the soldiers stepped in and seized her arm.

The imperial guards leaped to their feet, ready to intervene, even without weapons. Throwing their lives away, for her. The boys, too, all pushed forward.

Kaiya raised a hand. "Stand down. I will meet with Lord Tong."

Her guards hesitated, yet their every muscle twitched.

Hardeep staggered up. He stomped a foot on the ground. "Stop." His voice echoed in the cavern, the vibration shaking in Kaiya's core.

Around her, everyone froze in place.

He looked from guard to guard, then to the boys. "There is no need for anyone to die. Trust your princess."

He had spoken in Ayuri, but the imperial guards and the boys all shrank back. The tension in their postures melted.

Kaiya exchanged a smile with Prince Hardeep. "Thank you. I will end this war now." She walked out of the prison surrounded by traitors. If only she felt as confident as she let on.

They marched her out of the tunnels, and she gulped the fresh air. No matter what happened, at least it would happen above ground. Through the yard, they headed to the five-story main keep. After passing through yet another gatehouse, they arrived in the inner bailey. Servants opened the double doors.

The nightingale floorboards chirped under her tattered slippers. The sound was meant to deter spies, but right now gave her comfort. It was also a rhythm that she might be able to borrow. Another set of double doors slid open, revealing an audience chamber.

Two men guided her into the room, where she was greeted by the scrutiny of several important-looking warriors. At their head sat a middle-aged man with a round face and flat nose. A flabby paunch poked out from under his green robes. Failing to sing him into surrender would mean enduring him, acting out the pictures of the pillow book. Her shudder was interrupted when he reached down and placed a musical instrument on his lap.

The Dragon Scale Lute.

His goons must've recovered it while Hardeep was trying to protect her.

A grin formed on his lips. When he spoke, it sounded like rocks rattling in a sack. "Do you like it?"

Her eyes must have betrayed her.

"Of course you do, since you stole it." He looked past her. "Isn't that right, Little Li?"

Kaiya followed his eyes.

Wringing his delicate hands, Chamberlain Li met her gaze before averting his eyes to the floor. With his powdered face, he was as pretty as he'd been back in Huajing. "Yes, *Jue-ye*."

Lord Tong grinned. "Ever since receiving the instrument that could repel Avarax, I've tried many different types of strings and searched for a true Dragon Singer to play it."

Kaiya lifted her chin. "I'll never play it for you."

His gravelly laugh sent a shudder down her spine. "Foolish girl. You can't. Only a Dragon Singer. Which I happen to have." He nodded toward Chamberlain Li.

Just as she had feared. Was that why he'd been practicing with a lute that night? Kaiya gawked.

The uncertainty on Li's face shifted as he tightened his lips and straightened. He made a tentative bow.

"Taught by the elf lord Xu, no less." Lord Tong sighed as he patted the Dragon Scale Lute. "Yet it seems I rushed him here for nothing. The lute's magic is gone."

Kaiya's head spun, even as her chest ached. Chamberlain Li was a Dragon Singer? Taught by Lord Xu? All her dreams of proving her worth by reviving the dead art melted. Lord Tong had brought the Lute here, probably to use on the imperial troops, but now it seemed she'd used the last bit of its magic in the Temple of Heaven.

With a feral grin, Lord Tong gestured toward a cushion in front of him. "Now, *Dian-xia*, sit."

Brushing her shredded inner dress to her shins—well, the hem didn't reach that far anymore—she knelt. "Lord Tong—"

"Master. You may call me Master."

His men chuckled. Heat flared in her cheeks. Not like they were even married yet. She opened her mouth to protest.

"We will be wed at midday, before your brother's wedding. I will marry into the Wang family and invest my ancestral tablet into your family temple."

In less than two hours. Why so urgent? And why would a powerful lord wish to forsake his ancestors and take on his wife's name? She raised an eyebrow.

"You are wondering about the immediacy, wondering why. Before your brother speaks his vows before Heaven, my allies will slaughter him, the Crown Prince, the *Tianzi*, your paternal uncle and his sons. The old Lord Peng and his heir are dead, and the current Lord Peng is in my custody. All heirs to the Jade Throne will be dead, leaving only you, a girl, with imperial blood."

Kaiya's head spun. How could this even be possible?

He grinned "You will obey me. Otherwise, your men will die. The imperial expeditionary army is trapped, and functioning Dragon Scale Lute or not, we will crush them."

Her blood ran cold. Not because of his threat, but because his finger rested on one of the lute strings.

Her shoulders froze; her heart hurt so badly it must have stopped. If he strummed...

He did. The finger flicked across the string.

The sound came out flat, lifeless, even duller than a regular musical instrument. How could that be? When she'd played, its song had radiated out in eerie desolation and sent warriors into a panic. Now, it merely vibrated, perhaps only loud enough for her keen ears to pick up. It was true, its magic had been depleted.

He grinned so the edge of his lips nearly touched the flabby crinkles in the corner of his eyes.

Straightening her spine, tilting her chin, she locked gazes with him. The lute string still buzzed, lending her strength she didn't have on her own. Like the interplay of her music teachers' duet, she'd merge the lute's frequency with Lord Tong's heartbeat.

Rooted to the ground, your spine aligned, let your heart impel your voice. Listening for Lord Tong's pulse, she rose and gripped her feet to the floor. Where was his pulse? In this room, with poor acoustics, it hid among the other sounds. Still, she had to try, had to guess. She hummed to the frequency of the lute string.

His fingers quivered. His men rocked on their feet. It was working! The rebellion, put down by a girl! Chamberlain Li stared at her, wide eyed.

Her vitality guttered. Her already depleted spirit wavered, unable to sustain the hum. It began to crack.

Then her energy failed. Her knees buckled, and she dropped to the floor.

Lord Tong straightened. He lifted his chin to one of the soldiers. "Start the attack. Crush the imperials." He then turned to her. "Let me show you where you will be spending most of our married life."

CHAPTER 38

Explosive

While an attacking army had little chance of scaling the ravine walls to the castle walls, a single *Moquan* could do so with ease. At least, that's what Tian had thought at first. Exhausted from a whole night of riding, swimming, climbing, and jogging, he found the task more daunting once he started.

He'd chosen a sparsely patrolled west side of the castle, now shadowed in the early morning. Still, if anyone actually spotted him on the descent, he'd make for any easy target. Hand under hand, foot after foot, his fingers and toes ached. He glanced back at the castle several times, freezing at any flash of color on the battlements.

At the bottom, sixty-two *chi* below, he rested next to the churning rapids of a hundred-some-*chi* river. Boulders stuck out in places, but they lay too far apart to jump. Dark as twilight at the ravine's bottom, he had no sense of the depth while slogging across. Halfway through, the frigid waters only came to his waist.

Then his foot slipped on a slime-covered stone and he went under. The swirling current swept him at least a dozen *chi* before he clung on to a shrub growing between some rocks.

Gasping for air, freezing from the chill waters, he floundered across and heaved himself onto a cold boulder. Once he caught his breath, he stripped off his wet clothes and moved around to generate warmth. If an enemy arrow or freefall didn't claim him, hypothermia might. As he waited to regain a semblance of energy, he looked up at the daunting task ahead. The castle side of the ravine rose higher than the other, and then there was the climb up the walls to the battlements.

He shook his arms and legs to limber them up before starting the treacherous climb. His muscles screamed for every foothold and handgrip. His body seemed to weigh more than usual, demanding more of his knees, shoulders, and elbows as he struggled to find purchase on the ravine wall.

It was seventy-two *chi* to the top of the cliff, another twenty to the top of the castle's outer walls. With no signs of patrols, he slunk over the side and pressed up against the inside parapet. Supposedly, the half-sized Madaeri in the Eldaeri northeast thought of his last twelve grueling hours as *fun*. If he ever met one, he'd tell them just how insane they were.

Tian turned around and peeked over the parapet. From this vantage point, it appeared as if the entire complex was divided into three walled-off sections, with watchtowers at the intersections of the walls. The sole entrance stood at the center of the south wall, with a gatehouse leading into an outer bailey. In times of peace, the soldiers might drill there. Today, however, it was a deathtrap. The imperial army, or at least those who survived the charge across the bridge, would take fire from all sides before having to file through the second gatehouse.

In the northeast corner, protected in the inner bailey, stood the main keep. Green-tiled roofs demarked its five levels. Jie's palanquin had entered an hour and a half earlier, so by now, she had either neutralized Lord Tong or been captured. Or killed. His gut twisted. No, Jie didn't die easily.

Just below him was the main ward, stretching the length and breadth of the outer walls. Twenty-seven wooden buildings of varying sizes would provide cover while he searched for Jie. The banging of metal from one of the twelve stone structures suggested at least one smithy. Despite being six and a half times as large as the rest of the castle, this section was nearly abandoned at the moment.

He was about to climb down, when a squad of men in lamellar armor ran across the yard to meet another now coming out of a nearby wooden building. Tian ducked down below the parapet and listened.

"The girl who escaped is still unaccounted for," one solider said.

Jie, no doubt. If anyone could escape an ambush—

"Find her! She can't be more than ten," said another.

Too young to be Jie. The handmaiden, then. Which meant she was a Black Lotus member. Likely an initiate and not a full adept. If she were too young and inexperienced, she would be frightened and forget her training. But since they hadn't found her yet, she had probably found a way to blend in.

A good idea for himself, and the easiest way to hide in plain sight. And to keep warm. When the voices faded and the footsteps trailed away, he shimmied down the wall, jumping the last ten *chi* to save time. Landing lightly on his feet, he dashed to the closest building. He peered into an open window.

Sixteen cots lined both the east and west walls. At the fifth one from the right, a young man struggled with his lamellar tunic. A broadsword lay on his bedding. Tian leaped through the window, rolled across the floor, and landed on his feet just behind the hapless man. All without a sound. A very easy kill, which would save time looking for armor.

Hold the dragonfly with care. Princess Kaiya's voice prodded him from where she stood in Sun-Moon Castle, seventy-two *li* away and four thousand, twenty-three days in the past. Instead of breaking the soldier's neck, Tian stepped through the young man's knee and wrapped an arm around his throat.

The soldier struggled, hands flailing, but then fell limp. In linking motions, Tian shimmied the tunic off the man and lowered him onto the bed. He then shrugged the armor on, tightened the buckles, and retrieved a T-slot helmet and the broadsword. Not his preferred weapon, but it would have to do.

Now to find the *Moquan* girl. If she'd tried to infiltrate the castle, she would probably take the guise of a servant. Right now, those girls would be in the kitchens rolling rice balls or cutting strips for bandages. Leaving the barracks, he headed to the closest stone building.

Sure enough, inside, several women and girls gathered around a table, laughing and chatting as they pressed balls of rice in their hands. None of them seemed familiar. He made his way toward the castle, poking his head into kitchens and barracks.

Halfway to the inner bailey, he spotted a girl kneeling by a stone-lined circle, working a winch. A well, in all likelihood, though it must have gone at least seventy-two *chi* to reach the aquifers. Tian marched at an angle to get a look at her face. She kept her head down, and even turned in such a way that revealed less of her face as he passed. She was either shy, or...

Tian came up behind her and placed a hand on her shoulder. He'd started to tap a code when she seized his arm and twisted. He reeled toward the opening and would have careened down the well had he not had the sense to hook the edge with a foot and catch the winch with his free hand.

Still, she had superior leverage. She'd be able to send him over with a simple sweep of her leg.

"Black Water," he said. Hopefully, even in the heat of the moment, she'd recognize one of the many code words that allowed Black Lotus members to identify each other in disguise.

Her pressure relented. "Who are you?"

"Zheng Tian."

"Oh!" Eyes wide like cups, she helped him up.

Armor jangled from behind them, enough sound for two men. "What is going on there?" a gruff male voice called.

Tian spun and pressed a fist into his hand. "I tripped. Thank the Heavens. She saved me."

The taller of the two soldiers waved. "Well, get your water and hurry to your post. Lord Tong will order the attack soon."

Soon. Tian's guts knotted as he watched the two soldiers march toward the outer bailey. He turned to the cute girl. She looked familiar. Right, she'd come to the temple five years earlier... Feng Mi was her name, and he'd taught her the *Ghost Echo* technique. "What happened?"

"Lord Tong knew we were coming. Clan traitors helped ambush us in the first gatehouse, but I escaped."

"I don't think they're traitors. No, they're a new clan. Now what about Jie?"

Feng Mi shook her head. "They attacked her first, and she never even moved. From where I hid, I saw them take her, unconscious, into the main keep."

From where he'd watched on the bluff, he knew there had been at least seven more soldiers, plus the eight porters with Jie. "What about the others?"

"The imperial guards couldn't fight in the dark. Lord Peng surrendered and was escorted to the inner bailey. His aide escaped. He told me to find the princess, but I haven't seen him since."

"Which way...wait, the princess?"

Feng Mi shrugged. "I suppose he meant Jie. As for the guards, I overheard Lord Tong's men saying they were taken into the caves below."

Tian tapped his chin. "Where is the entrance to the caves?"

She pointed to the sluice gutters on the roofs. "I think they feed into the underground cisterns, and there might be an access point from this well." She leaned over and called into the hole.

Indeed, the echo sounded like there might be a side passage at the bottom. Still, "They took the guards in through the well?"

She shook her head. "There's an entrance near the second gatehouse, but it is guarded."

"The prisoners need water, too." He grinned.

"They were looking for me." Her shoulders slumped.

He patted her on the back. "You escaped. You gathered information. Now there are two of us. Come, let's find the—"

A horn sounded in a sequence of blares, two long, one short.

Tian tracked it to its source. The main keep. He looked to Feng Mi. "What was that?"

She frowned. "I haven't learned their signals yet."

A cannon boomed from the front walls. More blasts followed, eight in total. Then musket fire crackled. Muted yells and screams carried from Wailian Town.

He met her eyes. "Lord Tong has started the attack. We need to hurry, or the entire imperial procession will be destroyed."

Together, they jogged toward the outer bailey. At the rear gatehouse, she pointed to another stone-lined hole, this one wide enough for eight men to enter abreast. The two guards with swords and spears stepped aside to allow them to enter. After sixteen steps, the rough-hewn passage descended at a sixteen-and-a-quarter-degree incline, with columns supporting the cave every fifteen *chi*. The walls rocked with each cannon volley. Hopefully, the tunnels wouldn't cave in, at least not until they got out.

A hundred and forty-two paces in, they came to a metal door with a guard outside. He held a spear in one hand, while a broadsword and dagger hung on either side of his waist. In the narrow tunnel, it would be easy to get inside the arc of the spear. Still, there might be an easier way.

Rehearsing the line in his head, Tian pressed a fist into his palm. "Lord's orders. We are bringing water to the prisoners now. Before the fighting gets too intense."

The guard unlocked the door. It groaned open as he pushed it.

"Come on. Make sure the prisoners don't attack." Tian drew his sword and gestured for the guard to enter with him.

Inside, several expectant faces looked up, including a familiar imperial guard: Chen Xin, the one who'd played a minor role in Tian's banishment. Who knew if he'd recognize Tian eight years later?

No time to consider such a trivial matter. Yanking the enemy soldier's helmet off, Tian smashed the sword pommel into the back of his head. When he collapsed to the floor, Tian took his own helmet off. "Lord Tong has our troops surrounded. We need to neutralize the cannons. And open the gates." Not like five guards, one barely-conscious foreigner, eight porters, and twenty-seven boys, all unarmed, stood a chance.

Chen Xin raised a hand. "Our duty is to the princess."

Tian gawked at him. Surely, he knew Jie'd been a decoy.

"The real princess," Chen Xin hissed. "She's here. Not like you care about her."

Turtle's egg! Tian glared at him. Still, Princess Kaiya was *here*. His childhood friend, the girl who promised to marry him. His shoulders tensed. "You will never make it to the main keep."

"At least we can try," another of the guards said.

Tian pointed at Feng Mi. "She is the most equipped to try."

A particularly testy guard with flat knuckles growled. "Give me your sword."

Leave it to an imperial guard to think he was a better swordsman. It wasn't a fight worth contesting. Tian passed it over and pointed to the soldier he'd knocked out. "There's another sword, spear, and dagger—"

Two of the guards, one with a triangular head and the other with a scar on his chin, wrestled over the sword. Chen Xin glared at them, then let out an exasperated sigh and turned back to Tian.

"—plus two guards at the entrance to the tunnel. Feng Mi and I will take care of them and bring their weapons."

Chen Xin favored him with a tight expression. "You have three minutes. If we don't hear from you, we'll do it our way."

Such a desire to get themselves killed. Tian rolled his eyes. Beckoning Feng Mi, he said, "Approach in silence. I'll take the one on the right, you, the left. You have weapons?"

She nodded. Given her size, she'd have to use lethal force to neutralize her target. Who knew if her target had a family who would miss him?

Cannon bursts, musket shots, and repeater clicks volleyed in succession, all growing louder the closer they came to the mouth of the tunnel. Behind the two guards, he motioned for her to stop. Beyond them, soldiers ran into the gatehouse, carrying crossbow bolt bundles and rolling kegs of firepowder. None looked in their direction. Just before the next cannon volley, he jabbed a finger forward. He leaped behind his man, yanked off his helmet, and hook-punched him in the temple. For good measure, he continued with an elbow to the other side of the head. His victim collapsed, just as Feng Mi's did, blood spurting from his neck.

Taking ahold of both men's arms, Tian dragged them back into tunnel. Unsurprisingly, Chen Xin and the imperial guards were approaching the entrance.

Tian raked a gaze over them. "I told you to wait."

"I gave you three minutes." Chen Xin bent over and retrieved one of the swords.

Tian ground his teeth. "Most of Lord Tong's men are on the walls. Repeaters and muskets. Get in close. Their weapons lose their advantage."

Flat Knuckles grunted. "We are going to rescue the princess."

Tian's own knuckles must be white. He loosened a fist to point at the outer walls. "Loyal men are dying."

"You are right, but our first duty is to the princess." The youngest-looking guard pressed a fist into his hand.

Curse their sense of duty. Reversing the roles Tian had planned meant he'd storm the walls and fail; while the imperial guards would attack the main keep, and likely not make it past the gatehouse. There were two wild cards. "Feng Mi, go with the imperial guards. Find Jie— Wait." The only way he stood a chance of surviving the wall alone was to become a remorseless killer with singular focus and no fear. In short, *The Tiger's Eye*. Use it on me."

Eyes shifting from the already-running imperial guards back to him, Feng Mi's face blanched. "I...I am not good at it."

"You have to try." He stared at her hands.

With a sigh, her scowl hardened. She arranged her fingers in a web and then twisted them into a loop and hook. "Your mission is to take the wall."

Tian waited for a second. The technique's effect did not wash over him. Still, Feng Mi didn't know that. He flashed a hand signal, which she'd hopefully mistake for success.

With a smile, Feng Mi spun and took off after the imperial guards.

He turned and beckoned the twenty-three able-bodied young imperial soldiers, with two spears and three daggers among them. Wait. "Where is Lord Peng's aide?"

One of the boys thumbed back the way they'd come. "He couldn't move. He's with our own wounded."

Tian scanned the yard, where the imperial guards decimated the enemy soldiers carrying supplies. He pointed. "Scavenge a weapon. Follow me into the gatehouse. Once you are all inside, close the door. Don't let Lord Tong's men through. Now go."

He raced toward the gatehouse. The armed boys followed close behind. As long as they stayed in the gatehouse, they could cut off one of the supply lines and keep themselves relatively safe.

At the entrance, three men raced out. Stepping inside the arc of the first's swing, Tian seized his attacker's arm and twisted him into the chop of the second. Snatching the first's sword, he ducked under the hack of the third while slashing through his knee tendons. As he rose, he stabbed into the face of the second. He swept up a second sword and charged into the gatehouse.

Sunlight from the doors on the second level silhouetted soldiers now coming down stone steps. Tian engaged; bobbing, cutting, and sidestepping as he worked his way up. One, four, six enemies lay dead or incapacitated by the time he reached the second level. He yelled to the boys, "Hold the gatehouse."

On the top of the walls, he scanned the outer bailey. At the center, stone-filled glass jars surrounded three kegs, one open, exposing a black powder. A firepowder trap. It would rain glass shards and stones onto an invader as they tried to file through the second gatehouse bottleneck. Somewhere, there was a way to ignite the open barrel.

He looked up to the outer wall, about three hundred *chi* long, from where the castle defenders coordinated the deadly barrage on the imperial army. He poked his head back into the gatehouse, to find four of the boys right there. "Stay here. Don't come out. You'll get yourselves killed. And open the inside gate... Wait." He pulled the closest one out and pointed at the firepowder trap. "Roll the barrels to the inside gate of the first gatehouse. Put those glass jars between the barrels and the gate. Then find a way to light it. From a distance."

The boy ogled him. "But..."

"Just do it. For your comrades stuck outside the castle." Without waiting for an answer, Tian sprinted around the inner walls to the outer parapet. If he had been tired earlier, he was now functioning on nervous energy alone.

He emerged at the rear of the lines and attacked with broadswords in either hand. The first nine men with muskets and crossbows never had a chance; they either fell fumbling with their swords, or without knowing what hit them. Others took close shots at him, near enough for him to knock their muskets or crossbows off-line so the projectiles would hit their own men. Still, it was a sea of enemies. His two swords meant nothing, and his second wind began to wane.

He dared a glance over the outer walls. Imperial soldiers crowded the bridge below, caught between the defenders on the battlements and the ranks of enemies in the town, closing in around them. It was hopeless.

Then several of the boys joined in, following the path he'd blazed, their own swords and spears flashing. A cannon fired, and it was all he could do to get out of its way as it recoiled back on its two wheels. A musket barrel swept toward his head and he ducked, nearly ramming into the soldier cleaning the cannon muzzle, but coming to a pause with a crossbow in his face. He dropped to the floor just as the string twanged, and hacked at the wielder's legs. The musketman behind him grunted.

When he popped back up, they were loading the cannon. The gunner held a torch, ready to light the fuse once his crew of two pushed the artillery into position. Thwarting the cannon team meant protecting a dozen imperial soldiers in the town. Tian slashed at the pair, dropping them. Spinning out of the way of a barrage of bolts, he finished his twist beside the gunner. They stared at each other for a split second before Tian cut through him with both blades.

The cannon... Tian dropped his left sword and caught the torch as it slipped from the gunner's hand. He beckoned the boys. "Help me turn it!"

The gun balanced over the wheels, making it easy to rotate. Two of the boys pushed the barrel while Tian shoved the breech in the opposite direction. It now pointed along the battlements. Enemy soldiers screamed, gesticulated, and gawked.

"Clear!" Tian swept his sword back and forth, gesturing the boys to the side. He lit the fuse right near the barrel. The muzzle flashed, sending a ball into the crowd. The cannon recoiled, grazing Tian and knocking him down. His head slammed into the parapet. The world spun. A dozen men charged into him—or was it just one?

An explosion below rocked the front walls, sending his attacker—only one—lurching into him.

Jie's ears twitched as the walls of Lord Tong's playroom shook with each cannon volley. Between the booms and the staccato of musket fire, it sounded like there were eight cannons and over a hundred muskets. More importantly, she was underground, albeit close to the surface.

There was nothing saving the imperial army from total annihilation, unless she could find a way out. She fiddled with her bindings again. Getting out of the rope would be easy, except—

"Stay still," the Bovyan said.

Except him. He'd clung to the shadows, and besides the rope dart, there was no telling what other weapons and tools he had at his disposal on top of his *Moquan* skills.

Maybe the cursed Bovyan race's lustful streak could be used against him. Conjuring her most alluring pout, she twisted to the source of his voice; or maybe not, if he'd used a *Ghost Echo* to throw it. With little slack to work with in the rope, she widened her stance, arched her back, and exposed her rear.

He gulped, revealing his position to be just where she'd thought. If he got close enough...

A knife rasped out of its scabbard and he stepped into view. "I warned Lord Tong you were too dangerous to leave alive."

CHAPTER 39
Songs of Despair

Hands still bound above her, and with only her toes on the floor of Lord Tong's playroom, Jie had only seconds before the Bovyan gutted her.

Grabbing the rope, she sprung up into an inverted position and pulled herself hand over hand to the rafter. She hung there, upside down like a bat.

"Fool, you're still in my reach." He leaped after her, slashing toward her neck.

She flipped back down and pulled the rope into the path of his cut. His dagger shredded through the fibers, and she landed in a squat, one hand on the floor.

His snarl resembled the Black Lotus Temple dogs when they'd cornered a fox by the well. Get in his head and he'd make a mistake. She flashed him her most irrepressible smile and shrugged.

He growled and stabbed again, but she spun out of the way and snatched up the flaying blade from the table. With back and forth thrusts, she cut though the last of the bindings. Warmth rushed into her hands, sending tingles down her fingers.

She stuck her tongue out at him. "Can you defeat a naked girl with a shorter weapon?" Probably so, but she was probably twice his age and four times as experienced. "Though maybe your weapon isn't so long."

Dropping into an offensive stance, he twirled the dagger into an underhand grip. One on one, in these circumstances, she didn't stand a chance in a fair fight.

Which was why she wouldn't fight fair. With a *Mockingbird's Deception* to imitate Lord Tong, she used a *Ghost Echo* to throw her voice to the room's entrance behind her. "Bovyan! Look out behind you!"

He spun.

She darted in and slashed the tendons of his dagger hand. His fingers slackened and the weapon slipped from his grasp. She caught it in her other hand. As he gawped at his useless limb, she plunged the dagger into his gut and raked it through his intestines. With the other hand, she drove the flaying blade up under his ribcage.

Blood spurted from his liver. Gasping, crumpling to the floor, he tried to keep his insides from spilling out. He bowed his head. "It is my honor to be defeated by a better foe."

Enemy or not, he didn't deserve to suffer. Tian had always said as much. Darting in, she slashed his carotids with the flaying blade. Then she spun and ran. Behind her, his body thudded to the floor and his wheezes stopped.

The corridors appeared otherwise abandoned, though perishable food supplies lay in crates. She listened for the cannons, felt for breezes on her bare skin. The floors felt rough and cold beneath her feet. Then, something piquant caught her nose. Firepowder. Sniffing, she followed the scent through a few twists and turns. At last, she came to a room with dozens and dozens of barrels.

To think this escapade had started with Tian's suspicions. Here was the proof. Proof she was about to destroy, so as to turn the tide of what had to be a hopeless battle. Who knew how much damage it could do underground? Maybe Tian. By now, he probably would've calculated the volume of the cave and tunnel space, counted the kegs and estimated their combined blast pressure.

Definitely not her skillset. She cracked a few of them open with punches and kicks. With several back-and-forth rocks, she managed to heave one onto its side. Luckily, it didn't ignite and blow her to tiny bits. Following the breeze and sniffing for the fresh air, she rolled it down the corridor. The farther away she got from the arsenal and the closer to an exit, the better chance she'd have of surviving her plan.

Then, the last of the barrel's firepowder spilled out. Kneeling, she struck her blade against the stone floor in a shower of sparks.

The cannons boomed and musket fire crackled in the distance as Kaiya pressed her palms to the floor and tried to push herself up. With supreme effort, she brought a hip under herself. Trying to channel magic into her voice had left her limbs languid, her core as flaccid as egg custard, and her head muddled like heavy fog.

And she'd failed.

Now, loyal men died at the castle gates because of her vanity, her belief that she could sing Lord Tong into submission. Instead, he devoured her with his eyes, his pig face contorted into a feral expression reminiscent of a wild boar about to feast on truffles.

His cushion hissed as he rose from the gaudy chair and set the Dragon Scale Lute onto the seat. He knelt down beside her. "What's wrong, my slave? No magic on your lips?"

She gawked at him. How did he know?

He placed two fingers under her chin and lifted it. "Of course Little Li and my spy both told me about your efforts."

Spy...no wonder he knew about the music. About the trap.

"I am just glad you didn't give yourself to that foreigner. I will be your first. Your only." He withdrew his hand. "Now, kneel before me. Show me you have at least a remote semblance of grace."

No. No matter her shortcomings, she still had her dignity. She glared up at him.

He clucked his tongue. "My, my, you do have some spirit, after all. I will have to break you of that. Now kneel, and maybe, just maybe if you are fast enough, I'll spare the foreigner."

Kaiya's chest scrunched. She brought her knees up under her.

"Avert your gaze. You will not make eye contact with your master."

All the better to hide the tear forming in her eye.

"Now, kowtow before me."

She shook her head. An imperial princess could only show such complete submission to the *Tianzi* himself.

"Hurry, and I will call off the attack. Think of the lives you will save."

What choice was there? He held all the leverage. She pressed her forehead to the floor, completely defeated by this vile traitor. To think he'd use marriage to establish a legitimate claim to the Jade Throne. Tears trickled down her cheeks and plopped onto the floor.

He snapped his fingers and one of his men shuffled over, then waddled back. Kneeling over, the closeness of his large body muffled the sounds around him. His breath tickled her ear. "I am your master now." Something cold and smooth wrapped around her neck. It tugged and twisted at her nape.

A collar?

"You belong to me." He stood and laughed; a taunting chortle, reducing her to something small and insignificant. How mortifying.

But maybe there was a chance. Head still to the ground, Kaiya eased open the fingers of her tightly balled fist, forced her tired legs to relax. Every nerve fiber tingled. Ready to spring.

"Now," he said. "Your decoy is an exotic little treat. A true beauty compared to you. You will watch me do to her what I will do to you. Come."

His feet treaded past her.

He was making it easy! She leaped forward towards his chair.

"Foolish girl," he said. The collar around her neck wrenched her to a stop. He gave it a tug and she stumbled backward onto the floor. "Apparently you aren't so compliant after all. Captain Zhu, go to the dungeons and cut out the foreigner's right eye."

No! What had she done? Tearing at the collar, she scuttled back from him, toward the Lute. The soldier marched toward the doors.

An explosion rumbled from somewhere not far in the distance, rattling the walls.

Lord Tong yanked the leash again, forcing her to her feet and nearly twisting her fingers. With another jerk, she staggered toward him.

A second blast swelled out from near the front of the main keep, underground. The floors quavered and rocked. Lord Tong slipped, and she bowled into him. They tumbled to the floor, with her landing on top of him. Rafters above cracked and splintered.

Ears ringing, she set a hand down to the floor to push herself back up, but found his dagger instead. Pulling it from its sheath, she cut the hand that held the leash. He grunted and let go, and she snatched up the frayed end and backed up. The soldiers closed in around her. She spun and ran the last four steps to the chair. Her hands wrapped around the Dragon Scale Lute, which, like before, seemed to throb with heat. She placed her fingers over its strings. Perhaps she could coax the last of its energy out.

Lord Tong lumbered to his feet. "Go ahead. It is a useless piece of junk. I regret wasting the resources to bring it here. If you even try it, I'll have your foreigner tortured before your eyes."

Her hand froze. What if it didn't work? Hardeep would suffer even more. No, Lord Tong couldn't be trusted to keep his word. Chamberlain

Li huddled in the corner, a look of horror on his face as he stared at the instrument.

She strummed out a few notes. Just as when Lord Tong had plucked it earlier, only a barely audible sound came out.

He shrugged. "I told you so."

In the corner, Li's posture relaxed as he blew out a breath.

"Now," Lord Tong said, "I will have to deliver on my promise. Guards, go stop Captain Zhu, so my bitch can watch her lover lose an eye. Then his fingers, one by one. Then his skin. I'll have the tanners turn his brown flesh into a suit of armor for her."

Her stomach roiled. Her failure was complete, and Hardeep would die an agonizing death because of it. To think she'd resented her fate as a political tool; now she was a rebel's pet, his means for gaining power. This was the most dismal moment of her life.

Her eyes strayed to the dagger, blurry through her tears, which she'd left in the chair. One last choice. Die here, and Lord Tong would have no reason to harm Hardeep. He'd lose his tool for gaining the throne. All it would take is a stab to the—

Let your heart impel your voice. The words of the book sounded suspiciously like Hardeep's voice in her head.

Of course, Lord Tong had plucked the string while gloating. When she had used the Dragon Scale Lute before, it had been under times of duress or fear. Guilt-ridden for strong-arming Chamberlain Li. Scared of assassins. Worried about trespassing in the Temple of Heaven.

And now, resolved to end her life. His attention on the knife, Lord Tong took a step toward her.

She thrummed out a chord. The bass strings keened like a beast led to slaughter. The treble notes wailed like a mother mourning her dead baby.

Lord Tong's next step faltered. The fingers of his hand, outreached to do something horrible to her, slackened. Then, his rounded eyes squinted.

Maybe it wouldn't work. He didn't care for music, beyond its potential power.

Unlike her, who reveled in music and had received a lesson from the mysterious Lord Xu. *It is not the strength of the pluck that matters, but the intensity of your emotion,* the elf had said. *Only the power of your intent can compel the sound beyond its physical limitations.*

Gripping the floor with her toes, straightening her spine, Kaiya grasped her sense of hopelessness and despair and plucked out the few bars Hardeep had taught her. Beneath her fingers, the Lute emitted a chorus of screams, like horrified children fleeing Avarax's fiery breath.

Lord Tong stilled, his lips quivering. His breath rasped through his thick nose. Li cowered behind him, but his expression also betrayed an emotion she recognized too well in herself: disappointment in one's self.

Her next chords moaned like a man trapped beneath a collapsed building as Avarax descended. Stuck, unable to flee. Only able to watch.

Covering his ears, Lord Tong stumbled. His quavering men backed away. Then, they clawed at one another to reach the entrance first. Li disappeared with them.

She continued the song, with the change in pitch now moaning like souls rising from their graves on Ghost Day.

The power of the world coalesced through her, and again, her belly felt like hundreds of thousands of worms writhing over each other. Her energy flagged. The room spun around her, fading at the edges and closing into blackness.

CHAPTER 40
Sunset Over Wailian

Face to the sky, Jie's chest heaved as she took in deep breaths. She'd barely cleared the tunnel before the underground stores of firepowder exploded. With the rumbling fires giving chase, her bare feet scraping on the rough ground, a leap and forward roll saved her from the column of fire that belched from the hole. A few other bursts of flame spat out from other tunnel openings. Anyone in the caves would be incinerated.

Then, the eerie music had radiated from the main keep, like the collective wails of prisoners led to execution. Jie's heart rattled in her chest, and every nerve fiber screamed for her to flee. It felt just like the horrendous song from the Temple of Heaven two nights before.

Cannons and muskets fell silent, and even the yells of bloodlust quieted. She sat up and scanned the outer walls. Many of Lord Tong's men lay cowering on the battlements, even after the desolate music came to an abrupt end.

The main keep creaked and groaned. Jie sat up and twisted to see. The inner bailey's western walls now lay in rubble. The same side of the keep gaped open, with flames licking the interior walls. Men ran out, yelling and screaming.

Her bare skin prickled in the cool breeze and she stood up.

"To me, soldiers of Hua!" Lord Peng's voice cracked at first, and then settled into a tone of command. He marched out of the second gatehouse, broadsword pointed forward. How gallant he looked at the head of a small but growing band of imperial troops.

More yells drew her attention. Lord Tong, unmistakable with his pig nose, wandered out of the main keep. His pale face and distant stare might have belonged to a ghost. His shaking men groveled at his feet, but when he didn't respond, they pulled at his sleeves and begged him to take command.

At the inner bailey gatehouse, Salt-and-Pepper Chen Xin, Fox-Faced Zhao Yue, Lefty Li Wei, Boy-Faced Ma Jun, and Flat-Knuckle Xu Zhan were dispatching the handful of Tong's soldiers who kept a semblance of resistance. The imperial guards' fighting was deadly and efficient, beautiful to watch. Little Feng Mi slunk behind them, her hands trembling too much to be of use.

Out of disguise and with such distinct features, Jie's identity would be compromised. She hurried over to mingle with the people who already knew her. Feng Mi's eyes widened and she bent over to retrieve a cloak from a fallen man. She draped it over Jie's shoulders.

"Thank you." Jie pulled the hood over her head.

Feng Mi pointed. "Look."

Lord Peng's gait grew more resolute with each stride, his commanding presence rallying his men. They charged toward Lord Tong's soldiers, who dropped to their knees and placed their hands on their heads. Lord Tong himself just stood, staring blankly past his captors.

Lord Peng pushed past friend and foe alike. He took Lord Tong's hair and yanked it back. "For betraying the *Tianzi*, your punishment is death." He raised his sword.

Jie surged toward them, nearly tripping on the long cloak. "Wait! We need to find out his co-conspirators."

Too late. Lord Peng's sword chopped into Tong's neck, sending blood spraying. The body slumped to the ground.

The last holdouts fighting the imperial guards lowered their weapons. The imperial guards did, too. Perhaps it was better this way, to end hostilities as quickly as possible.

Peng beckoned to one of the soldiers. "Remove Tong's head, mount it on a spear, and parade it before his men. That will ensure their quick surrender."

The man pressed a fist into a palm. "As you command, *Jue-ye*."

Lord Peng gestured toward other imperial soldiers. "Form up and disarm Lord Tong's men. Spare the rank and file, but his senior retainers must be immediately executed to discourage future treason. Do not allow them any last words."

Chen Xin marched over, his comrades behind him. He gestured toward the burning castle. "Lord Peng, please spare some men to help us search for the princess."

Jie followed Lord Peng's gaze to the fires. "So Princess Kaiya joined the procession after all?"

Feng-Mi nodded. Lord Tong had been telling the truth about Princess Kaiya, and now she was likely trapped inside.

Shaking his head, Lord Peng put a hand on Chen Xin's shoulder. "No one could survive that. I cannot spare men on a futile mission. I do not command you, but I highly suggest you do not throw your life away."

Jie looked back at the fortress. Flames blazed on the outer walls. It would soon become a conflagration. Lord Peng was right. She turned to Feng Mi. "Why didn't you sneak in earlier instead of slinking behind the imperial guards?"

The girl stared at the ground. "I wanted to, with Zheng Tian, but the imperial—"

What? Jie put both hands on Feng Mi's shoulders, not caring if the cloak blew open. "Tian is here?"

Feng Mi nodded and pointed toward the outer walls. "The imperial guards insisted on saving the princess and left Tian to attack the outer defenses."

If that fool got himself killed, trying to take the walls all by himself... Jie tightened the cloak around her and dashed toward the outer bailey.

Punctuated by sharp twangs and a loud crack, timbers splintered and walls groaned in a song just as doleful as the one Kaiya had played on the Lute. Her body rocked to its rhythm.

No, someone was shaking her.

"Wake up!" The voice filled her.

Energy trickled into her limbs. Her eyes fluttered open. Blue irises encroached on her visual field, for the third time in as many days. Hardeep's soot-covered expression melted from concern to relief.

She bolted up into a sitting position. "Where are we?"

"Thank Surya." Hardeep smiled at her. His cape was gone, and his was armor singed. "We have to get out of here. The castle is burning."

No wonder it was so hot. With his help, she scrambled to her feet. "What about the Dragon Scale Lute?"

"Ruined." He pointed at the smashed resonator. The strings sprawled unwound in a tangled mess. Even the scale soundboard lay shattered from the center out, looking much like a spider web. "Ruined beyond repair."

She cast a last glance at the cinnabar-red scale, the instrument of a rebellion's undoing. Was a shard missing? "We should take what's left of the scale."

"No." He shook his head. "Leave it buried beneath the rubble. Now come."

She searched his eyes. Perhaps he was right. Better to leave it here, forgotten, lest it fall into the hands of someone with less-than-noble motives. She took the hand he extended.

Limping along, he guided her through the smoke-filled halls. The soot in her lungs forced out ragged coughs. Flames leaped from side passages. Burning beams crashed in their path. Each time, Hardeep with his Paladin skills pulled her out of harm's way. Still, her energy wavered.

"Up ahead!" He pointed to where the castle's entire outer wall had collapsed.

Behind them, more columns and beams cracked and fell. They didn't have much time.

Eyes dry and aching, throat singed, her energy guttered. She could never pick her way through this rubble. Her vision faded and her wobbling knees gave out. She would just hold him back. "Go...on. Save yourself."

He swept her up into his arms and staggered through the debris.

Pain shot through Tian's ribs as he pushed an unconscious man off of him. Limbs protesting, he sat up and looked.

Lord Tong's soldiers all knelt with hands on their heads. Seventeen of the boys under his charge stood among them, weapons at the ready. A path of bodies started from the intersecting walls of the outer bailey and ended at him. All these men whose lives he had taken, just because of some lord's greed and ambition. Imperial soldiers, some just boys, dead as well.

And for what? The realm was weaker for all the precious lives wasted.

"Tian!" Jie's voice rang from somewhere on the walls.

He turned to see the half-elf, clasping a cloak—and apparently, all she wore was a cloak—running among the bodies and kneeling men. Little Feng Mi trailed behind her.

Ignoring the searing pain in his ribs, Tian groaned to his feet.

Jie shot into him, wrapping her arms around him, and igniting a new surge of agony through him. "You fool. What did you think you were doing, attacking a wall by yourself?"

"I had help." Grimacing, he unwound her arms. He'd have to check to see if she'd picked his pockets later. "Uh. The boys are staring. You ought to find some clothes."

She stepped back and pouted. Behind her, Feng Mi giggled.

A loud crash drew his attention to the main keep. Flames wrapped around it like a torch head, consuming it. If anyone were still in there, they'd be ashes by evening.

He sucked in a sharp breath. The princess had been taken there. He looked at Feng Mi. "Did you find Princess Kaiya?"

Casting her gaze down, she shook her head in slow arcs.

Oh no. His first love. Once a dear friend, though they hadn't communicated in three thousand, one hundred and forty-nine days. A pit sank in his gut and his shoulders slumped.

Jie squeezed his hand.

"Look!" One of the boys pointed toward the main keep.

Tian spun.

A man emerged from the west side of the main keep, carrying...

Tian squinted. In the man's arms, he cradled a girl in a tattered dress.

Jie blew out a sigh. "Thank the Heavens. The princess. She is moving."

If only his vision were as sharp as a half-elf's! His hand tightened around Jie's. "Are you sure?"

She nodded. "No mistaking that acne-riddled face."

The man set the princess down. Her gangly legs wobbled. Had she always been so skinny? Tian had always remembered her as being graceful and beautiful as the weeping *danhua* tree in Sun-Moon Castle. He started toward the closest steps down.

Jie tugged. "No, you must not compromise your identity."

Tian's chest squeezed. Jie was right. After all this time, Princess Kaiya was a *biao's* heave away and she might never know he was there. Just like Jie and Feng Mi, his name would never appear in the histories of the Battle of Wailian Castle. Not that it mattered.

"Come," he said. "Let's go home."

CHAPTER 41
Enemies Far and Near

Peng Kai-Long stood atop the tallest watchtower, watching the sun set over the mineral-rich hills between Walian County and the Nothori Kingdom of Rotuvi. The foreigners had withdrawn their troops from the border, their deal with Lord Tong now moot.

Still, Hua was weak. No lord would have dared rebel against the throne just a decade ago. Foreign nations wouldn't have presumed to meddle in Hua's affairs. The *Tianzi*, so shrewd and decisive in his earlier years, had grown soft. The two princes would never command respect. It was up to Kai-Long to lead Hua back to greatness.

And Heaven must have smiled upon him for everything to work out the way it had. That, and Kai-Long's own ability to gauge the shift in winds. He looked down at the Hua chessboard, the pieces positioned where he'd last left off with his mysterious opponent. His new advisor, no less, who was late.

"Right cannon moves right three," a male voice came from the ceiling.

Kai-Long's soul must have jumped out of his body. He searched for the source.

The Water Snake clansman kicking his legs from the rafters appeared to be of middle age, his eyes so sunken his head might be mistaken for a skull. "Greetings, Lord Peng."

Kai-Long studied the spy. "We meet at last."

The man shook his head. When he spoke, it sounded like the voice of a particular serving girl in Sun-Moon Castle. "We've met. The night Miss Yi helped you smuggle Princess Kaiya out of the protection of the palace. That was me. I drugged her and took her place."

Kai-Long nodded in slow bobs. Yi was an expert liar, which is why he'd chosen her. It turned out, it hadn't been her at all. Still... "You made a mistake, leaving the illusion bauble where it could be found."

"Who said it was a mistake?" The clansman's shrugged and turned to the chess board. "This is the first time I have actually seen the board."

Boastful snake. Kai-Long was just two moves from finally winning. He shifted the piece over to where the man indicated, and then moved his own elephant up and over. "It has been interesting playing this game by messenger." Which had also been their means of coordinating through coded letters.

The man nodded. "Your strategy has been unpredictable."

"The Founder wrote that a good leader must ride in the winds like a kite."

The man grinned, his gaunt face now looking like the symbol of the Pirate Queen. "As did Lord Tong. Still, he failed. Games, unlike life, are played with rules."

Kai-Long scoffed. "Real life is about preparation." He should know. He kept every heir to the Dragon Throne ahead of him sterile through a simple toxin. With spies in the right place, he'd known about Lord Tong's plan for years, and used his company, Victorious Trading, to stockpile firepowder for when Tong made his move.

The man yawned. "And you certainly prepared. Would you have really helped Lord Tong?"

Kai-Long looked around, making sure no one was within earshot. "He kept up his end of the bargain by having my father and brother killed. Had the *Tianzi* sent the bulk of his armies here, as we had hoped, then I would have joined Lord Liang and led my own armies to attack the imperial rear, trapping them between the Great Wall and here. Just as I promised." Actually, he had planned to occupy the capital with the help of Lord Tong's allies in the South, but some things were better left secret, at least until this advisor earned unquestionable trust.

"And yet, you betrayed Tong. Why?"

"Once his allies abandoned the attack on Prince Kai-Wu's wedding, he had already lost." Fool that he was for keeping the princess' decoy alive, even after Kai-Long's warning. "He would have revealed all the conspirators."

The man shook his head. "No, earlier. Why push for marriage to Princess Kaiya instead of the original plan for encouraging a siege of Wailian Castle?"

Because it was a last-ditch effort to get her killed. "I didn't expect her to suggest marriage, for the *Tianzi* to approve it, or for her to show her worth." Though really, she was like a rat, surviving where she shouldn't have. First, on the night he'd smuggled her out of the castle into an ambush, where it could have been pinned on the Madurans targeting Prince Hardeep; and then when he told Tong to wipe out the supply brigade that he'd lured her into joining.

"I see. Well, as promised, the Water Snake Clan is at your service, though we must lay low until the Black Lotus clan forgets about us."

Kai-Long grinned. He was one of the privileged few to know that *Moquan* were more than just imaginary child snatchers. Furthermore, beside the *Tianzi* himself, he was now the only lord

to have them under his employ. "We will maintain contact through our normal channels."

"As you command, *Jue-ye*."

"What shall I call you?"

"My former comrades in the Black Lotus knew me as the Surgeon." The man melted into the shadows, but then his voice came from the general on the chessboard. "Chariot moves left three. Checkmate."

Flanked by an aide, Haros Bovyanthas marched toward his office in the Assembly Hall of Telesite to wait for the election's results. Because of his birth to a virgin, his promotion to First Consul of the Teleri Empire was a foregone conclusion. After all, the Keepers of the Shrine of Geros all believed the prophecies proclaiming that he would be the one to end the first of the three Bovyan curses.

He chuckled to himself. The prophecies hadn't kept his rivals in the *Directori* from assigning him to the inconsequential duty of administering relations with the kingdoms of the northwest. Until now, it didn't matter. Let them bumble over the futile invasion of Eldaeri lands. Brute force alone would not prevail, and that was all the Bovyans knew.

Except him. As a youth, he'd read the Cathayi Founder's work, *The Art of War*. Wang Xinchang was a warrior genius, even if his descendants were nothing more than petty merchant princes. Incorporating his strategies, Haros had used his position to cultivate relationships and turn his spheres of influence into profitable income streams and new tactical tools. How ironic that all of these would be turned against Cathay when the time was right.

Warriors all thumped their chests in salute as he passed. His steward opened his door and Haros walked in.

And gawked.

Sitting in *his* chair was the Altivorc King himself, with feet kicked up on *his* desk. Bedecked in a dapper uniform and crowned with a silver circlet, the King of the Orcs held a message addressed to Haros in his filthy paws.

"How did you get in here?" Haros jabbed a finger at the King.

The King lowered the missive and bared his fangs in a patronizing smile. "Now, now, Haros, there's no need to be rude."

Frowning, Haros turned back to the aide outside the door. "How did he get in here?"

The steward's mouth hung agape. So unsightly for a Bovyan. "I...I don't know. The door was closed from the time you visited the Shrine and the Conclave."

"I come, I go." Shrugging, the King flicked the paper over. "It looks like you have bigger problems than pest control, though."

Amazingly, the message flew in a straight line. Haros snatched it out of the air and skimmed it. He then looked back at the Altivorc King. "Everything proceeds as planned."

The Altivorc King lowered his feet and leaned forward on the table. "Lord Tong is dead. Without him, you can't influence Cathay."

Apparently, the thousand-year-old King wasn't as all-knowing as the legends proclaimed. Haros laughed. "Lord Tong would have never succeeded. My agreement with him was all a ploy to plant my operative in their country. Cathay will not be taken with the sword alone. It will take eight years to undermine them from within."

"How old are you now? Thirty?" The Altivorc King counted off on his fingers. "If the curse remains in place, you'll die in three years."

Haros crumpled up the message. "You were the one who identified my mother. You must know I will be the one to end the curse."

Boots clopped to a stop at the entrance. Haros turned to see the messenger, dressed in the robes of the Keepers of the Shrine of Geros.

He pounded a fist to his chest. "Your Eminence, congratulations. You have been elected First Consul."

Haros turned back to gloat. "You see—"

The Altivorc King was gone, the chair empty as if no one had been there.

With a snort, Haros turned back to the courier. "When is the Eye-plucking ceremony?"

"Tonight. Once you will receive the Eye of Solaris and Pin of Geros, you will formally take the name, Geros Bovyan, XLIII."

Haros dismissed the man with a wave of his hand, then covered his right eye. All the previous First Consuls claimed they could see through the Eye of Solaris. Then again, men were liars.

He lowered his hand. Losing an eye was worth the chance to become the greatest Bovyan since their progenitor, the mortal son of Solaris. He smoothed out the message and read it again.

Perhaps this Peng Kai-Long, who had captured the impregnable Wailian Castle, would prove to be a more worthy adversary than Cathay's emperor. Haros would have to tell his spy to keep close eye on this upstart lord.

In the meantime, while Haros plot to undermine Cathay simmered, it was time to turn his attention to the Eldaeri Kingdoms. His spy there had already gotten into Tarkothi Prince Aryn's good graces, and seeded discord between Tarkoth and Serikoth. Haros would succeed where his political adversaries had failed.

Humming *Whims of Fate* as he untangled the imperial stallion's mane, sixteen-year old Li Bin considered the strange twists and turns his life had made. Born to his town's most famous musician, who'd once entertained the *Tianzi*, he would've never expected to become Lord Tong's chamberlain and pillow boy. Now he'd managed to join the army, by mingling with the injured imperial troops in the aftermath of Wailian Castle. He'd since been reassigned as a groom in Sun-Moon Palace.

"*Dian-xia.*" The pretty face of Lady Lin Ziqiu peeked around the horse and flashed a radiant smile. "Oh, Li Bin, it's you."

Li Bin swallowed hard and looked down at his feet. A niece of the *Tianzi*, Lin Ziqiu was beautiful, even in riding clothes. Indeed, with the exception of Princess Kaiya, every imperial family member and close relative was good-looking.

He bowed and stammered, "My Lady."

"Have you seen Princess Kaiya? I am supposed to go riding with her." She extended a hand.

"No, my Lady." Li Bin shook his head. He proffered the reins.

"Thank you." Her hands felt surprisingly rough and calloused for a noblewoman's.

He hazarded a glance up to find her studying him. Lines creased her brow. He jerked his head down.

"If you see Princess Kaiya, please tell her I am at the cavalry field."

"Yes, my Lady," Li Bin lied. He was good at it.

Good enough to trick Lord Tong into believing he had the skill to play the Dragon Scale Lute—which was why he'd happily acquiesced when Princess Kaiya had demanded it that night. He might be a talented musician, but he was no Dragon Singer. He'd known when the elf had given up teaching him.

"You know, you have a beautiful voice." Ziqiu giggled. As she led the horse out, he held a low bow.

Then his gut clenched.

Princess Kaiya would arrive any moment to get her horse. If she were alone, he might be able to take vengeance. For her role in the death of Lord Tong. For realizing *his* dreams of reviving Dragon Songs.

But no, a complement of imperial guards always accompanied her. And, even without all the makeup Lord Tong had insisted he wear, she might recognize him through the dirt on his face.

It would be better to hide now, and bide his time for a better chance.

EPILOGUE
Diverging Paths

Jie found Tian in the corner of her eye as they walked along the docks of Jiangkou Harbor. Two weeks had passed since the Battle of Wailian Castle and the foiled attack on Prince Kai-Wu's wedding. Plots uncovered by Tian and her, respectively. While Lord Peng received the accolades for his improbable victory, in Black Lotus fashion, she and Tian headed to receive their rewards.

"Here's my steed." Jie jerked her head at the Tarkothi ship *Indomitable*, where sailors prepared for departure. It was far easier to watch them work than to make eye contact with him. Her heart might have been a rock in her chest, if a rock weighed more than a dwarven anvil.

Tian turned and looked up at the hulking black ship. "Make sure Prince Aryn keeps his hands off of you."

She grinned. "What if I want to put my hands on him?"

Tian's expression betrayed neither concern nor jealousy. "As long as it doesn't cloud your objectivity."

Was that it? Jie sucked on her bottom lip before letting it go with a pop.

Tian's face hardened. "I should be going with you."

While she might appreciate the sentiment, "As the Founder said, *Never send a man to do a woman's job.*"

"Did he say that?" He cocked his head.

Jie giggled. "No, that's *my* proverb. Will you miss me?"

"I will always miss my little sister. Just be careful. You are going into a foreign land and you barely speak the language."

Jie's chest squeezed. Still the little sister. "I will have at least a month immersed with the Eldaeri sailors. I'm sure my Arkothi will be fine by the end." If *fine* meant laden with chauvinism and curse words.

His eyes and mouth made perfect circles. Perhaps he was thinking the same thing. The surprise melted and he started turning toward his own berth on the *Wild Orchid*.

She tugged at Tian's official robes to take out some of the wrinkles. "You need to make a good first impression, Junior Clerk Zheng. See you in a few years."

While she was off tracking the Water Snake Clan to its source in Arkothi lands, what kind of man would he grow into? And when they met again after those few years, her body still wouldn't have matured into a woman's.

Tian cast a surreptitious glance back at Jie as she headed up the dock to the *Indomitable*. She was just a girl, all alone with a bunch of sailors.

Then, she'd go on a lonely, deep reconnaissance mission into Serikoth and the Teleri Empire itself.

Perhaps they were chasing their tails. In the end, Master Yan had only been able to uncover two *Yu-Ming* lords conspiring in the failed attack on Prince Kai-Wu's wedding, and none of the foreigners Jie suspected even attended: the altivorcs had wandered into restricted areas of the palace and been expelled the night before the wedding. No Golden Scorpion ever surfaced. With Lord Tong dead, they hadn't been able to confirm any of the alliances he'd established, either foreign or domestic.

The only reliable leads were the large boys of the Water Snake Clan, who Lord Tong had referred to as Bovyan. Never mind that the ruling race of the Teleri Empire were huge and fair-skinned. Still, the Teleri's vassals in Rotuvi had threatened the imperial army in the North, preventing General Lu from helping in the siege of Wailian Castle. It couldn't be just a coincidence.

Which was why Tian was now headed for a new position as a trade official in the Kingdom of Iksuvi. In reality, he would serve as head of information in the Northori Northwest, as a reward for his uncovering of Lord Tong's plot. Farther than ever from Princess Kaiya.

Kaiya listened to the songbirds warbling outside the Hall of Bountiful Harvests, her hands trembling. This was where her unlikely adventure had begun when she first greeted Prince Hardeep.

Here too, it would end. Father had allowed one last meeting with Prince Hardeep, a reward for her role in subduing the North and for his in saving her.

Servants opened the doors. Chen Xin and Ma Jun snapped into a salute.

Secretary Hong bowed and extended a hand inviting her to enter. "The *Tianzi* will allow you to meet Prince Hardeep alone."

Alone. She smoothed out her court gown. If only she had a mirror. She'd spent hours preening, in hopes of giving Prince Hardeep a perfect last memory of her. Taking a deep breath, she stepped over the high threshold.

Prince Hardeep pressed his palms together and bowed his head. Dressed in a ceremonial *kurta*, he looked so handsome. So perfect. It was hard to imagine that just two weeks before, as he carried her out of the burning castle, his face had been covered in soot. Even then, his hair never seemed out of place. He looked up and smiled at her.

Her heart fluttered. How could she have ever suspected he might be a Maduran Golden Scorpion, using foul magic to influence her? In retrospect, her own insecurities had planted seeds of doubts over his noble intentions, when all he'd done was encourage her to act on her morals.

"Princess Kaiya, thank you for seeing me off."

He made it sound so...trivial. A simple parting, after everything they'd been through. She bowed her head. "It is my honor to do so. I am sorry I could not do anything for your homeland. The treaty with Madura remains in place for one more year, and the remains of the Dragon Scale Lute are buried beneath Wailian Castle." Not that Father would allow her to go to Ankira, anyway.

He shook his head. "It doesn't matter. You have given me something more precious. Hope."

Tears threatened to ruin her make-up.

"Will you sing for me? As a memory of our meeting."

An audacious request under normal circumstances, but there was nothing normal about the two of them. He had guided her to the power of Dragon Songs, made her find her purpose beyond political marriage. She cast a glance out of the Hall, where her guards and Secretary Hong stood. Who cared what they thought? She owed Hardeep this courtesy. "I've put words to your lute song."

His eyebrow lifted and his lips quirked into a smile. She'd spent the last two weeks composing the lyrics. Toes gripping the floor, spine straight, she let her spirit guide her song about an uncertain girl who'd found purpose beyond the circumstances of her birth. Jubilation coursed through her, sending each nerve tingling. Even if he wouldn't understand the words, he would feel her intent.

"So much emotion," he intoned.

She drew inspiration from his voice, pouring her soul into words. With each note, her spirit floated higher until it reached a crescendo. His irises sparkled back at her. No matter what anyone else thought, she felt truly beautiful in his eyes. Finishing her song, she looked up at him through her lashes.

In three quick steps, he stood before her and clasped her hands. Warmth surged through her. He leaned in, breath hot on her neck.

"Thank you, Princess Kaiya. Your voice, just like the legendary Yanyan's, could enchant the dragon Avarax. I may return home empty-handed, but my heart is full." He withdrew, his lips tracing across her neck. Electricity coursed through her, every nerve on edge.

He turned toward the door.

No! He was leaving. It was too soon.

"Wait." She loosened several dwarf-forged platinum pins binding her voluminous hair, sending unruly locks tumbling down to her waist. Fiddling with an errant tendril, she proffered the jewels, each worth a soldier's annual pay. Hopefully, he wouldn't be insulted. "Prince Hardeep, please accept these as my personal apology for not being able to help you."

He plucked the simplest hairpin, her favorite. The brush of his finger across her palm sent a jolt of excitement up her spine. He pressed the jewel to his breast. "I will keep this one as a bittersweet souvenir of you and your voice."

Kaiya started to speak, but no words came out.

Lips trembling upward, Hardeep unpinned from his shirt a shard of cinnabar, shaped into the likeness of Ankira's nine-pointed lotus. He pressed the trinket in her palm and closed her hand around it. His large, strong hands wrapped around hers. "Please accept this as a symbol of our meeting. When you gaze at it, remember that no matter how far away I am, I will be thinking of you."

Warm like his smile, the lotus jewel buzzed, sending pleasant pulsations through her.

He turned and left. When he reached the door, he bent his head with a sidelong glance at her. "Once you have grown in your music, I am sure you will come to me." Without waiting for a response, he marched out of the hall.

Was it her pulse or the lotus jewel vibrating so rapidly? Kaiya reached back toward a column to steady herself. Yes, when she was ready, she would go to him.

PRELUDE TO ORCHESTRA OF TREACHERIES

Holding the music in her head, Kaiya arched back under the sweep of her *jian* straightsword and lifted her leg into a kick with the point of her toe. The blade passed within a hairbreadth of her cheek as she transitioned the movement into a precise stab. She held the nearly inverted pose, grateful for not nicking her now-pretty face with the complicated technique. Until today, she'd held back on the *Dance of Swords* for fear of marring her now smooth skin with a self-inflicted scar.

It'd taken a year of drinking bitter herbal medicines to finally quell her rebellious complexion. Vanquishing thoughts of Prince Hardeep had proved more difficult. Since then, the *Tianzi* had arranged a dozen introductions to self-absorbed sons of first rank *Tai-Ming* and second rank *Yu-Ming* lords.

None could compare to Prince Hardeep's charm. Those three days, a year past, still twisted her stomach into cartwheels when she thought about them.

Which was too often.

Kaiya tried to cope with unfulfilled love by immersing herself in dance and music. At times, it worked. At other times, she would stare at his lotus jewel for hours on end. After all, why did she practice, except for the secret hope of Hardeep returning?

Applause from the doors interrupted her concentration. With a *jian* in either hand, Kaiya pirouetted into a cross-legged low stance to avoid tumbling into an embarrassing heap. Her gaze fell on her sisters-in-law Xiulan and Yanli, whose floral outer gowns trailed across the gleaming wood of the training-hall floors. Several handmaidens followed them.

Crown Princess Xiulan's dark eyes danced with mirth, reminiscent of the whimsical gardenia motif of her pink outer gown. "Kaiya, you're hiding here to avoid a second meeting with Lord Chen."

Kaiya shuddered at the thought of the *Yu-Ming* heir from Jiangzhou Province, the latest in a long line of rejected suitors. "Young Lord Chen may be handsome, but he's as dumb as a rock. And he wouldn't stop looking at my chest." As if there was much to see.

Yanli sighed. The gold pine branch design of her green robes suited her usually subtle pragmatism. Today, her tone bordered on irritability. "Don't be so picky. Some counties of Jiangzhou grow restless, and your marriage to one of their *Yu-Ming* would go far in reasserting imperial authority there."

Kaiya twirled to her feet, flipping the pair of swords together. The lightweight *jian*, considered the marriage of elegance and practicality, at first seemed like the perfect metaphor for her purpose in this world. Yet even if she could choreograph the exact movements of the blades, her own life was more like a cherry blossom petal, carried on the whim of fickle political winds. "Is that why you married my brother? So your father could proclaim allegiance to mine?"

She held the swords out. The imperial guard Zhao Yue, up to now as motionless as a statue, strode forward. Bowing, he received them in two hands and shuffled backward to his unassuming place by the door.

Yanli opened her mouth, but Xiulan cast a furtive glance, silencing her. The Crown Princess smiled. "Oh, Kaiya... Yanli's situation was different. How could the *Tianzi* deny such a torrid mutual love?"

How could he deny *her* love for Hardeep? And *torrid*? Sappy would be a more accurate description of Kai-Wu and Yanli. At any other time of the month, Yanli would've waxed poetic about it.

Today, she pursed her lips. "It was just as much a reward for our province's longstanding loyalty." Her eyes bored into Kaiya's, pushing her point. "Yes, our love was enabled by the unprecedented leeway your father allows his children. But that indulgence has left you unmarried at fifteen! Please, stop being selfish and think about his poor health. It would ease his mind to know the imperial bloodline was secure."

Xiulan looked down at the ground.

Kaiya sighed. With the White Moon Renyue's passage toward new, her sisters-in-law's normally cheerful demeanors turned first to nervous anticipation and then invariable melancholy. Xiulan had been married for three years, Yanli for one, and neither had conceived.

That left her, a girl with skinny hips and no husband, to conceive a son and ensure the continuation of Wang family rule.

Yanli's eyes narrowed as they followed Kaiya's hand straying to the lotus jewel inside her sash. "You're still pining over Prince Hardeep, aren't you?"

Kaiya's cheeks burned. Telling Yanli about the prince had been a mistake. "No," she lied. She was older and wiser now. Of course the foreign prince had tried to manipulate a naïve girl. Maybe even used his Paladin powers. Oh, but his smooth voice, those blue eyes... She mentally chastised her younger self for venturing into the present.

Shaking her head with a knowing smile, Yanli took Kaiya's hand. "Kaiya, even if Ankira weren't occupied and its royal family scattered in exile, their prince would never be a match for you. Don't let an idealized memory set the standard for a suitor."

Kaiya nodded. It was true. He was a foreigner, after all. She would forget about him. This time, the thousandth time, it would work.

Xiulan took her other hand. "Yanli is right. Your brother and I were arranged to marry, and yet we fell deeply in love. It's not impossible."

Yanli gave her hand a gentle tug. "Come. Lord Chen is waiting."

"Like this?" Kaiya freed a hand and waved at her plain robe and unmade-up face. Her appearance was more suited for, well, someone practicing a dance.

Yanli's eyes sparkled mischievously. Her dear sister-in-law was still there, buried under the disappointment of another failed cycle. "It will send Lord Chen a message, won't it?"

Kaiya rolled her eyes. "I did say he was as dumb as a rock, right?"

They shared a giggle before straightening their postures into epitomes of imperial dignity. It had been so hard in the years preceding that fateful encounter with Hardeep, so easy just a year later.

With Xiulan in the lead and trailed by imperial guards and handmaidens, they glided through the alleys toward the Phoenix Garden. A year after Xiulan had shown Kaiya the pillow book, she still hadn't made use of it.

At the edge of the garden, they paused. In the pagoda where they'd dined the night before the fall of Wailian Castle, the handsome Young Lord Chen was talking to another man whose posture looked familiar. He made a gesture, and Young Lord Chen bowed...and left? Without so much as acknowledging he'd seen her.

Kaiya exchanged glances with Xiulan, whose brows furrowed. With Young Lord Chen's departure, there wasn't much point—

The other man turned around and met her gaze. Cousin Kai-Long! It had been almost a year since they'd last met. He'd returned to his home province of Nanling, and apparently had instituted land and trade reforms.

Kaiya nodded toward Xiulan and Yanli. "I am going to greet Lord Peng. Perhaps we can have tea later?"

"An hour, in the *Danhua* Garden." Xiulan smiled, and then she and Yanli, along with the bulk of the imperial guards and handmaidens, shuffled out of the garden in a flash of color.

Watching them leave, Kaiya glided over the arching footbridge to the pagoda. Chen Xin, Zhao Yue, and Han Meiling kept a respectful distance.

"*Dian-xia*." Kai-Long bowed his head, addressing her formally. Even though he was an elder cousin, her position as a princess from the direct ruling line ranked her above him.

Kaiya smiled at him. "Cousin, you do not need to stand on formality."

"As you command, Kaiya." He grinned back.

They'd repeated the same exchange, almost verbatim, for years now. She covered a laugh. "What brings you to the capital?"

"I am here brief to the *Tianzi* on my progress in governing Nanling Province. It has been wildly successful." Kai-Long's smile faded. "Unfortunately, I am also reporting on the latest incursions from Madura. Since our trade agreement expired, they have sent even more of their Golden Scorpions across the Great Wall to steal firepowder."

A note of sadness laced his voice. He still suspected the Golden Scorpions of assassinating his father, even if Lord Tong had taken credit for it. She placed a sympathetic hand on his arm.

He nodded at the gesture, smiling wryly. "Madura's greedy ambitions will turn our way before long. I am going to beseech the *Tianzi* to finance the Ankiran resistance, which has fallen into disarray since Prince Hardeep was gravely injured."

The prince! Blood rushed from her head and she stretched a hand out onto the balustrade to keep from falling. Hadn't she just banished the prince from her heart? Yet mention of his name alone nearly caused her to faint. "Will the prince survive?"

He nodded. "Yes, he escaped to Vyara City. He is under the care of the Ayuri Paladins."

Kaiya covered her mouth to bury her shocked exhalation. She quickly lifted her chin and composed her expression into one of distant concern.

Her cousin drew in close, reaching into the fold of his robe. He pressed something into her hand and whispered in the secret royal language, a tongue which none of her retinue would understand. "A message for you, from the prince. He recently initiated contact with me to ask for my province's aid."

She kept herself from looking at her trembling hand and fought the urge to unwrap the tightly folded parchment. Not in front of prying eyes. Did he remember her after all this time? If so, did he feel the way she hoped he did?

As he left the garden for his audience with the *Tianzi*, Peng Kai-Long kept his face composed to hide his delight. From watching Princess Kaiya's reactions to the simple mention of a name, he confirmed what he'd suspected from her rejection of so many eligible young lords: Prince Hardeep still held sway over her heart, even if they hadn't spoken or corresponded a year.

Before stepping into the castle, he stole one last glance over his shoulder to see the princess. So poised moments before, now reduced to a pathetic ball of female emotion. This was why women weren't fit to rule. Governed by their feelings, they lacked objectivity.

And were easily manipulated.

Walking through the castle halls, Kai-Long congratulated himself for his quick thinking. After his spies had told him of her second meeting with Young Lord Chen, he'd moved swiftly. He gave her the forged letter in hopes it would shatter any budding romance between her and the handsome young man. Her trembling hands told him it had worked.

With a scholar of Ayuri poetry and a master of written magic in his pay, Kai-Long could pass on as many letters as it would take to keep the princess yearning for a foreign prince—one who must've forgotten her after all this time.

Perhaps he might even offer to smuggle a message for her. It would help him control the princess further. Through her, perhaps even influence the *Tianzi* himself. More importantly, it would keep her unmarried.

Servant girls knelt and slid open doors. New ripples in his plan occurred to him. Sun-Moon Palace had many eyes and ears. If word leaked that the princess was corresponding with the exiled Prince of Ankira, the Madurans would have a motive to intervene. When the Madurans acted, they rarely did so with restraint. At least, that was what the Hua Court believed, thanks to the rumors he spread.

The nation's beloved princess, murdered by agents of the rogue Kingdom of Madura.

He liked the idea of it, even if making it happen would require careful planning. It would extinguish one source of potential heirs to the Dragon Throne, and stir up enough outrage for Hua to take punitive action. He would just have to wait and see how well he could control her, and then decide whether she was worth more to him dead or alive.

End of Book 1

ORCHESTRA OF TREACHERIES

A LEGENDS OF TIVARA STORY

JC KANG

ORCHESTRA OF TREACHERIES

PROLOGUE:

Rude Awakenings

Waking up without wings perplexed Avarax even more than the purple light that flashed at the entrance to his cave. The glimmer danced among the precious metals and gemstones, which towered above his uncharacteristically small size. A rumble shook the cavern walls, punctuating the rude awakening.

It had been a pleasant nap. Now someone would die for disturbing him.

He looked among his horde, searching for his most valued treasure.

The girl was gone.

Her scent lingered, yet in impossibly minute traces.

He thought back. Her voice had resonated with the universe, harmonizing with the vibrations of his own life force. Its vibrant tempo, like the torrent of river rapids, lulled to the dripping of a melting icicle. Heavier and heavier...

She must've sung him to sleep! But how?

He wrapped his consciousness around The dragonstone in his core, the almost-infinite source of energy all dragons had. Its pulsations meandered lazily, like a winter stream before the spring melt.

It didn't seem possible for a small human to affect him so much, no matter how special her voice.

And why?

Surely she'd adored him, as much as he did her.

It was time to learn the answers to this question, even if required more conventional means of drawing them out. Uttering a word of magic, his bipedal form morphed. His size swelled as arms bent into forelegs, and wings sprouted. Hands and fingers became talons, while his tail thickened and elongated.

Ah, it felt great to be a dragon again! He stretched his limbs and spine to work out tight muscles. Sufficiently limbered up, he snaked towards the cave opening. Night hung over the land, cloaking the world in darkness.

Another flash lit up the sky. He tracked it to its source, hundreds of miles to the southwest. A column of purple fire streaked down from the heavens, annihilating stretches of a sprawling port city of domes and minarets.

A city that had not been there when he went to sleep.

How long had he slumbered? Shrugging his shoulders a few times, Avarax loosened his wings. His claws tore into rock as he coiled his hind legs and then vaulted skyward. Higher and higher he flew, reacquainting himself with a land drastically different from the one he remembered.

Cities and towns. Hundreds of them within his far-reaching sight, oases in wide expanses of farmland. Not ghastly orc outposts, which glared out from the mountains, nor even the graceful spires of elf citadels melding with their surrounding forests. But rather, the centers of human populations he had seen as a younger dragon, back when their civilization was upgrading from collections of mud huts.

Their rebellion against their orc masters must have succeeded. Like all bottom feeders, humans had a way of proliferating when left unfettered.

The dragonstone in his chest sank. There was no way they could've expanded so fast within the girl's lifetime. Given how little of her song echoed in the pulse of the world, hundreds of years must have passed. The one whose voice connected with him more than any other must be long dead and withered to dust.

Still far in the distance, another blast of energy pulsed down on the city, obliterating the levees restraining the Western Ocean. An inexorable tide crawled across the low-lying lands and swallowed up towns and villages.

Hell rained down from the heavens. Destruction and suffering. Avarax laughed, belching blue sparks from his snout.

In that moment, he caught a faint whiff of her, in the direction of her homeland. Maybe, just maybe, if he could recover a strand of her hair, or a bone, he could recreate her.

He accelerated northwest, in the direction of her scent.

Flight! The cool night air streaked over his wings. The last time he had flown, he'd held her in his claws.

Over the mountains he soared. In the distance, a town had risen up where her village had been.

There, to the left, was Celastya's lair. From the scent, the only other dragon in the world still lived. Even if the slave girl's ward on his dragon stone allowed him to draw on a trickle of energy, he was more than a match for Celastya. He would rip her open and swallow her Flaming Pearl. The thought had crossed his mind over the millennia. Instead he had regularly mated with her and ate her clutch of eggs to gradually increase his potential power. He did not have the luxury of time now.

Ignoring the sporadic flickers of purple in the skies behind him, Avarax scanned the landscape below. The plains first rose into rolling hills before vaulting higher into mountain crags. Nestled in a valley, Teardrop Lake glimmered a pale blue, even in the dark of night. The light from the three moons gamboled in its ripples, the reflections dancing across Celastya's hidden cave entrance.

He hovered by the opening. Stronger or not, it would be foolish for him to fight in her lair. He would have to coax her out. His voice echoed across the valley, shaking the mountains. "Celastya, out with you! It is time to mate again."

She was inside. Avarax could hear her shrink back, smell her fear. He would roast her alive and pick through her charred remains for her Pearl. He took in a deep breath and belched into the cave.

Only a few sparks fizzled out— enough to incinerate a human, but only a tickling to a dragon. His frustrated wail sent the mountains shivering. He clawed at the cave mouth, ripping rock away.

A burst of reds and oranges erupted high in the heavens, just above the Iridescent Moon. A roar tumbled across the lands, the shockwave pushing him back from the cave.

Celastya darted out. She glanced at him with her luminous blue eyes. Her wingless, slithering form undulated past as she levitated close to the ground. Light from the White Moon sparkled off of her silvery scales before dark clouds billowing out from Mount Ayudra blotted out their sheen.

Avarax gave chase, the gusts from his wings splintering trees below. He barreled into Celastya, sending her careening into the loathsome Tivari pyramid still standing by the shores of the lake.

Its stones cracked as she rebounded off the walls. He drove his claws toward her, but she darted away, and he ripped into the pyramid's stonework instead. His talons lodged into something deep in the rock, sending a searing shock through body. Curse the Tivari for ever building the vile structures!

Avarax tore his claws free and resumed his pursuit. Celastya flew over the mountains and towards the shore, and then skimmed the ocean as she streaked towards Jade Island.

The fool thought she could channel the island's latent energy. Of course, he could, too. Perhaps it would energize his dragonstone, reinvigorating it a little more.

Mountains along the closed end of the horseshoe-shaped island shielded a port town at the head of the bay. A smooth metal arch, engraved with runes of elven magic, spanned the mouth of the harbor. Celastya coiled herself around the arch. Her eyes glowed a brilliant blue.

As he approached, she unwrapped herself, freeing herself just in time to avoid a swipe from his foreclaw. With a graceful spin, Celastya twisted around him and tangled up his wings. The air dropped out from beneath them. Wind roared past as the ground rushed up to meet their tumbling bodies.

They crashed into the shore with a jolt that shook the island. Her strangling grasp around him eased. She seized his forelegs in her own claws, but Avarax was still much stronger. He raked a talon across her neck. Bright blue blood spurted out. They struggled for dozens of minutes, toppling statues and buildings as they thrashed around.

"Avarax!" A bold voice called his name, and he turned to see a puny elf. He radiated power far out of proportion to his size.

Though smaller than one of Avarax's fangs, the golden-haired elf dared to lock gazes with him. He began to chant. The vibrations of his voice, similar yet different to that of the slave girl from before, rolled over him.

The power of the dragonstone lurched inside of him. A dull ache blossomed into searing pain as his bones broke and reformed. Hulking muscle shrank and impenetrable scales softened. His forelegs and claws withered into arms and hands, his hindquarters transmuting into legs.

Several excruciating minutes of transformation later, Avarax rose on wobbling humanoid legs, a scant head above the elf whom he had dwarfed just minutes ago. He looked down at his naked, frail body.

A human! The most pathetic of sentient beings.

Avarax scoffed. The silly trick might buy them time, but he would pay them back tenfold. He uttered the words to restore his dragon form.

Nothing happened.

What? His morale melted away. Instead of a roar that would compel a mortal to obey, his voice merely shouted. "What have you done?"

"Made you wish you had stayed asleep for another seven hundred years." The elf whipped out a narrow longsword.

Avarax felt its power, knew that it held a magic enchantment. His new tiny heart rattled against the narrow confines of his scrawny chest. Was it in fear? He had not experienced that emotion in several millennia.

He closed his eyes as the tip pushed into his chest. The blade made a divot into the thin flesh covering him, not even cutting the skin.

It barely tickled.

A magical elvish blade should have stabbed through a human with ease. Avarax held the elf's shocked gaze. In that second of silence, Avarax sensed the dragonstone inside of him. It pulsed as feebly as before, yet it still held all the potential energy of a dragon. He spoke a word of power, sending the elf hurtling back into the sand.

He spun to see Celastya bearing down on him. He slammed his fist into her swiping claw. She recoiled and winced.

Avarax laughed. Even in this pitiful form, he was still a dragon. He punched again, hitting nothing but air.

Celastya, the elf, and the horseshoe island were all gone, replaced by wind-driven snow on a mountain top. Ice sizzled and melted beneath his feet.

He evaluated his dragonstone. The elf's ward dammed it up. The trickle of vitality would not sustain his dragon form, at least not for more than a few minutes.

Condemned to be a human!

No matter. *Find opportunity in disaster*, the tribe of black-haired, yellow-skinned humans said. Before him lay a new world infested by inferior beings. Even without his dragon form, his superior intellect would allow him to rule over a weak-willed, borderline intelligent species.

And when he did, he would find the slave girl's bones and recreate her.

Celastya snaked her head around. A second before, she had been ready to rip Avarax's human form apart; the next, he and the elf were gone. Before she had time to consider what had happened, the elf reappeared out of thin air. He collapsed into the sand.

"What happened?" she asked.

The elf staggered to his feet. "We were lucky to take him by surprise. I froze time and transported him to the other side of Tivaralan. Though I forced him into human form, he still has all the vitality of a dragon. It took all of my energy to move him."

Celastya scratched her whiskers. She never imagined a mortal could be so strong. "He will return."

"Yes, but he will have to walk. It will take him years, unless he finds a way to unlock his dragonstone."

A shudder sent ripples down her serpentine form. Nothing left in this world could stop Avarax at full strength. "And when he does?"

"Let us hope I have time to teach someone with the right voice to sing him back to sleep."

CHAPTER 1:

Chance Meetings

Princess Kaiya fled Sun-Moon Palace, hoping to escape the dragon's imminent arrival. Not Avarax, who supposedly heard the magic in her voice from afar; but rather General Lu, a human who could pass as a cold-blooded lizard. What the self-proclaimed Guardian Dragon of Hua lacked in height, he compensated for with an ego that cast a long shadow over her mood.

Her identity hidden by a hooded cloak that roasted her on this unseasonably warm day, she wandered through the busy city streets. Well, not exactly wandered, since she had a destination in mind.

Her five most trusted imperial guards, likewise disguised, kept hands on their *dao* hilts. Chen Xin walked a few paces ahead, ensuring no citizen got too close. More grey streaked his black hair now, perhaps because of such frequent forays into the city. From the way their eyes darted back and forth, one would've thought a new insurrection was brewing.

Covering a giggle with a hand, Kaiya beckoned them to a stop in a quiet intersection. "Chen Xin, if it were dangerous out here, the Ministry of Appointments would have never let us out." Two years ago, they wouldn't have, but Father had given her some leeway after her role in putting down the rebellion in the North with the power of the Dragon Scale Lute.

"*Dian-xia*," he said, using the formal address, "We should turn back. Your meeting with General Lu..."

Kaiya suppressed a shudder and looked up at the Iridescent Moon Caiyue, never moving from its reliable spot to the south. It waned past its second crescent. "What time is the meeting?"

"Just *short* of the third crescent." Ma Jun grinned, emphasizing his boyish looks.

Chen Xin's lips pursed. "If we turned back now—"

"We'd still fall *short*." Ma Jun stared at the sky, ignoring the elbow Zhao Yue jabbed into him.

She scanned the surroundings, trying to get her bearings. It couldn't be much further. If only she had a better sense of direction. Had they gone straight there... "Just a few more minutes."

Ma Jun shook his head. "General Lu has a *short* temper."

Whether or not the Guardian Dragon deserved ridicule, it wasn't appropriate to mock him. She fixed Ma Jun with a glare until he cast his gaze down. Satisfied, she found the Iridescent Moon again. If it was to the south, that meant east—

"That way." Zhao Yue jutted his prominent chin at the next street corner.

Heat rose to her cheeks. Of course they knew the destination. To hide her embarrassment, she headed in the way he indicated.

At the intersection, sunlight enveloped her in warmth, a reminder that spring was only a week away. It'd been two years ago, around this time, when Prince Hardeep had begged for her help. Her hand strayed to the lotus jewel, Hardeep's token, under her sash.

Heart fluttering, she hummed. With the resolute pulse of the world beneath her feet, she raised the volume. The sounds of walking feet, haggling merchants, and gossiping housewives guided her as she used the hum to bring harmony to the disparate sounds. Around her, commoners going about their daily drudgery smiled. Even dour Chen Xin's stiff shoulders loosened.

Her chest swelled. After two years of practice, her mood flitted through her music. It affected a larger audience now, even without the use of a musical instrument. Perhaps she could finally help Prince Hardeep liberate his homeland from the Madurans. *Once you have grown in your music, I am sure you will come for me*, he'd said. If only there was a way to convince Father.

The scent of turmeric wafted from a street up ahead. They were close. The bright yellow, orange, and red streamers beckoned her. They turned another corner into the Ankiran ghetto, where angry cacophony drowned out her hum.

"You brownies go home!" a male voice bellowed.

"Leeches!" said another.

"Steal someone else's job."

Two dozen burly Hua men, muscles bulging from threadbare shirts and pants, massed in a boisterous wall of antagonism in the middle of the street. On the other side, a group of darker-skinned Ayuri folk, mostly women and children, cowered.

The guards formed a protective shield around Kaiya, even as she craned her neck to get a better view.

A lanky fellow in fine silk robes pushed to the front of the Hua men. His slicked-back hair contributed to an appearance oily enough to lubricate a dwarf siege engine. A guild boss, no doubt. "Look here, we don't care what kind of work you do, just as long as you stay out of the construction of the outer wall."

A middle-aged woman pressed her palms together and bowed her head. She spoke in fluent but accented Hua. "Kind sir, that's all our young men can do. We would starve—"

He waved a hand at the surrounding row houses, painted in lively purples and blues. "Maybe you should use your money for food instead of ruining our city with your garish customs."

The woman touched her ear, an Ayuri sign of apology he wouldn't understand. "We were only able to beautify our neighborhood with the generosity of Lord Peng and Princess Kaiya."

Kaiya twirled a lock of hair, loosened from where she'd already removed gold pins, the ones she regularly gave to Prince Hardeep's people. It was good to know Cousin Kai-Long had been generous with them, too.

The guild boss apparently had different ideas. He threw his hands up. "You see? The *Tianzi* allowed your kind to live here, and now you waste money taken from our national coffers."

Three young Ankiran men jostled their way to the front line. One jabbed a finger into the Hua leader's chest. "It's your country's fault we are refugees. The least you could do—"

The leader punched the teen in the jaw, and then jerked his thumb toward the homes. "It's about time we taught you freeloaders a lesson. Men, ransack the place."

Kaiya's eyes widened. This couldn't be happening. Not in Huajing. She started forward.

Chen Xin blocked her way. "*Dian-xia*, you cannot risk revealing yourself. There are only five of us to protect you."

With their swordsmanship, two was more than enough. She gestured toward the construction workers, now shoving through the women. "The city is safe. The only violence in the last three hundred years was the attack on these refugees two years ago! You saw the aftermath." Dozens had been murdered in cold blood.

Chen Xin dropped to his knee, fist to the ground. "*Dian-xia*, please." The other imperial guards followed suit. If they were trying not to reveal her identity, they weren't doing a good job.

With the guards bowing down, she had a better view. The young Ankiran men lay on the ground, curling up against kicks. More of the hooligans ripped down the streamers and decorations that marked the Ankiran ghetto.

"Stop!" Kaiya yelled.

She might have been a statue for all the attention anyone paid. Not a single Hua or Ayuri even looked in her direction. And if the fighting didn't stop soon, the ruffians would ruin the refugees' efforts to make their Hua houses feel like an Ayuri home.

Two years. It'd been two years since she'd used a Dragon Song for anything of consequence. This situation might pale in comparison to a rebellious lord slaughtering unarmed young men, but these downtrodden foreigners' livelihoods were at stake. The screaming grew louder.

Do not use magic as a crutch, Father had said. Even more ominously, the mysterious elf Xu claimed that powerful musical magic was a beacon for the dragon Avarax. Yet right now, there was no other recourse.

Through her slippers, she gripped the pavestones with her toes. The resolute pulse of the earth coursed into her, rising though her core as she straightened her spine. She raised her voice in song. *Spring Festival*, a favorite for this time of year, celebrated magnanimity. Her notes merged the rhythm of her countrymen's angry jeers with the cadence of the Ankirans' sniffling cries. Her arms grew heavy and her legs wobbled.

The commotion silenced. Everyone turned and looked at her, their eyes glazed over in reverie.

"Please," Kaiya said, catching her breath. "The Ankirans are our guests."

The workers' leader shook his head, sending his oiled hair into disarray. The sharpness returned to his eyes. Chest puffed out, he strode over. "Who are you—"

Dao rasped out of scabbards as her guards rose. Their cloaks swooshed open, revealing their distinctive breastplates. The etched lines of the five-clawed dragon flashed in the sun, evoking awe in those not used to seeing it. Save for their leader, the Hua workers skittered back, dropped to their knees and pressed their foreheads to the ground. The Ankirans pressed their palms together and lowered their heads.

The guild boss' face shifted from her to the others and back again before he, too, dropped to his knees. "*Dian-xia*."

Identity compromised, Kaiya lowered her hood and adopted a tone of imperial authority. "Citizens of Huajing, I understand your concerns. I will present your case to the Ministry of Works."

The leader pressed his forehead to the ground. "Thank you, *Dian-xia*."

"You may go." She waved a hand, dismissing them. Such a flashy motion. Father could have accomplished the same effect with a mere tilt of his eyebrows, no words required.

"Yes, *Dian-xia*." With a jerk of his chin, the boss guided his men away.

Head still bowed, the Ankiran matron stepped forward. "Your Highness, thank you. Men like that harass us on a daily basis."

Daily? Kaiya's stomach tightened. How awful it must be to be far away from home, treated like vermin. She'd never know. She switched to the Ayuri tongue. "I will speak to the city watch." The day's itinerary now included visits to the Ministry of Works, the city watch, and General Lu, not necessarily in that order. To think that two years ago, her only duty had been to get married.

One of the young men spat. "You'd *better* talk to the watch. It's your fault we are stuck here. If you hadn't sold firepowder—"

Whether they understood the Ayuri language or not, the imperial guards stomped forward. The man shrunk back.

"Enough, Ashook." The matron waved him back. "Do not blame the princess for a decision made before she was born. She has tried hard to support us."

"Not hard enough," he muttered under his breath. Quiet, but loud enough for Kaiya's keen ears to catch.

She turned to the matron. "We no longer sell firepowder to Madura. Maybe with the help of the Ayuri Paladins, Ankira will expel them."

The matron teared up as she shook her head. "The Paladins are too afraid of Avarax."

The Last Dragon's name sent a quiver down Kaiya's spine. He guarded against anyone gaining the power to sing him to sleep, like the slave girl Yanyan had done before the War of Ancient Gods. After Kaiya's use of the Dragon Scale

Lute, Father had sent spies to keep an eye on Avarax's lair. In the last two years, he had yet to leave the Dragonlands. She shook the worries out of her mind. Perhaps he hadn't heard the lute—now destroyed—or he knew her paltry music was no threat to him.

Behind her, a door to one of the row houses slid open. The guards tightened their circle around her. She spun around.

Standing in the doorway of a house near the end of the block was Cousin Kai-Long's courier. The rugged soldier from Nanling Province delivered Prince Hardeep's secret messages. What was he doing in the Ankiran ghetto? His eyes met hers and widened. He dropped to a knee, fist to the ground. "*Dian-xia*, I was just coming to see you. I have a letter from...Lord Peng."

Kaiya's stomach fluttered. That letter most certainly wasn't from Cousin Kai-Long. She shuffled over to the messenger and, casting a glance back at the guards who trailed just a sword's reach away, received the folded paper cover in two trembling hands. She pressed it against her heart, which pattered like spring rain on roof tiles. The ink's scent invited her to rip the cover open and look.

No, not in front of prying eyes. She turned to Chen Xin. "General Lu must be waiting. We must return to the palace posthaste."

If her guards' jaws could hang open any wider, Avarax himself might grow jealous. Ma Jun opened and closed his mouth several times before he found his words. "Such *short* notice..."

CHAPTER 2:

Love Letters

The shuffling of the imperial guards outside the Hall of Righteous Hearts barely registered in Kaiya's ears as she pressed the latest letter from Prince Hardeep against her chest. Her grasp of the Ayuri language had improved through their regular correspondence, and the poetic imagery of his words became more vibrant with each note. Her stomach twisted in pleasant knots, imitating the graceful loops and whorls of his script.

She looked down and read it again.

Kaiya, my love, I gaze across my war-torn homeland and see immeasurable suffering. The only thing that gives me hope, brings me joy, is the memory of you. The fullness of the lips so close to mine. The gentle curve of your chin which I still feel beneath my fingers. And your voice, so melodic that it still carries me now. Alas, how I wish I could be at your side. The liquid brown eyes that truly saw me.

If only he *could* see her now. She was no longer an awkward, lanky girl with enough pimples to make a topographical map of Tivara. He'd—

"*Dian-xia,*" an official outside the door called. "General Lu is here."

Kaiya stuffed the letter into the sash behind her back and squared her shoulders.

The doors opened. General Lu stepped over the ghost-tripping threshold and into the hall. Glossy black hair framed his oval face, and his light complexion, chiseled jaw, and nose all spoke of Hua's north. He would have cut a dashing figure in his formal blue court robes if he weren't so short. Behind him, her handmaiden Meiling and imperial guard Ma Jun exchanged raised eyebrows, while a secretary from the Ministry of Household Affairs bowed low.

"*Dian-xia.*" General Lu dropped to his knee, fist to the marble floor.

She nodded, allowing him out of the salute. "General, please forgive my tardiness."

"The princess has important matters to deal with." Though he lowered his head in respect, his acerbic tone suggested otherwise. No doubt he still held a grudge from two years before, when her music had reduced him to tears; and then, not a day later, she'd put down the rebellion in the North with the Dragon Scale Lute before his own nearby army even arrived. Behind his back, some even called the Guardian Dragon the Sleeping Dragon.

She knew. He knew she knew, and yet, the annual ritual continued. As if one day, she'd finally relent and he'd succeed where all the other suitors had failed. She conjured a smile as contrived as his tone. "General, I understand you have kept the North tranquil."

A grin formed on his lips, even as his gaze strayed to her cleavage. "You have followed my exploits?"

Using muskets to defend fortified higher ground against barbarians armed with primitive single-shot crossbows hardly constituted an exploit, but there was no need to antagonize him. She crossed an arm over her chest to brush an errant lock of hair from her face. "I heard that you rebuilt Wailian Castle."

His eyes shot up to meet hers. "Yes. The main keep no longer stands above old mines. We won't have a repeat of the last invasion."

Her hand strayed to the lotus jewel at her hip, concealed by a sash. Prince Hardeep's token. He'd rescued her from the burning castle before it collapsed into the network of tunnels. The magic of the Dragon Scale Lute had ignited the firepowder stored down there. "You undoubtedly learned from Lord Tong's mistakes."

"Well, I was the one who suggested he store the firepowder there, just in case we would ever have to take it from him." He flashed a smug grin. "The castle was only impregnable in name before; now it is fact."

Kaiya kept from pursing her lips. Like all her other suitors, the general's favorite topic was himself. The only men who ever cared about what she thought were Prince Hardeep and her childhood friend, Tian. Who knew where either were now?

She met the general's gaze. Prompt him along, and perhaps he'd use up all his allotted time bragging without bringing up marriage. She said, "I understand the *Tianzi* plans to elevate you to *Yu-Ming* status and grant you full authority over Wailian County."

His smile spread even further, the edges of his lips nearly reaching his ears. "The citizens are content, the borders secure. The saltpeter mines surpass quotas. All the castle needs now is a lady."

Kaiya cringed. He'd weaseled his way into broaching the topic of marriage. She'd virtually given him the opening, and no doubt his military mind seized the advantage. It was time to redirect. "Many eligible girls are coming of age this year. Chen Meili, Fei Qing, Chu Yingying are beautiful *Yu-Ming* daughters. They'd all be appropriate brides for a newly-appointed *Yu-Ming* lord."

"The *Tianzi* suggests I aim higher." If only his focus, fixed on her chest again, aimed higher.

She made a show of pondering, scrunching her forehead and nose. "*Tai-Ming* Lord Lin's daughter Ziqiu, Lord Peng Kai-Long's sister Naying or Lord Liu Yong's daughter Lili are all eligible." Ziqiu was sweet, if flighty, though Naying was

something of a bully, and statuesque Lili stood a head taller than General Lu.

His eyes lifted and bored into hers. "I had someone else in mind."

Kaiya looked up at the dwarf-made water clock. "Oh! General, forgive me, but I have an appointment with my doctor."

"At half-past the fourth crescent?" General Lu cocked his head.

In her haste, she hadn't actually noted the time. At least the appointment was real, even if it was much later. She raised her voice in hopes that the officials, her guards, anyone, would hear her. "It is back in the castle, and I have to change."

Wrong words. His gaze roved over her body, likely plotting out a battle plan with her curves as the terrain. How much easier life had been two years ago, when she was flat and acne-ridden. At least then, the suitors didn't leer at her like wolves.

General Lu sank to a knee. "Princess Kaiya, I have asked the *Tianzi* for permission to marry you."

How presumptuous! It was all Kaiya could do to keep from gaping. Hopefully, Father had not promised anything. He had, after all, given her plenty of leeway in this matter since the fall of Wailian Castle. She placed a hand on her chest. "General, I am flattered by your request. However, I am afraid there is another." Hardeep, whom Father would never approve of, but this half-truth would at least extricate both of them with dignity intact.

"I was unaware of a leading candidate."

She flashed a smile. "As the Founder said, *Knowledge of a combatant's disposition is the key to victory.*"

"*Which can only be obtained with use of spies,*" he finished. "The *Tianzi* has the best spies in the world, and yet, he is apparently as unaware of your disposition as I."

Kaiya searched his expression. His roundabout responses suggested Father hadn't promised her hand. No, General Lu was baiting her. She tilted her head, intentionally exposing the side of her neck, and covered a contrived giggle. "The secrets of a woman's heart could not be uncovered by even the fabled *Moquan*, let alone the *Tianzi's* spies."

He snorted. "Probably because the *Moquan* are too busy kidnapping naughty children. In any case, the *Tianzi* said he would be amenable to a union of our families. I humbly request that you take the proposal into consideration."

She dipped her chin. "I am honored by your attention," now on her breasts again, "and I will consider it."

Considered and denied. Though if Father had said *amenable*, perhaps she no longer had the choice. It might very well be a done deal.

Her reply letter to Prince Hardeep could wait. First, she'd visit Father to discern his intentions.

Sitting on the bloodwood chair in Sun-Moon Castle's Jasmine Room, *Tai-Ming* Lord Peng Kai-Long poured another cup of tea for the *Tianzi*. Imperial guards stood by the sliding doors, which opened out on a terrace overlooking Sun-Moon Lake. Annoying bird chirps twittered in on a warm breeze, which presaged an early spring. A historically monumental spring, if his plans went well.

Hand trembling, the *Tianzi* reached for the kettle. "Nephew, please drink."

Kai-Long shook his head. Using the formal address, he said, "*Huang-Shang*, I wouldn't dare. This tea is reserved only for the Imperial Family."

"No need to stand on ceremony." The *Tianzi's* laugh devolved into a coughing fit. "You are my sister's son and grew up with my children."

Which gave him a close-up view of their incompetence. Kai-Long bowed. "I am of your blood, but I do not belong to the Wang line."

"It would be a shame if you never tasted the imperial tea."

Kai-Long suppressed a smirk. At the end of spring, he would. For now, though: "In this, I must refuse your invitation."

"And if I command it?" Phlegm rattled in the *Tianzi's* throat.

Kai-Long withdrew his curved dagger. Hand on their *dao* swords, the imperial guards strode forward, only to freeze and melt back when he set the blade on the table. He lowered his head again. "If you give such a command, *Huang-Shang*, I will cut my own throat."

"My most loyal vassal." The *Tianzi's* laugh came out as a labored wheeze. He was only the husk of a once-great man, and wouldn't last much longer. Perhaps no more than a year, even if Kai-Long didn't arrange for an earlier death.

A good thing, too, since Hua grew weaker by the day under his increasingly timid leadership. Once Kai-Long ascended the Dragon Throne, he would strengthen the nation through economic and military reform, just as he had his own province. Just as the *Tianzi* had done a generation ago, before age and sickness sapped his vitality.

The door slid open, revealing a kneeling minister. "*Huang-Shang*, Princess Kaiya requests an audience with you." He pressed his forehead to the ground, revealing the princess, who knelt behind him.

"Enter," the *Tianzi* said.

Cousin Kaiya rose with the grace of a weeping cherry and glided into the room. How elegant she'd become. And beautiful, too. Just two years ago, she'd been woefully plain and flat, though that had done little to stem the tide of ambitious suitors. Her gaze met his and a smile quirked across her lips for a split second before her attention shifted to the *Tianzi*. She sank to her knees and pressed her forehead to the floor. "*Huang-Shang*."

"Rise, my daughter."

She straightened. "*Huang-Shang*, I met with General Lu. He informed me that you are amenable to a marriage between our families."

Kai-Long hid his shock. Her tone was too neutral, with no hint of defiance. Perhaps she'd grown used to the magic in the letters she believed came from Prince Hardeep. And the *Tianzi* was *amenable*. That might as well have been order.

The *Tianzi* locked his gaze on Kaiya. "Your brothers have yet to conceive an heir. I would rest assured knowing your future son would be third in line to the Dragon Throne."

Third in line—the position Kai-Long currently occupied based on the patrilineal laws of succession. He kept his face impassive. After all...

"You have one month to choose an appropriate suitor," the *Tianzi* said. "Otherwise, you will marry General Lu."

Kaiya's lips trembled for a split second. Then her eyes darted to all the guards, and her expression settled. She bowed. "As you command, Father."

One week. Her obedience to Uncle trumped even the magic of the fake letters. All the plans Kai-Long had set in motion two years prior might crumble around him. If he couldn't keep Kaiya from marrying, he'd have to get rid of her for good.

And with his foresight, he had a plan in place to accomplish that.

CHAPTER 3
Challenges

Kaiya stared blankly out one of the solarium's dozen windows, distracted by thoughts of Father's ultimatum and Prince Hardeep's recent note. With Cousin Kai-Long's help, they'd secretly exchanged letters for a year. Their relationship had matured through their correspondence, and at eighteen, she now realized how idealistic and lovesick she'd been as a sixteen-year-old. Now, it would never be. Not unless she found a way to make it happen.

"*Dian-xia!*" Doctor Wu's voice rattled her out of her thoughts.

Kaiya blinked, her focus shifting to the grey-robed woman. Nobody knew Doctor Wu's age, though some speculated the Master of the *Dao* had discovered the secret to immortality.

Pulled up into a tight, austere coil, her long silver hair had a faint bluish tinge to it, perhaps reflected from her eyes when the light hit it just right.

Those eyes, unlike any other Hua woman. Luminescent blue, like the pale Blue Moon Guanyin's Eye itself. Their depth and serenity evoked a soothing calm rivaling Sun-Moon Lake on the clearest of days.

Kaiya probably deserved the reprimand for daydreaming. She bowed her head, contrite.

"Recite what I just said," Dr. Wu said.

Kaiya twirled a lock of her hair. What *had* she said? Something about the Tivari, who had enslaved humans for millennia until the War of Ancient Gods a thousand years ago. "Altivorcs and tivorcs have an extra energy point on their Conception Meridian, between... between..."

Doctor Wu poked two points on Kaiya's belly. "Between these acupuncture points, *Juque* and *Shangwan.* What happens if it is blocked?"

Why did it matter? The Tivari were now little more than disorganized bands of mercenaries that Kaiya would probably never see. She shook her head.

"Nausea. Vomiting. Headaches." Doctor Wu's tone remained calm, devoid of accusation. "You are more distracted than usual. Your thoughts are scattered, unfocused. You will meditate."

And by meditation, Doctor Wu meant standing in an unladylike stance and staring out the window. They'd done it so many times in the last decade. Kaiya obediently rose and strode over to the spot facing east out the latticed windows toward Jade Mountain.

"Now, focus on your breathing, anchor yourself with the energies of Mother Earth."

The same words, as always. Kaiya sank into a deep horse stance, thighs parallel to the ground, spine straight and gaze locked forward on the snow-capped peak. As ugly as the posture was, the stance had helped her channel the magic of Dragon Songs.

"Still not right after all these years." Doctor Wu furrowed a brow. With a nudge of a hand, she lifted Kaiya's chin to further straighten her back. Her voice softened. "Now breathe. In through the nose, letting your stomach expand; out through your mouth, pushing your stomach in."

Kaiya could have quoted the words verbatim.

Doctor Wu afforded her a cursory glance. "Good. Now visualize your weight sinking deeper and deeper into Mother Earth as you exhale. Draw her life-giving energy through the *Yongquan* points in your feet as you inhale and bring them to your *Dantian* below your navel."

Slowing her breath, Kaiya settled her mind. Her toes gripped the stone floor through her shoe soles. Thoughts of marriage and foreign princes melted away as the resolute vibration of the earth filled her.

A snort came from the right, just outside Kaiya's peripheral vision. "My dear doctor, shouldn't the princess be nurturing musical talents instead of playing with energy fields?"

The voice and flippant tone could only belong to the elf, Lord Xu.

Kaiya kept her attention forward. Turning around would invite a rebuke from Dr. Wu.

Xu walked around and faced her, blocking the view of the mountain. His glossy gold hair sparkled in the sun. It'd been two years since he'd last appeared, yet his fine, ageless features remained the same. Youthful, even if his eyes glinted with wisdom.

And perhaps, mischief.

Concentration broken, thoughts of Hardeep's written words flooded back. And it wouldn't do to let the elf see her in such a crude pose. She straightened and bobbed her head in a show of respect.

He didn't return the salute and looked her directly in her eyes. "After all," he said, "she has shown a knack for Dragon Songs."

"Perhaps you should teach her," Doctor Wu said with a hint of amusement in her voice. "Just as Aralas taught his Hua lover Yanyan. Princess Kaiya will be singing dragons to sleep in no time."

Xu laughed, his tone mocking. "Aralas was Elestrae, an elf angel sent by the Sun God Koralas. She was—"

"*He*," Doctor Wu said.

"Yes. He was master of all magic and none like him have walked Tivaralan since."

Doctor Wu scoffed. "Then if you can't do it, you must trust me to teach her to connect with the energy of Mother Earth. Just because the elves did not teach humans about the *Dao* does not mean it's useless."

Kaiya's eyes shifted between doctor and elf. The barbs they stabbed into each other sure *sounded* mirthful, but who knew? Xu seemed affable enough, but he was still a high lord and could order Doctor Wu's execution for her impudence.

"But she is a busy girl," Xu said, "and I would think her time would be better spent fusing magic into her music."

"What is magic, but a link to the energy of Mother Earth?" Doctor Wu's tone sounded like a verbal jab to the elf's ribs.

Xu scoffed. "Nonsense."

The doctor flashed a playful grin. "A wager then, my Lord. Show us something you think is beyond our princess' musical abilities, and if she cannot replicate it, I will give you one herb from my collection of rare tonics. But if she does, you will acquiesce to one of my requests."

Both their eyes turned to her, all but forgotten until now. The argument over her training had been mundane enough until this challenge. How could she possibly compare to the powerful Lord Xu? "But Master, my skills are trifling com—"

Doctor Wu silenced her with a hand. "You recently held an entire audience enthralled by your *guzheng* zither performance. What is the connection between performer and audience, if not a manifestation of energy?"

Kaiya shook her head. "You should not gamble on something beyond my small abilities."

The old woman winked. "Lord Xu will be kind with his challenge, and I won't ask for something like a Starburst when you win."

"A Starburst?" Kaiya gaped incredulously. Though if anyone had one of those mythical relics from when elves and orcs battled for supremacy over Tivara, it would be Xu.

Lord Xu laughed. "Shall I ask her to invoke another Hellstorm? Or the Wrath of Koralas?"

With a grandmotherly grin, Doctor Wu rubbed her hands together. "Lord Xu is having delusions of grandeur. Does he think he is the equal of Archangel Aralas?"

Kaiya's mind swam. Everyone else spoke in awe of the devastating magic that'd obliterated a mountain and ripped a new sea in the continent. Lord Xu referenced it with the same nonchalance as the as he'd flippantly mentioned the genocidal vengeance of the elvish sun god—magic that was never invoked during the War of Ancient Gods. Meanwhile, her teacher bandied about the name of the elf hero from that conflict as if he were a dear acquaintance.

Doctor Wu offered her a reassuring pat on the shoulder. "Easy, *Dian-xia*. This is just idle banter among old friends."

"Old friends, indeed." Lord Xu snickered. "As long as we understand the stakes, I will keep my challenge simple." He beckoned the imperial guards Chen Xin and Ma Jun, conveniently tucked away in the background. "You two, over here."

Neither so much as flinched, their attention set forward.

Kaiya covered a laugh. "If that is all, then it is quite easy. Chen Xin, Ma Jun, please come."

The two guards dropped onto a one-knee bow, fist to the ground. "As the princess commands," they shouted. They stood up and marched over in unison.

Chen Xin eyed Xu. "Do you wish us to remove the lord?"

Unsurprisingly, Lord Xu ignored the threat and sang in the musical words of elf magic. The melody might have been a chorus of angels. Her heart soared.

At the end of the five-second chant, Chen Xin and Ma Jun both started sniffling. Blinking, their lips twitched in a futile attempt to contain emotion. Within seconds, both sobbed uncontrollably.

Lord Xu turned toward the doctor with a smug expression. "Can your breathing exercises accomplish something like that?"

"*Dian-xia*," Doctor Wu said, "make them stop. Use your flute."

How did one stop magically-induced crying? Kaiya withdrew a four-inch *dizi* flute from the folds of her robes. Playing a joyous tune, she looked up.

Her guards still sobbed. Uncertainties grew. Her melody wavered.

"Focus," the doctor said. "The nature of grief is metal, which cloys the lungs. It can be tempered by the fire of the heart."

Heart. Fire. High stances and erratic tones. Kaiya nodded, shifting in her stance and letting her weight sit lightly over her toes. She shook her hair out, sending the precious gold, silver, and jade clips and pins jingling to the ground. Her music became more volatile and whimsical as she drew her breath from her heart.

Ma Jun and Chen Xin's crying came to an abrupt stop. They organized their expressions into their typical stoicism.

Lord Xu clapped. "Nicely done, *Dian-xia*. I concede there is something to what the doctor says. Had you not broken my spell, they would have continued blubbering until I released them or they died of starvation. Perhaps you can move beyond parlor tricks and actually replicate the exploits of your musicians from the War of Ancient Gods."

Kaiya's heart fluttered. She might have grown in the lost art of Dragon Songs, but... "Stopping men from crying is trivial compared to singing the Last Dragon to sleep."

"Do you think Yanyan's first feat was confronting Avarax?" He favored her with a raised eyebrow. "And yet when she did, he slept for seven hundred years, setting the stage for humans' ascendance after overthrowing the orcs."

Kaiya cocked her head. Avarax had only woken three decades before. Surely the powerful Lord Xu could do simple math. "But Avarax slept for a thousand years."

Doctor Wu scowled at Lord Xu, and then laughed. "*Dian-xia*, Lord Xu has lost his edge in his old age."

"Yes, I was thinking of the Hellstorm. To think, not even a rain of fire roused him."

Doctor Wu poked him in the ribs. "In any case, my Lord, you lost your wager."

"Indeed, I did. Since I gave the princess an easy task, I hope your demand is of commensurate value."

Easy? Kaiya shuffled on her feet.

Doctor Wu chuckled. "Am I anything but fair, my Lord? I ask that you teach the princess *The Ear that Sees*."

Kaiya snorted. A fictitious technique from martial arts novels, *Seeing Ears* allowed boogeymen spies to fight in the dark. The stories might be fit for entertainment or scaring little children, but not much else. "I don't see how that will help my music."

The elf chuckled. "In the beginning stages, *The Ear that Sees* is simply a means of separating all sounds from each other." He nodded at the doctor. "Perhaps it is not such a bad idea. I've always implored this girl to listen."

Kaiya fiddled with a lock of hair. What was the use of such a skill? But Doctor Wu had recommended it, so... "Very well. With the *Tai-Ming* Council and reception tomorrow, this lesson will have to wait for a few days."

"Alas, I will be returning to Haikou before the reception," Lord Xu said. "But, the fundamentals are quite simple, won't you try now?"

Kaiya looked out of a south-facing window. The Iridescent Moon Caiyue waned to its Fourth Crescent. "The Crown Princess is expecting me in an hour..."

Lord Xu laughed. "More than enough time, then. Send your guards out."

When Chen Xin and Ma Jun left the room and took up places outside of the doors as Kaiya commanded, she searched Lord Xu's eyes.

What would she learn this time? His lesson on the castle wall two years before had opened her ears to the possibilities. She'd since surpassed all her teachers and was now considered one of the best musicians in Hua. No one else could evoke magic through sound.

And here Xu was again, suddenly interested in her development, after not so much as mentioning Dragon Songs since.

He opened his hand and spoke a melodious word of elf magic.

Kaiya gasped as a long musical instrument appeared in his hand. The *sanxian* was ancient by the look of it, perhaps magical. An unknown animal skin stretched over the round resonator. Three strings ran over the fretless wooden neck.

"This belonged to your ancestor," he said with a wistful tone, "Queen Yuxiang, the consort of the founder of the Wang Dynasty, and later Regent." His fingers danced over the strings, the short melody a flittering combination of short pentatonic notes, ending with a long note. "She adored the sound of it, brought it from her home on Jade Island. It is my gift to you." He held it out.

Kaiya hesitated before reverently taking the priceless artifact in her hands. It was light, the resonator rough and the neck smooth. Unlike the Dragon Scale Lute or Yanyan's *pipa*, it didn't seem to pulse with a life of its own. "I do not know how to play this."

"Which is exactly why I gave it to you. Now, pluck one of the strings and listen."

Kaiya did as she was told and a deep, rich hum emanated from the instrument. It was hard to believe such an ancient *sanxian* could create such a crisp twang.

His hand swept over the room. "Do you hear how the sound fills the room? Play more and ponder how that compares with the acoustics of the Hall of Pure Melody."

She thought back to all the performances there in the past two years, in the hall's acoustically perfect room. And of course *that* time, with Hardeep. She plucked different strings, experimenting with the notes as she pressed on the neck.

He made a subtle gesture and a chair whispered across the floor of its own volition, stopping right in front of her. "Concentrate on how the sound wraps around the chair and reflects back."

Tearing her attention away from the chair, which no one had touched, Kaiya obediently plucked the strings.

Her eyes widened. The quality of the *sanxian's* sound had changed, albeit subtly, from the seat's new position.

The elf nodded at her. "Your ears are keen. You understand. Now close your eyes and play long, slow notes."

Strumming, she peeked through narrowed eyelids. Objects flew through the room: the desk, chairs, cushions, scrolls and wall hangings. In the corner of her vision, she saw Doctor Wu, yawning as if the orchestra of flying objects was no more than a street illusionist's trick.

"Close your eyes!" Lord Xu barked from behind. "Focus on the sound."

How had he seen her eyes? Kaiya acquiesced. The subtle changes in the *sanxian's* vibrations became clear. Some objects seemed to create their own sounds while others reflected or absorbed the notes. After several minutes, the sounds leveled off. The suddenly steady modulation startled her into looking.

Xu had rearranged all the furnishings with the expertise of a *Feng Shui* geomancer.

"Do you understand?" he asked.

"I think so."

"Good. Today, I just wanted to open your ears to the possibilities. This somewhat resembles the way bats in the night sky and dolphins in the ocean depths can sense things around them."

Such preposterous statements! Kaiya twirled a lock of her hair.

The elf turned to Doctor Wu. "Is my wager sufficiently fulfilled?"

The doctor flashed the same devilish grin as before. "No, you will teach her more."

He laughed. "Very well, when I return to the capital before the New Year."

Kaiya nodded politely to Lord Xu, and then bowed toward the doctor. "Thank you both for your lessons."

Her sixteen-year old cousin Lin Ziqiu poked her head into the solarium, her face bright. "Hurry up, Kaiya! Lord Peng's messenger is here with a letter for you!"

CHAPTER 4
Theoretical Conspiracies

Minister Hong Jianbin's dark blue court robes absorbed the heat of the late winter sun, warming his old bones as he hobbled through a garden in Sun-Moon Castle. The carefree laughter of young ladies flitted out from beyond a grove of weeping plum trees. The emerging blossoms formed parasols of white fluff, blocking his view.

He followed the blissful chatter, which beckoned him through a wide terrace covered in red tiles. Beyond a white latticework guardrail of interlocking round and square patterns sat five of the realm's most beautiful ladies.

They gathered around an hourglass-shaped pedestal of red porcelain, painted in a gold carp motif and topped with a glass disk. Four were settled on bloodwood chairs, whose gently twisting lines and thin struts belied structural resilience.

Crown Princess Xiulan stood, holding a calligraphy brush in her right hand, and the hanging sleeve of her gown with the left. She finished her work with a flourishing twist. The other ladies leaned back and clapped. A dozen handmaidens joined in the applause.

Ignoring the Crown Princess, Hong fixated on Princess Kaiya, the most stunning of the five. She covered her full lips with delicate fingers as she shifted in her seat and laughed with her friends. In the two years since he had last seen her, when he had taken the plain and gangly girl to meet the Ankiran delegation, she had blossomed. Gone were the blemishes, leaving her natural complexion as flawless as a pearl. Her curves filled out, borne with a nonchalant grace. Lustrous black locks rippled down to her waist.

Her gaze found his as he shuffled toward them, her dark brown eyes so large a doe would envy them.

Two imperial guards blocked his way. The magic etched into their breastplates' five-clawed dragons radiated out. His legs wobbled beneath him and his hands trembled.

The ladies fell silent as their stares bore down on him.

"Minister Hong." Princess Kaiya's melodious voice stopped his heart, making him forget his dread.

She knew his name. His knees protested with a pair of hollow popping sounds as he sank down into a kneel. "Princesses. Forgive my intrusion. The Chief Minister summoned me here."

"Rise." Crown Princess Xiulan spoke as the highest ranking of the five.

The imperial guards parted. Hong clambered to his feet and hobbled toward them. He caught the Crown Princess' withering glare from the corner of his eyes when he admired her calligraphy.

The script for *spring*, written in a brisk, wispy style tangibly whispered over him like a cool spring breeze. The calm stood in stark contrast to the time he saw her magical handwriting on the army's banners. The character for *fear* had evoked an uncontrollable urge to cower.

The Crown Princess turned back to her writing, but Princess Kaiya beckoned him.

"Do you wish to join us while you wait?" She extended a hand with the refinement of a dancer, offering a paintbrush. Her red outer robe with gold embroidered borders flashed open with the motion, revealing a high-collared white inner gown held together with a broad pink sash.

How he longed to receive the brush and perhaps innocuously graze a finger against the smooth skin of her hand. He looked down at his own dry and gnarled hands and thought the better of it.

The other noblewomen's expressions proved less inviting, though none as hostile as sixteen-year old Lin Ziqiu, who regarded him with a disdainful glare. The imperial cousin's scrunched up nose and curled lip marred an otherwise beautiful face, and proved even more of deterrence than the Crown Princess' banners or the imperial guards' breastplates.

He bowed. "Thank you for your kind consideration, but I must beg off your invitation."

Lin Ziqiu blew out a long breath, and the weight of the princesses' stares lifted.

"As you will." Princess Kaiya flashed him a demure smile.

Hong's heart hopped erratically like a tentative rabbit. Repeatedly bobbing his head, he shuffled backward off of the terrace and turned. He ambled toward one of the plum trees, congratulating himself for his lie. *He* had requested Chief Minister Tan to meet him there, knowing the princesses gathered in the adjacent garden, and hoping to catch a glimpse of Princess Kaiya.

He afforded himself this last look at her as a gorgeous young woman. The curve of her neck, the slender high nose, and those eyes. The next time he saw her, he would think of her as a mere tool for his plans.

"Hong, my friend, you asked me to meet you here, of all places?" Chief Minister Tan called from the garden path.

Hong bowed. "Yes. The *Tianzi* ordered me to vet another potential suitor for Princess Kaiya. I cannot join you in the Floating World tonight."

The Chief Minister laughed. "Ah, old friend, had I known your promotion to Minister of Household Relations would eat so much into your time, I would have never recommended you!"

Hong bowed again. "Of course, I am grateful for—"

Tan waved a hand. "I jest, of course. We have come a long way together. I just feel sorry that Princess Kaiya is so...particular. I do not envy your duty of finding a suitor for her."

"It is my honor. Again, I apologize about tonight."

Tan clapped him on the back. "Always responsible. That is why I have always supported you. Well, I have another meeting to attend. Perhaps another time?"

"Yes, sometime soon." Hong watched as Tan strolled back through the garden. He owed his title to the Chief Minister's patronage over the years.

After five years of waiting and watching, he had the unenviable task of repaying kindness with betrayal. With all conditions aligned, Hong just needed Tan to start a cascade of events which would leave the Chief Minister position vacant.

Once Hong claimed the highest office a commoner could achieve, he might even dare to ask the *Tianzi* for Princess Kaiya's hand. When their future son ascended to *Tianzi*, a fishmonger's son could rule as regent.

Heavily cloaked to hide his identity, *Tai-Ming* lord Peng Kai-Long jaunted through the Guanshan Temple grounds with a confident gait. A particularly cold winter now gave way to unseasonable warmth, and his fur-lined coat was stifling. As if to punctuate the heat and the early start of spring, *tianhua* flowers burst free from the confines of their dark green sepals, carpeting the garden borders in cloying white fragrance.

It was the perfect setting for the exotic young woman there. Her features bore a slight roundness, unlike the more angular lines of typical Hua women. She wore an inner gown resembling the gray luminescence of the White Moon Renyue; and above that, an outer robe with long hanging sleeves. Its sapphire color was reminiscent of the Blue Moon Guanyin's Eye, accentuating her cinnamon skin—the union of the honey-toned Hua and the walnut colored Ayuri people.

She knelt on a cushion by a knee-high marble table, across from Minister Hong Jianbin's repugnant form. The servile old man sat, gnarled hands on knobby knees, as he contemplated a chess board. Sallow cheeks hung on a face which might have resembled a weasel had it not been so wrinkled. Wisps of white hair clung to his mottled scalp. Hong easily appeared two decades older than his fifty-some years. His presence sullied all the beauty of the meticulously landscaped garden.

Kai-Long lowered his hood and leveled his eyes at the repulsive man. "Minister Hong, I have come in secret at your request."

Hong turned on his porcelain garden seat and bent his aged frame low. The beauty placed her hands in her lap and lowered her head, revealing the smooth curve of her nape.

Kai-Long's attention lingered on her before a quick glance at the chessboard. A sad imitation of Hua's own chess, the Northerner's game was the latest fad gripping the aristocracy. He'd taken little interest—foreign barbarians had nothing to offer Hua's great empire, beyond land to occupy and resources to control.

His focus settled on the old man. "Rise."

Hong creaked out of his bow and met Kai-Long's stare. He ran his hand through his thin white hair. "Lord Peng, I am honored you came. I trust you are enjoying this wondrous late winter evening?"

Peng Kai-Long had not become the youngest provincial ruler in their wealthy nation by wasting time on idle talk. He withdrew a metal-rimmed monocle with curved grills running through one half of it, and held it up toward the Iridescent Moon Zhuyue, floating inexorably in its reliable position to the south. "A new timepiece, dwarven make. The convex glass magnifies the image to accurately measure a fifth of a phase of

Zhuyue. I grant you five minutes of audience and suggest you not waste it on useless pleasantries."

Hong bowed again. "Forgive my disregard for your valuable time, my Lord. I understand why your fellow *Tai-Ming* respect you so. How long has it been now since you inherited Nanling Province?"

A better question would be, *when would the fawning stop?* Kai-Long fidgeted with his sword hilt. "It has been two years since the Madurans ambushed my father and brother on the docks of Jiangkou."

The woman cast her gaze down, shoulders trembling.

Hong shook his head sympathetically. "Forgive Leina. She is from Ankira, her Ayuri mother left behind and slain when her Hua father fled the Maduran invasion."

"Then we are kindred spirits." Kai-Long leaned over and lifted the beauty's chin. Rude in polite circles, for sure, but he was a high lord and she was just some half-breed bastard. In the corner of his eye, he saw Hong's obsequious smile slip into a frown for a split-second. "With the *Tianzi*'s permission, I hope to one day lead my armies to liberate Ankira and avenge my father and your mother."

Hong spoke, his flattery knowing no limits. "You are the *Tianzi's* favorite nephew, the son of his beloved sister, and the most accomplished of the *Tai-Ming*. But even if the *Tianzi* tolerates your disregard for centuries' old laws, I do not believe he would condone open conflict with Madura."

Flatterers, like rats, tickle first, then bite, or so the old proverb claimed. Kai-Long continued with his demonization of Madura, his regular strategy for hiding his true goals. "We cannot stand idly by and continue to repel Madura's incursions against us without retribution."

Hong shook his head. "But you will not change the mind of the *Tianzi*. His thirty years of rule have been marked by policies of free trade and non-aggression, leading to unprecedented peace and prosperity."

Kai-Long stifled a snort. Hong would hum to the tune of whoever was singing. These little men all wanted something, and sometimes it took the right song to draw it out. "Everyone," Kai-Long said, "from the *Tianzi* and the *Tai-Ming* lords down to the commoners has grown fat on trade and gold, secure with our guns and the Great Wall. We have fallen into complacency. Hua stagnates while the Teleri in the North and Levastya in the South build their empires. It will only be a matter of time before one or the other appears on our doorstep."

Hong nodded repeatedly. "The Royalists on the council are too strong, convincing the *Tianzi* his policies are right."

Kai-Long regarded the minister, thinking back to his meeting with Chief Minister Tan two years before. Hong was Tan's toady, who in turn was secretly invested in the Expansionist faction. "We are the only naval power in the West, and through trade, we have brought all of the best ideas to Hua and made them better. We have improved upon the repeating crossbows of the Eldaeri in the east. We forge steel as strong and sharp as the dwarves. We grow bumper crops on otherwise barren mountainsides."

Leina scowled. "And you monopolize the secret of firepowder."

"There is nothing keeping us back from expansion," Hong said.

Kai-Long ignored the venom in Leina's words, and instead feigned excitement as he held Hong's gaze. "Yes! Old Hong, for the longest time, I had believed you to be just another one of the sycophants currying the *Tianzi*'s favor."

Hong bent over. "I have only the best interests of the motherland at heart."

All it took to get a nightingale to sing was a little seed. Kai-Long decided to reveal some of what he knew. "So these secret meetings with the *Tai-Ming* you have been holding... are they meant to garner support to petition the *Tianzi*?" He raised an eyebrow. "Tell me, how do we change the mind of my dear, but stubborn uncle?"

Minister Hong lowered his voice to a whisper. "To paraphrase the Five Classics, sometimes it is harder to change the mind of a *Tianzi* than to change a *Tianzi* altogether."

There it was, the offer clearly stated. Or a trap.

Kai-Long placed a hand on his sword, just in case it was the latter. "What are you suggesting? It sounds like treason."

Hong shook his head, his eyes wide and defensive. "Patriotism. You would make a stronger *Tianzi* than either of his sons."

Kai-Long suppressed a smirk. He'd spent plenty of time in his youth with cousins Kai-Guo and Kai-Wu, and agreed with the minister's assessment. Though the two princes were undoubtedly intelligent, the elder suffered from indecision and the younger displayed little interest in national affairs.

Kaiya was the proverbial mystery egg. The ugly duckling had transformed into a swan. Kai-Long couldn't allow her to become a phoenix. He'd manipulated her fragile emotions with forged letters from a man she'd only met once; but with her imminent betrothal it was time to take more drastic measures. It might very well tie into what Minister Hong tacitly proposed. He shook his head, pretending to need convincing. "I do not aspire to such a lofty position."

Hong sunk to his knees again. "You are the only one of the *Tai-Ming* to have met an enemy in battle, and in just two short years, you have diversified the economy of your historically modest province. We need a man like you, a man of vision like the Founder. Somebody who can guide our country by marrying our technological innovation with our cultural refinement."

Kai-Long laughed to himself. The old man's words echoed his own self-evaluation. "Hypothetically speaking, if I were *Tianzi*, what would you be?"

The corners of Hong's lips almost connected to the crinkles around his eyes. "Hypothetically speaking, I would be Chief Minister." After a pause, he added, "And I would also like the hand of Princess Kaiya. Hypothetically speaking, of course."

Kai-Long cringed, trying not to envision the decrepit old man bedding his cousin, whose beauty was said to come along once every three generations. "You have obviously already expended a lot of thought on the hypothetical. I wonder if you have a plan in place?"

Minister Hong lowered his gaze and spoke. The meticulous details, including steps starting five years before, plans within plans and conspiracies hijacking others' plots— it was all impressive. It worried him, even, because the old man somehow knew bits of Kai-Long's own scheme. He concluded their talk with a newfound respect for Hong, and assurances that he would play his part.

Smiling to himself, he could guess the eventual, untold outcome of Hong's plot. As someone who'd engineered the demise of his own father and brother, Kai-Long had a nose for treachery. Nonetheless, the first part of the plan was a good one; it just needed a few changes toward the end to make sure *he* sat on the Dragon Throne and Lord Hong was left hanging.

After a quick glance at the chessboard, Kai-Long surmised the treacherous minister would never recognize his own peril. After all, Leina was disguising her inevitable victory in a losing position.

Leina watched as the young *Tai-Ming* lord disappeared down the path. She turned her attention back to the chessboard. With a trembling hand, she moved her Knight into danger, faking a careless attack on Hong's king. "Check."

"Ha!" Hong Jianbin pounced on her diversion, capturing her knight with a pawn.

It opened a path in his line, and she slid her queen through. She clapped her hands together with a delighted squeal. "Checkmate!"

Jianbin's mouth gaped, his wrinkled brow furrowing even more. With eyes darting from her to the board, he used his crooked finger to trace the sequence of moves that led from an apparent victory to sudden defeat.

While he shook his head in disbelief, she thought back to their discussion before the clandestine meeting with Peng. Jianbin had prattled on about Cathay's incomparable resources and ingenuity, eldarwood trees and the need for a great leader. To her, it was a soulless nation without morals. Their sale of guns and firepower to Madura had led to the occupation of her homeland. If the *Tianzi* ruled with the Mandate of Heaven, then the gods must have a sick sense of humor.

Leina had spared herself the boring history lesson by prompting the old man along, ignoring his biased conclusions. The Wang Dynasty's history, as told by men, always extolled the genius of its founder. Wang Xinchang had invented the gun and taken advantage of the chaos following the Hellstorm and Long Winter to pacify All Under Heaven. Little did the historians talk of his consort, who set Cathay on the road to prosperity during her eighty-year rule as regent after his death.

Now after observing Peng Kai-Long's interaction with Hong, she wondered. Was he indeed the caliber of leader Hong believed? To her, he was just another man who spent too much time admiring his own reflection.

Hong still contemplated the board. Just like in chess, he missed the glaring flaw in his plan to seize power: it relied on a stupid opponent.

"You are right," she said. "Lord Peng is a dynamic man. But would you really allow him to become *Tianzi*?"

Old Jianbin looked up and laughed. "Dear Leina, you may be good at the Northerner's version of chess, but you do not have an eye for real strategy."

"Of course not, dear Jian." Leina hated having to feign stupidity and affection for the wretched old man. It was nearly as bad as being his lover. "Then why do you need him at all?"

Jianbin favored her with the same patronizing smile which she always pretended not to notice. "Because he has what I do not. Youth, handsomeness, charisma, and more importantly, the right bloodline," Hong virtually spat the word, "he is the figurehead who can rally our allies. He also has a motive to murder the *Tianzi* and his sons, and will be the perfect scapegoat after the firework show."

Leina crinkled her nose. Lord Peng had surely seen through Jianbin's plan, but that was something the old minister need not know. Because if she manipulated the situation correctly, both men would be dead and the nation thrown into chaos. She only hoped that once she'd fulfilled that task, her employer would keep his promise and free her mother.

CHAPTER 5:
Change of Heart

Kaiya usually found the absolute silence in the Hall of Reflection's inner sanctum almost as unsettling as the countless criss-cross coffering on the walls, floors, ceiling, and door. Acoustically, it was the exact opposite of the Hall of Pure Melody, the Yin to its Yang.

Yet now, even after the whimsical sensation from Xiulan's calligraphy had worn off, even with Father's ultimatum to choose a husband, even inside the otherwise unnerving chamber, Hardeep's latest letter sent her heart skittering to the same frequency as his lotus jewel in her sash.

Cousin Kai-Long's messenger stood outside the building, rarely used among the nine thousand nine hundred and ninety-nine rooms on the palace grounds. Her cousin had been generous in facilitating the clandestine written exchange, and it wouldn't do to let his personal messenger wait so long.

Setting the letter down, she took up a brush and jotted a hasty response. How excited Hardeep would look when he read it, that broad smile beaming, those blue eyes sparkling. She scanned the page, searching for any mistakes.

Perfect.

She stood and poked her head out the door with the note in hand, heedless of her own mischievous grin.

The smile melted.

Second Brother Kai-Wu, Yanli's husband, plucked the letter out of her hand. Behind him, a minister bowed. Several imperial guards, including her own Chen Xin and Li Wei, along with Peng's messenger, all knelt on one knee. The Hall of Reflection's sound-absorbing qualities had masked their approach, even from her keen ears.

Kaiya reached to take the letter back, but Second Brother thrust it behind his back.

His eyes narrowed. "What is this?"

"Nothing important. Just a message to Cousin Peng." As always, she'd written Kai-Long's name on the cover sheet, so it wasn't exactly a lie.

To her dismay, Second Brother unwrapped the cover and unfolded the letter. His gaze raked over the text, his brow furrowing. "You are writing to Peng in Ayuri?"

Kaiya tried to snatch the letter again, but Second Brother passed it back to the minister. She clenched her jaw. Hopefully, the minister could not read the foreign script.

Oh, no. The official's shifting eyes widened. He looked up at her before dropping his chin. "*Dian-xia*. It is a, uh... note... to whom, I do not know, but the message is... well...."

Kaiya's heart lurched in her chest as she clenched and unclenched her clammy hands. Her year-old secret, carefully concealed from all but Lord Peng, exposed.

Second Brother stared at the minister, who withered under her brother's glower. "Speak."

"*Dian-xia*. It is a love letter."

Kai-Wu's mouth dropped open. He turned to the imperial guards. "Take Peng's messenger into custody. Find Lord Peng and command him to present himself before me at once."

"As the prince commands!" The imperial guards snapped to attention before hurrying to fulfill his order.

Second Brother took Kaiya's arm and pulled her back into the hall's inner sanctum. He closed the doors behind him and leveled his glare. After several long minutes, he spoke, the chamber rendering his voice oddly flat. "Is this why you have rejected so many suitors? For some secret affair? I pray to the Heavens you have not given yourself to a man."

Kaiya's cheeks flushed hot. Did he just...as if... "No...no, of course not."

"So you are not having an inappropriate liaison with the messenger?" Brother Kai-Wu asked.

The messenger? Her breath caught in her throat. "No. Of course not," she repeated.

Searching her eyes, Kai-Wu exhaled sharply. "Very well. A rumor circulates among the palace servants that you have been secretly meeting with one of Lord Peng's men whenever he visits the capital. If not him, then who is it?"

Kaiya sighed. There was no use in hiding it. They would find out soon enough. "Prince Hardeep."

Brow furrowing, Kai-Wu cocked his head. "Who is he?"

"The Prince of Ankira."

"Ankira? Aren't they in a war or something?"

Kaiya nodded. "Occupied. Prince Hardeep leads their resistance."

"So a foreigner. This is most inappropriate."

It was true. Yet up to now, the suitors all saw her either as a stepping stone to greater power and influence or, since her blossoming into a woman, an object to possess. Only Prince Hardeep had ever *seen* her, starting from their fated meeting two years ago and growing through their furtive correspondence. None could match his wit or charm. She pressed the lotus jewel in her sash, feeling its steadfast warmth against her waist.

A slot in the door opened and a voice called in. "*Dian-xia*. Lord Peng is here."

Second Brother's brow furrowed. "You are to end this relationship. We will find you someone appropriate." He then pushed the door open. "All of you, enter."

Lord Peng strode in with a confident gait, followed by the imperial guards, the minister, and the messenger. All sank to one knee.

"You may face me." Though the otherwise aloof Kai-Wu rarely used it, his voice carried the tone of command bred into the Imperial Family. When all looked up, he raised the letter. "Lord Peng, explain this."

Peng bowed. "*Dian-xia*. I have long been in contact with Ankira's Prince Hardeep, since his embattled nation shares a border with my province. I send the Ankiran resistance supplies. I have passed messages between the foreign prince and princess for a year now."

"You did not deem it inappropriate?"

Kaiya started to speak, but Second Brother held up a silencing hand.

"They could be writing about anything," Peng said. "It is not my place to judge the Imperial Family."

Of course Cousin Peng would sacrifice her to protect himself. What had she expected? Kaiya bit her lip. She was by herself in this.

Second Brother's voice rose just a little. "Lord Peng, you will cease your intermediation between Princess Kaiya and the foreign prince."

Peng lowered his head again. "As the prince commands."

"The rest of you: you will not relate what occurred here today. The *Tianzi* must never find out. Am I understood?"

All of the assembled men bowed and spoke in unison. "As the prince commands."

A wave of relief washed over Kaiya. At the very least, Father wouldn't have to worry about her exposed secret.

Second Brother gestured the men out of the room. "Shut the door and wait outside."

The men rose and shuffled out.

When the door closed behind them, Kaiya spoke. "Thank you, Second Brother."

"You are lucky Eldest Brother did not find out about it. He has a good heart, but he lacks discretion as much as you."

Kaiya bowed her head, contrite.

"Now, forget about this Prince Hardeep. There are many great lords in this land who will make fine husbands. In fact, I have someone in mind."

Hardeep's lotus jewel's near inaudible buzz seemed to intensify as Kaiya held it over the bloodwood box. It hadn't left her person in the two years since their parting, even when she slept or bathed.

Her heart squeezed. She couldn't do it. She couldn't put the jewel away. It felt too much like giving up on Hardeep.

No, giving up on *herself*.

When everyone had scoffed at her music, he'd been the only one to believe in her potential.

She'd proven herself. She'd grown in power with Lord Xu and Dr. Wu's lessons. As much as she wanted Hardeep, her music was her own. Putting the jewel away wasn't giving up.

Settling in Dr. Wu's horse stance, Kaiya gripped her bedroom's wood floors with her toes. She took a deep breath. The cool night air filled her lungs. Outside, birds chirped and frogs trilled. The symphony of spring calmed her thoughts and eased the dragonclaw on her heart.

Prince Hardeep had encouraged and inspired her, but now it was time to sing with her own voice. She would free Ankira, not because she loved Hardeep, but because it was the right thing to do.

She had thirty days.

Kaiya waited until the light breeze off Sun-Moon Lake subsided, then loosed the arrow. The man-shaped straw target standing thirty feet downrange had nothing to fear. Indeed, it seemed to be enjoying the view of melting snow caps reflected in the lake's placid surface on this unseasonably balmy afternoon.

She sighed as the arrow missed by the worst margin in years. Her hand strayed to Hardeep's lotus jewel. Gone.

Right. It hadn't been easy leaving it on her make-up table four days ago, after Second Brother uncovered the relationship. Each morning it beckoned her, sending her heart racing and palms sweating. She needed Dr. Wu's breathing techniques to resist its tug on her heart. She now plodded back to the communal quiver, head tilted down to avoid the gazes of her four friends.

Crown Princess Xiulan looked back as her shot brushed over the target's armored shoulder. "Thinking about your meeting with Lord Shun yesterday?"

Kaiya shuddered. "He was boring." And not a fraction as amazing as Hardeep.

"But he *is* handsome." Her cousin, Wang Kai-Hua, stroked her fingers through an arrow's fletching. The glow of her recent marriage to Young Lord Liu, the heir to Jiangzhou Province, had yet to wear off. She seemed even more radiant these days. It was good to see her happy, at last, after two years of family misfortunes.

"Oh, Lord Shun is delicious," squealed her other cousin, Lin Ziqiu. The naïve sixteen-year-old stood beside Kaiya, her eyes wide. "I could watch him all day and not grow bored."

All the other ladies covered laughs with their sleeves, hiding their amusement at the girl's youthful bluntness. Yanli glowered at her, though Ziqiu didn't seem to notice.

"There's more to a man than his looks," Kaiya said. "He could not hold a conversation beyond one-word answers."

Xiulan giggled. "A handsome face can sometimes be ruined by too much talking. That's why the Crown Prince and I rarely discuss anything of deep import."

Ziqiu loosed an arrow, which joined her others in the target's head with a dull thud. "That's because you talk with your hips."

Yanli scowled and poked Ziqiu. Sleeves flashed up again, this time covering laughs *and* blushes. If Xiulan's cheeks could burn any brighter, it might seem like a recurrence of the Year of the Second Sun from antiquity.

A smile tugged at Kaiya's lips, though she fought it off. With her chambers next to Eldest Brother's, there was no arguing with Cousin Ziqiu's assessment.

"If you want someone who talks," Ziqiu prattled on, "then maybe you should consider my cousin Lin Ziqiang. He never shuts his mouth! I know my father has been discussing it with the *Tianzi*."

A rumble of galloping hooves interrupted the girl's blabbering.

Kaiya spun around.

A soldier in dark green court robes bent down from his warhorse and pulled a few arrows from the communal quiver as he cantered by. His glossy black locks whipped behind him. Was that the scent of *shouwu* berries? Like most ladies, she used them herself to maintain healthy hair.

All eyes followed the newcomer as he put two shafts between his teeth, fitted an arrow, twisted back and shot.

The arrow lodged dead center in the target's head.

Kaiya turned back to the rider, just in time to see him shoot again.

It hit the target in the center of its chest, driving through the leather cuirass.

The man wheeled around and spurred his horse back toward them. He floated the last arrow upwards. She tracked its lazy arc into the target's neck.

The horse slowed as it approached and the rider swung out of the saddle. His large eyes briefly met hers before veering toward the ground as etiquette demanded. Who was he? There was something familiar about him.

It might've been easier to remember without Ziqiu's tight clutch squeezing the sensation out of her arm. The girl pressed up against her shoulder. "Who is that?" she whispered, breathless.

The archer strode over, his posture straight. His beautiful hair, which rivaled her own, obscured the family crest on his left breast.

A dozen imperial guards, who undoubtedly appreciated his showmanship more than the princesses' mediocre archery, now interposed themselves with hands on swords.

A deep voice from the opposite direction drew her attention away from the visitor. "The *Tianzi*! The Crown Prince and Second Prince!"

Father and both brothers, all wearing official blue robes, approached on horseback. Dozens of imperial guards trailed them, their burnished breastplates flashing in the late afternoon sun as they jogged in exacting formation. At their head, iImperial guard commander General Zheng held the Broken Sword, a symbol of the *Tianzi*.

Father hadn't ridden a horse in years. Nor did he ever come to this section of the palace grounds, generally limiting his visits to the Hall of Supreme Harmony. If not for affairs of state, he would've sequestered himself across the moat in the castle. Now, he slouched in the saddle, wheezing.

In unison, the princesses pressed their practice robes down to their shins and dropped to both knees. Spreading their arms out horizontally to straighten out the sleeves, they placed open hands at the front of their knees and bowed their heads at the approach of the *Tianzi*.

"Rise," he said.

Kaiya looked up.

Age hadn't treated Father kindly. Whenever she saw his many care lines, wispy white hair, lusterless eyes, and listless gait, a lump formed in her throat. Kaiya knew well the other culprit.

His thirty-two-year reign had been marked by unprecedented prosperity for Hua, spurred by his benevolent wisdom and policy of expanded foreign trade. In recent years, some of the *Tai-Ming* lords had let their newfound affluence transform into avarice, and the *Tai-Ming* Council had become increasingly divided by the lords who wanted to expand the national borders and those who were content to maintain the status quo.

Expansionists versus Royalists. The final arbiter and decision maker, the *Tianzi* had been physically and mentally drained by the contentious situation. After the death of Kaiya's mother two years earlier, he'd declined rapidly.

As the *Tianzi's* gaze brushed over them, his burdens seemed to melt away. He nodded at each, his eyes speaking of fatherly admiration. His voice wheezed. "My daughters, it looks like it will be a beautiful evening with both Renyue and Guanyin's Eye looming large in the sky tonight. I would be pleased if you would join me in the *Danhua* Room for dinner, so I can enjoy myself before next week's council meeting."

It wasn't a request, and Kaiya and the others bowed again in acquiescence. As senior, Xiulan answered for everyone. "We would be honored to join you, Father."

"Rise." The *Tianzi* motioned toward the horseman, who shifted from a kneel to a one-knee, one-fist salute. "This is Captain Zheng Ming, the heir to Dongmen Province. He is visiting the capital from the northern border to defend his archery title at the New Year's Tournament. Rise, Young Lord Zheng."

Zheng. Zheng Ming was the eldest brother of her childhood playmate, Tian. They had met once, ten years before, while she and Tian practiced swordsmanship together.

He stood and now met Kaiya's gaze again. His complexion hinted at time spent in the sun. Strong, chiseled features rivaled General Lu's handsomeness, though he stood a head taller. It probably made him even more of a narcissist.

A sweep of Zheng Ming's head sent his hair over his shoulders with a whiff of the *shouwu* scent again. He almost purred when he spoke. "Princesses, it is my honor to meet you."

The five ladies nodded in acknowledgement, though young Ziqiu followed a split-second late, and her face flushed. She batted her lashes at him.

Ziqiu's reaction might be amusing, but Kaiya forced herself not to roll her eyes. The lordling was just the latest among the dozens of handsome lords and generals she'd met over the last two years, with nothing beyond a title and a pretty face to distinguish them. None could compare with Hardeep.

"Young Lord Zheng came to visit Kai-Wu," the *Tianzi* said. "When I heard you were all practicing archery, I commanded him to come share his expertise with you."

Zheng Ming bowed. "*Huang-Shang*, I hope my poor skills can meet your expectations."

The *Tianzi* let out a shallow, breathy laugh. "Your bow has defended the realm against Lord Tong's rebellion and the Kingdom of Rotuvi's incursions. You have earned numerous distinctions. I have no doubt my daughters will benefit from your guidance."

Such praise, as if it would impress her. Kaiya nodded with the others nonetheless.

"Now, I have other matters to attend to." The *Tianzi* turned his horse around.

All bowed low and held the position until the sound of his horse and marching imperial guards faded.

Xiulan smiled, exchanging glances with the others. "Well, I must freshen up before we dine." She motioned for her imperial guards.

Zheng Ming bowed. "Perhaps I will have the honor to speak with you another time, Crown Princess."

"I, too, must be getting ready." Yanli winked at Xiulan and beckoned her guards. She glared at Ziqiu, who had missed the tacit message and still gazed at the dashing cavalry officer.

"And I, too, must be returning to my own residence," added Kai-Hua. "And so should you," she growled lightly at Ziqiu. "You should be getting back to your father's pavilion before dusk. A lady should not be out after dark, lest she be mistaken for a Night Blossom of the Floating World."

Zheng Ming laughed, a warm laugh. "What a shame. I am always surrounded by soldiers and yes-men, and never by so many beautiful ladies."

Ziqiu's brows furrowed, an annoyed look falling across her pretty face. Her attention still lingered on the handsome soldier. "I am certain the page will call me when my guards arrive."

Xiulan took Ziqiu's hand. "You can wait in the main courtyard. I will accompany you."

Frowning, Ziqiu offered a reluctant bob of her head. The dancing colors of a dozen vibrant handmaiden robes departed like spring blossoms blown from the trees.

After a few minutes, Kaiya was alone with Young Lord Zheng, save for the imperial guards Chen Xin and Li Wei.

Such a blatant set-up. Zheng Ming was probably the lord Brother Kai-Wu wanted to introduce, with Xiulan and the others complicit in the *chance* meeting.

With no time for her to prepare.

In all of the previous appointments with potential suitors, Kaiya had worn the finest silken gowns like armor to protect her from the choreographed farce. Now, training robes and wits were her only weapons against this new opponent. She bowed her head, deferring to the man as convention dictated, waiting for him to speak.

His lips curved upward like the stroke of a calligrapher's brush, sweeping away the awkwardness of the situation. "You may not remember, but we have met before, when you were still a child of seven."

"I do remember, though not clearly."

He nodded. "You shared the same swordmaster as my younger brother Tian. You were fencing with him at the time. And beat him, if my memory serves me well."

"It does." She smiled at the mention of Tian's name and the fond recollection. "He was a dear friend...until that unfortunate misunderstanding. I have not heard from him since he was sent to the monastery. I trust he is doing well?"

"I have only spoken to him once in the last several years. My mother tells me he is a trade official, serving at our embassy in the Nothori Kingdoms."

She covered her laugh with a hand. "Fancy that, a monk becoming a diplomat. But enough about Zheng Tian. I am sure my father did not bring you here for us to reminisce about your brother."

Zheng Ming grinned. "Nor to teach you the finer points of archery, I presume."

Kaiya tilted her head, placing a hand on her chest in mock indignation. "Do you presume to know the mind of the Son of Heaven?"

He pressed his hands over his own chest in exaggerated contrition. "I know the mind of a father with unwed daughters."

She raised an eyebrow. "So you are an expert at this type of meeting?"

"If rumor is to be believed, the princess is much more experienced than I in such matters." Zheng Ming stared at the sky.

Heat rose to Kaiya's cheeks. She lowered her head to hide her blushing. "Rumors proliferate like spring blossoms after a storm."

"Unfortunately, for every blossom there are a dozen weeds."

Kaiya maintained a demure smile, stalling. The weeds *had* to refer to all the lousy suitors. Right? *She* was the one who usually had *them* on their toes. This blossom, however...he spoke like a poet, reminding her of Prince Hardeep's written words. Yet whereas the prince's script simmered for months between new letters, Zheng Ming's wit had a fulfilling immediacy to it. She tilted her chin toward her guards. "The imperial gardeners carry sharp shears."

Zheng Ming ran his hand back and forth over the side of his neck. "I empathize with the palace weeds, then."

The palace bell tolled, and both looked up to see the Iridescent Moon waxing toward half. The nine-star constellation of E-Long, the evil dragon, seemed to wrap around it.

Kaiya lowered her hand. Heavens, she was playing with a lock of loose hair.

"I am afraid I must depart. I dine with the *Tianzi* tonight. It seems like we will have to cut our discussion of landscaping short."

Zheng Ming lowered his gaze, peering up through half-lidded eyes. "I would not be averse to continuing our debate over the merits of flowers and weeds at some other time."

Up to now, no suitor had survived her questioning, let alone asked to meet again. Kaiya's heart skittered a few beats. For the past two years, she'd held on to an idealized memory of her meeting with Prince Hardeep. Zheng Ming was here and now, and her belly's somersaults felt real. She looked up at him through her lashes. "I would not be averse to considering it."

His grin slipped for a split second, but returned, brighter than before. "I might be inclined to wait here for a more definite answer."

Kaiya smiled coyly, lifting her chin toward the imperial guards. "Do I have to summon the gardeners?"

Zheng Ming dropped to one knee and brushed his hair to the side to expose his neck. "You decide."

CHAPTER 6:

Seeds of Insurrection

After picking out the distinct breathing patterns of fourteen different men, Liang Yu flung open the sliding doors to the private room. Now at middle age, his eyes adjusted slowly from the bright lights of the Phoenix Spring Inn's common area to the candlelit interior room.

Even before the thirteen dark shapes at the knee-high table came into focus, he already smelled the mix of sweat and weapon oil. He was greeted by the rasping of five broadswords, two straightswords, and four knives from their sheaths, as well as the cocking of two repeating crossbows.

Liang Yu admired their enthusiasm. Once upon a time, he would have gone to any end to impress his master. But when he was presumed killed on a mission thirty-two years before, had his master even cared?

He reassured the rugged men with a secret hand signal. All bowed in response, rustling their dark clothes as they returned to their knees. Without looking back, he slid the door to an exact, silent close with a quick sweep of his walking stick.

"Thank you for coming. Make yourselves comfortable." Liang Yu surveyed the former Hua soldiers as they shifted from their knees to sitting cross-legged. With their experience in the army and later as mercenaries, their skillsets were suited to the upcoming task. He shifted his attention to the one man, the disowned son of a minister, who had remained calm as he entered. "Little Song, why didn't you reach for your weapon when I entered?"

Song bowed. "I heard you outside the door."

"You knew it was me?"

"Yes, from the walking stick on the floorboards."

Liang Yu nodded. At least one of the young men had passed the test. He ran a hand through his greying black hair, wondering how he had gotten so old. "Very observant. And a cool head is a sign of discipline. You will lead the attack."

Song shifted up to a one knee, keeping his gaze lowered. "I am honored."

Straightening his black robes, Liang Yu sat cross-legged at the head of the table. He passed out several sheets of folded rice paper. Each bore the sketch of a handsome young man, with words written in the Ayuri script.

As the men unfolded the paper, he leaned over the table and spread out his crudely-drawn map of the capital. It did not do justice to Huajing's precise gridded layout, designed by Feng Shui masters at the behest of the Queen Regent three hundred years ago to ensure national prosperity.

Liang Yu indicated the Phoenix Spring Inn on the map, in the northwest near the city's walls. "We are here."

He then tapped his finger on a narrow bridge nearby, which arched over a stream. Houses with first-floor shops lined the street near the bridge—bustling during the day, but almost everyone would be retiring or already asleep when they attacked. "Our target is Captain Zheng Ming, the heir to Dongmen Province. He will be passing over this bridge on his way back from a meeting with Minister Hong Jianbin. My sources say he has two guards with him."

One man grinned. "The capital has always been safe. The high-and-mighty lords aren't prepared for a surprise attack. This should be easy if he only has two guards."

Song shook his head. "Don't underestimate him. He is an excellent, battle-tested archer."

Liang Yu nodded. "We can't let him past this bridge." He pointed out several landmarks near the bridge, assigning hiding spots for each of his men. He then traced a line of approach that would flush Lord Zheng into an alleyway where Liang Yu himself would be waiting.

The men smiled, heads bobbing at each point. Of course they were impressed; his planning skills had once earned him the nickname the Architect. At his side, Song's gaze shifted over the map, undoubtedly drinking in the details. Sharp mind, that kid. Maybe as observant as the other pupil Liang Yu had recruited two years earlier.

"Young Lord Zheng must not be killed," Liang Yu said. "I leave the guards to your discretion, though we should avoid unnecessary bloodshed of our own countrymen. Regroup here after the mission."

All the men bowed again. They stood and departed.

Liang Yu relaxed and called to the proprietress for some rice wine. In two hours, it would be time to incite a war.

Zheng Ming studied Minister Hong Jianbin and decided a monkey would look more dignified wearing blue official robes. Nonetheless, he bowed to the knobby-kneed minister as protocol demanded. The old man struggled to his feet and tottered across the receiving room's dark wood floors.

Ming sighed, his mind swimming with Hong's requests. The minister had revealed Peng Kai-Long's plans to take punitive actions against the Kingdom of Madura. Without significant pressure and resources from the *Tai-Ming* lords, the *Tianzi* would never approve. Hong wanted Ming to convince his father to switch sides to the Expansionists.

Ming should've never come to Huajing for the New Year Tournament. Court intrigue was eating up all the time meant for carousing with the more sophisticated and promiscuous women of the capital.

It was too much of a headache. Perhaps he could still withdraw from the tournament and return to his cavalry unit in Wailian. With the possibility of dying in combat looming over each day, *they* knew how to have fun.

Emerging from the secluded official pavilion, he looked up to the south at the Iridescent Moon Caiyue, never moving from the same position in the sky. It now waxed to its fourth gibbous, just two bells before midnight.

Much too late to be discussing politics, but perhaps not too late to pay a visit to one of the ladies he'd captivated with his charm.

He walked out into the courtyard, now bathed in the pale blue light of Guanyin's Eye. It struck an odd hue with the dark green court robes his two waiting guards wore. Both had sheathed swords tucked in silver sashes. One bowed and presented Ming's cavalry saber, the other his bow and quiver.

Ming glanced back to the pavilion.

He could almost hear Minister Hong's joints creak and pop from the way he bent into a plain wooden palanquin. A dozen guards surrounded it— quite a lot for the capital, and overkill for the nobles' quarter.

Blowing out a long breath, he motioned for his men to mount up and set out for the ride back to the Dongmen provincial pavilion.

He rode with little focus, his mind wandering over the meeting and Hong's appeals. The obsequious toad lacked ambition, so someone must be pulling his strings. He did, however, have a level of influence as Minister of Household Relations. In return for Ming's support, Hong had promised the hand of Princess Kaiya.

Ming chuckled. The princess had rejected over two dozen fine suitors. Though beloved by the general populace, she'd acquired the nickname *Ice Princess* among the young noblemen. Theories abounded, with rumors ranging from a secret liaison with a servant, to her desire to dally with ladies rather than marry a lord.

As much as Ming might enjoy his defenses being flanked by a coordinated onslaught from Princess Kaiya and another beauty, he doubted the validity of *that* rumor. No, if anything, she probably still harbored feelings for his youngest brother Tian, the black sheep of the family. The two had shared some foolish romance as children.

He snorted. Regardless of her reasons, it had become a virtual rite of passage for the young lords, to be offered up as fodder for the Ice Princess. One friend alluded to his meeting with her as akin to a torturer's interrogation. Another compared it with going into battle; never mind that the closest he'd come to a battlefield was the first Wang Emperor's treatise on the Art of War.

With that in mind, Ming had taken his own meeting with the princess a few days before as mere formality. He played her game, with the expectation of adding the most interesting story of rejection to the rumor mill.

Now, Hong suggested he could not only arrange a second meeting, but almost guarantee a betrothal. As the old man insinuated, marriage to the *Tianzi*'s daughter would place his own future son somewhere in line to inherit the Dragon Throne of Hua.

Ming laughed out loud. Not that the rules of succession mattered to him. More interesting was the challenge of melting the heart of the Ice Princess. She would—

The horse in front of him screamed. The guard tumbled from the saddle as it collapsed.

A crossbow bolt protruded from the flailing horse's neck. The beast lay squirming, obstructing his path forward off the bridge...bridge? When had he reached it? He reined back his own mount, only to find the rear guard struggling with his own horse.

"Back off the bridge!" he bellowed, as if it would make his retainer move faster.

The rhythmic clicks of repeating crossbows echoed from nearby buildings. Bolts lodged into his guard's horse in quick succession. Both collapsed. Several men swarmed toward the bridge from both sides, brandishing broadswords.

His mount panicked, its head thrashing about as it looked for a means of escape. If only he'd ridden his own reliable warhorse instead of a skittish palfrey borrowed from the Dongmen compound. Another bolt whistled by, missing his face by a ridiculously safe margin.

"The watch," he yelled, "Call the watch!" Trying to control his lurching horse, Ming unslung his bow. Though the court robes restricted mobility, he nocked an arrow and let it fly. It hit its mark, dropping one of the men. He loosed a second arrow, but the pitching of his horse sent it flying errant.

Unfazed, Ming took aim at one of the four assailants hacking at his lead guard, who was pinned under his horse. If not for his panicky mount, Ming might've targeted the man's eye. Instead, he shot the arrow into his center of mass, knocking him to the ground from point-blank range.

As he withdrew another arrow, he glanced around. Lights flickered and shutters opened as the commotion drew the attention of curious citizens.

Ming drew his string for another shot. The horse reared. The arrow slipped from his fingers as he swiped for the reins. A bolt hit his mount's flank, just barely missing his own leg. Another lodged into the beast's skull.

The horse tumbled. Ming leaped from the saddle to avoid getting crushed, and landed hard on his side. He rolled out of the way of flailing hooves.

Sword raised, an attacker bore down. Ming rolled, then staggered to his feet. Though more accustomed to fighting from horseback, he swept his blade out with a smooth rasp, cutting into the assailant before the man could start his chop.

The narrowness of the bridge trapped Ming, but also slowed the advance of his foes. In front, two tried to skirt by his sprawling horse. He glanced back to see his rear guard injured, but holding his ground. The four attackers held back, goading the guard to pursue them off the bridge.

Another several bolts thwacked into the bridge, and then abruptly stopped. These had to be the worst crossbowmen ever.

An assailant in the front clambered over Ming's dead horse. Before the man found his footing on the other side, Ming cleaved him shoulder to chest with a two-handed cut. He yanked the saber free.

Click, click, click. The crossbows resumed their barrage, persuading him to kneel beneath the cover of the guardrails.

His guard's harried voice rasped, "We are surrounded, *Xiao-ye.* Jump off the bridge and escape."

The ambushers held back, affording Ming a momentary respite. He shuddered at the potential blow to his reputation. Stories of his brave death would live on forever. Soldiers would raise their cups to him, and women might dream of him while they lay with their men. On the other hand, abandoning his guards for a midnight swim would brand him a coward well past a quiet death at old age. What woman would have him?

The ones attracted to wealth and power. Ming's family had plenty of both. He gritted his teeth. Time to throw himself over the bri—

"The watch, the watch, fall back!" The villains scattered, leaving their dead and wounded behind.

Ming caught his breath. He'd survived unscathed. Both he and his reputation would live on. A quick survey of the scene revealed his lead guard lying dead among four foes. At the rear, one attacker had perished, and another crawled away. His surviving guard fought to remain standing as blood spurted from a gash to his leg. Ming loped over and knelt. Tearing a strip of cloth from the guard's robe, he bound the wound.

"*Xiao-ye.*" A commoner bowed low before him. "Allow me to help."

Ming looked around. Townsfolk emerged from their homes, with several racing over and others calling for help.

He rose and strode over to the survivor. "Who sent you? Why did you attack me?"

The man stayed silent, feebly lifting his sword in defiance.

Credit the man for courage. Ming might do the same, even if he ultimately planned on surrender. "I am asking politely, but I am sure the *Tianzi* has many a good man who can get an answer out of you with much less courtesy."

Too late did he recognize the man's look of resolve—that of a soldier facing certain death. Ming thrust his saber forward to interpose it between the man's sword and neck. It arrived a fraction late, as the man jerked the blade across his own throat.

"Smart Son of a Turtle," Ming said. Better to die quickly now than slowly and painfully. Rifling through the man's possessions, he found some silver coins stamped with a scorpion and crown, and a crumpled sheet of paper with a very accurate drawing of himself. Not bad at all! Making sure no one was watching, he stashed it into his robe. Although he couldn't read the foreign script, he recognized it as Ayuri, the language of the South.

Of the countries in the South, only the Madurans would engineer such a brazen attack. As much as he would have liked to believe they had targeted him for his value as a leader, he assumed there must be another reason.

Perhaps they knew of Minister Hong's efforts to start a war against them.

Liang Yu strolled through deserted streets back to the Phoenix Spring Inn. People stuck heads out of windows as patrols of the watch scurried toward the scene of the attack. He kept to the shadows, secure in his stealth.

The plan had worked as intended. Without adversity, he could never effectively evaluate the mettle of his recruits. Those that survived would emerge stronger for their troubles. Some of them might be worthy of further training. Young Song had survived, saved from Young Lord Zheng's aim by his careful angle of approach. He might make a fine lieutenant, to go along with his special pupil.

Too bad neither of the two would ever begin to compare to his former brothers and sisters-in-arms. Nonetheless, his men were skilled enough for the scare tactics he planned to orchestrate over the next several days. The attacks on the nation's ruling class would implicate the Kingdom of Madura. Fearing for their pitiful lives, they would be clamoring for a punitive invasion.

No doubt the *Tianzi* would mobilize Liang Yu's former comrades first, before rushing to war. If they knew he was alive, the mindless pawns he once called friends would label him a traitor.

He saw himself as a patriot.

Sometimes, a patriot had to sow seeds of insurrection, lest the nation succumb to its own complacency.

And if pressure from the nobility couldn't sway the *Tianzi* to act, perhaps the assassination of the beloved princess would.

CHAPTER 7:

Dragon in the Room

Kaiya listened to the warbling songbirds in the adjoining garden. If only she could be out there, instead of stuck in the stifling council of hereditary lords. Unlike daily administrative functions held across the moat in the Hall of Supreme Harmony, this quarterly meeting convened in Sun-Moon Castle.

As the residence of the *Tianzi* and his family, the castle was Kaiya's retreat from official responsibilities. Now, the *Tai-Ming* and *Yu-Ming* lords invaded her refuge. Her ancestor had established the tradition, before his consort and later Queen Regent commissioned construction of the surrounding palace grounds.

The only woman to attend these meetings since the Queen Regent, Kaiya's too-conspicuous place next to her brothers invited the only slightly less conspicuous glances of the three dozen great lords facing her. Dressed in court robes, they sat cross-legged in a three-row semicircle, some peeking at the curves she'd lacked just a year ago.

She tightened her outer robe over her bust. Unlike the Queen Regent, or the *Tianzi*, she couldn't order a lord to take his own life with the curved dagger resting on the floor in front of him. By the time the Queen Regent died at the unprecedented age of one hundred and twenty-four, her figure might not have attracted many leers, anyway.

The sliding doors of the Celestial Flower Room stood open to the garden, taunting Kaiya with a cool spring breeze off Sun-Moon Lake. To be out there...

The *Tianzi* cleared his throat. He slouched on a bloodwood chair encrusted with jade fish and mother-of-pearl bats. His yellow silk robe, embroidered with symbols of health and prosperity, sagged from his gaunt form. A long necklace of jade ornaments hung from his neck, and a square black hat with dangling jade beads adorned his head. His voice rasped when he spoke. "What is next on the agenda, Minister Fen?"

Throughout the morning, the minister had avoided the topic on everyone's mind: the recent ambushes in the capital. He now bowed from his place at the end of the first row, where the nine *Tai-Ming* lords sat. "*Huang-Shang*, we are receiving an envoy from the Eldaeri Kingdom of Tarkoth. The Foreign Ministry has vetted their request."

Kaiya perked up and looked to the interior doors, curious to catch a glance of the visitor. Though human, the Eldaeri had escaped to a distant continent and mingled with elves five millennia ago. With ships rivaling Hua's, they had returned to Tivaralan in the chaotic aftermath of the Hellstorm and occupied much of the Northeast. Though Tarkoth maintained a trade office in Huajing, they usually conducted businesses through lower ministries. The last time any Tarkothi of consequence had visited was two years ago, when their prince attended Second Brother Kai-Wu's wedding.

Murmurs broke out among the great lords. They apparently didn't share her enthusiasm for the guest.

Father silenced them with a raise of his eyebrow. "I will receive Tarkoth's emissary. Send them in."

The doors to an antechamber slid open. Foreign Minister Song strode in and bowed low. He spoke in perfect Arkothi, the common language of the North. "I present Lady Ayana Strongbow, representative of the Eldaeri Kingdom of Tarkoth."

Strongbow? A strange name for the Arkothi-speaking Eldaeri. To get a better view, Kaiya shifted as much as decorum would allow. The lords turned craned to face the antechamber.

A slender old elf woman with sharp features glided in. She floated across the room in a light blue gown and diaphanous green shawl. Her dull gold tresses and fair complexion stood out among the black-haired, honey-skinned Hua. A rope of silver hung around her waist, and a matching silver anklet graced a bare foot. A twinge of jealousy pricked at Kaiya. How could someone so old still be so ethereal and beautiful?

With delicate grace, Lady Ayana curtseyed in the manner of the North. "Greetings, Your Imperial Highness. Thank you for receiving me." Her voice sang like a nightingale as she spoke lilting Arkothi.

The *Tianzi* answered, his own Arkothi heavily accented. "Greetings, Lady Ayana. How is it that an elf comes to represent the human Kingdom of Tarkoth?"

"Your Majesty, I am in the employ of Prince Aelward Corivar of Tarkoth, captain of the Tarkothi Royal Ship *Invincible*. The prince sent me because I can travel much faster than anyone else aboard his ship, which is currently anchored in the port city of Sodorol."

The elf's voice carried a resonance, similar to...the conspicuously absent Lord Xu. Perhaps she could pop in and out of places, just like him. While the lords murmured about how she'd gotten here, Kaiya fought the urge to speak out of line.

Foreign Minister Song bowed and presented a parchment envelope. "The Tarkothi trade mission presented Lady Ayana to the ministry yesterday. The wax seal on her missive matches our records."

Ayana nodded. "May I present Prince Aelward's request?"

The *Tianzi* waved for her to continue.

"The *Invincible* will be provisioning at your port of Jiangkou in about two weeks, and Prince Aelward requests an audience with the Emperor." She gestured toward the *Tianzi*. Kaiya clenched her jaw at the impudence.

He leveled his gaze at the elf. "It will be close to the New Year Festival, and your prince is welcome to join the other dignitaries that will celebrate in Cathay at that time. I cannot promise I will have time to meet with him."

Ayana took a step forward. "Prince Aelward wishes to discuss an alliance. Tarkoth's nemesis, the Teleri Empire, is allied with your enemy, the Kingdom of Madura. The prince will be conducting raids and supplying insurgents in Madura. He hopes we might coordinate our efforts against our mutual foes."

Murmurs broke out among the lords. All eyes turned toward Father. Kaiya sucked in a breath. The Expansionists would jump at the opportunity. If only they had been so enthusiastic two years ago, when Prince Hardeep needed it.

Kaiya's stomach...did nothing. Once upon a time, just thinking about Hardeep sent it into flutters. And she hadn't even thought about him for the last few days. Had the charming and heroic Zheng Ming so quickly replaced Hardeep in her heart? And here she was, daydreaming while the lords discussed sending men to kill and die.

The *Tianzi* raised his hand and the room fell into silence. "Lady Ayana, I was not aware that Madura was our enemy. Cathay's position for the last three hundred years is one of neutrality. Tell your prince we do not take sides, and we trade with all. We only resort to arms when attacked."

Cousin Kai-Long rose from his seated position to one knee. "*Huang-Shang*," he said in the Hua tongue, "Madura has created troubles at your borders for years, even while we sold them firepowder. They slip raiding parties in, circumventing the Great Wall and ignoring your law. Certainly it would be wise to join forces with the Tarkothi and squelch this threat."

Lord Liang of Yutou Province and Lord Lin of Linshan Province both rose into one-knee salutes. "*Huang-Shang*, we agree with Lord Peng."

Chief Minister Tan scowled. "Order! Sit."

Cousin Kai-Long continued undaunted in the Hua language. "My armies in Nanling stand ready to descend from the Wall. We could liberate the Maduran-occupied Kingdom of Ankira in two weeks, especially if Madura's troops are diverted to the south by the prince's ship."

Ankira, Prince Hardeep's homeland. Kaiya's hand strayed to the lotus jewel's place in her sash. Left on her make-up table. Forgotten. Yet no matter what her feelings for him, his people still suffered because of Hua's past trade agreement with Madura.

"And what of the Golden Scorpions, Little Peng?" boomed Lord Han of Fenggu. At sixty-five, he was Father's brother-in-law and a staunch Royalist. "As castoffs and traitors to the Ayuri Paladins, they are a formidable army."

"Not even a Paladin can dodge a bullet," Chief Minister Tan said from his place at the other end of the first row.

"Fool," Lord Han muttered under his breath, though loud enough for everyone to hear it.

Kaiya bit her lip. Lord Han was a grandfatherly figure who spoke his mind, oftentimes forsaking etiquette. She looked toward Chief Minister Tan, whose face burned red, marred by a nasty frown.

Zheng Ming's father, Lord Zheng Han, rose to one knee. "We must not spread our own armies too thin. The Kingdom of Rotuvi also threatens us, especially Wailian County outside of the Wall."

Kaiya shifted uneasily. Her role at Wailian Castle two years ago was the only reason she was in this council. Rotuvi's armies had forced General Lu to hold his position, robbing him of glory.

Lord Liang scoffed. "We have guns."

With an emphatic nod, Lord Lin said, "We can free occupied Ankira and bring them the prosperity we enjoy."

Kaiya twirled a lock of hair. Hardeep had prophesized that she would liberate Ankira with a Dragon Song. The Expansionists proposed military might, at the cost of blood and gold. And ultimately, the Ankirans would trade one occupier for another.

Crown Princess Xiulan's father, Lord Zhao, wagged a finger at the Expansionist lords. "You will exploit their resources as the Madurans do. We know that is your goal, coming from such a poor province."

Lord Lin rose to his feet, and many others followed suit. General Zheng edged forward to the *Tianzi's* side, the Broken Sword in hand. The rest of the imperial guards closed in, hands on their swords.

Such disorder was unheard of. A quick glance at Father revealed his face flushing red. Kaiya prodded Kai-Wu, hoping he'd intervene, only to find him dozing off. On the other side of the *Tianzi*, Kai-Guo wrung his hands as his head swept back and forth over the unprecedented commotion.

If only she'd been born a boy. Her brothers, both kind and doting, provided no leadership. It only increased the burden on Father, who now aged before her eyes. If neither spoke...

The tension in the room sounded like a thick taut chord, vibrating in a slow bass, drawing in anger from all the men. Altering that could change the tone of the room.

Almost singing, Kaiya infused her short burst of laughter with a lighthearted and sincere tone, modulating it to unwind the underlying tension.

All eyes turned to her, wide with wonderment. Lady Ayana cocked her head and smiled.

Kaiya pressed her forehead to the floor, partially to recover from the loss of energy from the magic, and then straightened. She framed her rebuke innocuously so as not to make it seem like an accusation. "My Lords, forgive me for breaking protocol and speaking out of line."

The men stared at their feet. One by one, they settled back onto their cushions.

Kaiya switched to Arkothi so Lady Ayana could understand. "The prince of Tarkoth has asked to meet the *Tianzi*. The Classic of Rites expects the ruler to provide hospitality for foreign nobility. The *Tianzi* has two weeks to decide whether or not he wishes to grant an audience. After that, he has more time to decide—with your wise counsel—how he will approach Tarkoth's campaign against Madura."

Chief Minister Tan nodded. "Princess Kaiya speaks with wisdom beyond her years. Might I suggest we defer our decision to meet until the *Invincible's* arrival in Jiangkou?"

The *Tianzi* coughed before speaking in a wheeze. "Sound advice, Chief Minister. Lady Ayana, return to your prince and inform him of our disposition."

Lady Ayana curtseyed again. "Thank you for considering our request, Your Highness." She met Kaiya's gaze and winked before taking her leave.

Once she'd drifted out of the room, the *Tianzi* cleared his throat. "We will adjourn for the day and conclude the council meeting tomorrow morning."

Kaiya searched his eyes. Hopefully, Father was only rebuking the lords for their outburst, and not exhausted by the commotion.

"*Huang-Shang,*" Lord Peng said, "what of the attacks in the capital?"

The *Tianzi* pushed himself out of his chair and to his feet. "Tomorrow, Little Peng."

All in the room bowed low, holding their position until the *Tianzi* left with his imperial guards.

Minister Hong Jianbin kept his attention on the floor along with the rest of the councilors, until the princes and Princess Kaiya departed. His back protested when he straightened. Around him, the Royalists and Expansionists stood and gathered in clusters.

Hong pushed himself to his feet and took a step toward the garden where he had requested to meet the princess. Over the last few days, he had worked to gain her trust, running her little errands

and gathering information about the council members' political leanings. Now he had some news to share.

"Minister Hong," came a familiar voice behind him.

Hong turned around. Lord Peng Kai-Long stood alone by a window, beckoning him. After a quick glance toward the garden, Hong tottered over.

Lord Peng leaned in. "See how easily the princess diffused the tension? She may only be a girl, but she could disrupt our plans."

"Maybe. In order to get what we want, we must find a way to temporarily remove her from the picture. I may have a way, though it might take a couple of weeks to arrange."

Lord Peng rubbed his chin, his face a study in stoicism. "Well then, I won't keep you." He turned and joined the Expansionists Lin and Liang.

Peng was hiding something. Clenching and unclenching his fists, Hong headed toward the garden.

He found the princess waiting under a budding pear tree, with two imperial guards hovering nearby. He creaked into a low bow. "*Dian-xia,* I have found out what you requested."

The princess glanced back at her guards and then drew closer. His muscles locked up as she leaned in and whispered, "Please tell."

The heat of her closeness sent his heart lurching. She was beautiful and enchanting, but Hong reminded himself to see her as a mere tool. "Young Lord Zheng Ming is quite famous for his wit and charm. He has enticed many a young lady into his bed. And he has been particularly busy since his arrival in the capital a week ago."

A half-truth, but one which the princess believed, if the curling of her full lips into a frown was any indication. After a second, she spoke, her voice hitching. "Thank you, Minister Hong. You may be excused."

Hong bent as low as his body allowed, hiding his grin by staring at her feet. "As the princess commands."

He looked up after he heard her robes rustling away, deeper into the garden. Each time the princess had met an eligible bachelor, Hong worried she might agree to wed. Up to now, he had nothing to be concerned about.

Young Lord Zheng was the only suitor the princess had ever shown any interest in, and he seemed to be doing his best to disqualify himself.

This afternoon, Hong would make sure to remove Zheng Ming from the picture altogether.

Peng Kai-Long stewed in his palanquin as he rode back toward his compound. Like the other great lords, he now travelled with an escort of three dozen guards, even if he knew he was safe. Façades had to be maintained. Nonetheless, their noisy boots rattled his concentration.

Minister Hong apparently had a plan to remove Princess Kaiya from the picture temporarily, but Kai-long preferred a more permanent solution. Now that she'd moved on from Prince Hardeep, she was beyond his control.

He slid open the window and called for his aide-de-camp. "Little Yi. Initiate Operation Scorpion."

The Ayuri thugs whose services he retained through several layers of intermediaries would finally earn their keep. With them, and the disaffected insurgents he anonymously funded, he could use suspicions of Madura to get rid of Princess Kaiya *and* guarantee war.

He just had to lure dear Cousin Kaiya out of Sun-Moon Palace.

CHAPTER 8:

Second Chances

The last time Zheng Ming crossed a bridge accompanied by two guards, he had ridden unawares into an ambush. This time, staring at the arched stone bridge between the Sun-Moon Palace grounds and the *Tianzi*'s castle, he *knew* he was walking into an ambush, albeit one of a different kind.

He looked up to the sloping, tiled eaves of the fortress across the moat. It loomed seven stories above him, standing in silent vigil over the capital and surrounding plains. With tiers and vaulting eaves, its triangular shape stood out from the rest of the imperial compound's standard block buildings of white plaster walls and blue tile roofs. If the rest of the palace suggested organized elegance, the central bailey boasted military might.

In the late morning, Minister Hong had sent him an urgent message. The old man had called in several favors and arranged a formal invitation to meet Princess Kaiya. Up to now, no suitor had ever been invited back for a second visit with the Ice Princess.

With a deep breath, Ming smoothed his formal robes and donned his battle face. His two guards followed as he strode across the bridge.

A palace valet, flanked by eight imperial guards, waited on the other side. The valet bent at the waist. "Welcome to Sun-Moon Castle, Young Lord Zheng. Your guards must wait here. Please allow me to care for your sword."

Ming bowed his head and offered his sheathed *dao* to the valet.

The man bent at the waist and received the weapon in two hands. "Follow me. Princess Kaiya awaits."

Narrow paths between steep walls wound clockwise and upwards toward the central bailey. Arrow slits, murder holes, and battlements gave defenders an insurmountable advantage. Even if an invading army made it through the palace grounds, assaulting the castle would result in devastating casualties. Proof of the Founder's genius. Though in these times of peace, it was little more than a relic from the turmoil following the Hellstorm and Long Winter.

At last, without even entering the main keep itself, he came to one of the gardens and emerged onto a veranda. The mottled trunk of a weeping *danhua* tree curved up thirty feet, its willowy branches cascading downwards in strands of red blooms. Almond blossom bushes formed a circle around the tree, their own pink flowers pooling at their bases. A fragrant scent wafted through the air, borne by petals drifting on the early spring breeze.

The blossoms seemed to slow their descent, as if listening to the bright and rapidly varying notes fluttering from the *pipa* nestled in Princess Kaiya's lap. Similar in appearance to the lute played in the North, it was a hollow, pear-shaped wooden instrument with ridged frets along its neck and upper body.

Her long fingers swam swiftly across its four silken strings. Some sounds roared like a pouring rain, others whispered as the sweet secrets passed between lovers. Sitting at the edge of an ornate bloodwood chair, surrounded by three handmaidens and two imperial guards, the princess appeared lost in her music. She wore a light blue inner dress under a dark blue outer gown with hanging sleeves. With her eyes closed and an angelic expression, she appeared oblivious to his arrival.

Mesmerized by the sound and snowing blooms, Ming's steps faltered. A cool calm washed over him as he drew near. The perfect curve of her lightly rouged lips edged upward into a dainty smile, like a benevolent spirit.

He'd conquered many women in the past with his looks and charms, including several since his near brush with death on the bridge; but in that instant, he regretted his past, and swore to make himself a better man, worthy of her.

After a moment, he woke from the whimsical reverie. The emotion of the music changed. Unease and uncertainty crept over him.

As she neared the end of her song, Kaiya noted the change in the *pipa*'s sound. It wrapped around a newcomer on the veranda, whose own breath fell in step with her rhythm. With the fleeting bond between performer and audience established, she smiled.

Kaiya looked up through a half-lidded eye. Young Lord Zheng Ming stood on the veranda. What was he doing here, uninvited? Her throat tightened and the music's power slipped from her fingers.

A couple of days before, she'd felt an instant attraction, like none other since Prince Hardeep. Perhaps it'd been the full White Moon Renyue clouding her judgment. With that in mind, she'd sent Minister Hong to find more about him.

His reports of Ming's philandering should've come as no surprise. All strapping young lords engaged in such behavior. Why was it so... disappointing?

Minister Hong's confirmation of these reports only strengthened her resolve. She wouldn't be just another conquest, no matter how handsome and charming he might be. Nevertheless, there was no reason to be uncivil.

No sooner did Kaiya finish her song than Zheng Ming dropped to his right knee, right fist to the ground. "*Dian-xia*, thank you for sharing your practice with me."

With a nod, she allowed him out of his bow and beckoned him over. She passed the *pipa* to the handmaidens, and then motioned them to withdraw to the veranda. "Thank you for listening, Young Lord Zheng."

He strode over, withdrawing a kerchief from the fold of his robe. He held it at her forehead. "May I?

Audacious. Charming. Her stomach fluttered. At her nod, the imperial guards relaxed. Zheng Ming dabbed her skin.

Heat stirred within her. "I...you are first to hear me play this piece, *Eye of the Storm*. Can you offer me any critique?"

He pressed the kerchief into her hand. "Unfortunately, I am just a simple soldier, and I have no technical skill in music, and—"

"Surely you have some artistic talent? The Five Classics implore the gentleman to be skilled in both the sword and the arts."

"I consider myself a decent poet, though you did not give me an opportunity to show off last time we met." He grinned.

Intrigued, she flashed a smile. "Here is your chance. Tell me what is on your mind."

He dropped to his knee again. "As the princess commands." He looked up, his eyes sparkling with mischief. "But I implore you not to be too critical!"

Kaiya caught herself playing with a loose lock of hair and abruptly dropped her hand. She covered a laugh, which sounded too flirtatious to her ears. "I am no more a poetry expert than you are a music critic."

Zheng Ming took a deep breath and his gaze swept over the garden. He then spoke:

"Storm clouds gather on the horizon,
Dark shades of fear and pain.
Travelers lost without direction
Pelted by unforgiving rain.

A melody hums through somber shade
A shining beacon to guide their way
The path ahead opens to sheltered glade
Beckoning back those led astray."

Heat warmed her cheeks. He must be alluding to her and the state of the nation. "Is that poetry or politics? You must have heard what transpired in the council this morning."

"*Dian-xia*, you said you would not be a critic!" His lips drooped into a facetious pout, sending a swarm of butterflies fluttering in her stomach. "You *did* command me to say what was on my mind."

"It weighs heavily on the minds of all the hereditary lords and ministers." And poor Father. Kaiya sighed. "And on the *Tianzi*'s as well."

He plucked a flower and tucked it behind her ear, sending a shiver up her spine. "We stand at a crossroads, facing uncertainty for the first time in the three hundred years of Wang family rule. The intrigue of internal politics has intersected with the machinations of foreign powers. It is a shame that the *Tai-Ming* have sunk to infighting and scheming instead of rising to ensure stability."

"I believe all the *Tai-Ming* have the realm's best interests at heart," she said. "Unfortunately, they do not agree on whose policies will ensure future prosperity."

"As long as the Wang family controls Huayuan Province, the *Tai-Ming* will have no choice but to obey the decisions of the *Tianzi*."

Kaiya stopped fiddling with her hair. "I wonder." The audacity of the lords during the council meeting suggested otherwise.

He nodded emphatically. "It is quite simple, really. With the exception of Huayuan, all of the other provinces are economically interdependent. None could survive on their own."

Kaiya's lips pursed. Cousin Kai-Long's domain had broken conventions. Nanling province could sustain itself. Luckily, none could question his loyalty.

"Furthermore, since Huayuan has half the number of soldiers as all of the other provinces combined, it would take most of the *Tai-Ming* allying against the *Tianzi* in order to pose a military challenge. And the *Tai-Ming* can only meet together in the presence of a council minister. This is how your illustrious ancestor Wang Xinchang established stability in the realm. The political climate may be unsettled, but we are far, far away from a tipping point."

She looked up at him through her lashes. "I did not think a simple soldier could have such deep thoughts."

"Even a carp dreams of becoming a dragon." Zheng Ming's lips twitched.

"Perhaps that is why you were targeted the other night. I am glad you managed to fight off your attackers."

He raised an eyebrow. "Because if something happened to me, you would have one less person to discuss politics with?"

Her belly buzzed like a dragonfly's wings. Why did he have to be so witty? He would be so much easier to dislike if he were stupid. She placed a hand on her chest and tried to imitate his sarcastic tone. "No, because you are a key witness, and we need to uncover who is behind all of these recent attacks. The capital is on edge."

Zheng Ming flashed a disarming smile. "Well then, based on the evidence gathered by the watch, those who attacked me the other day were financed by the Ayuri Kingdom of Madura." Doubt weighed in his voice.

Madura occupied Hardeep's Ankira, as well. "But you do not believe that is the case."

"No. There was too much evidence, and no motive for the Madurans to attack me. I suspect there is something more insidious. I had just met with Minister Hong Jianbin, who wanted my father to support the Expansionists. Then I was ambushed. It leads me to believe the Royalists tried to silence me."

She leveled her gaze at him. "So where do you stand, Young Lord Zheng? Royalist or Expansionist?"

His eyes widened in mock surprise. "So direct! Usually, my peers try to coax me into revealing my affiliations with wine and sweet words."

She found herself playing with her hair *again*. Bad girl! Kaiya straightened, lifting her chin. "I am the princess, and command you to speak." Despite her order, her own lips quivered as she fought to suppress a grin. "Where do you stand?"

Zheng Ming bowed his head. "I stand on the Great East Gate of the Wall in my home province, and look out on the vast untamed lands of the Kanin Plateau. Its pristine beauty, so unlike the manmade splendor of this palace, seems to be a metaphor for our debate. To expand into it means to tame and bring order; but that in itself will destroy what makes it beautiful."

"Spoken like a politician!" She caught herself exposing the side of her neck with a tilt of her head. "I want a straight answer, Simple Soldier."

His lips quirked up. "The Wall protects our land borders, our dominant navy defends our shores from a sea invasion. I see no need to expand as long as the people are content. Enlarging our borders beyond the Wall means stretching resources thin to protect them, as I can tell you firsthand from my experience in Wailian County. So you can say I am an anti-Expansionist though not necessarily a Royalist."

"Is that supposed to be a straight answer?"

He laughed. "Had I known we would be discussing politics, I would have come better prepared. I was led to believe that we would share poetry and tea." He gestured toward a gazebo overlooking the lake. "Shall we?"

Led to believe? He wasn't supposed to be there. Still, poetry and tea in the gazebo sounded appealing. She looked up at the Iridescent Moon. Hopefully, time constraints would give her an excuse to get away from him before she forgot all about his reputation and succumbed to his charm. "Alas, I am afraid I must beg off your invitation.

Lord Peng invited me to watch a shower of shooting stars from his pavilion tonight. I do hope the skies clear."

"All of the great hereditary lords and their families will be there," Zheng Ming said. "Perhaps I will see you."

Her jittering stomach leaped into her chest, and words slipped out in spite of her better judgment. "Then maybe you would ride with me? An escort of three dozen imperial guards will surely offer better protection in these unsettled times."

"I would be honored. I shall meet you at the moat in two hours."

Kaiya clapped her hands together. "I look forward to it. It will be my first time leaving the palace grounds since all the chaos started."

CHAPTER 9:

Audacity

The nearly-full White Moon Renyue hung low in the early evening sky, lighting Liang Yu's path to *Jianguo* Shrine. To think, a shrine dedicated to national peace was where he received instructions that undermined the *Tianzi's* authority.

Such paradoxes didn't matter to a patriot. Hua had grown complacent and weak. As the Founder once said, *the gourd that rots within is easily smashed from the outside.* The Expansionists must prevail, lest foreign powers enslave the motherland.

As Liang Yu walked, he took mental note of the changes since his last visit: Fewer birds now nested in the plum trees. The scent wafting from the shrine spoke of cheap incense. The white pebbles' scatter pattern suggested the groundskeeper had been distracted when raking the path. Had he skimped on incense quality, pocketing silver to afford a gift? A new lover, perhaps?

This ability to notice a thousand details and draw connections between them resulted from years of rigorous training at the legendary Black Lotus Monastery. Liang Yu had been one of the *Moquan*, the mythical Black Fist Warriors who, according to frustrated mothers, would kidnap disobedient children in the middle of the night.

In reality, they were the *Tianzi's* fiercely loyal spies, whose skills in stealth and swordsmanship bordered on the impossible. One of the three most talented *Moquan* in his youth, Liang Yu had been betrayed and left for dead during an operation in the Ayuri City-State of Vyara thirty-two years before.

He'd returned to Hua five years ago as an importer, under an assumed name. It turned out spying skills translated well to business, and Hua's aggressive trade policies didn't hurt either. Yet it also exposed him to the dark underside of immoral mercantilism: the bribes, corruption, and greed that would drag the country into decline.

Now forty-nine, Liang Yu pondered these things, all the while assessing potential danger along his route. Nothing amiss. He continued until he reached the grove of plum blossom trees that surrounded the temple grounds. The flowers had passed peak, and now only a few stragglers desperately clung to limbs as they watched their fellow petals fluttering like warm spring snow. Hundreds of pieces of folded paper competed with the blossoms for space on the low branches, tied by those who hoped their written wish would come true.

He silently recited the one-hundred-twenty-third poem from the popular book *Poetry Anthology of the Yu Dynasty*. Comparing it with a numbered code his anonymous employer had provided, he came to the correct tree and branch and looked for the specific type of paper his benefactor always wrote on. He retrieved the correct note and squirreled it in the folds of his robes, then set a brisk pace back to the Phoenix Spring Inn.

Liang Yu found the inn especially empty this night. With few prying ears, its location made for a perfect meeting place. That, and the attractive proprietress who sometimes shared her bed with him.

A glance around the common area revealed nothing suspicious. He continued on to the private room. Settling on one of the cushions arranged around the table, he unfolded the paper and read the first few words of the sloppy script.

The scare tactics have not done enough. It is time to make a louder statement with an assassination implicating Madura...

He continued reading. His employer was moving quickly, ready to take a bold step. An actual kill. Liang Yu pursed his lips. Not enough resources to make this brash move. Perhaps if he made the kill himself. The order gave meticulous time and location details.

Up to now, all of the missives had been unerringly accurate. Liang Yu, in whom suspicion was well-trained, often wondered how. By consideration of means and motives, he had already narrowed his employer's identity down to eight possibilities. He would find out soon enough.

In the meantime, he had an assassination to plan.

Hong Jianbin peeked out from his palanquin, baffled at Princess Kaiya's weak resolve. He had been certain she would order the imperial guards to expel the philandering Young Lord Zheng from the castle after his unannounced visit. Yet there she was, riding with the fop as the imperial procession made its way toward Lord Peng's pavilion.

Perhaps Peng had been right about women's lack of willpower. The princess went so far as to forgo the propriety and safety of a palanquin to ride by Zheng's side. Had her brothers

been there, they would have ordered her to use it; but on this night before the full White Moon, they were most certainly busy in their futile attempt to conceive an heir.

The imperial guards had remonstrated her, citing the unsettled climate in the capital. Zheng Ming also insisted she ride in the palanquin. Even Hong protested, though more for show: he knew of every ambush, and the imperial family was never targeted. Nor were any of the attacks ever fatal to anyone save for a hapless guard or two.

His concerns, along with those of the imperial guards and Zheng Ming, had all fallen on deaf ears.

The princess disguised herself as one of the imperial phoenix riders in court robes. Her decoy, the beautiful handmaiden Han Meiling, rode in the imperial palanquin.

Hong could not help but admire the princess' courage, even if it bordered on recklessness. He slid his palanquin window shut and closed his eyes, thinking of his impending meeting with Royalist *Tai-Ming* Lord Liu in Lord Peng's renowned garden teahouse. He would pledge the princess to Lord Liu's second son in exchange for the Chief Minister position, just as he had promised her to Young Lord Zheng.

Zheng Ming. Just thinking the name brought a bitter taste to his mouth. If the princess still favored the young man even after hearing of his reputation, Hong would have to find another way to remove him from the picture. It was just a matter of timing.

A loud crack jolted Hong in his palanquin. He turned to see an arrow protruding from the wall, the head just inches from his nose.

The grim voice of General Zheng carried over the commotion of men and horses outside. "Ambush. Protect the princess."

Hong fought the rising panic and tried to concentrate. There was supposed to be an attack on Lord Han tonight, not here. This was never part of the plan, nor did it make logical sense. The only scenario he could imagine was the possibility of other disaffected partisans taking advantage of the political climate. That, or perhaps Lord Peng had decided to take things into his own hands.

No, it was still too early for Peng to make a move like this. If the princess were harmed—

A female scream rent the air.

Zheng Ming scanned the line of tiled rooftops where two dozen enemy archers bobbed up, sniping at them. He couldn't believe the audacity of an attack on an imperial procession, let alone the foolhardiness of engaging a contingent of a hundred imperial guards.

His cousin General Zheng remained calm, issuing orders. A column of imperial guards on either side of the procession knelt and loaded their muskets. Others snapped into a protective formation around the princess' palanquin. Her personal detail formed a line around her horse.

She made for an easy target.

She rode high above the rest of the procession, though the archers ignored her. The disguise? He admired her composure, even as her startled doe eyes darted from place to place. A hand strayed to the curved dagger in her sash.

Ming swung out of the saddle and placed himself between their two horses. He reached up to her. "*Dian-xia*, you are an inviting target. Please, come down."

Her gaze settled on his, recognition blooming in her face. She took his hands and slid from her horse. Ming grasped her shoulders. Her slight body trembled.

He gestured downward. "Stay low, between the horses."

Armed only with his own dagger, he pulled the *dao* from her sash. It wasn't much better, given the distance, and he silently lamented the ban on weapons near the Imperial Family. Were he allowed to carry his bow, he could give the assailants a reason to keep their heads down.

A barrage of gunfire rang out, followed by the cracking of wood and tile as musket balls struck

them. The horses stirred and shuffled, nearly crushing him and the princess between them. Sulfur hung in the air.

The volley of arrows stopped, and the sound of men skittering across the rooftops faded in the distance.

"Wolf and Lion Companies, pursue the rebels," General Zheng said. "We are not far from Lord Peng's pavilion. The princess' detail, along with the Dragon, Tiger, and Phoenix Companies will escort her there. Captain Tu, run ahead to Lord Peng and order him to send a contingent of his guards to meet us. Commander Ling, take a horse back to the palace with word of this brazen attack, and assemble half of the imperial guards to come to Lord Peng's pavilion. The rest of you remain here, tend to the wounded, and gather evidence."

Ming turned to the princess. "Are you all right?"

Her wide, startled eyes met his. She straightened, her voice firm as she called out, "General Zheng, is Meiling unharmed?"

Ming could not help but gawk in admiration at the sudden transformation from frightened girl to imperial princess.

"Yes, *Dian-xia*," the gruff soldier replied. "Shaken, but uninjured."

"Then let us proceed to Lord Peng's pavilion."

Ming didn't like the idea of splitting their guard. He turned to General Zheng. "Cousin, what if this was merely a diversion, to thin our defenses and draw us into a more dangerous trap?"

General Zheng nodded. "Your concerns are noted. However, Lord Peng is close by and we will be much safer in his compound until the rest of the imperial guard arrives."

Ming only hoped Cousin Zheng was right.

Frogs croaked and trilled in the large pond of Lord Peng's Four Seasons Garden, oblivious to the dangers beyond the compound walls. Having survived an attempt on her life, Kaiya knelt in the teahouse, listening to the serene night sounds in hopes they would calm her rattled nerves.

She'd travelled the width and breadth of the empire, always greeted by an adoring citizenry. To her, the imperial guards were just a formality, a symbol of imperial splendor. Besides the single incident in Wailian two years ago, she'd never considered they might be actually called on to protect her.

Tonight, they had performed admirably, holding a tight protective formation as the procession marched to the Peng's estate. Cousin Kai-Long suggested she sequester herself in the safety of the main keep's inner sanctum; but at General Zheng's insistence, Cousin Kai-Long cancelled his appointment in the garden teahouse so the imperial guards could appropriate it.

Situated on a peninsula jutting into the pond, it was the most defensible position in the pavilion. Her senior-most guards, Chen Xin and Zhao Yue, stood inside by the door, while a dozen others kept watch over the narrow path.

Kaiya's frantic heart slowed as she took deep breaths and wiggled her toes in the slippers Cousin Kai-Long had provided. As her worries over safety faded, other concerning thoughts filled her mind.

Zheng Ming had seen her scared and trembling, the antithesis of imperial grace. She shuddered at the prospect of having to face him, now that he knew she was not a Perfect Princess.

Right now, he might very well be enjoying wine with Cousin Kai-Long—or worse, Kai-Long's pretty sisters—laughing at her expense.

She looked down to find her fists clenched tight around the kerchief he'd given her. She was holding her breath. With a sigh, she closed her eyes and reprimanded herself. Doctor Wu's *Cool Spring Rain* breathing technique quieted her mind.

By the door, Chen Xin's and Zhao Yue's breaths synchronized with each other.

Three other breathing patterns, slow and muffled, emanated from beneath the woven straw floor panels.

Her eyes fluttered open. "Chen, Zhao, intru—"

Two floor panels flung open. Three men emerged just beside her.

Clothed in long *kurta* shirts of the Ayuri South, they all wore expressionless metal masks with eye slits and a nose opening. Each brandished a guardless broadsword with a wide tip resembling a scorpion sting.

The mask, the sting. Madura's Golden Scorpions, the castoffs and deserters from the Paladin Order which defended the Ayuri South. They were banned from Hua, so she'd never seen a Scorpion with her own eyes, let alone been attacked by one.

She twisted to her feet and glided to the side, just as the heavy blade crashed down where she'd been sitting. Another sting whipped toward her neck.

With a technique from the *Dance of Swords*, her foot swept up as she bent back under the swing, and her toes connected with her assailant's chin. Yet the silken slippers Cousin Kai-Long insisted she wear provided little traction. Her planted foot slid out from beneath her.

The collapse to the mats knocked the air out of her. The third attacker raised his blade. Unarmed, fighting for air, there was nothing she could do. She closed her eyes. Tonight, a Scorpion's sting would cut her life short.

A loud clang rang out inches from her nose, followed by cloth tearing and a male scream. To the side, a *dao* whistled through the air and cut through muscle and bone. Two heavy swords and a body part thudded to the ground in quick succession. Someone shuffled across the floor toward the corner.

Kaiya opened her eyes. Chen Xin stood above her, his blade reflecting light from the lamp. One of the Scorpions leaned against the wall, clutching at his spilling intestines. Another lay headless at her side. Zhao Yue held his *dao* raised, ready to fall on the third Scorpion, who pressed his back to the wall.

At the entrance, her guards Xu Zhan and Li Wei rushed in. A third presence breezed in behind them, and Kaiya could hear its quiet breathing. Try as she might, she didn't see anyone else.

As Xu and Li interposed themselves between her and the remaining Scorpion, Chen and Zhao surged forward with a coordinated attack. The would-be assassin huddled down, his sting quivering in a feeble defense. Without a doubt, both of her guards' blades would find their mark.

Their *dao* clinked against metal without reaching the cowering man, though all she could see was a dark blur and a flash of short blades. A shadow darted across the Scorpion with a tearing rasp. The man yelped and his sword clunked to the floor.

"Keep him alive for questioning," the shadow chirped in a girlish voice. A familiar voice, but from where? The shape swept out the entrance before Kaiya could ascertain any other detail.

She picked herself up off the mats with as much grace as she could muster and lifted her chin. "Take the survivor into custody." She waved toward the one man, whose guts hung out of his abdomen, and then met the terrified gaze of a disembodied head.

Her belly lurched and bile rose to her throat. She collapsed to her knees and watched in horror as she threw up.

By the first gibbous, two hours before their planned ambush, eleven of Liang Yu's hired swords had arrived. Song came first, wide-eyed and eager as always; and then a new recruit surnamed Fang who claimed to be a marksman with his repeating crossbow. If he lived up to his boasts, he would be the key to Liang Yu's daring plan, able to eliminate their target from a distance regardless of an army of guards. A clean escape would prove more difficult.

Liang Yu lifted his brush and sketched a simple map on a sheet of rice paper. "Our target is Lord Han of Fenggu, whose heir nominally supports our employer's cause. He could be pushed

toward war by his father's death. Lord Han should leave Lord Peng's compound at the fourth gibbous."

He began handing out copper coins from Madura when the sliding door crashed open, causing all to look up. His twelfth man, surnamed Fu, straggled in.

Something was out of place, something wrong about the man's smell: the sweet scent of *yinghua* petals, a contact poison causing intoxication in males.

That flowering weed grew in only one place in the world, the Black Lotus Monastary. Home to the Black Lotus *Moquan*.

Liang Yu frowned. "Song, go out into the common room and mingle with the other patrons."

With an inquisitive cock of his head, Song left the room.

Liang Yu turned to Fu. "You are late because of a woman, aren't you?"

Fu ran his hand through his dark hair, biting his lip.

"Hurry up and answer."

Fu nodded. "She was such an exotic little sprite, barely yet a woman."

Liang Yu modulated his voice, changing the pitch and inflection to imitate the accent from Hua's rural South. "Were you able to bed her?"

Fu chewed on his lip.

"She claimed some sort of reason she couldn't, didn't she? Answer truthfully."

Fu's words slurred as he spoke. "She kissed me on the neck, then got up and left."

Liang Yu sprang to his feet, his walking stick already in hand. "Abandon the plan. Regroup at *Long-An* Temple in three days."

An excuse. *If* there were any survivors, they would be followed. He only hoped Young Song had made it out of the room early enough to avoid being associated with the rest.

It was time to recruit a new collection of disaffected soldiers and insurgents.

With confused murmurs and shrugs, his men headed toward the exit. Liang Yu slipped into the low closet door behind him and into the dark. He released the secret exit in the back of the closet and slid into a hidden corridor that ran from the inn to the adjoining bowyer's workshop.

He finished shutting the hatch just as his hurried men opened the sliding doors. The muffled sound of murmurs and ruffling clothes instantly fell into deathly silence.

Suspicions confirmed. A female *Moquan* had drugged the hapless Fu with a contact poison; and then a group of them followed him as he stumbled to this meeting. Sudden and precise in their assault, only they could operate with such surgical efficiency and then disappear into the night. Not even the proprietress or other inn patrons would realize what had happened, though it occurred right in front of them.

Liang Yu retreated quickly through the corridor, listening to the silence of the *Moquan*. Emerging in the bowyer's workshop, he heard the subtle breathing of one of the warrior-spies, likely assigned to this spot to watch for anyone who might escape out of the inn's kitchen backdoor.

Reaching into his robe, Liang Yu snatched three *biao* throwing spikes and flung them at the sentry. The young man contorted himself so that two blades whizzed by, but the third lodged into his throat.

Liang Yu bounded over to both silence his scream and prevent his blood from staining the floor. Too young, too inexperienced, too confident. How unfortunate. The boy might have one day made a fine warrior.

Covering his trail the best he could in the urgent escape, Liang Yu collected his weapons and headed toward his special pupil's home. He could put his gardening skills to use for a couple of days, while hiding in plain sight. The *Moquan* would not think to look for insurgents in a *Tai-Ming's* villa.

Then again, the *Moquan* had identified Fu. But how? The only unpredictability in his infallible planning was employer betrayal.

Of course! The order to assassinate Lord Han had been too audacious. It must have been a ruse. His employer had likely decided their group had outlived their usefulness, and needed to clean his hands.

Liang Yu growled. It was time to root out whoever it was and pay him back.

CHAPTER 10:
Aftermath

Hong Jianbin passed another cup of rice wine to *Tai-Ming* lord Liu Yong, surprised the aristocrat could be so talkative. The forty-eight-year-old ruler of Jiangzhou province never spoke during council meetings, always siding with the Royalists, always listening to the lecherous Treasury Minister Geng.

Close to the capital, with a cool climate and fertile valleys, Jiangzhou produced bountiful crops of wheat and millet, and its wooded mountainsides supplied timber and silkworms. The Liu family had faithfully served the Wang Dynasty for centuries, and the current lord was no exception.

Hong suspected his support came not from loyalty, but expectation. As a second son who was never cultivated to inherit, the unimaginative Lord Liu did nothing but follow the status quo. Luckily for his province, the systems left in place by his late father, as well as the aggressive trade networks established by the current *Tianzi*, had bolstered Jiangzhou's prosperity.

Liu drained yet another cup. His brand of aristocrat was the most contemptuous: he enjoyed wealth and status by virtue of noble birth, with no appreciable skill of his own. He was, as they said in the North, cut from the same cheap cloth as the *Tianzi*'s two sons. These men would run the nation into the ground.

According to Hong's spy, Liu had started his battle with wine right after the council meeting. By the time he joined Hong in a private room at Lord Peng's villa, Liu was already quite drunk.

Liu turned to applaud for a young lady dressed in a peach-colored robe. She played the *guzheng*, her hands running over its twenty-one twisted silk strings.

"She is quite good." Hong poured another cup of wine for Liu.

Liu shook his head. His words slurred. "Not nearly as good as Princess Kaiya."

"Nobody in the empire can rival the princess' musical talent," Hong said. "She could probably sing Avarax to sleep."

Lord Liu laughed, raising his wine cup. "A toast to the princess!"

Hong lifted his cup. "To the princess." He then lowered his voice. "Speaking of which, this is the exact reason I wanted to meet with you tonight. Your second son, Liu Dezhen, is of marriageable age, is he not?"

"Yes, he is already twenty-four, and becoming a fine man!" Liu clapped his hands.

Hong forced himself into an enthusiastic nod. If young Dezhen was anything like his father, he still had a long way to go to become a fine *man*. "Just like your first son, who married the *Tianzi*'s niece, Wang Kai-Hua. What would you say if I told you that I might be able to arrange another match with the *Tianzi*'s family?"

Liu's brow crinkled. He tapped the cup.

How dense could he be? There was only one eligible girl. Hong hid his frustration with a friendly smile. "Princess Kaiya."

Lord Liu choked on his wine. "Impossible. She is such a choosy girl. She has already rejected a couple dozen suitors, and Dezhen is only a second son."

Hong shrugged. "Once I am Chief Minister, and the indecisive *Tianzi* faces a united voice from the *Tai-Ming*, he will have no choice but to force his sister to marry your son."

"You, the fishmonger, becoming Chief Minister?" Liu's voice rose in laughter. "I can't imagine that!"

As expected, the dunderhead missed the insinuation. Minister Hong clenched his jaw, promising retribution for the insult. It had been a mistake to make veiled suggestions to such a dense person, especially after alcohol had muddled his mind. "Then imagine this: your grandson, sitting on the Dragon Throne."

Liu's forehead scrunched. "How do you plan to accomplish this?"

"I have secured four of your brethren *Tai-Ming* who will support my candidacy as Chief Minister once Minister Tan retires." Hong continued in a low voice, as if the walls could hear, "The *Tianzi*'s health has deteriorated so quickly in the last few years, I do not believe he has much more time left. His son has little interest in state affairs. He will be easy to manipulate."

Liu cocked his head. "Crown Prince Kai-Guo is sufficiently capable, and certainly takes an active role in the council."

"That is not the son I had in mind."

Lord Liu burst out laughing. "What, you think Prince Kai-Wu will ascend the throne? Then you have my full support, just so I can see if you can make all those pieces fall in place. And of course, I want you to pledge that Princess Kaiya will become Dezhen's bride."

"You have my word of honor, my Lord. In the meantime, I need you to at least nominally support the Expansionists while we set things in motion."

"What will be set in motion?" Liu's eyes glazed over.

Without a doubt, in the debate between the Expansionists and Royalists, Lord Liu had little intellectual depth to consider the merits of either side. He would blindly follow the *Tianzi*, since his province had always benefited from imperial favor. Liu might not even know which side the *Tianzi* supported.

Hong suppressed a sigh. "Troop movements. Huayuan Province troops will move away from the capital and toward the northern border with Rotuvi. Dongmen troops into the Kanin Wilds. And of course, a grand invasion force to liberate Ankira from its Maduran occupiers."

Liu shook his head. "The *Tianzi* will never authorize that!"

So Liu did know more than he let on, though apparently not much more.

"Remember, my Lord, we do not necessarily refer to the wise *Tianzi* Wang Zhishen." Hong again stifled a groan, hoping—perhaps unrealistically—that Liu would at least remember his pledge to support his candidacy for Chief Minister.

The doors slid open, and one of Lord Peng's men entered and bowed. "My Lords, for your safety, please come to the audience hall immediately. The *Tianzi*'s agents foiled a plot on Lord Han's life, and there was another attack on Princess Kaiya here, in the compound."

Hong's heart skipped a few beats. More attacks he had not heard of... "Is the princess safe?"

The man nodded. "Yes, Minister."

Hong relaxed his clenched fingers. His entire plan hinged on Princess Kaiya remaining unmarried. And still breathing.

Perhaps he should initiate the second phase of his plot earlier than he intended. Chief Minister Tan's early retirement could not come soon enough.

But before he could do that, he would need to have Princess Kaiya sent away. It would remove her calming influence from the council, *and* keep her safe from whoever was trying to kill her.

Peng Kai-Long mused that his villa's audience hall currently bore all the trappings of a council meeting. With the exception of the enigmatic elf Xu, all the *Tai-Ming* sat there, along with several of the *Yu-Ming*. As host, he relaxed on a cushion at the front of the room, just as the *Tianzi* would in Sun-Moon Castle. As he would, when he became *Tianzi*.

Then, Princess Kaiya glided in.

As protocol demanded, he yielded his seat.

Even if his blood boiled.

The incompetent assassins had foiled a plan he had in place for years. Not only that, they effectively closed the window of opportunity for killing Princess Kaiya, since the *Tianzi* would arrange near-impenetrable security around his family.

He might not even let them out in public at all. The Imperial Family could very well hole up in Sun-Moon Palace until the *Tianzi*'s spies uncovered the conspirators.

Kai-Long did not worry about himself in this matter. His funding of insurgents in the capital passed through many hands, leaving his own clean while falsely incriminating the Madurans.

The princess nodded as she slithered by, wearing the slippers that should've sent her tumbling to her doom. He smiled at her. His cheeks hurt from smiling so much.

No matter; he was safe from scrutiny. Many layers of disinformation insulated him from those pathetic Ankiran boys masquerading as Maduran Scorpions. Indeed, for all the surviving assassin knew, Kai-Long himself was the target in the teahouse. The convincing interrogation performed by the *Tianzi*'s agents would implicate Kai-Long's gardener, a spy for the insurgents whom Kai-Long had hired years ago, just to be sacrificed at a time like this.

The only weak link was Minister Hong, who now tottered in and creaked to his knees. Did the wretched old man still serve a purpose? Kai-Long looked over to meet his supposed ally's gaze. Minister Hong glared daggers at Young Lord Zheng, the heir to Dongmen Province.

Zheng Ming, in turn, repeatedly exchanged winks and grins with Princess Kaiya.

Kai-Long ground his teeth. Hong had given assurances she would reject Zheng Ming, but that certainly didn't seem to be the case. Kai-Long cursed every orc god and goddess he could think of. Cousin Kaiya was not only alive, but maybe even one step closer to finally choosing a suitor and pushing out an heir.

He consoled himself with the old adage of finding opportunity in disaster. Even if some of his plans crumbled around him, at least other aspects of his scheme were working. With the failed attempt on Lord Han's life, the *Tai-Ming* would make a scene during tomorrow's council meeting. After the princess' own brush with death, even she wouldn't object to punitive action against Madura.

The princess lived, but he would still get the war he wanted.

CHAPTER 11:

Unwelcome Bedfellows

From inside the narrow confines of her palanquin, Kaiya heard five hundred imperial guards marching in tight formation. Like a funeral procession. Perhaps she'd died and now took her last journey in a coffin to a funerary pyre. The walls closed in around her. Her brush with death wove in with the terrifying childhood memory of being locked in a cabinet.

The pitching roiled her stomach, confirming she still lived. A deep breath of hot, stuffy air reassured her of the fact. At least the palanquin allowed for privacy. In the first hour after the attack, she'd forced herself to project an undaunted image. Now hidden from prying eyes, she allowed salty, hot tears to trickle unchecked down her cheeks.

The procession lurched to a stop. Kaiya used Zheng Ming's kerchief to dry her tears. Her eyes felt heavy and swollen. Outside, a herald called, and large gates swooshed open. They had arrived at the palace.

"*Dian-xia*," Chen Xin called from outside. "We have passed the palace's front gates. Would you like to alight?"

Her act must have worked, for him to think she'd want to walk the rest of the way to the castle. Not tonight. The White Moon neared full, ready to cast her vulnerability in its bright light. "No." She cleared her throat. "Take me to the Jade Gate. No need to rush."

Kaiya shuddered. The cracking of her voice revealed weakness. At least the trip from the main gate to the imperial family's residence would provide time to regain her composure. In a way, the ride felt like déjà vu, like the time she'd faced Father after trespassing at the Temple of Heaven with Hardeep.

Just like then, when she had coped with the prospect of certain punishment, she now emotionally distanced herself from near assassination by envisioning the path: Past the Hall of Supreme Harmony. To the Dragon Bridge between the palace grounds and the castle. Through the winding alleys of the castle compound.

The porters stopped and lowered the palanquin to the ground. The doors slid open and a hand—the chamberlain's, from its phoenix feather-like smoothness—took hers and helped her out on to legs as wobbly as a newborn foal's. Imperial guards by the gatehouse dropped to one knee, fist to the ground.

The chamberlain released her hand. "*Dian-xia*. The *Tianzi* will receive you immediately."

With a nod, Kaiya forced herself into a semblance of grace as she crossed the covered stone bridge from the keep to the imperial family's walled-off, hilltop residence. Moonlight sparkled off the gold leaf of the one-story pavilion's tiled eaves. Surrounded by moats, the building was further protected from magical intrusion by an ancient ward.

As she approached the gatehouse connecting the bedrooms to the rest of the residence, her entourage of guards and handmaidens halted and knelt. Ahead of her, eight imperial guards stepped aside to reveal a familiar face.

The old nun from Praise Spring Temple raised a light bauble lamp to Kaiya's face. To guard against magical disguises, like the illusion bauble from Wailian Castle, she spoke in the Imperial Family's secret language to verify Kaiya's identity. "Where did the Founder come from?"

"Great Peace Island."

"What was the Founder's motto?"

"*All Under Heaven Swathed By Might*"

The nun nodded. "What was the name of his castle there?"

A trick question, since he'd had many. "Which one?"

"The last."

"Peaceful Earth Castle."

The gatekeeper turned around and rapped a code—changed hourly—on the heavy ironwood doors. They slid open, revealing nine bowing nuns who straightened and formed up around her.

With them as an escort, Kaiya walked to the *Tianzi*'s quarters. Like her imperial guards, the protection had always seemed like needless formality. Before today.

Her brothers, both kneeling on cushions, met her gaze as she stepped into the bedroom antechamber.

Eldest Brother Kai-Guo motioned her to a cushion. "Doctor Wu is attending to Father."

Kaiya knelt and bowed. Safe! Truly safe, for the first time in hours. A spring breeze off Sun-Moon Lake wafted in through open windows, cooling her down and calming her nerves.

Father's wheeze rasped from the other side of the gold-painted sliding doors. From her place in the anteroom, she tried listening for his heartbeat. Her own pounding heart drowned out the sound of his.

Sick fathers, assassination attempts. Kaiya looked up to focus on something else. Lanterns with bloodwood frames around paper-thin white jade and dangling red silk tassels hung from the ceiling, providing a soft light from Aksumi light baubles. The ceiling was coffered, with jade insets carved to depict scenes from the Wang Dynasty's glorious history. Lacquered wooden panels with mother-of-pearl inlay adorned the red walls.

The doors to the bedchamber slid open and Doctor Wu emerged. She cast a reproachful glance at Kaiya. "The *Tianzi* is weak. Worrying about his headstrong daughter riding exposed on a horse taxed him further." She passed a scroll to Eldest Brother Kai-Guo. "Have him drink a decoction of these herbs twice a day."

As Kai-Guo withdrew his hand, the old doctor snatched it up and pressed fingers to his pulse. She then beckoned Second Brother Kai-Wu over, who offered his right wrist as well.

Doctor Wu's brow furrowed. "The same toxin courses through all of your veins, though it affects the *Tianzi* differently. I don't know why I didn't feel it in your pulses until today."

Kaiya gasped. A toxin. How, with all the precautions?

Eldest Brother Kai-Guo frowned. "Doctor, I thought you knew everything about the body."

The old woman shook her head. "There is no one thing that could cause this ailment, and I suspect most of the ingredients come from abroad."

Lowering her voice so Father wouldn't hear, Kaiya asked, "What is the *Tianzi's* prognosis?"

The doctor answered in a low whisper. "The stresses of state tire him. He must rest, if he is to see the cherry blossoms bloom next year. You must ensure he does not hear any startling news." With a stern glance at Kaiya, she bowed and slipped out of the room.

Eldest Brother Kai-Guo sighed. "With the New Year's Festival fast approaching and the capital falling into chaos, we must share the burden of Father's duties."

Second Brother Kai-Wu pursed his lips. "We have to convince him to rest, first."

Their eyes turned to Kaiya, prodding her to go speak to him. Her eyebrows knitted together, but her silent refusal was met with chin jerks in Father's direction.

He broke the silence with a throaty voice coming from his bedroom. "My children, enter."

They all rose and approached the entrance to the dimly-lit sleeping chamber, heads lowered.

Father eased himself up into a sitting position.

Hurrying over to help, Kaiya propped him up with cushions and pulled fur blankets to his gaunt chest.

"My children, I am very concerned about your safety in light of tonight's events. I have decided you will have, in addition to your complement of imperial guards, an adept from the Black Lotus Temple accompanying you at all times. This is a secret order known only to a handful of the most senior imperial guards and Praise Moon nuns."

Kaiya's childhood friend Tian had been sent to the Black Lotus Temple. Mention of it usually tempted her to bring up the taboo subject. However, the idea of a man—even a celibate monk—watching over her sleep invited protest instead. What was the benefit in having a scholar or accountant as a protector? "Father, Chen Xin and Zhao Yue have protected me since youth, and they are unparalleled swordsmen—"

He raised a hand to silence her. "Yes, the imperial guards are the most skilled swordsmen in the nation. However, the *Moquan* adepts can recognize potential threats before they happen. I have one with me at all times, yet you have never even noticed."

"*Moquan*?" Kaiya twirled a loose strand of hair. Perhaps the legendary thieves in the night were more than a mother's tool for controlling unruly children. Maybe the *Moquan* guards explained all the times something sounded out of the ordinary around Father. Or the unexplained bumps in the night. "So they are real."

Eldest Brother Kai-Guo nodded. "Yes, they are a secret only the *Tianzi* and his heirs know of."

Male heirs, at least. So they existed. The strange shadow at Cousin Kai-Long's teahouse. Perhaps a *Moquan* had rescued her. Even so, the idea of one watching over her sleep... She shook her head. "I don't want one in my bedchambers."

Father's brow furrowed. "We suspect these recent attacks are the work of a renegade *Moquan*.

You need those who understand their methods, even in your room. Your new guard will remain silent unless ordered to speak, or if there is imminent danger."

It made sense. Still, the thought of someone besides her one familiar nun attendant violating the sanctity of her personal space... As if this night couldn't get worse. Father clapped twice as Kaiya started to protest.

Three shadows dropped from the dark ceiling corners, landing soundlessly on the sablewood floors. They sank to one knee, fist to the ground. All were small, wispy figures, wearing black utility suits and masks.

As Father spoke, each of the dark shapes bowed their heads in silent acceptance of his order. "The Crown Prince and Princess will be protected by One. Two, your duty is to Prince Kai-Wu and his wife. Three, you must safeguard the Princess Kaiya. My command supersedes any they might give you."

Kaiya scowled at the *Moquan* assigned to her, but Three's body language showed no signs of intimidation. She tried to keep the irritation out of her voice. "Goodnight, Father. Let us speak again about this in the morning."

With a curt bow, she spun on her heel and fled the room, closing the door before Three could follow.

After a quick jaunt through the halls, she came to her sleeping chamber's anteroom. Her usual nun attendant bent at the waist as she entered. Kaiya quickly shut the doors, just in case Three hadn't gotten the message earlier.

With dexterous fingers, the nun untied Kaiya's sash and eased the outer robe off her shoulders. Later, she would take it, and the inner gown, to the private dressing room just outside the restricted bedroom wing.

Kaiya's gaze swept across the room to the stand where her plain white sleeping robe hung. What was that? A flash of black? She turned back.

A girl in black clothes sat in the corner near the door.

The nun gasped and interposed herself between Kaiya and the intruder. She raised her hands in a defensive position.

How had someone slipped in? Kaiya glanced toward her bed where she kept a curved dagger. "Who are you? What are you doing here?"

The girl bowed her head. "Forgive me, *Dian-xia*. It was not my intention to surprise you. I am...Three...whom the *Tianzi* assigned to protect you."

Kaiya studied Three carefully. The girl had seemed little more than a tangible shadow in Father's dimly lit room. Now in the bright light, she didn't look to be much older than a young teen, short and lithe. Her dark hair was pulled back to reveal a slight point to her ears and particularly large eyes, belying a hint of elven blood. Though pretty, the girl lacked the ethereal exquisiteness of elves.

And the voice. It sounded so familiar. "Three, how did you get in?"

"I was right behind you, *Dian-xia*."

Maybe the myths about the child-snatching *Moquan were* true. "Impossible. I closed the door right behind me."

"Yet, I am here." Three's tone was blunt as a chopstick, with a hint of amusement. From behind her back, she produced a long knife—Kaiya's own.

The nun snapped back into a defensive position, only to tentatively receive the blade when Three handed it to her.

"Remove this from the bed chambers," Three said. "It is something that could be used against the princess. As long as I am here, no harm will come to her."

Such bravado. Kaiya frowned. "You will not always be here. I am going to change into my bedclothes, so begone, until I tell you to return."

"Forgive me, *Dian-xia*. My orders are to be with you at all times."

At least the *Moquan* guard was female, but such impertinence! "I will speak to the *Tianzi* about this arrangement in the morning. Do not make yourself too comfortable here. You will be gone by tomorrow night."

Three sucked on her lower lip. "*Dian-xia*, it is for your own protection. If you command it, you shall not even know I am here."

"Then humor me, and at least pretend to leave." With an exasperated sigh, Kaiya snatched up her sleeping gown and went behind a folding screen to change. On the other side, the *Moquan* girl stomped across the room to the door, opened it, stomped out, and closed it behind her. Her footsteps echoed down the hall.

Kaiya emerged from behind the screen. No sign of Three. The nun unpinned her hair, allowing her luxurious locks to tumble down to her waist. Taking up the inner gown, the nun bid her goodnight and slipped out the door. As always, a clean inner gown would hang on the anteroom stand first thing in the morning.

Now alone, Kaiya slid her window open and looked out. A cool breeze brushed across her face, and she smoothed her silken tresses with her hands. The constellation of E-Long loomed high above, a reminder of the evil dragon who supposedly hung over her destiny—if an assassin didn't get her first. Below it, the Iridescent Moon waxed to mid-gibbous. Only three hours to midnight. She would need a good night's rest to deal with the inevitable arguments in the council the next morning. And the confrontation with Father over the *Moquan*.

Blowing out a long breath, Kaiya closed the windows, shuttered the lamps, and rolled into her bed. She drew up the silk sheets and fur covers, allowing them to envelop her. After a few minutes of deep breathing, her annoyance subsided and her mind settled.

She'd been insufferable with Three, and the guilt gnawed at her. After all, Father only wanted her to be safe. And Three had done nothing wrong, save for her tone, which bordered on mocking insolence.

Something felt wrong in the room: an extra sound in the voice of the night. It seemed oddly familiar.

Kaiya called out softly, "Three, are you there?"

Silence was her only reply, and she spoke again. "Three, I command you to speak if you are here."

Three's voice, coming from a mere ten feet away, sounded surprised. "Yes, *Dian-xia*."

"I guess I will not be rid of you, will I?"

Mirth danced in Three's tone. "I am afraid not."

Kaiya sat up in her bed. "Three, come here, and bring a light."

Although Kaiya could always hear most movements in her room, Three reached the lantern and opened its shutters in complete silence. Bright light flooded the room.

Squinting, Kaiya beckoned Three over. "Come. Closer."

Three approached, head bowed. When she raised it, their gazes met.

Kaiya examined the girl's features. "You are very beautiful, although not in a classic sense. It is...exotic. You have elven blood, do you not?"

"Yes, *Dian-xia*." Three answered concisely, though Kaiya had asked in a way that prompted for more information.

"It is not often elves mate with humans," Kaiya said, waiting for an explanation of Three's origins. Elves very rarely left their secluded valley realms. The few half-elves in history were the result of violent circumstances, and oftentimes met tragic ends. To her frustration, the girl remained laconic. "What is your story?"

"It is not what you think," Three finally answered. "From what I have been told, my father is an elf and my Hua mother died in childbirth. Since my adventuring father could not raise me alone, I was left in the care of the Temple as a babe long ago."

Long ago? "How old are you?"

Three fell silent again, gaze cast down in avoidance of Kaiya's. She looked up again. "Forgive my rudeness, *Dian-xia*, but may I speak freely?"

Kaiya nodded.

Three sucked on her lower lip before speaking, almost inaudibly. "Do you typically ask your servants their age, even before you know their name?"

Kaiya paused in surprise before shaking her head. "I apologize, that was rude of me. I—"

"How long has your nun attendant served you? Do you know her name?"

Heat rose to Kaiya's face, and she turned her head down and to the side. The way it exposed the curve of her neck would buy her time in the company of men, but the half-elf's eyes merely narrowed. "My apologies. What is your name?"

The girl grinned. "Jie. My family name is Yan, the same as the Master of the Black Lotus Temple, who adopted me. I'm thirty-one."

Yet she appeared no older than twelve, thirteen at best. If the half-elf had spent so much time at the temple, then... "You must know my childhood friend, Zheng Tian. He is a cloistered scholar."

Jie, whose eyes had sparkled with mischief just seconds before, choked on a cough. "Cloistered scholar? There are none of those at the Temple, only *Moquan*. Even the cooks and scullery maids can kill a dozen different ways. Tian is a deadly swordsman and an unparalleled planner. The best since the fabled Architect."

Her reference to the Architect meant little to Kaiya, but Tian as a swordsman... The idea would be comical if it weren't so perplexing. As children, he wasn't much better than her with a sword, despite being older and a boy. Her archery skills had surpassed his. Even when Father revealed the *Moquan* were real and came from the Black Lotus Temple, Kaiya assumed Tian must've held some clerical role there. How could her gullible, adorable friend be a warrior and spy? "He was like a big brother to me."

"As he is to me, too. He calls me *Little Sister*, even though I'm ten years older." Jie's tenor dropped to a drone, but there was a hint of adoration in her voice.

The girl was cute, insolence aside. Kaiya covered a giggle with her hand. "Then we are almost sisters. Very well, Yan Jie, when we are in private like now, I command you to speak freely as my sister. Also, from tomorrow, you'll dress as one of my handmaidens. I'll feel more comfortable that way."

Kaiya rose from her bed and treaded over to her writing table. From an ornately carved rosewood box, she withdrew a jade hairpin and offered it. "We must exchange hairpins to sanctify our bond of sisterhood. It'll make a much more convincing disguise as my handmaiden, as well."

The half-elf tentatively extended her hand, and bowed her head as she received the jewel. She then plucked a flat, tapered pin from her own hair and proffered it in two hands. "This is all I have. Be careful not to stab yourself."

The black-lacquered metal hairpin had a wicked-looking tip. Kaiya tried not to gawk as she received it. "I...I shouldn't take my bodyguard's weapon."

Jie smirked. "There are a lot more where that came from."

Once the princess had returned to bed and her breathing became shallow, Yan Jie settled into an alert meditation. It would allow her to forgo sleep for a while, even as she reflected on the dramatic turn of events.

Just a day ago, she'd returned to Hua after an unsuccessful two-year mission abroad. No sooner had she stepped of the ship, than she was tasked with rooting out the anti-imperial insurgency. No rest for the weary; at least no more than her current meditation.

This evening had started innocuously enough, with tracking a careless rebel and kissing him on the neck with a contact toxin. That had been followed with her both disabling an assassin *and* protecting him from certain death at the swords of predictable imperial guards. All in a typical day's work.

And second nature for her, compared to her new assignment.

It was far easier to slink in the shadows than to act like a proper handmaiden.

Protecting a headstrong princess was already proving to be difficult. Doing so in a dress would be even more so. Hopefully, the princess wouldn't ask who had spoken to her from the shadows two years ago, before the attack on Wailian Castle.

CHAPTER 12:

Sweat in Times of Peace

Zheng Ming watched as his arrow sang through the cool morning air, its path undeterred by a light breeze off Sun-Moon Lake. It smacked into the small wooden target with a satisfying thud, just barely audible over the pounding of his horse's hooves and the applause of watching soldiers.

He looked skyward. Hopefully, the thick clouds would break. He planned on visiting the princess soon, to see how she fared after the ambush the night before. Excitement tingled up his spine as he thought of her, so brave and yet so vulnerable.

Ming turned his horse and trotted back to the starting point on the archery course. His long-time friend, Xie Shimin, waited with several other riders.

Xie grinned. "I see you have kept up with your training since I left the border."

Watching the next rider begin his run, Ming nodded. "As the first Wang *Tianzi* said, *more sweat in times of peace...*"

"*...means less blood in times of war.*"

They both leaned back in their saddles and shared a chuckle.

Xie's laughter settled. "I shouldn't have invited you to practice on my province's equestrian field." He waved a hand at the uninhabited stretch of land in the capital's northwest, nestled among wetlands and manicured parks. "These extra practice sections will help you win the national tournament again this year."

Ming yawned. "I guess I should give your delegation a chance, since you have provided me this opportunity."

"Yes, Princess Kaiya would be happy to see her home province win, wouldn't she?" Xie leveled his gaze at him. "How are things progressing with her?"

"Certainly one of my most challenging campaigns ever."

Xie snorted. "All that sweat, and you are still bloodied. Come now, Brother Ming. You can't expect the Princess of Hua to easily surrender to your charms like all of your other conquests."

Ming shrugged. Usually, a woman would be warming his bed after an hour of sweet talk. Then again, this was the *Tianzi's* only daughter. "And if she did, I would end up like a Yu Dynasty court eunuch. Nonetheless, a man has urges."

Xie clapped him on the back. "Nothing a discreet foray or three into the Floating World can't solve."

"I have decided to save myself for her." Ming lifted his chin in mock defiance.

Xie grunted. "Let's see how long you'll last."

"It'll be worth it." Ming tracked the next archer.

"If you can accomplish it! But yes, just think about it: your son could be a potential heir to the Dragon Throne."

There it was again, the same bait everyone dangled in front of him. Ming turned to watch a

Huayuan province soldier make his archery run. "That's the least of my worries."

"It should be your foremost consideration, especially if Prince Kai-Guo and Prince Kai-Wu fail to plant their seeds."

Ming gawked. Some things were better left unsaid. He started to respond.

Xie gestured for him to remain quiet. "These are perilous times. If your future son sat on the throne, you could be regent until he comes of age."

Regent? As if ruling his own province would not be difficult enough. "I'm not sure I want that responsibility."

"In times of need, I'd rather trust the unwilling hero who rises to the occasion, than the greedy official who wishes to take charge." Xie locked his gaze on him. "We need leaders to contain the barbarians in the North and an aggressor to the South who seek to carve Hua up."

Ming's eyes darted about. His friend's words bordered on treason. "In any case, even though the *Tianzi* is in poor health, he still rules. Crown Prince Kai-Guo will rule after him. Even if they remain without child, it would be many, many years before my yet unconceived son would ascend the throne."

Xie fell silent, nonchalantly brushing the fletching of one of his arrows.

Ming shifted in his saddle. Enough talk of politics. "Now if there's anyone who needs a wife and child, it's you!"

Xie shook his head. "Unfortunately, a soldier's pay can't cover both the costs of a sick mother's medical expenses and a bridegroom gift for the right bride."

"So your mother's condition hasn't improved?"

Xie sighed. "The herbs are helping to keep her from deteriorating further, but she's not getting any better."

"I'm sorry to hear that. Perhaps she would be heartened if her only son finally married. If you need a bridegroom gift, then let me know how I can help you."

His old friend faced him, blinking away what looked suspiciously like a tear. "I appreciate the gesture, my friend. We're a proud family, and I will not accept charity for this. You need not concern yourself."

Ming placed a hand on Xie's shoulder. "We served together for years in Wailian. It would be my honor to help my comrade-in-arms."

"And I thank you for the offer. But I plan on winning a purse from the national tournament, and taking care of it myself." Xie flashed a broad grin.

"Just know that in this matter, I will not yield." Zheng Ming grinned at his friend. "But otherwise, let me know how I might help. I must be going now; I will soon be engaging another opponent at the palace."

Xie smiled slyly. "I'm afraid I'll have to embarrass you in front of her at the tournament this year."

Peng Kai-Long avoided the downward slash, turning to the side and cutting to his opponent's midsection. The satisfying crack of the bamboo sword on the man's armor echoed through the courtyard.

Both combatants stepped back and bowed.

Kai-Long kept his expression stoic, hiding his satisfaction. He was a fair swordsman at best, using pre-engagement analysis and deceit to compensate for his admittedly mediocre physical skills.

His villa steward shuffled out onto the veranda. "*Jue-ye*, Minister Hong is here to see you."

"I will meet the old man in private. Send him to the teahouse."

The prior night's ambushes had visibly shaken Old Hong. Those who thought they knew everything failed to plan for uncertainties. The minister's lack of foresight and preparation would be why Kai-Long ultimately prevailed once it was time for them to betray each other.

He reached back. One of the squires placed a silk towel in his hand, which he used to dab the sweat off his forehead. More sweat in times of peace.

Peaceful times would be ending soon, for the good of the realm. If only the *Tianzi* and his Royalist yes-men saw it. Kai-Long took his time walking, not bothering to strip off his padded cuirass. Hopefully bloodstains remained on the teahouse mats. That would be sure to intimidate Old Hong.

A servant opened the sliding doors, revealing Hong sitting cross-legged on a cushion. Sweat trickled down his leathery face. He bent over low.

Kai-Long took a seat across from him, taking note of the new mats. "Rise."

The old man creaked out of his bow. "Good morning, Lord Peng. You look well in spite of the chaos last night."

Kai-Long shrugged. "The *Tianzi's* agents have questioned everyone. From what I have been told, the attackers on the road between here and the palace used arrowheads forged in the South. The assassins were Maduran Scorpions. One was captured alive."

Hong lowered his voice. "You decided to attack the princess?"

So, the old man correctly suspected his involvement. Kai-Long scowled and shook his head. "Of course not. The princess will be yours, as we promised— if we can keep her alive."

Hong's eyes narrowed. "Then this was not your doing?"

Kai-Long glared at the minister, wrapping his next lie in indignation. "No. The prisoner revealed that *I* was their target. They didn't know the imperial guards would appropriate the teahouse. In any case, I need her alive so that *you* can continue using her as your bargaining chip, and *I* can get what I want."

Hong's mouth gaped. "Are you suggesting there are real Maduran Scorpions in Huajing?"

"It appears so. The *Tianzi's* agents are paying courtesy calls to all of the Ayuri nations' trade offices, to root out infiltrators and spies. I suspect word of the princess' romantic correspondence with the Ankiran prince got out."

Hong nodded, understanding blooming on his monkey face. "That would make sense, then. Killing the princess would prevent her from sealing an alliance with the Ankiran freedom fighters; assassinating you would silence the greatest of our lords and the loudest proponent of punitive action against them."

Kai-Long wondered if the old man was truly convinced. He needed the minister for a little while longer, just until he could get the Expansionist policies approved by the *Tianzi*, as well as measures that would aid with his eventual coup.

Once the obsequious toad delivered on the third stage of their plan, he was a loose thread that could unravel his carefully-knit plans. A loose thread that would be clipped, at the neck.

After wasting time being fitted for her first silk dress, Yan Jie watched from a covered veranda as her ward shed an extravagant gown in favor of simple cotton robes.

Jie snorted, drawing the stares of the handmaidens beside her. The princess now looked not unlike the young nun who guided the group of noblewomen in their martial arts practice. Fashionable hairstyles were abandoned in favor of simple pony tails, giving them an austere appearance befitting the White Sand Courtyard. Bordered on the east by the Praise Moon Temple, the courtyard's only defining features were the fine white gravel for which it was named, and a dragon-shaped well.

The Praise Moon nuns practiced a secret style developed by the Founder's consort after witnessing a fight between a snake and a crane. Jie suppressed a yawn. The nuns should probably stick to their duties of harvesting a unique species of tea leaves reserved for the Hua Imperial Family.

On this overcast morning, the princess, along with her sisters-in-law, her cousin Wang Kai-Hua, and the yappy Lin Ziqiu, all tied up their sleeves, exposing slender white arms. Wrist-to-wrist, they engaged in the pair exercise of *Sticking Hands,* supposedly to learn how to feel a partner's intention through tactile sensation.

Eschewing elegance, the techniques appeared direct and efficient, not unlike *Moquan* fighting arts. Its economy of motion and relaxed power suited a woman's smaller stature. Perhaps it was a worthy fighting style after all.

If only the princesses took it seriously.

Besides the otherwise flighty Ziqiu, they all laughed and chatted, much to the visible chagrin of their teacher. Heavens forbid they would ever have to defend themselves.

"I can't believe the Madurans would be so bold as to attack you," Lady Kai-Hua said as she deftly redirected one of Princess Xiulan's punches.

Princess Kaiya's technique was sloppy as she engaged Princess Yanli. "Cousin Peng believes it is because they feared our support of Ankira."

"Lord Peng would like nothing more than to invade Madura." Crown Princess Xiulan's skill was no less clumsy against Lady Kai-Hua. "The attacks last night may turn the *Tai-Ming* to the Expansionist cause."

Backing away from the Crown Princess, Lady Kai-Hua held up a hand and covered her mouth. "From what my husband tells me, Minister Hong has been working hard to push the Expansionists' agenda."

Lin Ziqiu's lips curled. "Ewww. He's gross." Her hands moved like a maelstrom through the nun's defenses, yet never seemed to be able to land a blow as her partner's leisurely, nonchalant movements warded off all attacks. Jie appreciated how the nun cut through Ziqiu's guard and slapped her on the shoulders with both hands like the whipping of a silk sash. Despite the seemingly innocuous movement, the blow struck with a loud hollow thud, sending Ziqiu staggering back four feet.

"Less haste, less emotion," the nun droned with neither haste nor emotion.

Ziqiu stepped back toward the nun, ready to reengage, a frown contorting her otherwise pretty face; but the nun held a hand up, motioning for the ladies to relax.

"We must not judge people by the way they look." Kaiya disengaged and regarded the girl. "Minister Hong is not all that he seems. In fact, I have summoned him to meet with me in two hours."

"Whatever for?" Xiulan and Yanli spoke in unison. If their eyes could open any wider, they might actually be able to see their partner attacking.

"He has been my ears among the *Tai-Ming.*"

At Jie's side, the handmaidens all murmured. Jie would make use of the princess' *speak freely* command later to remonstrate her on trusting a minister to do spy work.

From the corner of her right eye, she saw a young page pattering along the far veranda. When he reached the steps, he dropped to his right knee, fist to the ground. His voice was high-pitched. "Minister Hong of the *Tai-Ming* Council requests an audience with Princess Kaiya."

The princess bowed her head at the nun. "I did not expect the minister until after practice. Please allow us to finish early today."

The nun placed a fist into her palm, and all the ladies returned the salute.

"I will receive him here," the princess told the page.

He rose and scurried away, while the nun disappeared into the temple. The ladies straightened out their robes and alighted the temple's veranda on Jie's left. They knelt in a U-formation with Crown Princess Xiulan at the head, Yanli on her right, and Kaiya on her left. For Jie, it was a fascinating insight into imperial court rituals of rank and seniority.

Presently, Minister Hong tottered along the far veranda with his chin respectfully lowered. His gaze swept over the ladies, lingering on the princess just long enough for Jie to notice. Dirty old man.

He climbed down the steps into the courtyard and shuffled over to where the ladies sat. He stumbled to both knees and bowed. "Crown Princess, Princesses."

Ziqiu rolled her eyes in a look of disgust that Jie needed no special training to discern.

"Rise." As the highest-ranking lady, Xiulan dipped her chin once, allowing the old man out of his bow.

Princess Kaiya afforded him a tight smile. "You are early."

"Forgive me, *Dian-xia*." Hong's straightening resembled a tortuous stretch Jie remembered from her youth. "I wanted to speak to you before the council meeting begins."

The princess opened a palm toward him. "Speak."

"As you commanded, I conferred with many of the hereditary lords last night. Most of them now want war with Madura."

The princess twirled a lock of her hair, a subconscious habit Jie had already seen a few times. "I hoped we could avoid armed conflict. It puts undue burdens on the citizenry, and little on the ruling class."

Hong's head bobbed like a seal's. "As the son of a fisherman near the border, I admire your concern for the commoners. I believe there may be a way for you to stop the march to war."

"Me? They will not listen to a girl." The princess' already large eyes rounded.

The minister placed a hand on his chest. "You are far more than that. Yesterday, you disarmed angry lords with a laugh."

Only a laugh? Jie favored Princess Kaiya with a discerning eye. Perhaps she'd grown in the last two years. Perhaps protecting her wouldn't be such a waste of time.

"Even if that is true, what do you suggest I do?" the princess asked.

"The ambassador from the Kingdom of Bijura is an old friend, going back thirty-two years to the days when I was posted in Vyara City as a trade officer. They have relations with Madura and

may be willing to mediate for us. In today's meeting, please offer to negotiate with the Madurans on neutral ground."

The princess twisted a stray tress. "It sounds like a promising idea. Why don't you suggest it yourself?"

Hong placed his hand on his chest. "I am just a minister, one whom the hereditary lords disdain. They will reject it out of hand if I propose it. However, they will listen to you, as will the *Tianzi*."

The princess stopped playing with her hair and let out a deep breath. "If that is the only way to avert hostilities, I will try."

Hong beamed, exposing perfect teeth. "Very good, *Dian-xia*. However, there is still unrest in the capital. I ask that you consider another proposal: allowing the great lords to bring in more protection from their provinces. It will make them feel more secure, and more patient on punitive action against Madura."

"That sounds reasonable," the princess said, even as Jie wondered just how many soldiers Hong considered to be *sufficient*.

Hong bowed low again, forcing Jie to hide a grimace at the motion's awkwardness. "The princess is wise beyond her tender years. With your leave, I must talk to a few lords who may yet be swayed from war."

After Minister Hong's departure, the ladies gathered around the well to wet their throats and wash their hands.

"What did you think about the minister?" Princess Kaiya asked.

Young Ziqiu's lip turned up. "Disgusting! His groveling makes my stomach turn."

Jie couldn't disagree.

Lady Kai-Hua shook her head. "He is adequately respectful, and seems to have the best interests of the nation at heart."

Jie wondered about the accuracy of that. She would send one of her *Moquan* brothers to learn more about Minister Hong's comings and goings.

The Crown Princess apparently agreed. "I would not trust him fully."

Princess Yanli nodded. "You must be careful when dealing with him. As the Five Classics say, a wicked heart with good intentions is still wicked."

Princess Kaiya sighed. "For the time being, I will assume the best. His suggestions *do* make sense, after all."

The valet appeared again, dropping to his knee. "*Dian-xia*, Lord Zheng Ming wishes an audience with Princess Kaiya."

Head jerking to the far veranda, the princess shot a hand up to her mouth. She fumbled with her sleeve, trying to loosen the cords that held it up.

The other princesses covered their giggles, trading knowing smiles. Crown Princess Xiulan beckoned in the direction of the royal retinue. "Handmaiden, bring a towel and assist Princess Kaiya."

Jie watched the handmaidens from the corners of her eyes. One of them was supposed to respond. None moved.

The Crown Princess' thin-painted eyebrows rose, like dagger points, her gaze stabbing into Jie.

It left little doubt who was responsible for Princess Kaiya's towel. Gaping, Jie dropped to her knee, fist to the ground.

A soldier's salute.

It lacked the refinement of a lady's dainty bow at the waist, and the handmaidens exchanged glances which somehow combined shock and amusement.

Heat rose to the tip of Jie's ears. She stood and attempted a bow, which even the stoic imperial guards reacted to with quivering lips.

Jie sucked on the right side of her lower lip as she straightened and descended toward the courtyard. When her foot touched the first of three steps down, her robe's hem maliciously reached over and tangled up her ankle. She took the last two steps with a leaping butterfly twist and landed lightly in a *Dipping Crane* stance.

Who knew working in a dress would be so difficult? The gown would need modifications to allow for better mobility.

All eyes widened and mouths hung agape, none more so than those of Lady Ziqiu. "*That* is no Praise Moon Fist technique..."

The imperial guards reached for their swords, but were assuaged by Princess Kaiya's glare.

The morning couldn't get any more embarrassing. Jie shuffled over to the princess and offered her favorite silk kerchief, the one with a musky, manly smell.

"Thank you." The princess received it and dabbed the sweat beading on her forehead. The way she cherished that rag...

Princess Yanli favored Jie through slitted eyes. "You are new. What is your name?"

"*Dian-xia*, my name is Jie."

Princess Xiulan also stared at her. "What family do you come from? You do not honor them with—"

"It's all right," Princess Kaiya said. "Please help me with my sleeves."

Jie nodded and moved behind the princess. The delicate knots *looked* impractical, but she pulled the wrong end, causing them to tighten.

"*Dian-xia*, Lord Zheng Ming is here," the page said.

All attention shifted to the handsome lord, and Jie used the opportunity to flick out a knife from beneath her sleeve and slash through the cords. The sleeves tumbled down the princess' thin arms, and Jie let out the breath she'd been holding.

The princess bowed, affording a view of Lord Zheng Ming. He knelt in salute, his topknot hanging over a shoulder. Most ladies would probably find his wolfish grin charming, even if it looked like a wild beast stalking prey.

Though not close to his eldest brother, Tian had always idolized him. After seeing him in person, Jie could not fathom why.

"Princesses, forgive me for interrupting your practice. Again."

"We were just adjourning." Crown Princess Xiulan's tone bordered on flirtatious.

Yanli took Ziqiu's hand. "Yes, we will leave you to speak with Princess Kaiya." Her up-to-now stern voice softened. She, too, sounded enamored.

Zheng Ming bent over in a sweeping bow. "Yet again, I do not get to enjoy the pleasure of all of your company."

Such a fop. Jie caught herself shaking her head in disdain. Luckily, she stood behind the princesses and had her back to the rest of the entourage. No one would see it. Her cover disappeared as all present but Princess Kaiya's own imperial guards made their way to the veranda like a Spring Festival procession.

The princess leaned over and whispered. "We need to work on your etiquette. For now, go change into your utility suit."

"I am supposed to be with you at all times, *Dian-xia*."

The princess' lips quirked. "And your skill is compromised in that dress. I am sorry to put you through this."

Jie shook her head, almost contrite. "I have embarrassed you."

"Not at all," the princess said. "Go, change. I doubt Lord Zheng is a threat."

Threats came in many forms. Not all of them caused physical damage. Jie shot a quick glance at the beaming lord. "Better for me to practice in this gown now, while there is no real danger."

The princess narrowed her eyes. "I command you to change."

To obey both the *Tianzi* and the princess, Jie would have to change right there.

It was a good thing she wasn't shy about nakedness.

CHAPTER 13:

The Best Laid Plans

Hong Jianbin admired the princess seated on the dais beside the vacant Jade Throne. She looked beautiful as always, despite her ordeal the night before. After years of finding and sabotaging potential suitors, all of his planning would give him the standing to marry her himself.

A thump jolted Hong from his reverie.

Seated on the floor with the other hereditary lords, Lord Peng slammed his palm on the floor in an unsightly breach of etiquette. The young man must have been a stage actor in a previous life. His contrived rage at last night's ambushes would be convincing to anyone unaware of his likely involvement.

"Perhaps," Peng said, "the attempt on Lord Han means nothing to you. Nor the plan to take my life. But how can you ignore the targeting of your own sister?" He nodded toward Princess Kaiya.

Had he been present, the *Tianzi* would have cowed Peng or any other lord into silence with a tilt of his chin.

Crown Prince Kai-Guo, sitting at the front of the council next to the *Tianzi's* empty throne, adamantly shook his head in a slip of imperial comportment. "The Five Classics say we are all children of the *Tianzi*, and he treats us as such. He does not place his daughter above you in his policy-making decisions."

Lord Han, always a supporter of the throne, now jabbed an impertinent finger at the prince. "Pretty words, but the Five Classics also say a ruler's actions must reflect his thoughts. What does the *Tianzi* plan to do about this?"

Prince Kai-Guo stared at Lord Han for a few seconds until the old man lowered his gaze. "He will pursue punitive action once we know who to punish."

"Is it not obvious?" Lord Liang of Yutou, an Expansionist, snarled. "The perpetrators of the princess' attack used Ayuri-made arrows. One dropped a purseful of gold coins stamped in Madura. Maduran Scorpions targeted Lord Peng and ended up attacking the princess. We *know* who the enemy is."

"Excuse my impropriety in speaking out of line." The princess' voice carried over the murmurs, a melodic wave which drowned out all others. She bowed her head as the hereditary lords turned to face her. "I appreciate Lord Liang's concern for my well-being. However, I will be the first to say Hua must tread with caution. My father's spies foiled an attack perpetrated by our own people."

"As were the other ambushes, starting with the one on Lord Zheng's son," Peng said, tilting his chin toward Lord Zheng. "Plenty of evidence indicts Madura. Madura's money is behind this. As the Founder said, *Cut off the head, and the demon will die.*"

Prince Kai-Guo shook his head in an unsightly fashion again, making Hong wonder if the boy would ever have the composure to be *Tianzi*. "There is almost too much evidence. If we assume Madura is behind this, we may be overlooking something more insidious."

"Forgive me, Cousin, for contradicting your wisdom," Lord Peng said. "Only the paranoid ignore the obvious in favor of conspiracy theories. Again, I say, allow me to take my armies into Madura."

The Crown Prince's face burned an angry shade of crimson. He opened his mouth, but no words came out.

"No." The word flitted off Princess Kaiya's tongue like the warble of a songbird. "My father's legacy is one of peace. He would never stand for war if it could be avoided. He has commanded me to negotiate with the Madurans. Minister Hong, I understand you have a contact who can help arrange a meeting in Vyara City, a neutral site."

How sweet his name sounded on her lips! Hong's chest tightened. How could the girl have such an effect on him? He could only nod in response.

More murmurs rumbled through the room, as the Royalists and Expansionists considered the impact of this new measure on their position. It didn't matter. As long as they perceived his support of their cause, Hong would benefit.

Chief Minister Tan cleared his throat. "Minister Hong, while we appreciate your enthusiasm, it is hardly the role of the Household Minister to make such arrangements."

The princess raised a hand, looking every part the *Tianzi*, even as she sat by his empty throne. The effect was the same. The room fell silent and all attention turned to her, a girl of only eighteen. "My father has already approved the measure. He deemed Minister Hong appropriate because of his experience in the Ministry of Trade. You were Minister of Trade back then, and specifically commended his performance, did you not?"

The Chief Minister stared at her a few seconds before bowing a fraction. "Yes, *Dian-xia*. However, surely you can appreciate that each ministry has specific duties and roles. This task should be the provenance of the Foreign Ministry."

The princess locked stares with him and placed a delicate hand on her chest. "Forgive my poor understanding of government, Chief Minister. I had always believed that all duties and responsibilities were the provenance of the *Tianzi*, delegated at his pleasure. Was I wrong to assume he could assign this task to Minister Hong?"

Hong squeezed his lips shut to keep from gaping. The girl had outsmarted one of the most seasoned, highest officials in the realm. He stole a glance at Chief Minister Tan, whose mustaches quivered. His old friend was barely containing his anger.

The Chief Minister bowed, lower this time. "The princess is correct. However, we should not honor the Madurans by sending a scion of the Son of Heaven to discuss a matter that is beneath her."

The princess brought her slender fingers to her lips, covering an innocuous laugh. "I did not think maintaining peace was beneath me. Is that not the primary mandate of the *Tianzi*?"

The hereditary lords demurred, with even the Expansionists nodding.

Lord Peng met Hong's gaze and raised an eyebrow, yet otherwise his expression remained inscrutable. Peng must have been behind the attack on the princess, but if the young lord was disappointed his quarry would escape his reach, it didn't show.

Then Peng spoke up, his voice transformed into anger. "Negotiation? Will we wait again for another attack? Who will be targeted next?"

Lord Han, a longtime Royalist, bobbed his head. "How long will it be until you meet with the Madurans? In the meantime, something must be done to ensure not only the safety of the *Tai-Ming* and their families, but also to prevent the citizenry from descending into chaos."

"If I may speak?" Unlike the others, Lord Zhao asked to be recognized, as protocol demanded.

The Crown Prince beamed and nodded, again forgetting the dignity of the *Tianzi's* office. "You may, Father-in-Law."

Such familiar terms were meant to stay outside of official functions. Hong would have rolled his eyes, if not for the need to stay in the Crown Prince's good graces. For now.

Lord Zhao said, "Regardless of what action we take, we must increase security around the capital."

Hong congratulated himself for not only convincing the Royalists to push his plan, but getting them to believe it was their own. He was further reassured when Lord Liu, drunk during their conversation the night before, spoke up.

"If I may speak?" Lord Liu waited for the Crown Prince to recognize him with a tilt of his chin. "In the three hundred years of the Wang Dynasty, the capital has never faced security issues. The general populace is already uneasy because of these unheard-of attacks, and there may very well be a new insurgency brewing."

"There has been some discussion among the *Tai-Ming*," Lord Lin of Linshan said, speaking out of line. Perhaps the princess' young friend Lin Ziqiu had learned impertinence from her father. "In these unprecedented times, we wish to petition the *Tianzi* to allow each province to bring five thousand of our own soldiers to the capital. They would assist in our personal security and help the watch maintain order."

Hong peeked at the Crown Prince, who gawked in a manner unbefitting the future *Tianzi*. Always suspicious, the Founder had stipulated that the *Tai-Ming* could bring no more than two hundred soldiers into the capital at a time. Although five thousand soldiers—a number that Hong himself had whispered into the ears of the Royalist *Tai-Ming*—would never pose a serious challenge to the national army garrisoned in Huajing, the suggestion bordered on treason.

The princess, too, regarded Lord Lin with an unseemly gawk. Apparently, her support for Hong's request earlier that day only went so far. Despite her apparent shock, her voice remained serene. "Lord Lin, the defense of Huajing is the responsibility of Huayuan Province, the jurisdiction of Prince Kai-Guo. A sudden, dramatic increase in outside provincial troops would certainly raise the anxieties of the people."

Hong had underestimated her. Nonetheless, he could find opportunity in failure. The best-laid plans rarely survived first contact with the enemy. As long as all sides got what they wanted in the end, he would still benefit from a change in tactics. "If I may speak?" Hong said, and waited to be recognized. "It is two weeks until the New Year Festival. There will be increased shifts of the watch and more soldiers from other parts of Huayuan Province deployed to the capital to maintain order. Perhaps more could come?"

From the corner of his vision, Hong saw Peng trying to get his attention, his eyebrows clashing together. This new suggestion would be perceived as a betrayal.

The Crown Prince dipped his chin a fraction, the motion more becoming and regal. "A good suggestion, Minister Hong. We can divert an extra two thousand men from the Rotuvi border, and another three thousand from Jiangkou. The *Tianzi's* spies are also mobilized. We will make the capital safe."

All anger drained from Lord Peng's voice. Perhaps the man had a touch of insanity to go with his flair for drama. "What would the *Tianzi* think of a compromise? Allow the *Tai-Ming* to increase their military presence by five hundred men, limited to the city's northeast?"

True to form, the Crown Prince wavered. The princess silently prodded him with her eyes, yet she remained quiet. Good, a sign that she remembered a girl's place beneath her brother. At last, he nodded, again the motion coarse and unbecoming. "Very well, start making arrangements, though the *Tianzi* will have to approve the plan himself."

Hong ran calculations in his mind, pondering the timing of all of the plans in place. Some would have to wait until after the New Year's Festival, when the princess departed for Vyara City. In the meantime, he would need to keep her out of Peng's reach, without Peng realizing that was his goal.

The next step of his scheme, to become the princess' groom, now ran well ahead of schedule. It was almost time to oust Chief Minister Tan.

Just after the council meeting adjourned, Peng Kai-Long excused himself before any of the other Expansionist lords could corner him. Now he lay in wait, ready to ambush Old Hong on his predictable visit to the privy. The treacherous minister, likely knowing of Kai-Long's involvement in the attack on Cousin Kaiya, was now trying to protect his ultimate prize.

With the *Tianzi's* spies lurking in the shadows and increased imperial guard presence, the girl was out of harm's reach anyway. Kai-Long had already committed himself to a less satisfying backup plan: rendering her infertile with a steady dose of the right herbs. Or, if he did not want to get his own hands dirty, perhaps push for the marriage with the soon-to-be Chief Minister Hong. The wretched old man's repeating crossbow probably had an empty magazine anyhow.

No, the princess marrying and conceiving a son was the least of his concerns right now. More pressing was whether or not he could still count on Hong in other aspects of their plan. Especially after the outrageous proposal to move more of the *Tianzi's* own men into the capital.

The old bastard turned the corner, and stopped in his tracks when their gazes met. The minister's fearful look was immensely gratifying.

"So old man, are you backing out of our arrangement?"

"What?" A broken smile appeared on Hong's face. "Of course not."

Kai-Long scrutinized Hong's expression for any sign of a lie. "We did not discuss any of what you proposed in council."

Hong shook his head. "We underestimated Princess Kaiya. I had to adjust our strategy in light of that."

Kai-Long glared at the minister. "When she meets with the Madurans, she will learn they have nothing to do with the attacks." Not to mention she might meet with Prince Hardeep and find out their year of correspondence was all a lie…

"We can always incriminate the Kingdom of Rotuvi, which has threatened us for years, and is a weaker opponent anyway. It will also give you reason to move your armies north. Most importantly, she will be out of our way in two weeks. It will be easier for us to attain our final goal."

"I wonder if we are speaking of the same goal." Kai-Long noted that Hong was regarding his own expression with just as much scrutiny.

"Of course. You as *Tianzi*, me as Chief Minister. We will do great things for Hua."

Kai-Long pursed his lips. At least Hong got half of it right. "Regardless of whether or not Cousin Kaiya is around, five hundred of my best men are not enough to stage a coup. Especially with all of the additional Huayuan troops you proposed."

"Your men just have to be present for contingencies. Once everything has played out, you will be the legitimate heir. Then you will have a new five hundred best men: the imperial guard."

It did make sense, except for how Hong undoubtedly planned on betraying him in the end. Kai-Long forced a smile. It was two weeks until the New Year Festival. After that, Cousin Kaiya would leave. With her out of the way, everything would fall into place.

CHAPTER 14:

Resonance

By the second night, Kaiya could lie in her bed and reliably pick out Jie's breathing from the chorus of spring sounds. Like a shallow whisper, each of the half-elf's inhalations lasted over a minute, followed by an equally-long exhalation. Try as she might, Kaiya couldn't replicate the marathon breath cycle.

Kaiya fiddled with Zheng Ming's kerchief, unable to sleep. As intrusive as the *Moquan* girl was, it was still nice having someone there. "How do you breathe like that?"

Jie's breathing returned to normal. "It's part of our training. It's called the *Viper's Rest*. At the highest levels, we can slow our heartbeat so as to appear dead."

What a strange technique, with little obvious use. "What other special skills do the *Moquan* possess?"

Pride radiated in the girl's voice. "We are masters of stealth. We can infiltrate an enemy. We make excellent information gatherers. If need be, we can be untraceable assassins."

"You will not need to make use of *that* skill in my service." Kaiya shuddered. To think, sweet little Tian, sneaking around in the dark, murdering. Maybe some things were best left unasked.

Apparently, Jie would be answering those unspoken questions. "It's not something I've had to do. The clan cultivates us according to our abilities. The best assassin in recent memory was the Surgeon, who died thirty-two years ago on a mission. His friends, the Architect and the Beauty, perished with him." Awe carried in her voice. "Tian might be as good a planner as the famed Architect."

Kaiya had a good idea where this was headed. "And you?"

"Like the Beauty, in more ways than one." The girl had to be grinning. "My specialization is infiltration and information gathering."

"What information did you gather from watching the council meeting?"

"May I speak freely?"

"Speak, my Insolent Retainer."

"Then forgive my audacity, but I fear the Crown Prince is not ready to be *Tianzi*. The Second Prince, even less so. He ignored the entire meeting."

"Kai-Guo has plenty of time to grow into the role." Did he? Kaiya tried to sound convincing. Father might not have much time left.

"He'd better have. Lord Peng waits in the wings."

"Cousin Kai-Long? He has always been my father's favorite nephew. Even if he is intent on invading Madura, he does so with the country's best interests at heart."

Jie's silence spoke loudly about her distrust of Lord Peng. When she voiced her concerns again, it had nothing to do with Cousin Kai-Long. "Be wary of Minister Hong. When you're not paying attention, his eyes undress you."

After enduring the lewd stares of boorish suitors, it didn't come as a surprise. "Most men are governed by their base desires."

"Yes, but the minister goes beyond leering. He hides it so well, it makes me wonder what other treacherous thoughts bounce around in his head."

Kaiya shuddered again. Hong was old enough to be her father, perhaps even grandfather. Nonetheless... "He has proven reliable up to now. Unless your elven senses detect something else?"

"The only legacy of my elf blood is a father who abandoned me." Whereas Jie had spoken in an objective tone about treacherous cousins and lecherous old men, her voice now sounded like she'd taken a bite of raw bitter melon.

How awful! Kaiya propped herself up on her elbows. "There must have been a good reason." She beckoned her bodyguard over. Court conventions might frown on physical contact, but here, in the privacy of her room, she would give Jie a reassuring hand squeeze.

Not moving from her seat, Jie sighed. "According to the note he left, it was because he couldn't care for a baby while he adventured. Little good elf-blood has done for me, beyond making me look a third my age. I—"

A cackle broke out in the corner of the room. "When you are ninety, you will be happy for that."

Kaiya shot straight up. A third presence in the room had evaded her hearing. She fumbled for the knife hidden under an extra pillow. Gone. Of course. The nun had removed it at Jie's order. She tightened the sleeping gown around her. As if that would help.

Jie leapt to her feet and flung something, or perhaps several things, in the direction of the laugh. Something flashed in her hands as she interposed herself between Kaiya and the intruder.

Then the half-elf froze in place, her defensive stance silhouetted by light from the full White Moon Renyue.

Kaiya peered past her to where a dark shape stood.

Jie felt like a disembodied soul. She had no command over her muscles, nor could she feel a thing. Yet all of her senses worked.

Her elven vision clearly painted the cloaked intruder in olive shades as he walked around her. A thin longsword hung at his side.

A male voice invaded her mind. *You can also thank your elven blood for the vision that allows you to see me now.*

The same voice spoke aloud. "*Dian-xia*, your *Ear that Sees* improves, yet it still did not detect my arrival."

The renegade *Moquan*! Perhaps the one who taught the rival clan she'd unsuccessfully tracked for two years. His presence evaded even Jie's own keen senses, and he spoke of *Seeing Ears*, a *Moquan* technique that helped adepts fight in the dark. The great masters could paralyze an opponent by merely touching energy centers, and there were supposedly secret techniques of striking an enemy without actually making physical contact. Yet, projecting thoughts was beyond even fanciful legends.

The lamp shutters flapped open, throwing the room into bright light.

The princess stumbled over her words, her tone a mixture of fear and anger. "Lord Xu. This is my personal chamber. How did you get past the magical wards?"

The elf lord! If only Jie could see the interaction behind her.

"Who do you think put them in place?" Xu's tone sounded harmless enough, and he had no reason to attack the princess.

Try as she might, Jie couldn't turn.

"What did you do to Jie?" the princess demanded.

"I had to protect myself. Her barrage of spikes and stars almost hit me, and I would wager she is handy with those knives...and probably all of the other weapons she hides."

Jie would've shuddered if she could. Perhaps nakedness did bother her. And she was fully clothed.

"Release her." The princess' tone of command, bred into the royal family, would make most people think twice about disobeying.

Jie wasn't one of those people.

Apparently, neither was Lord Xu. He came back around and stood in front of her, examining her with dispassionate eyes. How satisfying it would be to gouge them out. And then spill his guts for good measure.

He looked over her shoulder to the princess. "Your bodyguard wants to dig my eyes out with the hilt of her knife, and spoon out my intestines. You will have to command her to behave."

If Jie could gawk through her paralysis, she probably would. Her first up-close experience with a real elf was proving to be quite memorable.

"Jie, I command you to leave Lord Xu alone."

It is for your own safety. Xu's smug voice grated.

As much as that order begged to be disobeyed, what chance did anyone stand against who'd paralyzed her as an afterthought?

You are still young. Perhaps with more experience and training.

He was listening to her thoughts. Jie blanked her mind, using an anti-interrogation technique.

Lord Xu chuckled, and then uttered a foul-sounding syllable, worthy of an altivorc oath.

The sudden return of sensation nearly sent Jie tumbling to the ground, yet she managed to regain her balance before suffering further injury to her ego. Now if only Lord Xu would get out of her mind.

My apologies. I will not violate your privacy again, unless you attack me. "Now, withdraw from the chambers. I have secrets to share with the princess."

He was unravelling her, puncturing even her mental armor. Jie crossed her arms. "I cannot. My orders are to remain with her at all times."

Lord Xu's almond eyes, almost a mirror of her own, narrowed. "I *could* teleport you to the other end of the realm, but you would probably just

kill yourself for dereliction of duty. It would be a waste of such talent." He walked past her to stand at the head of princess' bed.

Such arrogance. Add arrogance to abandonment to the long list of elven shortcomings. The princess retreated to her headboard and glared at him. "So why do you invade my room at this late hour?"

The elf grinned like a schoolboy. "You will be negotiating with the Madurans. I thought I should teach you one more skill beforehand."

"Can't it wait until morning?" The princess pulled the covers up higher. It was tempting to join her beneath the blankets, like Jie's favorite dog at the Black Lotus Temple would.

"I am to perform a ritual magic spell when Renyue is full. I will be returning to Haikou as soon as I am done teaching you."

With a low sigh, the princess bowed her head. "Yes, Master." She pushed her legs over the side of her bed.

Still smiling, the elf drew his longsword. Jie reached for her knives. Before she drew them, he tossed his weapon toward the princess, hilt first.

The princess cowered back, moving out of its flight path, but the sword suspended itself in mid-air, just outside her reach. She tentatively seized it by the hilt. The nonchalance with which he performed these impossibilities didn't seem to be simple theatrics.

The show continued. Lord Xu reached behind him, and a lute from the anteroom flew across the bedchamber and into his grasp. He turned it over in his hands, examining it. "None the worse for its tumble onto the castle parapet two years ago. Now, *Dian-xia*, place your hand on the sword blade, so as to be barely touching it."

When the princess had done as she was told, the elf strummed several notes. He peered at her as he did so. "Can you feel the change in vibrations?"

She nodded.

"Sound can be a weapon," the elf lord said, "as deadly as the sword you hold."

Jie snorted. To a *Moquan*, almost anything could be a weapon. But sound?

"Though perhaps even more deadly is the heart," he added. "Half-elf, come here."

She crossed her arms over her chest. No way would she surrender any more of her pride to this pompous ass.

"Your loss." Xu shrugged before gliding over to the princess' bedside. He took her hand and placed it on his chest.

She recoiled, her head shyly tilting to the side. "That... This is inappropriate."

With a chuckle, Xu jerked his chin in Jie's direction. "It's either me or her. Your choice. Or hers, as the case may be. Or, just lose the chance at a valuable lesson."

The princess looked up at Jie, her eyes pleading. The expression was reminiscent of that temple dog waiting for attention. At least the princess hadn't commanded it. With a harrumph, Jie strode over.

Xu smirked. "Good girl. Now, *Dian-xia*, put your hand over her heart."

The princess did as instructed. Her hand felt cold, even through Jie's shirt.

"Now, feel the change in your little friend's heartbeat." Xu improvised a long series of notes on the lute.

Little friend, indeed! The elf lord could take his little—

As understanding bloomed on the princess' face, her hand resonated against Jie's chest. The vibration changed as the elf picked up the tempo. Maybe a *Moquan* master's delayed death strikes worked in a similar manner.

"You understand, too, don't you, half-elf?"

Jie hesitantly nodded.

"And you, *Dian-xia*, have you experienced a connection with your audience when you play? Something you *knew* was there, even if you did not know exactly what it was? Of course you have, when you saved the boys from slaughter two years ago in Wailian. Here is how: everything has a unique resonance, which can be changed by the cleaving of a sword or something simple as the right musical note. Now sing."

Her eyes glazing over, the princess lifted her voice in song. Both the vibration of Jie's heartbeat and the princess' hand sped up. Joy and happiness welled up in her.

"If you can make that connection, you can bend a sentient being to your will. Now, withdraw your hand and sing a one-word command."

The princess' hand dropped away, her fingers relaxing into gentle crescents. "Sit." The word trilled out like an opera singer's line.

Her voice washed over Jie like a rolling wave, compelling her muscles to obey. She found herself seated at the edge of the bed. The temple dogs again came to mind. Perhaps this was what they experienced. Unlike the dogs, however, she was not rewarded with a tasty treat.

The princess' shoulders slumped, and she gasped for air.

Xu clapped his hands. "Very good, *Dian-xia*. It will feel draining at first, but as you get better, you will be able to string longer commands together with less fatigue. Lesser beings and those of dim wit" —he grinned at Jie— "will succumb easily to your voice. But with enough practice, you might one day be able to affect even Avarax."

Sucking on the right side of her lower lip, Jie glared at the elf.

He returned her stare with a wink. "My, my, if looks could slay a dragon..." *Listen well, Little One. Now that you know how it feels, you can counteract the effect by knowing how to control your own heart's frequency. You may very well need to resist the Siren's Song in defense of your princess. I am sure she will give you many opportunities to practice.*

"Practice more, *Dian-xia*." His gaze bored into Jie. "You will need it soon."

The air popped and Lord Xu was gone.

The princess met Jie's eyes. "I wonder how *soon* soon is."

CHAPTER 15:

Another Foreign Prince

The last time Kaiya greeted a foreign prince, the duty had been foisted on her at the last minute. She fell hopelessly in love and was taken advantage of. Now two years older and wiser, she went armed with feminine wiles and ten days of practice using the power of her voice. If anyone would have the upper hand in today's engagement with Prince Aelward of Tarkoth, it would be her.

She examined her smooth complexion in the mirror of her dressing room. Though the supposed Once-In-Three-Generations beauty batted eyelashes back at her, the gangly, hesitant teen hid beneath.

Perhaps a touch of rouge would help.

The faint sound of a rustling gown was followed by a brief flash of color in the mirror. She turned to see Jie slinking toward the door, dressed in a court robe. Embroidered in a spring flower pattern, the extravagant silk befitted an imperial handmaiden.

However, the lines of the gown had been awkwardly modified, with raised hems and jagged stitching.

Kaiya covered her gawk with a hand. "Who altered your gown?" The tailor would face reprimand for ruining the beautiful dress.

Her Insolent Retainer cast her gaze down. "I did. It constrained my mobility and I needed to sew in hiding places for weapons."

Kaiya raised an eyebrow. "Have you ever stitched before?"

"Only wounds." Jie shrugged a shoulder out of her inner gown and turned to reveal a thin scar, barely noticeable, above her shoulder blade.

Kaiya tried to banish the unsettling image of the half-elf sewing up her own laceration. However... "That is immensely better than what you did to your clothes."

The edge of Jie's mouth quirked up. "How would I reach the back of my shoulder? Someone else stitched that one."

"Tian?"

Jie burst out laughing. "He's far better at cutting flesh than stitching it back up."

Yet another childhood memory of her gentle friend, ruined. She patted Zheng Ming's kerchief, tucked away in her outer gown's pocket. "In any case, we cannot have you seen in *that*. There is not much time to fit you with a new dress, so it looks like you will have to be my shadow again today."

Relief danced across Jie's face before vanishing as quickly as it appeared. "As the princess commands."

"I will need your eyes when we venture out into the city."

Jie nodded. "To watch for danger, I know. That is my job."

"The danger I speak of is the Prince of Tarkoth, and his weapon will be his words."

Hiding in the shadows of the princess' dressing room, Jie shed the annoying gown and slipped into her stealth suit. The princess' primping was so meticulous, her tone so grave when referring to the visiting dignitary.

Jie tried to keep a straight face. From her mission to the East, she knew all three princes of Tarkoth, one intimately. Only one was a particularly dangerous diplomat; but as Crown Prince leading a war effort, he wasn't going to be the one travelling all the way here. Nor would it be the second prince, whose heart she'd broken.

No, it would be the bastard, Aelward, and no amount of the princess' feminine charms would work on him. It would be so fun to watch her try.

After having not seen the princess since the attempt on her life nearly two weeks prior, Zheng Ming looked forward to a quiet chat over tea. Instead, she invited him to accompany her on a carriage ride to the Huajing's West Gate, to greet some foreign prince.

Ming had never heard of a member of the Imperial Family leaving the palace to receive an envoy. A foreign dignitary climbing the steps of the Hall of Supreme Harmony to bow before an imperial representative was standard protocol, a symbolic gesture of subservience to the *Tianzi*.

Waiting for her by the palace carriage house, Ming admired the glossy finish of the two imperial coaches. The stable master and his assistants hitched the covered carriage to four jet-black stallions, imported from the horse-breeding Kingdom of Tomiwa.

"We will take the open coach." The princess' melodious voice caused Ming's legs to buckle.

Still, even though the ambushes on the hereditary lords had abruptly stopped, it was an insane order. He turned around.

The princess glided through the courtyard, stunning in a light blue dress with a cloud design. Two handmaidens and several imperial guards followed.

Ming dropped to his knee, fist to the ground. "*Dian-xia*, perhaps the covered carriage would be safer."

The stable master and imperial guard captain nodded in agreement.

The princess tilted her head. "Young Lord Zheng, thank you for your concern. However, there has not been an attack in ten days. On this glorious spring morning, we should reassure the populace with our confidence."

Ming bowed. "*Dian-xia*, please consider your safety."

She covered a laugh with her hand. "My Lord, we must be considerate of Prince Aelward as well. He should be able to see our city at its finest, just before the Spring Festival." She locked eyes with the stable master. With a sweep of her hand, she gestured to the open carriage. "Switch," she said, the single syllable warbling out as a song.

To Ming's surprise, her straight posture sank for a split second, and she reached out to a handmaiden for support. Her thin eyebrows knitted together.

The stable master, on the other hand, gawked at her before looking at the captain for permission.

Frowning, Kaiya sung her order again. "Switch...rides."

She wobbled, and Ming stepped forward, ready to catch her if she collapsed. He couldn't let her fall, even if it meant tempting the death sentence for touching a member of the Imperial Family uninvited. "*Dian-xia*, are you all right?"

The imperial guards looked askance at him, but did not reach for their swords.

The stable master, on the other hand, bobbed his head, and motioned for his assistants to help him re-hitch the horses to the open carriage.

"I will be all right. The fresh air will help." The princess offered him a weak smile.

He helped her into a seat and sat across from her. Two dozen mounted imperial guards formed up around the vehicle, bearing the sky-blue banners of the Wang family and the Hua Empire. At the driver's command, the carriage set off, passing through the main gates of Sun-Moon Palace.

Ming's eyes darted back and forth, constantly looking for danger as they travelled down Prosperous Hua Boulevard, the main north-south thoroughfare, lined with now-blooming cherry trees. At Grand Square, they turned west onto Eternal Peace Boulevard, where past-bloom plum trees boasted their purple spring foliage.

His concern for the princess' safety, and the constant clopping of horse hooves, made conversation difficult. His words faltered as he tried to identify potential threats among all the colorful New Year's preparations.

Strings of red paper lanterns fluttered along all the major streets. Shops hung red scrolls of auspicious poetry over their doors. The smell of burning incense percolated throughout the city, combining with the sweet aroma of New Year's pastries cooking in almost every home. Huajing's population swelled as local soldiers and merchants returned home to spend time with family for the most important holiday of the year. Those not tidying up their homes swarmed the streets as they paid off debts, visited public baths, and got their hair cut to start the New Year on a lucky foot.

Throngs gathered at the side of the road, bowing as the carriage rolled by. For the last couple of years, the citizenry had speculated about whom their beloved princess would choose as a husband. They now pointed at Ming and whispered among themselves. As excited rumors passed ear-to-ear, he would probably go from unknown provincial heir to household name by the end of the day.

Thirty-six *li* and two hours later, they arrived at the West Gate. There, Hua's Foreign Minister Song chatted with the Tarkothi ambassador and his contingent of embassy guards. The latter all wore green surcoats over chain hauberks. A silver, nine-pointed star—the shared symbol of the Eldaeri Kingdoms of Tarkoth, Serikoth, and Korynth—was emblazoned on their chests. Ming stifled a yawn.

Minister Song and the several dozen Hua soldiers flanking him all dropped to a knee in unison. The Tarkothi crossed their fists over their chests and bowed their heads, showing deference to their host's ruling family.

Outside the gatehouse, the sound of horns and marching feet approached. The billowing green flags of Tarkoth came into view as Prince Aelward's party marched through the urban outskirts of the city. Commoners lined the streets, pointing and chattering about the brown-haired men.

Ming chuckled. The prince himself sat awkwardly astride a white horse, led by several walking Hua officials and followed by two dozen Tarkothi marines in dark green coats. At his side rode a matronly elf, the first of their kind Ming had seen up close.

The entourage came to a stop just outside the gate. All of the Tarkothi crossed their fists over their chests. The Hua, with the exception of the princess, bowed when the prince dismounted, though he nearly got tangled in his stirrup.

The Tarkothi ambassador cleared his throat. "May I present Prince Aelward Corivar of Tarkoth, Captain of the Tarkothi Royal Ship *Invincible.*"

It was Ming's first experience with foreign royalty. At the edge of his visual field, he saw the princess' eyes widen, rapt with interest. He gave the prince a thorough examination, wondering what intrigued her.

Sure, he was good-looking, with a bronze complexion and long brown hair tied into a pony tail. His sharp, refined features and shorter stature was typical of the Eldaeri—long-lived humans who had intermixed with elves in millennia past, on a distant continent.

From what little Ming knew of them, they had arrived on the northeast shores of Tivaralan not long after the Hellstorm, on daunting black ships. With those ships and an ingenious repeating crossbow, they had taken advantage of the Long Winter chaos and carved out their own empire. They treated their Arkothi and Estomari subjects as second-class citizens.

Foreign Minister Song spoke in what sounded like flawless Arkothi, the language of the North. "I present Princess Kaiya Wang, daughter of the Son of Heaven."

In Arkothi fashion, Prince Aelward dropped into a rigid bow, reminiscent of his inept horse riding.

"Greetings, lass." He took her hand and pressed his lips to it, making Ming cringe at their uncouth customs. "You're even more beautiful than the stories say."

The princess tilted her head and looked shyly away. She then curtsied with the grace of a weeping willow bending in the wind, surprising Ming with her knowledge of the foreign etiquette. "I am delighted to meet you, Prince Aelward. This is my escort, Lord Ming Zheng."

Ming stammered with his poor Arkothi. "Pleased to meet you, Prince."

The foreign prince grinned and turned to the elf woman. "This is my bodyguard, Ayana."

With no visible weapons and a frail build, it didn't look like the old elf could guard much more than a rocking chair. Whoever these people were, to deserve the attention of an imperial princess, was beyond Ming.

The princess curtseyed again. "Prince Aelward, it is my honor to conduct you to your audience with my father, the Son of Heaven." She extended an open hand toward the carriage. "Please join me in this carriage, a gift we received from Tarkoth ten years ago."

Taking her hand in one of his and gesturing with the other, the prince bowed again. "In our culture, a lady boards first."

With a dip of her chin, she accepted his help stepping into the carriage. Ming rolled his eyes, glad the prince wouldn't be able to see him.

Not to be outdone, Ming took the old elf's hand and helped her onto the seat next to the princess. Prince Aelward slid across the bench opposite Kaiya, and Ming followed last, facing the elf.

When the carriage set off, the prince stared at the architecture and people with wide an unseemly gawp. The princess played the perfect hostess, pointing out landmarks and their history. He would nod, say a few words, and smile. She would smile back.

The prince's Arkothi was downright unintelligible when it wasn't uncouth. Yet the princess tilted her head and looked up through her lashes at him.

Ming sat there, all but forgotten. He could only put on his best face, leaning back with his arms crossed. Even if he barely spoke the language, he could certainly best this arrogant prince in archery or swordsmanship. As a prince, and one who showed neither royal comportment nor riding skill at that, this Aelward probably got his officer's commission as a result of his high birth.

Even though only two phases of the Iridescent Moon passed, the ride back to the palace felt like it took ten. On the order of a palace official, Ming waited at the first moat before entering the palace grounds. He could only watch as prince and princess strolled over the bridge to the front gates, laughing like lovers.

CHAPTER 16

Half-Truths and Misdirections

With two-year-old scars firmly in her mind, Kaiya had steeled herself to resist more manipulation. Prince Hardeep had entranced her with his golden tongue and hypnotic eyes, each poetic word of their encounter sparking foolish dreams.

Prince Aelward, on the other hand, had barely spoken at all on the carriage ride back to the palace.

When she pointed out landmarks and spoke of their history, he only responded with one-word grunts. Maybe he didn't understand her accented Arkothi. She turned to Ming for help, but the usually witty lord seemed preoccupied with staring off into space.

Even her body language, which typically mesmerized men, failed to capture the prince's attention. A shift of her foot exposed a bare ankle, yet he never looked down. She tilted her head and batted her eyelashes as she spoke. He seemed more interested in the scenery.

As she guided his entourage toward the bridge over the first moat, Kaiya cast a glance over her shoulder toward the carriage. Zheng Ming stared back at her with a most curious expression. Perplexed, she pressed his kerchief beneath her sash. Maybe Jie, slinking somewhere unseen, would have more insight. Then again, the girl probably had little experience in the game of courtship.

Kaiya turned back to Prince Aelward. He'd paused a few steps behind her, in the middle of the gently arching marble bridge that crossed eighty feet over the first palace moat.

She followed his gaze to the towering white-plaster front walls, looming fifty feet above, capped with dark blue eaves and stretching nearly five thousand feet from east-to-west.

From her study of his homeland, she knew the curiously-shaped Tarkothi castle was miniscule by comparison, with rounded towers and elliptical footprints. Small, but an architectural marvel all the same. "I am embarrassed to say that our palace is not as unique as yours," she said.

He harrumphed. "Bah. I rarely go to that court of stuffed shirts, sycophants, and backstabbers."

She covered a laugh. Perhaps on the inside, the Tarkothi castle wasn't so unique.

On the other side of the bridge, they came to the marble plaza running eighty-eight feet from the moat to the base of the walls. Following the protocol of a royal visit, two hundred imperial guards drew their *dao* swords and held them over the left side of their chests.

Prince Aelward was awfully quiet.

Kaiya guided him and his retainers on the central path, lined with guards and gold-plated dragon statues. The front gates were painted dark blue, with hundreds of silver nubs. Above the gates hung a black sign, emblazoned with the words: *Gate of Heavenly Justice.*

Prince Aelward looked up at the sign and then lowered his head. Penned by a master calligrapher hundreds of years before, the magic imbued in the characters evoked a sense of awe and reverence in those unaccustomed to seeing it. The prince couldn't possibly read it, yet his shoulders trembled.

Kaiya gestured him through the gates. On the other side, she swept an open hand toward the central courtyard, where petals from hundreds of espaliered fruit trees drifted across the white flagstones. "Please forgive the unsightly appearance of Sun-Moon Palace as we prepare for the New Year."

The palace bustled with activity. Servants wiped down the floors, walls, ceilings, windows, and doors. Craftsmen came to repair or refurbish anything that might have broken over the year. Gardeners worked hard to ensure the palace landscaping looked its best. Seamsters sewed up tears in cushions and bedding. Somewhere in the palace, Crown Princess Xiulan directed all of these duties. In two days, every building within the Sun-Moon Palace grounds would sparkle in its full glory.

Prince Aelward gawked as he spun in place, his gaze raking from the imperial archives on the right to the Hall of Pure Melody on the left.

"Come with me to the Hall of Supreme Harmony, where the Son of Heaven will receive you." She dipped her chin toward the enormous stairway, rising up over a hundred feet. Ministry buildings flanked the stairs at tiered landings.

At the top of the one hundred sixty-eight steps, before the doors to the Hall, Prince Aelward hunched over, panting. "Damn, lass, no wonder yer so thin."

Kaiya gestured north. "Only one structure in the realm stands taller: Sun-Moon Castle, on the other side of the Hall of Supreme Harmony. It was originally the centerpiece of the capital, providing a full view of the surrounding basin."

With an open hand, she pointed him toward the entrance, where the doors had been flung open to greet the warm spring breezes. Prince Aelward bowed and continued walking, with Ayana and his ambassador at his side. He nearly stumbled over the high threshold, meant to trip malevolent ghosts if they dared enter.

Inside the Hall, the prince walked down an aisle formed by dozens of bowing ministers, officials, and nobles. Father sat on the Dragon Throne, flanked by her brothers, as well as General Zheng with the Broken Sword. It was the first time the *Tianzi* had been seen in public for weeks. After regular acupuncture and herbal tonics, he looked a fraction healthier.

Still too pale. Kaiya came around and stood on the other side of Father, opposite her brothers.

Prince Aelward and Ayana bent over low, holding the bow until the *Tianzi* signaled for them to rise. When he straightened, Aelward recited words in Arkothi at a dignified, measured cadence, so different from the way he'd spoken to her. "Your Highness, I bring greetings and wishes for your health from my father, King Elromyr of Tarkoth, and thank you for receiving me today."

Father's faint voice wavered as he answered in his accented Arkothi. "Welcome to Huajing, Prince Aelward Corivar, youngest son of King Elromyr. Your eldest brother visited us ten years ago, your second brother, two. I remember them very well."

Prince Aelward clenched his teeth. "My half-brothers. I'm the unwanted get of a mistress, n'er raised with royal graces." He paused to take a breath. When he spoke again, it was reminiscent of young boys, reciting proverbs by rote. "As I am sure you are aware, the Teleri Empire has spread like a disease through what was once the ancient Arkothi Empire, subjugating the Arkothi people under its tyrannical reign."

Kaiya's ears twitched at the sudden switch from sailor slang to diplomatic jargon.

Father's eyes narrowed in the tone of his response. "I shall be blunt. Did your own ancestors not do the same three hundred years ago?"

The prince stared at his feet. Having studied Tarkoth's history and customs in preparation for the visit, Kaiya knew the conquering Eldaeri had seen other humans as inferior and ruled with an iron hand.

Prince Aelward raised his head. "Aye, I can't deny it. But Tarkoth has changed. Its rule is considered benevolent, and both Arkothi and Estomari folk within our lands have the same opportunities as the Eldaeri."

Kaiya searched his expression. He spoke in half-truths. A century ago, clashing views on racial purity led to civil war, sundering the Eldaeri Empire into three separate kingdoms. Perhaps the same disagreements would tear Hua apart. As the Founder wrote, *A nation divided within falls victim to predators without.*

Prince Aelward lipped several syllables, then looked up to meet Father's gaze. He again fumbled over obviously-rehearsed words. "The Teleri's First Consul Geros Bovyan has focused his attention toward our peaceful nations. His armies now occupy a quarter of our sister Kingdom of Serikoth."

Eldest Brother Kai-Guo leaned over and whispered to Father, "Serikoth has changed very little. It still has a rigid class system that benefits the Eldaeri at the expense of other humans living there."

Never shifting his gaze from Prince Aelward, Father raised his hand to silence Eldest Brother. "These are affairs in the East. They have very little bearing on Cathay's peace and prosperity."

Prince Aelward turned to his ambassador, who nodded. "The Teleri Empire has formed strategic alliances with the Levanthi Empire, cowed the Nothori Kingdoms into subservience, and bought off the Ayuri Kingdom of Madura. It will only be a matter of time before they attack Cathay. I am in the Western Seas to form mutually beneficial alliances on behalf of Tarkoth."

Kaiya tried to picture a map of Tivaralan in her mind, to no avail. Still, Cousin Kai-Long saw Madura as an immediate threat; and of course they'd invaded and occupied Hardeep's Ankira.

"We are well apprised of the state of international affairs," Father said. "Since we trade with all, including the Teleri, it is of the utmost importance that we remain fair and neutral. We can only extend the same hospitality to you as we do to all of our trading partners."

Prince Aelward opened and closed his mouth, his eyes staring up. "Your true enemy is the Teleri Empire. Madura and Rotuvi only threaten you at their bidding."

Father tilted his head a fraction, the equivalent of a shrug. "These countries are small. They are no more than a nuisance, one we will be dealing with shortly via diplomacy."

"I hear you will be negotiating with Madura in Vyara City soon," the prince said.

Her assignment. How had he known? The gathered officials and nobles murmured among themselves. Only the *Tianzi* remained unfazed.

Cousin Kai-Long, up to now hidden among the rest, stood up, cutting into the clamor. "*Huang-Shang,*" he said in the Hua language. "As I said before in council, this is a perfect time to end the threat from Madura once and for all, by sweeping into the occupied Kingdom of Ankira. Although I oppose our meeting with the Madurans, I suggest that if talks break down, we ally with Tarkoth."

More murmuring, though Prince Aelward's blank expression suggested he didn't understand their tongue.

Father's tone provided no hint of what he was thinking. "Nephew, your suggestions are better suited for the *Tai-Ming* Council. In the eyes of our distinguished guest, we must always show a united front."

Lord Peng dropped to his knee, fist to the ground. "Forgive me, *Huang-Shang.*"

Father raised a hand. "I will speak with Prince Aelward alone, with only my children in attendance. The rest of you will withdraw."

The assembled audience again broke out in low whispers. Father very rarely entertained a foreign guest alone, and usually in one of the palace's pavilions. It was unheard of for him to do so in the Hall of Supreme Harmony. Nevertheless, they all filed out without protest.

Kaiya looked around. With only the imperial guards, Prince Aelward, Father, and Brothers Kai-Guo and Kai-Wu, the cavernous room felt virtually empty. Jie and her *Moquan* brethren were likely hiding somewhere as well.

Father turned to Prince Aelward. "Our traditions stipulate we must act with propriety lest Heaven forsake us. We cannot forego negotiation. Yet if history is any lesson, the Madurans will reject our peace overtures. If our talks fail, we will provide material support to Tarkoth's cause."

Kaiya stifled a gasp. Father was sending her to foreign lands, with the expectation she would fail.

Father lifted a hand. "Would you consider as act of Tarkoth's good will, to take my daughter to Ayudra City on *the Invincible*?"

Kaiya's brow furrowed. The imperial flagship, the *Golden Phoenix*, might not rate with the Eldaeri black ships, but it was still a symbol of Hua's wealth and power.

Prince Aelward bowed deeply. "Aye, it'd be my pleasure. Not only that, but the *Invincible* can't navigate the Shallowsea between Ayudra Island and Vyara City. I offer my own personal guard Ayana as protection for your daughter when she transfers to the Shallowsea skiffs."

"Her transport will be conducted in the utmost secrecy." Father smiled, breaking imperial decorum. "The meeting is set for when the White Moon waxes to full, just over fifteen days from today. In the meantime, please enjoy our hospitality, especially during the festive New Year season. My daughter will guide you to your guest house after I speak with her. You may be excused."

Prince Aelward bowed to the *Tianzi* and left with the elf and the Tarkothi ambassador.

Father motioned for Kaiya and her brothers to step off the dais and face him. "My children, you are wondering why I asked the Tarkothi prince to take Kaiya to Ayudra. It was actually the suggestion of Minister Hong Jianbin, and his logic is sound."

Kaiya looked to her brothers to see if they shared her shock. Minister Hong had gained favor with Father, bypassing regular channels to his ear. She turned back to find Father's gaze bearing down on her.

"First," he said, "there are those who would seek to derail the peace talks in hopes of promoting Expansionism. They would never expect you to go aboard *the Invincible* while we send the rest of your entourage on the *Golden Phoenix*. If there is any treachery, you will be safe."

He rose to his feet and swept his hand through the empty hall. "Secondly, we do not know who is behind all of these attacks. As much as I want to trust the *Tai-Ming* lords and ministers, I will take all precautions with your safety."

The *Tianzi* returned to his seat. "Finally, I wish to see the extent of Tarkoth's good will. Our trade routes must remain protected. Remember that when the elf appeared before the council, she said that Prince Aelward is here to harass Teleri's allies. If we continue trade with the Teleri, perhaps the *Invincible* will target our ships."

Kaiya's mind spun. "*Huang-Shang*, am I being sent to Vyara City, not to push for peace, but rather to ensure war with Madura?"

Father shook his head, something he would only do around his family. "No, Kaiya. I have faith that you will avert war. However, in order to get Prince Aelward to agree to take you, I had to make it seem like failure was the inevitable outcome."

"You lied, then." Kaiya couldn't keep the accusatory tone out of her voice. Heat rose to her face.

Father's lips formed a tight line. "No. I said that *if history is any lesson.* I trust you have the wit to rewrite history."

Eldest Brother Kai-Guo nodded. "The last week administering national affairs in Father's stead has shown me that the *Tianzi* must make decisions in the best interest of the nation. If those choices are not the most moral, they must be articulated in half-truths and misdirection."

Kaiya gawked at Eldest Brother. Such cynicism. Her eyes shifted to Kai-Wu, who as always seemed to be busy with his own thoughts.

Father's gaze still fell on her, reading her. Did he really expect her to succeed against the odds, or was that just encouragement wrapped in a half-truth and misdirection?

She looked back toward Prince Aelward, who waited outside of the Hall. If anyone knew about his agreement with the *Tianzi*, he could very well be Madura's next target.

CHAPTER 17:
Patriot Games

Jie tugged at her dress, almost satisfied with the tailor's alterations. Cut from bright red silk with gold embroidery, the gown allowed her to blend in with the aristocracy gathered to watch the New Year's Tournament. They milled among the stone-tiered seating on the western side of Qingjinghu Amphitheatre, chatting and pointing at contestants.

Unlike the nobles' garments, Jie's afforded plenty of mobility and had several secret pockets for tools and weapons. She was better armed than the dozen imperial guards surrounding the Imperial Family's box. Their *dao* were tucked in golden sashes, which matched their festive red robes.

Replacing the conspicuously absent *Tianzi*, Crown Prince Kai Guo presided over the final day of the tournament. His wife and siblings joined him in the box abutting the grassy field in the three hundred-foot basin. Across from them, tens of thousands of commoners covered every last inch of the basin's grassy slopes, cheering for their favorite competitors.

Jie shifted her attention from Princess Kaiya to the adjoining box, where foreign dignitaries sat. Yappy young Lin Ziqiu circulated among them, flirting with handsome men.

"Kayane elestrae arasti tu?" called a flitting voice from behind.

Jie spun to meet the gaze of the matronly elf woman Ayana. She responded in Arkothi. "Excuse me?"

The elf leaned back. "I was asking your name, Little One."

Jie glared at the old hag. "It is *not* Little One."

Ayana placed a hand on her chest. "Forgive me, our forms of address do not translate well into Arkothi. Please believe me, in our language, it is a term of endearment for young elves."

Lord Xu had used the same address, but he didn't come off as particularly endearing. And after three decades of life, the constant references to her tender years grew annoying. "I am not as young as you think."

The right side of Ayana's lips quirked up. "I was a child during the Hellstorm. To me, you are quite young. "

"It shows." Jie regretted the words as soon as they left her mouth. She bowed. "I'm sorry. I am so used to being called *little* and *young* by people younger than me."

"It is to be expected. You are one of us, living among humans."

Jie pursed her lips. She'd *never* be one of them, but she forced herself to mind her manners. "My name is Jie Yan. How may I be of service?"

The left side of Ayana's lips joined the right in forming a smile, sending rays of fine crinkles by her eyes. "I was just curious. My magic tells me this basin is called Clear Crystal Pond. I don't see any water."

Jie sucked on her lower lip. How did the history go? "It was once a reservoir. The Founder used castles to stimulate urban development and economic growth. As the city grew—"

"It needed water."

Jie pointed to the north end of the basin. "A streambed paved with rocks fed into the reservoir."

"What happened?"

What did it matter to an elf? Jie's forehead scrunched up. "I think an earthquake damaged the streambed and choked off the water supply. Grass took over, and now it's used for recreation, military training, and events like this tournament."

Ayana nodded. "Ah, humans and their competitiveness." She pointed to the horses gathered in the field. "Is this a polo?"

A polo? Jie chuckled. For someone three hundred years old, Ayana should've been an expert in Arkothi grammar. "No, these events are military in nature. Fencing, archery, wrestling...right now it's mounted archery. That's why Princess Kaiya is here."

"Yes, Kaiya has a special rooting interest." Lin Ziqiu appeared at her side, giggling.

The princess glared back. "Lady Ayana, you mustn't believe my naughty handmaiden or cousin."

Naughty! Jie stared back in a subtle show of insolence.

Prince Aelward, seated beside Ayana, leaned over and grinned. "Aye, she is. Put 'er on my ship, and we'll have 'er scrubbing the decks. That'll teach 'er to mind 'er tongue."

Scrubbing the decks? Jie snorted. Maybe using his tears.

The princess covered a laugh. "I merely enjoy watching mounted archery. Even as muskets supplant bows in our armies, there is still an elegance to a man who can shoot a bow from horseback."

Jie coughed. A man. Riiight. *The* man. Her eyes strayed to the kerchief clenched in the princess' hands.

A dark-haired, ruddy-skinned man in the same box as Prince Aelward chortled. He wore a flaxen coat with tassels of braided horsehair along its borders. Brightly-colored bird feathers adorned his hair. A Kanin plainsman from the Kingdom of Tomiwa, he spoke Arkothi with a rich accent. "If you want to see *real* mounted archery, come to my homeland. Our children can ride a horse without a saddle and still shoot."

The princess tilted her head a fraction. "Is that an invitation, Prince Tani?"

He winked. "Only as my bride."

Jie pointed out in the field. "Young Lord Zheng Ming might have something to say about that."

The princess' cheeks flushed a red to match her gown, but her gaze followed Jie's finger all the same.

A parade of the twenty-seven archers, three from each province, circled the green in single file. As reigning champion, Lord Zheng rode in the lead, wearing a light tunic of pale green with the golden circle *wen* emblem of the sun rising over twin mountains on his chest and sleeves. He waved at the crowd to raucous cheers. With the rumors swirling around the capital, the dashing lord's ego had likely swollen large enough to shift the tides. The three moons would be jealous.

He approached the royal box as per custom, to be greeted by the Crown Prince. He drew close, and Princess Kaiya leaned forward and tied a white silk ribbon with the sky-blue stitching of the imperial dragon around his forehead. The break in tradition sent the audience into louder applause. Even if Zheng received it with cool calm, her blush could've competed with the sun. Jie just yawned.

When all the contestants finished saluting the Crown Prince, they gathered at one end of the field. From there, they would circle the course and shoot at twenty wooden targets of different sizes. The number of targets hit would determine the winner, with the quickest time on a dwarf-made water clock as a tiebreaker. Zheng, the reigning champion, would ride last.

Jie scooted forward, rapt with interest. On firm ground, she was a fair archer at best. Maybe mounted archery was impractical, but it certainly took skill. The event started to loud cheers. Each participant seemed better than the last, hitting more targets in faster times.

The princess sat at the edge of the imperial box, right next to Prince Aelward in the adjoining box, pointing out the riders and describing their home provinces. On occasion, her regal demeanor would slip as she gasped and clapped her hands.

At Prince Aelward's side, Kanin Prince Tani shrugged. "What's the challenge in riding around in a circle?"

A rider in a light blue tunic came to the line. With her sharp eyes, Jie picked out the silver *wen* crest of a nine-petal flower, symbol of Huayuan Province. Smiling, the princess rose to her feet and clapped. Prince Aelward, looking at her, followed suit.

The princess gestured with an open hand. "That is Xie Shimin, a decorated soldier and provincial champion. He is a crowd favorite, a strong contender every year."

Xie spurred his mount forward, shouting a salute that carried across the basin. None of his first shots came close to their targets.

Prince Tani scoffed. The crowd buzzed with talk of the hometown hero's poor performance.

Jie sucked on her bottom lip. Something felt wrong.

Besides the imperial guards and her two *Moquan* brothers, none of the spectators had weapons. The contestants, on the other hand...

Jie inched forward, straining to get a better view of Xie Shimin as he rounded the final bend. He urged his horse into a full gallop, no longer even looking at the remaining targets. The audience pointed and shouted, many launching jeers at their own soldier.

With an arrow fitted, Xie approached the center of the tiered seating, far past any of the clay targets.

Around Jie, the imperial guards surged past her toward the front.

Xie leveled his bow, took aim and let his arrow fly.

The audience let out a collective gasp as the arrow streaked toward the dignitaries.

Jie reached across the stone divider into the adjacent box and snatched the arrow out of the air with her left hand, just before it could hit the unsuspecting Prince Aelward. With her right, she whipped out a *biao* throwing star from her sleeve and hurled it at Xie.

The would-be assassin had already nocked another arrow and shot just as the *biao* lodged in his gut.

In Jie's peripheral vision, Lady Ayana raised her hand and spoke a guttural syllable. The air in front of them shimmered like a hot summer haze. The arrow careened into an invisible barrier and fell to the ground.

In front of her, the imperial guards Chen Xin and Li Wei formed a protective shield in front of Princess Kaiya, their naked blades held forward.

Xie took aim at a target higher up, seemingly unfazed by the throwing star in his belly. Jie followed his line of sight.

Chief Minister Tan stood alone, unprotected, sweat trickling down his forehead and drenching the armpits of his robes.

The arrow smacked into the stone wall behind him with a loud thwack.

Jie spun back to see Xie fit another arrow. He aimed at Lord Peng Kai-Long, who stared impassively at the instrument of his own impending doom.

Zheng Ming spurred his horse into a full gallop across the field. He'd watched his friend Xie's bizarre run, wondering about the challenge Xie had promised. Each of his shots had been sloppy. On the final stretch, he didn't take a shot at all.

At least, not until his friend started shooting into the dignitary box. Not once, but twice.

Leaning from his saddle, Ming plucked an errant arrow from the ground as he closed the gap. He whispered a prayer to any god that would listen and let his arrow fly.

It struck Xie in the back of his left shoulder, just before he loosed his fourth shot. The shock of the blow jolted him forward. The bow skidded from his hand and snapped back into his face. The arrow dropped to the ground.

Wobbling in his saddle, Xie withdrew one last arrow and placed the edge on his neck. Ming closed quickly. He would never reach his friend in time.

"Stand down." The princess sang the words, her voice carrying across the field and above the chaos of frightened spectators.

Xie hesitated.

The elf woman pointed a finger at him and grunted something.

Xie slumped in his saddle, the arrow slipping from his fingers. He pushed against the neck of his horse, his body rocking as he righted his balance.

On the slopes, the watch swam through the panicked audience toward the field. The nobles and ministers in the seats pushed and shoved their way toward the exits. Several imperial guards spilled over the balustrades and charged toward the horse and rider with weapons drawn.

Crown Prince Kai-Guo pointed at Xie. "Take him alive!"

Zheng Ming trotted up to Xie's horse and seized its reins. The imperial guards pulled the limp man from his saddle.

He bled profusely from wounds to his abdomen and shoulder, his complexion pale as they laid him on the ground.

Crown Prince Kai-Guo climbed down, surrounded by wary guards, and pushed his way to the would-be assassin.

Behind him, the exotic little handmaiden pulled on Princess Kaiya's sleeve, even as the princess slipped between her two imperial guards. She glared at her handmaiden, and the servant relented.

Such courage! Not only that, she could make something as awkward as jumping from the stands look graceful. Ming dismounted and came to her side.

The Crown Prince stood over Xie. "Why did you attack the Tarkothi prince? Who sent you?"

Xie Shimin, his eyes fluttering, choked on his words. "Forgive me, *Dian-xia*, I am sworn to secrecy. It was not treason. I did it to protect our great nation."

"Protect the nation?" The Crown Prince gestured back to the stands. "You attacked a foreign dignitary. How will that do anything but tarnish our great name? I command you to answer. I would prefer not to subject one of our soldiers to an interrogator."

An imperial guard shook his head. "*Dian-xia*, he will not survive this wound, let alone interrogation."

Ming made his way to the circle of men surrounding his friend.

"*Dian-xia*." Xie coughed blood as he spoke. "These are not times for talk, but for action. Foreign enemies seek to swallow up Hua."

The princess touched Ming's arm. "What can you tell me about Xie Shimin?"

Ming bowed. "We served in Wailian County at the border. His father passed away several years ago. His only family is a sick mother. He has no siblings, no wife."

Without any acknowledgement of his words, the princess pushed forward through the guards. Even as they tried to stop her, she knelt by Xie's side and took his hands in her own. "Brave soldier of Hua," she said, "you have been misled by those who seek to destroy our peaceful country from within. Please, let us know who your co-conspirators are, and I will personally ensure that your parents' graves are tended to."

Xie looked up at her, inner struggle mingling with pain on his face.

"Tell me." She sang her words again.

Xie's shoulders relaxed. "I have sworn on my family's grave not to reveal the origin of the order... When you go to my barracks, you will find a lot of evidence meant to mislead you..."

That answer was no less a riddle than anything else Xie had said. Ming exchanged glances with the others gathered around. Eyebrows were raised, lips were pursed. At least he wasn't the only one who was confused.

Crown Prince Kai-Guo straightened and addressed the guards. "Reestablish order, calm the citizenry. The tournament will be cancelled for now. Send someone to the soldier's barracks and gather all of his belongings. The *Tianzi* must not be told about this. I will not worry him more before New Year's prayers at the Temple of Heaven on the morrow."

Ming dropped to his knee. "*Dian-xia*, please allow me to accompany your investigator to Xie's barracks. He was my friend, and never once did he say anything treasonous."

The Crown Prince peered at him for a few seconds before nodding. He motioned for a member of the watch. "Accompany Young Lord Zheng to the Huayuan Provincial Cavalry barracks."

Ming turned to check on the princess. She would be shaken from yet another attack, and a few sweet words would comfort her. He'd reassure her he would ride with her during tomorrow's New Year's procession.

She already stood at the base of the stands, smiling and chatting with the Eldaeri prince.

Kaiya still felt the cold of Xie Shimin's grasp, even as she held a low bow before Prince Aelward. She hadn't wanted to release the dying soldier's hand, but the prince's choking in the stands was a poignant reminder of her duties as an imperial representative. If a foreign dignitary died at the hands of an assassin, the repercussions could range anywhere from trade embargos to war. It would also scuttle her own mission of peace, perhaps leading to more unnecessary deaths in Hua.

She did not deign to meet Prince Aelward's eyes. "I cannot apologize enough for this breach in security."

"It's okay, lass," he said, voice gruff. "No need for theatrics."

With effort, Kaiya straightened. After expending the energy needed to get Xie to talk, her limbs felt like dwarf anvils, and a haze fogged her mind. Such power came with a price, apparently, and the limit of her commands seemed to be two syllables. "Again, I am sorry. I hope you are uninjured."

"Aye, lass. Only a scratch when I slipped on the step. Your chippy handmaiden has quite the hands. Saved me from an arrow." He nodded toward Jie, whose sleeves concealed her hands, and who knew what else. "I owe you a blood debt."

Jie started to drop to one knee, but twisted with the grace of a cat into an Arkothi-style curtsey. "I will remember that."

Kaiya clenched her jaw. "Perhaps we should retreat to the safety of the palace now."

"Nay, I think I've enjoyed enough of your country's festivities. I'll be heading back to the *Invincible*. She'll be ready to sail when you embark on your mission."

From the embankment on the opposite side of the basin, the renegade *Moquan* Liang Yu used a dwarven magnifying scope to watch the dying soldier. He had to twist and crane his neck to get a good view through the swirling crowds.

Though he did not know of this plan, he had suspected his former employer would strike here. Without Liang Yu to do his dirty work, he had blackmailed Xie Shimin, using the leverage Liang Yu had uncovered months before.

He sighed. Alas, yet another patriot sacrificed, all to ensure Hua's continued greatness. Certainly the *Tianzi* would now move beyond purely defensive measures and take decisive action.

His special pupil flashed a hand signal, confirming Liang Yu's suspicions. Snapping the dwarven scope shut, he rose to his feet. He now was certain of the identity of his former employer. Once the war started, he would exact his vengeance for the betrayal at Jade Spring Inn.

Near the back of the stone seats, Minister Hong Jianbin feigned panic, even as he struggled to hide joy at his luck. Even if his spy had bungled, his plans might work out better than he imagined. With the princess to depart on her trip to Vyara City in two days, he might very well be Chief Minister in less than a week.

CHAPTER 18:

Idle Pursuits

Zheng Ming lay awake on silken sheets, in a room whose luxury might have rivaled an imperial pavilion. Not that he'd know.

He stared at the ceiling tiles, admiring how the late afternoon light played on the intricate dragon and phoenix carvings. His thoughts wandered, bouncing between the investigation into his friend Xie Shimin, and the princess' affection for the foreign prince.

A search of Xie's personal effects earlier that day revealed Maduran coins and a letter in Ayuri script. Though Ming couldn't read it, he had little doubt it had come from Madura as well. Yet Xie had also told the princess something about not believing all the evidence.

Ming rolled over, only to be pulled into the bare arms of some minister's daughter or niece or something. The walnut-toned beauty, who looked to have some Ayuri blood in her, had virtually thrown herself at him after his exploits at the tournament. He'd succumbed to her charms, having grown frustrated at the princess' coy flirtations. A man needed release, after all.

It hadn't taken much to coax the exotic young woman into joining him at this high-end establishment, which specifically catered to discreet meetings. A frequent visitor on his trips to the capital, Zheng Ming often wondered what secrets the proprietress knew, given the patrons included all manner of lords and high officials.

Yet right now, even as the girl kissed his neck and ran her hands over him, all he could think about was his guilt. Of course the princess would not be like other women. She was too bound by court conventions to openly shower affection on a man. Her token before the tournament was already a bold statement on her part.

And here he was, with a girl whose name he couldn't even remember.

Her kisses stopped abruptly and she pushed him away. She pulled the sheets up to hide her magnificent nakedness, eyes glinting in accusation. "You are thinking of *her*."

Ming flashed a well-trained smile at her. Her lips quivered. A strategically-placed finger on those full lips caused her to inhale sharply, eyes closed.

"If by *her*, you are referring to our motherland of Hua," he said, "then yes. I'm thinking of her. I'm sorry. But if you are implying some other woman, then the only one I'm thinking of is you."

His response was so glib, he almost believed it himself. He kissed her forehead. Her hands reached into his hair. The sheet covering her slipped, forgotten.

So naïve, these city girls. Ming tried to ignore the guilt tapping on his shoulder, and focused on pleasing her. The afternoon ambled on, their lovemaking leaving him spent.

When he awoke, the woman was gone. All his worries and guilt flooded back to him. He dressed and slipped out of the guest house. Above, the Iridescent Moon waxed to its fifth crescent, giving him an hour before the New Year's Eve feast began at his provincial compound.

The streets bustled with people rushing home for their own holiday feasts. With his *dao* tucked in his sash, most recognized him as a lord and made way. He ground to a halt just before he reached the stable where he'd left his horse.

A dozen members of the city watch were questioning the stable boy. A couple of other men milled among them, nodding and pointing.

Just when Ming was about to approach, a plainly-dressed man with a walking stick barreled right into him, nearly knocking him to the ground.

Ming growled. "Hey! Are you blind? Watch where you're going!"

The boor just snickered and kept walking. The gall!

The horse and commotion could wait. Ming spun around and jogged to catch up with the man. "I'm talking to you! Do you know who I am?"

The man's shoulders shook as his pace quickened. The bastard was laughing!

Indignation rising, Ming followed the man around a corner.

He found himself dumped onto the ground. A knife pushed against his throat. Ming's eyes darted around to get his bearings. He'd turned into an alley, never suspecting a trap. After all, who would attempt such an audacious attack in broad daylight, in a fairly busy part of the city?

"Young Lord Zheng Ming," the man whispered. "That should answer your question, I *do* know who you are. I am going to let you get up, and I want you to follow me. Swear to me now you will not call for the watch."

"I swear," Ming whispered his answer, now more intrigued than angry or frightened.

His assailant had long black hair with streaks of silver, and worn features that bore evidence of a hard life. Besides that, he was incredibly plain. He offered a hand, and Ming took it.

Pulled to his feet, Ming followed the stranger deeper into the alley. Who was this guy? And what did he want? With the man's back turned, it would be easy to run away, call out— though not for the watch, since he'd sworn—or even attack—

"You will be dead before your sword leaves its scabbard."

Ming's hand had unconsciously strayed toward the hilt of his *dao*. He thrust his hands behind his back.

The man chuckled. "Do you know with whom you have been sharing a bed?"

Heat burned in his cheeks. "Have you been following me?"

The man looked over his shoulder at Ming. "I am watching you for your own sake. You, my friend, are being set up. What do you suppose will happen if your pretty princess finds out you are spreading your seed while actively courting *her*?"

Ming shrugged. Years of smooth talking yielded a lie he almost believed himself. "It doesn't matter. It's over between us."

The man grinned. "Good. Now that we've gotten that out of the way, don't you wonder why you were set up? Or did you just assume your handsome face was enough to get any girl into bed?"

Ming had, in fact, assumed that. He bit his lip. "Why?"

"If you knew *who*, then the *why* might be easier to guess."

"Would you stop talking in riddles?" Ming glared at the man.

The man's smirk deepened. "My problem is I know *who*, but not *why*. Maybe you can help me."

Ming threw his hands up. "Just say it!"

"Minister Hong Jianbin. The girl is his pawn. Or maybe even his lover."

Ming winced. Had he just slept with... "Hong's lover?"

Another chuckle. "I can only surmise. If I were in your boots, I'd be more concerned that Hong was setting you up."

Ming's mind swam. "Whatever for?"

"And we circle back to the first question. I would think he is either trying to ruin any chances you might have with the princess—"

"He *wanted* me to court her." Ming scratched his head. Maybe there was more to that.

"—or use it as leverage against you," the man continued.

"What kind of leverage?" Ming asked.

"Almost certainly not the same *I* am going to use on you."

Ming reached for his sword, but found the walking stick pressed against the guard, preventing him from drawing it.

"Young Lord Zheng, you have much to live for. Don't throw your life away in this alley. I can make your death look very embarrassing."

Ming hid his cringe. The idea of death did not seem particularly appealing. Dying with everyone thinking him a coward, or worse, even less so. He spoke through gritted teeth. "What do you want?"

The man raised a silencing hand. He then reached and plucked a red envelope from the folds of Ming's robe.

"Hey!" Ming swiped for the packet, but the man shifted just out of his reach. It was only a poem he'd written for the princess before the tournament, a gift for the New Year's procession tomorrow. Hadn't he given it to one of his men to take back to the compound? Now some stranger had his dirty paws on it.

The man withdrew the folded paper and snapped the letter open. His eyes darted over the script before he looked up. "Love letters—to the Crown Princess, no less."

Crown Princess Xiulan? That would be a capital offense. Ming snatched the letter from the man's willing grasp and read. "This isn't even my handwriting." Not to mention... "The poetry is horrible."

The man shrugged. "Has the princess ever seen your script?"

No. Ming clenched his jaw. "Why would Hong do this?"

"Scuttle your budding relationship with the princess? Have you branded as a traitor? Undermine the Crown Prince and Princess?"

"Hong is going to pay for this."

The man held up a hand again. "Young Lord Zheng, let the Founder's words guide you. *Knowledge is power.* Perhaps Hong is up to something more insidious. If it were me, I would make Hong think you have fallen into his trap and

see how he reacts. You might very well dig up more than you imagined."

Ming closed his slack jaw. "So you want me to give this to the princess?"

"No, just don't meet with her at tomorrow's procession. Hong will think she spurned you."

Ming's heart sank, even if he kept his face impassive. Standing the princess up would destroy any chance of winning her back from Prince Aelward. "No, I have to go."

The man grinned. "Well, let's not forget about my leverage. I have means of reaching the princess. I will expose your infidelity myself. I know where you went and who you were with."

This man was some mousey commoner. How did he have access to the princess? Perhaps it would be better to risk exposure of his dalliances. After all, young lords were expected to have an occasional tryst or three.

The man shook his head. "If that's not enough persuasion, let me give you another reason to heed my advice. I can make you a hero."

Liang Yu sat quietly at the Jade Teahouse, his new meeting place in the Floating World in southeast Huajing, close to where he'd ambushed Zheng Ming.

Stealing the poem from the young lord's messenger outside the amphitheater had been easy. Planting and then revealing the fake letter was even easier, like pulling a coin from a child's ear. Liang Yu took only mild offense at Zheng's insult of his poetry and handwriting.

He leaned back from the table and chuckled. The provincial lord's naïveté was amusing. Even an initiate *Moquan* could have seen through Zheng Ming's pathetic attempts to hide his emotions. His affection for the princess and his own vanity made him simple to manipulate. Promised with the chance of again being the hero, he'd willingly embarked on a trail which would—

with Liang Yu's help over a few weeks— expose his former employer.

Of course, it meant keeping Zheng Ming in Hua until the betrayer pushed the war with Madura to inevitability.

The only uncertainty was whether or not Young Lord Zheng's servant would confess to losing the poem. A betting man would gamble that the man would not come forward with his guilt, and the naïve young lord would assume Hong's woman had swapped the letters.

Gambles only won wars half the time. The messenger would be yet another necessary casualty for Hua's greatness.

The door to the teahouse opened. His special pupil stood there, back from spying on Minister Hong.

Minister Hong Jianbin looked at his naked form in the full-length mirror, not really liking what he saw. It had little to do with the sagging leathery skin, sallow complexion or thin whitening hair that came with his advancing age. Rather, he wondered when and where he had become obsessed with power, willing to do almost anything to obtain it.

He was not ambitious by nature, but his family had sacrificed much to get him into the civil service and on the path to rapid social mobility. He had been a good government bureaucrat at every level, quickly rising through the ranks and gaining the trust and friendship of the man who would become Chief Minister.

Hong turned around and studied his back, all covered in splotches. When had his inside become as horrible as the outside?

Chief Minister Tan had brought Hong up with him. At each level, from dutiful provincial clerk to trade official, and now to Household Minister, he had tasted new heights of wealth, power, and privilege. He might have been satisfied,

had the opportunity to progress even higher not serendipitously tumbled into his hands.

"My Lord," a sweet voice sang from outside at the sliding door.

Hong smiled, gathering his robe around him and forgetting his misgivings. One of wealth's perks was the keeping of a concubine. "Come in, come in."

The doors slid open, revealing Leina, his half-Hua, half-Ayuri beauty, now wearing a translucent vermillion inner robe. The hot bath they'd shared together left a pink flush on her walnut cheeks. With no family in the capital, he would spend New Year's Eve with her. She closed the doors behind her and swept across the room to a low table where she kneeled again. Her every movement reminded him of the graceful fluttering streamers of the ribbon dance. Tonight, she practically sparkled with bliss.

Leina poured some tea for him. "My Lord, are you ready to play chess?"

Minister Hong tottered over to the table. He eased himself down into a cross-legged position, his old knees protesting. "I have never beaten you, have I?"

"No, my Lord, neither in Northern nor Hua chess. But there is always a first time." Leina beckoned him with an enticing lift of her eyebrow. "You look particularly naughty this evening. Perhaps you should take the black pieces while I take the white."

As always, her sense of humor made him forget his own troubles and uncertainties. He admired her delicate elegance as she glided her pieces across the board in response to his own moves. Her intelligence and charm just added to her exotic beauty, and Hong often wondered if he should just give up his plans, forget about Princess Kaiya, and take Leina as his official wife. Of course, she continually pressed him to pursue the princess, claiming it would make her the second most important woman in Hua.

Leina shifted her chariot into a defensive position. "Sending the princess to meet with the Madurans will be disastrous to your prospects of becoming Chief Minister. She'll learn they had nothing to do with the insurgency. The Expansionists won't get their war."

Hong tried to concentrate on the implications of her move. Although Leina rarely used the same strategy twice, or any strategy for that matter, the one constant was her lulling voice. "I had to send her away," he said, "or Lord Peng would kill her."

"You will never have her if you cannot become Chief Minister in the first place."

Hong sighed. He realized the limits of his ambition when he placed the princess' life ahead of his own plans. "I gambled that I could push the Chief Minister issue before the princess meets with the Madurans. The Expansionists would still support me because I have done everything they asked. The attack on the foreign prince all but guarantees the war they want. I also have the backing of the Royalists, who want the princess as a bride for their sons."

The rise of Leina's thin eyebrow prompted him to continue.

Hong grinned back. If she had to think it out herself, she would be less focused on her game. His first victory was close at hand.

At last, she shrugged.

Hong laughed. He could always outwit her in conspiracies, even if he could not beat her at chess. However, that string of defeats looked to change in a few minutes. "It won't be long before the *Tianzi's* agents learn about Xie Shimin's immense debts from paying for his sick mother's treatment."

Tears glassed over her eyes; the sentimental weakness of women. "Oh, the poor thing."

"Yes, the honorable Xie Shimin, duped into believing there was patriotism in assassinating a foreign dignitary under the *Tianzi's* protection, and exploited by his financial needs. The trail will lead back to the mastermind, and I control the timing."

"What a stroke of genius!" Smiling, Leina clapped her hands together. Then her perfect brow crinkled. "But by sending the princess to Vyara City, you are putting your prospect of marrying her into jeopardy. No telling what the treacherous

Madurans will do, especially if they are unjustly accused of meddling."

"Dear Leina, you mustn't let your own biases cloud your judgment." Hong used the distraction to put pressure on one of her advisors, which would open up a line of attack for his elephant. "I know your mother was Ankiran—"

"But my father was from Hua, the trade official to Ankira," she interjected, a wounded look in her dark eyes.

Hong looked up from the board to contemplate her exotic features. He knew her history well: her father had been posted in Ankira for many years, arranging official sales of outdated, first-generation muskets to Ankira; her mother an Ankiran dancer whom he had taken as a lover despite his family back home. Leina had grown up in Ankira. When Hua ultimately closed its trade office after Madura's occupation ten years before, she had been left behind and her mother killed. How horrible life must have been for her before escaping to Hua two years ago in search of her father. "Would *you* rather marry me instead?" he ventured.

She threw her head back in laughter, such a refreshing show of emotion compared to reserved Hua ladies.

Heat rose to Hong's face, maybe enough that the redness showed through his thick, tough skin. "I...I would be honored to take you as my wife."

"And give up on your ambitions?" Her amusement carried an underlying tone of rebuke. "I would be selfish to have you do that. After all, you are just one move from becoming Chief Minister, two moves from marrying the princess."

"And three moves from finally beating you!" Hong smacked his cannon down in direct line to her general. "*Jiangjun!*" Check.

"No, just one move from losing," Leina said, moving her rider back between his cannon and her general. It opened up a line for her chariot toward his general, where his own cannon had just vacated. "Checkmate," she exclaimed with girlish excitement. She had unwittingly disguised her offense and defense, and he had stumbled into the trap.

Again.

He reached across the table and placed his hand on hers. "Let us celebrate your victory, the New Year, and my imminent appointment as Chief Minister."

If Hong Jianbin weren't already so dismissive of her, Leina would feign stupidity and play strategy games to lose. As it was, beating him time and time again provided small consolation for having to tolerate his patronizing.

She now peered through the darkness at him, fast asleep from their long and vigorous lovemaking. His always surprising virility had allowed her to close her eyes and imagine it was Young Lord Zheng again.

Maybe in Zheng's mind, she was just another conquest. Still, he could dissemble convincingly enough with his pillow talk to stir a rush of excitement. And she'd sacrificed him. A lump formed in her throat.

Hiding out as they were in the Floating World, news of Zheng Ming's arrest wouldn't reach old Hong's ears until the next morning. She'd hidden a letter in the young man's scabbard, implicating him in the insurgency. The city watch, tipped off by her informants, would find it when he went to get his horse.

She rolled over to face the window, away from Hong. He would never know of her involvement, and yet he would benefit: with Zheng out of the picture, the princess would remain unwed just a little longer, and Hong would stay motivated.

At the same time, Leina would move closer toward completing her assignment of weakening Cathay from the inside. All the easier with Princess Kaiya about to leave. Without her soothing voice balancing out rivalries, the hereditary lords would be at each other's throats.

She sighed, considering Hong again. For so long, she'd stoked his ambition, helping him overcome his natural lack of motivation and tenacity. She'd manipulated him, making him believe her scheming was his own. Though he showed remarkable adaptability to Peng's change in plans, his lack of foresight validated her choice of him as a tool.

Just as in chess, when playing a long game, forward thinking and planning overcame reaction and countermeasure. As Chief Minister, Hong would never foresee the long-term implications of the decisions she made for him. With two and a half years left in her assignment, his actions would leave Cathay weak, ripe for invasion.

In the meantime, sharing the old man's bed was the price she would pay. It was far preferable than staying in Ankira, to be used by countless foreign soldiers. She could only hope that when everything was said and done, her employer would hold up his end of the bargain and free her mother.

CHAPTER 19:

It Will Be a Good Year

For Kaiya, the staccato bursts of firecrackers in the distance punctuated the most somber New Year's Day she could remember. The *Tianzi's* annual procession to the Temple of Heaven was her favorite ritual and usually a lively affair. In previous years, crowds had lined the streets to watch and perhaps catch a glimpse of the Imperial Family among all of the lords and ministers.

Given the current security concerns, the city watch and national army kept the citizenry blocks away. Storefronts, while bedecked in celebratory red, remained shuttered and idle. Strings of lanterns and banners hung limp and lifeless. Without cheering crowds, the procession seemed like a wedding banquet with no guests.

No spectators enjoyed the one-hundred-and-sixty-eight-foot dragon, embroidered in gold silk and borne by eighty-eight of the most handsome imperial guards. The only people to see the flashing colors of silken robes and horse brocades were those marching in the parade.

Kaiya sighed. Perhaps in the distance, the citizenry could hear the beating drums or tinkling saddle bells. They would certainly see the imperial aviary's eight earth phoenixes circling above the procession. Nearly fifteen feet with a wingspan of twice that, they made for an impressive sight, despite being a tenth the size of the mythical phoenixes. They had heads that resembled pheasants, but tails that fanned out like peacocks. Their legs stretched long like cranes, while their wings flapped like swallows. Brightly colored gold and silver feathers sparkled in the sunlight.

Female imperial guards rode astride the phoenixes. Like all imperial princesses past and present Kaiya had trained to ride, but with her fear of heights, she was happy her New Year's duties kept her on the ground.

Father rode in an open carriage. The High Priest of Hua's patron god, Yang-Di, sat beside him; though Jie had told her that today, the man was the half-elf's adoptive father, Master Yan of the Black Lotus Monastery, who sometimes posed as a minister at court. In any other year, the citizenry would sink to their knees and press their foreheads to the ground as the *Tianzi* passed, wishing him a life of ten thousand years. Today, there was no one.

The rest of the Imperial Family followed the carriage in gold-painted palanquins; though at her insistence, Kaiya rode a horse, as she had for years. Her vantage point provided an excellent view of the inactivity. Her keen hearing told her that beyond the confines of the main boulevard, New Year's Day went on as usual for everyone else.

People flocked to the temples to wish for health and prosperity, and neighbors visited each other bearing auspicious gifts of fruits and candies. Despite the Hua people's worldwide reputation for frugality, not even beggars went hungry this day, as they were given leftovers from the feasting the night before. After all, generosity on New Year's Day would be repaid tenfold throughout the year.

Martial artists performed lion dances in front of stores and homes to scare away evil spirits. The sounds of drums and children laughing floated on the winds. Kaiya even imagined she could smell the burning incense drifting in from afar.

And here, the imperial procession marched, detached from the vibrancy and vitality of the annual celebration. Were these precautions really necessary? No one would stage an attack during the Spring Festival—nobody in Hua would use anything sharp on New Year's Day, for fear of cutting their luck during the coming year.

Kaiya looked to her side, where her senior-most imperial guard Chen Xin rode awkwardly in the saddle, his knuckles white around the reins. It should've been Young Lord Zheng Ming beside her, the invitation having been extended and accepted weeks before.

She pouted. As if the funerary atmosphere of her favorite holiday wasn't bad enough. She *liked* him. *Really* liked him. Problems dashed every opportunity to meet. Assassination attempts. Gruff foreign princes. Now sickness.

She pressed at his kerchief, stashed in the fold of her robe. A courier had arrived earlier that morning with news of Zheng Ming's illness. He'd been fine just the day before, when he heroically saved ministers and lords from assassination at the hands of his own friend. If illness kept him from accompanying her to Vyara City tomorrow, it would be at least a month before they met again.

"Halt!" The announcement by the Minister of Rites jolted Kaiya out of her thoughts.

She scanned the area. The procession had arrived outside the walls of the Temple of Heaven, an eight-tiered stupa. Painted red with blue gables, it housed a chunk from a fallen star, brought to Hua by the Wang Dynasty Founder at the bidding of the Gods. It was here she'd played the Dragon Scale Lute for Prince Hardeep.

The *Tianzi* descended from the carriage with the help of Ming's cousin, imperial guard general Zheng Jiawei. With an entourage of ministers in tow, he plodded through the gates and onto the Temple grounds.

Kaiya and her brothers followed at a respectful distance. It was only two years ago, after her exploits at Wailian, that she was allowed to enter. The white marble walls followed the elliptical outline of dragon bones, with the temple itself at the far focus. It stood on a circular, three-tiered marble base. She'd played the Dragon Scale Lute on the identical base at the near focus. Father negotiated the steps to the base with some difficulty before disappearing inside the stupa.

Vibrations, strong and rapid, emanated from the tower. She'd first noticed them when she came with Prince Hardeep, but now...the frequency sounded so clear, and a slower, deeper pulse harmonized with it. How had she never noticed it before? Lord Xu said sounds changed based on their relative location; but now, no matter where she stood, the resonance sounded the same. If not for the solemnity of the rites, she would've raised her voice in song.

Instead, she gazed into the heavens. At exactly noon, when the Iridescent Moon Caiyue disappeared from the sky for a few fleeting moments as it phased to new, on this day of the Spring Equinox, the *Tianzi* would pray to Hua's patron god Yang-Di for the nation's continued prosperity.

To mark the time, the Minister of Rites struck a standing gong, which rang much louder than it should have. The *Tianzi's* voice emanated from inside the stupa, sounding as awe-inspiring and powerful as she remembered from her youth.

Despite her earlier melancholy, Kaiya's spirits rose. Every fiber of her being resonated with excitement. This *would* be a good year. She would make it so. Starting with a visit to sick Zheng Ming, whose villa was fairly close to the temple.

From her place behind the princess, Jie found the *Tianzi's* voice pleasant, in an almost fatherly way. If her real father had ever sung to her, it might have sounded something like the Emperor's prayer.

Why everyone else seemed genuinely enraptured by his words, Jie couldn't fathom. She made a mental note. Give—no, proffer—a handkerchief to the princess so she could dab off the drool.

The princess' eyes glinted with a new focus. If Jie's experiences from two years ago were any guide, there was an idea forming in that pretty head, and thus far, nothing good had ever come of her impulses. Riding in open carriages, jumping into the fray surrounding the would-be assassin Xie Shimin, riding a horse today—the princess always got her way. It was a miracle she was still alive.

Jie watched her charge with a careful eye, recognizing a subtle fidget as the entourage departed the temple grounds.

As when they left Sun-Moon Palace, Chen Xin dropped to all fours to allow the princess to use him as a footstep to mount her horse. No sooner had she settled in the saddle did she spur her mount out of parade formation and into a fast lope.

Insane princess!

While the rest of the procession gawked, Jie pop-vaulted off Chen Xin and onto his horse. She urged it into pursuit.

Now who was insane?

Though Chen Xin's riding had been laughable, Jie had next to no experience with a horse, the last time she'd ridden being two years ago under the similar circumstances of rescuing an impulsive princess. *This* impulsive princess. The gown, while modified for fighting, further hindered her questionable equestrian skills. She clutched the reins, her balance keeping her from bouncing out of the saddle and into an embarrassing—and potentially dangerous—rendezvous with the ground.

Despite her misgivings, Jie quickly got the hang of it. Luckily, the crowds of well-wishers made way for the princess, giving their horses a relatively straight path. Jie ventured a quick glance behind to see no one else giving chase. Above, the phoenixes still circled over the Temple of Heaven.

She quickly banished the wistful thoughts of riding a phoenix— *that* would never happen. It was up to her to protect the princess. Their direction left little doubt as to where they'd end up.

There, Princess Kaiya would face a threat beyond Jie's ability to defend.

Sure enough, the princess slowed her horse to a stop outside of the Dongmen provincial pavilion. She gingerly dismounted, and Jie followed. Her foot nearly caught in the stirrup, causing her to stumble. Her thighs burned and her rear ached, just from the ten-minute canter. Forget phoenixes. If she never rode a horse again, it would be too soon.

The princess approached the solid wooden gate. "I am here to see Young Lord Zheng Ming."

The gate guards gaped and bowed. Perhaps they recognized her, but even if they didn't, her regal carriage and tone commanded respect. One raised his head. "The young lord is not here right now."

The princess raised an eyebrow. "Is he not convalescing? Open the gates."

The guards looked among themselves, confusion creased into their brows. The same one as before bowed again. "Do you have an invitation?"

Jie snorted, only to be silenced by the princess' glare. Jie composed her expression and stepped forward. "Princess Kaiya gave you an order."

The guards dropped to a knee, fist down. "*Dian-xia!*"

One stood and rapped on the gate. A slot slid open, revealing a pair of eyes. "Princess Kaiya is here to see the young lord." The slot snapped shut, and the guard turned back and bowed.

The gates opened at a tortoise's pace. A middle-aged gentleman knelt at the threshold, his forehead touching the ground. "*Dian-xia*, please be welcome. I am the villa steward. If you would like to wait for Young Lord Zheng's return, allow me to convey you to our teahouse."

The princess looked at Jie, her brows furrowed, before glaring at the steward. "So he is truly not here?"

The steward's face contorted into confusion. "No, *Dian-xia*. He had urgent business to attend to this morning."

"On New Year's Day?" the princess said.

"Yes, *Dian-xia*."

The princess spun on her heel, all excitement drained from her face. She wobbled toward her horse.

Jie's belly hollowed. Until this moment, she never empathized with a noblewoman over trivial matters of courtship. She reached her hand out, for once at a loss of words. The princess was making her soft.

The steward hurried to the princess' side. "*Dian-xia*, it is not safe in the city. Please come inside the compound and I shall send a messenger to the palace."

Ignoring him, the princess put her foot in a stirrup and climbed onto her horse.

The reality of Jie's assignment quashed her short-lived sympathy. By now, word of Princess Kaiya's mad dash could have reached whoever wanted her dead. They were out in the open, with no protection. She dropped to her knee, fist to the ground. "*Dian-xia*, please listen to the steward. You must not risk your life."

The princess looked down from her mount, her expression forlorn. "I do not wish to be here when Zheng Ming returns."

Jie rose and took the reins, holding firm even as the princess tugged back. "Lord Steward, please send your messenger to the palace. We will wait here."

The princess' eyes narrowed into a deadly glint. "Yan Jie, I command you to let go."

Jie turned and started leading the horse into the compound.

"Let go." The princess sang the order. Her angry voice seemed to shake the walls, and the guards dropped their spears. Even the old woman tending to a small garden down the street by the Linshan provincial villa dropped her walking staff.

Having experienced the power of the princess' voice several times already, Jie let it ripple over her and continued walking toward the gates. Glancing over her shoulder and seeing the princess slumping in the saddle, she waved toward the wide-eyed steward. "Prepare that tea. If your young lord returns, I would suggest—"

Guards murmured and pointed. Jie followed their gazes.

Down the street, Zheng Ming rode side-by-side with a plain young woman, chatting and laughing and oblivious to the unexpected visitors ahead of him. Hopefully, the princess hadn't seen them. Jie hazarded a glance up.

Sitting stiffly, the princess scowled in Zheng's direction. With a jerk of the reins out of Jie's limp grip, she turned the horse around.

Zheng Ming looked up and brought his own horse to a stop. If his mouth hung any wider, a fist would fit in it. It was a tempting thought.

Instead, Jie could only watch as the princess set her chin and rode her horse at a walk toward Zheng. Jie scrambled to catch up.

Zheng Ming bowed his head. "*Dian-xia*. I...I am sorry. But it's not what you think."

The princess didn't stop the horse, or even deign to acknowledge him as she rode past.

"*Dian-xia*. Please, let me explain." He might as well have been talking to the Great Wall.

Jie trotted past him, casting the reproachful glare the princess was too proud to express.

As for the young woman...too much perspiration glistened on her forehead for this cool day, and up close, the smile she wore looked too contrived.

Very little surprised Liang Yu, but the turn of events in the last ten minutes reminded him of how little he could actually predict.

He had been there, pretending to weed a small garden plot at the side of the Linshan provincial villa, just to see if Young Lord Zheng had followed the instructions he provided. Little did he imagine that Zheng would bring Xie Shimin's prospective bride back to the Dongmen provincial villa.

Even more surprising was Princess Kaiya's unannounced visit, with a handmaiden who seemed familiar, despite the fact he had never seen a half-elf up close before. From the way the latter moved, he guessed her to be *Moquan*. She was probably the same one who had saved the foreign prince from Xie's arrow the day before. Curse his old eyes.

Liang Yu looked up from under the brim of his wide straw hat, assessing. His former employer had suggested he might need to assassinate the princess if all of their other plans failed to shake up the ruling elites. Now, she made for an inviting target, guarded only by a handful of provincial guards and a *Moquan* hindered by a court dress. With the city on edge, he wouldn't get a better chance to find her so unprotected.

Her death, if pinned on Madura, would ensure war. Against a *Moquan* and a battle-tested, champion archer, Liang Yu doubted he would live to see that war. Maybe he could have overcome them in his youth— though even then, he had been defeated and left for dead by a different elf.

He tightened his grip around his walking stick, ready to draw the blade concealed within. The smooth wood jarred the memory from just a few minutes before. The power of the princess' voice, even from twenty-three feet away, had compelled him to drop his walking stick.

The day before, she'd also braved the chaos and fearlessly approached a would-be assassin. Perhaps the princess was not such an easy target after all. Perhaps she might be a worthy leader.

Liang Yu went back to weeding, wishing his ears had not deteriorated so much with age. What he would give to be able to hear what Zheng Ming would say once he caught up to the princess.

Zheng Ming couldn't believe how quickly good luck could turn bad. His hands shaking on his reins, he waved toward the handmaiden's horse. "Lord Steward, bring the other imperial stallion."

He then turned to Li Feng, the common girl whom his friend Xie Shimin had been secretly courting. "Ms. Li, please accompany my steward into my province's compound. You will be safe there."

Ming took the reins of the imperial horse the handmaiden had left behind and set out in pursuit of the princess.

On horseback, it didn't take long to catch up.

He found them in a quiet alley, where the princess leaned into her horse, one arm draped over its neck and her face in its mane. His fault. The handmaiden rested a hand in the bend of the princess' elbow, even as her head shifted left and right.

She must've caught a glimpse of him peeking around the corner. Her eyes locked on his and she marched toward him. If his guards were as alert as this girl, he'd never have worry about ambushes. He stepped into the alley.

The handmaiden blocked his way. Her elven features seemed all the more exquisite in her anger. "You have done enough to ruin the princess' New Year."

Ming didn't have time for a girl, even a unique one such as this. He extended an arm to push past her.

His hand never reached her.

She brushed it aside and somehow managed to stay in front of him. He used his other hand, only to find himself spun around with his arm wrenched behind his back. A shove into his shoulders sent him stumbling a few steps.

Ming spun back around, hand on his *dao*.

The insolent girl stepped forward, pressing herself against him, her hand on his wrist. It probably would've excited him had she not been so young. She grinned. "It is bad luck to draw a blade on New Year's Day."

Though not a superstitious man, he hesitated. It would look bad if he cut down an unarmed handmaiden. It would look worse if he were bested by an unarmed handmaiden. He raised his hands and took a step back.

She kept pressuring him backward, only stopping when they reached the main road.

"*Dian-xia*," he called, craning his neck around the girl's omnipresence. "It is not what you think. I will explain on the way to the ship tomorrow."

He scowled down at the half-elf again. She smirked. With a turn on his heel, he stomped back to his compound.

Not far from the gates, a stooped old woman, straw hat concealing her features, stood by a garden plot next to a house. She beckoned him over, and he came to a stop, not wanting to be rude on New Year's Day.

"Did you win your princess' heart back?" Her voice creaked with age. "Or was she too disgusted by your womanizing?"

The impertinence! As a noble, Ming had every right to slap the old hag. Yet it was a New Year. He settled for a glare.

The eyes of his mysterious informant twinkled back at him from beneath the hat's brim.

Ming let out a sigh. "You!"

"Why did you bring Li Feng back here? You deserve the princess' scorn for your stupidity."

Ming's jaw clenched at the insult. "I will explain everything to her tomorrow."

The man shook his head. "No, you won't."

"I made a promise to accompany her to Vyara City." Ming could not believe the desperation in his voice.

"If you want her to live," the man said, "you will have to break that promise."

"Are you threatening her to secure my obedience?"

The man chuckled. "I already have your obedience. No, you will break your promise because in doing so, you will protect her and also come closer to exposing the perpetrator of the insurgency."

CHAPTER 20:

Mirrors and Warnings

Twenty-year old Wang Kai-Hua looked across the table at Kaiya, Yanli, and Xiulan, all gathered for a special New Year's game of mahjong. They played several times a month, as a pretext for sharing the latest gossip among the hereditary lords. Unlike in the opium-filled gambling dens of the city's seedier parts, where family fortunes could be lost in a drug-induced stupor, the noble ladies typically bet favorite pieces of jewelry or clothing.

Kai-Hua sighed. She missed her father the most around the New Year. The younger brother of the *Tianzi* would have been fifty this year, had he not died from the sudden onset of asthma two years before. Not long after, her two brothers also perished from respiratory illnesses which even the renowned Doctor Wu couldn't treat.

Her mother, the sister of *Tai-Ming* Lord Liang of Yutou Province, returned home in grief, not wanting to stay in Huajing with all the memories of her family. She'd only come to the capital once since, for Kai-Hua's wedding to the *Tai-Ming* heir to Jiangzhou Province.

The Liu family, into which she'd married two years before, was full of obedient but narrow-minded men. Though she hoped her own husband Dezhen, the heir, would spend more time in his province learning how to rule better than his father, Kai-Hua was also happy he resided in the capital. It allowed her to frequently visit Sun-Moon Castle, where she'd grown up with Kaiya.

The atmosphere of the game room in Sun-Moon Castle felt more like a funeral than the New Year. As expected. Although she hadn't lived in the palace for two years, she knew her cousins' rhythms well—everyone had synced up with Yanli when she moved in two years prior. Without a doubt, another month had passed without the conception of an heir to the Dragon Throne.

Xiulan and Yanli were somber as usual. More surprising was that Kaiya, who usually helped comfort the others, seemed the most downcast. Never looking up from the square bloodwood table, she didn't speak a word through her pursed lips. Perhaps she'd forgotten to take Doctor Wu's herbs that month.

Kai-Hua rubbed her belly, still flat two months into her pregnancy. Even if her friends knew nothing of it, it felt wrong to try to comfort them when the Heavens had blessed her while denying the others.

Through two hours of silence, broken only by clicking mahjong tiles, Yanli won most of the games in ruthless fashion. That was not out of the ordinary, but on any other night, she would teasingly gloat after each victory.

At last, Kai-Hua pushed the tiles in. "It's late, and Kaiya should get some rest before her journey tomorrow. Do we even need to calculate the winners and losers tonight?"

Xiulan wordlessly tossed a jade bracelet into the tiles. Kaiya added an embroidered silk kerchief.

Kai-Hua sucked in her breath. "Isn't that a gift from Young Lord Zheng?"

Without meeting her eyes, Kaiya nodded.

"Is that why you've been so quiet tonight? Did he say something during the procession this morning?"

"He didn't show." Yanli hadn't spoken for so long, Kai-Hua had almost forgotten what her voice sounded like.

Kaiya glared at Yanli before focusing on Kai-Hua. "He lied to me. He was with a woman."

"Are you sure?" Kai-Hua raised an eyebrow.

"I saw them riding together."

Xiulan let out a long sigh. "Oh, Kaiya. Men will do that. Even the Crown Prince. The Floating World wouldn't exist otherwise."

Kai-Hua nodded. Though the Founder's consort had broken with the traditions of previous dynasties by outlawing polygamy and disbanding the imperial harem, laws failed to change male nature. Kai-Hua allowed her husband an occasional dalliance, just so long as he remembered who his wife was. Especially now, while she was pregnant. Even so, her spy kept careful tabs on just how many times Dezhen visited the half-Ayuri beauty in the Floating World.

Kaiya frowned. "I had hoped he would at least control himself while we courted."

"You're right, Kaiya." Yanli snorted. "I don't know how you two tolerate it. Our husbands should be saving their seed for making heirs."

Heat burned in Kai-Hua's cheeks. Xiulan shot Yanli a scowl.

Yanli threw her hands up. "What? It's true. The *Tianzi* would rest easier knowing there was an heir after our husbands."

"Which is why," Xiulan said with a nod toward Kaiya, "you should give Young Lord Zheng a chance to explain himself. The *Tianzi's* health deteriorates quickly. It would set his heart at ease to see you married before…"

Nobody wanted to finish her sentence, least of all Kai-Hua, who had lost most of her family already. After a brief silence, she spoke up. "Did Young Lord Zheng say anything?"

"He said he would explain himself tomorrow. I don't think I will allow him inside the gates."

"Hear him out." Xiulan turned the kerchief over in her hands before pressing it down in front of Kaiya.

"But make him grovel first," Yanli added.

Kai-Hua chuckled. Despite their shared sadness, Xiulan and Yanli had resumed their roles in Kaiya's love life. Xiulan, the enabler who encouraged her to follow her whims; and Yanli, the practical voice of reason. Kai-Hua imagined them as mirror images of Kaiya's psyche.

Kaiya stared at the kerchief before tentatively retrieving it and sliding it into a fold in her robe.

Silk gowns rustled as handmaidens folded the dresses and wrapped the jewelry Kaiya had chosen to take on her mission to Vyara City. They stacked lacquer boxes near the doors to her dressing room. Porters would take them to the *Golden Phoenix*, even if she herself would travel on the Tarkothi ship *Invincible*. Worried that Jie might make inadvertent alterations to her wardrobe, Kaiya had ordered the half-elf to stand back and take inventory.

Still dwelling on Zheng Ming's betrayal, Kaiya glanced at the brocade box on her make-up table. It sat apart from her cosmetics, next to the table's oval mirror. Holding her breath, she opened it, revealing Prince Hardeep's lotus jewel and Tian's river pebble.

She lifted the lotus jewel and held it up to the lamplight. It seemed to vibrate in her hands, slow and sluggish. So swept up with Zheng Ming's wit, she'd all but forgotten Prince Hardeep in the past few weeks. Cousin Peng had said the prince was in Vyara City. Perhaps she would see him there, and she could apologize for the sudden end to their correspondence. She tucked the jewel into her sash. Though it had always seemed like part of her, it now felt oddly foreign after a long absence from its familiar spot.

With a sigh, she grasped Tian's pebble, the cool smoothness reminding her of his sweet, genuine affection. His had been a childhood love. He never used her as a tool, like Prince Hardeep had; nor as a conquest, like his older brother Ming.

Perhaps *conquest* was too harsh. She played the scene back in her mind yet again, for the hundredth time that day. The girl, cute in her own way, looking up through her lashes at him; Ming, flashing that infuriatingly charming grin. Kaiya couldn't have misjudged the situation. Or had she?

She turned to see Jie, attention fixed on the pebble. Kaiya closed her hand around it. "Jie, what did you think of the girl riding with Young Lord Zheng?"

The half-elf sucked on her lower lip. "Desperate, *Dian-xia*."

It wasn't the word Kaiya would've used. "How so?"

"She was not particularly adept at riding, and she was quite nervous."

"But she was smiling."

"Contrived. Her eyes darted back and forth, and her brow glistened with sweat on a cold day."

Kaiya kept her jaw from dropping. Her Insolent Retainer's ability to notice details and draw connections was amazing. Perhaps it would be worth giving Zheng Ming a chance to explain himself tomorrow.

A male voice said, "You should be less concerned with philandering lords and more focused on important things."

Kaiya jerked her head around.

The elf Xu leaned against a wall, fiddling with a hand-sized rectangular mirror.

One handmaiden gasped, while another dropped a jewelry box. Trinkets jingled on the floor. Others stared wide-eyed at the intruder. Jie's lips tightened, even as her hand, tucked in the fold of her gown, strayed behind her back.

Kaiya glared at him. "Must you always make such dramatic appearances?"

"I am impulsive." Lord Xu yawned. "Here, a sending-off gift." He tossed the mirror at her.

Kaiya caught it in both hands. It was light, lighter than it should be based on its size. It displayed a perfect image of her face, instead of a mirror image. It was rather disconcerting. Curious, she tilted it side to side, and then over. "Thank you."

"You do not seem impressed. It's magic."

She turned it over in her hands. "I assumed so. What does it do, besides reversing my reflection?"

"Brush your finger across it." He pantomimed the motion.

Kaiya raised an eyebrow. "Won't that smudge it?"

"I said it was magic, didn't I?"

Kaiya glanced sideways at Jie. Maybe impertinence was inherited among elves, like their pointed ears. Nonetheless, she did as she was told. Her reflection disappeared, replaced by text written in a skilled hand. She sucked in breath. "What is this?"

"A gift. Rather, part of the bet I lost with Doctor Wu. She bade me to give this to you: a book of songs and music theory. It may entertain you during your voyage."

"A book?"

"Keep brushing it, back and forth, and it will turn the pages. It is a copy of a tome Doctor Wu, with the help of myself and your music teachers, used to treat one of your father's maladies, thirty-two years ago. Unfortunately, it is missing four important pages, lost when three of his best agents retrieved the original." The elf's eyes gleamed through his otherwise inscrutable expression.

Kaiya stared at the book...mirror. "Thank you."

"It does one more thing: If you need me, call my name into it. I will try my best to respond. And as long as you hold it, I can transport you through the ethers if you need to escape danger."

A sudden hope swelled in her. Perhaps she could avoid seasickness in the tight confines of a ship cabin. "Could you just send me to Vyara City?"

"I could." He grinned again. "But that would rob you of the chance to reconcile with Young Lord Zheng."

Heat rose to her cheeks.

Lord Xu's face hardened. "A warning, before I go. Limit using the power of your voice while in Vyara City. Just as I warned you about that power two years ago, the mirror interacts with all the sounds of the universe, rippling out from you. It would be like a beacon to those who can detect it."

In the past, he'd warned her about Avarax sensing the effect of her music from afar. However, the Last Dragon's treasure hoard was rumored to be enormous, so he probably wouldn't care for a little mirror. "Who would be listen—"

The air popped, filling the space where the elf had just stood.

CHAPTER 21:

Bait and Switch

Waiting in the pre-dawn darkness, Zheng Ming finished his mental countdown. It gave his men time to cover the dimly lit inn's side and rear doors. Several others gathered with him at the front. According to his mysterious informant, insurgent leaders converged there, preparing to attack Princess Kaiya's procession to Jiangkou. Their assault would commence once they saw Ming marching in the procession, so as to finally kill both him and her.

He would surprise them with an early appearance. He whipped his *dao* out. "Attack!"

A sheet of paper fluttered away from where it had been wrapped around the base of his blade. He skidded to a halt and retrieved it, leaving thirty of his men to surge across the street toward the building's front entrance.

His eyes widened as he scanned the letter, which implicated him as a traitor. The informant must've set him up! Had he not drawn his sword now, he would've sauntered into the inn, possibly to square off against government troops. But why would the man do this to him? How had he gotten ahold of his sword?

And who was really in the inn? Ming started to call off the attack, but his men had already stormed in. Sounds of struggle broke out.

Letter revealed or not, his own men had just attacked imperial troops. Who else could it be? He took his time slogging toward the main door, savoring his last minutes of freedom. How humiliating it would be, striding into the building in full dress uniform, only to be escorted out in chains.

Inside the common room, his soldiers stood with bared blades. A dozen men knelt with hands on their bowed heads. Ming studied each, scanning for some identifier.

As long as the planted letter remained secret, he could pretend his intentions were legitimate. He turned to his aide-de-camp. "Did they have weapons?"

"Yes, *Xiao-Ye*." His man pointed to a table where broadswords, crossbows, and daggers formed a heap.

Ming stifled a cringe. Maybe those weapons had government marks. He picked up a dagger, checking for any tell-tale sigils. None. He pointed it at the captives. "We have foiled your attack on Princess Kaiya."

They looked among each other, confusion scrawled across their expressions. One murmured under his breath, while another shook his head in response.

If they were government soldiers, they would surely be protesting now. Putting on his best gambling face, Ming stepped forward and glared at one of the men, who looked more like a sailor than a warrior. "I know you are part of the insurgency. Who do you work for?"

Heads drooped in silence. Perhaps they were insurgents after all. He thought back to his encounter with the informant. At no time had he taken Ming's sword. But if he hadn't planted the letter, someone else was plotting against him.

Perhaps one of the jealous young lords who resented Ming's success with women.

In the distance, a bell tolled six times. Princess Kaiya's procession would depart the palace very soon. The foiling of this attack on her had taken too much time. There was no way he could keep his promise to meet her at the main gate.

There was still a chance to redeem himself. He turned to his aide-de-camp. "Call the city watch to take these men into custody."

On horseback, Ming might still make it to the palace in time.

Jie looked from the princess to the fog-shrouded Iridescent Moon and back again. Even if she could barely make out the moon, she knew valuable time slipped away. Horns at the main gate blared again, echoing through the early morning quiet and into the palace garden where they waited.

The drums and horns marked the departure of the princess' palanquin, flanked by a hundred imperial guards and followed by her baggage train. It would take the main road to the port city of Jiangkou, where the princess' decoy, Meiling, would board the *Golden Phoenix*.

Jie touched the princess' hand. "*Dian-xia*, we must make haste."

Her focus fixed on the veranda, Kaiya shook her head. "A few more minutes. He will be here. He promised."

Jie exchanged glances with Chen Xin, the senior-most of the five heavily cloaked imperial guards.

With a nod, he spoke: "*Dian-xia*, we have arranged for a cargo boat to take us downriver. They have a tight schedule to keep and will not wait for us."

The princess turned around, jaw set. In her hands, she squeezed the kerchief. "Zhao Yue. Go to the main gate and leave word with the guards there. When Young Lord Zheng arrives, send him to the *Songyuan* quays."

Standing behind the princess, Jie waved her hand to countermand the order. Zheng Ming's flamboyance would certainly attract attention to their clandestine trip.

Zhao's gaze met hers, and he tilted his chin a fraction before dropping to a knee. "As the princess commands." He rose and jogged toward the veranda.

"We shall depart." The princess waved a hand toward a spot on the garden wall.

Chen Xin's fingers probed the wall. He glanced back at the rest of them and then used his body to conceal which stone he pressed. It wasn't too hard for her *Moquan* eyes to see past his efforts.

A slab of stones slid back without a sound, a testament to dwarven engineering. Chen Xin disappeared into the opening, followed by Ma Jun and then the princess. Jie went next, trailed by Xu Zhan and Li Wei.

Steep stairs, illuminated by Chen Xin's light bauble lamp, descended into the musty bowels of the castle. Jie counted eighty-eight steps, which placed them about sixty feet below ground.

Ahead of her, the princess walked stiffly, her shoulders hunched as if she were hugging herself. Jie sighed. Unrequited affection was a heavy burden, but one which should never interfere with duty. She should know.

The four imperial guards—five, once Zhao Yue caught up to them—clopped over the passageway's stone floors. Luckily, they were far enough underground that no one would hear them. In any case, anyone who considered foiling their diplomatic mission was probably preoccupied with the public procession.

After ten minutes, they emerged from the passage into a building in the secluded *Tiantai* Shrine, just outside the palace walls in the city's northwest quadrant. The princess let out a monumental sigh, as if she'd somehow held her breath the whole time underground.

Hooded cloaks concealed their faces and the men's short swords. The brittle light of dawn filtered through the cool morning mist, further obscuring their identities. Trailed by a dozen *Moquan* brothers and sisters, they set off on a brisk, ten-minute walk to a freight dock not far from where the Jade River emerged from Sun-Moon Lake. Despite the secrecy of their departure, Jie maintained careful vigilance.

Princess Kaiya seemed detached, staring down at her feet while they walked through the warehouse-lined streets. When they arrived at the quay, she craned her neck, looking among the dozens of sailors and workers bustling along the wooden docks, loading and preparing cargo boats. There was little doubt whom she searched for.

Jie didn't have the heart to say Young Lord Zheng would not be joining them. It was for the better. Whether she admitted it to herself or not, the princess repeatedly fell prey to his charm. Given a week at sea with his forked tongue beguiling her, it might be more than the waves rocking the ship.

Chen Xin flagged down a middle-aged pilot, who'd been contracted through anonymous intermediaries. His river boat, laden with cargo, would take them through the wide but shallow waters of the lower Jade River to the sea docks in Jiangkou. Two dozen brawny rowers looked over their group with little interest, while the quartermaster kept peering through the mist at the Iridescent Moon.

The princess didn't accommodate him, raising a hand. She spoke in an unmistakably regal tone, which might unwittingly blow their cover. "Wait a moment." Her eyes swept across the docks several times, and then focused on the road.

Jie followed her gaze. Maybe Zheng Ming had somehow found them. No, the philandering lord didn't seem to be among the dockworkers and sailors. She tugged on the princess' sleeve. "We must get underway. Our hosts in Jiangkou are following an unforgiving schedule."

The princess glared at her from underneath her hood, but after a few seconds, turned on her heel and motioned for her entourage to board. With Li Wei's help, she climbed onto to the boat.

Jie held her sigh of relief until the boat pushed off. They would be on time, and she

wouldn't have to suffer through Zheng Ming's presence.

Kaiya listened to the oars swishing through the water, following the cadence of the drum situated at the long river boat's aft. Perhaps it wasn't too late to order a full stop and head back. What if Ming had been attacked by the insurgents again? And hurt, unable to meet her in the palace? He'd better be hurt, to not show up.

Forget Zheng Ming. She stared at the lazy waters of the Jade River. Melting winter snows first filled up Sun-Moon Lake before emptying into the wide channel that flowed out to sea. With the river being too shallow for ocean-going vessels, swift row boats and slower pole barges plied the waters, transporting goods and people from Hua's largest port to its capital.

Since the transformation of Huajing from a muddy fishing village to the national capital, other villages along the river banks had blossomed into towns, catering to the barges as they pushed their way upstream.

For the first time, Kaiya saw these towns from the meandering river. Normally, she bypassed them on the main highway. Merchants sold wares directly from docked barges, while fishermen took small craft out for the day. Women washed clothes in the shallows, sharing gossip with broad smiles and laughter.

Even though she frequently traveled through the country, it was always meticulously choreographed. It was rare for her ever to see the common folk going about their daily lives. How relaxed their lifestyles were compared to the rigid routines of court life! Her hand strayed to Tian's pebble.

The boat arrived at Jiangkou's docks in the early afternoon, and the party disembarked. Ma Jun went to search for the *Invincible* while the rest of the group waited by one of the many large warehouses near the busy docks.

On previous trips, Kaiya had gone directly to a wharf just outside of the city and a little further upstream in a private cove, where the *Golden Phoenix* moored. Now in a public area, she could hardly hear herself think over the buzz of activity as sailors, dockworkers, and merchants all played their respective roles in Hua's vibrant international trade.

The smell of fish and sweat mingled with brackish water to assault her nose. Her stomach turned at the sight of huge crates writhing with live shellfish, on their way to the sprawling Jiangkou fish market. Perhaps the open sea wouldn't be so bad compared to this.

Thankfully, it didn't take long for Ma Jun to return. He beckoned them to follow, and within minutes, the *Invincible's* sablewood hull and five masts loomed large over the three-masted Hua cargo ships around it.

Kaiya had never seen such a gigantic vessel. If only Zheng Ming could be here to see it! Fair-skinned sailors rarely seen in these waters prepared the ship for departure. They laughed, shouted, and relayed orders as they worked the rigging and moorings. Their Arkothi was laced with colorful metaphors which might as well have been gibberish.

Their catcalls, as Jie approached the gangplank and pulled down her hood, needed no translation.

Better to keep her own hood up. Perhaps for the duration of the weeklong trip.

Four stout marines armed with cutlasses eyed them suspiciously. After the attempt on Prince Aelward's life two days prior, he'd returned to his ship, and it stayed under heavy guard. No supply crates or cargo went unchecked.

Soon the prince, along with the elf Ayana, came to greet them. He took Kaiya's hand to help her aboard. "Welcome aboard the *Invincible*, lass. I hope to be as fine a host as you were for me."

There was no sarcasm in his voice, despite what had happened at the arena. Kaiya searched his eyes and found nothing but sincerity. She bowed her head. "Thank you. Your ship is beautiful. Though we take pride in our ships, even the Son of

Heaven's flagship cannot compare to the *Invincible*."

With grace he couldn't imitate on land, Prince Aelward sidestepped some sea foam carried on the wind. "Impressive as she be, yer *Golden Phoenix* is built fer speed, not fer power. Our ancestors arrived on the Tivaralan coasts as conquerors three hundred years ago in these ships. Even now, they are the technological pinnacle of sea-going vessels. We still build them with sablewood, which is only found in Tarkoth."

Li Wei, known more for his left-handedness and pessimism than his eye for woodwork, ran his hand over the rail. "The wood is beautiful but clearly well-worn."

"The *Invincible* is nearly two hundred years old, one of just eight Intimidator Class ships ever commissioned." Beaming, Prince Aelward patted a bulwark. "None have been lost to battle or to the sea, and the three originals on which our ancestors arrived are still in service."

Kaiya clapped her hands together, in awe at the age of the ships. "I always believed we in Cathay were the best sailors, but it seems that the Eldaeri are masters of the sea."

"Saltwater runs in our veins." Aelward motioned them to follow him across the deck toward the aft. "Now come with me to your quarters."

Xu Zhan pointed at four light cannons, two each at the bow and stern. "You have fitted your ship with guns."

Kaiya twirled her hair. No Hua ship was similarly armed. What if Father was right about the Tarkothi being a threat to Hua shipping?

"Wrought-iron cannons," Aelward said, gliding across the deck, "bought from your country a hundred years ago. Your modern cast-iron guns are too heavy and unbalance the ship."

"Our ships don't have guns at all." The pugnacious Xu Zhan never shied from an argument. He might very well get them thrown off.

She bowed her head. "Please forgive my guard."

Aelward laughed. He was a different man on a ship. Relaxed. Confident. "Not at all. Our circumstances are different. You have no seafaring rivals in the West, but Tarkoth and Serikoth have been nominally in conflict with each other for a hundred and twenty years. Now we face the even greater threat of the Teleri Empire. We use ships not just for trade, but to project our might from the seas."

They arrived at the door to an aft cabin beneath the poop deck, and Aelward held the door open. "It is very rare that we have women on board." Aelward grinned with what could only be described as nostalgia. It would be worth asking Jie about later.

"Princess Kaiya and her handmaiden will stay in my cabin. I will bunk with the senior officers. Unfortunately, we only have space for your guards in general crew quarters."

Kaiya bowed. "Thank you for your consideration. I am sorry to inconvenience you." Though not sorry enough to bunk in the ship's guts.

Jie emerged from the cabin— Kaiya hadn't even seen her go in—and bowed her head. "It is secure," she said in the Hua tongue. "The only thing out of place was a single strand of frizzy red hair."

Red hair. It was unheard of among the Eldaeri, and rare even among other Northerners.

Peng Kai-Long mingled in with the peasants on the bluffs overlooking the restricted cove where the *Golden Phoenix* docked. Though Jiangkou city guards kept a watchful eye, he was confident they would not see through his disguise. He regretted, however, that they had confiscated his spyglass at the cordon.

Nonetheless, he saw Cousin Kaiya about to board the *Golden Phoenix*. Once it was out on the open seas, he would finally be rid of her.

For good.

Through three layers of agents and influence, he'd managed to get two insurgents on board. Somewhere on their journey, they would ignite the muskets' gunpowder magazine and sabotage the lifeboats, scuttling all hope of negotiations with Madura and forever drowning the secret of Prince Hardeep's fake correspondence. And of course, consigning another source of heirs to the Dragon Throne to a watery grave.

The *Golden Phoenix* sparkled in the sun. How regretful to sacrifice the realm's magnificent flagship. It would have been his once he ruled. No matter, he would commission an even grander vessel, even better than the Eldaeri's *Invincible*.

Below, an imperial messenger, clearly marked by his dragon banners, interrupted Kai-Long's daydreams. The rider galloped toward the cove, kicking up dust along the access road. When his horse reached the dock, the rider jumped off and dropped to a knee before the ship's quartermaster.

He pointed toward the ship and held his arms out as if he were embracing a bear. The quartermaster shook his head, then threw up his hands and traipsed up the gang plank.

Around Kai-Long, the rustics murmured and pointed. Before long, Cousin Kaiya appeared at the the gang plank and disembarked.

Had his agents been uncovered? How was it that all of his supposedly foolproof plans failed? Kai-Long loosened his fists, even as heat rose to his ears.

He listened to the chatter of the people around him. Something about sabotaged water barrels. What was happening?

Against his better judgment, Liang Yu waited around to see Lord Peng's reaction to the princess disembarking from the ship. He had not expected to see the lord of Nanling disguised among the crowds of well-wishers, and now wondered what his stake in this game of intrigue was. Up to now, he had only suspected Peng as one of the serious players. Here was proof.

Somehow, Liang Yu had become a player as well, instead of just a somewhat independent game piece. As he surmised, his former employer had hired new agents to scuttle the princess' mission to Vyara City; and Liang Yu had tricked Young Lord Zheng into revealing them.

The results were better than he planned. Negotiations would be delayed. He did not have long to wait now. Once war began, he would trick Zheng Ming into exposing his former employer. In the meantime, it was time to investigate Lord Peng Kai-Long a little more carefully.

CHAPTER 22:

Song of Ayudra Island

With a large porthole looking out onto the sea, Kaiya's cabin was the *Invincible's* most spacious and luxurious. Nonetheless, the tight confines, combined with the rocking of the ship, stirred her stomach to rebellion.

Though Jie and Chen Xin implored her to stay indoors and avoid the foreigners' leers, she spent most of the week on deck. To her relief, the sailors and marines of Tarkoth's elite navy proved to be disciplined, and none so much as spoke to her beyond polite greetings. With no interruptions save for the half-elf's constant nagging over safety issues, she delved into the mirror-book Lord Xu had given her.

Acoustic theory came to life through tales of legendary musicians and their songs. To think music could stir armies into bloodlust or send enemies into a panic. Kaiya might be able to invoke a two-syllable command, yet that paled compared to singers who beguiled large audiences with only their voice.

The book also recounted the first part of Kaiya's favorite story: how the slave girl Yanyan sang the dragon Avarax to sleep. How she would love to learn that song! Unfortunately, four of the pages were missing.

Using what *was* there, and what she'd learned of vibrations and vocal commands, Kaiya experimented on her guards. Getting Li Wei just to yawn drained her; and even then, it might not have been the impact of her voice, but just the lulling waves.

Such a basic skill, beyond her grasp. How could she ever hope to attempt some of the book's more unbelievable feats, like stirring gale winds or causing the ground to quake?

On the fifth day, the seas pitched with a curious regularity. Kaiya stumbled across the deck to the prow, grasping the cool metal of the cannon to stabilize herself. Facing into the winds, she listened.

The waves sang in rhythmic ripples.

Ears tracking the sounds to their source, her eyes followed a long line of small islets. Their contours curved toward the horizon, finally ending at a large island rising out of sea. It seemed to whisper to her through the symphony of ocean sounds.

"You feel it, too," came a melodic voice behind her. "Ayudra Island."

Kaiya met Ayana's gaze. The elf woman pointed back toward the prow. "Those are barrier islands, which separate the Western Ocean from the Shallowsea. Beyond them, Ayudra Island. On it, the ruins of Ayudra City and the hill that was once Mount Ayudra."

Kaiya knew the history well. Ayudra City had once been capital of the Ayuri Empire, a vibrant and prosperous port of magnificent spires and domes built up around an ancient orc pyramid. The Hellstorm obliterated it, and reduced Mount Ayudra to a hill. The city's levees failed and the hungry ocean swept in, swallowing ten thousand *li* of low-lying farmland and the millions of souls inhabiting it. Those that survived, along with everyone else on the continent, suffered through the Long Winter. Empires fell, chaos ensued. It was in the ashes of the old world that her own ancestor, and those of the Eldaeri and Teleri, forged a new world.

"How is the island *speaking* to me?" Kaiya asked.

Ayana smiled. "One of the pyramids dedicated to the worship of the ancient Tivari gods stood in the shadows of Mount Ayudra. Even though the Hellstorm annihilated it, the energy of the world wells up there. Some humans can feel it."

"Then elves can hear it, too? What is it saying?"

"I *feel* it," Ayana answered, "but no one experiences the energy in the same way. I can tell you this: our oral histories, ancient even to us elves, say that our civilization sprang up tens of thousands of years ago in the same places where our Tivari conquerors later built pyramids as monuments to their vile gods."

Kaiya nodded. Human civilizations, as well, flourished in these areas. "Why?"

"All those areas resonate with the energy of the world. Especially here, where the physical manifestation of Magius, God of Magic, appeared," she pointed to the Iridescent Moon, floating much higher and larger than usual, "to help my people hide from the Tivari's attempts to exterminate us. That is why the Ayuri Paladins constructed the Temple of the Moon over the ruins. Perhaps you should visit the Oracle there."

A visit to the Oracle...it might answer more questions about this energy bubbling in her core. Kaiya turned back to contemplate the island, which grew larger as the *Invincible* approached. By late afternoon, the island's docks came into view. With seagoing Hua ships incapable of navigating the Shallowsea, and the Ayuri skiffs unable to handle the open sea, those docks served as a gateway for trade into the interior Ayuri kingdoms. Hopefully, they could arrange transit and leave enough time for a detour to the Temple of the Moon.

She looked up at Caiyue to gauge the approximate hour. As when Ayana pointed it out before, it no longer hung in its reliable position to the south. Instead, it floated much higher, almost directly overhead. How bizarre—but not nearly as strange as its hum.

The humming joined with the ever-rising chorus of seagull caws and ocean waves. The finger-length *dizi* flute in the folds of her robe found its way into Kaiya's hand. She played, allowing the harmony of the island to guide her just as she'd learned from Lord Xu two years before during the Wailian debacle.

The flute resonated clearly, its sound louder and fuller than she could imagine. Sailors paused and stared.

Ordered back to work, they returned to their duties, and the *Invincible* lumbered into port. There, the Arkothi-speaking sailors and Ayuri-speaking dockworkers began tying the ship down to the moorings, communicating through the universal language of seafarers.

Oh, to feel solid ground again! Kaiya shifted her weight left to right, peering down a single stone-paved boulevard running several *li* to the broad, low-lying hill. Two-story buildings of white mud bricks topped by flat roofs lined the wide road. Save for the Ayuri architecture, it might have been any street in Hua for all the bustling activity.

However, on the other side of the buildings lay the ruins of the once-great city of Ayudra, as far as her eye could see. She shuddered. Hundreds of thousands of unfortunate people perished here during the Hellstorm. The piles of rubble stood as their grave markers.

Once the gangplank lowered, Kaiya disembarked with Jie and the five imperial guards. Prince Aelward and Ayana followed with ten marines. Around them, Ayuri dockworkers began unloading cargo under the watchful eye of a harbormaster and the ship's quartermaster and boatswain. The call of sea birds mingled with the buzzing of the Ayuri language, swarming in from all directions.

As the party advanced toward the head of the wharf, they were greeted by an Ayuri man, not much older than her, wearing a lightweight, white cotton tunic that hung to his knees. The *kurta*'s high neck was embroidered with symbols indicating he was an official, and he sported a short beard of coarse black hair. He spoke in heavily accented Arkothi. "Your papers, please."

Prince Aelward produced a scroll with wavy Ayuri script. The official skimmed over it before regarding the group. "Welcome, Prince Aelward of Tarkoth. You, the elf lady, and your crew may come ashore, but only within six blocks of the harbor." He then narrowed his eyes at the Hua. "These people do not look like Tarkothi crew. Unless you can produce proper identification and permissions, I am afraid they will have to stay on your ship, at least until we can arrange escort tomorrow morning."

Kaiya searched the harbor for the *Golden Phoenix*. The faster vessel should've arrived earlier, and certainly they would've made arrangements for her. It was nowhere to be found.

Uncompromising bureaucrats! There had to be some way to persuade him, even it meant identifying herself. She lowered her hood. "I am Kaiya Wang, daughter of the Emperor of Cathay. I have business at the Temple of the Moon."

Behind her, the imperial guards and Jie shuffled on their feet. She wasn't supposed to reveal their identities, let alone break from their rigid itinerary.

The official paused to gape at her. "We were not informed of your visit, and without any kind of identification, I am afraid I cannot let you off this wharf."

He began to motion for several local soldiers to come over and help enforce his judgment, when an adorable young boy of about ten years scampered up. He wore a white *kurta* with a light-yellow embroidered collar. Kaiya searched her memory, and recalled that his clothes marked him as a trainee of the Ayuri Paladin order.

The boy bobbed his head. "The Oracle wants the Cathayi woman with the flute to visit the temple tomorrow at dawn. The Paladins will allow her to stay in one of the guest houses."

Kaiya looked back at her people, who all gawked at the boy. She turned back to the beaming child and withdrew her flute. "How did he know I was coming?"

The official harrumphed. "He is the Oracle, after all. It is his business to know. Very well, the lady may come ashore. Did the Oracle say anything about her friends?"

The boy stared at Kaiya with wide eyes and shook his head. "He only mentioned the one with the flute."

The official peered at them with a smug grin. "I am very sorry, but only the princess may enter the city."

"That is not acceptable," Chen Xin said in Arkothi. "The princess must be protected at all times."

The official laughed. "This is the spiritual home of the Ayuri Paladins, the greatest warriors on Tivaralan. As their guest, she is safer here than anywhere in the world."

Kaiya summoned her most charming voice. "At least allow me to bring my handmaiden."

The official looked down at her feet. "I am sorry, but we must follow protocol."

Kaiya sang her request. "Let her come." Three syllables, yet it didn't drain her energy at all. The boy's eyes widened.

The official pressed his hands together and bowed his head. "Very well."

"I protest, *Dian-xia*," Chen Xin said in the Hua language. He dropped to one knee. "It is our duty to protect you, always. Please stay on *the Invincible* one more night."

"I will not stay on the ship tonight. I will be safe with Jie and an island full of Paladins." Kaiya lifted her chin and scowled.

Chen Xin immediately stood up, took two steps back and bowed down again. Turning to the boy, she smiled graciously and said in Ayuri, "Please, little friend, take us to our quarters."

Since the night Lord Xu popped into the princess' bedchambers, Jie had felt the power of the princess' voice dissipate around her with no effect. Yet here, on this island which pulsated at a low hum, the princess' command swept over her like a tidal wave. She stood mesmerized, just like all of the men, and trailed after the princess like an automaton. It took a few minutes of walking in a daze before she regained her focus.

The boy skipped down the boulevard, between warehouses, trading offices, inns, and shops. He, too, seemed to recover his wits and spoke with puppy-like enthusiasm. "This part of the ruins was rebuilt. Ayudra is now a transit point for people and cargo. Lots of merchants, sailors, and passengers. But not everyone is allowed here. And there is a nighttime curfew."

Jie suppressed a cough. For a purportedly safe place guarded by the supposedly most powerful warriors in the land, there sure were a lot of rules.

The crowds thinned and they came to a short stone wall crossing the road. It had an open gate large enough to allow a cart through. On the left stood a handsome young man, on the right an attractive young woman. Both wore the same white *kurtas* as the boy, though their high collars were embroidered in gold. Postures relaxed, their hands rested on the guardless hilts of curved *naga* swords hanging at their sides.

Paladins. Jie eyed them. Had she not witnessed their fighting skills two years ago in Tokahia, she wouldn't have believed their martial prowess. Then again, the Golden Scorpions she'd fought hadn't impressed, and they supposedly underwent the same training as Paladins.

The boy pressed his hands together and bowed his head. "This is the Cathayi lady who is allowed to enter."

The two saluted her with folded palms and stepped to the side.

The princess nodded in response. Jie followed her and the boy past the checkpoint.

"Welcome to the sacred inner city. The spiritual home of the Order of the Ayuri Paladins." The boy waved his hand at the boulevard ahead, which looked just like the harbor side of the city. It continued toward the verdant hill, with two-story, flat-roofed buildings on either side. An occasional dome or spire or minaret topped a few buildings.

There were less people here, and all were uniformly dressed in the garb of the Paladin Order.

More evident was the change in sounds. The commotion of commerce gave way to orderly marching footsteps and the rhythmic pounding of metal—all woven into the rustling of the wind in the willowy paperwood trees and the song of the ocean behind them. It should've been a cacophony raucous enough to scare off evil spirits, but Jie found it oddly soothing.

The princess wore a serene expression, perhaps for the first time since Zheng Ming's betrayal. With those sharp ears of hers, she probably noticed the sounds, too.

"You feel it, don't you?" said a male voice from behind them.

Jie's stomach lurched into her chest. Someone had snuck up without her hearing. She whirled around, her hand instinctively reaching into the folds of her cloak for a *biao* throwing star. Before she could get her fingers around it, a hand pressed firmly on her elbow, pinning it down. Try as she might, she couldn't free her arm.

"Please, do not be alarmed." The older man's grandfatherly voice rippled through her, calming her nerves and relaxing her muscles.

He had long, graying hair tied into a pony tail, and wore a white *kurta* with a gold-embroidered collar. Unlike the sentries at the wall, his shirt also had gold-embroidered cuffs.

The boy bowed low, hands pressed together. With even the princess bowing, Jie followed suit.

"Master Sabal," the boy said. "I am taking the Cathayi lady to the guest house, as instructed by the Oracle."

The Paladin master waved the boy off. "Run along, young Gayan, back to your studies with the Oracle. I will take them from here."

Gayan pouted, but then pressed his hands together and skipped off down the boulevard toward the hill.

"You." Master Sabal's focus locked on Jie. "Have you come back for more training?"

More training? Jie's brows scrunched up. "I've never been here before."

"You were here two years ago, spying on our training." The Paladin master's lips pursed.

If only. Jie cast a sidelong glance at the princess, and then shook her head. "No, I've never set foot in Ayudra before." She'd only seen it from a ship on the way to her mission in the North.

"I see." Master Sabal scratched his chin. "Perhaps my old eyes failed me. Still, there aren't many half-elves in this world. Maybe you all look alike."

The nerve! Jie's cheeks must have flushed an interesting shade of red.

Turning from her, the master examined the princess, so different from the way any other man looked at her. "Young lady, for years I have been charged with identifying children who can feel what you feel right now: the vibrations of the world itself. It is a shame that our mandate only extends to the borders of Ayuri lands, for we will miss rare gems like you. Perhaps one of your parents is Ayuri?"

The princess shook her head.

"Please pull down your hood."

To Jie's shocked disapproval, the princess did as requested.

The old Paladin sucked in his breath. "By the Sun and Moons, I have never seen such a perfect face. Perhaps it is a good thing we never found you. We are still dealing with the repercussions of a beauty who threw an entire class of Paladin students into chaos."

Enough of the princess' beauty, already. It wasn't like Tian hadn't raved about it all the time, even before she was actually pretty. Jie tried not to roll her eyes. "How did you know what my hand was doing?"

"We learn to surrender our conscious thought and let the vibrations of the world guide our actions and amplify our own abilities beyond normal physical limitations. My hand moved to stop you from reaching your weapon, even before I consciously recognized the threat." The man smiled disarmingly.

She would have to try again, though maybe not on a master the next time.

"In any case," he continued, "follow me to your lodgings. You will find your answers...or perhaps just more questions...when you visit the Oracle yourself."

He brought them a little further down the boulevard, where they came to one of the ubiquitous two-story mud-brick buildings. Unlike the other structures, the guest house had a metallic domed roof that reflected the swirling colors of the Iridescent Moon, now waxing to its half phase. The sun hung low in the sky, gilding the Ayudra hilltop in gold.

The princess' stomach rumbles joined the other harmonized sounds. Her cheeks flushed red in the late afternoon sun.

"There is food, and a hot bath." Master Sabal opened the door and gestured for them to enter. "Rest well tonight. If you are so inclined, come to the temple before dawn tomorrow to join our morning meditation." With a bow, he bid them farewell.

Jie followed the princess into the two-story foyer, overlooked by a second floor balcony wrapping around three sides. Her feet sank into the wool Ayuri carpet, intricately woven in patterns of red, cream, and gold. She walked under a glass chandelier of light baubles that hung from the ceiling, illuminating the room.

Twirling in a circle, she took in the cloying scent of incense. The bright light brought out the colors in two large paintings of pre-Hellstorm Ayudra, which hung on either side of an arched opening.

An older boy, wearing a simple cotton *kurta*, emerged from the opposite archway, between a pair of golden banners with a twenty-one-pointed black sun. He bounded up the flight of steps at the far end of the foyer and beckoned them. "Follow me, mistresses."

When they reached the landing, he motioned to a door with an open hand. "That will be your room for the night. Please let me know if you need anything. We are serving dinner right now on the first-floor room to the left. There is a communal bath off of the room to the right."

Jie looked at the princess. An internal struggled played in her expression. In all likelihood, the hot bath after a long journey would win out over the aroma of roasted chicken wafting out of the dining room.

The princess' eyes drifted to the bathing area, then back to Jie.

If she thought Jie would help her bathe like a real handmaiden, she was in for a surprise.

CHAPTER 23:

What Happens in the Floating World

Minister Hong Jianbin's hands sweated, though not from the warm moisture billowing off the baths and percolating through the halls. The bathhouse was one of many in the Floating World, nestled among gambling dens, theatres, brothels, and teahouses. The district was secret in theory only, providing a haven for those who might seek temporary escape from the rigors of daily life.

Floating and ephemeral, like a waking dream. Commoner and noble alike visited, anonymously brushing shoulders on their way to enjoy pleasures for every budget. While the *Tianzi's* law ostensibly extended into the Floating World, it was more governed by convention and custom. As long as nothing spilled into the *real* world, and the businesses continued paying taxes, the authorities left well enough alone. What happened in the Floating World, stayed in the Floating World.

Or so the maxim said.

The effects of what would happen here tonight would ripple throughout Hua and usher in a new era of greatness. At least, that's what Hong told himself. Again.

His gaze returned to the dressing room's full-length mirror. His old skin glowed pink from a young woman's vigorous scrubbing. Yet no matter how much dirt and dead skin came off, the blackness of his soul reflected in that mirror. Were power and prestige worth betraying a friend? A friend who had helped him rise through the ranks?

Yes.

It would have never come to this, had the opportunity not fallen into his hands. The impossible aligning of so many circumstances could not have happened unless Heaven willed it.

Years ago, when he was still a minor palace official, he had recommended a new maid for Chief Minister Tan as a favor to an old hometown acquaintance. Little did he know how much the grateful girl would overhear: a plot to start war, in order to rectify the Chief Minister's past mistakes. With the maid as his eyes and ears in the Tan household, Hong knew almost everything.

At the same time, his father's former business connection told him of an exotic weed surreptitiously imported from Ayuri lands, delivered in small amounts to Lord Peng Kai-Long's Huajing estate.

Through a little investigating, Hong found out that the weed rendered a man's seed sterile. He would have exposed Lord Peng's treason right then and reaped a small reward, had he not met Leina. She inadvertently convinced him to keep the knowledge for himself and wait for a more opportune time to reveal it.

Up to now, he had just ridden on the wave of plots and plans, positioning himself to benefit when it crashed. He would have waited even longer, had the bumbling Young Lord Zheng not begun closing in on Tan's treachery.

Hong took in a deep whiff of the flowery air, which did little to cover the stink of betrayal. Peng and Tan were neck deep in seditious moves, with plenty of evidence waiting to incriminate them. Meanwhile, Hong's only treason was testing an herb interaction on the *Tianzi's* brother and nephews two years ago. Nothing linked him to those deaths.

Hong draped a thin robe over his frail body and approached the sliding doors. A scantily clad young woman opened them for him. He banished thoughts of his own treachery and walked across the wooden floors. The hall was empty. In an effort to protect the anonymity of her patrons, the proprietress always ensured that only one customer was in a passage at any given time.

Another door opened ahead of him and he turned and entered a private bath room. Chief Minister Tan was already soaking up to his chest in an enormous wooden tub, two beautiful young women sitting naked on either side of him. The water level tantalizingly hinted at the cleft between their breasts.

"Little Hong," the Chief Minister said, "thank you for inviting me."

"It is always my pleasure, Elder Brother." Hong addressed the Chief Minister as he always had in the many years they had known each other. He removed his own robe and settled into the hot water. One of the women waded across the tub, keeping her soft curves provocatively submerged, and sidled up next to him.

Tan draped an arm over the girl beside him. "It has been years since we enjoyed a bath together with such lovely ladies. To what do I owe the pleasure?"

"I want in." Hong eschewed all secrecy— they could discuss classified affairs of state here, since the ladies of the bathhouse were sworn to confidentiality. What happened in the Floating World, stayed in the Floating World.

Tan yawned. "What exactly do you want?"

Hong leaned forward, out of the arms of the beauty, and kept all hint of accusation out of his voice. "I know Xie Shimin visited you in secret before his unlikely assassination attempt."

"Yes, he did," Tan answered casually, without even a trace of worry or concern. "I suppose my maid told you? What of it?"

So he knew about the maid. "Just that I know. And I support you in your work to punish Madura. I was a part of that trade mission thirty-two years ago, too, and bear the same responsibility for Ankira's occupation. I want to help you."

"You already have." Tan disentangled his arm from the girl and leaned forward, hands steepled to his chin. "Did you ever wonder why so many of the attacks on the *Tai-Ming* occurred after their meetings with you?"

Hong paused, thinking back to each of the attacks.

"It is because you always informed me whom you were meeting with," Tan continued. "But given the circumstances, it certainly does not look good for you."

Blood rushed from Hong's face. Minister Tan had been setting him up to take the blame in the event his plot failed! But why?

Tan grinned. "Do not worry, my old friend. I withheld this piece of information from investigators. I merely wanted to let you know, to ensure your good behavior."

"Of course." Relief washed over Hong. "I only share your vision of Hua's prosperity."

"Good. Because the prerequisite for being a part of my plan is dedication to our great nation." Tan shook his head. "I am sad I had to go to such great lengths, but the *Tianzi* will not change his ways in his old age, at least not without significant provocation."

Hong hid his scoff. Chief Minister Tan, as one of the *Tianzi's* favorites, probably believed he would be awarded a fief and *Yu-Ming* status if new lands came under Hua rule. "If I may ask, why did you want to assassinate the Tarkothi prince? It does not seem to have any relevance to our goals of expanding the nation, and if anything, would make Hua look very bad in the eyes of our trading partners. And there are those, such as Lord Peng, who wanted to ally with Tarkoth."

Tan waved his hand dismissively. "He was simply a necessary casualty, an expendable target that would not needlessly kill one of our own lords. We needed to create the appearance that nobody was safe; that Madura, Rotuvi, and their allies were meddling in our affairs. That is why we have tried to implicate Madura time and time again."

"Which explains why you had the *Golden Phoenix*'s water barrels sabotaged." Hong feigned sudden epiphany. "To keep Princess Kaiya from travelling to Vyara City. As soon as she talked to the Madurans, she would find out they had nothing to do with our own internal problems."

"Exactly!" Tan said, beaming. "I should have recruited you earlier, since you seem to have an eye for conspiracy."

More than Tan realized. Hong raised an eyebrow. "And all of the attacks on the lords? Your doing?"

Tan shrugged. "All but the debacle in Lord Peng's compound that night. None of my planned attacks, save the attempt on Lord Han, were meant to be fatal; just enough to scare the *Tai-Ming* into pushing for punitive action against Madura. I was worried when you began to propose troop movements, especially away from the borders, since that is where we will eventually launch our expansion."

Sweat beaded on Hong's head. It was hot, and not just because of the steam. "How were you able to recruit the insurgents?"

"Insurgents?" Tan's brow furrowed. "I had nothing to do with them. I procured the services of patriots. There are enough former Hua soldiers who are tired of hiring themselves out to foreign armies, who share our vision of Hua's greatness. All it took was the recruitment of one of the *Tianzi's* agents, a real *Moquan*, I believe. He did the rest."

Moquan? Hong's forehead scrunched. Tan really believed they existed.

The girl massaging Tan's neck paused momentarily and Tan smirked. "Do not worry, my sweet, you have nothing to fear from the *Moquan*. They only kidnap babies. And do the *Tianzi's* dirty work."

The girl smiled nervously and returned to her kneading.

Hong lifted his hand, letting the warm water slither off. "So there really is no foreign threat, is there?"

Tan scowled for a split second. "There is no *imminent* foreign threat. However, our neighbors covet our wealth. Mark my words, it will only be a matter of time before the Teleri Empire and its satellites pressure us. We must expand our buffer territory, to protect the Hua heartland from their machinations."

"Certainly you have shared your concerns with the *Tianzi*? He is a reasonable man."

Tan sighed. "I have. But he has become too tentative with age. He will not budge in his mindset without significant pressure from the hereditary lords. His sons are too weak-willed to do anything. The realm will stagnate and fall to ruin under them."

"But if the princess negotiates a lasting peace with the Madurans—"

"She will not." Tan slapped his hand down on the water's surface. "She has been ill for two days, and the *Golden Phoenix* would not sail even if she were well."

Ill! Hong's chest tightened. His ultimate prize, sick.

Tan continued, "I have many ways to keep the ship anchored. If we do not show for our meeting with the Madurans, they may take offense. Perhaps they will attack us first."

"When do you plan on pushing Expansionism? The *Tianzi* dismissed the notion at the last *Tai-Ming* Council."

Tan leveled his stare. "The next council meeting, in three months. By then, all of my pieces will have fallen in place, and I will remonstrate the *Tianzi* to come to a resolution."

Hong grinned. Tan had effectively incriminated himself, and it was time to deliver the coup-de-grace. "I would like to remonstrate the *Tianzi*."

"That is not your place as Household Minister." Tan glowered at him.

Hong's grin curved into a toothy smirk. "But it would be, if I were Chief Minister."

"The only way for you to become Chief Minister..." Realization bloomed on Tan's face. He turned to the girl beside him. "Go, summon my guards!"

The sliding doors to the room crashed open, revealing six shadowy figures brandishing lacquered swords. Unlike the brash Young Lord Zheng, who had tried to win all the glory by uncovering one plot himself, Hong had gone to the *Tianzi* and secured the help of imperial agents.

"Yes, the position will be vacant," Hong said. "You, old friend, have revealed enough tonight to seal your fate."

"Ungrateful cur!" Tan bolted up in the tub. "You will not have the satisfaction of seeing my downfall, and I will not have to suffer witnessing a fishmonger's ascension to Chief Minister!" His eyes flashed, the infuriated look of a man whose lifelong dreams had just been quashed. He started to lunge across the tub toward Hong, arms outstretched as if he would choke the life out of him with his bare hands.

Yet before the Chief Minister had even had a chance to launch himself, the young woman beside him tangled up his legs with her own, and he floundered unceremoniously, face-first into the water.

She yanked his head out of the water by his hair, and placed him in an unrelenting choke hold. Tan clutched desperately at her slim arms, frantically trying to break her precise grip, fighting the inevitable shutting down of his brain.

Hong laughed to himself. He would never be allowed in this bath house again. It did not matter. It was time to start calling in the *Tai-Ming* lords' agreements to have him named Chief Minister.

CHAPTER 24:

Visions

Kaiya woke to the sound of frog trills and bird chirps outside her open window, still singing in orchestra with the ocean rumbling in the distance. She yawned. How refreshing! Never again would she take for granted a comfortable bed which didn't rock with the seas.

She blinked away the unladylike gunk from her eyes. Outside, the black of night faded to an inky blue at the horizon. Dawn, and with it, the Paladins' morning meditation, fast approached.

Kaiya jumped to her feet and flashed a disdainful eye at her travelling clothes, still inundated with the stench of brine and—she shuddered—sweat. With nothing else to wear, she threw them on nonetheless.

On the other bed, Jie might have been hibernating. The poor girl needed her sleep, and it would take time to wake her, anyway. Precious time. Scarlet lined the horizon.

Kaiya flung the door open and dashed out. She almost careened into a boy on the mezzanine, who nonchalantly sidestepped her just outside the door. Not even the Insolent Retainer could have reacted so fast.

Or could she? Back in the room, the half-elf's feet padded on the floor. Kaiya looked down at the boy.

Gayan, their guide from the day before, stared back with bright eyes. He placed a yellow flower in her hand. "No need to hurry, miss. The Oracle said you wished to speak to him. He sent me to meet you here."

"How did he know?" Kaiya stared at the boy.

He giggled. "He is the Oracle, after all. Come, follow me to morning meditation." He took her hand with a blush.

The touch might have been impertinent if he weren't so cute. She let him guide her down the steps, out the door and into the street.

Outside, Master Sabal towered over a dozen boys and girls, all dressed in white *kurtas*. "Good morning, Your Highness. I am glad you could join us." He pressed his hands together and the children followed suit.

Kaiya imitated the greeting. "Good morning, Master. Thank you for guiding me."

They set off at a brisk walk with Master Sabal leading. He didn't speak a word, and it seemed inappropriate to break the silence. Behind her, the entourage of children trailed like a line of ducklings, so unlike her usual retinue of handmaidens and imperial guards.

After a few minutes, they came to a life-sized statue of a handsome, middle-aged man in the center of the road. Sitting in a lotus position, he held a shattered *naga* sword in his left hand, out to the side with the tip down. Over his heart, his right hand cupped a fist-sized gemstone with countless facets, round at the bottom and tapered on top. The statue itself was made of a greyish blue metal and pulsated with the same energy as the island.

The children each added a yellow flower to the hill of yellow blossoms on the stone base. They then pressed their hands together and bobbed their heads, like pecking baby chicks.

"This is part of our morning ritual: to salute Acharya, the first Oracle." Master Sabal prompted her to add her own flower to the pile.

As she knelt to do so, she saw the shards of the sword at the figure's feet. "I did not think an Oracle would need a sword."

"In his younger years, when the chaotic aftermath of the Hellstorm and Long Winter still gripped Ayuri lands, Acharya led a band of *Bahaadur* mercenaries."

The term, to Kaiya's understanding, implied heroism—she'd always associated it with Prince Hardeep, who must have trained at this very island. A mercenary hardly evoked the image of honor. "He fought for money?"

Master Sabal smiled. "In desperate times, people do what they must."

Definitely not the image of heroism. Her lip twitched into a curl. "I guess I had a different understanding of the term *Bahaadur*."

"You speak our language well," he said, "but this word has a long history. It is a thousand years old, from when the elves taught the gifted among our ancestors to channel their *prana* life force into superhuman martial abilities. We used those skills to overthrow our orc masters during the War of Ancient Gods."

"Just as elves trained Cathayi girls how to evoke magic through the arts." Kaiya watched the children shuffle away.

He nodded. "The Cathayi and the Ayuri people share a similar history of consolidation. The *Bahaadur* played a major role in ours. For seven centuries after the War of Ancient Gods, tribal chieftains used them to carve out kingdoms; kings sought them out to build an empire; and the Emperor of the Ayuri organized them in the Hundred Years of War against the Arkothi Empire in the North. To our people, they were heroes."

"Even the mercenaries?" Kaiya pursed her lips.

Master Sabal leveled his gaze at her. "Our life experiences can help us transcend our origins. In his middle years, Acharya made a pilgrimage to

this island, where he received his first vision. It inspired him to systemize *Bahaadur* training methods and lay the groundwork for the Paladin Order. It brought peace to most of our lands."

Kaiya contemplated his words. Her own ancestor had reunified Hua, sometimes through brutal methods. Yet, historians described him as a heroic figure, and she accepted it without question. Who was she to judge the leaders who had lived through the upheaval of the Hellstorm?

Master Sabal gestured toward the *naga* shards. "Acharya took up residence here and became the first Oracle, living to be one hundred and twelve years old. He shattered his own sword, to represent the precedence of wisdom over martial skill. Our young students are reminded every morning. Speaking of which, look, they have already continued without us. Come, perhaps the current Oracle will tell you more if he sees fit."

It was a short distance to the Temple of the Moon. Cathayi books and scrolls had never described the famed temple itself. Expecting a magnificent structure of spires and domes characteristic of ancient Ayuri architecture, Kaiya was sorely disappointed. She found nothing but a broad stone-paved park facing a flat-topped mesa, with Ayudra hill's cliff face as a backdrop. A semicircle of several dozen megaliths surrounded the plaza. Above her was the open sky.

And the Iridescent Moon, now waning to half. It appeared larger than ever, its soap-bubble colors swirling more vibrantly than usual.

Picking her way through the couple hundred sitting Paladin students, knights, and masters, Kaiya found an open spot and settled into a lotus position. She looked up to contemplate the mesa.

It jutted up some fifty feet. A cone of pale blue light sprayed from the top, upwards toward the Iridescent Moon. This had been the core of the ancient Ayuri pyramid, which originally towered some four hundred feet above the low-lying delta in the shadows of Mount Ayudra.

Kaiya closed her eyes and listened. The Paladins breathed in unison, synchronizing with the wind in the trees, the twittering of birds, and the ocean waves in the distance. She joined her breath to theirs, the thump of her heart slowing to beat in time with the island.

She opened her eyes. Sounds flashed in a multitude of colors, coalescing with one another and painting fleeting images, both beautiful and grotesque. The unworldly pictures should've evoked emotional responses, yet the sounds lulled her into calm.

Minutes passed as seconds, and before Kaiya realized it, morning meditation had ended. The images slipped from her memory. Master Paladins dismissed students, sending them to their next tasks. The handful of Paladin knights talked among themselves.

Beside her, Jie rose to her feet, expression serene. When had she arrived? She'd never looked so calm.

Gayan beckoned. "Come, the Oracle awaits you. Your maid must wait here, though."

Kaiya nodded at Jie, giving her the tacit order to stay. Surprisingly, the Insolent Retainer actually complied.

The boy took Kaiya's hand and pulled her along through the dispersing throng of Paladins and students, toward the cliff behind the mesa.

They came to steps hewn into the cliff face and climbed. Halfway up, Kaiya peeked over the edge, only to hug the side the rest of the way. At the summit, a white-bearded man draped in long white robes sat in lotus position.

Looking at him, Kaiya bent, hands on knees, to catch her breath. Cathayi records placed his age at eighty-one, but he didn't seem a day over fifty. Yet when he gazed at her, his eyes bared her soul with an ancient wisdom.

She bowed low, respectful of the mysterious man's dignified aura. He was only the fourth Oracle in two hundred years, and there might not be another in her lifetime.

"Go back to your studies, young one," the Oracle said to Gayan. "Though I know you will be back soon." He laughed with a wink.

Once the boy departed, the Oracle stood with a swirl of his robes and motioned to a stone bridge that crossed over to the mesa. "Come with me, young lady of Cathay."

She followed him over the bridge, to the top of the rock column. From this new vantage point, she saw that the almost perfectly flat top of the rock was about thirty feet in diameter. In its center was a circular hole, the size of her fist, from which the ray of pale blue light emerged.

"You have questions," he said just as she was opening her mouth to speak.

"I feel as if the island is trying to speak to me."

He laughed. "When a Paladin apprentice finishes his service with his mentor, he often comes here to meditate and feel the vibrations of the world. What he experiences becomes a vision of his life's work. Throughout his career, he receives assignments from the Council of Elders of the Crystal Citadel in Vyara City, yet ultimately, it is the vision that guides his path."

"Where does the vision come from? The island?" She waved her hand from horizon to horizon.

He gestured for her to sit near the hole. "There are other places in the world where people have been documented to have received these types of visions. Around all of the pyramids. In the valleys of the two elven realms. Wild Turkey Island on the Kanin plateau. Around Haikou Island in your own country. Supposedly the Forbidden Island of the Eldaeri."

Sitting, she contained a scoff. "Then the Paladins place a lot of trust in architectural ruins, if their vision guides their life."

"What can we trust more than that which comes from within ourselves?" He sat down across from her, on the other side of the hole. The light cast his complexion in turquoise hues.

She must've looked the same to him. Her brows furrowed as she considered her words. Did the vision come from oneself, or from the location?

He smiled and placed his hand over his heart. "The vision is what separates the Ayuri Paladin from the Maduran Golden Scorpion, for power without guidance leads to a selfish sense of superiority and self-righteousness. Even worse is power which is manipulated by dogma. The Bovyan Knights, who inspired Acharya to form the Paladin Order, deferred to the Keepers of the Shrine of Geros, who interpret their Founder's last will. They are now the Teleri Imperial Army, whose very existence is sustained by institutional rape."

"Is the Paladin's vision so clear? I do not understand what I heard." She stared into the cone of blue light.

"Understanding the vision requires special training in harmonizing one's own life force to the vibrations of the world. All Paladins begin this study when they are children and practice as you saw them do today. Yet even with this life-long training, they oftentimes come to me to help them make sense of what they feel." He ran his hand through the light. "You said the island *spoke* to you, that you do not understand what you *heard*. This is different from how we describe what the Paladins *feel*. What exactly are you hearing?"

They were speaking a different language, it seemed. "All of the sounds around me are harmonized, from the beating of your heart, to my breathing, to the sounds of the ocean waves. It is a symphony of sounds. During the morning meditation, I could almost see these sounds as colors, coalescing into fleeting images."

His lips formed a perfect circle. "This is why you played your flute yesterday. You were answering the call of the island."

"How did you hear my flute from all the way over here?" She gawped at him.

He laughed again. "Have you not been listening? I did not *hear* it, I *felt* it. The notes you played merged with the vibrations of the world and came to me. So, you saw the sound as colors this morning?"

Kaiya nodded.

"Fascinating. I have heard that in ages past, your people could do astonishing things with the fine arts, whether it was music, dance, sculpture, or painting. This warrants further investigation by the Paladin Order." He reached across and took her hands in his, pulling them into the light. "Now, perhaps I can help you understand your images. Please, tell them to me."

Kaiya's skin tingled in the light. The forgotten images flooded back. The emotional content, lost in her meditative state, now engulfed her like a tidal wave. Tears blurred her vision. Choking with sobs, she crumpled over. "The most perfect lotus flower transformed into a venomous snake. The rest, I can't remember clearly. A plucked phoenix. Scorching sun. Shattered jade."

The Oracle's hands pulled her up. His eyebrows scrunched together. "Is that all you remember now?"

Kaiya nodded. "What does it mean?"

"It is your near future."

Such a terse answer, after all the loquacious stories! Kaiya straightened, trying to regain her composure. Her voice sounded desperate in her ears. "What is my not-so-near future, then?"

His lips and nose wiggled. "Let me preface my answer about the future by telling you about the past. Something that happened thirty-two years ago, not long after my mentor passed on and I became the Oracle."

Kaiya nodded. If nothing else came from this visit, at least she would get a history lesson.

"The dragon Avarax, who had disappeared from history during the War of Ancient Gods a thousand years before, suddenly reappeared and descended upon the Temple of the Moon. He demanded the Lotus Crystal, which hovered above the Font." The Oracle waved at the hole in the ground, from which the light sprayed out.

Kaiya shuddered. Avarax! He ruled from his mountain lair in the Dragonlands; the mere threat of his fiery breath kept his subjects cowed. With so many of their numbers deployed at the border with Ayuri lands, the Paladins hadn't been able to assist Prince Hardeep's Ankira when Madura invaded.

The Oracle bowed his head, sending his white hair and beard cascading. "Many Paladins died in its defense that day. He threatened to immolate the island with his breath. I surrendered the precious stone and he left. Ever since then, Paladin students have needed deeper training to gain a more complete picture of their visions. A beginner cannot possibly sense much, let alone hold on to what he felt."

Was that why she couldn't remember the vision clearly? Did she need more training? Kaiya prompted him with a tilt of her chin.

The Oracle stroked his beard. "What I mean is, in order to see further into your future, you would either need more training, or the Lotus Crystal would need to be returned to its rightful place over the Font."

"So you cannot tell me anything?"

The Oracle shook his head. "I never tell, just guide."

She bowed. "Then guide me, please."

"I believe the lotus flower represents something you treasure. Its transformation into a snake could mean that it becomes something onerous. Or perhaps it never was what you thought."

The Oracle's *guidance* seemed just as perplexing as the image itself. Kaiya conjured her most gracious smile and bowed. "Thank you."

He gazed at her. "Master Sabal will be setting off for Vyara City later today to greet some young Paladin recruits. I will see to it that he takes the same skiff as you, and that he teaches you a simple exercise to help you feel—or hear—the vibrations of the universe. When you are ready, come again and meditate with us. Perhaps then you will get a deeper insight into your future." Without looking back, he gestured toward the bridge. "Ah, here is Gayan to deliver some news."

Kaiya glanced past the Oracle. The boy hurried across the bridge on his short legs. He stopped just short of the mesa. "Master, the Dragon—"

"—is sending an envoy to Vyara City."

The boy nodded. "The Council of Elders wants to—"

"—know if I will take my seat and greet the envoy with them. Young Gayan, surely even without your gift of foresight, you know what my answer will be. What it has always been." He then turned to Kaiya. "Though they do not yet know, the council will be asking you to meet the Dragon's envoy."

CHAPTER 25:

Token from Ayudra

To Kaiya's ears, even the hammering from the dwarven smithy in the distance seemed to beat in tune with all of Ayudra's other sounds. She regarded the stone building with a dubious eye. According to the Oracle, the Blackhammer dwarf clan would help her find a focus—a tie to the energy of Ayudra.

Cross-armed, Jie tapped her toe. Apparently, she agreed it wasn't worth the delay.

Two teenage Ayuri, a boy and a girl, sat outside sharpening their *nagas*. Beyond them, the stone building had an open front, allowing a clear view of the two dwarves in goggles and leather aprons.

Sparks flew as a dwarf with rust-colored hair and beard struck a blue-hot metal rod with a large hammer. A wrinkled, white-bearded dwarf held and flipped the rod over an anvil with a pair of tongs. They both hummed what sounded like a marching tune, the beat set to their hammering.

Kaiya gasped. Dwarves were famous for their inventiveness and craftsmanship, not their music. The sound was beautiful. But what were they making?

"Paladin *nagas*," Gayan yelled over the pounding, answering her unasked question. He waved at the younger dwarf, who paused and lifted his goggles.

Tugging off his gloves, the dwarf stomped over. He stood a head shorter than her, nearly as tall as Jie. Soot covered his face, except where the goggles had protected his eyes. He thumped his chest with his fist. "Ashler Blackhammer, at yer service, lass," he said in Arkothi. "Or should I say, Yer 'ighness?"

Even a dwarf she'd never seen before recognized her. Kaiya returned his salute, bringing her fist to her chest. "Well met, Master Blackhammer," she spoke in the manner of the North.

He favored her with irises as black as coal. "So up the hill we go, t'fetch ye a rock of istrium alloy."

"A rock?" She raised an eyebrow at Gayan.

The boy nodded. "To make your focus."

Master Blackhammer tilted his chin to the elder dwarf and wiped his hands on his apron. He then led them down the street.

At the flower-covered statue of Acharya, they turned right off the main road and onto a side street that ran through the three-hundred-year-old ruins of ancient Ayudra.

Kaiya shuddered. Nothing in Hua spoke of the Hellstorm like the crumbling buildings and rubble-strewn streets before her. A city built over seven hundred years, reduced to ruins in just a single night. Hundreds of thousands of unfortunate souls, immolated or drowned.

Following a cleared path through the debris, they circled the Temple of the Moon at a distance and began the gentle ascent onto the hill.

The dwarf raked an open hand over the land. "Keep yer eyes open fer somethin' that catches yer fancy, lass." He then started to hum, continuing his earlier war song. Every now and then, he would pick up a stone and thrust it into a coarse cloth bag.

Bewildered, Kaiya looked around at the heap of blue-grey shards scattered as far as the eye could see. She bent over and picked up a smooth pebble.

The dwarf laughed. "That's just a rock, lass."

Kaiya held him in her gaze. "What am I searching for?"

"A rock ye kin feel belongs to ye."

Gayan's head bobbed several times. "When the Hellstorm obliterated Mount Ayudra, the istrium dust fused with iron deposits. Paladin students come here to find a piece that *feels* right to them, and the Blackhammers incorporate that into a *naga*. Rumor has it a Golden Scorpion melts his *naga* sword to make his mask to symbolize their break from the order. Still, it's their connection to the spiritual home of the *Bahaadur*. The Oracle wanted you to have a tie as well."

Master Blackhammer raised a bushy eyebrow at Gayan. "Ye sure she kin do it? She's got no trainin' in yer meditation."

The boy nodded enthusiastically and the dwarf shrugged, going back to his humming.

"Sing," Jie said. "Just like Master Blackhammer's hum. The Paladins *feel*, you *hear*."

The suggestion was as good as any. With a deep breath, Kaiya banished impatience and uncertainties from her mind. She raised her voice in song, letting the orchestra of the island guide her as she improvised.

Around her, shards lit up in soft blue light.

The dwarf stared at her, eyes wide. The boy just grinned ear-to-ear.

Among all the scattered rocks, a cherry-sized stone sang back to her. Kaiya knelt down and picked it up. Its coldness gave the impression of a stream infused with snowmelt.

"That's yer stone, lass," the dwarf said. "Give it t'me, and I'll craft a nice ring for ya. Come t'my uncle's forge next time ye visit so ye kin sing t'it again. Yon voice o'yers will work much better than a pair'o dwarves a'hummin'."

The next time she visited, he said. If the Oracle's predictions were true, a lot would be happening between then and now.

CHAPTER 26:

Song of Swords

The wide sailing barge cut through the Shallowsea's mangrove-dotted expanse, sailing farther and farther away from Ayudra. As the island disappeared in the distance, Kaiya needed to focus harder to perceive the soft wind in the mangrove branches singing in concert with the ripples of the placid waters.

"Concentrate!" Master Sabal's tone had become strict after leaving behind his role as guide and taking up the mantle of mentor. "You can feel, and to some extent control, the vibrations of the world. You must now learn to surrender to them. You laugh, half-elf?"

Kaiya opened her eyes and whipped her head around.

Jie covered her mouth with a hand. "Sorry, Master. The way you spoke brought visions of one of my teachers."

The master Paladin pursed his lips. "I hope he was handsome."

Jie grinned. "She was."

His eyebrows clashed together as he glared at the Insolent Retainer. "You want to challenge my *naga* skills. You have, since the day we met. Well, let us have at it. I forewarn you, you will get wet."

Kaiya stared from Jie back to the master. The kind man from just a couple of days before was nowhere to be found on this barge. In his place, a strict teacher stood ready to tongue-lash her each time she failed to *feel* the so-called vibrations of the world. Now, she stood forgotten as he turned his ire toward Jie.

The *Moquan* girl placed her right fist in her left palm. A snap of her wrists brought a knife into each hand. "Please teach me."

Kaiya twirled a lock of her hair. The Hua politeness before a duel might be lost in translation.

The master pressed his palms together and then drew his *naga*. Made of a bluish-grey metal, the single-edged broadsword had a wide tip and no guard. "After y—"

Jie lunged at him with a torrent of slashes. The older man avoided each one with subtle body shifts before his *naga* whistled toward her in a single horizontal cut. It glowed with a blue tinge.

She barely dodged the blow by jumping backward; but the Paladin pressed the attack. Her next step back sent her over the edge of the barge, flipping head-over-heels into the sea.

Water sprayed upwards with a loud splash. Kaiya flinched. It had all happened so fast. Her ears had captured it all, but her eyes still processed the image.

"You felt it! Good!" The Paladin beamed at her. He then looked toward where Jie had gone overboard. "Not bad on your part either, half-elf."

The imperial guards rushed to the edge. Jie's fingers gripped the rim while she vigorously kicked up water.

Master Sabal laughed. "Try standing, girl. There is a reason we call it the Shallowsea."

The babbling water quieted and Jie's head popped up. Only her pony tail was wet. "It's just waist-high!"

"Yes," the master said. "Just below the brackish waters lie the fertile flood plains that once made up the heart of the Ayuri Empire. Most of the Shallowsea's depth is knee-height. The barge captains follow the old river beds, which rarely go deeper than the height of a man."

Ma Jun helped Jie back on board. Wet clothes clung to her lithe form, outlining several small weapons and tools.

Master Sabal turned to Kaiya. "What you saw me do, Your Highness, is what happens when you surrender to the vibrations of the world. You move—not with intention, but because you are moved. Combat slows down in your mind's eye, and your own motions become subconscious."

Kaiya nodded, even if it didn't make sense. Her music teachers always emphasized the power of intent...though Lord Xu had mentioned something about improvisation before.

"You do not believe me." He motioned for the guards. "You three, attack me."

Xu Zhan whipped his short sword out, ready to take up the challenge. His enthusiasm for fighting might get him killed one day.

Zhao Yue, on the other hand, responded cautiously. He looked over the boat, then back. "When you send us for a swim, I am afraid the ghosts of the millions who died in the Hellstorm will drag us under."

Master Sabal harrumphed. "There are no ghosts. The energies of the living join the vibrations of the universe for a time, only to be reborn and die again. The cycle has repeated itself many times since the Hellstorm. Now draw your weapons. Fight as if you are defending your princess."

As if defending her? Zhao Yue and Ma Jun turned to her, and Kaiya nodded in silent authorization. Hopefully, they would be careful.

The two joined the more enthusiastic Xu Zhan. They saluted with right fists in left palms, and then bared their blades.

The Paladin pressed his hands together. "Now come at me."

The three imperial guards fanned out as much as the boat would allow, interposing themselves between the Paladin and her. On Ma Jun's shout, they engaged Master Sabal in a synchronized attack that very few would escape alive, let alone unscathed.

The master Paladin whirled in a blur among their buzzing swords. His deadly dance was reminiscent of when Lord Xu had approached her through a cordon of imperial guards on the castle wall years before.

Unable to track his movements, she turned her ear to listen. Jie appeared in her line of sight. The *Moquan*'s eyes darted back and forth, tapered ears twitching as she watched the melee.

The noises were unlike those of any other duel Kaiya had witnessed. The swishing of blades and bodies through the air replaced the typical clinks and clanks of metal on metal.

When the sound stopped, Master Sabal's presence radiated next to her. She met his solemn gaze.

"Your guards fight in harmony with each other," he said. "Their form is intricately choreographed, with excellent changes according to situation. Nonetheless, it needs to harmonize with the vibrations of the world if they are to have a chance of defeating a seasoned Paladin."

The three all sank to one knee, heads bowed, swords proffered to her. "We have failed you, *Dian-xia*. If it is your command—"

Kaiya waved them into silence, even as she gazed at Master Sabal. The sounds of the fight replayed in her ears, giving clarity to the blur of motion.

He narrowed his eyes. "Do not just *feel*. Be *moved*."

Kaiya sighed. She'd never felt so inadequate, even as an awkward tween pretending to be Perfect Princess. "I will try."

He jabbed a finger at her. "*Trying* is the first step to failure. Your conscious mind cannot *be moved*."

"I will meditate on it more." She bowed.

The master smiled. "Good. You, handmaiden, get some dry clothes or you will catch a cold."

The journey across the Shallowsea took three days, giving Jie plenty of time to watch and listen to the lessons meant for the princess. It gave her reason to ignore the badgering old elf wizard Ayana, whom Prince Aelward had sent along as extra protection.

At times, Jie would convince one of the imperial guards to play with her at the other end of the skiff, in the games they excelled at.

As much as Black Lotus clansmen mocked the imperial guards behind their backs, the only *Moquan* who could go toe-to-toe with one in a swordfight was Tian. She was certainly no match for an imperial guard in a *fair* fight. Which was why she rarely fought fair.

These days, however, with Master Sabal's lessons to the princess taken to heart, Jie refrained from tricks and found herself performing better and better with each successive loss. The master, whose line of sight was blocked by the center cabins from his side of the deck, shouldn't have been able to witness the duels. Nonetheless, he would tell her almost exactly how a fight had unfolded and where she'd gone wrong.

In the afternoon of the third day, she and Chen Xin squared off against each other in a light drizzle. After returning her salute, he surged forward with a quick stab of his curved short sword. She sidestepped and cut toward his hand with a knife, but he raised his weapon to parry.

A stray clump of seaweed on deck begged to be kicked into Chen's face, but that wouldn't be fair. She followed through with a thrust of her other knife. He parried that blow as well and swept his blade around. She stepped back out of reach and sank into a defensive stance.

He was fast, even though he approached middle years for a human.

"Feel his intention," Ayana said, uninvited.

Jie turned to spit out a retort, just as Chen Xin pressed his attack with a lethal combination of slashes. In that second of inattention, she knew everything he planned. His sword seemed to move through honey, and it took little effort to avoid.

She moved in to deliver the winning blow when he paused and looked toward the bow of the ship. She followed his gaze to a sparkle on the horizon.

"The Paladins' Crystal Citadel," Ayana said, "on Vyara City's central hilltop."

Hair matted with sweat, Chen Xin backed away. He put his fist into his palm and grinned. "We'll call it a draw."

She would've won. Nonetheless, Jie ignored him and instead squinted to see a thin line of land in the distance, separating the pale blue sky from the dark green sea. Yet even her sharp elven sight couldn't make out any detail of the famous city-state.

Vyara City intrigued her not for its famous network of beautiful canals, nor for its importance as home to the Paladin Order. Rather, the city played prominently in recent Black Lotus history, when on a mission a year before her birth, one of three young *Moquan* masters perished while retrieving a secret artifact for the *Tianzi*. The other two died within the year; and the next generation of *Moquan* conjectured fanciful theories of how the mysterious artifact had been cursed.

The names of the three had been expunged from the monastery records, and all adepts who knew the young masters were forbidden to speak of the mission or their real names. Master Yan had gone so far as to block off the memory of some *Moquan* with the *Tiger's Eye* technique. In tales of their other exploits, the three deceased masters were known by the code names Beauty, Surgeon, and Architect.

Though the ill-fated mission had occurred before her birth, it always piqued Jie's interest. If circumstances permitted, she would investigate the three-decade-old cold case. Perhaps she could find someone in Vyara City, not bound by the *Moquan* rules of secrecy, who might tell her more.

CHAPTER 27:

A Hot Welcome

A barrage of sound assaulted Kaiya's ears as the barge approached the wharfs, which reached far into the waters like several dozen spindly fingers. Seagulls screeched in lazy circles above, occasionally swooping in to steal fishermen's daily catches. Sailors joked and cursed as their barges jockeyed for docking positions. Even the din emanating from the city itself echoed over the water. If Jiangkou Port had been cacophonous, the Hua language didn't have a word to describe the level of noise and chaos of Vyara City's harbor. She rubbed her ears.

Master Sabal laughed. "You will find no noisier place on Tivaralan than early morning Vyara City."

A smile! It befit him better than the gruff role of teacher. Kaiya nodded in time with the gently rocking boat. Jie edged up next to her.

Master Sabal gestured toward the skyline. "Vyara City was already quite a commercial center before the Hellstorm. Located at the confluence of two great rivers, where ocean-going vessels could no longer pass upstream, it prospered as a transit point between the river barges upstream and the sailing ships downstream. In one night, the ocean came all the way to its doorstep and transformed it into a peninsular seaport."

Kaiya tried picturing the city as an inland river city, but the noise addled her imagination.

"Concentrate, young one." The teacher's tone returned, if only for a second. He pointed to other cityscapes in the distance. "When smaller nation states emerged from the ashes of the Ayuri Empire, they established national capitals there, there, and way over there. Each is less than an hour's ferry ride from Vyara's harbor. That is how it supplanted Ayudra as the economic and cultural heart of our people."

Grasping the bulwark, Kaiya looked at the other cities before scanning Vyara's waterfront. Block-shaped, flat-roofed shops, warehouses, and trading offices stretched as far as the eye could see, broken only by canals going inland. People crowded the streets, yelling and gesticulating as they went about their business. The noise rose to a roar as their barge docked. Her heart rattled at the dissonance. Reading about Tivaralan's largest city was so different from experiencing it.

She disembarked, followed by her guards. Humid heat rolled over her almost as soon as her foot touched the quay. Paintings did the city little justice. A hill rose in the background. A single road spiraled its way up the slope, lined by dozens of white mansions with graceful columns and arches, and topped by elegant domes, spires, and minarets. At the very top, the Paladins' Crystal Citadel sparkled in the morning sun.

If the Oracle truly knew the future, Kaiya would be visiting the citadel soon enough. "Why do the Paladin elders meet here, instead of Ayudra Island?"

"Ayudra may be the spirit of the Paladin Order, but Vyara City is its brain. It is in the center of Ayuri lands, within a week's travel of every nation within the Paladins' mandate." Master Sabal gestured to the dock. "Here is where we part ways,

Your Highness. It has been a pleasure. I hope our paths cross again."

Hopefully. With the imperial guards drawing up around her, Kaiya pressed her palms together and bowed her head. "Thank you for teaching me, Master."

He returned the gesture and disappeared into the crowds.

Without the foreign ministry official who was supposed to have met up with them on Ayudra, they were on their own. Kaiya drew her hood up, despite the stifling heat.

Jie's shrill voice answered her thoughts. "Shall we go to our embassy?"

"That would be the best course of action," Chen Xin added. "Where is it?"

All eyes turned to Ayana, who shrugged. "It is *your* embassy."

Jie sucked on her lower lip, and then pointed. "Near the hill. We could probably take a canal boat and avoid the masses."

Not another boat. Kaiya shuddered. Her feet were just getting used to solid ground after so many days at sea. People jammed the canal boat quays, making the proposition even less appealing. "We shall walk, since we know the general direction."

Despite their prior instructions, her imperial guards all knelt, fists to the ground.

Jie hissed. "On your feet, dunderheads! Don't betray the princess' identity!"

The men tentatively rose, heads bowed. So much for secrecy.

They set off toward the hill, pushing their way through the mass of humanity. Unlike the unified sounds on Ayudra Island, Vyara City was a disjointed screaming of Ayuri and Arkothi languages, with several other tongues mixed in.

Kaiya's mind spun. Countless light-brown skinned Ayuri people negotiated trade terms with the many darker-toned Levanthi. A handful of fairer Nothori, Estomari, and Arkothi from the North mixed in with the crowd as well. The heavy scent of sweat, fish, and curry powder joined in with the bewildering sights and sounds to overwhelm her senses.

It didn't help being bumped and jostled by people hurrying by, despite the imperial guards trying to provide a shield. Jie clasped her hand, like a mother keeping hold of her frightened young child.

A press of people pushed back from the middle of the streets, shoving her against the walls of a building. A firm hand rested on her shoulder, providing a comforting warmth. She turned to see Ayana looking back at her with knitted eyebrows. Heat flushed Kaiya's cheeks. This three-hundred-year-old survivor of the Hellstorm was handling the crowds better than she.

"Make way, make way." A voice shouted in Ayuri and accented Arkothi, carrying above the quieting crowds.

Kaiya pouted. Had they come with the rest of the diplomatic staff from the *Golden Phoenix*, they would've enjoyed the privilege of right-of-way, instead of being swept along in the tide of people. She craned her neck to see above bodies and heads. Rust-red banners emblazoned with a golden scorpion fluttered in her line of sight.

The Ayuri Kingdom of Madura. The rogue nation behind the attacks in Huajing. The ones who had invaded and occupied Prince Hardeep's homeland of Ankira. She was supposed to meet with them the next day, and perhaps the one riding on the litter was her counterpart.

"Make way, make way for Prince Dhananad of the Kingdom of Madura!" the crier yelled again.

Copper coins rained from above, flung from the procession. Kaiya raised her hands to protect her face, but Li Wei snatched one out of the air. He handed it to her, revealing a scorpion stamped on one side.

She flipped it over. A faded image looked back at her. Despite the lack of clarity, there was something unsettlingly familiar about it.

Jie recognized the name Dhananad as a piece of the thirty-two-year-old puzzle—a survivor of the *Moquan* plot devised by the famed Architect in their quest to retrieve a secret artifact. She left the princess' side, slipping through the wall of people to reach the front.

The procession stretched half a city block, with a crier at the fore, throwing coins into the crowds. Several dozen soldiers and ministers wearing rust-red *kurtas* followed, surrounding a gold-cloth litter.

Jie snorted. Such ostentatiousness. Still, it didn't begin to compare to the man in his late thirties reclined on his side in the litter. Long dark hair hung loosely about his shoulders, merging with a pointed beard to frame a somewhat handsome face. Embroidered with gold borders, his rich burgundy robes brought out his light-brown complexion. A curved *talwar* sword dangled from his left hip.

At the side of the litter, standing almost a head above the other guards, marched six imposing men, all fair-skinned and fair-haired. Chainmail jingled beneath black tunics with gold-embroidered collars. A yellow sun was embroidered onto each left breast, and straight longswords hung from their sides.

Bovyans: the rulers and soldiers of the Teleri Empire. Jie sucked on her lower lip. After her last mission, she'd never expected—or wanted—to see one of those brutes again. Descended from the mortal son of their Sun God, the all-male race had devolved into conquering thugs and gang rapists.

One beggar apparently didn't know of their reputation. He stepped toward the litter with an open palm, only to be launched back into crowd with a nonchalant shove of a meaty Bovyan hand.

Jie pulled up her hood and pushed back through one rank of spectators, then knelt to look between the people in front of her.

Interspersed with the Bovyans marched four smaller Ayuri humans. Their grace reminded her of the Paladins' fluidity; but instead of white, they wore open-faced surcoats in a light bronze tone with intricate borders. Dark bronze-colored *kurtas* peeked out from underneath the surcoats. Most distinctive were their featureless masks, made of a bluish-grey metal. The *nagas* at their sides ended in the shape of a scorpion sting.

Maduran Scorpions.

Real ones.

Body language alone suggested they were more skilled than the three incompetents in Peng's teahouse. The latter's masks had been cheap facsimiles of the ones she saw now. Who were those three, and who had sent them, if not Madura? And as castoff Paladins, how deadly was a true Golden Scorpion?

After the procession passed, the crowds thinned enough to provide some breathing room. Jie headed back to where she'd left the others.

Chen Xin's gaze was locked on the princess, his expression contorted with concern. "The princess looks pale. We should get out of this crowded area."

It was a sound idea. There'd been a less busy side-street not far back, and Jie beckoned them. "Follow me. It's only a couple minutes' walk until things clear up."

"If we aren't crushed to death first," muttered Li Wei.

The suggestion proved to be good. They made their way northeast toward the city center, with the density of moving bodies thinning the further they travelled from the docks.

Before long, Chen Xin called for a halt. He was looking at the princess again. He'd served her since she was a child, and even if all the imperial guards adored her, his paternal affection showed in small gestures like this. "Do not worry, *Dian-xia*. Once we reach the embassy, we should enjoy the same right of way afforded other dignitaries. We won't have to wade through the masses."

The princess afforded him a wan smile. It hid whatever silly ideas might be bouncing around in her pretty head.

Jie could guess, though. The princess' expression was similar to when they had walked through the castle's escape tunnel. Jie snorted, and then scanned the area to reorient herself.

White block buildings rose two stories above them, their first floors being storefronts. The Crystal Citadel still glittered from the hilltop, serving as a landmark. The Iridescent Moon hung high and to the southwest.

Ma Jun pointed northeast. "I believe our embassy is only half an hour away on foot."

Li Wei shook his head. "The last time we trusted you with directions—"

Chen Xin shot Li Wei a glance, and all the guards chuckled. Perhaps they had shared some misadventure in the Floating World. Or maybe they were just being men.

Though showing no signs of fatigue in her old age, Ayana threw her hands up. "Have any of you been here before?"

Ma Jun grinned. "If we get lost, *you* can ask for directions. Now, with the princess' permission, I will lead the way."

Just like a man. For now, Jie would have to trust Ma Jun with directions. Her skillset was better used for another problem.

Someone was following them.

CHAPTER 28:

Stalker in the Shadows

Humidity hung in Kaiya's lungs and her heart pounded in her ears as they headed from the docks toward the embassy. Throughout her life, she'd always been shielded from the masses—metaphorically by Hua conventions toward their royalty, physically by a line of imperial guards. She was just about wilting from the close quarters and incessant noise. Yet she put on her best face, mortified by the idea of her people seeing her as anything less than a Perfect Princess.

To hide her fatigue, she lifted her chin and lengthened her stride. If she was no longer a living metaphor for nonchalant grace, let them remember her gritty determination. Kaiya channeled her younger self, envisioning the inconvenience as one of the imaginary adventures she had shared with her childhood friend, Tian. A smile tugged at her lips.

With Ma Jun ostensibly in the lead, they stuck to the main streets, crossing several arched bridges which spanned the numerous canals. She observed the Ayuri people going about their daily lives and stole glances at stands outside storefronts.

Women picked through fruits of exotic colors and shapes lying perfectly stacked in bins, making her wonder about their flavor and texture. Young ladies ran their hands through multicolored *sari* dresses that hung from poles, piquing her imagination. How beautiful she'd look in a dress like that! Perhaps this negotiating trip wouldn't be so bad, after all.

On a couple of occasions, Paladins walked by, marked by their white *kurtas* with gold embroidery on the cuffs and collar, and the curved *naga* sword hanging at their side. They paid the Hua no mind.

Bins of deep green tea leaves lined the front of one store, and a dark trail of smoke billowed from its open door. The merchant standing by the entrance beckoned them in. "Come in, come in! Take a puff of the finest gooseweed you will find in all of the Ayuri Confederation."

Despite their haste, Kaiya approached, curiosity getting the better of her. The dried weed's curled appearance and sweet aroma seemed almost identical to the leaves from the tea shrubs on Jade Mountain, picked by the nuns of Praise Moon Temple for the Imperial Family.

"Do you drink this?"

The man's eyes widened. "No, no. It will kill a man's seed. No. It is for smoking. Very rich flavor, and incomparably relaxing! Come in and try it!"

Images of emaciated addicts straggling out of opium dens formed in her mind. With a bow, Kaiya backed away.

"Please, try!" The man moved to follow, motioning toward her.

Hands on sword hilts, Chen Xin and Li Wei formed a wall between them.

Scowling, the merchant raised his hands and retreated several steps. "Who do you think you are, the Queen of Vadara? Don't smoke, then!"

Kaiya glanced back at him before they resumed their walk. He stood halfway inside the store, talking to someone while pointing in their direction. It was too early in the day to make an enemy.

Almost three-quarters of the way to the Hua embassy, Jie inserted herself between Kaiya and Chen Xin. "Keep walking, don't look back, don't act surprised," she whispered in the Hua language. "We are being followed, by someone who knows how to follow without being noticed."

"*You* noticed him." Chen Xin kept his attention forward, but his tone carried an audible smirk.

Jie grinned. "You should know I'm better than he is. He is trailing about a hundred feet behind us, on the other side of the road, trying to keep lots of other people between us. A large Ayuri man wearing a *dhoti* skirt and shawl."

Kaiya fought the urge to look back, and twirled a lock of her hair instead. Someone sent by the scorned gooseweed merchant, perhaps.

Chen Xin nodded. "This is a good time to take a break." He opened his pack and drew out a waterskin, which he offered to Ma Jun. He whispered a warning about the stalker. Ma Jun passed both canteen and message to Li Wei.

Jie sucked on her lower lip. "I am going to find out why he is following us."

"How do you plan on doing that?" Kaiya raised an eyebrow.

The half-elf pointed down the street. "Keep walking and turn onto a quiet side street. In the meantime, I will go back to the last fruit seller, let him pass me, then tail *him.*"

Li Wei coughed. "That seems very elementary. Are you sure he will fall for it?"

Jie shrugged. "Only one way to find out. If it doesn't work, at least he'll stop following us."

Kaiya played with her hair. "Very well. Proceed as you see fit. Meet us at the embassy if we get separated."

Jie bobbed her head and turned back. So cavalier. The half-elf's confidence bordered on foolhardiness.

From the corner of her eye, Jie watched the spy's reflection in a storefront window as they passed each other on opposite sides of the street.

He continued walking with almost admirable stalking skills.

When she reached the fruit store, she took her time choosing a perfect mango from the stands out front, all the while keeping an eye on the interloper. It was time to practice her Ayuri.

And the fine art of haggling.

She scrunched her nose and held a fresh mango up to the vendor. "How much for this rotten one?"

"Rotten?" The man placed his hand on his chest. "It was just picked today. You cannot get any fresher. Ten copper rupayas."

"Ten?" Jie feigned outrage. "This fetid piece of slime would only bring three coppers in Cathay."

"But you can't get it in Cathay," the vendor said with a sly grin. "However, the gods favor the magnanimous. I offer it to you for eight."

Jie spat. "Magnanimous is five. Eight is waterway robbery."

The man wagged a finger at her. "My boy fell down from the tree picking this very mango this morning, and broke his leg. I need at least seven to pay the doctor, or he will never walk again."

A bare-chested boy of about ten skipped out of the door, smiling. "Mother wants me to run to the South Market to pay the mango farm's distributor."

The man's face flushed red. "Did I tell you I have two sons? Six coppers, no less."

Smiling victoriously, Jie handed him an Ayuri silver rupiya, worth ten coppers. Before the man reached into his purse to make change, the spy had almost reached the side street where the princess had turned. Jie hurried after him, mango in hand but change forgotten.

In the game of espionage and counterespionage, the man was overmatched. Jie had learned his trailing and stalking techniques years before, and her smaller size allowed her to melt into the crowds.

Before turning the corner, he looked back toward the fruit seller. His eyes widened as he scanned the crowd. Though his gaze swept over her several times, he didn't seem to have noticed her. He ducked into the alley.

Time to sneak up behind him and choke him into unconsciousness. Jie dashed to the alley and turned the corner.

The man waited there, curved dagger brandished in an underhand grip. He seemed even larger up close, with broad shoulders and square features. Huge for an Ayuri, small for a Bovyan. Just like the renegade *Moquan* clan members in Cathay; just like the operatives she'd fought in Eldaeri lands.

Jie took a few steps back, hands raised. "Why are you following us?"

The man snarled and slashed down at her.

Jie jumped out of range, and then tossed the mango up in a high arc.

His eyes tracked the fruit, and in that instant, she darted in and yanked the *dhoti* skirt from his waist.

All he wore underneath was a loincloth. A well-bred Hua lady would've averted her eyes, but Jie wasn't well-bred. Instead, she twisted the rectangular cloth into a rat-tail as the man recovered from his initial embarrassment.

His cheeks red, he stabbed at her again.

She spun around him, catching his arm in the cloth. In a split-second she was behind him, and yanked so the blade was now pinned against his throat. With another twist, she wrapped one end of the cloth around his free hand and squeezed tight, while stepping into his knee.

He buckled to the ground.

"Now, let's try again," she said in his ear. "Who are you?"

His voice trembled. "I'm sorry, miss. Just a petty thief, casing some unsuspecting victims."

Jie gave the cloth a slight tug and the blade nicked his chin. "I tried to shave my brother's beard like this once, but I ended up rearranging his face. I'm not stupid. Thieves don't choose groups of people to rob."

"Jie!" The princess approached from around the corner, the imperial guards close on her heels. "There is no need to torture him," she said in the Hua tongue, "even if he is a spy."

"Forgive me, mistress," Jie answered in Ayuri, to make sure he understood the misinformation she was about to feed him. Then again, *mistress* tasted kind of funny compared to *Dian-xia*. "He won't speak unless given the right encouragement."

Ayana stepped forward and looked the man over. "Teleri Nightblade. They've been trained in your people's art of spying and assassination, and played an instrumental role in the Teleri Empire's invasion of Eldaeri lands."

Jie cocked her head. So the students of the renegade *Moquan* she'd tracked through Eldaeri lands and the Teleri Empire had a name…if the old elf was right.

Chen Xin frowned. "He's a little short for a Bovyan."

"He's Ayuri." Xu Zhan pointed at the man. "Bovyans aren't so dark-skinned."

Ayana shook her head. "No, Bovyans are all male, and they will always look like their mother's race. This one's mother was undoubtedly some unfortunate Ayuri or Levanthi woman." She glared at the man and said, "But you never knew your mother, did you? No Bovyan ever does, because of your despicable rape and breeding programs."

The man spat. "My mother is the Teleri Empire. In time, it will be your mother as well." With a flick of his wrist, he tried to slash his own throat.

Jie jerked part of the cloth so that he missed completely. She launched her knee into his back, right between the shoulder blades, knocking the wind out of him and driving his face into the ground.

"Jie!" The princess scowled at her.

"Sorry, mistress," Jie said without the least amount of sincerity. She twisted the man's dagger out of his hands. "But we had better do something about him."

Zhao Yue pointed. "Bystanders are gathering at intersection to the alley. It would not be good if they called the Paladins to enforce the law here."

Jie withdrew a vial from the folds of her robe and dabbed it on her wrist. A fruity smell almost like perfume wafted through the air.

The princess raised an eyebrow. "What is that?"

Jie wiped her wrist across the back of the Nightblade's neck as he struggled. "It is a contact toxin made from several secret plants. This combination will induce a state of euphoric intoxication in human males."

The imperial guards took two steps back. The spy wriggled for a couple of seconds before relaxing.

Chuckling, Jie loosened the cloth. "Come on, big boy, up on to your feet."

With a ridiculous grin, the spy eased himself into a sitting position.

"Why were you following us?" The princess flashed that infuriatingly alluring smile.

He just smiled back for a moment. "You are such a pretty lady! How about you join me for a drink of delicious Ayuri *thara*."

Jie frowned, lifting her hand to backhand him, but the princess' preemptive lip pursing stopped her. "The toxin is not truth serum. But we can safely leave him here without fear he'll follow."

Ayana shot a reproachful glance at Jie. "I can make him talk without having to resort to barbaric means or unreliable coercion." Chanting in the flowery language of elven magic, she waved a hand over the man's face.

"You could have said so sooner," Jie mumbled under her breath.

The Teleri's ridiculous grin broadened even wider. "My friends! Shall we have that drink now?"

Ayana beamed. "Not now, dear friend. My name is Aya. What is yours?"

"Toran."

"So Toran, could you tell me why you were trailing us?"

"Well, Grandma," he started, drawing a look of ire from the elf, "we had heard there might be some Cathayi dignitaries coming through." He nodded amiably at the rest of the party. "And they might be trying to strike some sort of deal with the Madurans. Our embassy staff needs to know what that deal is, because, well, you know, the Madurans are our friends. We've been staking out the waterfront, keeping an eye on all of the passenger barges coming in."

"We? How many of you are watching the docks? How many staff in the Teleri embassy?" Ayana asked. Whatever else Jie thought about elves, at least Ayana knew what questions to ask.

"Six of us scouring the docks. Eighty-some people working in the embassy."

Ayana smiled at him. "Thanks, dear friend. Now why don't you run along back to your embassy? And just for old time's sake, tell them that we are just merchants."

Toran pouted. Nonetheless, he stood and moped off, head hanging.

Jie sighed. "You should have had him spy for us."

Ayana shook her head. "A charm spell can convince someone to do something they would not ordinarily consider, but it's hard to change their true nature. I didn't want to test the limits. We may still be able to find out more through him if we cross paths again."

Chen Xin watched him turn the corner. "That would be handy. It would be good to know why the Teleri are so concerned about our dealings with Madura."

Ayana wagged a finger at him. "Prince Aelward already told your Emperor: Madura is an ally of the Teleri. They would not meddle in your country unless the action was either condoned or even instigated by the Teleri Empire."

Ma Jun chuckled. "Too bad. I bet he knew the fastest way to our embassy."

CHAPTER 29:

For Every Answer, Two New Questions

Zheng Ming sat cross-legged at his father's seat in the council, warmed by the sun which bathed the *Danhua* Room in morning light. Around him in the hastily-called meeting, ministers and hereditary lords shuffled and murmured among themselves.

Such an influx of youth! Due to the urgent summons, several *Yu-Ming* and *Tai-Ming* lords had been unable to come from their home provinces. Sons living in the capital came in their stead. Like him, most had never attended a council meeting, and didn't know whether their position was determined by their fathers' seniority or their own age.

Lord Zhao's son sat stoically, yet sweat beaded on his brow. At the other end, Lord Han's son fidgeted uncontrollably. Even the usually debonair Lord Peng seemed nervous, playing with his sleeves. To think, the assembled faces might well be a preview of the *Tianzi's* future advisors.

They all pressed their foreheads to the ground as sliding doors opened and the *Tianzi* entered, flanked by General Zheng, bearing the Broken Sword, and another imperial guard. He creaked onto the throne between his sons.

"Rise." His voice rasped before being overtaken by a fit of coughing.

Ming straightened, avoiding eye contact as protocol demanded. Nonetheless, he noted that the *Tianzi's* eyes seemed more sunken, his face more sallow, than just a few weeks before at Ming's first meeting with Princess Kaiya on the archery field.

The *Tianzi's* coughing subsided. "Thank you all for coming on such short notice to this emergency gathering of the *Tai-Ming* Council. Such a meeting has only been called a handful of times in the three centuries of Wang rule, so I do not summon you here without cause."

Everyone bowed.

"When Hua is threatened, her sons are ready," Peng said.

The *Tianzi* nodded with a smile. "Thank you, Nephew. Now, I am pleased to report that we have apprehended the mastermind behind the attacks on our lords."

A collective sigh of relief was followed by excited chatter.

"*Huang-Shang*," Lord Peng said, "who was it? Who had so much information that he was able to orchestrate so many attacks?"

The *Tianzi* seemed to age even more with his deflating sigh. "It is my utmost disappointment and sadness to announce it was Chief Minister Tan."

The Chief Minister! Ming steepled his hands to his chin. He'd been so close. With his dying breath, Xie Shimin had referred to his attack as an *order*. His betrothed had mentioned his meeting with a high official before the tournament. The insurgents Ming captured had been able to board the *Golden Phoenix* and sabotage the water barrels. All the clues, right there in front of his nose. His informant might as well have spelled it out for him.

Lord Wu shook his head. "Why would he do such a thing?"

"It was his hope," Crown Prince Kai-Guo said, "that the implication of Madura would push us toward the liberation of Ankira. He felt guilty about his role in selling guns and firepowder to Madura thirty-two years ago."

Lord Liu scratched his chin. "But Xie Shimin tried to kill the Chief Minister. The letter of command we found included the order to kill him."

"But he missed," Ming said. On purpose, without a doubt. "Xie Shimin was one of our best archers, shooting from point-blank range."

Minister Hong bowed. "It was likely a diversion, so he would not be implicated."

Lord Liang of Yutou, an Expansionist, narrowed his eyes. "I cannot believe the patriotic Minister Tan could do such a thing."

"Minister Tan's patriotism is not to be questioned," the Crown Prince said. "His means were misguided. Never did he order any of our lords killed. He just wanted to scare us into action. Even a gentle dog will bite when poked."

Lord Han's son bent his neck and stammered. "*Huang-Shang*, he tried to kill my father in his treasonous plot. His family should be executed to five generations."

Ming stared at Young Lord Han. With no descendants to follow proscribed rituals, Minister Tan and his ancestors would starve in the netherworld, and be forced to wander the land as hungry ghosts. It was too cruel a punishment, one which hadn't been handed down since the time of the Wang Dynasty Founder.

Heads nodded, accompanied by low murmurs.

The *Tianzi* raised his hands, silencing all. "Chief Minister Tan was a loyal servant. He confessed to his crimes and provided information for rooting out the insurgents. I have commuted his death sentence. He will live the remainder of his life under house arrest."

Minister Hong put his forehead to the ground. "We are blessed by your benevolent mercy."

Lord Peng stroked his chin. "How was the Chief Minister able to organize an insurgency without anyone noticing?"

"He recruited a merchant, who we believe was once one of the *Tianzi's* agents," the Crown Prince said. "Minister Hong laid a trap for him, which he did not fall for."

All attention turned to the beaming old man. Minister Hong would likely reap grand rewards.

The *Tianzi* straightened. "In the meantime, his former clan is piecing together information about him so we can learn his true identity."

Perhaps this was Ming's mysterious informant. If he surfaced again, Ming would turn the tables on him. In the meantime... "Is this renegade a threat?"

Prince Kai-Guo shook his head. "Now that he knows his patron is gone, he no longer has the information he needs to carry out his attacks."

Lord Peng slapped his hand on the floor. "Until the insurgency is completely wiped out, there will always be a threat."

"Yes, Nephew." The *Tianzi* coughed. "The insurgency remains, with or without Tan. In his confession, he claimed he was not behind them, but merely sought them out in hopes of controlling their excesses."

Lord Peng snorted. "As long as the insurgents live, the Madurans may try to use them to destabilize us."

"Chief Minister Tan was behind the attacks, not Madura," the Crown Prince said.

Ming's eyes widened. Of course. "Then thank the Heavens Tan sabotaged the *Golden Phoenix*. Otherwise, Princess Kaiya would be in Vyara City by now, demanding they cease their meddling. If falsely accused, there is no telling what an unreasonable and aggressive nation like Madura would do to her. I do hope she is recovering?"

The Crown Prince looked down at the floor while the *Tianzi* sank forward in the throne. Ming hadn't been allowed to meet with her since the day she'd been supposed to depart. From their reaction, maybe she was more ill than they had let on.

"What?" Peng sucked in a sharp breath. "Is she getting worse?"

The *Tianzi* sighed. "The princess is in Vyara City already."

Ruined! All of Peng Kai-Long's plans slipped through his fingers like fine sand in the wind. Princess Kaiya was in Vyara City. When Madura confirmed their non-involvement in the recent attacks, the fake Scorpion attack would raise questions. It might even cast doubt over the circumstances of his own father's murder. Then, if she sought out Prince Hardeep, she would learn he'd never written a single letter to her.

Gaze raking over the council, Kai-Long knew he had to distance himself from any of the plots he'd hijacked to his own purposes. Otherwise, he would need to flee the capital and consolidate his power in the South. "The princess lacks sufficient protection. We must find some way to send word to her not to agitate Madura. They are belligerent and unpredictable." Or so they all believed, thanks to his disinformation.

"Are you not the one who wanted war?" Lord Liu stared at him. The unimaginative sycophant certainly chose an inopportune time to find his tongue.

"Ask Lord Xu." Young Lord Zheng, perhaps the most incompetent buffoon in the room, somehow came up with the best suggestion. "His magic could summon her home."

Crown Prince Kai-Guo shook his head. "My sister is also tasked with visiting the Sultan of Selastya, who lives in exile near Vyara City. She will request that an Akolyte come to Hua and heal the *Tianzi* with their Divine Magic."

Kai-Long gritted his teeth. If a true Akolyte healed his uncle... "Perhaps Lord Xu could send a message to the princess, warning her against meeting with the Madurans. They did not hesitate to kill my father and brother."

The *Tianzi* sighed again. "I already asked as much. He said it is beyond his power, based on the distance of Guanyin's Eye in the Heavens."

"Then the princess walks into danger." Kai-Long placed a hand on his chest. "I could not bear to see my cousin harmed."

The *Tianzi* beamed at him. "I appreciate your concern, Nephew. But now, I need your advice. All of your advice, for that is the reason I called this meeting."

All bowed, pressing their foreheads to the ground.

"The position of Chief Minister is vacant," the *Tianzi* continued. "I have narrowed my candidates to Household Affairs Minister Hong and Foreign Minister Song."

Kai-Long hid his scowl behind a pleasant smile. Hong had wheedled and cajoled himself into consideration. He needed reminding that his road to the Chief Minister seat depended on Kai-Long being *Tianzi*.

Kai-Long bowed toward the throne. "Foreign Minister Song has served for many years at the highest level of government and proven to be an excellent administrator." He narrowed his eyes at Hong, holding his gaze. "Minister Hong is capable."

Leave it at that; let Hong simmer a little. Both he and Minister Song bowed when Kai-Long had finished his endorsement.

The Expansionist lords followed Kai-Long's lead, praising Foreign Minister Song with glowing praise and leaving nice but less enthusiastic words for Hong. The old man's weathered smile seemed to sap him each time he rose from a bow.

Surprisingly, the Royalists favored Song as well. Although the *Tianzi* would make the final decision, if the *Tai-Ming*'s words held any weight, Hong's candidacy was dead in the water. Just like Cousin Kaiya should've been.

Young Lord Zheng spoke last, all the while staring at Minister Hong. "Minister Hong's hard work led to the arrest of Chief Minister Tan. Despite his lack of experience compared to Minister

Song, I believe he has shown creativity and initiative."

Kai-Long studied Zheng. *Hong must've promised him something amazing.* The upstanding Zheng family was known for honoring its word to the point of stubbornness. Kai-Long had used their sense of honor to manipulate Zheng Ming's youngest brother Tian many times when they were children, and would do so again when Zheng Ming inherited his father's seat.

"Kai-Guo," The *Tianzi* said. "I do not have much time left, so whoever rises to Chief Minister today will likely serve you. Therefore, I entrust this decision to you. Choose well, for the Chief Minister is one of the Dragon Throne's greatest assets."

Such trust! Kai-Long hid his surprise.

In contrast, the Crown Prince's mouth hung open in a manner unsuited to rule. He bowed low. "Thank you for placing this great trust in me. Based on the advice of our esteemed lords, I choose Foreign Minister Song."

Minister Hong was the first to congratulate Chief Minister Song, yet he must've been stewing inside. *Two years of maneuvering for naught.* In this, the old man could share Kai-Long's despondence. *It would make it easier to get him to skip to the final stage of their plan.*

The *Tianzi* raised his hand, silencing the hereditary lords. "Chief Minister Song, your first duty will be to ensure the *Golden Phoenix* is ready to set sail for Ayudra Island with a full complement of imperial guards and diplomatic officials."

The new Chief Minister bowed. "As the *Tianzi* commands."

Young Lord Zheng bowed low. "*Huang-Shang.* The princess had asked me to travel with her, and I was unfortunately delayed by the insurgents. I ask to join in on the journey to Ayudra."

Kai-Long considered the implications of Zheng Ming's blooming relationship with the princess. *Even if he could convince Hong to go through with the final stage of their plan, he still had to do something about her.*

Hong Jianbin's face hurt from forcing smile after smile. His cheeks burned even more than his old knees, which buckled with each step toward the main gates of Sun-Moon Palace.

The day could not get any worse. *If only the Tianzi had decided himself, instead of leaving the choice to his foolish son, Hong's merits would have reaped rewards.* Instead, the Crown Prince caved to the *Tai-Ming* lords, as Hong knew the weak boy would.

Years of planning, all gone to waste. All of the backroom deals, for nothing. Only Young Lord Zheng had kept his word. And how ironic would it be if Hong's role in arranging Zheng's second meeting with the princess actually led to the philanderer winning her?

A hand clamped his shoulder and yanked him into one of the many small buildings on the palace grounds. His heart jumped into his throat as his vision adjusted to the dim light.

Lord Peng. Hong would expose Peng's treason, as soon as he could figure out a new way of doing so without revealing his own complicity.

"*Household Relations Minister* Hong," Peng hissed. "I am sorry things did not work out for you today. However, there is still a chance for your dreams to come true."

Hong searched Peng's eyes. "How is that?"

"When I am *Tianzi*, you will be my Chief Minister." Peng patted him on the shoulder. "Even though things did not unfold as we planned, we can skip to the end of our plot. You deliver stage three of the poison. The *Tianzi* and his two sons will be dead. The Expansionist alliance currently has enough men in the capital to support my nominal claim to the Dragon Throne."

CHAPTER 30:

A Position of Strength

The symphony of peaceful sounds energized Kaiya as her entourage made its way through the upper city. The low strums of the sitar radiated from one mansion, while fountain chimes rang from another. Birds twittered and chirped as they hopped among the hanging vines and flowers on villa walls.

If she had to live outside of Hua, this is the place she would choose! Unlike the raucous waterfront and downtown, which were virtually devoid of vegetation, this district of Vyara boasted graceful trees and manicured shrubs along the broad avenues.

By mid-afternoon, as Caiyue had waxed just past its middle crescent, they arrived at Hua's embassy. At last! Walls nearly twice Kaiya's height connected several adjoining block buildings, each two stories with tiled flat roofs. It certainly wasn't as elegant as the neighboring villas, though it was nice enough not to shame Hua in the eyes of its Ayuri trading partners.

Two embassy guards, dressed in dark blue robes and armed with broadswords, stood by the main entrance.

Chen Xin stepped forward and displayed the unique silver ring that signified him as imperial guard. "By order of Princess Wang Kaiya, summon Ambassador Ling."

Kaiya lowered her hood and shook out her hair. Though still clad in simple travelling clothes, she brushed off the persona of tired traveler and did her best to project the image of imperial grace.

"*Dian-xia.*" The embassy guards dropped to a knee, fists to the ground. "Welcome to the *Tianzi's* office in Vyara City," they said in unison.

She allowed them out of their salute with a nod of her head.

One jumped to his feet and ran inside. The other beckoned to the entrance and followed them in.

Kaiya took in the foyer with curious eyes. A fusion of several cultures, it didn't resemble any room back home. A mosaic floor of white, brown, and green tiles depicted a map of the Hua Empire. An Estomari-style framed oil painting of the *Tianzi* in his youth hung on the wall opposite the entrance. The two scrolls flanking the portrait were unmistakably written in Xiulan's bold hand. The broad strokes of Hua script sent a shiver of awe through Kaiya's spine.

The embassy guard guided them to a side room.

Now this felt much more like home! A Hua silk carpet with colorful symbols of health, longevity, fortune, and prosperity covered the tile floor. Brush paintings of famous landscapes in Hua adorned the walls on brightly bordered scrolls.

Kaiya settled on the edge of one of several elegant bloodwood chairs, and ran her fingers through some exotic Ayuri plant that grew in a white porcelain planter with a blue dragon motif. The imperial guards took up defensive positions around her.

Without any invitation, Ayana sprawled into another chair and let out a long breath. So much for the legends of elvish dignity.

Commotion erupted from deeper inside the building. A middle-aged man in dark blue court robes emerged from an arched doorway, flanked by several similarly-dressed officials. It was Ling Xiaomin, a distant relative who had visited Sun-Moon Palace several times in her childhood.

He bowed low. "*Dian-xia*, it is our honor to receive you here in Vyara City. We had originally expected you two days ago, but since we had heard no word of the *Golden Phoenix* ever arriving in Ayudra, we were unsure how to proceed."

Kaiya's heart sank. The *Golden Phoenix* carried her wardrobe, personal effects, and official documents. Negotiating with the Madurans in salty rags would embarrass Hua, not to mention her.

She allowed him out of his bow. "Thank you for receiving us, Ambassador. We are pleased to be your guests. I would like to receive a briefing on the Maduran situation once my retinue and I have settled in."

"Of course, *Dian-xia*." The Ambassador bowed again. He motioned a girl forward from behind the wall of aides. "This is Meixi. She will take you to the guest house and assist your handmaiden in attending to your needs."

Kaiya glanced at Jie from the corner of her eyes. The half-elf wore a half-smirk that told Kaiya she would be washing herself. Again.

The girl, probably no older than Jie's apparent age, cast her wide eyes downward as protocol demanded. Her hand shook as she extended it toward an arching exit. "Th-this way, p-please, D-Dian-xia...."

Meixi kept her head lowered as she led them to a house within the compound. "We reserve this only for important visitors."

Kaiya's second-floor quarters were decorated with bloodwood furniture and fine silk carpets. Fresh fruit, cut into narrow slices, sat in a bowl on a center table. Narrow windows allowed a glimpse of the street, where activity was now winding down for the day. The house had its own private bath on the first floor, which Meixi had

started preparing. Cowed by Jie's narrowed eyes, Kaiya waved the servant off and washed and dressed herself.

Though the simple shirt and dress on hand were more suited to a commoner, at least they were clean. With that small improvement, Kaiya felt a little more like herself. When her reflection in the dressing room mirror looked more like an imperial princess and less like a ragged traveler, she was ready to receive the ambassador.

Her entourage of imperial guards, all looking and smelling clean, joined her in the first house's audience room. Kaiya ascended the far dais and settled on the edge of a central bloodwood chair carved in the shape of a dragon's claw. Unlike a formal room in Sun-Moon Palace, where visitors would kneel on floor cushions before the *Tianzi*, chairs were arranged in a semi-circle facing the dais.

Niches in the walls displayed samples of Hua's most treasured goods: bolts of silk, porcelain wares, and tins of tea leaves. A second-generation Hua musket, less accurate than the current model and therefore allowed for export, occupied the most prominent spot behind the central chair.

Kneeling, Ambassador Ling motioned toward a slender man in blue robes. "This is my Information Minister, Yi Minshou."

"A *Moquan* brother," Jie whispered in her ear.

How did Jie know? Had she exchanged some secret message with the gaunt, middle-aged man? Kaiya allowed the two out of their bows and motioned them into chairs facing her. "Ambassador, what have you learned about Madura's relationship with the Teleri?"

The ambassador took a seat. "*Dian-xia*, Madura is a staunch ally of the Teleri Empire. Any meeting that occurs between Madura and other nations will invariably be attended by a Teleri advisor."

"Do you believe that the Teleri Empire, not Madura, is behind the unrest in Hua?" Kaiya asked.

Yi Minshou bowed. "*Dian-xia*, if I may speak. The maharaja of Madura believes he can manipulate his relationship with the Teleri. It certainly seems that Madura has a free rein with regards to its aggression."

Ambassador Ling nodded. "We think the Teleri chose Madura as an ally because of its belligerent nature toward its neighbors."

"However," the *Moquan* said, "there is nothing to suggest that Madura instigated any of the trouble in Hua."

Kaiya twirled a lock of her hair. If it wasn't Madura behind the unrest in Huajing, then who was it? "Are you certain? And if not, how much of a threat is Madura to Hua?"

Li bowed his head. "We can never be fully certain. We only have limited reach into Madura's inner workings. Their Golden Scorpions root out our spies with ease."

The ambassador unfurled a map. "As for the threat, Madura has occupied Ankira at our border for ten years. Though much of the populace still pines for the return of their own maharaja, the land is mostly subjugated."

Ankira. Prince Hardeep. Kaiya's hand strayed to the lotus jewel, concealed in her sash. Yes, they would make time for a visit to the Ankiran villa here.

The ambassador pointed out locations on the map. "Madura will not directly confront the Ayuri Confederation because of its Paladin protectors. The wild lands to its east between Madura and the Kanin Kingdom of Tomiwa are controlled by the dragon Avarax. Therefore, Hua is the most available target."

A full-on assault? Unthinkable. Kaiya straightened. "The Great Wall and thousands of muskets stand between us and Madura. Are their Golden Scorpions so formidable they could breech the Wall?"

The ambassador gave a slow half-nod. "If Madura could deploy half of its two thousand Golden Scorpions, then Lord Peng's provincial army would have a difficult time defending the Great Wall's south gate. However, many Scorpions are stuck in Ankira to stifle a potential insurgency."

Minister Yi raised his hand. "The Teleri have been breeding an auxiliary Bovyan army in occupied Ankira for almost ten years. Within another four or five years, they may have enough numbers to control the populace and escalate the threat to us."

Kaiya shuddered. The Maduran army, bearing down on the Great Wall. Tens of thousands would die on both sides, and if the Scorpions could fight half as well as Master Sabal... And to think Minister Hong wanted to bring so many soldiers into Huajing. She might not have a mind for strategy, but even *she* knew such moves would leave the defenses in the south thin.

She stood and glided over to the map. She ran a finger from Hua north to the Nothori kingdom of Rotuvi. An aggressive neighbor and independent tributary nation to the Teleri Empire, they had tried several times to recapture Wailian County, where Ming had served.

Her eyes turned south to Madura, another friend of the Teleri. Prince Aelward had insisted that there was an unholy alliance among the three nations, and Ayana insisted the Teleri were pulling the strings. Their encounter with the spy earlier in the day lent credence to those assertions.

She looked up from the map. "It seems, then, that even if Madura is not a threat now, it may be one in the future. We must gain the support of those who might help us deter Maduran aggression—either current or future."

The ambassador bowed. "The princess is wise. Just remember that it is our national policy not to enter into alliances with other nations, so that we may trade unfettered with all."

"Of course, Ambassador," Kaiya said. "Yet the perception of an alliance can be just a powerful tool as an actual one. Please make arrangements for me to meet with representatives of the Ayuri Confederation." Another thought crossed her mind. "And Ankira's exiled maharaja."

"What about the meeting with the Madurans tomorrow?" the ambassador asked. "You are supposed to dine with their prince at the half-waxing crescent."

If the Madurans weren't behind the insurgency in Hua... "I do not see the urgency. Let us delay the meeting for one week. By then, my retinue will hopefully arrive on the *Golden Phoenix* and I will have met with potential foreign friends. When we negotiate a non-aggression treaty with Madura, it will be from a position of strength."

The ambassador shifted in his chair. "Prince Dhananad has been pestering us about the meeting for the last several days. It would be unwise to offend him with a postponement."

She twirled a lock of hair. "Then I will have lunch with him, and relay our desire to negotiate a non-aggression pact at a later date."

The ambassador gazed at her, a smile forming on his lips. "As the princess commands. I will send messengers to all of the embassies at once."

Kaiya raised a hand to stop him from leaving. She pulled the Maduran copper rupiya from her sash and passed it to him. "Who is this?"

Ambassador Ling held it up to the light before passing it back. "This is old Maduran coinage. You can tell by how worn the images are. I would guess it is Madura's former Grand Vizier Rumiya."

The name sounded familiar. Kaiya received the coin and stared at it. "Who was he?"

Minister Yi tapped his index fingers together, a symbolic gesture to ward off bad luck. "He was an evil magician who rose to power in the Maduran court a century and a half ago."

An evil magician! As if elf wizards and Oracles weren't enough excitement for one lifetime. Kaiya twirled a lock of hair. "He must have been influential to have ended up on a modern coin."

Minister Yi nodded. "It was his idea to recruit castoffs from the Paladin Order and establish the Golden Scorpions. In a few short decades, Madura tripled in size, until it reached the border of the Paladin mandate."

And then north into hapless Ankira. Kaiya's hand strayed to the lotus jewel in her sash.

"Rumiya himself," the minister said, "used black magic to suck the life force from others to preserve his own. Until thirty-two years ago, he remained young and hale."

Evil magic. Kaiya shuddered. "Then what happened?"

The ambassador paused a second. "He just disappeared."

Disappeared? She rubbed her finger over the image on the coin. Perhaps the familiarity came from having seen it in a history book before. "Do you have any paintings of him?"

"No, but I am sure the Maduran embassy does. He would be a national idol if their current maharaja didn't downplay his role in their history."

Kaiya pushed the coin into her sash, joining Tian's pebble and Hardeep's lotus jewel. She hadn't wanted to request anything of Prince Dhananad in tomorrow's meeting, but she felt compelled to see a painting of Grand Vizier Rumiya.

CHAPTER 31:

Even a Carp Dreams of Becoming a Dragon

Though not an accomplished poet like that fop Zheng Ming, Hong Jianbin felt inspired to compose. It was not the full White Moon Renyue reflecting in the carp pond of his courtyard garden that stirred him, though he watched it as he sat on the adjacent veranda on this warm spring evening. Without a doubt, his muse was the deflating feeling of failure. The poetry he wrote tonight would sing of unfulfilled dreams and monumental disappointments.

The only path he could see to Chief Minister now travelled through Lord Peng. The treacherous lord might very well have him executed instead of promoted. He had always planned on poisoning the *Tianzi* and his sons, but on his own terms, not Peng's.

Now, the *Tianzi* might be the only one who could keep him alive. All those years getting into Prince Kai-Wu's good graces would also be meaningless if Crown Prince Kai-Guo inherited.

Hong let out a long sigh. He was to meet Leina tonight in the Floating World—not for the celebratory lovemaking he had planned, but for advice. He could not count how often great ideas came to him through her idle banter. If the silly girl had an eye for political maneuvering, perhaps *she* would be a high official.

He studied the rocky stream that fed the pond, thinking of the ancient story of the carp that swam up a waterfall and transformed into a dragon. Chief Minister was still within reach. If he played his game carefully, if he courted the right people and betrayed them before they realized what was happening, he could very well become father of the future *Tianzi*.

"You will need help," the stone dragon overlooking the pond said.

Hong's heart jumped into his throat as he gawked at the sculpture. Had it read his mind? His first impulse was to call for the guards posted just outside his pavilion.

They would think him insane.

"No need to call your guards," a frog on a rock said in the same voice. "If you did, I would be gone long before they arrived."

Hong found his wits. "You are the renegade agent. Tan's asset."

"One and the same," said a just-opening blossom on a cherry tree, forcing the minister to turn again in confusion. "I am impressed you know me."

"Will you stop doing that?" Hong wagged a finger at the blossom.

A painfully plain, middle-aged man with a walking stick melted out of the shadows, a bemused tone in his voice. "As you command, Chief Minister."

"Apparently, your information sources have failed you for once."

The man smirked. "Oh, no. My information is *early*. The title...and all its benefits...can still be yours."

Being beholden to a traitor didn't seem much better than having to trust Lord Peng. "What do you want from me?"

"First, let me thank you. You knew of the former Chief Minister's method of contacting me, and warned me of the trap, did you not?"

"I did not," Hong said, now thoroughly mystified. He had *set* the trap.

The man shook his head. "Oh, but you did, though perhaps you had intended the opposite. No matter. Which brings me to the reason for my visit. I am here to accept your assignment."

Hong's confusion grew, though he tried his best to hide it. "What assignment?"

"The unwritten one." The upturn in the man's lips almost connected to the crinkles at the side of his eyes. "The removal of Chief Minister Song."

Hong stared at the man through narrowed eyes. "How would you do that?"

"First, you must promise to pursue war with Madura once you become Chief Minister."

The man was perplexing. Hong threw up his hands. "Everyone now knows Madura had nothing to do with the insurgency."

"You are a smart man. Make it happen. If you go back on your promise with me, I will not be as incompetent as Minister Tan when *I* try to throttle you."

Was he referring to the bathhouse incident? Hong could not keep the incredulousness out of his voice. "How do you know such things?"

"It is my business to know," the man said. "For example, I know how Peng has been rendering the *Tianzi* and his sons sterile for four years now, by replacing the imperial tea with Ayuri gooseeed."

Hong had learned this from a business associate long ago, which was one of the reasons he had approached Peng with his plot. How did the renegade agent know? Perhaps he would spill his secret. Let him monologue.

"Your contact inside the imperial kitchens orders from your business acquaintances in Yutou province, and that acquaintance in turn procures a certain Levanthi spice through my shipping company, Golden Fu Trading. The otherwise harmless spice, which goes into the *Tianzi's*

longevity elixir, interacts with gooseweed to cause respiratory distress."

The man knew of Hong's actual treasonous actions, even more than Peng did.

"That on your command, your kitchen contact will mix that spice into the palace meals so that the princes will consume it as well. And lastly, you knew the asthma-treating herb *Ma Huang*, when mixed with gooseweed, will cause heart failure."

He *knew*. Did he know about—

"Just as you did to the *Tianzi's* brother and nephews two years ago."

He *did*. Aching face muscles told Hong he must have been wearing the most ridiculous expression.

"You see, Minister Tan's plot was simple; yours more subtle and entertaining. Mine is even more complicated, and ultimately, you will be one of the main beneficiaries if you play along."

Though always ahead of his political opponents, Hong was completely baffled by this man. "What is your stake in this?"

The man shrugged. "I have nothing to gain personally. I only wish to make Hua strong before its neighbors swallow us. Tan was my greatest hope for success until he betrayed me, which is why I led Young Lord Zheng to him."

Whatever made him think Tan betrayed him? Still, his goals seemed noble enough, and were very much in line with Hong's. He would at least reap benefits until he found a way to tie up this loose end. "Very well. I swear to press for Expansionism once I am Chief Minister. Now, how do you plan on killing Chief Minister Song?"

"Killing?" The man glared. "I have no such plan. He is a good man whom Hua still needs. But he will resign in embarrassment when he learns his son is an insurgent."

If Hong's jaw could drop any further, he would have to pick it off the ground. "How do you know that?"

"Because he has worked for me for two years."

Hong's head spun. "And what do you need me to do?"

"First, let us remove Lord Peng from the picture. Left unfettered, he is conniving enough to thwart our plans. Go through with your plan to poison the *Tianzi*."

CHAPTER 32:
An Audacious Proposal

Yan Jie's sharp eye caught the small scar on the side of Maduran Prince Dhananad's neck. The Architect's intricate plan from thirty-two years before had called for kidnapping the young prince. The Surgeon had nicked him when the brave boy fought back.

Adult Dhananad covered the mark with a thick layer of cosmetics—part and parcel of a flamboyant package. It did little to compensate for the toll age had taken on a mildly handsome face.

Gold pins held up his hair in a twist the Hua would consider feminine. His rust-red *kurta* of fine cotton hung to his knees, embellished with a repeating pattern of gold scorpion symbols. Gold-threaded slippers graced his feet, while a cloying musk hung about him, competing with the sweet incense burning in the brazier. All told, Prince Dhananad's vanity could challenge even Princess Kaiya's.

"Absolutely stunning!" He brought both of his palms together below his chin in a typical Ayuri greeting. "Truly, you have come prepared to impress us!"

The princess covered her laugh with a slim hand. She pressed her palms together to imitate his greeting. "We say, *When in Vyara, do as the Ayuris do.*"

Jie suppressed a snort. Although the Hua expression was liberally translated, the pretext was a white lie: the princess *had* planned to wear a priceless Hua silk court robe, lost aboard the still unaccounted-for *Golden Phoenix*.

Refusing to meet dignitaries in simple clothes, she'd recruited the young and enthusiastic Meixi, who had grown up in Vyara, to help her choose something local and presentable. At first light, she visited a tailor to alter a local dress to reflect her own conservative tastes.

Even with little fashion sense, Jie had to admit the result was stunning. A *langa* petticoat wrapped around the princess' legs and to her ankles, the most modest part of the ensemble. A long, broad strip of bright blue Hua silk, embroidered with white cranes and bamboo, swathed around the princess' waist and draped over her left shoulder much as the local women wore their *saris*. It partially covered a tight-fitting white cotton *choli* blouse with short sleeves and a low neckline. It completely covered her back and midriff, contrary to local fashion trends—thank the Heavens, as if the neckline didn't reveal enough! The unaltered *choli* looked like the Hua bust supports Jie never needed, except to stash weapons.

With none of her handmaidens around, and dubious of Jie's hairstyling abilities, the princess let her hair cascade freely down to her waist. That girl certainly loved her hair. How long before she fiddled with a stray lock, *again*?

The prince's eyes roved over her like a starving man at a royal banquet. Jie wouldn't mind helping the princess bathe tonight, if it would help wash off the stains his leer left.

He extended his hand toward two matching chairs made of a maroon wood. Topped by plush burgundy cushions, the chairs stood on either side of a knee-high oval table. The tabletop's pink marble matched the color of the dome above them in the Bijuran embassy.

Following his gesture, the princess glided across the red and gold carpet, whose high-quality wool and Ayuri craftsmanship were prized throughout Tivaralan. She settled on the edge of the chair while Ambassador Ling stood to her right. Chen Xin, the only imperial guard in attendance, stood behind him. He wore the light blue robes of the embassy guards, his own armor and ceremonial clothes aboard the missing *Golden Phoenix*.

Jie knelt on the princess' left, dressed in a standard *choli* and *langa* that bared her midriff, with a bolt of Hua silk matching the princess' wrapped around her as a *sari*. She stole yet another glance at her reflection in the silver lamps. She looked good! If only Tian could see her like this. Though he'd probably focus more on the numerous small weapons the *sari* concealed.

Prince Dhananad took a seat on the chair opposite the princess. To his right glowered a giant of a man with fair hair and fair skin, dressed in a *kurta* of black with gold embroidery. The size and emblazoned sun symbol marked the brute as a Bovyan from the Teleri Empire, though he stood even taller than the prince's escort the day before.

To the prince's left stood a Golden Scorpion, obvious from the dark bronze *kurta*. Dark brown eyes stared out from beneath the oval slits of the otherwise expressionless mask. As the Bijurans had stipulated, no weapons were allowed in the embassy, and so the Scorpion didn't bear the curved sting of their order.

The prince clapped his hands together, summoning servants as if they were his own. Several Bijuran girls, dressed in light green *saris*, emerged from the door and hurried over to place food and drink on the table. The centerpiece was an enormous oval dish made of Hua white porcelain with four-clawed blue dragons—audaciously denoting *Tai-Ming* status—with two dozen matching rectangular bowls nestled within.

Each held a unique Ayuri delicacy: colorful sauces and pastes filled some bowls, while chicken, pork, rice, and vegetables filled others. Saffron, curry and other exotic spices provided a symphony of delectable aromas. A piece of *roti* flatbread wrapped in a white cotton napkin on a silver dish, a single silver spoon, and a crystal glass graced each setting. A matching decanting carafe filled with a yellowish liquid sat on the side of the table.

"Is this your first time in Vyara City?" The prince flared his fingers toward the dish; according to Meixi's primer of Ayuri etiquette, an invitation to eat.

"This is my first time leaving Cathay." The princess tilted her head and imitated his gesture. Thank the Heavens it was her manners on display instead of Jie's!

"Ah!" He clapped his hands together. He made each gesture intricate, even the crude act of eating with bare hands. "You must allow me to show you around this magnificent city!"

"If time permits," the princess said.

"And sometime, hopefully in the near future, I would like to personally give you a tour of my hometown of Maduras." Dhananad flashed a broad smile of straight white teeth and turned his palms up. According to Meixi, each refined movement denoted some deep meaning, but Jie had lost track of the lesson in the first few minutes. In any case, it would be far more interesting to see what that masked Scorpion could do.

The princess predictably brushed a lock of hair out of her eyes. "I have heard that while Vyara City's skyline is a testament to Ayuri cultural beauty, that of Maduras bears witness to Ayuri cultural might. Is it true that your entire capital is a virtual fortress?"

He grinned ear-to-ear. "The fortifications are impregnable. Yet within hides a true architectural gem, befitting a jewel such as yourself. It is certainly worth seeing."

"Yet fortresses hold little interest for me, for I have seen so many crenellations and battlements along our Great Wall."

Jie stared at the princess is admiration. The naïve girl who'd chased after Prince Hardeep now delicately broached the issue of Maduran aggression.

Prince Dhananad frowned, leading to seconds of palpable silence. He then gestured to the table. "Are you enjoying this fine sampling of Ayuri food?"

She nodded. "It is delicious. By comparison, Cathayi cuisine varies widely by region, and some of the foods in the west have very bold flavor. But most of what we eat in the capital has a very subtle taste. I am afraid you would find it bland compared to Ayuri fare."

"Any food would be like sweet nectar from Heaven when shared with an angel." His grin was as smooth as a baby's bottom, and probably just as toxic.

All discipline lost, Jie shuddered. The silky delivery of his responses resembled Zheng Ming's charming tone. All the more reason to dislike him.

The princess placed a hand on her chest. "Then you should come to Cathay to enjoy our food, for we treat all of our *invited* guests as royalty."

A warning, wrapped in pretty words. Jie glanced at the men across the table. The prince's eyes shifted back and forth, and his lips jiggled into a somewhat gracious smile. The metal mask hid the Golden Scorpion's thoughts, but the Bovyan official's displeasure was evident from his silent scowl.

Conversation over lunch between prince and princess continued along these lines. Seemingly mundane topics about the New Year and weather all carried unspoken suggestions and refusals. Prince Dhananad repeatedly extended invitations for her to visit his homeland; while she repeatedly rebuffed him, packaging her refusal in flowery language. He was either annoyingly tenacious or inordinately dense in his persistence.

Kaiya drew strength from the high whine of the sitar and rhythmic beating of drums, which an ensemble of Bijuran musicians in the far corner of the room played as background music. Without

it, she might have withered under Prince Dhananad's ogling. At least most men tried to hide their peeks. The elegant Ayuri body language would've been easier to imitate if not for the need to conceal all that the local clothes tried to expose.

As they finished eating, a serving girl came to the table and reached for the decanting carafe.

The prince held up his hand to stop her and motioned for the Golden Scorpion to serve. Agile as a cat, the warrior knelt and poured the yellow fluid into the two glasses, and slid the drinks in front of her and the prince.

Like a happy wolf, the prince bared his teeth. "This nectar is extracted from several different rare flowers, and served only to royalty. Please, drink."

Kaiya took up the wineglass in her hands and lifted it toward him. "In Cathay, it is our custom to toast friendships."

His eyes tightened into slits, but he raised his glass as well.

With a smile, Kaiya brought the carafe to her lips. Her rouge would leave a mark, and there was no telling how the pervert would—

Jie took a step and tripped over her skirt. Her light weight plopped into Kaiya's lap, her *sari* sweeping across the table. Dishes clattered noisily onto the floor. The glass was knocked from Kaiya's hand, its precious contents spilling out onto the fine carpet.

"Clumsy fool!" The prince bolted to his feet, his hand reaching to his left hip, where a *talwar* hung the day before. Not finding a weapon, he stepped over and cocked his arm back to strike Jie.

The girl cowered, covering her head with her arms.

Recovering from her initial shock, Kaiya leaned over to protect her Insolent Retainer. Jie must've seen something; she was far too dexterous to fall like that.

The prince growled, his glare bearing down on the half-elf. "If you caused such a scene and wasted the nectar in Madura, we would pluck your eyes out. You are lucky your liege is more forgiving than I."

Jie picked herself off Kaiya, took several steps back and sunk to her knees, forehead pressed to the ground. "Please forgive me," she pleaded in halting Ayuri.

Jie could speak better than that. Kaiya extended her hand, which the ambassador took and helped her to her feet. She bowed deeply at the waist. "Gracious Prince Dhananad, please forgive my handmaiden's clumsiness. Let us not allow this unfortunate accident ruin what has thus far been a pleasant afternoon."

The prince pressed his palms together. "As you wish, dearest Kaiya. Your magnanimity is truly admirable." He invited her to return to her seat with a wave of his hand.

So presumptuous, addressing her by name! She settled on the edge of the chair. Jie shuffled back, holding a low bow. Oh, to be able to ask what she saw. But no, one of the prince's entourage might be able to speak Hua. It would have to wait.

"So, Kaiya," Dhananad said, "it came as a great surprise when your nation approached glorious Madura through the Bijurans to propose such a high-level meeting. Since our past trade agreement expired, we have had little contact. To what do we owe the pleasure of your visit?" His focus dropped to her bust, which the cut of the *choli* embellished and revealed too much of.

It was no furtive glance, but rather the most unabashed stare yet, less subtle than her childhood lapdog waiting for a treat. Kaiya brought an arm across her chest, feigning to adjust the *sari's* position at her shoulder. Dhananad's gaze shifted up to meet hers.

She lowered her hands to her lap and bowed her head. "Benevolent prince, my father sent me to express Cathay's desire to maintain amity between our peace-loving nations."

Confusion, which could only be genuine, contorted his expression. "I did not realize there was anything but peace between us."

Perhaps Lord Peng's accusations were unfounded. Kaiya searched Dhananad's eyes. "Of course. The Ayuri Kingdom of Ankira—"

The Teleri official cleared his throat, the sound commensurate with his Bovyan size.

"Certainly, Princess Kaiya, Cathay recognizes that Ankira is not a kingdom, but merely a province of Madura."

Kaiya's hand strayed to Prince Hardeep's lotus jewel, concealed by the band of her *langa*. It warmed her palm, even through the cloth.

Prince Dhananad nonchalantly waved off the Bovyan's comments. "It goes without saying that Ankira is an indivisible part of Madura."

"And as Princess Kaiya knows, Ankira Province sits at the border of Cathay." The Bovyan's stare bore into her. "You would not come all the way here unless you were concerned about the potential sting of the Golden Scorpions. So perhaps the question should be, what token of goodwill is Cathay willing to offer to ensure lasting peace with glorious Madura?"

The prince laughed and waved a hand. "Our lunch was virtually ruined by the clumsy handmaiden. There is no need to leave a bad taste in our mouths by spewing unveiled threats."

The Teleri glared at Dhananad, but remained silent as the prince turned back to her. "Though our friend brings up a good suggestion: we must certainly endeavor to ensure continuing good relations between our two countries."

Kaiya bowed her head. "I could not agree more with your wisdom. Though our past trade agreement expired, perhaps we could negotiate a new one?" One that didn't involve firepowder.

A devious glint shined in the Dhananad's eyes. "Yes. Perhaps we could trade nuptials among a prince and princess of our realms. I believe this is a custom our cultures share, to strengthen relations via marriage? The Wang family marries its princes and princesses to the sons and daughters of your hereditary lords, does it not?"

Ambassador Ling's robes rustled behind her, and Jie's gaze bored into her back. Maybe they worried she didn't understand the tacit message, though Dhananad left no doubt where the conversation was headed. All of his previous flattery and invitations had been a game to set up this question. With both of her brothers married, there was only one princess to barter.

Dhananad would probably not take no for an answer, and the Madurans hopelessly outnumbered the Hua in Vyara City.

Kaiya stole a glance out of the window. From the bright sun and position of the shade, the Iridescent Moon had probably waxed to mid-crescent, and there were only a little more than three hours until sundown. In order to avoid replying to Prince Dhananad's audacious proposal, she decided to mimic Ayana's charm spell the only way she knew how.

CHAPTER 33:
Shifts in Winds

Peng Kai-Long sat in his tea room, reading and rereading the imperial missive which summoned all *Tai-Ming* and *Yu-Ming* to the palace.

The *Tianzi* was dying, Crown Prince Kai-Guo was bedridden. Prince Kai-Wu was already dead.

Hong's poison, as promised during their secret meeting at Guanshan Temple six weeks earlier, had worked. The old fool's ambition to become Chief Minister must've blinded him to the perils in trusting the soon-to-be *Tianzi*. It wouldn't be the Chief Minister's medallion around his neck when everything was said and done.

Kai-Long unfurled a map of Huajing, picturing where his soldiers and those of his allies were deployed in relation to vital government centers. It was a precautionary measure. Once the *Tianzi* and Crown Prince joined Prince Kai-Wu in the netherworld, he would meet little resistance.

The Dragon Throne was his.

How long would the old man linger? The uncertainty raised other uncertainties. Cousin Kaiya might visit the Ankirans any day now. If Prince Hardeep were there, with no knowledge of his correspondence with her, she was smart enough to realize who was behind the fake letters. Perhaps smart enough to unravel his entire role.

A grin came unbidden. Information travelled at the speed of ships, and the *Golden Phoenix* would depart for Vyara today. It would be best to make sure she remained anchored in Jiangkou for as long as possible, to give him more time to consolidate his power before the girl returned. He already had a hundred men not far from the docks.

Kai-Long hastily drafted a letter. He then rose and threw open the doors to the tea room. A glorious afternoon awaited him, sun shining in the bright blue skies. Surely it was a sign from Heaven. He was destined to rule.

His steward waiting outside bowed. "Your horse is ready, *Jue-ye*."

"Excellent." He pressed his handwritten message into the steward's hands. "Have this letter conveyed to our provincial trade office in Jiangkou. Use our *own* horse relays. Nobody is to see this except Lord Tu."

Dismissing the steward, Kai-Long strode toward the stables and found his horse already saddled. An entourage of his best guards, dressed in formal court uniforms, sat astride their mounts.

He swung into his saddle and beckoned them forward. "Come. Destiny awaits."

The horses trotted toward the main gates. They opened to reveal a heavily-cloaked woman.

Undaunted by the horses, she sank to both knees and set her forehead to the ground. "Lord Peng, might I have a word with you in private?"

That voice, the foreign accent. Hong's concubine, Leina. Likely here to secure her lord's favor in the new regime. It might be entertaining, and rewarding, to see what she might offer for the old man's life. Rewarding enough to delay departure. "What do you wish to tell me that my own loyal men cannot hear?"

She looked up. "You are riding into a trap. Do you want to know why?"

Leina knelt on the tea room mats, recalling what old Hong had told her. In his own clandestine meeting with Lord Peng here, he'd been shaken by the attack on Princess Kaiya. Worried that Peng was ready to betray him.

Not even a month had passed, yet how long ago it seemed. Each player's plot had surged into motion from that point, sometimes hiding in another's shadow, sometimes amplifying, sometimes crashing head-to-head. The first round of winners would soon emerge from the mess of entangled plans.

With one of his underlings kneeling behind him, Peng eyed her like a bird of prey. "Hong had the *Tianzi* and his sons poisoned, did he not? The Dragon Throne sits empty. How am I walking into a trap and not to glory?"

He had less foresight than it seemed. To think she'd picked him out as one of the initial victors. She bowed her head again. "Prince Kai-Wu still lives, unharmed, with the authority of the *Tianzi* vested in his hands until either his brother or the *Tianzi* recovers."

Peng pulled out and unfurled the imperial missive with a whip of his hand. "This says Kai-Wu is dead. It is stamped by the imperial correspondence seal. Do you deny its authenticity? A lie stamped with the seal would mean the *Tianzi* losing the Mandate of Heaven." Despite the outward show of confidence, his trembling voice hinted at uncertainty.

She pointed. "Look carefully. There is magic of distraction embedded in the words, so much that you missed that the seal is a fake." As his eyes roved over the page, she continued, "Minister Hong convinced Prince Kai-Wu to send these out to find out who is loyal to the Wang family."

"I *am* a member of the Wang family!"

"But through a maternal line, so your claim is in question. You will be branded as a usurper, taken into custody the instant you try to claim the Dragon Throne."

Peng's eyebrows bunched together. "Not if I don't claim the throne. Not if I swear loyalty to Kai-Wu. The weak-minded boy will be easy to manipulate until I can get rid of him altogether."

She shook her head. "Hong's mole in the kitchen staff fingered you as the procurer of the offending spice, since it came up through Nanling Province, on your ships."

Peng paled, forcing her to hide her satisfaction. His lip quivered. "My province is loyal to me. I will retreat there and reconsolidate my power. Yutou Province is my ally. They can defend the west road into Nanling while my armies defend the north pass."

Men. Always too confident. She shrugged. "Your fief is forfeit. Lord Liang will desert you, making Yutou Province a staging area for an invasion instead of a buffer. That is, if you even make it home in the first place. A full division of the imperial army waits on the road south to capture you."

The young lord jumped to his feet and turned to his lieutenant. "Send word to all of my men stationed in Huajing. Order them to march east to Jiangkou. Have our men already in Jiangkou begin operations to capture the *Golden Phoenix*."

He then glared down at her, the hand on his sword sending a cold shiver down her spine. "Why are you helping me?"

If there was one thing a man believed, it was his own genius; none more so than Lord Peng. As long as she sang the song he wanted to hear, she could deceive him and she would live. "You are a capable leader. If you survive, you will make an unparalleled *Tianzi*."

And create enough chaos inside the nation to weaken it...

Minister Hong Jianbin knelt close to the Dragon Throne, where Prince Kai-Wu sat for the first time. The exalted spot, reserved for the Chief Minister, provided an excellent view of all the other ministers and hereditary lords who sat in rows facing the throne. It made the trip up the steps to the Hall of Supreme Harmony worth the toll it took on his old knees and lungs.

Prince Kai-Wu fidgeted, his attention shifting from person to person. Sweat matted the hair peeking through the *Tianzi*'s hat of office. Never expecting to inherit, the poor boy was in over his head. It was fortuitous—or at least well-planned—that Hong had put himself in the prince's good graces to become his advisor. Once the *Tianzi* and Crown Prince died, his power would know no bounds.

"He will show," Hong said. At least he hoped the soon-to-be ex-Lord Peng would show. It would be far easier to take him into custody inside the palace, unarmed and lightly protected. He looked at the hundred imperial guards deployed around the room, each more than a match for Peng and a pair of guards. Malleable Prince Kai-Wu's first decisive act would be a public humiliation of Peng.

Unless the wily young lord had sniffed out the trap.

Hong had distinguished himself in Prince Kai-Wu's esteem with his infallible wisdom and accurate predictions. To have this plan fail would undermine his credibility, though he had also advised Prince Kai-Wu to surround Peng's compound.

A messenger appeared at the threshold, quieting the murmuring lords. He stepped into the hall and dropped to both knees, forehead to the ground. "*Dian-xia*! Horrible news! Our troops surrounded Lord Peng's villa, but he already escaped. He is moving on Jiangkou Port!"

Blood rushed from Hong's face. "He is going to try to steal a ship. Maybe even the *Golden Phoenix* herself." How could he have not foreseen such a move? Where was the opportunity in *this* disaster?

There it was. Zheng Ming, soon to embark for his reunion with Princess Kaiya, might already be on the *Tianzi's* flagship. Maybe Peng would kill him. Or better yet, hold him hostage and expose him for the weakling he was.

Hong met Prince Kai-Wu's gaze, trying to speak as quietly as he could. "Send word to Young Lord Zheng to defend the *Golden Phoenix* from the traitor's imminent attack."

CHAPTER 34:

The Perfect Dance

As a collector of unique and beautiful objects of art, Prince Dhananad looked forward to possessing this stunning girl whose every move embodied grace. Even without the use of the intoxicant-laced nectar, Princess Kaiya had fallen for his charm. Yet she still kept up the charade of innocent misunderstanding.

How cute! She surely understood his wedding proposal. He had made it obvious with the talk of binding royal families.

"As always, you are well-informed," Princess Kaiya said. "My ancestor Wang Xinchang used many methods to ensure civil stability and lasting peace, political marriage among them. He was also famous for the cultivation of the fine arts, especially among our nobility. Beyond economic, political, and military acumen, all of our hereditary lords are well-versed in some form of art. Is that not the same in Madura? I have heard that you are an excellent dancer."

She knew of his dance! He waved a nonchalant hand. "I have been told that my dancing is passable. Certainly not on par with one such as yourself."

Her eyes twinkled mischievously. "It is rude in Cathay to directly ask someone to perform, but I would be honored if you show me an Ayuri dance."

"By all means, Sweet Kaiya." He returned her coy smile. "But it is our custom that if I dance at your request, you must dance for me as well."

She covered her mouth with delicate fingers as she giggled. "This is *not* our custom, but, *When in Vyara, do as the Ayuri do.*"

Dhananad laughed. "Then it is a mutually beneficial situation, much like a union between our two illustrious families would be." He beckoned toward the musicians. "Play *The Scorpion King Vanquishes the Twelve-Armed Demon.*"

The Teleri official—what was his name again?— shuffled petulantly beside him. Cursed with a short life, Bovyans lacked patience. That was why their soulless empire would never achieve greatness compared to Madura. If this uncultured boor could not appreciate fine art, that was his problem.

He stood and sauntered to the middle of the room. The music, which had been barely perceptible while they ate, now resonated clearly in the domed room. The rhythmic beat energized his solo, which he knew to be the epitome of Ayuri male dance: distinct poses with rapid transitions to the music's cadence. Perhaps she would find it jerky, but no more than their dance between the bed sheets would be.

At the end of his display of technical mastery and physical flexibility, she wholeheartedly applauded. "Prince Dhananad, I am embarrassed to follow such an amazing performance."

As she should be; but at the very least, it would allow her dress—irritatingly altered to befit a virgin priestess of Shakti—to expose more of her smooth skin. He grinned. "Yes, but you promised!"

"And it would not reflect well on Cathay if I go back on my promise, would it?" She blinked with captivating eyes. "But since we do not have any of our instruments, please forgive me as I improvise to your music."

Casting him an apologetic smile, Princess Kaiya spun and glided over to the musicians. She approached the drummer, whose various-sized *tabla* hand drums stood in a semicircle around him. She tapped out a long sequence on the drums at a moderate tempo. "Please play this as your *tala* refrain." She then turned to the rest. "And please, let your inspiration guide you."

The musicians nodded, and Dhananad could not help but be impressed with her knowledge of Ayuri music theory.

She returned to the center of the room and bowed. "I will dance *The Loves of Prince Aralas*. It recounts the story of the elf angel who fell in love with eight human girls, thereby establishing the alliances that helped overthrow the Tivari during the War of Ancient Gods."

A dance of love! Albeit with a tragic ending, at least as recounted by the Ayuri storytellers. Perhaps the Cathayi had a different take. At the very least, the theme was obvious: she was dreaming of their marriage!

The girl drifted into a pose, forming an elegant curve reminiscent of an elephant tusk. Her right arm floated upwards with her palm facing to the heavens and delicate fingers gracefully bent. Her other arm sank low as if cradling a giant ball. Both the free end of her makeshift *sari* and her hair cascaded behind her. The shift in the *langa* exposed the perfect arc of her calf, and the *choli* rose to allow her navel to peek out. Had he been sitting in the right place, he could have snuck a glance at the luscious valley between her breasts. Soon enough.

She gave no signal, yet her movement and the tune started in perfect synchronicity. Had the musicians reacted so fast, or had she been moved by the melody? The flavor of the dance was decidedly foreign, and yet harmonized with the local style of music.

The *langa* around her legs should've restricted her mobility. Yet she seemed to swim through it as she wafted across the floor, like a fluffy cloud on a perfect day, blown by the strumming of the sitar and transforming to the beat of the drums. It seemed gravity itself had paused to admire her, allowing her to achieve impossible feats of balance and flexibility.

The symbiosis between musicians and dancer caused the seconds to blur into minutes, minutes into hours. Dhananad sighed. It was like experiencing the legend firsthand, through the eyes of the dashing elf angel (how appropriate!). His beauty, reflected in the enchanted eyes of the ancient human princesses; the ecstasy among lovers; and at last, the melancholy as they aged and died while he remained youthful.

The music slowed to a stop, guiding the girl to the floor in a tangle worthy of a yoga guru.

Yet it was Dhananad whose stomach twisted in knots. His heart hammered in his chest. A few minutes of utter silence followed, interrupted only by an occasional bird chirp and the shifting of the Golden Scorpion. He looked out the arched window toward the Iridescent Moon, which had passed through two phases in the blink of an eye. It would have required a monumental reserve of stamina to dance as the princess had for so long. He rose from the chair, ready to help the girl to her feet.

To his surprise, she spun up unto her toes, appearing as energized as if just waking to the morning sun. When she batted her lashes at him, he knew then he would do anything she asked.

He applauded, followed by the musicians and even the Teleri troublemaker. Dhananad said, "I have never experienced such a dance. You, my lady, give sound a shape, a tangible form."

Sweet Kaiya bowed again before returning to her seat. With dainty grace, she took up a glass and sipped some water. When she smiled again, he thought his heart would stop. She gestured toward the west windows. The sun, now meeting the Shallowsea, flooded the room with red rays of dusk.

"Alas, Prince Dhananad," she said, her very inflection of his name sending sparks up his spine. "Time is short, for I have been invited to dine with the maharaja of Vadara tonight."

Dhananad waved his hand, even if his chest felt squeezed by her imminent departure. "Well then, I look forward to seeing you again."

The Golden Scorpion prodded his back. "The Princess of Cathay did not respond to your proposal," she said, voice silky. "She should not leave until she answers."

Kaiya's eyes widened at the Scorpion before turning back to him, where they belonged. She looked up at him through her lashes. "Matters of peace are important, but please give us some time to consider details."

"No," the Scorpion said. Dhananad hoped it would be now. They could exchange private vows at the local Temple of Surya now, celebrate in each other's arms tonight, and then hold a grand wedding in Maduras within a month.

Princess Kaiya shook her head, sending her voluminous tresses prancing. "My next several days are marked by meetings with officials from other Ayuri Kingdoms to discuss trade and docking rights. Let us meet in seven days, when the White Moon wanes to its half-phase."

The Bovyan wore a stupid grin on his face, nodding. "One week, very reasonable."

One week! It was too long not to be graced by her beauty. Still, waiting made good things even better. "Very well. I had planned to return to Madura before then, but I shall delay my departure."

She dipped her chin. "Then let us host you at our embassy as a means of compensating you for the time you have lost."

Dhananad clapped once. "Of course! I would be delighted to enjoy Cathayi hospitality."

The Golden Scorpion—what was her name?— poked him again. "We will make arrangements to meet here, at the Bijuran embassy."

The Scorpion's voice tugged at him, pulling at the fog in his mind.

The princess shook her head. "We have troubled the Bijurans too much already. We are more than happy to have you as our guests." Princess Kaiya locked her gaze on the Golden Scorpion. Their eyes waged a silent battle of will.

Dhananad wavered. His logical brain understood the Golden Scorpion's intervention: it was better to talk at a neutral site instead of giving the Cathayi a territorial advantage. Yet his heart could not bring him to oppose the princess' will. Finally, he waved off the Scorpion. "The princess is right. We have already asked much of the Bijurans. Let us meet at the Cathayi Embassy in seven days. I hope to hear some good news then."

Sweet Kaiya stood. She motioned for her retinue, and they all followed her lead, standing and bowing. The imperial guard led them out of the room, with the infuriating handmaiden in the rear.

Standing at the window above, Prince Dhananad watched her entire entourage of two dozen guards form up. The haze shrouding his mind lifted. Why had he let the princess dictate terms to him?

He waved toward the musicians, who whispered among themselves as they packed up their instruments. "You, drummer. How did you know when to start playing?"

The drummer exchanged glances with his compatriots. "We were just discussing that, Your Eminence. We felt the princess' movements guided our hands. We may never put on such a wondrous performance again."

The Golden Scorpion and the Teleri official came up on either side of him. Both stared out the window.

"Your Eminence," she said, her voice soothing. "Do you not find it curious that the Princess of Cathay travels with such minimal protection? Among her guards, I can count the truly skilled warriors on one hand."

The Bovyan nodded. "Our spies say she arrived in Vyara in secret, with a very small retinue and no baggage. Usually, Cathayi royalty travel abroad with at least a hundred of their elite soldiers."

Dhananad slapped the window sill. "Curse the clumsy handmaiden. May the many arms of Yama drag her down to Hell! Had my Lotus Blossom drunk the nectar, we would be making wedding arrangements now. It would only be a matter of years before we could take Cathay without drawing a sword."

"It was no accident," the Scorpion said. "The handmaiden intentionally knocked the glass out of the princess' hand."

He turned to the woman, trying to read her expression. "Could she have seen you slip the aphrodisiac into the princess' drink?"

"Only one with natural talent and trained in the *Bahaadur* fighting arts could have perceived the speed of my motion."

Dhananad looked to the Bovyan. "Bring out your Nightblades. Have the princess followed, find out what she is doing over this next week."

"Your Eminence," the man replied. "The Teleri embassy must attend to many issues in Vyara city. We cannot commit all of our resources just to chase this latest infatuation of yours. I will certainly speak to our ambassador about it, though."

Dhananad spat. "Bah. To control Cathay would mean monopolizing the supply of guns and firepowder. Your enemies in the East and ours in the West would soon fall before us. My marriage to Princess Kaiya, combined with your empire's machinations in their country, will put my future son on their throne."

"Do not underestimate the princess, Your Highness," the Scorpion said. "She could very well be Madura's undoing if you do."

Dhananad held her gaze. "That is why you will follow her moves, especially if the Teleri will not."

The Ayuri music still echoed in Kaiya's ears. Her arms and legs screamed to move to the beat of her guards' marching boots. Her energy should've been drained after such an epic performance; but instead, she felt invigorated, as her vitality surged against her corporeal bonds.

The Loves of Prince Aralas was the longest solo dance she knew. The entire suite, when performed by an ensemble of dancers, lasted nearly two hours; the abridged solo version took ten minutes and tested the limits of her endurance.

Yet when the music had started, Master Sabal's lessons on the barge came to her. She lost all volition as the melody guided her body's movements and tangibly held her up in positions she had never achieved before. Each enunciation of a musical note pulled or pushed her, while her classical training allowed her to effortlessly articulate perfect postures.

When at last she had eased to a stop, having decided to leave out the tragic ending in favor of one of bliss and fascination, over two hours had passed— impossibly longer than the stamina of the stoutest warrior. Never in her life had she performed such a perfect dance.

She thought back to her audience, all enthralled by *her*, lulled into complacent reverie. Even the Bovyan, who as a race cared little for mundane pastimes, watched with rapt interest. She'd formed a connection, not with her voice as Lord Xu had taught her, but through motion. The beating of their hearts, nudged into harmony with hers. Just as Ayana had done with her elven magic to the Teleri spy.

Only the Golden Scorpion had seemed bored, and, like Master Sabal's *naga* when he fought, her mask had emitted a soft blue light during the dance. The woman had resisted the connection, shrugged off the enchantment. Perhaps Paladins could do the same. If Madura indeed had two thousand of the Golden Scorpions... What an ingenious move it had been to recruit them.

Kaiya gasped. She'd forgotten to ask to see an image of Grand Vizier Rumiya, the man who had formed up the Golden Scorpion Corps.

CHAPTER 35:

A Prince by Any Other Name

After several days in Vyara City, Kaiya had grown accustomed to the bustling cacophony of its main boulevards. It made the district around the Ankiran maharaja's villa seem quiet and eerie. It was as if they had crossed a bridge into a different city.

Worn boots clopped on the uneven pavement as several dozen soldiers in threadbare uniforms marched around the weathered white walls. The villa's crumbling minarets cast shadows across a fetid canal, making the entire compound appear dark and cold. She tightened the sari around her shoulders, as if it would provide warmth.

In a city of spotless buildings, manicured boulevards, and sparkling canals, it seemed like they were visiting a castle that had been held under siege for the year. Poor Prince Hardeep. He'd come to this ramshackle building to recover from his wounds a year before. From his letters, he was still staying in Vyara City.

Maybe she would see him today. The lotus jewel felt warm at her waist. Her heart quickened and her palms sweated. Had her feelings for him been there all this time, tucked away by Zheng Ming's attention?

A steward in a faded blue *kurta* guided them into a receiving room which spoke of desperate times. Light bauble lamps were three-quarters shuttered, perhaps to avoid illuminating the Ankiran royal family's plight.

The steward pointed her toward a rickety-looking wood chair. Kaiya's bare feet slid across the thinning rug. She gingerly settled on the edge, worried it might collapse beneath even her light weight.

Jie, despite her even slimmer build, eyed her own seat dubiously. Though invited to sit, Chen Xin and Ma Jun remained standing, either from protocol or their own doubts about the chairs.

A girl in Ankiran blue livery, if it could be called that, brought a large bowl with cracked enamel, filled with *roti* flatbread. She placed it on a low table with splotchy varnish.

Several guards watched her from the periphery of the room.

"*Dian-xia,*" the half-elf whispered in the Hua tongue. "How much clout do you think the Ankiran maharaja has?"

Kaiya glared at her Insolent Retainer, cowing her into silence. Let her believe it was all about alliance building. Soon, very soon...

The valet called out from the entrance, "His Majesty, Maharaja Bahir II."

Kaiya turned back to the doors. An old man strode into the room, shoulders square and head held high. Just behind him walked a youth whose face looked not much older than Jie, but whose broad shoulders and barrel chest could have belonged to a fierce warrior. He entered the room cradling a middle-aged woman's hand in the crook of his arm. A dozen guards flanked them as they walked to the front of the room and sat.

"Greetings, Princess Kaiya of Cathay," the maharaja said. Like the boy, he wore a royal blue *kurta* with a gold lotus emblazoned on the left breast.

Kaiya pressed her hands together and bowed her head. "Thank you for receiving me, Your Eminence."

The maharaja motioned toward the woman. "This is Queen Shariya."

The queen shifted the blue *sari* on her shoulder. Her eyes narrowed to slits. "We are something of outcasts to Vyara City's high society. To what do we owe this royal visit?"

Cold and blunt. Kaiya sucked her breath in. "I bear greetings from my father, the Emperor of Cathay."

The queen's tone went from unfriendly to downright hostile. "Does he wish to gloat at Ankira's occupation? Your trade mission's decision thirty-two years ago to sell guns to Madura doomed us."

Guilt yanked at Kaiya's heart. The ugly side of unfettered mercantilism enriched Hua at the expense of others. She would've never considered the implications if not for meeting with Prince Hardeep. She folded her hands in her lap and bowed low. "I... We—"

The queen thrust an obtuse finger at her. "And there you sit wearing fine silk and the latest fashions and rubbing our misfortune in our faces. I should have my guards hold you down and rip your dress from you and share you many times over, before cutting your pretty head off and sending it back to avaricious Cathay on a spear so that your Emperor will know how Ankira suffers because of his selfish decisions." The queen panted to catch her breath. Tears ran down her weathered cheeks.

A chill raced up Kaiya's spine. Embassy robes ruffled as the imperial guards tensed. Jie reached into the band of her *langa*. They were hopelessly outnumbered.

Fixing his attention on Kaiya, the boy raised an open hand. He spoke in a deep voice which matched his build but not his face. "Please calm down, Grandmother. You cannot blame the Princess of Cathay for something that happened before she was even born. Princess Kaiya, please forgive the queen. All of her sons were lost in defense of our homeland, her daughters married off to secure alliances which never materialized."

Lost? *All* of her sons? Kaiya met his gaze. The lump in her throat strangled her words, and she had to clear it before continuing. "Does Prince Hardeep still live?"

The queen burst into sobs. The boy prince looked at her with sympathetic eyes.

Oh Heavens, no. Kaiya's spine might have been made of jelly, the way her body wanted to fold in on itself. "I am sorry for your loss." Her loss. She slipped off her chair to her knees and touched her fingers to the rug. Her retainers dropped to a knee as well. "I was very touched by my meeting with him two years ago."

Queen Shariya wiped her eyes and cocked her head.

"That is impossible," the boy said. His brow creased.

Impossible? A presumptuous kid she just met was judging her emotions! Kaiya straightened. "He came to our palace to request an alliance against Madura."

The queen choked on tears. "Two years ago would have been too late, anyway."

The boy whisked his hand to quiet his grandmother. He nodded at Kaiya to continue.

"We exchanged correspondence up until just a month ago," Kaiya said.

Queen Shariya pursed her lips and snorted.

The boy shook his head. "That is just *not* possible."

The gall of the little brat, questioning her emotions. Heat flared in Kaiya's cheeks. She reached into the band of her *langa* and withdrew the lotus jewel. It pulsed with a warmth in her hands. "He gave me this lotus jewel."

The queen and the boy gaped at it. The maharaja leaned forward, squinting. Perhaps now they would believe her.

At last, the boy spoke in a low monotone. "That is *not* a lotus jewel. I don't know what it is, but it is not a lotus jewel."

Kaiya stared at the trinket in her hand. For two years, she'd gazed at it, stroked it, held it to her heart many times, all holding on to the memory of her prince. "But what about Prince Hardeep? When did he die?"

The prince cocked his head. "My uncle Hardeep died in infancy. Before you or I were born."

The world spun and Kaiya thrust a hand back against the chair for support. This could not be right. She'd seen the royal registries in the foreign ministry archive herself. No death date for Prince Hardeep had ever been entered. He'd been there, before her eyes.

Who had visited her?

And if Hardeep was dead, who had she been exchanging letters with?

Jie had seen Prince Hardeep from a distance at Wailian Castle two years before, but was curious to see what he was really like. She knew Princess Kaiya had a thing for transparent men like Young Lord Zheng...but a ghost?

She laid a hand on the princess' shoulder. Her trembling body radiated an unnatural heat as she staggered to her feet and slumped back into the chair. Which creaked, but by an act of the Heavens did not collapse into a tangle of firewood and princess.

Jie's focus shifted from the maharaja to the queen and back. The woman crumpled onto herself, crying inconsolably. The old man's face might as well have been frozen, like a *Moquan* brother under interrogation, revealing less than a Golden Scorpion's mask.

The boy was the real king, setting up the old man as the primary target for Madura. Though no doubt, the child was no safer than the decoy. Which was why the royal treasury must have been strained to finance so many guards protect the sole heir to the Ankiran throne.

No point in revealing her suspicions. Jie turned to the old man. "Your Eminence, I am sorry to ask in light of the sad circumstances, but an impostor with full credentials visited Princess Kaiya back then, requesting assistance in your fight against Madura. Who from Ankira authorized the visit?"

The decoy remained impassive, but the boy stroked his beardless chin. "I do not recall any missions to Cathay. Two years ago, it would not have mattered anyway. It could have been anyone looking to make mischief."

Princess Kaiya found her voice. "He had pale blue eyes, unlike any other Ayuri I have ever seen."

The boy maharaja exchanged looks with the others and the soldiers murmured among themselves.

His grandmother set her hand so the pinkie and index finger stuck out, the *mudra* for warding evil. "Only one Ayuri in history has had blue eyes, though he disappeared thirty-two years ago. Madura's Grand Vizier, Rumiya."

Jie hesitantly looked back at the princess.

Her knuckles were white around the armrests. Tears glistened in her eyes. She mouthed *painting*, but only a gasp came out.

Jie bowed toward the old man. "Do you have a painting of Rumiya?"

The boy motioned toward a female servant and pointed toward the entrance. "Go to the library. Retrieve the *Chronology of Madura*."

The girl disappeared and the room fell into a nervous hush, broken only by the princess' and Queen Grandmother's occasional sniffs. Jie used the awkward silence to ponder the bigger picture. If Prince Hardeep was really the evil wizard Rumiya, where had he been for thirty years before visiting the princess? And who had she been corresponding with? Oh, to be as good as Tian at drawing connections!

Tian. The answer dawned on her and she turned to draw the princess' attention, only to find her looking back, mouthing the same name.

Peng. It fit what Tian had said: several years after the fact, he realized Lord Peng had set him up to take the blame for the horrible mistake that got him banished. Peng was a snake to be sure, and this was certainly the same sort of vicious prank that inevitably hurt others.

Unless Peng had more sinister reasons beyond pure maliciousness.

When the servant returned, the boy motioned for her to deliver the heavy bundle of scrolls into the princess' hands.

Kaiya sat in her room at the Hua embassy, fingers trembling as she flipped through the sheaf of yellowing scrolls the Ankirans had loaned her. Her focus settled on an entry.

When the Hellstorm and Long Winter laid low the first great human empires, dynamic individuals forged new nations with strategic skill, diplomatic acumen, or the sheer force of will. In the region that would become the Kingdom of Madura, that individual was Madukant, who had been a captain in the Ayuri Empire's armies.

A masterful military tactician, Madukant made up for his lack of charisma with a combination of brute force and cutthroat political maneuvering. He ensured his soldiers survived the Long Winter by plundering the land of all its value. He set himself up first as a regional warlord. After absorbing nominal friends and crushing enemies, he declared himself maharaja.

His descendants inherited his ambition but not his skill, and had barely expanded the borders of the original Kingdom for a century and a half. That all changed when the sorcerer Rumiya rose to Grand Vizier.

See Illustration on the next page.

Kaiya tightened her hand into a fist. Was it worth seeing what this Rumiya looked like? It was bad enough she wasted two years of her youth pining for an imposter. If that imposter turned out to be an evil wizard...

She closed her eyes and flipped to the next scroll. With a deep breath, she looked down.

The full-color painting captured her Hardeep's dark bronze features just as she had remembered. How often had she dreamed about the line of his jaw and the thin curled beard? And of course, the luminous blue eyes which *saw* her.

The image blurred as hot tears clouded her vision. He had never truly loved her. Her own genuine feelings, wasted. A single drop splattered on the painting, causing the rust-red in his *kurta* to run.

Why had Rumiya come to Hua? Surely not to free Ankira, as he claimed. Why the interest in her music and the Dragon Scale Lute? And why had he rescued her from Wailian Castle?

Kaiya dabbed the tears, grateful for the solitude of her room. With magic involved, there was one person who might be able to tell her more. She unwound Lord Xu's magic mirror from its silk wrapping.

Her reverse reflection gazed back at her, eyes rimmed in red. It would not do to let Xu see her like this.

After a few minutes, she cleared her throat. "Jie, please bring me some water."

Presently, the door swung open and the half-elf slunk in, a decanter in hand. With a rare look of sisterly concern, she sucked on her lower lip. A squeak escaped when she opened her mouth to say something, but she then fell silent.

The very fact that Jie had actually done something handmaidenly, without protest, made Kaiya feel a little better. She flashed a bittersweet smile. "Close the door behind you, Jie. I want you to be privy to this conversation."

"Conversation?" Jie raised an eyebrow, but turned and did as she was told.

Kaiya waved her hand over the mirror. "Lord Xu, please answer me." She waited until her impatience got the better of her. "Lord Xu?"

At last, her own reflection faded and the ageless elf shimmered into view. He peered back with half-lidded eyes, and his hair looked as if birds had recently nested in it. "*Dian-xia*. How may I be of service?"

"What can you tell me about Madura's Grand Vizier Rumiya?" Her voice choked on the man's name.

Xu yawned and scratched his head. "He claimed he would expand Madura to Hua's Great Wall. But Madura spread too fast, and its armies were stretched too thin, suppressing rebellions in its north and defending the east against the Paladins." His brow furrowed.

"Then what?" Kaiya prompted.

Xu eyed her for a second. "When the Dragon Avarax awoke from a thousand years of sleep, many of the Paladins stationed at Madura's border redeployed to the edge of the Dragonlands. It allowed Madura to resume its northward expansion into Ankira. However, Rumiya was not around to see his dreams realized."

Not around? "Where did he go?"

Xu shrugged.

A shrug? Kaiya glared at him through the mirror. "Rumiya visited me as Prince Hardeep. Why didn't you tell me?"

Xu's brows scrunched together. "I know a lot, young lady, but I did not know it was him. He might have cloaked his energy signature. From what I know, his magic resembled the sorcery of the Aksumi humans, which in itself is beyond the capability of an Ayuri human. And much more powerful. No human should wield so much power."

Kaiya sighed. Xu supposedly knew *everything*. Could do virtually *anything*. Yet now, he told her no more than the scrolls.

Xu looked beyond her. "Half-elf, you are smarter than you look, I'm sure. Use that pretty little head to piece together everything you know. A lot happened thirty-two years ago..."

Why did Xu always speak in riddles? Kaiya started to complain when his image faded out, revealing her own perplexed expression.

CHAPTER 36:
Titles Bestowed, Titles Earned

From his command tent near the cove entrance, Zheng Ming counted his blessings. Had he not received the imperial missive to return to the capital, he would've boarded the *Golden Phoenix* and been trapped after Peng's men captured it. The dead bodies of sailors caught on board bobbed in the harbor, a feast for the birds, victims of Peng's brutality.

Now, by order of the acting *Tianzi*, Ming was elevated to *Dajiang* and tasked with the immediate recapture of the flagship. He examined a rough map of the cove and its surrounding bluffs. With Princess Kaiya's escort of a hundred imperial guards, joined by a thousand infantrymen with a hundred guns, they had superior numbers. Yet despite what Prince Kai-Wu might think, numbers alone wouldn't prevail in this situation. If only he had the services of the *Tianzi's* mysterious agents, he could send them aboard under the cover of darkness.

Ming swept his gaze over the officers. Their hard expressions spoke one message: storm the cove, there and now.

Of course, very few of them had actual combat experience. Ming knew better. He'd charged into a situation before, at the inn, only to find he'd been tricked.

Since their initial assault, Lord Peng's faithful soldiers had swelled to five hundred men. At least a hundred occupied the *Golden Phoenix*, while the rest held strategic points near and around the sandy cove where the ship was moored. More importantly, the enemy controlled the cliffs above.

The dock was a bottleneck, much like a certain bridge from Ming's recent past.

Ordering his men to assail such a fortified position was practically a death sentence. It was safer to just wait them out. Without a crew, Peng wouldn't be going anywhere. Yet the imperial messenger in the tent crossed his arms and looked askance. Why the urgency on Prince Kai-Wu's part?

Ming stepped out of the command tent and glanced up at the bluffs overlooking the cove. An indeterminate number of Peng's archers held a ridge above the bluff's rear access path. Any chance at victory depended on securing that spot. It would provide a good view of the enemy's deployment and a line of sight to the flagship.

If the imperials wanted a fight, at least Ming could keep them busy with something that wouldn't get many killed. On his command, the infantry commander formed up a phalanx of muskets, three ranks of thirty-three men each, facing Peng's archers.

The first volley from the lower ground did little more than kick up dirt around the archer's entrenched position. Peng's men retreated out of sight and returned an arcing salvo of arrows.

The barrage pushed the musketmen out of range; nonetheless, it had done its job. From the number of arrows, Ming estimated about three dozen men defending the ridge.

He pondered the conundrum. The angle of the rise rendered muskets useless. A charge up the narrow path would only get his men killed. Unless the archers above had a reason to keep their heads down... like the night the princess was ambushed on the way to Peng's. The attackers' barrage had kept them hiding between the horses. "Commander, set your musketmen in ranks of six men—"

"Six men at a time?" The commander looked at him as if was insane. "Not concentrated enough. We won't hit much."

Ming nodded. "That is not the point. Each group will approach, fire their volley, then fall back and allow another group to replace them. I want non-stop shooting to lay suppressing fire. It will cover my horses' charge."

All ten of them. Only the officers rode horses, and Ming doubted their cavalry skills. No one else could lead the charge. What had the Founder said? Men respect a title earned, not bestowed? Now if only the cover fire would keep the archers' heads down until he led his makeshift cavalry to the top of the bluff. He beckoned a captain of the imperial guard. "I want you to follow our horses and engage any surviving enemy at the top."

The captain placed his fist in his open palm. "As you command, *Dajiang*."

The musket squad commander shook his head. "It's never been done before. I can't guarantee the rebels won't return a volley."

Such insubordination. Ming gritted his teeth. "I will take it into consideration. Now, let us ready our horses. Begin firing on my signal."

When his line of horses and the imperial guards behind him were ready, Ming drew his *dao* and raised it to the sun. "Charge!"

The musketmen discharged a staccato patter of gunfire, six shots every two seconds. Wind rushing through his hair, Ming dared a glance up. Could it be? None of the archers poked their heads up from behind cover, though some took blind shots that flew toward the source of the musket fire.

Ming's horse galloped up the path, rounding the bend and breaking out into the archers' line at the top of the ridge. He charged through, cutting as many as possible with one run. He wheeled around. The survivors drew swords,

even as the rest of the mounted imperial soldiers crashed through them.

Unslinging his bow, Ming cantered back the way he came. With aimed shots in the gaps between his troops, he dropped five of Peng's men.

The imperial guard reached the top of the bluff. Their gleaming breastplates, with their scowling dragons, radiated dread. Peng's surviving men threw down their weapons and cowered.

Ming turned to a lieutenant. "Our losses?"

His aide-de-campe beamed. "Four musketmen killed, seven wounded. Two of your riders were also injured."

Ming nodded. A sad sacrifice, but one made for the sake of superior position. And certainly better than the blind charge the imperials wanted. "Redeploy the musketmen along the bluff, facing the cove. Send the imperial guards to the access road to await my orders."

"What about the prisoners?" His aide lifted his chin toward Peng's defeated men, who knelt in a line with hands on their heads.

Ming strode over to them, twenty-one in all, mostly uninjured. Several prostrated themselves, perhaps hoping to avoid the penalty for treason. But no, the princess had treated the dying Xie Shimin with dignity and kindness. "Soldiers of Nanling. You have risen up in arms against the Son of Heaven. You know the punishment."

One man whimpered. "It was Lord Peng. He ordered us to do so. Said it was for the good of the nation."

"You obeyed orders. For that, I give you two choices." Ming held out his curved dagger. "You may cut your own throat and die with honor. Or, I will organize you into our army." Heaven knew they needed archers, even if the imperials preferred guns.

All twenty-one rose into one-knee salutes.

"Traitors," the imperial commander muttered.

Ming flashed him a sharp glance. "Assign a dozen men to watch over them, ready to run them through at the first sign of treachery. Provide bows only if we need their service."

Lips pursed, the commander placed a hand in his fist. "As the *Dajiang* commands."

Letting out a long breath, Ming turned around and used the new vantage point to reassess their situation. Peng's men held the cove's beaches and the dock. The *Golden Phoenix* remained anchored about four hundred feet away from where he stood, making it difficult to pick out Lord Peng from the other men on deck.

He turned to the musketmen's commander. "Can any of your sharpshooters find Lord Peng and hit him from here?"

The commander gawked. "Not from this range, no. We would splinter the *Golden Phoenix* with all of the misses."

Ming looked back at the ship. From this range, it was an impossible shot with a bow, even if they could locate Peng among the defenders. He waved toward the newly appointed commander of the archers. "Bring your unit here. When we storm the beach, I want our new recruits to prove their loyalty by raining arrows on the ship's deck."

He then turned to the musketmen's commander. "On my order, lay down volley fire into their units on the beach and dock."

Orders passed from unit to unit. Soldiers brought the command tent to the top of the bluffs. Within two hours, everyone was deployed.

When the fusillade of muskets tore into the beach, many of the enemy threw themselves into the sand or cowered behind the docks' pylons. Arrows from his new archery unit arced into the ship, sending Peng's men below deck.

The imperial guard swept in. Ming had seen combat in Rotuvi before, but never the beautiful but brutal efficiency with which the imperial guard fought. The defenders put up little resistance, many throwing down their arms and begging for mercy.

The beach was theirs in just minutes.

A volley of musket fire roared from the *Golden Phoenix*'s portholes, ripping into the imperial guards' efficient lines. Ming gritted his teeth. There had been no report of Peng's men having guns.

"Sound a defensive withdrawal," he told an officer. "Without a crew, their only escape is by the beach. Have our men fall back and guard the access road. Do not let anyone through."

Another officer shuffled on his feet. "What about the *Tianzi's* command to take the ship?"

Ming sighed. "As long as they have guns, the ship is a floating fortress with one point of access. I will not needlessly sacrifice our men in a futile attempt to take it." Even with his archery skills, the portholes were a near impossible shot given the range and angle. Which left... "How many days of food and water do they carry?"

The officers chattered among themselves before a quartermaster spoke up. "I don't know much about ships, but it takes six days at best to reach Ayudra. If it were me planning, I would provision for ten days."

Ten days. A long time, but hopefully, the stark reality of Peng's situation would set in sooner: a soldier's bravado would last only as long as his stomach was full.

Ming pointed toward the city. "Procure lumber from the port and construct cover fortifications that bring us closer and closer to the ship. Then we will wait."

They waited three days. Ming imagined the ship's occupants must be growing unsettled, wallowing in their own stench and perhaps rationing food.

He drew up a letter:

Brave soldiers of Hua, your loyalty to your lord is admirable. However, you now stand in rebellion against the Tianzi. *Surrender Lord Peng, and your death sentences will be commuted.*

He tied the note to an arrow and shot it onto the deck.

Nobody went up top to retrieve it.

He rewrote the letter and had a messenger deliver it under the flag of parley. The unfortunate man made it halfway down the dock before falling to a barrage of musket balls from the ship.

The imperial soldiers shouted and cursed. Ming stared wide-eyed. To kill a man walking under the flag of parley was unthinkable. Let Peng starve. The *Golden Phoenix* would bake under the sun, all those below deck boiling in a stinking cesspool of disease and misery.

On the fourth day, the enemy soldiers lowered the gangplank and began filing off one by one, weary, unarmed, and hands on their head.

Ming rode down to accept Lord Peng's surrender.

Instead, he found himself talking to *Yu-Ming* Lord Tu, the young heir to one of Nanling Provinces' more prosperous counties.

"Where is Lord Peng?" Ming demanded.

Lord Tu shook his head. "Dead. Killed by one of your arrows on the first day."

Not totally unexpected. Nonetheless... "Why did you not surrender at that time?"

"It would have been dishonorable."

And yet, they had slain a man approaching under the flag of parley. Ming raised an eyebrow. "You surrender now."

Lord Tu cringed. "Your agent onboard murdered several of us each day. I was faced with a mutiny."

Agent? Ming scowled. Why had he never heard of this?

Voices stirred Liang Yu out of the *Viper's Rest* technique and back into the world of the living. He instinctively remained still and kept his breath near imperceptible as he tried to piece through the disorientation and memory loss the technique caused.

At least he remembered his identity—*Moquan* who were not true masters like himself might even forget their very name.

Beside him laid dead corpses, cold, but not yet rancid with the stench of death.

The memories trickled back.

He was the one who killed those soldiers.

Days before, he'd melted in with Lord Peng's troops as they marched to Jiangkou.

He made sure he was part of the boarding party that initially captured the *Golden Phoenix.*

That first night, he hypnotized Lord Tu with the *Tiger's Eye* and learned the attack on the flagship was meant as a diversion for Lord Peng's escape over the border into Rotuvi.

Liang Yu focused. Why was that so important to him?

Because he intended to kill Lord Peng, lest he became a threat. Yes, Peng had pushed Expansionism, but according to Minister Hong, it was mostly as a way of garnering support among the Expansionist lords. What he would do after actually capturing the Dragon Throne was anyone's guess.

Though now, it turned out Peng was quite clever. Perhaps he would be worth keeping alive a little longer.

Liang Yu peeked out of a nearly closed eye once the voices faded into the distance. He was still below deck on the *Golden Phoenix*, lined up among the dead. A blade of fading afternoon light cut through a partially open porthole.

He withdrew a slender bamboo reed from his hidden pouch. Though not as supple as he had been in his youth, he could still squeeze out of a sea-side porthole, and then swim below the water, undetected.

He had done as much thirty-two years before when an elf pushed him off a bridge and left him for dead.

Unfortunately, Lord Peng had escaped his reach. And apparently the *Tianzi's* as well.

For now.

CHAPTER 37:

Rogues Gallery

Prince Dhananad disliked visiting the Teleri embassy not just because of the vermin inhabiting it, but mostly due to its spartan décor. It seemed that even in Vyara City, a magnet for culture and refinement, the Bovyan Scourge prided itself on its bland lifestyle. The sooner his country ended its alliance with the Teleri Empire, the better.

The huge guards, dressed in black surcoats that must have left them roasting in the South's sun, stepped to the side and let Dhananad and his Golden Scorpion escort pass.

Dhananad stormed through the halls and slammed open the metallic double doors to the audience room. The Teleri ambassador sat straight-backed and cross-legged on a dais, holding audience with several— Dhananad skidded to a halt.

Leisurely nestled in a mountain of cushions was a turquoise-skinned altivorc dressed in a dapper military uniform. Dhananad knew this particular specimen. Unlike the rest of his kind, this one was handsome, with refined, almost elf-like features. No one was sure how old he was, or even if he was the same person over the centuries. He had first appeared in history a millennium ago (but who was counting?) as his people were losing the War of Ancient Gods. Nobody knew his name, and Dhananad joined everyone else in addressing him as the King of Altivorcs.

Humph. King of what? A pack of ugly humanoids of little consequence. The Tivari might have once controlled all of Tivaralan, enslaved all of humanity; but now they hid away in subterranean cities sprinkled throughout the mountains of the Northwest. Both the altivorcs and their more hideous, stupider cousins, the tivorcs, worked as mercenaries for the highest bidder. Dhananad's homeland of Madura had nothing to do with them. If he had anything to say about it, they never would.

Dhananad avoided the altivorc's gaze, and instead turned to Ambassador Piros di Bovyan. Like all of the Teleri Prospecti—the upper echelon of Bovyans who ruled their empire—he was an imposing man, with dark hair and grey eyes. He had been in Vyara for six years, and Dhananad tired of having to pander to him.

"Is it true?" he asked. "Did Princess Kaiya really meet with the Ankiran insurgents?"

The Bovyan brute Piros shrugged and cocked his head. When he spoke, his Ayuri reeked of the North. "If by insurgent, you mean their former maharaja, then yes. Perhaps you should have paid heed to our advisor, instead of falling for the girl's charm. She was obviously misleading you."

Dhananad spat. "Bah. A meeting with some outlaws means nothing. Perhaps the filth begged her to speak to me on their behalf."

Another familiar face sneered. With Lord Benhan's light-brown skin tone and dark hair, a Northerner might have mistaken him for Ayuri; but Dhananad (and any other Southerner!) recognized him as Levanthi. This dolt hailed from the Empire of Levastya, which, unlike Madura's other ally, at least had a semblance of high culture. Albeit inferior to the Ayuri.

Dhananad glared back. "Do you find something funny?"

Benhan laughed. "Do not assume Cathayi women are as easily cowed as those in Madura."

Dhananad cast him a disdainful glance. It wasn't worth acknowledging the comment. "Her meeting with them means nothing."

Piros scoffed. "Don't you find it suspicious that she also met with the Vadarans, Bijurans, and Daburans? While not your enemies, they certainly aren't your friends."

The Altivorc King let out a yawn a lion would envy. "I would be more concerned with her visit to the Paladins' Crystal Citadel in two days."

Dhananad was about to respond, but found himself uncharacteristically at a loss for words. His mouth hung open as the others afforded him patronizing grins. When he found his tongue, his voice squeaked. "Your Nightblades are following her, then?"

Piros shrugged again. "Of course. We must know what she is up to. It is ultimately our goal to bring Cathay into our alliance's sphere of influence, though our plan could take a decade to accomplish."

Dhananad stomped his foot on the marble tiles. "Then you must see the importance of my marriage to her? Our son would have a claim to rule Cathay, which could move up your timeline by many years! Imagine, my infant son on the Dragon Throne, with me as Regent! It would give us access to more and better guns, and limitless firepowder. Not even the Paladins are fast enough to avoid a bullet!"

He glanced back to see his Scorpion shifting on his feet, in denial of the truth.

The Altivorc King cackled. "Humans! Always concerned about short-term gain. It is ironic that the Bovyans, the shortest-lived of your kind, seem to be the only ones who understand the effectiveness and subtleties of long-term planning."

Lord Benhan shared Dhananad's scowl, but before either of them could speak, the King wagged a finger at the Levastyan. "Don't try to deny it. Even though your ruling priests in Levastya now worship the Ancient Gods of Tivara, they do not seem to have embraced the wisdom of long-term thinking that we teach. Otherwise, you would not be threatening the Estomari in Korynth without having fully subjugated Selastya."

Prince Dhananad regarded him curiously. "What do you mean by *short-term*, oh wise King of the Orcs?"

The Altivorc King waved a dismissive hand. "Your entire plan rests upon the princess agreeing to marry you. You are obviously not going to accomplish that with your good looks, so you resort to the threat of force. Yet she is evidently befriending those who might be your enemies, and more importantly, those who can attack you on another front. Your threat of force will be neutralized." He smirked. "What part of your plan is it that you consider good?"

Heat rushed to Dhananad's cheeks. Nobody mocked him! Had he carried his *talwar*, he might have attacked the King, even though he would certainly have no chance of surviving if the legends of the King's physical prowess were to be believed. "Then it is quite simple. If the Paladins do not agree to help Cathay, then Bijura, Vadara, and Dabura will not be in a position to oppose our Scorpions. All we have to do is prevent her from meeting the Paladins."

The altivorc's yellow eyes narrowed as they locked on Dhananad's. "What do you intend?"

Dhananad turned his back on the altivorc to face Ambassador Piros. "Your Nightblades have surely noted that Princess Kaiya travels with little guard?"

Piros responded with a slow, dubious nod.

"My Scorpions say that her best protection is an ancient elf wizardess, five imperial guards, and a half-elf girl."

"Half-elf?" The Altivorc King leaned forward and turned toward Piros, who nodded. Dhananad knew the Tivari had tried to exterminate the elves millennia ago, but the King's sudden interest seemed to go beyond mere hatred.

He ignored the altivorc's query and continued. "When she departs from the safety of her embassy, a force of my personal guard, assisted by several of the Scorpions, will take her. And then she will be mine. Cathay relies too much on their Great Wall and does not have the seasoned soldiers to attack Madura to take her back. In due time, we will have a son, and when that happens, we will lay claim to Cathay."

Piros stroked his chin thoughtfully. "You would take her by force and despoil her against her will?"

Dhananad snorted. "I would think the Teleri would appreciate such measures."

"And if your men fail to capture her?" Piros asked.

"Then they will be disavowed. They will not wear the markings of Madura or the Scorpions. We will leave no evidence that we were ever involved."

Piros and Benhan both seemed to be in deep thought (at his brilliance, no doubt!), so much that he swore he saw smoke coming out of their ears.

The Altivorc King clapped. "Ingenious, Prince Dhananad! It is a sound plan, one that I am willing to support. I will supply several of my soldiers to assist you. Perhaps Cathay will fall within your alliance's grasp sooner than we expected."

Dhananad beamed at the compliment. He would be gracious and forget the previous insults. "Thank you, King of the Orcs. I will take my leave to prepare the specifics of the attack. Have your men come to the Maduran embassy under the cover of darkness."

After Prince Dhananad had spun on his heel and left, Piros sighed. He lamented spending the twilight of his allotted thirty-three years of life stuck in this city, dealing with fools like the prince.

He looked toward the beneficiary of his short lifespan, the Altivorc King. The ancestor of all Bovyans had made a deal with the altivorc gods, surrendering the collective life force of his descendants to sustain the Altivorc King's. The King promised to end the curse when the Bovyans gave him control of the three remaining pyramids in the north. That was not likely to happen in Piros' lifetime.

In the meantime, they remained strange bedfellows. Piros could not fathom why the Altivorc King decided to throw his weight behind a brash attack, especially after sparing no expense to stay unannounced in Vyara City. He had remained holed up in the Teleri embassy since his sudden arrival a few days before. Perhaps suffering clowns like Dhananad was easier than fathoming mysterious allies like the Altivorc King.

"It is a foolish idea," Piros said to the King. "One that has too many ways to fail."

The altivorc laughed. "Of course it will fail. Prince Dhananad does not realize the power of the old elf who protects the Princess of Cathay. But whether his plan succeeds or fails, it will not interfere with our goals. Let the prince put on a show; it will distract the Paladins from my work here."

What work, Piros could not guess, nor would the Altivorc King tell if asked. Piros had a hunch that it related to Lord Benhan's Levastyans, who sought to bring about the return of the Orc Gods on their flaming chariots.

Piros regarded Benhan, doubting the wisdom of the Levastyan's zealotry. Before their gods were vanquished, the Tivari wielded powerful magic which they used to enslave humanity. Worshipping those gods did not seem like the brightest idea.

Yet when it came down to it, they were all just using each other toward their own ends, ready to abandon alliances if they became too burdensome. Of the Levastyans, altivorcs, Madurans, and Teleri, only his own people had a truly noble goal: lasting peace for the world.

Lord Benhan smirked. "Perhaps we should inform the Paladins about an anonymous threat on the princess, to ensure Prince Dhananad's failure. We just have to know when."

The King bared his fangs. "I will let you all know the timing of his ill-advised plans."

CHAPTER 38:
Ulterior Motives

As the princess dressed with Meixi's help behind the screen, Jie considered the coincidences. The last time the *Moquan* had conducted a mission in Vyara City, they had a secondary assignment, executed under the guise of diplomacy. Following the Architect's plan, the Beauty had seduced a Maduran official, allowing her access to the young Prince Dhananad.

At least this time, their party's ulterior motive was noble. Today, they would cross the river to Vadaras to visit the government-in-exile of the Sultanate of Selastya. Selastya had been absorbed by its neighbor Levastya two decades before, after the Akolytes of their Sun God Athran lost their power to channel Divine Magic. Rumor had it some of the faithful had regained their abilities, and the princess hoped to convince the deposed sultan to send one to Hua in hopes they could cure the *Tianzi.*

As noble as their intentions were, Jie questioned the timing. The princess had shown remarkable resilience after learning of Rumiya's deception, and gone on four days of whirlwind negotiations.

She'd charmed each of the maharajas of the Ayuri Confederation nations with charisma and wit, and received several wedding proposals, which she graciously deflected. In addition to arranging several trade agreements, she secretly secured mutual protection pacts. It now rested in the hands of the *Tianzi,* who would ratify Hua's side; and the Paladins' Council of Elders, with whom she would meet the next day.

Calling from the anteroom, Chen Xin vociferously agreed with Jie about the timing. "*Dian-xia,* we still lack sufficient protection. I humbly suggest this visit wait until after your full complement of imperial guards arrives. There is no need to recklessly expose yourself to danger."

The princess' voice sang out from the other side of the screen. "We do not know when that will be. In any case, with the Paladins' omnipresence, there is virtually no petty crime in this city, let alone violence."

Jie sighed. Nothing good ever came of the princess' stubbornness. "Teleri Nightblades are constantly following us. And in any case, we will be taking the ferry over to Vadaras, where the Paladins' presence is less evident. If Madura or its allies suspect your audience with the Paladin elders in two days, there is no telling what they would do."

Hushed whispers and giggles emanated from behind the screen. Meixi came out, beaming.

Then Princess Kaiya emerged. "You are worrying needlessly."

Jie sucked her lower lip. If anyone should worry, it was the *Tianzi.* His daughter, dressed like *that*, with a degenerate Maduran prince lurking around somewhere. The white silk outer robe, embroidered with green dragons, hung from her shoulders. Open in the front, it revealed a sleeveless, strapless inner gown of light green silk, whose neckline dipped just low enough to suggest the curves beneath. A blue silk sash tied tightly around her slim waist accentuated the contour of her hips. Intricate gold pins held her obsidian hair tied above her ears.

By comparison, Jie's own flat body would've made that dress look like a war banner on a windless day. "I would remind you, Prince Dhananad tried to poison you at your last meeting."

The princess' lips quivered as she maintained her smile. Her tone turned indignant. "I appreciate all of your concerns. However, my father's health is now my priority. We will proceed with our trip to Vadaras. Prepare the guards for departure."

Chen Xin and Jie exchanged worried looks. "As the princess commands," he said.

Within a half-hour, the five imperial guards and two dozen embassy guards formed up around the princess and Ayana, who rode side-by-side on horses. The skies were overcast, and the hot and muggy air hung in her lungs. Jie knew the route well now, and watched every convenient place to lay an ambush.

Just ten minutes from the Hua embassy, the procession ground to a stop as an argument between a merchant and a miffed customer drew a crowd of spectators ahead of them.

The procession's crier yelled, his voice booming louder than his size would suggest: "Make way! Make way for Princess Kaiya Wang of Cathay!"

Despite his appeal, nobody cleared the streets. Instead, more bystanders crowded in to point and gawk at the beautiful princess in their midst. The soldiers, despite a week of drilling from the imperial guards, still lacked discipline. They broke their attentive stances, and instead bobbed and weaved to get a better view of the argument.

From her position next to the princess' horse, Jie noted the location: in a long lane between rowhouses. A perfect spot for an—

Several metal discs sliced through the air toward the first rank of embassy guards. Screams. Blood. Jie was on her feet at once. Her eyes tracked the discs back in the direction they came from. People ran every which way, yelling and pointing.

Sitting side-saddle on her horse, the princess now clenched its mane with both hands as it shied. Her mouth hung open in a silent scream as it reared. Avoiding flailing legs, Jie reached up, snagged hold of the princess' long sleeves, and yanked. The two tumbled way too close for comfort to the horse's stamping hooves. The princess covered her head with her arms.

Above them, Ayana's horse panicked and shoved its way backward despite the elf's protestations, crushing several of the guards who had been to slow to react.

Jie sprang to her feet. She took the princess' quivering hand and pulled her up. Face pale, with the eyes of a startled doe, Kaiya trembled.

Chen Xin's voice boomed over the commotion. "Form up your lines! Move forward! Protect the princess!" He and the four other imperial guards backed in around them with naked *dao* swords.

The clang of metal on metal mingled with the cries of wounded men and the screaming crowds. The embassy guards fought valiantly, streaming forward to move between the princess and the pack of rugged assailants in front of them. Ayana yelled something from behind, her voice trailing farther and farther away.

The princess straightened and motioned back in the direction they'd come. Voice calm, she said, "Pull back, back toward the safety of the embassy."

Jie shook her head. Not without knowing what was in that direction. Tall men blocked her view. Being short came in handy sometimes, but not now. Added to which, this confounded dress hindered her movement. She tugged on the princess' sleeve. "Let me go first. They might be trying to flush us into the open, out of the ring of guards."

The princess nodded, and Jie slunk through the few rear guards. On the other side, the streets blurred in chaos as citizens ran for the cover of shops and homes. The road continued for several hundred feet before intersecting with a cross-street. Two-story rowhouses lined either side, providing no escape routes.

Something was wrong; danger lay in that direction. Or at least, that's what every instinct screamed. Jie scanned windows, doorways, and rooftops. Sounds of skirmishes approached from the direction she'd just come, and she stole a glance back. Their front line of soldiers had collapsed under the onslaught. No choice now. She motioned for Chen Xin to fall back.

Chen pointed with his sword. "Zhao, help hold the line! The rest of you, surround the princess and head back toward the embassy."

Jie took one step. Six turquoise-skinned humanoids charged toward them. Protected by chainmail, they brandished heavy broadswords in their left hands. Orcs. The intelligence gleaming in their eyes suggested altivorcs, not their stupid cousins, the tivorcs.

She whipped out a handful of *biao* throwing stars and flung them. The first altivorc fell to his knees, clutching his throat, but the next was on her with a downward chop of his blade.

Jie sidestepped the blow. In the same motion, she thrust the heel of her palm under his outstretched arm and into his unprotected chin, while stomping through the back of his knee.

Even as the second altivorc collapsed, two broadswords swept at her, one toward her neck and the other at her waist. Jie sprang between the two blades while hurling two spikes at each of the orcs' flanks. She landed in a forward roll, but tripped on her hem as she tried to regain her feet.

Stumbling to the ground, she twisted over, just avoiding the hack of another sword. It sent showers of sparks by her head. Yet the roll positioned her prone in front of the sixth altivorc. He cocked his broadsword back, ready to run her through.

Jie hooked his ankle and leaned into his shin with her shoulder. He sprawled backward, and she used her momentum to flip over him. The dress prevented her from straddling him in a controlling position, so she continued her roll. Finger-jabs in his eyes vaulted her back into a stand.

She took two steps back to reassess the situation. The first altivorc lay dying, the second was incapacitated by torn knee ligaments. The second pair appeared undamaged by her spikes, regrouping with the fifth altivorc to continue their attack. The sixth staggered to his feet, clawing at his black-bloodied eye sockets.

Past them, the guards still formed a protective ring around the princess, and pressed toward Jie. Luckily—at least as far as duty was concerned—the altivorcs seemed more concerned with her than the princess.

Jie whipped out a pair of knives and sheared slits down her dress to allow more mobility.

The altivorcs closed in a coordinated attack, cutting in three different directions. Jie twisted away toward their phalanx's left flank, putting one between her and the other two. As he spun at her with a backhand chop, she sank her knife into his exposed throat.

Before either of the remaining two could attack, the imperial guards came up from behind. Ma Jun decapitated one in a spray of black blood, while Chen Xin drove his *dao* through the other, punching through the chain armor as if it were cloth.

The escape path was clear—

Two figures with curved *talwar* swords stepped in and blocked their way. They wore plain brown *kurtas*. Scarves wrapped around their faces, revealing only their eyes. One leapt past Jie before she could react and began cutting through the guards with blinding speed.

The other fixed her focus on Jie. Those eyes...they belonged to the female Golden Scorpion who'd tried to slip poison into Princess Kaiya's wine.

Jie unleashed her last *biao* spikes and stars with a single sweep of her hand.

Impossibly, the Scorpion evaded most and deflected the rest out of the air with a flash of her *talwar*, then lunged forward to close the distance. The speed with which she covered fifteen feet bordered on the unbelievable.

Jie flipped her knife into an underhand grip. There was no chance she could survive against such a skilled swordfighter.

In that second of resignation, the Scorpion attacked. The intention behind the dozen superhumanly fast slashes was as clear as if the Scorpion had whispered them beforehand. Pressed back, Jie suffered only a few nicks, though the sleeves of her beautiful gown were shredded to ribbons.

The Scorpion disengaged, her gaze flicking behind Jie.

In that direction, Ayana's voice growled, followed by the sound of dozens of weapons clattering to the ground. Jie didn't dare risk a glance back.

When they set out, Kaiya's stifling court gowns, more suited to a cool spring in Hua, had made the hot and humid day downright miserable. That was a mundane concern now. She should've listened to Jie and Chen Xin's advice.

A blindingly fast swordsman darted back and forth around the perimeter of her own protective ring, stabbing and slashing with a rapid tittering of clashing blades. He engaged Li Wei and Ma Jun, who fought in unison. Neither the swoosh of one blade nor the clanging of another deterred his onslaught. A flash of his curved sword would've ended Li Wei's life had he not deflected it with a last-second clank.

Li Wei reeled back, his boots pattering on the pavement. The enemy closed, stepping toward Chen Xin's thrust and the swish of Ma Jun's horizontal slash. He spun out of the attacks like a gush of air, and the pommel of his sword met Ma Jun's skull with a crunch.

Xu Zhan's sword tolled as it received the blow which would've finished off Ma Jun. The assailant's foot brushed through the air, thudding into Xu's temple. He tumbled into Zhao Yue, and both clattered to the ground.

Chen Xin backed off, keeping himself between the assassin and her, while Li Wei pressed the attack on wobbly feet. The man slammed his fist into Li Wei's nose, sending him sprawling.

"Princess Kaiya." The attacker raised his blade over Li Wei's inert form. "Come with us peacefully, and we will spare your guards."

Far behind her, Ayana's voice sang in the melodic language of elven magic.

Chen Xin lunged forward, his sword whipping through the air; but the man evaded the attacks and elbowed Chen in the temple, knocking him to the ground. He looked to make good on his threat, raising his sword and chopping down.

Kaiya swept out the long sleeve of her gown, entangling his blade before it finished Chen Xin.

The attacker twirled the sword, wrapping the priceless fabric around his weapon. He jerked her forward, but she spun her way out of the gown and grasped the other sleeve in her hand.

As he stood and gawked at her bare shoulders, she coiled the gown around his sword and swept it from his hands and onto the street. His eyes widened further for a split second.

Moving faster than she could see, he lunged. His fingers clenched around her wrist.

Years of Praise Moon Fist training allowed her contact reflexes to take over. She turned her wrist out of his grip, and he reached with his other hand toward her neck. Without conscious thought, she covered the opening with her free arm, intercepting his hand and guiding it downward. Still, her tactile responses couldn't keep up with him.

Ayana's voice sang out again, closer now, and the man's speed slowed to almost normal. With this change, Kaiya gained the advantage. She pinned the man's hands close to his body while delivering an onslaught of punches, strong enough to send him reeling back. He ducked into a roll back toward his sword, still wrapped up in the remains of her outer gown.

A warm palm pressed on her shoulder at the same time a single, guttural syllable echoed in her ears. Her head swam with blurring colors before all went black.

The female Scorpion launched another flurry of attacks at Jie, making her give more ground than she had left. She would be bumping up against the princess soon. She started to reengage.

Behind her, Ayana uttered a foul-sounding word. The air popped.

Her opponent lowered her sword, eyes wide in the slits of the cloth. Jie shot a quick glance back.

Princess Kaiya and Ayana were gone.

Recovering from her surprise, Jie reached down and claimed Li Wei's *dao*, easily hefting its balanced weight in her right hand while brandishing the knife in her left. She grimaced at the pain in her flank—only now did she realize she'd been cut across the ribs. Her legs wobbled and her vision blurred for a second.

She raked her gaze over the area.

Besides spectators who kept their distance, only the two Scorpions were left standing. The Hua guards and several other attackers lay on the ground, incapacitated, killed or...sleeping?

Both Golden Scorpions advanced on her.

Even the improved reach the *dao* gave her would do little to help her against one, let alone two, of these astounding warriors. She resigned herself to the inevitable. Regrets threatened to break her already-fading concentration. Never learning who her parents were. Never telling Zheng Tian she loved him...

"Paladins!" The words passed from mouth to mouth among the distraught crowds. When the Scorpions looked past her, Jie glanced back as well. A dozen men in white *kurtas* with gold embroidered necks ran at astonishing speeds toward them, their curved *naga* swords drawn.

The two villains ran off, leaving Jie to curse herself for thinking such silly thoughts. She bent down to check on the closest imperial guard, Xu Zhan.

He was alive. Thank the Heavens.

When she started to stand, everything faded to black.

CHAPTER 39:

Interlude

Kaiya was cold, and her head ached. Her forearms stung and her knuckles burned. The soft surface beneath her was cool and damp. Grass. A sweet and nostalgic smell of evergreens hung in the air. Nearby, water rustled over rocks. Beyond the stream, beautiful voices spoke softly in a wondrous, musical language.

Her eyes complained as she forced them open. Gradually, the dappled sunlight peeking through the spindly tendrils of pine needles came into focus above her. What had happened? Where was she?

Her head protested at the effort to ease herself up, but she at last managed to sit upright. She looked toward the voices. A stone's throw away, a short, lithe silhouette gesticulated. The size, her voice... Ayana.

The ambush, the fight with the Scorpion. Her guards, fallen. Her priceless outer gown, lost. Maybe that's why it was so cold. Though it certainly hadn't been so chilly outside before.

"Ayana," she called. "What happened?"

The shadowed form moved toward her, revealing a second thin figure, who remained behind. Ayana stepped into the sunlight, which cast her face in a pale sheen.

Her voice sounded weak. "Princess Kaiya, you are finally awake. You fainted and have been unconscious for three hours. It is a typical reaction, the first time you travel through the ethers. I imagine your head must feel as if it were split by a dwarf's axe."

Travelled through the ethers! Like Lord Xu, though she had never expected to ever do it herself. They could be anywhere. "Where are we? Where are my guards?"

Ayana pursed her lips. "I have sworn not to reveal our location, and in fact I am not entirely sure. I used an emergency spell that transported us to an anchor held by a friend of mine. Suffice to say, we are safe for now."

Safe! But what about... "The guards, Jie...we need to get back to them."

"I don't have the energy." Ayana sighed. "The Shallow Magic incantation is very taxing, especially when I transport someone else. Not to mention all the energy I used to protect you in your ill-advised escapade."

"We need to get back." Kaiya's voice sounded like a petulant child's to her own ears, but her retinue was her responsibility. Her fault.

"I am sorry, Princess Kaiya, but it is just not possible. We will have to wait until this evening, after I have rested."

The second shadow spoke in a mellifluous male voice. The words sang like a chorus of nightingales, reminiscent of Lord Xu.

Ayana shook her head adamantly, but he protested. She harrumphed. "My friend has agreed to send us back to Vyara City, although not to the same spot. He can only transport us somewhere he has been before. I would advise against it, since I am too weak to protect you now."

"I cannot just wait here and do nothing."

Ayana's brows furrowed. Despite the angry expression, her tone remained calm. "It is that self-assured attitude, that foolhardiness, which got you into that ambush in the first place. How many people have died because of your vanity?"

Kaiya's face flushed hot, partially from anger at the audacity of the rebuke, but mostly from shame. The elf was right. Kaiya placed too much faith in her own abilities of persuasion, never considering that that alone might be insufficient.

Ayana continued, merciless. "Do you realize what could have happened? Had I not been able to get back to you in time, the Golden Scorpions would have captured you. Prince Dhananad would be deflowering you right about now."

Kaiya shuddered. She pushed the image of the musky prince's leer out of her mind.

The other elf emerged into the clearing. A longbow hung over his shoulder, and a thin straight sword, similar to Xu's, dangled at his side. Handsome, with fine features and shiny golden hair, he wore a poncho of forest-green.

No, not handsome; he was gorgeous. Kaiya straightened out her inner gown and ran a hand through her hair.

When he spoke in Arkothi, it was tinged with a sensually exotic elvish accent: "Ayana does not speak out of maliciousness. You will not find a more caring person."

Ayana's eyebrows sunk into a scowl. "I—"

He flashed a devilish grin at the matronly elf. "She has been alive since before the time your ancestor General Shyaotian established the Wang Dynasty, and carries three centuries of experience on her shoulders. She knows the human strengths that lead to the rise of nations, and the human weaknesses that have led to their collapse. Take her wisdom to heart."

Kaiya shuffled in place. "I understand. But my retainers are my responsibility. I cannot just sit here and do nothing."

He held her gaze. "Think carefully about what you can do in your condition. I can tell you firsthand that Vyara City is not as safe as you think.

You should know this already. But if you believe it is that important to go back, I will send you."

Kaiya nodded. Still, she had to do *something.* "It is. Please send me back."

He shrugged. "Very well, if you are so insistent." He chanted several whimsical words of elven magic.

Kaiya's eyelids grew heavy, her head faint. Just before she slipped out of consciousness, he reached over with elegant grace and caught her.

Ayana frowned at Thielas Starsong for a dozen reasons, past and present.

He was too busy admiring Princess Kaiya to notice her scowl.

"Always a fool for a pretty human face," she said.

Thielas lowered the foolish girl to the ground at Ayana's feet. He then looked up with the grin that had disarmed so many in the past. Herself included. "The ephemeral nature of their beauty makes it all the more precious. I don't think you would understand."

She rolled her eyes. "I don't. Are you chasing that redheaded princess now? The fetish for headstrong human girls runs in your family."

His lips twitched. "You almost broke me of it, so long ago."

Ayana paused to think back on her middle years, when the strapping elf prince had reminded her of what it meant to be *young* again. A smile quirked on her lips, unbidden.

He locked his gaze on her, then looked away. "I have not been to Vyara City in thirty-two years. I don't have fond memories. It's the site of one of my two greatest mistakes in life. However, I will send you back to the Crystal Citadel. It is the safest place I know there." He studied the silly girl. "She is strong-willed and has a lot to learn. She may or may not remember much of this brief interlude, though I hope your lecture sticks."

Grinning, he sprinkled flower petals in a circle around her and the princess. His eyes flashed up to meet hers. "It was good to see you again, Ayana. Don't you find it interesting how often our paths have crossed in the last year, after a hundred years of separation?"

She shrugged. "Our involvement in human affairs has led to these unexpected reunions."

"We elves are too few. We must guide the humans so *they* can prevent the Tivari from reconquering Tivaralan."

"Nonetheless, I never expected nor hoped to see you again."

Thielas laughed. "You would hold the indiscretions of my youth against me?"

"No, only that I would hope you always remember me when I was as beautiful as she." Ayana lifted her chin toward Kaiya's sleeping form.

He laughed again. "You have always been older than I, and although you were wildly stunning then, I was mostly attracted to your wisdom." He winked suggestively at her. "I have to admit, that has seemed to grow only more in the last century."

Despite her many years and resistance to such charms, Ayana still felt the flush in her cheeks. She stared down at the ground, and then lifted her eyes to speak.

Thielas began a long chant in the flowery words of elf-magic. She knew not to interrupt his song, lest they reappear before the Altivorc King's throne or a Teleri breeding site. She fell silent, waiting patiently for the scenery to shift around her.

As he inflected the last syllable, her body began to slip through the ethers. The colors coalesced and reformed into an enormous chamber of marble with light blue streaks of istrium. A magnificent dome above swirled with color, like the Iridescent Moon itself. Princess Kaiya slept peacefully at her feet.

Gasps of surprise echoed through the Crystal Citadel's audience chamber, followed by the rasping of a dozen swords sliding from their sheaths.

CHAPTER 40:

Awakenings

Birds chirped in harmony with the low hum around her. Cool and light, the soft touch of fine linen sheets brushed across Kaiya's bare skin. The refreshing sensation stood in stark contrast to the humid heat hanging in her lungs. Muffled sounds of a distant conversation coaxed her into consciousness.

Though feeling fully revitalized, she eased her eyes open tentatively. They focused on large windows from which sunlight streamed in at a low angle, casting long shadows across the white, undecorated room.

Kaiya bolted up into a sitting position on a soft, unfamiliar bed. Her chest tightened. There was something eerily familiar about waking up in a strange place. Her brow scrunched up as she tried to recall her last memory...the ambush.

Guilt flooded over her. She looked frantically around the white-walled room. First locating the heavy wood door, her gaze then settled on a red *sari* draped over a simple wooden chair. The only other furnishings were the bed and a basin of water.

The breeze on her skin... She was naked, save for underpants and some musky-smelling gauze wrapped around her forearms. Kaiya pulled the sheets up to cover herself. Had she been captured? An image of Prince Dhananad's foul hands on her sent a cold shiver up her spine. Quickly banishing the notion, she eased herself from the bed, pulling the sheets along to stay covered in the event some rogue barged in through the door.

The window would give an idea of where she was, but it would also give anyone walking by a good look at her bare skin. She went to investigate the red fabric on the chair. Unsure of how to drape the *sari* correctly, she put on the *choli* shirt and *langa* petticoat first. Its open back, low neckline, and bare midriff was too immodest, resembling undergarments, but it was certainly better than exploring a strange place in nothing more than bandages.

Now dressed, if it could be considered dressed, she walked over to the window. She gasped. The red sun perched not far above the Shallowsea, which in turn merged into a bustling waterfront far down in the distance. The canals and streets fanned outward in a tangled web, cutting through flat white buildings cast in the setting sun's red sheen. Without a doubt, this was Vyara City. Given the vantage point, higher than anything else, this was the Paladins' Crystal Citadel.

Had the Paladins rescued them from the ambush? And if so, why had she awakened almost completely undressed?

Kaiya padded across the room to the heavy door and pulled it open a crack. The muffled sounds transformed into conversations in the Ayuri language; talk about the Hua wounded.

Her men, injured because she insisted on a trip that could have waited.

Without hesitation, she strode out of the room to find herself in a hallway, dimly lit through several windows by late afternoon sun. A dozen feet down the hall, a Paladin and an older Ayuri man stopped their discussion and turned to face her.

The young maid, Meixi, was sitting quietly on a wooden chair just outside the door. Her eyes widened. The girl dropped to the floor and into a bow. "*Dian-xia*, I'm so glad you are awake. I was so worried." The girl stood and adjusted Kaiya's *sari.* "I'm so sorry about your outer robe; it was lost in the attack. Your inner gown was filthy, stained with grass and dirt. I sent it back to the embassy."

Grass and dirt? Kaiya cocked her head.

The Paladin approached and pressed his palms together. "Good afternoon, Your Highness. I am glad to see you awake."

Forgetting her manners, Kaiya blurted, "How did I get here? Where are my men? How long have I been asleep?"

"About seven hours ago, your procession was ambushed. By all accounts, the elf woman Ayana Strongbow sequestered you away through time and space, reappearing almost three hours ago in the audience chamber of the Crystal Citadel. You have been asleep this whole time, unresponsive to the healer's attempts to wake you."

Time *and* space? How was that even possible?

The older man added, "We received an anonymous tip about the attack. The Paladin patrols came to your rescue, but we were too late to save all of your guards. Several were killed, and most of the rest received wounds of varying severity. Because of your status as a foreign dignitary, the Paladins took the extraordinary measure of bringing the wounded here for treatment and protection."

Several killed! Kaiya bit her lip, feeling a pang in her chest. She pressed her hands together. "Thank you for your kind consideration. Please take me to them."

"I will take you to the half-elf." The Paladin gestured for her to follow.

As they walked down the hall, she asked, "Who was behind this?" As though it wasn't evident.

"We captured several of the assailants who were put to sleep by the elf's magic. They claimed to be hired mercenaries, but we are investigating their backgrounds."

Kaiya had a good idea where that trail would lead. "Two of the attackers were Maduran Scorpions."

The Paladin shrugged. "Perhaps, but witnesses did not see the telltale mask and sting. There are also some disaffected former Paladins who work as independent mercenaries."

Kaiya fell silent, mulling over his words as they came to another door. An Ayuri woman emerged from the room just as they were about to pass, pulling up short before she ran into them.

The woman's voice sounded too cheerful. "Your Highness! I am glad you are finally awake! Let me look at your arms." Without waiting for permission, she took Kaiya's wrist and unwrapped the bandages, revealing yellowing splotches. She rewrapped the gauze. "Good, good. You are healing quickly. You had no major wounds that I saw, just bruises on your arms that the liniment is taking out nicely. Are they painful at all?"

For the first time, Kaiya considered her own physical condition. Her arms did hurt a little, but the pain was a minor compared to her guards' injuries. She shook her head.

"Good. Your other maid and the elf are inside." The woman gestured toward the door she'd just exited. "Won't you come in?"

Kaiya nodded.

The woman guided Kaiya into another plain room. Two beds with simple wooden frames flanked a single window. Beneath the sheets of one, Ayana slept peacefully; on the other, Jie laid with her bare shoulders and arms above the sheets. Like Kaiya, her arms were wrapped in gauze, though black splotches peeked out through the white mesh.

Jie bolted up, holding the sheets up around her. Her face contorted into a wince. Kaiya's fault. "*Dian-xia*, I heard that you had been brought here, but they wouldn't let me visit you. Or even tell me where you were. Where did you go? Ayana didn't say anything, she just came in and tumbled into the bed."

Kaiya ignored the question. "I'm so glad to see you are alive. Are you hurt badly?"

Jie shrugged, evincing another grimace. "It's just a few scratches. I've been hurt worse."

The Paladin healer's lips squeezed tight. Her tone was stern. "You were cut across the side. Had the angle been more oblique, it might have sliced between your ribs and punctured your lung. You are either very lucky or very skilled."

Jie pouted, mouthing *skilled* in the Hua tongue.

Kaiya suppressed a smile. "How long will she take to recover?"

"We have stitched the wounds and wrapped them in a liniment that will speed the healing process. If your handmaiden is strong, she should be mobile in a few days and fully recuperated in two weeks. In the meantime, she should remain on bed rest."

Not likely. Kaiya bowed her head. "Thank you. How about my guards?"

"They are in other rooms, and I am not allowed to enter," the woman said. "But from what I have heard, their injuries vary in severity."

"I would like to visit them. Would you please let them know to make themselves presentable?"

The woman hesitated before nodding and leaving the room.

Kaiya turned back to Jie. Before she could even ask her question, Jie answered it: "All of the imperial guards have concussions. Chen Xin also has a broken nose, Xu Zhan a dislocated shoulder, and Zhao Yue a sprained knee. Of the twenty-four embassy guards, six were killed and another thirteen wounded, three seriously."

Her fault. Remorse gripped her chest. Kaiya's voice cracked. "The Paladins don't think the Madurans are involved."

Jie shook her head. "It was undoubtedly the Madurans. The woman I fought was the Golden Scorpion who tried to poison you. I suggest you call off your meeting with Prince Dhananad."

"If my audience with the Paladin elders tomorrow goes well, then we will be in a very strong negotiating position with Madura. We will take extra care. I will even ask for a Paladin escort if need be."

Jie glared at her for a second of insolence before turning to Meixi. "Can you find me some clothes? I must accompany the princess to the men's room."

The girl flushed. "The Paladin healer explicitly ordered us not to bring you any clothes, until your wound was better healed."

Kaiya covered a laugh. Maybe, just maybe, the embarrassment of nakedness would keep Jie from trying to return to duties. "I am going to visit the others. If I see a healer, I will persuade them to bring you clothes." The lie would keep the half-elf in one place, at least for a while. Kaiya spun and glided out of the room, Meixi on her heels.

Outside, the male healer waited. With him stood a young Paladin not much older than herself, and a dignified-looking older man, with a darker complexion and graying black hair and beard. His white *kurta* had gold embroidery not just on the neck, but along its borders as well.

The older man put his hands together. "Greetings, Your Highness. I am Devak of the Paladin Council of Elders. I was told you were awake now, and came immediately to inform you that the council wants you stay in the citadel under our protection until we learn more about who attacked you and why."

Kaiya pressed her palms together. "Thank you for your consideration, but I do not wish to intrude."

He shook his head. "It is our honor to host you here. The Oracle of Ayudra sent us a message that your personal safety is of the utmost priority. There is no safer place on Tivaralan than the citadel."

They had said the same of Ayudra. She stifled a snort. "That, I am sure. However, I can certainly tell you the identity of the likely culprit, as well as their motivations. In the meantime, I would rather return to my country's own embassy to prepare for our audience with you tomorrow morning."

The elder shook his head again. "Although I cannot force you to remain here, I can only hope that you see the wisdom in staying."

His voice rippled into the space between them. Meixi and healer shuffled on their feet.

Wisdom. The word weighed on her like a dwarf anvil. "Very well. However, I must send my maid back to our compound to retrieve some things that I will need for the night. I request that you assign some of your courageous Paladins to escort her."

"Of course. It is our honor to have you with us," the elder said. He motioned toward the young man with him. "This is Sameer Vikram, who has just recently finished his apprenticeship and awaits his final tests. He will take you to your quarters in the guest wing tonight, and also assist you with anything you might need during your stay." With that, he spun on his heel and strode down the corridor, disappearing around the corner.

Kaiya turned to Sameer. Handsome, with a light-brown skin tone, he had perfectly coifed long black hair and a short pointed beard. His eager expression would have put a puppy to shame.

He pressed his palms and bowed his head in salute. His voice purred, "I am at your command."

Kaiya smiled graciously and clasped her hands together. "Thank you." She then turned to the Paladin healer. "Before we go, I would like to visit my guards who are in your care."

The Paladin healer motioned for her to follow and guided her down the corridor to another room.

It was significantly larger than the two other rooms Kaiya had been in, but just as plain. Two dozen cots were laid out, almost all occupied by her guards, some quietly talking among themselves. So many wounded! All her responsibility. The guilt made her head spin more than the musky smell of herbal medicines that permeated the air.

News of her arrival circulated through the room. Some soldiers jumped to their feet before sinking to one knee. Others crawled off their cots and stumbled to their knees. All were in extreme stages of undress. Poor Meixi flushed bright red and excused herself from the room. Kaiya averted her gaze.

Chen Xin, his nose covered with plaster, spoke sonorously. "Men, cover yourselves."

Her own face must have glowed as bright red as Meixi's. Still, the men had paid for her foolhardiness. She raised her hand. "As you were."

Chen Xin bowed. "I was afraid you were.... We are overjoyed to see you are safe."

"I am glad to see you are, too." She glided over to one of the men, who struggled through his injuries to rise. Hesitating for a split-second to touch an almost-naked man, she nevertheless placed a gentle hand on his shoulder. "At ease."

"We failed to protect you," Chen Xin said. "If it is your command, we—"

Kaiya silenced him with a shake of her head. "My dedicated guards, I want to express my gratitude for your hard work...and also to apologize. My own recklessness brought about this disaster. I promise not to risk your lives so callously in the future."

She bowed low at the waist. It was unheard of for a member of the Imperial Family to admit fault or apologize to guards, let alone bow so low.

The men returned to their knees.

Xu Zhan looked up. "It is our honor to serve you."

"It is our honor," all of the men repeated in unison.

Kaiya wiped away a tear. "We will stay here overnight, under the protection of the Paladins. Rest well and await my orders."

She turned to leave, and Chen Xin and Ma Jun quickly rose to follow her. She raised her hand again, giving them a silent order to remain. "As the Paladins told me, there is no safer place on Tivaralan. Focus your energies on recovering."

Kaiya glided out of the door. Hiding in the threshold where no one could see her, she hung her head. All the injuries. And the dead. Hot tears slid down her cheeks.

Meixi cleared her throat.

Kaiya wiped her eyes and straightened. As unfair as it was to those who suffered for her, she couldn't afford to dwell on it right now. With her audience before the Council of Elders, tomorrow would be an important day, one which could affect the lives of millions. She would need as much rest as the men injured in her defense.

CHAPTER 41:

Victory without Fighting

Kaiya woke to light drizzle pattering on the outer walls. The refreshing scent of spring rain wandered in through the latticed window, mingling with the aroma of fried twisted bread, rice porridge, and hot soy milk—all brought by young Meixi from the Hua embassy.

With a few hours before her appointed audience with the Paladins' Council of Elders, Kaiya ate at a leisurely pace, mentally practicing her speech and formulating answers to the questions the elders were bound to ask. If she succeeded in winning the endorsement of the Paladins, it would go a long way to deterring the Maduran threat to her homeland.

She donned the multiple layers of a Hua court robe with Meixi's assistance, and wrapped the broad sash around her waist. The maid arranged her hair with fine jade pins, while Kaiya preened in a full-length mirror so that everything down to the last eyelash was perfect.

When at last a page summoned her to the main audience chamber, she was fully prepared. Rumiya's fake lotus jewel caught her attention, beckoning from its place on a table. Its audible hum, louder than ever, assailed her mental armor. She afforded it a last glance and left it there.

Ambassador Ling joined her outside the door. She glided through the Crystal Citadel's white marble hallways, admiring the breathtaking beauty of the carved columns, painted ceilings, and elaborate scrollwork.

At last, she came to a pair of doors made of the same light-blue metal as the Paladin's *naga* and Golden Scorpion's mask. With a deep breath, she composed her expression into one of serenity, to hide her nervousness.

A collective gasp from the numerous Paladin masters and Ayuri lords greeted her on the other side. Several craned their necks to get a better view.

Yet if they were admiring her beauty, Kaiya couldn't help but marvel at the grand chamber. White marble floors, streaked with pale blue imperfections, stretched the length and width of the enormous room, with smooth columns vaulting toward the ceiling. A dome soared high above, its colors swirling like a soap bubble. How small she was compared to this.

The room emitted a faint, pulsing hum. Could anyone else hear it? Kaiya's heartbeat echoed its call, sending a cool sensation through her body.

She made her way through the crowd to the front of the room. Thirteen chairs faced her, arranged in a semi-circle on a dais. All but the center were occupied by middle-aged and older men. Most had long, narrow beards and fine mustaches, and each wore a white *kurta* with a gold embroidered collar and border, denoting their status as an elder.

She nodded toward Elder Devak, whom she'd met the day before.

A page announced her in a clear, resonant voice, carried by the perfect acoustics of the hall. "Princess Kaiya Wang, representing the Empire of Cathay."

Kaiya brought her hands together and bowed her head in typical Ayuri fashion. The elders did so in return.

One with a split beard spoke. "Greetings, Princess Kaiya. We are honored to have you as our guest today. I believe it is the first time that a representative of your nation has spoken before the council."

The resonance of the hall magnified her voice. "Thank you for your generous hospitality, and for granting me this opportunity to speak."

Elder Split-Beard favored her with a curious expression. "The Oracle of Ayudra sent word that you would seek audience with us and recommended that we listen. Yet, as is his wont, he did not explain your business. Your activity in the city hints at a request. Please, speak."

She swept a demure smile over the assembled elders, satisfied they all seemed sufficiently captivated and speechless. When she began her long-rehearsed speech, each syllable echoed back to her as music. "I come to you on behalf of my father, Emperor Wang Zhishen, who has ruled Cathay for three decades of unprecedented tranquility, stability, and prosperity. We are a peace-loving nation, one which respects its neighbors and builds lasting friendships through mutually-beneficial trade."

Several of the elders nodded, while whispers tittered through the chamber.

Kaiya shook her head in choreographed sadness. "Yet there are those who seek to subjugate our people and plunder our wealth. They threaten us unprovoked, rattling their sabers at our borders. While our Great Wall and guns will surely repel an invasion, my ancestor once said, *vanquishing an enemy without fighting is the pinnacle of skill.* We do not wish to needlessly draw blood, even from those who seek to spill ours."

She peeked up through her lashes. Was the preamble working? Hua had committed unconscionable actions in the name of free trade and the Mandate of Heaven. Surely they knew that. One elder stroked his beard; another's brow crinkled.

She kept her voice level, letting the acoustics magnify it. "It is for this reason that I have come to Vyara City: to negotiate directly with one of the aggressors, Madura. Yet our overtures for peace were met first with an attempt to poison me, and later an ambush on my entourage."

Murmurs passed among the assembled guests, many bobbing their heads. Madura's historical aggression toward its neighbors, though held in check since its occupation of Ankira, had earned it enough mistrust.

The youngest elder raised an eyebrow. "Those are serious charges. Do you have proof?"

Kaiya smiled defensively. Since when did Paladins defend Madura? This young one might prove troublesome. "Only what my guards have told me about both attacks. My people have no motive to implicate the agents of Madura."

"Nonetheless," the youngest elder said, "it is a serious accusation to make without evidence. But please, continue."

She lifted her chin. "With these incidents, and also its history of aggression and betrayal, we realized that Madura did not negotiate in good faith. Therefore, I have spent the past week meeting with those who might put pressure on them to curb their hostilities."

Kaiya paused momentarily, brushing her gaze across the room to gauge the elders' reactions as her words sank in. Behind her, murmurs of approval rippled among the dignitaries.

She turned and gestured toward the representatives as she named their countries. "The maharajas of the Ayuri nations of Vadara, Bijura, Dabura, Sanura, and Ebura have all provisionally committed to stand with Cathay. We have agreed that an attack on one is tantamount to an attack on all, and we will use all means—economic and diplomatic, military if necessary—to contain the Maduran threat. I humbly ask the Paladins, as guardians of the Ayuri Confederation, to endorse our mutual defense agreements." She bowed her head and held it, clasping her hands together.

The youngest elder cleared his throat. "Princess Kaiya, although I see the wisdom in your actions, I wonder if you have considered this:

Madura has allied itself not only with the Teleri Empire far away in the North, but more importantly the Levastyan Empire which stands at our doorstep." He spread his arms wide. "This level of brinksmanship could very well throw Tivaralan into a chaos unheard of since the Century of War between the Ayuri and Arkothi Empires. Is that something peace-loving Cathay really wants to risk?"

Such sarcasm. Kaiya shook her head. "Of course not, Elder. The rulers of Madura may be brash, but they are not foolish. They certainly know that the Cathayi guns, Ayuri swords, and Paladin righteousness will lead to their expedient defeat, before their friends in Tilesite and Levastyas can come to their aid."

He laughed. "Paladins are protectors, never aggressors. Our mission is to maintain the peace, not to escalate war."

If the elder's logic became any more circular, she would rip her hair out. Nonetheless, Kaiya raised a hand to her mouth to cover her own laugh. "Forgive my idealism, but I believe that it is merely the perceived strength in unity that will deter Madura and hold its aggression in check. Is that not a means of keeping the peace?"

He smirked. "That may be so. I certainly admire your idealism. Where was your righteous enthusiasm when Ankira fell to the Madurans?"

Elder Devak raised his hand. "Peace, Elder Mehal. I can appreciate your courage to express yourself, especially for someone so new to the council. However, the princess speaks wisely: it is our cloak of protection over the Ayuri Confederation that has prevented a Maduran invasion of Vadara thus far. Furthermore, it is our responsibility to keep careful watch over the Golden Scorpions, who use the powers of the *bahaduur* for their own personal gain instead of for the betterment of all."

Elder Mehal pursed his lips and leaned back in his chair.

A balding elder lifted his chin toward her. "Although I admire your wisdom and poise, especially for someone so young, I must admit my disappointment." He nodded toward the empty chair. "The Oracle suggested that you will play a very important role in the fate of this world."

An important role in the world? The Oracle had never said such a thing. Kaiya opened her mouth, but no words came out.

"And yet," Balding Elder continued, "you do not look beyond the borders of your own nation, to see that our world is in a state of flux. We teeter on the precipice of a new Age of Empires. It threatens to set us back three centuries, into an era of perpetual war." He squared his jaw at her. "You come asking for protection, yet offer nothing in return."

Kaiya gazed at the floor to emphasize her remorse, before looking up and meeting his eyes. "Cathay honors its agreements. If it is within our power—"

Elder Devak silenced her with a raise of his hand and smiled at his balding colleague. "It may be. We will retire to deliberate your request. In the meantime, I implore you to consider what Elder Kairav has said."

The elders rose and withdrew to their meeting chambers atop the citadel. When the last one left the audience chamber, applause broke out. Several lords approached to convey their respects.

Kaiya smiled so many times, her cheeks hurt. Through it all, she dwelled on Elder Kairav's words—what role did she have to play, beyond the protection of her own country? What would they ask in return? She glanced back at Ambassador Ling, her eyes tacitly begging him to help her withdraw from the mob of admirers.

She didn't have to endure the adoration long. In short measure, the elders returned. The room fell into silence. Kaiya examined each of their faces as they took their seats, yet they hid their intentions better than a Golden Scorpion mask. She placed her hands together again to salute them.

Balding Elder Kairav spoke. "Princess Kaiya. After an unprecedentedly brief deliberation, we have decided to provisionally endorse the agreements between Cathay and the Ayuri Confederation. At this time, our endorsement does not necessarily mean that Paladins would be deployed for punitive action. It is our hope that the united front amongst our nations will be enough to deter Maduran aggression."

Such a lack of commitment! Kaiya bowed her head. Hopefully, it would hide her disappointment. "I appreciate your consideration. Is there something I might offer to demonstrate Cathay's sincerity toward this pact?"

"There is." Elder Devak gestured toward the back of the hall. Kaiya turned to follow his motion. The room rose into nervous chatter as the gathered dignitaries parted down the middle, starting from the rear, as if a giant dagger sheared the audience in half.

A slow vibrating wave pushed forward, sluggish but powerful, clashing with the low pulsating of the room. Fighting her curiosity and wanting to maintain a dignified mien, Kaiya forced herself not to stand on her tiptoes to get a better view over all of the heads.

The last row of men split, revealing a tall figure in armor of red scales from shoulder to toe. A matching horned helm revealed only luminous light blue eyes. A black cloak hung from his shoulders.

Never making eye contact, the man strode to her side. He pulled off his helmet, tucked it into the crook of his elbow, and lifted his chin toward the Paladin elders.

She tried to get a good look at his side profile from the corner of her eye; but when he turned toward her, she felt compelled to return his gaze.

Prince Hardeep.
Rumiya.

CHAPTER 42:
Ultimatums

Anger. Sadness. Self-doubt. Kaiya could hardly sort out her clashing emotions over the rapid pounding of her heart in her ears. The sluggish pulsing that Hardeep—no, Rumiya—emitted clashed with the low hum of the chamber, adding to her internal chaos.

"Princess Kaiya," Elder Devak said, interrupting the chastising voice in her mind. "I introduce the Dragon's Envoy, Girish, who wishes to convey his master's message to you."

Girish? How many names did this deceiver go by? Kaiya clenched and unclenched her fists.

The Dragon's Envoy flashed a feral grin. His canine teeth extended past his incisors and ended in sharp tips. To think she'd once been hopelessly in love with whomever this man was.

When they had first met, Prince Hardeep's voice had sounded like honey spilling from his mouth; Girish's tone slithered like a snake's tongue wrapping itself around her. "Princess Kaiya, I *knew* this day would come."

Discarding all sense of poise, Kaiya wrapped her arms around herself, as if that could provide armor against an evil wizard. She had to know how deep his ruse went, even if it would make her look silly in front of the elders and dignitaries. "Prince Hardeep, for two years of separation, I *hoped* this day would come. My hope was kept alive by your letters."

The elders leaned in and whispered among each other; the audience around them chattered in a low voice.

"Letters?" Girish's conceited smile slipped for a split second.

So it was true, the suspicions raised after her meetings with Ankirans. The ones she didn't want to believe. Rumiya had nothing to do with the letters. In that, at least, he was innocent. Her chest tightened and she placed a hand over it.

So if not Hardeep—Rumiya—then who? Peng, who kept up the charade. How easily he'd duped her! She didn't even want to fathom why. It was too painful. Too fresh. Almost as fresh as the pain of Zheng Ming abandoning her. She was a fool, but at least she was now a fool with eyes opened wide.

"Never mind," she said. "You expected me. How did you know I would be here?"

The lotus jewel materialized in his hand. "This token I gave you, a flower carved from Avarax's scale. It sparked the magic within you. It even made you beautiful. Everything you have done over the last two years has been put in motion by *me*, culminating now with our inevitable reunion."

Was it true? Did she owe her power, her very beauty, to a piece of an evil dragon? Around her, the dignitaries echoed her thoughts in hushed whispers.

Her voice choked. "Why?"

"I knew you were the one," Girish said. "When I first heard your voice, and then when you played the Dragon Scale Lute."

Kaiya forced the indignation in her tone. "My voice?"

Girish's head swayed as he nodded. "It had a unique quality, though raw, in need of tempering. And you had a potential teacher in the elf Lord Xu."

So Girish had manipulated her, and possibly tricked Lord Xu, as well. Doctor Wu, the Oracle, and Master Sabal had all deepened her understanding of sound manipulation. Perhaps he'd caused all of it to fall in place. "What do you need with my voice?"

"My master wants you to sing the song promised to him by Aralas."

What? Kaiya brow furrowed. "Yanyan's song? Does Avarax *want* to sleep for another thousand years?"

Girish stared at her, and then laughed. "Silly girl. The song Aralas promised and the one Yanyan sang were different."

Kaiya's eyebrow rose, unbidden. This little detail never appeared in the histories. "Where am I supposed to find this song? Aralas returned to the Heavens a millennium ago."

"I have it." The wizard patted his chest. "But only your voice can sing it correctly."

"What does the song do?"

"I don't know." Girish shrugged. "Dragons are fickle beings."

Didn't know? Or wouldn't tell? After all the deceptions, his words stank as a lie. "Why should I comply?"

Girish turned to the audience. "As I told the council yesterday, if Princess Kaiya does not sing for him, Avarax will burn the city of Palimur to the ground. He will melt the stones to magma and immolate the hundred thousand souls living there."

Murmurs erupted throughout the hall. The elders sat in silence, regarding her with knowing eyes. They knew about this ultimatum. They needed a political agreement as much as Hua, yet acted as if they were granting her a favor.

They'd tricked her, too. Still, Kaiya shuddered. All those people would perish in dragonfire, the horror recounted in ten-thousand-year-old elven legends of the Fall of Istriya. Dragonfire hadn't been seen since. After nearly wiping elves from the face of Tivara, the orcs had betrayed their dragon allies in the Dragonpurge. Only Avarax survived, his immense power such that the orcs, even armed with the magic of their gods, had no choice but to come to an uneasy truce with him. Until Yanyan sang him to sleep with a Dragon Song. There was no record of Avarax using his fiery breath since awakening thirty-two years before.

Kaiya hung her head. "Where is this song?"

"Actually, I had a different song in mind." Girish tugged off his scaled gauntlets, revealing leathery hands. He reached into his cloak and withdrew a few sheets of paper, all ripped at one of the long edges. "This is the music Yanyan sang at the start of the War of Ancient Gods."

That song. Kaiya's heart thudded. A betting princess would wager the tears lined up with the lost pages of Lord Xu's book. But why did Girish want Avarax to sleep? Perhaps so that he, himself, could rule over the Dragonlands?

There was more to the story. "Won't Avarax recognize it?"

"The differences are subtle. When Yanyan sang, Avarax did not notice the treachery until it was too late." He passed the sheets to her.

She received them in two hands and flipped through them. There were four pages in all, detailing a song the likes of which she'd never seen before. Rapid changes in pitches. Vocalized chords. An extreme range in keys. It might very well be beyond her ability to sing, let alone invoke the magic involved.

"Try it." Girish's blue eyes searched hers, mesmerizing in the way they danced—like she'd danced for Prince Dhananad, like they'd danced when they'd met two years ago.

Heavens. Just like then, his eyes compelled her. Kaiya sang the first three notes. The blue streaks in the hall's marble surfaces sparkled faintly. The Paladins' *nagas* shed a dim light. Even Girish's eyes pulsated, the slow resonance he emitted quickening. His grin widened. Power, like a jolt of lightning, energized her arms and legs.

Something wasn't right. She feigned exhaustion, staggering back a step and tumbling to the floor. He'd seen her faint from channeling a Dragon Song thrice before; would he believe it this time? In the corner of her eyes, Girish's smile faded.

She cleared her throat and coughed. "I need time to practice this. Maybe weeks, if I am to have a chance of singing it correctly."

Girish counted on his fingers. "You have four days before Avarax casts his shadow over Palimur."

She shook her head, pretending shame. "Even if I can learn it, I am not Yanyan. I was not taught by the elf angel Aralas. Even those three notes drained me."

He leaned over her, so close that his hot breath washed over her. "I don't believe you."

His proximity felt like centipede feet crawling over her skin. Yet perhaps there was an opportunity here. A chance to see her future, with the Oracle's help. "If Avarax wants to hear me sing, I want the Lotus Crystal from the Ayudra Pyramid, which he stole."

Murmurs roiled throughout the hall again.

"Palimur City is in no position for you to make demands." Girish roared with laughter.

Kaiya could claim a foreign city of a hundred thousand people didn't matter to her, but could she bluff a wizard nearly two-hundred years her senior?

Those blue eyes would see right through her.

Jie had crept into the audience hall, surprised at how easily it'd been to escape confinement in the medical ward and sneak through the corridors of the Crystal Citadel undetected. Perhaps the pure white robe she wore blended in with all the goodness around here. Or maybe it was because most of the Paladins were now crowding the audience hall.

Beyond the wall of their tall backs, Girish's power had screamed louder than the energy of all the Paladins combined, and even greater than the energy of the citadel itself. His voice raged like a wildfire as his patience with her princess grew short.

For Princess Kaiya's part, she had dared to face down an evil wizard and make ultimatums. *Now* who was insolent?

Jie winced at the pain in her ribs as she rose to her tiptoes, trying to see over all of the Paladins and Ayuri lords. Meeting with little success, she slipped through the cracks in the wall of human bodies in hopes of getting a better view.

The princess' tired but melodic voice called from the front of the hall. The fatigue in her voice sounded off, almost contrived. "You want me to sing to him, you convince him to bring the Lotus Crystal."

Jie made it to the front just as Girish gripped the princess' face with a hand and chanted three foul-sounding syllables.

Reaching for her throwing weapons, Jie found none. She liberated a curved dagger from a bystander's belt while the Paladins surged forward with *nagas* in hand. The Paladin elders jumped to their feet, some leaping toward the evil wizard.

The princess tore at his arm; but then her body wilted, arms drooping to her sides. Girish wrapped his arm around her and guided her limp form to the floor.

As the Paladins encircled Girish, Jie edged behind them toward his back for an easier killing blow.

Girish's cackle sounded like flint striking steel. He stomped the floor. Jagged blue light flashed up from the imperfections in the marble to form a wall of energy around him.

A cold wave shoved Jie back. Around her, Paladins staggered away.

Looking around the room, Girish lowered his hand. The blue light dropped back into the stones. "At ease. I was merely confirming the princess' energy for myself. She did not tell the entire truth. No, she is not powerful enough on her own to sing my master to sleep, but she has more vitality than she claims."

With visible strain, the princess eased herself up on an elbow. Jie padded to her side and knelt.

Girish wagged a finger at them. "Feed her well, make sure she rests and cultivates her energy. And practices the song. The resonance of the world is strong at the Temple of Shakti in Palimur. She had better be there in four days, when the Sawarasati's Eye is open."

He must be referring to the Blue Moon, which would be at its largest for the year. He spun on his heel and stalked back toward the doors. People made way, flashing ward-evil *mudra* hand symbols.

Jie gave his back one last glance. The unarmored spot at the base of his neck made an inviting target, and indeed, there was an oval scar there from a previous wound, but...Jie turned back to the princess, whose eyes fluttered and closed.

CHAPTER 43:

Enemy of My Enemy's Enemy

Proud Prince Dhananad trudged into the Teleri embassy's audience chamber, his minions keeping a safe distance behind lest they become targets of his temper. Enraged at the audacity of Ambassador Piros' curt summons, he had considered not coming at all. When he became maharaja, he would cut off relations with the Teleri on the day of his coronation. In the meantime, he would suffer through this indignity.

Dhananad skidded to a stop in the middle of the room. He raised his hand to shield his eyes from the sun streaming in through the west windows. If only his vision hadn't adjusted. The patronizing grins from the ambassador, the Levastyan Lord Benham, and the Altivorc King greeted him from their cushions. Even the motley collection of guards did not bother to hide their smiles.

Without bothering to rise from his seat, Ambassador Piros beckoned him over, as if he were calling a servant. Or a dog. "Come, Prince Dhananad."

Damn Bovyans. Dhananad spat on the floor in front of the Teleri ambassador. "What was so important that you interrupted my dinner?"

"We received news from our couriers." Piros frowned. "The Paladins have endorsed a pact of mutual protection between Cathay and the Ayuri Confederation."

Shifting into a relaxed stance, he modulated his tone to amused boredom. "Yes, yes, my own agent was there at the time. Surely you understand that I know everything that goes on in the Paladin Council."

Benhan glowered at him from his cushion. "And you are not disturbed?"

"Why should I be?" Dhananad cocked his head. "Madura never had any plans to attack Cathay. *That* was the Teleri Empire's goal once your expansion reached their Great East Gate. As per our many redundant agreements, Madura has maintained a semblance of a threat, to keep Cathay's attention on our shared border."

Piros jabbed an impudent finger at him. "Your clumsiness has set us back. First, the futile attempt to kidnap the princess—"

"It was not futile!" If the Bovyan wanted to engage in a shouting contest, Dhananad could play. "We timed it perfectly, so the Paladin patrols would be nowhere nearby. It was just bad luck."

"And bad planning, and even worse execution." The Altivorc King taunted him with a laugh. "After that fiasco, Cathay won't see your vaunted Golden Scorpions as a credible threat."

Behind him, the two Scorpions' anger was palpable, even if hidden behind their expressionless masks. Dhananad shuffled in his place, waving an annoyed hand at the King. "It might have worked if your stupid altivorcs hadn't totally ignored the princess."

"It was poor communication." The Altivorc King returned his glare, the deadly glint in his eyes making Dhananad second-guess his insult. "A competent leader would ensure his allies understood the plan."

Dhananad shrugged. "What is done is done. A good leader adapts."

The Altivorc King grinned, revealing his fangs. "I agree. With that in mind, you will delay your meeting with Princess Kaiya tomorrow. Wait until after she sings to the Last Dragon."

"Bah." Dhananad spat in the altivorc's direction. "You are not my king, you are not even Madura's ally. I will dine with whom I please, when I please."

The Altivorc King leaned deeper back into his cushion. "Then you are a fool, walking into a diplomatic trap. Your father will disown you, and your stupidity will go down in the annals of Tivara."

Heat rushed to Dhananad's cheeks, and he could only imagine what shade he must be. This insult would not go unavenged. With a jerking motion of his hand, he ordered his Golden Scorpions to arms. "Kill the Altivorc King's guards, and then disfigure his pretty face."

The Ambassador and Lord Benham's jaws dropped, eyes wide. Their shock would have pleased him had the Altivorc King not worn an amused look—the kind that screamed at Dhananad's instincts of self-preservation.

The pair of Golden Scorpions jumped into action, their stings flashing as they closed the gap and cut through three of the altivorc guards before their weapons even left their sheaths. The two survivors had managed to draw their own giant broadswords, but fell before taking a swing as the Scorpions slashed through them. Black blood sprayed on the floor and walls.

They closed toward their final target, but the Altivorc King did not seem the least bit concerned. He leisurely shifted on his cushions as he withdrew a grey metal wand, pointed it at one of the Scorpions, and spoke a guttural syllable.

A bolt of blue lighting sizzled from the tip, hurling the man back a dozen feet through the air with a scream of agony.

In that split second, the other Scorpion reached him and stabbed. Dhananad barely registered the motion, but the final result stood out clearly. The Scorpion screamed and clawed at the King's hand, which seized his wrist in a bone-crunching grip.

Rising to his feet, the altivorc drove the would-be assailant down to his knees and plucked the weapon away. He threw it at Dhananad's feet. "I am very forgiving, and will forget this reckless transgression." He released his hold on the Scorpion's wrist. "Your life is spared...for now. Go ahead and meet with the princess if you are still so thick-skulled. You will see I am right."

The Scorpion gasped, clutching his hand, which bent at a strange angle. He fared better than his companion, who lay in a smoldering heap near the entrance.

Dhananad cringed, deciding once and for all he would never tempt the Altivorc King again. He turned on his heel and left, his entourage scurrying after him.

Ambassador Piros watched Prince Dhananad storm out of the room. Once his angry footsteps had faded out of the embassy, Piros motioned for his men to deal with the bodies of the five slain altivorcs and the Golden Scorpion. "Why did you goad the prince like that? Look at this mess...and your own men."

The Altivorc King laughed. "My soldiers will lay their lives down for me without question. It was a necessary measure, to remove that royal fool from the picture. Tomorrow, you will send word to Madura to demand Dhananad's recall. It will make our plans much easier."

"But the damage is already done." Lord Benhan threw his hands up. "The Ayuri Confederation and the Paladins will now be keeping a scrutinizing eye on Madura, and by extension, the rest of us."

Piros hid his scoff. Benhan had much more to worry about because of Levastya's proximity to the Paladins.

"As the Cathayi say, we must seek opportunity in adversity," the Altivorc King said.

"When the timing is right—maybe not this decade, even— we shall incite an incident that implicates Madura. All of the mutual protection pacts the princess arranged will draw the Paladins' efforts in that direction. That will give your sultan the perfect opening to move into Ayuri lands."

Piros doubted the Altivorc King had Levastya's best interests in mind, and wondered what the altivorcs had to gain. "Madura has always been the weak link in our alliance. Sacrificing them for the sake of creating other opportunities will be of no consequence."

"And they will not go down easily," the King said. "Contrary to your taunts, the Golden Scorpions are a formidable force that will keep the Paladins occupied. It will provide a chance for you to attack Cathay and for us to capture Ayudra."

Piros chewed on the inside of his cheek. From a human perspective, Ayudra was a strategic port, controlling commerce into the Ayuri heartland. Yet to the altivorcs, who cared little for trade, it was a rock full of ruins. Perhaps it had to do with the King's obsession with the pyramids, the ancient monuments to their departed gods. "Avarax once attacked Ayudra. We should send an envoy to see if he might join our cause."

The Altivorc King burst out laughing. "Avarax is a shadow of his former self, still weakened by the Cathayi girl's song from the War of Ancient Gods. He can't use his breath. When he attacked Ayudra thirty-two years ago, all he wanted was the Lotus Crystal, and he bluffed to get it."

Piros nodded slowly, wrapping his head around the idea. Trickery was such a foreign concept to him, but apparently one that worked.

The Altivorc King yawned. "In any case, even if Avarax were a real threat, he serves only his own cause, which has minimal benefit to us. Let him rule over and expand the Dragonlands. It will keep the Paladins busy. Our goals would be better served if he never sets claw on Ayudra again. And my instincts tell me, this ploy to get Princess Kaiya to sing is another attempt to strengthen himself."

CHAPTER 44:
Pieces of a Puzzle

The four pages taunted Kaiya from where they lay neatly on her bed in the Crystal Citadel's guest chambers. She could see the notes, hear them in her mind, and yet the underlying power escaped her. The City of Palimur, along with all of its hundred thousand inhabitants, depended on her grasping the music's secrets.

Her languid legs protested as she traipsed back from the dresser to the bed for another look. After she woke from Rumiya's magic, her energy guttered in her belly. Fog shrouded her mind. It seemed like dwarf anvils hung from her shoulders. She looked down to confirm that it was, indeed, her own slim arms there.

Ayana leaned back in the plush chair. "You should sleep, especially after the way the wizard drained you. Maybe you will see the answers clearly when you are rested."

The door whispered open behind her, and Jie's soft but distinct footsteps treaded in. Ayana didn't seem to notice the half-elf's arrival, reassuring Kaiya that at least her hearing still served her well, even when the rest of her body did not.

"*Dian-xia*," Jie said, her voice strained. Her forehead furrowed. "As you commanded, I checked on the men. They are recovering well. The imperial guards are in no condition to protect you, but still wish to stand watch outside your chambers."

Kaiya turned and held her Insolent Retainer with her gaze. "While I appreciate their dedication, I would be happier if *all* my guards focused more on their own recovery."

The message seemed lost on Jie, who just sucked on her lower lip— a telltale sign the half-elf was thinking something she wouldn't say.

Unless prompted. "Speak your mind."

"Perhaps your guards' princess should heed her own words. She is having dinner with a rake of a prince tomorrow, after all."

Kaiya sighed. "I will sleep when Meixi returns with the magic mirror. I want to speak with Lord Xu about magic."

"*I* am pretty well-versed in magic; perhaps I can answer your question." Ayana's wounded pout belonged on someone a hundredth her age.

With a contrite nod, Kaiya smiled. "It would save me from the embarrassment of groveling before Lord Xu, thank you. I was considering something. When I invoke a command through my voice, short wording tires me. Yet when I lulled Prince Dhananad with a two-hour dance, I felt energized. Why would that be?"

Ayana put a finger to her chin. "I am afraid that my grasp of Artistic Magic is poor at best. Perhaps your voice is similar to Shallow Magic, which is quick to invoke but draining; while the dance is like Deep Magic, time-consuming and ritualistic, but less tiring. My friend you met in the woods might have been able to tell you more."

Jie sucked her lower lip again. "In the woods? What friend?"

A musical voice, along with gold hair and eyes of molten purple, flashed through Kaiya's mind, and she swore she could smell evergreen needles. The fleeting memory disappeared before she could grasp it. She shrugged.

Meixi burst into the room before Jie could complain, embracing the wrapped-up magic mirror as if it were her first lover. She bowed before Kaiya, proffering the bundle in two hands.

At last. Her body screaming for rest, Kaiya unwound the silk wrappings and found her reverse reflection looking back at her. "Lord Xu, I have questions about Avarax and Artistic Magic."

Ayana crowded in behind her, an expression of wonderment showing on the reflection of her face. "What is *this*?"

How could she not know? Kaiya turned her heavy head back. "A magic mirror."

"I have never seen one so…small and portable." Ayana's usually wise and knowing voice held a child's fascination.

To think that something could amaze even the old elf, who must've seen countless magical artifacts. Kaiya looked down to find her reverse reflection still staring back at her. She sighed and flung herself onto the soft bed, her legs dangling off the side. "Lord Xu keeps his own schedule."

Jie snorted. She slunk over to the side and peered at the pages of music. Her eyes bobbed up and down. "*Dian-xia*, can you summon the image of the book, to the torn-out pages?"

"Book?" Ayana asked excitedly.

"I guess he will appear if he decides to answer." With another tired exhale, Kaiya brushed her hand over the mirror's cool surface. The book shimmered into view. With several rapid brushes that made her tired wrist ache, she came to the ripped-out pages and lifted the mirror up.

Jie held the first sheet up to the image. The story of Yanyan's mastery continued from the picture on one half of the mirror to the sheet. "See? The tear line is close, but not exact."

"What?" Kaiya sat up as quickly as her complaining body would allow and looked. Jie was right: the tear lined up, but not exactly. A gasp escaped her. She turned to Ayana. "What do you know of Yanyan's story?"

Ayana shook her head. "Not much more than you, I assume. It occurred some seven centuries before I was born, and our written records emphasize the heroism of our own people during the War of Ancient Gods. Our Sun God Koralas sent his Archangel Aralas down from the heavens to teach the remnants of our people how to invoke the *Wrath of Koralas*, a ritual spell that would turn the air to fire and kill all animal life."

"Wouldn't that kill the elves, as well?" Kaiya shuddered at the idea of mass genocide.

Ayana shook her head. "During the years it took for our ancestors to sing the spell, Aralas travelled the width and breadth of Tivaralan, planting Trees of Light. Our people were to gather under the canopies and remain protected when the magic took effect."

Jie plopped down in a chair. "What does this have to do with Yanyan?"

"In his journeys, he encountered humans. Not wanting to murder guiltless sentient beings, he called off the ritual spell. Instead, he bade our people to teach humans different forms of magic, according to their ethnic affinities. The most talented of the Cathayi, Yanyan, went to sing Avarax to sleep so he could not ally himself with the Tivari."

Kaiya nodded. "Our own official history comes from several oral accounts told in the small states that made up modern-day Cathay before the first unification of the Yu Dynasty. To us, Yanyan was Aralas' lover."

Ayana's coughing objection rivaled Jie's eye-rolling protest in drama.

Kaiya peered at the old elf. "Do you not believe an elf can love a human?"

"Oh, no, that's not what I meant." Ayana waved both hands defensively. "Aralas' daughter became the first ruler of Aerilysta, the Queendom of the Moon. His son was the first sovereign of Aramysta, the Kingdom of the Sun. We call them high elves because of the divine ichor flowing in their veins. Yet Aralas', um, *interest* in human women has appeared in a handful of those descendants."

Jie rolled her eyes. Again. By now, she likely knew what the inside of her skull looked like. "I don't see how any of this has to do with Avarax, or the fact that the pages Girish gave you don't line up."

Kaiya twirled a lock of her hair. What had Lord Xu said when he gave her the mirror? "When did he say Doctor Wu obtained the book?"

"Thirty-two years ago." Jie shrugged.

"A lot happened thirty-two years ago," Kaiya thought out loud. "He said it was retrieved by the *Tianzi's agents.* Could that be the *Moquan?* Do you know if they might have been involved?"

The blood drained from Jie's face. It was hard to imagine anything surprising her. "I...it did not occur to me until now. There was a mission—famous among our clan because of the secrecy surrounding it, even now—by three of the most promising young masters: the Architect, the Surgeon, and the Beauty. Besides taking the young Prince Dhananad as a hostage, they retrieved a secret artifact. Maybe the book?"

So the *Moquan* had taken Prince Dhananad hostage. Perhaps it explained the man's quirks. Kaiya set the thought to the side, returning to more pressing questions. "And the missing parts of the book are in either Avarax's or Rumiya's possession."

"Grand Vizier Rumiya disappeared from history right around that time," Jie said, "only reappearing once over the next three decades: two years ago, to meet with you."

Ayana scratched her chin. "Rumiya says he wants Avarax to sleep again. He planted a seed in you so that you would be able to do it, and now produces the music that can accomplish that goal."

Kaiya's cheeks burned at the mention of planting seeds, since apparently, that was all anyone wanted of her.

"But he gave you a fake song." Jie held up the pages and poked them.

"What does this music do, then?" When she'd sung the first three notes, the energy of the audience chamber crackled with power.

Ayana stared at the pages. "Most importantly, what will the music do to Avarax?"

"It doesn't matter. I don't even have the energy to invoke the power of the song."

"In four days," Ayana said, "the Blue Moon's Eye is larger and more open than at any other time this year. The resonance of the world also wells up on the hill of the Temple of Shakti. That should help you."

Kaiya sighed. "That must be why he insisted on four days. He has already waited thirty-two years, I don't see why—"

"Thirty-two years!" Jie jumped to her feet. "Avarax woke up thirty-two years ago. He went to the Pyramid on Ayudra to steal the Lotus Crystal, which magnifies the energy of the world."

All of the details began to make sense, coming together like a web of interconnections. Thirty-two years ago, Rumiya acquired the book of music for Avarax, who was looking to magnify his power. Kaiya's voice droned slow and hollow in her own ears. "Rumiya wants to make Avarax *stronger.*"

Jie's brows furrowed. "Why would he want that? What does Rumiya get in return? Besides maybe a trip down a dragon's gullet?"

The real missing pages of the book likely held the answers. However, it was unlikely she would see Rumiya—Girish—again, let alone convince him to give her the *real* song. Kaiya was on her own, with only four days to figure out those answers and get to Palimur in time to save the city and its people.

CHAPTER 45:
Checkmate

Prince Dhananad held his chin high as he sauntered through the ranks of Paladins guarding the entrance of Cathayi embassy. Even if they knew he was behind the attack on the princess, they would not dare touch him with the proverbial flag of diplomacy fluttering above his head. Two of his Golden Scorpions marched behind him. He imagined them grinning beneath their masks, their very presence a taunt to the Paladin Order that abandoned them.

His third Scorpion, the pretty girl, whatever her name was, walked at his side, shedding her maroon *kurta* and mask for a *sari*. Her beauty would make Princess Kaiya jealous.

Because no matter what the Altivorc King and his yes-men said, Dhananad would win the princess over. The dinner tonight would help her remember his charm and seal their betrothal.

Cathayi Ambassador Ling greeted him with hands pressed together and guided him through the first house into an adjacent building. Servants knelt beside the double doors, on which two long scrolls hung.

Though the wavy script might have been gibberish, it felt as if someone had lodged a spear of ice down his spine when he looked at it. His knees wobbled and hands trembled. When the doors opened, he had to gasp for air.

He turned slightly to see one of his Scorpions through the corner of his eye, likewise quivering. With a deep breath, he stepped into an anteroom.

Princess Kaiya waited there, the long sleeves of her translucent outer gown hanging to the floor. Jade jewels pinned up her hair. The pink inner gown, stitched with white plum flowers, exposed her delicate collarbones, while accentuating the perfect divot at the base of her neck. It just barely hinted at the softness of her bust. Even her austere *choli* from a week before had revealed more.

The impertinent little maid stood by her side, looking no thinner from the punishment the princess had promised. She locked eyes with his companion, and both reached for their hips. He shifted his head from one girl to another, enjoying the duel of their razor-sharp gazes.

The princess bent slightly at her waist, and Dhananad stole a glance at the luscious valley between her breasts.

"Greetings, Prince Dhananad," she said, voice as placid as the Shallowsea. "Please be my guest tonight, in appreciation for your hosting me a week ago."

Dhananad clasped his hands together. "Thank you for your hospitality, My Orchid. I hope that after what promises to be a delectable Cathayi meal, we can conclude our discussion from last time."

She raised a perfect eyebrow, playing coy confusion. Such a cute girl. "Of course. I also invited some friends to share dinner with us, since it would be a waste to share our best cuisine with just one person. I hope you do not mind."

Friends? It was supposed to be a private dinner. Dhananad kept his expression jovial nonetheless. "Certainly not! It is always enjoyable to share a meal with many. Though I would have far rather had you all to myself." For the first several months. After that, perhaps other beauties could join them.

She smiled demurely and motioned for him to follow as she glided through the doors. He kept his eyes fixed on the elegant sashay of her hips.

His Scorpion drew in a sharp breath.

Dhananad looked up and raked his gaze across the room to find friendly grins on the faces of those he would not consider friends.

Fire raged in his face, but he remained silent as Princess Kaiya gestured toward a rectangle of embroidered silk cushions, each with a small table in front of it. The maharaja and queen from each of the three largest Ayuri Confederation states sat on one side, and three Paladin elders in white *kurtas* on the other. Most galling was the presence of the exiled old maharaja of Ankira and his plump queen near the head.

Princess Kaiya guided him to a cushion across from the Ankirans, next to her at the head of the table. Was it a place of honor in their culture? Or subservience?

He hesitantly sat. His own girl Scorpion stared at the floor, turning her head so her cascading hair screened her face from the Paladins. They, in turn, whispered among themselves.

The princess had such poor taste in guests. Things couldn't get much more awkward. With a wave of her open hand, she motioned for food to be served. Servants hurried in and out, bringing in trays filled with aromatic foods on exquisitely thin white porcelain dishes.

She gestured toward the first dish: a soup, made of a fish stock and soybean paste, with bean curd cubes and seaweeds, garnished with chopped green onions. "This simple soup was a favorite of my ancestor, Wang Xinchang, who founded Cathay as you know it today. He served this on the occasion of his first great alliance with the elf Lord Xu on Haikou Island, sealing their security pact. Tonight, our cook used seaweed from the

Shallowsea around which Madura and the Ayuri Confederation lie."

Dhananad turned the porcelain spoon over in his hands, his heart racing. *Sealing of security pacts* suggested she had already decided on marriage! His rivals must have been sweating!

A porridge of black rice and golden grain, split in half to resemble the Cathay yin-yang symbol, came next. "We call this Yin-Yang Porridge: it symbolizes the fusion of the disparate elements of nature," she said. "In Cathay, we prefer to use a special short-grain rice grown in the southern province of Yutou, with millet from the northern province of Dongmen to signify the unity of disparate places. Today, we have chosen a black rice grain from my home province of Huayuan, and wheat grains from Dabura."

Daburan wheat? Though the servant offered a new spoon, Dhananad's fingers would not loosen around the first. If the princess was serious about marriage, she would have used Maduran wheat.

Heavier dishes began arriving. Servants brought in a large steamed fish with a reddish skin, covered with ginger, scallions, and peppercorns, and garnished with fruit slices. From the middle of the rectangle, they carved up individual portions and presented them to each guest. And what was this? The Ankirans were served first! They wondered at the straight sticks supposedly used for eating. Others struggled with the awkward utensils as they ate.

"A whole fish symbolizes prosperity," the princess said. "When served among new friends, it represents the hope that by working together in harmony, we will reap bountiful rewards."

Reaping bounties. Perhaps a child who would rule Madura and Cathay. Soon, soon enough Dhananad would need to start the arduous work of making that baby. In his excitement, he fumbled with the bizarre sticks the Cathayi used to eat with.

Then, a roasted turkey, skin brown and crispy and permeating the room with a savory aroma, was placed in the middle of the rectangle, its head pointing at Dhananad. Exotic squashes and root vegetables ringed the bird. It smelled wonderful, but such a hideous face staring at him! Surely this was inappropriate! Servants began slicing it.

"To us," the princess said, "chickens represent opportunity, and it would typically be served on such an auspicious occasion. But today, we were very lucky to find this wild turkey from a Kanin merchant. In our language, we refer to it as a *wild fire chicken*, and we dip it in a tangy sauce made from its own juices. To us, it means that if we wildly grasp for all opportunities, we will end up consuming ourselves in our own passions."

What? Dhananad almost snapped the chopsticks in his hands. Was the princess insulting him? The symbolism of the turkey left little ambiguity. Maybe she was *not* considering marriage, maybe all of these enemies—

A sliced barbecued pork loin, with a pungent sauce, came last, surrounded by stir-fried leafy greens. It was a commoner's dish, well below the expectation of royalty.

Princess Kaiya smiled. "Late in the Yu Dynasty, before the Hellstorm, the armies of Cathay defeated a small army led by an Arkothi Empire general who invaded and occupied some of our land. Far from the capital, the soldiers feasted on barbecued pork provided by the local farmers who were happy to be freed from the tyranny of that general."

Normally, the aroma would make his mouth water; but his appetite had fled. She was comparing him to a tyrant. Dhananad turned his nose up, not deigning to taste the pork.

As the distinguished guests finished the main course, the princess motioned for the dessert, it too bearing an unsubtle message: cut melons from each of the nations of the Ayuri Confederation, mixed together, lay in the hollowed rind of a Maduran melon.

Dhananad stared at the bowl. All of them, filling Madura. The Altivorc King had been right. The girl had set a diplomatic trap for him. The identity of the guests alone sent the explicit message that Madura's neighbors stood against it; the blatant selection of dishes, delectable as they probably would have been under different

circumstances, had merely hammered home her point.

He blanched. The only uncertainty he held was whether Madura faced imminent invasion, or if his rivals had merely formed a defensive alliance.

Kaiya watched Prince Dhananad from the corner of her eye. He wasn't the only one not enjoying their meal. The Golden Scorpion woman, stunning in the rust-colored *sari* that complemented her light brown skin, demurred. The ruthless warrior who'd nearly killed her Insolent Retainer now looked less like a daunting foe than an ashamed and embarrassed young girl who had just been castigated by her parents.

Coming from a culture that emphasized proper etiquette, even when treating with enemies, Kaiya worried she'd overreached with her message. Prince Dhananad held his lips tight, his expression reminiscent of her own seasickness on the *Invincible*. She leaned over and whispered in his ear, careful to keep any hint of malice out of her tone. "Prince Dhananad, are you not well?"

"Unfortunately, I am afraid that something has not agreed with me," he answered in a low voice. "I will have to retire early tonight."

She'd gone too far. It would reflect poorly on Cathay. "And our talks that were to conclude tonight?"

The prince raised his voice. "I believe you have made your position abundantly clear. But know now that Madura will not suffer an invasion quietly. Those who dare tread on Maduran soil uninvited will meet the Scorpion's sting!"

Kaiya leaned back, hand on her chest. Nothing in the choreographed dinner party had been meant to suggest an invasion of Madura. "Prince Dhananad! Cathay is a peace-loving nation, we have no intention of infringing on Madura's sovereign territory."

"Yet it is obvious you do not recognize the province of Ankira as an inseparable part of our nation." The prince jabbed a finger in the direction of the Ankiran rebels.

She lowered her hand from where she'd been twirling a lock of her hair. "It is my concern—and I imagine that of all those present today— that a certain dignity be afforded all people. I am concerned about the women living in Ankira who, at your behest, are subjected to the depravations of Bovyan soldiers and their country's breeding program. I believe if you were to cease this cooperation with the Teleri, then your neighbors would think...more highly of you."

The prince leaped up and stormed out the room. The female Scorpion looked up for the first time that night, and then quickly dropped her head again as she staggered to her feet and shuffled out after him.

The room fell silent. All attention turned to her, some in admiration, others in disbelief.

The Queen of Ankira broke the silence, her eyes glinting. "What have you done? Have you sold us out?"

Paladin Elder Kairav, who'd criticized her the day before, scowled. "You still have not learned to look beyond your own borders."

Kaiya fiddled with her hair. Jie placed a reassuring hand between her shoulder blades.

Despite her embarrassment, she straightened her carriage. "Now that Prince Dhananad has seen that his neighbors oppose Maduran aggression, they will be more circumspect about meddling with any of us. I did this for the benefit of all." She turned to the Ankiran queen, hoping to appease her. "I did what I could for you. It is beyond our capability to liberate Ankira. At the very least, there will be fewer Bovyan soldiers garrisoning your homeland in the future."

The queen climbed to her feet as quickly as age would allow and stomped out of the room. The one Paladin elder stood up and departed as well, leaving his two companions behind.

Elder Devak afforded her a reassuring smile. "I believe you had the best intentions. I think you will prove it when you sing for Avarax in three days."

CHAPTER 46:

Interview with Evil

The enthusiastic twitter of birds roused Kaiya from a fitful slumber, one where she dreamed of Rumiya's glowing blue eyes, snakes entangling her, and the gush of beating dragon wings. She sat up in her bed and dabbed the sweat from her neck and face. Looking down, she found Zheng Ming's kerchief in her hand, damp with her perspiration.

Despite her restless sleep, energy coursed through her limbs, at last recovered from Rumiya's draining two days before. The fog clouding her mind had fully lifted and her focus returned.

Jie's chirpy voice mingled with the excited birds outside her window. "*Dian-xia*, good morning. Hurry, get dressed; the river barge for Palimur departs soon."

Images of her childhood nursemaid, now replaced by the half-elf, danced in Kaiya's mind. Tucking the memory away, she smiled and kicked her legs over the side of the bed. She had little time to react when her Insolent Retainer tossed travelling clothes into her lap.

As she tugged on the cotton pants and squirmed into the shirt, Jie chattered away nonstop. "The Paladins have assembled quite a flotilla to escort us. There will be a hundred knights and masters travelling as honor guard, though I am not sure Avarax will be impressed. Speaking of Avarax, I talked with Minister Yi, my *Moquan* brother, last night. His hometown legends claim the dragon flew over the night of the Hellstorm."

Having just started to fasten her cloak, Kaiya paused. "If it was Avarax, why did he wait three centuries to reclaim his lands? He could have taken advantage of the Long Winter to seize more territory. Maybe it was another dragon."

"Avarax was the only survivor of the Dragonpurge." Jie sucked on her lower lip.

Kaiya finished pinning her cloak. "Then maybe it was just a fanciful story. There are so many legends and myths surrounding the Hellstorm." She bound her voluminous hair into a pony tail and strode toward the door.

Jie opened it, revealing Elder Devak with Sameer at his side. The young knight's ear-to-ear grin suggested he was happy to rejoin them, after not having accompanied them to the Hua embassy the night before.

Then his eyes fell on the Insolent Retainer. His jaw dropped. "Jie. It's been a long time."

Jie grinned. "Not long enough. You've grown."

"In two years?"

Kaiya looked from one to the other. There was a story here, one that would warrant a melodramatic novel given the unspoken conversation in their eyes.

Clearing his throat, Elder Devak pressed his hands together. "Good morning. I am here to escort you to your boat. And to apologize." He bowed his head lower.

Kaiya had a good idea of what he was going to say next and stayed silent, waiting.

"We knew of Avarax's ultimatum and we still made you present your case before the elders. We also knew that Girish was once Rumiya, Grand Vizier of Madura, though we did not know he had visited you in the past. Otherwise, we would not have granted his demand to have us introduce him as Girish."

It was no use being angry. Kaiya returned his salute, pressing her hands together. "To save so many people, I would have chosen to sing, regardless of our agreement."

The elder's lips twitched. "I believe you are well on your way to becoming the hero the Oracle foresees." He then beckoned for her to follow.

Hero? The Oracle had said nothing of the sort to her, nor did she want such a burden. A quiet life in a peaceful country seemed much more appealing. Her hand strayed to Zheng Ming's kerchief in her sash. Maybe he would be part of that picture.

Still, now wasn't the time to think of love or marriage. A city depended on her. She looked up from her thoughts to see her five imperial guards, each on one knee before her.

"*Dian-xia*," Chen Xin said in the Hua tongue. "I object to this ill-conceived quest. It puts you in needless danger and gains nothing for Hua."

Kaiya had expected resistance from her loyal guards. "Chen Xin, is the *Tianzi* the Son of Heaven, who rules with the Mandate of Heaven?"

Chen looked among his comrades before turning his gaze back. "Of course, *Dian-xia*."

"And the agreements he endorses are the Will of Heaven?"

Chen Xin nodded.

She lifted her chin. "I am the Granddaughter of Heaven, and negotiated with the full faith and backing of the *Tianzi*. My words are his." It wasn't *exactly* true, since only an imperial plaque— presumably carried on the *Golden Phoenix*—could unquestioningly represent the *Tianzi's* word.

The imperial guards looked among themselves, their lips pursed and brows furrowed.

They weren't convinced. She cleared her throat. "Chen Xin. Li Wei. Ma Jun. Zhao Yue. Xu Zhan. You are my senior-most guards. Some of you have protected me since I was a babe in my mother's arms. I have trusted you with my safety. Will you trust me?"

More dubious expressions. She continued anyway. "Ayana will whisk me away to safety if it looks like I will fail, though unfortunately, she will probably not be able to save you as well."

Smiles bloomed on their faces.

Kaiya straightened her carriage. "We will go to Palimur, and you will protect me. That is my command."

The five guards lowered their heads in unison. "As you command, *Dian-xia*."

Countless Paladins greeted them outside of the Crystal Citadel, escorting them down to the river quays. Dockworkers and sailors finished preparing flat-bottomed barges, just wide enough for three men to sit abreast, for departure. A lizard the size of an elephant was hitched to each boat.

With Li Wei's assistance, Kaiya boarded the assigned boat. She turned back toward the quay, where Meixi bowed. When the girl rose, her lip quivered. "*Dian-xia*, it has been an honor to serve you. I wish I could accompany you."

The girl's dedication—and bravery—was heartening. Nonetheless, failure meant condemning a thirteen-year-old to death by dragonfire. "I thank you for your service here in Vyara City. Your knowledge of the local customs provided invaluable expertise to our mission. Not to mention much needed help with my hair and make-up when I had none." She ignored Jie's poke in her back and continued. "I will require your aid again when we return from this quest."

Meixi flushed a scarlet that would have made the setting sun jealous.

Holding the image of the girl in her heart, Kaiya took a seat toward the front, looking inland up the river. The boat slid forward, imperceptibly building speed as the lizard tacked in effortless zigzags through the waters. The hitching mechanism barely whispered, its mesmerizing undulations converting the beast's swaying into forward momentum. Dwarf-made, in all likelihood.

After two hours, during which Kaiya paid more attention to the scenery than deconstructing Rumiya's song, they stopped at a small port upriver. Without coming to a complete stop, the pilot unharnessed the lizard, which dockworkers guided into a corral, while other workers hitched a fresh lizard. The whole process took just a few minutes.

Time to focus. Kaiya pulled the pages of the song from her pack. With her head clearer, the music made much more sense than any time over the last two days. At times she would hum it, only to stop when the Paladins' *nagas* began to glow.

A sluggish but powerful surge, like a deluge held back by a weakening dam, emitted from the Paladin sitting in front of her. She looked up as he turned around and lowered his hood.

Rumiya.

He still wore the scaled armor, and his eyes glowed blue.

Kaiya sucked in her breath, while at her side, Jie whipped out a knife. Paladins rose with drawn *nagas*. Whatever good that would do.

He grinned, sending snakes writhing across her skin. "Greetings, Your Highness. I come in peace. I thought you might need help with the song."

In peace? Not likely. Kaiya motioned the Paladins back. She lowered Jie's hand and forced herself to smile. "Thank you for your offer. But first, may I ask a question? About you?"

He laughed. "Come now, princess. Do you still have feelings for me, even though you now know I am Grand Vizier Rumiya of Madura, and Girish, the Dragon's Envoy?"

Heat pounded in her cheeks. "Where have you been all of these years? Not from when we last met, though I would like to know, but from the time you left Madura."

As he considered the question, Rumiya's hypnotic gaze seemed more like snake's eyes than those of the beguiling beauty from two years before. "Control of nations and men was of little consequence when the power over cosmic laws lay at my fingertips. When I had a chance to learn from the most knowledgeable and powerful being on

Tivara, I took it. For years, I gleaned his secrets. In return, I went where he could not, in search of the one who could please him with her voice alone."

His boasts coiled around her like a serpent, forcing her to choke her words out. "And in all of your travels, I am the only one who saw you in the last thirty-two years?"

He cackled like metal on flint. "I have more than one face, though this is the one I grew used to. I am ironically quite fond of it."

"What will you do to advance your power once your mentor sleeps? Assuming I am able to accomplish that."

His eyes searched hers. "I have learned all I can from him, and he only has one thing left to offer. Let me tell you a secret about dragons. Do you know how in your people's depictions of dragons, they are always chasing a flaming pearl?"

Kaiya shook her head, not to answer his question, but in denial of his comparison between the harbinger of death and destruction and the auspicious protectors of Hua. "Our dragons are creatures of good. They are nothing like Avarax."

Rumiya growled, a low rumble that shook the boat. "Ever seen one to make a comparison?"

Kaiya lowered her head, chastised. Though she'd never seen Avarax, either.

Vindicated, he continued in a smug tone. "Though only legends, your images hold a grain of truth."

Rumiya's rough hand took her chin. He held her in the slits of his terrifying gaze. No! Not again!

Kaiya's chest ached, as if he'd ripped her heart out. From the corner of her eye, she saw Jie jump to her feet. Swords rasped from scabbards, where the imperial guards stood behind her.

Leaning in, the wizard let go and thankfully broke eye contact. His hot voice burned in her ear. "The pulsations of a magical dragonstone in a dragon's belly are the source of his power. When Avarax falls asleep, I will slay him, cut him open, and take his."

Kaiya shuddered. *If* he were telling the truth, her actions would replace one evil magical being with another. At least the Last Dragon was ostensibly predictable. There was no fathoming what a human with so much power would do.

Metal snapped with a clink. Beside her, hand shaking, Jie gawked at her knife, broken at the guard.

Rumiya laughed as he stood and raised his right hand. A blue flame flared in his palm, burning without a sound.

Kaiya rose and interposed herself between him and Jie. "Please. Stop. She won't do it again."

The wizard seized her shoulder in his left hand, sending heat searing into her body. He shoved her back into her seat, even as he glared at Jie. "Foolish girl, a mortal weapon has no chance of penetrating my armor. Now die."

"If you harm her," Kaiya shouted, spreading her arms, "I won't sing for your master. You will have to resume your search for someone with the right voice."

Rumiya stepped back, again locking her with his serpent eyes. "Would you sacrifice hundreds of thousands of lives and Cathay's mutual protection pacts for one stupid girl?"

Kaiya pulled the black-lacquered hairpin from the base of her pony tail and pointed the tip at him. "For my blood-sister, yes."

He'd seen through her bluff in the Crystal Citadel; or rather, tested her with his magic. Yet this time, he closed his hand, snuffing out the flame. He sat back down. "You, half-elf, are of little consequence. If I killed everyone who tried to slay me over the years, their bodies would litter the length and breadth of the Shallowsea. Now, princess, tell me how the song escapes your puny intellect."

Kaiya let out the breath she held. "I understand how the notes' modulation can affect the resonance of things. I just don't know how to magnify it to impact something as immense as Avarax."

Rumiya's brows furrowed. He spoke as if the answer was childishly simple. "Focus not on the dragon, but on his dragonstone."

What was that supposed to mean? Kaiya shook her head. "What if I don't have enough energy? How do wizards use powerful spells? How

is it that magic which drained them when they first learned it becomes easier as time goes by?"

He gave her a blank stare. "Power is innate. The more you need, the more you draw from your surroundings. But I see now that even though you have the right voice, you just aren't talented enough on your own. Perhaps Avarax will consider *loaning* you the Lotus Crystal."

A chance to see her future. If she survived. She bowed at her waist. "I thank you for that."

"I shall be off. In the meantime, practice well." With a harrumph and a scathing glance at her, Rumiya blinked out of existence. The air popped as it filled the space he'd departed.

Kaiya slumped in her chair. If she never saw him again, it would be too soon.

Ayana sidled up next to her. "I have never heard such an explanation for how magic becomes easier to use. It just takes time and practice. And I have never seen anyone teleport without using words to manipulate magic."

Jie held up her shattered knife. "I stabbed into the bare spot on the back of his neck. I am sure I was nowhere near his armor."

When they'd first met, Jie didn't take the princess' talk of blood-sisters seriously. Hairpins or not. Yet time and time again, from shielding her from Prince Dhananad's rage to allaying Rumiya's threats, the princess proved herself a liege worth serving. Two years ago, she'd offered herself as a bride to Lord Tong to avert a civil war, and then later secretly joined the expeditionary force tasked with capturing the rebel's castle. Perhaps a moral compass, and not mere flightiness, guided her impulsiveness.

Now left undisturbed, the princess immersed herself in two days of meditation and study. Convinced she could deconstruct and alter the song to really sing Avarax to sleep, she experimented with the sounds to see the effect on Paladin *nagas*. She paused only to eat, drink, and rest. Her dedication rivaled that of a *Moquan* trainee.

In spite of all the effort, it was unlikely the princess could actually succeed. Their journey to Palimur could very well be a one-way trip.

At least Jie could learn something during their travels. At times, the enthusiastic Paladin Sameer would point out places of historical or architectural interest along the riverbank. They passed famous temples, battlefields, and even a maharaja's old palace. His happy-go-lucky nature hadn't diminished in the last two years, despite all that had happened back then.

The moons rose and set, though it was Guanyin's Eye that Jie watched the most. If only she could slow its inevitable approach, to delay their confrontation with Avarax. Perhaps with more study and practice, the princess would actually be able to accomplish the task at hand.

Early on the second day, their travel upriver slowed. Boats clogged the waterways as refugees fled Palimur. Apparently, she wasn't the only one who doubted the princess' abilities. A torrent of people crowded the riverbank highway; some in horse-drawn carts laden with all their possessions, some on bare feet with babies slung across their backs. Many stared and pointed at the princess and whispered.

By midday, the hill of the Temple of Shakti in Palimur loomed into view.

Kaiya turned to Ayana. "I can hear the energy radiating from the hill."

Sameer nodded enthusiastically. "Palimur is a holy site, built on the delta where the Kaveri River washes into the Palimur River. The former is fed by several other rivers, including three flowing out of the Elf Kingdom of Aramysta, the valley of the old Kanin Pyramid, and Avarax's mountain. The area resonates strongly with the vibrations of the world."

Ayana added, "The hill is one of the Glittering Caves sites. During the Twilight of Istriya, our ancestors uncovered a Starburst there. Starbursts magnified the power of elven magic and turned the struggle for supremacy over Tivara in our favor... until the Year of the Second Sun, when the Orc God Tivar appeared in the heavens as a Red Sun, burning day and night, and rendered our magic useless."

Jie realized her mouth was hanging open. Elven legends had never interested her, yet she dwelled on Ayana's every word. She rearranged her expression into detached boredom and stared at the hill ahead.

They docked not far from the temple. The procession of a hundred Paladins marched through broad avenues of block buildings with domes and spires. It would've made for an impressive sight had anyone been present to watch.

The hill sloped up on a gentle incline. Its rocky ground harbored a few sparse shrubs and short grasses, but was otherwise devoid of trees. Jie scanned the flat, oval top, which she estimated to be a third of a *li* wide, one *li* long. A single mound rose some thirty feet above the rest of the hill near its east end.

The Temple of Shakti stood opposite the mound. Made of white marble, its multilayered steppes formed a dome supported by arched columns. As Jie understood it, Shakti represented the female energy of healing and creation. Though her own dismally flat chest was far from the perfect specimen, the symmetrical domes perhaps symbolized the female form.

She turned a jealous eye toward the curvier princess, who somehow made a squat appear graceful. Her eyes were closed, and her hand touched the hallowed ground. She opened her eyes, her previous look of doubt gone. "I hear it. The energy of the world bubbling in this point. I might be able to do this."

Jie flashed her an encouraging smile she didn't believe. This was such a lost cause.

Then, the hairs on the back of her neck stood rigid and her legs began to shake. Around her, Paladins and Priestesses of Shakti gathered, pointing toward the north. Jie followed their gazes.

An ugly blotch of red marred the horizon, floating inexorably toward them.

Avarax.

CHAPTER 47:
Verbal Jousting

Kaiya winced as the air roared with the slow bursts of Avarax's beating wings, even at a distance. Perhaps the dragon was in no hurry to hear her sing, since he was taking his time. Or maybe his enormous mass could only travel so fast. His slow approach gave her several minutes to listen to her surroundings.

The priestesses of Shakti chanted mantras to their goddess, their voices cracking under the fear Avarax evoked, even from so far away. The Paladins breathed in unison, slow inhalation followed by a slow exhalation, balancing out the priestesses' trepidation. Jie's heart beat calmly, palpable through the half-elf's hand on her shoulder. Ayana hummed to herself. The hill itself droned a serene, steadfast canticle.

Kaiya drew strength from the others, calming her own nerves. She could do this. After these last couple of days, Rumiya's song made sense, and altering it should be easy. If Lord Xu had ever contacted her, he would've surely confirmed that her alterations to the music would send Avarax into a deep slumber.

Down in the city below, horns blared, their low keen a background to the percussion of heartbeats and breaths around her. People who lacked the means or foresight to flee Palimur ventured into the streets, only to run back into their homes upon seeing the dragon. Her stomach tightened. Their lives, and the livelihood of all those who had escaped, depended on her.

Avarax loomed closer, a shard of cinnabar flashing in the blue sky. He grew unbelievably larger each minute, the slow pounding of his beating wings threatening to drown out all other sounds.

Around her, even the Paladins began to shuffle, the synchronicity of their breaths choking into disarray. Jie's hand pulled back. Ayana's hum faltered.

Her own heart gathered speed, cold fear crawling up her back and turning the blood in her arms and legs to ice. She shook her hands out, fighting the primal urge to panic. Death. She, and everyone else would die today.

Of all the sources from which she drew strength, only the hill's resonance remained.

Now, focus on your breathing, anchor yourself with the energies of the earth. Doctor Wu's words, repeated over and over again throughout her childhood, rang in Kaiya's mind now. She straightened her spine and gripped the ground with her toes.

It wasn't working! Her eyes locked on the dragon in dread fascination. His red scales and white talons came into focus. The glinting claws and teeth promised death. Every fiber in her body screamed at her to flee.

Close your eyes. Focus on the sound. Lord Xu's first lessons on the magic of sound repeated in her ears. The chorus of the hill rose into her soles, chanting in slow rhymes to her heart. With a deep inhalation, she sucked in the energy of the air. When she let the breath out, the Paladins' breathing lurched back into harmony.

The sounds around her slowed. The presence of Avarax loomed above. She opened her eyes.

His immense size blotted out the sun. From snout to tail, he might be even larger than the grounds of Sun-Moon Palace. His eyes glowed bright blue, boring into her soul. Death on wings, able to kill her a dozen different ways with less effort than it took for her to draw a breath.

Keeping her toes gripped to the ground, Kaiya bowed her head. "I am here, as you commanded."

"Then sing for me." Avarax's voice bellowed slow and powerful, his breath hot and reeking of charred flesh. "I have waited a thousand years to hear you."

Had she deconstructed Rumiya's music correctly, rearranged it to repeat Yanyan's feat a thousand years before? If not... No, better not to sing at all. Avoid the risk. She dared to meet the Last Dragon's gaze. "I do not think you want to hear the song your envoy provided. He seeks to betray you."

Hovering high above, Avarax regarded her for a few seconds. "All this is known to me. Little did Rumiya know that I tricked him and he gave you the correct song. He will suffer his due punishment soon enough. Now sing."

Hardeep...Rumiya, evil as he was, didn't deserve that. And what punishment *she* might face if her plan failed? She summoned all her courage to make her own demand. "Only after you deliver what I asked for."

The weight of a hundred stares fell on her. The priestesses and Paladins must think she was insane. Maybe they were right.

Avarax echoed the sentiment. "Foolish girl. Sing, or you will burn in fire hot enough to melt stone."

Could he see her legs trembling beneath her gown? Hear the anxiety in her voice? Smell her terror? Drawing on the energy of the earth, Kaiya forced herself to project confidence. Now if only her queasy stomach would play along. She laughed. "Then you will have to wait another thousand years to hear the song you requested."

The dragon snarled. The slow vibration shook the ground, which resisted with its own tune. Around her, several priestesses and Paladins struggled to keep their feet.

Avarax opened his maw and bared his teeth, each sharper than a *dao* and as large as the imperial guard who wielded it. He extended a claw and flicked something from his jaws.

Though only a flake of snow compared to its enormous dragon backdrop, the object pulsed with a deep sound, stronger than any Kaiya had ever heard. It glittered as it escaped the shadow of the dragon and caught the rays of the afternoon sun, growing larger in its descent.

Jie stepped forward and caught it in two hands, her eyes wide with wonder. She knelt and proffered it.

Kaiya drew a sharp breath. Had she just bluffed a *dragon*? Maintaining a straight posture to hide her surprise, she received the jewel.

It was a colorless crystal, the size of a man's fist, but light as air. Round at the bottom, tapered toward the top like a lotus. The number of tiny facets was beyond fathom. It sang in her hands, forming a symphony with the sounds of the hill, the chanting of the priestesses and the breathing of the Paladins.

Avarax roared again, sending the air cackling like sparks. "Now, mortal, sing."

Can you feel the change in vibrations? Lord Xu had asked her the night before her departure for Vyara City. Avarax's voice had modulated. It echoed with something deep in his chest, sluggish yet powerful. Different yet familiar, now that the Lotus Crystal was in *her* hands.

Kaiya bowed low, holding the position as she contemplated the sounds. Before singing her planned modifications to the music, she had to first test her theory.

Raising her head, she lifted her voice in song, the exact melody which Rumiya had given her. Each note reverberated into Avarax, the frequency of the dragonstone at his core increasing. The dragon's eyes glowed a brighter blue, though the shade remained the same...the same as...

Those vibrations. Lethargic, with immense power behind them. Like a mighty river held back by a dam. Exactly matched to Rumiya's. The blue of his eyes, which filled her dreams, were the same. The scales of Rumiya's armor hummed at the identical frequency as Avarax's. Rumiya had disappeared when Avarax awoke.

Rumiya was Avarax.

Avarax was Rumiya.

It all made sense now. Two years before, he'd tested her voice. Tried to get her to sing. And when that didn't work, he conveniently recovered the Dragon Scale Lute and restrung it for her to play in the acoustically perfect Temple of Heaven. When he realized it wouldn't work, he probably shattered the instrument himself and made sure it remained buried beneath Wailian Castle's ruins.

And now she was making Avarax more powerful with the song, just as she'd feared days before. He'd tricked her once, two years ago. Not this time.

She just had to undo what she started, using the variation she'd devised over the last three days. She transitioned into her new hymn. As long as he didn't notice...

Avarax's dragonstone buzzed a little faster, like a swarm of angry bees. No! It wasn't working! Maybe she'd misinterpreted the music. Or perhaps he *expected* her to make the modifications, shaped her actions. Just like with the fake lotus jewel years before.

What can we trust more than that which comes from within ourselves? The Oracle had said as much. She had to trust herself. If her music could make Avarax stronger, it could also make him weaker. She renewed the effort, pouring her heart into the next notes.

The steady rise in Avarax's energy wavered. Maybe...

Then it redoubled, even stronger than before. Inexorably building toward a crescendo. His triumphant roar echoed across the plain, shaking the city below. Her voice cracked. If she couldn't reverse what she'd started, they would all die here.

Harder. She had to try harder.

Trying is the first step to failure, Master Sabal had taught on the Shallowsea. *Your conscious mind cannot be moved... Do not just feel. Be moved.* She abandoned the song she'd meticulously planned over three days and now let Avarax's pulsations guide her voice, just as when the music had propelled her during her perfect dance for Prince Dhananad.

The Lotus Crystal glowed bright blue in her hands, and all the courage of the Paladins joined with the energy of the world and surged into her. Power welled up in her chest.

She sang new notes, and his immense body answered with a symphony of its own. Dozens, if not hundreds, of different sounds worked in concert inside of him, like the cogs of a dwarf clock. The torrent of vibrations hid a quiet sound: Yanyan's lullaby, soft and soothing like falling cherry blossoms dabbing into placid water. Its residual echo barely held Avarax's energy in check.

Strengthen those, and he would sleep. Kaiya slowed her tone, softer and softer to match the ancient verse.

Another rhythm flared somewhere inside of him, blocking the impact of her voice. No, worse! It weakened Yanyan's lullaby, diffusing it around them. A grin, if a dragon could grin, formed on Avarax's face.

Many of her honor guard cowered, some even throwing themselves into the dirt and covering their heads. The Lotus Crystal's glow guttered. The power inside her dwindled. The barrier of sounds constraining Avarax's energy began to collapse. It was hopeless.

Jie's hand pressed against Kaiya's back, evoking an image of the half-elf in her mind. Resolute. Courageous. Dedicated. Abandoning Yanyan's song, Kaiya sank her voice into a deep bass.

Around her, the faltering imperial guards and Paladins straightened in a wave radiating out from her. Young Sameer was first to recover.

"Form up, form up!" he said, even if he must be among the most junior compared to the masters.

The Lotus Crystal flared back to life, sending power coursing from her hands into her core. Yet despite the surge, how could her tiny voice possibly affect all of those interacting songs within him?

Focus not on the Dragon, but on his dragonstone. As Rumiya, he'd revealed the key to his own defeat. Kaiya sang directly to his dragonstone, his very source of vitality, using a different frequency to reinforce the remnants of Yanyan's lullaby.

Again, the same vibration flared inside of him, dispersing the effect of her voice. Yet this time, another verse revealed itself, whispering from deep within. Just like the stanza which kept her from renewing Yanyan's song, this was some sort of defense...but against what?

Listen. Sing. Be moved.

His defensive verse mingled with Ayana's hum, disrupting it. Had an elf voice vanquished him sometime in the past? Inverted, the sound would have an erratic beat and rapid changes, like nothing she'd heard before. She modulated her voice to create it...

The dragonstone responded with a sudden jolt.

She had him.

Subtle note by subtle note, she unwound Avarax's vibrations and bound them up with her own. Slower and slower, weaker and weaker, until he would be no more powerful than a manipulative, deceitful man who preyed on naïve princesses.

The dragon snorted. His brightly glowing eyes faded to a dull blue, lids sagging around them. He bobbed in the air as his wings echoed his dragonstone's slowing beat.

He opened his maw, teeth bared to roar, yet only music came out.

Her music.

His eyes widened, but the remaining blue within shimmered and then faded. With two rapid wingbeats, he pushed himself back half a *li*. His wings cocked one more time...and withered. The hulking muscle of his forelegs and hindquarters shriveled, the limbs compressed.

As Avarax plummeted, his entire form shrunk and shifted. Red scales smoothed out and melded into soft flesh. His snout rounded and his horns shortened. Looking human, he splashed into the river—naked, foundering, writhing. The current carried him away.

Around her the Paladins rushed down the slopes toward the splash.

"Capture him!" a Paladin master yelled.

Kaiya gasped and brought both hands to her neck. What had she just done? How was it even possible?

Jie squinted, her sharp elven vision straining to get a better look at the man who was Avarax before the river swept him away. It happened so fast, it was hard to make out his features. She turned to Ayana. Maybe the elf had gotten a better view, even with her decrepit old eyes.

Beside her, the princess' legs wobbled. Before Jie could react, her charge collapsed.

Sameer, chivalrous as always, jumped and caught her before she crumpled to the ground.

Predictably, the imperial guards stepped forward to intervene.

As soon as the princess found her feet, the Paladin retreated three steps, head bowed and hands pressed together.

She afforded him a grateful smile. "Sir Paladin, thank you for your assistance."

Sameer bowed. "Your Highness, it was my honor. But I am not yet a full-fledged Paladin, just an apprentice."

The princess smiled. "Yet I could feel the power of your *Qi* supporting me as I sang. Surely you are one of power. Jie, give the apprentice the gemstone."

The Lotus Crystal! They had re-liberated it from Avarax and would now apparently be returning it to its rightful owners. Jie bobbed her head and presented it with two hands.

Sameer looked toward a Paladin master, who nodded. He received the stone in both hands, his eyes wide.

The Paladin master bowed toward the princess, hands pressed together. "Your Highness, young Sameer was wrong. He is a Paladin now. "

If Sameer's mouth could hang any wider, he would be able to stuff the Lotus Crystal in it.

"We have another visitor at the Crystal Citadel," the master said, "an Aksumi Mystic who is well-versed in the lore of the pyramids."

Jie gaped wider than Sameer. It couldn't be! Not thousands of *li* from where they'd parted.

The master continued, "Once she confirms the authenticity of the Lotus Crystal, you will complete your mission by delivering it to the Oracle of Ayudra, and return it to its rightful place at the pyramid."

The princess' breath caught in her throat. "The Pyramid. The Oracle. Sir Sameer, when will you take it back?"

Jie sighed. Perhaps the princess would now get a better view of her future. Hopefully, it would be one she wanted.

CHAPTER 48:
Return to Ayudra

Cheering crowds greeted Kaiya in every village and town the Paladin procession passed through on their way back to Vyara City. Returning refugees showered her with gifts, all of which she politely accepted, but then made sure were donated to those in need.

None of the fanfare compared to her reception in Vyara City, where they toasted her as the Dragon Charmer. She received more marriage proposals in a day than she had in four years back home, all of which she politely deflected.

Her unlikely quest accomplished, she didn't linger long in Vyara. With a continued heavy Paladin guard, she spent two days meeting with prominent Hua families in the region, and looked for gifts to bring back to her family as was the Hua custom.

Most importantly, a week after her encounter with Avarax, she made it across the bay to Vadaras, to complete the task which Madura's ambush had cut short. Unfortunately, in her meeting with the deposed Sultan of Selastya, she learned that the senior-most Akolyte of their god Athran had recently died. None of the other Akolytes had regained the ability to channel divine power into healing.

Maybe that was the *Tianzi's* last chance. In this, her journey was a failure.

With a heavy heart, Kaiya, along with Jie and the imperial guards, headed back across the Shallowsea to Ayudra Island. Going with the gentle currents, the voyage took half a day less than the inbound journey. Their barge arrived mid-afternoon on the second day. The familiar synchronicity of sounds echoed in her ears. The *Invincible* remained in port, towering high above all of the barges.

The same official who had made a fuss about her lack of identification papers the first time now received her entire entourage with a broad smile. "Welcome back, welcome back!" He gestured into the city. "The Paladins have opened Ayudra to you. This is an unprecedented honor. Though there is not much to see beyond the central boulevard."

Young Gayan skipped down the street toward them, reminiscent of the time she'd disembarked from the *Invincible*. He greeted her with a toothy grin. "Please come! The Oracle instructed the guest house to expect you."

He seemed even more carefree than the last time. After the experiences of the last two weeks, those days were forever gone for her.

Kaiya smiled back. Though the answer would be the same as always, she asked, "How did he know I would arrive today?"

The boy cocked his head. "He is the Oracle, after all."

"Then he would also know I would like to see him at once." She flashed him a playful pout.

Gayan giggled. "The Oracle said you would say that, word for word. He suggested you come first thing in the morning, when you are rested and your thoughts are clear. He said, *less haste, less emotion* would mean something to you."

Thoughts of the Praise Moon nun admonishing her young cousin Ziqiu came to mind.

Apparently, the Oracle knew not only of the future, but the past as well. She bowed her head in acquiescence to the boy. "Very well. Please guide us."

The imperial guards and Jie followed Gayan down the street. Once they passed the wall separating the waterfront from the Paladins' district, they stopped at the surprisingly quiet smithy. A different pair of teenagers sat outside, sharpening their *nagas* while the young dwarf Ashler peered over their shoulders.

He glanced up as they approached, a broad smile forming across his bearded face. The dwarf turned and entered the smithy, beckoning her to follow.

Inside, the heat sang its own song, billowing out in waves from the anvil, where a thin ring glowed blue-hot. The old dwarf paused from stoking the bellows and lifted his goggles. "Welcome back, lass. Ye come t'sing for yer Focus?"

Kaiya looked to Gayan, who bobbed his head enthusiastically. She tentatively repeated his nod.

"Very good then, lass. Listen t'its purr, and sing back t'it." Ashler gestured toward the band, glowing ever brighter with the rising temperatures.

The ring's hum echoed the rhythm of the island, vibrant and alive. So unlike the sluggish pulsing of Avarax's dragonstone. She sang back to it, letting her heart fall into beat with the rest of Ayudra.

The metal glowed brighter, as did several of the rough *nagas* hanging on the walls. Both dwarves stared with wide eyes and wider mouths.

"By Dirkan's Beard," muttered the old dwarf. "The God 'imself must've forged yer pipes. N'er before 'ave I 'eard the like."

Ashler beamed. "Aye. Let 'er cool down. I'll etch a symbol in'er, make 'er yers, though I'm sure she knows already. What be yer fancy, lass?"

Several images flashed before her mind. Dragons. Phoenixes. Musical notations. None of those seemed fitting anymore. Kaiya took up a piece of charcoal and drew the ideograph for Heaven, *tian*. Surely it was the Will of Heaven that

had brought her there. *Tian* for *Tianzi*, and ironically the same word as her childhood friend's name. If only she could write it as beautifully as her sister-in-law Xiulan.

"I'll bring it to yer lodgin' t'morrow, when I'm done," Ashler said.

Kaiya placed a fist on her chest and bowed her head. "Thank you, Master Blackhammer. I look forward to seeing you tomorrow."

Tomorrow couldn't come soon enough, not because of the ring, but because of her appointment with the Oracle.

They returned to the guest house. Despite her command to rest, the imperial guards took turns standing watch outside her room instead of enjoying a full night's sleep in a comfortable bed. Jie, apparently, had no such compunctions.

Nonetheless, the half-elf was awake and by her side when Kaiya again woke to the harmonious interplay of morning sounds. Energy surged in her heart from what must've been the most restful sleep in a long time.

"*Dian-xia*, the *Golden Phoenix* arrived in port late last night. Young Lord Zheng Ming," Jie said the name as if she'd just sucked on a lemon, "was aboard and asks to see you."

Zheng Ming. Part of her, the one which longed to disengage from court life, yearned to see him, regardless of his shortcomings. No matter how much he disappointed her, his wit always made her heart race; his smile made her stomach flutter. It was *real*. She could grow to love him as Sister-in-law Yanli, ever practical, suggested.

Nonetheless, a visit with the Oracle came first. "I am not ready to receive him."

Jie grinned. "The Paladins wouldn't let him past the wall."

"You don't like Zheng Ming, do you?"

The half-elf's lips snapped shut.

"Speak freely. Not that I have needed to give you permission in the past."

Jie shrugged. "My expertise is protecting you, and you do not tend to heed my opinions anyway. I see no need to comment on matters of the heart."

Kaiya held up the half-elf's lacquered hairpin. "As my sworn sister, I *ask* you to sp—"

"You will never be first for him," she blurted, like pent-up waters breaking through a dam. "Young Lord Zheng is in love with himself." Jie's sigh sounded like she'd just set down a load of bricks.

Kaiya suppressed her own sigh. When had she ever been first with anyone? The monster posing as Hardeep had only wanted her voice. All of the young lords in line to marry her wanted prestige. As for Prince Dhananad...she shuddered. Perhaps the only time when she had been first for anyone was with Ming's brother Tian, and they had just been naïve little children. Nonetheless, Father's deadline for her to choose a suitor fast approached.

"What about you, my sworn sister? Where is your heart?" Kaiya met Jie's gaze, knowing the half-elf would never confirm her suspicions.

True to form, Jie's face went blank for a second. Her eyes then sparkled with a mischievous glint. "I am in love with serving you, *Dian-xia.*"

Kaiya covered a chuckle. Some questions might be better left unanswered. "Come, we must hurry to morning meditation."

They left the guest house, all five imperial guards in tow. Kaiya collected a handful of yellow flowers and set them by the statue of Acharya as they passed.

Gayan greeted them when they arrived at the semi-circle of megaliths at the Temple of the Moon. "Your entourage may join the meditation, but the Oracle bids you come to the Font by yourself."

Her guards grumbled, predictably, but obeyed her command to wait. They all remained outside the megaliths, save Jie, who worked her way through the crowds of seated Paladins.

Following Gayan up the steps, Kaiya arrived at the landing near the Font.

The Oracle looked into her soul as he welcomed her with palms pressed together. "You have grown in these short weeks."

Kaiya bowed. "If so, it was only with the help of the Paladins."

He beckoned her toward the bridge to the Font. "Come see...no, *hear* the fruits of your labor."

She crossed over to the mesa. Unlike the first time, when faint blue light sprayed out of the font, the ray now seemed to suspend the Lotus Crystal several feet above the hole. Its facets refracted and dispersed the light, bathing the entire area in a dim blue. A single beam emerged from the tapered tip of the gemstone, shooting straight up to the Iridescent Moon.

He nodded. "Your Paladin friend Sameer returned the stone last night. I can feel the energy of the world more strongly than ever. Can you?"

Kaiya closed her eyes and listened. The symphony of sounds rang louder than the first time she visited. The waves seemed almost palpable.

The Oracle beamed a smile at her. "I look forward to feeling the difference in today's morning meditation. As for you, it is my understanding that your people practice a form of moving meditation, similar to our culture's yoga."

Kaiya had taken lessons in *Taiji Fist*, the *Supreme Ultimate*, from Doctor Wu, though it certainly wasn't her forte. Nonetheless, when the Oracle folded his legs into a lotus position, she assumed a high stance, rooting her feet to the ground. She closed her eyes and cleared her mind, letting the song of the island lull her into emptiness.

Do not move, *be* moved. Master Sabal's admonishment formed the first verse of the song in her head. The series of waves lifted her out of her stance and sent her feet teetering across the top of the mesa. Her hands moved of their own accord, much like when she danced for Prince Dhananad. Gravity seemed to release its hold on her as she accomplished feats of balance that should not have been possible.

When the Oracle clapped once, she found herself twirled into a cross-legged squat, back arched and arms bent like weeping willow branches. The Iridescent Moon had moved a phase, though unlike the first time, she didn't recall any images or visions.

She turned to the Oracle. "I...I don't understand. Everything *sounded* perfect. My movements *felt* perfect. But I didn't see anything this time."

The Oracle peered at her, his face wrinkled as his eyes, nose, and mouth all scrunched up. "Your movements articulated your future. You may not want to know how I interpret it."

Why had she come, if not to learn her future? She returned his stare. "Please, tell me."

He sighed. "You will be tested. You will suffer. You will lose a part of yourself. Yet in the end, you will gain more than you ever lost."

Kaiya found her lips pursed. The Oracle spoke in such broad generalizations; his words were more a riddle than the answers she sought. "Is there anything specific?"

"As I explained the first time, everything is symbolic. But what I can tell you from watching your dance is this: you will find love, hot and fierce enough to melt snow and ice. You will lose love, nay, have it burned away as if by the sun itself. Your homeland, weakened from within, will be invaded and occupied. You will be faced with a choice that can free your country, and the impact of that decision will ripple throughout Tivara."

Hua, invaded and occupied. Like Ankira. Maybe she'd end up as bitter as Ankira's exiled queen. Her own choices would figure into the outcome. The inexplicable despair Kaiya remembered from her first visit to the Oracle flooded back over her now. "How will it happen? What choices must I make to avoid this future?"

The Oracle gazed at her as if she were asking how to switch day and night. "Your expression of the world's vibrations are only symbols. It becomes clearer and more exact the sooner into the future, and the cloudier the further you go. Remember, the future is not carved in stone, but rather billowing in the mist. The collective choices we make blow it into new shapes. What you manifested were merely possibilities. Sometimes, the decisions we make to avoid a certain future bring it about."

Kaiya frowned. If this was the type of guidance the Oracle gave the young Paladins, how could they possibly base their life's work on it? "Then what should I do?"

"Remember, a vision comes from within yourself. It is for *me* to give you guidance and for *you* to reflect on. Continue meditating on it, using the ring the Blackhammer Clan forged for you. It is a part of Ayudra, for you to take with you."

Kaiya wasn't sure of her own sincerity as she bowed low before him. "Thank you for your guidance. Farewell."

As she crossed back over the bridge, the sound waves of the Temple amplified his whisper. "The Bovyans as a race are very susceptible to the vibrations of the world, yet they cannot harness them. Therein lies the weakness of the Teleri Empire."

Since he'd whispered, perhaps he hadn't meant for her to hear him at all. As such, she didn't acknowledge his words, but continued down through the plaza.

Jie waited expectantly. Whatever vision she'd seen apparently made her beam ear to ear.

Kaiya nodded a greeting. "Where is Young Lord Zheng?"

"I understand that he has been waiting at the gate to the Paladin district all night and into the morning." The half-elf's lip twitched.

Kaiya sighed. How Jie could dislike the brother of the man she liked so much? "Let us see what Zheng Ming has to say for himself."

They continued back toward the harbor, their walk to the barricades taking just a few minutes. Zheng Ming sat quietly on the wall, mutually ignoring the Paladin sentries. His gaze met hers, sending her stomach into a routine of twists and tumbles that rivaled her latest dance. The girl she'd left behind in Hua decided to replace the Dragon Charmer.

He jumped down from the wall and sank to both knees, pressing his forehead to the ground. "*Dian-xia*, please forgive me."

An apology. He probably didn't even know how he'd wronged her. "Young Lord Zheng, rise." Her voice came out as a timid squeak.

He lifted his head, his crooked grin making her heart race.

It was only when Jie poked her in the back that Kaiya realized she was playing with an errant lock of her hair. She let go of the tress and folded her arms together.

Zheng Ming climbed to his feet. "*Dian-xia*, allow me to explain my very late arrival."

So he did understand at least one of his offenses. She raised an eyebrow. "In front of everyone?"

His cautious smile sent her head spinning. "It seems due penance." Then his expression turned grave. "However, there is more pressing news I must tell you. The *Tianzi* fell deathly ill nine days after your secret departure from Hua. The Crown Prince, too, was bedridden. Both poisoned by Lord Peng. Prince Kai-Wu sits on the Dragon Throne for now."

Nine days after... The pleasant dizziness disappeared. In its place, shock and confusion. Blood rushed from her head. Father, Eldest Brother almost dead. Poisoned by Cousin Peng, whom she'd trusted for so long. Perhaps he had his eye on the throne all these years. She reached out with a hand, as if it would keep her from fainting.

Jie's firm hand pressed on the middle of her back, supporting her. Zheng Ming took a step forward to catch her arm. If she weren't so concerned for Father's health, she'd be embarrassed at Ming seeing her so vulnerable. She couldn't worry about that now. She could be the Perfect Princess later, when she returned to Hua. Right now, she afforded herself a brief moment to be daughter.

"What...what happened?" The tightness of her throat clawed at her voice.

Ming held her in a sympathetic gaze. "The *Tianzi's* heart weakened and his entire body swelled up."

Wise and gentle Father, so strong when she was a child, now laid low by a traitor's ambition. Why hadn't she heard of this until now? Her mind tried to count the days between Father's illness and now, yet failed to grasp any number. Even the current date escaped her. "The *Golden Phoenix* is the fastest ship in our fleet. It could have been here within six days. Why are you just arriving now with this news?"

He bowed. "Lord Peng's men captured the *Golden Phoenix*. We thought they planned to whisk him home to Nanling. The crew refused to sail and were slain, to the man. It took us several days to recapture it, repair their sabotage, and redeploy new sailors."

Peng again. He'd deceived her time and time again, poisoned her family, murdered so many. Maybe even had Tian banished when they were children. The man knew no limits to his evil. Her only consolation... "I trust Lord Peng was brought to justice?"

Zheng Ming sighed. "He escaped over the Rotuvi border."

Her hands trembled as she tried to contain her anger and keep the desperation out of her voice. "We must return to Hua at once. When will the *Golden Phoenix* be ready to depart?"

Zheng Ming shook his head. "We took a beating in a freak storm off Haikou, which caused further delays. The captain says repairs will take a week or more."

Kaiya looked to her handmaiden. "The *Invincible* was in port. Do you know where Prince Aelward is staying?"

The half-elf nodded. "Follow me."

CHAPTER 49:
Journey's Bounty

A cacophony of surprised gasps buzzed in Kaiya's ears, while the colorful court robes of hereditary lords swirled before her eyes. Head spinning from the disorientation Ayana's magic caused, she might have fainted right there in front of the kneeling ministers and nobles. She lifted a hand to cover her mouth and stemmed the rising nausea, her other hand reaching out for support.

Two images of her brother Kai-Wu, sitting around the central spot of the dais, undulated back and forth. Several imperial guards behind him drew their *dao* and advanced.

"Kaiya?" His voice combining incredulity and relief, both Kai-Wus lifted their hands and stayed the guards.

"*Dian-xia.*" A baffling chorus of voices spoke in unison. A mob of oscillating colors surrounded her.

With a few blinks, the ringing in her ears subsided and the images around her came into focus. Instead of a mob, four ranks of seated men held low bows in a semicircle around her. They raised their heads in a wave rippling out from the inside ring. Over half the lords of Peng's Nanling Province were absent.

As she suspected, there was only one Kai-Wu, and he wore a broad smile which didn't match the *Tianzi's* dignified yellow robes. "Kaiya, you appeared...quite suddenly."

She nodded toward Lord Zheng Han, Ming's father. "Young Lord Zheng told me of the situation, and I came as soon as possible."

Which was quite fast. She bowed toward Ayana. The old elf, after a ten-minute song which sounded like angels singing, had transported the two of them through the ethers back to Hua. It worked out much better than the weeklong sea journey she'd asked of Prince Aelward.

Kai-Wu sighed. "The *Tianzi* and Crown Prince are both on their death beds. Doctor Wu is with them, delaying the inevitable."

The lords' expressions betrayed loyalties and ambitions. All had kowtowed before Father, sworn oaths when he was in his prime. Kai-Wu, while liked by all, did little to inspire confidence. Would they swear fealty to him?

Expansionist Lord Lin of Linshan pursed his lips. The people of his rugged forest province were well known for an independent streak. Lord Liang of Yutou, friends with the snake Peng, smirked, perhaps counting the hours. Hua was about to throw itself into civil war.

Kaiya bowed, showing deference to Second Brother as she would the *Tianzi*. "With your leave, I would like to visit Father."

"Of course, of course. They are in the solarium." Kai-Wu made to stand, stopping when she gave a slight shake of her head. His place was here, in front of the hereditary lords.

She turned around, heads again bowing low. Pages slid the doors open and she glided through and strode toward the residential wing of the castle. Two imperial guards fell in behind her, along with Ayana.

They passed through Jade Gate and onto the covered bridge separating the castle from the residence. Halfway over the bridge, Ayana's pace slowed. "What magic is this? I have never seen wards so powerful."

Kaiya smiled, but preferred to keep the secrets of the castle to herself. She walked through the gate and continued into the residence.

Just outside the archway to the solarium, the usual guardians of the sleeping quarters' wing greeted her. Eight imperial guard sentries stepped to the side, allowing the old nun to approach with light bauble lamp raised.

Her wrinkled features creased further in surprise. "*Dian-xia.*" She then switched to the secret imperial language. "How old was the Founder when he arrived in Hua from Heaven's Gate?"

"Forty-nine. He came from Great Peace Island, not Heaven's Gate."

The nun nodded. "Where was the portal on Great Peace Island?"

"Original Mastery Temple."

"What was his castle's name on Great Peace Island?"

"Pacified Lands Castle."

The gatekeeper switched back to the Hua tongue. "Welcome home, *Dian-xia*. I apologize for my impertinence, but your friend may not accompany you into the solarium." Her narrowed eyes showed no sign of apology.

The imperial guards stepped forward, barring Ayana.

Kaiya frowned. "Lady Ayana has helped me on numerous occasions. I—"

"It is all right, Kaiya," Ayana said. "I must be returning to Prince Aelward...just have someone get me outside of this magic bubble, and I will be on my way."

"Then thank you for all of your help and guidance." Kaiya bowed at the waist to express her gratitude. She straightened only when Ayana made

her way back through the residence with an imperial guard escort.

Kaiya studied the archway. How would Father, already ravaged by age and the burdens of rule, look now? And Eldest Brother Kai-Guo, just twenty-five...could she cope with seeing him near death? She took a deep breath and strode in.

Sunlight streamed in from the half-dome of glass, bathing the room in brightness. Despite shining on the dark-tiled floor, the sun couldn't warm the cold presence of impending death.

Xiulan, leaning at Kai-Guo's bedside, and Yanli, standing behind her, both gawked at her.

"Kaiya," Xiulan said, while Yanli beckoned her.

Beyond them, Eldest Brother laid motionless, his chest struggling with labored breaths. His ashen pallor stood in contrast to his usually healthy complexion. Kaiya's heavy heart weighed her steps, and she couldn't will her feet to move.

Sitting in a chair beside Father's bed, Doctor Wu held one of the *Tianzi's* limp wrists in her weathered hands, taking his pulse. She turned her head, her blue eyes delving deep into Kaiya's. "You have returned. Your journey bore fruit."

Indeed, if only Doctor Wu knew the whole story. She would undoubtedly appreciate hearing how her lessons helped vanquish the dragon. But now wasn't the time to tell the tale.

Doctor Wu smiled, the creases on the side of her eyes radiating out. "Come, child, bid your father and brother farewell."

Bid them farewell...it was that bad. Kaiya choked back a tear and stumbled forward. She fell to her knees by Father's frail form. Once, he'd been young and robust. Carried her on his back and threw her up in the air and caught her. But now...when she took his free hand in her own, the cold almost caused her to drop it.

"Sing to them. Let your voice escort them into the next life." Doctor Wu placed a surprisingly soft hand on her shoulder.

Warmth radiated into her from the doctor's hand, giving her courage. Kaiya started humming a lullaby, one Father had once sung to her. Slow and comforting, the words all but forgotten.

The *Tianzi's* eyebrows fluttered, their arrhythmic pulses threatening the harmony of her hum. His frail and stuttering heartbeat protested, jerking feebly at her melody. Behind her, Eldest Brother's faint and wobbling breaths magnified the amplitude of Father's imbalances.

"The combination of toxins," Doctor Wu said. "It breaks the natural resonance of their bodies, weakens them."

Perhaps it was no different than the vibrations of Avarax's dragonstone. Maybe she could influence their health and the toxins as well. Guanyin's Eye had already receded, however, and there was no army of Paladins, no priestesses, no elf wizard, no Lotus Crystal to lend her strength.

No. The power of two dying men did not begin to compare to a mighty dragon.

Kaiya rose from her kneel and gripped the solarium floor with her toes. With a deep breath, she cleared out all the other sounds besides her own hum, and the reply of her father's and brother's life forces. In the distance, the pulses of the Temple of Heaven reached even here. Doctor Wu, too, still projected immense power through the palm on Kaiya's shoulder. At her sides, Xiulan and Yanli breathed in harmony with each other. Her Ayudra ring. Kaiya might be able to borrow all of these, using her body as a conduit.

Continuing the lullaby, she raised her voice, accepting the irregular vibrations from Eldest Brother and Father's life forces, and harmonically nudging them closer to their correct course with musical notes.

Father's resonance was weak. Too weak. The toxins in both pushed back. It wasn't working. Despair threatened to overtake her, and she stuttered on her words.

No, she couldn't give up. A poison was nothing compared to a dragon dragonstone.

She let the toxin move her, pulling its vibrations to her instead of pushing them within Father and Eldest Brother's bodies. Their healthy energies filled in the space between the venom's wave pattern.

Behind her, Eldest Brother stirred. When she turned, his eyes were open and color was returning to his face. He propped himself up on his elbows and spoke, voice rasping. "Kaiya. You are home."

Continuing her hum, Kaiya nodded at him and shifted her attention to Father. The frequency of his vibrations remained feeble and irregular, though improved from when she'd started the song. Her energy, on the other hand, began to flag. Listless and heavy, her arms and legs protested the effort, and her concentration waned. She wouldn't be able to keep it up much longer.

"*Dian-xia*," Doctor Wu said. "Enough. This is far beyond the scope of musical power. Any more and it could cripple the power of your voice. It might even kill you."

Kaiya forced her voice louder. Just a little more, for Father, for the nation that might very well tear itself apart if he died today. All on her shoulders. She was alone.

No. Not alone.

Maintaining the melody, she sang to her sisters-in-law. "Eldest Sister, write...the words for health, power, and harmony. Second Sister, perform a tea ceremony."

Xiulan and Yanli exchanged dubious glances.

"Do it." Doctor Wu nodded toward her brush and prescription paper.

Xiulan took the brush and wrote the character for *power*.

The authoritative strokes of her hand invigorated Kaiya, sending a surge through her body. Her flagging energy provided one last push in her voice.

The *Tianzi's* eyes flew open and drifted onto her. A wan smile formed on his face. "My daughter. I did not expect to see you again in this life."

Kaiya gasped out the last note. The weight bearing down on her shoulders pushed her toward the floor. With supreme effort, she forced herself to remain standing.

Xiulan grasped her elbow, providing support, while Yanli brought a chair.

"Although he is still weak, he will live." Doctor Wu released Father's wrist and turned around to take Elder Brother's pulse.

The *Tianzi* pushed himself up into a seated position and beckoned a page. His voice still sounded weak. "Summon Kai-Wu, the *Tai-Ming*, the *Yu-Ming*, and the inner ministers. I will receive them here now."

The page dropped to his knees, then stood and hurried out of the room.

Doctor Wu finally came and took Kaiya's wrist in her hands. Her lips pursed as she held Kaiya's gaze with a stern glare. "Silly girl. Almost killed yourself, only to delay the inevitable."

The inevitable? Kaiya's heart tightened in her chest. "They will still die?"

Doctor Wu's expression softened into a grin. "Everyone dies. From the instant you leave your mother's womb, you are beginning to die. Yes, child, everyone dies."

"Even you?" Kaiya flashed a coy smile.

Doctor Wu harrumphed and stood. "*Huang-Shang*, I am going to prepare another herbal medicine for you. Do not exert yourself." She pushed her way through the stream of hereditary lords, brushing them aside like an autumn breeze through leaves.

To think a doctor could command the Son of Heaven...

All the lords, starting with the *Tai-Ming*, dropped to a knee as they approached the *Tianzi's* bed. Soon, they crowded the solarium.

The *Tianzi* cleared his throat and spoke with a stronger voice. "Great lords of Hua. The nation prospers, yet we are not at peace. A rebel, one who once sat among you, hides on the other side of the Great Wall while his province descends into chaos. I command you each to provide soldiers to assist the imperial army in its pacification."

The lords all answered in rote unison. "Yes, *Huang-Shang*!"

Such resolve, such obedience! A tingle of excitement surged up Kaiya's spine. Even so, the idea of potential hostility was disheartening.

"In the meantime, I command you to concentrate your efforts into maintaining stability in your own provinces to ensure they do not follow Nanling into insurgency."

"Yes, *Huang-Shang*!"

Father lifted the Founder's Broken Sword. "Peng Kai-Long, once my treasured nephew, must be brought to justice, to be made example of lest others follow his lead. Now, reaffirm your oaths of loyalty to the empire."

"I swear!" All repeated.

The chorus of voices reverberated in the room. Kaiya smiled. For now, the hereditary lords would hold the line. Now if only something as simple as a vow could secure the return of Cousin Peng. Who could convince the Kingdom of Rotuvi to extradite him?

Father's eyes fell on her.

EPILOGUE:

All Good Things

T

he sounds of Sun-Moon Lake lapping up against the castle walls comforted Kaiya with their familiarity. She sat atop the ramparts, letting her feet dangle over the edge as she listened to the waters' song.

Whereas none of her personal imperial guards would dare protest, her current detail of dour men virtually ordered her to come down before night made it too dark to see.

Convincing them otherwise gave her more opportunities to practice the power of her voice.

She needed the quiet time to contemplate what had unfolded, and her unlikely and mostly unwanted place in this world.

In the two weeks since her return, the *Tianzi* and Eldest Brother had continued to improve, with Doctor Wu's constant ministrations.

Court life resumed as usual. Her sisters-in-law welcomed her home with open arms.

Yet nothing was the same.

The hesitant girl who left Huajing had returned a confident young woman, scarred by betrayal and wiser because of it. Court gossip seemed trivial compared to the story of facing down a dragon.

The only ones who could understand that— Jie, and her guards Li Wei, Zhao Yue, Chen Xin, Ma Jun, and Xu Zhan—all remained behind in Ayudra until the *Golden Phoenix* could bring them home.

Zheng Ming—the one she most wanted to hear her story—was likewise stranded with the others.

Kaiya reached into her sash and withdrew Tian's pebble. As always, the cool smoothness reminded her of a carefree childhood, one that she could never relive. She started to cast the stone into the lake, sending it back to whence it came, but pulled her arm up short. With a sigh, she returned it to its place at her side. Some ideals were worth holding on to.

Her other thumb toyed with the Ayudra ring on her index finger. Its vibration mingled with the lake's waves, neither synchronized nor discordant.

"May I?" An open palm, like a beggar's, appeared before her, blocking the view of her lap. "I would like to see the ring that sings the song of Ayudra."

Kaiya's heart must've skipped three beats. She twisted to find Lord Xu sitting beside her on top of the wall, his legs hanging over the edge. His sad smile replaced the impish grin she'd grown accustomed to.

Angry questions welled up from her heart. "Why didn't you tell me? When you said someone would hear my song, you *knew* it would be Avarax, didn't you? Did you know Avarax was Hardeep? Why didn't you answer me when I called for you in Vyara City?"

His eyes searched hers for a few seconds, stirring her impatience. He then lifted the magic mirror and held it up to the skies. With his other hand he pointed.

She followed his finger, to a spot in the vast expanse of speckled night sky where a tiny red dot blinked.

"What can you tell me about that star?"

His question did nothing to answer hers. She responded in hopes of coaxing a reply from the fickle elf. "It represents the God of Conquest, Yanluo."

"Or in the language of the orcs, *Tivar*." He pointed to another a twinkling blue star. "How about that star there?"

"Wu-Long, the Dragon Protector of Hua." Curiously, it shined brighter than usual.

"She has appeared twice since the War of Ancient Gods, when great generals in Hua's history reunified the nation." The elf's finger shifted to the nine-star constellation facing the blue star. "And who does Wu-Long oppose?"

"E-Long, the Evil Dragon."

"Now receding. Who do you imagine that represents?"

A spark of understanding dawned on her. "Avarax."

"The Powers of Good are on the rise, though Evil always seeks opportunity. The Oracle of Ayudra is not the only one who can divine the future, though he is infinitely better than an Estomari tarot-card reader." A hint of mischievousness twinkled in his eye. "Or an elf astrologer."

Had Lord Xu arranged her meeting with the Oracle? Or set it in motion as Hardeep had influenced the path of her life? "So you can divine the future?"

Shrugging, the elf laughed. "Perhaps. The dilemma of knowing the future is our desire to change it. Sometimes, an attempt to alter our destiny only hastens its arrival. If you had known you would confront Avarax, would that have influenced your choices?"

Kaiya twirled a lock of hair. It was one of the many questions which had weighed heavily on her these past few weeks. Even as people hailed her as the heroic Dragon Charmer, she might not have willingly confronted Avarax if she'd truly had a choice in the matter.

She was no hero. Her hand caressed Tian's pebble.

Lord Xu's eyes were on that hand until he looked up and smiled wryly. "To answer one of your questions, no, I did not know Hardeep was Avarax, though I knew he always watched Hua in hopes of finding someone to sing to him. I told you as much, when you played the Dragon Scale Lute. I suspect he was responsible for the deaths of past magical music masters."

Yet he'd spared her. Used her. And more troubling, "Is it true that his Lotus Jewel awoke my magic and made me pretty?"

"You were born with the magic of music, as well as the intuition to face the Last Dragon. That is why I did not respond to your summons. Sometimes, you have to find the answers within yourself."

He'd avoided the whole question, specifically the more troubling half. She placed a hand on her cheek. "And my beauty?"

All mirth disappeared from the elf's expression. "You were not meant to be beautiful."

It sounded a whole lot like destiny again. "So everything that happened, and will happen, is my destiny?"

Lord Xu shrugged again. "You fulfilled your destiny when you vanquished Avarax. From here, you make your own. The stars just predict it. Resist the temptation to know it, since it may not always unfold as you hope. Worry not about what might be; concentrate on the present, the task at hand. That task now is to demand Lord Peng's extradition from Rotuvi."

With a melodic word, he disappeared, the air popping as it filled in the space he'd departed.

The future may not unfold as hoped. Ominous words, made all the more so coming from both an enigmatic elf and a mysterious oracle.

Threads of a Tapestry

H

ong Jianbin stroked sleeping Leina's cheek as they lay in her new Floating World abode. He had purchased the single-story wood building with his greatly increased stipend as Chief Minister.

It was well worth it.

The secret entrance from the adjoining Jade Teahouse allowed him surreptitious access to his mistress, away from prying eyes.

To think, without the encouragement of a foreign refugee and the help of a renegade spy, this fishmonger's son would have never risen to the exalted position of Chief Minister.

His native Nanling Province now lacked a *Tai-Ming* lord to rule it. Once the imperial armies rooted out minor lords loyal to Peng and pacified the countryside, the *Tianzi* would replace the province's leadership with those he could trust. Faithful generals and ministers would be elevated to hereditary lords.

Which would be better? To become a hereditary lord would improve his chance of marrying Princess Kaiya. As Chief Minister, he would have plenty of influence beyond the reach of a single province.

He gazed at Leina. Perhaps he already had everything he needed.

Leina feigned sleep, hoping old Hong would soon unwrap his leathery arms from around her. His proposed celebration for his promotion to Chief Minister was something she did not enjoy.

He'd been particularly virile tonight, and she feared his old heart might not be able to keep up with his manhood. His death, just when she'd gotten him to a position where he could influence national policy, would be disastrous. Everything she'd endured in her assignment as his mistress would have gone to waste.

As always, he surprised her. Just like when he outlasted Peng in their game of power. Or talked his way into Prince Kai-Wu's good graces.

The Chief Minister, hers to manipulate.

At the cost of her body and pride.

It was too much to bear.

Besides the herbs which poisoned the *Tianzi*, she knew of others that would kill quite quickly. One of those, hidden in her nightstand drawer, would be tempting to take right now.

But then there was her mother, trapped in Ankira, relying on Leina to succeed in her mission

to undermine Cathay from the inside. The house's secret entrance would allow her to covertly meet with the surviving insurgents and other lords and ministers she could bend to her will.

The most important key was to keep the imperial armies bogged down in Nanling Province. Then, the northern borders would be less defended once her employer was ready to invade. But how to sustain a provincial uprising without good leadership?

Peng Kai-Long.

She would think of a way to sneak him out of exile in Rotuvi Kingdom and back home where he could cause the most damage.

Geros Bovyan XLIII, First Consul of the Teleri Empire's ruling Directori, paced back and forth. The stone floors of his stark quarters in Tilesite were cold beneath his feet, in contrast to the anger which raged hot in his head.

The unlikely alliance of Eldaeri Kingdoms had recaptured some of the lands his armies occupied in Serikoth. The Bastard Prince Aelward of Tarkoth had broken his ingenious blockade of Bullhead Lake, allowing the cowardly Eldaeri to harass Teleri supply lines from the safety of the waters.

Apparently, Geros' commanders could not win a war without him.

The face of one such incompetent appeared at his door and thumped his fist against his chest. "Your Eminence, an official message from Cathay."

Cathay was a pig he planned to roast later, after sufficient marinating. He ripped the folded rice paper out of his underling's hands and whipped it open with a flick of his wrist.

To the Directori of the Teleri Empire:

Your vassal state, the Kingdom of Rotuvi, currently harbors the criminal Kai-Long Peng, former Great Lord of Nanling Province, within its borders. We will be dispatching Princess Kaiya Wang to meet with you and discuss terms of his extradition and continued trade between our great nations. We would request this meeting to take place in the port city of Iksuvius at your earliest convenience.

> *From Zhishen Wang*
> *Son of Heaven, Emperor of Cathay*

Geros harrumphed. How ostentatious a title for a pathetic nation of merchant princelings. Nonetheless, it would be a chance to meet the Dragon Charmer herself, who had foiled some of the Altivorc King's plans. Princess or not, Dragon Charmer or not, she was just a girl. And supposedly a beautiful one at that.

Geros turned to his lieutenant. "Have the rest of the consuls seen copies of this letter?"

"Of course not. You were first."

"Good. Draft my response, to be presented for the Directori's approval. I will personally meet with Princess Kaiya, on the occasion of the Northwest Summit."

His crowning moment, and one rife with underlying messages. To have her meet with him, in front of the eyes of foreign friends and foes, would symbolize Cathay bowing before him.

Now he just had to find out why he had not heard of Lord Peng Kai-Long seeking asylum in Rotuvi. And also get an update from his spy in Cathay.

Stirring the dying embers of his fire, Peng Kai-Long gazed out onto Guanyin's Tear Lake. After a month of travelling disguised as migrant farm workers with two of his most trusted guards, he'd reached the halfway point home in Nanling Province. To avoid a checkpoint in the staunchly Royalist Fenggu Province, they had veered off the main roads and now camped in the shadow of the old orc pyramid.

Despite what his officers aboard the *Golden Phoenix* had confessed under the *Tianzi's* agents' persuasive techniques, he never slipped over the border into Rotuvi. He hadn't even gone to Jiangkou, instead revealing himself to the insurgents in the capital as their anti-imperial

benefactor. After a month of letting his hair and beard grow roughshod, he headed south, trailing the expeditionary armies meant to quell any resistance in *his* province.

The lake stretched for several *li*, glowing a light blue. Legends claimed it was the single tear of the Blue Moon Goddess Guanyin, shed when the Sun God Yang-Di presented the mortal world to her as a gift. Many people visited each day in hopes that the holy waters would cure their ailments.

Kai-Long snorted. The *Tianzi* had drunk twice his bodyweight in the water over the years and still never recovered from his poisoning.

Yet Kai-Long did believe one legend.

Hua's guardian dragon once appeared somewhere in this valley. Though one local legend reported her sighting during the Hellstorm, most stories said she hibernated through the orc's Dragonpurge and would serve whoever woke her.

Kai-Long spat into the water. Who was to say hateful Cousin Kaiya couldn't charm *that* dragon as well?

No, he would have to rely on his own wits if he were to reconsolidate his power. The satisfaction of watching the Dragon Charmer suffer a slow death was motivation enough.

Liang Yu leaned against an Eldarwood tree, keeping watch over the funerary potter's shop. The rhythmic clanging of metal in the nearby blacksmithy all but drowned out the spring chirping of songbirds.

His search for Lord Peng, which had taken him to the border of Rotuvi and back, had proved fruitless. The devious lord had sunk so low as to feed his own loyal men disinformation. Despite what everyone believed, Peng had to be somewhere in Hua.

Which brought Liang Yu here, to one of the information relay points for his former clan. Even with a *Moquan* renegade at large, they didn't think the location was compromised. Of course. They never considered that the Architect, one of the few masters who knew of this drop spot, might still live.

The latest message he'd intercepted accused the renegade—him—of treason, for helping the Teleri Empire train spies.

Treason!

He clenched his fists. He was no traitor. If the ruling elite weren't so corrupt, they'd recognize his patriotism. And the only two people whom he'd trained in *Moquan* ways were Young Song and—

There was a light tug on his pouch.

Liang Yu spun around, curved knife ready to slash the young lady's throat.

She raised a metal hairpin, stopping the arc of his cut, and then bowed her head. "Master."

His special pupil, Lin Ziqiu, daughter of a *Tai-Ming* lord. Her skill had improved so much. She had tracked him here, and even succeeded in sneaking up on him. Used the noise of bell-making to mask her approach. Clever. Or maybe his hearing declined with age.

Though she was still not smart enough to realize his deception. He smiled. "Have you tracked Chief Minister Hong's mistress?" he asked.

She nodded. "Yes. He bought her a house in the Floating World."

The Floating World! It might be a better place to gather information than even the bell foundry. Liang Yu reached over and brushed hair out of her pretty face. "Pose as a Night Blossom, get close to her."

Her lip curled. "But I wanted to accompany Princess Kaiya on her mission to demand Lord Peng's extradition."

It was a pointless mission. A dangerous one, too, since the barbaric kingdoms to the north might not take kindly to accusations of harboring criminals.

Liang Yu shook his head. He couldn't expose his student to needless danger. But if he told her Peng was still in Hua, she might warn the princess. "Hong's mistress is more important. My control over him is nominal at best, but if we can find a way to manipulate her, it might give us extra leverage."

Her expression lit up and she clapped her hands together. Always in search of adventure, this one.

Colors flashed in the corner of his eye. He pulled the girl back behind the cover of the tree and peered back toward the potter's shop. The mute worker from the bell foundry dropped several messages into a worn funerary urn.

Within a quarter hour, a *Moquan* trainee, hypnotized to forget his task after completion, would retrieve the specially-folded messages. Which gave Liang Yu a quarter hour to send his student on her way, and then find out what his former clan knew.

For what must've been the hundredth time, Jie opened the small magic pouch Ayana had given her, marveling at the massive interior space. If only she could fit Zheng Ming through the opening, she wouldn't have to listen to his constant complaints about the heat and humidity.

She looked up from the pouch and toward the back of the river skiff.

The imperial guards sat back in their seats, their rigid discipline softened in the princess' absence. They chatted and joked with Sameer, revealing actual personalities. The belligerent Levanthi mercenary, on the other hand, sat apart, always staring ahead toward the homeland he hadn't seen for two decades.

The chocolate-skinned Askumi Mystic Brehane, with whom she'd shared an adventure two years before in the Teleri Empire, also kept to herself. She ostensibly studied her sheaf of magical scrolls, but was more likely trying to avoid Zheng Ming's flirtatious banter in his ever-improving Ayuri tongue. By now, he must've heard a dozen different ways to say *no*. Rounding out the motley crew was the dwarf Ashler Blackhammer, who constantly tinkered with some contraption he planned to market.

Rumor had it that Avarax, now limited to two legs, was making his way to Selastya. With the repairs to the *Golden Phoenix* expected to take much longer than the initial estimate, she'd convinced the imperial guards that the princess' future safety relied on foiling whatever nefarious plans the dragon had.

They now travelled with Sameer, on his quest to investigate the magical dead zone surrounding the Levanthi Pyramid.

Seven Hua warriors, an Ayuri Paladin, a Levanthi mercenary, an Askumi sorceress, and a dwarven weaponsmith in a boat. There had to be a punchline in there somewhere.

Avarax huddled among the beggars near the docks of some river city. It had taken him weeks for his two legs to bring him here, and he was not sure how much farther he had to go to reach Selastya.

Princess Kaiya's music still reverberated through his dragonstone, holding his immense reserves of energy in check. Though he was still virtually invulnerable, his magic remained locked away. Somewhere in her song, the tapestry of musical notes had destructively interfered with the frequency of his dragonstone. It was something only her voice could do.

Two years of planning, only to have a naïve girl grow into an insightful woman and deconstruct the fake song he'd given her. No, she could *not* again, and make Kaiya his own.

circumvent the magical ward designed to protect a human voice from singing him to sleep, as the slave girl had a thousand years ago. But she had reverse-engineered the other ward, the one set to prevent an elven voice from forcing an involuntary transformation.

Xu had done so during the Hellstorm, trapping him in human form for nearly three hundred years. Only when he tricked one of Aralas' descendants into playing the Dragon Scale Lute had he been able to regain his dragon form, if not all his power.

Never did he imagine that a human whelp—not even one with the voice of the slave girl—could accomplish the same as Xu. It should not have been possible.

Though fond of Rumiya's form and all of the entertaining adventures it afforded him when he chose, he was not pleased at the prospect of being stuck as a human for another three hundred years.

Decades were not long for an immortal. Another chance would present itself. Maybe not today, maybe not in a century. But it would happen. If one thing was reliable, it was that mortal beings had failings which his fifty-thousand years of experience could find ways to exploit.

The first step would be tapping into the energy of the pyramid to restore his magic. Now if only he could find his way to the closest one, in Selastya. It wasn't that easy. Everything looked a lot different at ground level.

It didn't matter. Soon he would look down on   the   world

DANCES OF DECEPTION

A LEGENDS OF TIVARA STORY

JC KANG

DANCES OF DECEPTION

PROLOGUE:

Childhood Scars

Sweat rolled off Zheng Tian's forehead and stung his eyes as he fumbled with the tiny key.

"H-H-Hurry up, Tian!" Kai-Long hissed.

Tian's hands trembled even more than his companion's voice. The loose robes and pants usually afforded ample mobility, but now seemed as restricting as a silkworm's cocoon.

He shot a panicked glance out the circular window, where his friend stood on lookout. Beyond, two men wearing dark blue robes hurried down the garden path.

Kai-Long's shoulders quivered. "Come on! We're dead if they catch us!"

"Shut up! I can't focus." Tian took a deep breath and eyed the rectangular golden lock. It taunted him as it dangled between the double doors of the eldarwood armoire. Everyone knew Dwarves forged the sharpest blades and strongest armor, but who knew they could also make such intricate locks?

And in truth, it hadn't been that difficult to unlock the first time he opened the armor cabinet. Now his fingers had minds of their own. He again tried to ease the spindly key into the hole, praying to all his ancestors. If they would please, please just let him open this lock, he'd place incense at their altars every day, both morning and—

Behind him, the training hall doors crashed open. Tian's heart leaped into his throat, and he stumbled backward, his legs tangling in the mess of armor pieces strewn at his feet. He tumbled onto his behind. Face hot from panic and embarrassment, he looked up.

The two imperial guards approached, marching in unison across the worn wooden floors. Etched into their burnished breastplates, a five-clawed dragon—the symbol of the ruling *Tianzi*—glowered down at him. Already racing, ten-year-old Tian's heart now hammered like a drum at a New Year's Lion Dance. His stomach twisted in knots.

"What are you doing, Young Lord Zheng?" Though lanky with a boyish face, the newly minted imperial guard Chen Xin still radiated intimidation.

Cowering, Tian whipped the key behind his back. "I-I...nothing..."

Chen Xin leaned down and clamped Tian's concealed wrist in an eagle's grip. The guard dragged him to his feet, revealing the key in the same motion. He looked from Tian's hand to the lock. "Silly boy. This is the wrong key."

How had that happened? Tian shrugged with a sheepish smile. "Oh, what do you know..."

Chen Xin's jaw tightened. His comrade's shoulders shook as he tried to swallow a laugh.

Behind the guards at the door to the master's study, thirteen-year-old Peng Kai-Long scowled at him. He held up the correct key and mouthed, *Get them out of here.*

The guards followed Tian's gaze back towards Kai-Long. The boy stood there gaping, key out for everyone to see. The older guard gestured him to come, and Kai-Long's head sank as he moped over. Chen Xin swiped the key away.

"What are you doing in the swordmaster's armoire? Trying on his armor?" Chen Xin scowled as he looked at the mess on the floor, and then began fiddling with the lock.

Oh, no. Tian tried to open his mouth to say *something*, but his tongue refused to move. He had been clenching his teeth. What had seemed like a harmless joke three hours ago might now have serious consequences. If the guard opened that chest, even Father wouldn't be able to save him from banishment, or even death.

His mind raced for a good answer until he caught sight of the hanging scroll with the character for *calm*. The magic imbued in its tranquil script rippled over him, slowing his heart and cooling the heat in his head. "No, no, the master. He ordered us to oil his armor. We were just putting it back. We can take care of—"

The lock yielded in Chen Xin's hands with a whispering *click*.

Oh, no.

The armoire doors swung open, revealing an eight-year-old girl standing as motionless as a statue. She wore the same cotton robes as Tian and Kai-Long, suitable for martial training. Her typically porcelain complexion blanched into an ashen pallor. Her fists squeezed so tightly her knuckles whitened, and her brown eyes, too large for her head, stared straight forward, unblinking.

"*Dian-xia!*" both imperial guards boomed in unison, using the formal address for an imperial princess. They sank to their right knees, right fists to the floor.

The princess steadied herself on the armoire wall and took a tentative step out, limbs stiff as the corpses that the bronze-skinned Southerners embalmed. After having spent a few hours in the equivalent of a coffin, all of her delicate grace seemed lost. Chen Xin rose and hurried over to support her, while the other guard fixed his glinting glare on the two boys.

Tian and Kai-Long both dropped to their knees and placed their foreheads to the ground, hands splayed in front of them.

"Forgive us, *Dian-xia!*" Tian's own voice sounded wrong to him, almost a squeak.

"Us? It's not my fault, it was *your* idea!" Kai-Long peered over, expression almost mirthful.

"Liar," Tian muttered under his breath. It *had* been Kai-Long's idea, but there was no use protesting. He was the *Tianzi*'s favorite nephew and would escape blame.

The princess' catatonic expression remained unchanged for a few seconds before her eyes welled up with tears.

"I'm sorry, Kaiya. It was just a stupid prank." Tian sobbed as Chen Xin grabbed him by the collar and hauled him to his feet. Was he crying because he faced certain, and possibly severe, punishment? Or because he'd hurt his best friend— and if he admitted it, his love? He'd spent almost half his life with her, learning archery, swordsmanship, literature, and the other educational foundations of the noble houses.

Stumbling to keep up as Chen Xin dragged him along, Tian craned his neck to catch one last glimpse of the girl who'd promised to marry him. Kaiya was now weeping inconsolably, while her cousin Kai-Long comforted her with reassuring pats on the head.

He didn't want this to be his last image of the princess. Would she only remember him as the one who locked her in an armoire? Servants scurried past him, obscuring his view of her. Attention forward, Tian shuddered as Chen Xin prodded him through the grounds of Sun-Moon Palace for his inevitable audience with the *Tianzi* himself. The other guard ran ahead.

All Tian could do was count, like he always did: His paces. His breaths. The number of flowering fruit trees.

Tian climbed the one hundred and sixty-eight white stone steps to the entrance of the Hall of Supreme Harmony. The final step, the knee-high spirit-tripping threshold, took the last of his strength. Inside the cavernous room, eighty-eight gold-lacquered columns vaulted upwards to support a tile ceiling mosaic of circling dragons.

Inebriated by the cloying incense hanging in the air, Tian stumbled down an aisle between ninety-two seated ministers in blue robes. His footsteps clicked on the white marble floors, faltering as he came to a bloodwood dais carved with countless auspicious symbols of bats and lotuses.

Two thrones loomed above him. One was chiseled from a gigantic chunk of jade to resemble a coiled dragon; the other was gold, worked to resemble a resting phoenix. Seated on the larger jade throne was a man of middling years, dressed in yellow robes with blue-and-red dragon heads on the breast and sleeves.

The *Tianzi*.

Tian gulped. Despite spending much of his time at the palace, he'd never seen Kaiya's father, the man who would pass sentence on him.

His gaze strayed to the Broken Sword, borne by the commander of the imperial guard, who stood behind the *Tianzi*. Maybe they'd use it to behead him, or run him through; or maybe order him to cut his own throat.

Tian threw himself to his knees, nearly knocking himself unconscious as his forehead hit the ground. He knew his history well: three centuries before, the first *Tianzi* had executed five generations of an entire family over a child's mischief.

"Raise your head, boy."

Despite Tian's fear, the man's tone of command compelled him to rise into a kneel. He stared downward, keeping his eyes averted from the *Tianzi*.

"You convinced the princess to hide from her guards, and then locked her in an armoire for three phase-hours of the Iridescent Moon. What have you to say in your defense?"

Tian's words stuck in his throat. He opened and closed his mouth, but only a squeak came out.

"*Huang-Shang*," a new voice from behind said, using the formal address for the *Tianzi*. "May I speak?"

"You may."

"Young Lord Zheng, face me." The same voice now came from the opposite side of the room.

What? Tian shifted his position and looked in the direction of the voice. He found only pitying stares. No one acknowledged him. He turned again, back in the direction from which the voice had initially originated.

A minister with one knee down, fist to the floor, gazed back at him with dark eyes that seemed to be looking into his mind. "You were counting the number of guards on your way in, weren't you? It's okay, answer freely."

Tian nodded. He *had* counted them. Counting was a compulsive habit with little use.

"How many?"

"Thirty-six," Tian said.

"On your way to the Hall of Supreme Harmony, did anything seem out of the ordinary?"

These questions had nothing to do with the princess. Why was he asking? "There was an enormous palanquin. With wheels. Borne by large horses instead of porters."

"And?"

"The door was dark green. With a nine-pointed star of silver."

The minister's lips twitched. "As you entered the hall, who was standing where you are now?"

"A barbarian from the East."

"Where in the East?" The minister was smiling now.

Where? How was he supposed to know? Just as he was about to shake his head, he remembered his heraldry lessons. Tian swept his gaze towards the area he thought the man's voice had come from the second time.

A teenage boy with a slim build and sharp features looked back at him. Unlike the honey-colored skin and black hair of the Hua, this boy had an olive skin tone and a long brown mane. And although he wore silken court robes, the *wen* emblem on his chest was the same foreign-looking star he had seen on the palanquin.

He was an Eldaeri human, part of a tribe that had mingled with elves thousands of years before. The circlet indicated nobility, and the crest belonged to the Kingdom of Tarkoth. "He is a prince of Tarkoth."

"Crown Prince Elrayn, to be exact." The *Tianzi* nodded a fraction. "Impressive."

"*Huang-Shang*," the minister said. "With your permission, allow me to decide his sentence and administer the punishment."

Fear had partially given way to curiosity, and Tian now spoke with no thought to his predicament. "Will I see the princess? Before my punishment?"

The minister shook his head. "No. Where I am taking you, you might never see her again."

CHAPTER 1:

Value of a Dragonfly's Life

Zheng Tian knew many ways to kill the smuggler, but none to ease his own conscience.

A column of sun streamed in from the dusty warehouse's skylight, reflecting off his target's seventeen glittering rings. All it would take was a signal to assassinate him and his two bejeweled henchmen.

Hold the dragonfly with care, eight-year-old Princess Kaiya's voice chimed in his head, quoting an old Hua proverb. *For even their fleeting lives have value.*

What was the value of a *man's* life?

Now twenty-one, Tian banished memories of the gentle girl to the recesses of his mind. Time to focus on the most distasteful of his duties. Just eleven feet away, the olive-skinned Estomari merchant walked from crate to crate, checking items off a cargo manifest and barking orders.

The twenty-four wooden crates contained legitimate trade goods, for sure. However, Marcus Larruso also trafficked in the local girls, sending them to the South, where their fair complexions and blonde hair would fetch a handsome price. Perhaps he deserved death.

Tian's goals weren't particularly noble, either. As much as he wanted to, he wasn't here to rescue impoverished girls from a short and miserable life of exploitation, far away from home.

Larruso reached the last of the two crates, while one of the heavily-armed bodyguards stepped onto the spot where he would die.

The power of life and death, in Tian's hands. Perhaps that burden was a form of punishment, one which widened the gulf between his carefree youth and the ruthless spy he had become.

He flashed the hand signal from his vantage point.

Six *Moquan* Black Fist spies fell upon the three unsuspecting smugglers in clinical silence.

Old Tong, the most experienced of them, darted from between the last two crates. He covered Larruso's mouth and slashed his throat with a black-lacquered knife.

At the same time, Pockmarked Zu dropped from the rafters. He stomped through the largest man's knee and applied an unremitting chokehold. His victim's frantic clawing only hastened his demise.

The most recent arrival to their embassy in Iksuvius, Cheng, burst out of the shadows and hacked at the third henchman's neck with his curved sword. Blood sprayed, and the man let out a choked screech before falling dead.

"Clear." Six voices echoed the word in quick succession. Lives, so easily snuffed out.

Pockmarked Zu eased the body to the hard-packed dirt floor. "Brilliant plan, worthy of the Architect."

"And executed with the precision of the Surgeon and the Beauty." Young Cheng's eyes crinkled as he opened one of the many crates.

Tian snorted. His plan had not been much more than picking a hiding place, and choosing the right timing against overmatched thugs.

"Now which one of you is the Beauty?" Old Tong looked from Young Cheng to Pockmarked Zu before shaking his head. He was old enough to have known the three legendary masters, all struck down in their youth a generation ago. Under clan orders, he never spoke their names, though he animatedly recounted their exploits when given a chance. "Neither, you're both too ugly."

Like the rest of his comrades, Tian held the deceased masters in awe. Nonetheless, he silenced the men with a scowl. "Cheng. Use a more effective technique. He made a sound. Others could have heard."

The boy hung his head. "But you timed it so the rest of them—"

"It's all right. Just learn from your mistakes." Tian swept his gaze around the warehouse. "Now. Where's our primary target?"

Old Tong motioned him over. "Here."

Larruso lay dead, his curly brown hair matted in a pool of blood. The Pirate Queen's agent in the frigid Northwest, Larruso was a known associate of Tian's former friend and current fugitive, Peng Kai-Long.

Tian sighed. Three more murdered, bringing the total he'd arranged to eighteen, on top of thirty-two he'd killed with his own hands. All necessary to protect the homeland. He gestured towards Young Cheng. "What's in this shipment?"

"Just fine glassware." The boy shrugged.

"And wool," Pockmarked Zu added, looking up from another crate.

Tian tapped his chin. They'd tracked Larruso for weeks after receiving word of increased weapons orders. With a Hua trade ship coming into port later today, it would be the perfect opportunity to smuggle his cache. "No weapons?"

Old Tong looked up from a table and waved a blood-smeared sheet of paper. "Here is a diagram for repeating crossbows."

Tian nodded. Without access to firepowder for muskets, Peng would need Hua's other great invention. Or innovation rather, since the Repeater design had originally come from the Eldaeri people of the Northeast.

"Here are the parts," Shun said from the far corner. "Uncrated."

Uncrated. So they weren't being shipped home to Hua, to arm the dwindling insurgency. At least not yet.

Tian took the diagram from Old Tong and scanned it. He then traced the cocking mechanism with his finger. "This is an Eldaeri crossbow. Not one of ours." Just like the ones he'd seen two years ago when the Eldaeri attended the wedding of Second Prince Kai-Wu.

"You're right." Shun tossed over the trigger component.

Tian swept it out of the air. "Dockworkers will arrive later. Shun, impersonate a merchant. Make sure the crates get loaded. The rest of you. Dispose of the bodies. The locals won't miss this criminal. Then regroup in my office."

"As you command," his men responded in unison.

Three knocks rapped on the skylight, the prearranged signal from their lookout that someone was coming in.

The *Moquan* melted back into shadows, dragging the bodies with them. The door opened, revealing a young man with a repeating crossbow.

He took a tentative step in. "Master Larruso?" A thick local accent weighed down his Arkothi.

Tian raised a fist, ordering his men to stand down. No point killing a hapless servant who had the bad luck of walking in at the wrong time. He stepped out into the light. "Master Larruso is indisposed."

The man looked at him, his eyes intermittently glancing to the space behind him. "Who are you?"

"Feng. Trade officer. From the Cathayi embassy." Tian motioned to the crates behind him. "I am here to make sure everything is in order. This shipment is going out tonight."

The man licked his lips. "By yourself? That's not like him."

"Oh yes. Lord Larruso had another matter to attend to. He told me to make arrangements." Tian covered the bloodstain on the cargo manifest as he held it up. "Wait here. If you want. Or I can pass your message to him."

The man presented the crossbow. "I can't read. I just wanted to make sure I assembled this correctly."

Tian flipped it over in his hands. Hua had improved upon the inefficient magazine and unwieldy cocking mechanism a century ago. To think the most advanced weapon in the North was almost obsolete back home.

He looked back at the man and held the weapon as if it were a venomous snake. "I'm only a clerk. I don't know weapons. But I will leave this...*thing*...on his table. How about I write a note for you?"

The man nodded enthusiastically. "Just let him know the workers are confused and need directions."

"I will do that." Tian flashed him a warm smile as he walked the man to the door. As the fellow walked out, Tian flashed a signal to Tong. *Follow.*

Old Tong zipped through, and Tian closed the door and let out a long sigh.

"Why'd you let him go?" Young Cheng emerged, shaking his head.

Tian held the boy's gaze. "Shun, was he an immediate threat?"

"No, the crossbow was uncocked," Shun said.

Tian nodded. "Zu, was he close to Larruso?"

"No, Larruso's lieutenants are all literate and wear their wealth," Pockmarked Zu said. "He was just a local peasant, looking for work."

Cheng cocked his head. "But shouldn't we tie up loose ends? He didn't matter."

"What did you make of his bracelet?"

"Crudely woven, with faded colors," Cheng said. "Fraying in spots."

Tian nodded. "Very good. What does that tell you?"

Cheng's forehead furrowed.

"The poorest cannot afford rings. When they exchange wedding vows. Unlike Larruso, he would be missed."

The young *Moquan* shrugged. "What is one life worth?"

"A dragonfly. Now, clean up here. Then meet back in my office."

With a last glance, Tian slipped out the door and into the bright afternoon sunlight. He blinked a few times to let his eyes adjust, and then set off for the embassy, just on the other side of Iksuvius' western marketplace.

Guilt pricked at him, even more so than the marketplace's scent of oily foods, fresh vegetables, and salted fish. Had they needlessly killed those men? He'd lost his innocence many times over since his banishment from the capital. What would his ten-year-old self think of who he had become? Princess Kaiya would be disappointed.

Her *again*. He'd last seen her from afar on the battlements of Wailian Castle, eight hundred seventy-eight days ago. She'd rarely visited his thoughts in the last four thousand and twelve days; maybe only on the several occasions when he'd had to kill an enemy of the state. Otherwise, there was no use wondering about someone he'd never see again. Or who'd undoubtedly forgotten about him. His chest squeezed. There were more pressing matters.

Tian started to pick his way through the crowded market. After two years, he'd grown accustomed to being surrounded by the large, light-skinned, fair-haired Nothori folk. Even so, their sweat stank of raw onions and goat's milk. He weaved through them with careless grace, loath to brush up against their hairy bodies.

Along the way, he cut the purse of a brothel owner, and later slid a copper Iksuvi *kroon* into the pocket of a destitute boy. When asked by his spies about this peculiar habit, he always shrugged it off as an exercise to keep his skills sharp. And if a child happened to notice his handiwork—or even tried to pick *his* pockets—he or she might be recruited as another set of eyes and ears for Tian's information network.

A network whose information he'd misinterpreted. The weapons weren't meant to arm the insurgency back home. A pit formed in the bottom of a stomach. He'd ordered an unnecessary murder.

What had he missed? Tian stood before the spongewood board that took up the entire northern wall of his second-floor office. The setting sun peeked in from the windows, splashing the middle of the room with gentle light. It left the walls cloaked in shadows, concealing his Black Lotus brothers.

A cool breeze wafted in, bringing with it a breath of salt water off of Cold Harbor. It dislodged the crossbow diagram from one of the strings crisscrossing the room, and sent it fluttering. Tian plucked the page out of the air as it drifted by, without looking at it or creating a whisper of sound.

He snaked through the organized tangle of zigzagging lines like a contortionist, and tacked the diagram to a new spot on the southern wall board. Satisfied, he stepped back and pondered. The carelessly scribbled notes, objects, and twine connections formed a chaotic net of interrelations between events, people, and evidence.

The embassy staff referred to his office as the *Cobweb*. If the embassy as a whole presented the face of his homeland's commerce with its northern neighbors, this room was the brain. Here, twelve *Moquan* gathered information on potential enemies who otherwise masqueraded as trading partners.

The systematized mess of data mirrored the rest of the room, from the cluttered wooden desk to the random positioning of the chairs, bookshelves, and even the richly-colored wool rugs on the dark wood floors. In the middle of it stood Tian, his mind the calm eye in the storm of facts and figures, bringing logical order to the chaos.

He pointed out a single strand of curly red hair, which Old Tong had retrieved from the crossbow workshop, dangling on one of the threads.

"There," he said, keeping his voice just loud enough to carry over the din of the late afternoon bustle in the western marketplace. "Only Northerners have red hair. This strand is coarse. It probably belongs to an Eldaeri. There was a huge order for Eldaeri crossbows. Not from the rebel Peng. Maybe the Eldaeri are planning to disrupt the summit."

Gliding untouched through the web of strings, he traced that particular thread back towards the northern wall board, to a note labeled *Northwest Summit*.

"An assassination attempt?" queried a voice from the dark corner of the room.

Tian tapped his chin. He'd been wrong about Larruso. He spoke slowly, making sure not to trip over the words. "Maybe. It would be their best chance. The Teleri Empire's First Consul will be here. With less protection. They can split the Northwestern alliance. Between the Teleri and the Nothori Kingdoms. And we would benefit. Stay on the lookout for the Eldaeri. If they are here, we will make contact. To help them."

"Understood," answered a chorus of voices from the shadows.

He waved his hand, dismissing them. The sounds of their breaths disappeared, indicating they had melted away.

Tian smiled to himself. His spies might now consider him the second coming of the Architect, but when he had first been posted here, as a young man who couldn't speak in complete sentences, they probably thought it was because of his family connections. As if any aristocrat would choose to work in these barbaric lands. He returned to the tendril of hair, rubbing it between his fingers.

An unfamiliar young man appeared at the door, guided by the Mistress of Chambers.

"I have just arrived on the *Wild Orchid*," he said, "and have been instructed to bring you to the docks."

"Me?" Tian snorted. The cargo that would fatten Hua's coffers mattered little to him. "You're looking for Trade Minister Zhang."

"I was explicitly ordered to summon you." The messenger reached into his robes and drew forth a thin jade plaque. Carved in the likeness of a five-clawed dragon, it symbolized the *Tianzi*, ruler of Hua.

As protocol demanded, Tian sank to his right knee, head bowed, right fist to the floor. It was strange to see a plaque here. "Please. Take me to the ship."

The two descended through the main residence, a three-story mansion of wood and immaculate white stone with sloping eaves of blue tile, which stood at the center of the embassy compound. Situated on a low hill and encircled by a twelve-foot-high stone wall, the spacious grounds overlooked the only deep-water harbor in the Northwest of the continent.

With the arrival of a cargo ship, the embassy buzzed with activity. On his way through the courtyard to the main gates, Tian weaved around trade officers, guards, and porters, who all hurried between the two-story trade office building, the stables, the barracks, and a warehouse.

Monks' chants and the cloying smell of burning incense emanated from the East Light Temple in the southeast corner of the compound. Dedicated to Hua's patron god Yang-Di, the wooden temple rose to the height of six men and boasted sharply pitched, yellow-tiled eaves. Sailors from the *Wild Orchid* already streamed in to thank the Lord of the Sun for the ship's safe arrival after a week at sea.

Tian paused at the wrought iron gates and looked back to see the messenger still near the residence, stutter-stepping through the crowd. There was no need to wait; they both knew where to go. He continued out of the embassy, and maintained a brisk pace through the bustling streets. Near the docks at the far end of the marketplace, now shrouded in the long shadows of late afternoon, a crowd of locals gathered to witness the arrival of a Hua trading ship.

They jostled each other to catch a glimpse of the black-haired, honey-toned Hua people, whom they referred to as Cathayi. Many gawked at the giant ship, and fought to get first pick of the gadgets and wares imported from all over the continent. In this, they would be disappointed. With lords and kings visiting for the quinquennial Northwest Summit, this particular shipment contained luxury items far beyond commoners' means.

When Tian reached the head of the quay, a stocky Hua sailor nodded and waved him past the cordon. As Tian waited for the less dexterous messenger to catch up, he studied the dark planks of eldarwood that made up the *Wild Orchid's* hull.

It was eldarwood that made the otherwise small, mountainous nation of Hua so rich. The straight-trunked evergreen was the only tree thriving on the west coast which could be made into ocean-going ships, and it grew in abundance in Hua. Hua's navy and trading fleet dominated the western seas, making it the envy of its neighbors.

The messenger arrived a moment later, interrupting his musings. Tian followed him up the gangplank to the main deck, where the bright light of the setting sun caused him to squint. Here, their roles reversed—the messenger's sea legs allowed him to jaunt across the deck towards the aft cabin, while Tian lurched after him.

The man stopped at the door, placed the imperial plaque in Tian's hands, and then gestured for him to enter.

The door closed behind him, plunging him into darkness. He instinctively reached into a secret pocket in his vest, withdrawing a twelve-pointed, razor-sharp *biao* throwing star. A year spent blindfolded prevented Tian from panicking. His other senses kicked in.

Incense had recently been snuffed out. A man breathed at the far end of the cabin, near a closed porthole.

"Young Lord Zheng, thank you for coming." The man's sonorous voice carried a certain tone of command bred into the royalty of Hua. It belonged to Crown Prince Kai-Guo, the first son of the *Tianzi*, whose voice Tian had heard only once, a decade ago.

Tian sunk to his right knee, right fist to the floor, head bowed. Yet suspicions tugged at his mind: why would the Crown Prince be here? Unannounced? In the dark? Why the secrecy? There had been no imperial guards on the ship. "Your servant obeys," he answered nonetheless.

"You are being recalled to Hua, to inherit your father's place on the *Tai-Ming* Council."

Tian's mind swam at the implications. Something had happened to his father and his brothers. Dead? Branded traitors? He took a deep breath to settle his grief.

The scent of incense had faded, and a different smell, a more flowery fragrance, percolated in. The Crown Prince's breathing changed in depth.

Tian whipped the *biao* toward the voice. Metal clanged, the tone of the reverberation suggesting a small knife had deflected his throwing star. He bounced up onto his feet and into a half-hearted defensive stance. There was no real threat.

"Hey! That was dangerous." Gone was the prince's deep, commanding tone, replaced by a familiar high-pitched, girlish voice, with a hint of laughter wrapped around the complaint.

Tian snorted. "My aim isn't so bad. It would've missed you."

The imposter giggled. "I still would've deflected it, had your aim been any better."

Light flooded the room as the half-elf Yan Jie opened her hand to reveal a magical Aksumi light bauble. Half the households on the continent owned one, but the sprite-like girl might have a dozen hidden in her black linen dress. Unarmed to the untrained eye, she was a walking arsenal.

She bounded across the cabin to envelop him in a warm hug. He fought off her affectionate embrace and stepped back. Making a mental note to check his pockets for any stolen items, he took a good look at his best friend.

Short and lithe, she hadn't changed in eight hundred and ninety-two days, her father's ageless elf blood giving her the appearance of a tween. It also accounted for her particularly large

brown eyes and slightly pointed ears. Her pulled-back dark hair framed sharp features.

She flashed an impish grin. "How'd you know it was me imitating the Crown Prince?"

"Your *Mockingbird's Guise* technique couldn't deceive my *Seeing Ears*. Or maybe that was the most outrageous command. About me inheriting. I *do* hope my family is well?"

"Yes, of course, your father was never better. Your eldest brother Zheng Ming, in fact..." She shook her head. "But I forget why I'm *really* here. I've come by imperial command."

He smirked. "What mischief have you been wreaking? On the imperial court?"

"Oh! It's been so exciting, you'd never believe it. I was assigned to protect Princess Kaiya—"

"You're right. I wouldn't believe it." The shock of hearing the princess' name stirred not so much memories, which had faded with time, as a sense of nostalgia for innocence lost a decade ago.

"It's true! And she's nothing like your childhood memories. She's not fun or playful. She's very serious, very proper, very guarded."

"*Really?*" Serious, proper, and guarded would never describe the girl he'd grown up with. She'd been adorable then, and stories said she was now a once-in-three-generations beauty. How could she have changed so much? "Now I really don't believe you."

"Have I *ever* lied to you?" Jie cast him a wounded look, which he dismissed.

"Maybe stretched the truth. A little..."

Her mouth spread into a toothy smile. "Well, if I told you everything that happened, you'd think I was a golden-tongued storyteller inspired by the old tales from the War of Ancient Gods. Like how she vanquished a dragon and enchanted the entire Ayuri Paladin Council of Elders."

"So, if you were the princess' prized bodyguard. Why are you here? Telling me tall tales. Instead of enjoying more adventures?" Tian raised a suspicious eyebrow.

"Oh right. It's a long story, but basically, I was sent ahead *by imperial command* to deliver a message to Ambassador Wu—"

Tian rolled his eyes. "So why all the secrecy? Why have me come here? So urgently?"

"Oh, I was just having fun with you." She grinned and winked at him.

"Impersonating royalty. It's a capital offense."

Her lip twitched as she fought off another grin. "I risked my life, hoping you wouldn't report me."

"I don't understand. Why do you have an imperial command? Just to deliver a message? Why didn't the court just send it? With the diplomatic packet?"

"You never did let me get to that." Or rather, she'd kept changing the subject. "I'm also supposed to learn about the operations here and arrange security. The princess is coming in a month."

CHAPTER 2:

The Games We Play

If there was one thing Jie knew better than spying, interrogation, and dirty fighting, it was the psychology of Zheng Tian.

His eyes widened and lips parted for a split second. Then his face blanked as only a *Moquan's* could. If he thought the clan's empty expression could hide his thoughts, or make him look objective...

Objective indeed! There she was again, lingering on his lips. He probably knew exactly how many days had passed since they'd last seen each other, though more out of habit than for any affection he might have for her.

Jie arranged her own expression into playful nonchalance, while Tian's face reverted to his sometimes endearing, always infuriating *Older Brother* look.

His voice droned in trained disinterest. "Why is she—"

She held up a hand to silence him. "You're on a need-to-know basis, and—"

"I don't need to know," he said, finishing their oft-repeated exchange.

"Actually, you do." Heavens, it was fun to mess with his head. It had been too long. "Just not this second. It's been a long journey, and I would really like to put my feet on solid ground. More details when I settle in, I promise."

Before he could press the matter, she dropped a few boxes of her personal effects in his hands and ushered him out of the cabin and onto the deck. After disembarking from the ship, he placed her things on a wooden cart, atop carefully crated and stacked trade wares. They then joined the two dozen sailors and porters heading back to the embassy compound.

Their group drew so many stares from the locals, they might have been a circus troupe, with a pointy-eared half-breed as star of the freak show. She'd need to cover her ears to move anonymously through the city.

No sooner had she set foot in the marketplace than the foreign culture began its assault on her senses. The drab colorlessness of Iksuvius only emphasized the confounding diversity of foul smells. The spoiling crustaceans had chosen long-dead fish as dancing partners, with rotting onions and garlic as an audience. Did the gamey odor come from the squalid goats tethered to a vendor's dilapidated wooden stall, or from the unwashed vendor himself? She'd seen splattered human brains and disemboweled entrails without flinching, yet now had to fight down rising bile.

"You get used to it." Tian's crooked smile made her stomach flutter in a completely different way.

He always knew what she was thinking. Heavens, she was becoming just as sappy as Princess Kaiya around a certain flamboyant lord. Her lips curved into a grin of their own accord. "When?"

"Winter. When it cools down."

"It's already chilly enough, and it's still summer!" Jie tightened her shawl around her shoulders. It wasn't just her. Beggars in tattered woolen clothes huddled together by weathered storefronts to soak up the last rays of afternoon sun, while shopkeepers and merchants donned flannel and wool jackets.

"Oh, it gets worse. In the dead of winter. The cold will freeze you to the marrow. Unfortunately it will do the same to the homeless and destitute. "

They continued down the packed dirt road. Although her training emphasized detached observation, the abject poverty was appalling. Hua had been stable for almost three centuries, and wealthy her entire lifetime. Sure, there were still many poor people, but it didn't begin to compare to here. So many beggars in one place! A toothless girl in rags crouched near a squat wooden building, gumming down a crust of moldy bread.

"Abandoned child." Tian must be reading her thoughts again, or at least following her eyes. "Taxes are so high. Parents can't afford to raise more than a few children. Many girls are sold into brothels. Or simply kicked out onto the street."

Abandoned! Jie shuddered. She might have shared the same fate as these discarded girls had her father not left her as a bawling babe at the front gates of the *Moquan*'s Black Lotus Temple. Master Yan had raised her as his own, though he had lost the only hint of her identity. The letter pinned to her swaddling blanket spoke of a human mother who died giving birth and a father too busy to be burdened. Jie would always carry that resentment towards her father—and the aloof elves in general.

She sucked on her lower lip. There were no elves to be found here. They were too prim and prissy for a stinking backwater like this. Up ahead, a group of ruffians extorted protection money from a protesting baker. Yet the greasy-looking man and his half-dozen thugs wore the light blue and yellow uniforms of Iksuvi soldiers. Longswords hung at their sides.

"Tax collector," Tian whispered. "Iksuvi pays a king's ransom in tribute. To the Teleri Empire. They call it an alliance. It places a heavy burden on the citizenry. Still, the Iksuvi commoners are generous. That baker will give leftovers to the beggars."

The shopkeeper bobbed his head and proffered a purse.

The tax collector swiped it away, though his grin transformed into a scowl as he looked inside. He started to say something, when one of his henchmen leaned over and whispered in his ear. Both men turned and looked directly at Jie. Nothing good would come of this.

A lurid smile appeared on the tax collector's face, and he gestured for his men to follow him as he approached. "Who is in charge here?" He spoke in Arkothi, the common language of the North, though it was heavily laced with a Nothori accent.

A young trade official strode forward and offered a few papers with a curt nod. "You will find that all documentation is in order," he said in his own accented Arkothi.

The tax collector waved the papers away while his attention edged towards Jie. "I am sure they are. But I have heard *vicious* rumors that you Cathayi are smuggling in contraband. Certainly you will not mind if we take a quick look to dispel this hearsay?"

Tian leaned over and whispered, "This is a common occurrence. We have to bribe them. Otherwise, they'll keep us here for hours. Young Zhu has a few silver coins ready. Just for these contingencies."

Just as Tian said, Zhu reached into his wide sleeves and produced a dozen Hua coins, strung together through square holes in their centers. "I am sure this more than covers any import duties."

The tax collector shook his head, his expression wounded even as he took the coins. "No, no, I am not that kind of man. I take my responsibilities very seriously." On a hand signal, the Iksuvi soldiers began to move among the carts, while he himself sauntered over to Jie.

And not to give a warm welcome, no doubt. She cast her gaze downwards, assuming the role of a servant, even as she mentally prepared for confrontation. Tian sidled closer to her.

"Do you have papers, girl?" The man lifted her chin, his hand reeking of a musk which did little to cover his pungent sweat. His pigeon-like eyes leered at her. It would be easy to dislocate every joint from his elbow to finger tips in two seconds. Still, she feigned nervousness, trembling at his scrutiny.

Tian's hand closed around hers, the electricity of his touch breaking her concentration. Angry at herself for the lapse, she refocused on the situation.

"My wife," Tian said. "Just arrived from Cathay."

A lie to counter a lie. Still, her heart fluttered.

"She looks too young to be married." The man turned her head to the side, jolting Jie out of her fantasy. "I need to see documentation for all females. We do not want those of an...unsavory profession...coming to our noble kingdom."

Noble, indeed. If anyone was unsavory—

"I've never heard of such rules," Tian said.

"New guidelines. She will have to come with us." The tax collector shrugged and drew Jie closer.

The games adults played. Jie made a show of turning her head. She'd play along until an opportune moment to escape presented itself, then find her way to the Hua embassy.

Tian stepped forward. "I will accompany her."

"I am afraid that is out of the question." The tax collector's tone was apologetic. His grin was anything but. "You are in our country and will follow our laws. Now step back before I have all of your cargo impounded."

Tian's grip loosened, while his weight shifted. He was readying himself to fight! Over such a trivial matter, no less.

She clasped his hand tighter, leaving her index finger free to tap on his palm in a *Moquan* code. *Don't. Only seven. I have this. Not here. Non-lethal.*

He relaxed and turned to her, eyebrow raised. "Are you sure?" he asked in their native tongue.

"It should be easy to slip away from these oafs."

A male with a deep voice boomed from behind her, in perfect Arkothi: "That is no way to treat a married woman."

Everyone turned to the half-dozen Teleri soldiers in impeccable black tunics emblazoned with a nine-pointed golden sun on their chests. Onlookers gave them a wide berth as they approached in precise formation. The ruling race of the Teleri Empire, the Bovyans stood half a head above even the tall Nothori folk. With the exception of their even taller leader, whose dark locks fell to his shoulders, they all sported close-cropped hair.

Jie gritted her teeth. Her own experiences with Bovyans—a two-year mission in the Teleri heartland, as well as several run-ins with the Bovyan spies in Vyara City, and Bovyan charlatan Akolytes in Selastyas—had been less than cordial.

The tax collector stiffened, his hand slipping from Jie's chin. He looked around for his men, but they conspicuously kept their distance. He licked his lips. "As if a Bovyan knew the first thing about marriage. This is an Iksuvi state matter, and none of your business."

The young Teleri leader, a general by the sun insignia on his collar, stepped closer to the cowering man. His chiseled features might have belonged to the Arkothi Sun God Solaris, from whom the Bovyans descended. "It *is* our business. The Teleri care deeply about how our allies treat our trading partners. Now, run along and harass your own citizens. I would hate to see an incident mar our nations' relations on the eve of the Northwest Summit."

The tax collector scowled as he backed out of the general's shadow. Turning on his heel, he snapped his fingers at his men. Heads down and shoulders slumped, the lot of them slunk towards another shop.

What a surprise; a noble Bovyan. Jie dipped into a curtsey. With Tian still clasping her hand, they might have been about to start a Northern-style dance. "My deepest gratitude for your intervention on my behalf."

The general dipped into a sweeping genuflection reminiscent of the old Arkothi Empire. When he straightened, he was grinning. "It's me, Marius di Bovyan. I am only returning the favor from two years ago. You can always find me at the Teleri Embassy in the city center."

Jie maintained a smile, even though she had no idea what he was talking about. Perhaps all half-elves looked alike, because obnoxious sailors, a Paladin Master, a fraudulent fortune teller, fake Akolytes, and now a Bovyan general all claimed to have met her. Sometimes in places she'd never visited.

One of the Teleri cleared his throat. "General, we are late."

"Of course." General Marius winked. At his command, the column marched out of the marketplace with the same precision they had entered.

"Well. That was interesting." Tian released Jie's hand, scuttling any hope that he'd maintain the act.

She nodded. "Yes; he was more the image of the Bovyan Knights of old, and not like the Teleri brutes and rapists they have become. And I have no idea what favor he is referring to."

The caravan proceeded without further incident, and arrived at the embassy.

Jie stared wide-eyed at the amount of white stone that had gone into its construction. It gave the grounds the feel of a northern-style fortress, even if the sloping blue roof tiles hinted at a Hua architectural influence.

Tian led her to the main residence, through the vaulting foyer and up the broad wooden steps to the second floor. Her room had a window facing west towards the harbor. The red sun hovered just above the water, bathing the room in a fiery glow.

"So. Why is the princess coming here?" Tian's tone was impatient.

Let him squirm a little. Jie placed a few boxes by the foot of the bed.

"Especially during the Northwest Summit," he added.

It was more fun to keep Tian in suspense. Jie walked across the room and leaned her elbows against the window sill, looking out onto the city. The side streets, which a drunkard must have laid out, provided many bottlenecks, ambush points, and escape routes.

Tian shuffled behind her. He was close to his bursting point.

She turned around to face him and spoke with detached nonchalance. "The princess is to be betrothed to the Teleri First Consul." It was a *Moquan* interrogation trick: glibly throwing out nonsense to gauge a reaction.

The twitch of his lips, flashing before he buried it under years of training, betrayed his disappointment. Yet, he didn't miss a beat. "Bovyans don't marry. They *breed*. Prolifically. To sustain the Teleri war machine."

Jie forced a laugh. "Zheng Tian, you have become gullible since we last met. Has the cold frozen your brain?"

Again, his mask dropped briefly, the brow above his high-bridged nose relaxing.

So he still had feelings for the princess after all these years. Now it was her turn to hide disappointment behind an inscrutable expression.

"Why is she *really* coming?" He locked eyes on her. Beautiful, intelligent eyes. Her heart skipped a beat.

Where to start? She could write a novel. Jie withdrew a lacquered box from her things. "Here, an imperial edict. I was instructed by the *Tianzi*'s own order to deliver this into the hands of Ambassador Wu."

Frowning, Tian bowed to the edict as protocol demanded. He then extended his hand towards the door. "Come. Let me introduce you to the ambassador."

Ambassador Wu Liming's office was on the other end of the mansion, on the second floor, a spacious anteroom to his personal quarters. Two large windows looked east out onto the Alto River. Hanging scrolls with brush-and-ink style paintings and calligraphy adorned the walls.

The ambassador sat behind a meticulously clean sablewood desk, between the windows and facing the doors. Stocky and middle-aged, he wore a blue silk robe. His long hair, drawn back into a pony tail, was as white as his short mustache and thin beard.

Jie had visited the Foreign Ministry archives in Hua before her departure, and had already learned about him. He'd been assigned to establish the embassy in Iksuvi twenty years ago—ostensibly to bolster trade, but more importantly to keep an eye on this crossroads between the Nothori Kingdoms and their Teleri masters.

Tian guided Jie across the plush Ayuri carpet covering the hardwood floors, and cleared his throat. "Godfather," he said, "the *Wild Orchid* carried some unwanted cargo." He coughed as Jie jabbed him in the back with her finger. "This is Yan Jie. My sister from the temple."

Jie bowed, putting her right fist in her left hand.

A broad smile crossed Ambassador Wu's face as he rubbed his knees and eased himself out of the chair. He spoke with a warm, fatherly voice. "Welcome to Iksuvius, my dear. Unwanted cargo? Little Tian! Such a beautiful girl, it looks more like a surprise gift!"

Jie fought back a smile. "Thank you, Ambassador Wu. I—"

He shook his head. "I insist you call me *Godfather*. Since Tian is your Temple-Brother, and he calls me Godfather, we are virtually related."

Jie nodded. "Thank you, Godfather. However, I am no ordinary stowaway here to see the sights. I have come by order of the *Tianzi*, to personally deliver this message into your hands."

Opening the lacquer case and withdrawing a scroll, she approached the desk and dropped to a knee. Head bowed, she extended both arms to offer the imperial edict.

The ambassador received it with both hands, bowing. He unfurled the scroll, revealing the large, dark red mark of the *Tianzi*'s imperial seal. His pupils swept across the text before he passed it to Tian.

Of course, she'd already read it. Princess Kaiya would meet with First Consul Geros Bovyan of the Teleri Empire and negotiate the rebel Peng Kai-Long's extradition. Ambassador Wu would be tasked with making all arrangements. And she'd be responsible for security.

The ambassador leaned back and sighed. "The timing is bad. The First Consul is here to bask in glory. He won't acquiesce to the demand, let alone to a woman."

Jie shook her head. This was the Dragon Charmer he was talking about. "Princess Kaiya is no ordinary woman. She vanquished the Last Dragon with only her voice."

"Very well." The ambassador didn't sound convinced. "We will prepare for the princess' arrival in a month. Little Jie, you have had a long journey and need some rest before you begin your duties here. Settle in, avail yourself of the bath house. If you need anything, please don't hesitate to let me know."

"Thank you, Godfather. I will be taking my leave, then." Jie held a bow as she backed out of the room, with Tian not far behind.

Walking back through the halls towards Tian's office, she hid her smile. Her first duty had been accomplished: delivering the edict. Now came the interesting part, reminding Tian how amazing she was.

Tian patted her on the head. "My little sister. All grown up. Protecting princesses."

Curse her elvish blood: at thirty-two, she was eleven years older than Tian, yet still looked like an adolescent. She forced a coy smile. "My big brother, still hasn't grown up, still in love with princesses."

Where he'd normally have a quick retort, his silence and pursed lips spoke louder than words. She quickly changed the subject. "Remember how we used to play blind Hua chess, without a board?"

"Of course," he answered, almost before she finished asking. "Do you want to play again?"

"I want you to teach me Arkothi chess."

He nodded. "The pieces are fairly similar. The game reflects our cultures' differing mindsets. The Arkothi play between the lines. Controlling space. We play around the space. Controlling lines."

She laughed. "Seems simple enough. Let's start. I learn best by immersion."

"Very well. I will be white. Since your soul is obviously black. Queen's pawn forward two."

How appropriate a move. For the princess' pawn.

CHAPTER 3:

Plant Expectations, Reap Disappointment

Standing on a balcony of the Hua embassy's main residence, Tian gazed out across Cold Harbor. A warm, early autumn sun settled over the shallow waters, its yellow shimmer in the waves dancing among the fishing boats. In the distance, a larger, three-mast, phoenix-headed ship approached, flying the sky-blue flag of Hua. His pulse quickened.

The oars slid through the waters, rhythmically following the hollow drum beat and accompanying shouts that echoed over the bay. It would take at least another half-hour for it to navigate the deeper sections of the inlet. Smaller boats zigzagged by, coming and going from the dozens of shallow landings. Only one dock could accommodate the deep-drafted vessels, which the Hua and the Eldaeri nations alone could build.

At last! For the past several days, Tian had stolen a few minutes from his duties to come here and scan the horizon for the ship. Now it was here, his unexpected reunion with Princess Kaiya close at hand. An unlikely chance to relive, if only for a moment, childhood memories and an innocence cut short by his training at the Black Lotus Temple.

Jie's voice from the balcony door interrupted his nostalgia. "Knight takes pawn. Check."

"A daring move," Tian said, turning towards his best friend. "You're exposing your knight to danger. Though it takes pressure off your queen."

"That's the knight's duty, right?" Jie emerged from the shadows. A pink ribbon held her dark brown hair in a bun. She wore a simple linen gown, pink with black floral borders, looking very much the servant.

"You're beginning to think like a Northerner. Your move is strategically questionable, though. Hua chess and Arkothi chess share one goal. Protect your king. Capture your enemy's. Every other piece is expendable."

Jie remained silent, and Tian surreptitiously studied her empty expression. The message in her move was obvious. She was still goading him over his *childhood* relationship with the princess. For someone who was a decade older than him, Jie still looked and sometimes acted like a girl just into the awkward years before womanhood.

"So, what news have we gathered?" he asked.

"The Teleri First Consul has crossed over the Alto River and just passed through the marketplace by the eastern gate. His retinue includes three thousand heavy infantry, armed with spears and longswords, and two hundred heavy cavalry with sabers and spears."

Tian tapped his chin. So many soldiers. The First Consul didn't need that much protection in an allied nation. It was quite an investment, feeding and lodging so many men. "They can't all be staying at the Teleri Embassy. I'll send Old Tong to learn where the rest will be. In the meantime, let's join the princess' welcoming party."

"Like that?" She laughed and pointed at his head, proffering a jade comb that appeared in her hands. "Your hair's a tangled mess! You haven't been sleeping well lately, have you?"

He took the comb, drawing it through his hair from crown to shoulder, noting a passing rise in the right corner of Jie's lip. She offered him a pink ribbon, which he ignored, and instead withdrew a black tie from his dark-blue silk robes. His palms sweated. A reunion, four thousand and fifty-one days in the making, was close at hand.

She ushered him inside and through his office, tugging the wrinkles out of his robes. His white silk vest was embroidered with four-clawed, blue-and-gold dragons, a symbol of his family's standing as *Tai-Ming* lords. His heart pattered. Soon. He gathered up his curved *dao* sword as he passed the door, and both went down to the courtyard to join the princess' welcoming escort.

Twenty embassy guards dressed in dark blue cotton tunics and black leather breastplates assembled there, joining four horses and a stable boy. Each soldier was armed with a broadsword and a spear with red horse hairs near its head. A single sky-blue banner emblazoned with a five-clawed golden dragon, held by the lead soldier, fluttered in the light breeze.

Jie fell in behind twelve runners who carried an elaborately carved palanquin on their shoulders. Another pair of men pulled a cart with two mounted drummers on either side of a three-foot round drum. A hundred musketmen watched from the top of the white stone walls.

Ambassador Wu arrived, wearing his own formal robes and a black square hat. He mounted a horse, and Tian and two ministers bowed and followed suit. Wu's voice, still strong despite his advancing age, carried through the courtyard. "To the docks. Our princess will be disembarking soon."

Turning to Tian, he whispered, "Little Tian, we are entrusted with one of the *Tianzi's* most treasured jewels. What movements are we seeing thus far?"

Keeping his voice low so that only Ambassador Wu could hear him, Tian said, "The kings of Lietuvi and Rotuvi arrived several days ago. They have small contingents of a few hundred

each. They are staying in their own embassy compounds in the city center. The Teleri First Consul just arrived within the hour. With three thousand foot soldiers and two hundred cavalry. I have sent men to investigate."

Wu nodded, then signaled the party to depart with a wave of his hand. They left in exacting formation, led by the four mounted officials. The palanquin went next, followed by the foot soldiers. The drummers took up the rear, setting a slow, thunderous beat as the gates swung open.

As the procession made its way down the hill and through the market, citizens cleared the road and pointed and stared. The deliberate pace extended what would normally be a five-minute walk into a fifteen-minute parade. Other Hua residents of Iksuvius joined in, faces solemn. Tian's heart beat twice as fast as the drum. It wouldn't be long now.

By the time they arrived at the head of the dock, the sun cast a red glow from low on the horizon. Coming to a stop, the foot soldiers moved to secure the quay and prevent any of the gathering crowd from approaching.

The drummers slowed the beat to half-time. Tian joined the officials, dismounting from his horse and walking to the landing. The palanquin bearers followed close behind, with Jie in tow. Dockworkers bustled about, tying down moorings and extending a ramp to the second deck of the ship.

At a distance, the *Golden Phoenix* was impressive. Up close, it inspired awe. The figurehead resembled a regal phoenix surging forward in flight, making the ship seem in motion even when stationary. It towered above them, dwarfing all of the other nearby vessels and casting shadows across the docks. As the *Tianzi's* flagship, it was the fastest ship in the fleet.

Tian slowed his breath to calm his excitement. The drummers on deck sped up to double-time, and those on shore responded to match the pace. Members of the imperial guard, in their sky-blue silk tunics and immaculately polished steel breastplates, appeared on the deck.

They lined up eight in a row on either side of the ramp.

General Zheng Jiawei, Tian's cousin and commander of the imperial guard, stepped to the head. Dropping to one knee, fist to the ground, he announced, "Princess Wang Kaiya from the Empire of Hua."

The drummers on shore and on deck ceased simultaneously. With a jangle of armor, the other imperial guards sank to their right knee, heads bowed, right fists touching the ground. All the Hua people on the dock and shore followed suit, a wave of color rippling down the procession.

Tian stole a glance up. A single figure stepped onto the ramp and billowed down at a deliberate pace. Here she was. His stomach leapt into his throat. He quickly lowered his head. The soft rustling of her heavy linen gown approached. A single red brocade slipper covering a delicate foot came to a stop just in front of him.

"Rise." Just one single word. It was resonant and melodious, so unlike the voice from his childhood. Tian looked up, avoiding direct eye contact as protocol demanded.

He suppressed a gasp. Even in the waning light, it was clear the stories were true: the gangly child he knew a lifetime ago had blossomed into an unparalleled beauty. Her waist-length hair, braided into a single queue, hung over her shoulder. Large, doe-like eyes accentuated her high-bridged nose, the perfect curve of her lips, and her pearly complexion.

Ambassador Wu labored to his feet, maintaining a bow, and spoke: "Welcome to Iksuvius, *Dian-xia*. I am Wu Liming, the *Tianzi*'s representative in the Northwest. I yield that honor to you." He motioned to the officials as he introduced them, and as she nodded to recognize each one, they bowed deeply in response. "Lastly, this is Zheng Tian, Chief of Information."

The princess tilted her head at a slight angle, revealing the elegant line of her neck. Looking up at him through her lashes, she smiled with a radiance that brightened the afternoon shadows. She spoke in a gentle, yet clear and mellifluous voice, which a nightingale would envy.

"It has been many years since we last met, Young Lord Zheng. You have grown into a fine gentleman. I trust you have been doing well."

Tian's voice caught in his throat. "I am, um, honored. That you...remember me. *Dian-xia*." Somewhere behind him, Jie was undoubtedly laughing at his expense.

She tilted her head. "I do not forget my friends."

Warmth rose to his face, and he cast his gaze at her feet. Hopefully the late sun would prevent her from seeing him blush.

Luckily, Ambassador Wu relieved his awkward moment. "We should get back to the compound before the sun sets. Perhaps you can reacquaint yourselves over the princess' week-long stay." He motioned the palanquin bearers over.

A handmaiden shuffled forward, knelt, and opened the palanquin door. Nearby, Jie's lips quivered in a half-laugh.

"I shall ride a horse." The princess waved the handmaiden away. "It is not often that I leave Hua, and I will see this foreign city."

The officials looked at one another in confusion. For a member of the Imperial Family to ride exposed in a foreign country was unheard of. Jie stared at the sky.

Someone had to say something. Tian cleared his throat. "*Dian-xia*. That is not wise. We must ensure your safety. The locals have never seen one of your stature. Our enemies' agents may be among the crowds."

"Nevertheless, I will ride." The last three words trilled like a song.

Her voice washed over Tian like a wave. All his misgivings now seemed inane, and he found himself compelled to obey. Around him, the ambassador, all of the officials, and even the imperial guards nodded. Jie sucked her lower lip, perhaps too concerned with protocols to entertain the princess' completely reasonable command. Nonetheless, she kept silent.

As an embassy soldier went for a horse, General Zheng sidled up to Tian. "It was like this on the *entire* journey. She insisted on doing *everything* her way. Kicking the captain out of his quarters on the poop deck so she could move in. Constantly getting in the way of sailors on deck. She is so headstrong, and nobody can defy her."

"It sounds like she gave you quite a headache," Tian whispered back.

"Now your headache, too, Cousin." General Zheng swallowed a laugh, motioning to one of the imperial guards to accompany the horse. "Zhao Yue, come!"

With his triangular face, Zhao Yue looked familiar. Of course; he'd been at Wailian Castle two years ago. Now he knelt, and the princess used his knee as a footstool to mount the horse. The Nothori on the shore pointed and laughed at this humiliation, too ignorant to know that any of the Hua would consider it an honor.

Tian took the reins to guide the horse, but the princess pulled them away. The procession, now joined by a hundred of the imperial guards and three handmaidens at the rear, began their return to the compound. Though it was almost dusk, the Nothori commoners clogged the streets, jostling to catch a glimpse of the Cathayi princess. Excited shouts and chatter erupted as she passed.

Tian scanned the crowds for potential threats. Why had he ever conceded into letting her ride high on a horse, exposed to danger? This was such a bad idea.

Maybe he had little to worry about. The imperial guards radiated an aura of awe. Commoners, and even Iksuvi soldiers, shrank back as the procession passed. When they reached the compound, the gates opened.

Once inside, a stable boy took the reins of the princess' horse and guided the mount towards the mansion. She looked back and flashed Tian a demure smile as she rode off.

Tian's mouth gaped. Was the pounding in his ears the echo of the drum, or his own heart?

"Queen takes knight," Jie muttered under her breath.

He turned to glare at her, and caught sight of a large Hua youth watching from between two buildings across the street. As their gazes connected, the boy darted back into the dark shadows of the alley.

It was not someone he recognized, and he knew almost every one of his countrymen living in the city. And his size...it was reminiscent of the boys who'd assassinated Old Lord Peng two years ago.

CHAPTER 4:

Heart of a Princess

Kaiya suppressed a laugh. Zheng Tian, with his mouth agape, oblivious to onlookers, stirred nostalgic feelings of their carefree childhood. Despite what Jie had said about him being a deadly swordsman and incomparable spy, he seemed just as innocent as he was ten years ago. She rubbed the river pebble he'd given her back then as a token of his affection. After all that had happened in the past two and a half years, it was nice to remember the idealistic girl she'd once been.

His bewildered expression vanished as quickly as it had appeared.

She would have traded an armful of jade bangles to see that look again, to remember a life before court intrigue, putting down rebellions, and singing to dragons. Before being manipulated by both Avarax and Cousin Kai-Long. If only she could be that girl again. Heavens, there was that ugly bitterness invading her thoughts again.

She gazed at Tian. If anyone could restore her faith in humanity, and reassure her of her worth, it would be him.

The moment passed, and Kaiya composed her countenance to one of regal aloofness. She slid off the horse near the steps of the main residence. Solid ground. Open space. Fighting to keep her legs from unsightly wobbling, she looked up at the building. It was quaint, almost reminiscent of a Hua noble's villa with its steeply-pitched tiled eaves.

The ambassador bowed low. "We attempted to recreate the architecture from back home, but I am afraid all the stone gives it a cold appearance."

The steward, bowed on one knee at the entrance, echoed the ambassador's apologetic tone. "We have reserved the entire south wing of the second floor for your use. I am so sorry we cannot do better."

The kneeling Mistress of Chambers was equally contrite. "We have tried to train the servants in proper court etiquette, but I am afraid it will never meet the standard you are used to."

As if to emphasize the point, a porter bearing one of her ornately-carved rosewood boxes nearly ran into her. He sank to his knees, forehead touching the ground, almost dropping the box in his haste. Other servants followed suit, bowing abjectly.

She fought off the impulse to reassure the porter, since such displays would only embarrass him more.

Everyone was making such a big deal out of trivial matters. No, it was enough just to escape the stifling cabin that had been her home for a week at sea, to be out of the narrow confines of the ship.

"We have prepared a bath for you." Bowing, the Mistress of Chambers invited Kaiya inside with an open hand. "I will take you there while the servants bring your train to your suite."

A bath! It would have been her first order of business as well, had she set the itinerary herself. A chance to wash out a week of travel. Sea salt seemed to clog every pore. Worse was the awful stench of the filthy harbor and marketplace, which clung to her like a grimy second skin. She hid her enthusiasm as she followed the Mistress of Chambers through the foyer to a side door.

A short walk across a raised, covered walkway through an enclosed garden brought them to the embassy's wooden bathhouse. Kaiya's nose crinkled at the fresh varnish that made the wood gleam. Along with the manicured shrubs and combed white gravel, it was a clear sign the staff had prepared for an imperial visit. Her most faithful imperial guards, Chen Xin and Ma Jun, kept watch outside the door, while several others blocked the two access points to the courtyard and patrolled the perimeter.

A kneeling maid slid the door open, bowing low as Kaiya entered. Although the enormous soaking tub inside could tightly hold a dozen men at once—and probably did on busy evenings—the entire building had been cleared. Maids swarmed around to assist her. Waving them off, she sat on a stool outside the bathtub and scrubbed the salt out of her skin and hair until she glowed pink. She then stepped into the tub and sank into the steaming waters.

They warmed her to the core, chasing away the cold sea breezes that had lodged in her bones. To think it was already so chilly in early autumn! Why was *she* the one sent to this frigid wasteland to negotiate Cousin Kai-Long's extradition?

Beyond the bathhouse walls, the imperial guards shared her complaint in low whispers. They should have known her keen ears would hear them.

"I could have sworn it was summer when we left Hua," Chen Xin grumbled.

"And it will still be summer when we get back," Ma Jun said cheerfully.

"Well, I can see my breath."

"At least we will be able to see it coming before we have to smell it."

Kaiya choked back a giggle. No one bantered with her like that.

"My breath doesn't smell bad," Chen Xin said.

"Compared to this city, no. It *is* cold, but at least you're not posted here like the embassy staff. We get to go home soon enough." Ma Jun could always see the bright side of things.

"Yes, but who knows where they will send us next? The last trip almost got us killed."

"You got to see a real dragon...the last one in all of Tivaralan."

"We were almost his dinner. And I suppose getting diced up by the Maduran Scorpions is your idea of adventure?" Chen Xin was no longer complaining as much as bragging.

"Well, as the classics say, *Travel is worth more than a thousand books in cultivating wisdom.*"

"If you survive..."

Kaiya smiled. Oh, to have a deep camaraderie like those two enjoyed. Like the one she and Tian once shared. Playing the Dragon Scale Lute almost three years ago had changed everything, burdened her with unwanted responsibilities in the imperial court. Vanquishing Avarax with a song had elevated her to legend. Nobody could relate to that, and now her closest confidante was an impertinent half-elf whose idea of opening a heart was more literal than figurative.

With a sigh, Kaiya sprawled out in the tub, sinking beneath the water. Her hair floated on the surface, filtering light from the baubles on the ceiling. In the three hundred years of the Wang Dynasty, the Founder's consort—who had reigned as Dowager Regent for eight decades—was the only woman who had played a more important role in the Hua court. She must have felt so isolated.

Kaiya emerged to catch a breath, brushing hair and water out of her face while affording herself a moment to daydream about the dashing *Tai-Ming* heir who'd been courting her. She'd rejected a dozen suitors before him, but his quick wit and charm made her entire body tingle. A delightful fluttering erupted in her stomach. Maybe after marriage, people would forget about the Dragon Charmer, and life would regain a semblance of normalcy. Maybe it wouldn't feel so...*lonely.*

Quickly banishing these thoughts, Kaiya mused over her reunion with Zheng Tian. Despite the assurances that he had become a magnificent swordsman, he seemed just as adorably awkward as ever. His puppy-dog reaction to her smile! Just like when they were children. Apparently, the right facial expression or gesture could still evoke his response. A laugh escaped her, but she covered her mouth. If the guards heard her outburst…

A maid opened the doors and shuffled in, head bowed and eyes averted. She presented a towel with both hands. "*Dian-xia. Zhuyue* waxes to half. The reception is at the second gibbous."

Sighing, Kaiya reluctantly left the waters' warm embrace. She stepped out of the tub and into the open towel, again fighting off a maid and wrapping herself. Perhaps other Hua nobles expected servants to do all the work of washing and dressing them. After a particularly insolent retainer had admonished her, Kaiya took more responsibility for herself.

Barefooted, she glided across the room and to a private changing area. While maids fussed at drying her hair, she donned a simple white silk robe and draped a heavy fur shawl over her shoulders. She slid her feet into fur-lined sandals. Kneeling maids opened the sliding doors.

Kaiya stepped out and tasted the brisk night air with a deep breath. The Iridescent Moon Zhuyue floated a little more south from its usual position, waxing halfway towards its first gibbous. There was only an hour and a half until the reception for the senior embassy staff and prominent Hua families living in Iksuvius.

Her nose wrinkled at her imperial guards' odor. To think she must have smelled just as bad just half an hour before. She shuddered. "Ma Jun, Chen Xin, be sure to bathe before the banquet."

Both guards dropped to their right knee, heads bowed. "As the princess commands," they both bellowed.

Satisfied, Kaiya nodded and strolled down the walkway, handmaidens in tow. The other half-dozen imperial guards fell in behind her, keeping a respectful distance.

A shallow breathing hid in the muffled sounds of the city, buried among the quiet footsteps and swishing robes of her maids and guards.

Kaiya paused mid-stride and raised a hand, signaling all to stop. The guards behind her placed their hands on their *dao* and deployed into defensive positions around her.

"Jie," Kaiya said.

The Insolent Retainer melted out of the shadows and dropped to her right knee, right fist to the ground. "*Dian-xia.* As always, I am amazed that you can hear me."

Kaiya covered her laugh with a hand. The half-elf's straightforward nature and witty banter were always endearing. No one else dared speak freely to her. "Maybe I just guessed you would be lurking the halls. Either way, I am pleased to see you again."

"Me too." Jie rose to her feet at Kaiya's hand gesture and followed her down the walk and through the side door into the embassy. The guards again fell in behind.

"So," Kaiya said. "You have already been here a month. What are your impressions?"

"The people are big and standoffish," Jie said. "The level of poverty crushes their collective soul. It is amazing that the nation has not collapsed under the weight of civil disorder."

Kaiya sighed. "It does not sound like a very hospitable place. The sooner we are done negotiating with the Nothori Kings and their dreadful Teleri masters, the sooner we can leave this land. You have made security arrangements?"

"Yes, *Dian-xia,*" Jie said as they arrived at the foyer's grand staircase. "Taking your itinerary into account, I have selected the safest routes and ensured that the *Moquan* will be watching for potential threats. Zheng Tian has been helpful in organizing them."

"Tian." Kaiya tasted the name and decided it was the flavor of nostalgia. "What do you think of him?"

The usually quick-witted half-elf was unusually slow to respond. Within those three seconds of silence, the average *Moquan* could probably plan the invasion of a small country. When Jie finally answered, her tone carried forced objectivity. "He has an exceptional grasp of the situation here. He sees connections between seemingly unrelated pieces of information. You will find his insight and advice invaluable."

"Yes." Kaiya covered her laugh with her fingers, deciding to test her theory. "But what do you think about *him*? You have not seen Tian for three years. I have not seen him for ten. But he has hardly changed at all. Still awkward, despite his good looks."

Even if Jie did not betray an emotion in her expression, she was again uncharacteristically quiet for a few seconds. "There's a lot going on in his head, all the time."

A hint of defensiveness floated in the answer. Could Jie actually have affections for a boy? *That* boy? How could such a pretty and talented girl fall for a boy so...*Tian*? Kaiya rubbed his pebble. No, Tian was a man. Not the gullible ten-year-old, despite initial impressions. Though surely, he'd always be the reliable ear to keep her secrets and a solid shoulder to lean against.

Jie's ears twitched. Outside, bird calls rang out. Fake bird calls.

CHAPTER 5:
Things That Go Bump In The Night

From Tian's vantage point on his office balcony, the marketplace in the near distance appeared an oasis of light in a desert of dull grey, lit by Aksumi glass baubles brought by the citizens socializing there. The nearly-full White Moon Renyue blanketed the city in dim light, while the larger Blue Moon Guanyin's Eye was almost closed.

Muted sounds of laughter diffused from the market and filled the otherwise empty city streets. Farther out, individual lights from fishing boats bobbed in the harbor, like fireflies dancing in Hua's gardens at midsummer.

He and seven-year-old Princess Kaiya had once caught fireflies in one of the many gardens of Sun-Moon Palace. It seemed like a lifetime ago; a time of innocence, before the realities of duty and responsibility took over.

Tian looked up and south to find the Iridescent Moon in its usual place, swirling in translucent pinks and purples like an opaque soap bubble. It waxed towards its first gibbous. Just an hour remained until the reception. With so little time, he returned to the office to ponder his convoluted web of information.

Just as he was about to pin a note about the strange boy, the annoying squawks of peacocks erupted in the courtyard below. The fake caw, a *Moquan* code indicating an intruder, repeated twice from different parts of the compound. Old Tong and Shun.

The little hairs on the back of his neck stood on end. An intruder, just when the princess arrived, couldn't be a coincidence. Sheathed sword in hand, he slipped out onto the balcony. A quick search along the perimeter revealed nothing. Perhaps it was related to the young man in the alley a couple hours earlier.

At a spot near the middle of the western wall, two drunken Nothori ruffians argued, loud enough to scare ghosts away. At the top of the wall, half a dozen Hua musketmen pointed and laughed.

The lack of discipline! Especially with the princess visiting. Tian clenched his jaw as he raked his gaze back and forth over the grounds. Maids and servants hurried about, preparing for the reception. Beyond his line of sight, a caller announced the names of prominent Hua families at the main gate.

Young Cheng's bird call shrieked from the north, then Pockmarked Zu's answered from the east. Intruders. At least three. Any could be a threat to the princess. Tian's hands clenched. He started to leap down into the courtyard, but paused with a leg over the railing. Something didn't add up.

Ducking back into his office, he closed the door and locked it behind him. He shuttered the Aksumi light-bauble lamp. The room blinked into dim darkness, with only the feeble rays of Guanyin's Eye filtering in through the window. Tian sank into a crouch in the darkest shadow of the southwest corner.

Settling his gaze without focus on the middle of the room, his field of vision encompassed the entire space. His right hand rested on the wooden floors, while another pressed against the wall to feel for the vibrations of someone's approach. His hearing reached out beyond the floors and walls and ceilings.

The sounds above and below suggested nothing out of the ordinary, beyond preparations for the princess' reception. On this level, a large group climbed the central stairs and then passed through the east corridor, heading south. It was likely the princess and her retinue heading to her spacious quarters, oblivious to potential danger.

Outside where the Nothori ruffians had been arguing, the ruckus increased. Embassy guards yelled at them to quiet down and leave. Yet hidden in the commotion was a faint new sound just outside his balcony, the unmistakable scraping of the cat-claws the *Moquan* used to scale walls. Tian's heart squeezed. His own men wouldn't come up the walls like that, not without announcing themselves.

Feet landed on the balcony with almost inaudible sound, followed by the indistinct clicks of the door lock being picked. None of his men would do that. Every nerve stood on edge as Tian gripped his sword.

A blink of light and shadows under the threshold of his hallway door broke his concentration. Just outside, Princess Kaiya's unmistakable voice spoke in muffled whispers. What was she doing here? Right when a possible attacker was nearby, no less.

Both doors simultaneously opened.

At the balcony, the intruder stood taller and broader than any of Tian's spies. Dressed all in black and wearing a hooded mask, the man remained at the half-open door, surveying.

In the same second, the princess glided into the room, light from the hall flooding in.

Tian vaulted through gaps in the twine, simultaneously flicking three *biao* throwing stars behind him.

The *biao* arced between the strings and whistled through the space of the closing balcony door. Behind him, a youth's muffled shriek pierced the night. Tian hit the ground shoulder first, rolled, and sprang again through more openings in the twine. On his descent, he tackled the princess, shoving her back into the hall. He twisted to soften her fall, so that she landed on top of him.

Six *dao* rasped from scabbards as the imperial guards closed on him. He ignored them, signaling instead to Jie who slunk behind the princess' group. *Intruder, balcony.*

Jie responded even before he'd finished. She charged into the office and swam through the web of twine with effortless dexterity. And then she was out of his line of sight. The balcony door crashed open, followed by a loud thud. Then silence.

Tian's stomach clenched as he craned his neck to see through the Cobweb. Had Jie taken care of the intruder? Or had he—

Hands pressed against his chest. He looked up. A beautiful woman lay on top of him. Wearing only a silk inner gown. His arms were wrapped protectively around her. Her warmth and fragrance and softness smothered him. His armor of martial and mental training failed.

She was trying to push herself off of him. Five, now six, of the realm's deadliest swordsmen pointed the sharpest swords in the world at him.

"Unhand the princess," snarled one, the belligerent, flat-knuckled guard from the Wailian battle.

"Let go of me!" the princess panted, her face flushed, regal bearing lost in her panic. She took a deep breath. When she spoke again, it was with the imperial tone of command. "Zheng Tian, release me."

The confident voice woke Tian from his own state of shock. Heat rose to his face. He'd just touched a member of the Imperial Family. Ended in a compromising position, no less. Such a trespass, even to protect her, might invite a death sentence.

He let go.

With a sharp push on his chest, the princess extricated herself. Her luxurious locks cascaded over her face as she staggered to her feet and stumbled back. She tightened her gown around herself and brushed the errant hair away, revealing a flushed face and glinting eyes. In that moment, she seemed less like the elegant princess and more like the child he remembered.

An imperial guard charged, *dao* raised.

Tian sprang to his feet with a windmill kick, just before the sword came down. He sidestepped the follow-up thrust, caught the guard's wrist, and twisted. As the man's grip loosened, Tian plucked the blade free. In the same motion, he wrapped up the guard's elbow into a lock and started to slash his throat. He stopped himself. Heavens, his automatic reactions almost killed one of Princess Kaiya's personal guards.

The other guards closed in around him, naked blades held in defensive positions. He was skilled enough with the sword to confront one of the vaunted imperial guards in a fair fight; but had very little chance against five, regardless of what underhanded tactics he might use. Even now, the magical aura of intimidation from their breastplates sent his heart racing.

"Stop," the princess said, her voice shaking. She stared, her gape one of shock and horror.

He dropped the sword and released his hostage.

CHAPTER 6:
Plots Unraveled

Jie had finished binding the intruder on the balcony when she heard the sounds of warriors assuming fighting stances in the hallway.

Imperial guards, always late. She twisted through the Cobweb, coming back to the hall.

Her jaw slackened. Five of the princess' personal imperial guards—whom she had come to appreciate, despite any jokes she made at their expense—surrounded Tian with naked blades. Face red, Xu Zhan was climbing to his feet. Princess Kaiya stood near the wall, gown clutched tightly around her, tears glistening in her eyes.

It had happened so fast, the others must not have known about the infiltrator. Jie dropped to her knee, head bowed. "*Dian-xia*, Zheng Tian was protecting you. An intruder is bound, out on the balcony." She glanced up to see the princess' cold stare, tears gone. Had she imagined them?

All attention turned to the princess. After two seconds, she motioned the guards with a wave of her hand. "Zheng Tian, the prisoner is yours. In the future, do not dare touch me without my permission."

There was the princess Jie knew. Afraid to show vulnerability, hiding embarrassment behind regal carriage.

"Understood, *Dian-xia*." Tian sank to both knees and pressed his forehead to the ground. He held himself in this most contrite bow.

The princess lifted her chin and straightened her back, not deigning to afford Tian another glance.

It was time to diffuse the awkwardness. "*Dian-xia*," Jie said, "allow me to go ahead of you and check your rooms. There might be more than one intruder. Please wait here."

The princess cast a sidelong glance in Tian's direction. "I shall not wait here. I am well protected with you and my guards." Despite her defiance, her voice carried a hint of embarrassment and her hand trembled.

"Forgive my insolence, *Dian-xia*," Jie said without a hint of sincerity, "but if there is someone in your rooms, I want to apprehend them. If they hear you coming, they will try to escape. Unfortunately, Chen Xin and Ma Jun could not sneak up on a deaf man. If anyone, send Li Wei several paces behind me." She flashed a grin at the imperial guards.

The princess nodded. "As you suggest, Jie. The rest of us will take the north hall, which should give you plenty of time." With a flourishing sweep of her robe, she turned and glided up the corridor, guards and handmaidens scurrying to keep up.

Only after the princess had disappeared around the corner of the hall did Tian lift his head. He wore an expressionless look, save for his rigidly set jaw and twitching neck muscles.

When had he ever had such a reaction before? Was he angry or humiliated? She grinned. "You did the right thing. At first, that is."

Without ever making eye contact or acknowledging her comment, Tian slipped into his office and closed the door.

Attitude from him, too. Jie snorted and turned back towards the princess' suites in the south hall. She drifted lightly along the hardwood floors, motioning for Li Wei to wait at the corner.

Another imperial guard, Zhao Yue, stood at the door to the suite. She signaled for him to stay put as she approached. The crack beneath the door was dark. She placed a hand and an ear to it. Even if her father had abandoned her, at least he had left her with superior hearing.

Inside, there were almost inaudible sounds of activity. Whoever was in there was good. *Moquan*-good.

Jie looked first at Zhao Yue and then back towards Li Wei at the junction of the west and south halls, and then made simple hand gestures. *I am going in. You*, she pointed to Zhao Yue, *follow. You*, she nodded at Li Wei, *go down and to the other side.* A three-year-old would understand. An imperial guard was another matter.

She withdrew four magical light baubles from a pocket concealed in her dress sleeves. A quick push on the door opened it a crack. Grasping a knife, she tossed the beads through and burst in.

All had been in order when Jie had checked the suite an hour earlier. Now, several ornate lacquer and brocade boxes were open, revealing extravagant gowns, musical instruments and jewelry.

A large fair-haired youth, his face darkened by pitch, rose to his feet near one of the boxes. He screened his eyes with one hand and reached for a shortsword with the other. Beyond him, at the double doors leading out onto the grand balcony, a young Hua male squinted at her.

With her left hand, Jie reached into the fold of her dress and flung a throwing spike at the man near the balcony doors. In the same motion she surged towards the youth by the box.

He swung his sword with such precision, his vision must've already adjusted to the sudden light.

She whipped out another knife from her sleeve with her left hand, leaving her left flank exposed to bait him. As he lunged with a thrust towards the opening, she twisted out of his line of

attack and slashed through the tendons in his wrist.

Even before the sword slipped from his limp fingers, Jie passed under his arm and severed his knee ligaments with a backhand slash. She finished the motion with a shoulder butt to his floating ribs. Despite being more than twice as large, he tumbled to the ground with a grunt.

Zhao Yue and Li Wei charged in. Both of them. Jie kicked the sword out of the youth's reach before turning her attention towards the young man near the balcony doors.

Her spike had lodged on the right side of his chest, likely puncturing a lung. It had him keeled over on all fours, gasping for breath. As Jie approached, he lobbed a knife at her. Thrown with little force, it was easy to sidestep. The blade clattered harmlessly along the floor behind her.

In two steps, she kicked his hand out from under him. Cocking her foot back, she drove her heel into his temple. He collapsed in a heap with a muffled groan.

Not wasting a beat, Jie edged over to the door into the sleeping chambers and peeked around the corner. Empty.

However, one of the eastern windows overlooking the bathhouse courtyard stood open. After a quick glance into the dressing room, she went to the window and screeched out a birdcall that would notify her *Moquan* brothers of potential danger.

Jie returned to the antechamber, where the imperial guards kept a watchful eye over the intruders. "I will take the princess to the east-wing guest room until we clean up this mess. Get one of the embassy guards to bring these prisoners down to the storerooms, and tell them to bring the doctor. This one needs help if we want him to survive long enough for interrogation."

She slipped out of the room and up the east hall, where she found the princess and her entourage.

The princess' posture was straight and her pace deliberate, her regal bearing suggesting that she'd put the awkward incident with Tian behind her. However, her jawline quivered and her eyes locked forward, unfocussed. Hiding her embarrassment, no doubt.

Jie dropped to her knee. "*Dian-xia*, we are dealing with a security issue in your quarters. I will report to you when the entire picture is clear. Until we resolve things, please use these guest quarters, next to the ambassador's suite." She motioned with an open hand towards a door.

The princess simply nodded, and Jie went to listen at the door.

Satisfied that it was empty, she opened it and took a quick look in. Her night vision—another legacy of elven parentage—penetrated the darkness, casting the bed and table in hues of green. Nothing seemed amiss.

Meiling, the princess' handmaiden and decoy, glared at her. "The princess will require appropriate attire for the reception tonight."

Jie motioned for Meiling to follow her as she turned back towards the princess' suite. It had transformed into a beehive of maids and guards in the short time she was gone, with the Mistress of Chambers directing cleanup efforts. Embassy guards carried out the prisoners.

Jie smirked as Meiling blanched. "Which robe did the princess intend to wear tonight?"

"The plain white silk, hanging in her changing room." Meiling waved an open hand towards the sleeping chambers and the dressing room that lay beyond.

Jie slunk in and examined the robe under the bright illumination of a light bauble. She sniffed and ran her hands over the luxuriant fabric, which felt almost like mist made solid. Undraping it, she handed it to Meiling. "This is safe. Wait while l check her cosmetics."

Face powders of crushed pearl, rouges of *danhua* flowers, jade combs and make-up brushes of phoenix feathers lay neatly arranged on a rosewood table with ornately carved borders. Jie caught herself looking at her reflection in the large silver mirror, imagining herself made-up, wearing a silken gown. What would Tian think of that?

The reflection of Meiling, lips pursed in amusement, brought her back to the present. How silly, to think of such vanity. She returned to the make-up, again smelling and taking the minutest of tastes.

"This lip rouge might have been tainted." Jie held up a small mother-of-pearl case before stashing it in her sleeve. "The others are safe. You may take these to the princess so that she might prepare."

She dismissed the handmaiden with a jerk of her head and returned to the antechamber to examine the boxes. Suspicious powdery residue clung to the three finest court gowns. Those she placed in a box, which she had embassy guards take to her own quarters.

After an exchange of fake bird calls to confirm the compound was secure, Jie descended into the network of tunnels and rooms beneath the grounds.

Originating from the warehouse, the network had started as cold storage, hewn into the subterranean rock. It had been further excavated over twenty years to include several rooms and two escape routes into the city sewers.

She found Tian in a musty room filled with wooden crates. Two of the intruders, now bound and blindfolded, sat motionless in deceptively flimsy-looking bloodwood chairs.

Unlike other young Hua males, the tall, brawny youths sported the close-cropped hair favored by mercenaries and Teleri soldiers. Balcony Boy's knee and ankle wounds had since been bound, using strips of cloth torn from his loose-fitting black pants. Those pants were part of an ensemble that resembled the utility suits the *Moquan* wore on night missions.

Blond Boy was similarly dressed and coifed, his face now washed to reveal the fair skin of a Nothori. The last, also Hua, lay on a blanket, hands bound in front of him. His breathing was labored and blood flecked his lips. With wounds like that, he wouldn't last the night.

Tian would not look at her, and instead made himself busy rummaging through the prisoners' effects: climbing cat-claws, a kit of lockpicks, Aksumi light beads, straight shortswords, small flasks, various small throwing weapons, hemp twine, and other tools.

In almost every respect, they appeared *Moquan*. However, the Hua youths did not resemble any of the warrior-spies and recruits who had passed through the Black Lotus Temple in the last three decades Jie had been there.

After an up-close examination, it was clear *what* they were. If only Tian would acknowledge her so they could confer. He was still keeping to himself, sulking from his encounter with the princess.

"Knight takes queen, and looks stupid doing it," she said.

Tian looked up from the tools, scowling.

She flashed her most innocent smile, and his expression softened.

Not wanting the prisoners to overhear, Jie used the *Moquan*'s silent body signals. *Teleri Nightblades. Bovyans trained by* Moquan *traitor. I was tracking. You fought one in Jiangkou.*

Tian pointed at the two who looked like their Hua countrymen. *These not Bovyan. Are Hua.*

Jie waved her hands back and forth. *Bovyans always look like mother. See, huge for Hua.*

After another look at the two, Tian shrugged. *But small for a Bovyan.*

Jie nodded. *Small ones do other military specialties. Spies. Logistics.*

"You should've told me. Earlier," Tian said.

Jie shrugged. *Not many Nightblades at all. All in East.*

At least three here. Tian pointed at the two bound boys, and the dying one.

"I will find out more," Jie replied. *You prepare for reception.*

A sheepish grin appeared on Tian's face. "That will be awkward. I am sorry. About earlier."

She waved him off with a smile, though saying in her most lethal voice, "You had better be."

The tone was for the benefit of the prisoners, to whom she turned her full attention once Tian disappeared from the room.

Balcony Boy sat, seemingly unfazed by his predicament, his breathing calm and shoulders relaxed.

Jie had many ways to unsettle a man.

She reached into the sleeve of her dress and withdrew a single-edged knife with a sharp rasp. Slowly, she ran the blunt side across the top of the boy's lip, pausing for a brief second of pressure in the divot under his nose.

His knuckles whitened around the chair's delicately curved armrests, and he let out a sharp breath of air. Despite his initial calm, he was not trained as thoroughly as a Black Lotus *Moquan*.

She leaned over and whispered in his ear, "You *will* talk. Save yourself the misery."

He laughed, but it was half-hearted, forced. When he spoke, his voice straddled the divide between puberty and adulthood. "Do what you will, bitch. I won't talk."

"You were trained by a Black Fist spy. I can tell." Jie took out a small flask and uncorked it. A sweet fragrance diffused through the small room. She held it under his nose. "So tell me, what is this?"

He bit his lip.

"I suspect you know quite a bit about contact toxins, since you put a powder in the princess' cosmetics. And staged toxins, since I found some deer horn velvet in her dresses. So you know that if I took the first powder and mixed it with *yinghua* flowers instead of the deer horn, it would make a male-specific toxin instead of a female-specific one. Like what is in this bottle."

He cast his gaze downward. He knew.

Dabbing a small amount of the fluid onto her lips, she slid behind his back. She then lightly pressed her chest against his back and brushed her lips across his neck. Feminine wiles would probably be enough to bend a hot-blooded teen boy to her will. The euphoric intoxication he would feel from the toxin would make him soft clay in her hands.

Now why would the Teleri want the princess in such a state?

CHAPTER 7:

Princesses Unraveled

First the humiliation of being manhandled into a compromising position; then enemy spies rummaging through her clothes and jewelry. Throughout it all, Kaiya had maintained her composure, had tried to seem aloof even if her heart had raced. Now, with her handmaidens and imperial guards waiting outside the guest room, the privacy afforded her a chance to unravel.

The worst part was seeing the awkward, gentle boy from her fondest memories transform into a brutal killing machine. Letting out a long sigh, she threw herself down in a chair in front of the writing desk that now served as a make-up table. In the mirror, her straight carriage slumped back and her placid expression contorted into distress. Tears welled in her eyes. Her hands trembled freely, matching the rhythm of her fluttering heart.

She shook hair into her face, as if it would hide her shame. It was her fault. After years of having no real friends, here was a rare chance to reconnect with her one-time confidante. Perhaps even share secrets like they had as children. She should've waited until morning to call upon his cobweb sanctuary instead of visiting unannounced.

Tian had been trying to protect her from what he perceived to be a clear and present danger. She *knew*. Even so, Tian holding her down on top of him was too reminiscent of Rumiya seizing her face.

With the need to always project the image of control, it was hard to feel so powerless. The memory of dark confinement rushed back, threatening to unravel her at a time when Hua needed her resolve. She was holding her breath. Her chest tightened.

No, she wouldn't go there. She wasn't that helpless girl anymore. She'd secured a mutual protection pact with the Paladins. Transformed a dragon with her voice. She was in control of her own destiny.

She closed her eyes and took several deep breaths.

Her heartbeat slowed. Kaiya opened her eyes and looked in the mirror to find the lines of weakness gone from her face. The Dragon Charmer had replaced the scared little girl. Tilting her neck at just the right angle, she tested a demure smile, a mischievous rise of an eyebrow, an innocent blink, a flirtatious pout—all tools that could be just as useful as the magic of her voice.

One more deep breath, and she rose to her feet. She slipped on an outer robe with long hanging sleeves.

As she brushed her hair, a light rap on the door was followed by her handmaiden Meiling's voice. "*Dian-xia*, Zhuyue has waxed well towards its third gibbous. Your guests have been waiting almost half an hour."

How had the time slipped away from her? She must seem like a spoiled brat to everyone around her. Her heart quickened a beat, but she fought back the rising flustered feeling with another deep breath.

"Enter," she commanded.

The door swung open, revealing her handmaidens in silken floral gowns, kneeling. Her most trusted imperial guards stood behind them, now immaculate in their dark-blue robes and burnished breastplates. The five-clawed dragons etched into the steel seemed to wink at her with their gleaming eyes.

Confidence building, she smiled. They might be late, but at least they wouldn't dishonor Father with their appearance!

Ambassador Wu stepped forward from behind the imperial guards and bowed. "*Dian-xia*, please follow me to the banquet."

With a nod, she glided out of the room and fell in behind the ambassador, following him down the grand stairway and into the central hall.

If the rest of the embassy compound felt like an imitation of Hua, the enormous banquet room was nothing but. Modeled on ancient Arkothi-style architecture, it took up the northern end of the building, vaulting two stories with an overlooking mezzanine. A dozen windows on the northern wall, made by Estomari glassmakers in Iksuvius, reached nearly to the ceiling and looked out onto a meditative rock garden. Color brush-paintings and black-and-white calligraphy by some of Hua's most famous masters graced its walls.

Prominent Hua families and senior embassy officials alike had arrived well in advance. They formed a rectangle on the dark hardwoods, each person kneeling on a cushion of light blue silk with gold-colored embroidery. As she entered, all bowed, bringing their foreheads to the ground, open hands on the floor in front of them. If only they knew she'd been a quivering mess of nerves just half an hour ago.

There—Tian sat in the far corner of the rectangle. Although all avoided direct eye contact with her as etiquette demanded, he was doing a particularly good job at it. Maybe it was for the better. She glided to her place at the head of the rectangle, then settled to her knees onto a cushion.

She nodded her head. "Please sit comfortably."

All bowed again. The male guests switched into a cross-legged position, while the women shifted their weight to relieve pressure on their knees. General Zheng of the imperial guard took a seat on her left. Ambassador Wu, on her right, motioned for the servants to bring the food.

They placed a low, small table in front of each person. Chopsticks rested at exacting angles on every table, accompanied by a bowl of rice, a plate of boiled Nothori clams, a small saucer of soy sauce-braised pork belly, a low-rimmed bowl of stir-fried Nothori greens, a small plate of fried Nothori squash, and a lacquer bowl of turnip soup.

Several porcelain flasks of rice wine were passed around, to be poured into small white cups. Thinking back to that humiliating brush with wine and a drunken traipse through Huajing with Avarax, Kaiya waved it off.

"Unfortunately, many of our leafy vegetables are past harvest in this cold climate," the ambassador said. "However, we import some of our spices and seasoning and use local produce to imitate cuisine from home. It is quite delicious if not authentic. Please, try some."

Kaiya had been clenching her jaws. She must have quite a dreadful expression. With a shy smile, she took her chopsticks in hand and extended them towards the only dish she recognized: the braised pork. Hand cupped beneath, she lifted it.

The entire room had fallen quiet. Everyone was trying to hide the fact that they were watching her. When she slid it into her mouth and nodded graciously, the collective sigh of relief was silent but obvious.

How ironic. Her recent flare-up of food allergies was a state secret, to prevent tarnishing the image of Perfect Princess. As hard as it was to maintain that façade, her countrymen tried even harder to accommodate her.

Pretending to ignore their stares, Kaiya raised her rice bowl and scooped out a small clump with her chopsticks. She took a few small bites, and the weight of attention gradually fell away. Thank the Heavens for the reprieve from the guests' scrutiny. She tentatively picked at the unfamiliar dishes.

The evening wore on, with the slow trickle of individuals coming to introduce themselves with deep bows soon building up to a torrent of bobbing heads. It became the perfect excuse for ignoring the food. Even if socializing was tiring and not particularly enjoyable, at least she excelled at it. Her neck would certainly be sore in the morning from all of the nodding. After the ritual exchange of pleasantries, she committed each person's name to memory.

Tomorrow's welcoming reception at the Teleri Embassy would be more of the same, albeit with a bewildering plethora of foreign names and faces. Among those would be First Consul Geros Bovyan of the Teleri Empire, and she'd be relying on Tian to guide her.

Tian. She'd have to apologize to him in private, and then share her biggest secret: the imminent announcement of her betrothal. He'd want to know.

She looked towards his corner, only to find that his seat was empty.

CHAPTER 8:

A Losing Game

Summoned by Jie, Tian was grateful to escape the reception and focus on something other than the slow and tortuous death of his childhood memories. From the shadows of the hall, he shot a last glance back at the princess. How could she be so picky? She wouldn't so much as look at the clams, an expensive delicacy and the main course of the meal.

The girl he remembered was open-minded and adventurous. He was just now coming to grips with the notion that that girl was gone, transformed by years of extravagance in the Hua imperial court. How different from the austere life and demanding training he'd endured. Hopefully, she would return home soon, before the memories of his youth were completely poisoned, leaving him only with the realities of the present.

"King's rook forward three," Jie said even before he set foot in his office. "Check."

"Interesting move. You've played an unorthodox game so far."

Jie shrugged, her expression blank.

Tian absently ran a hand over one of the Cobweb lines. "Did our prisoners have anything to say?"

"If he's to be believed, one said that their goal was to catalog this office, to see what you knew."

"You don't believe him."

Jie smirked. "I have no doubt he was telling the truth. But I couldn't get them to say why they'd placed a staged intoxicant in the princess' lip rouge and gowns."

Tian nodded, pondering. "They breached our security. How?"

"They're recent arrivals, hired by the Zhou family as bodyguards." She traced relative locations in the air. "After escorting them here, they told the gate guards they would wait in the barracks to meet some friends. That is when one tried to access the Cobweb and the others snuck into the princess' chambers. Hired hands and some other Teleri soldiers made a concerted effort to create distractions outside the walls."

Tian scrunched his nose. Such poor planning, and even worse execution. "Where are the prisoners now?"

Jie pointed down. "Still in the warehouse tunnels. I was waiting to see what you wanted to do with them."

"Find out more about the Nightblades. Who trains them. How many there are here. This might be our best chance. I trust that you can do that? Given a little more time?"

Jie brushed a lock of hair behind her ear and looked up through her lashes. "Unfortunately, with my limited tools, teenage boys are a difficult lock to pick."

That seductive look! It made perfect use of her exotic elf-influenced features. Heavens, Jie was quite beautiful. How had he missed it all these years? Maybe calling her *Little Sister* so many times had consigned her to the *inappropriate* category in his mind. Or perhaps idealized memories of a child princess had blinded him to the young woman right in front of him.

Jie wasn't just cute. She was beautiful. Such a novel concept.

She looked up, one eyebrow raised. He had paused for more than a beat, and she was waiting on his answer.

"Um, good." What was the question again? Tian quickly changed the subject. "Now. What about the Teleri? Their troop movements?"

Jie produced a map of the city from the fold of her dress. It depicted Iksuvius' location between the west bank of the Alto River on the east and Cold Harbor to the west, with city walls surrounding the Old City on the north, east, and south sides.

She pointed to the center of the city, close to the Teleri compound. "Their cavalry are stabled here." She then indicated a spot near the Hua embassy. "Here, off of the western market, are five hundred soldiers; and near the northern and eastern gates are three hundred soldiers each. Another three hundred at the southwest and northwest gates. The rest are staying on Teleri embassy grounds."

"That's not protection for the First Consul. That's an army. Three thousand additional Teleri soldiers. That triples the number of Bovyans in Iksuvius."

Jie sucked on her lower lip. "A simple show of force? The Northwest Summit is when they demonstrate that they are the real masters of the region, to show they are the inheritors of the Arkothi Empire."

Tian glanced up at his nest of notes, then back at the map. "Look at their positions. They control all of the main gates into the capital. Except the southern gate."

Jie's eyes widened. "The summit is a distraction. They're staging an invasion. The capital is their prize. "

"Four thousand Bovyans. Against twenty thousand Iksuvi soldiers and city guards." Tian shook his head. Was it possible? Bovyans weren't just the most physically imposing men in the world, but also the best trained. From six months

of age, when a Bovyan was weaned from the breast, he'd be raised by men in a warrior culture.

Jie made a show of counting on her fingers, though she'd likely run several scenarios through her head already. "Almost an even match, but it would leave the First Consul exposed. And with the Nothori nations already paying an exorbitant tribute, what would the Teleri have to gain from an invasion?"

Tian tapped his chin. Of course. If anything besides brutal training and constant warfare kept the Bovyans' population in check, it was the Orc God Tivar's curse on their ancestor. Because of it, their race had no females, and women of other races would miscarry a second Bovyan pregnancy. They procreated through the institutionalized gang rape of every last flowering girl in their vast territory. Tian's face scrunched up. "Breeding stock."

Jie fidgeted. No doubt she'd seen it played out during her deep reconnaissance into the heart of the Teleri Empire. How could it not be unsettling, especially with the Teleri Empire's inhumane process? After giving birth, a new mother would never even hold her own baby. He'd be taken away, so that the empire was the only mother he'd ever know. Meanwhile, the young woman would serve as a wet nurse for a different lot of boys before being sent back to her life. To marry, give birth to more girls. To continue the inhumane cycle.

"Ignore the motives," Tian said. "For now. Can four thousand Teleri soldiers take the city? I don't think so."

"There's another piece of the puzzle. We believe there is a Keeper from the Shrine of Geros," Jie said, referring to the Bovyans' most sacred temple in their capital of Tilésité. It housed some of their progenitor's personal effects—most importantly, his final testament, which laid down his vision for establishing peace and stability. The Keepers were trained to read and interpret its arcane language, and provide guidance as to how the Testament should be applied to the modern Teleri state.

Tian sucked in his breath. "Keepers don't leave the Shrine. Let alone Tilésité."

"There's something much bigger going on than just the Northwest Summit," Jie said. "We have proof they tried to poison the princess. Even if it seems more like a prank than a threat, the Teleri are up to no good. We should call off her meeting with the First Consul and send her home sooner."

Tian shook his head. "Hua would appear weak. It's a drastic decision. We need to find out more. Tomorrow's reception at the Teleri embassy. It's the perfect opportunity. Every dignitary will be there. The princess gives us a reason to be there, too. I've never been inside."

Jie glared at him. "Be careful how you use the princess. She's not just a chess piece to set out as bait."

Chess piece? Tian grinned. Jie's unusual strategy had given him the upper hand, but maybe he was missing something. "Speaking of which. Queen takes rook."

"King's knight to king's three. Check."

Tian sighed. He could sacrifice his knight now to save his queen, but it would only prolong the inevitable. "It's just as I feared. My queen is hopelessly lost."

"Your move."

CHAPTER 9:

Rogues' Gallery

With spears in their left hands, the black-clad soldiers thudded their right fists against their chests as First Consul Geros Bovyan XLIII passed. The sound of their salute and his own heavy boots echoed down the bare stone halls of the Teleri embassy, the rhythm reminding him of cocking Eldaeri repeating crossbows.

A titan among giants, he absently nodded down to his fellow Bovyans, thinking more about the impending meeting with his spymaster.

The embassy steward shuffled toward him, his impeccable dress coat rustling with his incessant bowing. A balding Nothori man of middle years, he barely came up to Geros' chin. "Your Excellency, you have a visitor in the audience hall."

Already. Geros harrumphed. The local sycophants were so pathetic. Without slowing his pace, he waved a hand. "Yes, yes. The Nothori kings undoubtedly heard of my arrival and are coming a day early to kiss my feet. However, I gave you specific instructions that I was not to be disturbed by outsiders tonight."

The man's head bobbed, and he licked his lips. "Your Excellency, it is not the kings. This one... I could not keep him out. He just...appeared."

Geros paused mid-stride. "Appeared?"

"Yes, Your Excellency. He was in the audience hall, demanding to see you. He is...is...sitting on your throne."

On his throne! Someone would die tonight. Geros suppressed an angry snarl, looking back to see if his shadow was still following him. He lengthened his gait towards the audience hall, motioning for the guards stationed along the walls to follow. "My men did not remove him?"

"They are trying..."

Geros slammed the double doors open and stalked into the spacious audience chamber. It was almost as he remembered it from five years before: stone, cold, and bare, save for the banners of the Teleri Empire and each of its army divisions hanging from the walls.

One difference was the sight of his soldiers littering the floor, all alive but nursing wounds with low groans. The other difference was on the throne directly in front of him.

Slouching back with legs splayed sat the King of the Altivorcs himself. Bedecked in a sharp dress uniform and sporting a thin silver crown, he lazily twirled a magic wand around a finger. A half-dozen stocky, turquoise-skinned altivorc guards in chain tunics flanked him with arms crossed, though their broadswords remained sheathed.

With a shout, one of Geros' guards surged forward, lowering a spear.

Geros' vision flashed with lines of yellow as the Eye of Solaris in his skull processed the guard's vector of attack. It would hit the Altivorc King's chest.

The wand stopped spinning and settled in the King's hand. Pointing it at the guard, he grunted a grotesque-sounding syllable that the human mouth probably couldn't imitate. A blast of blue energy burst out from the wand and slammed into the guard.

Knees buckling, his man crumpled to the floor in a heap. The spear clattered away.

Two more guards roared out challenges and stepped forward with weapons lowered, but Geros raised an open hand. "Enough!"

Both soldiers snapped to attention, while the King grinned and resumed the twirling of his wand.

"You." Geros regarded the King of the Orcs through narrowed eyes, evaluating. No one was sure how old he was, and some suggested that he was not even the same individual over the centuries. He had first appeared in history almost a millennium ago, as his people were losing control of Tivaralan during the War of Ancient Gods. Unlike other altivorcs, whom humans would consider short and quite unattractive, the King combined the handsomeness of an elf with the frame of a Bovyan.

"Thank you for answering my summons so promptly." The King grinned, revealing his fangs.

Heat surged into Geros' head, but he held his tongue. Only this pompous boor could lift the curse the first Geros—the mortal son of the Sun God Solaris, and progenitor of the Bovyan race—had submitted to. In return for strength, he had sacrificed his descendants' life force to sustain the Altivorc King. Until the King relinquished this benefit, all Bovyans would expire just past their thirty-third birthday.

A date in Geros' near future. He clenched his jaw.

The King stood and stepped down off the dais, laughing. "Geros, Geros, forgive my bad joke. We're all friends here." He sheathed his wand and sat down on the edge of the dais, patting a spot for Geros to join him.

"Of course." Geros didn't bother to disguise the disdain in his voice as he walked over and sat. "To what do I owe the pleasure of your company? I am sure you have more important matters to attend to."

"Nothing is more important than giving an old friend advice. Especially on the eve of, shall we say, his crowning moment."

Crowning... How did the King know so much? Geros scowled, the underlying messages in that one statement not lost on him. "And what advice is that?"

"Bovyans have a propensity to underestimate what you humans would call the fairer sex. My counsel is this: do not take the princess of Cathay lightly. Your allies in the South did and fared the worse for it. So did Avarax." The King produced a grey metal collar and tossed it at Geros' feet. "Put this around her neck, if you have a chance."

Geros laughed. "I was not elected First Consul by my peers in the Directori for my charm. Nor have I defeated all of my enemies by looking down on them. Your advice is duly noted. But rest assured, I have taken measures to ensure the girl's capacities will be impaired."

"Your Excellency." A small Bovyan soldier in dress uniform stepped forward, pounding his fist against his chest. Fair-skinned with short-cut blond hair, he was clearly of Nothori stock. "I am your chief of spies in Iksuvius. Might I discuss the matter of Princess Kaiya in private?"

"No need," Geros said. "We are all friends here. Speak."

The spymaster's gaze darted from the First Consul to the King and back again. "I am afraid the outcome of our attempt to influence the princess with an intoxicant is uncertain."

"Uncertain?" Geros frowned, and the spymaster shrunk under his glare.

"Our insertion into the Cathayi embassy was countered. The lone survivor reports that the intoxicants were delivered into the princess' effects, but that they might be discovered by their Black Fists."

The Altivorc King chuckled. "Black Fists? What ever happened to the Black Fist traitor we recruited for you, what—twenty, thirty years ago? The Surgeon? It sounds like he'd do a better job of planning than this fool."

The spymaster snorted. "With due respect to Master Feiying, he is not Bovyan."

The King burst out laughing again. "Neither were the ones who *countered your insertion*."

Geros snapped his fingers.

A shadow by the throne coalesced into a slim humanoid shape, dressed all in black. In the light, the short, wiry man was revealed to be Cathayi, with a honey-toned skin coloration that emphasized the sharp cheekbones and sunken eye sockets in his gaunt face.

The spymaster's eyes widened, and he hit his chest with his right hand. "Master Feiying."

Feiying's expression seemed frozen in a perpetual frown. "I may not be Bovyan, but as the King of Orcs says, I would not have been so foolish as to plant Nightblades in a place protected by Black Fists. You may have the physical assets, but not the right mentality."

"Which is exactly why I brought Feiying with me from Tilésité." Geros frowned at the spymaster while jerking his head towards Feiying. "Debrief the master—and the rest of us—while you are here."

The spymaster bowed his head in acquiescence. "A dozen Black Fist spies operate out of the Cathayi embassy. They mostly function as information-gatherers. However, since a half-elf girl joined their ranks a month ago—"

"A half-elf Black Fist?" The King sat up straight, his aloof demeanor jolting into one of keen interest. He and Feiying exchanged glances.

The spymaster continued, ignoring the King. "—their duties have shifted towards security. We assumed that was in preparation for their princess' arrival. After our failed attempt to penetrate their security, only two of our Nightblades remain. "

"Then it was truly foolish to attempt an infiltration," Feiying said. "It would be difficult to get in and out of a place protected by a Black Fist cell without being noticed, unless you had superior numbers and skill."

The Altivorc King rose to his feet and turned towards Geros. "It looks like you have your hands full with your plots, so I won't bother you any more with idle chatter. One of my sons will coordinate with you regarding our deal." He looked again towards Feiying.

Geros stood. He hid his relief at the King's imminent departure behind a broad smile. "Have no doubts, the Teleri always honor our arrangements. If you provide the support you promised in our Northeast Campaign, the pyramid in Lietuvi will be yours to administer."

"Farewell." The King of the Altivorcs grinned again. He barked a series of harsh syllables, and his guards fell in behind him. Geros watched as the King led his entourage out of the hall, their clopping steps the only sound.

Once the orcs had disappeared, Geros turned to the steward. "Summon the healer to attend to these injured men."

The steward bowed and hustled out of the room, leaving Geros alone with his soldiers. He threw himself down onto the throne and motioned the spymaster and Feiying over. "I want you to combine your great minds and come up with a plan that will give us an upper hand when negotiating with Cathay. I don't want the princess harmed in the process."

After all, he was looking forward to seeing if the Dragon Charmer was really as beautiful as the rumors said. He picked up the collar and turned it over in his hands. The metal resembled the Teleri imperial crest pinned to his chest, which blocked magic.

CHAPTER 10:
Battle of Wills

Tian's heart felt like a chunk of ice as he weaved new lines into his web early the next morning. The names of each person working in the Hua embassy—all of whom he knew, liked, and trusted as much as a *Moquan* could—dangled from those threads. The list even included the ambassador, his spies, and Jie. None escaped his scrutiny as suspects in abetting the attack the night before. The only person whose innocence he was absolutely certain of was himself.

The task had taken much longer than expected, but after the better part of a morning of subtle questioning, he was now relieved to have torn down over half the names. Nothing he could think of even remotely implicated any of the other half, with the exception of Jie.

Jie. She was unaccounted for in the minutes before the attack. The very thought of her betraying the princess was ludicrous. Nonetheless, evidence exonerated a suspect, not personal feelings.

And just what were those personal feelings? Tian was not even sure anymore. Adopted Sister. Best Friend. Unexpected Beauty. He laughed at this last and newest revelation. How stupid he'd been all these years. As he stood amid the zigzagging lines, his mind was more tangled than his convoluted web of information.

Fresh air would help restore clarity. He huffed out onto his balcony, accidently dislodging several of his threads in the process. He didn't bother to tack them back up.

Tian settled down with his back to the door, looking out onto the harbor. No sooner had he eased into a comfortable position than a crisp sound cut through his troubled thoughts. What was it?

A torrential resonance of the *guzheng*, a Hua zither, drowned out the late morning din of the western marketplace. Not only that, there were no other sounds. Not because the *guzheng* was *that* loud. Rather, it seemed that even the birds had stopped chirping to listen.

Tian rose to his feet and looked past the compound walls. Hundreds of people gathered outside, held spellbound by the mystical quality of the music.

Curious, he leaped down from the balcony and followed the song to the southern side of the main residence. To a spot below the princess' suite. The placid melody seemed to tangibly billow out of her window, wrapping tendrils of sound around him and settling his scattered thoughts.

The princess' renowned music! It had vanquished a dragon, and now, like the ocean's lullaby, it calmed him. Worries forgotten, he stood entranced for several minutes before returning to his task of rooting out the traitor. His efforts took the rest of the day, and ended with more names removed from his list.

As dusk approached and the Iridescent Moon waxed to its fifth crescent, Tian put aside his work. He descended into the courtyard to join the official procession to the Teleri Embassy. Like Ambassador Wu and the other officials assembled there, he wore a dark-blue silk robe, with his pony tail hanging from beneath a square black hat.

Sixty-four of the imperial guard stood at attention. The dragons etched on their sparkling breastplates glowered, inspiring as much fear as the *dao* swords that hung at the guards' sides. Drummers and palanquin bearers all wore shiny blue coats with high collars embroidered in gold. A porter carried a *guzheng* in a silk brocade bag.

The princess was conspicuously absent. Her music had continued through the day, but no one had seen her. If it were up to him, he wouldn't have to look at her again. Minutes passed, though all hid their impatience with irreproachable decorum. Maybe his wish was coming true.

When she finally emerged from the residence with her handmaidens, all in the courtyard bowed in unison. The sound of ruffling clothes and clinking armor stuttered through the ranks.

"Rise." Her voice could have shamed a nightingale.

Tian stood and gasped. The entire embassy staff gasped as well. Even the ambassador stood with his mouth agape. While the princess may have been stunning after a long journey the day before, her appearance now, after an afternoon of preparation, was nothing short of divine.

She wore a sleeveless, strapless pure white silk inner dress, with an undecorated bust that just barely gave a hint of the soft curves beneath. From her waist down, the white silk was embroidered with a bright blue dragon-and-plum-blossom pattern. An open-face outer robe of translucent sky blue, bordered by a thicker dark-blue silk with gold embroidery, trailed behind her lightly on the courtyard stones. Its long sleeves hung to her ankles. A broad, dark-blue silk sash encircled her slim waist, accentuating the curve of her hips.

Her lustrous black hair, which had been straight and tied back the day before, now appeared in full-bodied tresses, fragrant and curled into a slight wave by *shouwu* berry juice and adorned with simple platinum jewels. It fell nearly to her waist and just partially obscured her delicate neck and collarbones. Her pearly complexion was now slightly tinged with light rouge from *danhua* petals.

Tian blew out a breath. In ancient times, wars would be fought over this beauty.

Behind her stood three of her handmaidens dressed in dark-blue gowns, holding the train of the outer robe so that it would not touch the ground. Although all would be considered beauties in Hua, they didn't warrant a second glance in the company of their princess.

Yet Tian did linger on one. Jie, in disguise, would use this opportunity to enter the Teleri Embassy. He'd never seen her in such elegant dress or exquisite make-up. Though she'd always seemed like a girl not quite to the edge of womanhood, tonight she had transformed into a delicate blossom, rivaling the princess herself. If she felt awkward primped up as such, she hid it well.

The princess interrupted his moment of admiration. "My horse," she commanded.

The order was audacious, even from her. For such an official function, dressed as she was, it was absurd to consider.

The officials and guards looked among themselves, but none dared speak. Tian dropped to one knee, rehearsing his lines in his head. "*Dian-xia*, it is unwise. Even your father, the *Tianzi*, would have ridden in a palanquin."

Her large eyes glinted as sharp as a knife. "I am not my father. I *will* ride a horse." Her voice took on a musical quality and tugged at his mind.

Expecting the tone of suggestion, Tian braced himself. His resolve weakened, yet her voice didn't wash over him as it had the night before. He glanced around for support, but even Ambassador Wu just shuffled on his feet. "Please *Dian-xia*. We must protect the image of Hua."

"What better show of confidence is there than a procession with a member of the Wang family at the head, in full view?" She raised a perfect eyebrow.

"It is not just image." Tian kept his tone less than deferential. "Consider your safety as well."

She waved a hand at the procession. "Will the foreigners dare attack when we are protected by the imperial guard?"

The ambassador stepped forward and bowed. "Please, *Dian-xia*, I humbly recommend following Zheng Tian's advice. He has been monitoring troop movements, and he thinks it is best for your own protection."

"If we were truly in danger, would it not be better to be on a horse so that we can escape quickly?"

Ambassador Wu fell silent, head bowed.

So stubborn! In this, Princess Kaiya had not grown up. Tian clenched his jaw. "If we do not set off now, we will be late. An imperial princess, of all people, should understand protocol. Being late, riding in the open, allowing the common foreigners to behold the daughter of the Dragon Throne. It would be unacceptable."

Her eyes flashed.

Though he withered under her glare, he stood resolute. In this battle of wills, for her own good, he would not give in. And Heavens, he'd probably just uttered the longest sentence of his life.

Behind the princess, Jie flashed a grin unbecoming a handmaiden, while the rest of the procession shifted nervously.

The seconds dragged by before Imperial Guard Captain Chen Xin stepped forward and dropped to his knee. "Please, *Dian-xia*. We must trust the judgment of the embassy staff, who know this area. After we return to Hua, we will see to it that this uncultured cur be reassigned to the most uninhabitable, forsaken excuse for a country with which we have relations."

"Which would be here," the princess said with a sigh. She afforded Tian one last contemptuous glare, which he returned with detached nonchalance, before ducking into the ornate palanquin.

He'd prevailed. For now. No doubt there'd be more struggles to come. The tomboyish streak and unrelenting stubbornness from their childhood was still there, even if it were wrapped in a pretty package.

The gates swung open and the procession embarked on the half-hour march down a tree-lined boulevard to the Teleri embassy in the city center. Along the way, crowds gathered, marveling at the Hua, whose colorful regalia still stood out in the light of the full White Moon, Renyue.

Tian broke formation on his horse and fell back to be closer to Jie, who walked with as much grace as the other handmaidens behind the palanquin.

Little Sister beautiful, he signaled.

Her cheeks flushed slightly, all the way to the tips of her pointed ears. He chuckled.

Beautiful like your princess? she gestured back.

What kind of question was that? He just smiled and spurred his horse back towards the front of the formation. Though not before seeing Jie sucking on the right side of her lower lip.

Arriving at the Teleri embassy, the procession passed through the heavy steel gates, set into twenty-foot walls of grey-speckled stone. The compound looked more like a fortress than an embassy, with battlements and crenellations manned by hundreds of stoic Bovyans.

Tian tapped his chin. Getting in or out, without permission, would not be easy.

The front wall stretched hundreds of feet, with guard towers at regular intervals. Flanking the vaulting metal-and-glass reception hall stood an equally impressive official residence that easily dwarfed its Hua counterpart. Several stone barracks were on the left.

The procession came to a stop in front of the reception hall. The bearers lowered the palanquin and a handmaiden dropped to one knee as she opened it. Ambassador Wu extended his hand to meet the princess', and she glided out with his help.

Was her hand trembling? Did her face seem somewhat paler? Perhaps their earlier confrontation was still on her mind. If so, all of those signs of nervousness instantly disappeared when she met Tian's eyes.

She faced forward, and Tian hurried to take his place on her right side. With the ambassador on her left, she glided up the dozen stairs. How elegantly she moved; the embodiment of grace. Her handmaidens followed, stiff in comparison.

Four enormous Teleri guards with close-cut dark hair and bronze skin flanked the top of the landing. Their formal black overcoats had gold-embroidered cuffs over high-collared black shirts, accentuating their strong, chiseled features. They stood unmoving as statues, longswords held at their chests in salute. Tian's fists clenched as he passed between the hedgerow of blades. These were the people who tried to intoxicate the princess, and now she was walking into their stronghold.

Two equally imposing men greeted them near the doors. The Teleri ambassador to Iksuvi on the right had long blond hair and a short beard that covered his sharp jawline. Fair skin and blue eyes marked him as local Nothori, except for the telltale Bovyan height and muscular frame. He bowed in grand Arkothi fashion. "Ambassador Wu, welcome."

Hands at his side, Ambassador Wu returned the bow. "Thank you," he said in perfect Arkothi. "Allow me to present Princess Kaiya Wang, daughter of the *Tianzi* of the Heavenly Empire of Cathay."

"Delighted to meet you," the princess said in Arkothi with a lilting Hua accent. She afforded the Teleri ambassador the slightest of nods as he took her hand to kiss it. Her fingers looked so small and delicate compared to his. No telling how many other hands his lips had touched already. Still, she didn't appear taken aback by the barbaric custom of the north.

The uncouth greeting didn't begin to rate with the boorish leer of the man on the left. Towering a head and a half above Tian, he undressed her with sharp eyes, one the color of anodized steel, the other brown—The Eye of Solaris. Streaks of grey in his tied-back hair suggested he was not far from his inevitable

expiration day. A scar over his right cheek marred what was otherwise a perfectly smooth olive complexion.

The Teleri ambassador gestured towards the larger man. "I present Geros Bovyan XLIII, First Consul of the Teleri Imperial Directori, King of the Arkothi Three Lakes Province, and Prince of the Western Plains."

Tian assessed the famed Geros Bovyan, elected by his peers as head of the Teleri Directori two years ago. Supposedly, he was born to a virgin, begotten by the Arkothi Sun God, Solaris. His military, political, and economic acumen had expanded the empire to its historic pinnacle. A giant among men. No doubt, Princess Kaiya was overmatched. She'd likely make a fool out of Hua tonight.

The First Consul bowed ever so slightly, sending the medals on his left breast jingling. One curious pin stood out. Circular, with irregular squiggly lines etched into it, its dull grey surface absorbed all light.

As he snapped out of his bow, Geros drew up to his full height, towering above her. "Enchanted to meet you, Kaiya. We are pleased at Cathay's participation tonight. You will enjoy yourself." With an unwavering stare, he took her hand in his and pressed his lips to it.

Tian stiffened. The First Consul hadn't even bothered to address the princess by her title. Beads of sweat gathered on Ambassador Wu's brow. Behind them, Jie shuffled while the other handmaidens quivered. If the princess panicked now, like the rest of them...

Yet she stood steadfast beneath the First Consul's hulking frame and overbearing stare. Her gaze remained on his, impassive, and she barely nodded in acknowledgement. "Many thanks for your gracious invitation. We look forward towards fraternal relations and eternal peace between our countries."

Tian bit his lip. She was goading him! An ill-advised game of indiscreet messages, meant to let the First Consul know that Cathay saw the Teleri as equals. He'd earned a reputation for quick wit, and his retort would slap her down, taking Hua's honor with her.

The First Consul's mouth open and closed, while tight lines in his brow faded and the arrogant smirk melted. His eyes, only seconds ago sharp and penetrating, now softened as the princess held him with her gaze.

Seconds passed as other dignitaries queued behind them. Finally, she smiled coyly, and spoke in a playful tone with the same lilting voice. "My hand please, First Consul..."

With a gape, he released her hand and bowed to the waist in a show of deference. A diplomatic faux-pas. The most powerful man alive, outwitted by a delicate blossom.

Tian hid his smile while their entourage passed the humbled First Consul. He'd misjudged her. As introductions continued behind them, all who witnessed the encounter would think that in the game of statesmanship, the Cathayi had won the first engagement.

All because of Princess Kaiya. No longer the naïve eight-year-old of his memories, nor the willful diva from the last two days, she was the *Tianzi's* envoy. A well-honed weapon of diplomacy.

Tian looked out into the banquet hall beyond. If he were the one planning a Teleri invasion of the Northwest, this is where he'd start: a gathering of prominent leaders.

CHAPTER 11:

Change of Fortune

The buzzing of a hundred conversations quieted to a sudden hush as Kaiya stepped into the grand reception hall, with her retinue in tow. A thousand eyes met hers, though all of them combined were not as disconcerting as Geros' brown one.

The Eye of Solaris. According to everything she'd read, a new First Consul would gouge his own eye out and replace it with the glass orb, which contained a spark of the Arkothi sun god's divinity.

Suppressing a shudder and shaking the thought out of her head, she held the gathered dignitaries with a gaze for a brief second, before tilting her head a fraction down and to the right and offering a shy smile.

Whispered murmurs erupted, all echoing the same sentiment: never before had they seen such beauty. Whether it was the power of theatrics or the gullibility of males, a glance had captured the room more effectively than a thousand musketmen could with their guns.

Her head spun at the dizzying swash of national colors: an explosion of blues, scarlets, yellows, blacks, and golds. Yet the vibrant mélange of livery paled in comparison to the majesty of the prism-shaped hall itself. Spaced at regular intervals, arching metal columns framed the building. They vaulted some forty feet towards a central spine, with stained glass forming the walls.

The glass panels might have been a history lesson if not for the propaganda. The first few depicted stories from the Arkothi Empire, which had collapsed after the Hellstorm three hundred years before. The next showed their Sun God Solaris impregnating the mother of the first Bovyan, Geros I. The rest celebrated the Bovyan Knights of old, then the soldiers of the modern day Teleri Empire.

Kaiya suppressed a snort. While not known for their appreciation of fine art, the Bovyan rulers of Teleri sent a clear message in the awe-inspiring architecture: they were inheritors of the ancient Arkothi Empire.

Yet there was something more, something deeper than just the view. She closed her eyes and listened. A subtle resonance hummed with an uncanny familiarity. Where had she heard it before?

Perhaps the Temple of Heaven back home. Or Shakti's Hill in Palimur, where she'd confronted Avarax.

She opened her eyes to meet a familiar face. Light-brown in complexion, with flowing black hair and a short, pointed beard, Sameer Vikram approached with a fluid grace. It'd been nearly half a year since they'd parted ways at the Temple of Shakti.

"Sir Sameer," she said, switching to the Ayuri language. After months of not speaking it, her accent lilted in her ears. "I did not expect to see you here."

"Nor I. What an unexpected pleasure." Sameer pressed his hands together and bowed his head. A white cotton *kurta* shirt and matching surcoat hung to his knees. The gold embroidery on the collar and hems, along with his curved *naga* sword, all marked him as an Ayuri Paladin. A weariness clung to him, one that hadn't been there just months before.

"I cannot thank you enough for your support when we faced Avarax," she said.

"Support?" Sameer laughed. "I was merely a bystander. You were the only one who did not wither under the dragon's stare. To be honest, I have never been so frightened in my life."

"Your presence gave me courage." Kaiya pressed her hands together. "But how is it that you are in Iksuvius? I did not hear of you taking a Cathayi ship. I would have ensured the most comfortable berth at no cost to you."

He chuckled. "Your Highness, you assume that Cathayi ships are the only way to travel from my homeland to here. But to answer your question, I am en route to the ancient pyramid in the Kanin Wilds, by command of the Paladin Council. It will be the fifth I have visited. Perhaps Jie or your, uh, male friend, told you about our journey to Levastya?"

Male friend. Kaiya's belly fluttered. Neither said male friend nor the Insolent Retainer had mentioned anything about a side trip. Tian shuffled beside her.

She turned to glare at Jie, who was apparently admiring the architecture.

With an eye on the others who jostled toward her, Kaiya turned back to Sameer and talk of pyramids. There were several different architectural styles, one for every region of the continent, dating back to ancient times. Her ancestors, slaves to the altivorcs, likely worshipped the Orc Gods at the pyramid in Hua. "If your duties find you in Cathay, I would be delighted to take you to our pyramid. However, in Iksuvius, I can only offer you a room in our embassy compound."

Sameer waved a hand. "I appreciate the gesture, but I am staying with my father, who is the Ambassador from the Ayuri Confederation to the Nothori lands. Allow me to introduce you." He beckoned over a dignified-looking gentleman with a darker skin tone. Streaks of white punctuated his long black hair, which was pinned up in an intricate braid. Unlike the white *kurta* of the

Bahaduur, the older man's clothes shone with a copper hue.

The ambassador approached with a broad smile of white teeth. He placed his hands together and bowed his head. "Princess Kaiya, it's a pleasure to meet again."

Kaiya pressed her hands together and bowed her head. "Ambassador Vikram. The honor is mine."

"You know each other?" Sameer cocked his head.

The older man laughed from his belly. "I attended the wedding of her brother, Prince Kai-Wu. Her cousin, Lord Peng, introduced us, and a fabulous Blind Musician."

Kaiya's chest tightened. One was a traitor, her reason for coming to this frigid land; the other, Avarax in disguise. Both had made a fool of her. Never again. She took a deep breath to calm her nerves. "I hope you found Sun-Moon Palace hospitable."

He pressed his hands together again. "First rate. Please do me the honor of paying a visit to our embassy during your stay in Iksuvius."

She turned towards Ambassador Wu, who'd been deflecting well-wishers. "Please see if there is time on my schedule." Hopefully not, if Ambassador Vikram intended to reminisce about traitors and dragons.

Ambassador Wu bowed at her command and stepped forward to take over her conversation with the Ayuri. On her other side, Tian talked animatedly with Sameer, the first hint of warmth she had seen in him since their reunion.

She looked around the hall, her gaze pausing at the group of a dozen stout altivorcs who stood away from the conversations and crowds. Their coarse black tunics and large broadswords did little to enhance their blunt noses, huge foreheads, and blocky faces. The altivorc prince they protected, however, would put a human to shame with his good looks.

Kaiya shuddered. Her previous encounter with these ferocious humanoids involved a Maduran prince who'd tried to kidnap her. She turned towards Jie and whispered, "Find out who they work for."

Jie nodded and slunk in their general direction. Despite her worry, Kaiya suppressed a giggle at the thought of Jie trying to be discreet while dressed in a gown designed to draw attention.

Indeed, it did. Before Jie had even taken a dozen steps, a gigantic Teleri general intercepted her with a friendly smile on his face. He leaned down and whispered in her ear. Kaiya barely picked out his words from the background noise. "Where is your husband tonight?"

Husband? That had to be a mistake. Had Tian and Jie eloped without anyone knowing?

Jie looked down and to the side, covering her mouth with her hand. It was a cute gesture, though with better execution, it might overwhelm a man's willpower. Kaiya had practiced it enough.

A uniquely accented male voice from behind interrupted her thoughts. "Princess of Cathay. Well met."

She turned to see a rough and wrinkled face with a ruddy complexion. Greying black hair hung freely from his shoulders, decorated with brightly colored bird feathers. His flaxen coat had tassels of braided horsehair along its borders, and was covered in the front with a rectangular plate of interlocking shells painted in red and blue.

A Kanin plainsman, famous for their magnificent horses and equally amazing equestrian skills. He placed his worn right hand over his heart and swept it out in an arc. He spoke in Arkothi with a heavily nasal accent. "The stories of your beauty do you no justice."

She imitated his salute. "Well met, sir. I'm afraid you have me at a loss."

"Yes, there are far fewer tales of my beauty." He chortled with an endearing sincerity.

She leaned in with a conspiratorial grin. "The secret is to shower the storytellers with gold and jade. Before long, everyone in Tivara will know your name. How many of my platinum hairpins must I part with to learn yours?"

"My name is hardly worth a strand of your lustrous hair. So I will settle for a kiss." His eyes sparkled mischievously as he patted his cheek.

She turned her head and covered her lips with a hand in mock modesty. "I am afraid these lips have never touched a man before, and as much as I would like for you to be the recipient of my first friendly kiss, my future husband would not be pleased." She plucked a strand of her hair and proffered it. "Since you say your name is not worth a single hair, then I expect to hear your entire family tree for this."

"I would have preferred the kiss." He pouted, not at all looking his age.

Tian came to her side and ruined their banter. "He is Ambassador Manuwaya from the Kingdom of Tomiwa. He is renowned for the role he played in the unification of their tribes a generation ago."

"I can see why. He has quite a way with words."

Manuwaya grinned. "In those days, words alone were not enough to unite the plains. I was better at negotiating with a spear than my mouth."

Kaiya bowed her head. "I apologize for being presumptuous."

His laugh was infectious. "That was then. Now I am just an old man trying to impress a pretty face with tall tales of past martial prowess. And you cost me a kiss, Mister Zheng. You will have to let me win our next game of mahjong."

Kaiya pressed a hand to her chest. "Mahjong? I did not realize our national pastime had found its way so far north."

"Oh no, Mister Zheng taught me, and we occasionally play over your country's delicious rice wine. I presume he is trying to get me drunk while we discuss trade."

She looked towards Tian, eyebrow raised.

"Military supplies," Tian said. "Our guns to arm their palace guard, their corn wafers to feed our soldiers when they travel."

Manuwaya waved him off. "Of course, we are interested in cultural exchange as well. Please ask your father to send a trade mission to Tomiwa, hopefully with you at the head. Our king is a connoisseur of fine teas and teacups, most of which he acquires from the Ayuri Confederation. However, the Cathayi teas are the most famous, and very hard to obtain. He owns one single Cathayi teacup, which he treasures above all others for its exquisiteness. I know now after meeting you, my dear, that your country, besides teacups, produces other unique beauties as well."

Kaiya turned her head to the side and smiled. "For our teas and cups, we would certainly hope to acquire some of your peerless horses. They are renowned throughout the world—strong, intelligent and courageous, much like their masters, the Kanin people."

"They are headstrong, brash, and difficult to break," he responded, his tone proud.

"The people? Or the horses?" She flashed a hint of a smile.

Ambassador Manuwaya burst into a loud guffaw. Turning to Tian, he said, "Mister Zheng, I have been completely disarmed! Our king's son is a debonair and spirited warrior, who is indeed hard to control. But perhaps your princess could tame him!"

Spirited, to be sure. Prince Tani had visited Cathay the past New Year, and made a proposal of a different nature. She looked to Tian to gracefully extricate her from the sudden shift in topic.

His face remained devoid of expression, making Kaiya wonder if an Aksumi necromancer had switched out her childhood friend with a zombie.

First Consul Geros' commanding voice, booming over all conversations, rescued her instead. The room quieted and all eyes turned to where he stood on the dais. "Greetings, distinguished guests. Take your seats. We have prepared several courses of Nothori and Arkothi delicacies for you to enjoy."

More strange foods. Her poor skin might erupt with ugly red blotches by the end of the night. Kaiya's stomach twisted in dread anticipation as dozens of male servants circulated through the crowds and ushered guests to assigned seats. There must've been over forty tables, each

surrounded by ten heavy wooden chairs with armrests and black upholstery.

From the livery, dress, and military symbols, it seemed that the kings of Northwest countries—participants in the Northwest Summit—sat at the front center table. Other guests sat at distances commensurate with their importance. It appeared that everyone who was anyone in Iksuvius was there. Teleri generals, influential Iksuvi families, government officials, and ambassadors. As representative of a sovereign state, no doubt she'd sit somewhere in the middle.

A servant placed a hand on her elbow—so rude! No one else was getting grabbed—and guided her toward the front. After several steps, she looked over her shoulder.

Other servants guided Tian, Jie, Ambassador Wu, and her handmaidens toward the back. The ambassador protested. He moved to follow her, only to be blocked by a Bovyan soldier.

Her own usher kept an insistent tug on her elbow, pulling her along until he came to a halt. Kaiya turned to see where they had stopped, only to find a wall of elite guards in the livery of their respective nations. Standing in stoic attention around their rulers, they parted to make space for her to pass. Her eyes widened.

She stood directly across from First Consul Geros himself.

To his left, seventeen-year-old King Arvydas of Lietuvi rose to his feet. He wore a dark-blue jacket over a scarlet, high-collared shirt. Like most Nothori nobles, he was tall and well-built. Sandy blond hair, coifed flat with oil, framed his heavy features. Wisps of light-colored hair shadowed his upper lip and jaw line. Despite his youth, he exuded an air of confidence, perhaps bordering on foolhardiness. "What a pleasant surprise that such a jewel will adorn our table."

"There must be some mistake," Kaiya said. To sit here would suggest Hua was joining the Northwest alliance—and becoming a vassal state to the Teleri.

"None at all," the Teleri Ambassador Thieros said. "The First Consul wished to give the

Cathayi princess all due respect and place her here, with her noble peers."

Or rather, make it look like she was submitting. Kaiya waved off the suggestion with a sweep of her hand. "That is not necessary. Cathay is a mere observer to this gathering and would not deign to aspire to more significance." Gripping her toes to the ground and borrowing the pulsating energy of the chamber, she sang, "Please allow me to join my countrymen."

Ten syllables of command, necessary to maintain the formal wording of diplomacy. Far more than she'd ever tried. Her vitality guttered. She thrust a hand out to the chair to keep from collapsing.

Still, the dignitaries all nodded.

The magic had worked! Now to return to the safety of—

"Nonsense," Geros said. "Take it as my atonement for being such a boor at the gates. Now, I insist you be seated."

Kaiya kept herself from gaping. The First Consul had somehow resisted her power.

The usher pulled out the empty chair, right next to King Gunvyldas of Rotuvi, who harbored Cousin Peng. With hair and long beard greying, he bore lines of care drawn by a lifetime of failed dreams. His light-blue coat seemed as dreary as his demeanor.

Had they intentionally chosen this seat for her? Two years before, Rotuvi's soldiers had pinned down General Lu at Wailian Castle, necessitating her use of the Dragon Scale Lute to subjugate Lord Tong's rebellion. Now, King Gunvyldas protected Cousin Kai-Long.

The First Consul, at eye level with her despite being seated, again motioned for her to sit. Behind her, soldiers moved closer.

There was no other choice, besides embarrassing herself and Hua by making a scene. Kaiya settled on the edge of the chair, next to Queen Ausra and King Evydas of the host nation, Iksuvi. Both were young, fair-skinned and blond; both tall and attractive by Nothori standards. The queen wore a white satin dress that spilled loosely down to her ankles. Its plain neckline plunged low,

revealing a lilac-colored topaz necklace that matched her violet irises.

King Evydas' light blue eyes glinted, his face held tight in uncontained anger as he exchanged glares with King Arvydas. Ambassador Wu had mentioned something about an attempted coup in Lietuvi a year before, rumored to have been staged by Iksuvi, but more likely financed by the Teleri. Who knew for sure? Even if these kings squabbled among each other, their countries remained ostensibly independent only through the tribute they sent to the Teleri Empire each year.

Kaiya shifted the outer gown over her shoulders, as if it would warm her from the frigid stares the young rulers exchanged.

"Such a beautiful dress!" Queen Ausra ran her hand over the silk, again demonstrating the Northerners' disregard for personal space.

Kaiya offered a gracious smile. "Thank you. Your gown is lovely, as well."

"Do you like it?" Ausra beamed. "We buy the silk from your country, and the dyes from Vyara City. Of course, it all comes in on Cathayi ships."

The First Consul brushed a hand over the table, which was carved from a single cross-section of a tree trunk. He met Kaiya's gaze. "Greywood trees, brought in from the Kanin Wilds. When we establish an easier way to bring them here, we will build a fleet of ships to rival yours."

Kaiya acknowledged Geros' impossible daydream with a curt smile, then turned back to the queen and their talk of fashion. "Yes, the Ayuri have an eye for vibrant colors. I bought several *sari* on my trip to Vyara City."

Ausra clapped once in excitement. "Vyara City is so beautiful. I went one time with my father, years ago. He exports the Nothori snow crab that the Ayuri so love. Those old memories are still so fresh in my mind! The Crystal Citadel is simply amazing, both in sheer size and design. The architecture is so beautiful."

Kaiya nodded. "As are buildings here in Iksuvius, which I could not help but admire last evening when I arrived. They are nothing like the ones we build in mountainous Cathay. Yours are constructed to withstand the bitter cold sea winds, and yet they are aesthetically beautiful in their simplicity. It is reflective of the Nothori people's practicality."

Lietuvi's boy King Arvydas snorted. "It is a practicality borne from centuries of combating bitter cold, both from the Heavens and our fellow man." He glared at King Evydas.

Iksuvi's king scowled back. "I could not agree more. The bitter cold causes crops *and* the human spirit to wither, especially in the absence of benevolent leadership."

Arvydas pointed his fork at his counterpart. "Though, as the famed Lietuvi historian Istorikyas wrote, *Nothing is more frigid than the cold corpse of a dead king.*"

Evydas' eyes narrowed and his hand strayed to a butter knife. The soldiers of the three Nothori kingdoms edged closer, their hands resting on sword hilts. The First Consul smirked. Had he instigated the hostilities to keep his vassals divided and ruled? His smug grin suggested he would not be intervening any time soon.

Which left her, lest these boys come to blows, with her and Queen Ausra caught in between. "*Nothing is more frigid than the cold corpse of a dead king,*" Kaiya repeated. "One of my favorite quotes from the Chronicles of Vydas. From the twelfth chapter. A hundred years after the War of the Ancient Gods, when the great Vydas defeated a neighboring tyrant in single combat and founded the Nothori Empire. I have read that your royal families all descend from Vydas."

Arvydas' hands relaxed, fork returning to its place. Likewise, Evydas' bitter expression melted away. The table was momentarily silent, and all the kings' gazes fell on her.

Geros Bovyan, however, frowned. "The Nothori *Empire*? I would not consider a rogues' gallery of petty princes and chieftains, held together by political marriages, adoptions, and hostage exchanges, an empire. Even your modern day *kingdoms*"—he spat the word in disdain—"would fall apart if your childish squabbles were not held in check by the protection of Teleri imperial order."

The table fell into an awkward silence, all the Nothori kings cowed by their powerful neighbor. Behind them, servants held trays, ready to deliver the first dish of the seven-course meal, but none dared approach the table after the First Consul's tirade.

Kaiya placed a hand over her mouth to cover a soft laugh. "First Consul," she said, channeling her most disarmingly sweet voice, "we in Cathay believe that brotherly love holds people and nations together more than fear of the sword. Was that not also the belief of your ancestors, the Bovyan Knights," she gestured with an open hand toward one of the stained-glass panels, "who protected the Arkothi states following the Hellstorm and Long Winter?"

The First Consul scowled, and Kaiya imagined his brain was overheating as he searched for a rebuttal to her question.

She forced her expression into serenity, even if her nerves were strained tighter than the coiled strings of her *guzheng*. Had she gone too far in confronting a man who could probably break her in half with his bare hands?

With a cold stare at her, he stood and raised a hand.

CHAPTER 12:

Distractions

Jie never made it to the table at the back of the hall.

She knew a set-up when she saw one, having engineered many in her life. The Teleri planned to embarrass the princess by isolating her from counsel and surrounding her with enemies. Ambassador Wu could protest until the vanquished Orc Gods returned to Tivaralan on their flaming chariots, but the dozens of armed Teleri soldiers would not be changing the seating arrangements any time soon.

Tian met her gaze, his nod conveying their mutual understanding. Any attempt to intervene would risk the princess' safety.

Jie looked toward the front of the hall, where the First Consul stood, staring daggers at the princess. Elf ears notwithstanding, the buzz of a hundred quiet conversations drowned out whatever Geros was saying.

He took his seat, and servants began setting down plates of food. It was a perfect opportunity for them to poison the princess. They had already tried once, after all.

Jie glanced at Tian, flashing a simple hand motion to convey her intent. *I handle it.*

She turned towards her usher. Rising on her tiptoes, she whispered in his ear. "Where might I go to freshen up?"

The young man craned back and gaped at her. His confused look might have been amusing if not for the urgency.

"The privy," she hissed.

His face flushed an interesting shade of red. "Oh. My apologies, miss." He gestured toward the right side of the hall. "Outside that door, to your left."

With a curt nod, Jie swept towards the door, taking note of its relation to the kitchen exit. In the corner of her eye, young General Marius di Bovyan was watching her.

He rose to his feet.

Jie had spent the afternoon modifying her gown to conceal weapons and tools in the sleeves and hems, but now regretted not doing anything about improving its mobility. Lifting her skirts, she quickened her pace.

She burst through the door and out into the cool night air with a sigh of relief, her admirer left behind. Jie took one step, only to stop and marvel at the banquet hall's exterior. The bright lights from inside sparkled through the stained glass, shooting colorful blades of light up into the night sky. It had to be a coincidental byproduct of the garish interior. No Bovyan would intentionally create such an aesthetic view.

"Mrs. Zheng," Marius called her from behind.

Jie cursed under her breath. The combination of his longer stride, her restricting gown, and a temporary distraction had resulted in a needless delay. She spun around in a swift twist more befitting a warrior than the lady she meant to portray. So careless on her part! Hopefully he wouldn't notice. Channeling her inner Princess

Kaiya, she flashed her most alluring smile. "General Marius, shouldn't you be accompanying your comrades?"

"I am around them all the time. As I am sure you can imagine, the company of a dozen taciturn Bovyans becomes quite dull."

Jie suppressed a shudder. Being among a dozen Teleri would mean something completely different for *her*. "I guess you spend hours discussing the most efficient way to split a skull?"

He placed a hand on his chest. "You know us too well. But in all fairness, we are not all so one-dimensional."

Doubtful, but then again, the sparkling view of the hall supported his claim. She tilted her head. "I've been told a Bovyan's appreciation of art is limited to blood splatters. Yet I couldn't help but notice how beautiful this hall is from the outside. Did your people design it?"

General Marius' expression lit up like Wailian Castle's firepowder stores. "I am happy you noticed! Actually, the framing is quite ancient. Legends say it is the bones of the ancient dragon Venorax, who allied himself with the orcs in their conquest of Tivaralan five thousand years ago. The elves slew him with their Deep Magic on this very spot. The first Nothori king, Vydas, built his castle here. First Consul Geros personally redesigned it a dozen years ago, when he was still just Junior Consul Haros."

Right, the First Consul. There was a princess to rescue. Jie opened her mouth to speak–

–

"Of course you know the real reason I followed you. I'd hoped to reminisce about the old days." He flashed a broad grin.

Old days? And that smile. The man must think his appreciated but unnecessary rescue was worth reminiscing about, and that a month ago was the *old days*. Jie channeled her inner Kaiya, tilting her head. "I'd love to catch up sometime. Perhaps I can join you at your table?"

Marius' eyes widened, the corners of his lips curling up. "I would be honored."

"The stuffiness in there overwhelmed me. I will join you after I cool down." Jie's hand lingered

on a throwing spike in her sleeve before withdrawing a sandalwood fan. She snapped it open and fanned herself, pausing for a beat to conceal part of her face, while she batted her lashes.

The general's cheeks flushed. Maybe it *was* possible to make a Bovyan swoon. Princess Kaiya would be proud.

His smile broadened. "I'll be waiting."

A long time. Jie watched as he disappeared down the hall. Finally. She turned and tottered towards the kitchens as fast as the gown would allow.

The activity in the outdoor space between the hall and kitchen resembled the entrance to an ant hill, with servants bustling back and forth with trays in their hands. Scents of roasting meats and unfamiliar, pungent spices hung in the chill air.

Jie crept closer and peeked into the hall, immediately locating the main table and identifying the young Nothori server assigned to the princess.

"Excuse me miss, are you lost?" An unfamiliar voice said from behind.

She turned around to find a short, blond servant. "No, no. I was just admiring the efficiency of the kitchen staff. You don't mind, do you?" She squeezed her chest between her arms, trying to conjure the feminine curves that the Heavens had thus far denied her. She tilted her head and looked up through her lashes.

The servant loosened his collar and gulped. "Uh, sure. Just be careful."

It was too easy. No wonder the princess got her way so often. Jie brushed a loose lock of hair behind her ear, just as she spotted the princess' server. Closely bunched with several others, he approached with choreographed precision, platter in hand.

"Of course. I'll be so careful, you won't know I'm here." She offered a shy smile and bobbed her head. Then, with a short step backward, she conveniently tripped on her inner gown and careened into the closest server in the phalanx.

As his tray slipped from his grip, Jie caught it in one hand. She spun and exchanged the platter with another servant, before lifting the dragonshell lobster on the princess' tray and swapping it out with the same dish from the second server. In a final display of dramatic clumsiness worthy of an accomplished stage actor, she launched herself into the princess' server. His tray clattered to the hard-packed ground, sending chunks of spiced red potatoes and stewed baby carrots tumbling in a cascade of color.

Ugh, the humiliation of it, even when planned. No need to put any more of an act than necessary. She caught hold of another servant's arm to keep herself from flopping into the mess. "I am so sorry!" she whispered in as distraught a tone as she could muster.

She squatted, picking up the vegetables piece by piece and taking surreptitious sniffs. Nothing. She rolled her eyes, stewing more than the carrots. Why worry? Even if something were poisoned, the princess wouldn't eat any of it anyway.

"Do not concern yourself, miss." A servant bent down next to her, offering a reassuring smile as he joined her in cleaning up.

"I'm so sorry." Jie bowed her head yet again.

A set of boots came to a halt in front of her and she looked up to meet the hard scowl of the kitchen manager. He pointed a finger towards the hall. "Begone!"

"I'm sorry." If Jie had to say it again with so much sincerity, she might actually convince herself that she meant it. She bowed her head a last time, her neck more sore than the time she'd wrestled an altivorc. Picking up her skirts, she took the service entrance back to the reception.

The hall was silent. At the front table, Princess Kaiya was locked in a staring match with the lobster. Spectators watched the duel enthralled, wondering in low voices if the princess was not so perfect after all.

With a snort, Jie stalked over to the main table, deftly avoiding a hulking Bovyan guard who tried to block her way. The princess clenched and unclenched her hands under the table, her face

blanched. Across from her, the First Consul wore a gloating smirk.

Jie hurried over and bowed deeply at the princess' side. "Your Highness," she said in Arkothi so that all could understand, "you must not eat shellfish now." She turned to face the First Consul and bowed again. "Your Eminence, Princess Kaiya hoped to play the zither for you on this auspicious night. In Cathay, it is taboo to eat shelled animals before a performance. Too much of an imbalance between hard and soft, cold and hot."

Murmurs broke out among the guests.

Jie sucked on her lower lip. How ridiculous a lie was that? She could come up with better—

Geros' smirk disappeared. "Play for me? Yes!" He rose to his full height, towering over all. Even across the table, his presence was unsettling. He waved servants over. "Clear the dais."

This had to be a dream. It had actually worked. In the middle of a formal banquet, no less.

The princess offered Jie a frail smile. She floated to her feet and spoke, her melodic voice carrying across the hall. "Ambassador Wu, have my *guzheng* brought over and prepared."

Servants scurried to obey the First Consul and princess' command. As she fit silver picks on each of her fingers, the handmaidens brought forth an antique *guzheng*. A resonant half-tube wood cavity over five feet long, the instrument had thirty-six twisted silk strings with moveable bridges. They placed it on a carved wooden stand, and set a gold-embroidered cushioned stool behind it.

With the planned distraction in place, it was time for Jie to slip out. Now if only she could get Tian's attention.

From his seat at the back of the hall, Tian had ground his teeth as he watched the princess embarrass herself and Hua. Over a crustacean, of all things. Without Jie's intervention, the guests would still be chattering about the spoiled Princess of Cathay. Instead, they were now admiring the craftsmanship of the antique *guzheng* as the handmaidens set it up.

The princess glided across the floor to the dais. Settling on the stool with her back perfectly straight and hands resting in her lap, she raised her head and swept her gaze over the audience. Gracefully raising her arms, she extended her delicate fingers. The picks glittered in the light. The sleeves of her outer gown settled down around her elbows, revealing slender, porcelain-like forearms. A hush settled through the room, everyone's focus transfixed on the dais.

All except the altivorcs. With a look of disdain, the orc prince rose to his feet. Chairs rattled across the stone floors as his guards stood as well. The prince spun on his heel and stalked out the main door, his entourage in tow. Only a handful of heads turned at their blatant departure.

One of those was the Teleri general who'd been sticking to Jie like a wet leaf. He also rose and headed towards a side door.

The sound of the *guzheng's* first elocution yanked Tian's attention back to the front, as if the note had tangibly wrapped itself around his head and turned it. The slow, deliberate strum through pentatonic notes caressed his cheek like fanning fingers. The vibrato alternated between jubilant, short high notes and long, pensive low notes, eventually transitioning into a melancholy tremolo. He closed his eyes, basking in the sound's embrace.

Something hit him in the ear, jolting him from his reverie. Tian jerked his head toward the source. Jie scowled, motioning towards the mesmerized audience.

His logical mind awoke from its torpor. The song, *Between Heaven and Earth,* was a particularly long piece about man's smallness compared to the wonders of the Heavens above and the world around. If the First Consul understood that the princess was rebuking his ambition through the song's symbolism, he might become even more adversarial. And indeed, the Bovyan seemed less entranced by the rise and fall of the notes, and more by the rise and fall of the princess' chest.

Still, the length of the song afforded Tian plenty of time to reconnoiter before anyone missed him. He nodded at Jie, who slipped out a side door. With everyone else captivated, he stood and slunk out the front. The enthralled guards didn't move to block his way.

The cool night air greeted him. He crept through the shadows towards the rear, taking note of the compound's layout. At the back of the main residence, the jingle of chain armor sent him ducking behind a thick hedge. He peeked up from the bush.

The altivorc prince and his guards came to a stop near the building's back door. Apparently, Tian and Jie weren't the only ones using the musical distractions towards nefarious ends. He crouched, motionless. Hopefully, the bright moonlight would dim the altivorcs' heat vision.

Jie's Teleri general arrived next, approaching the orcs with a nod of his head. "Do we still have a deal?"

"Will you still deliver on your side of the bargain?" The prince bared his fangs as he grinned.

"Of course. The Teleri do not renege on their treaties and promises."

"Good," the prince said. "Three thousand of my foot soldiers have descended from the Nothori Mountains and are heading up the main highway from the south. Five thousand of our men, garrisoning the southern border for Iksuvi, abandon their post as we speak."

What were the altivorcs up to? And how could they know troop movements hundreds of *li* away?

The general nodded, showing no sign of surprise. "Then you will allow the Lietuvi army to attack western Iksuvi?"

"The garrison will join in the assault," the prince said. "Another ten thousand of our soldiers have joined up with the Rotuvi army to invade Lietuvi while they are distracted attacking Iksuvi. If your First Consul wanted to destabilize the Nothori Kingdoms—and why, I cannot fathom, since you have them well under control—then you will get what you wished for."

Blood rushed to Tian's head. Jie had been right. The Teleri were staging an invasion. The princess was caught in the middle.

The general shook his head. "These pathetic wretches live in constant fear of their incompetent rulers. When the Nothori Kingdoms are no longer simply tributaries and become integral parts of the Teleri Empire, all will prosper from peace and stability. We are still under treaty with those petty kings until midnight the day after tomorrow. After the treaties expire, we will begin our attack. By the third day, the Kingdom of Iksuvi will be no more, and the other two will be in chaos. Now if only we could liberate Cathay as easily."

"You will control all exits to the city soon enough. Take their whelp hostage and watch her daddy sing." The altivorc prince shrugged.

Tian clenched his jaw. The princess embarrassing herself over a lobster now seemed trivial.

The general harrumphed. "Now is not the time. The First Consul has other plans for Cathay."

The altivorc laughed. "You may lose a golden opportunity. Just know that our king is amenable to assisting you, if you wish to assail their embassy."

CHAPTER 13:

Symphony of the Gods

Jie looked for a place to change. Sneaking around in a gown worked just about as well as hiding the moons on this cloudless night. The White Moon, Renyue, hung full and low in the sky, shedding a soft light over the compound. The larger Blue Moon tilted sharply, its rings at their smallest and dimmest for the year. The Iridescent Moon Zhuyue waxed towards half gibbous. Though their interplay cast enough shadows to hide in, the guards would be sure to see the flash of silken colors.

Blending into the deepest shadow, Jie withdrew a pouch from her silk sash. She pulled out a lightweight black shirt, pants, and mask. They would have never fit into such a small space if not for the enchantment placed on the pouch by the elf Ayana. She shrugged out of her gown and shimmied into the outfit, then wiped a black cream over her face and the backs of her hands.

She crept towards the residence, pausing at the sight of a Teleri soldier standing guard at the main entrance. Not an easy access. However, a small balcony on the shaded side of the building offered an alternate insertion point. She slunk along the base of the wall and stopped right below. With spiked hand straps and feline dexterity, she scaled the wall and swung over the balcony.

The door was unlocked. She opened it a crack and slipped in.

The large, undecorated room was furnished with two single beds and a wooden armoire. Two sets of armor—each consisting of a chainmail tunic with a leather cuirass—rested on stands at opposite sides of the room. Large rectangular shields and longswords completed the set. The markings indicated that they belonged to high-ranking infantry officers. Nothing interesting here.

Jie opened the interior door and peeked out into the moonlit hallway. Empty. The muffled conversations downstairs didn't seem relevant. Most of the important people were probably attending the reception. She slid soundlessly through the halls, checking doors and sparsely furnished bedrooms. Nothing of consequence.

After several minutes, she came to her first locked door. Perhaps this room was more important. It easily yielded to the lockpicks from her pouch. Pushing the door open a crack, she peered in. Even her elf vision couldn't penetrate the darkness.

She slipped in, closed the door behind her, and produced one of her Aksumi beads. Her vision adjusted to the sudden change in light.

In the center lay a large table, over three times her height in diameter, its entire surface a scale model of the Iksuvi kingdom. Blocks of various colors dotted the map, likely indicating troop strengths and positions. Blues, the most numerous in and around the city, probably represented Iksuvi soldiers. The Yellows...

They corresponded with known Teleri troop locations inside the city. But there were many,

many more just on the Teleri side of the Alto River. If each block denoted two hundred men, then there must be over twenty thousand in the border town of Altogrina. And who were the Blacks?

Someone outside the room pushed a key into the lock.

Jie stowed her light bead into a pocket and slid under the table, just as the door opened. Heavy footsteps paced across the floor. His weight and length of stride, as well as the type of boot, all betrayed his identity. General Marius, her admirer. A flickering candle approached the table.

His feet came to a stop. Several blocks brushed across the table top.

Not even her newly discovered feminine charm could convince him she was a simple handmaiden if he saw her now. Jie kept her breath slow and silent. As long as she didn't give him a reason to look under the ta—

One of the blocks clattered to the floor.

Was there enough light for him to see her? She crept back, deeper into the table's shadow.

He squatted down and plucked up the piece between two fingers, his head never dropping below the table line. Thank the Heavens for Bovyans' tall stature.

The block cracked down on a spot near the edge. He then turned and left. His footsteps trailed out and the door locked.

Jie ducked out from under the table and looked at the changes in troop positions.

She sucked in a sharp breath.

Tian waited until well after the Teleri general and the altivorcs parted ways, contemplating the situation. With the entire region about to descend into chaos, they had to get the princess to safety.

Picking himself out of the hedgerow, he brushed himself off and slunk back to the reception with his head swimming. The princess was still playing as he peeked in. There was no sign of Jie.

Taking advantage of the captivated guests, he crept into a chair near the rear.

The melody trailed off and came to an end, and the princess bowed from her seated position. The audience rose to their feet, and thunderous applause swept through the room. Tian stood and joined in, even if his thoughts were elsewhere.

The princess made some adjustments to the bridges of the guzheng. She raised her arms, and the audience fell silent in anticipation of an encore performance. Her slender fingers danced over the strings, now plucking on a heptatonic scale reminiscent of Northern lutes.

It was a Nothori folk song, popular in the drinking halls Tian visited to trawl for information. It celebrated the perseverance of a nomadic Nothori tribe on the Eastern Plains, which had refused to submit to the Arkothi Empire three hundred years before. They outlasted the empire's attempts to wipe them out, surviving through the Hellstorm and ensuing Long Winter that led to the fall of the agrarian Arkothi nation.

The Teleri—who saw themselves as inheritors of the Arkothi Empire—would certainly understand the significance of the song. Tian had never seen anyone dare hum it in the presence of the Bovyans. Was the princess trying to encourage the Nothori kings? Or intentionally agitate the Teleri, not knowing that they were about to be entangled in a warzone?

Around him, the Nothori people responded with nods and smiles to the princess' unique rendering of an otherwise simple song. Even the musically disinclined Teleri grinned and bobbed their heads to the beat.

And then she began to sing.

If her speaking voice was melodious, her singing voice was nothing short of celestial. It resonated with clarity through the deep hall. Tian closed his eyes, as his heart floated. Perhaps this was like the music Guanyin sang when her consort Yang-Di presented the newly-forged world as a gift to her.

The princess' voice softened, and the *guzheng* took over again, repeating the refrain in different keys, becoming lighter and lighter until the hall reached complete, reflective silence. Time passed before deafening applause filled the room. Only the First Consul himself refrained, a contorted smirk on his face.

Kaiya lifted her head and cast her gaze across the room. Guests stood, applauding. She had won them back, after losing their respect with her hesitance to eat their food. She suppressed a shudder, remembering the dragonshell. The dead eyes had gaped at her from its stalks, controlling her much as she had captivated the hall with her entrance. Her stomach had rebelled, and it took all of her power to conjure a smile at the expectant faces.

Those faces now beamed, entangled in the magic of her song. She stood and bowed. Languid and fatigued, she took tentative steps towards the closest seat. After settling on the edge of a chair, she closed her eyes and listened.

There it was: the subtle but unmistakable resonance from when she'd first entered the hall. It sang louder than the Teleri ambassador's booming announcement of a dance, and the ensuing sounds of servants clearing tables and chairs from the floor.

The reception hall must've been built over a deeply magical location. The first hint had been the colors. As she had played, the music appeared as swirls of iridescence, wrapping radiant light around her audience. The circumstances of resonance and visible sound bore an unmistakable resemblance to her experience at the Pyramid of Ayudra, and later, Shakti's Hill in Palimur.

However, none of the dancing lights ever reached the First Consul. The curious metal pin on his chest absorbed all her music's luminescence before it could touch him. What did it mean? Her eyelids fluttered open.

And there he was.

Her heart lurched. Pushing through the crowd, First Consul Geros approached, his mouth curled into a smirk. The mismatched colors of his eyes made them look all the more predatory. He towered above her, his very shadow chasing away her bliss.

He clapped his hands together several times. "Absolutely amazing. You have surprised me time after time tonight. When I heard your father was sending you to meet with me, I expected nothing more than a pretty face to distract us. However, you are certainly no ordinary girl."

If only she were. She rose to her feet despite her knees' protests. "First Consul, my ambassador tells me that Bovyans do not care for art or music, but I am glad that you appreciated the zither tonight. We Cathayi believe that underneath prowess with a sword or technical knowledge of shipbuilding lie the cultivation of the spirit through creative endeavor. The arts form the foundation of our culture, and it is the hope of noble and commoner alike to honestly express himself through art. To do so allows us to find a quiet amid all of the background noise of daily life."

He cocked his head, eyebrows clenched together.

She gestured to the *guzheng*. "With this is mind, I would like to offer my zither to you as a gift, in hopes that you may find some peace through it. It is hundreds of years old, made during the Long Winter when the trees of the world grew slowly and densely, by one of our most famous craftsmen. Its value to our people surpasses even the fastest ship in the west, the *Golden Phoenix*."

The First Consul harrumphed. "You are correct. We care little for creative endeavor, because our austere lifestyle makes the Bovyans strong. Our contentment comes from the satisfaction of our basic needs, not from idle pursuits. A musical instrument may be beautiful, but it is easily smashed with a club. An artist's hands may create fancy things, but her fingers can be severed with a blade. The zither means little without the musician to play for me." Extending his hand, he added, "I wonder if this musician would join me for a dance."

Fear clamped iron claws around her heart. Forcing a demure smile, she said, "First Consul, the last time you took my hand, I was not sure when I would get it back. Although I am honored by your invitation, I do not have the energy after performing so long."

"Princess, the style of dance in the North requires no energy on the lady's part. All you have to do is follow the man." Geros took a step closer.

It took all of the willpower she could muster to keep from shrinking back. "I will meet you in two days at the appointed time to discuss more weighty matters than art. Perhaps after we establish our countries' eternal bonds of peace, we might celebrate with a dance."

The First Consul grinned. "If your terms for a dance are so stringent, I wonder if we will be able to negotiate an accord."

"Regardless of the outcome of our meeting, I promise to share one of our dances with you before I return to Cathay."

Geros' grin contorted into a frown. He raised a hand and motioned for some of his soldiers.

Tian and Ambassador Wu closed in behind her. But where was Jie?

CHAPTER 14:

Plans Never Survive First Contact With The Enemy

With the First Consul intimidating the princess at the front of the hall, Tian reached into his sleeve. He palmed a stack of star-shaped *biao* as he took note of enemy numbers and positions. The closest escape path was through the door to the kitchens, and for the moment, no Bovyan blocked it.

He could hold the First Consul and his guards here long enough for the princess to escape the hall, but with his old knees, Ambassador Wu wouldn't be able keep up. Even if he could, he didn't have the skill with a sword to protect her against one soldier, let alone the entire Teleri embassy. He mouthed to the handmaidens, *Bring the imperial guard.*

And where was Jie? She didn't seem to be among the dignitaries who watched the face-off in silence.

The princess kept her chin up, her expression inexplicably calm. She must have been oblivious to the danger. If she gave the First Consul just one dance, they could walk out of there and then get her aboard the *Golden Phoenix.*

Six enormous Bovyans closed in, and Tian eased forward. If they took two more steps, he'd put throwing stars into their faces. Would Sameer come to his aid? His Paladin skills made him worth a dozen Teleri.

"Allow us to retire for the night," the princess sang.

Stern expressions softening in unison, the soldiers took two steps back and bowed.

Her legs wobbled, and she reached out and took Ambassador Wu's sleeve. She'd saved them for now, but it appeared as if the power she wielded came with a cost.

The First Consul's gaze shifted from his men back to her, his frown turning up into a calculating grin. "My men will escort you to your palanquin. I look forward to our meeting in two days."

Tian kept a grip around his *biao*. This was too easy to be true.

The princess nodded her head at a shallow angle. "Thank you again for the pleasant evening. I am sure our negotiations will bring new opportunities." Posture straightening, she beckoned the handmaidens to join her. She turned and glided leisurely towards the entrance and out the door. Heavens, she was confident, and thoroughly unaware that there were a thousand more Bovyans.

The cool night air prickled at Tian's damp neck. Had the First Consul called more men and barred their exit, there was nothing they could've done about it.

At the base of the steps, the Hua procession stood at attention. Without protest, the princess took the ambassador's hand for support and ducked into the palanquin.

Her hand, previously concealed in her long hanging sleeves, trembled.

She did understand the danger. And she had the sense to hide her fear.

The entourage passed through the dark, quiet streets of Iksuvius without incident, their drums and lanterns breaking the sleeping city's tranquility. Upon their arrival at their own embassy, the princess shuffled through the halls toward her suite without a word to anyone.

Tian turned to Ambassador Wu. "Please meet me in your office. In a few minutes." He then headed toward Jie's room. Perhaps she had already come back.

There was no sign of her, so he went next door into his own office.

He hastily tacked up a few notes about the altivorcs and reorganized the relational positions of the three Nothori Kingdoms. Grabbing a map, he went to the ambassador's office.

Ambassador Wu slouched in his chair, sweat beading on his uncharacteristically pale brow. He let out a long sigh. "Little Tian, I was concerned back there."

Tian nodded. "So was I, Godfather. We have more reason to be. The Teleri Empire is plotting. To overturn the balance of power in the Northwest. They are no longer content to collect an annual tribute."

Ambassador Wu frowned and sat up.

Tian snapped out the map and spread it over the ambassador's desk. "They are pitting Rotuvi and Lietuvi against each other. They will gobble up Iksuvi for themselves. The altivorcs will help. Iksuvi will fall by the end of the month. Lietuvi within a year. Rotuvi will stand alone as Teleri's ally. Threatening our border."

The ambassador looked from the map to Tian, then back down. He pointed to the east. "The Teleri are too bogged down in their Eastern Campaign."

Tian nodded. "So we thought. But if I'm right, they will be a direct threat to us. In three years. Maybe even two. Then there's their monstrous breeding program. In fifteen years, they'll have produced enough troops. To fully pacify the Northwest. And they have gained this city. The only deep-water port in the region."

Wu's eyes narrowed. "They are not far off from a navy, then. For now, the embassy is about to be caught up in a conflagration. What is our best strategy? What do we accomplish with our meeting in two days? What about tomorrow, when the princess meets with Rotuvi? Perhaps we should delay until after the summit so we know where the Empire stands in the Northwest. Or just send the princess away as soon as we can provision the *Golden Phoenix*."

"The summit is just a diversion," called a soft voice from the door.

Tian turned around to see Jie, her face black. Thank the Heavens she was safe. "Where were you?"

Jie smirked. "In the Teleri embassy war room, and I've seen their plans. An army of fifty thousand regular soldiers and another ten thousand of their homeguard are about to cross over the border. There is also a large battalion of altivorcs moving up from the south."

Tian tapped his chin. "That might be why they left the southern gate open—it's a trap to make the Iksuvi believe there's an escape route."

"That's not all," Jie said. "A Lietuvi army of forty thousand has already crossed the border into southwestern Iksuvi. The bulk of the Iksuvi army will be pinned down west of the mountains."

Ambassador Wu sucked in his breath. "Is our mission here in any direct danger?"

"No," Tian said. "I overheard their general. He said we are of no consequence. They have little to gain from attacking us." Except maybe a pretty princess.

Ambassador Wu stroked his beard. "Would it benefit us to tell the Iksuvi of the imminent threat?"

Tian shook his head. "The Teleri might take punitive measures. They could declare an embargo on our goods. Their influence is strong enough that it might hamper trade."

"It is our moral imperative to warn them." The princess' voice protested from the door.

Tian turned to see the princess dressed in a double-layered white sleeping gown. She looked weary but resolute. And alone.

He scowled at Jie. How could she make the mistake of leaving the door open?

The princess locked her gaze on him. "We know their process of subjugating a country. They will slaughter the male members of the royal family, and subject the women to rape. I like Queen Ausra, and shudder at the thought of her fate."

Tian bowed his head. "If I may. That is Iksuvi's problem. Not ours. Our concern is your safety. We must put personal feelings aside. And look at the implications of an unsettled Northwest."

The princess' eyes glinted.

Before she could reply, the ambassador said, "*Dian-xia*, it is late, and you have a long day ahead of you tomorrow. Please, let us formulate a strategy, and we will present our recommendations when you are fresh in the morning."

"Whatever that strategy is, it must include assistance for the Iksuvi royal family, even if we will not aid the nation itself. That is my command." She turned on her heel and stomped back to her room.

"She is idealistic," the ambassador said in a low voice.

"And stubborn." Tian shook his head.

"And she has good ears," Jie said. "We have less than two days before the Teleri plot comes to a head. We need to demand Rotuvi turn over Lord Peng, and then get the princess out of here."

Their final plan ensured the princess' safety. Whether she heeded their counsel or not was another story.

After tossing and turning through the night, Tian rose well before dawn. He donned simple training robes and slipped out into the courtyard to practice a meditative martial form. Jie was already there, swimming through the very set of slow, deliberate motions that he planned on doing himself. No longer made-up as a handmaiden, nor face-painted for espionage, she was simply Jie.

What did that mean anymore? For so long, she'd been just a clan sister. A best friend.

She didn't pause in her form, even as she greeted him with a smile. Her long dark hair was tied back in a pony tail, fastened with a pink ribbon that dangled over her own plain white robes. As her hand stretched out to *Part the Wild Horse's Mane*, he approached and paralleled her position, his wrist crossing hers. She pressed her body structure into his stance, and he twisted his hips to redirect her force. He then turned to push his own energy back into her.

In this partner exercise of sensing intention, Jie had always surpassed him at harmonizing energy, even if he was better at planning attacks. Yet on this morning, their interchange was perfect, her *Yin* intermingling with his *Yang*. At a neutral position, with hands crossed between them, their gaze met for what must have been the ten thousandth time in their lives.

In that second, he *saw* her. For the first time. His image reflected in her half-lidded eyes, as if their lucidity had ensnared a part of him. She was more than just a skilled fighter and spy. More than a little sister. Perhaps—

Her other hand slapped down on his crossed hand as her first came forward. It landed with light force, though enough to knock him back half a step. A maelstrom of fluid strikes in the span of a second followed, and none of the set responses in the form prevented him from getting hit. Her leg slipped behind his as she twisted his torso, sending him tumbling to the ground.

He looked up. Where had that come from?

Her grin might have reached her ears. "It works, even on you!"

"Huh?"

"The princess gains the upper hand in her interactions because she knows how to use her body language. Everything from the tilt of her neck to the way she looks at you. You fell for it."

"Well, you cheated. You didn't use the motions. From the form."

"When did I ever play fair?" Jie raised an eyebrow, yet it was her eyes beneath that were captivating. "I bribed one of the princess' cousins to teach me their *Praise Spring* style, the one that all the noblewomen learn. It's simple and practical for those who don't have time to train anything in depth."

"Bribed her with what? You don't own anything. Nothing an aristocrat would want." Not that it mattered where she learned a new trick. He just continued gazing at her.

"Information. She's a gossip-monger, who would make a great *Moquan* if she didn't talk more than she listened. Stop looking at me like that, it's distracting."

From his spot on the ground, Tian threw out his legs and caught up Jie's in a scissor kick. She stumbled on top of him. They pitched into the gravel, neither gaining the upper hand for a few seconds until Tian finally ended up on top, pinning her hands on the ground beside her head.

Their faces were no more than a breath away. Their gazes met again, her playful look melting into one of longing. She closed her eyes and parted her lips, inviting him. They'd walked the path that had been expected of them, brother and sister in a clan of warrior-spies. But a new path lay ahead, determined not by where they had taken the first step of the journey, but rather from where they chose to walk now. Tian leaned in.

"Minister Zheng, Ms. Yan." A male voice from the residence door called.

Tian's head jerked up before his lips met Jie's.

Standing next to the main entrance was the ambassador's young aide, his face red. "The princess will be ready to receive your briefing in a fifth of a phase of Zhuyue."

Tian pushed himself off of Jie and stood, brushing himself off. He extended a hand to help her up. When hers met his, something felt...different.

Standing in Ambassador Wu's office, Jie wistfully tugged out the wrinkles in her training robe. What had that been about? It couldn't be happening. Years of affection, never destined to go anywhere, now becoming something more? And just before she would be returning to Hua. She reached over to give Tian's hand a squeeze.

Then Princess Kaiya glided in with nonchalant grace, wearing a light-blue, long-sleeved silk inner gown. A fur shawl covered her shoulders, and her hair hung in a ponytail. Even without make-up, she looked stunning. Jerking her hand back, Jie suppressed a jealous pout. All bowed low, holding that position until the princess ordered them to rise.

She alighted on the edge of a chair. "What plans have you considered, Ambassador?"

The ambassador bowed. "First of all, a messenger from Rotuvi arrived, insisting we move your meeting with King Gunvydas to Iksuvi's royal palace. He suggested it was a more appropriate venue for royalty than the Iksuvi Trade Ministry."

"Do you see any reason to deny the request?" The princess swept her gaze to each person.

"It's more heavily defended," Tian said. "If we needed to escape, it would be difficult." He then gave Jie a meaningful stare, his unspoken message clear. The princess would likely ignore the potential for danger, so it would be best to prepare.

Jie nodded at him. She'd take another look at the palace's schematics after the meeting adjourned.

"I understand your concern, Young Lord Zheng," the princess said. "However, in this foreign land, we are never completely safe, even here in our own embassy. Furthermore, this is our one chance to demand Lord Peng's extradition. Ambassador: relay a message to Rotuvi that we will meet at the palace. Now, what is your advice regarding negotiations with the Teleri?"

The ambassador bowed again. "With the Teleri Empire's intended power grab in the Northwest, the region will be embroiled in chaos. They will not pose a threat to us for the time being. We have no reason to meet with them."

"We should call off the meeting," Jie said, wondering if the princess would disagree. "It is safer that way, especially after the way the First Consul treated you last night."

Ambassador Wu raised a hand. "Little Jie speaks from her standpoint as head of your personal security. However, from my position as a diplomat, I must also consider Hua's interest. Whatever else we may think of the Teleri, they take their treaties very seriously. Our mission here stems from our agreement with Iksuvi."

Jie peered at the ambassador. He'd made no mention of this the night before.

He continued. "In two days, this will be Teleri-occupied land. Since we do not have any formal relations with them, there is nothing to prevent the Bovyans from seizing this embassy. However, if you successfully negotiate a treaty with them, you will ensure our trade and information mission in the North continues unhampered. You bear the *Tianzi's* plaque. It is your decision to make."

Trade Minister Zhang nodded. "We must ensure that trade continues. If we anger the Teleri, they may pressure their allies and tributaries to restrict our exports. Also, this may be a good opportunity to sell our first-generation muskets. In times of conflict, there is profit to be made."

This, too, was a deviation from the script. Jie stared back and forth between Zhang and Wu.

"We should not be profiting from the misery of war." The princess' withering scowl caused Zhang to lower his head. "If anything, my meeting at the Iksuvi palace will be a chance for us to pass on the message about their imminent danger."

"Respectfully," the ambassador said, "we should not meddle in these affairs. We are neutral in these matters, and will only make enemies if our interference is discovered."

The princess shook her head. "Ambassador, Iksuvi will fall to a surprise attack, and Lietuvi will be weakened as well by underhanded scheming. The Five Classics—which you and your ministers studied to join the ranks of the civil service— implore the ruler to act morally, even at risk to himself."

"We are far away from home," Tian said. "Among uncivilized people. They have never heard

of the Five Classics. Would you put yourself at risk?"

It wouldn't be the first time. Jie sucked on her lower lip.

The princess' stare bore down on him, and poor Tian lowered his gaze. "Ambassador, during our visit to the Iksuvi palace, you will warn King Evydas of the impending invasion. Offer him and his family safe haven on the *Golden Phoenix*."

The ambassador bowed his head. "As the princess commands."

A slight smile formed on her lips. "Young Lord Zheng, your concerns are duly noted. Therefore, I will not meet with the First Consul." Though she kept her back straight, her hands trembled. "I will depart for Hua as soon as the *Golden Phoenix* is ready to sail. It must be provisioned before the Teleri lock down the city. I am told that you are an unparalleled planner, so you and Jie will make preparations for our early departure."

"As the princess commands," they said in unison, bowing.

All bowed as she rose to her feet. "I will be in my quarters preparing for the meeting with King Gunvydas."

Tian watched her drift out of the room, then shook his head. "She has a kind and just heart, but that is not an asset so far from home."

"Don't worry so much." Jie laughed. "She masterfully cornered the Maduran prince in her negotiations there. She is much sharper than you give her credit for." If only she felt as confident as she pretended.

CHAPTER 15:

Bait and Switch

Jie looked back towards the embassy as she followed the princess' procession of a hundred imperial guards towards the Iksuvi palace. Tian, who was staying behind to plan the princess' escape, offered her a farewell smile from the gates. She returned it with the tilt of a head a Hua wife might use to send her husband off.

What had passed between them earlier that morning? As she walked at the palanquin's side, Jie thought back to the warmth of his body, the closeness of his lips. She'd let down her guard and surrendered to him. Then, duty interrupted. Whatever had budded between them was left unresolved.

How *unsurprising*. She frowned. Years of unrequited affection, about to be returned. Only to have responsibilities get in the way. And now, she might be leaving as early as tonight. The gods sure had a cruel sense of hu—

She looked up to see a palace of white stone and stained glass, looming high above the squat buildings surrounding it.

Several weeks before, Tian had shown her the floor plans and brought her here. Despite the aesthetic modifications made over the centuries, the original architect had intended it to function as a fortress. Even if elegant white stone walls and graceful towers now replaced battlements and anti-siege defenses, the interior layout of the main keep included bottlenecks, murder holes, and long halls with arrow slits. The defenses not only kept invaders out, but could also prevent *guests* from leaving.

Outside the entrance stood dozens of officials and armed soldiers in precise formation, all dressed in the light-blue and yellow livery of Iksuvi. Porters set the palanquin down, and Jie moved forward to open its doors. A distinguished-looking Nothori man of middle years, dressed in a long formal coat, stepped forward and took the princess' hand.

She wafted out of the palanquin with the grace of a dancer. A dark-blue silk outer gown, open in front to reveal a light-blue inner dress, trailed behind her. Held up with silver pins, her hair was wrapped upward and to the left into a coil, with the last feet of straight hair cascading to her shoulder. A dark-blue *qinghua* flower nestled on the left side. No matter how pretty Jie felt today, she could never compare to the princess.

"Princess Kaiya," the man said with a sweeping Arkothi bow. "I am Lord Jonyas, steward for the Iksuvi royal family. I bid you welcome to the palace. Please follow me to the throne room to meet with King Evydas."

She cast him a demure smile. "My thanks."

"You may bring two of your guards, while the rest wait outside in the palace courtyard." Jonyas licked his lips.

A telltale sign of nervousness. Jie shot a glance at young Cheng, disguised as the flag-bearer. The boy gave a near-imperceptible shrug.

"Of course." The princess motioned toward her two personal guards, Chen Xin and Zhao Yue. Excellent choices. Both were exceptional swordsmen who could best Jie in a fight. Or at least, in a *fair* fight. With confident strides, the pair fell in behind the two other handmaidens and the ambassador. The princess then nodded towards the steward.

With a flourishing bow, he turned and walked through the nine-foot-high, silver-gilt double doors. On either side of the entrance, two large guards in light-blue dress uniforms held stiff bows as the princess' entourage passed.

They were too big, their movements too awkward. Jie tugged the princess' sleeve. "We should—"

"Princess Kaiya!" Queen Ausra met them in the airy foyer, taking the princess' hands in her own. "I am so glad to see you! Come, come!"

Sweat glistened on the queen's forehead despite her broad smile. Behind her enthusiasm, her tone sounded forced. Jie pulled on the princess' sleeve again, and looked back towards the doors just in time to see them close.

The princess ignored the tug, and instead nodded. "Queen Ausra, thank you for personally greeting me."

"Oh. As we say in the Northwest: *a lady who greets her guests adds warmth to the house*," Ausra said with a giggle. "It applies to the queen in the palace just as much as to a peasant in her hovel. Come, come!"

As they passed through the halls, the queen's excitement bubbled into her stories about the palace décor. But while she was busy telling them that the colorful carpets had been imported from Ayuri lands aboard Cathayi trade ships, Jie's pulse quickened.

There were deep footprints spaced far apart in the plush wool rugs. Even though famous painters had rendered the Arkothi-style oil paintings of Iksuvi's past monarchs, two hung off-balance on the walls. They concealed interior arrow slits, if her memory of the castle floor plans served her well. And the musky scent of Levanthi incense?

It *almost* covered the metallic smell of well-oiled weapons.

Even more concerning were the palace guards—all too large for their uniforms—who occupied strategic bottlenecks. Sweat gathered on Ambassador Wu's forehead, and both Zhao Yue and Chen Xin sized up potential enemies. Only the princess, still chatting with Queen Ausra, seemed oblivious to the warning signs.

Jie leaned in and whispered in the Hua tongue. "*Dian-xia*, this is a trap."

Not breaking stride, the princess turned. "I know. I assumed you were coming up with an escape plan." She turned back to Queen Ausra and smiled. "My handmaiden was complimenting your taste in carpets. It helps muffle the sounds of soldiers' footsteps."

The queen blanched. Her smile looked forced. "It helps, but not when there are two hundred and thirty-seven inside clanking around in their chainmail. Thank the gods the other thousand outside didn't insist on coming in."

Jie sucked on her lip. There was no escaping. Now, was Queen Ausra threatening them? Or warning them?

They passed through heavy wooden double doors and into a windowless antechamber. Sunlight flooded in from the throne room, which lay directly across the chamber, through another set of double doors. Copper lamps with Aksumi light beads were shuttered in the corners. Antique tapestries of scenes from the Nothori Empire's storied past hung on the walls, and a light-blue carpet covered the stone floors.

Why was King Evydas *here* in the antechamber, and *not* in the throne room? He glared daggers at young King Arvydas of Lietuvi, who sat at the opposite end of the room. Around them, ministers and soldiers of Rotuvi, Lietuvi, and Iksuvi stood, wearing the bright court colors of their respective countries. Hands squeezed sword hilts, eyes darted back and forth, and the air reeked of male sweat.

The voice of Rotuvi's ambassador echoed in from the throne room. He was pledging a long list of tribute: ten thousand bales of red wheat, a hundred barrels of red wheat liquor, a thousand pounds of salted fish, a thousand pieces of gold—the list went on.

Ambassador Wu's jaw dropped. He leaned over and whispered to the princess. "This is the Northwest Summit! The tribute list from Rotuvi is almost twice normal." Probably since they would be the last Nothori kingdom left standing.

The princess shot a glance back at him. "Ambassador, you were supposed to arrange our meeting before the summit."

Sounds of struggle erupted at the entrance. Jie turned around. One of the large palace guards seized Queen Ausra's shoulders and pulled her away.

The steward remained there, his attention first following his queen, then turning back to the princess. With a trembling hand, he motioned towards one of the velvet-upholstered chairs. He stuttered over his words. "Please be seated."

"Lord Steward," Ambassador Wu said, "what is happening? We came today to meet with King Gunvydas of Rotuvi. We understood that the summit would be held tomorrow."

"Ambassador, please forgive the misunderstanding." The young Bovyan General Marius stepped forward with an unapologetic smile. "The First Consul had an urgent change in plans, and moved the summit up to today."

Jie sucked on her lower lip. No doubt those plans were nefarious; probably involving this trap.

Kaiya bowed her head. "Then we would not deign to interpose on these important proceedings." She turned to her retinue. "We shall be leaving now."

"It is but a small matter," General Marius said. "We hope you will stay." With one hand, he motioned the princess toward a cushioned arm chair, while with the other he made a not-so-subtle gesture. Behind them, chainmail clinked as half a dozen Teleri soldiers moved to block the exit.

The princess scowled. "General, are you detaining me?"

"Of course not, Your Highness," the general said. "We are merely providing protection for you. The palace is not safe right now."

Because it was infested by Bovyans. Two hundred and thirty-seven of them, if Queen Ausra was to be believed.

The princess met Jie's gaze with a raised eyebrow.

She shook her head. No, no way to escape. With only her knife and a dozen throwing *biao*, fighting the heavily armed Bovyans—even with Chen Xin and Zhao Yue's formidable swordsmanship in support—would only delay the inevitable. For the moment, they were trapped.

CHAPTER 16:

Demands Unmet

Kaiya's heart pounded in her ears, drowning out all other sounds. They'd been tricked into attending the summit, but why? Now they were trapped and separated from the rest of her guards. With no other recourse at the moment, she glided to the chair and perched on its edge. The Teleri general afforded her a curt nod before returning to his position by the double doors to the throne room.

Concealing her worries behind a calm façade, she sat serenely amid the two young kings' unbridled hostility. Like two grasshoppers locked in a duel, they ignored the bird waiting to devour them both. King Evydas looked as if he were ready to leap across the room and choke his rival with his bare hands, not knowing that Teleri troops massed on their side of the Alto River, waiting for their treaty to expire. King Arvydas' smug grin revealed that he had no idea that his own Lietuvi would soon be invaded from the south by Rotuvi and their altivorc allies.

Kaiya turned her attention to the throne room, where the First Consul sat on the king's throne, looking down at Rotuvi's King Gunvydas and his ambassador. He was supposed to meet with *her* today, not the First Consul. And yet—

The king stepped forward to perform the sword presentation ritual, an old practice that dated back to the times of the Arkothi Empire. In an act which represented allegiance and obedience, he knelt with a bowed head and offered his sword with two hands. The First Consul received it with one hand and flipped it over. When he passed it back, King Gunvydas received it again with two hands.

"The Teleri Empire recognizes your allegiance," the First Consul said. "Our treaty shall stand for three years."

The Rotuvi entourage in the antechamber mumbled among themselves, while Gunvydas cocked his head.

Ambassador Wu leaned over and whispered. "Usually, their treaty lasts for five years. The Teleri must assume it will take three years to conquer the other two."

Weakened from their invasion of Lietuvi, and bankrupted by their tribute to the Teleri, Rotuvi wouldn't stand a chance when the Bovyan pointed their spears at them. Which would put the Teleri Empire at Hua's border. Kaiya suppressed a shudder.

The First Consul dismissed the king with a wave of his hand. "Return to your seat and wait quietly until your counterparts have likewise submitted. You will not receive the Princess of Cathay today."

Kaiya's palms sweat. The First Consul wanted her here, and not to negotiate for Cousin Kai-Long's extradition.

"As the First Consul commands." Gunvydas bowed again before turning on his heel and marching back out into the antechamber. As he passed the threshold, his perplexed expression transformed into a grin. He paused to cast a haughty glance at the other Nothori kings. His two guards assumed positions around him as he took his seat.

It was time to get some answers from Gunvydas. Kaiya started to rise.

The Teleri general spoke. "The First Consul Geros Bovyan XLIII summons King Arvydas of the Nothori Kingdom of Lietuvi."

The young king rose to his feet and strode through the double doors. His ambassador stood and followed him.

Gunvydas could wait. Kaiya used the distraction to glide over to the chair beside King Evydas. Leaning over, she whispered in his ear. "Your nation is in grave danger, Your Highness. The Teleri will not extend your treaty. They plan to invade once it expires. We offer your wife and family refuge in our embassy."

He turned to her, mouth agape. Without a word, he bolted up and darted out of the antechamber and into the hall. The Teleri soldiers at the door made way while his soldiers stumbled out after him. Everyone in the room exchanged confused glances.

"What did you say to him?" King Gunvydas' eyes narrowed as he regarded her.

Kaiya ignored the question. How easy it had been for Evydas to leave! She stood and headed toward the door. Chen Xin and Zhao Yue followed.

The Teleri guards closed ranks, forming a cordon of steel. Her own guards strode forward, hands on their swords. Brave and skilled as they were, they were hopelessly outnumbered. Chen Xin and Zhao Yue would die, and she would be no closer to escape.

Kaiya drew upon the power of her voice, singing her command. "Stand aside." Heaviness crept into her arms and legs as her vital energy transformed into magic.

The Bovyans' blank expressions jumbled into confusion before all six opened a path to the door.

"Men!" the general barked from behind her.

Kaiya started towards the door, her listless limbs protesting with each step. Four more Teleri swept in from the hall.

They might succumb to the power of her voice as well, but how many Bovyans stalked the palace, ready to *protect* her? The draining effect would leave her exhausted before they made it halfway out of the castle.

Kaiya looked toward Jie, only to find the half-elf wasn't standing in her previous spot. Her eyes swept over the room. No sign of the Insolent Retainer. Kaiya fiddled with a lock of her hair. For now, the only recourse was to persevere. She returned to her seat.

In the throne room, King Arvydas now stood before the First Consul, bowing. When he lifted his head, he spoke in the ritualistic language of the defunct Arkothi Empire. "I, the embodiment of the Nothori Kingdom of Lietuvi, present myself to the First Consul."

Kaiya sighed. The poor boy didn't realize what was happening.

"King Arvydas," Geros said, using plain Arkothi, "the last time you swore allegiance to the Empire, you were a boy of twelve, with your regent playing you as a puppet. Now, five years later, you make your own decisions. Do you understand the ramifications of today's agreement?"

Arvydas bowed his head. "Yes, Your Eminence."

"Very well, then." The First Consul grinned, and returned to the old language. "It pleases the Teleri Empire to embrace the Nothori Kingdom of Lietuvi as brothers. What does Lietuvi present as goodwill to us?"

The Lietuvi ambassador stepped forward and bowed before unfurling a scroll. He began reading off a long list of gifts. With the comparable climates and geography of the Northwest, the annual tribute was similar to that of Rotuvi, though the amount was only about half. At the end, Arvydas stepped forward to perform the sword presentation ritual.

"The Teleri Empire recognizes your allegiance." The First Consul handed the sword back to the boy king. "Our treaty shall stand for two years."

Around her in the antechamber, the Lietuvi entourage exchanged glances and muttered their shock at the short duration of the agreement. If only they knew what was about to happen. Kaiya looked back into the throne room, where King Arvydas remained stoic.

Geros gestured him out with his hand. "Return to your seat and wait there until your counterparts have likewise submitted."

Counterparts? There was only one, King Evydas of Iksuvi. Unless that meant—

Arvydas bowed again and returned to the antechamber. He looked around the room, pausing momentarily on Evydas' vacant seat. He offered the princess a respectful nod.

General Marius gestured towards his men at the doors. "King Evydas should have been back by now. Do you see him in the halls?"

The soldiers shook their heads. He stepped into the throne room and approached the First Consul. Kaiya strained to hear his whisper. "King Evydas left and has not returned. How long shall we wait?"

The First Consul's own voice was barely audible, even to Kaiya's ears. "Perhaps he suspects something. Send your men to find him. Drag him back here if need be. In the meantime, send the Princess of Cathay in, so that the other kings will think she is here to submit."

Kaiya pursed her lips. So this was a game of image. Tricking her into attending the summit and make it seem as if Hua was proclaiming its loyalty.

The general strode back into the antechamber. "Princess Kaiya, the First Consul is ready to receive you."

Kaiya stared at the wall. Let the Rotuvi and Lietuvi see she was being forced. "If the First Consul wishes to see me before our appointed date, he will have to come here."

Two Teleri soldiers squared their shoulders and strode towards her. Chen Xin and Zhao Yue stepped forward, hands on their sword hilts. Around them, the other kings jumped to their feet while their own guards formed up around them.

Kaiya raised her hand to stay the guards, and rose from her chair. As long as she got her message across, nobody needed to die. She glided into the throne room, Ambassador Wu stumbling behind her.

The room jutted out from the rear of the palace, and was well lit by windows that overlooked the bay to the west and the Alto River to the east. More light streamed in from the skylights, illuminating faded tapestries on the walls. She continued down a rich burgundy carpet that stretched down the center of the room, ending at Iksuvi's throne.

There First Consul Geros sat, his leer on her bosom.

She tightened her outer gown over her shoulders and met his gaze.

He was flanked on his left by a scribe, and on his right by his ambassador. A dozen armed guards in black-and-gold Teleri uniforms stood on either side, while another two stood by the entrance.

And somewhere in the room, there was an impossibly slow breath mingled in among all the others.

Jie's.

Kaiya smiled. She had extra protection.

The heavy blockwood doors closed behind her, muffling her guards' protests in the antechamber. She looked up.

The First Consul watched like a bird of prey, all the more disconcerting for his mismatched eyes. "Princess Kaiya, thank you for visiting. You are certainly much more pleasant on the eyes than those boring kings who came before you." He laughed before clearing his throat. "Today, for the first time, I am extending the Teleri Empire's cloak of protection over Cathay. What does Cathay offer in return?"

Kaiya smiled, even as she eyed the First Consul's pin. It would protect him from the power of her voice, as it had twice last night. That left only her wits and charm to extricate herself and her countrymen from the situation. "Most gracious First Consul, on behalf of the Heavenly Empire of Cathay, I thank you for your generous offer."

He started to open his mouth, but she raised a hand to stop him. "However, we owe allegiance only to the Sun God, Yang-Di, to whom my Father the *Tianzi* is but a faithful servant. Yang-Di's Jade Palace may be far away in the reaches of the Western Sea, yet that is where we deliver all of our tribute."

His grin melted. "I—"

She held up a hand again. "Under his watchful eye, we have remained at peace with our neighbors since the War of the Ancient Gods ended a thousand years ago. While Teleri protection comes at a steep price, our Great Wall and rifles are economical."

Geros gritted his teeth. "Your defiance comes as no surprise. However, this chance will only be offered once. I advise you to give it some thought, since walls and rifles may not deter all of your enemies."

The enemies the Teleri sent. She smiled innocently. Let him think she misunderstood his threat. "Up to now, they have effectively deterred your friends in Rotuvi and Madura, who make noises at our borders. I believe if we can arrange a treaty of non-aggression, we can ensure lasting peace that will benefit all."

The First Consul crossed his arms over his chest. "I am afraid that the Directori would not approve of anything short of recognizing your country as a protectorate. However, in the interest of peace, I will use what little influence I have to persuade Rotuvi and Madura not to trouble you for a while. However, I do have a price for this."

Ambassador Wu stepped forward and opened his mouth, but the First Consul silenced him with a glare. "I do not ask much. Just one of your renowned dances that so enchanted Prince Dhanannad in Vyara City."

Kaiya's skin prickled at the name. The way Prince Dhanannad's eyes had roved over her still felt like a violation, half a year after the fact. She forced a reply. "Such a magnanimous gesture. Very well then. A dance, tomorrow afternoon, since your summit was moved to today."

"My guards will escort you to my embassy to stay the night." Geros' lips twitched into a slight smile. "For your protection, of course."

The audacity! Kaiya veiled her protest with an innocuous smile. "I would prefer to prepare for tomorrow in the familiarity and comfort of my own embassy."

The First Consul's grin broadened. "Since we simple Bovyans cannot master the delicate refinement with which you speak, I shall be blunt. I need an assurance you will actually come tomorrow."

Finally, the demand clearly stated. Yet why did he want to see a dance? With her focus locked on the First Consul, she used a tone of command. "Ambassador Wu, the plaque of the *Tianzi*'s office."

A gasp preceded his words, which he spoke in the Hua tongue. "*Dian-xia*, if you give him the plaque, you cannot back out. It, like the Broken Sword, is the embodiment of the *Tianzi*."

As if she didn't know. "There is no other way. My virtue, your life, and Chen Xin and Zhao Yue's lives depend on it." She switched back to Arkothi, motioning him forward without ever looking back. "The plaque, Ambassador."

She extended both arms toward the ambassador, never breaking eye contact with Geros. The reassuringly cool jade met her hands, and she closed her fingers around it. She pressed her forehead to the surface, and then extended it towards the First Consul. "This plaque represents the *Tianzi* himself. My own word of honor *should* be sufficient, but this surpasses even that."

The First Consul glanced towards one of the tapestries, and Kaiya followed his gaze, listening. There was the extra breath from before. Geros nodded ever so slightly and his attention returned to her. Who was hiding there?

Not Jie.

"I accept this as a token of your word." He reached with one hand to take the plaque.

Kaiya did not let go. "First Consul, please receive it with two hands."

His smile twisted into a smirk, and he pulled a little harder. She stumbled a few steps forward. Her heart lurched. His manipulations and contempt for her, she could endure for the sake of her retainers' lives; but disparaging the embodiment of the *Tianzi* was insufferable.

He laughed and took it in two hands. No matter how important the symbol, a wave of relief washed over her as she released it.

With a last glance at the tapestry, she bowed her head. "Tomorrow morning, I will send word of the time and place for our meeting."

The doors flung open, revealing King Evydas. Sweat glistened on his forehead, and his fair face looked even paler than usual. His hands tightened into fists. One step behind him, his foreign minister gripped a sheathed sword in trembling hands. A wall of Iksuvi guards held the outnumbered Bovyans at bay in the antechamber beyond.

What was he planning? Kaiya dug her nails into her hands.

Around her, the Teleri reached for their swords and started forward, but Geros raised his hand. The synchronized clop of boots echoed in the hall as his soldiers snapped to attention.

"King Evydas," the First Consul snarled. "You are late."

The young king strode forward, pausing at Kaiya's side. "It was a pleasure to have met you, Princess of Cathay." He then leaned over to whisper in her ear, "Please make sure my family is protected."

Her eyes widened. He didn't intend to leave the throne room alive. She grabbed ahold of his arm, just as he took another step. *Value your life,* she mouthed.

He offered a wry smile before continuing towards the First Consul.

Ambassador Wu tugged at her sleeve. Audacious. Urgent. At the throne room entrance, the imperial guards clenched their jaws.

She frowned and furrowed her brows to let her will be known. They would stay. Ambassador Wu loosened his grip and she turned to watch First Consul Geros and King Evydas.

The king stood several feet away from the First Consul, his posture stiff and dignified. He reached back with his left hand. After a second, he made an emphatic gesture.

The foreign minister, trembling and sweating, tottered forward and placed the sword in his king's hands.

Evydas held the weapon on either side of the sheath and lifted it. "This sword, *Tamskelti*, was forged by dwarven smiths in antiquity, and holds an edge imbued with elven magic so that they could oppose the armies of the ancient Orc Gods. My forefathers used it to protect our people against the expansion of the Arkothi Empire. Iksuvi will terminate our alliance with the Teleri Empire, and I present this sword as prescribed by ancient rituals."

Before he could take a step forward, the First Consul halted him with a raised hand. "By tradition, you must present the sword with the hilt on your left."

King Evydas froze for a second. Then, with a brusque nod, he flipped *Tamskelti* over, strode forward and extended it towards the First Consul. As Geros reached to take the weapon, the king switched his grip and whipped it out with his left hand. The edges of the intricately etched blade glowed a luminous blue, and its hum resonated in Kaiya's core.

The sword swished toward the First Consul's midsection. Evading the attack, Geros ripped the grey metal pin from his shirt with a rasp. Evydas transitioned into a stab toward his chest. The Bovyan twisted away and used his pin to slap the blade with a muted clang.

A minute pulse of energy rippled out from the impact, percolating through Kaiya. The luminous glow of the blade went dull. Evydas gasped.

Chainmail clinked as two of the soldiers on either side of the First Consul sprang into action, lowering their spears. Geros drew one of their swords with his left hand. The weapon whooshed as it cut toward Evydas' head. The king lifted his own blade, but it shattered with a clank on impact.

Iksuvi soldiers flooded into the room. A wave of jingling armor and rustling cloth surged past Kaiya as they joined in the fray. One of the

Teleri charged and thrust with his spear at the king. Evydas evaded the stab with a quick spin, and simultaneously caught the weapon's shaft in both of his hands. The turn pulled the Bovyan soldier forward, into the foreign minister, and both went crashing to the floor.

Spear in hand, the king faced off against the First Consul. The Teleri guards at the door joined in, their own spears flashing. The one guard picked himself up off the minister, and a compatriot threw him a sheathed sword.

Having listened to the cacophony of crossed swords, Kaiya snapped out of her dread fascination.

Ambassador Wu was pulling at her arm. His voice was hoarse and insistent. "We must leave now!"

Her two guards Chen Xin and Zhao Yue shoved through the crowd to protect her, holding their *dao*. Another dozen of the Iksuvi guards burst into the antechamber from the hall, heading toward the throne room.

The broken sword's shards vibrated, pulsing through her. Kaiya pushed past her own men. Pulling the hand-length *dizi* flute from the fold of her inner robe, she approached the throne. She played four melodic notes, which cut through the tense air more sharply than the flashing blades.

The king, his foreign minister, and all the soldiers on both sides lowered their weapons. Only the First Consul held a defensive stance, eyes darting around the room. He lowered his sword.

Kaiya edged forward. Brushing her gown down to her shins, she kneeled on the plush carpet. She spread her arms horizontally to straighten the sleeves, then brought two open hands to the front of her knees and bowed her head. Such a bend was two levels from the deepest bow in Hua culture, those highest levels of respect reserved for their own royalty. "My Lords, please desist."

The imperial guards gasped. They dropped to a knee, right fists to the ground with heads bowed. Ambassador Wu pressed his forehead to the rug.

King Evydas raised his spear again. "I appreciate your consideration, Princess Kaiya, but this must end now. Please withdraw to your embassy for your own safety. And remember my earlier request."

She shook her head. "My Lords—"

"Forgive my rudeness," the king said. "Guards, remove her."

Iksuvi men darted in, putting blades at the Hua imperial guards' necks and yanking the swords from their hands. A third soldier ignored her protests and pulled her to her feet.

Interrupted *and* manhandled! Kaiya tore her arm away from the soldier and lifted her chin. "Chen Xin, Zhao Yue, ambassador, come."

Iksuvi soldiers hustled the Hua contingent out of the throne room, through the antechamber and into the hall, where Iksuvi and Teleri soldiers paused in their conflict to let them pass.

Turning a corner, they ran into a company of two dozen Hua imperial guards with naked blades, General Zheng at their head. "Unhand the princess," he demanded, his Arkothi heavily accented.

The Iksuvi palace guards, who probably wanted nothing more than to go back to their own king's defense, released her not unkindly and bowed. They returned the weapons to Chen Xin and Zhao Yue before racing back towards the throne room.

"*Dian-xia*," General Zheng said with a bow of his head, "please follow me." He escorted them outside, where they were greeted by the bright light of late morning. The remainder of the imperial guards stood in ranks, ready to storm the palace if the need arose. There was not a single Iksuvi uniform around.

Ambassador Wu turned to face her. "There is nothing else we can do for the king; his fate lies in his gods' hands. We must hurry back to the embassy before we get caught up in the chaos."

Kaiya nodded. "Let us be gone from this hornet's nest as soon as possible. I hope the *Golden Phoenix* is provisioned. Where is Jie?"

The procession's flag-bearer stepped forward and dropped to his knee. "*Dian-xia*. My clan sister drew off the gate guards and signaled for us to go in and find you. She must still be inside."

"We shall wait a few minutes for her." Or perhaps it would be better to storm back in. Kaiya wrung her hands.

The ambassador sunk to his knee. "Jie can take care of herself. We must get you back to the safety of our own embassy."

All of the imperial guards dropped to their knee in perfect unison.

They were right. Jie could take care of herself.

Kaiya nodded, looking around for a horse. Seeing none, she cast her palanquin a frown before curling in. She slid the window open.

Horns blared from the palace, and their call echoed throughout the city. The procession headed east towards the embassy with the imperial guards' formation tightly packed around her palanquin. Commoners frantically rushed through the streets. Several squadrons of Iksuvi soldiers marched towards the city center, their leaders ordering the citizenry into their homes. Gone was Ambassador Wu's typically calm and collected composure, replaced by trembling hands and quivering lips.

They arrived at the compound as the barely visible Iridescent Moon waxed to its first crescent. When Kaiya emerged from the palanquin, she found Tian waiting there to greet her on one knee, fist to the ground. "*Dian-xia.* We have urgent business. Come to the receiving room."

CHAPTER 17:

Price of Insolence

Tian searched the faces among the returning procession without satisfaction. He drew aside the flag-bearer, Cheng. "Where's Jie?"

"She's in the Iksuvi palace, I believe to latch on to that Teleri general."

Him again. For a Bovyan, the general seemed inordinately interested in one girl. And what about Jie? Surely she couldn't like him. Why put herself in so much danger?

Unless she was the mole who'd helped the Teleri the night of the princess' arrival. Jie was unaccounted for on another instance, as well—in the Teleri embassy. Right after the general had parted ways with the altivorcs. And of course, there was the mysterious past relationship between the two, which Jie repeatedly denied.

No, that couldn't be. Tian sighed and hurried to catch up with the princess, who was nearly to the receiving room.

He waited outside as the doors opened, revealing Queen Ausra perched on a delicate-looking bloodwood chair. Evydas' two teenage sisters sat beside her. A wet nurse held the king's infant nephew, the next in line for the throne. All wore simple cotton traveling clothes, their satin gowns abandoned in their haste to flee the palace through a secret tunnel. Their escort of a dozen Iksuvi guards had also disguised themselves as commoners, though their swords would have marked them as soldiers to anyone who took a second look.

Queen Ausra stood and curtseyed as the princess entered. She stumbled forward, blinking away tears. "Princess Kaiya, I am so sorry to have betrayed you at the palace. We were forced."

The princess smiled and motioned for the queen to sit. "I understand, Your Highness. It is already forgotten."

So magnanimous. Tian buried a snort.

Queen Ausra bowed her head and sniffed.

The princess placed a hand on her shoulder. "I do not wish to be the bearer of bad news, but I am sure you would want to know. When we left the palace, your king and his men were fighting for their lives. He was very brave in ensuring that I escaped."

The queen crumpled back in her chair, her voice cracking. "I..." She wiped a sleeve across her eyes, cleared her throat and straightened. "Before we parted, my king asked me to convey his deepest appreciation. His brothers and uncles are preparing for war. However, he has asked that you shelter his sisters, for they will endure horrors if they are captured. And of course his nephew, the heir."

Tian tapped his chin as he watched from the entrance. This was not their problem. One of his spies slipped a note into his hand, and he glanced at it. The latest report.

"...and we are not at war with Teleri," Ambassador Wu was saying, "so you are safe in the embassy for now. Nonetheless, I suggest that you board the *Golden Phoenix* tonight, under the cover of darkness. Although it is not as comfortable as our embassy, the situation here is dire. It may be necessary to make a hasty withdrawal to Cathay in the event that Iksuvius falls."

Iksuvius would fall, and Tian had little doubt who would be responsible for escorting the queen to the ship.

The princess nodded. "Please, make yourself comfortable. You must be tired from your harrowing escape. If you need anything, please let me or the Ambassador know." She rose to her feet, nodded to the guests, and glided out.

Tian dropped to his knee as she emerged. "*Dian-xia*, Ambassador. I have information from my brothers."

With the princess and senior embassy staff surrounding a map, Tian pointed out landmarks. "King Evydas was seriously wounded in the castle. He managed to escape. We are not sure of his current whereabouts. His younger brothers have taken command of the army. They have set up headquarters at the Ministry of War. The Teleri are sweeping throughout the city. Searching for the king's family. They don't know they are here. They've closed all the city gates. Except the southern gate."

"I imagine there are a lot of people trying to get out through that one gate," the ambassador said.

Tian nodded. "And into the hands of the altivorcs. They are coming up the southern road."

The ambassador turned to his chief of staff. "The sun will set in a couple of hours. If the princess is in agreement, send a message to the captain of the *Golden Phoenix*, informing him of Queen Ausra's arrival tonight. Also instruct the embassy staff to ensure the queen and her family are spared no expense for their comfort until then. After night falls, Tian and his men will take them to the ship."

Of course. Tian suppressed a snort.

General Zheng dropped to his knee. "*Dian-xia*, I suggest you board the ship as well."

All of the assembled officials and soldiers followed suit and knelt in a rippling rustle of robes and clatter of armor.

The princess shook her head. "I have promised to dance for the First Consul. To go back on my word, especially to the Bovyans, who value honor, would reflect poorly on Hua."

"*Dian-xia*," Tian said. "Your safety takes precedence. Over honor. I will take you to the ship. By force if necessary. When you are safely on board. I will cut my throat for my impudence."

The princess glared at him, but he raised his head and broke protocol by making direct eye contact. Her expression hardened even more. She motioned towards her imperial guards, Xu Zhan and Ma Jun. "General Zheng, have your men remove this insolent cur from my sight. If he dares lay a hand on me, cut it off."

General Zheng, still on his knee, removed his sheathed sword and held it above his bowed head with two hands. "When you are safely aboard the ship, I will cut my throat for disobeying your order."

All of the soldiers repeated his motion, while the unarmed officials dropped from one knee to two, foreheads pressed to the ground.

Ambassador Wu sighed. "She has given the First Consul a plaque of the *Tianzi*'s office as a guarantee."

The collective sucking in of breaths told Tian what he already knew: like the Broken Sword, a plaque was the embodiment of the *Tianzi*. Not to honor one would be tantamount to the *Tianzi* forsaking the Mandate of Heaven. The last emperor of the preceding dynasty had reneged on his plaque-bound obligations three centuries prior, and the gods had punished the world with the Hellstorm and Long Winter.

There must have been other options than using the plaque! "How could you take a symbol of state so lightly? There—"

"Little Tian, desist." The ambassador's voice was low. "What is done is done."

The princess glared at him. "I do not need to explain myself to an impertinent boor like you, but I will. We were surrounded with no chance of escape. By promising to meet with him later, I may have exposed myself to danger again; but I will do so at a time and place of our choosing, with an opportunity for the *Moquan* to plan my defense. But perhaps I have overestimated your ability." She afforded Tian a last scathing glance before whipping around and marching out of the office. Xu Zhan and Ma Jun hurried after her.

An apology was in order. Tian rose to follow, but the ambassador warded him off with a hand. "Little Tian, your intentions were noble, but you have made the princess lose face. Give her some distance."

Kaiya strode through the halls towards her suite, all trace of poise forgotten. Her imperial guard Chen Xin opened the door for her as she came to her room.

Handmaidens and servants were crating up her personal belongings, just as she had commanded upon her return from the audience with the First Consul.

"Out!" she ordered, her choking voice sounding wrong in her ears.

The servants and handmaidens' eyes widened, but they all bowed low and scurried out.

Kaiya slammed the door behind her. The Northern-style doors made the most satisfying sound.

She walked across the room and slumped into a chair. Using the imperial plaque had been a mistake. Had she waited just a few minutes, King Evydas' attack on Geros would have provided an opportunity for them to escape.

That didn't excuse Tian for scolding her like a child. He'd always been her support in all things, her confidante. Instead, now he publically humiliated her. To think her eight-year-old self wanted to marry him.

Kaiya sniffed. She could order him to cut his own throat, but she did not want that burden any more than she wanted to risk herself by dancing for that brute of a First Consul.

If only she could leave behind the power of life and death, the traditions that placed honor over life, and the loneliness that only someone in her position could understand. She looked into the mirror, to see her reflection blinking away tears.

Tian poked his head out of the Cobweb several times to see if Jie had returned. By nightfall, there was still no word of her. Most of the other *Moquan* brothers *had* returned, bringing strategic updates and the news of a mass exodus of citizens through the southern gate.

He sent some of his men back out to spy on Teleri positions, but organized six to escort the Iksuvi royalty to the *Golden Phoenix*. When his team arrived at the receiving room, they found the queen and her retinue dressed in dark robes, ready to depart. A handful of servants milled about, attending to their needs, while the ambassador and princess bade their farewells.

She looked up as he entered. Her expression instantly hardened, as if she had found a raw turnip in her imperial soup. He dropped to his knee as protocol demanded, but she'd already turned away.

Perhaps there was nothing he could do to make amends. Their constant verbal duel over the last few days had cut through whatever childhood threads connected them.

That wasn't important right now, anyway. He rose and bowed before Queen Ausra. "Your Highness. We must leave now. Before the White Moon reaches its zenith. And brightens the night sky. My team needs your guards' swords. If we need to use force. It needs to look like part of the conflict. Between your nation and the Teleri."

Queen Ausra nodded towards her men, and they reluctantly surrendered their swords. Her smile was frail. "Please lead on. Our lives are in your hands."

Tian bowed. He and his *Moquan* led them out of the compound through the warehouse tunnels. The secret passage went under the walls and connected to the city's sewers. Walking as quickly as possible through the muck, they emerged not far from the docks.

Eight Teleri soldiers stood at the head of the deep-water dock, checking the few people who passed. It would be impossible to sneak the Iksuvi royalty past them, and equally unlikely to draw them away from their post. That left one option, expedient but distasteful.

Tian motioned for the queen and her family to stay back, then used hand signals to assign targets to his men. On his mark, his brothers slipped through the darkness in utter silence, hanging at the edges of the Bovyans' light bauble lamps.

As he strode towards the soldiers, Tian collected a few rocks and flung them at their heads. Once he came into their light, he drew an Iksuvi longsword and brandished it at them.

One of the men pointed. "Lucius, Cyril, Augustas, and Sciro, execute the rebel."

As if taking the life of a faceless enemy wasn't hard enough, their leader had to name them. Four of the soldiers lowered spears and approached in tight formation. Tian tightened his grip on the sword.

His own men slid in behind the soldiers holding the dock and slashed their throats with knives. They caught two of the advancing Bovyans from the rear and slew them as well. When the two living ones turned to see what happened, Tian came up from behind and ran one through. The remaining soldier quickly fell to a coordinated onslaught. As always, efficiency took precedence over honor.

Tian frowned. His master had told him that killing became easier each time, but that never seemed to be the case. "Arrange the bodies so it looks like they died fighting regular infantry."

After seeing the Iksuvi royals safely onboard, his team slunk back to the embassy without incident. There was still no word of Jie, so Tian went to his own room and threw himself into bed. Maybe Jie *had* avoided kissing him because she was the traitor.

CHAPTER 18:

Escape Plans

Tian's eyelids fluttered open as a red haze filtered in through his window. A blurred image came into focus.

Jie looked back at him, elbows on his bed and face propped in her hands. Her lips curled into a grin, reminiscent of the dolphin he had seen on the voyage over. She still wore the blue court gown from the day before, though it was as ruffled as her unkempt hair.

He bolted upright, wiping the gunk from his eyes. "Where've you been?"

Jie's lips twitched, and her gaze roved over what must be his disheveled hair, but her expression quickly transformed into one of seriousness. "I spent the night in the Teleri embassy. I entered on the arm of General Marius, then made sure he enjoyed a long slumber. I am sure he is waking up with a bad headache and a very poor recollection of yesterday's events."

Heat rose to his face. She couldn't have...

"N-no. I-I did not." Her face flushed bright red.

"Sorry," Tian said. He'd made too many assumptions. He'd even believed Jie was a mole. What was he thinking?

"Never mind. I learned from Marius that the senior-most Keeper of the Shrine is here, though I couldn't find out why."

Was she really on a first-name basis with the general? "The senior-most? Important. Was it worth it? Risking yourself and worrying me...us...all night? Why didn't you slip out earlier?"

Jie gesticulated in exaggerated stabs and circles. "I was hiding and got stuck in the war room as their officers came and went. The bulk of their army is less than a day away, and they are moving soldiers to strategic points in the city."

Tian rose to his feet, pulling the wrinkles from the sleeves of his stealth suit. "The noose is closing around the city. I'd hoped to get the princess aboard the *Golden Phoenix* last night—"

"Let me guess, she refused?"

If only his simple nod could convey what had transpired.

Jie sighed. "I also overheard the First Consul talking about her last night. He hates her for her defiance, and he wants to possess her. He told his officers to draw up plans for her capture once the city is secured."

"What? Does he not know we have guns? We have enough provisions to hole up in this compound. For a year if need be. Plus the imperial guards. We are safe here."

Jie shook her head. "What do we do after a year? They outnumber us here, and our homeland is too far away to be a credible threat."

"You're right. However, we are still more powerful at sea. Let's get her aboard the *Golden Phoenix*." Hopefully, the *her* didn't sound as acidic enough as it tasted in his mouth.

Jie shook her head again. "The Teleri have secured the docks with over two hundred men. They are allowing us to bring cargo aboard, but they are checking everything."

Tian sighed. They'd lost the one easy opportunity to get the princess aboard. Of course the Teleri would bolster security after his team's attack last night.

Jie sucked on her lower lip. "Our compound is under constant watch. If we raise suspicions that we know of their plot—"

"Time is short," Tian said. "Assemble the senior staff. In the ambassador's office. I will inform the princess myself."

After Jie left, Tian changed into robes and combed out his hair, then headed to the princess' quarters.

Even at that early hour, music emanated from behind the closed door. The short strumming sounds of the *pipa*, a Hua lute, melded with the long hum of the *erhu*, a two-stringed bowed instrument. Not wanting to disturb the music, he quietly pushed the door open and slipped in.

In the corner of the anteroom, two of the handmaidens plucked at *pipa*s, while another played the *erhu*. In the middle of the room, the princess glided through classical movements, seemingly lost in her dance. She wore a simple white sleeping robe, her hair cascading loosely over her shoulders to her waist. Even without her make-up, she was stunning.

Tian stood mesmerized by her grace, forgetting why he'd come.

Though the music continued, she froze in a perfect stance: back slightly twisted, neck tilted at a gentle curve, and arms above her head in a smooth bend. One bare foot was rooted to the ground, while she held the other leg weightlessly with her toes on the floor. A shapely calf peeked out from the slit of her gown.

The musicians stopped, all eyes on him as he gawked at the angle of her neck. The princess straightened from the pose, brushing her hair behind her ears. Her severe look locked on him. Her cold voice doused any fascination. "Yes, Young Lord Zheng?"

Tian dropped to his knee in salute. When he spoke, an *I-told-you-so* tone slipped out. "*Dian-xia*. Geros plans to take you hostage." And probably

more. "We will be convening a meeting in a half hour. To discuss how to expedite your escape."

The princess backed up and collapsed into a chair by a window. Hair curtained her face, and her shoulders trembled. "How I wish I had never been sent to this godforsaken land. That I never met that demon of a First Consul."

Tian hadn't expected vulnerability. Perhaps his tone was too harsh. He bowed his head.

Pushing her hair back, her gaze met his, searching for something. Perhaps a word of consolation.

In that moment, she was the child he remembered, not the uppity princess she'd become. He took a step forward, hand outstretched to comfort her.

With a lift of the chin, her expression hardened, the cold look returning as if it had never changed. Her voice was icy. "I hope you have come up with a plan."

Kaiya couldn't forgive herself for showing weakness in front of Tian. She was too embarrassed to look at him when she came to the ambassador's office a half hour later. Let him believe it was anger.

More importantly, Jie was back. Safe. She knelt among the senior staff.

Kaiya paused to smile and clasp the half-elf's calloused hands as she glided towards the ambassador's desk. A map of the city lay unfurled there.

"*Dian-xia*," Tian said. "The *Golden Phoenix* is under tight guard. From eight soldiers last night. To two hundred now. We cannot get you aboard. Not if they choose to stop us."

Another reprimand? Kaiya squared her jaw and refused to make eye contact.

The captain of the *Phoenix* bowed his head. "*Dian-xia*, if we can get you aboard, the *Golden Phoenix* is provisioned and can be ready to sail in two hours."

Tian shook his head. "As long as they maintain that troop level at the docks, escape by sea will be impossible."

Kaiya snorted. Perhaps Zheng Tian was not such a great planner after all. "Can we charter a boat to take us to the ship?"

It was Jie's turn to shake her head. "Charter, no. Maybe we can steal one."

"The docks are crawling with Teleri," Tian said. He pointed to the Alto River on the map. "Captain, how far upstream can the *Golden Phoenix* go?"

"At low tide, we can pass under the Great East Bridge, maybe as far south as the docks at Aremarela." The captain pointed at a fishing town about twenty *li* south of Iksuvius, on the Teleri side of the river.

Jie gawked. "You can't simply sneak the *Golden Phoenix* up the river."

The captain laughed. "Who said we would sneak? *If* they even realize what we are doing, there is nothing they can do to stop us. They can't float anything larger than a fishing boat, and my hundred muskets will keep their heads down."

Tian's eyes darted back and forth across the map. "Speed will be of the essence. And a level of deception. We have to leave through the eastern gate. Pass through the crowds on the eastern bridge. Into the Teleri Empire. Then take the road to Aremarela."

"Into Teleri?" Kaiya covered her gaping mouth. Tian was supposed to be the second coming of his clan's fabled Architect, and this was the best he could do?

The captain nodded. "There are no other docks deep enough for the *Golden Phoenix* on this side of the river."

"However," Jie said, "we need a very good reason to leave the embassy compound. They have us surrounded."

Murmurs broke out, but Kaiya silenced them with a raise of her hand. "We have a good reason. I have promised to perform for the First Consul. Choose a time and place."

Jie sucked her lower lip and let it go with a pop. "Wait. We must reach Aremarela before sundown, because the Teleri western army will be passing through as they move to occupy Iksuvius."

The captain tapped the bridge on the map. "The tide will start coming back in, so we need to be on the northern side of the bridge not long after sundown."

Escape seemed less and less likely. Kaiya's chest constricted.

Tian placed several Hua coins on the map. "The princess dances for the First Consul as promised. However, we move the time up to the Zhuyue's second waxing crescent. Move the location to the northern suburbs. We pass back through the northern gate. The wall is deep there. There is a long tunnel. We create a diversion. Stop the palanquin in the tunnel. We switch the princess out. Then she and an escort will take her through the eastern gate. We will need some fast horses waiting on the east side. You can reach Aremarela. One hour at full canter. In the meantime, the *Golden Phoenix* will sail out of the harbor. Up to the mouth of the Alto River. Then down to Aremarela. That will take three hours. So the ship must be ready to disembark by Zhuyue's waxing mid-crescent."

Several of the officers nodded.

Kaiya shook her head. It was amazing how quickly he calculated everything, but there was a one glaring problem. "The palanquin is narrow. You will need a long diversion and very simple clothing if you expect me to be able to change in there."

General Zheng cleared his throat. "How do we keep the First Consul from detaining the princess at their meeting?"

How could they? One answer immediately came to Kaiya's mind, though she wondered if she had the ability or will to go through with it. No, it had to be done, and perhaps it would avert the invasion of Iksuvi.

She took a deep breath. "I will kill him myself."

CHAPTER 19:

The Dance of Swords

In the momentary silence that hung over the room, Jie considered the possibility. The princess had never killed anyone before, at least not that she knew of. Then again, she had vanquished a *dragon* with her song. Not many people could say that. Only one other, in fact, in the history of Tivara. She exchanged a look with Tian, whose pursed lips almost distracted her from the slight shake of his head.

"*Dian-xia*," he said, "forgive my impertinence. Have you ever killed anyone before? You need technique. You need resolve. King Evydas had both. He failed to slay the First Consul."

The princess nodded. "I will perform the *Dance of Swords*. I should be able to hold his attention until it is too late. Between then and now, I will find the resolve."

Jie chewed on her lower lip. A surprise attack. Hardly honorable, but practical. Perhaps being around *Moquan* was rubbing off on the princess. Still... "The Eye of Solaris will warn him of an attack."

"Not if I disguise it." The princess stood. "Trust me with the dance. You will handle the small details."

All knelt in acquiescence.

After she glided out of the room, Tian and Jie again exchanged glances. All the things she wanted to say to him would have to wait.

Despite her bravado, Kaiya questioned whether she had the skill or resolve to kill the First Consul with an underhanded knife in the back. The procession departed the embassy as the Iridescent Moon waxed to its first crescent, with all hundred imperial guards escorting it. She rode astride a horse through the city, even as porters toiled at carrying her palanquin. In the hour it took to reach Iksuvius Heights, a sanctuary reserved for nobility, the doubts Tian had seeded in her mind grew to worry.

Kaiya dismounted and straightened out her maroon gown, while handmaidens fussed over an errant thread in its gold-embroidered borders. As planned, the colors coordinated with the tall wispy trees that flaunted their autumn raiment on either side of the white stone pathway. Her hair was pulled back and fastened with a golden comb, and her cheeks were lightly rouged by *danhua* flowers, her lips tinged a deeper red.

With her imperial guard taking up posts halfway up the hill, she accompanied her handmaidens to the white marble open-air pavilion whose columns crowned the hilltop. Her stomach twisted. Could she really do this?

She twirled around to drink up the panoramic view of the harbor to the west, the Old City to the south, and a long stretch of the Alto

River as it twisted from the southeast to its mouth several miles to the north. Two of her ladies set up a *guzheng* outside the circle of columns, while another prepared hot water.

The tightness in her stomach juddered into somersaults.

Below, the First Consul and his contingent rumbled in on warhorses. Dismounting at the base of the Heights, he ambled up the hill. His white toga fluttered behind him. On his command, his retinue of a hundred guards halted halfway up.

Kaiya stole a glance at the Iridescent Moon, now waxing past its second crescent. The plan relied on a narrow window of time, one which Geros tightened more by his slow pace. Ignoring his mismatched eyes, she greeted him with a demure smile. "First Consul, you are late! Please, enter and sit. Unburden yourself from the weighty matters of state."

"You actually came." With a smirk, he presented the plaque.

Thank the Heavens. Bowing her head, she received it in two hands. After passing it to a handmaiden, she motioned toward a pair of plush blue cushions on either side of a low rosewood table in the middle of the pavilion. A hammered iron kettle of water boiled over a small, contained flame at the side of the table, a wooden ladle resting inverted on the kettle top. Next to the kettle, a silver tray held two eggshell porcelain cups, two matching bowls, a tea brush, a sky-blue silken handcloth, a silver tea scooper, and an eight-inch octagonal brocade tube. On the other side lay a pair of lightweight straight swords.

"I am sorry you had to witness the hostilities yesterday." His tone managed to be at once smug and flippant. "Sometimes, our vassals do not agree with the equity of our arrangements."

Kaiya frowned but said nothing, following the First Consul toward the cushions. From behind, his monstrous frame brought into question the wisdom of her plan. He rounded the table, pausing midstride to look at the swords. He glanced back at her, and then shook his head with a grin.

So dismissive, so rude. Her resolve strengthened. She brushed the gown down to her shins and settled to the cushion on both knees. With her left hand holding the end of her long right sleeve, she extended her open right hand in an invitation for the First Consul to sit.

He dropped into a cross-legged position, the thump of his weight on the floor causing the ladle to fall. Kaiya swept it up before it hit the ground and returned it to its position. Distasteful as it was to defer to the tyrant, she bowed low, as ceremony demanded.

As she straightened, she cast a glance at the matching pair of ceremonial straight swords. The blades lay sheathed in a double scabbard on the marble floors, just within reach.

The instruments of murder. How could a musician, who'd never hurt anyone, become a cold-blooded killer? Her stomach twisted as all resolve faltered.

Kaiya lifted her gaze to the other side of the knee-high table, where the hulking dictator lounged. His white toga exposed sculpted arms, and provided little protection from the cool breeze blowing through the gazebo. He yawned, his bored expression suggesting he didn't mind the cold. His eyes followed hers from the weapons, until they met. He snorted. Daring her to try.

So dismissive. And why not? He loomed a head and chest taller, his enormous frame at least twice her size. He'd likely killed hundreds of enemies in battle even before her birth. Her pulse skittered like a tentative rabbit. Forget resolve. Maybe she didn't have the skill to hurt him.

Still, she couldn't betray weakness to this despot. Kaiya closed her eyes, letting the gentle thrum of the handmaiden's zither settle her racing heart. Both his and her guards waited outside the hilltop gazebo, halfway down the slope. They could see everything, but stood too far away to intervene. In here, it was just her and two handmaidens.

And two ceremonial swords.

Without magic to balance out his advantages in size, skill, and experience, the odds looked bleak. No, it would be foolish to even try. There had to be some way to escape, without gambling on a desperate attack—one which would leave a stain on her soul even if she somehow succeeded.

Kaiya opened her eyes to find his leer on her. His wolfish grin left no doubt as to what he wanted. His gaze roved over her, as if formulating a plan of attack with her curves as the battlefield. Her only defense was a gown, and the gold comb which held up her hair.

And the two swords, which weren't meant for actual combat.

She was powerless and trapped. Stomach hollow, Kaiya shook the terrifying thoughts of being pinned beneath him out of her head. *Disguise strength in weakness*, her ancestor had written. In these dire circumstances, it meant acting demure and deferring to the male ego. It was all part of her upbringing anyway. She could do this.

But first, he needed to lower his guard. What better way than to serve? With her left hand holding the end of her right sleeve, Kaiya leaned forward to the tea set on the table. She lifted the kettle and poured into his eggshell cup. "Please," she offered with a bow of her head. "Admire the tea's color and savor its aroma before taking a sip."

Eyeing the cup with a frown, the First Consul pushed it back across the table. "You first, My Lady."

Such vulgar behavior. Still, the situation required hiding her disgust and fitting his image of the weaker sex. Kaiya lowered her head while still maintaining coy eye contact through her lashes. She covered her mouth with a hand and softly laughed. "First Consul, it is not our custom to poison even our most hated foes when serving them tea. And while Cathay and the Teleri Empire have our differences, we are certainly not enemies. But if you insist."

Kaiya took up the cup in both hands, reveling in its warmth. She closed her eyes and took in a long sniff. Her shoulders relaxed and her concerns unwound. Bringing the cup to her lips, she took a sip. With a smile, she returned the cup to the table, with an unfortunate hint of red from her lip balm.

As Kaiya reached for the kettle to fill the unused cup, Geros snatched up the one she'd just sipped from. The contrast of his large, rough hands emphasized the dish's delicate lines. It was a miracle he didn't crush it between his stout thumb and forefinger. Holding her gaze the entire time, he emptied it into his mouth and gulped it down without so much as pausing to savor its scent or flavor. He wiped his mouth with his sleeve, and then thrust the cup onto the table.

Barbaric. To think such uncultured thugs ruled over the world's largest empire. Looking up from the two swords, she forced her expression into indifference. "First Consul, how can you enjoy the tea if you wolf it down like so? Appreciation of tea reflects our appreciation of life. Without simple pleasures, what is the purpose in living?"

The First Consul scowled. "As I told you, we have little use for extravagance. Ultimately, as your own ancestor said, *the world will be brought to peace and order by the sword*. I have studied him in depth, and highly doubt tea, or your haughty manners, could achieve the same results."

"Yet the Founder was highly cultured and known for appreciating fine tea."

He slammed his open hand onto the table with so much force that the cups fell over. Kaiya's stomach jumped into her throat.

"My patience wears thin, Princess. There are lands to bring under Teleri order. Enough of this idle talk. Let us see your dance so we can continue with more enjoyable endeavors."

Kaiya hid her sinking heart behind a pleasant smile. There were no redeeming qualities in this brute. No signs of repentance for his empire's evil deeds. His death would save countless others. Would Heaven take that into account when it judged her for the evil deed she was about to commit?

She waved towards her handmaidens to clear the floor of the table, cushions, and tea set. After bowing as etiquette demanded, she smoothed out her dress and picked up the scabbard.

The First Consul leaned forward and grabbed her forearm in an iron grip. His huge hand seemed large enough to wrap around her slender wrist twice. He yanked her toward him with a menacing glare, and she thrust her free hand down to keep from falling on her face.

With his other hand, he withdrew one of the swords to half its length. It was a thin, supple blade meant for ceremony and performance. Though it held a sharp edge, it lacked the tensile strength for thrusting.

Her calm façade slipped. He'd never intended to watch the dance. Heavens, he was going to take her now, before she could even attempt to kill him. Fear coursed up her spine like a spear of ice. Her arms and legs froze, ignoring every instinct which screamed to pull away and flee. Her words came out in a stuttered squeak. "Please, First Consul, you are hurting me."

The two handmaidens at the edge of the pavilion shuffled over in their own restrictive gowns, though not even the three of them would be able to overpower the man.

"Would you try to assassinate me?" He drew the sword to its full length and wiggled it with a patronizing grin. "With these toys? You have been eyeing them this whole time."

So he'd suspected a trap, despite her best efforts to disguise it. Kaiya's pulse galloped. Again she spoke, her voice sounding like an eight-year-old version of herself. "Please... I just need these for my performance, the *Dance of Swords*." As if he cared about her plea.

Geros smirked. If he intended to intimidate her, it was working. Rising to his feet while forcibly dragging her up, he pulled her close. Her heart pounded up against his hard belly, while something unpleasantly firm pressed against hers. He brought his face down close. His breath burned hot against her face. "Very well. Dance!" He pushed her arm as he let go of her, and she stumbled back.

Her handmaidens came to her side and supported her by the arms. Her entire body shook of its own accord. Heavens, no one had ever manhandled her like that.

At least she'd been wrong. For whatever reason, he was letting her dance before proceeding with the worst kind of assault. Maybe he had some sick fetish. She had to remain calm, if only to reassure her handmaidens. With a deep breath, she willed her pulse to calm and motioned them off. "It's all right," she said in the Hua tongue. "Return to your places. Play the music on my signal."

Bowing low, they shuffled back. They'd share the same fate if she failed.

Rubbing her sore wrists, Kaiya turned to face Geros. She gestured towards the cushions on the eastern edge of the gazebo. With a few more calming breaths, her voice settled. "Please, First Consul, sit facing the west. That way, the harbor below and the autumn trees above may serve as a backdrop for my dance."

The Bovyan flashed a grin before strutting over to the cushion and dropping into a cross-legged seat. He crossed his arms. "Get on with it."

Kaiya motioned to the handmaidens. One strummed a slow, tremolo tune on the zither, while the other joined in with the plucking of a lute. Borrowing the music's vibrations, she forced her hands to stop trembling. She unsheathed the swords and took up a position in the middle of the floor. Curving her body like an elephant tusk, she held both blades behind her back in her left hand with an underhanded grasp. Even if she couldn't use musical magic against him directly, she could borrow it to lend her strength.

Her heart beat with the resolute rhythm of the zither, while her breath united with the plucks of the lute. With the energy of the duet coursing through her, Kaiya swept her arms up to meet one another and split the swords into either hand. Weightless as clouds, she twirled in an arc.

From this opening, Kaiya continued her dance, transitioning from position to position with graceful precision, orchestrated to the varying tempo of the zither. She never held a pose for more than a split second, making it appear as if she were in constant motion, moving and transitioning as if she were a wisp of smoke, seamlessly transformed by a gently shifting breeze.

Losing herself in the performance, she let the vibrations of the world propel her effortlessly through the dance. She was safe in this state, the fear and humiliation of the First Consul's physical intimidation melting away. The blades became one with her, swirling and shaking in harmony with the music.

In the corner of her eye, the First Consul sat spellbound. Not through the magic of music, but rather through the connection between performer and audience. For a few fleeting seconds, they shared that bond, where both found spiritual calm.

There it was, his humanity. Just a moment prior, he was an evil monster responsible for the misery of millions. One intent on violating her and her handmaidens. Now he was simply a living, breathing man. How could she kill him?

Him or her. He would have no reservations, but that was what separated them. Her window of opportunity was closing quickly. Time to make a decision.

Coming from a culture that considered women to be little more than breeders and objects of carnal pleasure, First Consul Geros Bovyan found Princess Kaiya to be an enigma. On the one hand, he found himself begrudgingly admiring her for her poise and quick wit; yet he despised the girl because she challenged all of his assumptions of the *weaker* sex. More than anything, he wanted to punish her for embarrassing him.

When he had seized her in his grip, he had broken her spirit. It was obvious from the fear in her eyes, the tremble in her hand. From then on, he assumed a bored expression, waiting for her to finish this silly performance so that he could get on with showing her just what a woman was good for in Teleri.

Yet now, as she willowed through her dance, Geros could not contain his respect for her. Though a Bovyan would care little for elegant style or intangible beauty, he found himself appreciating the martial aspects of the dance—the exacting cuts and thrusts, the sweeping parries and redirections, the elusive slips and weaves. The Eye of Solaris, usually reliable in predicting attack vectors with red lines across his vision, mis-identified movements on several occasions. It was so different from the brute power of the Bovyans' fighting style!

And yet, the subtlety so mirrored his own strategy of deception, which had broken the long stalemate with the Eldaeri Kingdoms and opened the Eastern Campaign. It would soon engulf the Northwest as well. Within a few years, it would put the empire on the doorstep of Cathay itself, which would be ripe for the picking because of the spy he had planted there years before. How ironic that these were the lessons he had learned from studying the military, diplomatic, and economic acumen of Princess Kaiya's own ancestor, Wang Xinchang.

The combination of the gentle strumming of the Cathayi musical instrument, the mesmerizing motions, and the warming sensation of the tea lulled him into a state of tranquility. For this brief moment, he forgot all about the world events that he was shaping, and cared little for his own ambitions.

Time seemed to slow. The princess and her swords flattened into the surroundings as if she were the moving subject of an oil painting. The wispy trees in the background gently waved at the clouds drifting above.

She lunged at him with her sword. Sun reflected off the blade, flashing into his eyes and blinding him. Though the Eye of Solaris adjusted, it was all he could do to scuttle backward out of her reach.

The blade tip in her right hand sword cut though the cloth holding his pin in place. With a surgical spin and reverberating shake, the blade sent the pin flying high into the air. The left followed instantly with a precise, shallow insertion of the tip into the center of his sternum. The right blade whirled in a circle, cut through his boot and nicked a spot on his left little toe; and the left arced back to scratch yet another spot on the outer part of his right wrist.

The entire sequence must have taken no longer than a second. The princess ended in a cross-legged squat, her left sword again held behind her back in an underhand grip, and her right blade tip planted shallowly in the divot at the base of his neck.

Time resumed its normal flow as she withdrew her right sword with a smooth flip and passed it behind her back into her left hand to join its twin. Gaze locked with his, she extended her right arm out again. His pin dropped neatly into her outstretched hand.

She'd attacked! Yet all he could do was focus on her elegant pose. Geros could not help but admire her. Had she been born a Bovyan man, perhaps she would be First Consul, soon to be Emperor, instead of him.

Nonetheless, she had disengaged, leaving him uninjured. Nothing hurt. Now to end this charade.

He moved to stand. His muscles refused to respond. He tried to clench a fist, to no avail. What was happening?

Geros looked at the areas her toy sword had struck. They felt numb and heavy, though there did not seem to be much blood. One more attempt to stand. Nothing!

He called out for his guards, but no words came out. Only a hissing whisper.

"I have spared your life today," the princess said as she spun to her feet. "I have closed off four energy centers of your body: your Yin reserves are obstructed and pooling at *Tian-Tu* on your neck and *Dan-Zhong* on your chest; your Yang vitality is locked and stagnant at *Wai-Guan* on your wrist and *Lin-Qi* on your foot."

It was all gibberish, but the effect left no doubt: he was helpless. Devious whore!

Her expression remained grave, devoid of satisfaction. "You will not be able to move, nor speak louder than a whisper, until you are treated by one who understands the *Dao*. There is such a doctor at our compound's temple. I suggest you make use of his services by sunrise tomorrow, or your injury shall likely be permanent."

Lying helpless, Geros envisioned all of his well-laid plans slipping from his grasp. This visit to the Northwest should have cemented his place in Teleri lore. The edict he had forced through the Directori, with pressure from the Keepers of the Shrine of Geros, would have crowned him First Emperor. These were now meaningless. He was an invalid, spared by the mercy of a girl.

"Treacherous bitch!" he croaked. "You had better kill me now, or else I will surely hunt you down and force you into a life of misery, fear, and humiliation. I shall make the crushing of Cathay my sole reason for living."

She shifted back a step, lips quivering and eyes wide. Her knuckles whitened around the sword hilt. Yes—he had intimidated her, sown the seeds of fear in her. Perhaps that would be the final pleasure he would enjoy in this life.

As quickly as it came, her fearful expression flickered away, replaced by a pity that only infuriated him more. "Until you cherish life, starting with your own, you will never truly find inner peace." Picking up the scabbards, she sheathed her weapons and motioned for her handmaidens. "Leave it all, we must make haste."

They walked past him, beyond his line of sight. Unable to turn his head, he lay stranded on silken cushions. Hatred stewed inside him, roaring louder than the Cathayi musket volleys from the slope.

CHAPTER 20:

Escape from Iksuvius

Shouts and jingling armor greeted Kaiya as she emerged from the pavilion. Her imperial guards were deployed in three ranks halfway up the hill, standing between her and the advancing Teleri phalanx. Spears protruded between the enemy's shields as they approached, trampling down the grass as they came.

She might not have an eye for strategy, but it was clear: the wider Teleri line could envelop her own men.

The imperial guard were all armed with muskets, which had been hidden in her palanquin. *Her* idea.

"Fire!" General Zheng's command was answered with a rumble of musket fire from the first rank. The volley tore through the wall of shields and into the Teleri line. Several gaps opened as men fell with grunts and screams. Kaiya shuddered, memories of her few brushes with combat roiling her stomach.

With the precision of a dwarf water clock, the Bovyans in the rear line lifted their spears. Wherever there was a hole, a soldier stepped forward to fill it, while several men on either side of the front line fell back to the back line. They reset their spears. Some injured men rose to form a reserve in the rear. Astoundingly, the wall's advance continued during the entire position shift.

At the same time, the front line of Hua soldiers stood and retreated to the rear to reload while the second rank knelt and took aim. On General Zheng's command, they unleashed another volley and stepped to the rear. Kaiya's heart raced. Would the imperial guard be able to stop the Bovyan advance? Hundreds of armies had fallen to their charge.

The continuous barrage of musket fire took its toll. The Bovyan ranks began to falter as the injured men slowed their approach. Smoke and the stench of gunpowder hung in the air. Bodies littered the ground. In just two minutes, half the soldiers lay dead or incapacitated.

A Teleri officer bellowed the order to charge. The Bovyans broke rank and surged forward. Kaiya's hands ran cold and clammy.

General Zheng's voice carried over the din as he raised his *dao*. "Fire and form a single bow!"

Kaiya watched in dread fascination. The first rank of imperial guards unleashed a final volley and fanned out into a half-ellipse. The third rank followed them as they formed a single curved line, with the second rank occupying the center as they finished reloading.

"Take aim!" General Zheng's voice boomed, and all the imperial guards lowered their rifles. As far as Kaiya could tell, only a third held loaded weapons.

The Teleri officer barked out a command. The remaining Bovyans halted their advance and formed up into a tight square, shields facing outward. Perhaps only twenty remained within the main group, while others littered the blood-soaked hillside. Kaiya blew out a breath. General Zheng's bluff had worked.

He now stepped to the head of his troops. "Brave Teleri soldiers, you are hopelessly outnumbered and outgunned. Do not needlessly waste your lives. Surely we will meet on the battlefield again so that you might have a chance to avenge your brothers."

The spears jutted out from the defensive square, and the formation resumed its advance, albeit more slowly. Even if General Zheng's trickery had deceived them, apparently they were willing to walk into certain death. Maybe not so certain, unless the imperial guards could reload.

Kaiya pushed through her men, fighting the rising nausea from the sight of blood and gore. She pointed back to the gazebo. "The First Consul lies at the top of the Heights, helpless and dying. If you die here, on this hill, he will certainly perish as well. Surrender now, and we will send someone who can heal him. You have my word."

A Teleri officer stepped forward, spear held aloft. "The First Consul would rather die than to live at your mercy."

Kaiya closed her eyes and listened. His voice carried across the hill, its strong resonance picked up by the steadfast beating of his men's hearts. Behind her, the imperial guards' heart rates stuttered. They might win with superior numbers, but not without serious casualties. Gripping the ground with her toes through her slippers, she channeled the world's resolute pulse. Modulating her voice to interfere with the frequencies of the Bovyans' heartbeats, she sang her command: "Surrender."

The Teleri line wavered. The officer lowered his spear. "Stand down. Drop your arms."

Kaiya's shoulders sagged as she let out another sigh. In the three centuries since the Bovyans appearance in Tivaralan, had any ever laid down their spears or shields?

General Zheng turned to her. "*Dian-xia*, this is the first time the Teleri have seen our battlefield tactics. Though it pains my honor as a soldier, I recommend that we execute them to the man so that none can speak of it."

Eyes wide, Kaiya shook her head. "I gave my word."

"You gave your word to send someone to heal the First Consul." He stared at her feet.

If they resorted to such technicalities, they'd be no better than the Teleri. Kaiya shook her head. "You will spare them. Let them take their wounded to the Heights, and tie the able-bodied to the columns so they cannot follow us."

"That will take time."

Kaiya looked up at the Iridescent Moon. Her sense of morality clashed with her instinct for self-preservation. "Then hurry."

On the general's orders, the imperial guards helped the disarmed soldiers bring their wounded to the top of the Heights to join their Consul. Uninjured Bovyans were tied to the columns, while the imperial guards tended to the wounded. Kaiya helped over the protests of her men since, as General Zheng had said, valuable time was slipping away. It was not until twenty minutes later, halfway between the Iridescent Moon's mid- and fourth crescents, that the procession was ready to return to the Old City.

Kaiya now rode in the palanquin, struggling in the tight confines to strip off her gown. Had they really hidden a hundred muskets in here? Her fingers trembled as she wrapped a broad cloth around her bosom several times to flatten it out as best she could. Lastly, she squirmed into the simple brown robes of the Hua monks who wandered the lands.

The light filtering in through the palanquin windows darkened. Her soldiers' footsteps echoed on stone floors. They must have entered the long tunnel through the northern gate. Shouts erupted from up ahead.

Then the procession ground to a halt.

Jie looked up at the ninety-foot watchtower above the northern gatehouse. She had snuck up there one afternoon and enjoyed the spectacular view of the northern coast. Yet today, it cast a shadow over the bustling northern marketplace.

She shivered and returned to the task at hand, wondering why the princess' procession had not yet arrived.

Jie had come at dawn to set up a stand selling pork buns, right by the side of the main road. It provided a good line of sight into the gatehouse tunnel, where Tian waited, dressed as a wandering monk.

The Nothori people apparently had little interest in pork buns, a favorite among the Hua. Even if hawking fattening snacks wasn't her real purpose in being there, the slow business was disappointing. It did, however, give her plenty of time to glance over at Tian. Once the princess had safely boarded the *Golden Phoenix* and he returned to the embassy, they'd have plenty of time to sort out whatever it was between them. Her heart fluttered.

They had to get the princess on the ship first, though, which meant focusing on the task at hand. Just after giving a repeat customer a generous deal, Jie's ears perked. The boots of marching men approached. At last! They were behind schedule. She craned her neck to get a clear line of sight on Tian.

There was his signal. Jie grabbed ahold of a citizen who had the misfortune of passing by at the wrong moment. Who cared if he had little interest in pork buns? "You! Give it back! That's eight copper *kroon*."

"What? What are you talking about?"

Jie shoved him. "The pork bun. You took one of my pork buns!"

The man stepped back, hands raised. "I didn't. I wouldn't eat that junk anyway! And it's not worth eight coppers."

Bystanders gathered around and pointed, while Iksuvi soldiers tried to clear the way.

Jie only argued louder. She deftly kicked out the legs of her stand, sending pork buns rolling into the road. Street urchins scrambled forward to capture the delicious prizes.

General Zheng marched to the head of the procession, now stalled by Jie's show, to snarl at her in the Arkothi tongue. "Clear the road, woman! Your princess is passing through."

Jie cursed him and all of his ancestors with Arkothi vulgarities that surpassed the limitation of Hua's sterile language. A large crowd pushed forward to watch, pointing and laughing at the fracas.

Jie smiled. Mission accomplished. The Teleri Nightblade she'd been eyeing had missed the exchange.

Tian had waited in the northern gate tunnel with a real Hua monk, begging for alms as people passed. Both wore long, round straw hats whose brims sank down to eye level, though Tian's long hair made it difficult to secure. Besides a walking staff, the only other weapon he carried was a concealed dagger and several throwing *biao*.

Travelers were sparse, donations even sparser. If he had to wait much longer in the musty chill, he'd catch a cold. Not to mention the princess might not make her ship. She was already an hour behind schedule.

At last, her procession came through. It stopped and she stepped out of the palanquin. The monk handed her his hat, revealing his bald head. She put it on, tilting it forward so that her face was slightly covered. All performed with admirable precision.

When she'd finished stuffing her hair in the cone, she placed a letter in his hand. "Have this delivered to the ambassador immediately."

The monk nodded as he bent into the palanquin. Tian looked through the tunnel, into the city.

Just in time. Up ahead, the Iksuvi soldiers had restored order. With loud shouts and a little jostling, they cleared a path through the streets and the procession continued. As the crowds dispersed, Tian guided Kaiya through the northern gate and into the city.

He looked up at the Iridescent Moon, already waxing to its fourth crescent. They were running well behind schedule. Not a word passed between them as they walked toward the eastern gate, briskly heading south along the main road that ran from the northern gate to the southern gate. They turned east on a ring road that bypassed the city center and intersected with the main east-west road.

Tian stole glances at the handful of people they passed along the way. They didn't pick up any followers; at least this part of the plan was working. Not only that, they were making up for lost time. They would make it.

Waiting at the intersection of the ring road and the east-west road were the princess' five most senior guards, all dressed as monks: Chen Xin, the leader, followed by Zhao Yue, Ma Jun, Li Wei, and Xu Zhan. They dropped to a knee, right fists to the ground.

Unbelievable. Eyes darting left and right, Tian beckoned them to their feet. Leave it to an imperial guard to expose their disguise. Luckily, the streets were nearly deserted.

Chen Xin bowed his head. "There are rumors that the Teleri western army is about to pass through Aremarela. If it is true, they must have moved their timetable up."

Tian shook his head. They couldn't risk crossing the bridge into Teleri and running into an army. Picturing the area in his head, he drew up a new plan. "We pass through the southern gate. There's a fishing village on the Iksuvi side of the river. About fifteen *li* south. Not far from Aremarela on the opposite bank. We can commandeer a fishing boat. Then row back up."

Xu Zhan growled. "We need to meet up with the stablemaster, who is waiting with horses outside of the eastern gate." Always pugnacious, Xu would likely prefer to test his sword against the entire Teleri division instead of running away from them.

Li Wei counted on his fingers. "It will take too long to row from the village to Aremarela. Our horses wouldn't be fast enough to ride from the eastern gate to the southern gate, and then down to the village anyway." If there was anyone who expected anything and everything to go wrong, it was him. The unforeseen change only validated his bleak outlook on life.

The princess sighed. "Your plan has failed, Zheng Tian. We should just head back to the safety of the embassy."

Tian's mind ran calculations. "We can't hole up in the embassy indefinitely. The Teleri will lay siege. We must press on with this plan. Let's hasten to the Kanin Embassy. They're no friends of the Teleri. And the ambassador was impressed by the princess. If they loan us some of their horses, we can make it."

Ma Jun, the opposite of his best friend Li, was always optimistic. "*Dian-xia*, the idea is sound. We will make it."

All attention turned to the princess.

"We will never make it in time." Li Wei shook his head.

Tian pursed his lips. It was a sound plan. It would work.

The princess' eyes searched his. "Very well. To the Kanin embassy."

The Kanin compound was located just off of the ring road, in the southeast section of the Old City. It took fifteen minutes, and they arrived as the Iridescent Moon waxed halfway between its fourth and fifth crescents. Still more than enough time.

Except for the gate guards doubting that the ragged monk before their eyes was the Princess of Cathay. She removed her hat and shook out her hair, and the gaping guards allowed them entry. Tian glanced back at the handful of passersby. Hopefully, no one had seen her.

They were brought to a comfortable receiving room, where Tian planted himself by a window. The floors were uncarpeted stone, and oil paintings of scenes from the Kanin plains hung on the walls. The princess examined the portrait of their rugged king, whose likeness gazed over the entire room.

Tian fidgeted. Zhuyue was passing its fifth crescent. This was taking too long. Perhaps Ambassador Manuwaya had already started drinking.

The old man shuffled in with a red face and a wide smile. Tian gritted his teeth. Suspicions confirmed.

"Welcome, welcome!" the ambassador said. "We are honored by your visit. Though you are certainly curiously dressed. To what do I owe this pleasure?"

The princess stood up and bowed. "Ambassador, I have some important information, and also a humble request of your great kingdom. The Teleri Empire will be invading Iksuvius with overwhelming force tonight, while the Kingdom of Lietuvi will cross the southern border in support. Iksuvi's days are numbered."

Ambassador Manuwaya stared at her, his eyes shifting to Tian.

Tian nodded. Of course the ambassador would trust him. They'd worked together many times. Now if only the princess would hurry up with that humble request.

"In addition," she said, "The Teleri First Consul is plotting to take me hostage, and plans for my escape have run into unforeseen obstacles. I beg you to please provide us with horses, since your great steeds are the only ones fast enough to reach our rendezvous point in time."

The ambassador nodded his head. "Of course, of course, my dear. We certainly cannot allow a precious jewel like you to fall into the hands of the Teleri! No telling what demands they will make of your father."

Tian shuffled on his feet. The First Consul probably had other plans for the princess. The leverage he wanted had little to do with politics.

The princess bowed at the waist. "I will never forget this. When I reach the safety of Cathay, I will ask my father to send me personally to Kanin to deliver a set of our finest teacups. I extend my deepest thanks and appreciation for your help."

The ambassador provided them with seven horses. The Hua packed away their monks' clothes, then donned black-lacquered leather jerkins and painted red Kanin symbols on their face. Armed with borrowed cavalry sabers, lances, and short bows, they would hopefully pass as a Kanin patrol.

It helped that the Hua and Kanin people looked similar to the untrained eye. Tian's were not untrained, however—to him, each difference was glaring as a noon sun. Someone would notice. And the Iridescent Moon had already waxed past its fifth crescent. Almost no margin of error.

"It is not too late to turn back to the embassy," Li Wei said.

Tian eyed his enormous horse, famed for its speed. "It's not too late to make it, either." Even with the time wasted at the Kanin embassy.

CHAPTER 21:

Personality Clashes

Kaiya's ears rang from the constant pounding of horse hooves on the paved highway. In fact, her entire body vibrated after an hour of hard riding. Their Kanin guide looked none the worse for wear, unlike her tired guards. He'd had to stop several times to allow them to catch up.

She cast a jealous eye at him as the journal of the famous Minister Deng Liansu came to mind.

In all my travels, I was aided by the Kanin and their thoroughbreds. Though trapped between the Ayuri and Arkothi empires, the Kanin empire has maintained its nominal independence through a series of shrewd, if brazen, switches of allegiance. None of Tivara's people can raise the horse like they, born in the saddle, learning to ride before they walk. A Kanin, it is said, stands on his own four feet.

Wherever this ride ended, she probably wouldn't be able to stand on *two* feet.

Despite Tian's concerns and Li Wei's pessimism, they didn't encounter any problems, either in the city or the fields and woods on the way to the village. A windswept wooden sign at the outskirts named the community as *Gaukaimos*. Dirt roads crisscrossed the paved highway, lined by some hundred squat homes with thatched roofs.

Kaiya wrinkled her nose. From what Tian had told her on the way, the locals farmed mollusks and fished for a living. The stink of shellfish left little doubt of that.

When they came to a stone bridge over a stream, Kaiya looked up. Zhuyue was waxing to half-crescent. Her hands ached from gripping the reins so tightly, and her heart raced. There was very little time left.

Tian led them down a dirt road to a stone-lined embankment. The top, some six feet above the water, gave a commanding view of the river. On the banks, children played and collected shells. Their laughter carried over the whisper of small waves lapping against the shore. Numerous boat landings jutted into the channel.

Kaiya gasped. Plenty of fishing boats plied the waters, but none were moored to the docks. No way to cross the river to Aremarela. Maybe there was a boat within earshot. She scanned up and down the river.

There, maybe five *li* southeast in Aremarela, the *Golden Phoenix* lifted anchor. With sails down and oars extended, it began heading downriver. Towards them! Sticking to the deep channel which cut unseen through the middle of the river, the ship's course would take it right by. Maybe more than a *li* away from them, and closer to the Teleri shore, but surely the captain would send a boat out.

Without waiting for her permission, Tian and her guards dismounted and ran down the closest dock. Kaiya's heart soared, though she kept her demeanor calm as she followed. As the *Golden Phoenix* approached, they waved and yelled. Someone onboard would just have to see—

Musket fire cracked, echoing across the water. Smoke rose from the ship. Another volley. Who were they shooting at?

Tian patted at his leather jerkin, then withdrew a spyglass. He brought it to his eye, but then lowered the instrument and examined it. He shook his head. "Broken lens."

Broken lens? How could the supposedly brilliant planner not check his equipment? Kaiya looked back towards the ship, now speeding northward. "Can the horses swim out?"

Their guide raised a hand. "No; even our best thoroughbreds would not make it before your ship passed."

"With the tide coming in," Tian said, "the *Phoenix* would be stranded on the river for six hours. By then, every Bovyan within fifty-two *li* will know of your attack on the First Consul. The captain has no choice. He has to escape to open seas. And use the last rays of sun to help navigate the deep channel."

Li Wei threw his arms up. "I told you this wouldn't work. Now they know we are here."

"No," Tian said. "Not necessarily. The *Golden Phoenix* fired at the Teleri side of the river. It was anchored at a Teleri town. They would assume the princess was there. If not already on the ship."

Maybe. Still, Kaiya watched in despair as her means of escape disappeared north through the river, racing against time. For now, they were stuck in this backwater, fetid village, caught between a city in turmoil and the contingent of altivorcs approaching it.

Sore all over, she sighed. They'd wasted too much time on the Heights, a half hour that could've been used to flee. Her decision. Her fault. A lone tear trickled down her cheek. She wiped it away, the coarse sleeve of the Kanin tunic scouring her skin.

It wouldn't do to let her retainers see her like this. Heavens, she'd confronted Avarax without melting into a quivering mass of tears. Straightening her back, she composed herself before facing them.

"Be strong, *Dian-xia*." Tian must have seen her crying. His encouraging tone rang with patronization, and his smile was forced. *Be strong.* Easy for him to say. *She* was the one who'd almost been violated, just three hours before. Who still faced that risk. The memory of the First Consul pressing against her sent a shudder through her body.

Tian continued, inconsiderate and undeterred, "We should be safe here. For now. There was an inn. Near the entrance to the village. Let us rest there. Think of a new plan. At least there...we will avoid the chaos in Iksuvius tonight."

Kaiya bit her lower lip, fighting back more tears. Oh, to be safely home, where the food wouldn't make her sick. Out of the reach of a Bovyan tyrant who planned to take a very personal revenge on her. Tian couldn't understand. At least as a child, he would have tried.

She nodded at his suggestion nonetheless. She couldn't summon a dignified tone, and her voice sounded childlike in her ears. "Lead the way to the inn."

The Kanin Rider swept his hand out from his heart. "I will take your leave and return to the city. Do you wish me to bring any message to the ambassador?"

She forced a brittle smile. "Please convey my gratitude to him."

"May the wind ever be at your back, Princess." Waving his hand out in an arc, he spurred his horse north at full gallop.

With Tian leading, they rode their borrowed horses towards the inn. Their motley crew attracted curious looks. They arrived as the sun winked out over the horizon.

In the fading light, the inn appeared to be a decent size—the only two-story building in the village thus far—and made of wood planks that had weathered years of brackish winds. A faded sign hung above the door: *The Hard Shell.* The Arkothi words were painted in a simple hand below brightly colored images of various crustaceans and mollusks.

Kaiya fought back the rebellion in her stomach. The name might refer to the food or the quality of bedding. Maybe both. Not much different from being aboard the *Golden Phoenix*, really, except for the danger of being captured and raped. Her insides twisted again. This danger... she'd invited it by doing the right thing and sparing Geros and his men. It was too unfair.

A second look at the sign evoked another obvious shudder, her vulnerability on display. She lifted her chin and hid fragility behind stubborn conceit. "I can't stay *there*. There has to somewhere else."

"*Dian-xia*. It's dark now." Tian shook his head, his tone reminiscent of a nursemaid. "The closest inn is back in the city. This will have to do."

Her shoulders trembled against her attempts to square them and suppress the sobs wracking her body. She let a cascade of hair hide her weakness.

Tian dismounted and came to her, extending his hand. "Please. Let's go in. Rest a while." His short sentences, so endearing as a youth, now sounded like a rebuke.

Refusing his hand, she clasped the reins tightly and turned to look down in the other direction. There had to be another option. Keep moving, find somewhere to hide. Just not here.

He seized her wrist firmly and tugged.

The impudence! Kaiya resisted and tried to withdraw her hand. Her despair transformed into anger, and she found her voice. "Guards!"

It was an unequivocal order, yet the five imperial guards looked among each other without moving from their places. Finally, Chen Xin bowed his head and his juniors followed suit. She was alone in this battle of wills.

"Please," Tian said.

A little late for a request. She'd already lost face. She pulled back away from him.

Tian's growl was nothing like his childhood sweetness, and he gave her a push. The nerve! She leaned back towards him so as not to fall off the horse. A sudden pain bloomed in her wrist as he twisted it and caused her to lurch sideways. With a sharp gasp of protest, she tumbled into his arms. He dumped her unceremoniously on her feet and pulled her toward the door of the inn.

It was worse than when the First Consul had grabbed her. At least then, it'd been an enemy.

At least then, her handmaidens had supported her. Now, even the imperial guards refused to intervene.

Humiliated and defeated, she surrendered and allowed Tian to drag her toward the inn. Hair curtained her face as she hung her head, but anyone could tell she was crying from the unconstrained sobs. So much for maintaining a dignified façade.

At least he could be less rude. If he only had a fraction of chivalry, like his sophisticated, charming brother.

Tian motioned toward the guards. "You four come with us. Don't show the princess any extra attention. Xu Zhan, you stable the horses. Keep guard outside the main entrance. One of us will relieve you. Soon."

The stench of steaming shellfish assaulted her nose as soon as the door opened. Her stomach churned. Kaiya covered her mouth.

The Hard Shell, despite its weathered exterior, was actually quite comfortable on the inside. About twenty round tables, each surrounded by several empty chairs, occupied the spacious main room. Covered in soot, a large unlit hearth stood at the far end. A balding barkeep paced behind the smooth bar, drying off tankards and ignoring the four locals who sat there. While they laughed over mugs of red wheat beer and shared fish stories, a fifth man folded his arms on the bar and cradled his head face-down.

Kaiya didn't resist as Tian pulled her to a table close to the hearth. He motioned her to a chair so that her back faced most of the room, while he plopped down across from her. The four guards took up other chairs, two on either side of her.

"Let's eat something," Tian said. "I need to think."

He should have thought things through before. Kaiya gnawed on her lip.

An uncomfortable silence hung over the table until a barmaid came and listed what was on the menu for that night. Kaiya's skin prickled. All the main dishes included some sort of shellfish.

Without even asking her, Tian ordered a cheap clam dish and potatoes for each of them. She didn't have the energy to protest. Only Zhao Yue, who loved to eat, seemed pleased by the choice.

She beckoned the barmaid over. "Please bring a quill, ink, and paper."

The server shrugged. "Will you be staying the night?"

Tian's eyes flicked toward the bar for a second before turning back. He nodded. "What's available?" His gaze shifted back to the bar.

Kaiya focused her hearing in that direction, picking out the deep, slow breathing of one of the men. He was pretending to be asleep.

The barmaid's screechy voice interrupted her concentration. "We have two small singles, four doubles, and three large common rooms that sleep eight."

The jingle of Tian's pouch under the table sang of copper coins. There was disappointment in his voice. "We will take seven beds. In a common room."

Share a room with men? How could the son of a prominent family be so inconsiderate and uncultured? That, after he treated her like a child and ordered food for her. And he'd told her guards to ignore her. Who was *he* to punish *her*? She shot Tian a furious scowl.

He returned it with an aloof rise of his eyebrow, and then turned away.

That was too much. "Young Lord Zheng—"

Tian's livid glare bore into her, and his hand signal made it clear that she was not to talk.

Heat flared in her cheeks. Who was the princess, and who was the half-rate spy?

The barmaid grinned at them, muttering "lover's quarrel" under her breath. She thrust a charcoal pencil into Kaiya's hands. "Sorry, we don't have a quill or ink down here, though there should be one in the room."

Kaiya glowered at Chen Xin, sure that he would understand her silent order. *Go get the writing instruments, or there will be hell to pay later.*

Chen Xin looked from her to Tian and back before standing, bowing his head, and hurrying towards the steps.

Kaiya turned her head to watch him go. The sleeping man at the bar shifted on his stool.

An awkward silence hung over the table. Kaiya crossed her arms and turned her head to the side, while Tian leaned back in his chair and stared at the table. She would glance back at him, only to find his eyes on her, and jerk her head back.

Chen Xin returned and interrupted their battle of wills, placing a quill and inkwell in front of her with a bow of his head. His voice trembled. "There was no paper."

It was all she could do to keep from throwing her hands in the air. With a sigh, Kaiya withdrew the love letter from the dashing lord from her tunic.

Tian couldn't believe that this petulant girl had once been a stately and confident princess. When future historians extolled the legendary charmer of dragons, he hoped his own ancestors would be around to tell his side of the story.

The letter could have been an imperial heirloom, the way she gazed at it. She unfolded the rice paper coversheet, with her name written in a confident script. Flamboyant even. Whoever penned it was undoubtedly ambitious and vain.

Brow furrowing, she smoothed out the cover sheet and jotted a long letter in Hua script. She folded it in half twice. On the back, she signed her given name in lieu of the stone name chops that had been sent ahead on the *Golden Phoenix*. On the front, she crossed out her name and wrote *Ambassador Wu*.

She then unfolded the letter. As her eyes roved over it, a smile tugged at her lips. With a deep breath, she closed her eyes, and then tore it in half. On the back, she wrote another letter in Arkothi print. She folded it in half twice, and then wrote a second message on the other half. Folding it in half twice, she looked up. And scowled at him.

Tian cast his gaze down. Whatever she was up to, it was bound to get them in trouble.

She turned to Chen Xin and proffered the first letter. "After you finish eating, return to Iksuvius and deliver this letter to Ambassador Wu."

Chen Xin received it in two hands, head bowed until Tian cleared his throat.

The princess snorted and held up the second letter. "Take this to the Lietuvi embassy at first light tomorrow, and deliver it into the hands of King Arvydas. After he reads it, he will hopefully ask you to bring him here. Do so, unless you suspect treachery."

She then showed him the third letter. "If the king refuses to see you, then allow yourself to be caught by the Teleri with this letter. If you are caught before delivering the messages, do everything necessary to destroy the letter to the King of Lietuvi first, then Ambassador Wu's next; but make it seem that you are trying to destroy the third letter without actually doing so."

Bowing his head, Chen Xin received the three letters in two hands.

Still acting like an imperial guard! Surely even the yokels would find it amiss. Tian glanced at the bar, where the patrons ignored them. Thank the Heavens. Still, she was sending a soldier to do a spy's job.

Their food came. He and the guards virtually inhaled it, all propriety forgotten after a long, grueling day. The princess just nibbled at the potatoes.

More people entered and joined the party at the bar. At least some people here were enjoying themselves.

Chen Xin wiped his mouth and took his leave. Tian stood, too. There was no point in escalating tensions with her, but his instincts screamed to read the content of those letters.

"I will relieve Xu Zhan." Tian followed Chen Xin out. He quickly caught up. "Let me see the messages."

Chen Xin hesitated, his uncertainty so unlike the brash young imperial guard who'd brought his ten-year-old self before the *Tianzi* a decade before.

Tian extended his hand. "This is a matter of security. The princess might endanger herself.

And in any case...she didn't seal them." Chen Xin probably wasn't so gullible as to believe such flimsy reasoning, but it had been worth a try.

"The princess didn't have anything to seal them with...but although I hate to say it, you are the more level-headed right now." Chen Xin handed Tian the letters and continued towards the stables.

Tian scanned quickly through the letter to Ambassador Wu, picking out the key points without actually reading it in its entirety.

... did not succeed in boarding Golden Phoenix... make sure sets sail for Hua immediately... ensure safety of [obscure character for Iksuvi] queen... did not succeed in killing First Consul... will seek revenge on our country... Teleri probably believe I am in compound, use to your advantage, but do not sacrifice yourselves needlessly... [obscure character for Kanin] has provided aid, please extend thanks... am sending a message [obscure character for Lietuvi] king asking to meet... not revealing current location in case messenger intercepted... am entrusting Zheng Tian to protect me... will send word from safe location... inform the Tianzi.

A smile pulled unbidden on Tian's lips. She might be acting like a child, but the princess still had a clear head. She told enough without giving away too much, and it did seem she understood he was trying to protect her. But what about the letter to Lietuvi, who was complicit in the events that would unfold tonight? She could get herself in trouble with it. He folded up the first letter and unfolded the letter to the King of Lietuvi.

Your Royal Highness, King Arvydas of Lietuvi:

By now, you have probably heard that Cathay and Teleri are at war. We know that you have conspired with Teleri to occupy and annex the Kingdom of Iksuvi, and are therefore an ally of our enemy. However, Cathay and Lietuvi are not at war with each other, and it may be that we share a common foe. We also have information that may make you reconsider your agreement with the Teleri Empire. Please meet with me tomorrow morning at the fourth waning crescent, at a location that you will be led to by my messenger. The city should be in pitched battle in the east, leaving our position unguarded."

Princess Kaiya Wang of the Empire of Cathay.

Tian nodded. There was no denying her reasoning. She kept the door open to dividing the Teleri and Lietuvi alliance, thereby helping to protect Iksuvi. It might also provide a possible escape route for them. Finally, he read the third letter, the one which Chen Xin should reveal in the event he was captured:

Your Royal Highness, King Arvydas of Lietuvi:

As per our arrangement, we will be supporting your alliance with Iksuvi, which will ultimately envelop the Teleri western army. We have five thousand musketmen and twenty warships which will be sailing up the Alto River and landing at Altogrina. With this defeat, the Teleri Empire will lose its foothold in the Nothori region.

Princess Kaiya Wang of the Empire of Cathay

Tian blew out a breath. She'd planned better than him, especially with the instructions she gave Chen. If all went perfectly as she planned, then the young Lietuvi king would meet with her here. The princess would presumably tell him of the deal between the Teleri Empire, altivorcs, and Rotuvi. They would make a new friend.

However, if Chen Xin was caught, it would make it seem that Lietuvi was in collusion with Cathay and Iksuvi against Teleri, and would at the very least cast suspicion on their alliance, if not completely divide them. Tian had started to fold up the letters when he again noticed the writing on the back.

The letter to the princess: it bore the red chop mark of Zheng Ming—his first brother and heir to his home province of Dongmen.

Tian had once idolized his brother, but it had been ten years since they last met. As a first son, Zheng Ming would most likely be married to the daughter of an important family. He'd been trained as one of the few remaining cavalry officers in Hua. His skill at mounted archery had gained him fame during the annual Spring Festival tournaments held in Hua. Flamboyant and charming, he was well known for his quick wit and oratory skills. A perfect match for the princess.

And this was a personal letter. It had nothing to do with either national security or the princess' safety. There was no need to know about her personal matters. Tian sighed. It was none of his business. He began to fold the letters back up and return them to Chen Xin in the stables.

Then, unable to contain his curiosity, he put the two pieces together and read.

CHAPTER 22:

Unexpected Visitors

Lying helpless on Iksuvius Heights, all Geros could do was watch the Iridescent Moon pass through two phases. His muscles tightened and joints locked up more and more as time dragged on. Around him, his soldiers shuffled and struggled to loosen their bindings, to no avail. He would miss out on leading his invading army tonight. Worse, he might never move or speak again, cursed to live out his few remaining years as an invalid.

Geros was about to give up all hope when a young Cathayi man dressed in yellow-and-red robes reached the top of the Heights. He wiped sweat off his forehead and bowed deeply. When he spoke, his accent was thick. "Your Eminence, my princess sent me to care for you."

Care for him! The thought of being indebted to her was demeaning. Geros opened his mouth, but only a croak escaped. He had been able to speak in a whisper right after the girl ambushed him. His condition must have since deteriorated.

The priest bowed, before kneeling down to examine his wounds. "The princess did this to you?"

Yes! The bitch! That priest wouldn't be grinning like that once Geros cut his head off and stuffed it on a pike. He did his best to nod, but his head weighed more than a warhammer.

The Cathayi placed three fingers on Geros' wrist. His brow furrowed. "Show me your tongue."

His tongue felt like sand and barely moved. What could this priest do to undo the princess' craven attack?

"The princess has blocked the flow of your life energy. I will restore it." The priest withdrew several thin needles from a silk brocade box, and without ceremony inserted them in Geros' arms and legs. Each spot felt like a jolt of lightning racing up his limbs and into his core. The heaviness immediately diminished.

"Your constitution is strong. You will make a full recovery. Rest for now." The man turned toward the wounded Bovyans and began examining and adjusting their bandages. In some, he inserted more thin needles.

While the Cathayi worked, Geros' energy gathered, a drip at first, then a trickle. Relief washed over him. He would not be crippled for the rest of his life. Furthermore, despite this setback today, he could still move forward with his plans tonight.

He rose and shook out his limbs. Though languid, at least the feeling had returned to his hands and feet. In three steps, he bounded over to the priest and seized him by the throat. The effort nearly winded him. "Where is the princess now?"

The priest's eyes rounded and his voice choked. "Back. At. The. Embassy..."

Geros released him, shoving him back. He hid his wheeze for air, lest his men see him weak.

"You saved my life today, and for that, I will spare yours. I suggest you flee the city now, because I will raze your embassy and kill everyone there."

The priest's face blanched, and he scuttled backward with bobbing bows. When he reached the edge of the pavilion, he turned around and fled in a flash of red and yellow.

Geros snorted derisively as the man escaped. Coward. Just like the princess and the rest of her ilk.

With no blades immediately available, he fumbled at untying his aide-de-campe. "Go to headquarters. Convey my order to surround the Cathayi embassy and kill any man who tries to leave."

In the fading sunlight, Jie counted the Teleri soldiers amassing around the embassy walls. Inside the compound, two hundred musketmen watched from the battlements, while imperial guards armed with repeating crossbows deployed behind a line of shields at the main gate.

Only a skeleton staff remained—just enough to give the guise that the princess was still there. The ambassador had ordered all non-essential personnel to flee, both for their own safety and also to reduce the number of mouths to feed in the event of a protracted siege. With the princess disguised as a wandering monk somewhere in the city, the temple priests had been sent out as decoys.

Jie returned to the main residence foyer. There, Ambassador Wu paced, with sweat trickling down his head.

"Godfather, you summoned?"

He nodded. "Little Jie, I know your primary responsibility is to the princess and not to the embassy. However, I need your help now. I am going to meet with a Teleri general who waits outside the main gate. Accompany me as I listen to his demands, see what you can pick up. Of course,

we must maintain the deception that the princess is here."

Jie bowed her head. "As you command."

She followed a step behind him as he trudged towards the main gate, his slow pace seeming even more labored than usual. Yet he held his head high, like the captain of a sinking ship, the honor of his two decades of service in Iksuvius radiating in his dignified expression.

The imperial guard parted, opening a path for the two to walk. Up ahead, General Marius stood cross-armed on the other side of the gate, flanked by two gigantic officers. His eyes widened as he caught sight of her. Having shed a court gown in favor of utility clothes that she could fight in, Jie grinned at his shock. He probably still believed they'd slept together the night before.

Marius composed himself before they arrived at the gate, stiffening in his stance. "Ambassador Wu, the First Consul demands that you surrender the embassy and turn Princess Kaiya Wang over to us."

Ambassador Wu smiled grimly. "You know what our answer will be. You also know that your shields and armor cannot stop our firepowder. We have stores to last us a year."

"And what happens after a year, Ambassador? The First Consul is patient."

Ambassador Wu laughed. "Do you think the Son of Heaven will stand for you holding his beloved daughter hostage? Within a couple of months, expect an armada of warships on your coast with a flight of phoenixes ready to extract her."

Jie sucked on her lower lip. Hopefully, Marius would believe the bluff. Although Hua kept a handful of lesser phoenixes in the imperial aviary, they had limited endurance and range, and only flew during the New Year's parade. The highly sensitive birds would never survive a trip by sea.

Marius swept his arms outward. "We will flood the harbor with fire and fill the sky with enough crossbow bolts to blot out the sun."

"Then it looks like our negotiations have reached an impasse." Ambassador Wu bowed his head.

"I suggest you reconsider. I will give you until dawn." Marius cast Jie one last look, his eyes round and wounded. Was it a sense of betrayal? Or pity? Or even concern? It was hard to tell in the twilight, where her elf vision didn't work.

As he turned around, she caught a glimpse of his shadow shifting out of sync with his movement.

It was a Teleri Nightblade. And unlike the young men who failed to infiltrate the embassy, this one was very skilled. By the time she focused on the area, he was gone.

CHAPTER 23:

A Chance Meeting

Dearest Kaiya,

I never knew what it meant to be truly alive before I met you. During your diplomatic mission to Vyara City, when we were separated for a month, I felt so empty that the finest food and wine seemed flavorless, the most melodious music sounded flat, the most radiant painting colorless.

I promised I would always follow you and protect you, and it pains me that duties in my province prevent me from joining you on your trip to the Nothori lands. Not just because I must break my promise, but because you are like the air to me. Please be safe on your journey. I am consoled by the hope that each morning I awake brings me a day closer to being with you again.

Zheng Ming

Tian had never thought of his brother as being truly romantic, beyond the dashing façade he presented. Nor was it typical for Hua people to express themselves in such a...personal manner. Did the princess feel the same way? She must, since she had kept the letter with her all this time. And why had he not heard about this already from Jie or his cousin, General Zheng?

Tian could never expose his soul like that. If he *did* write something like that to Jie, she would probably punch him. Pondering the relationship between Eldest Brother and the princess, he went back to the inn.

The suspicious man who'd been sleeping at the bar was gone. Tian pushed past the drunken revelers, approached the barkeep, and pointed to the empty seat. "Where did that man go?"

The barkeeper looked around before beckoning Tian closer and whispering, "It was an altivorc. He went upstairs, where he's staying in a private room. I hear from our patrons that there have been several altivorcs passing through this last week. Though for all I know, maybe it's just one individual. They all look the same to me."

An altivorc! Likely an advance scout for the battalion, on its way to aid the Teleri in the subjugation of Iksuvi. While the Hua and Kanin peoples shared enough similarities that the locals probably couldn't tell the difference, an altivorc scout would. He might not know their identity, but he would surely think it strange that there were Cathayi people masquerading as Kanin horsemen.

Tian tapped his chin. If the altivorc knew about what had transpired on the Iksuvius Heights earlier that day.... No, impossible—the altivorcs were coming from the opposite direction.

He pointed at the stairwell. "Are there any other ways to access the second floor?"

The barkeep shook his head. "No, those steps are the only way."

"Besides us, who is staying here?" Tian produced a shiny silver coin to entice an answer.

The coin disappeared into the man's palm. "Besides your party in a common room and the altivorc in a private room, there is also a trifle guide and his three dark-skinned friends in two of the doubles."

Tian swept his gaze around the room to take stock of the patrons. *Trifle* and *halfling* were derogatory terms for the madaeri people, a short but good-looking race of non-humans. They were known to be excellent guides, scouts, and foragers, with ravenous appetites and something of an inferiority complex. Hailing from the Eldaeri Northwest, this one was a long way from home. As for the dark-skinned clients, could they be the mysterious Aksumi people? Or the pious Levanthi? Or perhaps the Ayuri? They probably wouldn't be in league with the altivorcs.

Tian motioned Ma Jun over. "There's an altivorc scout. Staying here. He might know who we are. Keep watch on the stairs. Let me know if he comes down. Or if anyone else goes up. The rest of us shall retire. In two hours, someone will come down to relieve you."

Ma Jun nodded. "We should allow the princess to sleep by herself."

So loyal. And impractical. Tian shook his head. Since they'd planned to board the *Golden Phoenix*— "We don't have much money. Not enough for a separate room. She'll have to make do."

"The men are willing to exchange our rings for their finest private room." Ma Jun held up a thick silver ring cast with the dragon crest of Hua, the mark of the imperial guard.

Tian stared at the symbol, which a guard would never sell, even if he came on hard times. To think they would sacrifice it for the princess' comfort. Sadly, in Nothori lands where the significance meant nothing, their rings would be no more valuable than their weight in silver. Not to mention it would draw undue attention to them.

"That will not be necessary," the princess said, approaching from behind. The squeak in her voice was gone, replaced by a regal, albeit tired tone. "I would not sacrifice your badge of honor just for my own privacy for one night. I will retire for the evening. Please give me some time to myself before following."

The imperial guards, who had gathered around, reflexively bowed despite Tian's orders.

She disappeared up the stairs, the graceful float in her step replaced by a defeated trudge.

There was still the altivorc up there. Tian gestured for Ma Jun to follow. "Stand guard. Outside the door."

The rest returned to their table, mood somber amidst the merriment of a growing crowd. Tian leaned back and watched the entire room, noting comings and goings, and paying particular attention to the stairs.

Before long, a short figure descended the steps. At first glance, a child; but on further observation, undoubtedly the madaeri guide the barkeeper had spoken of. The diminutive fellow climbed up to a barstool and ordered a long list of food. Patrons shifted away from him.

Even if his group had no relevance to their current predicament, a guide would know more about the area. Tian motioned for his companions to wait at the table. Withdrawing his map of the region, he slipped through the boisterous villagers and sidled up to the madaeri.

The little man was no different from most of his kind: fair, with short-cropped hair that emphasized his pointed ears. Light skin and sharp features gave him a passing resemblance to a certain half-elf. A long dagger was tucked into a broad leather belt, which held up black cotton pants. A greenish-brown traveling cloak draped over a dull brown shirt.

The madaeri turned and faced him. "I've walked from one coast to the other," he said in very loud Arkothi, "been to the icy rim in the far north and the sweltering heat of the deep south. Never in my life have I seen a Cathayi looking so ridiculous wearing a mismatched suit of Kanin armor. Even your sword is on the wrong side!"

Tian gaped, and then looked down at his sword, sheathed on his left. "Um, I'm left-handed," he said, his voice about two decibels lower than the guide.

The madaeri laughed from his belly. When he spoke, it was in a big voice that did not seem to match his size. "No, you're not."

Some of the bar patrons now looked in their direction.

Heat rose to Tian's face. Usually, it was *he* who prodded information out of people, either through trickery or by not-so-friendly means, not the other way around. "Lower your voice a little. We are trying to keep a—"

"Low profile?" the madaeri whispered, lifting his shoulders and ducking his head. "You're not doing a good job of that, at least not to someone who has any amount of world experience. Luckily, I am probably the only one in this room with that. You could do better, but you would need some actual training."

Tian held back a retort. "My name is Tian. Come join us at our table. I have a proposition for you. I would like to discuss it in confidence."

"My name is Fleet, short for a much longer name that you won't be able to pronounce or remember, so we'll just keep it at that. Any chance I could get you to pay for my meal here?" Fleet jerked a thumb toward the kitchen.

Tian cringed. It would be expensive, but worth it. Madaeri were compulsive information-gatherers. Dangle some rumors in front of him and they would find out plenty in return. "Let's talk first. I have earth-moving information."

Fleet turned to the barkeeper. "Bring my food to this fine gentleman's table." He hopped off the stool and extended his hand. "Lead the way, friend!"

"So where are you taking your clients?" Tian asked on their way to the table.

Fleet's jovial tone turned grave. "I'm not allowed to speak regarding these types of business transactions. Wouldn't you expect your privacy protected if the roles were reversed? Perhaps you can ask them directly."

Arriving at the table, he looked around. "Interesting, Cathayi imperial guard, also in poor disguise. Which one of you is the dignitary?" He cast a glance at Tian, scrunched his forehead up, and then shook his head. "Not you, obviously."

The guards shuffled uncomfortably but remained silent, all glaring at the madaeri.

He pointed to the princess' untouched clams. "Anyone eating this?"

Tian nodded "Help your—"

The clams disappeared into the madaeri's mouth, shells and all. The entire table gawked at him.

"What?" With a wounded expression, Fleet shrugged. "I grew up in a big family where we had to fight for the food. You learn to eat fast."

Tian waved off the madaeri's protests. "No, eat. We need to confirm the accuracy. Of a map. Your people are the best mapmakers." He unfurled the paper and spread it out on the table.

Fleet munched on potatoes, his eyes darting over the markings. He shook his head and looked up. "Was this map made before or after the Hellstorm?"

Tian scowled. The final episode of the conflict between the Ayuri and Arkothi empires, three centuries prior, had drastically transformed the landscape. His map couldn't be *that* bad. He opened his mouth to answer.

"It was a rhetorical question," Fleet said. "Your map is definitely outdated. I can certainly spruce this sad rag up...for the right price." The quill the princess had used now twirled between his fingers.

Tian pursed his lips. "We are short on funds. Is there something else?"

"A woman, perhaps? This quill sure smells nice." The madaeri took a long, deep sniff of the feathers.

All three guards sprang to their feet, hands on their weapons, knocking chairs over and startling all the patrons into silence. Fleet didn't flinch. Tian put his hands up, tacitly telling the soldiers to stand down.

Fleet chuckled and fanned himself with the map. "A dead madaeri can't fix this antique for your pretty princess."

"Princess?" Tian feigned shock.

"Why else would Cathayi imperial guard react that way?"

The madaeri was good. It was useless trying to hide anything from him. Might as well confirm it. Tian leaned in. "Our guards are devoted to their princess. I implore you. For your own sake. Don't speak ill of her." He motioned again for the soldiers to sit down.

Fleet scratched his head. "Alright, how about this: you tell me something interesting, and I'll make revisions to the map based on the value of what you tell me."

Tian nodded. "That's fair. Here's a tidbit: Teleri will invade Iksuvi tonight."

Fleet whistled. The guards gritted their teeth, probably because of the Hua belief that whistling at night attracted ghosts. Unfazed, he inked the quill with several blots, and extended a road that ran from Iksuvius along the coast of Cold Harbor.

Tian smiled. The road reached all the way to the head of the bay, which might be a place they could catch up with the *Golden Phoenix* if they rode hard enough. "The First Consul of the Teleri Directori. He's here himself."

Fleet nodded, and put a dot and notation on the map, in the woods they had passed through earlier today: *Good mushrooms here.*

"Come on! That information is valuable!"

"But something I'd already guessed." Fleet grinned and rubbed his hands. "All the Teleri activity, plus the amazing procession at the Great East Gate a couple of days ago... But you get the idea: the quality of your information begets the quality of mine."

The back-and-forth continued for a while, with the madaeri adding all kinds of notes, roads, and information to the map, while Tian shared intelligence about troop strengths and movements.

At last, Fleet said, "Look, I can add so much more to this map, but at this rate, we won't be done until the Orc Gods return on their blazing chariots. Stories say that the only daughter of Emperor Wang is an unparalleled beauty, who sang a dragon into a stupor. Let me see her face, and I'll update everything I know."

Was it worth the risk? There was little they could do to keep the madaeri from hanging around and seeing her anyway.

Something flashed by the staircase. Fleet's head turned, and Tian's followed.

Another figure descended the stairs. He wore a dark cloak which covered nearly his entire body, with a hood pulled over his head.

The madaeri and his requests could wait. Tian motioned towards the guards with hand signals. *Block exit, flank, I take.*

None of the imperial guards budged.

Of course not.

Fleet's jaw dropped. "No, no, that's my client. She's no threat to you." He beckoned her over.

The cloaked figure approached the table, lowering the hood to reveal an attractive young woman with a light chocolate complexion and piercing dark eyes. She had coarse, wavy black hair which fell to the middle of her back. Aksumi. They rarely left their city-states in the south, and Tian had never seen one before.

The imperial guards, however, rose to their feet. In unison, they each pressed a fist into a palm.

"Lady Brehane," Li Wei said.

"Wei," she said with a toothy smile and a thick accent. "And Yue."

Tian's gaze shifted from Brehane to the imperial guards. How could this be? From the way Fleet's eyes bolted back and forth, he must have been just as surprised.

The Aksumi woman counted on her fingers. "But where are Jun, Xin, Zhan, and Ming? And little Jie?" Her eyes locked in on Tian.

Such a piercing stare. Tian shuffled on his feet. Brehane extended her open hands towards him, and he looked at Fleet with a raised eyebrow.

"It's their custom to clasp hands at their first meeting." The madaeri encouraged Tian with a tilt of his head.

Tian tentatively took Brehane's hands in his own. "I am Tian Zheng. I am honored to meet you."

Brehane held his hands and showed no signs of letting go. "Mister Tian, the honor is mine. I trust you and your family are doing well?"

What a strange question. "We are all well," he said. Eldest Brother most of all, apparently.

Another smile bloomed on her face. "You are Ming's brother, aren't you? I can see the resemblance. Which means you're the one Little Jie..."

Tian's face flushed hot enough to fry an egg. Usually, he knew more about people than they did of him. And the unspoken part about Jie. He turned to see the imperial guards' lips quivering into half-grins. "Yes. Ming's brother."

"Better looking, too. I can see why Little Jie—"

Tian coughed. "How do you know my brother? And the imperial guards?"

She nodded in the direction of the men. "We shared an adventure not four months ago." She placed a hand on her chest. "I am deeply indebted to them. Their swordsmanship, Ming's bow, and Little Jie's charm," she winked, "saved our mission."

Tian turned to the imperial guards. The smiles disappeared and they snapped to attention. There was a story here, one that he would pry out of the tight-lipped men. He looked back at her. "What brings you so far north? You are far from home."

Brehane sat down uninvited at the table and regarded him with curious eyes. She then turned to Fleet, who nodded. "What do you know about my people?"

Tian shrugged his shoulders. "Your people are the greatest magicians. You can bend the laws of nature. To suit your needs."

Brehane clasped a clear crystal that hung from a silver chain around her neck. "Some of what you know is true. Almost all of our women can sense the energy of the universe. Most only dabble. However, there are a very small number of truly wise and wondrous Mystics. I am an initiate into the Order of Mystics."

Her words sucked Tian in, the rest of the room and revelers fading into the background. "Both my order and the Order of Ayuri Paladins have noticed that there are places in the world where our connection to the world's energy has weakened. My Paladin companion and I are charged with visiting the holiest places, where magic has always been the strongest—"

"The pyramids," Tian said. It all made sense, at least from what he'd learned at the

reception the other night. "Your companion is Sameer Vikram."

Brehane nodded. "Yes, he is with me, along with the Akolyte Cyrus Estazadeh."

"A true Akolyte?" Tian kept himself from gaping. It was impossible. "Didn't they all lose their abilities to channel the divine magic of the gods?"

Brehane shook her head. "After the Levastyan Empire conquered Cyrus' homeland and took control of the pyramid there, the Akolytes lost their most powerful magic—but only in their homeland. The few who fled to other lands found their powers restored. When your friends and I infiltrated that pyramid, we found its font blocked."

Tian looked again at the imperial guards, then back. It would explain their camaraderie with Jie. "Where are you going now?"

"Fleet is guiding us to the ruins of a pyramid in the Kanin Wilds."

But how? Tian recalled the map. "Wouldn't it have been easier to go upriver from the Shallowsea?"

"Can I tell him?" Fleet jumped up and down on his chair. "Please?"

Brehane laughed. "Of course."

Fleet whipped a map out from who knew where and snapped it open across the table. It depicted the Kanin Wilds, with meticulous detail and all kinds of notations about landmarks, flora, fauna, and tribe names. He pointed to a ring of mountains right in the middle, which had several notes scribbled around it. *Tivorc City. Kanin Pyramid.*

Tian shook his head. "But how do you get there?"

"We will follow the north-south highway to the source of the Alto River, where the Nothori Mountains branch off into the Everwhite Mountains." Fleet traced a route on the map with his finger. "There is a secret pass near there, which will open into the Kanin Wilds near one of the branches of the North Kanin River." He pointed at one of the small tributaries. "There is an old, almost overgrown stone road that dates back to the first Kanin Empire over six centuries ago, which will go through the wooded hills before opening up to the mountains of the pyramid."

Tian considered the route. From here to the edge of the Wilds, it was two weeks by horseback on the main roads. If they found one of the ancient roads along the North Kanin River, they could follow it right to the East Gate of Hua. It would take another two weeks, at most. At the latest, they would have the princess back in Hua not long after the Mid-Autumn Festival. "How safe is the area? Around the North Kanin River?"

"There are many tribes of Kanin hunter-gatherers there," Fleet said. "Nothing like their horse-riding brethren in the Kanin Kingdom." He jerked a thumb at their armor. "There is also at least one tribe of wild elves, as well."

"Wild elves?" Thoughts of Jie crept unbidden into Tian's imagination.

Fleet gesticulated wildly. "Those elves that did not believe Aralas was the angel from their prophecies, and therefore didn't rise up during the War of Ancient Gods. They are the least of your worries. Ogres, on the other hand..."

Plans formulated in Tian's head. The most dangerous leg of the journey would start now. They would have to stay ahead of messengers coming from the north, who would be spreading the news of the princess' escape; and also avoid the altivorcs coming up from the south. He turned to Brehane. "May we accompany you? To the confluence of the North Kanin River and its tributary? We can provide six extra swords. We'll help pay for the madaeri's services."

She was about to answer, when Zhao Yue motioned to the stairway. The altivorc was coming down.

CHAPTER 24:
More Unexpected Visitors

As night fell over Iksuvius, Geros slouched on his throne in the Teleri embassy. His energy still guttered in his limbs, and it took significant effort to maintain the façade of strength. Patrols had taken control of several strategic points, yet had met with unexpectedly stiff resistance at others. Progress might have stayed on schedule had he not redeployed hundreds of troops from the eastern gate to the Cathayi embassy.

Reports came in, each relaying another objective captured. His western army was scheduled to arrive within an hour. Soon, very soon, his dreams would be realized.

First Emperor of the Teleri Empire. It sounded wonderful in his ears, no matter how many times he repeated it. Fulfillment of the prophecy of his virgin birth, begotten by Solaris himself.

An unexpected visitor spoiled his anticipation.

Through the throne room doors, an altivorc prince marched in, surrounded by an entourage of guards in chainmail. Like the Altivorc King, he was handsome, especially compared to his hideous minions.

Without so much as a bow, the prince spoke. "First Consul, we are ready to assist you in the siege of the Cathayi embassy. I have three hundred men inside the city at my command."

Geros forced himself to sit straight and glared at the prince, wondering where he got such strange ideas. "That won't be necessary. I have sent my most trusted general to negotiate their peaceful surrender. The princess is too compassionate and weak. She will surely sacrifice herself for her people. I will take that girl and punish her for her insolence."

The prince grinned, revealing his fangs. "That is unwise, First Consul. Mark my words, she will only bewitch you."

"I do not need your counsel. She is only a girl, one whose spirit I will crush with a night in bed."

The prince's grin froze on his face. "Do not be so sure. Despite my king's warnings, you take her too lightly. You do so to your own detriment."

"Be gone from my sight." Geros waved his hand at the altivorcs. Even that simple motion was tiring.

The prince shrugged and turned on his heels without further comment.

Once the mercenaries disappeared, Geros motioned towards an officer who stood by the door. "Has General Marius sent word?"

The officer bowed his head. "No, Your Eminence. There have been no new reports from the Cathayi embassy."

"Send a runner to convey my orders to the general. Master Feiying and his Nightblades will infiltrate their embassy to find out where the princess is hiding, and capture her if the opportunity presents itself. If there is no movement by dawn, commence the attack."

Jie and ten *Moquan* brothers gathered in the Cobweb, though it no longer deserved its nickname. The intertwined strings which Tian had meticulously connected over two years now lay on the floor, the notes and evidence all boxed up and ready to be hidden.

Old Tong, now in command in Tian's absence, turned to her. "Sister Jie, you are the most talented at setting the *Tiger's Eye*. Use it on us now and take command."

Jie offered a bow. Such responsibility! The *Tiger's Eye* locked away all emotions and moral compunctions, and drowned out all perception of pain. It would transform a *Moquan* from a deadly adversary to a heartless killing machine who wouldn't stop until he was dead or his assignment was completed.

The brothers focused on her as she arranged her hands in a secret sign. When all sense of humanity faded from their eyes, she issued her command. "Your mission is to protect the embassy until daybreak, whereupon you will return to this room at first opportunity."

They flashed the answering hand signal, one that only their subconscious minds remembered.

Jie addressed the two youngest. "Fen and Cheng, relieve your brothers at the warehouse escape route and send them here." With the tunnel secured, there would be a means to flee if the embassy fell.

Both bowed their heads and slipped out of the room through the balcony doors. No sooner had they left than red peacock caws emerged from the warehouse. The fainter, more distant set of screeches stopped mid-caw, almost as soon as it had started, while the other faded away in the

distance before getting cut short as well. Had an enemy discovered the escape route? Had she sent the boys to their deaths?

"Sheng, Lu, and Yang: go to the temple and protect the princess' decoy. The rest of you come with me to the warehouse." The shadows shifted as they drifted from the room, and Jie beckoned the remaining *Moquan* to follow her to the balcony.

Cool, reassuring air washed over her as she stepped out. Along the outer walls, none of the musketmen had taken up defensive positions, nor had the Teleri moved from their own ranks outside the walls. If they'd penetrated the secret passage, why weren't they attacking from the outside as well? Or was it a diversion?

Leaping down to the ground below, Jie swept through the courtyard. The imperial guard remained motionless at the main gate. Maybe there was no attack, despite the bird calls. She motioned her brothers to continue towards the warehouse, while she paused and searched the ranks for General Zheng.

There he was, near the front gate. She sprinted over. "General Zheng, what's the enemy doing?"

"Nothing. They just stand like toy soldiers."

It made no sense. Attacking from inside and out would work better. No matter; if they wanted to use a stupid strategy, that was their choice. "There is a threat on the embassy, coming from the secret escape passage. Have some of your men defend the temple. We want them to believe the princess is there."

General Zhang nodded and bellowed orders.

Jie caught up with her brothers. They crept through the darkened warehouse, fanning through before converging at the hatch that dropped into the underground tunnels.

It was open. The clang of swords echoed from below. The passage was compromised. Jie tapped orders on the men's backs. One went to warn the general, while the rest dropped down into the passage.

She trailed several steps behind, listening. The sounds of combat had been replaced with the pounding of heavy boots, their spacing much too close to be Bovyans, but too heavy to be Nothori humans.

Altivorcs. Her second encounter with them in her defense of the princess, her sixth in all. Each time, they seemed to have a personal vendetta against her.

In the pitch black, the *Moquan* would lose their blind advantage, since the altivorcs would see their heat signature. In these depths, her elf vision would be useless as well. "Lights! Lights!" She yelled down the hall, pressing her back against the roughhewn walls at a turn in the passage. Someone would have to be rear guard.

Up ahead around another corner, the passage lit up. Jie stayed in the dark, well outside the reach of the light, readying her throwing stars and spikes. Again, swords reverberated against each other, mixed with the inhuman grunts of altivorcs.

Tong and Cheng fell back toward the corner and into her line of sight. One of Tong's arms hung limply from his body by a strip of flesh, while the boy had suffered several deep gashes. Yet they took a stand at the corner, fighting on as altivorcs crowded the passage.

Blades flashed, and altivorc bodies began to drop at the sides; but at last, Tong fell from the slash of a broadsword. Despite his mortal injuries, he grabbed at the closest enemy and bit into his unarmored thigh. Cheng fought on with a shattered *dao* in one hand and a knife in the other, even as his lifeblood spurted from a cut to his neck. After a few seconds, he collapsed, unmoving.

Her brothers! Jie had not received the *Tiger's Eye*, and their deaths wrenched her heart. There was no time to grieve their loss. The altivorcs crunched the light baubles under their boots, plunging the tunnels back into darkness.

She pushed herself off of the wall and hurled at least a dozen *biao* in the direction of the orc grunts. Several bellowed in pain. She turned the corner back towards the hatch and waited, her own *dao* now held in both hands. The boots thudded in her direction, punctuated by exclamations in their guttural tongue.

As she planned, a few paused to hack at the spot on the wall where she had been leaning. Jie turned back around the corner and cut through three altivorcs in a quick combination of deadly slashes. A fourth swung at her with a broadsword, but she ducked under its whistle, while slicing through his abdomen with her *dao*. Ahead, more heavy feet stomped in her direction.

So many bloodthirsty voices! Jie was vastly outnumbered. No way to hold the passage by herself. She turned and raced towards the hatch. Scrambling through the opening, she slammed the trapdoor shut and barred it with a heavy blockwood board. She dropped the smallest of her light baubles by the hatch and looked up.

Perfect. The light didn't reach the ceiling, some twenty feet above.

Jie darted towards the corner and pop-vaulted against the walls until reaching the worn rafters. Crawling inverted, taking care not to slip in the dust, she arrived at an overhead door, installed just for these kinds of emergencies. Below her, the hatch door buckled as the altivorcs below slammed into it.

A few minutes of pounding. The hatch held.

Jie blew out a sigh—no! With a last shove, the altivorcs crashed through and tromped up the ladder into the warehouse. They bloomed out from the opening, taking in their surroundings, but never looking up. Two hundred seventy-nine in all, crowding the warehouse, several wounded. Among them marched a prince, a begotten son of the legendary Altivorc King himself.

Just as she began to inch towards the escape door, a last figure emerged, taller than the altivorcs, but gaunt. He looked around and up, and would have seen her had she not been concealed by the dark.

Jie chewed her lower lip. He was a Hua man, much too small to be a Bovyan Nightblade, and certainly too old. A *dao* hung on his back, and he was dressed in the manner of *Moquan*. Yet he was no one she had ever seen in her three decades at the Black Lotus Temple.

When he spoke in Arkothi, he barely had an accent. "She will go to the most defensible position. I suspect that's the temple, but I recommend sending several of your men to sweep through the rest of the compound. I will wait here to guard the escape route."

The altivorcs stampeded towards the door, their boots and armor rumbling and clanging like an earthquake. After several dozen exited, the thunder of musket fire roared through the night sky. Jie waited patiently until all of the altivorcs had departed and the sounds of hand-to-hand skirmishes resumed outside.

Now alone, the man picked up her light bauble. Before she could react, he threw it in her direction and looked right at her. His eyes bore a hint of sadness. Whatever; no time to dwell on it. The roof would provide a better view of the battle. Jie popped out of the hatch.

In the courtyard below, a large group of altivorcs charged through musket fire towards the lines of imperial guards defending the temple. Another regiment was locked in mortal combat with a detachment of imperial guards at the main gate. Yet a third force stormed the main residence. A reserve had formed by the warehouse, shooting black-fletched arrows at the musketmen, who in turn discharged their weapons and passed them back to their partners for reloading. Several lay at the base of the wall, felled by altivorc arrows.

Jie raced along the rooftop and leapt to the battlements along the outer wall, timing her jump with a lull in the volleys. She peeked out of the compound.

The Teleri still held their position. Their officers, however, argued among themselves.

No time to think about it. She continued along the wall, dodging several well-aimed arrows...they really must have a personal vendetta against her! She didn't recall ever insulting an altivorc before, at least none that lived to tell about it.

Reaching the closest point to the temple, Jie vaulted across the gap and caught the bottom edge of the pitched roof. After flipping up, she teetered along the edge to the sole entrance and swung down. One last glance at the courtyard.

Outnumbered, the imperial guards were losing ground to the altivorcs.

She passed through the double doors. Inside, she was greeted by bright light shining from the huge statue of Yang-Di at the rear of the temple, sparkling off the gold paint on the red ceilings high above. Kneeling there in prayer were Ambassador Wu and Meiling. The last of the princess' handmaidens, she was a stunning beauty in her own right, now serving as a decoy.

"Godfather," Jie said.

Ambassador Wu turned to face her. His shoulders slumped, and his eyes now betrayed his age. "Little Jie, what is happening?"

"The Teleri haven't moved, but altivorcs have stormed in through our escape passage. An older Hua man assists them."

The ambassador shook his head. His voice was calm and melancholy. "We cannot hold the compound against an attack from the inside. All is lost. When the embassy falls, make sure all the firepowder is detonated. Without a sample, the Teleri cannot study it, nor use the guns they will capture tonight."

Outside, the roar of musket fire stuttered to sporadic shots, then stopped altogether. Shouts and cries grew louder, and a dozen imperial guards backed into the temple as the altivorcs pressed their advantage.

"Hold the door, hold the door!" General Zheng yelled as he took a protective stance by the decoy's side.

Keeping two of her throwing stars in reserve, Jie drew her *dao* and charged into the fray. Around her, the imperial guards fought brilliantly, dispatching more of the altivorcs than they lost. But before long they were pushed back, as they succumbed to fatigue and overwhelming numbers.

Jie found herself not far from the door, isolated from her countrymen, forced to fight half a dozen altivorcs on her own. In fact, it looked like they'd intentionally isolated her. As she evaded deadly slashes and struck back at her attackers, she shot a quick glance back. The imperial guard had formed a protective circle around the ambassador and Meiling. A contingent of altivorc archers stood at the door, arrows trained on the decoy and her protectors. The prince stood at the fore with a wicked broadsword raised, his head protected by a T-slot helm.

He snarled a few words.

Jie gasped.

The altivorcs loosed their arrows into the group. Imperial guards fell, and others rushed forward to take their place as their circle tightened. Meiling screamed.

Ambassador Wu's voice of command carried above the pounding in her ears. "Jie! It is lost here. Remember what I said!"

Remember. Remember. Rage at the altivorcs washed over her. Her pulse thrummed in her head. What was she supposed to remember?

The firepowder.

Jie lobbed her sword at the closest enemy and dove into a roll between two altivorcs, popping up in front of the prince with knives held in underhand grips. He hacked at her with a two-handed swing, but she twirled around him while stabbing at his midsection. The prince turned just enough that his rib stopped her thrust, and he bellowed in pain as black blood oozed from the wound. He tried to spin with her, but she abruptly stopped her turn, slicing upwards across the back of his wrist. With a roar, he cocked back to chop at her again, but she pressed her attack and slipped a knife into his neck.

He gurgled and choked on blood. Jie didn't stay to gloat, instead cutting her way through the archers that stood between her and the door. She stabbed and slashed at them in rage, killing all that blocked her way.

Cool air and the coppery stench of blood greeted her as she made it out onto the terrace. With a quick glance, she appraised the situation. Bodies—both human and altivorc—littered the courtyard. Outside the temple, the altivorcs ushered the surrendering musketmen and wounded imperial guards into a corner of the compound. A dozen imperial guards still fought another group of orcs, pressing their way towards the temple.

An arrow zipped by her head from behind her. Jie withdrew a flash-powder packet from her belt and hurled it against the ground. Hopefully, the bright flash and smoke would provide enough cover for her to make it through the courtyard to the armory without getting hit in the back.

Bounding through the courtyard, arrows buzzing by her head, she somehow arrived at her destination unscathed. The door to the armory was unlocked; she pushed it open and slipped in. At the far end, past the muskets, swords, and armor, sat a dozen kegs of firepowder. Heavens, this was just like the caves beneath Wailian Castle over two years ago.

Jie pushed and shoved the heavy barrels, to no avail. Gritting her teeth and squeezing her eyes tight, she thrust her heel into the midsection of the centermost keg. The wood yielded with a splintering crack. She opened her eyes, thankful not to have blown herself to oblivion. Black powder gushed out from the hole. She grabbed a broom and swept the powder in a line towards the door.

A peek out revealed a fierce fight between the few surviving imperial guards and altivorcs at the temple doors. The rest of the Hua knelt with hands on their heads in the corner of the compound as the altivorcs trained arrows on them. One of the orcs barked a guttural order. Arrows flew into her unarmed compatriots.

Their screams filled her ears. Her chest tightened. Jie turned her head away, grief flooding over her. Why had she not been placed under the *Tiger's Eye* instead?

The same accursed orc syllable repeated, followed by more screams of Hua men.

A tear ran down her cheek. With a deep, choked breath, she opened her eyes to survey the situation again.

Nobody between here and the warehouse. Only one old man to fight there.

Despite her vast knowledge of weaponry, despite having almost blown up Wailian Castle, Jie had no idea how large of an explosion the powder would cause. She slunk as far as she trusted her aim, and hurled another flash packet at the line of firepowder at the door.

It caught. A fizzling flame tracked down the line.

She bolted toward the warehouse.

She crashed through the door and just barely avoided a barrage of throwing stars that came hurtling at her. Two knives were in her hands as the old renegade *Moquan* charged with a *dao* raised above his head.

Jie twisted out of his chop. Slipped the follow-through stab. Slashed at his forearm, but he jerked his own blade up with a flick of his wrist, deflecting her cut. With a subtle twist, the sword sliced towards her throat. A killing blow.

Jie had presence of mind to jump forward. Pain bit at her shoulder. Just a nick, instead of decapitation. She wrapped one arm around both of his and cut towards his throat with her other hand.

The force of the explosion rocked the walls and floors. Her body lurched forward. Jie's ears rang and something slammed into her head. All went black.

CHAPTER 25:

The Resonance of the Universe

The altivorc shot a quick glance at their table before hurrying towards the door. Tian signaled the imperial guards to stay in place. Seeing their blank stares, he said, "Stay here. I'm going to follow. And watch the altivorc."

As he got up, Fleet also rose. The two trailed the altivorc out of the inn and around the corner. Tian paused at the turn. On the other side, the altivorc breathed lightly and rapidly, ready to ambush him.

Tian smirked. Even if altivorcs fought well, apparently subterfuge did not come as easily. Time to spring a poorly set trap.

Feigning carelessness, Tian turned the corner.

A knife flashed in a deadly thrust toward his side. It was a quick, well-aimed shot that would have passed between the ribs and punctured the lung of an unsuspecting victim.

Tian wasn't unsuspecting. He caught the altivorc's knife hand, pulled his arm, and twisted it upwards. The altivorc's fingers loosened and the knife slipped from his hands. With a spin on his hips, Tian drove him face-first into the ground and kneeled on him. "All right—"

Fleet smashed a ceramic plate over the altivorc's head, knocking him out and shattering the dish in the process.

Tian scowled. "What did you do that for?"

The madaeri meekly shrugged his shoulders. "I thought you were in trouble."

"Now we're just going to have to wait for him to wake up."

"It can't be helped, so let's see what he has on him." Fleet grinned, snatching up the altivorc's belt pouch and shaking its contents onto the stable floor. After stashing away a few silver *kroon*, he held up a crude, hand-drawn map. "Even worse than yours, though not by much."

Tian snatched up a finger-length metal tube just before the madaeri's hand could reach it. Popping off the cap, he eased out a piece of parchment and unfolded it. The strange runes bore no resemblance to any language he'd ever seen.

He handed it to Fleet, whose large round puppy eyes shifted into foxlike focus as he quickly glanced through it and shrugged. "Maybe Brehane can help us. What about the altivorc?"

Tian frowned. "We can't have him spreading news. Of our presence." *Hold the dragonfly with care.* Did it apply to monsters? And did the princess still believe it? He took the altivorc's knife and brought it to his throat.

"Wait!" Fleet whispered. "If he goes missing or turns up dead, it'll raise suspicions. There's another way." Reaching into his pouch, he pulled out some dried red mushrooms, which he crushed into a coarse powder. "Open his mouth!"

Tian watched dubiously. "What will that do?"

"These fungi have a sedative effect on altivorcs and tivorcs. Legends say that before the War of Ancient Gods, the altivorcs enslaved my people to serve as watchdogs to warn against dragon attacks. What they don't say is that we also harvested these mushrooms so they could use them for leisure. After he eats them, he'll be out for hours with sweet dreams, and have only a vague recollection of what happened." The madaeri grinned. "So don't say my notes on your outdated map are useless!"

They drugged the altivorc, and then half-carried him back to the inn. Locals turned their heads, but most quickly returned to their socializing. At the table, the imperial guards seemed uncharacteristically...relaxed. Their usually hard eyes were softened, their gestures animated. And they were smiling.

Two newcomers sat on either side of Brehane, their backs to him. Zhao Wei made eye contact and tilted his head in Tian's direction. Everyone's attention, including that of the two recent arrivals, fell on him.

Sameer. Dressed in the Ayuri Paladin's traditional *kurta*, he stood and pressed his palms together in greeting. The other young man, dark of skin with a bald pate, remained seated, his posture straight. Likely the Levanthi Akolyte Cyrus, if he was with Brehane and Sameer.

Tian greeted them with a nod, and then sat their unconscious guest down at an open chair.

Cyrus' tone was harsh as he addressed the madaeri in what sounded like the Ayuri tongue.

Fleet grinned at the Akolyte and shrugged, while binding the altivorc to the chair with confounding knots. After he finished with his handiwork, he swept his gaze over the room. He grinned at the few patrons who gawped. "Our dinner guest."

Their stares awkwardly returned to their drinks, and Tian withdrew the altivorc's letter. "Miss Brehane. Fleet said you could translate this letter. Do you read the altivorc language?"

She shook her head. "I only learned a little about the magic they lost millennia ago. However, I may be able to help."

Tian handed her the letter, which she opened and placed on the table. Producing a crystalline prism from a pocket in her cloak, she set it atop the sheet. She then spoke a three-second string of guttural words, whose harshness did not match her appearance. The prism glowed, and the words on the paper swirled into a different script. The Akolyte and Paladin joined Tian and Fleet in crowding around.

The wavy script of the Ayuri was still just pretty gibberish. "What does it say?" Tian asked.

Brehane translated: "Have been watching activity outside Iksuvius.... Cathayi ship docked at Aremarela... Cathayi here dressed as Kanin Riders... appears to be princess, six guards... await your orders..."

Tian looked at the altivorc, who was smiling in his sleep. "The scout saw through our disguise."

"We should kill it." Xu Zhan slashed a finger over his throat.

Tian tapped his chin. "He was going to pass this message on. We need to find out to whom. When will he wake?"

Fleet chuckled. "A couple of hours. Aren't you glad I didn't let you kill him?"

So much for restful sleep tonight. Tian turned to Li Wei. "We'll have to rotate watches. You take first."

Li Wei was just starting to stand when the miserable but beautiful tone of a flute floated down the steps. The princess! Clear and resonant, the melancholy sound pulled at Tian's heart, constricting his chest. Around him, the spirited conversations guttered to a hush. All the revelers' expressions contorted into sadness.

Brehane clasped her necklace. Her eyes closed, but then flapped open. "What magic is this? So beautiful and serene, yet I can feel the resonance of the universe."

"That's our princess," Tian said. "She came to Iksuvius in peace. Now she's pursued by the Teleri Empire. I failed to expedite her escape by ship. Let us travel with you. At least to the madaeri's pass. It could save us weeks of danger."

Brehane ignored him, turning instead to Sameer. "Is this the princess you spoke of, who transformed a dragon with her voice, and captivated kings and generals with her music?"

Sameer nodded.

She turned back. "Mister Tian, please introduce me to your princess."

Tian raised his eyebrow at the imperial guards. Zhao Wei shrugged, and the others remained expressionless. They were leaving it in his hands. At least they didn't object to it, and apparently they trusted each other. Sameer was honorable as well. And regardless, there weren't many other choices. If he were to take the princess over the land route, he'd never find the mountain pass without Fleet's help.

He rose from his chair and beckoned Brehane. He shot Fleet a warning glance as the madaeri moved to get up and follow them. Climbing the steps, they came to the cracked door to the common room. Ma Jun stood beside it, his eyes tearing and lips sagging as the despondent tune floated out from within.

Tian peeked into the small room. The princess sat on a chair by a writing desk between two windows, wearing the simple pants and shirt of the Kanin uniform. Poor girl. He'd been too harsh. This had to be the most downtrodden place she'd ever slept in her life. But there would probably be harder days to come.

Kaiya had trudged up the creaking stairs, unable to remember the last time her limbs felt so listless or her heart so heavy. All sense of grace forgotten, she plodded through the narrow hall to the common-room door and pushed it open. The stench of sweat blew over her like a wave. She cupped her mouth to fight back the rising bile and stumbled over to the closest of eight cots.

The bed jolted her tired body as Kaiya threw herself down on its coarse woolen blanket. Tears pooled in her eyes, unbidden. Not so much from the pain of the rock-hard bed, nor even the inevitable vermin that hid there; they only seemed like the final insult in the worst day of her life.

She allowed herself a moment of self-pity.

Having wiped the tears away, she sat up and looked around the room. The cots lined both sides like sarcophagi in an Arkothi sepulcher. A crude writing desk and chair encroached into what little open space there was. With the two windows shuttered, it seemed even more stifling than the ship's cabin.

The leather cuirass, though not actually that tight, contributed to her sense of confinement. Kaiya stood and struggled with its buckles. When her trembling fingers failed her, she tried squirming out of it. Designed for and by a man. She paused in her futile efforts and caught her breath. With persistent twisting and turning, it finally came loose. She flung her tormentor onto the cot and glared at it.

With a sigh, Kaiya inched through the room and collapsed into the chair. She withdrew her flute from a pocket and began to play, the memories of the day flooding back to her. Geros pulling her to him. The hopelessness of missing the ship. Tian humiliating her. Her own guards betraying her. And finally, this lice-ridden inn.

"*Dian-xia.*" Tian's hated voice interrupted her self-pity, calling from outside the door.

Kaiya shuddered. She'd left the door open a crack. Had anyone seen her wallow?

"You have a visitor. She might be able to help us. Would you meet with her?"

Her? Had Tian brought some woman warrior like Jie to show just how useless she was in comparison? Very well, let him try to humiliate her more. She attempted to compose herself, straightening her carriage and lifting her chin. "Send her in."

Tian opened the door and fell to one knee, head bowed. "*Dian-xia.* I present Brehane. An Aksumi Mystic."

A chocolate-skinned woman strode in with the gait of a man.

"Leave us." Kaiya didn't even look at Tian.

He turned on his heel and left. When his soft footsteps lightened as they went down the steps, Kaiya turned back to Brehane. She'd never seen an Aksumi person so close. The woman's dark skin and coarse hair would be considered unattractive by the Hua standards of beauty, but she was pretty all the same.

Brehane walked over to the desk. Locking a penetrating gaze on her, she extended her hands and clasped Kaiya's.

Such strange customs, rude by the conventions of the Hua court. Kaiya fought the urge to break eye contact, to pull back.

Brehane spoke with a heavy lilt. "I am Brehane, daughter of Dahnay of Bahir. I am honored to meet you. I hope that your health is well in this chill autumn air?"

Never before had a complete stranger addressed her so! And the Mystic's hands were so hot. Comforting, actually. Kaiya nodded.

"And your family is all well, too?"

How to answer such a question? Father's health worsened by the day, and her two brothers remained heirless. Kaiya rose out of the chair. "I am Kaiya Wang. My health, and that of my family are all well, thank you. To what do I owe this visit?"

Brehane smiled and released her hands. "My friend Sameer spoke of you, saying you were the most beautiful woman he had ever seen, and that your words alone disarmed a tyrant. I had to see for myself what kind of woman that was."

Kaiya's shoulders stiffened. As the old Hua proverb said, *A stranger's flattery is often followed by a knife in the back.*

The Mystic's eyes searched hers, and she spoke again in a soothing voice. "Yes, your inner spirit is strong, strong enough to tame the Last Dragon. But a deluge of events beyond your control has crushed it. Even now, you deplete what is left in a tenuous maintenance of your mask. Let go; you are safe with me."

The audacity! Yet she couldn't deny the truth in the Brehane's words. Even now, it took all of her control just to hold back tears. She shook her head, all the same. "You are mistaken. Perhaps you should question the strength of your magic."

Brehane laughed. A sincere laugh, devoid of mocking or rebuke. "Miss Kaiya, my words have nothing to do with magic, and everything to do with being a woman who has also had her confidence shattered. As a girl, I was considered a prodigy. But my natural gifts could not surpass less

talented people who practiced harder. That realization forced me to question my very understanding of my place in the world. Is that much different from how you feel?" She reached out with both arms, inviting Kaiya into an embrace.

Kaiya stiffened and took a step back. It would not do for the Princess of Cathay to show weakness, or allow herself the close contact that foreigners engaged in so freely.

"I've had my spirit crushed, as well. I lost the man I loved. I was forced to give up our child." Brehane beckoned her closer.

How reassuring it would be to confide in someone. Someone who would disappear from her life just as quickly as they had come. That someone was supposed to have been Tian, but now, perhaps it was this stranger. Her resolve faltered. She stumbled into the Mystic's arms. Empathetic warmth enveloped her, and tears flowed down her cheeks as the Aksumi stroked her hair.

Kaiya's shoulders relaxed. She drew away, wiping her eyes on her coarse sleeve and lifting her chin. The sisterly hug hadn't been too awkward or embarrassing. It was pleasant, even, though the last time she'd found comfort in a hug was with a dragon in man's clothing.

Brehane smiled. "You are not alone."

Kaiya nodded.

"Now, Miss Kaiya, might I ask you to play your musical instrument?"

Though it would be considered rude to make such a request in Hua, Kaiya withdrew her flute. Why not? She had already *hugged* a stranger. She brought it to her mouth and started a peaceful tune, the previously melancholy sound all but forgotten.

"More emotion," encouraged the Aksumi.

Kaiya complied, allowing her renewed sense of serenity to float on the notes.

Clasping a jewel which hung from her neck, Brehane closed her eyes. "I can feel it. The resonance of the universe." She started a slow chant in a guttural language. It rippled through Kaiya's music.

The Aksumi intonated one last syllable. Several crashing sounds came from downstairs, followed by silence.

Kaiya lowered her flute, while Brehane came out of her trance and looked around.

"What was that?" Kaiya asked.

"As you were playing, I could sense the energy of the world coalescing, similar to the vibrations surrounding the ancient pyramids—though not as strong. I tried to help put you into a state of relaxed sleep with my magic, since I was so certain your scattered thoughts would prevent you from resting well tonight. Yet you are still awake. How is that?"

Kaiya's emotional armor reformed. The Mystic had tried to put her to sleep without her consent. She glanced at her pack on the bed, where she'd stowed the Teleri imperial crest. Certainly, it couldn't protect her from magic from so far away. And no matter how compassionate Brehane had acted, it was not worth the risk of revealing it. "I do not know," she said. "Let us go downstairs and see what all the noise was."

Down in the main room of the inn, everyone from the revelers to the barkeep to the imperial guards slept: some on the floor, others at the bar, some at their tables.

Heavens. Kaiya turned to Brehane. "Did you do this?"

Brehane's eyes rounded. "My skill is not so powerful as to cause an entire building of people to fall sleep. I believe that your music amplified my spell. However, you remain completely unaffected. Where did you learn how to manipulate magic?"

"We do not manipulate it, as much as evoke emotion through our art."

Brehane waved her hand at the sleeping room. "This is more than just stirring emotions."

Kaiya shrugged. "It is a long story, which starts with an elf lord who serves as my father's advisor. He taught me to feel that all things vibrate. He also gave me a book explaining how music affects those vibrations."

Wonderment danced in Brehane's expression. "Do you have this text with you?"

Technically, it had not been a book, but rather a magic mirror which displayed text. Kaiya shook her head. "I left it in Cathay, with the elf lord."

"It is said that during the War of Ancient Gods, the elves taught us magic based on our peoples' natural affinity. But perhaps my people's sorcery and your artistic mysticism are not so different." Brehane clasped her necklace. "I would like to meet your elf, so that I might listen to his invocation of ritualistic Deep Magic. I have heard that it sounds almost musical. Maybe it, too, is similar to your own music."

If she ever made it home. Kaiya forced a smile. "I will give you the text and do my best to introduce you. I warn you, however, that he is a private person with strange whims, coming and going as he pleases."

"Then I will do my best to make sure you make it home. In the meantime, we should wake these people. Though maybe it would be better if we did not tell them what happened." Brehane winked at her. She spoke again in the harsh words of magic, and everyone started lifting their heads and rubbing their faces.

Tian, who'd been asleep with his head resting on their table, looked around through half-lidded eyes. "What happened? Is everyone all right?"

After his involvement in this horrible day, it was impossible to resist a petty jab. "Everyone is fine, thanks to your watchful vigilance." She regretted it as soon as the words passed her lips.

His expression blanked.

Brehane furrowed her brows at Kaiya before turning to him. "Mister Tian, considering your men's past assistance, we would be happy to escort Miss Kaiya to the Nothori Mountain pass. It will be a long, hard journey, so we had all better get some rest. Miss Kaiya will stay with me in my room; Fleet, you sleep with the Cathayi boys."

Fatigue crept back over her, and Kaiya did not bother to hide her relief. Not only did she have more protection, she would also not have to share a room with men.

Her relief was short-lived.

Tian looked around. "Where is the altivorc?"

CHAPTER 26:

Rude Awakenings

The pounding of a fist on a breastplate jostled Geros awake. His eyes fluttered open, and he dragged himself out of his slouch on the throne. His limbs felt listless and heavy, the effects of the princess' brazen assault still weighing on his energy.

All around him, officers stood at attention. A soldier stepped through the doors, and Geros acknowledged him with a half-hearted nod. "The city center is ours, First Consul!"

He had almost slept through his moment of glory. "What time is it?"

A general on his flank spoke. "The Iridescent Moon wanes to its first gibbous, Your Eminence."

Well past midnight. Geros frowned. "We are a phase behind schedule."

Another general thumped his chest. "Your Eminence, because of our redeployment of men to the Cathayi embassy, we did not have enough troops to completely secure the eastern gate. Even now, the Iksuvi soldiers are mounting a counter-attack along our flanks."

Cathay. The princess. Had Feiying captured her? Or at least located her? "What is the latest report from the Cathayi embassy? Did Feiying succeed?"

The first general shook his head. "No, Your Eminence. Feiying is unaccounted for."

"Unaccounted for? What about the Nightblades?"

"Also unaccounted for."

"Tivar take them!" Geros pushed himself up out of the throne, towering to his full height despite his tiredness. "Never mind that for now. Prepare my horse. We will set out for the eastern gate to greet our armies. In the meantime, move the cavalry from the northern gate to the eastern gate, and order them to prevent the Iksuvi from setting an edge on our flanks."

Fists pounded against chests as the Bovyan soldiers hastened to fulfill his command. Geros strode out of the throne room, his honor guard keeping pace behind him. It took all his will power to maintain the façade of strength. When he reached the courtyard, a column of cavalry awaited him. He mounted up on a horse, drew his sword, and held it aloft. "To the eastern gate to join our brothers! Iksuvius will be ours!"

His soldiers roared as they pounded their chests in unison, and followed his horse as he rode out. The streets were devoid of citizens, though the sounds of skirmishes carried from many different directions. On the eastern edge of the city center, a messenger caught up with them.

The soldier ran to the front of the column and saluted with a fist to his chest. "Your Eminence, the altivorcs attacked the Cathayi embassy from the inside."

Geros gripped the reins as he clenched his jaws. "What? After I told them not to? From the inside? How? What did Marius do?"

"We are not sure how they got past our cordon. Marius sent me to receive your orders."

Geros pounded his fist into his open hand. "Tivar curse them! Guards, come with me. The rest of you, keep up." He wheeled his horse around and spurred it on, cantering in the direction of the Cathayi embassy. His dozen mounted guards followed him, with no semblance of their typically precise formation.

No sooner did he split off from the column than Geros regretted his impulsiveness. Their handful of mounted Bovyans would not be able to counter any more than a platoon of thirty. He could not afford to show any weakness now. He pressed his men onwards, and under Solaris' watchful eye, they rode unopposed.

Not far from the Cathayi embassy, a series of explosions rang out. Red and orange lights flashed above the squat buildings, and the ground shook. Geros yanked on his reins, though he hardly needed to as his horse shied at the loud sounds.

Their horses calmed and the Bovyans approached the embassy. Several of the buildings had erupted in flames, glowing in the night sky. Around the compound, Teleri soldiers stood in exacting lines, even as they looked on with wide eyes.

"The First Consul has arrived!"

Heads turned to face him and fists pounded on chests. The men parted in perfect synchronicity to create a path for Geros to ride through.

Young General Marius greeted him. "Your Eminence, the altivorcs appeared inside the embassy compound and attacked the Cathayi. We held our position, unsure of what to do in this unforeseen circumstance."

Geros dismounted with some effort and looked through the gates. The raging flames consumed the graceful Cathayi architecture, mirroring the anger that burned in his heart. "General, storm the embassy and take any survivors into custody. If you find any altivorcs, engage and kill them."

Marius bowed his head. "As the First Consul commands!" He turned back to the soldiers. "First, second, and third companies, prepare to breach the gates!"

The soldiers formed up in the center with drawn spears, just as dozens of altivorcs appeared on the other side of the walls. Their apparent leader flung open the gates and sauntered through. "First Consul Geros, I bring you a present."

With a wave of his hand, two altivorcs marched forward, dragging a limp body in bloodied, light-blue robes. Hair hung over her face. She yelped as they flung her down at Geros' feet.

His anger at the altivorcs' betrayal faded as a new rage at the princess boiled over. He grabbed her by the hair and jerked her head back.

Though beautiful, the girl was not Princess Kaiya.

"Fools!" Geros spat at the leader. "I have no use for this girl. Where is Princess Kaiya?"

The altivorc grinned and shrugged. "They all look the same to me. There were no other females inside, save for the half-elf girl who is burning in the flames as we speak."

Without breaking eye contact with the altivorc leader, Geros snarled orders to his men. "Enter the embassy, search for any survivors and bring them out. Collect their rifles and firepowder."

The altivorc laughed. "What do you think caused the explosion? All the firepowder was ignited, and the rifles destroyed. Maybe you can salvage some after the fire burns itself out."

"You. Get out of my sight before I change my mind and have you join the half-elf in the inferno." He looked down at the girl, whose teary eyes were wide with fear.

The sounds of stomping boots marched in perfect rhythm with the throbbing in Jie's head, jolting her awake. The straw mattress prickling her back beckoned her to sleep, but willpower pried her eyes open. The orange haze beneath her eyelids gave way to blurry sunlight, filtered through a small, partially shuttered round window. She went to rub her aching head, only to find her wrists bound tight above her head. Her ankles were likewise tied down with silk rope.

The stifling air hung in her lungs. She lifted her head to get a feel for her surroundings, realizing then that the only thing she wore was a bandage around the cut on her shoulder. Some dust in the center of her chest sparkled in the brittle sun. Jie regarded her nakedness with a detached apathy and returned to taking in her surroundings.

The cot barely fit into the tiny room, whose pitched ceiling and exposed rafters suggested an attic space of some sort. There was a familiarity to it, but why? Her black clothes lay neatly folded by a trapdoor in the floor. Next to them, a crude ceramic cup on the floor taunted the dryness in her throat.

"You're awake." The male voice behind her was aged and hoarse, and spoke in the Hua tongue.

Jie craned her neck to get a better view, to no avail. "What happened? Where am I? What day is it? Who are you? Why am I naked and bound?"

The man cackled. It was a melancholy laugh, filled with contagious sadness. "I will answer the last two questions first, with a question of my own. If you captured a *Moquan* master, how would you secure them?"

Sedated, naked, and bound, with no tool that they could use to escape.

The man's face came into view. It was the one who had helped the altivorcs assault the embassy. Up close, he was gaunt, with sharp cheekbones and sunken eye sockets. White streaked his thinning black hair. Rage should have welled up within her, but oddly, she didn't care.

He held her head up and brought the cup to her lips. She drank greedily, not caring if the cool water was poisoned.

"You are in one of the Black Lotus safehouses," he said. "They won't have use for it anymore. I brought you here after the explosion. It is the next morning."

A safehouse. The next morning. "What about my comrades?"

"As far as I know, dead to the last man, slain by the altivorcs."

Though her logical mind knew she should be angry, she felt nothing. "Why'd you help them?"

"I swore to avenge my broken heart. When I heard about you, heard that you were so close, I couldn't pass up the opportunity. And when I saw you, you looked just like *him*. I hated you in that instant."

What was he talking about? Who did she look like?

"But after I knocked you unconscious, with your eyes closed in peaceful sleep, you reminded me so much of *her*. I couldn't bring myself to kill you."

Emotion broke through her apathy. Jie's heart raced, the urgency in her voice sounding odd in her ears. "What are you talking about? Who do I look like? Who do I remind you of?"

The man uncapped a bamboo tube, and the heavy scent of deer musk percolated through the small room. Everything came together now: the dust on her bosom, the subtly sweet taste of the water, and now the musk. A staged euphoria toxin, exactly the same as the one the Nightblades had tried to use on the princess, similar to the one she'd used on General Marius two nights before. Her captor could tell her the answer to the Unanswerable Riddle from Eldaeri folklore, and she'd never remember.

He brushed his finger across her neck. A pleasant buzzing replaced the aching in her head.

"Who do you remind me of? Why, your parents, of course. But as you've probably surmised, you won't remember much of this conversation anyway. Trust me, I am doing you a favor; you're better off not knowing."

"My parents?" The dead mother she never knew, the elf father who abandoned her. "You knew my parents?"

His voice no longer seemed tired, seemed to carry a lighthearted tone. "Oh yes, very well. Now, tell me about your father."

Who didn't have father issues? This guy, probably. She giggled. "He left me at the gates of the Black Lotus Temple with a letter asking for them to take me in."

The man inhaled sharply. What was *his* problem? It was *her* father, not his. So much tension in those shoulders. "So you never knew him?" he asked. "Nor he you?"

"No. Nope. Nada." Hah! On a normal day, mention of her father would nudge her into a carefully concealed anger. Was she usually so uptight? It wasn't like she was the first one to ever be abandoned. Her face must've now been wearing the most ridiculous smile.

"Well, that changes things. Not only can I not bring myself to kill you, it wouldn't achieve anything anyway."

Kill? That would sound like a threat if the guy didn't look like a grandfather. Not like death was scary anyway. She'd always faced it with a sense of resignation to fate. She let out a sputtering giggle. "What did you hope to achieve, anyway?"

The renegade tapped his chin, almost like Tian. "It's said that loss of a child is the greatest pain. I thought I could hurt your father by killing you. But he must not care, if he abandoned you."

"Yes. I would kill him myself if I ever met him." Would she? Maybe. It seemed like the right thing to say. "Gouge his elf eyes out and cut off his manhood!"

"Now there's an idea... I do hope you will remember parts of what I am about to tell you." He grinned.

Good, a grin. This guy really could stand to smile a little more.

"So, enlighten me," he said. "How do you think your father delivered you to the gates of the Black Lotus Temple?"

The question jabbed into her euphoria. The temple was well-hidden, and nobody could find it unless they had been shown the way. Jie had asked herself this question time and time again, but trusted Master Yan's word so implicitly that she'd always dismissed her nagging suspicions. Her goofy smile dissipated, replaced by knitted eyebrows.

"This letter, what did it say?" he continued.

"I never saw it. Master Yan lost it."

The man burst out laughing, and Jie found herself giggling with him. He choked as he forced himself to stop. "When does even a *Moquan* apprentice *ever* lose anything? Let alone the great Master Yan? What did he say was written in the letter?"

Jie stopped laughing. Yet another buried suspicion, vocalized by someone else. "That my mother died in childbirth, that my father cared more about his adventures than me. That I would just be a burden, so he left me there."

The man's eyes were wide now. "Well, it seems I don't have much to do here. Yes, your father was a selfish dastard who didn't care for you or your mother. He only cared about making a half-elf by bedding a human. You have every right to hate him."

Jie didn't hate him, at least not right now. She just smiled. "So who's my father?"

"Royalty, from what I understand. Master Yan knows better than I, in that regard. If you remember our little talk, do ask him about your birthright."

Royalty? She wasn't just an abandoned child, whose elf blood the *Moquan* thought would come in handy? And how could Master Yan, her adopted father, *ever* deceive her like that? Despite her euphoria, she protested. "I don't believe you. You're lying."

"Hush, hush. It is true. And unlike your father, I loved your mother. We were in love, before that Turtle's Egg came along. Now that I look at you, you really do resemble her. The beauty." The man brushed his hand through her hair, which sprawled loosely over the bed.

Even through her euphoria, his touch felt wrong. Jie struggled with her bindings, but they were even more secure than she could tie herself.

"She loved me." Her captor came around the cot and leaned over her, his body heat and musky smell suffocating. He brought his face to her neck. His hand brushed up her thigh. She squeezed her eyes shut and turned her head. No, this wasn't right. The rope dug into her wrists and ankles as she fought to free herself.

And then the hot weight above her drew away. Jie forced her heavy eyelids open again, and gasped for breath.

Above her, the man wore a sad expression. "You are not her."

She shook her head, wondering for the millionth time in her life what her mother must have been like.

He slid a finger into her mouth, bringing a touch of sweetness. "Sleep now, my dear."

Jie fought the fog that settled over her mind, and mumbled one last question. "Who was my mother?"

The sadness of his voice added to the heaviness in her head. "She was—"

And then blackness.

CHAPTER 27:

Last Details

Tian shook his head. The altivorc couldn't have gotten far, and yet their search proved fruitless. With no other recourse, he questioned the drunken locals for news of altivorc activity over the last several days, only to be greeted by blank stares.

Certainly they would've heard about the battalion if it were within a few days' march. If they didn't have to worry about a few thousand altivorcs, it was better to take advantage of sleep here, instead of moving to a different location. Especially since Chen Xin would be returning in the morning.

Yet even with rotating watches, Tian slept restlessly, waking at the slightest sound. At first light, he pulled himself off of the cot to prepare for their departure.

The chill morning air greeted him as he stepped out of the inn. With precious little money, he was pleasantly surprised to find the Kanin Rider who'd guided them the day before, waiting by the stables with gifts from his embassy: a month's supply of Kanin cornbread in backpacks, more feed for the horses, the monks' clothes they had left behind, and thirty gold *kroon*.

Just before the Iridescent Moon waned to its fourth crescent, Chen Xin returned. Beside him rode Arvydas, the young king of Lietuvi, with a contingent of twenty mounted guards. Tian scanned the road behind them. Perhaps it was a trap. Perhaps a hundred enemy soldiers waited in the tree line outside the village. It was surprise enough the boy king had come at all. Unless it was

to capture the princess. If only she would listen to reason.

Keeping his gaze on the king, Tian bowed. "Your Majesty. Princess Kaiya will be pleased. That you came."

Arvydas' mouth curled into a lopsided sneer, the fuzz on his upper lip reminiscent of a caterpillar rearing its head. He spoke with a contrived brashness that did little to hide the insecurity of youth. "Make haste. I have important matters to attend to in the city."

Tian made eye contact with Chen Xin and tilted his head back towards the inn. The guard nodded and headed in that direction. While they waited, the king and his knights took in the surroundings.

The princess emerged from the inn, walking as regally and straight as if the day before had never happened. Her hair was tied back tightly, and she wore just the leather cuirass of a Kanin soldier. The uniform did nothing to highlight her physical perfection, yet she still carried herself as if wearing silken gowns.

Around her, the imperial guards held their sword scabbards, their free hands never straying far from the hilts. Their eyes evaluated the king's guards. Tian palmed several *biao*.

For their part, the Lietuvi guards sat upright, hands on the pommels of their swords. Their gazes shifted between their king and the Hua.

King Arvydas' jaw remained rigid, though his glare softened when her gaze met his. His lips twitched, and his eyes roved over her with the hot blood of early manhood. He raised a hand, and his knights drew their swords and fanned out.

Oh, no. Though not unexpected. Tian stepped in front of the princess while the imperial guards formed up around her.

Though she wore pants, she gracefully dipped into a shallow, Northern-style curtsey. Her voice remained calm. "Your Majesty, thank you for meeting with me. Please, be at ease." The last four words warbled like the song of a nightingale, but Tian shrugged off the power of her voice as it rippled over him.

The Lietuvi contingent, however, relaxed in their saddles. The king's expression twitched again, settling into an obviously forced scowl. His tone was accusatory. "You do realize the risk I am taking to come here? Speak."

"Your Majesty, these are words privy only to your royal ears. Please, walk with me, alone." She sang the last three words, power radiating from them.

The king's brash façade melted. Motioning for his shocked guards to stay behind, he joined her in a stroll toward the river's shoreline.

The princess turned to Tian, her silent order clear: *do not follow us.*

Foolish. All it took was for the king to resist her voice once, and she'd be alone, defenseless against him. Tian fought the urge to trail them, and just watched as the two descended to the riverbank. He pulled Chen Xin away from the semicircle of knights. "Did you deliver all the messages?"

Chen Xin shook his head. "Our compound was completely surrounded, so I went to the Kanin embassy and spent the night there. Their ambassador pledged to send supplies to the princess."

The embassy. Hopefully, Jie was there, safe behind the compound walls. "What about the *Golden Phoenix*?"

Chen Xin frowned. "Rumors say she has gone out to open sea."

"Out to open sea? How could they leave the princess behind?"

"She ordered the captain to return to Hua, even if it meant leaving us behind." Chen Xin sighed.

Selfless, but ill-advised. It was Tian's turn to shake his head. "And you let her?"

"When has she ever listened to us?" Chen Xin threw his hands up. "I went behind her back, but I couldn't convince the captain to disobey her order."

Tian sighed. Stubborn girl. Noble, stubborn girl. There was no point in blaming Chen. "Did the Teleri take the city?"

"This morning, the Teleri captured the eastern gate and occupied much of the eastern portion of the city. The Iksuvi army puts up a valiant resistance in the city center, but it's only a matter of time before the Iksuvius is completely occupied."

Tian lifted his chin at the king's twenty knights. "And so the Lietuvi agreed to meet. I don't trust them."

Chen followed his gaze. "Give the princess more credit. She may be stubborn, but she has manipulated older and more experienced rulers than young King Arvydas."

Perhaps. Tian looked down towards the river, where the princess and the king talked, just out of earshot. "Let us hope she finishes her parley soon. We need to stay ahead of the news coming out of Iksuvius."

The early morning sun danced on the ripples of the lazy river, while small white birds floated on the light breeze. Standing by the sandy riverbank beneath the weathered seawall, Kaiya scrutinized the king.

Younger than her by two years, and having just taken the reins of power after years of being a puppet king, King Arvydas took long strides with his chest puffed out. His own insecurities, youthful ardor, and brashness would make him soft clay in her hands.

His lips were pursed. "The First Consul sent a message to his allies, saying that you have committed crimes against the Teleri Empire. He offered a substantial reward for your capture. I wondered what offense would warrant such a bounty."

Kaiya flashed her most disarming smile. "I wonder as well. I am just a girl, defenseless and far from home. There is little that I could do to the great Teleri Empire."

He jabbed a finger in her direction. "You fled the city, so you must be guilty of something. Tell me, or our discussion is over and I will deliver you to the First Consul's bedchamber myself."

Kaiya tilted her head and placed her hand over her heart. "I did nothing more than defend myself. Perhaps the First Consul cannot accept that he was bested by an untrained girl a third his size."

Mouth agape, Arvydas lowered his hand. He looked at her, his eyes appraising more than her curves. He snorted. "So...why did you ask to meet me?"

She looked up through her lashes. "I wish to discuss your new alliance with Iksuvi."

His mouth again hung open for a few seconds before he burst out laughing. "Why would I ally with those weasels? They tried to set up their own puppet to usurp my throne. That snake Evydas will receive his comeuppance soon enough."

"I think you will rethink your position after you hear about an even greater betrayal." She edged closer and lowered her voice. "My informants have told us that the Teleri have made several deals aimed at conquering the Nothori region. While your troops move into the south of Iksuvi, the altivorcs guarding your border with Rotuvi have abandoned their post and have left your rear unguarded. Rotuvi has made a deal with the Teleri to invade you from the south, while you are preoccupied with your invasion of Iksuvi."

The king frowned and waved a hand. "Preposterous! Why would the Teleri double-cross us? They have nothing to gain, nor the resources to fight a war on two fronts."

Kaiya chose her words carefully to avoid offending Arvydas. "I am only a girl, with no mind for military strategy, but I wonder why the First Consul set your alliance for just two years instead of five. After they conquer Iksuvi, who will be next? How long would it take them to conquer your kingdom if you weakened yourself by dividing your troops between occupying Iksuvi and defending your southern borders from Rotuvi?"

Arvydas paled, though he still spoke with bravado. "You *are* just a girl. Old Gunvydas is a coward. But if Rotuvi *does* attack us, we have enough soldiers in the south to repulse an attack. Why are you telling me this now? What do you have to gain from us joining forces with Iksuvi?"

At least he was entertaining the idea. Her real reason—to cover her own escape—would remain unspoken, replaced by a half-truth. "I do not care to see the Bovyan scourge sweep through the Northwest, for that will put them at Cathay's border. Iksuvi and Lietuvi standing together have a better chance than either one alone."

King Arvydas cast a sly smile. "Are you so confident in your information that you would be willing to come back to our embassy?"

Diplomatic words spilled off her lips on reflex. "I am confident in our information, but not so assured in the safety of returning to Iksuvius, even under your protection. The Teleri are bringing a sizeable force, and could easily surround your embassy if they learn of my presence there. It would be unfair of me to put you in that situation."

The king's peach fuzz danced back and forth as he visibly pondered her words. "What do you plan to do now?"

Of course this question would come. She'd prepared more half-truths to gauge King Arvydas' trustworthiness. And protect them if he decided to betray her. "I am heading south to winter in Kalenai City, as far away from the invading army as possible. I do not care to share a bed with Bovyan soldiers. Come spring, my father will send warships to press the Teleri for my safe return."

The king shook his head and offered a smug grin. "You are cornering yourself. You do not realize how quickly a Teleri army conquers. The only way out of southeast Iksuvi is either across the river into Teleri itself, or through altivorc tunnels in the Wilds. You should turn west at the highway crossroads and head toward Laramies."

Right where his armies were heading. Kaiya nodded her head and smiled coyly. "Thank you, Your Majesty. I defer to your military mind. I have no eye for strategy or map-reading."

Arvydas beamed. "Laramies is close to the border of my kingdom. You will find safe haven with us."

It was too fast a change in attitude. Still, it was better to play along and preempt his next suggestion. "Thank you for your kind offer. We do not know the way. Would it be impertinent to ask that you send one of your men with me as a guide?"

Surprised satisfaction flashed across his face, as evident as the sun on a cloudless day. "We are pressed for able-bodied soldiers in these times of uncertainty. Nor can I give the Teleri the impression I am helping you."

She raised an eyebrow. "And what about your alliance with the Teleri?"

His feral grin returned. "If your information is wrong, then I will tell the First Consul where you are headed. If it is right, then we still have two years to prepare a defense against them."

Kaiya curtseyed again. "Then we will both be safe. For the time being."

Tian appeared at the top of the seawall. "*Dian-xia*," he said in the Hua tongue. "We must make haste. A swifthorse relay messenger just passed through. Iksuvius has fallen. Bovyan scouts are headed this way."

CHAPTER 28:

A Journey of a Thousand Li Begins With Trouble

Once they passed the exodus of refugees on the first day, Tian knew his plan would work—as long as they stayed ahead of the news from the north. The altivorc column coming up from the south would have no reason to stop a small patrol of Kanin Riders if they didn't know about the disguise.

The first three days of the journey went smoothly, with sunny weather and unseasonable warmth for early autumn. The highway ran along the river through pastoral farmland, passing through several villages and a few small towns. Farmers and townsfolk afforded them only an occasional curious glance. Even the usually pessimistic Li Wei seemed to be less gloomy than usual.

Across the river, which narrowed to about a *li* in width, lay several Teleri towns and villages. Yet from what Tian could see, life went on as usual, with no hint of the war that raged to the north. Fleet, regularly rode ahead to scout, coming back with reports that all remained calm in the south. More importantly, there was no sign of the altivorc army.

They stayed in the swifthorse highway lodges, though the message relay system had ground to a halt in the last week after horses started falling ill. As a precaution, Tian insisted on paying farmers to stable their own horses, away from the swifthorses. Despite that inconvenience, easy access to food and soft beds made their journey feel more like an outing than an escape.

The change in terrain matched the transformation Tian saw in the princess. Now out of immediate danger, she seemed happy as she rode side-by-side with Brehane.

The two exchanged hairpins, declaring themselves sworn sisters. They chatted and giggled like farmers' wives with few cares in the world. The Mystic frequently spoke of the son she so missed, while the princess provided empathetic encouragement. She began to actually resemble the girl from his youth. But on occasion, the princess caught him looking at her. She would lift her chin and turn away, dispelling any illusions.

Around noon on the fourth day, they arrived in the river town of Kalenai. The friendly faces from previous towns and villages gave way to suspicious glares, and the townsfolk refused to sell them food or feed.

Fleet frowned as they came to a stop in the middle of the town. "I've been here many times and have never received such a cold reception."

Tian tapped his chin. They were riding well ahead of the news out of the north. "No one could possibly know. That we're being pursued. And even if they did know... The people of Iksuvi wouldn't help the Teleri."

"You!" a loud, unfriendly voice called out in Arkothi.

Tian turned.

A burly town constable approached, pointing at them. "You there, what business do you have in Kalmies?"

Tian had prepared a story before they'd even set out, just for these occasions, and had rehearsed the long sentence over and over again in his head. He gestured towards Sameer and his friends. "The Kingdom of Tomiwa has asked these Southerners to investigate a haunting at our villa in Kalenai."

The constable regarded him through narrowed eyes. "You're going to have to come with me."

Tian frowned. "Sir, we cannot be delayed."

"You are foreigners on Iksuvi soil—"

Brehane chanted a string of guttural syllables, while crushing some flower petals in her hands.

The constable's expression softened, and he beamed with outstretched hands. "My friends! Forgive me for my rude behavior just now. These are unsettled times."

Brehane smiled back at him. "My companions have said this town was always warm and hospitable; but today, we get nothing but suspicious stares. What has happened?"

The constable shook his head sadly. "I'm so sorry. An altivorc came to our station yesterday. He said that a party of seven Kanin Riders might pass through. He also said that Iksuvi would soon fall to Teleri, and that whichever town captured the Riders would be spared the Mating indefinitely. An entire squad of my men are coming to detain you. You must flee now. Be careful. There's a rumor of a large regiment of altivorcs heading north along the highway."

Tian gritted his teeth. How could their escaped prisoner have spread the news so fast? "Thank you. Tell your comrades that we fled. North along the highway." He then turned to his companions. "We must move quickly."

As they cantered through the streets and out of town, the locals whispered and pointed. They didn't pause until the town was well in the distance, and the next village was just within sight. With tired horses, hungry humans and a famished madaeri, they left the road, descending to the Alto River bank to break for lunch.

The river flowed lazily north, its glittering ripples reflecting the sun high above. Birds flew south against the flow of the river, heading toward their winter nesting grounds. For the first time since the onset of their journey, they had to eat some of the Kanin corn bread. An uneasy silence hung over the group.

Akolyte Cyrus broke the silence. "Brehane, our own mission is in jeopardy now. We must split and go our separate ways."

Tian would do the same if their roles were reversed. He kept his voice measured. "We won't find the pass into the Wilds. Not without Fleet's help. You'll be condemning the princess to capture."

Cyrus kept his voice equally level. "As cruel as it sounds, the nature of Brehane and Sameer's duty impacts everyone on Tivaralan. I'm sorry to say that your princess is—"

Brehane touched her head. "Here, you are right." She then covered her heart. "But sometimes, we must decide *here* what is right. I will not abandon my sworn sister in her time of need."

Cyrus tapped his head several times with his finger. "Consider this. From what we know, we must be at the Kanin pyramid during the full White Moon. If we stay with the Cathayi, we'll be slowed down as they ride around towns instead of through them. We also risk capture. Your own mission must take precedence."

The Akolyte's reasoning was sound. Still, there had to be a way to convince them. Tian looked from Brehane to Sameer.

Sameer intervened. "Our mission is important, but I'm honor-bound to help protect those who need it, especially when we assured them of our swords. Remember that the imperial guard and Jie helped us in Levastya, too, when our magic failed."

Tian blew out a breath.

Cyrus sighed. "As long as you know where I stand. I hope we don't regret this."

The princess rose to her feet. "Thank you, my friends. Once upon a time, I would have been too proud to let my own problem impose on others.

However, you have seen me as none have before; I can never be the resolute and unfailing princess in your eyes. I admit I am afraid. I truly appreciate your help." She bowed low.

The imperial guards all dropped to one knee in a salute.

Fleet piped up, his voice cutting through the reflective silence. "Does anyone have mustard seeds? This bread is quite bland."

The princess glared at him for ruining the moment, and he lowered his head in mock shame.

As they finished up their lunch, Tian gazed over the madaeri's map. They'd reach the crossroads of the east-west and north-south highways by the end of the day. Soon after that, they'd be able to see the northernmost mountains of the Nothori range to the west. The altivorcs must have come from that direction. After reaching the highway, their battalion would turn northward toward Iksuvius. How far away were they now? Who would reach the crossroads first?

Chen Xin said, "The altivorcs are looking for seven Hua disguised as Kanin Riders. If we change back to monks' robes, it might throw them off."

Li Wei shook his head. "Wandering monks don't ride warhorses, and nobody will confuse a Kanin charger for a farm nag."

Fleet jumped up and down, waving his hands. "We'll be able to see the altivorcs on the river basin well in advance. We can leave the highway and ride through the woods a few miles west of here."

"We should split up," Cyrus said. "The Kanin horses are faster anyway, and they're not looking for the three of us."

Tian tapped his chin. Maybe the Akolyte was trying to abandon them again.

Fleet shrugged. "Whether we are seven and four or eleven, we don't stand a chance confronting an army of altivorcs. But in smaller groups, it'll be easier to bypass them. We can meet in the town of Issemies, at the confluence of the Alto and Noto Rivers. It's about two days from here."

It made sense. As long as they saw the altivorcs first, they could avoid them. Tian exchanged glances with Chen Xin, who nodded his approval. All eyes shifted expectantly to the princess, who consented with a tilt of her head. With reluctant farewells, the Hua rode ahead.

That night, they camped under the stars for the first time on their trip, not far from the crossroads between the two main highways. After eating a dinner of cornbread, they fed the horses with the feed they'd bought in Gaukaimas.

Despite the pleasant evening weather, the princess' cheerful demeanor tumbled into silent petulance.

Tian hid his scoff, thinking about how some people actually enjoyed the outdoors. He and the five imperial guards rotated watches, allowing the irritable princess to sleep.

He woke the next morning to find that the horses were bloated, and refused to be ridden. They pressed on nonetheless, pulling reins and cajoling their mounts for a couple of miles before their pace ground to a halt.

Tian called for a break. Removing everything except the horses' saddle blankets and bits, they sat at the roadside and snacked on cornbread. After an hour, the horses' condition deteriorated.

"We might have to leave them behind," Tian said, fiddling with the straps to his armor.

Cornbread crumbs dribbled from Li Wei's mouth as he spoke. "If we do, it'll be the dead of winter before we reach the rendezvous point."

Ma Jun shook his head. "We can buy horses in the next town. We should have enough for seven horses."

Tian tapped his chin. They only had thirty gold *kroon*. Maybe enough for horses.

"What about riding gear?" Xu Zhan pointed at their sick horses. "We can't carry it all—"

"Altivorcs!" Chen Xin scrambled to his feet, pointing with his sabre towards the river.

Tian turned his head. Fifteen altivorcs surged up the riverbank, armed with curved broadswords and spiked shields. Apparently not even the princess, with her keen ears, had heard them above the water splashing among the rocks. The altivorcs fanned out, encircling them.

Kanin spears and sabers in hand, the imperial guards formed a protective circle around her. Taking up a horse bow, Tian came to the princess' side. It'd been years since he'd shot, and as children, she'd always been better. Had she ever shot at live targets before? Her hands trembled as she fitted an arrow to her own bow.

The enemy circled, using their superior numbers to flank each of the guards.

Tian nudged the princess. "Do that thing with your voice."

Kaiya shook her head. "They're resistant to it."

The leader spoke in thickly accented Arkothi. "Turn the princess over to us, and the rest of you will be spared."

"Set spears!" Chen Xin ordered. In response, the guards all took a step back to tighten their circle and lowered their spears.

With a laugh, the leader barked an order in a foul-sounding language. Five of the altivorcs broke away from the group and trotted towards the sick horses.

Tian and the princess both loosed several arrows at the pursuing altivorcs, but they lifted their shields and continued towards the horses. None of the arrows found their mark.

Tian lowered his bow. The enemy could wait them out until they tired or reinforcements came. If someone didn't act now, the altivorcs would be eating horsemeat tonight. He dropped his bow and vaulted into a flip over the protective line, drawing his saber with a simultaneous cut toward the leader.

The sudden attack caught the altivorc unawares, and his head rolled into the dirt. The other altivorcs froze and gaped at the black blood which rhythmically spurted from the severed neck.

Using their shock to his advantage, Tian slashed through the knee ligaments of the next closest.

The imperial guards, perhaps sensing the shift in momentum, surged outward in unison. Spears flashed towards the closest enemy. Just as swiftly, the men spun back into a protective circle around the princess. Their vicious coordination and efficiency was jaw-dropping.

Tian glanced around, evaluating the results of the imperial guards' split-second attack. Chen Xin's lightning strike had impaled an altivorc in the throat, while Zhao Yue thrust through the eye slot of another's helmet. Three altivorcs had suffered injuries.

Those three had no time to fall back. The circle flared out again, this time in a crossing burst of precise thrusts, before reforming around the princess. One second, three more altivorcs down. No wonder Jie had come to respect them.

Behind Tian, the horses cried out. He turned to see two of the altivorcs hacking at their mounts, while the other three rushed back to join in the fray. The princess wept, her fingers fumbling at fitting another arrow.

All-out melee broke out, with one-on-one duels, man versus altivorc. Spears flashed, sabers glinted. Red blood splashed against black. In the half-minute that it took for the other three altivorcs to arrive, the Hua had killed or incapacitated the first group. Tian, along with four of the imperial guards, set upon the last three and quickly finished them off.

The two surviving altivorcs, near the slaughtered horses, bolted. Ma Jun and Li Wei scrambled after them.

"Don't let them get away!" Tian yelled. Why hadn't the princess shot them already? "They will reveal our position. And bring reinforcements."

His orders seemed to unfreeze her. The princess let arrows fly. Even as her hands shook, her aim was true: one altivorc fell, shot in the back, and the other one was slowed as another arrow lodged in his leg. Ma Jun quickly caught up and decapitated it.

The princess sunk to her knees. She turned away from everyone and threw up.

Tian afforded her a quick glance. It must've been hard on her, being so close to combat. He turned his attention to his second victim, the altivorc whose knee he had cut in the opening seconds of the encounter. He knelt, brandishing his broadsword.

Tian disarmed him with a deft twist of his saber, and then wrenched the altivorc's arm back in a lock. "Why did you attack us?"

The altivorc's voice cracked. "We knew to be on the lookout for Cathayi disguised as Kanin Riders, and were ordered to capture you. We knew it was only a matter of time before your horses ate the poisoned feed, and that we would be able to catch up with you."

The sleeping altivorc must have passed the message on. But how? "How did your message get ahead of us? How many of you are coming up the highway? Where are they now?" Tian cranked the lock a little more.

The altivorc chortled and sealed his lips tight.

"Speak, and I will spare you!"

The altivorc set his gaze forward, a grim look forming on his hideous face.

Spewing foul language, Tian placed more torque on his lock. The tearing of ligaments and the dislocating of a joint made a wet popping sound.

The altivorc unleashed a guttural scream. His free hand yanked a dagger from his belt and jerked the blade across his own throat. Black blood gurgled from his mouth, and he collapsed into the dirt.

It was suddenly silent, save for the princess' sobbing.

Tian turned to her. Poor girl. She must have never experienced this type of carnage before. He then realized how wrong he was.

The pounding in Kaiya's ears drowned out all other sound. How she wanted to spit out the sour taste in her mouth!

She'd watched in slow motion as an orc spear floated through the air. Had it been aimed at her? Or Chen Xin's back? It should have hit one of them. But then Xu Zhan was there, in front of her.

He wasn't Tian or Jie, able to use some *Moquan* trick to turn aside projectiles. He blocked the spear the only way he knew how.

With his life.

Now, through the tears in her eyes, his unconscious form was blurry, lying in a pool of his own blood. She knelt beside him, using her shaking hands to try to staunch the profuse bleeding from the gash in his neck.

She wiped away the tears and looked up as Tian approached. What did his tight lips mean? Disgust at her for their predicament? Scorn for Xu Zhan, whom he'd scuffled with when they first arrived in Iksuvius?

Kaiya looked back down. Less of Xu Zhan's blood slipped from between her fingers as his pulse faded. Though belligerent, he'd always been the first to step up to her defense in times of need. How sadly ironic that he loved fighting, and his passion had claimed him. He was only twenty, twenty-one? She clasped his cool hand. Hopefully, that would warm his spirit as he returned to Yang-Di's embrace for a temporary respite. She whispered a prayer that he be reborn into a better world.

As she knelt with a heavy heart, Tian helped the guards bind open wounds. His expression never changed, the loss of a comrade-in-arms seeming more like an inconvenience to him than a tragedy. Words more bitter than the bile's aftertaste threatened to spill out of her mouth.

Chen Xin came forward and knelt. "*Dianxia*. We must bury Xu Zhan. We cannot let carrion birds and other wildlife desecrate his body."

Kaiya nodded in solemn agreement, though it was clear calculations were running through Tian's mind.

His voice droned like a failed poet. "We must hurry. We can't waste much time."

Waste time! How could he consider honoring the dead a waste? Despite his cruel words, he grabbed an altivorc shield and dug into the soft ground near the river. Chen Xin, Ma Jun, and Zhao Yue joined him. Li Wei, even more somber than usual, helped her collect large stones along the banks to form a cairn.

"Let us create more cairns," said Ma Jun, "to make it appear as if we have lost more than one of our own. Since we don't have the horses anymore, we should disguise ourselves as wandering monks, as Chen Xin suggested earlier."

Kaiya shot a glance over at Tian, who in turn looked at the Iridescent Moon. Still thinking about time!

"Very well," he said. "Keep it simple."

They made two more shallow graves, stacked rocks in a ring around the mound, and placed a Kanin suit of armor and sword on top of each.

When they were finished, the imperial guards all bowed their heads.

Kaiya followed their lead, saluting Xu Zhan. "If we make it home, I swear we will one day return in force so that we can take you back."

They threw the rest of the Kanin armor into the river, and dressed in monks' robes with broad conical straw hats. They kept the spears in hand and packed away three sabers, as well as her pair of straight swords. Saying their final farewells to Xu Zhan, they continued south down the highway on foot, keeping a quick pace and drawing the curious stares of passing travelers.

Kaiya sighed. They stood out like a bride on her wedding day.

CHAPTER 29:

Sacrifices

The princess and her imperial guards trudged down the road in front of Tian. Xu Zhan's death weighed heavily on his mind, clouding all the other questions that raced through it. Pugnacious and curt from their very first meeting, Xu had nonetheless earned Tian's grudging respect over the past few weeks.

Indeed, all of the imperial guards had proven more mentally capable than he'd given them credit for: Chen Xin's recognition of King Arvydas' dissembling; Li Wei's observation about their mismatched disguises; Ma Jun's suggestion to mask their losses with multiple cairns. Their precise and ferocious attacks when defending the princess. How many more of them would perish from his failed escape plan?

With a sigh, he tried to focus on their current predicament. Without horses, they couldn't outrun the altivorcs if they encountered a large regiment. He would have to find a way to buy or otherwise liberate some horses in the next town. If there were any healthy horses there.

By dusk, they had only walked about thirty *li* in somber silence. Tian glanced at the princess again. Her jaw had been rigidly set and eyes focused straight ahead the whole time. His stomach clenched. Did she blame him for the death of Xu? The loss of their horses? At this rate, it would take around three days to reach Issemies, while Brehane and the others would arrive in less than two. Would they pass each other on the road sometime

tomorrow? If they missed each other, would Brehane wait, over Cyrus' inevitably vocal objections?

Mercifully, they made it to a town before night fell. They stayed at an inn and ate warm food. The mood was solemn, with the imperial guards' sorrow at the loss of their comrade drowned by the local ale. Tian abstained, instead concerning himself with the stares of the innkeeper and patrons as they pointed and joked about the Cathayi monks with long hair.

Early the next morning, Chen Xin and Zhao Yue set out to look for horses. Though they returned unsuccessful, they were able to procure larger packs to carry the supplies.

After a quick breakfast, the group set out as the Iridescent Moon waned to its second crescent. Walking in silence, it didn't take long for them to reach the town limits. Before the third crescent, it was well behind them.

When they took their first break around the fourth crescent, Tian worked up the courage to say what he had been thinking since the night before. "We're dressed like monks. But we still have hair. Even the locals can tell."

Ma Jun ran a hand through his hair. "What do you suggest?"

Tian braced himself for their reaction. "Shave it off."

Zhao Yue grasped a lock of his hair. "Only monks, newly inducted soldiers, and convicted criminals shave their heads."

Li Wei snorted. "Or have it shaved for them."

Tian threw his hands up. He'd expected resistance. After all, long hair was a badge of pride in Hua. But this...

"For the princess' safety." Chen Xin stepped up and extended his hand toward Ma. "I will go first. Ma Jun, your razor."

Thank the Heavens someone saw reason. Tian glanced at the princess. Her arms were folded over her chest, her eyes set forward above her frown. This one would be harder.

Li Wei snorted again, but headed down the bank. "At least Xu Zhan got to keep his hair."

Tian descended the riverbank with the guards close behind. The princess tentatively followed. The imperial guards helped each other cut their hair with a dagger, while Ma Jun shaved everyone close with his razor. When it was Tian's turn, he watched as his hair floated downstream.

When the last guard finished, Tian looked expectantly at the princess. "Now you."

She turned her head like a petulant child. "Never."

Tian looked towards the imperial guards for support, but they all edged back and stayed silent. "*Dian-xia*. Locals have been staring. At least cut your hair close. To hide under your hat. You don't have to shave it."

She scowled at him with a glare sharp enough to shear steel. "I will *not* look like a slave or prisoner."

Perhaps she wanted to be the First Consul's bed slave. Tian clenched his jaw. "On foot, we can't outrun the altivorcs. We can't fight any more than ten."

"My hair will not be touched. That is my order."

Where was Jie when he needed her? Maybe the princess would have listened to her. "Xu Zhan sacrificed himself for you. The rest of us will do the same. Is your own vanity more important than our lives?"

The princess' face hardened. She spun around and walked back towards the road.

Tian opened and closed his fists. His life would be forfeit if they ever reached home. She would resent what he was about to do, but she would live to realize it was the right decision. He might be the villain today, but he would not be the fool in history.

Kaiya stood by the riverbank watching the waters drift northward. Though she wouldn't admit it aloud, she took greater pride in her hair than even her voice. Even when she'd been a woefully plain child, her hair had been beautiful. And now, the silky, lustrous locks could be pinned, braided, or curled. The very thought of cutting them made her heart seize up.

She didn't have to listen to this incompetent cur's demands. She turned to climb up the bank.

The guards had already reached the road, a couple dozen feet away. When had they departed? And where was Tian?

Her head jerked back. She gasped at the burning pain in her scalp from the yank on her hair.

"*Dian-xia*, forgive me. I do this for you." Tian's voice choked, even as he seized a larger handful of her beautiful tresses. He used them to tug her along, ignoring every tearful threat, curse, and plea she could muster.

With her feet unable to grip the ground, the power of her voice died on her lips. All grace and martial technique forgotten, she twisted around and flailed at him. Her long hair allowed him to stay out of reach as he dragged her inexorably towards the river.

At the bank, he spun her hair into a thick coil around his hand. She frantically tried to hold on to her precious locks, but her hands only became entangled.

Holding the dagger in an underhand grip, he slid his arm up the coil, pushing her fingers back through the mass. With a lightning twist of his wrist, the blade slashed through her hair. The sudden cut sent her tumbling to the ground, butt first.

They both stared at the long, voluminous bundle in his hands.

Her hair.

He had cut her hair.

Kaiya screamed. Staggering to her feet, she lurched over to Tian and repeatedly battered him with her hands. In her rage and sorrow, she barely noticed that tears streamed unchecked down his cheeks as well.

Too late, the imperial guards appeared at the top of the bank and scrambled down. Where had they been?

Chen Xin lunged forward, seizing Tian's robe. Tears glistened in his eyes. "What have you done?"

Tian flopped to the ground when Chen Xin threw him down.

Still weeping, Kaiya turned around and clambered up the riverbank. She stumbled to the road and collapsed against a boulder. With short, ragged breaths, she ran her hands through the remains of her hair, finding the cut rough and jagged. Only a finger-length towards the back of her head, it lengthened to an uneven hand-width towards the top.

Her hair.

Zhao Yue and Ma Jun staggered after her and bowed, watching in silence.

They pitied her.

She raised her head.

Both guards dropped to their knees, offering their sabers forth in two hands. "Forgive me, *Dian-xia!*" they shouted in unison.

Kaiya looked back down towards the river.

She was the daughter of the *Tianzi.* The blood of the gods coursed through her veins. A ruler should not shed a tear over personal loss. Tian did what he had to, did what she could have never done herself.

Setting her jaw, she wiped the tears from her face. The chafing fibers served as yet another reminder of how far she had fallen. With a deep breath, she rose and marched back to where Chen Xin and Li Wei detained Tian. Zhao and Ma trailed a respectful distance behind.

Choking on his own sobs, Tian knelt down, hands on top of his bowed head. His heart pumped guilt through his veins. It was surprising, actually. He shouldn't feel guilty for something that gave them the best chance of survival. So why did it feel so *awful?*

Better to die, here and now, than carry the shame of hurting his childhood friend.

Chen Xin and Li Wei both stood cross-armed in front of him, though neither held a weapon.

Tian barely recognized his own voice through its hoarseness. "I'm so sorry. It had to be done. For her sake."

Chen Xin let an exasperated sigh escape. "We are just as guilty for letting it happen. We're soldiers, and we understand the need. You may look down on her vanity, but it's her armor against what she faces every day of her life. Try to empathize. Here she comes now."

Empathize. All the other women in his life were *Moquan.* Practical. Like Jie. Who he'd probably never see again. If only she were here now. Tian looked up.

The princess approached, her carriage straight and regal as always, even if her scraggly hair didn't match the image.

He cringed. He'd done that to her. Already on his knees, he touched his forehead to the ground. "It had to be done, *Dian-xia.* I will take my life now. If you so command."

Her tone was icy, biting with a hatred that chilled his bones more than a Northwest winter. "I have already lost Xu Zhan. We will not sacrifice anyone else needlessly. But know that from this day, your life belongs to me, and you will give it when I ask."

"As you command, *Dian-xia*." Tian raised his head, not daring to make eye contact.

The princess took a few steps along the rocks and glanced down at a tidal puddle. Her face was frozen in composed perfection, like an alabaster statue, as she stroked the remnants of her hair back. She then turned to Ma Jun and extended a hand. "Your razor."

Ma Jun withdrew his razor and held it up to her in both hands with his head bowed. She took it and lopped off what was left of her hair. After shaving five heads already, it had dulled and it did not cut evenly. Every couple of seconds, the princess winced.

It was a ragged job. Ma Jun clasped her hand and took the razor. While he worked at finishing the job, she silently took up a long lock of her hair and started braiding it. She finished quickly and stashed the braid away into the fold of her monk's robe.

When Ma Jun stepped back and bowed his head, the princess stood and gazed into the river again. She took a deep breath and then let out a long sigh. She didn't look at any of them.

Tian gritted his teeth. His fault.

On her hoarse and rasping command, they resumed their trek. After two phases of brisk walking in silence, Tian called on the party to halt. In the distance, open farmland gave way to wooded hills, which stretched from the riverbank to as far west as the eye could see and would obscure any approaching threats.

Tian tapped his chin. They could hide off-road behind the trees if they heard armored Altivorcs traipsing through the woods.

As long as they got there quickly. He beckoned the others onward. "Come on. We need to hurry."

A hundred feet. Fifty. Twenty.

Twenty altivorcs emerged from the trees, resembling spears thrusting out between shields in an Arkothi phalanx. Oh, no.

Tian motioned for the imperial guards to stay calm. They were about to test their disguise.

With the precision of a dwarf-made clock, the altivorcs' long line merged into a three-man wide column that took up the width of the road. At the head, their leader bared his fangs at them. "Off the road, peasants!"

Tian waved the imperial guards and princess off the road. All bowed their heads as the column passed without further word.

Vindicated! Tian blew out a sigh of relief. He dared a glance at the princess, but her hard expression hadn't changed.

When the sounds of marching altivorc boots faded in the distance, they resumed their journey, following the road through the woods. Tian scouted ahead, seeing only a couple of travelers and hunters. Before long they emerged on the other side into open farmland.

After a few phases, the clopping of three horses approached from behind, at a walk. Tian turned around.

It was their friends from the South, minus the madaeri. The three soon overtook them and passed.

Tian waved his hands wildly. "Brehane! Sameer! Cyrus!"

Sameer reared his horse and wheeled around. "By the Gods! What happened to you? Where is Xu? Where are your horses?"

"Our horses were poisoned. We were ambushed." Tian was loathe to tell the whole story.

Brehane's eyes sought out the princess', but the princess turned her head and refused to meet the Mystic's gaze.

"We must keep going," Cyrus said. "Now that the Cathayi don't have horses, they'll only slow us down. A full White Moon draws near."

The rapid pounding of hooves from the south interrupted Tian's rebuttal. He threaded past the horses to see Fleet coming down the slope in the road, bouncing in the saddle with his horse at full gallop. As the madaeri approached, he waved them off the road. Once he was within earshot, he started yelling. "Altivorcs! Thousands of them marching down the highway!"

Tian scanned the road ahead, but the rising ridge obscured his line of sight.

Yet as if to punctuate Fleet's warning, deep, ominous drums echoed from beyond. The madaeri pulled up and the clop of his galloping horse quieted. The sound of thousands of heavy boots rhythmically thumped on the hard-packed road.

Another series of drumbeats thundered up ahead, frightening dozens of black birds out of a tree on the downslope.

"It would be bad for us to be seen together," Cyrus said, his voice flat and emotionless. "Especially if news from the towns up north has reached that our group—which stands out in this land of the fair-skinned—is traveling with yours."

Brehane nodded in agreement. "Cyrus is correct. There is no way we can fight thousands of altivorcs, and the plains are too open for us to find cover. We'll withdraw to the north toward the closest farm and wait for them to pass. Princess, come with us. Fleet, hide and keep an eye on the Cathayi. You may be our only chance to link back up. We will meet at the next town."

Tian nodded. The princess should be safe with the others. With the altivorcs soon upon them, they could test out their disguise, but without risking her safety.

Chen Xin bowed deeply towards Sameer. "If something should happen to us, I humbly request that you deliver the princess to Cathay after you have completed your duties."

Sameer pressed his hands together and bowed his head, while Fleet slid out of the saddle. He flashed a grin at Tian and helped the princess up onto his horse with a little too much enthusiasm. Where had he put his dirty paws? The imperial guards glared at the madaeri, but if the princess was offended, she didn't show it.

They knelt in salute, and she looked at them sadly. "Thank you for your service up to now. I am sure this will not be our final farewell."

Maybe it would be. And despite all their conflict now, they'd once been best friends. Tian tried to make eye contact with her, but she looked away. The Mystic, Acolyte, Paladin, and princess all turned and galloped north. It would make a great

opening to a bad joke, if the consequences weren't so severe.

Fleet winked at Tian before scrambling down the riverbank and into some shrubs. Even Tian's sharp eyes couldn't find him among the brush.

He turned to the remaining four guards. "Continue walking. It will look suspicious. If we just stand here. Waiting for them."

They continued down the road. The altivorcs reached the crest of the hill and started the gentle descent. They marched in a tight formation, six abreast, shoulder-to-shoulder, taking up the entire road. At their head rode a single mounted officer. Their black flags hung lifelessly on the windless day.

They drew nearer and nearer in neat ranks, trailing each other like a line of ants. When they were about fifty feet away, the mounted altivorc waved them to the side of the road.

Tian and the guards complied, moving to the side closest to the river. They removed their hats and bowed their bald heads. He could see the altivorcs clearly now, with their chainmail, spears, and curved broadswords, looking straight ahead and marching in precision. The leader guided his horse—was it a horse? It was covered head to toe in armor, yet barely made a sound—off the side of the road to meet them, while his troops kept moving forward.

He spoke Arkothi in a thick accent. "You there. Have you seen riders from the southlands, riding large warhorses? Seven total, perhaps with a woman."

Chen Xin shook his head. "No sir. The highway has been more or less empty for about two hours, with the exception of a small group of your kind who passed by half an hour ago."

The altivorc officer turned and rode south toward the back of the column. Not long after, drumbeats emanated from that direction. Several seconds later, a series of drumbeats answered, echoing from the north.

They must be communicating with drums. Tian memorized the beat pattern in hopes that he could decipher the code in the future.

Minutes stretched into an hour, and at last the rear ranks passed. At the end of the line, an enormous packhorse, over twice as large as a warhorse and clad from head to hoof in plate armor, took deliberate steps like a dressage show horse. Despite all the metal, it moved quietly, pulling a train of wooden wagons.

The first dozen were no more than cages on wheels, several filled with young Nothori women. With wide, desperate eyes, some reached towards Tian. Others sat listlessly, resigned to their fate.

The first wave of rape victims for the Teleri breeding program. Was there any way to help them? Five men and a madaeri against an army of altivorcs? Maybe trail the column and raid their encampment at night? No; if they weren't careful, Princess Kaiya would be joining these unfortunate women.

He watched as the last wagon passed, bearing a huge drum, cut from the cross section of a greywood tree. "What was the count?" Tian asked.

"I counted five hundred ranks," said Chen Xin, "so about three thousand."

They looked among each other and confirmed the count with nods.

"All right. Let's keep moving south. The princess will catch up. They'll go around the altivorcs. On the horses."

Fleet picked himself out of the brush and rejoined them by the road. "Well, that was fun. Been a long time since I've seen one of those beasts." The madaeri pulled errant twigs out of his hair as they started up the slope in the road.

Once they reached the crest of the hill, Tian and Fleet took advantage of the higher ground to look back to where their companions had fled.

Fleet squinted. "Oh no…"

CHAPTER 30

A Bitter Homecoming

The sounds of heavy boots stomped in rhythm with the pounding in Jie's head, jolting her awake. A straw mattress pricked her back, further prodding her eyes open.

Feeble rays of sun trickled in through a shuttered round window, barely illuminating a stifling, narrow room. The sharply-pitched ceiling with exposed rafters told her she was in an attic space somewhere. But where? And how?

Through the quickly clearing fog in her head, Jie fought to recall her last memories. She'd been about to slash the renegade *Moquan*'s throat when an explosion unbalanced her. He'd head-butted her! A dirty trick she could appreciate.

Jie pushed herself up, despite complaints from her listless limbs. The plain brown cloak that was draped over her slipped, revealing her nakedness. She looked down and sighed at her boyish form, made even flatter by weight loss. The cloak found its way back up, covering a bandaged shoulder wound she did not recall wrapping.

She rubbed at her chafed wrists as she wobbled to her feet. Concentrate. This was one of Tian's hideouts. Above a warehouse near the west marketplace. She let out the breath she'd been holding. One of her comrades must have brought her here. Or...the renegade? That couldn't be right.

A ceramic cup filled with water beckoned her to a neatly arranged pile of supplies. She greedily quenched her thirst with the tepid water while examining the items. A hunk of cornbread. A single-edged knife. Brown woolen clothes, suited for a peasant. A knitted wool hat with flaps that would cover her pointed ears. Her black utility suit, its tears well-stitched. Most importantly, her magic pouch. She picked it up, revealing a sheet of crinkled parchment underneath. Hua words were written with a quill in an unrecognizable hand.

Iksuvius occupied. Citywide curfew at sundown. Hua embassy gutted. Blend in with the locals. Don't do anything stupid.

A Friend.

When did she ever do anything stupid? That was Tian's job, especially when Princess Kaiya was involved. Maybe he was back in the city, looking for her. Her heart swelled.

Chewing on the cornbread, Jie teetered to the window and pried the shutters open a crack. The marketplace below, typically buzzing in the late afternoon with the chatter of young women and the laughing of children, was quiet. Shopkeepers edged back into their stores as a patrol of Bovyans marched through. Though it'd taken her some time to get used to the stink of the marketplace, she'd always appreciated the overall liveliness. Now it was just filthy.

The brittle light would soon give way to night, and darkness would allow her to venture out. In the meantime, she ate, rehydrated, and stretched out her muscles. The pounding in her head felt less like a hammer on a dwarf anvil now, and more like a dull ache. She looked at the letter again. Now why would a *Moquan* brother use a quill and parchment?

Dusk came. Dressed again in her black clothes, Jie ventured out, drinking in the cool night air. The White Moon Renyue's waning gibbous marked two days since the attack on the embassy. Tian *had* to be back by now.

In the marketplace, doors were barred and windows shuttered. It was so quiet she could hear the waves in the harbor lapping up against the seawall. The silence also allowed her to hear patrols well before they came close, and she slunk unmolested through the shadows towards the embassy.

The damage was obvious even from a distance. The main residence and temple, which had once vaulted gracefully above the walls, were now nothing more than burnt-out shells.

A hollow sensation settled in her stomach that had nothing to do with hunger. The embassy had been home for only a month, but it had been an enjoyable month, which *almost* culminated in a kiss.

A pair of Bovyans stood guard just inside the gates, ready to ambush anyone who tried to enter. Jie almost pitied their lack of stealth. She crept along the walls to the east side, where the bathhouse courtyard—if it was still there—would conceal her insertion.

The wall felt cool beneath her hands as her fingers found nooks between the stones. In short order, she made it to the top and peeked over. All clear. Creeping between the crenellations, she dropped down onto the walk. The vantage point afforded a wide view of the damage.

Where the armory had stood, there was now nothing but a dark splotch in her elf vision. The debris radiated out from the blast site, with blackened stones lying in a clearly-defined circle starting a dozen feet from the epicenter. Fire had claimed the warehouses, leaving only roofless, charred shells of stone. The main residence itself fared no better—flames must have consumed the wooden beams, leaving only the stone façade and western walls intact.

This place was where she had reconnected with Tian and almost fulfilled a decade of unrequited affection. Now rubble was all that remained. Jie swallowed the nostalgia and returned to her task of information gathering. There were the two sentries to interrogate.

Dropping down to the ground, she snuck along the walls toward the temple. It remained untouched by the destruction, probably due to its distance from the blast. Inside, the statue of Yang-Di still glowed. The green hues of her night vision burst into full color.

She almost wished they hadn't. The dark bloodstains stood out on the white stone floors and the red-painted walls. Memories flooded back: the slaughter of the ambassador, the imperial guards, and the princess' decoy, Meiling. Her scream was haunting— handmaidens rarely left the sumptuous confines of Sun-Moon palace, and none in the history of Hua had ever been lost to violence.

Jie shook the thought out of her head and came to the long rope that sounded the temple bell. She gave it a gentle tug: light enough so that its ring would hopefully stay within the confines of the embassy grounds.

She then rushed to the entrance and peeked out. As expected, the guards looked up at the bell. One broke from his position, drew a longsword, and marched towards the temple.

With a silent prayer of apology to Yang-Di, she climbed to the broad beam above the main doors.

The Bovyan clambered up the steps and strode through. She pounced on him, jabbing her knife through his subclavian artery and possibly into his lung. His sword clattered to the ground as he buckled to his knees.

Jie glanced toward the main gate. Her ambush would've stood out like a stage play to the other sentry. Her friendly wave jolted him out of his blank look. She turned to her gasping victim, whose blood now spurted in rhythmic bursts. It joined the altivorc blood she'd spilled in the very spot days before. "Why are you here?" she demanded, on the off chance that he might actually reveal something with his dying breaths.

"Die, Cathayi snake." The words tumbled out of his mouth with his last moments of consciousness.

Jie looked back towards his companion. He took the temple steps two at a time. She retreated deeper inside.

To her dismay, the jaunt up the steps didn't seem to tire him at all. She ran to the side of the statue to lure him in.

The soldier approached, pointing his sword at her. "Surrender."

He was taller than the other, and the suns on his collar marked him as an officer. With another quick apology to Yang-Di, Jie turned and pop-vaulted onto the statue's base, just at the edge of her adversary's reach.

"You're the female Black Fist spy! You're supposed to be dead!" He swung his sword at her, and she danced away from the blows.

She stopped and raised an open hand. "Shhh... Can you hear that?"

The man paused, but kept his sword raised. His brow furrowed. "What?"

She grinned at him. "Absolutely nothing. None of your patrols are within my very long earshot." She pointed behind him. "It's just you and my partner there."

The man turned his head. In the split second before he could turn back and raise his sword, she leapt down and slashed his wrist tendons. His sword slipped from his fingers. Before it hit the floor, she ducked low and severed the tendon in back of his heel. Working her way around to his other leg, she hooked his ankle and pushed into the back of his knee.

The Bovyan hit the ground face-first with a loud bellow.

Jie swung around and sat on top of him, still cranking his knee. "You won't live to see the sun rise. If you don't answer my questions, you will survive to just before dawn, but you'll wish you hadn't. So why're you here?" She added a little more torque, just enough to get him to yelp.

He spoke through gritted teeth. "We are rounding up all the Cathayi in the city as enemies of the state. Some come back here."

"Where are you keeping them?"

He didn't answer. She twisted a little harder, evoking a grunt.

His words spilled freely. "The men, in the city jails. The women, at the Teleri compound, entertaining us. That one girl, the treacherous princess' little bitch, she was real good."

Meiling. She must've survived. Jie leaned back a little, adding just a little more pain. "She's at the Teleri compound?"

"No, she's at the palace now. She's a noble, so she is servicing the officers. Her child will be part of your country's new ruling class."

Jie decided to punish his gloating with another sharp twist. Ligaments tore, the knee joint popped. She spun around on top of him, took control of his left arm and began wrenching it behind him. "Why are you keeping the Cathayi prisoner? What use are they to you?"

He laughed past his pain. "We torture one man to death each day, in public. If your princess weren't such a coward, she would come out to spare her people. Tell her that."

So they believed the princess was still nearby. "You deserve a slow, painful death, but I'm not so cruel."

Despite what she led others to believe, killing wasn't fun, not even a Bovyan or altivorc. With surgical precision, she slid her knife into the space between his spine and skull. His body went limp.

What a mistake! Even at full strength, it would be strenuous and time-consuming to dispose of the bodies. The *Moquan* traitor—assuming he was still at large—would be able to identify her work. Her only advantage now was stealth and surprise. Sucking on her lower lip, and yet again apologizing to Yang-Di and the dead men, she took a longsword and began mutilating the bodies.

To take her mind off the unenviable task, she began plotting her next move: rescuing Meiling from the Iksuvi palace, where the Teleri officers had apparently taken up residence. And she knew one Teleri officer very well.

CHAPTER 31:

Off the Beaten Path

The wind blew over Kaiya's scalp as Fleet's horse galloped behind the Southerners. The sensation served as a reminder that her head had been shaved; the periodic booming of altivorc drums proved it had been the right move.

Before long, they came to a tree-lined dirt walkway that cut through vast rows of leafy green vegetables. It ended at a one-story farmhouse some five hundred feet up a gentle slope. Brehane pointed them toward the path.

They followed it to the weathered house. Behind it, broad fields of red wheat swayed a head above her. Kaiya turned back and looked down towards the highway, which stretched along the river. Back south the way they had come, the altivorcs seemed like a line of black, inching their way up the white road.

Brehane gestured past an empty wagon towards a wooden stable, next to a chicken coop. "We'll hide there till they pass."

"I don't suppose we have time to tell whomever lives here that we are squatting?" Sameer's shoulders rose in a shrug.

A smile formed unbidden on Kaiya's face. Sameer, polite even in a crisis.

"No time!" Brehane pointed down towards the army making its way up the river road. Still far away, but there was certainly a risk of being seen. She clasped Kaiya's clammy hand and pulled her along to the stable. Inside, they found four old plow horses.

Hiding with the animals. Kaiya instinctively went to twirl her hair, only to find it gone. She shrugged off her pack and crouched, watching as the altivorc column passed along the road. She peeked out. Cold sweat beaded on her forehead as the first ranks marched by.

An hour of waiting trudged by. The last ranks passed, trailed by an enormous armored draft horse, effortlessly pulling a train of wagons. All those young women in cages. That could've been her. A chill crept up her spine.

She was about to let a sigh escape when a mounted altivorc wheeled and pointed towards the farm. Six soldiers broke off from the rear of the column and hustled up the path.

At the entrance to the farmhouse, an altivorc rapped on the door. He yelled in heavily accented Arkothi, "This region now belongs to the Teleri Empire. We are taking a census and collecting tribute."

Kaiya pushed herself deeper into the stable, her heart pounding.

The altivorcs waited for a few seconds, and then one kicked in the door with a loud thud. Within seconds, the sound of furniture and dishes breaking mixed in with the crude laughs of the altivorcs. Kaiya bit her lip. Whoever lived there—

One of the altivorcs laughed. "No tribute? Then we will take your daughter, instead!"

A woman screamed.

Sameer sprang to his feet, his curved *naga* in hand.

Brehane urgently waved him down.

Cyrus hissed at him. "Remember the mission! Remember the princess!"

Focus set forward, the Paladin strode out of the stable and toward the farmhouse.

Brehane sighed. "Not again..."

Again? Kaiya searched the Aksumi's eyes. "Shouldn't we help him?"

Brehane clasped her necklace. "He will have no problem with six altivorcs. He may be a newly-minted Paladin, but they are easily worth ten trained men. We just need to make sure none of them escapes to tell their friends."

Kaiya looked back at the road. The distance between them and the altivorc column increased at a crawl. How long before they would send someone to find out what happened to their comrades?

Grunts emanated from the house. Loud crashes followed. Kaiya craned over the others at the stable door, just in time to see two altivorcs burst out of the house at full sprint.

Brehane jerked her head back, but then began a guttural chant. Streaks of glowing arrows appeared out of thin air and darted towards one of the fleeing altivorcs. He let out a shriek as the energy tore into his back. He stumbled into the dirt. The other dashed down the walkway, waving his arms and yelling.

From the rear of the column, an altivorc turned his head in the direction of the farm. Brehane mumbled something in her language. The tone could only be a curse.

Six ranks—three dozen altivorcs in all— peeled off the back of the column and charged towards the path. The sound of drums echoed down the river.

Cyrus shook his head and drew his scimitar.

"Sister, your flute," Brehane said as she reached down to pick up some dirt. "Play the tune from the other day!"

With trembling hands, Kaiya fumbled for her *dizi*, which was tucked in the folds of her robe. Bringing the flute to her lips, she played.

The sound warbled out disjointed, without clarity or resonance.

"More control! More soothing!" Brehane's forehead crinkled as she rolled the soil between her fingers.

The altivorcs covered the distance quickly. They were no more than twenty feet away.

Kaiya sank her toes into the ground and took a deep, calming breath. What were forty altivorcs compared to a dragon? The flute's sound leveled off.

Brehane seemed to inhale the musical notes and started invoking harsh words, finishing her incantation by tossing dirt at the closing altivorcs.

They collapsed to the ground with a loud clatter of armor and steel weapons. All deep in slumber.

"How did you do that?" Cyrus stared at Brehane with rounded eyes. "I've never seen you affect so many."

Bent over panting, hands on her knees, Brehane nodded at Kaiya. Before the Mystic could open her mouth, a black-fletched arrow lodged into the stable wall, just a handbreadth from her head.

Kaiya lowered the flute and tracked the arrow back to its source. A line of altivorcs stood on the highway, loosing a volley of arrows.

Cyrus grabbed her wrist and pulled her back into the stable. Both huddled near the ground as multiple thuds rained into the walls outside.

"Quickly, get your things." Cyrus scrambled on all fours and grabbed his and Sameer's saddlebags. Kaiya and Brehane also shouldered their own packs.

Cyrus peeked around the corner. "We can't stay here, we'll be trapped! Brehane, can you create some sort of diversion?"

The Mystic shook her head as if it were an anvil. "I'm depleted. I need some rest before I can call on the resonance of the universe."

"Princess?" Cyrus raised an eyebrow at her.

Kaiya bowed her head. "Maybe if I could reach the altivorc drums."

Cyrus snorted. "It would be easier to run in the *other* direction."

Kaiya stood straight and squared her shoulders. "I will surrender myself, and try to barter my freedom for yours."

Outside, Sameer's voice rang out. "Altivorc fools, your archery is horrible, see if you can hit me!"

Brehane peeked out and then turned back. "They are taking aim at Sameer. Run! Into the fields behind us! They will have a harder time targeting us in the wheat."

Kaiya opened her mouth, but Cyrus took her hand and pulled her along. Before they turned the corner, she stole a glance towards the front of the house, where Sameer stood.

Dozens of arrows streaked towards him. He moved inhumanly fast, a blur to her eye. His sword seemed to glow a light blue as he effortlessly weaved around arrows that should have hit him. It might have been unbelievable if she hadn't witnessed his master fight on the trip to Vyara City. To think Sameer was only an initiate into his order.

Cyrus pulled her into the rows of wheat, where the stalks growing above their heads would hide them.

Within minutes, Sameer caught up, grinning.

After a while, their running slowed to a brisk walk. In the distance, the muffled yells of the altivorcs grew fainter and fainter.

Cyrus breathed heavily. "We can run faster, but the altivorcs have better endurance. They'll catch up. We need to find a way to lose them."

Sameer nodded. "Beyond the fields to the west are some woods, and several miles beyond that, wooded hills that start to rise into the mountains. Those should provide cover from their arrows. We can find a place to hide there and then return to the main road in a couple of days."

Kaiya's lungs and legs burned, unaccustomed to long stretches of physical exertion. Discarding any notions of propriety, she dropped into an unladylike squat, one hand on the ground. Each breath was a struggle. Afraid and useless, a burden on strangers. The pack slipped off her shoulders. "I can't go on. It's me they want, so

I will wait here and try to buy you more time to escape."

Cyrus shook his head. His voice was flat, conveying no emotion. "No, Your Highness, we have attacked them and they will come for us, regardless of whether you are with us. There's another way."

He withdrew a gold disk that hung from his neck. The symbol of Athran, the Levanthi God of the Sun. She'd seen it during her visit to Vadaras, while searching unsuccessfully for an Akolyte to cure Father.

He placed his hands on her shoulder and began chanting in a musical language.

A cool wave washed over her, and the aching in her muscles faded. Her lungs lightened and the air felt cool and fresh. It was like waking from a peaceful night's slumber.

His dark eyes searched hers. "How are you now? Can you go on?"

She nodded.

He smiled. "Athran favors you."

"Let's keep moving!" urged Brehane.

From near the crest of the hill, Tian saw the altivorcs in the distance break ranks and advance on a farm. There was no way the Southerners could defend the princess. His plans had failed. Again. To think his *Moquan* brothers once considered him the second coming of the Architect.

He motioned for the imperial guards. "Come on. We need to rescue the princess."

"Wait." Squinting, Fleet raised his hand. "Our friends are safe for the time being."

Tian strained his eyes. How could the madaeri know?

Fleet pointed. "They are fleeing west-southwest through the fields of red wheat, towards the woods beyond."

The other group should have never run into trouble at all. Tian threw his hands up. "We need to help them."

Fleet held his stubby fingers up, framing a spot in the woods. "If they're smart, they will start heading south once they enter the woods. If we head due west, we might be able to intercept them. If not, I can track them. Follow me."

The madaeri dashed toward the hills. Tian and the imperial guards hurried to catch up, setting a brisk pace westward through the Iksuvi farmland. Fleet would occasionally look towards where they had last seen the other group, but otherwise kept moving forward. After an hour, they neared the woods.

Fleet raised his fist, calling for a halt. "I think we're still slightly ahead of them, based on the pace they were keeping. Wait here while I look for tracks."

The others squatted to catch their breath while their diminutive guide disappeared into the tree line. How did he have so much energy? Tian fidgeted. He had to do something. Not just sit here.

Fleet returned soon. "There were no fresh human tracks, and certainly not a dozen altivorc boot prints." He motioned them in a north-northwesterly direction into the woods, and they had to hurry to try to keep up. Despite his short legs, he moved swiftly and lightly through the underbrush, leaving the Hua behind.

Tian yelled, "Fleet, slow down!"

"No time!" the madaeri called back. "I'll whistle like this..." he let out a very shrill sound, unbelievable that someone so small could make it, "...every few minutes to let you know where I am. You do the same."

The whistles drifted farther and farther away over the next half-hour. The trees grew denser and denser, until they came to a clearing. Exhausted, Tian threw himself down on a fallen log. He motioned for the imperial guards to join him.

It was hopeless. They'd never reunite with Fleet, let alone the princess. He was a failure.

The madaeri yelled back through the trees. "I found them. Stay where you are."

Tian's heart soared. The madaeri was incredible.

Before long, the Southerners emerged from an animal path, with Fleet in the lead. The princess glided straight and regal, with no sign of fatigue. The Hua dropped to one knee in a bow. "*Dian-xia*," they shouted in unison.

Fleet shot them an annoyed glance, cutting his hand in front of his mouth.

"It is a miracle," Chen Xin whispered, "that we were able to find you in these woods."

"No miracle, just exceptional wilderness skills." The madaeri grinned.

Kaiya bowed deeply to Brehane. The Hua followed suit. "I am so sorry. Because of me, you lost your horses, and you will not be able to reach the Kanin pyramid in time."

Cyrus shook his head. "What is done is done. There is no point placing blame. We must just continue forward. The White Moon is full once a month."

Fleet pointed west. "The main road will not be safe for the next couple of days. I suggest we head up into the hills and keep heading south. About three days south of here, the river bends. We can descend there and return to the road. We travel by day, to take away the altivorc's advantage with their night vision." Without waiting for discussion, he started down a path heading southwest.

Tian tapped his chin. What other choice was there but to follow? At least for now, they were safe.

With about three hours of daylight left, the group forged ahead, following paths worn by animals. When they came across streams, Fleet insisted that they walk through them until they found new paths.

By the time the sun sank to just above the Nothori Mountains, they had reached the foot of the hills. The trees thinned. For the time being they found themselves well ahead of the altivorcs, with cold feet and in desperate need of rest. While the others stopped to catch their breath and drink some water, Fleet backtracked to cover their trail. How did the madaeri get his endless energy?

Upon his return, he reported that the altivorcs had lost their trail. Even so, it would be safer to keep up a fast pace and head into the hills where they might find shelter.

After spending the last hour of sunlight marching, Fleet left the party again to search for a campsite. He returned with the news of a small cave not far up a nearby hill.

Tian wiped the sweat from his brow and turned to the princess. In the low light, the princess' features twisted. What now?

They climbed a winding path to the entrance to the cave. The Southerners entered first. The Hua sank to their knees and waited for the princess to go in, but she turned her head to hide behind hair she no longer had. "I can't stay in there. If they come this way, they won't think to look up. I can stay outside."

Fleet shook his head. "The altivorcs have excellent night vision. Your body heat would be a beacon. Better not to risk it."

Chen Xin looked up. "*Dian-xia*, we should get a good night's sleep."

After all that had transpired between them, Tian was glad someone else was pressing the princess.

Nevertheless, she folded her arms across her chest and turned her back to the cave entrance. What happened to the strong and resolute princess from earlier?

Tian began to rise, when Chen Xin shot him a warning glance. No, somebody had to talk sense into her, and the imperial guards would only go so far. "*Dian-xia*," Tian said. "You must get used to this. Our trip will take many months. You'll spend many uncomfortable nights. On hard floors. In tight quarters."

The princess pouted and her eyes welled up. Without another word, she stomped into the cave.

Exasperated, Tian shook his head. He peered through the cave mouth. Too dark to see. What was the princess doing? At this rate, they wouldn't survive the night, let alone rest of their journey.

Fleet gathered up some branches and brush to cover the cave entrance. "We need to set single watches. One-hour rotations. Let the princess have her beauty sleep. We should be moving at sunrise."

Tian's limbs screamed for rest. He ducked into the cave, which was barely large enough for them to spread out all of their bedrolls. The princess insisted on sleeping closest to the entrance, even if it meant that people would have to step over her when their turn to stand watch came. Whatever. Tian fell asleep in seconds.

Zhao Yue jostled him awake. "You have this watch."

Tian rubbed his face. It felt like he had only slept for a few minutes. His body still ached. It would be a long day, unless they died early. He sat by the cave opening, thinking. Hopefully, Jie was faring better than they were. She must be safe and sound behind the embassy walls, worried about *him.*

Fleet crept past him. "I'm going to scout out the altivorc position. If I don't make it back by breakfast, head due south without me."

Disappearing again? Tian opened his mouth, but the madaeri slipped out of the cave and into the night.

When the ink-black of night gave way to black-blue hues, Tian woke the others. They rolled up their bedding and ate a breakfast of Kanin cornbread in silence.

Fleet poked his head into the cave. "The altivorcs are breaking camp, about two hours behind us."

Tian tapped his chin, now covered with stubble. The madaeri had been gone two hours; how did he know where the altivorcs were? "Have they found our trail?"

Fleet shrugged. "Hard to say. We have to keep constant watch to the west. This area is crawling with altivorc tunnels. Not even *I* know where they all are." He grinned.

Tian rolled his eyes. "We can eat while we travel. It will save time."

Fleet shook his head. "Eat first. I don't want you leaving a trail of cornbread for them to follow."

Tian kept his expression blank. The madaeri was regularly leaving the group, and now he was keeping them in one place.

When the sun peeked through the autumn foliage, they set off. The princess was testy, refusing help from the guards and refusing to talk to anyone.

Tian shook his head. To think this girl had bedazzled kings and generals just a week before. They would spend another few months travelling like this, assuming her attitude didn't first get her caught and the rest of them killed.

Barely an hour had passed before altivorc drums echoed through the hills. The faint sound from a smaller drum answered from the direction the party had come, well in the distance.

Tian glared suspiciously at Fleet, but before he could say anything, another drumming pattern answered the first, this time originating from the hills ahead of them.

Fleet's eyebrows furrowed. Was that steam coming from his ears? "Our pursuers have discovered our campsite. Another band in the hills above is descending on an intercept path."

CHAPTER 32:
Confrontations

More drums, echoing through the wooded hills. Tian glared at Fleet. Was he leading them into a trap?

The madaeri pointed to the line of mountains to the west. "The Nothori Mountains are dotted with entrances to underground altivorc cities. Altivorcs are all over the place."

Tian blanked his expression. No point in vocalizing his misgivings at this point. Otherwise lost, they had little choice but to follow their supposed guide.

Fleet led them to the southwest, taking them closer to the mountains and apparently out of the altivorcs' intercept course. Yet after an hour of hiking, they stumbled upon another patrol. After a brief but fierce engagement, they backtracked and followed a tributary of the Alto River upstream toward the mountains.

Tian scratched his chin. It seemed like they were spiraling into a smaller circle. If only he could see the Iridescent Moon through the trees, he could get a better sense of direction. The wilderness was a lot harder to navigate than urban environments.

The arduous path bent upwards, with the river rustling ever to their right. On their left, the terrain rose, the thick woods now thinning from spindly deciduous trees to straight, fresh-smelling evergreens. The only signs of animals were intermittent bird chirps. The princess wore complaints on her hard expression, but thankfully kept quiet.

After several hours, the gentle rise in elevation on either side jutted sharply upwards, forming a gorge. The cliff walls were rocky, with an occasional shrub breaking the monotonous white clay.

Tian eyed the entrance. "There might be more altivorcs. On the other side. We'd be trapped. We should turn back. Look for another path."

"There are no humanoid tracks here." Fleet pointed down to the ground. "This path was formed by animals, not by altivorcs. And even if we have a lead on them, they might still catch up to us if we turn back now. Our best chance is to forge ahead."

Tian looked up at the cliffs that now towered sixty feet above them, their tops lined with rocks and trees. Just like ambushes he had set from rooftops. They might be walking into the jaws of a trap. "Can we be sure the path continues? Might it dead-end?"

"There's always that possibility," Fleet conceded. "However, if you look at the freshest deer tracks, there are more going in than out."

How could the madaeri tell? The tracks were bewildering. Maybe he was lying. Tian stole a glance at the princess, who somehow maintained an air of elegance even as she squatted to catch her breath.

She met his eyes and stood. Her weary voice still sounded melodious. "Young Lord Zheng, I don't like this either, but we have no choice but to trust Fleet. We will continue through the gorge."

Tian kept his face from twisting into a scowl. She was right. Without Fleet they'd be wandering aimlessly into one altivorc patrol after another. "As the princess commands."

After a few minutes of rest, they refilled their water skins in the river and pressed on. Had there been no sense of urgency, the ravine would have been picturesque, with occasional waterfalls and deep azure pools among broad mossy boulders. The rustle of the water dancing over the rocks drowned out all other sounds.

The path, which had started off wide enough for four of them to walk abreast, narrowed as it rose high above the water line. Tian glanced at the others. They all wore concerned looks—all but Fleet, who merrily hopped along, undaunted by the prospect of a dead end.

The ledge abruptly narrowed to just a few feet at a sharp corner around a river bend. Oblivious to danger, Fleet effortlessly skipped around the corner. Tian and the princess, too, had little problem negotiating the left-hand turn. The ledge widened on the other side.

Yet for the rest of the party, it became a heart-stopping endeavor. Brehane, in particular, squeezed the hands of Sameer in front of her and Cyrus in back of her as she inched around the corner, face pressed against the cliff wall. "I won't make. I'll never see my son again."

Such dramatics. Tian assessed the position. A perfect bottleneck, easily defendable for a left-handed warrior. He looked at Li Wei, who was already passing his gear to Ma Jun. The two exchanged knowing nods. Tian bowed his head.

With sweat beading on her bald head, Princess Kaiya pushed back through the others. Ma Jun bowed low and allowed her to pass, and the rest of the imperial guard gathered up behind her.

"Captain Li," she said in a low but severe voice, "why have you stopped? Are you abandoning your duty to protect me?"

Li Wei dropped to his knee, fist to the ground. "Never, *Dian-xia*. I can slow the altivorcs' advance here, especially since I am left-handed and can attack them as they turn the corner."

She frowned. "Do not needlessly sacrifice yourself. I command you to walk at my side."

He bowed his head lower. "Forgive me, *Dian-xia*. The punishment for disobeying your command is death. I will accept that now as I hold this position to give you a greater lead."

"And if I say we will all fight together?" she asked. Her sincerity was touching, if misplaced.

"Then we will all die together," Li Wei said. "We cannot hold it indefinitely. They have superior numbers and will eventually come around the other side. I would not be able to face Xu Zhan in the next life if I let that happen."

Tian took her by the crook of the elbow. They had to go. For *her* safety. "*Dian-xia*. It is our highest honor. To die for you. Come, so that Li Wei's sacrifice will not be in vain."

She stubbornly struggled against his pull, tears in her eyes, while Li Wei remained bowed.

"Stop resisting and conserve your strength," Tian said. She would need it.

Finally, the princess allowed herself to be led away, casting one final glance at her loyal guard. Despite his pessimistic demeanor, Li Wei was well-liked by everyone. Tian would miss him.

The river's water rustled in Kaiya's ears as she walked wordlessly down the paths. Despair squeezed at her heart. All these sacrifices made by her guards, handmaidens, and others, for her. Li Wei, despite his droning pessimism, had been the most chivalrous, helping her on and off of boats and carriages. If only she'd killed Geros when she had the chance.

At the next break, she crouched on a rock, sighing as she studied her reflection in a mud-clouded puddle. Her once waist-length, lustrous black hair now bristled as coarse stubble, suited to a solider recently pressed into service. Dirt and blood streaked her pearly complexion. Instead of the finest, vibrant silk gowns that floated on her like mist, she now wore faded brown hemp robes whose coarseness chafed her milky skin. They did little to warm her in the chill autumn breeze.

In the puddle's reflection, the brilliant reds, yellows, and oranges of autumn foliage, and the azure sky above, provided a breathtaking backdrop to her tattered appearance.

What should have been an easy, week-long journey by sea had warped into a perilous trek that might take months—if they eluded capture and survived. They'd lost two already. Her fault. A lone ripple floated across the puddle, radiating out from a single tear she allowed to fall from her cheek.

"*Dian-xia.*" Tian's hated voice interrupted her moment of self-pity.

He thought he knew everything. Where was the sweet, awkward boy she once adored? She clenched her teeth and wiped her tears away. He would not see her cry, not see that she was anything less than a princess of Hua. Even if she no longer looked the part.

Rising, she lifted her chin, focused on him and forced a regal smile. No matter how ragged her outward appearance, command had been bred into her blood.

He instantly averted his gaze, showing proper deference. Yet when he spoke, his tone was patronizing, like a teacher admonishing an unruly child. "Fleet is back from covering our tracks. He says we need to keep moving if we want to keep a safe distance from the altivorcs."

Before it was over, even more would perish. Because of her. Guilt and despair threatened to overcome her voice, so she kept her words simple. "Then move." She bent down and gathered her pack before turning away from him so he wouldn't see her tears.

It took all of Tian's discipline to conceal his contempt for the princess. She was wallowing in self-pity again. That much was obvious from the smudged streaks across her filthy face. *Then move?* What was that supposed to mean?

His concerns about the madaeri could wait. "As the princess commands."

The trilling and chirping of birds ceased, as if in reproach for his cold voice interrupting their songs.

He'd been harsh, but it was for her own good. He turned so she wouldn't see his regret, his eyes finding the three surviving imperial guards. Gone were their stoic expressions, silk blue robes, and burnished breastplates, replaced by haggard sadness and monks' robes. Even if they didn't look the part, they'd still happily give their lives to protect the princess. It didn't make Tian feel any less guilty for putting them in this position.

His attention shifted to their diminutive guide, who slouched on a moss-covered log, munching happily on a chunk of cornbread. He sat up straight and looked around, furrowed brows and tight lips marring his usually jovial expression. Plotting something, perhaps. Yes, time to tell the princess.

"*Dian-xia—*"

He turned his shoulder and reached out to snatch the shaft of a black-fletched arrow that whizzed past the princess' head. It would have hit him in the chest had his reflexes been any slower. He looked towards the source of the shot, using the arrow in his hand to swat away another one with a crisp sweep of his arm. Above them, along a ridge just fifty feet away, several altivorcs fitted arrows to their bowstrings.

Sameer whipped his *naga* from its sheath and charged up the ridge. The imperial guards bolted up, forming a living shield in front of the princess.

Not like she needed it. They wanted her alive, unharmed.

The others scrambled among the boulders along the side of the trail. Tian glared at the madaeri. "You said they weren't far behind!"

Fleet jumped out from cover and loosed an arrow from his bow. It flew true through the eye of an altivorc. "It's not *my* fault." He ducked back behind a boulder to avoid an answering volley of deadly arrows. "These are *ahead* of us!"

Right. Tian drew his saber. He couldn't leave Sameer to fight alone. He stepped out and looked up the ridge.

The Paladin had drawn the altivorcs' fire. He nimbly, almost impossibly, dodged some arrows while cutting others out of the air with his blade. Such recklessness!

Tian followed him up the slope, albeit with more caution, picking his way around trees, boulders, and fallen trunks.

Behind him, Brehane uttered foul gibberish. Her chant concluded with a hard inflection. A thunderous blast of sound reverberated from the altivorcs' position. The shockwave nearly knocked Tian off his feet.

The deadly rain of arrows ceased.

Tian sighed. The unnatural sound would reveal their location to other pursuers, but at least they were out of immediate danger.

Sameer sheathed his sword and headed back down the slope, grinning and patting Tian on his shoulder as he passed.

Tian's gaze followed Sameer down. Just beyond, Cyrus' brow furrowed in concentration as he bound Ma Jun's wounds.

"The altivorcs will be incapacitated for several hours," Brehane called. Her voice sounded exhausted. "That will give us some time to gain more ground."

Hold the dragonfly with care. It'd be easy to permanently put the unconscious altivorcs out of their misery. They'd take great pleasure in doing the same if the roles were reversed. "I'm going up to collect some of their bows. They can't follow us that way. You all continue down the path. I will catch up with you."

He clambered to the top of the ridge. The trees around them stood splintered by the sound wave. Twelve altivorcs lay unconscious.

Going to the nearest, he bent the soldier's knee, locked it between his forearm and shoulder, and twisted. It let out an involuntary grunt. The torque would sprain the knee joint, thereby preventing it from walking for several days. Tian repeated the process on each of the altivorcs. He then picked up four bows and several quivers of the steel-headed arrows, and hurried to catch up with the rest of his company.

How many more such encounters could they survive? The others came into sight. The princess lagged behind, her shoulders drooped. She'd been too busy looking at her reflection, and hadn't eaten while they were resting. He suppressed a growl.

Yes, she was infuriating, but he could only blame himself for their predicament. The original escape plan had been his. So had several of the subsequent alternatives. All failed. His plans never failed. Perhaps it would've been better to fortify the embassy in Iksuvius while sending the *Golden Phoenix* back home to bring ships and musketmen. Maybe even ask for a real phoenix to fly the princess home.

Certainly, things would have been different had he finished off the altivorc spy in Gaukaimos. Now Xu Zhan was dead, Li Wei missing. As he caught up to the others, he quickly wiped his eyes. For the time being, lamenting the past would do them no good.

Kaiya trailed behind the others, though Chen Xin, who'd guarded her since she was a child, often slowed down to help her through the rough terrain. She'd always taken him for granted. She'd never truly appreciated the imperial guards' dedication to her. Now, one had died to protect her, and another had probably shared the same fate. Even Tian would sacrifice his life for her, if for nothing more than pride. It wouldn't make her feel any less guilty.

And then, beyond her own people, there were the four others, who owed no allegiance to the *Tianzi*, yet assisted her to the detriment of their own quest. Tears blurred her vision. Maybe they'd all share the same fate as Li Wei and Xu Zhan. Heavens, she was pathetic.

She had little time to cry before Tian caught up to her. Their eyes met, and Kaiya was surprised to see that his were red and swollen. Had he been crying, too? Maybe he was a human after all. She forced a smile at him, which he returned, equally forced.

"*Dian-xia*. I just caught this in a stream." He held up a miniature lobster, still squirming. "Please eat it. It will help your endurance."

Her stomach churned. Kaiya recoiled and covered her mouth.

Tian scowled, all sense of propriety gone. He jabbed a finger in her direction. "The comforts that *you* have been asked to forfeit—your hair, a soft bed in a spacious room, the finest food prepared by imperial chefs—they are an inconvenience compared to the sacrifice that Brehane and her group have made. And nothing compared to the ultimate sacrifice that Xu Zhan and Li Wei made."

He was talking to her like a little girl. He'd never spoken to her like that, even when she *had* been a little girl. Kaiya raised her voice, loud enough that any altivorc within three *li* could've heard. "Zheng Tian, do you think I don't understand this?"

Up ahead, the others stopped. Chen Xin sighed and started heading back.

Kaiya lowered her voice just a little. "I don't mind discomfort, but I can't handle narrow confines...and that's your fault." She pointed at him. She never pointed at anyone, as Hua custom considered it rude. Her voice shook, dropping to almost a whisper. "Ever since you locked me in our swordmaster's armoire, years ago, I can't think or even breathe in tight places."

Tian gawked, eyes wide, and then hung his head.

Chen Xin rubbed his bald head thoughtfully.

Hot tears trickled down her cheeks. She sank down, her back to a large boulder, and drew her head to her knees. Her voice wavered. "I don't eat shellfish, not because of the taste, but because I'd be throwing up for hours. Even the smell of it brings on nausea. But as princess, I have to hide weakness."

Tian stared at the ground. He dropped to one knee and bowed his head. "I'm sorry. I didn't know."

Brehane came back and offered Tian a reproachful glance before sitting down next to Kaiya and putting her arm around her.

Tian bowed his head. "I am sorry."

Kaiya looked up from between her knees and smiled a bitter smile. "It is also my fault. I assumed I could confide in you like we did when we were children. But we aren't children anymore."

An awkward silence ensued, broken only by the shrill voice of the madaeri. "I'm all for sentimentality, but we need to get moving again and cover more ground before sundown. I hear altivorc drums in the distance."

CHAPTER 33:

First Consul No More

Jie spent a week regaining her strength. She avoided physical exertion, instead disguising herself as a Nothori peasant child and mingling with Tian's network of local spies. For once, looking like a kid came in handy.

Learning of Chen Xin's visit to the Kanin embassy, she surprised their ambassador with a midnight call. Ambassador Manuwaya, knowing of the roundup of Cathayi nationals, offered asylum to all of them, as long as they could be brought in without drawing suspicion. The old man also gave her the princess' letter, where Jie learned about her escape into the Wilds—with Tian.

Alone, stranded, and with no one to report to for the first time in her life, she made it her mission to rescue the princess' handmaiden, Meiling. She didn't doubt she could get *into* the Iksuvi Palace undetected, but getting *out* with an untrained and now traumatized girl would be another challenge altogether. She stalked General Marius, thinking he could be the key to her plan.

Marius di Bovyan had the strangest habits for a Bovyan. Whereas most of them spent at least some of their time in the company of unwilling women, the general never visited his assigned mating compound at the Iksuvi Palace. He kept regular routines, though Jie would swear that he seemed almost sad these days.

One late afternoon, she made her move.

As Marius led a patrol through the marketplace, she joined in with a gaggle of street urchins and ran across the Bovyan column's path.

She stumbled, careening into the general and slipping a note into his boot. With a quick bob of her head, she sped away, ignoring the Teleri soldiers' reprimands.

That night, she returned to the eastern marketplace in hopes that he would accept her invitation to meet. Arriving early, Jie scouted out the area to ensure he hadn't laid any traps for her. She found none, and hid in a weathered wooden stall which provided a full view of the area.

Just as the Iridescent Moon waxed to its mid-crescent, exactly at the appointed time, Marius ventured in—alone, as far as she could tell. With the White Moon near new, her elf vision gave her the advantage.

Jie threw her voice to make it seem like a nearby goat had spoken. "General Marius, thank you for meeting me."

The general frowned as he approached the goat. "Miss Jie, I was intrigued by your letter. Why did you want to meet? I suspect it has nothing to do with two years ago."

That again. Before the invasion, he'd babbled something about how they'd shared some adventure in Arkos, but she'd assumed it was just the effect of the euphoria toxin she'd given him.

As he walked by, she jumped onto the stall's counter behind him. She yanked his hair back and stuck a knife point to his carotid artery. "Hands up and away from your sword. Slowly."

Marius lifted his arms at a safe speed. "This is not necessary. I came in good faith."

"I did not. Needless to say, I'm not too happy about my people being imprisoned and murdered."

"Miss Jie, your princess attacked the First Consul. What did you expect? That he would not exact justice?"

Justice, eh? She pressed the knife into his neck, ever so slightly. "My princess knew his plans to kidnap her and acted in self-defense. Now, tell me, why is her handmaiden being held separately?"

"This is how things have been for a hundred and thirty years, since the Bovyan Edict. The ruling class of the Bovyans—our Prospecti—mate with the ruling class of nations with which we ally and protect. The offspring become a bridge between our nations."

Occupied allies, rape as a bridge. Jie shuddered at Marius' rationalization. She leaned in and whispered into his ear. "What you call *mating*, civilized people call gang-rape."

"It is necessary, lest our race die out. Even if you hate him, the First Consul works to end Tivar's Curse so that our mates might bear more children, both boys and girls. Until then, the prophecies state that a Bovyan who knows his true mother and father will bring an end to the Teleri Empire. We can't let that happen. Without the order we bring, the world will plunge back into a darkness unseen since the Hellstorm."

More excuses. Jie scoffed. As for prophecies— thank the Heavens they did not govern *her* life. She released a little of the pressure on his throat. "I have noticed that you don't participate. Why is that? Injury down *there*?"

Marius sighed and eased himself into a seated position on the counter. He set his hands down on the edge. "Because I love someone. Someone I shouldn't. By Solaris, we aren't supposed to *love* anyone."

Heat flared in Jie's cheeks. He liked her. *Really* liked her. Not like she was particularly interested in a Bovyan, reformed or not. If only she could see his face, to read his expression. She kept her guard up nonetheless. "I hope you do not mean me, because—"

"No, no. I've always been fond of you." Marius started to shake his head, but stopped, probably because of the knife point at his artery. "However, this one is *really* married. I tried to forget her by rekindling what we had."

Always second best. Jie sucked on her lower lip. Even if the only thing she'd want to rekindle was his head—ideally with another cache of firepowder—it was a blow to the ego. She pressed the blade a little harder into his neck. "Don't bring up our past again." Especially fictional pasts.

"Of course." Marius sighed again, wistfully. "Anyway, she is gone now, escaped like so many others."

"Did you force yourself on our handmaiden?"

"No! No. After my love, I don't think I could ever sleep with another, especially not through the Mating."

He sounded sincere enough. But trust a Bovyan? "Perhaps, then, you can fathom how much poor Meiling is suffering. I want you to help her escape." She lowered the knife, ready to spring away if he tried to attack her.

Marius spun around, hands behind his back, mouth agape. Jie tensed, but did not jump away. He did not make any move towards her, instead shaking his head. "I could never betray my people."

Jie snorted. "Then you are no better than any other Bovyan. If you don't do the right thing, how can you expect your comrades to do the same when your own love is captured? "

"I...I..." His lips sagged into a frown, and his eyes shifted. Then he sighed. "Very well, I will help you."

Jie offered him a smile, even though he probably couldn't be trusted. "In return, I'll help your own love escape."

Marius shook his head yet again. His head would probably wobble off before the end of the night. "There's no need. Your people have already helped her. She's aboard the Cathayi flagship, already beyond the reach of our empire."

Now Jie gawked. The only married woman onboard the *Golden Phoenix* was Queen Ausra. She recovered from her surprise, composing her emotionless mask. "I want to initiate a rescue as soon as possible. When would be the best time?"

"Tomorrow," he answered. "When most of the Teleri will be at the Temple of Solaris."

If only she had a cache of firepowder. "Whatever for?"

"The Keeper will coronate First Consul Geros as Emperor."

Geros stood at the entrance of the Temple of Solaris, ignoring the ceremonial blathering of the Keeper, who spoke platitudes in a long-dead language. On this day, he had forsaken his typical dress uniform in favor of a silk toga befitting of an ancient Arkothi emperor. He looked every bit the part in the Arkothi-style temple, whose ornate white marble columns supported a massive dome.

In the center towered a gilded statue of the god, anointed with a crown of sun and bearing a striking resemblance to the First Consul. Holding a sword aloft, its right arm stretched out of its robe, revealing rippled muscle. Its other arm nestled a book: the Last Testament of the Founder.

Geros fidgeted as the Keeper droned on. He remembered posing for the statue, basing it on an image his ancestor had sketched in the Last Testament. That had been ten years ago, when he had ordered the construction of the temple on this hill, razing the ramshackle hovel that had passed for the temple of the Nothori god Deivos.

The Nothori folk insisted that he would be struck down by the god's own hand for this transgression. He stifled a laugh, lest he taint the sanctity of the ceremony. Here he was, standing; just a little tired as he recovered from his closest brush with death—not by the wrath of a god, but at the sword point of a girl.

With the exception of that minor setback, the schemes he'd set in motion that day had all unfolded as planned, leading to his well-deserved reward. He looked up at the hole in the center of the dome.

A narrow blade of sun shone through; it would not be long now.

He swept his gaze around the temple, where Teleri officials and soldiers stood in solemn silence, forming perfect rows in their meticulously kept uniforms. Under the statue stood the senior-most Keeper of the Shrine of Geros, there to consecrate the rites unheard of in the three centuries since the end of the Arkothi Empire.

The Keeper switched from the archaic language to modern Arkothi. "First Consul Geros, approach the altar."

Chin held high, Geros marched towards the statue, down a central walkway formed by the Teleri ranks. He knelt and looked up to see the sun almost at the center point of the dome's hole. His attention shifted towards the Keeper.

The Keeper bowed his head. "The Last Testament of the Founder obligates the Bovyan people to the duty of bringing peace to the world, and ushering in an era of harmony and prosperity unseen since the Hellstorm and Long Winter ended the Arkothi Empire three centuries ago."

Yes, yes, old history. Geros forced himself to stay still. He'd soon make a new history.

"To these ends," the Keeper prattled on, "we have always evolved. Our First Ancestor and his sons defended the village of Lagrina, and the next generation was the palace guard of Tile. As our mandate grew, we remade ourselves into the Bovyan Knights. When we brought more lands under our protection, we became the Teleri Empire. We now enter a new era, one where we require stability in succession, as outlined by the Edict of Blood Inheritance, agreed upon by the Keepers and the Directori early this year."

All of this was known. Geros clenched his jaw. He had bent the Keepers and Directori to his will. Now hurry up and—

The Keeper looked towards the entrance. The Teleri soldiers broke into low murmurs. Geros fought the urge to follow the Keeper's eyes.

A boy from the Shrine came up to his side, holding a black velvet cushion. On top rested the antique crown of the Arkothi emperors. Made of a bluish-grey metal, its tip held a starburst jewel—an artifact used by the elves a thousand years before in their losing war against the orcs.

Geros grinned in spite of the solemnity of the coronation. Unlike the elves, he would not lose a war.

The Keeper lifted the crown from the cushion and raised it just as the sun reached its zenith, bathing the statue of Solaris in brightness. The rays caught the starburst, showering the dome above with pins of light.

At last. The Keeper placed it on Geros' head.

Despite its bulk, it weighed very little. A surge of excitement roared through him.

"By the power vested in me by the Keepers of the Shrine and the Imperial Directori, on this day of the Autumn Equinox in the year 913, I crown First Consul Geros Bovyan, Forty-Third of his name, as Emperor Geros Bovyan the First."

Geros rose.

The Bovyans chanted his name, over and over again.

The chorus continued until the Keeper raised his hand, calling for silence.

"Bring forth the consorts of the imperial harem."

From the entrance, three dozen young women dressed in Arkothi robes came forward, walking in unison. It was a mélange of pretty faces, chosen from the nobility of six of the ten human races.

The olive-skinned Arkothi girls, descended from the last Arkothi emperors, had been conscripted from within the Teleri Empire. Nothori princesses were never mentioned in the Northwest Summit, but were tribute all the same. Daughters of Estomari merchant signores were there as well, bartered as part of trade rights and protection of trade routes.

From Teleri's allies in Madura, Levastya, and the barbarian tribes of Kanin, Geros had secretly negotiated girls from the ruling families, with the promise that one day, grandsons might become Consuls in the Teleri Directori; of course,

he foresaw them as rulers of their own ancestral realms.

It was like a Levanthi sultan's harem, to breed a pool of potential heirs. Each consort would be discarded and replaced after they bore a son, to avoid tempting the prophecies of the end of the empire. The boys would never know their own mother. Yet unlike the Consuls, who were elected by the Prospecti—or the First Consul, who was elected from the Consuls—the next emperor would be personally chosen by Geros from one of his future sons.

Unrepresented were the Eldaeri, who falsely claimed to be the chosen tribe of Solaris, and thus deserved extermination for their blasphemy; the chocolate-skinned Aksumi, despite Geros' efforts to secure their females by diplomacy and other means; and the Bovyans themselves, who had no females. The fourth, the Cathayi—well, Geros knew very well who he wanted to bear his son, even if it meant inviting prophetic doom.

The Keeper placed a circlet of silver on each of the consorts' heads; and they, in turn, knelt before Geros and kissed the back of his hand.

Once the rituals ended, an honor guard escorted Geros out of the temple, to lead a grand parade back to the Iksuvi Palace. Typical Bovyan disdain for flamboyance was momentarily forgotten. Teleri soldiers marched in perfect formation, holding black banners with the nine-pointed sun of Solaris aloft. Each of the consorts was afforded her own litter, curtains open to the chill autumn air to further boast the grandeur of the empire. Geros himself rode astride a Kanin black stallion, waving to the crowds who threw autumn flowers in his path.

Geros wore a smile, even if he didn't feel it. There was still the matter of Princess Kaiya, tarnishing what should have been a crowning moment. She'd be his. She would suffer for her treachery. But for now, she was out of reach.

The steward Jonynas, the Nothori man who had previously served the Iksuvi king, greeted him with a deep bow at the palace gates. "Your Eminence, your bed chambers have been prepared for your long afternoon. Which of your consorts will honor you with her visit?"

Geros snorted. "I want the Cathayi handmaiden."

A look of confusion bloomed on the steward's face. He looked back towards the litters, then opened his mouth to say something.

No, there were no Cathayi among the consorts. Geros scowled, silencing his unspoken words.

Jonynas turned back towards a servant. "Bring the Cathayi girl to His Eminence's bed chambers." He offered Geros a weak smile and bowed.

Geros pushed past him, taking his time as he made his way towards the king's former suite.

A servant met him halfway, his face pale and dripping with sweat. The man fell prostrate. "Your Eminence, the Cathayi girl is...gone."

CHAPTER 34:
Orc Gods and Flaming Chariots

After their confrontation, Kaiya tried her best to be civil to Tian, even rebuffing his suggestion to break away from Brehane's group without criticizing the stupidity of the idea. Even if the madaeri was acting suspiciously, they were lost without him.

Over the next three days, the weather was cloudy and chilly. Frigid nights forced them to huddle close together. Altivorcs seemed to be everywhere, but Fleet had taken them off the main path and through a wide stream, higher into the hills. Cold, wet feet put a damper on everyone's mood, tempered only by the miracle of avoiding their pursuers.

At dawn on the day before the Autumn Equinox, Kaiya unwrapped a pack of herbs prescribed by the enigmatic Doctor Wu. Cyrus watched with wide eyes as she soaked the twigs, roots, and dried flowers in Fleet's copper bowl.

Kaiya's nose scrunched up as she sipped the bitter draught, but she couldn't contain a laugh at Cyrus' contorted face after he insisted on tasting it. Tian offered her a mysterious look, but no rebuke for her laugh, which any altivorc within five *li* could hear.

Cyrus choked on his words. "What do you drink this for?"

"Poor Cyrus." She giggled, deflecting the question. "My doctor tells me that adding dawn-blooming everblossom would improve both the taste and the effect. Unfortunately, there was a shortage in Cathay because of the exceptionally hot summer."

Fleet grinned at her. "There's plenty around here. I'll point it out if we come across it."

After they at last set off, the day dragged on as they seemingly wound in circles. Throughout the day, Kaiya would swear she had seen a boulder or tree or other landmark that they had passed earlier. Fleet, however, was resolute in saying that they were headed more or less south. By nightfall when they set up camp under a large rock outcrop, they had encountered no enemies.

Tian sprang to his feet, sword sheath in hand, as a shout tinged with pain jolted him from sleep. He peered around the campsite, barely lit by the slivers of the White Moon and nearly-closed Blue Moon. The dark shapes where Chen Xin and Ma Jun had settled down for the night pushed themselves into seated positions. Sameer, Cyrus, and Brehane stirred on the ground. Where was Fleet?

And the princess?

"Wake up! Altivorcs!" Zhao Yue's voice mixed with the clang of metal on metal.

Tian shook off the tight grip of sleep as Chen Xin and Ma Jun rose. At the head of the path to the outcrop, Zhao Yue was fighting off altivorcs, even as his left arm hung limply at his side.

Pulling a saber free of its sheath, Tian charged over to help the embattled guard. He stopped in his tracks. Arrows darted in front of him, shot from dark shapes by the trees. With his left hand, he took hold of two *biao* from his forearm strap and hurled them toward the attackers.

Behind him, Zhao cried out. Tian turned to see an altivorc yanking a broadsword out of him. Yet Zhao fought on, swinging his saber.

Brehane uttered a guttural syllable, and the area flooded with bright light.

Tian squinted as his vision adjusted. The altivorcs seemed even more blinded. Behind him, metal weapons clanged, and Cyrus' distinct voice called on his gods.

With everything now clearer, Tian worked his way toward Zhao. Drums rumbled somewhere to his side, but stopped mid-sequence. The altivorcs, no longer shading their eyes, swarmed in again. He shot a quick glance behind him. His companions were backing under the outcrop, with Sameer striking and retreating with inhuman speed.

Saber in hand, Tian deflected an incoming hack that would have finished Zhao Yue. He grabbed the guard by the shoulder, fighting off attackers as he dragged him back to the relative safety of the outcrop.

A sea of altivorcs surged around them, broadswords bared. Behind them, a new line formed with bows trained on them.

Brehane held Sameer back. She barked foul words in the language of her people's magic.

The altivorcs loosed arrows at her as she chanted. Tian leaped forward. He should be able to catch at least one. Instead, they slammed into a spot in the air and ricocheted harmlessly to the ground. More altivorcs shot from all around the semicircle now, with the same results.

A single foul syllable from behind the line of altivorcs carried over Brehane's chant. The barrage of arrows stopped. What now? Tian tightened the grip on his saber.

The lines parted and a tall altivorc, in a black tunic and with a golden circlet on his head, strode forward. He resembled the altivorc prince from the Teleri Embassy, though he was even taller and more handsome. When he spoke, it sounded like honey spilling out of his mouth, in perfect Arkothi. "How long can you maintain your shield, Mystic? Even now, you are weakening. If you want to live to see your child again, surrender now."

Tian turned to Brehane. Her face contorted. Sweat gathered on her forehead and trickled down. The strength in her voice faltered.

So this was the end of their ill-advised journey. Tian bent down towards Zhao Yue. "You were on watch. What happened to the princess?"

Zhao choked on his words, blood pooling around his lips. "She and Fleet left camp, half an hour ago. Said they would be back by sunrise."

Tian looked up. The star-speckled blanket of night's black gave way to deep blue on the horizon. Where had they gone?

The altivorc leader drew a wand from a sheath at his hip and lowered it at them. He uttered a hideous word and a bolt of red lighting sizzled forth, outlining a flickering dome between their groups.

In the instant that Brehane collapsed, the leader barked again. Another energy bolt struck Sameer. The Paladin buckled to the ground, writhing as his eyes rolled upwards.

The leader twirled the wand on his finger and shoved it back in its sheath. He grinned, baring his fangs at Cyrus. "Now, Acolyte, tell me where the Eye of the Pyramid is."

What? Tian lowered his weapon. They weren't looking for the princess?

Kaiya strained her eyes in the predawn dark, waiting for the everblossom to burst open. They would be the most potent if harvested in that instant. Fleet leaned up against a tree, yawning.

Deep altivorc drums rumbled in the distance. Heart leaping into her throat, she looked up. Fleet's ears twitched and his forehead crinkled.

There was a distinct rhythm to the beats. Signals. They seemed to be coming from the direction of their camp. She exchanged glances with the madaeri.

The beating stopped short.

"The altivorcs found our campsite," Fleet whispered. "And there are a lot of them, too many to fight. We need to get as far away as possible."

An emptiness crept into Kaiya's chest. It was her fault that the Southerners were facing capture. "No. There must be a way that we can help our friends."

"Your Highness, you should be more concerned about your own safety." The madaeri had never looked so serious, even when their journey had taken turns for the worse.

There had to be a way. Joining her music with Brehane's, they could put dozens of altivorcs to sleep. She shouldered her pack and started heading back towards camp.

Fleet darted in front of her, holding his arms out. "No, Your Highness. That would be foolish. Your men would want you safe."

Kaiya moved to brush him aside, but he deftly avoided her hand every time and managed to stay in her path. She glared at him. "If you aren't going to help me, at least get out of way."

He grinned, sending a wave of anger rushing to her head.

"Back off." She sang the words, using the power of her voice. Tiredness crept into her limbs.

Fleet yawned. "Save your energy for running. Come on."

Kaiya poked him in the chest. Heavens, that was rude of her. "Brehane and the others might just be clients to you, but I care about my people."

The madaeri sighed. Loudly. "You don't understand. Once I get you to a safe place, I'm going to go back and help them. There are much greater stakes here than a princess fleeing a tyrant. Even greater than wars between nations. When Brehane, Cyrus, and Sameer's story is told, you will be a footnote."

"What are you talking about?"

The usually jovial madaeri's jaw squared, his eyes intent. "Do you know how the saying *'when the Orc Gods return on their blazing chariots'* means something will never happen? Well, there are those who would very much like to see that happen. I, for one, don't want to go back to the time when my people were slaves to the altivorcs. When I decided to help the Southerners, it wasn't because I needed the money."

The madaeri's sincerity was surprising, but what was he talking about? She crossed her arms. "What do they have to do with the Orc Gods?"

Fleet offered her a bitter smile. "The pyramids. If the orcs ever control all of the pyramids again, they can summon their gods."

Kaiya listened in disbelief. "I'm well-versed in the history and lore of Tivara. I've never heard of such insanity."

He laughed. "Tall folk don't remember like we do, nor can you seem to put together all the small images to see the big picture. What was the last episode in the War of Ancient Gods?"

Kaiya shrugged. "Easy. The dwarves stormed the Temple of Tivar—"

"No, afterwards. The Elf Angel Aralas' Last Command."

The madaeri spoke in thousand-year-old riddles. Kaiya forced the impatience out of her tone. *"Keep well the Pyramids, reminders though they may be of your enslavement."*

"Exactly." He gave a triumphant nod. "What do you think that means?"

She sighed. They were wasting time, debating folklore and long-departed Elf Angels. "How should I know? I will ask him next time I see him."

Apparently, her sarcasm was not lost on him. Fleet threw up his arms. "Never mind. You don't have to believe me or my people's lore. Just know that I will find a way to free our friends, because it's that important."

Kaiya shook her head at him. "I can help."

Fleet scrutinized her, eyebrows furrowed. "All right, follow me. Tread as quietly as you can."

They picked their way back through the woods, the only sounds being bird chirps. When they came within eyeshot of the outcropping, the morning sun revealed their ransacked camp. A single body lay among the ruffled bedrolls, while several others sprawled in a disorderly circle around the camp. Kaiya's heart lurched into her throat. Who was it? Kaiya started forwards, but Fleet grabbed hold of her sleeve.

"It might be a trap," he whispered. "You wait here, I will investigate."

She nodded and he disappeared into the brush. Even her keen ears couldn't tell where he went. She kept her focus on the body.

It flinched. Still alive.

Kaiya fought every nerve that screamed for her to run to whoever it was.

After what felt like an eternity, Fleet appeared at its side. He looked towards her and beckoned.

Kaiya picked her way through the brush and dead altivorcs. It was Zhao Yue, face pale and lips wan. He opened his eyes a crack and offered her a frail smile. "*Dian-xia*, you should not have come back... flee... while you can."

She looked at Fleet, who shook his head. Another person to die because of her. Her chest constricted and she fought back tears. She had to be strong, for him.

She forced a smile at Zhao and clasped his cold hand. "I release you from your duty to the *Tianzi*. Rest."

"I will watch over you until I die and am reborn," Zhao answered. "It would be my honor to serve you in the next life."

Fleet patted Zhao on his bald head and looked at her. "You stay here; I'll track the altivorcs. Pay attention to your surroundings. If there's any sign of danger, flee back to the everblossoms. If you aren't here, I'll look for you there." With that he disappeared.

Zhao did not linger long. Kaiya held his hand until his soul drifted from its corporeal bonds.

Alone, Kaiya cried freely as she went to look for stones to build a cairn. Through her tears, she caught sight of a hip drum under an altivorc body. An idea began to coalesce. She kicked at the corpse to make sure it was truly dead; then, with some hesitation, pushed it over to retrieve the drum.

Fleet returned an hour later. "Our friends are being held uphill, at an altivorc campsite. I counted about thirty of them."

Kaiya showed the madaeri the drum. "How well do you know their signals?"

A devious grin formed on the madaeri's face. "Well enough."

Tian subtly worked at the ropes which bound his hands behind his back, even as an altivorc guard glared at him. His companions all sat in a circle with their backs to each other, with the exception of Cyrus and Brehane.

Though he couldn't see them, their screams emanated from the rocky clearing behind him. Brehane repeated the name *Fassil* over and over again.

Sameer's unconscious form slumped against Tian's back. Their weapons lay out of reach, but tantalizingly close, amongst their packs—which the altivorcs had emptied and now rummaged through. On occasion, the sounds of the Southerners' torture were broken by an unintelligible tirade from the altivorc leader, followed by one of his minions beating out some pattern on the large drum. Try as he might, Tian couldn't decipher the code.

Escape, though unlikely, was still possible. With the bulk of the altivorcs already departed, probably to search for the princess, the imperial guards and Sameer might stand a fighting chance...if only they could break loose and get to their weapons before the altivorcs hacked them to pieces.

A break in the screams was followed by the altivorc leader's heavy footsteps coming up behind him. Tian twisted and caught a glimpse of Cyrus and Brehane. They stood about thirty feet away, their hands bound above their head, suspended from a tree limb.

The leader kicked at Sameer's feet. Then he stomped around to face Tian. "So, how did you come to join the Southerners?"

Tian licked his lips, feigning fear, even as he loosened the bonds a little more. "We were just travelling and ran into each other. It is always nice to have company on the road."

The leader laughed, pointing at Chen Xin and Ma Jun. "Don't lie. These two wear signets of the Cathayi imperial guard. You were protecting your princess."

Tian kept a straight face, even as he let a stream of curses explode in his head. "We split up. To draw you away from her."

"So she is with the meddling little halfling?"

Maybe Tian had misjudged Fleet. "You'll never catch her."

The leader laughed. "She's inconsequential, beyond being bait to dangle in front of my friend Geros. Tell me which way she went, and I'll let you go. I'll let her go, too, even escort you through our cities into Rotuvi. That's close to home."

Tian gauged the possibilities. Even if he didn't trust the altivorcs—he and the guards would be dead the second she was captured—he could at least pretend to comply. He let his features soften. "They fled towards—"

A beating of drums from the south interrupted him, and the leader held his hand up. "Oh, too bad. It sounds like my men are already on her trail." He unleashed a barrage of harsh-sounding syllables. An altivorc beat on the big drum, while several others formed up.

The leader grinned at him. "Well, duty calls. Savor your last breaths. It won't be long now." With another snarling command, his soldiers followed him out of the camp.

The leader was gone. Tian craned his head to see that a dozen altivorcs stood guard. Their chances of escape began to improve, albeit just slightly. He continued to fiddle with the ropes. If only Sameer would awaken.

Kaiya crouched at the edge of the clearing, Fleet by her side. She counted fifteen altivorcs: one by the large drum lying on its side, not far from them; six surrounding her people and Sameer; two where Brehane and Cyrus stood with hands bound above them; and six standing guard at points around the perimeter.

Fleet shook his head, likely seeing what she did: their friends were split up and the altivorcs were too dispersed. It would be impossible for the two of them to rescue both groups of their companions before their enemies slaughtered them.

Kaiya pointed to her drum. Maybe they could draw more altivorcs off.

Fleet shook his head violently. He pointed downhill, in the direction that the other group had departed. They would also hear any drumming.

Minutes passed. Fleet's scrunched-up forehead and suggested he was either at a loss for plans or, like her, suffering from menstrual cramps. More likely the former. It was up to her. She pointed him towards Brehane and Cyrus, and gesticulated. *I will break for the big drum, you rescue those two.*

His jaw dropped, but before he could protest, she rose and ran.

Altivorcs lifted their heads, their gawps as wide as the madaeri's. She made it halfway to the drum before they even started towards her. The drummer lurched forward and caught up her sleeve in his huge paw.

Her Praise Spring fighting style reflexes took over on contact.

She coiled her hand back on her sleeve, changing the angle of his grip. As he gave her another sharp yank, she drifted forward into his pull and swatted him with *Silk Whips Like Thunder* palms. The altivorc staggered back. The sharp rasp of ripping stitches and the sudden cool air on her bare arm indicated he'd taken her sleeve with him. She kept driving through his stumbling form, landing a chain of straight punches to his face.

He swiped at her again, but she slipped under his swing. He might have seized her hair had she still had any. Coming up on the other side of him, she reached the drum.

Rooting herself to the ground, she listened to the altivorc heartbeats. One ferocious palm strike in the middle of the drum hide sent a sound wave reverberating outward. She raked her gaze over the clearing to see the effect. Everyone, save for Fleet, cowered.

Straightening her spine and digging her toes into the ground, she summoned ferocity in her heart. She pounded out a combination of beats worthy of the best war drummers in Hua. It echoed through the hills, shaking the ground with its resonance.

Birds scattered from trees. Altivorcs fled. Fleet tentatively held his ground.

Kaiya changed the beat, softer this time, channeling all of the courage she could muster in hopes that it would hearten her friends. Without stopping to catch her breath, she ran towards her bound guards and picked up a knife from their scattered belongings.

Tian looked at her, eyes rounded in awe. "Well done," he murmured.

She leaned in and gingerly cut through the ropes behind his back. As soon as he was free, he snatched the knife from her. With swift strokes, he cut through the others' bindings.

Kaiya looked towards Brehane and Cyrus and realized the hole in her hastily drawn-up plan: Fleet was too short to easily reach the ropes above their heads. The madaeri was climbing up Cyrus like a tree, putting a foot in his face as he reached out and cut the bonds. As the two Southerners crumpled to the ground, Fleet leaped down and landed on his feet. He arched his back, tilted his head backward, arms raised in victory.

Such theatrics. Kaiya looked down towards her knuckles, where pain blossomed. Red blood—hers, not the altivorc's black blood—trickled over her hands. Yet she had little time to think about her own wounds as her companions hastily gathered their belongings and stuffed them in their packs.

Cyrus clasped his gold medallion with one hand while grabbing Fleet by the collar with the other. "Do you have them?"

"Relax. Of course. All accounted for." Fleet opened his bag, and withdrew a clear gemstone. It resembled the Lotus Crystal from the pyramid of Ayudra in size and shape, except a grey metal coated its flat top.

Kaiya's eyes widened. It was the same strange material as the First Consul's pin. Which was in her... "Where's my pack?"

Chen Xin presented it, but looked in Fleet's direction. "We helped the Southerners recover that from the pyramid in Selastya."

So that was the story no one was telling her about. Still, there was no time to find out more now. Once the altivorcs recovered from their initial shock, they'd be coming back in force.

CHAPTER 35:

End of the Highway

Kaiya clenched her sleeves with clammy palms as she watched blades flash faster than her eye could see. Only her keen hearing picked up on the otherwise indistinct clinking of blades as Sameer's *naga* clashed against Tian's saber.

Metal flashed. Tian tumbled to the ground. His sword clattered across the clearing in the woods.

Cyrus, Chen Xin, and Ma Jun all laughed, though none of them had fared any better.

Sameer grinned and offered Tian his hand to help him up. "Best four out of seven, then?"

By Jie's accounts, Tian was one of the finest swordsmen in Hua, yet he could last no more than a few seconds against Sameer's extraordinary speed.

"One more time," Tian said, his expression sour. If nothing else, he was persistent. Failures didn't seem to discourage him from trying again.

Kaiya rolled her eyes. Brehane shared a knowing nod.

Men. Their ego grew in proportion to the size of their sword.

It had all started over the last several days. After a week of tension-filled marching with little rest, they'd finally managed to escape altivorc pursuit. They eased their frenetic pace, and their spirits rose as much as they could, given their losses. Danger gave way to monotony. With little else to do, Fleet pointed out the flora and fauna to Kaiya.

Not to be outdone, Tian taught her strategies for improving her observational skills. Gone was the cold and unforgiving automaton. He even smiled on rare occasions, with the innocence of his younger self.

The lessons in awareness escalated into occasional knife-fighting practice, which in turn got Sameer involved in theoretical discussions of swordplay.

By Kaiya's reckoning, on Hua's Double Ten Day—twenty-four days since they began their escape—they descended the mountain path by moonlight and set up camp. The ridge overlooked the walled city of Kalenai, the administrative seat for the southeastern region of Iksuvi, at the terminus of the north-south highway.

In the morning, while they waited for Fleet to return from scouting out the city, Sameer and Tian decided to test their martial theories out. All of the men were eager to join in, and yet, Sameer nonchalantly dispatched them all without any signs of fatigue. Tian had come the closest, though only with the use of trickery to clinch up with the Paladin.

He still lost.

Just as Kaiya began to worry Tian would hurt himself in a fourth bout, Fleet returned to camp and provided a welcome distraction. He reported that the city was still under Iksuvi control, and that neither altivorc nor Teleri soldiers had come this far south. It would be safe to rest there for a night and buy provisions for their trek into the Wilds.

After these weeks of slogging through the wilderness, sleeping outdoors, and eating bland rations, Kaiya's excitement rose as they approached the city. Nestled in the nook between two mountain ranges, the scenery was beautiful; year-round, according to Fleet. Numerous hot springs attracted visitors from as far north as Iksuvius, and aristocrats from the capital kept hillside villas here.

Farmers jostled alongside the group, bringing in the final harvest. Fishermen clogged the streets with carts of Nothori toothfish, which were now making their annual pilgrimage up the river to their spawning grounds.

They made it to the northern gate at mid-morning. The city garrison greeted them with stares, but allowed them to enter.

Fleet guided them through the streets, which bustled with citizenry preparing for what was predicted to be a particularly long, harsh winter. Before long, they came to a secluded hot-spring inn. The madaeri forewarned them it was upscale and expensive, but no one complained— least of all Kaiya. Accustomed to daily bathing, she hadn't enjoyed a bath in weeks.

A wave of warm mist enveloped Kaiya as soon as Tian opened the ironwood door for her. Lit by light baubles, the spacious common room seemed even brighter than the early afternoon sun outside. Fleet strode up to the bar, where the rotund and balding Nothori innkeeper favored the rest of them with a curious eye.

"Welcome back, Master Fleet. The Life Spring is always happy to have you. I see you have brought more...guests."

Fleet produced a silver coin, which he sent dancing through his fingers. "Two rooms—one large one for the men, a smaller one for the ladies."

"Very good, very good," the man replied with a toothy smile. "Though it seems strange that wandering Cathayi monks would enjoy the earthly pleasures of fine food and a luxurious bath."

Another silver *kroon* appeared between the madaeri's fingers, and Kaiya looked at her own hand, wondering if she could spin two coins. "As always, I appreciate a level of anonymity."

The innkeeper shook his head. "And what about the red-haired beauty's horses? I've stabled them for a few months now."

Red hair. Kaiya reached to twirl hair that wasn't there. Hadn't Jie found a strand of red hair on Prince Aelward's ship, over half a year ago?

A third coin joined the other two, twisting through Fleet's digits.

"I know you like information, and there is some that your friends might be interested in." The innkeeper tilted his chin towards her.

The silver coins disappeared, replaced by a single gold *kroon*. Fleet slapped it on the counter. Where did the madaeri hide his money?

The innkeeper flashed a greedy smile and leaned forward, beckoning them closer. "News is, the Teleri stopped their advance at the highway crossroads and won't continue their offensive until spring. Rumor has it that they will head west towards the interior instead of coming south." Though the common room was empty, he whispered. "However, I have it from a good source that there are a few spies wandering around the city. Also, there is another Cathayi monk hanging around here. Arrived about a week ago. He was asking for others of his kind." The innkeeper nodded in her direction.

"Thank you," Fleet said. "We'll bathe now. If you would, send your boy out to fetch us some clean winter clothes, preferably wool." He tossed another gold coin onto the counter.

"Very good. You can get your noon meal from the kitchens whenever you're done."

Kaiya couldn't reach the baths soon enough.

Carved out of rock to a depth of three feet, it looked like the pools could accommodate ten or more people at a time. They weren't much different than the bathing pools that were loved by the Hua people, from inexpensive public baths to the *Tianzi's* exclusive hot spring on Jade Mountain.

Kaiya scrubbed off the dirt, sweat, blood, and tears that had accumulated like moss. Already slender, she was now almost gaunt, exposing muscles toned from constant marching. Thank goodness for the high ironwood fence that separated the men's and women's bathing areas.

As they soaked together in the warm water, Brehane commented that she looked much more the part of a wandering monk now, even if her hair had already grown a thumblength.

Across the fence, the men, except for Cyrus who waited to bathe by himself, soaked together. They bragged about their scars, with Ma Jun and Sameer telling colorful, almost unbelievable stories about their war wounds. Compared to their embellished battle of one-upmanship, Chen Xin sounded like a farmer recounting his daily weeding.

An hour later, all emerged from the baths pink and refreshed, and met in the common room for their first hot lunch in a long time: chicken and potato stew with a side of bread. It had been too long since they'd eaten something other than cornbread.

They changed from the monks' robes to the heavier woolen shirts and pants. Though not nearly as fine as the silk gowns Kaiya was accustomed to, the clothes still felt comfortable after weeks of wearing coarse hemp. When the inn's servant asked if they would like the monks' robes washed, Kaiya thought she would just as soon see them burned. Tian had other ideas.

For the rest of the day, they split into pairs to procure provisions for the remainder of the last leg of their journey. Tian accompanied Kaiya, who'd volunteered to find fur-lined travelling cloaks.

As they wandered the streets, perhaps looking like a couple as they peeked in stores, a handsome young Hua monk with a walking staff rushed up to them. Even without his red and yellow robes, Kaiya recognized him up close. A disciple of her own Doctor Wu, Fang Weiyong was a palace physician who'd travelled with her on the *Golden Phoenix* to Iksuvius. Now that she was clean, her nose wrinkled at his gamey odor.

He dropped to his knees, drawing curious stares from the locals. "*Dian-xia*, I have been looking for you."

"Your Holiness, please stand," Tian said with an edge in his voice. "You're attracting too much attention."

The doctor rose, brushing the dust from his knees. "My apologies. I should have known better."

"What news do you have, Your Holiness?" Kaiya asked.

"Unfortunately, not much. I treated the First Consul, as you commanded. When I returned to the embassy compound, the ambassador ordered all Hua to flee the city. In my travels, I heard that you were also heading south. The Teleri offer a substantial bounty for your capture. I do not think it is safe for you here, even this far south."

Tian rolled his eyes. "Then don't draw attention to her again."

The doctor started to drop to his knees when Tian caught him. He bowed his head. "My apologies."

Kaiya nodded back. "Come, Your Holiness, join us for a bath and hot meal."

Tian's lips tightened, but he said nothing.

That evening, they gathered over a hot supper of roasted elk with seasoned potatoes and steamed vegetables. Watching their new companion eat, Tian wondered if the doctor didn't attack the food with as much vigor as the madaeri. He barely paused to breathe, answering questions with grunts.

Had he seen any other Hua? Grunt no.

Had he encountered any altivorcs? Grunt yes.

Nearby? Grunt no.

Could he wield a sword? Grunt kind-of.

Great. The last thing they needed was another mouth to feed and another body to protect. If only they had run into Hua soldiers instead.

Fleet had the unique talent of speaking clearly with food in his mouth. "Enjoy the hot food now, because it'll be Kanin cornbread again soon."

The princess shuddered. "I never want to see or taste that bland stuff again."

The madaeri chuckled. "And be sure to enjoy the warm bed tonight. It'll be a long time before you enjoy that luxury again."

Tian tapped his chin. The princess was probably up to the task. She'd weathered the journey better than expected. Proven her mettle.

Before retiring for the night, Tian beckoned her aside. "His Holiness will be a burden. In the Wilds. We need swords."

The princess shook her head. "He might not be able to heal with the divine power of the gods like Cyrus, but a priest and doctor may be useful in the Wilds once the Southerners go their own way."

Tian shrugged. Perhaps she was right, and even if he disagreed, she probably wouldn't change her mind. Despite his misgivings, he slept well that night.

The next morning, the air was decidedly colder, despite the bright sun. The princess gave the innkeeper a silver coin and two letters, signed with an alias and addressed to the ambassador in the Kanin embassy in Iksuvius.

The group left the city from the southern gate, where the road became nothing more than a worn dirt path heading south along the rocky section of river. After several miles of pasture where the farmers worked hard at their harvest, the road rose into wooded hills. It followed the bends of the river, which became noticeably narrower and narrower along with the road itself.

On the night of the second day, they camped by a lake, which was flush with spawning Nothori toothfish. While Tian and Ma Jun tried their hand at spear-fishing, Fleet taught the others how to make fires, with the expectation that they would soon be on their own in the Kanin Wilds. The princess learned quickly.

Toward the end of the third day, when the river shrank to a rapidly flowing stream, they split off the main road, which Fleet said continued to the Alto River's main source and the old, closed-off pass.

Instead, they walked through a rocky feeder stream, with the madaeri nimbly skipping from rock to rock without watching where he was going. Tian followed close behind. And the princess...with amazing balance and unbelievable grace, she darted among the uneven stones.

He stood gawking as she passed him, and she flashed a mischievous grin. Just like when they were children.

No, that wouldn't do. His clan would never let him forget it if he let a dancer beat him. He redoubled his efforts, speeding over the rocks.

Just as he was about to catch up to her, she pulled up short. Crouching, she rubbed her ankle and looked up at him. "I think I twisted it."

Oh no. Tian leaned over to look and—

Ooof.

He picked himself out of the stream, his shoulder stinging from where she'd shoved him. He looked up.

Far ahead, she sat on a boulder with Fleet, both laughing at him. Yes, just like the little girl he had once known.

After several *li*, they arrived at an old trail with lush overgrowth stabbing through the cracks between ancient stones. According to Fleet, following it for two days would take them through the hidden mountain pass and into the Kanin Wilds. With winter fast approaching, they had little time to complete the last leg of their journey.

CHAPTER 36:

Into the Wilds

Kaiya listened to the wind in the evergreen needles and the rustling of a nearby stream. The three Southerners, along with Fleet, Tian, Doctor Fang, and the two surviving imperial guards, sat with her in a circle around the crackling campfire in the madaeri's secret pass.

The last few days of travel had been pleasant as they chatted and hiked at a leisurely pace through idyllic woods. She frequently walked beside Tian, who could keep conversations going with insightful questions. Perhaps it was just his training as a spy and interrogator, or maybe he felt guilty and was forcing himself to be nice. Nonetheless, he seemed more and more like the childhood confidante he'd been a decade before.

Shared memories, current court gossip, philosophy, poetry: they'd talked about anything and everything. Well, everything except his brother, Zheng Ming. It should have been an easy topic to broach, yet it felt awkward to bring it up. And really, she hadn't thought much about Ming in the last month.

They reached the pass on the evening of the seventh month's full White Moon. Crisp, cold air and clear skies provided a spectacular view of the heavens, framed by the mountain summits above. Surrounded by countless stars, the White Moon Renyue shone larger and brighter than usual, bathing the pass in a soft light. The Blue Moon, Guanyin's Eye, hovered half-obscured by the mountaintops. Caiyue joined the others, its colors swirling in its eternal spot low in the southern sky.

With a renewed friendship and beautiful scenery, Kaiya should've been happy.

Yet this was the night of Hua's annual Full Moon Festival, her second-favorite celebration after the New Year's Spring Festival. Had the escape by sea worked, she would've been home already. At this moment, Father must be hosting a grand party for the hereditary lords on the shores of Sun-Moon Lake, where the placid waters mirrored the night sky.

Kaiya sighed. No fireworks, no mooncakes, no singing songs in tribute to Renyue this year.

"Here." Tian offered her a cube of moistened cornbread.

Yuck! Hopefully, he had used *water* to wet it. She raised an eyebrow and took it with two fingers. "What is it?"

"Try it." He grinned.

Locking a suspicious eye on him, she took a tentative bite. The subdued sweetness of the softened cornbread mingled with the sinewy zest of smoked elk. He'd made an imitation mooncake. How considerate! So what if it was unladylike to smile while chewing?

Tian spoke up, breaking through their companions' conversations. "Shall we sing?"

All eyes turned to him, and they offered encouraging applause.

Kaiya politely clapped at his best rendition of a Hua folk song, even if she shuddered inside. This was why he was a spy and not a court singer.

Everyone took turns, even the Southerners who didn't celebrate the Full Moon Festival. From Sameer's Paladin Canticle to Cyrus' hymns; from Doctor Fang's temple chants, to the imperial guards' chorus of drinking songs. Kaiya outshined them all, holding her friends entranced with her voice.

This was the best Full Moon Festival ever. She'd been isolated in the Hua court, yet here in the Wilds, with people who'd shared the same perils, there was a sense of belonging. Like when she was a child, with Tian. And unlike their first reunion, he was so considerate and sweet now.

And handsome.

Heavens, did she just think that?

With Brehane's tribal tune as a backdrop, she looked across the fire. The flickering light danced across his features. The defined jawline and high-bridged nose. And those eyes, so intelligent.

And looking right at her.

Heat flared in her cheeks. She cast her gaze down. Heavens, it must be the full moon addling her better judgment. She peeked up through her lashes.

He was on his feet now, working his way around the others.

Toward her. With an adorably timid smile, he sat down by her side. She fought the inexplicable urge to lean into him. How nice it would be for him to drape an arm over her shoulder. Bad girl, to even think this! It *had* to be the full moon.

He leaned in close.

Her heart pattered. What was he doing?

His hand reached out and plucked a stray twig from her short hair.

Her cheeks warmed. It might've been the first time he'd ever touched her without serious reason. She met his gaze. His normally expressionless mask contorted into self-admonishment, but she flashed him a reassuring smile.

His attention awkwardly shifted to the ground between his feet; but in that brief glance, she imagined a kindness in Tian's dark eyes. They were beautiful eyes, at least in that moment when he wasn't assessing a threat or planning an attack. Maybe that was what Jie saw in him.

If her cheeks burned any hotter, they might not need a campfire. Kaiya turned her head away. Beautiful eyes or not, he'd been thoughtless during the frantic escape from Iksuvius. Yelled at her. Humiliated her. Butchered her hair. No, she must just be conjuring up a resemblance to Ming.

Her musing did not last long as, one by one, the companions settled down for the night and let sleep overtake them.

The low light before dawn woke Kaiya from a restless, dream-filled sleep. It took her a few seconds to remember that she was in the pass straddling Iksuvi and the Wilds. Her breath misted, discouraging her from abandoning the warmth of her blankets.

Rolling over, she looked at Tian, who slept just a few feet from her. No, he didn't look like his brother. She pressed a hand to her heart, realizing that for the first time, it didn't flutter when thinking of Ming. Asleep, without carrying his worries, Tian might be more handsome.

What *was* she thinking? She banished the thought and forced herself up.

Ma Jun paced the campsite, sometimes stopping by the fire to warm his hands. He dropped to his knee at her approach.

Kaiya nodded him out of his salute. Stretching her legs and arms out to get the circulation going, she strolled over to the southern end of the pass to scan the path ahead.

The sun had just risen. Countless evergreens in the valley below stabbed up through the thick morning fog. Unlike the thin woods behind them, the lands ahead consisted of dense forest, teeming with life.

She had little time to enjoy the view.

Fleet returned from scouting ahead, as was his habit, and greeted her with a cheerful grin. "You're up early this morning. I've collected some bark from the sweet evergreen trees below. When brewed into a tea, it'll warm you up and give you energy."

He boiled some water in his copper pot over the campfire and added the bark. A sweet, aromatic scent wafted from it. After a few minutes, he filled a wooden cup and offered it to her.

She thanked him and took a long sniff. Fresh and fragrant, it sent her nostrils tingling. "It is wonderful! The aroma seems familiar."

"We drink this tea in Hua during the winter," Ma Jun said as he joined them. "Some people venture out of the Great East Gate into the Wilds to collect the bark. Maybe you had some at the palace."

That didn't seem to explain the eerily nostalgic scent. Perhaps—

"At least you only take the bark, and not the whole tree," Fleet said. "The sweet evergreen, which only grows on this plateau, has always been prized for its straightness and sweet smell. During Kanin imperial times, the Kanin emperors had the lumber hauled to their cities in the plains below to build great temples, castles, and fortresses. Much of the plateau was deforested and tilled for farmland."

Kaiya waved at the forest below. "It doesn't look like farmland to me."

The madaeri rubbed his hands together, maybe because they were cold, or perhaps because he simply liked to tell stories. "In the Long Winter that followed the Hellstorm, the land bore no crops. Many humans migrated off of the plateau and into the warmer plains. Those that stayed became hunter-gatherers by necessity. In the three hundred years since, nature has reclaimed the area with astonishing—some say mystical—speed. These forests stretch to the edge of the plateau."

Kaiya breathed into her hands. It must be difficult to live in the Wilds, away from any trappings of civilization. "What became of the people who stayed?"

"There are several tribes of Kanin folk who live here. They don't necessarily get along with each other, but will unite to fight an outside invader. They did so thirty-three years ago, when their plains-dwelling cousins invaded. However, the density of the forest made it difficult to move troops in formation. The locals repelled the invaders."

Thirty-three years ago. A lot had happened then. The secret Moquan mission to recover a book of songs. The dragon Avarax's awakening. Jie was thirty-two, her parents must have... Kaiya shook *that* thought out of her head and turned back to the forests. "Could the Teleri invade?"

Fleet shrugged. "The Teleri would have difficulty with their supply lines. Heavy snows starting in the middle of next month will clog the paths, closing them down until early in the new year."

Kaiya tried to picture a map in her mind. The Wilds stretched to Hua's northeast border. "Then the terrain, climate, and inhabitants make the Wilds a safe buffer between Cathay and the Teleri."

Fleet met her gaze. "Cathay can't afford to remain neutral and trade with everyone. The Teleri won't rest until they control the world. The Wilds can't hold them back forever."

"How could they move soldiers through it?" Ma Jun asked.

"In the old days, the few large stones in the Kanin region were used to build highways." Fleet pointed into the forest below. "Not even the mighty greywood trees can grow through those old roads. I know these paths, and will show you one that goes to the East Gate of Cathay. However, it's only a matter of time before the Empire discovers the same route if they continue westward expansion. Maybe not for decades, and the resources required to restore the old highway might not make them a threat in your lifetime. But you can never underestimate the ambition of the Bovyans."

The tone of his voice sent a chill through her. Memories of the First Consul seizing her wrist and pulling her against him surfaced, unbidden. She suppressed a shudder, and quickly changed the subject to something more lighthearted.

From where he feigned sleep, Tian watched the princess warming her hands over the fire, bantering with the madaeri. This Kaiya was much more likable than the princess. She was like the girl from his past, whom his ten-year-old self had childishly promised to marry. Her genuine smiles and girlish giggles had a charming appeal to them, even more so than the elegant courtly smiles and covered laughs that she'd used to win over kings and generals.

It was almost like Jie, but without the sarcastic sense of humor. Which was the real Princess Kaiya?

That morning, they began their descent into the Kanin Wilds. The next few days consisted of winding along worn animal trails, covered with the browning needles of the sweet evergreens. The forest was alive with the sounds of fauna, and a sweet aroma from the evergreen bark hung in the air. Nothing that Tian had ever seen in Hua or Iksuvi could compare to these pristine woodlands.

On the third day, they came to a stream. Beside that ran another trail, where flat rocks peeked out from under the ground. Lines of small broadleaf weeds marked their borders. In some places, the roots of the huge, spindly-leaved greywood trees had pushed some of these ancient stones up and exposed them to years of wind and rain.

Fleet pointed to the markings on one, noting that it had been cut by dwarves, and that this road once crossed through the original pass between the Kanin Empire and the Nothori Empire, now the Wilds and Iksuvi.

They followed the hidden road for five uneventful days, until the stream widened significantly into rocky river rapids. Fleet explained that it was a tributary of the North Kanin River, and following it downstream would lead to the East Gate of Cathay.

Tian's home province. He hadn't returned in a decade.

They continued south along the overgrown road, which ran along the western side of the river for another five days, until the road turned towards the southeast. It was at this bend that they parted ways with the Southerners.

With their own mission to pursue, the Southerners would continue along the old road towards the Kanin Pyramid, while the princess' group would follow the river. It was a tearful farewell. Against all cultural norms, Tian and his compatriots warmly embraced their traveling companions.

"Remember," Fleet said, "Continue following the river south until it meets up with the North Kanin River—it will also flow south at that point. Be sure to stay on the eastern side of the river to avoid hill ogres! Eventually, you will come to this overgrown road again. Follow that road west until it ends, then continue along the river. If you're lucky, you might even see wild elves."

"Wild elves?" Kaiya cocked her head. "How are they wild?"

Like the last time Fleet explained, in the *Hard Shell* in Gaukaimos, an image of Jie appeared in Tian's mind.

Fleet grinned. "Well, *wild* isn't necessarily fair. It's just a label given by their kindred in the two *civilized* elven realms. During the War of Ancient Gods, the ancestors of the wild elves didn't share their brethren's belief that Aralas was an Elf Angel, prophesized to lead them in their uprising against the orcs. After the orcs' defeat, the wild elves refused to acknowledge Aralas' heirs. They stayed in these forests, making their homes in treetop villages."

Elf matters. It had little bearing on Tian's current mission, except... "Are they dangerous?"

Fleet chuckled. "They'll be the least of your worries. In all likelihood, you'll probably never see them. No, the greatest danger is from the hill ogres in the northwest. As long as you avoid that area, your journey should be safe."

The madaeri handed Tian a brightly painted, thumb-length woodcarving, of a bird of prey with its wings tucked. "This is a token of the Kanin Tribal Council. Present it to any of the tribes, and they'll provide food and shelter. From here, you're less than a month away from home. It might be faster if you can trade for a canoe, though the waters may be too shallow this time of year—ask the natives. They're simple, honest people, especially in the western reaches of the plateau. Hurry, because once the snow starts falling, it'll become virtually impossible to travel."

Tian repeated the instructions to himself several times before bowing low. "Thank you. For guiding us. I hope we meet again. So we can repay you."

The madaeri just smiled. "I'm sure our paths will cross. Your enemy is mine, and I have no doubt that the winds of war will blow us back together. Remember, stay in the east. Ogres are in the west."

The princess bowed low as well, and all of her retainers dropped to one knee. "I thank you for your generous assistance, especially as it has slowed your own mission. If your travels take you to Cathay, rest assured that you will be given a warm welcome."

She then turned to clasp Brehane's hands. "You will always be a sister to me. I hope you will be reunited with your son soon. Please bring her to Cathay when you have a chance. I will be sure to introduce you to our enigmatic elf lord."

From a pouch in her robe, Brehane withdrew a small glass ball with a soft white light glowing inside. "Aksumi cities are all lit with these lights. It is the first incantation we learn, so there are plenty. I have made countless in my life. It will never go out, unless dispersed by magic. I hope this will help you on the rest of your journey. Be safe, Princess Kaiya!" She took her up in a long, warm embrace, finally releasing her with a heavy sigh. Both wiped away tears.

The Hua waited and watched as the other group continued down the road, waving as they disappeared into the trees. Now it was just the five of them: Tian, the princess, the doctor, and the two imperial guards, Chen Xin and Ma Jun. Tian hoped that Fleet's assurances of safe roads would hold true.

"It looks like we are on our own now," Chen Xin said.

"And we will be finding out just why the Wilds are so wild, I'm sure," muttered Ma Jun.

Hill ogres in the west, Tian repeated to himself.

CHAPTER 37:

Hill Ogres in the East

Kaiya awoke to Tian's gentle shakes. The sound of the babbling river next to their campsite coaxed her head to clarity.

The crackling fire sent flickers across Tian's face, the dancing shadows emphasizing his eyes. *Your watch*, he mouthed.

In the three days since they'd parted ways with the Southerners, the men always insisted she take either first or last watch, allowing her uninterrupted sleep. If not for her command, they would've taken longer intervals and let her slumber through the night. Kaiya smiled back at him as she abandoned the warmth of her bedroll.

He cast his eyes down, and then looked back up. His lips, glistening in the flames, formed the words, *Goodnight.*

Heavens, staring at his lips? Kaiya gazed at the nearly pitch-black sky, with the White Moon shining as a thin sliver, the Blue Moon almost hugging the horizon. When she looked down again, he'd settled into his bedroll. Shaking her head, she paced over to a boulder, just inside the dim circle of wavering firelight.

A cramp clenched her belly. If only she had more herbal medicine from Hua. Massaging her stomach, she closed her eyes and listened to the chorus of the night.

Gentle wind sang, set to the beat of crackling fire. Nocturnal animals danced in tune. The river rustled...

No.

Something was wrong with the sound of the waters. All the animal sounds fell silent.

The ache in her belly went from wail to whimper, almost forgotten as a chill crept up her spine. Gathering up her two straight swords, she crept toward the river to investigate. She held up Brehane's magical bead toward the inconsistent sounds, but the soft light only extended about thirty feet out into the dark waters.

Which meant that if something was out there, she stuck out in a mantle of light. Kaiya closed her hand around the light bauble, sending the surroundings into darkness. Eyes shut, she listened.

Something sloshed perpendicularly across the flow of the river, almost rhythmically...a dozen sets of sounds. Coming closer. Maybe fifty feet away.

She turned and raced back towards her sleeping companions. "Wake up! Something is coming!" Her voice rang frantic in her own ears. Behind her, the splashing footsteps sped up.

Tian woke first, having just fallen back to sleep. Saber in hand, he leapt to his feet and kicked at Chen Xin, who was closest to him. "Wake up, wake up!"

Chen Xin groggily rose to a seated position. Kaiya reached Ma Jun. Behind her, heavy steps crunched over sweet evergreen needles and dry greywood leaves, and fanned out around them. She desperately shook Ma Jun out of his deep slumber.

What was Tian doing? She looked over her shoulder.

He was prodding Doctor Fang. Chen Xin was now standing, naked saber flashing in the guttering firelight. He rushed to her side. Ma Jun sat up and fumbled for his weapon. Kaiya took up a bow and a quiver of arrows.

A huge figure stepped into the firelight. Wearing a fur-lined shirt and loincloth, he stood about seven-and-a-half feet tall. In the low light, his skin appeared mottled grey. Long, dark hair sprouted out of his head in all directions.

Pointing a gigantic spiked club at them, he barked in halting, heavily-accented Arkothi, "You drop weapons. You surrounded."

A hill ogre! Fleet had said they stayed on the western side of the river! Kaiya held up Brehane's bauble. White light radiated out in a thirty-foot sphere all around her.

Fifteen ogres encircled them along the edge of the clearing, all dressed and armed the same as their leader. Many shielded their eyes from the sudden bright light.

In that split second, Tian leaped in the direction of an animal path, swiping at the closest ogre with his saber. The blade cut across the ogre's throat, and the creature stumbled to his knees, clawing his neck.

Kaiya considered using a magical command. No, the ogres might not all understand Arkothi, while all her men did. Instead, she dropped the bauble, nocked an arrow, and let it fly. It hit the leader in the right shoulder. He shrieked, and the club slipped from hand.

Brandishing swords, Ma Jun and Chen Xin guarded her flanks. She fitted another arrow, took aim and shot at an ogre closing on Tian's back. It lodged in the ogre's spine.

Tian deftly rolled under the clumsy swing of another ogre, simultaneously cutting through his knee tendons. A gap opened in the ring of attackers. Tian beckoned her. "Run, this way!"

Chen Xin grabbed Kaiya's wrist and pulled her in that direction. Ma Jun backed up, keeping the other enemies in front of him. Tian ran toward her.

A high-pitched whistling sang from behind. Chen Xin collapsed, dragging her down with him. Kaiya staggered to her feet and tried to pull him, but he was too heavy.

Tian grabbed her by the shoulder. "Leave him. We must get to safety!"

"No!" She tugged at Chen Xin's inert body.

Tian reached under her arms and across her chest. He pulled.

Her sweaty grip slipped from Chen Xin's arm.

Tian's tone was insistent. "We must go! We can outrun them. In the dense woods."

Kaiya looked toward the fire, where Ma Jun and the doctor stood back-to-back, fighting valiantly. Four of the ogres turned and lumbered toward her.

Heart racing, she turned and ran, letting Tian pull her along through the darkness. Despite what he believed about the dense woods slowing them, the ogres loped with longer strides. The footsteps gained on them.

Tian pulled her down into thick brush with no warning. He threw himself on top of her, his hand on her mouth. His heat and weight smothered her. Images of Geros leaped into her mind. Her heart seized. She struggled for a split second.

No, this was Tian, trying to protect her. With conscious effort, she took control of her fevered panting.

The footsteps approached. Faster. Louder.

Then ran past them.

She held her breath, too scared to let it out. Her vision adjusted to the darkness and Tian withdrew his hand. All was silent, save for the ogres' pounding feet in the distance and the rustling of the river.

Motioning for quiet, Tian helped her up and guided her back towards their camp at a brisk pace. His hand on hers felt reassuring.

Then he dragged her down into more brush. In the far distance, the ogres spoke in their harsh-sounding language. Soon, that too faded.

"I think they're gone," Tian whispered. "You wait here. I'll go back. To check the camp."

She shook her head emphatically. "We stay together. We might get lost and separated."

He nodded in acquiescence, but his pursed lips, silhouetted against the dark, betrayed his opinion on the matter. He pulled her to her feet, and they crept back toward the sounds of the river.

When they reached the path by the water, the flickering of their campfire shone in the distance to the south. The sky had started to lighten, dark blues on the horizon merging with the black above. Slinking back as quietly as they could, they reached the site.

There, Chen Xin lay face-down. She stifled a gasp. He was bleeding from a horrific wound in the back of his head. Their gear had been taken. There was no sign of Ma Jun, Fang Weiyong, or the ogres.

Sobbing, Kaiya ran over and sank to her knees. She rolled Chen Xin over and nestled his head in her lap. Within seconds, his warm blood seeped through her pants. She stroked his short hair, and his eyes fluttered open.

Squinting at her, he offered a weak smile. His voice rasped in a strained whisper. "Princess Kaiya, it has been an honor to serve you all these years. I have seen you grow into a fine woman... I'm so...." He choked on his words and fell silent.

Tian knelt down beside him to feel his pulse. He looked up at her and shook his head.

Tears trickled unheeded down Kaiya's cheeks. Chen Xin had been with her for as long as she could remember, had borne the brunt of her forceful personality without complaint. Now he was dead, at just thirty-eight. Her fault.

Tian eased her up and folded his arms around her. She leaned in, draping her arms around his neck and burying her face in his chest. The warmth of his body was comforting, filling the emptiness in her heart. He stroked the back of her head.

"Poor human," a mocking voice said from the shadows. "Stupid human, come back for friend."

A trap.

Tian's body stiffened as he muttered some unintelligible curse.

She was running, Tian's hand wrapped around her wrist and pulling her on a mad dash down the river bank trail. When had he grabbed her?

An ogre stepped in front of them, only to be cut across the neck with a swift draw and slash of Tian's saber.

Jumping over the body, Kaiya looked back. Two ogres shambled behind them in close pursuit.

Despite her improved physical conditioning after two months of hard travel, her lungs burned. She panted as the path sloped upwards. Below, the river descended, the roar of water suggesting rapids.

A whirling, whining sound swooped in behind her. Something tangled her legs. She fell hard into Tian's ankles, knocking the wind from her.

He tripped over the ledge and into the river below with a loud splash.

"Tian!" Kaiya sat up and struggled to free herself from the bola entangling her legs. Her fingers trembled, her heart raced. Was Tian all right? She squinted. Dozens of feet downstream, Tian's inert form bobbed among the rapids.

A dark shadow appeared above her. Heart pounding, she looked up.

"Girl need help?" an ogre cackled. His huge, six-fingered hand wrapped around both of her wrists and jerked her onto her entangled feet. He smirked, revealing sharp yellow teeth. Rubbing some of her short hair between his fingers, he grunted.

Then, he reached toward her face. No! He lifted her chin in a tight pinch between his thumb and index finger and fixed her with a dull gaze. "Girl got ugly hair, but pretty face." His breath reeked of rotten raw meat, stirring her stomach to rebellion.

She tried to turn her head through his strong grip, to no avail.

He laughed. His hand strayed from her face and down her back, then around toward the front.

Oh no. What was he going to do? All her muscles seized up, fear freezing her in place. The horror of this situation surpassed her encounter with Geros, swallowing up her attempt to use the power of her voice. Unlike altivorcs, who found humans to be hideous, ogres had a well-known appetite for human women. In human societies, one might sometimes encounter one of the few half-ogres born to women who survived the experience.

A male behind her barked in an unintelligible language. The hand on the side of her ribs withdrew. Patting her on the cheek, he mumbled, "Chief say we go. Maybe us do fun later." He winked, sending a shudder wracking through her.

He lugged her up over his shoulder, still holding both of her wrists in his hand, and shambled towards their camp. Incoherent thoughts bounced through her head.

When they arrived at the campsite, three more ogres leered at her. Chen Xin's body lay there, though they'd taken his boots. Why, considering their feet were so much larger?

With a deep breath, she settled her racing thoughts. "Put me down," she sang. Power, held back by fear, sputtered inside of her. Energy drained out of her arms and legs.

The ogre's expression blanked and he set her on the ground.

Kaiya stumbled away, her limbs weighing her down like dwarf anvils.

She did not get far.

An ogre tackled her from behind, sending her careening face-first into the ground and knocking the wind from her. He scrambled up and straddled her, his weight crushing into her back.

Her captors exchanged a few more words in their language and then flipped her over. One gagged her with a stinking rag, which must have been used to wash a goat. Two others bound her wrists and ankles with rope. The frayed fibers bit into her skin. They ran a long pole through the ropes, and then hoisted her up like a deer carcass between two ogres. Kaiya's rattling heart bounced all rational thought from her mind. She wriggled and writhed, only to be rewarded with cruel laughs. Finally, all energy spent, she wilted.

The sky above flushed pink, as the crown of the sun glanced through the tree tops. The beasts began their march back through the river. Where were they taking her? At the deepest point, the water reached to the ogres' waists. Their massive bodies resisted the strong flow of the current.

Kaiya wiggled upwards as best she could, to keep from getting her back wet from the splashing waters. After several minutes, they emerged from the river onto another path through the forest. They came to a clearing, where Ma Jun and the doctor lay bound to poles, just like her.

Ma Jun's left eye swelled shut, flushing an ugly shade of purple. He looked at her with his good eye and shook his head. Another seven ogres sat there, slurping on some food. Four ogres lay dead.

The largest one's arm dangled in a sling, with a black splotch seeping through a clumsy bandage on his shoulder. The leader. The one she'd shot. He glared at her and stood. He lurched over, drawing a wicked, serrated metal knife with his good hand and yelling foul gibberish.

His words needed no translation. The knife announced his intentions. He was out for revenge, coming to cut her throat here and now. Then they would do horrible things to her body, robbing her of dignity even in death.

She squirmed to free herself. The other ogres lifted the pole off the ground, setting gravity against her. Before the enraged leader could reach her, two of his companions interceded, stammering with wild gesticulations. He snarled and sheathed the knife, spitting on the ground. He came closer and aimed a kick to her side—not strong enough to break anything, but sharp enough to send pain flaring through her ribs.

She yelped. Ma Jun resumed his struggle, only to be punched in the jaw.

The leader leaned in and yanked her head back. "You lucky you pretty. You bring good money. Else I gut you." He released her and stomped away.

Good money? Were they to be sold into slavery? Kaiya let out a long exhale. Warm tears flowed freely over her cold cheek.

After a while, the ogres hoisted her and the two others back up and resumed their march through the forest. Where were they headed? There couldn't be a slave market in the wilderness. Could there? Fleet had never mentioned anything about the tribal peoples keeping slaves.

The sounds of wildlife fell silent as they passed. The brutes lumbered on, and the sun rose higher, peeking through tree branches as the morning progressed. After three hours, they arrived at what appeared to be a permanent campsite in a large clearing.

Kaiya's arms and legs ached from the strain. Hopelessness overcame her.

Evergreen needles and greywood leaves covered the ground. Several large tents circled a bonfire. A couple of ogres milled about, but the loud sound of snoring from the tents suggested there were a few dozen more.

And from one tent came the sounds of a woman, crying and screaming. Kaiya's heart leaped into her throat. She fought against her bindings. It was no use. She looked to see where the ogres were taking her.

Four fifteen-feet poles were secured horizontally between trees. On either side of each pole, alternating from left shoulder to right shoulder, dark-haired humans sat quietly, their wrists bound so that the pole passed between their arms. There were thirty-eight in total, about ten to each pole.

The ogres carried them over to the other prisoners. Black-haired with ruddy skin, they were Kanin tribespeople, dressed in deerskin clothes and furs. All young adults, mostly men. No children or elderly. Some looked up, craning their necks and meeting her gaze. Eyes widened and murmurs passed through the lines.

Kaiya sucked in a breath. There were several sets of twins.

The ogres untied her feet, and then added her to one of the poles. They secured Ma Jun and Doctor Fang to different poles. One ogre stood guard while the rest stomped back to the center of the camp.

How could they possibly get away? She looked over at her countrymen. Fang Weiyong was talking to a tribesman, or at least trying to. Ma Jun met her eyes and nodded. He must be making a plan of some sort.

Several hours passed. Mouth still gagged, Kaiya looked at each of the prisoners within her line of sight. They must all have some sad story. Like her, caught by ogres for some nefarious purpose. And why so many twins? If not for the stinking gag, she would've asked.

When the sun shone high in the sky, two ogres approached. One looked fairly intelligent, his eyes seeming to comprehend things more deeply than the average ogre. His comrades all nodded respectfully at him. The chief, probably. His companion was the one she had shot, arm still in a sling. Perhaps a lieutenant of some sort.

Behind them, the chief dragged a comely young woman, tears streaked across her face. Her deerskin dress was torn, partially revealing her breasts and legs. The blood staining her thighs left no doubt as to what had happened to her.

Poor girl. Kaiya drew her knees to her chest. It probably wouldn't be long before she shared the same fate.

The other prisoners muttered and wailed. Others sobbed as the ogres tied the girl to a pole.

The chief came up and inspected them in a cursory manner. When he paused at Kaiya, her heart almost stopped. He bent over and clutched her chin in an iron grip between his thumb and index finger. Try as she might, she couldn't turn her head. He peered at her through sleepy eyes before turning to his lieutenant and grunting something.

The other ogre nodded and grinned.

Her entire body trembling, Kaiya scuttled back as best she could. The prisoner beside her yelped.

The chief snorted and released her, then stood and yelled back at the camp. One ogre brought a sloshing wooden bucket and lifted it to each of the prisoners' mouths. Water! It dribbled out the sides, and tantalized Kaiya's dry mouth.

Another ogre hand-fed them small chunks of some foul-smelling meat. The stench quelled the gnawing in her stomach.

The ogres approached. They would have to loosen the gag to feed her. And then the power of her voice... No. There must be at least thirty here, and without a musical instrument, she'd be exhausted after three or four commands. Her flute, in the fold of her robe...gone. The Teleri imperial crest, too. Nothing to do now but wait, rest, and look for another opportunity. And hope.

When offered, Kaiya gulped the water down. Its coolness ran down her chin and neck. The meat, on the other hand, stank so bad that she just turned her head. Those ogre hands were filthy, and what kind of meat was it, anyway?

The chief addressed them all, speaking in heavily accented but fluent Arkothi. "Rest well. You will be travelling in the late afternoon."

Then he turned to Kaiya, grinning. "Except you. We will keep you until our next group is ready. I'm sure the big bosses won't mind if we have some fun first."

Big bosses? Fun? Her heart resumed its pounding, but she nonetheless glared back at him in defiance.

Another several hours passed. Kaiya's wrists chafed from trying to loosen her bonds. Eventually, she gave up and closed her eyes, letting sleep overtake her. In what seemed to be minutes, loud clanging jolted her out of sleep.

Night had fallen, and the ogres were back with food. Again, she drank the water but refused the meat. After half an hour, the leader appeared again. "Now, get ready to leave. Stand up."

As the prisoners shuffled to their feet, he ambled over to Kaiya. "All but you." He laughed as he motioned his lieutenant to take hold of her. He pulled out a large knife and cut through her bindings. Kaiya kicked and struggled, but the ogre effortlessly lifted her in the air, far enough away from her flailing.

It wasn't long before she tired.

Ma Jun twisted and turned, disrupting his pole, but another ogre came and punched him squarely in the kidneys. Everyone cringed at the sound of cracking bones. He collapsed, almost bringing the entire line of prisoners down with him. The leader angrily barked at the offending ogre, who then yanked Ma Jun to his feet.

Kaiya's wrists were retied in front of her. An ogre shoved her to her knees, holding her down with enormous paws while the ogres prepared the others for departure.

A dozen ogres marched the prisoners out of the camp on a path to the south. Ma Jun stumbled along, slowed by his injury. Exhausted from her struggle, Kaiya could only watch them leave before the chief half-dragged her towards a tent.

CHAPTER 38:

Rescue with Red Hair

He lay flat on his back. The chill of the hard ground seeped through his wet clothes. Tian opened his eyes. Everything was blurry. He blinked to clear his vision, and listened. There was the rippling of the river, birds chirping, wind blowing through the trees...and talking.

His vision came into focus. Above him, the tops of sweet evergreen trees, swaying in the breeze, framed a bright blue sky. The Iridescent Moon was hidden from where he lay, but the sunlight suggested it was either early morning or late afternoon.

Where were those voices? He turned his head, sending a blazing pain searing through his temples.

Ignoring his body's protests, Tian pushed himself to a sitting position. With great effort, he looked from side to side, but the voices came from behind, in elegant, accentless Arkothi. His hand inched toward his saber, only to find that it, and his dagger, were missing.

"Well, well, General Shaotyan rises from the dead!" It was an unfamiliar but melodious male voice, butchering the name of the Wang Dynasty founder.

Tian twisted around, gingerly, fearing that any quick motion would cause his brains to leak from his ears.

Six people huddled in a semicircle on the ground, about ten feet away from him. Four men, most likely Arkothi from their olive skin and dark hair, nodded at him in turn. They wore camouflaged leather cuirasses and bore shortbows and longswords. Some sported short beards. Most looked to be in their twenties.

A fifth man, shorter, slimmer, and younger than the rest, regarded him curiously. He had pointed ears, fine features, and shiny golden hair, and wore a poncho of forest-green. An elf. Perhaps a wild elf? A delicate-looking bow was slung across his back and a long, thin sword hung at his side. "We were worried about you," he said. The accent, like the lilting of songbirds, marked him as the one who'd referenced the first *Tianzi*.

None were as striking as the sixth person: a young human woman about his age, she had tanned skin. Dark red hair cascaded in waves of curls down her shoulders. Her almost almond-shaped eyes twinkled a light green, and her beautiful features seemed to have an elvish refinement to them. The smile she directed at him was devoid of any warmth. Like the elf, she wore a forest-green poncho.

"Yes, thanks," Tian said, stumbling over the Arkothi words. "Where did you find me? And who are you?"

The elf pointed toward the sound of running water. "In the river, unconscious. You're lucky to be alive. You shouldn't go swimming in the rapids, you know."

As if he had planned it. Tian forced a smile.

The woman peered at him. "Who are you? What is a Cathayi doing in the Upper Wilds?" Her soft voice might have been cute, if her tone didn't cut like a knife.

"I..." What *was* he doing here? The princess... "What day and time is it? Where am I? Who are you?"

She pursed her lips. "I asked first, so you answer first."

There was no point wasting time in an argument. "I am Tian Zheng. From Cathay. I work in Iksuvius. I am escorting someone. Back to Cathay. Please tell me who *you* are."

Her bushy eyebrows rose. "Back to Cathay? Wouldn't it be faster and safer to take one of your ships?"

She was avoiding his questions. Meanwhile, the princess was out there, in need of help. "Yes. But we had no choice. We weren't able to secure passage. Now, can you answer me?"

The woman yawned. "Unable to secure passage on one of your own ships?"

He could lie convincingly enough to fool most people, but his half-truths didn't convince this woman. Tian stood up. His head pounded, but it didn't matter. "Am I your prisoner? Because if not, I must find my traveling companion. She may have been captured. By hill ogres. At least tell me what day it is."

"You aren't a prisoner." The elf shook his head. "It is the second day of the eighth month. However, given how clueless you are, I wonder if you even have a chance of tracking down your friend. Maybe you should tell us what happened. Perhaps we can help you." He turned towards the red-head. "Look, Allie, if his friend was captured by the ogres, then he is not our enemy."

Allie glared at the elf. "*If* he's telling the truth. The Cathayi are only interested in money. Who knows who the bastard has sold his sword to? Perhaps he works for our enemies and is tracking us."

Tian growled. As if anyone would send *him* into the woods to track experienced rangers. And the girlish voice did not suit her foul mouth. "I am guessing, Allie, that you are Eldaeri. That means the Teleri's imperial ambitions concern you. They

declared war on Cathay by trying to take our princess hostage. I need to find her now."

The six exchanged glances. Of course, out here in the wilderness, they couldn't have heard the news.

The elf scratched his head. "I've seen your princess before, half a year ago. Describe her to me."

Tian bit his lip. Where to start? Banishing all the negative things that immediately popped in his head, he gave his most objective evaluation of the princess. "Voluminous hair. With a vibrancy of its own," at least before he cut it. "Doe-like eyes. A high thin nose. Full lips," a perfectly symmetrical face, really. "Graceful like willow branches in—"

"You sound like a man in love," Allie said.

Heat stirred in Tian's cheeks. "A voice that could charm a dragon."

"And did charm a dragon, for which I owe her a personal debt of gratitude." The elf turned to Allie and nodded.

Allie flicked hair over her shoulder. "If the stories are true, she's beautiful beyond compare. We'll help you. Be warned, if it turns out you are lying, we will nick your fucking intestines and tie you up to a tree. The Kanin brushhogs will come and eat your shit."

Tian hid his cringe, not so much at her threat but at her dirty mouth. "I'm not lying."

Allie smiled without the least amount of sincerity. "In order to find your princess, you need to tell us everything you remember about how you came here."

Tian paused to recollect the order of events. "We camped on the eastern bank of the river. We were running south when I fell off a ledge. It was just before dawn this morning."

Allie nodded. "The trail should be quite warm, then. It's now near the fifth waning crescent, and we are not far from where the river starts to drop and the east bank rises. Hurry up."

They all stood and collected their gear. Within minutes, they were swiftly marching toward the river, with Allie in the lead. The peaceful chirps of birds and the rustling of animals in the brush did little to assuage Tian's anxiety.

Arriving at the river in ten minutes, he scanned the surroundings. The ledge on the opposite shore was about ten feet higher than this bank, which in turn was level with the water. They turned north, walking uphill with the river at their side. Tian regularly checked to see the height of the opposite bank.

After an hour, they came to a stop at a wide trail that ran perpendicularly to the river.

"Ogre tracks." Allie pointed to the markings in the muddy ground. The others fanned out to look for clues.

Tian fidgeted, though noting how they operated. "Any human tracks? She's only this high." He held his hand at his nose. "Small feet. We also had two other men. About my height."

The elf shook his head. "If they were captured by ogres, they would have been carried."

"There were ogres." Tian pointed at one of the large, deep footprints in the mud. "We should follow this trail."

The elf again shook his head. "There are ogres all over this region, and we don't want to recklessly traipse into one of their camps. By the way, it is always safer to travel on the eastern side of the river, especially at night."

Just like Fleet said. Tian rolled his eyes. They *had* camped on the east bank. Apparently, the ogres didn't get the notice.

One of the men pointed. "A braid of human hair, coarse and black, about thirty centimeters."

The princess' braid!

Another one chimed in. "Blood on this leaf, red and fresh."

Tian looked at the elf and Allie with an urgent, forced grin, silently prompting them.

Allie tilted her head down the path. "Follow the trail. We're now entering dangerous territory. Keril, you take point; Rami, you have rear guard. You, Zheng, stay close to me and try to keep quiet."

One of the men padded to the front with a bow in hand. Although he didn't even seem to be watching his feet, he made no sound as he stepped through the needles and around the dried greywood leaves. The rest fell in behind him, all walking with equal stealth. Allie took the middle of the line and motioned Tian to follow her.

After a few minutes, Allie looked back and smiled at him, this time quite genuinely. She pointed at his feet and gave him a thumbs-up signal.

It wasn't *that* hard, considering his own stealth training. He smiled back.

Before long they came to a clearing. Keril raised his hand in a fist, and they all stopped. After scanning the perimeter, he motioned for them to enter. The sun now sat high overhead, providing radiant warmth in the clearing. Allie motioned Rami to continue down the trail and the others to fan out.

The scout came back in a few minutes and whispered, "Clear."

A torrent of whispered observations erupted.

"Ogres were here, probably about three hours ago."

"Looks like about a dozen, four dead among them."

"A human was bleeding here, the shape and amount suggests blunt trauma."

"Another human was set down here. Probably a woman, with six centimeter black hair. There's a flute here."

Tian hurried over to look at the flute, with Allie close behind. "This is our princess'."

Allie knelt down to sniff dried blood on a leaf. "Then it seems we are on the right trail. Let's break for lunch and rest."

Tian grabbed her shoulder and spun her around. "We must keep going."

All of the men grinned at him. One shook his head in a '*he's in for it*' look.

Allie lifted her arm to lock Tian's and started to push at him with her other hand. She slid a leg behind his. It would have dumped an untrained man flat onto his behind, but Tian's reflexes instantly took over. He reversed her throw by pressing a hand into the small of her back, stepping laterally and twisting his own hip.

She fell backward, but with catlike grace put a hand down and rolled back into a stand. In the same motion, she drew her dagger and set it at his throat.

Tian turned and seized her hand, then twisted her wrist and swiped the dagger away.

Her companions reached for their weapons. The elf already had an arrow nocked and aimed at him.

Allie raised a restraining hand and flashed Tian a lethal smile. "You're more than meets the eye."

Tian pursed his lips. So, he'd gone from being the rear end of a mule to the front side of a male prostitute.

Tone softening, she added, "You remind me of another Cathayi. One I consider a friend, and to whom I owe a debt of thanks. If what you told us is true, you've not eaten breakfast, and since we're all hungry and tired, you must be even hungrier and more tired. How do you plan on rescuing your princess from a dozen angry ogres on exhausted legs and an empty stomach?"

"I'm sure you know...what the ogres will do to her." And it would be *his* fault for bringing her into this Heavens-forsaken wilderness.

Allie placed a hand on his shoulder. "Your woman is safe for the time being."

His woman? "How can you know that?" He flipped the dagger and offered it to her hilt-first.

"You'll have to trust me on this." Refusing the weapon, she flashed a wry smile. "Ogre superstitions will protect her."

Tian threw his hands up. "What does that mean?"

She rolled her eyes. "If you want to continue on your own, please feel free to get yourself fucked. It would certainly free us up to continue on our own mission."

Tian sighed. She was right. He *was* hungry and tired, and even at full strength, there was little chance he could defeat a dozen ogres in their home territory by himself. Defeated, he dropped into a seated position.

Something cold and hard bit into his butt. He popped back up. All heads turned to him, amusement dancing in their expressions. He looked down. A round piece of strange grey metal, a thumblength in diameter, lay partially hidden in the leaves. Picking it up, he turned it over in his hands and traced the etching: a circle surrounding a curious emblem of squiggly lines. A precisely cut scrap of black cloth was still attached.

Allie gasped. "The Teleri imperial seal. How did it get here?"

Tian furrowed his brow, trying to recall where he had seen it before. "I think the Teleri First Consul wore this."

Allie chuckled. "Of course he did, idiot. It's the heirloom of the Bovyans, passed down from the first Geros to every First Consul. If it's real. Let me see it."

Tian handed it to her.

After a cursory glance, she drew her sword and held the two objects close to each other. She sucked in a breath.

Tian craned over her shoulder. Both pin and sword seemed to be made of the same mysterious metal.

She handed it back to him. "I believe it's real. Both the seal and my sword were made from a falling star. There's so little of this metal in the world, and the skill for etching into it was lost long ago. It's impossible to counterfeit."

Tian nodded. "I remember now. When the princess faced the First Consul, she mentioned this pin. She must have cut it from his uniform." He stashed it in his lockpicking tool pouch, and put that in his pack.

Allie sighed and looked to Thielas. "So the First Consul still lives. Our plan to attack his entourage must've failed."

Tian tapped his chin. It all made sense now. The Eldaeri repeating crossbows his team had found in Larusso's Iksuvius warehouse must've been ordered by Allie, to attack Geros. Yet another mistake Tian had made.

He looked to Allie, who'd already set up he bedroll at the other end of the clearing and was fast asleep.

The elf came and sat down beside him, offering him some bread and dried fruit. "Forgive my rudeness for not introducing myself earlier. I am Thielas. Allie is right, you know."

Tian nodded, chewing on some of the fruit. "Who are you people? What're you doing in the Wilds?"

"That's not my place to say. I leave that up to her to tell you, but you have to earn her trust first. Still, she does seem to have taken a liking to you." The elf's smile looked forced, his friendly tone masking jealousy. "She has a wild spirit; that much I can tell you. Even more so than your average human."

Tian nodded again. There must be something between these two. "I've been rude, too. Sorry. I should've thanked you. For helping me."

"With the appearance of this pin," Thielas said, "this rescue may be tied up in our own cause. In any case, you had better get some rest."

Around them, the five others had finished eating and unfurled bedrolls. Sighing again, Tian leaned up against the back of a tree on the other side of the clearing, in the shade, and closed his eyes.

He was awoken just minutes later by a gentle shaking. He opened his eyes.

Allie hovered over him with a smile. "Wake up, Tian. You were the one in the rush." She giggled like a girl. Everyone else appeared to be ready to go.

"How long have I been asleep?"

"About two hours," she said. "You looked tired, so I sent Kori and Rami ahead to scout, to make sure we were on the correct path. There are hundreds of ogre tracks passing through here, but I think we have the right one." She extended a hand to help him up, which he gratefully accepted. Her fingers were coarse and her grip strong, so unlike the princess' smooth, delicate hands.

Thielas looked up at the sun. "It is midday, so we should be safe from the ogres for a little longer while they enjoy their beauty sleep. We can be a bit less careful for another several hours. Let's make the most of it."

They started down the trail, with Keril taking point.

As they walked, Tian started probing as only a good spy could. "I don't often see ladies with such good wilderness skills."

Allie laughed. "How would you know what good wilderness skills are? Yours certainly need some work."

Tian laughed nervously, and prodded her to continue with a raised eyebrow.

Allie said, "My parents wanted me to be an elegant lady, but I preferred to run in the forests. When I was twenty-four, I met Thielas, who taught me woodcraft. Then, I was sent to live with a distant uncle, in hopes that I'd learn proper etiquette. After eight years, no success!"

She was least thirty-two! And obviously Eldaeri, whose traces of elf blood allowed them to age more slowly. Time to coax more information from her. "I guessed you were Eldaeri. I've not met many." Except for two princes, both quite arrogant. "It seems odd. To be this far away from home. In this wild land."

She skidded to a halt and stared at him. "You talk like a stalking predator. Know that I am elusive prey. You won't learn more than I want you to."

Tian snorted. Smart woman. Who cursed like a sailor. No need to continue with the roundabout questioning. "What *can* you tell me?"

"You look smart." She flashed a feral grin. "How much have you already deduced?"

"The Teleri Empire expands to the east. Into the lands of the former Arkothi Empire. It will soon be on the border of the Eldaeri Kingdom of Serikoth."

Allie sighed. "Yes, my homeland. They have already captured Thundercloud Fortress, which guards the pass between the mountains and Bullhead Lake."

Capturing Serikoth would put the empire closer to Tarkoth and all of its resources, like... "Teleri wants shipbuilding lumber. And deep-water ports." Cold tingled up Tian's spine. Tarkoth wouldn't fall easily, but here in the Wilds... "That's why they captured Iksuvius."

"What? Iksuvius has fallen?" Allie came to a stop with a gasp, startling the rest of their group. She looked at Thielas and shook her head.

"Yes. That's why we took this route." Tian kicked a small rock. "The Teleri troops cut off access to our ship."

Allie's gaze followed the rock. She bent over and picked it up. "How would you know to take this route? The only pass between here and Iksuvi is very-well hidden."

"A madaeri scout guided us."

"Fleet." Her face relaxed, and she fell silent for a few steps. "You have more to worry about than he realized when he sent you this way. The Teleri have discovered the ancient highway through the Kanin Plateau. The bastards are using local slave labor to build fortresses and restore the roads. The terminus is a one-week march to Cathay's borders."

The web of correlations formed a clear picture in Tian's head. "You can't afford to have Teleri gain easy access to these forests. They will get wood. They will build ships. Challenge you at sea. That's why you are here. To assess the danger. Who are you? You lead men. Even at a young age. You must be of some importance."

Allie whistled. "I've already said too much. Perhaps, when we meet your princess, I can explain more."

They continued down the path. After an hour, the sun descended beyond the Nothori mountain range, casting long shadows. Allie gave the order to maintain silence. After another two hours, with dusk fast approaching, the trail opened onto the eastern side of the hill ogre camp.

CHAPTER 39:
Mixed Feelings

Despite his urgency, Tian knew it would be foolish to try and attack an enemy camp without getting an idea of their strengths and weakness. Just as he could do with his own network of spies, Allie issued several silent orders with her hands. Her men fanned out in admirable silence.

Allie motioned for him to follow her up a tree. The sweet evergreens grew straight and limbless to the height of two men, but the trunks' proximity to one another allowed him to spider-climb between them. At a height of about twenty feet, he and Allie perched themselves on branches, with a good view of the entire camp.

The clearing was about ninety feet in diameter, with an additional trail leading out to the southwest. Twelve large round tents, all ragged and dirty, surrounded a bonfire. Four long poles lay on the ground on the southern edge of the camp. Outside of the ring of tents, ogres worked at making rope, rendering meat, tanning skins, and sharpening rocks.

Tian counted eight ogres in the open. He named them based on their distinguishing features: Mop Head, Big Brute, and the like. After an hour, he identified thirty distinct individuals, all male, with one obvious leader and two secondary leaders. One of those lieutenants, shoulder bandaged and arm hanging in a sling, looked like the one who'd led the raid on their camp.

Allie signaled for him to come down. The other rangers rejoined them, and she motioned them deeper into woods, out of earshot of the camp.

In the darkness, she whispered, "What did we learn?"

"Thirty ogres," Rami said, "though the number of tents suggests that more live here."

"No prisoners. They must have already left with an escort," said Keril.

Thielas scuffed his foot in the dirt. "They leave a guard by the supply tent constantly."

"There's a tent," Tian said. "That none of them entered. Or left."

Allie nodded. "We can't attack now. They'd have the advantage with their night vision. Let's get some sleep. Two-hour watches, one person observes the camp, while another guards here. We'll strike at dawn."

Tian frowned. No telling what they'd do to the princess in that time. But Allie was right. A bad plan would get them all killed, without helping the princess at all.

They laid out bedrolls on the forest floor. Thielas took reconnaissance duty first, while Allie stood guard.

Tian couldn't sleep. His mind buzzed with thoughts. All the mistakes he'd made that had led to the princess' capture. He stared up into the sky, barely able to see the stars through the dense tree cover. Thick clouds rolled in from the west, completely obscuring his view.

He sat up and let out a deep sigh. Something hit him lightly in the back of the head, and he turned.

Leaning up against a tree, Allie beckoned.

He crept over.

"Can't sleep?" she whispered.

"Can't stop thinking. Everything that could go wrong went wrong. It's my fault. I've never failed at anything. I'm not used to this feeling." Why had he said so much to a stranger?

She patted him on the shoulder. "The first failure is the hardest."

Tian shrugged. "I feel so out of place. In this forest. In the wilderness. None of my talents serve me."

"Sometimes, you just have to...surrender." She reached behind his head and drew his face closer to hers.

Tian's heart pounded. His obsessive thoughts blurred out of focus. Surrender. Allie was beautiful, something that he'd missed behind her strong and commanding nature. Or maybe it was because her rugged exterior was so unlike the classical Hua beauties.

He closed his eyes, and their lips met. It was intoxicating. All his worries and concerns melted away. He pulled her closer to him, savoring her intriguing combination of toned muscle and feminine softness. Her lips parted, inviting him deeper.

Images of the princess crept into his mind. Heavens, here he was, losing himself in a stranger's embrace, while the woman he was responsible for faced untold violation and humiliation. Waves of guilt careened over him, dousing his fire. He opened his eyes and pushed Allie away.

She searched his expression.

"I'm sorry," he whispered. "I can't...surrender." Or maybe he was crazy about the princess.

There! He admitted it. How foolish. She hated him, anyway. And even if she didn't, he wasn't an appropriate match. She was courting his brother, for the love of Heaven.

Allie shook her head. "No, I'm sorry. It wasn't fair of me, to take advantage of you when you were feeling weak. Forget this ever happened."

If only he could. Tian hung his head. "I'm sor—"

Thielas appeared without a sound. "Ogres, coming this way, fifteen of them, about three minutes behind me."

Thoughts of princesses and brothers and ranger girls blinked out. Tian snapped into ready alertness. Allie handed him a dagger, then woke up the rest of her group. Though they were too far off the path for the ogres to accidentally stumble upon them, the rangers all took up arms and pressed themselves against trees.

Tian squeezed the dagger hilt, sweat beading on his forehead. The eight of them didn't stand a chance against twice as many ogres, except by surprise. He peered through the trees.

Shadowy figures lumbered by on the path, making plenty of noise. Several carried the long poles from the campsite.

The sounds disappeared into the distance. Allie beckoned the group together. "I know we're all exhausted, and we wanted to wait until dawn. However, this might be our best chance to strike, now that half of the ogres have left the camp."

Thielas nodded. "From their activity, I'd guess they've gone out to capture more slaves."

Allie nodded, drawing a rough schematic in the dirt with a twig. "We need to take either their leader or his lieutenants alive so that we can find out where they've taken Tian's princess." She pointed with the stick. "We'll form a ring around the camp, placing ourselves so that we have a line of sight on the bonfire between each two tents. On my mark, take down as many targets as you can with your arrows. Every time one is killed or incapacitated, yell out the count."

Eyes following Allie's stick, Tian looked for possible flaws. What if several stayed in the tent? What if they didn't have a full count? There were just too many uncertainties to come up with a good plan.

"Once they sound the alarm," she continued, "we can expect them to head into the tents to arm themselves. If there're eight or less at that point, we will close in on the perimeter of the tents, and only engage hand-to-hand if necessary. If there're more than eight, I'll enter into the camp and try to get as many of them as possible to chase me down that southern trail. The rest of you will engage the remainders. Any suggestions?"

Tian tapped his chin. Not the best plan, but he couldn't have made a better one with their limited information. At least Allie's made the best use of the terrain and resources... Wait. He raised his hand. "All I have is a dagger. What am I supposed to do?"

Though cloaked in the darkness, Allie's smile was clear in her tone. "Your job is to check out the tent near the northwest corner that nobody goes into. Make your move in the ensuing confusion, and with your stealth, I am sure you will be fine. If you can, take out the guard on the provisions tent, right next door. Everyone give him your dagger."

Tian stuffed a few sheathed daggers in his belt, and one in each boot. He followed the rangers back to the campsite and continued around to the opposite side while the others fanned out.

He counted six dark ogre shapes along the outside of the tent ring. Cloud cover obscured the starlight, making it darker still. He waited for the signal, visualizing the path he would take between the supply tent and the unknown tent.

Allie's shrill call echoed in the night sky. Chaos broke out. Ogres bellowed in pain.

Shouts erupted around the perimeter.

"One down!"

"Two down!"

Crouching low to stay below the line of arrow fire, Tian broke towards the tent.

"Five down," called Keril from the east.

Disorganized ogre wails.

"Six down," Thielas yelled from the south.

Arrows whizzed above him.

"Seven down," another ranger called, again from the east.

Allie shouted out orders.

"Eight down," came Rami's yell from the west.

Now inside the tent ring, where firelight evened the odds between ogre and human, Tian assessed the threat. Fifteen feet away, the sentry at the provisions tent made direct eye contact. Tian hurled the dagger in his hand, and immediately followed with another at his belt. The first hit the brute in the throat, the second in the head.

"Nine down," Tian called.

Directly ahead, the injured lieutenant ogre ducked into the supply tent. The leader waved a huge two-handed sword, barking out orders from the front of his own tent. Two ogres emerged on the northern and southern side of the ring, both armed with spears.

"Ten down!" Allie's voice called from outside the tent ring.

Five enemies remained, one of them unaccounted for.

Tian threw himself towards the entrance of his assigned tent, staying low. Hopefully, the bonfire would obscure the ogres' view of him. He slipped in through the flaps.

Pitch black.

He listened carefully, trying to filter out the clashing sounds from outside.

"Eleven down!"

"Twelve down!" called Allie.

Only three threats left. This fight was won.

Inside, near the center of the tent, was quiet breathing. Human breathing. Probably a woman trying to hide the sound of her breath.

Please let it be the princess. No, it couldn't be, not this long after their capture. "*Dian-xia?*" he ventured.

Whoever it was in the center of the tent burst into sobs. "Tian!"

Tian let out a sigh. He crawled toward the middle to avoid tripping over anything. Halfway there, his hands found a thin cotton carpet. Past that, a fur blanket which covered the smooth skin of the princess' crossed legs. He jerked his hand back. He'd touched her.

"Tian." Her voice was choked, laced with uncharacteristic pleading.

He rose up onto his knees and wrapped his arms around her, and she rested her head on his shoulder, softly crying. Her upper body was clothed, and her hands were bound behind her back, tied to the tent's central pole.

He stroked the back of her head. "Are you okay?"

Her only answer was gentle sobbing. He traced a hand down her arm to her wrist, where he found the cold metal of manacles. He felt at his belt for his lockpick pouch.

The tent flap opened, casting a flickering light throughout the tent. Tian turned, making out the silhouette of an ogre with a huge sword in one hand.

A glaring light flashed from the other hand, washing Tian's eyes in a bright haze.

He sprang to his feet, simultaneously taking two daggers from his belt and throwing them. One clanged against metal, the other whirled out of the tent and tumbled across the ground. He squinted. A large blurry figure lurched towards him. It raised a sword with two hands to hack him in half.

Tian side-stepped the chop as he bent to pick up the blanket. The sword smashed against the dirt where he'd just stood. The blade then whistled towards him on an upstroke, rising at an angle with enough force to sever his head. Tian swept the blanket up into the sword's path while diving headfirst under its trajectory, into the ogre's knee. He seized the back of the ogre's ankle with both of his hands and drove his shoulder into its shin.

The leverage caused the brute to fall backward. The sword pitched across the ground. Tian finished with a forward roll, ending straddled on the ogre's chest.

He swept another dagger from his belt and stabbed downward with an overhand hold. The ogre caught his forearm in a powerful two-handed grip. Undeterred, Tian twisted his wrist, slashing the blade across the ogre's left wrist tendons. The grip from that hand went slack, and blood sprayed.

Tian bounced into a crouch and used his left hand to grasp his opponent's right arm—which still held fast to his own dagger hand. He twisted around and leaned back, hyperextending the ogre's

arm in an armbar. He arched his back. The tearing ligaments and rubbing bones made popping and grinding sounds. The ogre roared.

As his vision adjusted to the light, Tian gave the ogre a sharp kick to the side of the head, knocking him out. He climbed back up to his feet, blinked his vision clear, and looked down.

The leader.

"Thirteen down." Tian turned to the princess. Her eyes burned red from crying, and tears left dirt streaks down her cheeks. With the blanket gone, her perfectly-shaped legs were bare. His gaze involuntarily lingered, and she twisted her body in an attempt to conceal herself.

Ashamed of himself for so many reasons, Tian turned his head. He picked up the blanket and covered her. "I'm sorry..." he mumbled. "I, uh, will see if he has a key."

He leaned over and searched the unconscious ogre. A ring of four keys hung on its belt. The smallest one fit into the princess' manacles.

Hands free, she wrapped the blanket around her waist and held it together with one hand. She extended her free arm, tacitly asking him to help her up. Her legs wobbled as she stood, and she threw herself against him, burying her face in his chest. He embraced her warmly, protectively, as she pulled him closer and wept.

What could he say? There were no words of comfort he could offer. Maybe the *Moquan Tiger's Eye* mind-block could blunt the emotional trauma. No—no telling what it would do to someone not trained in *Moquan* ways.

"I'm so sorry, *Dian-xia*." He stroked her head. "It's my fault...that this happened to you. If only we'd gotten here sooner."

She looked up at him with furrowed brows. "We?"

Tian looked down at her with an equally perplexed expression. "We... Some friends I met. I wanted to storm the camp hours ago. We could've spared you...you know..."

She lowered her head, pressing her ear to his chest. Her words shook through the shuddering of her shoulders. "They didn't."

"But your…" He pulled her closer. It was too awkward to continue. Maybe Allie would say something appropriate. "Never mind."

Outside, the sounds of battle died down to only an occasional ear-wrenching death keen. The ranger Rami burst into the tent, nearly tripping over the ogre. He stopped in his tracks. "Sorry to ruin the moment." He turned around and jumped out.

Heat rose to Tian's face. What must Rami be thinking?

A couple of minutes later, Allie spoke in an exaggeratedly loud voice, just outside the tent opening. "You men, wait a few minutes so the lady can make herself presentable. Zheng: be a gentleman—if that's possible—and come out here."

Tian gritted his teeth and stepped back.

The princess looked up again, this time with a demure smile. "You heard her. Out you go." She turned him around and pushed him in the back towards the entrance.

A blast of cold night air greeted him. Allie's expression wasn't much warmer. Thielas stood by her side, while the other rangers investigated the tents.

"Your lady friend okay?" Allie asked.

"Traumatized. But it looks like you were right about…that…"

Allie chuckled and pushed past Tian into the tent. "Don't come in until I tell you."

Thielas shrugged. "Curious creatures, women. Especially human women."

"Especially human women?" Tian cocked an eyebrow. "Do you know this from experience?"

"More than you'd expect." The elf grinned back.

"Are all the ogres taken care of?"

Thielas held up two fingers. "There are two unaccounted for: the leader and one of his seconds. That one has an injured arm, so he's not an immediate threat beyond his ability to bring reinforcements."

Tian tilted his head towards the tent. "The leader is incapacitated in there. Did you check the provisions tent?"

"Yes. It looks like a lot of the possessions they took from captives, as well as a locked chest."

Tian produced the key ring from his belt. "Perhaps one of these will fit."

Allie's muffled voice called from inside. "Okay, you can come in now."

Kaiya felt exhausted to the core, her legs barely steady enough to support her lithe form. She'd used the power of her voice several times to fend off the ogre's repeated attempts to violate her, and it took a physical toll. At first, when she realized how thoroughly she could control him, it was almost amusing to watch him approach, only to be cowed by her command to back away.

She looked down at the unconscious leader and shuddered. Each time she'd used her voice, it drained her in alarmingly increasing increments. The effect of her command took longer to take hold and lasted shorter. As her fear grew, she found it harder to even find her voice. The last time, he had managed to rip her pants off, and only the hook of her thumb kept her undergarments from going with them. She shuddered to think what would have happened if he had had another chance.

She pulled her pants back on. After this torment, she'd never look at a male the same way again.

That changed when the tent flap opened.

Tian entered. A sense of relief washed over her. When had that happened? In two months, he'd transformed from an uncaring oaf to the dear friend she remembered from childhood. His embrace had felt…good.

Behind Tian followed the most gorgeous man she'd ever seen, with delicate features and large violet eyes that could've been the essence of a dawn cloud concentrated into a rich liquid. Vibrant golden hair tumbled down his shoulders. He seemed familiar.

Kaiya ran her hand through her own short hair, suddenly feeling naked again despite the warm woolen pants.

Tian's attention shifted to the semi-conscious ogre. Kaiya shivered. Its rough hands had rubbed her face. Even now, after Allie had tightly secured those same hands around the pole, behind his back, Kaiya edged away from the brute.

"Greetings, Your Highness. It has been a while." The elf's voice sung like the symphony of gods. Oddly, it sounded familiar, even if she'd never seen him before—and she'd certainly not have forgotten meeting someone so beautiful.

"Have we met?" She tilted her head at just the right angle and smiled.

He nodded. "At the time, we were not properly introduced. I am Thielas Starsong."

The name didn't sound familiar. "I am sure I would have remembered you." Heat rose to her cheeks. Had she just said that?

Thielas' grin was captivating.

Embarassed, she turned to where Allie and Tian knelt over the ogre leader.

"Nice handiwork," she was saying. "I don't know many people who could defeat an armed ogre with just a couple of daggers." Allie put a hand on Tian's chest.

An uneasiness sloshed in Kaiya's stomach. Jealousy? She shook off the thought, trying to replace it with more important matters. "We need to find out where they took Ma Jun and Fang Weiyong. They left the campsite around dusk, bound to poles."

Allie nodded. "That means they can't be traveling that fast." She gave the ogre a light kick in the leg. "Where do you take your prisoners?"

The ogre shot her a confused look and mumbled something long and drawn-out in his own language.

Allie scowled at him. "The people you captured."

"Me no speak you words."

If Kaiya didn't already hate the beast, she would now. "You do. Tell us where you took our friends."

The ogre chortled. "Whore, I won't tell! Since you'll kill me, I have nothing to gain. Unless you let me stab into your depths with my man-club!"

Kaiya winced, and he roared out in laughter.

His tone turned demeaning. "Of course, it'll have to wait until your girl-bleeding is finished."

Her face flared hot. All these men, learning her secrets. She fled the tent and stopped outside.

Inside, Allie whispered, though still loud enough to hear. "Don't follow. Just pretend you didn't hear or understand it."

The tent flap opened, and Allie emerged. "You okay?"

No. She nodded all the same.

Inside, the ogre bellowed. What was happening?

Tian's voice rose. "Poisonous fiend. You're right. You will die. Either quickly tonight. If you cooperate. Or very slowly overnight. If you don't."

Silence. Was the ogre considering the—

A roar of pain blasted out of the tent. Kaiya shuddered again.

Tian stomped out, Thielas close behind.

"It's no point in torturing the ogre." Tian shook his head with a look of frustration. "He won't tell us a thing."

Kaiya peered at him. "Get him to talk. Ma Jun and the doctor, and all those captives rely on that information."

Tian turned towards Allie. "Will you be able to track the others?"

"Not until daylight. Until then, I suggest that we get some rest. The tents reek, so I'm happy next to the bonfire." She beckoned her men over. "Two-man watches, two hours each. We'll let the princess sleep through. We should get moving before dawn, before the other ogres come back."

Sleep! After this horrific day, her body screamed for it, even if she was sure to have nightmares. Kaiya eyed the bonfire.

Tian headed towards one of the tents. After a short while, he emerged with their bedrolls and other supplies. He laid out Kaiya's bedroll for her, and then tightened the blanket around her, insulating her from the chill air. He really was like her childhood friend again.

A friend who might provide protection and comfort tonight. She pointed her chin towards the space not far from her and cast a shy smile. "Sleep there."

Tian's eyes widened, but he offered a tentative nod. He placed his bedroll where she indicated and settled in.

As she drifted into an exhausted sleep, she could hear his heart pounding.

CHAPTER 40:

Pursuit

At dawn, pins and needles skittered through Tian's left arm. He shifted slightly to relieve the pressure when Allie shook him out of sleep. He was lying on his side, something he never did.

Allie grinned as she pointed at his numb arm.

It was lying under the princess' neck, and wrapped around her shoulder. She also lay on her side, her back pressed to him, separated only by the thick blankets. His other hand... It rested on her hip.

Tian's eyes opened wide and he jerked his arm back. The princess rolled onto her front with a soft sigh.

His face burned hot, probably redder than the horizon. He'd just committed a capital offense, far worse than locking her in an armoire.

Allie chuckled. "She was crying in her sleep, and you reached over to comfort her. It was quite sweet, actually." She flashed him a sarcastic grin. "Your princess *is* very beautiful, though the legends of her luxurious hair are definitely overstated."

Tian's throat tightened. If only she knew. "Our secret, okay?"

"Another one?" Allie puckered her lips and grinned. "Anyway, we'll need to get moving soon." She nudged her head back. "The others are getting ready."

Which meant they probably all saw him with his arm around the princess.

"After waking your princess from her beauty sleep," Allie continued, "I suggest you take what you need from the provisions tent. Find something warm. It'll snow today."

Was that a tingling in his chest, where the princess' back had pressed into him? He shook the thought away and crawled out from the bedroll, his body reluctant to abandon the warmth. The air seemed much colder this morning, and clouds greyed the sky. He gently shook the princess, and her eyelids fluttered open.

Hands clenched, she frowned. Her gaze shifted back and forth until it settled on him. The scowl melted into a beautiful, innocent smile, one that sent his heart skittering. "Is it already time to get up? I had horrible dreams all night, and it seems like I only slept for a few minutes."

"Yes, *Dian-xia*. Allie says it will snow today. They need to start tracking. Before we lose the trail. Get ready. I'll bring you some hot water."

The rangers prompted them to go within half an hour. Tian retrieved the Kanin sabers, Kaiya's straight swords, two bows, two quivers of arrows, and their own packs from the supply tent. Most of the other items belonged to the native tribes: bows, stone-headed spears, furs, and the like.

One of the keys opened the locked chest. Inside were Teleri-coined gold *draka*s. They had little need for them in the Wilds, but he took two large handfuls just in case. He also retrieved Chen Xin's and Ma Jun's silver rings.

Rami discovered a rough map in the leader's tent. Some locations were marked in green, others in red, though no one could decipher the code. A small island at the confluence of the North Kanin River and the nearby tributary was circled in blue.

Markel and Kori had examined the tracks and concluded that the prisoners had been taken down the southern path. They set the tents ablaze, leaving only the supplies and the leader's tent untouched.

Which left the leader. They could've avoided this entire journey had they killed the altivorc in Gaukaimos. Tian didn't plan to make the same mistake again.

Surprisingly, the princess insisted on letting the ogre live. Allie added that a crippled ogre would face torment among his kind for the rest of his life. He'd never admit to having been defeated by just eight humans.

The rangers departed down the path, with Thielas at point and Rami taking up the rear. Tian walked near the front, the princess staying near his side. Her closeness sent a shiver up his spine. What was he thinking?

Within a couple of hours, light flurries began to fall.

Allie gave the sky a dubious look. "It doesn't usually begin to snow this early in the season. This might be a long winter."

Snow already? Tian started to look up when Thielas pointed at the ground. "A large amount of human blood here. I'm guessing it was vomited, maybe three hours ago?"

With a flash of Allie's hand signal, the rangers fanned out.

Markel knelt by the head of a trail. "The trail of blood heads east down this path toward the river, but everyone else continued south on the main path."

Kaiya placed a hand on her chest. "The ogres beat Ma Jun before they departed, when he tried to protect me. He could barely walk."

Four imperial guards, already dead or unaccounted for. Tian sighed. His fault.

Allie came up beside Markel and pointed at the ground. "We'll follow this trail of blood. Based on the ogre map, we're not far from the river, and there is a red circle here."

Tian tapped his chin. So much stubble; something he'd never allowed before this journey began. He followed Thielas as they veered off onto the smaller path. The rangers pointed out drops of blood. The sounds of the river grew louder and louder. After half an hour, the path opened up into a clearing by the water.

An irrigated field. They pushed south through a narrow field of corn, its crop past ripe and now rotting on the stem.

On the other side, the princess covered her audible gasp.

Tian shifted on his feet. The red circle on the map marked death and destruction.

Dozens of simple wooden frames, charred by flame, were all that remained of lodges. With no evidence of doors or windows, there was no way of telling the orientation of the burnt-out structures, but it looked as if they circled outward from a huge fire pit. The soft rustling of the river interrupted the otherwise eerie silence.

Tian picked his way through the huts towards the center of the abandoned village. The place stank of death. Hairs stood on the back of his neck.

Heart pounding, Kaiya clasped and unclasped her hands as she followed Tian past the scorched huts and into the center of the village ruins.

With a sharp breath, he jerked to a halt. He turned around and put a hand over her eyes.

Too late.

Around the fire pit lay nearly two dozen bodies, their advanced stage of decomposition preventing identification of gender. Crushed skulls suggested the manner of their horrific death.

Several smaller bodies could only belong to young children.

Kaiya's stomach lurched into her throat. She seized hold of Tian's arms so tightly that her knuckles went white. He drew her in close, pulling her head to his chest. His comforting warmth did little to melt the ice in her limbs. After a few seconds, she looked up at him.

Tears trickled down his cheeks as he looked past the gruesome scene. He hadn't shown so much emotion since their reunion. "Dragonflies," he whispered.

Dragonflies? Kaiya searched his eyes. He still remembered the old proverb she'd told him when they were children.

Allie came up beside them. "The ogres raid these villages for slaves, capturing healthy men and women, but taking savage delight in murdering the sick, old, and very young."

Horror and grief gripped at Kaiya's throat, choking her words. "But why? What do the ogres need slaves for?"

Allie tugged on her sleeves. "They sell slaves to the Teleri soldiers who have infested these woods."

Teleri? They weren't supposed to be in the Wilds. Kaiya shuddered. "How did the Teleri get here?"

Allie peered at her. "They spent years searching for the ancient roads from the Arkothi Empire into the Kanin Empire."

Which led right to the East Gate of Hua. Throat dry, Kaiya swallowed. "Who thought up such a plan?"

"First Consul Geros."

The First Consul. Kaiya's blood froze. He had seized her, pressed himself up against her. She hugged herself now, as if that would protect her from the memory.

Allie nodded. "Which brings us back to the Kanin. Since Teleri soldiers are only good at war, they need hands for construction, food preparation, and other services. In their satellite states, it takes the form of fair trade contracts—if you consider the Mating a fair part of the deal. But here, where there is no centralized rule to enforce Teleri law,

their goals can only be accomplished with slave labor."

Kaiya's heart ached. All the unfortunate tribal people, subjected to the cruelty of an evil empire. For too many years, Hua had enriched itself through trade with the Teleri, turning a blind eye to those it affected. Like Madura before. This needed to change. It would change, once she returned home.

From the distance, Keril called. "I think I've found your man."

Kaiya and Tian hurried in the direction of Keril's voice, on the eastern edge of the village, at the river's edge. He was there, kneeling over a human, who lay face up.

Alive? She gritted her teeth and looked down.

It was Ma Jun, her last imperial guard. His eyes were closed, and blood flecked his lips. Complexion wan, he breathed in rapid, shallow pants.

Kaiya knelt over him and stroked his cheek. He couldn't possibly survive.

Keril sighed. "He's bleeding internally and has lost a lot of blood. He doesn't have much longer. Unless Thielas can save him."

Kaiya looked up from Ma Jun. "Is he a doctor?"

Keril shook his head. "He can channel the divine power of the gods."

Like Cyrus, who'd given her energy when they fled the altivorcs. Kaiya nodded. She looked back toward the center of the village.

The elf knelt near the mass grave, head bowed in prayer.

She placed a hand on Tian's arm. "Please, bring Thielas here."

With a nod, he raced back toward the elf. She leaned over and brushed cold sweat from Ma Jun's forehead.

Thielas appeared at her side, his handsome features twisted into a melancholy expression.

Kaiya bowed low. "It is my fault my guard is mortally injured. Keril says that you have the power to heal. Would you please try?"

Thielas smiled wryly. "Only the gods have the power to heal; I am just their conduit into the realm of mortals. We can see if the gods have use for him in this life, or if they are ready to recall him to their bosoms." He closed his eyes, placed a hand on Ma Jun's forehead, and sang a prayer in the musical language of the elves. His chanting voice sounded familiar.

Inspired, Kaiya hummed with him.

The color returned to Ma Jun's face, and his breathing deepened.

Miraculous. Nothing Cyrus had done rivaled Thielas' healing powers. Kaiya reverently bowed her head and pressed her palms together. "Thank you."

Thielas smiled at her. "Thank Ayara, whom your people name Guanyin. Her compassion and grace restored him. He is safe now, but will require several weeks of rest in order to recover full strength."

"We still need to rescue the other prisoners," Kaiya said. "Will he be able to walk?"

"I am well enough to help, *Dian-xia*," Ma Jun answered in a weak voice.

Too weak; but conscious, at least. She looked down.

His gaze met hers and he tried to sit up.

Showing a surprising gentle side, Tian placed a hand on his shoulder.

"He needs to rest for another two hours," Thielas said. "Even then, he won't be able to keep pace with the rangers."

Tian lifted a water skin to Ma Jun's lips. "What can you tell us about the other prisoners?"

Ma Jun nodded and licked his lips. "Around dawn, the ogres caught another man. Since they needed more room on the pole, they released me since I was slowing them down."

"Was Doctor Fang all right?" Kaiya asked.

Ma Jun shook his head. "He struggled to help me, and the ogres beat him."

Allie appeared behind them. "The bastards will want to sleep during the day, and they'll be slowed by transporting the bound prisoners. It's been three hours since dawn. They can't be but so far ahead of us." She pulled out the map and pointed. "Princess Kaiya, stay here with your countryman and make him rest for two hours; then both of you head back to the main trail and turn south. Once we've taken care of the ogres, some of us will come back for you."

Could she do it? One girl, untrained in the ways of the wilderness, protecting an injured man?

Tian shook his head. "It's too dangerous. The ogre camp could house forty, maybe fifty ogres. We only eliminated fifteen. Fifteen headed west at dusk. Another dozen are escorting prisoners. There might still be some around here."

Memories of the leader's gigantic hands sent a shiver down Kaiya's spine.

Keril shook his head. "Ogres don't like to venture out during the day. It should be safe until at least the late afternoon."

Allie nodded. "We'll need your help, Zheng, to fight this group we are pursuing."

"My duty is to protect the princess." Tian crossed his arms.

Kaiya put a hand on his shoulder. "No, our duty is to protect the defenseless. Zheng Tian, just as they helped me when I needed it, we must help them. And remember, the doctor is with them."

He opened his mouth to protest, but she shot him a stern look that silenced him. She straightened, invoking her tone of imperial authority. "That is my command."

Tian dropped to his knee. "Forgive me, *Dian-xia*. I cannot obey your command."

She took his hand, so large and calloused compared to hers. "Will you obey my request?"

His eyes widened and searched hers, his pupils darting back and forth as if debating each other. He dropped to his knee. "As you...request."

Allie chuckled. "You have him well-trained."

Heat flared in Kaiya's cheeks. She caught sight of Tian in the corner of her eye.

He was blushing, too.

Pretending to ignore the comment, she sat down and laid Ma Jun's head in her lap. "It is settled then. We will meet you in a few hours."

Tian thought it foolish to leave the princess and an invalid guard behind. Still, she made no threats of punishment. No use of the power of her voice. Only a request—one which he now regretted acquiescing to.

The rangers marched quickly to try to catch the ogres, until the snow started falling harder and began covering the tracks. But as Allie had pointed out, there was only one direction they could possibly be heading at this point.

After another two hours, they stumbled upon the ogres and their prisoners.

They must've settled down for the day earlier than Allie expected.

Clad in deerskin clothes and furs, the prisoners sat in a square. Each side was formed by a pole, to which all their wrists were bound. A dozen ogres were laid out wherever they could find space. Two stood watch.

The rangers nocked arrows and shot. One of the ogre sentries yelled out. Screaming captives awkwardly jostled each other on their poles. Some, including the doctor, kicked at their captors. Thielas danced into the fray with his thin elven sword.

Tian gaped. The elf moved with a blurring speed, not unlike the Paladin Sameer. Recovering his sense of the present, Tian dashed to a groggy ogre and slashed his throat before he could stagger to his feet.

With most of the ogres bleary-eyed from sleep and slowed by the daylight, the fight ended quickly. None of the rangers or prisoners suffered injuries.

Tian picked his way through the captives, cutting bindings while searching for the doctor. Many patted him on his back, speaking words that he assumed were thanks. There were so many twins! One dignified-looking man hurried north up the trail without saying a word or waiting for company.

Young Doctor Fang's eye was swollen shut. Blood flecked his lips and chin. His words came out hysterically. "The ogres kept the princess at their camp! We have to rescue her before they do horrible things. Ma Jun, too, was dying somewhere back there." He gesticulated wildly to the north.

Tian rested a reassuring hand on his shoulder. "We already rescued her. And Ma Jun. Both are at a village. Back the way we came."

Doctor Fang glared at him through his good eye. "You left her alone?"

"She ordered me to."

The doctor's eyebrow shot up. "Since when did you start obeying her orders?"

Tian waved the comment off. "Are you well enough to travel? We'll race back. To rejoin them." Tian looked around for Allie.

The other rangers were busy binding wounds. Markel spoke some halting Kanin language and found out that the prisoners were all part of the same Maki tribe, though they came from three different villages. Ogres lived much farther north, and historically had not bothered humans this far south.

Tian nodded. It explained why Fleet had not known about the danger. The ogres had come to this region just six months before and started raiding smaller villages. Survivors sought refuge with cousins and distant relatives in other communities. Some of the larger villages now burst at the seams, stretching resources thin. Though these were relatively safer, the fear of capture generally kept people from venturing out in small groups, further straining the food supply of these hunter-gatherers.

More concerning to Tian was the news of the Teleri. Rumors from other tribes to the south and east told of a race of Metal Men, using the natives as slave labor to build new fortresses. Although there had been talk in the Kanin Tribal Council of allying to fight back, generations-old blood feuds and the upcoming winter season—predicted by their shamans to be the coldest and snowiest in years—had put those plans on hold.

At last, Tian found Allie, distributing what food they could spare. Other rangers were using their metal blades to sharpen crude spears from long, straight branches, so that the refugees could defend themselves on their return journey.

Tian placed a hand on her shoulder. "We should head back. To the burned-out village. The princess awaits us. Undefended."

She pointed to the blue circle on the ogre's map. "No, we're going to continue south, to find out where the ogres were heading. You escort the natives back north, at least until you meet up with your princess."

Undernourished and injured, the locals would slow him. Tian bowed his head in acquiescence nonetheless. "Thank you for your help. I have learned so much. From your example. About playing our role in the world. Thank you again."

Allie wrapped him in a tight embrace.

So strange, so uninhibited, these Northerners. Tian tentatively returned the hug.

Then she brought her lips to his. All he could do was freeze in shock, while bystanders pointed and whispered. The doctor grunted.

Releasing him, Allie flashed a feral grin. "I would like to say that is how you could repay me, but you aren't particularly good at it."

From the heat in his head, he must have been glowing an interesting shade of red.

Her coy tone turned serious. "So instead, remember that our nations share a common enemy, and that we may one day have the honor of fighting side by side. In these woods, I am Allie, but know that my true name is Princess Alaena of Serikoth, heir to the Kingdom of Korynth."

Royalty! She was royalty. Tian kept his face blank and nodded.

She continued, "The fate of my people, your people, and these people, may very well rely on the bridges we build today."

Tian nodded.

She winked. "Be sure to practice your kissing, and you may win your princess' heart yet."

The doctor gaped at him, his good eye wide and his mouth wider.

What could Tian say? The heat from his flushing reached his ears. All he could was stare as

Allie—Alaena—disappeared south down the trail with Thielas and her rangers. He turned to the Kanin people and motioned them to follow him north.

CHAPTER 41:

Opportunities

From her spot at the edge of the western marketplace, dressed as a street urchin, Jie eyed a dark-haired man with a cutlass concealed under his cloak. In a nation of farmers, occupied by a land army which confiscated anything longer than a knife, the typical sailor's weapon stood out to her trained eyes.

The bulge should have been obvious to Teleri patrols, and the man was a fool to be packing in the mid-afternoon sun. Maybe the Bovyans had grown lazy since Emperor Geros departed the city a month before with his concubines, leaving General Marius as governor.

When the stranger stopped by a nearby fruit vendor, Jie sidled up to him and began testing the apples. She'd learned—by some trial and plenty of error—that late-harvest apples this far north tasted better soft. Yet the man selected several hard ones with his worn, calloused hands. His face, from what she could tell from his profile in her peripheral vision, was tanned and weathered, punctuated by a stubbly dark beard.

"Don't go touching every last one and not buy anything." The vendor favored the two of them with a suspicious eye, though he wouldn't be running down any thieves with his clubfoot.

Poor man. His pretty daughter, who enticed customers with her flirting, had been taken by the Teleri not long after the occupation began. The thought of the poor girl saddened Jie, reminding her of her ambitious—and perhaps foolhardy— plan.

"Looks like a cold rain," the stranger commented in Arkothi. His voice was deep, his accent perfect.

Jie stole a glance up. There wasn't a cloud in the sky.

The vendor nodded, almost imperceptibly. "Oh, not for some time now."

Even more curious. A code, even. Perhaps an underground resistance forming? There hadn't been any acts of sabotage or attacks on Bovyan patrols.

Jie's instinct to find out more drove her to a hasty decision. A quick glance around the market revealed no Teleri patrols. Taking a deep breath, she tugged at the stranger's coin purse, yanking it free with enough force to let him know. She bolted off.

"Hey! Stop! Thief! Help!" The stranger ran after her.

Obviously a stranger. Though vendors might try to stop a petty thief, most of the locals left the street children alone.

Jie looked back to gauge his distance before turning into an alleyway between houses on a lazy street. With a pop-vault, she suspended herself a dozen feet up with outstretched arms and legs.

The man turned the corner.

She pounced, grabbing his cloak and wrapping him in it as they rolled on the ground.

She whipped a knife out and pressed it at his throat. "Quiet. Understand?"

Anger burned in his eyes, but he nodded.

"Now, who—" Jie cut herself short. She recognized the man. He was one of the marines aboard Tarkothi Prince Aelward's ship, when he had transported Princess Kaiya to Ayudra Island, many months ago. "Never mind. I know you're a Tarkothi marine." Easing the knife back to prevent him from trying to attack her, she pulled her hat off, revealing her ears. "I am Princess Kaiya's handmaiden. I'm going to let you get up, but do so slowly."

When a look of recognition bloomed in his expression, she sprung back out of cutlass reach, just in case he tried to attack.

He rose slowly, rubbing his lower back, where the cutlass had probably dug in during his tumble.

"Sorry about that." She grinned meekly. "Now I know who you are...or at least *what* you are. Is there a name to go with the beard?"

"Ciro." An Arkothi name. The marine glared at her, sizing her up as he extended his palm.

"Oh, yeah." She tossed his purse, which he caught with a quick snatch. "What are you doing here?"

His eyes remained narrowed. "I would ask you what *you* are doing here. Where is your princess?"

Jie looked him over. It wouldn't hurt to tell him generalizations. "She fled the attack on the city. I am stranded here."

"Well, maybe we can help each other."

Jie's ears perked up. "Go on."

"We are here—"

"We? Who is *we*?"

Ciro scratched his beard. "The TRS *Invincible*, captained by Prince Aelward, is off the coast. We are here looking for a band of rangers, led by a red-headed woman. Have you seen them around the city?"

Jie shook her head. Tian had mentioned something about a red-haired Eldaeri, had a strand of the hair dangling in his cobweb, but they hadn't uncovered the mystery before the Teleri invasion. More exciting was a friendly ship, somewhere off the coast. Perhaps it was a way home. After she'd

personally saved Prince Aelward from an assassin's arrow, he owed her a favor. "I would like to meet with the prince."

He scratched his beard some more. "On what business?"

"Mutual benefit, just like in the past." Jie imitated the princess' best smile.

Ciro looked at her for a few seconds. "Meet me on the coastal road, at the first cove outside the walls, when the Iridescent Moon waxes to half."

About three hours. Jie nodded. "Until then."

With little time to continue reconnaissance of the rape center as she had originally intended, Jie worked her way towards the coastal road. Well before the appointed time, she arrived at the meeting spot and descended on a path down the rocky embankment to a gravel beach. The waves roared as they came ashore, drowning out all other sound.

She hid herself among the boulders as the sky darkened, the setting sun giving way to the feeble light of the nearly-new White Moon. Her elf vision would surely give her an advantage if this meeting turned out to be a trap.

Not long after, Ciro arrived alone. Once he reached the beach, he looked around before peering out to sea and holding aloft a shuttered light bauble. He fiddled with it, sending flashes in long and short bursts.

A code. Jie tried to memorize it. She looked back towards the city walls and scanned the area. No threats.

Ciro paced, also squinting towards the walls. Before long, he took his cutlass scabbard in hand. He must have been quite nervous, but she would keep him waiting.

After a while, the dark shape of a boat came to shore, rowed by two men.

One of the men spoke. "Any word from the princess?"

Ciro shook his head. "No, our eyes and ears inside the city have not spotted her or her rangers."

"Then why did you call us ashore?"

Ciro sighed. "The Cathayi princess' handmaiden wanted to meet with Prince Aelward. However, she hasn't turned up."

Their conversation was reassuring enough. Jie used a *Ghost Echo* technique to throw her voice from a boulder. "I am here."

Ciro and both men jumped, startled.

Jie grinned. She emerged from her hiding place and approached.

"Hands up," Ciro commanded. When she complied, he patted her down, politely, finding two knives but missing her throwing spikes. He gestured toward the boat.

She turned to him. "Are you coming?"

He shook his head. "No, but you are in good hands with these sailors."

Jie saw the other men also had cutlasses at their side. She sucked her lower lip. On firm ground, she could dispatch a pair of armed men. In a boat, on the other hand...

She took one last look at them. Deciding they looked familiar, she boarded. One pushed the boat out into the water before jumping in himself. Ciro and the shore disappeared into the distance, the rhythmic sloshing of oars mixing with the roar of the surf.

Caiyue, never moving from its heavenly seat in the south, waxed to its first gibbous as the *Invincible*'s shadow ballooned. Before long, it loomed above them, even larger than Hua's own trade ships. Jie looked back to see the tiny dots of light in Iksuvius.

Climbing to the deck, Jie remembered how much she detested the rocking. All of the sailors looked wide-eyed at her. Prince Aelward approached, his long dark hair becalmed on the peaceful seas. His slim build and sharp features betrayed the hint of elf blood that flowed in Eldaeri humans' veins. She was about to extend a greeting, when he walked past her to the returning sailors.

"Where is Alaena?" Aelward's voice seeped with a longing that didn't take *Moquan* training to notice.

One of the sailors crossed his arms in an X over his chest. "Your Highness, there is still no news of her." He then nodded towards Jie. "Ciro bade us to bring this one aboard."

Jie removed her hat and attempted her best curtsey. "Your Highness."

"Handmaiden Jie?" Aelward cocked his head, favoring her with a raised eyebrow.

"The same." Jie held her clumsy curtsey, waiting to be released.

He clapped her on the back, nearly knocking her to the deck. "I barely recognized ye through all the grime. I thought ye were some boy the men recruited."

Jie channeled her Princess Smile, even as she stewed inside at the blunt reference to her curveless figure. "That's not the nicest way to greet someone who saved your life."

He laughed again. "True enough. So, handmaiden, what brings you aboard?"

"A favor. I need you to take urgent news to Cathay."

The prince's smile melted. "I can't do that, I must stay in these waters to retrieve...a friend. But fear not, we spotted a veritable armada from your homeland not one week ago on our way here. I would gauge from the prevailing winds that they will be here soon."

Jie sucked on her lower lip. Of course the *Tianzi* would retaliate for the assault on his daughter. However, what could warships realistically do that would affect the Bovyans? And with the princess escaping into the Kanin Wilds, the ships here did her no good.

At the very least, Hua ships offered Jie a means of getting home to deliver the news. And perhaps she could get Meiling to safety as well.

Meiling. The girl suffered in the throes of morning sickness. From what she said, Emperor Geros had kept her to himself, and hadn't allowed any other Bovyan to take her. Which meant she carried Geros' child.

The Teleri prophecy came to mind: a Bovyan who knew his true mother and father would bring an end to the Teleri Empire. If Jie could get Meiling home, they might have something to bargain with.

CHAPTER 42:

Little Friends

In the devastated village, Kaiya waited patiently as Ma Jun slept. With nothing else to do, she listened to the laughing of the river, the twittering of birds, and other sounds around her. The tall greywoods towered high above the forest floor, devoid of leaves. Across the river, cliffs rose some twenty feet above the banks, their white-colored faces crisscrossed by tangles of green vines. Prickly-leaved shrubs with large, bright-colored berries grew along the banks. Birds and squirrels chattered at one another as they ate the juicy treasures.

Kaiya's stomach rumbled. Laying Ma Jun's head on her pack, she rose and walked over to the shrub to try the bite-sized berries. Their pleasant aroma was reminiscent of cinnamon. She washed them off in the river before taking a bite. A sweet flavor exploded in her mouth, followed by pleasant warmth percolating through her.

A sniffling sound carried almost imperceptibly over the rustling of the river. Children's cries? Kaiya followed her ears, walking down the river, though occasionally looking back to see that Ma Jun rested undisturbed. The sobs grew louder.

Colors flashed by a grove of berry shrubs. Kaiya padded over.

Two children huddled together by the river. With their backs to her, they were oblivious to her approach.

Kaiya paused, composing herself. Using her most gentle voice, she addressed them in Arkothi. "Hello."

The children jerked around, startled. One was a boy and the other a girl, both about six years of age, and looked so alike, they had to be twins. They wore unadorned deerskin shirts and breeches, and had the ruddy skin tone of the Kanin people. Shoulder-length dark hair framed their little faces, the girl's braided in an unkempt queue behind each ear. Red berry juice stained their petite mouths.

Both jumped to their feet, eyes wide as they gawked up at her. The boy clutched his sister's arm and they turned to run.

It wasn't the reaction Kaiya expected. What *had* she expected? She couldn't even remember the last time she'd been this close to a child. Lacking even a drop of maternal instinct, her smile was probably more suited to manipulating a man. And men were probably far more gullible than children. She caught ahold of the girl's other arm.

The girl cried uncontrollably. The boy tugged at her.

Such dedication. Like Kaiya's own two brothers trying to protect her when she was young. Squatting down to eye level, she reached out to take the boy's wrist, and pulled them closer. "It's okay, I won't hurt you."

The boy let go of his sister's hand, and now swatted at Kaiya's arm. The girl wailed. Kaiya sunk lower, kneeling, and drew them close, wrapping her arms around them. The girl went rigid, but the boy continued to struggle.

The Dragon Charmer, confounded by two kids.

She sang a Hua lullaby while gently rocking the two in her embrace. Feet rooted to the ground, she projected the calm of the light wind.

The boy stopped struggling. The girl melted in her arms. After a few minutes, she shifted her weight back and returned to holding the children's hands. Maybe this was what it was like to be a mother? She smiled at them. Not a contrived court smile, but more like those she'd shared with Tian a decade before. And again, not long ago. "Are you lost? Where are your parents?" She spoke slowly, carefully annunciating each word.

The children looked at each other and then back at her, heads cocked.

They clearly didn't speak Arkothi. She placed her hand over her heart, and said "Kaiya. My name is Kaiya." She extended her open hand towards them. "What is your name?"

The girl's eyes brightened and she clapped her hands together. A smile creased her face. Pointing to herself, she said excitedly, "Nadi." She gestured back and said, "Kaiya."

"Yes." Kaiya smiled again. "Pleased to meet you, Nadi."

The boy, now bouncing on his toes, pointed at himself. "Waka." Both children giggled.

"Nice to meet you, Waka. You must be hungry." Rubbing her stomach, she put a finger to her mouth.

They both nodded eagerly while speaking in their own language, their trepidation now apparently forgotten.

Trying to pick out words, Kaiya took their hands and walked them back to where Ma Jun slept. Flakes started to flutter from the skies.

They looked at him with wide eyes, and then up to her. "*Kane ma taichoupu tezuga?*" the boy said.

Though the words might have been gibberish, their sounds and cadence seemed familiar. She kneeled down next to Ma Jun and covered him with her cloak. She took some cornbread from her pack.

The children eyed it. When she offered the bread, they snatched it and plopped down cross-legged to devour it, crumbs scattering onto their clothes. So cute! She handed them some dried fruit, which immediately disappeared into their little mouths.

At least for the moment, they were content. Kaiya watched them eat. What would she do with these two? She pointed at them, then toward the burnt-out village. "Did you live here?"

The boy tilted his head inquisitively. He asked something of his sister, and she just shook her head. He met Kaiya's gaze and shrugged.

A few more attempts at gesticulating, making faces, and otherwise trying to ask questions all met with the same frustrations. Perhaps her time would be better spent trying to learn some of their language.

It helped that many words sounded vaguely similar to the Hua court language, spoken only by the Imperial Family. Her new little friends were enthusiastic teachers. By the time Ma Jun woke up a phase later, her vocabulary consisted of body parts, animals, and geographical features. Fast learners, they had also learned the corresponding Arkothi words.

Ma Jun eased himself into a sitting position and bobbed his head as she brought a water skin to his lips. He took a few tentative sips before beginning to swallow large mouthfuls. He then shifted to his knees and pressed his head to the ground. "*Dian-xia*, I am mortified to have you serve me like this."

She ruffled through her pack and withdrew his imperial guard ring. "In Hua, I am the daughter of the *Tianzi*. Out here in the wilderness, we are just fellow countrymen, leaning on each other to survive. Think nothing of it. Are you well enough to walk?"

Receiving the ring with a bow of his head, he rose on wobbling legs and hobbled over to his pack. She lifted his arm over her shoulders to help him walk, and motioned for the children to follow her back down the trail to the west.

The boy and girl shook their heads violently. Refusing to follow, they pointed across the river, speaking animatedly. From the hour-long lesson in their Kanin dialect, the gist of their concerns seemed to be *there bad...river good.*

Kaiya looked up and down the bank. Her two new friends might know the forest better, but there was no way to cross. With the snow now falling fast enough to gather on her cloak, it would be wiser to head for the cover of the trees. Tian expected her at the head of the trail, anyway.

She emphatically motioned the children to come with her. After a few refusals, they reluctantly complied. Like ducklings, they pressed close, virtually tripping her as they clutched her pant legs. At their plodding pace, with Ma Jun's weight hanging on her, and slowed even further by the light accumulation of snow, it seemed like a full hour passed before the dead village disappeared from sight.

On they trudged. In the distance ahead, someone approached, their form partially obscured by the falling snow. Kaiya's heart lifted, her worries about progressing too slowly now melting away. Tian must have already reached the rendezvous point and was now heading up the trail to meet them. She called out to him. Was that *longing* she heard in her voice?

No reply.

What if it wasn't Tian?

The person drew closer, picking up pace. Too big. Much too big to be Tian.

Ma Jun pushed forward, saber in hand. His voice rasped. "It's an ogre...holding a shortsword in its left hand."

Left hand... Kaiya's heart skittered.

The children cowered.

Ma Jun shoved Kaiya in the back. "Run! Back to the village! I will stall him here."

Kaiya's palms sweated. At full strength, Ma Jun *might* be able to handle an ogre. In his weakened state, he didn't stand a chance. And the children. Even if she knew their word for *flee*, they could never outrun a loping ogre.

Pulling Ma Jun behind her, she unslung the bow from her back and quickly let two arrows fly in succession. The first grazed the ogre's right arm as he shifted out of the way, while the second lodged in his thigh. He staggered forward.

His arm hung in a sling. The ogre lieutenant from two nights before. The one *she'd* hit with an arrow. The one who'd promised vengeance. Not enough time to take an aimed shot.

Kaiya threw down the bow and slid her double straight swords from her sheath. One, she held underhanded in her left hand behind her back, the other in her right hand pointing forward. "Stop," she sang with her voice of command.

The ogre skidded to a halt and glared at her. His expression glinted with hatred. "Girl give up, others go. Or me kill all."

Ma Jun tried to step past her, but Kaiya, never turning her eyes from the ogre, swept her right-hand sword into his path. "Stand down, Ma Jun. Protect the children: they are your first duty now." He was in no condition to protect anyone.

Ma Jun bowed his head and backed off.

Kaiya turned the sword point towards the ogre. "You are injured and alone, and our friends are coming back this way. You cannot defeat all of us, but you can live to rejoin your own kind. I will command my people not to pursue you."

The ogre, whose grasp of Arkothi was probably not much better than the two children after her one-hour lesson, laughed. "No come, you die!" Holding the shortsword underhanded like a dagger, he lunged at her with a clumsy stab.

A sequence from the *Dance of Swords* came to her, unbidden. She glided to his left. Her right sword slashed into his attacking hand, and she turned her shoulder so that the left sword cut under his attack and across his gut.

As he tried to recover, she turned and stabbed back at his exposed left flank with her left sword. The blade slid with precision between his ribs. In the same turning motion, her right sword cut across his left shoulder, and the point thrust through his neck. Before the ogre hit the ground with black blood spraying from his wounds, she had withdrawn and flipped her left behind her back.

Had she really just done that? Behind her, both children sobbed.

With a quick flick of her wrists, Kaiya shook the swords, vibrating the black blood off before she sheathed them. She knelt down and wrapped her arms around the whimpering children, hushing them with her voice.

Ma Jun dropped to his knee beside her, head bowed. "I'm so sorry to be useless. I couldn't fight the ogre, I couldn't even comfort the children."

She pulled him into the group. "All that matters is that we are all safe. Let's find Zheng Tian."

The snow now fell heavily, clinging to branches like cherry blossoms. Despite the cover provided by the tree canopy, nearly a finger-length of snow accumulated on the trail. After another half-hour, they came to the trailhead. Kaiya pointed south, following Allie's instructions.

The children exchanged a few lively words. Their shaking heads and the numerous times they said *bad* suggested that neither liked the idea. They followed nonetheless.

Before long, another solitary figure approached, slogging through the snow. Though it was not large enough to be an ogre, Kaiya had learned a lesson from their last encounter. She eased Ma Jun down, unslung her bow, and fitted an arrow.

The man trudged closer.

"Stop. Who are you?" Kaiya drew the bowstring. If he took three more steps without announcing himself...

The newcomer knelt and stretched out his arms. The two children dashed out from behind her, crying excitedly. Their father, no doubt.

Kaiya lowered the bow and wiped away the few snowflakes that clung to her face.

Ma Jun nudged her. "That is the man whom the ogres captured before releasing me."

Kaiya nodded. Let the father and children enjoy their tearful reunion.

The boy and girl chattered with broad smiles, gesticulating wildly. On occasion, the tall, handsome man would look up and favor her with a penetrating gaze. Like the children, he wore beige buckskin breeches and shirts, with a heavier fur cloak about his shoulders. His long black hair fluttered in the breeze. A necklace of animal teeth and shiny rocks hung around his neck.

He approached, placing his right hand over his heart and bowing his head. A dignified pride radiated from him. He spoke in halting, heavily-accented Arkothi. "Thank you. You save my children."

She spoke slowly, hoping he would understand. "I am happy they could be reunited with you."

Nodding, he favored her with a curious eye. "Nadi say you beat beast. I think you too skinny for warrior."

"I am not a warrior. He was injured and I had superior weapons. Otherwise, you and I might have never met, and you would have never seen your children again."

The man nodded solemnly. Maybe he understood. "We wait, you friend, close to here. What you name?"

Her friend...Tian? She bowed her head. "Kaiya. This is Ma Jun."

He placed his open right hand in his left. A greeting? "I am Yuha. You already meet Nadi and Waka. We are Maki."

Kaiya nodded. Maki must be the name of their tribe.

"Why you here?" His eyes narrowed.

The short version would have to do. She pointed toward what she hoped was west. "We travel toward our homeland."

Yuha shook his head. "Land now very dangerous. Many beasts, many Metal Man build...big house. This season, snow very hard. Many White Moons can't pass. But, you save us. Please, come to village."

Beasts and Metal Men—ogres and Teleri, perhaps. And many White Moons...were they stranded here for *months?* She imitated his gesture of thanks, putting her right hand over her heart and bowing her head.

Faced with the prospect of wintering in the Wilds, she decided to learn what she could of the local language. Piecing together words she'd learned from the children, she said, "When my friend come?"

Yuha beamed. Using Arkothi, he returned her feeble attempt at conversation in the Maki dialect. "You try speak our mouth. Not like Metal Man. They take all, give none."

She continued in his dialect. "Your mouth, how say *man*?"

"*Odogo.*"

Odogo. It sounded like the imperial language for male. After half an hour of picking up new words and listening for grammar patterns, Kaiya looked up to the sounds of footsteps crunching in the snow.

Shouldering the doctor, Tian was leading a large group of natives up the path. Fighting the urge to run to him, she just stood there. His gaze met hers and his lips curved into a crooked smile.

Why did her heart flutter? Every step brought him closer, but seemed to last forever.

He sank to his right knee, fist to the ground. "*Dian-xia*, we have freed the captives."

"Where's Allie?"

"She headed south."

The doctor, too, tried to kneel, but almost fell. Despite his obvious pain, he still felt the need to salute, for nothing more than her title—one that meant nothing here in the Wilds.

Kaiya stepped towards him, and Ma Jun limped forward as well.

Fang Weiyong straightened. Still a doctor in spite of his own wounds, he pressed along Ma Jun's ribs, causing the imperial guard to wince.

"He might have a broken rib," the doctor said.

Kaiya sighed. "Ma Jun and Fang Weiyong are both injured. This man, Yuha, says the snow will fall heavily. He offered to let us stay in his village. It seems that the Wilds are also rife with dangers that we did not expect. It might be wise to rest well and consider our options there."

Tian nodded, though he did not hide his dislike of the idea. "Very well."

Kaiya turned to Yuha and tried speaking the dialect. "We go with you."

He nodded and pointed them back down the path towards the gutted village.

The entire band of Maki tribespeople joined them, helping the injured as they pressed down the snow-covered path. Large, wet flakes fell. What had taken Kaiya half an hour earlier lagged out to a full hour now. When they passed the ogre's corpse, the children chattered. Everyone favored her with wide eyes.

Tian turned to Yuha. "It's so dangerous. You travelled. With your children alone. Why?" The question *she* wanted to ask.

"I...healer... I visit holy place with two child. Take ten days. On way back, beast attack. I tell children run home."

Kaiya looked at the two young ones, clasping their father's hand. They were so brave, to flee on their own!

When they reached the burnt-out village, many of the Maki turned somber.

"Belong to same tribe." Yuha's face darkened. "Maki. Our cousins. Many missing."

Kaiya shuddered.

Coming to the eastern edge of the village bordering the river, Yuha led them south along the banks. Everyone picked the berries growing in the bushes. He lugged out three canoes from where they were hidden in the shrubs.

They were nothing like the planked hulls of Hua boats and ships. Dug out from the trunk of a sweet evergreen, each canoe held four people. Several of the men talked animatedly, pointing at various points along the river. It seemed most of their homes were downstream.

Kaiya studied Yuha's body language and inflection. Despite his foreign words, he radiated charisma. His opinion apparently carried weight, for the natives all complied with his decision to cross. After an hour of ferrying people back and forth, all four dozen had reached the east bank.

They hid the boats among the shrubs before continuing south in the shadows of the cliffs. Narrow and dotted with huge rocks, the banks made for a treacherous journey. Yet Yuha indicated that, not far to the south, they would find a path leading up to the top of the cliff. He let others take the lead, while he held his children's hands to help them jump from rock to rock. Kaiya and Tian also helped them negotiate the rocks, made slicker by melting snow.

At the top of the cliff, the group took a short break—just enough to rest tired legs and catch their breath. With words of farewell, they broke into three groups, each heading toward a different village. Standing at the head of a dozen tribespeople, Yuha motioned for Kaiya to follow him.

They walked until nightfall and camped off the path, where the trees provided partial cover from the falling snow. Kaiya couldn't remember ever feeling so cold. She leaned against Tian for warmth.

In the mid-afternoon of the third day, with the snow accumulating to her knees, several lodges thankfully came into view. Villagers pointed and yelled at their approach. Several came out to join them.

A stately older gentleman with long white hair fluttering in the breeze held his excited people back. Flanked by a dozen warriors armed with stone-headed spears, he marched forward. Like the others, he wore a buckskin shirt and breeches. A necklace of shimmering river stones hung around his neck, and bright feathers adorned his head. His wise eyes, which spoke of many winters, met Tian's before shifting to Yuha. Anger creased his already time-worn features as he pointed at them, barking out words that did not hint at a warm welcome.

Metal Men came out especially frigid. Kaiya's throat tightened.

The warriors lowered the spears at them.

CHAPTER 43:
Village Life

Tian gauged the warriors' skill by their stances and the way they held their spears. Hand drifting towards his saber, he spaced them out in his head, plotting a path to their grey-haired chief. The Founder's treatise on warfare espoused targeting leaders: cut off the enemy's head, and the body would surely fall.

The chief's brow scrunched up, adding lines to his withered skin. He barked out a string of syllables, the unfriendly tone leaving little doubt where the Hua stood with the natives.

The princess placed her right hand into her left and bowed her head. The natives' dialect spilled from her mouth, flowing in her distinctive voice.

Tian gaped. How had she learned it so quickly?

The chief cocked his head, the furrows in his brow smoothing and his frown softening. He turned and exchanged words with the shaman Yuha, and nodded.

Behind the chief, the villagers surged forward, greeting their lost fellows in warm embraces. They were so relaxed with affection, in stark contrast to the more rigid Hua decorum. Physical contact in the form of pats, hugs, and hair-rubbing seemed a natural complement to verbal exchange for these people.

The princess edged forward and rested her hand on the inside of his elbow. She leaned towards his ear. "The chief doesn't trust outsiders, but it seems he will allow us to stay."

For how long? Tian turned to her. "You speak their language. How?"

"A woman has her ways." She cast him a mischievous smile.

His heart skipped a beat, even if her deflection lacked conviction. He raised an eyebrow.

She rose to her tiptoes and whispered in his ear again. "All members of the Imperial Family learn a secret language, passed down from the Founder. The words are similar to what the natives speak here. The grammar is different, though."

He pulled away, reluctantly. "It sounded convincing enough."

"The chief probably thought I sounded like a cute toddler." She flashed a playful pout.

Cute, yes. He tore his eyes away from the swell of her lips. Definitely not a toddler.

Yuha beckoned them closer. "Meet Chief Nuwa."

The old man placed his right hand in his left hand and said something.

The princess responded, naming herself, Tian, Ma Jun, and Fang Weiyong, gesturing with an open hand towards each of them in turn.

The chief smiled broadly, though the friendliness seemed reserved only for the princess. He spoke again and gestured towards the village.

Tian turned his attention to Yuha and his children. They huddled in the collective embrace of an older man and woman, and two attractive twin girls about the princess' age.

Wearing a glowing smile, Yuha looked up from his family and gestured him over. "Follow me."

The village itself lay in a large clearing on the eastern side of a wide stream, not far from the North Kanin River. They passed through broad cornfields, which lay fallow for the winter. Only chickens tended the fields now, foraging with precise pecks reminiscent of Tian's master snatching flying insects with his chopsticks.

On the other side of the fields, he counted thirty domed lodges laid out in a circle. Framed in thick sapling trunks, with walls and roofs made of smaller branches, mud, and grasses, they looked to be about sixteen feet long, twelve feet wide. Animal furs covered the entrance and windows. Rustic, primeval—hardly practical for the cold.

Near the center of the lodge circle, a wooden platform rose to a man's height above the ground. On it sat two magnificent drums, set on their sides and facing each other.

Yuha gestured towards the larger, which was even wider than a man was tall. "*Gogorowa*. Heart of Village." He then pointed towards the smaller, which was just a little shorter than the princess. "*Gamiwa*. Soul of Village. Hundred winters ago, one big tree here. After fall, messengers of gods carved into drums for us."

Tian stared at the drums. Just who were the messengers of the gods? The princess pulled him along.

Not far from the platform burned a bonfire. Coming to a lodge facing the flames, Yuha pulled the fur door open. "Welcome my house. Bring friends here to heal."

The two children skipped in, and the rest of them followed. Tian's nose wrinkled at the pungent odor of dried herbs as he entered with Ma Jun's arm around his shoulder.

Thick poles supported the roof, which had a hole near the center. Several furs covered the lodge floor, surrounding a small fire pit lined with stones. Dried herbs dangled from the roof in one corner of the lodge, while clothes and other personal effects hung from the walls. Contrary to Tian's initial doubts, the interior was quite warm.

Yuha motioned them to sit, and Tian watched as an old woman stirred the simmering contents of a large but crude ceramic pot.

With a few words, Yuha sent his kids out. He then examined Ma Jun and Fang Weiyong, and applied a poultice to their injuries. Doctor Fang watched with curious eyes, sniffing and tasting the herbs.

Presently, the children brought the pretty twin girls in. Ma Jun and the doctor lost all interest in the herbs.

"My sisters," Yuha said. "Lana and Lahi. Kaiya stay with them. Men stay at other house. Now, we eat. Tell me your story."

The fire pit's flames crackled in the lodge that Kaiya shared with Lahi, Lana, and a few of the female refugees. She sat cross-legged, wearing a doeskin dress the twins had given her, watching as Lahi braided a queue behind each ear. The double queues marked her as unmarried.

As the village beauty, every unmarried man vied for Lahi's attention. Statuesque and elegant, she carried herself in fur and animal skins like a Hua lady would in silken gowns. In public, she played the boys off of each other with a demure act that belied her sharp mind.

Kaiya closed her eyes and recalled the entry of the famous Minister Deng Liansu in the *Encyclopedia of Peoples*:

The red-skinned barbarians on the Kanin Plateau, unlike their more organized cousins on the Plains, are beyond civilizing. It is hard to believe that before the Hellstorm, they were part of an empire, even if that empire lacked the enlightenment or sophistication of Hua's contemporary Yu Dynasty. Though some of their tribes live not far on the other side of the Great Wall, they did not warrant my visit. They have nothing of value to offer us.

She stared into the fire. Half a White Moon had passed since their arrival at the village, and her observations in those two weeks suggested that the late Minister Deng had been unfair in his assessment. If nothing else, these people had a vibrant culture. When she made it home, she'd write her own treatise, so that her future daughters would look at the Wilds with different eyes.

Yuha poked his head in through the flap. With her fluency in their language improving, he spoke in his native tongue. "Kaiya. Chief Nuwa invites you and Tian to his lodge for dinner."

She had a good idea why. Maki storytelling had a way of evolving; perhaps only they knew where their myths ended and history began. And one new legend was already in the making.

With each retelling of the captives' rescue, Tian had risen from minor participant to single-handed vanquisher of dozens of ogres. Apparently, his reputation had found its way into neighboring villages.

Kaiya rose and found him waiting beside Yuha, outside the tent.

"*Dian-xia*." Tian bowed his head. Old habits had died hard, and though he no longer dropped to a knee, he remained stubborn with these salutes.

She suppressed the urge to roll her eyes, and lifted her chin toward the chief's tent. Yuha grinned and led the way.

Just outside, in the village center, the chief's handsome seventeen-year-old son Hati and another young man practiced spearwork with the blunt ends of their weapons. Several other men surrounded them, watching and cheering.

They weren't the only ones. When she turned and looked at Tian, his eyes were shifting with the clashing spears.

The combatants paused and looked up.

Hati tossed the spear horizontally at Tian, who caught it. He then took the spear from his friend. "I hear you are a good warrior. Show me!"

Though Tian had supposedly picked up some of the Maki dialect, he turned to her, mouth agape. "Did he say I have a nice rear?"

Heat flared in her cheeks. He *did* have a nice rear. "No, he wants to test his skill."

Or more likely, Tian's skill. He raised his spear.

"Be careful." Kaiya sighed. Tian's competitive streak dated back to her childhood,

when she could beat him in swordplay and archery. It had gotten him in trouble before.

The old chief appeared at her side.

With a falsetto cry, Hati lunged forward with a stab.

Tian twisted out of the thrust and swept his own spear in an arc into the back of Hati's knees.

The youth tumbled to the ground, but leaped back onto his feet. He pointed the blunt end at Tian. "Now!"

He attacked again, and five other men surged in. To Kaiya's untrained eye, Tian moved like a blur, catching some weapons and using them to deflect others. He always positioned himself so one of his opponents shielded him against the others. Some, he threw to the ground, while others he knocked out of the ring.

Chief Nuwa leaned towards Kaiya. "Our tribal territories are well-defined and the resources are plentiful. There has been no armed conflict since our horse-riding cousins from the plains invaded a generation ago. Our weapon skills come from hunting, but downing a wild boar is different than fighting an ogre."

Kaiya met the chief's gaze. Had he arranged this confrontation?

The chief clapped his hands once, and the warriors backed off.

Tian extended his hand to help Hati up, and the young man hesitatingly accepted it.

Chief Nuwa placed a hand over his heart. "Young Tian, you are as good a warrior as Yuha says. Will you teach our men so that they might defend the village against ogres and the Metal Men?"

Tian looked to her, eyebrow raised.

She grinned. Even if his linguistic skills left a lot to be desired, he spoke the language of combat well. "He wants you to teach them."

After dinner with the chief, Tian walked the princess back through the snow. She leaned into him, huddling against the chill air. She must be cold. That's all it was. He tightened the fur around her.

"Don't let it go to your head, Tian." Her breath clouded in front of them.

Yes, she couldn't possibly feel the same way. He nodded. "Of course, *Dian-xia*."

She stopped in place, not far from her lodge. "Just because you beat a boy with a spear doesn't mean you can defend a village."

What was she talking about? He shook his head. "Oh, the training."

"What did you think I was talking about?" She raised an eyebrow.

"Nothing. I was going to recruit Ma Jun. To teach them about fighting in groups."

She resumed walking. "I saw him earlier today. Is he well enough for that?"

"He's improving. With Lana and Weiyong's attention." And especially Lana's. Whether it was her skill with medicinal plants and setting bones that did the trick, or her smile... Tian wiped the grin off his face. "Why don't you come and see?"

The princess turned her head and covered her mouth. "Visiting a man's lodge at night? I'm not sure that is appropriate."

Tian bowed his head. "Of course not, *Dian-xia*."

"I was joking." She pushed him in the chest.

"Oh."

With a small laugh, she took his hand and pulled him toward the lodge he shared with Ma Jun and Weiyong.

His hand tingled the whole way.

At the entrance, he pulled aside the flap.

Ma Jun sat by the fire pit, his chest bare. Lana stood behind him. Ma Jun's face flared in the firelight.

Had the princess seen? Tian closed the flap and turned to face her.

Blushing, she covered her mouth with a hand.

Tian stroked his chin. "I, uh, let me walk you back."

Ma Jun's voice called from inside. "Come in, it's not what it, uh, looks like."

Lana popped her head out and spoke. Even if Tian didn't understand the words, her tone carried no sign of apology. She beckoned them in.

The princess nodded and turned to him. "She was applying medicine to his ribs."

Tian grinned. Like her older brother Yuha, Lana had a knack for spiritual magic, and might have been a shaman if she were male. With her unabashed flamboyance, so different from her twin, the young men shied away. Ma Jun didn't seem to mind, though.

Kaiya turned her head from the chill wind, which rustled bare tree branches and sang its song to the babbling stream. Thank the Heavens her hair had grown back so quickly, protecting her from the chill. Like the other unmarried girls, she wore it behind her ears in two braided queues. Simple, compared to the lavish hairstyles in the Hua court. Just like everything else in the rustic village.

She looked down at the wild carrot in her hand. Dirt was caked in the creases of her fingers and clung beneath her nails. She smiled and set the carrot in a basket with some turnips and red-skinned potatoes. Life here was easy, carefree. No need to worry about appointments and appearances. Her next responsibility today would be to check the village chicken coop for eggs. And they said the winter months would be harsh.

"Kaiya." Lahi's pronunciation of her name sounded cute. The village beauty nodded her head sideways toward the forest path.

With the chief's son Hati playing the role of patient teacher, Tian tried walking through dry leaves. Crackle, crackle. While none of the tribesmen could touch Tian with a knife or spear, they had a lot to show him about the life of a hunter. He looked over to her and bowed his head.

Even here, where people admired his martial prowess, he felt subordinate to her. She smiled and waved.

Lahi giggled. "He likes you. Were you matched back home?"

The heat in Kaiya's cheeks made her forget how cold her toes were. "We were best friends." Were they again? Small, but considerate gestures brought out the adorable boy he'd been.

Lahi rubbed her belly. "Maybe you can make some babies, like Waka and Nadi."

Babies? Heat flared in her cheeks. Just a month ago, the twins had confounded her. After playing with them daily, she wondered if maybe she'd make a decent mother after all. Kaiya pointed at Lahi, such a rude gesture in Hua, but an essential part of the nonverbal communication here. "Maybe *you* have a better chance with Hati."

That was no secret. Lahi could choose any man she wanted, and while she made them all believe they were special, in private, with her sister Lana, she left no doubt that she liked the chief's son.

Lana's curt voice cut in from behind them. "Kaiya's still too skinny. You need more berries."

As if she hadn't eaten enough of them. Harvested throughout the winter months, the red berries supposedly increased virility. They found their way into the stews, along with rabbit, wild turkey, and other small game. The men would occasionally bring down a deer. With this diet and the relaxed lifestyle, she had already regained the weight she'd lost in their flight from Iksuvius. Apparently she still wasn't fat enough for this baby-loving culture, though.

Lana grinned. "Well, I must be getting back. Miwa just started labor." She headed back to the village. If Lana couldn't be a shaman, she would make a wonderful midwife.

Kaiya waved goodbye. The first birth she'd witnessed were twins, common in the autumn months, according to Lana. The next three were all singles. Miwa's would be the fourth, and like all the others, a cause for celebration. The entire village would erupt in day-long festivities. They doted on new mothers, with each household taking turns cooking for her.

Kaiya wanted to contribute this time, even though she'd never really cooked before. She

looked up to where Tian had been, only to find him gone. When he came back from hunting, he would be the first to try her dish.

Even if it tasted bad, he wouldn't complain.

Tian returned from an unsuccessful hunting trip—unsuccessful because of his poor wilderness skills. The chief's son Hati had taken special interest in him, helping him to build on the tracking and stalking he'd learned from Allie and her rangers. Still, it left a lot to be desired.

It also left a lot of animals alive, and for this, Hati just patted him on the back. The Maki had a great reverence for life, and whenever prey was killed, they thanked its spirit for the nourishment it provided. They used every part of the animal, nothing wasted. Yuha explained that all life was a treasure, and that the energy of all living things contributed to the balance and energy of the universe.

Just outside the village, he rounded the bend in the path and skidded to a halt.

The princess sat on a stump near the path by herself, sewing deerskin. He marveled at her delicate fingers dancing gracefully through the motions, reminiscent of her playing the *guzheng*.

She'd probably never sewed in Hua. What a stark contrast to the image of imperial perfection she projected before! Also so different from the spoiled girl he thought she'd become, oblivious to the danger she and her retainers faced during their escape.

Still, a princess of Hua doing menial labor was unacceptable.

Tian hurried over and dropped to a knee, fist to the ground. "*Dian-xia.* Let me do that for you."

The princess looked up from her work, and her lips curved into an innocent smile. It was so genuine, unlike the contrived mask she wore in Iksuvius, and Tian's mouth went dry.

She twirled the queue behind her right ear. "We aren't in Hua. You don't have to be so formal. Call me Kaiya, just like when we were children."

Tian looked down, mouthing the name to himself, silently tasting it. No, it wasn't appropriate. He looked up, arranging his face in *Moquan* blankness. "I will try, *Dian-xia*."

The princess' lips quivered, eyes laughing. With a tilt of her head, she beckoned him to a log, the beginnings of a dugout canoe. An unfinished pair of pants laid there, the seams of its legs unsewn. "Those are yours. You can finish them."

How embarrassing. And improper. The princess had been making *his* pants. Tian bowed his head low, the words tumbling out of his mouth automatically. "As you command, *Dian-xia*."

She smiled at him. "I have another command. I am cooking lunch for Miwa in a few days. I'm experimenting tonight. Will you eat with me?"

Tian kept his expression blank. Was she inviting him to a meal? They ate together frequently, though usually with Yuha's family, or occasionally the chief. Never just the two of them.

In the meantime, he had some pants to stitch. And a secret pocket to sew into his long-unused lockpick pouch.

Kaiya listened to the thin layer of snow crunching under their feet as she and Tian went fishing for the first time in their lives. A frigid breeze bit at her ears as they stepped out off of the forest trail and onto the bank of the river's pool.

Her attempt at cooking a stew had met with failure. Even if Tian praised the meal, his tentative chewing and forced smiles spoke volumes. Fish, at least, she'd roasted in the mountain pass between Iksuvi and the Wilds. And he'd devoured that fish.

Her excitement had made her forget about the bitter cold during the half-hour walk from the village, but now she looked dubiously at the flat boulder where they'd sit.

It looked freezing, jutting out over the expansive pool—famous for its large, succulent greyfish. The dozen tribespeople found places to sit, letting their legs hang over the edge.

Wait, they were broken into couples. Had Tian noticed that, too?

She studied his face.

He stared at the ground, chewing on his lower lip. He *had* noticed.

She glanced at Hati, who'd invited them along. From the spot where he sat with Lahi, he waved and flashed a broad grin. She smiled, too. *They* knew, for sure, and must've planned this.

Kaiya looked over her shoulder. Tian laid out a fur blanket for them to sit on. She suppressed a giggle at the uneven stitching of his pant legs, deciding that the only things he'd ever sewn before were battle wounds.

They cast their lines and waited. And waited.

The cold air bit through her doeskin and furs. Kaiya edged closer until she eventually huddled against his left side. He tensed up at her touch.

Tian inched away as he reached for another fur. "*Dian-xia*—"

"Kaiya."

"—your legs will get cold." He draped it over her lap.

Nothing would make her cold now, not with the warmth rising in her chest. It was so hard to imagine this thoughtful gesture came from the duty-driven, emotionless wizard's automaton who had forcibly shaved her head.

She leaned back into him and sighed, her breath hanging in the crisp air. He'd exacerbated her fear and sense of vulnerability months ago, but now provided nothing but a reassuring sense of safety.

Was it because he'd saved her from the ogres?

The fishing should've given her plenty of time to consider the question, but instead, his comforting nearness addled her thoughts. She stole a glance up at him through the corner of her eye, memorizing the angle of his jaw. He seemed to have achieved a meditative state, oblivious to her presence.

Pouting, she turned her attention to the dissonant interplay of noises around her: the river splashing lazily by, its waters low in the winter months; the drumming of a woodpecker; the rustling of underbrush as small animals foraged for food; the frequent chattering of birds. Yet beneath the cacophony was a primordial harmony, an unrealized symphony of sounds that lacked a glue to hold them together.

She began humming her own tune, linking the various sounds into a concert of nature. Her hum built up confidently, the undertone taking over as the main sound. As it reached its crescendo, all other noises stopped as if the wildlife had stopped to listen, leaving just her voice.

Her fishing pole jerked.

Kaiya fell silent and stared at the rod. She struggled to her feet, her legs wobbly from the long hours of sitting. The particularly resilient fish took advantage of her poor balance, and she found herself plunging into the icy waters.

She floundered wildly in the water. "I can't swim!"

No sooner did the words leave her lips than Tian jumped in after her with a splash. The water only came up to his waist. His mouth gaped.

The *Moquan* spy, gullible like when he was a child. Giggling, Kaiya stood and waded over.

The villagers' looks of concern transformed into laughs.

Shivering, she clasped his hand. "Are you all right?"

With a grin, he put a leg behind hers and twisted, dumping her completely into the water.

It was freezing! She let out a cry of surprise, which came out as bubbles. Getting her head back above the water, she wrapped her legs around his and twisted him back into the water as well.

Laughing, Hati urged them out of the pool. He held out dry furs. "Take off your clothes, or you really *will* freeze."

While Lahi built a fire, Kaiya wrapped the fur around herself and peeled off her wet clothes.

Tian apparently had no compunctions and stripped off the tunic clinging to his body. His belly was toned into six hard squares, his sculpted chest and arm muscles rippling as he flexed against the cold.

Her stomach fluttered like a dragonfly's wings, and heat flared inside of her.

Lahi winked at her, pausing before she draped a fur over Tian's magnificent body. Kaiya turned her head and loitered over to the warm flames. She held the furs tight around her as she sat.

Hati walked Tian over and pushed him down next to her. He pressed them close together. "You have to sit close, share each other's warmth."

Tian's face flushed an interesting shade of crimson. Hers must have been equally red. Beneath the fur blankets that separated them, they were naked.

Neither said a word while their clothes dried.

The walk back to the village was awkward, even as they huddled close together for warmth. With no fish in hand, only one thing had come from their fishing expedition: Yuha scolded them for getting their heads wet in the dead of winter.

She looked at Tian out of the corner of her eye. Maybe something more had come of it.

CHAPTER 44:
Wrestling

Normally skilled enough to slip through Hati's wrestling guard, Tian found his face pressed into the dirt ring, his arm twisted into a simple hammer lock. Not hard to get out of with patience and tenacity, but his heart wasn't in it today. He tapped on the ground, indicating his surrender.

Hati loosened his hold. "You're unfocused."

Tian accepted the chief's son's hand and clambered to his feet. Though his grasp of the language was improving, he still stumbled over some words. "Sorry I can't give you a better fight."

"You teach me a lot of tricks." Hati grinned. "Maybe I can teach you something."

Tian raised an eyebrow. The Maki excelled at wrestling. As one of the favorite pastimes among the men, they used it to impress women and settle disputes. Even so, his foreign *Moquan* grappling techniques always gave him the upper hand. "A new hold?"

"Yes." Hati puckered his lips and mimed hugging. "You will concentrate better."

The instigator of the fishing trip fiasco! Despite his knack for sniffing out ambushes, Tian had been caught flatfooted. Pressed up against the princess, with nothing more than two fur blankets between their bare skin, it had taken all of his discipline to stay calm. How mortified the princess must have been! He glared at the youth. "You don't understand. Where we are from, she is the chief's

daughter. I am her..." How could he explain? The Maki had no word for *servant* or *retainer*. "...piglet."

Hati swirled a finger around the side of his head, a Maki sign of confusion. "What's there to understand? Here, I am the chief's son. It doesn't matter who my favorite girl is."

With a sigh, Tian threw his hands up. If only things were that easy. "She only sees me as a piglet."

Hati puffed out his chest and pounded it with a palm. "I am an expert in these matters. Let me teach you."

Not that it would do any good. Tian pointed in the direction of the Iridescent Moon, obscured by the clouds. Hopefully, Hati wouldn't look. "It's almost time for weapons training."

Scrape, scrape. Kaiya sharpened stone arrowheads with Lahi. The Metal Men's encroachment into the forests had turned this man's job into everyone's responsibility. Though no hostilities had broken out, Kaiya's own experience with the Bovyan scourge told her it was only a matter of time.

She held up the arrowhead and ran a finger across its edge. Sharp. Dangerous enough to take down game, and even the ogres whose ambushes had dwindled during the winter. Teleri armor posed a greater challenge.

"You have to hit the heart." Lahi tapped on her chest.

Kaiya shrugged. "It has to get past the armor first."

Lahi laughed. "Very easy."

Was it? The Maki hadn't gone to war in thirty years, and even then, their opponents wore leather jerkins. Hopefully, they'd never have to test their stone weapons against steel. "I hope so."

Lahi peered at her. "You're a beautiful girl. His armor will melt with a smile..." She cast an alluring smile and twirled one of her braids. "...and body language."

Oh. That, Kaiya could do, and do well, probably better than Lahi. It wouldn't work, though—not on Tian. Even though he'd warmed up, too much damage had been done in Iksuvius. She was still his burden, and would be lucky if he considered her a friend again. But why did she *want* it? Want more?

And yesterday! It should've been embarrassing, being naked with nothing but a blanket between them. Instead, her heart fluttered even now, just thinking about it. Whatever she felt, it was real. More real than Ming's smooth words sending her head spinning, or Rumiya beguiling her with magic.

If only things were so simple. She was a princess, he was a spy.

Snow flew in her face. Lahi leaned back, laughing. "You look hot. Your face is red. You make too much of it. You are a girl. He is a boy."

Kaiya's eyes widened. Of course. In the Wilds, away from Hua's customs and conventions, they were just Kaiya and Tian. All it took was a Maki girl to remind her.

Pacing the village field, Tian scanned the young Maki men facing each other in two lines, all holding cloth-wrapped stone knives in a defensive stance. Like the last lesson two days before, a handful of new faces had appeared, likely from neighboring Maki villages.

After Chief Nuwa's test, Tian had immersed himself in teaching combat to the males. Besides their superior wrestling skills, the natives also excelled at archery, perhaps more than anyone back home, given Hua's shift from bows to muskets.

With no armed conflict since their cousins from the plains invaded a generation ago, their skill with spear and knife left a lot to be desired.

"Now," he barked.

The pairs all engaged in a fixed-pattern drill, quickly closing and disengaging. They were improving quickly, none more so than the chief's son. If not for the cloth wrapping around the knives, it might have turned into a bloody mess.

Clapping pattered from the edge of the field. Tian turned to look.

Ma Jun, ostensibly there to help teach tactics based on formations, leaned back against a fallen log, smiling and chatting with Lana. Whatever she'd clapped about had nothing to do with the training. She wasn't even paying attention. Meanwhile, her twin Lahi craned to watch the men. Or like as not, one man: Hati. Definitely a distraction.

Though none more than the impromptu swim the day before. Tian returned his wavering attention to the training. "Again."

The pairs repeated the same pattern several times, getting better each time.

"Good. Let's..." What was the word? "...spar." Tian circled his finger in the air and his students all sat cross-legged in a ring around him. "Who wants to go first?"

Hati jumped to his feet and pointed at Tian. "You and me!"

Tian smirked. Perhaps the young man thought his luck from the morning would continue.

The two circled and engaged in a furious exchange of cuts and stabs. Tian evaded or blocked all of Hati's attacks, while raking his knife across the young man's neck and wrists. When the opportunity presented itself, he poked him in the armpit.

Hati stepped back, bent over with his hands on his knees. Despite the thorough beating, he grinned.

Unwrapping the knife, Tian swept his gaze around the ring. "These knives will shatter on the Metal Men's..." They had used the word before, when describing the Bovyan's chainmail. Even now, the men scowled at mention of the big men whose voracious taste for meat had ravaged the large game supplies. "...skin?"

Hati shook his head. "*Roroi.*"

Right. "Backs of knees are open. Sometimes their hands are unprotected." He pointed at his face. "And their metal hat's openings. You must be fast and accurate."

One of the new men threw his arms up, speaking a mix of familiar and unfamiliar words in a strange order. Tian looked to Hati and raised an eyebrow.

"Our cousins, the Omiki," he said. "Their words are similar. He says it's impossible."

"Difficult, not impossible." Tian stroked his chin. "Use distractions."

A wide-eyed youth, Kosa, waved his hand. "How?"

How indeed? Tian opened his mouth, but then said nothing. Dozens of different ideas came to mind, yet none seemed practical given the tribespeople's resources.

Hati pointed toward the edge of the field. "Kaiya."

Heads turned. Tian ventured a glance. The princess stood next to Lahi...smiling? After their fishing misadventure, it should have been days before she so much as glanced at him. Yet here she was...

Tian hit the ground, with only his reflexes preventing the wind from getting knocked out of him. A heavy weight rested on his chest.

He looked up.

Hati sat on top of him with a grin, knife blade at his neck. "Distraction."

The men all laughed. Lahi clapped.

The chief's son learned well. Tian could have twisted past the knife and put Hati in an armbar, but decided against it. Let him savor his victory; let his people see him as a leader.

And Tian would save the technique for the village wrestling tournament.

The wind howled outside Yuha's lodge, reminding Kaiya that winter had yet to loosen its grip on the Wilds. Around the fire pit, the children Waka and Nadi held bowls of stew, chattering with their grandparents and aunties Lahi and Lana about the upcoming wrestling tournament.

Conspicuously absent was Tian, who always accompanied her when she ate with the shaman's family. He'd avoided her all day. Probably still embarrassed from the fishing trip. Kaiya looked up from her own bowl of stew.

Yuha was staring at her.

Returning his gaze, she raised an eyebrow.

"The world acts in cycles, guided by the spirits." He twirled his hand in a large circle. "In ancient times, even before the sky rained fire, the Turquoise Men enslaved our people."

Kaiya nodded. He must be referring to era before the War of Ancient Gods, when all humans were slaves to the Tivari. Still, it had nothing to do with village life or the upcoming tournament.

"And then, the Star Spirit, motivated by his love for the Willow Beauty, liberated us." He pointed up to the smoke hole. "The time will come again. The stars say in a year, when the Eye of Kannon greats the white and pearl moons. The spirits have spoken to me."

Kaiya followed his finger up to the night sky. Lord Xu had said as much, that the dance of the Heavens mirrored events among mortals. "Why do you tell me this?"

"I—"

The door flap opened. Kaiya turned.

Tian. He gawked at her, eyes wide. The flap started to close.

"Come in, come in." Yuha jumped to his feet.

Tian froze in place and stared at the ground. He must've been really horrified by their catastrophic fishing experience. He might need an imperial order to forget about it. With a tentative step, he crossed the threshold and looked up. "Why are the Omiki coming?"

With a laugh, Yuha motioned for Tian to sit. "They live south of the river, it's easy for them to paddle across and visit us."

"That's not what I meant." Tian plopped down next to the fire, about as far away from her as possible.

Yuha stroked the feathers in his necklace. "The spirits carry news on the winds. The Metal Men expand. The tribes are worried. But now, there is hope. Since the Warrior From Beyond the Wall arrived, the ogres have retreated."

Kaiya covered a giggle. Tian *would* get the fancy nickname.

"Of course." Tian threw his hands up. "It's winter and the trails are snowbound."

Yuha shrugged. "Perhaps. But rumors of your skills spread far and wide. Many wish to learn from you. Many in this village believe you are our tribal guardian. Like the Star Spirit a thousand sun cycles ago."

At last, Tian's eyes met hers. "I'm one man. There's little I can do. To stop the tide of Metal Men."

"One man can bring hope. Sometimes, to an entire people." Yuha's gaze shifted to her. "Sometimes to a woman."

Was Tian blushing? Or was it the play of firelight on his face?

Kaiya's face was probably just as hot and bright as the flames.

Yuha grinned. "I think that man should prepare himself for the wrestling tournament."

Nothing brought out village enthusiasm like the winter wrestling tournament, which Tian had entered at Hati's urging. Held under a new White Moon on the Winter Solstice, two months after their arrival, it would determine the village's representatives for the tribal tournament held in spring.

As was the custom, single women dipped their hands in berry juice and marked their favorite competitors with palm prints. Wearing a dozen handprints like a leopard wore its spots, Hati flexed his muscles to rampant cheers. The defending village champion's toned physique glistened in the flickering bonfire lights.

Lahi came last, claiming her spot over Hati's heart.

No other woman would dare make such a statement, on any man, let alone the chief's son. Tian grinned for his young friend. He looked around at the dozen competitors, all boasting a handprint or two.

Only his bare chest remained unmarked.

Not that it mattered. Even though the Hua had all been accepted as members of the tribe, most of the village held him in awe. The girls were all too timid, and there was only one girl that mattered.

A firm hand clamped on his shoulder and spun him around.

Hati stood there, smiling. He wrapped an arm over his shoulder. "Do your best. I want to fight you in the last round."

"I hope so." Tian grinned back.

"You might need some luck," the princess said from behind him.

Hati turned him around.

The princess stood there, a shy smile gracing her face. Looking down, she pressed her palm over his...heart. Around them, the tribe erupted in whoops and cheers.

Her hand lingered there, warm, sending tingles through him. Her dark eyes looked up through her lashes. "Win."

His heart pounded under her hand. He bowed his head. "As you command, *Dian-xia*."

"Kaiya," she corrected, dropping her hand and backing off.

Blanking his expression, he turned to watch the first bout.

After weeks of him participating in impromptu duels, *Moquan* joint manipulations had worked their way into the Maki repertoire of wrestling techniques. In his own first face-off, it took longer to defeat the man than it had in all previous meetings with him. By the bout with his third opponent, weariness began to creep into his limbs.

As Hati had hoped, he and Tian met in the championship. The chief's son looked just as winded, yet practice fighting through exhaustion would be important if the young men ever had to face an enemy on the battlefield.

At Chief Nuwa's signal, Tian and Hati circled each other.

Tian had tricked Hati time and time again with a wide arsenal of techniques. Tonight, Hati didn't bite on any of his feints.

Hati lunged forward for a two-handed grab, exposing his knees. An opportunity!

Tian shot in, taking hold of both of Hati's legs. He meant to drive his head into the young man's chest for leverage, but Hati turned his torso and caught Tian up in an underarm choke. As the two tumbled to the ground, Hati wrapped his legs around Tian's body, then arched his back to tighten the grip.

A technique he'd taught Hati! Blood rushed to Tian's head. He couldn't breathe, and his neck felt like it was being stretched a foot. Nonetheless, he held on. It was nothing compared to the strenuous training he'd endured as a youth.

Hati cranked his choke.

Something popped in Tian's neck, sending a flaring pain shooting down his arm. He tapped on the ground several times.

People cheered, drums beat.

Hati helped him to his feet. With his head tilted at a funny angle, Tian exchanged hugs, patting the victor on his back. Maybe they'd get a rematch at the spring tournament.

The princess beckoned him over and gestured for him to sit. As they watched the closing dance, a muscle spasm wracked his neck. He tilted his neck to take the pressure off.

"It's all right, you can't win *all* the time." She knelt behind him and massaged the knot in his neck. *She* was massaging *him*. He started to pull

away, but she wrapped her other arm around his bare chest. Her kneading fingers seemed to relax the muscle, but Fang Weiyong's acupuncture would work better.

She continued to twist into the knot. "You are becoming too predictable. Hati could—"

The drumming picked up, drowning out her words.

Tian turned his head awkwardly towards her. "I am sorry, *Dian-xia*. I couldn't hear."

She leaned in close, her soft voice tickling his ear. "Hati could guess what you were going to do. He gave you that opening on purpose." Her soft bosom pressed against his back.

Tian's heart hammered in his chest. What was she saying? Something about some match? Was that *her* heart, pounding against his back?

Her lips brushed the back of his neck; first low, then a little higher and more distinctly.

Her warm lips sent a cold shiver down his spine. She was no longer the adorable little girl, or the haughty princess. Here, she was just a woman. Sweet and smart and playful. More than he deserved.

Yet despite all of the barriers between them that had fallen in their months at village, his willpower and control would have never allowed him to say or do anything to act on his feelings.

Now, her soft body melted against his, her kiss warm against his neck. Ignoring the pain flaring in his neck, he turned and drew her to him. Her lips parted, inviting him.

The drums had stopped. Everything was quiet. Two hundred gazes hung on them. Their adopted tribe exploded in a cacophony of excited murmurs and cheers.

It didn't matter.

Sweet and intoxicating, her taste and smell overwhelmed his senses. She was the only one in his world.

But for how long? The specter of duty hung over his heart.

CHAPTER 45:
Obligations

Kaiya's pattering heart beat a dozen times for each of Tian's hot breaths brushing across her ear. Straddling him near the village stream, she lavished a kiss on his neck, marking him as hers for the hundredth time in the last two weeks. His arms enveloped her, pressing her body to his.

Wet with the heaven's dew that came each full White Moon, sweltering from months of longing, she drew her knees up, rocking against the hardness beneath his pants. She guided his hand to the hem of her undergarments.

His fingers froze in place; his breath hitched. The hand drew away.

Again? She raised her head and searched his eyes.

Lips tight, he refused to meet her gaze, instead looking past her.

Predictable. Kaiya pouted. "We aren't going any further than the other unmarried couples."

"We aren't like other unmarried couples, *Dian-xia*."

That title, again. She rolled off him and pulled the dress hem down over her knees. Apparently, someone hadn't bought into the Maki's lack of social hierarchy. Even if she were no longer the perfect princess, he was still the practical spy. She stared up at Guanyin's Eye, now at its one-quarter angle.

He turned to his side and draped an arm across her.

An empty gesture. She brushed it off. She was the one always initiating affection, guiding him to what he should want. She might as well have been a whore.

He propped himself up on an elbow and brushed an errant lock out of her face. "Yuha says that the snows should slow down by the end of the year. We may be able to go home at that time. We could probably paddle down the river with the spring melt and make better time."

He was in such a rush to get home. She sat up. "What about Ma Jun?" What about her? "He's doing better, but I don't know how well he could handle the trip. In any case, I'm not sure if he wants to leave." Because of Lana.

And her, because of Tian.

Tian stared at the ground. "Ma Jun is a member of the imperial guard. His duty comes before love."

Duty. The memory of that cage sent a shudder down her spine. She pushed away, almost afraid to ask the question that gnawed at her. "Is that how you feel? What about *your* duty?"

His jaw locked, silence conveying his thoughts louder than words. With him, responsibility first.

"Answer me."

He sighed. "These last months have been wonderful. But eventually...we will have to return to our duties."

She turned away from him, pouting, coming up with every rationalization to prove him wrong. "What about our obligations to these people? Think of the Teleri's advance into the Wilds and the burdens that will place on them. They've adopted us into their tribe; they are as much our people as the Hua."

Sitting up, Tian shook his head. "Even though I love them like my own brothers, my first responsibility is to Hua. You are its princess. You have your commitment to our people. I am a spy, and I have mine. No matter how I feel about the Maki, about you...I was born in Hua and owe allegiance to it."

Even if he spoke the truth, Kaiya wasn't ready to hear it. Not now, when she'd thrown off that yoke for the first time in her life. Her voice cracked. "What about *us*? If we go home, we could never continue like this, never marry."

A long silence.

"Answer me." She shoved him with a hand.

Tian blew out a long breath. "Then we must cherish the time that we have left. When we return, we can only treasure the memory of our short time together." His next words came out flat, emotionless. "Marriage to a suitable husband is also your duty."

Kaiya leaped to her feet, tears blurring her vision. Within an appropriately arranged marriage, she'd not relive the excitement of falling in love. Had she never known what it felt like, it might not have mattered. She might have eventually come to love her future husband. However, now that she'd experienced it, she despised Tian for allowing it to happen if he were so quick to abandon it. She tried to keep her voice steady, her words coming out as a whisper. "I thought you'd changed."

"I am sorry, *Dian-xia*."

"Stop calling me that." She turned and ran back to her lodge, leaving a trail of tears in the snow.

Watching the princess escape, Tian regretted his words. How he wanted her! More than anything. What man wouldn't, if he got to know her beyond her façade?

But no. There was no hope for them to be together. Hua's princess *had* to return to Huajing, and this banished spy was not allowed to step foot in the capital. Banishment would be nothing compared to the punishment he'd face for touching her the way he had.

Better to end things now before leaving even deeper scars.

For the next two days, the princess avoided him. If they were going to pass each other on the village paths, she would turn away without even making eye contact. When he sought her at her lodge, one of the women told him she was busy.

What had he done? Food tasted bland and he lacked the energy to even go through the training drills. Feeling more and more depressed in her absence, Tian sat down to eat dinner one night with Ma Jun and Fang Weiyong.

Still unaccustomed to using his hands to eat, Tian fiddled with his makeshift chopsticks. "How do you plan on telling Lana we are leaving?"

Ma Jun looked up from his meal, putting his own chopsticks down. "I've tried not to think about it." After a long pause, he amended himself. "That's not true. I've considered asking her to come with us."

"But you don't want to leave," Tian said.

"I know she'll refuse to come, and I'll miss her more. No, I'd far rather stay here, if I had the choice." Ma Jun's long sigh might have deflated the entire lodge. "I almost wish I had died at that burnt-out village. I would've never met her, never had to deal with the sadness of our inevitable parting."

The optimistic Ma Jun was channeling the spirit of his fatalistic friend, Li Wei. Tian gritted his teeth. How shallow their concerns were compared to Li's sacrifice.

A moment passed before Ma Jun spoke again. "What if we just stayed? By this time, Hua will assume we are dead." His hopeful tone, obvious to Tian's trained ear, suggested that this question had fermented in the back of his head for a while.

Outrageous. Yet tempting. Tian tapped his chin. He'd never fit in with the hereditary lords back home. He felt needed by the Black Lotus, but their disregard for life never sat well with him. But in this rustic village, among a different race of people, he *belonged*. "Can we abandon our duty? Just for our own selfish desires?"

Fang Weiyong snorted. Easy for him; he had nothing here.

Ma Jun poked at his food. "It goes against everything I was ever trained to believe in. Yet somehow, it seems that with the Teleri starting to expand on the plateau to Hua's doorstep, we can help both these people and our own by staying here."

Tian sighed. "The princess said the same thing. It sounded like rationalizing. I finally understand what the poets wrote. When they talked about lost love and lost hope. These last two days, without her. I've been walking in a fog... I'll be completely useless when we return to Hua."

He closed his eyes, envisioning their approach to the Great Wall. At the tree line, he'd let go of her hand. Her smile would tighten and her posture would straighten. Everything that had grown between them would fade into a haunting memory.

Since when had he become so melodramatic?

He opened his eyes to find Fang Weiyong and Ma Jun staring at him curiously.

Forget duty.

Had he just thought that?

Tian bolted up and ducked out of the lodge. He sprinted across the village as fast as he could through the snow, arriving at the princess' lodge within a dozen heartbeats. Standing at the doorway, he yelled in, "*Dian-xia.* Please. Come out and talk!"

Muffled sounds and indecipherable conversation came from within. The fur blanket covering the doorway opened.

Lahi appeared. "Kaiya does not want to talk to an idiot like you." Before he could reply, she turned around and the blanket closed behind her.

Undaunted, he called again. "Kaiya, I'm going to wait here. You have to come out sometime."

More muted sounds. The blanket opened and Kaiya was pushed through.

Without saying a word, Tian took her hand. She let out a gasp and pulled back, but then finally relented. He pulled her to the stream, their path lit only by the plump White Moon.

Arriving in the quiet fields on the southern end of the village, he turned around and took both of her hands. He repeated the words over and over in his head before finally speaking. "These last two days I have sunk into sadness. Unlike any other since we were first separated ten years ago. I had no desire to eat—"

Her brow furrowed. "Maybe because you cooked yourself?"

"—and could not sleep—"

She harrumphed. "Ma Jun's snoring?"

"—every day has been colorless and dull—"

"It *is* winter, after all." She rolled her eyes. She wasn't making it easy.

He sank to his knees. "Kaiya, my princess, my beloved. I realize now that I can't live without you. You are more precious than the air I breathe. Each morning I wake, my first thoughts are of you. I wonder when in the day I will be able to see you for the first time. I want to...wake up, and see you at my side every morning, forever..."

Her gaze bore into him. "What about duty?"

"My first duty is to you." Did he just say that?

The princess' eyes glazed over, hopefully with tears of joy. "Oh Tian, I'd decided never to talk to you again, to hate you forever. It was the only way that I could return to Hua. To hate you. I wasn't going to come out tonight. I was going to leave you freezing at my door. But then...you called me by name for the first time. I couldn't control myself."

She threw herself into his arms and wept. He brought his cheek to hers, relishing her hot, salty tears.

After a moment, she pulled back and pressed something hard and round into his palm. He looked down. It was a smooth river pebble, black with grey striations. He sucked in a breath. "Is this—?"

She nodded. "You gave it to me when we were children. When we promised to marry each other. It's always been a reminder to me, of when life was simple."

She'd kept it all this time. Bowing his head, he presented it to her, just like he had when he was nine.

Three weeks later, on the ninth day of the eleventh month, Kaiya's entire body quivered as Lana and Lahi helped prepare her for the ceremony. A princess of Hua would've worn the finest silks and jewelry to her wedding. Here, she was just another girl.

Her hair, now nearly five months removed from its unceremonious shaving at the hands of her groom-to-be, hung over two handlengths long. Although she had kept it in a child's style while living among the Maki, the women now straightened it out and decorated it with shell ornaments.

She wore a doeskin dress with tassels at the hem and sleeves, topped by a shawl of peacock and wild turkey feathers. A necklace of colorful river stones adorned her neck. Two horizontal red stripes were painted on her cheeks.

If only she had a mirror!

With Lahi and Lana serving as her maids, Yuha's parents guided Kaiya through the cheering villagers gathered around the drum platform. An imperial wedding would have been quiet and solemn, her face a carefully crafted mask of grace. Today, unfettered with joy, she smiled ear to ear. She looked up, and her heart rattled.

He was so handsome. Tian stood on the platform, wearing a buckskin tunic with tassels along the neckline and hem. A line of long shells hung from his neck. Two bright turkey feathers, held in place by a headband, adorned his hair, which was now about a handlength long. Chief Nuwa and his wife stood beside him, in place of his own parents. Ma Jun, Hati, and Fang Weiyong smiled there as his seconds.

Though the event was straightforward compared to elaborate Hua weddings, Kaiya appreciated the simplicity. She clasped the hands of Chief Nuwa and his wife, his steady gaze calming her. At her side, Tian did the same with Yuha's parents.

Then, Kaiya turned to face her groom. Hands trembling, she used her finger to paint two horizontal red stripes on his cheeks, then placed a bead bracelet she had made around his wrist.

He braided her hair back into a single queue, denoting her status as a married woman, and fastened it with a shell ornament he'd made and painted himself. His touch sent her stomach fluttering like a hummingbird's wings.

Yuha, as the village's spiritual leader, spoke: "Tonight, the waxing moon represents your growing love. Your energies have entered this circle separately, but will leave it joined. That which the spirits bring together cannot easily be undone."

A shiver ran up Kaiya's spine.

At Yuha's command, she clasped hands with Tian. Their adopted family members placed their hands on their shoulders, and then everyone in the village followed, radiating outward until all were connected.

One with each other. One with the village. One with the spirits.

They held a grand feast in typical Maki fashion, with each household bringing a favorite dish to share. All enjoyed a wine fermented from the red berries. Drumming and dancing lasted late into night, when the couple was led to their lodge.

Their lodge.

Many of the young adult Maki gathered outside. Following their custom, they'd raise a racket until they heard the marriage being consummated.

However, as the two had arranged, Fang Weiyong, dressed in his monk's robes, awaited them inside.

Despite not having all of the official trappings, Weiyong had scripted a highly-simplified Hua ritual which fused the legends of plain weddings—from the time when humans were slaves to the orcs—with current, more intricate symbolic marriages.

In the days prior, she'd painted a simple picture of Guanyin, Goddess of Healing and Fertility; while he drew a similar one of Yang-Di, Supreme God of the Sun. Both hung side-by-side on the far wall, above a makeshift altar—a long flat rock taken from the river bed—to their family ancestors.

Two round berries sat in a plain wooden dish in the middle of the altar, replacing the two oranges that would be placed in an elaborate porcelain bowl for a typical Hua wedding.

Weiyong motioned them to the altar. "Kneel."

Tian at her side, Kaiya dropped to her knees.

He gestured to the sketches. "Bow to the Heavens."

She and Tian faced the effigies of the gods and pressed their heads to the floor.

When they straightened, he nodded at the altar representing their ancestors. "Now bow to your families."

They bowed again. Kaiya prepared a cup of sweet evergreen tea, which they both shared. Finally, they bowed to each other.

"You may commit yourselves to each other."

Tian's gaze met hers, again sending her heart racing. "I take you as my wife, forever."

"I am yours forever, my husband," she answered.

Weiyong bowed low, and then held up their names, carved into wooden plaques. "I will invest these together in your new ancestral shrine, which I shall dedicate in this village. Having followed the rituals prescribed by the Emperor and Empress in Heaven, you now belong to each other."

He raised his head and grinned. "By the law of Hua, an official witness is required to confirm that a member of the Imperial Family's marriage is consummated."

Heat rose in Kaiya's face. She stared at the floor.

Tian stood up and unceremoniously ejected the chuckling Weiyong from the lodge. Outside, the gathered crowd gasped and laughed at his sudden appearance.

Returning to his knees, Tian stared at the floor, too shy to make eye contact with his bride. An awkward silence ensued. He knew that *she* knew what should happen next. Unlike their spontaneous kissing and touching before, the next part of the wedding was too scripted, too awkward.

Neither spoke, the silence exacerbating the playful taunts of the villagers outside.

He looked up.

Blushing in the flickering firelight, she looked down at her knees and started to unbraid her hair.

Kaiya was beautiful, even more so than in the finest silk gowns and bedecked in priceless jewels. His *wife*. To think that *she* loved *him*, the unworthy boy who'd once locked her in an armoire. He never thought he'd find love, let alone marry. She was more than he deserved.

She looked up at him through her lashes and offered a shy smile.

He'd wanted her for weeks now. All his passion, pent up by discipline.

It exploded now, like a spring river torrent bursting through a dam. He stood and pulled her to her feet. A surprised gasp escaped her. He brought her to him, fiercely kissing her neck, moving up towards her lips. Her sweet fragrance filled him as her soft body pressed against his.

Kaiya groped at his shoulders and back. He reached behind her and unfastened the ties of her dress. It fell to her ankles, revealing silken undergarments from Hua—her last vestige of vanity from a past life.

His hands had brushed across them before, and even ventured below, but never had he actually seen them. He paused momentarily to take it in, that which no man had ever laid eyes on before. A trapezoidal-shaped red silk bust binder, embroidered with green, blue, and golden flowers, accentuated her perfect curves and was held in place by thin laces tied behind her bare back at the neck and waist. Red silken arabesque underpants hid her most guarded place, hinting at what lay beneath.

Heart pounding, Tian pulled her back and drew her into a deep kiss. His dexterous fingers unraveled the ties of her top, and she undid the knot holding up his breeches. Finally, he loosened the strings that held her underwear. It slid down to her knees.

He stepped back to pull off his tunic, and then took in her nakedness in the dimming firelight.

She crossed her shapely legs and covered herself with her arms. She looked down demurely, causing her hair to fall over her face. But presently, she lifted her gaze and brushed the tresses out of her eyes. The coy smile was an invitation.

He took her hands in his, which revealed the treasures she'd been hiding, and brought her down onto the fur bedding.

Kaiya savored the ache after their first lovemaking. The darkness of the lodge mingled with the warmth of Tian's body, enveloping her in a calm sense of security. Naked under the thick fur blankets, she lay on her side with her head on Tian's chest, his arm wrapped over her.

He breathed lightly in shallow sleep, while she lay there wide awake. She brushed her free hand over his firm chest and abdominal muscles. A cold wind blew outside, rustling the door to the lodge, allowing the merged lights from the blue and White Moons to peek in. Beyond that, a wolf howled in the far distance.

Their first conjugal experience had been nervously awkward and over quickly. Her sisters-in-law had told her the first time would be. It didn't matter. After the brief physical intimacy, she now belonged to him, him to her. Two souls, two bodies joined as one.

She'd happily remain here forever, in this rustic village, away from Father's court and the associated burdens of duty, as long as she could share this life with him.

His embrace tightened. Was he thinking the same in his sleep? Allowing the darkness to hide her smile, she turned her head and kissed him on the chin, her hair brushing across his smooth chest.

The light touch must have woken him, because he slid his arm out from under her. He rolled her onto her back and buried his face into her neck, his breath hot and urgent.

Kaiya woke in Tian's embrace. High in the Heavens, the sun peeked in through the lodge's smoke hole. Languid, exhausted, and pleasantly sore, she rolled onto her side to look at her *husband*.

Sleep draped him in childhood innocence, exposing the gentle soul he hid underneath layers of discipline and duty.

She kissed him on the forehead and unwrapped herself from his arms. Dragging herself out of the blankets, she walked past her wedding dress, which laid in an unceremonious heap, to her plain doeskin clothes.

He yawned, and she turned around. His eyes creaked open and met her gaze.

And she was naked, hair tousled like a nest made by a drunken bird. With one hand, she covered her nether regions; the other arm, she crossed over her chest and brushed out her unruly tresses.

She fiddled with a strand of her hair. Silly girl. Not like she had anything to hide from her *husband*. Not anymore, not to the man she'd given herself to. Still.

Grinning, he covered his eyes. "I'll...uh, get dressed under here."

She turned back to her clothes and was about to bend down to pick them up, when she looked over her shoulder.

Tian still watched her, his expression yearning.

Should she be embarrassed? She cast him a mischievous grin as she shimmied into her underpants and slid into the dress.

With a pout, he disappeared beneath the blanket, emerging seconds later fully clothed.

He pushed open the flap and gestured her out.

Cheers and grins greeted them as they made their way through the village. Heat flared in her cheeks, hot enough to melt the snow. She'd spent too many years in Hua to acculturate to the Maki's open attitudes towards relations between men and women. Nonetheless, having abdicated her responsibilities, she looked forward to a life of simplicity here. Maybe one day, her children would assimilate fully into the tribe.

Children.

An old couple, hand-in-hand, grinned at them.

In thirty years, would they be like that, too?

Ma Jun ran up to them, dropping to one knee, first to the ground. "*Dian-xia*, the chief asks that you come to his lodge. A neighboring village reported seeing Bovyans."

CHAPTER 46:
Rude Awakening

Tian was relieved that the neighboring village's sighting of Teleri scouts was an isolated incident. At least for now. It wouldn't be long before winter loosened its grip on the plateau, and their patrols could move freely through the woods.

In the meantime, the idyllic lifestyle seemed like a dream, full of the joys and trials of new marriage. Living together exposed quirks he would've never imagined in her, and no doubt she found some of his habits no less strange. Passionate arguments, invariably leading to his capitulation, quickly gave way to passionate lovemaking.

Ma Jun married Lana late in the eleventh month. If Yuha was concerned about his sister wedding a foreigner, it was probably tempered by the relief that she had found someone who could tolerate her strong will and personality. They moved into a newly-constructed lodge right beside Tian and Kaiya's.

The snows petered out as quickly as they'd come that season. The red berries of the river shrubs reached their sweetest at the end of the eleventh month, and now, fewer and fewer clung to the branches. Tian's anxiety grew as the paths through the woods opened up with an early spring thaw.

Soon enough, the Omiki men who came to learn from Tian brought disturbing news. Ancient roads that had been long-lost to outsiders now teamed with activity. The Metal Men passed along the trails from east to west in ever-increasing numbers. Larger contingents carried supplies and tools. Horse-riders became more frequent.

Then, the slaves. Hundreds of people from the eastern Kanin tribes, chained together with collars around their necks. They cut swaths of greywoods along the main path, while others worked to restore the ancient stonework beneath.

Stories out of the east suggested that several large fortresses now controlled strategic points along the road. The Omiki observed from a distance, avoiding confrontation. They feared it would not be long before more and more of these Metal Men would become frequent visitors to their lands.

One day, as Tian taught spearwork to a group of Maki and Omiki tribesmen in the fallow cornfield, a squad of ten Teleri light infantry stumbled upon their practice. Chainmail peeked out from beneath their black tunics. Swords and daggers hung at their waists, and they all carried Teleri spears. A Kanin man from an unfamiliar tribe guided them.

Keeping an eye on the newcomers, Tian continued with his lesson. They huddled together near the stream, just outside of earshot to be clearly heard. After some discussion among themselves, the scout approached. He extended his right open hand, held in his left, in typical tribal greetings.

Hati motioned for a break and stepped forward.

"Hello, brothers," the scout said in a dialect Tian could barely follow. "These men are exploring the forest, and I'm their guide. Would you mind if we rested here?"

Tian would've rather they move along. Nonetheless, the chief's son glared at the scout and pointed towards the edge of the field. "Unseeded ground belongs to no one. You may sit."

The scout walked back to the Teleri soldiers, and the tribesmen around began muttering among themselves.

Hati leaned in. "He belongs to the Shaki tribe, you can tell by his marks. They are from the east, very aggressive. Nobody likes them."

Tian draped an arm over Hati and edged toward the Teleri, straining to hear their conversation.

The Teleri leader poked the scout in the chest. "Demand some food."

The scout returned, head hung low. "The visitors are hungry and want food."

Face flushing, Hati shook his head. "Tell your master it's winter's end, and food is scarce. We have none to spare."

The Shaki skulked back to the Teleri. "He say no food in winter."

The captain squared his shoulders and glared in their direction. "They're not scared, but that's because they've never tasted Teleri steel. Tell them we would like a challenge. Let's see what these barbarians are made of."

The Shaki came back with the Teleri captain. "It is not often that we see our Maki and Omiki kinsmen practicing together. The visitors would like a friendly lesson with your leader."

Tian had been around the tribe long enough to know the invitation was a thinly veiled challenge. He also knew that Hati was not one to back down from a fight.

Predictably enough, Hati thumped his chest. "I'd be happy to teach it." Scowling, the young man wrapped cloth around the spearhead. Tribesmen demarcated an area on the field, a square the length and width of three men.

Tian pulled him aside. "Brother, these men are trying to gauge our strengths and weaknesses.

You can't reveal all your techniques and strategies, but you must still win so they don't think we are weak."

Hati nodded, but the words didn't seem to be getting through.

With a sigh, Tian pointed to the Teleri spearhead. It was a new configuration, with multiple uses. "Look at the shape. The blade can be used to stab or slash. At the base of the blade is a hook, used to catch weapons or legs. On the other side, the hammerhead can break a bone."

The chieftain's son brushed Tian away and sauntered into the ring. He spun in a circle, pumping his fists. Amid the tribespeople's cheers, he thumbed his right fist over his heart.

The Bovyan returned the gesture, and then pointed his wrapped spear at Hati. The two circled each other. While the Maki yelled advice, the Teleri soldiers watched in silence.

The captain lunged with a skillful thrust.

Hati intercepted the spear with his own, guiding it harmlessly to the right, then swept down along the shaft and struck the Bovyan in the hand with the pole. Tian suppressed a grin. It was one of the early techniques he taught.

The Teleri wrung his hand, even though his gauntlet had probably absorbed a lot of the force. With the man's guard down, Hati landed a quick strike to his armored torso.

Grimacing, the Bovyan avoided Hati's follow-up, then came down with the hammerhead.

Hati lifted his spear up to block the blow, but the Teleri twisted his weapon on contact. With a quick pull back, the hook caught Hati's spear and yanked it from his hands.

The Teleri soldiers all roared taunts while the tribespeople fell silent. Tian sighed. The next lesson would cover counters to the hook.

The leader waved a condescending hand. "Not bad, for an untrained savage." He picked up Hati's spear, unwrapped the tip, and grinned. He threw it back into Hati's hands. "Unfortunately, I doubt this stone head could penetrate our armor."

Tian hung in the background. It was true, one of his greatest concerns. When the Shaki translated, Hati bristled with rage.

The captain twirled his own spear. "Perhaps we can civilize your people, and teach you how to make metal weapons. All you need to do is become our vassals, as your Shaki kinsmen have."

He was goading them. Tian kept silent. Yet on translation, Hati's face flushed an ugly red. Shaking, and despite Tian's silent pleading, he drew close to the captain, glaring him in the eye, even if he barely came up to the man's chin. "I will fight again!"

The scout translated and the Bovyan laughed. "I've already defeated you. If any others are brave enough to try my spear, then let them step forth."

Upon hearing the translation, the tribesmen started chanting. "Warrior Beyond The Wall!"

Tian drifted toward the back. Up close, the Bovyans would likely be able to tell he wasn't Kanin.

Hati, oblivious to the danger, pushed through his people and pulled Tian forward. "Brother, you must fight for the honor of the tribe!"

Tian shook his head. "I can't. I'll explain later. If these men find out...that Kaiya and I are here. They'll come back."

Hati shook his head, his eyes dancing with excitement. "Don't worry about that. You're our family now, and we'll protect you. Your enemy is my enemy. If they come to our village with ill intentions, they will feel the points of our spears!"

Tian cringed. The boy was overconfident and inexperienced. Though their spearwork had improved, they were still no match for the organized ruthlessness of Bovyan shock troops, fighting in an armored phalanx. "These men are just the beginning. Many nations have fallen before them."

The captain's laugh made Tian look up. "It's too bad that only your leader is brave enough to fight. If the rest of you are such cowards, then you aren't worth civilizing."

Tian feigned ignorance.

The Shaki scout approached, head bowed. "If you do not fight, they will think you are weaklings and it will only be a matter of time before you become their slaves. Learn from our tribe's mistakes."

Just like the Nothori Northwest, which Tian had witnessed firsthand. With a sigh, he crouched and rubbed dirt on his face. Then, he stepped into the ring, spear in hand. In the Kanin dialect, he issued his challenge. "You've said our spears won't pierce your steel skin. Let's see if that's true." He turned to the scout. "Tell him!"

Paling, the Shaki translated. "He want fight, open blade!"

The captain laughed, unwrapping the cloth. "Very well, let's see how long you last!"

Tian gave the Kanin salute.

His opponent returned the formality, and then dropped into a fighting stance. Without waiting, Tian stabbed at him with a clumsy, slow thrust, which his opponent easily deflected with his own spear. He twisted it and locked up Tian's weapon with the hook. However, Tian had set the move up, and before it could be yanked out of his hands, he thrust his spear downwards so that the Teleri's blade drove into the soft ground. Letting go of his weapon, he jumped forward and stomped on the shaft of his enemy's spear.

It slipped from the Bovyan's fingers. With two quick steps, Tian closed the distance, drew the shocked Teleri's own dagger and pressed the blade at his throat. "Yield," he ordered in the Maki dialect.

The message needed no translation. The captain held up his hands. The tribespeople all cheered.

Tian looked over his shoulder. A crowd had gathered, Kaiya among them. She shrank back behind the others. Hopefully the Bovyans hadn't seen her. Since the Hua and Kanin people shared some physical similarities, perhaps they'd go unnoticed.

He turned back to his opponent and presented the dagger. "Well fought."

After hearing the translation, the Teleri captain sneered. He yanked his sword back. "I am only one man, but the strength of the Teleri Empire is in the coordination of our troops. Perhaps you would like to try five of your warriors against three of mine?"

Tian narrowed his eyes. The Maki had very little experience fighting in formation. Ma Jun would have to drill them. There had to be another way. "I'll fight all three by myself."

Kaiya let out a startled cry, and the captain looked at her. She quieted and disappeared back into the crowd. As his counter-offer was being translated, the Maki began to chant, "Warrior Beyond The Wall."

The captain laughed, with no hint of mirth. "You're a confident bastard, aren't you? Very well then, this should be interesting." He motioned for three of his men to enter the ring.

Tian yanked his spear from the dirt. He feigned worry, letting his eyes widen and his hands tremble. Yet to himself, he smiled. The Teleri's confident grins told him they'd fallen for his act. With the versatility of Hua spear techniques and the element of surprise, there was little doubt who'd win.

After saluting his opponents, who returned the gesture, Tian held his spear one-handed and let the point drop to the ground. He waited as the three soldiers encircled him.

One let out a war cry, and three attacks thrust in at three different levels. With his spearhead still touching the ground, he lifted the shaft so that it stood straight up, and spun to the side, out of range of two of the spears while the third brushed harmlessly against his weapon.

With an open hand, he slapped down on the hammer part of the head, sending a vibration down the weapon. The wielder dropped it, staring at his shaking hands.

Tian kicked his spear up. The blunt end struck the unfortunate soldier in the face, knocking him to the ground. At the same time, he caught the Teleri's spear with one hand and swept it in a wide arc. The butt of the weapon deflected an incoming stab, and hit the second soldier in the head, crumpling him over. Three seconds, two down.

The Maki cheered loudly in the background. Even Kaiya applauded at the sudden shift in momentum.

The last Teleri disengaged and reset. Sweat gathered on his brow. Tian kicked his own spear up into his hands and advanced with multiple stabs and sweeps. The Teleri scuttled back to the edge of the ring.

"Attack, coward!" The captain stomped.

The soldier shouted and surged forward with the full arsenal of Teleri spear techniques: thrusts, slashes, and hammers. Tian nonchalantly evaded them all, backing up until he stood over one of the fallen men's discarded spears. He twisted his legs with the haft between his feet, and the spearhead slashed into his opponent's unarmored shins.

With a yelp, the Teleri limped backward, holding his spear up defensively. Tian lifted a foot so that the spear rose into his hands, and he advanced purposefully towards his wounded foe. He avoided one last thrust, and used the hook of the weapon to catch the Teleri's good ankle. A jerk sent the man tumbling to the ground, and Tian placed the point at his throat.

The villagers erupted in louder cheers. Silent, the Teleri soldiers went to help their fallen comrades.

The captain strode up to Tian and studied him. "You're good. I look forward to the opportunity to meet you again, when it really counts."

Which might be soon, after today's events. Tian stared at his feet. Hopefully, the officer wouldn't spot the features that separated a Kanin from Cathayi. He spun and walked back to the celebrating tribespeople.

Kaiya threw her arms around him, burying her face in his chest. "What were you thinking? Fighting against three?"

So little faith in his abilities. That was the least of Tian's concerns. He turned to Hati. "We can't let them leave the village yet. The chief needs to know the entire story. Let's invite them to rest and offer them some food."

Hati's lips tightened. Nonetheless, he went to talk with the Shaki, and the guide translated to the captain. From where he was standing, Tian could tell the prideful Teleri had refused.

Had the Bovyans recognized them? There was too great a risk to the village. As distasteful as it was, the Teleri and their Shaki guide would have to die, and their secret with them. The only question was how to wipe out the patrol and minimize casualties to the Maki.

Tian tightened his grip on the spear and pushed through his cheering compatriots.

CHAPTER 47:

Dilemmas

Kaiya's heart pounded in her ears, drowning out the excited villagers. What had Tian been thinking, taking on three men at once? And now...oh, no. His hard stare and clenched jaw was like the unfeeling automaton from their escape. He planned to kill the Teleri.

She placed a hand on his forearm. "No, Tian. Maybe they didn't recognize us."

He looked through her at first, and then his expression softened. He was her husband again. "All right." He turned to one of the young scouts, Noki, and pointed at the patrol hobbling out of the village. "Track them, find out where they are going."

Noki nodded and slunk off.

When Tian returned her gaze, he looked defeated. Had she made the wrong decision for them? The village?

"Come," he said. He waved Hati down. "We must tell Chief Nuwa."

In the confines of the chief's lodge, the Hua gathered with Hati, Lana, and Yuha around the fire pit. She told their story: she was a princess of Hua, betrayed while on a mission of diplomacy. They never expected the Teleri to be in the Wilds, never intended to bring harm to the village or tribe. At the end of her story, she pressed her forehead to the floor in apology. The Hua all followed suit.

"Rise," Chief Nuwa said after a moment of silence. "My children, you have nothing to apologize for. If the Metal Men are as ruthless as you say, and if the stories out of the east are true,

then we would have faced this threat eventually. On the contrary, you have enriched our lives, and perhaps taught us a means of defending ourselves. I am grateful that the spirits brought you here."

Kaiya shook head. If only it were so simple. "If they recognized us, then I'm afraid that we will have brought this threat sooner. The Teleri are efficient and vengeful. Their armored infantry have met little resistance in two centuries of conquest."

The wise chief stood and walked over to the wall. From the floor, he picked up a long object, shrouded in a fur blanket. He unwrapped it, revealing a spear, much longer than the typical Maki spear, with a steel head.

"When I was young," he said, "our horse-riding brethren in the plains tried to incorporate our lands into their kingdom. But the tribes joined together to fight. We knew these forests, we knew not to engage them head-to-head. I was just a boy, and I felled one of their generals with my bow, and took his lance as a prize."

So much dignity and pride! Kaiya smiled in spite of herself.

"If the tribes were willing to unite against our distant kinsmen, I have no doubt that they will put aside their differences to fight outsiders. I will send word to the Maki tribal council, and they in turn will reach out to the other tribes. Now return to your home and rest."

Kaiya looked at Tian. If the lines of worry etched into his forehead were any indication, the chief's inspiring words had done little to assuage him.

It was late afternoon as they headed back to their lodge in silence. Villagers all smiled and patted Tian on the shoulder, congratulating him for his performance. His own smile looked like that of a condemned prisoner resigned to his fate.

Kaiya leaned into him. It didn't make her feel any better. What made her think it would comfort him?

Five young warriors waited at their door. As was Maki custom, Tian invited them in, offering them a seat around the fire pit. Kaiya started a fire and began heating water to make some sweet evergreen bark tea for their guests.

"Your fight was amazing!" Kona, a wide-eyed sixteen-year-old, had developed good spear skills under Tian's tutelage. "Your techniques were so unpredictable. How did you think to use your opponent's weapons?"

Tian's expression brightened. Leave it to a martial discussion to make him feel better! "Beyond skill with your weapon," he said, "you also need to develop an awareness. Of your surroundings. You can use them to your advantage."

The youths nodded excitedly, soaking up his words. Kaiya hoped they would never have to make use of the lessons.

Tian grinned. "Know your enemy's weapon. Then you know his strengths and weaknesses. Kaiya's ancestor banned all bladed weapons in our homeland. Except in the armies. When his widow, the Queen Regent, had to put down a rebellion. She found the peasants had developed unpredictable fighting techniques with their farming tools."

Kaiya looked up from the boiling pot. Was it true? She'd never heard of a rebellion. Perhaps the *Moquan* knew more about these things.

Tian outlined the shape of the Teleri spear. "Their new weapon has four modes of attack. But at long range, the thrust is most common. It is the fastest way of covering distance. That makes the threat one-dimensional. Your response can be three-dimensional."

"So we can beat them!" Kosa, Kona's twin, clapped his hands.

Tian shrugged. "Each Teleri is formidable. However, their true threat is in formations. Ma Jun can tell you more."

Kona jumped to his feet and dashed out of the lodge. A moment later, he came back, dragging Ma Jun along with him. Lana followed close behind, smiling at Kaiya as she entered.

Thank the Heavens. Any more talk of fighting and weapons would be even more depressing. While she and Lana prepared dinner for four, the men continued with their discussion. On occasion, she would glance up to see Ma Jun and Tian working together to show how individual techniques worked in formation.

The teens all stared wide-eyed, so excited about combat.

Kaiya shuddered. All the sacrifices made for her: Xu Zhan. Li Wei. Zhao Yue. Chen Xin. Perhaps more she didn't know of since their escape. Had Jie survived? War was ugly business. Hopefully, these youths would never experience it.

After an hour, darkness fell and the youngsters were called back to their homes for dinner, leaving the four adults to eat in peace. Around her, Ma Jun and Tian wore somber expressions, habitually talking in the Hua language. Since Lana had picked up only a little, Kaiya tried several times to bring it back into the Maki dialect, to no avail.

Ma Jun poked at the food with his chopsticks. "If the Teleri recognized you, they'll be back with a larger force."

Tian sucked on his lower lip, almost like Jie. "We need to find where their base camp is. We can find out how many there are. And how soon they will return."

What was he thinking? Kaiya shivered. "Our presence here endangers the village."

Lana shook her head. "The chief is right, whether or not you are here makes little difference. Sooner or later, we will have to face this threat."

Ma Jun peeled back part of the rug and drew a map on the floor. "Strategically speaking, for them to come here would divert their attention from closer objectives. The only reason for them to come here in the short term is *us*."

And if the Teleri knew who they were...Kaiya shuddered. "Perhaps we should leave the village."

Lana frowned. "My brother never told you, did he? Last year, the spirits came to him in a vision, informing him that our people would soon face a great danger we could not overcome ourselves. He would find answers if he made a pilgrimage to the Land of the Spirit Messengers, on a night when the White Moon hid and the Blue Moon was half-lidded."

Kaiya calculated when that would have happened. Maybe several months ago, which meant—

"That is how you came to meet him on the trails west of the river."

Goosebumps rose on Kaiya's arms. "What did he learn?"

Lana locked her gaze on her. "He looked into the sacred pool and saw the reflection of the Blue Moon as straight swords. After Nadi and Waka told him how you defeated the ogre, he was certain the spirits brought you to us. You would save us from the danger. That's why Chief Nuwa accepted you into the tribe."

Save the tribe from danger? How was she supposed to do that? Kaiya looked at the floor. "I am no warrior. My encounter with the ogre was luck. I had to be saved from them the night before."

She leaned in to Tian, savoring his warmth, and he draped an arm over her. Why so hesitant?

Lana shook her head. "You do not need to be a warrior to protect others. The spirits do not speak directly, only in metaphors. Yuha's pilgrimage could be interpreted in many ways. Our people believe it is you."

Kaiya fell silent, lost in contemplation. They couldn't stay here, couldn't risk the village.

That night, after they'd gone to bed, she lay awake, unable to vanquish the thoughts clashing in her head. It was useless. She sighed and looked up through the hole in the roof at the stars.

Beside her, Tian whispered, "You can't sleep either?"

"I'm sorry, I didn't mean to disturb you."

"I was not asleep, *Dian-xia*." He shifted on his side, his gaze heavy on her in the darkness. His speech was so...*formal*.

And had he just used her title? She rolled over to face him. "I can't help but to think, if we returned to Hua, then the village would be safe. But if we go back, what will happen to *us*? I know that my father would never approve of our marriage. And I never told you this, but I was courting Zheng Ming before I departed for Iksuvius."

Tian's tone carried unusual shock. "My brother would not take kindly to our marriage."

"Even *if* they recognized our marriage. I couldn't continue living if we were forced to be apart." She nestled her head into his bare chest.

Tian rubbed his hand against her back. "Fang Weiyong would vouch for it. He administered our vows. He made sure it was all done correctly. We should return. If we stay here...it's only a matter of time. Before Teleri subjugates the Maki. The tribesmen know the forest. But the empire's armies would win. With overwhelming numbers. And superior weapons."

She looked up from his chest, into his eyes. They were pools of blackness in the night. "What if we just ran away? We do not stay here, nor do we return to Hua."

"Where would we go? We can't live on love alone."

Kaiya's chest tightened. How could he feel that way, after how far they'd come? She turned her head.

He reached for her, but she rolled onto her side, away from him.

"I'm sorry," he whispered.

She barely heard him over her own soft sobs.

Tian didn't sleep well that night. With her back to him, the princess' breathing suggested she barely slept either. All these people, his new family, faced danger because of them. The road back to Hua would mean their separation. His sense of duty nagged at him. The only way to ensure everyone's safety, the princess' included, was sacrificing his own feelings.

At dawn, when the pink and purple clouds drifted past the smoke hole, she rustled beneath the thick fur covers. Was the dream almost over?

Only if he let it. He sat up and leaned over. "I'm so sorry. I didn't mean what I said. Last night. Let's leave here. We can go anywhere in the world. I'll find work as a bodyguard. You can perform."

Kaiya turned and gazed at him. "We can't run from our responsibilities, and right now, our duty is to the Maki. I am sorry, I was not thinking well last night, but I see things very clearly now."

Tian studied her, amazed at how she could still look so beautiful, even first thing in the morning. He bent down to kiss her, and she pulled him down.

Her hands worked his pants off while he tugged the shirt over her head. He brushed his lips over her closed eyes and worked his way down to her mouth.

Emerging from under the blankets, no more reassured from their lovemaking, Kaiya looked up through the hole in the roof. Dust motes shone in the beam of mid-morning sun that streamed in. She tightened the covers over her shoulders, as if their embrace would strengthen her resolve.

Outside, Hati's voice rang out, frantic. "Hurry! Everyone to the village center!"

CHAPTER 48:

Clear and Present Danger

The village buzzed with rumor, the noise drawing Tian out of Kaiya's embrace. Hopping one-footed into his pants, he poked his head out of the lodge.

Hati ran up, grabbed his arm, and pulled him down the path. "Hurry, everyone is gathering!"

Kaiya emerged, sweat matting her hair to her forehead, and Tian beckoned her to follow. Not that she needed his prompting.

At the village center, most of the tribespeople crowded around the drum platform, their chatter drowning out all other sounds. Near the drums, the Teleri's Shaki guide, left arm in a sling, conferred with Chief Nuwa. The remaining villagers trickled in, including Kaiya, who sidled up and clasped Tian's hand.

The chief raised a weathered staff with wild turkey feathers tied to the end. The villagers fell silent.

"My people!" The chief's voice boomed, carrying through the assembled tribe. He always spoke softly, and it was startling to hear his tone of command. "We have ill tidings. Shoma, a Shaki tribesman enslaved by the Metal Men, stumbled into the village this morning, with an arrow wound in his shoulder. Yuha has treated him. However, he brought ominous news, which he will share with all of you now."

Shoma staggered forward. "My Maki kindred, I know that our peoples have not always gotten along—" Low muttering erupted, but the chief raised his staff again, quieting the crowd. "—we do not serve the Metal Men by choice, but only because they hold our women hostage. Seeing your warrior fight yesterday, I was given a glimmer of hope that we may one day be able to win our freedom." He paused, his eyes sweeping over the assembled Maki.

That seemed too easy. Tian tapped his chin.

Shoma tapped both hands on his chest. "When I heard of their plans, I came back here as quickly as I could, even though they tried to stop me. They are looking for her." He pointed at Kaiya, who sucked in a breath.

Tian stepped in front of her. So the Teleri had recognized her. Hopefully, young Noki, who he'd sent after the patrol, would return soon with more news.

"A runner headed back to their base camp, which is a two-day march for them in their metal armor. At the camp, there are three hundred warriors, much like the ones you saw yesterday. Their sole purpose is to find the girl. They'll be returning in force. You must be prepared to either turn her over, or fight."

The crowd murmured again. All expressed a desire to fight, to protect them as their own. Tian's pulse quickened. Though heartwarming, none of them had ever faced Bovyan infantry.

Shoma shook his head. "I forewarn you, three days beyond that, they've built a great fortress, which houses nearly two thousand of them. There, our women are forced to serve their soldiers while our men work like animals. If you resist and lose, you will share our fate."

Tian tapped his chin. It sounded like the Teleri way, but... "How can we trust you?"

Shoma placed his right hand over his heart. "I swear by the spirits that I speak the truth."

His oath was greeted by chatter. Yuha had told Tian in no uncertain terms that breaking a promise to the spirits had dire consequences: the oathbreaker's life energy would never reunite with the universe when he died, cursing him to forever wander the netherworld between life and death.

The chief raised his staff again, silencing the crowd. "My people. I wanted you to understand this threat before telling you that my decision has been made. Kaiya, Tian, Weiyong, and Jun may not be of the Kanin race, but they are members of our Maki tribe. We will never sell out one of our own. It will be war. We have three days to prepare. Heads of households, come meet with me. Everyone else prepare for our warriors' departure."

War chants resounded through the morning forest. Tian's heart sank. The village of almost three hundred only had about eighty men of fighting age. Even with the advantage of terrain, it would be almost impossible to defend against superior numbers and weapons. He exchanged glances with Ma Jun, who shook his head.

Tian looked to Kaiya. Maybe he had been right to begin with. It would be better to leave.

Hati pushed through the crowd to meet him, and hustled him towards the platform.

As soon as the war council convened, Tian stepped forward. "Chief Nuwa. We can't possibly defend this village. Not from their invasion force. Please do not throw your lives away for us. Kaiya and I will flee."

The chief smiled, his wise countenance the calm at the eye of a maelstrom. "Tian, who said we will defend the *village*?"

Tian fell silent. If not the village...

Chief Nuwa's expression returned to its usual gravity. "A wise warrior chooses the place where he does battle. A day east of here, along the river trail, is Omiwa Gorge. The north bank

between the cliffs and river is such that only two men can pass at a time."

The chief held up two fingers, then brought his hands a finger-length apart. "At its narrowest point, only one man can fight at a time. The river flows so rapidly that not even the great horses of our plains kindred can negotiate the current."

A bottleneck. The strategy could work, though it would only be a matter of time before the Teleri would send more men. It might prove to be a temporary reprieve.

The chief drew lines in the air with his fingers while the warriors nodded. "It is one of only three paths that lead to this village from that direction; one of the other trails is treacherous, winding up the cliff; the last is out of the way. We will also do our best to draw them away from those other paths with ambushes."

Tian frowned. What if the Teleri took one of the other paths? It wouldn't have been the first time an enemy did not stick to script.

The chief continued. "Our men will engage their troops in the gorge, at the narrowest spot. I will send word to our Maki kinsmen to the north to bear down on them from the cliffs above; and I will further request to the Omiki tribes in the south to rain arrows from the south bank of the river. Does anyone have any suggestions?"

Ma Jun, a household head like Tian, stepped forward. "What happens if we don't hold the gorge?"

Chief Nuwa smiled grimly. "Then we will fall back, with half the men returning to the village for defense while the rest of us harass them with arrows along the path."

And dozens would die for nothing. Rehearsing his words in his head, Tian stepped forward and dropped to his knee, fist to the ground as if he were addressing Hua royalty. "Chief Nuwa. I humbly request the honor to enter the gorge first."

The chief favored him through pursed lips. "Normally, that would be Hati's right. But if he is willing to relinquish that, then you may be the point of our spear."

Tian turned to Hati with pleading eyes. "Brother, please. It is Kaiya they want, and I will take the responsibility of being the first to fall."

Hati nodded. "It's been a generation since we went to war, and I had very much hoped to prove myself as my father did before me. I relinquish this honor, for you, my brother."

Fighting a tear, Tian extended his right hand in his left in the Maki motion for thanks. "I can't possibly face three hundred men, one right after the other. You will have your chance."

The chief clapped his hands once. "Depart after lunch. Let all the warriors prepare for this generation's struggle."

The men erupted in cheers. Still, Tian's stomach flipped. How many would die because of them?

As the group dispersed, Chief Nuwa motioned Ma Jun over. "Jun, you will stay behind and formulate a strategy for the defense of the village. Keep in mind that our most robust warriors will go with the war party."

Ma Jun opened his mouth, but no words came out. He simply nodded.

He must have wanted to join the war party, even if he was still not in fighting condition after these several months. Had the roles been reversed, Tian would have felt the same way, to be first to defend his family.

He placed his right fist in his left hand, saluting Ma Jun in Hua fashion for the first time since they arrived in the village. "Lieutenant, I temporarily relinquish my duty to protect the princess, and return it to the capable hands of the imperial guard."

Ma Jun straightened and returned the salute, bowing his head.

Tian placed his hand on his shoulder, in Maki fashion. "My brother, please protect my wife."

The next several hours blurred by as the frenetic activity around Kaiya bewildered her. Many small drums were set up in the village square around the two large drums. Mothers and wives painted the faces of their children and husbands. Grandmothers prepared food for the march, while grandfathers told stories of the last time an aggressor tried to invade. Middle-aged men beyond their fighting years sharpened spearheads and arrowheads, and children made good-luck charms of shiny river stones.

At last, the hour of departure arrived. Husbands and wives, mothers and sons all bid tearful farewells. Kaiya held Tian for a long time, memorizing the feel of his body against hers. He would surely sacrifice himself if the need arose. Was this the last time she would feel his warm embrace? Even after the call to march had been given, she pressed against him, unwilling to let go.

The chief presented Tian—as head of the column—a relic from the past war: a Kanin horse saber. Kaiya hid her smile. He already had one from their first disguise escaping Iksuvius. How long ago that seemed!

Tian hefted the weapon and smiled. With his free hand, he rubbed her on the back. "Don't worry, my love. These sabers will serve me well in a close-quarters engagement against Teleri spears."

He shouldered his pack and turned to leave. She held on to his strong hand as long as she could before he pulled away. His fingers brushed over her palm.

As the seventy-five warriors filed out down the path to the river, women played the drums to send them off. Wiping tears from her eyes and summoning up all the bravery she could muster, Kaiya joined them. The beating of her drum echoed from her heart, and the sound carried deep into the forest. The warriors answered the drums with a hearty cheer.

After several hours, the last rays of sun disappeared into the west, leaving a foreboding red glow on the horizon. The village grew eerily quiet, with even the littlest children seeming to comprehend the gravity of the situation.

To distract herself, Kaiya sought out Lana. She found her at the village center with Ma Jun, who'd already laid out plans for the village's defense. He was explaining the evacuation plan when a young scout rushed up.

Noki, a refugee from another Maki village, was one of Tian's original lodge mates. The one Tian sent to follow the Teleri patrol. Panting, he collapsed. "The Metal Men are coming! After they left the village yesterday, they split up at the river. One group headed east with the Shaki guide, and I followed the captain and two others west."

The villagers muttered among themselves. Kaiya's heart pattered.

"Where did they go?" Chief Nuwa's shoulders slumped.

"They stripped off their armor and ran to Wild Turkey Island, arriving around midnight. It was horrible. What was once our Uloki kinsmen's village, guarding the Shrine of Kahala, is now overrun with the Metal Men and ogres. Many tribespeople from all over the plateau were held in chains."

Where was that? Kaiya searched faces as a wave of upset murmurs rippled through the crowd.

Young Noki sighed. "As soon as the captain entered, their camp went wild with cheers, and it looked like even at that late hour, they were making preparations for war. I hurried back as fast as I could."

Ma Jun's face flushed. "A trap. The Shaki lied to us to draw our fighting-aged men in the opposite direction. He is with our warriors now, maybe ready to betray them as well."

Kaiya shuddered. They were undefended. "The men must be warned."

The old chief seemed to age even more. "All the able-bodied men are gone, and we're all tired from today's preparations. No one will catch up with them."

"Lana, then," Kaiya said. "She's a shaman, like Yuha. Can they communicate?"

Lana shook her head. "I've expended myself, coaxing thorn brambles to grow around the village."

Chief Nuwa shoulders slumped. "Spend the rest of the evening collecting what is dear to you, and rest well tonight. We evacuate the village at dawn."

CHAPTER 49:
War on Two Fronts, Part 2

After a forced march to ensure they would reach the gorge before the Teleri, Tian rested among fifty of the Maki men. With no word back from the vanguard, all seemed relaxed for the time being.

He looked at each of the inexperienced warriors' faces, looking for signs of frayed nerves. Perhaps it was the ritual Yuha led to help ward off harm, though Tian didn't feel the calm relief flood over him like the others claimed.

On the southern side of the path, the waters of the North Kanin River roared, fed by the melting snows. Cliffs rose twenty feet above them on the left, their white rock faces creating a glare off of the afternoon sun. At the top, Maki kinsmen from other villages, fifty in all, also waited. In the unlikely event that the Teleri took the higher, narrower path, they might very well have to fight for their lives. The more probable route would result in Chief Nuwa's villagers bearing the brunt of the attack.

On the cliffs along the south bank, a hundred feet away, fifty Omiki archers—many of whom had learned spear techniques from Tian—also waited. This was the first major conflict the region had seen in a generation, and none of the warriors here had fought in those wars. Indeed, many had not yet been born. A nervous excitement trickled through the ranks. All hoped to win glory.

Tian tapped his chin. Perhaps the Teleri weren't even coming. Something was off. A trap, maybe? This location was almost too easy to defend. Unless the Teleri came by a different route. Yet the path above them along the cliff would be too treacherous in armor. The path on the south bank was wider, but there was no place to ford further downstream.

No, this would be the route they would have to take. It was just a matter of waiting. He sat down with Hati and shared some cured elk meat.

He'd hardly eaten three bites when shouts rang out from the eastern reaches of the gorge. The yells came closer. It was their own advance scouts. They ran through the gorge, none looking wounded. Tian sprung to his feet, making way for the vanguard.

The last man through stopped and caught his breath. "One hundred Metal Men, with spears and shields, supported by fifty Shaki archers. Our arrows couldn't penetrate their shields. They're close behind."

The men cheered. Hati grinned. "Less Metal Men than we thought. A third of what Shoma predicted."

"I am happy to have been wrong." Shoma's smile spread ear to ear.

Tian bit the inside of his lip. Certainly the Teleri were not so arrogant as to think they could take a village in unfamiliar terrain with so few swords.

Hati motioned everyone to quiet down. "Signal our Omiki kinsmen to target the Shaki archers when they are in range. They're our most dangerous threat."

The sound of heavy boots echoed down the gorge, just above the roar of the river. Then the first Teleri troops came in sight. Heavy infantry, wearing dress uniforms and steel helms with T-slots. Their shields were made of heavy ironwood, reinforced with steel. They carried short Teleri spears, meant to be used one-handed.

Behind Tian, all bravado melted away, overcome by worried chatter. Tribesmen pointed and muttered.

Swords and daggers hanging at the Bovyans' sides clanked as they marched single file, in perfect unison. Black banners with the gold sun fluttered in the gentle breeze.

Tian looked back and took stock of the men. None seemed to have panicked, though many clutched their spears with white knuckles. "Steady, my brothers," he said. "They can still only fight us one at a time. Their peripheral vision is poor because of their helmets."

Yuha flashed him a smile and chanted an invocation to the spirits. The men behind him settled down. Tian felt no different, though perhaps it was because he had fought for his life before.

At about twenty paces, the Teleri leader raised his hand to stop his troops. He walked forward, the insignia on his uniform marking him as a commissioned officer. A Shaki man skittered along the narrow gap between the soldiers and the cliff face, trying to reach the front. Tian and Hati went to meet with them.

The officer spoke first. "Brave and noble savages, you are hopelessly outnumbered by a better-armed force. Withdraw now, and you and your villages will be spared."

The Shaki started to translate, but Tian interrupted him. "Teleri captain, your numbers are meaningless in this gorge, and your armor is not impenetrable. Return to where you came from, or meet the point of our spears this afternoon." He raised and shook his spear with a falsetto shout, and even if the tribesmen didn't understand what he had just said, they joined in.

The officer laughed. "You must be the Cathayi who defeated our men. *You* may have faced us before, but *they* will cower in fear as they taste Teleri steel for the first time."

"You speak in big words for someone who hides behind the rest of your men. Or are you brave enough to try my spear first?"

The officer laughed again, though now with a hint of anger. "That stone spearhead will break on my armor. It is hardly a challenge. But perhaps if I dispense with you now, the savages will surrender." Turning back to his own men, "I will fight the Cathayi first. If I fall, Lieutenant, you take charge and begin the assault."

He turned to face Tian and dropped into a fighting stance, left foot forward and spear cocked back in his right hand. Both sides cheered.

Tian motioned Hati back and assumed a relaxed side stance with his right foot forward. He held his spear at the ready, left hand at the butt and the right about two feet up the shaft in the power-thrusting position. Standing ten feet away, the Teleri officer saluted.

Tian returned the greeting.

The officer hurled his spear and charged as he whipped out his sword.

Tian swatted the spear out of the way with a subtle motion. He stepped forward with his left foot, and stabbed with only his left hand to reach maximum spear range.

The Teleri ran right into the unconventional attack. The surgical thrust slipped through the opening of his helm, and he collapsed to the ground in a loud clatter.

Both sides fell silent, the only sound the gushing river at their side.

"Archers, shoot!" the lieutenant shouted. "A virgin to the man who fells the Cathayi!"

Tian rolled forward and worked the fallen officer's shield off his arm. He hazarded a glance up. Arrows arced from behind the Teleri line and descended. He held the shield above his head like a parasol and slunk back towards his comrades. Several stone arrow tips ricocheted off the shield.

"Omiki archers, shoot!" Hati yelled. "Maki men, attack!"

The Omiki on the south cliff and the Maki above them emerged from where they lay under the Teleri line of sight. Arrows filled the air.

The barrage at Tian ceased and he dropped the shield to the side. Retrieving his spear from the head of the fallen officer, he strode towards the Teleri troops.

They adjusted their shields to cover themselves from the enemy volleys coming from the south. Though the Omiki arrows just bounced off the shields, some hit the soldiers in the legs, slowing them down. Large rocks and arrows rained down on them from above.

Tian knocked the helm off the next Bovyan before he could even lower his shield. The back swing slashed across his eyes. Screaming, he covered his face. Tian stomped through his knee.

A spear thrust past the collapsing man, at Tian's face. Tian dropped his own weapon, caught the incoming attack, and yanked the attacker into the first. The two collapsed into a heap. Tian punched the steel-tipped spear through the second's knees. Yet, more Teleri came, picking their way among their fallen comrades. Injuries from arrows and stones didn't deter them.

Tian was precise and efficient, oftentimes killing or incapacitating an enemy with a single thrust. He gritted his teeth. It was easy. Too easy. The Bovyans' attacks, though skilled, left openings they meant for him to exploit. Why? He shot a glance back, seeing if he could pick out Shoma from the tribesmen gathered behind him.

Each Teleri he faced seemed more tired than the last, having faced a constant barrage of arrows and stones in the bottleneck. His own limbs tiring, Tian yielded his position at the head and allowed Hati to take over.

With his improved spear technique, Hati dispatched several while suffering only a few cuts. When he tired, he gave way to the next warrior. The Bovyans barely tried to defend themselves. And within an hour, they had fallen to a man. The surviving Shaki archers fled.

With the Maki's respect for life, they treated the Teleri survivors. Yuha led a prayer that would help guide the spirits of the fallen to rejoin the energy of the universe.

The Teleri lieutenant had suffered an arrow wound through the leg and sat up against the cliff wall. Tian picked his way toward him through the carnage. Like the others with exposed heads, the lieutenant looked older. Perhaps older than First Consul Geros. With the ancestral curse over their head, perhaps they had volunteered to be part of a suicide squad. But why?

The lieutenant nodded at him. "You are truly a hero of the ages. I would be honored if you helped me end my life, for I cannot bear the shame of leading my men to defeat."

Hold the butterfly with care, Kaiya had said, *for even their fleeting lives have value*. Tian bound the man's wound. "You lost on purpose. Why?"

The lieutenant choked on his laughter. "This is but one battle, and we have served our purpose in fighting it. There are not enough bottlenecks in this godforsaken forest to dam up the flood of Teleri soldiers. Once we control this region, the story of your valor tonight will be nothing but a footnote in history. If it is remembered at all."

A Bovyan would not break under torture, nor would the Maki condone it. With no other means of coaxing an answer out of him, Tian shrugged. "Maybe we will meet again on the field. Until then, farewell."

He turned to rejoin the warriors, who finished collecting valuable steel weapons. He searched for Shoma and was met with blank stares and shrugs when he asked about the Shaki guide. Had he been injured? Tian would've noticed. Suspicion gnawed at his gut. Perhaps the Bovyans were just gauging the natives' strength.

Or perhaps it was a diversion? But from what? If what Chief Nuwa said was true, there was no other practical approach from the east; and there were no reports of Bovyans to the west.

A few of the warriors went east to scout, but the majority headed west out of the gorge, looking forward to returning home with the story of their victory. Tian couldn't blame them, though worry fluttered in his stomach.

It was nearly nightfall when the tribesmen left the gorge. Coming to a pool in the river, Yuha made them strip down and bathe. He held a ritual to cleanse their spirits of their deeds, which Tian found surprisingly refreshing. Afterwards, they set up camp and ate dinner before settling down for the night. They sent the young twins Kona and Kosa ahead to send word to the village.

Most fell into a well-deserved sleep, though some sat around the fire, recounting the fight.

Hati grinned ear to ear. "It will be remembered like the battles of my father's time."

"It will only be remembered," Yuha said with a frown, "if our people maintain their freedom."

Just like the Teleri lieutenant had said. Tian nodded. "This is just a single battle. It won't stop their soldiers forever. They are ruthless and relentless. They will come again, maybe within a matter of days after they learn of their defeat."

Hati pumped his fist. "When word gets out that we can win, the other tribes will join hand to expel the Metal Men."

"We need to prepare for the next wave." Tian sighed. "Their fortress is four days from here. It will take their Shaki archers two days to take news there. If they run without rest. Then another four days for them to reach the gorge. We must set up our defense there again. Within at least six days."

"I prayed for the spirits to bring rain," Yuha said. "Combined with the melting snows, the gorge will be inundated in five days and remained closed for two to three weeks. By that time, we will have held a tribal council so that we can set up a collaborative defense of the gorge."

Tian pictured the terrain in his head. "Are there any other means of them reaching us?"

"Yes." Yuha nodded. "But in order to move so many troops, they would have to follow the old road going northwest, then turn back south along the path which we took when you first came to us. It would take them nearly three weeks, and our kinsmen would harass them the entire way."

Hati's tone sobered. "If they had enough boats, they could go along the south bank of the river and then cross at Wild Turkey Island. But they would have to carry the boats to that point, at least until the melting season ended."

Tian blew out a breath. "Then it seems that for the time being, we are safe."

Doubts and worry kept Tian from sleep. The others woke by dawn, ready to return home to a hero's welcome. The trip at regular pace would take fourteen hours, but the weather was pleasant, allowing them to forge ahead.

Tian's mind raced the entire time. Something still felt wrong. There must have been a reason for the Teleri to lose on purpose. Had they sent soldiers on the longer path?

At least the others' spirits were high as they reached the path off the river trail that would take them home. They arrived at the village not long before midnight, fully expecting late-night revelry.

All were taken aback by the sobering quiet, as Chief Nuwa greeted them with tears in his eyes.

CHAPTER 50:

War on Two Fronts, Part 1

Tian's gut churned. The mood among the villagers was too somber as they waited to greet a father, son, or husband. More concerning was Chief Nuwa seeking him out, even before talking to Hati.

He placed a firm hand on Tian's shoulder. "My son, I have awful news. Kaiya fulfilled Yuha's vision. She saved the village by sacrificing herself."

Tian staggered back. In the past, he had lost comrades on missions without flinching, but this... He choked back tears. "Where is she? What happened?"

His friends all gathered around, putting their collective arms around him. The chief let out a heavy sigh, and began recounting the cascade of events from the previous day.

On the morning of the evacuation, dog barks jerked Kaiya out of sleep. She panicked when she did not feel Tian by her side, forgetting in her foggy waking moments that he had left the day before. She shook her head clear. Outside, the village drums beat wildly. Erratically.

Danger.

Knowing that they would leave at first light, she'd slept in her clothes. Her hair was unbraided, certainly not proper for a married woman in public. She reached for her double swords and peeked out the lodge.

Shadows in the dim light ran by. The drums beat urgently, and one of the older tribesmen appeared, running through the village yelling, "We're surrounded by the enemy! Go to the center and prepare to fight!"

Fight? The warriors were all gone.

She hurried to the middle of the village.

Ma Jun stood at Chief Nawa's side, giving instructions. Spears, bows, and arrows rested next to the drum platform. Middle-aged men, many who hadn't fought in thirty years, took up weapons and formed a perimeter around the village center.

Behind them, women also armed themselves with bows. Other villagers streamed in from all directions, many helping young children and the elderly. Arriving at the platform, Kaiya slung her swords over her shoulder and picked up a bow and a quiver full of arrows.

She waited for instructions, ignoring the drums, the murmurs of worried villagers, the crying of young children, and the barking of dogs.

Through the chaos, from the edge of the village, rang a loud voice with a distinct Shaki accent. "Surrender unconditionally, or face the wrath of the Metal Men."

Chief Nuwa raised his own voice. "We will not purchase our lives with our freedom, and you will not take either easily."

Mocking laughter echoed back. "Then prepare to die!"

A horn blared from outside the village, and the war cries and stomping boots approached from all directions. Children wailed as mothers tried to comfort them. Men on the perimeter faced outwards with deathly resolve. Women nocked arrows, waiting for the first enemy wave to appear among the lodges.

Kaiya's heart raced. How useless she was. The bow in her hand would do little to save the people upon whom she brought doom.

No, there was a way. She placed her bow and quiver on the ground and climbed up to the drumming platform. The higher vantage point afforded a view of imminent disaster. Hundreds of Teleri light infantry marched in orderly ranks, supported by Shaki archers. Their bootsteps stomped in steadfast rhythm.

Taking up a pair of drum sticks, she set herself between the two drums, *Nimewa* and *Himewa*. Taking a deep breath, she channeled the valor of King Evydas of Iksuvi when he faced the First Consul; Sameer the Paladin; her loyal guards Xu Zhan, Li Wei, Zhao Yue, and Chen Xin; and of course, her beloved Tian. She struck the Soul of the Village. The drum's bellow resonated through the village, its steadfast rhythm meant to encourage the villagers.

Kaiya spun to face the larger drum, and used a single beat to send an ominous tone into the enemy ranks.

The Bovyans jolted to a stop.

She turned, rapped three beats on the smaller drum, and then leaned back and struck the larger. The rhythm filled her heart. Her limbs moved of their own volition, much like they had when she danced for Prince Dhannanad in Vyara City and First Consul Geros in Iksuvius.

The tribespeople chanted war cries in unison with the smaller drum. The fearless Bovyans backed off a step. Then they faltered back a few more. Heavens, it was working! All discipline collapsed. Teleri soldiers fell into full retreat. Victory was in hand.

A single man stepped forward into the square. His feather and bead ornaments marked him as Shaki tribal shaman, and one of such power

that her drumming dispersed around him. He raised his staff, whose crystal head captured the red rays of the now rising sun, and yelled, "Spirits, hear me!"

The villagers shot, but their arrows caught up in a whirlwind around him. He slammed the end of the staff on the ground. A thunder clap blasted forth. The Maki tribesmen collapsed to the ground, covering their heads in fright.

The rumble met the drum beats and dissipated. Fatigue rippled into Kaiya's limbs.

The shaman's face contorted. He raised his staff again, and shouted in a deep voice, "Spirits, shake the earth!" He pounded the staff.

The ground trembled. The pitch of the drums softened. The larger clattered to the platform. Kaiya twisted out of the way, barely avoiding it. Quickly regaining her footing, she continued to beat on the smaller drum to restore the Maki's confidence.

Beyond the first ring of lodges, Teleri horns blew again.

Her heart sank. They were regrouping, ready to resume their attack.

A dignified-looking Teleri general stepped forward and spoke in Arkothi: "Princess Kaiya Wang of Cathay, surrender yourself to the Teleri Empire, and the village will be spared. Not just for now, but for as long as the Empire endures. It will pay no tribute, nor take part in the Mating. It will for all intents and purposes be independent."

Kaiya ceased her drumming and met his gaze. "If you will extend the protection to the entire Maki tribe, then I will surrender."

The general's brows furrowed. "You have no room to negotiate. You are outnumbered by the best-trained, best-equipped fighters Tivara has ever known. Your men, elderly, and children will die; the women will be taken to serve our soldiers. And in the end, we will still have you."

Kaiya's stomach clenched. Like at the Battle of Wailian, there was only one bargaining chip left. She unsheathed a sword and held it to her neck. "Then I will take my own life."

The general sighed. "Very well, we accept your offer." He turned to a Shaki warrior and shouted in Arkothi. "Let it be known that immediately following the surrender of Princess Kaiya Wang, the Teleri will cease hostilities with the Maki tribe, and its peoples shall remain outside of our control in perpetuity. We will only fight them in self-defense."

As the Shaki translated the words, the Maki murmured and wept among themselves. They made a path for Kaiya to walk through, many reaching out to touch her shoulder or thank her as she passed.

A figure stepped forward to block her way.

Ma Jun dropped to his knee, fist to the ground. "*Dian-Xia*, I will accompany you."

Kaiya found her tone of authority, long unused. "No, Ma Jun. This is my order. You must take care of Lana, your unborn children, and these people who have so generously accepted us."

She dropped her voice into a whisper and leaned in. Her voice hitched, forcing her to clear her throat. "Pass my message to Tian, these words that I could never say myself, even though we are no longer bound by the conventions of Hua. Please, tell him that I...love him. I love him so much, and want nothing more than to spend the rest of my life with him in this land and raise our children together. But I willingly make this sacrifice for something greater than me or him."

Ma Jun slid to the side, his head remaining bowed. Tears dripped down his cheeks.

A second person stepped in her way. "My daughter," Chief Nuwa said in his ageless voice. "We cannot trust that the outsiders will keep their word. We are willing to fight."

Kaiya shook her head. "Despite their evil ways, the Teleri are always true to their word. If they make this agreement, then they will abide by it. If you fight, you will surely perish."

He placed a heavy hand on her shoulder. "We will gladly die at their hands to spare you the indignities. You are one of us, and we never abandon our own."

Tears came unbidden, and she threw her arms around the chief. "As one of you, how could I allow my family to die at their hands? I gladly trade my freedom for yours."

Tearing herself away from his embrace, she strode towards the general. She then bowed, and extended her sheathed swords in two hands.

As the Teleri troops cheered, the general received the swords in one hand. He motioned for a captain. "The collar."

Collar? Were they already reducing her to a slave? Kaiya edged back.

The general locked eyes with her. "We will not consider you to have surrendered until you wear it."

Kaiya swept her gaze back at the villagers. Men too old to fight. Women, children. They'd all be slaughtered. She took a step forward and lifted her chin.

The captain bowed his head, and then affixed a hinged ring of grey metal around her neck. When he bolted it shut with a lock, the ubiquitous whisper of the world's energy was muffled in her ears.

"Now, General." Singing the next words, she said, "Withdraw your soldiers." The power surged in her chest, only to gutter at her throat. Energy trickled from her limbs. It didn't work!

"In due time, Princess," the general replied. "First, there is the matter of the Teleri imperial seal. Where is it?"

The seal? Kaiya stared at him in genuine confusion. In the escape from Iksuvius, she'd forgotten about it. It must have been months. "I do not have it. It must be lost."

The general's eyes narrowed. "Lost? I find it hard to believe you would misplace such a valuable relic. Lieutenant Espios, search her."

An unarmored Teleri man, whose features and ruddy skin tone suggested his mother was likely a Kanin human, stepped towards her. He was slightly smaller than the average Teleri, which made him a likely candidate for a spy. Kaiya shrank back a step. How humiliating, to be touched by a stranger, an enemy.

"I swear by the spirits that it is not on my person," she said, invoking the oath of the Kanin tribespeople.

"I am afraid that means nothing to me," the General said. "However, if you swear on your honor, then we will delay the search until the doctor at our base camp examines you."

A doctor examining her. Kaiya shuddered. "I swear."

The general smiled, not unkindly. "Very well. Lieutenant, take a detail to search the princess' home. Remember, she belongs to the Consuls. I will ready the troops for our return to camp."

Belonged...of course, this was what surrender meant. Kaiya's heart tittered. She forced a serene composure. At least her dignity was safe for the time being, since the Consuls must be far away in the Teleri homeland.

"As you command." The lieutenant pounded a fist on his chest. He turned to her. "Take us to your dwelling."

She led them to her lodge. They upturned everything, even the cinders of the fire pit. Although their family altar was a simple flat river stone, it symbolized her tie to her ancestors, and she couldn't bear to watch the soldiers casually defile it. They went through her clothes, humiliating her as they exchanged comments about her undergarments. The shell hair ring, which represented her marriage, was thoughtlessly crushed underfoot. By the time they were finished, tears clouded her vision.

The lieutenant motioned for the soldiers to leave. "We will give you two minutes to prepare what you want to take with you."

Left to herself, she cried. Was surrender worth it? Through tear-filled eyes, she gathered items of sentimental value and put them in her pack: among them, the remnants of her hair ring, her drawing of Guanyin, a head ornament of wild-turkey feathers, and the wooden bowl from the altar.

With a stick, she scribbled a message for Tian into the ground and covered it with a blanket.

After two minutes, the lieutenant pushed aside the door. "It is time."

Kaiya wiped away the tears. With one last look, she bid her home among the Maki goodbye.

It was still early morning as the Teleri troops departed the village. The Maki lined the path

back to the river, bidding her sorrowful farewells. Despite the foreboding that sent shivers through her spine, she carried herself with a long-forgotten pride and poise. The villagers greeted her with looks of awe and inspiration. Her life as a Maki tribeswoman was coming to an end, and she was once again, a princess of Hua.

Inside she shuddered. The dream was over, and a nightmare about to begin.

Tian hung his head, avoiding the gaze of the villagers. His wife, so courageous! Pride welled in his chest, even as his stomach twisted at the stark reality. Kaiya was a prisoner of the Teleri, enduring hell.

He squeezed his hands into bone-crunching fists. He would kill every last Bovyan, inflicting injuries that guaranteed a slow, painful death.

Chief Nuwa's voice radiated with a sad, fatherly pride. "Kaiya was so calm, so dignified. It brought inspiration to us all. Then, more than ever, we were so proud to consider her one of our own."

Tian shrugged the pack from his shoulders. It would only slow him down. "Where did they take her?"

"A scout followed them west to Wild Turkey Island. There used to be a holy shrine and a village of our Uloki kindred. It has since been taken over by the Metal Men."

"That is a twelve-hour march along the river." Yuha pointed west.

Tian straightened. He'd storm the camp alone if need be. "Then my brothers, I bid you farewell."

The chief placed firm hands on Tian's shoulders. "My son, you must rest. You will only be going to your death if you go alone and exhausted."

There was general murmur of agreement, but what else could he do?

He shrugged out of the chief's grip and took two purposeful steps before Hati crushed him in a bear hug. Tian twisted his hips, sending the chieftain's son to the ground. Three more warriors wrapped him up. Tian strained to break free, pulling them along. If they didn't give up, he might have to really hurt them.

Yuha placed a hand on him and chanted.

The energy of the spirits surged through Tian. A cool wave settled over him, the frenetic sensation of his rapidly beating heart and trembling limbs giving way to clear thought. The aches and fatigue weighed him down.

Yuha smiled at him. "There now, my brother, think with your head and not with your heart. Let us rest tonight. My prayer will calm your mind so that you will sleep well, and the spirits will show you a path if you allow them."

Every fiber of his body protested, but the spirits hushed their voice and lulled him into calm. Tian acquiesced and allowed Ma Jun to guide him to his lodge. Hati picked up the pack and followed.

Inside, it looked as though a storm had swept through. He ignored the clutter—even his compulsiveness to take stock of things was muted—and threw himself into his bedding, the one he would sleep alone in for the first time. Despite all the worries and concerns that should have nagged him, he fell into a deep slumber.

He woke up at dawn, feeling completely refreshed, as if the battle from two days prior and the hard march the day before had never happened. Yet, an unsettled feeling nagged at him. Had he dreamed? If so, he couldn't remember.

The morning light flooded in through the smoke hole, illuminating the mess made by the Teleri solders. Kitchenware was strewn haphazardly around the fire pit, bringing a bitter smile to Tian's face—although Kaiya now loved to cook, she was never good at cleaning up afterwards. It always fell to him to tidy up. Their clothes lay scattered about, each article bearing signs of a thorough search. What had they been looking for?

He turned to the long flat stone set up as their family altar. The wooden bowl they used for leaving a small daily sacrifice to their ancestors was gone. The altar's position seemed odd. He looked up. His crude sketch of Yang-Di, God of the Sun, looked at the empty spot on the wall where the drawing of his consort Guanyin once hung.

The blank spot on the wall! In his dream, Yang-Di had been looking down, pointing an open hand at the ground.

Tian turned toward the spot, covered by his bedding. He lifted it. Words were scrawled in the dirt, in beautiful Hua script: "I love you forever."

She must have written it, possibly in her last moments in the village. He choked on his tears. He should have told her the same, much like the young Maki lovers whispered in each other's ears.

The dream! In the dream, the words were not, *I love you forever.* What was written there? Try as he might, he couldn't remember.

He emerged from his lodge to find Ma Jun, Fang Weiyong, Lana, and the twins Kona and Kosa there waiting for him. They were packed.

Ma Jun bowed his head. "We will go with you, to Wild Turkey Island. Under the terms of their agreement with the Teleri, the Maki cannot engage the enemy, but they will be able to give us guidance."

Tian nodded, handing Ma Jun a steel Teleri longsword and dagger. "The Teleri troops have a two-day lead on us. However, it is light out. We can take a boat to the island. We'll arrive by mid-afternoon. I will free her tonight. Then we'll go by boat back to Hua. We can't return to the village. Not until the Teleri threat has ended."

Buckling on a longsword and dagger of his own, Tian went to visit Chief Nuwa and Yuha. Even if he succeeded in rescuing Kaiya, he might not see the Maki for a long time. If he failed...

The chief, along with several others, waited for him in the middle of the village. Despite Tian's urge to get underway, he took long moments to warmly embrace all of these people whom he had become so close to, and bid each a farewell.

To Yuha, he said, "It was fate that brought us together on that cold autumn day. Among your people, I learned so much about what was missing in my life before."

Yuha placed a hand over his heart. "May the spirits guide you, my brother."

He turned to the chief. "I've had many fathers. The one who gave me life. The master who taught how to take life. I consider you my third father. The one who showed me how to live."

The chief looked at him with grave eyes. "May the spirits guide you to your love, and find her unharmed. Regardless of where you float on the tides of war and peace, you may always return here."

Tian then embraced Hati. "My brother. You will become a great leader. Like your father. With spear in hand. Bravely and proudly defend our people."

Hati crushed Tian in his hug. "Thank you, Brother, for all that you have taught me. You are a hero of our people, and the Warrior Beyond The Wall will live on in our songs as long as we have mouths to sing them. I had hoped you would honor me by serving as second in my wedding to Lahi next month, but I know that's not possible. So go now, with the spirits as your guide."

With a final look at the people he had come to love like family, Tian left the village, greeted on both sides by the tearful farewells of the tribespeople.

CHAPTER 51:

Hope and Fear

As the enormous Tree of Light came into sight, the symphony of natural sounds sang in Kaiya's ears. The chuckling river danced with the rustling wind, waltzing in harmony to the myriad chirps of a dozen different bird species. Like Ayudra Island, where she'd met the Paladin Oracle; like Shakti's Hill in Palimur where she'd faced Avarax, magic permeated the area.

She tried to remember a Hua chronicle of the ancient Kanin Empire:

The land around Wild Turkey Island is one of the last forested areas on the Kanin Plateau. It is now the private hunting preserve of the Emperor of Kanin, an oasis of trees among farmland stretching as far as the eye can see. A giant Tree of Light grows there, planted by the Elf Angel Aralas himself, just before the War of Ancient Gods. Yet even before that, legend has it that beneath the island is one of the glittering caves, where the elves unearthed a Starburst to aid them in their struggle against the orcs during the Twilight of Istriya.

She sighed in frustration. The resonance of the world called to her, should have made her body tingle with power, but the grey metal collar walled the energy off, keeping it just out of reach.

The Teleri troops had left the village some twelve hours earlier, marching along the path with tireless efficiency. They rested for only short amounts of time, affording her a pack horse so that she would not slow the fast-moving, well-conditioned troops.

General Altos di Bovyan strode beside her and had proven to be a gentleman. He allowed her hands to remain unbound and treated her with the utmost respect. He certainly didn't paint the picture of a brutal rapist.

A member of the elite Teleri Prospecti—the military officers and administrators—he stood even taller than most of his men. He called for halt and extended a hand to help her off the horse. "Your Highness, this is our last break before we reach our destination. Please rest well."

With a last glance at the Tree of Light in the distance, Kaiya took his hand and slid down. She curtseyed in the manner of the Arkothi. "General, I thank you for your courtesy. I imagine you might have made a fine Bovyan Knight, bringing order to the chaos following the Hellstorm and Long Winter."

The corners of his lips tugged slightly upwards as he bowed his head. "I appreciate your compliment, though I do not deserve it."

Maybe she could appeal to his sense of honor. If only she could convince him to take the collar off. "From what I have read, the Bovyan Knights were a noble order, and you certainly honor their legacy."

"They were. Their code of honor was derived from the Last Testament of Geros, our esteemed progenitor Geros Bovyan, mortal son of Solaris. Nowadays, we are taught we are successors of the Bovyan Knights, but sometimes I wonder if the code hasn't been corrupted to fit state ideology."

She studied his earnest expression. Apparently, Hua's historians took an oversimplified view of the Teleri. "How did that happen?"

He returned her gaze. "In the time of our first ancestor, it was acceptable to take multiple wives. After the Hundred Years of War, the Hellstorm, and the Long Winter, there were so few men compared to women."

So it had been in Hua, until the Queen Regent banned polygamy—not even the *Tianzi* could take a concubine. Kaiya nodded, prompting him to continue.

"Within a century, the ratio balanced and monogamous relationships became the norm. But since we can only have one child, always male, our population declined with each succeeding generation. It would have led to our extinction."

"I would think the Bovyan Knights would have rather gone extinct than resort to institutionalized gang rape." Which would probably be her fate, at the hands of the Consuls. Kaiya shuddered.

General Altos sighed. "The North was in a perpetual state of chaos. Had the Bovyans died out, how many more people would have suffered? Solaris meant for his son's descendants to bring peace. It was the only way. "

Was it? Apparently, even good men could rationalize evil deeds. "It's a peace bought with the dignity of all the girls you violate." And they were just girls, just starting their monthly cycles.

Brow furrowed, General Altos pressed his lips together. "It is hard for the conquered, but within a generation of Teleri rule, participation in the Mating is considered an honor." The retort came out rote, forced.

"You don't sound convinced."

He sighed and lowered his voice. "I became close to a woman. She confided in me the horrors of our rule, forcing me to critically look at whether the peace and order we bring justifies the cruel means we use to achieve it. I began to question the Testament of Geros. It is written in a language that only the Keepers of the Shrine of Geros understand, so they control how it is interpreted."

"Surely there are others who share your sentiments?" If there were a rebellious faction, perhaps the Teleri could be changed from within.

He shrugged. "My views are in the minority, but there are those who idealize what the Bovyan Knights once were. Many of us were deployed to the Wilds instead of on a major front."

"It saddens me to think that even those who realize that the Teleri system is wrong do nothing to change it."

He gazed at her. "There is only one way to change us."

There had to be one. She raised an eyebrow.

He looked up to the sky. "An end to the Curse of Tivar, that cuts our life short at thirty-three, that bears us only sons, that keeps women from having but one Bovyan son."

If she could help end the curse... "How?"

"Fulfill our bargain with the Altivorc King. Or..." Altos regarded her with a curious eye. He leaned in and whispered, "There are some among us who believe an old story. When the Bovyan Edict was passed a hundred and twenty years ago, one young Keeper dissented, saying the methods were too brutal and that the Testament did not justify it."

Kaiya stared at him. At least some Bovyans took a moral stand. "What happened to him?"

"He was expelled from the Shrine of Geros. However, he used his newfound freedom to go on a pilgrimage to the pyramid in Arkos. The seer there prophesized that a Bovyan who knew his father and mother would take the Teleri imperial crest to the Tower of Light on the Eldaeri's Forbidden Isle. The knowledge he gained there would bring about the end of the curse."

Hope sprung in her. Jie had saved Aelward, an Eldaeri Prince and ship captain. He owed them a favor, and the Eldaeri would love nothing more than for the Teleri to leave them in peace. How hard could it be to find any number of Bovyans who knew their mother and father?

Altos shook his head, quashing her optimism. "Unfortunately, there are two sides to every story. The majority of the Prospecti dismiss the prophecy as a fairy tale; or worse, believe it prophesizes the world plunging back into a darkness rivaling the Long Winter. This is why magic is banned, why those with the gift of foresight are murdered. Bovyan boys who are born outside the Mating are quickly brought in, or hunted down and killed."

Kaiya's chest tightened. The murder of children, even Bovyan boys, was horrifying. Hua might've been immoral in its weapon sales, but it didn't compare to the evil of the Teleri Empire.

He held his hand out to her. "We must be going. I will do my best to protect you, but know that once we reach Wild Turkey Island, I will not be the highest ranking officer."

After three hours, they reached a fork in the river. A bridge crossed over a narrow strait onto an island stretching about a *li* from end to end. The gigantic Tree of Light blocked the view of the Iridescent Moon, but from the height of the sun, it was clearly getting late. Her heart raced, the foreboding looming over her even more than the tree.

Besides the dozens of wooden structures, the island had a familiar feel. A few shrubs peeked out from the flat, rocky ground. A single hill rose at the southern end, jutting out into the larger river. Its hum, perceptible from where they had taken a break, buzzed in her ears now, the frequency so similar to...Palimur, where she'd confronted Avarax. Even the shape resembled the island where the Temple of Shakti stood.

Holding her chin high as if it would hide her fear, she strode across the bridge. What had the elf wizardess Ayana said about Palimur? That it was a glittering cave site, a place where the energy of the world welled? Her hand strayed to the collar. If only she could tear the damned thing from her neck, maybe she could repeat the improbable feat that had earned her the title of Dragon Charmer.

On the other side of the bridge, a waiting Bovyan yanked her wrist from the collar. Another clamped a hand on her shoulder. Her chest seized. Together, they pushed and pulled her towards a squat wooden building. No! What was happening? Where was General Altos? Struggling futilely against their powerful arms, she looked back.

He stood there, head hanging as the rest of the column dispersed around him. He'd said he'd protect her. But now... Were these men going to violate her now? Pulse throbbing in her ears, she jerked against the men's grip, to no avail.

With her shoulders and head slumped, the Kanin woman standing by the entrance looked even more defeated than the general. She pulled back the animal fur door, the brown outline of a sun tattoo marring her wrist.

The two Bovyans shoved her in.

It was warm and humid compared to the brisk air outside, and dimly lit. Kaiya's heart skittered and her limbs froze up. Was this where she was to suffer a gang rape? She blinked away tears, and the room came into focus.

Steam drifted above a large wooden tub filled with water. The girl from outside—was it the same one, or was this a different girl? In her own panic, Kaiya hadn't noticed, but the body language was the same, screaming of hopelessness.

"They want you to take a bath," the girl said. "Please undress."

Kaiya looked back. The door had closed, the men out of sight. She blew out a long breath. The panic had been for nothing. As General Altos said, her rape would be at the hands of the Consuls themselves. Perhaps even the First Consul. She shuddered. Not that reassuring. Still, they would march her back to Tilésité, which might give her up to two months to preserve her dignity. And perhaps escape.

At least a tiny bit assuaged, she shrugged out of the dress, which the woman took before leaving. Once alone, Kaiya sank into the comforting embrace of the water. It'd been months since her last hot bath, going back to the hot spring inn in Iksuvi. Probably one of the happier times. The warm waters soothed her now.

Maybe it was no different than calming a farm animal before taking it to slaughter. While she soaked, a maid entered, bringing towels and a clean white robe that smelled of honeysuckle. Kaiya rose from the bath and donned the open-faced robe.

As she tied the robe in front, a young woman entered. Her broad features, fair complexion, and dark hair spoke of the Arkothi North. Her right wrist bore a sun tattoo, though unlike the girl's from before, it was filled in. She bowed her head. "Greetings, Your Highness. I need to ask you several questions."

Kaiya's insides quivered, but she nodded. There was little point in fighting.

"When was your last menstrual cycle?"

It shouldn't have been a surprising question, given the Bovyans' abhorrent customs. Still, heat flared in her cheeks. She counted back. "Thirteen days ago, on the new White Moon."

Taking notes, the doctor maintained a professional expression. "Are you having any discharge, like raw egg whites?"

Heaven's Dew. "For two days now."

The doctor's brows furrowed. "Is that normal for you?"

"Always for a few days, before the full White Moon."

"So you are very regular. Please forgive my forwardness. Have you lain with a man recently?"

She nodded. "Two days ago."

Eyebrows clashing together, the doctor searched Kaiya's eyes. Then her expression relaxed. "Thank you. Be strong." With a bow of her head, she turned and left.

What could the doctor's expression mean? It would be months before they'd reach Tilésité, where the Consuls would do the unspeakable to her. If it turned out she was pregnant beforehand, would they force her to drink a poison which would kill Tian's baby? Her belly churned. All sense of relaxation from the bath drained out of her.

Two soldiers came in. Anxiety gripped her heart. Kaiya took deep breaths to calm herself as they bound her hands behind her back.

Flanking either side, they took her to the largest building. Inside, it was octagonal, with knotted wood floors and animal skins covering the windows. The roof slanted upwards on eight sides into a tip. What was this place?

Her focus fell on a throne, perched on a wood dais across from the entrance. A sconce in each of the eight corners held a light bauble. Maybe two dozen Bovyans lined the walls, all eyes

undressing her. Ice crawled up her spine. She pushed her shoulders forward as much as her bound hands would allow, as if it would cover her any better than the robe.

"Kneel." One of the escorts prodded her toward the center of the black octagonal carpet, which covered almost the entire floor.

They would get no satisfaction out of her, at least not without a little resistance. She straightened and lifted her chin.

The other guard shoved her down like a peasant, the plush wool softening the blow to her knees. His heavy hand pressed down on her shoulder as she fought to rise. He was too strong. Exhausted, she gave up the futile struggle and choked up a breath. She stared at the carpet's gold lattice designs so as to focus on something else besides the men's leers.

"Salute!" a soldier by the throne barked.

All the Bovyans thumped a fist against their chest.

She refused to bow, not from a kneeling position. Only the *Tianzi* himself deserved that respect.

The soldier at her side rewarded her defiance by pressing between her shoulder blades, pushing her prostate. She gasped. She tried to straighten herself, but the man was unbelievably strong. Her nervousness and fear quickly gave way to anger.

From the entrance, heavy footsteps approached, stopping right in front of her. Kaiya tried to look up, but whoever it was placed a heavy hand on the top of her head.

Every muscle locked up. All she could see were large, bare feet, right by her face. He seized a handful of hair and jerked her head up. Fire flared in her scalp. Then every nerve went ice cold.

Geros Bovyan, First Consul of the Teleri Directori, glared at her.

Her heart leaped into her throat and she squirmed to back away. Her limbs wouldn't move. There weren't supposed to be any Consuls here. Least of all *him*. The one who'd sworn vengeance. Blood rushed from her head, and her vision dimmed. No, she wouldn't give him the pleasure of seeing her faint.

"Feisty as ever. I cannot help but admire your spirit." He patted her on the cheek before turning and strolling to the dais. Geros was dressed simply in a black, open-faced robe, which rustled as he walked. He lounged back on the throne, exposing a hairy chest.

On his right stood General Altos, still in uniform, his eyes downcast.

Kaiya winced. Geros wasn't supposed to be here. How? She forced herself to take a few deep breaths. Her heart slowed and her thoughts came into focus. Now upright, kneeling with a straight carriage, she returned his glare.

A long-term planner, Geros never expected his moment of vengeance to come so soon. He had left Iksuvius to personally oversee the restoration of the old Kanin roads, thinking the princess was trapped in the south of Iksuvi. Revenge had to be delayed in favor of starting the flow of shipbuilding lumber to his new deep-water port.

Or so he thought.

Geros now looked at the princess, proud but helpless as she knelt before him. No swords, no poison tea, the power of her voice bottled up by the Altivorc King's collar. Despite the image she tried to project, she reeked of fear. He savored the scent.

Her eyes shifted to a spot behind him. Geros had seen it often, when someone hid their intimidation by trying to look through him.

It was easy to shatter that façade.

"It was a surprise to hear you were here in the Wilds. Quite the gamble you took, braving the dangers here." He leaned forward, and her gaze met his. He grinned. "Welcome to our new capital in Kanin."

Her expression remained unchanged. How could she stay so poised?

"But I digress," he continued in a pleasant, contrived voice. "We really do need to catch up. What has it been, six months already since we last met? I love what you've done with your hair."

Still no reaction, save for a shift in her eyes. Was it at General Altos? A childhood friend, a capable man in his inner circle, but weak.

It was time to make the princess squirm, to let her know who controlled the situation. He made his tone threatening, enough to intimidate a Bovyan officer. "You took something of mine. Something valuable. Where is it?"

Her irises darted back and forth, her expression one of genuine confusion.

"The imperial crest. This is the last time I will ask nicely." He tapped the spot where the pin once graced his chest.

The princess remained silent, her face serene, but her hands trembled. Just a girl. A scared girl.

Geros sprung to his feet. He yanked a dagger from the officer at his left and bounded towards her.

Mouth open in a silent scream, she shrank back, her bound hands not finding purchase as she tumbled to the floor.

He was quickly upon her, straddling her stomach. He let his weight sink onto her slight frame, leaving her gasping for air. He grabbed at the lapel of her robe and raised a fist.

She flinched, and he reveled in her terror. Now she knew how *he* had felt, when she left him on the Heights. She turned her head to the side, and her voice came out as a hoarse whisper. "I don't know. I swear, it was lost."

He scowled. "Truly? When do you remember last seeing it?" Shifting his weight off of her, he wrapped a hand around her delicate neck and pulled her into a seated position. Her pulse fluttered beneath his grasp.

"It was here," she stammered. "In the Wilds, about five months ago. We were pursued by ogres."

Geros growled and tightened his grip. "Unbelievable. How could you lose the heirloom of our people? It has been passed down for three hundred years."

Her voice choked. "In the chaos of our escape, I forgot it was even in my possession."

He released his hold on her throat and shoved her onto her back as he rose to his feet. She gulped like a fish out of water.

"We will pursue this later." Stupid ogres. He turned to Altos. "At first light, send word to the ogres, find out when and where they captured this bitch. Our men will burn the forest down, if need be."

The girl struggled to sit up, freezing in place as he turned back to her.

He sat on the edge of the dais, leaning forward with elbows on his knees. "Next order of business. Since you have been gallivanting through the Wilds, I will forgive you for not knowing about my recent promotion."

He waited, taking in her bewildered expression.

"I am now emperor, in need of an empress. And while the Keepers of the Shrine tell me I must keep three dozen concubines pleased, I really only have one woman in mind." He winked at her.

She shuddered.

So satisfying! He grinned. "So quiet. Are you going to make me ask? Very well. I want you to be my consort."

The soldiers shuffled, their discipline lost. Many exchanged glances.

General Altos stepped forward. "Your Eminence, what about your agreement with the Directori and the Keepers? What about the prophecy?"

Geros did not bother to look at the general, quieting him with an open hand. "Silence! I want to hear her answer."

Altos withdrew, and the men straightened. She looked at the floor, her lips quivering.

"If you do not tell me the answer I want to hear by the count of three, I will send orders to Iksuvius to torture and execute all seven hundred and forty-two of your countrymen, women, and children in our custody there. If you agree, they will all be released."

A tear trickled down her cheek.

"One."

Her voice came out, barely louder than a whisper. "Coercing consent and wrapping violation in formality is no less a rape."

Pretty words, deserving a clever response. But not now; this was too much fun. "Two."

The princess slumped, her voice choking. "I have no choice, then."

"Is that a yes?" He leaned forward.

A tear trickled down her cheek. At last, she nodded.

Geros looked around the room, triumphant, pointing an open hand at her. "She accepts!" He strode over, squatted and lifted her chin with his hand. "I am overjoyed. Arrangements will be made tomorrow."

He then leaned in and whispered in her ear. "In Iksuvius, you left me helpless and vulnerable, just as you feel right now." He loosened the lapels of her robe, pulling them down to bare her shoulders as she tried to twist away. "Remember how I told you it was a mistake to leave me alive? What you would expect once I caught you?"

He dug his hands into her soft arms, relishing the fear and despair etched in her beautiful features. "I don't care about your consent. Whether you are my consort or my bed slave, you will suffer the life of fear and humiliation I promised."

CHAPTER 52:

Wild Turkey Island

The dugout journey downriver passed in a haze for Tian. The focus and observational skills he relied on were useless. His stare locked on the muddy waters kicked up by spring melt. On occasion, food would be put in his hands, or some tribesman along the shore would draw his attention with a wave. Otherwise, it was all a blur.

A gigantic cherry tree appeared on the horizon, its trunk as thick as a castle, its canopy vaulting far above even the towering greywoods. A similar tree supposedly grew near the Hua pyramid by Teardrop Lake, but Tian had never seen it himself. The sheer immensity jolted him out of his grief-induced stupor.

How much time had passed? He looked towards the Heavens. The afternoon sun nearly drowned out the Iridescent Moon, which waxed to its second crescent.

He turned to Lana. "How far are we from the island now?"

"Maybe two hours?"

And another four hours until nightfall. Tian tapped his chin. "Let's stop. Before we come within sight of the island. To scout the area out. The White Moon is full tonight. I'll only have a narrow window of opportunity. To penetrate the camp while it's dark."

Lana shook her head, pointing at the enormous tree. "No, when the sun goes down, the tree glows."

Tian favored her with a dubious eye, though he vaguely remembered hearing something about the tree in Hua glowing at night. He would soon find out, either way.

About three *li* away, they came ashore on the north bank of the river and stowed the boat among pink-budded shrubs. Avoiding Teleri patrols, they crept along the bank until they were close enough to observe activity on the island.

Tian pointed them in different directions to get multiple vantage points, and gestured for them to regroup at dusk.

Working his way through the brush, Tian came to a large tree. Its knotted trunk provided handholds and crevices. He slunk up, coming to a high perch with a view of the entire island.

Never before had he seen such an almost perfectly oval island, one-third a *li* wide and one *li* long. The western side bordered a swift-flowing tributary—the same one they'd had followed months ago just before the ogres captured them. Despite the name, there were no signs of turkeys.

The southern end of the island jutted into the North Kanin River, right where the riverbed made a hard turn south. Horns blared from a guard tower that stood atop an almost perfectly circular hill there. It probably provided a commanding view over the entire area, making a daytime insertion difficult.

Ogres led a train of bound Kanin tribespeople over a bridge at the northern tip of the island, which spanned over the tributary to the opposite bank. They wove through the dozens of tribal lodges and newer wooden barracks, and delivered the slaves to the stockade.

Black smoke billowed from two stone buildings, along with hammering that suggested armorers hard at work. Shaki tribesmen fished from the shores, while others rendered large game. Kanin women slaved at roasting the meat over large fire pits. And of course, Bovyans drilled in an open field in the middle of the island. They were holding Kaiya somewhere.

Fists balled tight, Tian shifted his gaze to the eastern bridge near the field, not far from his hiding place on the opposite shore. Narrower than the first, it spanned a strait of slow-moving water. With two guards at the bridge, rotating watches precisely on the phases of the Iridescent Moon, he'd likely have to swim.

When he regrouped with the others, they formulated a plan; one which had little probability of both him and Kaiya surviving. If he found her at all.

Late at night, after activity on the island died down, Tian stripped down to his underwear. Carrying only a dagger and his pouch of tools, he swam through the cold, dark waters of the strait. Though not a religious man, he could not believe it was just luck that storm clouds gathered above, blotting out the full White Moon.

Just as Lana said, tendrils of pale blue light trickled out from the tips of the gigantic tree's buds. Hopefully, it was not enough to expose him during his approach. He paused as he drew closer to the shore, waiting for a patrol to pass. When he gained the bank, he dashed towards a fire pit and covered himself in ash and soot.

Keeping to the shadows, Tian crept over to the cabin where female prisoners were held. A Teleri soldier paced the length of the building's front wall. Tian set himself up around one of the corners.

The Bovyan approached.

Hold the dragonfly with care. No, not tonight. Tian tightened his grip and—

Another solider stumbled out the door.

Relaxing, Tian waited and watched. The two soldiers exchanged greetings and the second ambled off into the camp.

The sentry reached the corner and turned on his heel. Tian stepped behind him, covered his mouth, and slashed his throat. After a quick glance to ensure no other Bovyans were around, he dragged the body inside.

Gasps greeted him. With their faces dimly lit by shuttered light baubles, a few Kanin tribeswomen covered their mouths. Their right wrists were tattooed in a brown outline of the Teleri sun. Their expressions spoke of fear and humiliation. Several others lay asleep on crude beds. To the far right of the entrance, crude animal skins covered four doorways. Behind one came the grunts and whimpering of forced intercourse.

His blood boiled. In all likelihood, it wasn't Kaiya serving the rank and file; it certainly didn't sound like her. Nonetheless, whoever it was deserved nothing less than a painful death.

Tian motioned for the women to stay silent. He pointed to the side rooms and then the dead soldier. Hopefully the women understood him.

The closest put up one finger and pointed at the occupied room.

He made a quick appraisal of each. Glimmers of hope peeked out from expressions of defeat and despair.

In the occupied side room, the sounds stopped. Tian bounded over and waited at the side with dagger in hand. When the Bovyan stepped out, Tian severed his carotid artery while muffling his yelp with his free hand.

A couple of the women sucked in sharp breaths. Luckily, none screamed.

He dragged the body into one of the empty rooms, which reeked of rape. When he emerged, most of the women were awake.

"Have you seen a Cathayi woman?" he asked.

One of the women nodded. "She was brought to the doctor two nights ago."

"Where's the doctor?"

The woman pointed east. "Two lodges over."

"Wake the rest of your sisters. Tell them to prepare to flee. I'll be back soon for you."

Tian ducked out of the cabin and slunk over to the doctor's lodge. Shadows cast by the flickering firelight in the pit indicated one person was awake. Waiting for the silhouette to move closer to the door, he burst inside. In the split second it took him to reach the person's back, he noted nobody else was there. He put a hand over the man's mouth and the dagger at his neck.

"Not a word," he whispered.

His now-rigid hostage nodded. The size and build...it was a woman. Likely another slave.

He spun her around, keeping the blade at her neck. She was...Arkothi, late-twenties, with dark hair and broad but attractive features. "Where is the doctor?"

"I *am* the doctor." Her voice was low and she showed no fear. "Who are you, and what do you want from me?"

Such bravery. And a doctor? Tian stared at her. "Where's the Cathayi woman?"

Her expression deflated. "Kaiya. She is gone. Such a nice girl, poor thing."

"What?"

"She was very fertile when I met her. You know what Emperor Geros did to her."

Emperor Geros? Emperor? Here? Tian's heart squeezed. It was all he could do to draw a breath. "I'm her husband."

The doctor's eyes narrowed at first, then softened. "I'm so sorry. They left yesterday morning by boat, en route to the next fortress downstream. After the threat of snow ends, they plan on taking her along the restored roads eastward, back to Tilésité."

Tian's stomach roiled. He was too late. He jabbed a finger at her. "How can you willingly be part of this?"

She looked down at the ground. "I'm from the city of Mirkos, conquered by the Teleri nearly fifty years ago. My grandmother was a noble there, subjected to the Mating by members of the Teleri Prospecti. After she gave birth and went home, she married someone of her station and my mother was born and suffered the same fate. Later, I was

born. When I was just fourteen, I too was taken by the Teleri." She held up her hand, exposing the nine-pointed sun tattooed in solid brown to her wrist.

Poor woman. Still, there was something she wasn't telling him. Tian stared at her feet.

"Though I never knew them, I have both a Bovyan brother and son somewhere. Maybe my unknown son is still alive after all these years of constant war. I have to hope the Bovyans are not all evil."

No telling who her brother or son had harmed. Tian snorted.

She glared at him. "The circumstances of my Bovyan brother's conception, according to my mother, gives me faith. He will end Tivar's Curse."

Fairy tales. Or rationalization. Tian leveled his gaze at her. "You act a lot on your faith in a story. To me, you are deceiving yourself. You're aiding an evil empire."

Her angry look melted. "My faith was rewarded by a kind Teleri general. As much as I abhor their practices, I came here to serve under that general, to see to the well-being of not just the soldiers, but also the prisoners."

Perhaps she was sincere. He pointed out the door. "I'm going to free those prisoners. Will you help me?"

Her eyes searching his. "Yes. If you can disable the guards at the stockade and women's quarters."

"Those at the women's quarters are taken care of."

She jabbed him in the chest with a finger. "No killing. Meet me by the eastern bridge in ten minutes. Take me hostage, and that will buy the prisoners some time to escape."

She seemed sincere enough. Could he trust her? If she could take a leap of faith about Bovyans, he could do the same for her. Not like there was any other choice, except to kill her now. *Hold the dragonfly with care.* Tian nodded.

Making sure nobody was outside, he snuck back to the women's cabin. All twelve women were prepared to leave.

He handed a woman the dagger from the slain Teleri soldier. "I'm going to free the men. In three minutes, head to the eastern bridge. As quickly and quietly as you can."

After another quick look into the camp, Tian moved on to the stockades and signaled the men inside to keep quiet. He rendered the guard unconscious with an artery block and took his dagger. Finding the key, he unlocked the chain securing the prison door. "Follow me to the eastern bridge. Quickly and quietly."

They didn't meet Tian's standard of quiet. It was such a large group. In the two-minute run to the bridge, horns blared throughout the island.

Near the bridge, two guards were talking with the doctor.

"Guards!" Tian yelled. It was the signal for Ma Jun to neutralize the sentries on his side of the bridge, and would hopefully attract the two guards with the doctor.

It worked. They rushed him, weapons drawn.

Tian flung two daggers, which hit each in the throat. The doctor screamed and ran over to the fallen men.

A voice roared to his left. "Spirits, hear me!"

Tian turned. A Kanin shaman strode towards him from thirty feet away. He held a crystal-headed staff in hand.

Only one dagger left, and no other choice but to use it on what could be a major threat. Taking the doctor hostage would have to wait. He charged, dagger ready to throw.

The shaman pounded the butt end of his staff into the ground. "Open the clouds!"

The storm clouds above flashed, and a bolt of lightning shot down towards Tian. Even a Paladin's superhuman reflexes wouldn't save him against the speed of nature. Yet the electricity sizzled and dissipated around him.

Tian stopped in his tracks, stunned but unharmed.

If he was surprised, the shaman looked even more so. His mouth stood agape, his eyes wide. Tian resumed his charge, coming within

fifteen feet. He hurled his weapon, just as the shaman raised his staff.

Instead of a chant, nothing but a muffled groan came out as the shaman staggered back, clawing at the dagger lodged in his ribs.

Tian scanned the area to reassess the situation. Prisoners flooded over the bridge, pursued by several Teleri soldiers. Horns shrieked, rousing the camp out of sleep. He picked the doctor out of the crowd—she still crouched over the fallen men, pressing on their wounds.

He bolted over to her, and she stood up with a bloody dagger in hand. Tears glassed over her eyes. "Why did you do this? We had a deal."

Tian shook his head. "No time to think. No other way to free the prisoners." Would she still play along with being taken hostage? He'd soon find out.

Her eyes darted behind him, and she clumsily stabbed at him.

Tian caught her arm, twisted it behind her back and swiped the blade away. He then turned to face the approaching Teleri, backing his way towards the bridge with the point of the weapon to her throat. Waiting until the last prisoner passed, he retreated to the middle of the bridge and stopped. The Teleri soldiers followed, keeping their distance. They stopped about ten feet from him.

Tian pointed the tip at them. "Bring your leader."

The Bovyans discussed his demand among themselves, but before they said anything, a handsome man, taller than the other soldiers, approached. His unbuttoned white shirt exposed firm muscles and his pants hung unbelted at his hips.

"I am General Altos, and I command this camp. Release the doctor."

Tian smiled tightly. "Only if you agree to let the prisoners go and to never take any more."

The general's lips pursed. "You know I cannot agree to such terms. However, release her and I will give the prisoners a one-hour start."

Tian shook his head. "Wait until first light."

"Very well." The officer nodded. "We are agreed. We would have a hard time tracking them in this dark night anyway."

"Back off to the island, and I will send the doctor across. If you show any signs of trickery, I will throw this dagger into her back."

"You have my word. We will not pursue the prisoners until daybreak."

"Nonetheless, back off the bridge." Tian repeated.

The general retreated, motioning his men with him.

"Thank you," he whispered into her ear. He pushed the doctor forward and let her get about thirty feet in front of him—about the maximum accurate range of his dagger—then followed her to stay in range. Once she reached the island, he turned and broke into a run towards the other side.

"Now, now!" he yelled.

On the opposite bank, Lana chanted. A deafening roar rumbled from upstream, and the bridge shook as the waters swelled beneath it. Tian teetered over the planks, his balance just barely keeping him from being pitched into the rushing waters in the strait below. The less agile Teleri soldiers, running behind him, lost their balance.

On the other end, Ma Jun and the twins waited in the dugout, and Lana was just climbing in. Tian leaped aboard, right as the deluge picked it up and carried it downstream.

Ma Jun stared in awe at his wife. "I didn't realize that your tie to the spirits was so strong."

"It was the island itself," she answered. "This is where our ancestor relearned the way of the spirits, when the lights of the Tree guided him here during the Long Winter. His invoking of the spirits began the transformation of the barren farmland around. The forest reseeded and grew at an accelerated pace. All shamans used to make a pilgrimage here, because the spirits speak louder here than anywhere else on the plateau."

Tian looked back towards the island, the sparkling tree above it disappearing in the distance. "I wonder why their shaman's lightning strike did not affect me."

Lana cocked her head, her eyebrows furrowed. When she spoke, she didn't seem convinced, herself. "At night, when the Tree lights up, the spirits cannot go under its canopy."

Tian nodded. However, he hadn't been under the canopy when the lightning struck.

Back on the island, General Altos looked over his assembled staff, his heart beating with excitement. "Get the Shaki to track the Cathayi. I need him captured alive."

The Doctor Myra turned to him, her hand over her mouth. "General, you have never gone back on your word! Were you not going to give him until daybreak?"

Altos was surprised that she would question him in front of his men, but grinned nonetheless. "I gave the *prisoners* until daybreak." He then turned to one of his officers. "Send word to all of our outposts, base camps and fortresses: the Cathayi man has the Teleri Imperial Crest."

Myra leaned in. "He is the one who slept with the princess before Emperor Geros."

Altos jerked his head back. "If she's pregnant, and Geros raises a non-Bovyan as his own..."

CHAPTER 53:

Impossible Mission

Tian looked up as the storm clouds parted, allowing columns of sunlight to shine through after days of continual rain. Though Lana's invocation of the spirits had transformed the downpour into a drizzle, the boat ride was far from pleasant. Each night, they camped on the eastern side of the river, to avoid the Teleri soldiers marching up and down the west bank.

Late on the fourth day after their escape from Wild Turkey Island, they turned a bend in the river. A massive tower rose high above the sweet evergreens, looming larger and larger as dugout approached. The bridge arching across the river was so big, Tian could see it from many *li* upstream. As they drifted closer, it became apparent the tower and bridge were all part of one massive fortress.

The one where the Bovyans held Kaiya, at least according to the doctor. Tian's every nerve stood on end. If they could see the tower, then anyone there with a dwarf scope could see them. Clearly.

They brought the dugout ashore on the east bank, far from the fort. Finding a dirt trail with no signs of human use, they hiked the rest of the way under the cover of the canopy. The path rose along a gradual slope, eventually opening up onto a thirty-foot-wide corridor through the forest. A broad road paved in stone ran through it.

Tian peeked around a tree. The road connected to the bridge, which in turn led into the fortress. Along the sides, slaves cut down trees, hauled lumber, and worked on the roads. Shaki hunters carried game back. Bovyans marched in formation to and from the fort. If the wilderness had claimed the stone roads after the Hellstorm, it looked like the Teleri were taking them back.

Across the river, the fortress looked like a feat of engineering. It sat atop an embankment the height of three men, on a peninsula formed by the bend of the river. A log palisade, twelve feet tall, encircled the mound. The single entrance, connected to the bridge and flanked by two guard towers, sat at a height of fifteen feet above the river.

Tian looked up. Though it was hard to tell from the lower vantage point, the central keep rose about three stories high, with a towering greywood growing out of the center. Wooden steps circled up and around the trunk, leading to a lookout post near the top, under its canopy.

The forest beyond the palisade had been cut down in a one-*li* radius, and the few small buildings in the clearing would provide little cover if someone tried to approach from that side of the river. It didn't look promising.

Tian looked among the men, evaluating. Ma Jun and the twins, Kosa and Kona, could fight, and Fang Weiyong could help tend their wounds. None would be helpful for scouting out the fortress interior, and it would be suicide to storm it.

He turned to Lana. "I need to find out about the inside of the fort. Most importantly, if Kaiya is there. Can the spirits do anything to help?"

Lana withdrew her talisman, a bright blue river rock, polished by time. "Spirits, hear me," she whispered. "Summon the eyes and ears of the forest to do my bidding."

Eyes and ears of the forest? Tian looked around, blanking his expression to hide his doubt.

Birds, squirrels, and other small animals trickled in by foot and wing, their chattering growing to crescendo.

Lana squatted down and smiled. "My little friends, tell me about the house over the river." She gestured toward the Hua. "Please find out if there is a female like these men inside."

Tian suppressed a snort. Most humans had a hard time differentiating between Hua and Kanin. How would a stupid animal tell?

Lana narrowed a critical eye at him. Were his thoughts that obvious? "A bird of prey can pick out a squirrel in a tree branch from high in the sky. The squirrel can sense the bird. Do not underestimate my friends."

The animals all glared at him. Tian placed his right hand over his heart in apology.

With more chattering, they scattered off towards the fortress.

After sending Ma Jun and Lana to survey the road, and assigning Fang Weiyong to watch the river, Tian and the twins climbed sweet evergreen trees to get a better view of what lay beyond the palisade. What he saw made the prospect of attack all the more daunting.

Besides the guarded entrance from the bridge on the east, there was another entrance on the western side, from which the stone road continued. The main keep appeared to be made partially of living trees, with horizontal log walls covered by dried mud. Soldiers milled around barracks, while slaves came and went from another large building. Kitchens, warehouses, a smithy, and a lumber mill all stood within the palisade walls.

Tian pictured the map in his mind. Right now, they were about one thousand, eight hundred *li* from the Teleri border, less than six hundred *li* from Hua. If at least some of what the Shaki guide said had been true, another outpost stood west of here, even closer to Hua. These old roads, which the Teleri worked hard to restore, must connect several fortresses so that the empire could project their power into the Wilds.

How long had the Bovyans been here? How had they built up the infrastructure so quickly, especially with so much of their attention focused on the Eldaeri kingdoms and Arkothi states in the Northeast? With Hua's distance from Teleri, their threat had never seemed imminent. Perhaps First Consul Geros truly was the genius the stories portrayed him to be.

Tian swallowed his sigh. Hua could no longer be content in its neutrality, resting secure behind its walls while promoting trade to fatten its own coffers. Beyond the practical need to maintain its own security, there was also a moral obligation to take a stand and choose a side. Being a member of the Maki, even for this brief time, had taught him that.

Yet to convince the *Tianzi* and the *Tai-Ming* nobles would be an entirely different matter. Perhaps Heaven had willed for the Teleri to capture their beloved princess, to wake them out of their complacency.

The vision from his last night in the village flared in his memory. The words on the ground in his dream were *accept fate*. Was he meant to accept this, the kidnapping and rape of the only woman he'd ever loved? Were they to make this sacrifice so that others would learn?

He tightened his hand around a tree branch. No. Forget Heaven, forget fate. He'd make his own destiny.

Night fell, and activity died down in and around the fortress. The group reassembled back at the dugout and used the cover of darkness to pass beneath the great bridge. Reaching the other side, and following the river as it bent west beside the fortress, they set up camp in the woods.

"I estimate their fortress can hold three thousand soldiers," Tian said.

"There are hundreds of our own people as well," Kona added.

Lana shook her head. "I can't imagine how horrible they must feel, forced to cut down the trees."

"Even if the tribes united, they couldn't take this fort," Kosa said.

Kona nodded. "And the rumors say there are other fortresses like this one throughout the plateau."

Tian tried to keep the agitation out of his voice. "Its defenses are daunting. Even if I had a layout of the main keep. Even if I knew where Kaiya was being held. I'm not sure I could get her out. Let's sleep on it, find out what Lana's forest friends learn."

Tian didn't sleep well. His thoughts were on Kaiya.

The next morning, Lana related what the forest animals had told her: a Cathayi woman was staying in a third-floor room on the northern side of the main fortress.

At least Kaiya was close. Still, she was beyond his reach, at least with the resources at hand.

Tian withdrew Chen Xin's ring, bowed his head to it, and pressed it into Fang Weiyong's hand. "Take the boat down the river to the East Gate of Hua. Show the ring to the imperial garrison. Inform them of our situation. Have a message delivered to the capital. Asking for twelve *Moquan*."

"*Moquan*?" Fang Weiyong raised an eyebrow.

Tian frowned. "Just do it. Take Lana with you so that she can guide you back to us. It will take a week for you to get there by boat. Two weeks to return by foot, at best. If there's any change in the situation, I will leave a message on this tree that my brothers-in-arms will understand."

Fang Weiyong nodded, though his pursed lips made clear what he thought of the plan.

As long as he did what he was told. Tian turned to the others. "In the meantime. We'll learn as much as we can. About the fortress and surroundings."

After the doctor and Lana pushed off, Tian sent Kona and Kosa east down the river to investigate the progress of the road, while Ma Jun watched the entrance. He, himself, scouted out the strengths and weaknesses of the fortress.

Over the next few days, he noted that several tribes besides the Shaki had allied themselves with the Teleri. All wore unfamiliar clothing styles and face paint, but they clearly served in support roles: as trackers, hunters, and archers. The slave overseers among them were lazy, and on the third day, Tian isolated a pair of Maki slaves sent to fell a tree.

He greeted them with a right hand in his open left, and spoke in their dialect. "I am Tian. From Swiftrun Village. Who are you?"

They gawked at him. "The Warrior From Beyond The Wall," one said. "I am Nala, from Blackhawk Village."

The other furrowed his brows.

Tian pointed toward the fort. "Is it true that a Cathayi woman was brought here?"

Nala bobbed his head. "Yes, the Willow Beauty. She arrived several days ago with the Metal Man chief."

"The chief?" Likely First Consul Geros himself. Tian clenched his fists.

"Yes, but different from other chiefs. He never leaves the main fort. The maids say he's always with the Cathayi girl."

Tian's face flushed hot. Damn Geros. He would die horribly. "Which tribes help the Metal Men?"

Nala clenched his fists. "The Pomaki from the west. The Lahoki and Shaki from the east, and the Komaki from the south. All made deals with the Metal Men."

Someone speaking a Kanin dialect yelled from the distance. "Hey! You lazy Maki get back to work!"

Tian backed into the trees. "Thank you. I will try my best to free you. In the meantime, please find a way to tell the Cathayi woman I am here."

Tian wasn't sure if the Maki passed his message on. He continued with his surveillance nonetheless. It was hard to fight the urge to go find Kaiya, but information could improve his chances of success. Thousands of Bovyans arrived from the east and departed west along the road. Undoubtedly they were building strength closer to Hua. Delegations of many of the Teleri-allied tribes arrived on the twenty-first day of the month, and left two days later.

By then, he'd learned the patterns for the changing of the guards, sending out patrols, mess times, and slave routines. The eastern wall, facing the river, was the least guarded... probably because the slope up to the palisade and river provided formidable defense against an attack.

Confident in this knowledge, Tian tried a few dry runs during the night, to see if he could get in unnoticed. The most daunting obstacle was trying to swim across the river, whose current flowed strong with snow melt.

Instead, he climbed under the bridge inverted, then landed on the narrow bank on the eastern side of the fortress. He crept to the south and found the earthen ramparts easy to negotiate. At the top, his cat-claws made scaling the palisade manageable. After two nights of experimenting, he was finally in. Still, as dexterous as she was, Kaiya would never be able to do the same.

It had been five days since the others had departed. If all went well, a team of *Moquan* would be there to assist him in two weeks.

The next day the twins returned, reporting that the restored roads stretched west for at least another three-day march, if not more. They witnessed plenty of activity, with slaves cutting down trees and dumping them into the river, and heavy infantry marching down the road.

For each of the next three nights, Tian infiltrated the fortress, identifying hiding places and locating potential access points to the main keep itself. There was just one entrance, facing south, flanked at all times by guards. The windows were all too small for him to fit through—if only Jie were around, she could squeeze in some of the upper windows.

On the second-to-last night of the twelfth month, the small sliver of the White Moon threw the fortress into darkness. Tian took advantage of the dark and scaled the western outer walls of the central keep to investigate the roof. With sixteen guards circling along the perimeter, he didn't climb all the way up, but instead peeked over the edge. Open space surrounded the single greywood tree tower protruding from the center of the building. Stairs spiraled down the tree to...another entrance. A way in, if only he could get by the sentries... Impossible without a diversion.

If Lana's forest friends were right, Kaiya was close. On Tian's descent, he edged across the third floor, listening at each fur-covered window he passed. The sonorous sounds suggested large, sleeping men.

Arms aching and listless, he somehow rounded the corner to the fort's north face. Fifteen window slots were spaced ten feet apart. If she wasn't in one of those rooms, his energy wouldn't last long enough to find her.

Heavy wooden slats blocked the twelfth window. The thick fur cover muffled the sounds inside, but...yes! Kaiya's familiar breathing. He reached between the slats—

Wood furniture creaked in rhythmic screeches. Geros Bovyan's voice, husky in a loud whisper, professed his love for Kaiya. Her heavy breaths sounded wrong in his ears.

Rage boiled in Tian's head. His foot slipped from one of the crevices, with only the cat-claws on his hands keeping him from falling. Kaiya was suffering. The man who caused it needed to die. Slowly, painfully. His vision dimmed at the edges.

Years of training brought his immediate impulses under control. His foot found purchase. Logically, what could he do? He had no leverage to break the heavy wooden bars, no way to slip in even if he could get past the slats. Anything he did now would just get him killed and leave Kaiya helpless at the rapist's hands.

No. His only recourse was to climb down and move far enough away that other noises would drown out the terrible sounds crushing his heart. Only then could he think clearly.

He fled the fortress as quickly as he could, trying to banish the memories of Kaiya's humiliation still echoing in his head. Muttering a terse greeting to Kosa and Kona, he climbed a tree to be alone with his thoughts.

After this foray into the fortress, two things were clear: even if he could break in, he wasn't sure how he could escape with her; and if Fang Weiyong had reached Hua in eight days, he would still have to wait another two weeks for reinforcements. Too long. And maybe still not enough resources to free Kaiya.

Though his strategic intelligence told him there was zero chance of success on his own, his impulse said otherwise. Tomorrow night, he would go in alone.

CHAPTER 54:

Realizations and Confessions

Kaiya was late. She was never late. Always as accurate as a dwarf-made clock, her monthly cycle reliably started when she woke the day of the new White Moon.

She'd looked forward to the debilitating cramps this morning, hoping it would provide her a temporary reprieve from the daily violations at Geros' hands. Now its failure to appear raised new fears.

What had Doctor Wu told her? *From when the flood waters receded, until about two weeks after it began, Heaven's dew would allow a seed to find fertile ground?* If only she'd listened more carefully instead of drowning out the graphic details. She counted off the days. Nineteen days since last making love to Tian. Eighteen since she surrendered to the Teleri. Sixteen since the emperor had taken her for the first time.

She choked back bile at the thought of Geros' calloused hands. Sitting on a soft bed in a narrow room, Kaiya brought her knees to her chest and wrapped herself tightly in her arms. A tear trickled unheeded down her cheek.

When her ordeal had begun, she'd forced herself into a state of denial, tried to emotionally numb herself to the humiliation of his assault.

It didn't work.

His insatiable lust dragged her down into depression. She considered throwing herself from the top of the fortress; but a bird came back day after day and sang to her. Its song perked her spirits up and gave her some resolve.

On several occasions, Teleri generals prodded Geros to go oversee construction of the next fortress downstream—one which would put them uncomfortably close to Hua, if her poor map skills were even a little accurate. She had to keep him here.

Without the power of her voice, all she had were her body and wiles. Like the tale of Lady Lanyu, concubine of a warlord during Hua's Warring States Period. He'd sent her to a rival king, ostensibly to seal an alliance. Really, it had been to break his enemy's focus as he became besotted with the girl. Still, a little part of Kaiya died each time she pretended to have fallen in love with the vile monster.

Then, word from a Kanin slave girl that the Warrior From Beyond the Wall was outside the fortress gave her a glimmer of optimism.

That was nine days ago. With each passing day, her hope guttered. Perhaps she'd have to keep up the act for the rest of her life.

The all-too-familiar sound of Geros' booted steps approached from down the hall. He only came to the third level to visit her.

A stifling sensation in her chest seized her breath. She rose from the bed and stumbled to the window for air. Outside, the first colorful buds began peeking out from the branches of trees and shrubs. In the past, these heralds of spring had made her happy. Now they were a reminder of this prison.

A lighter set of footsteps caught up to Geros.

"Your Eminence, Captain Miris in Fortress Ten expects you tomorrow. It is a one-week march."

She glanced back at the door. A week's journey from here must be at the Hua border. If only she was better with maps.

Geros' voice sounded bored. "Then I will take swifthorses after lunch and be there tonight."

"Your Eminence...certainly you know the road restoration and horse relays only reach Fortress Eight so far."

Kaiya frowned. From what she'd gathered, they were now at Fortress Nine.

"The captain is a smart man. I am sure he can build a fortress without me looking over his shoulder." His footsteps resumed, stopping right outside the door.

Shuddering, she turned back to the window.

The door swooshed open behind her.

He came up behind her and wrapped her in an embrace. With supreme effort, she kept every muscle in her body from locking up. He kissed the back of her head and turned her around, almost gently.

Kaiya composed her most adoring expression, and hated herself for doing so. "Your Eminence."

His voice was tender. "My love..."

Her stomach lurched into her throat, leaving a sour taste. Did he believe his words? To think, this might've been her fate had she gone through with marriage to Lord Tong in Wailian, three years ago.

He continued, "I was told your lunch was coming up soon, but I figured you might want an appetizer."

Kaiya winced. His idea of an appetizer was the reason she had no interest in food. Today, though... "Your Eminence, as much as I hunger for you, I cannot. Not today."

His eyebrows smashed together and his faced flushed red. He pressed himself against her. "What do you mean? Why not?"

She pushed herself back against the wall. She swallowed the fear choking her words. "I have good news, Your Eminence. I....my.... I am with child..." Was she? Hopefully, it wasn't... "Your child."

He staggered back, as if struck by a physical blow—one that didn't hurt, but caused confusion. His angered expression relaxed and his tone softened. "Are you sure?"

"You know there was no one else." She acted demure, casting her gaze at the floor. He'd either ignored or forgotten what the doctor on Wild Turkey Island had told him. "He will be third in line for the Dragon Throne of Cathay."

Geros turned toward the door. He paused and looked back. "A doctor will be visiting you shortly. You had better be telling the truth."

Kaiya shuddered again. She went to the washbasin to scrub where he had touched her, as if doing so would wash away his odor, which lingered in her imagination.

Before long, a middle-aged Arkothi man came and asked several questions. When was her last cycle, when her next one was due, when had she lain with the emperor, was she experiencing certain symptoms.

Though leaving out any mention of Tian, she answered honestly, wanting to know the result as much as Geros. After he finished taking notes, she asked, "Am I with child?"

The doctor's mouth shut like a trap and he rushed out the door.

Ill at ease, she turned back to the window, hand over her belly. Please let it be Tian's seed that had taken root in her. How devastating it would be to carry the spawn of a depraved rapist.

Presently, Geros' heavy steps approached, more rapidly than usual. He burst into the room, bounded across the floor and wrapped his huge arms around her.

Again, she fought to keep from shrinking in his embrace.

He then released her and leaned back. "Kaiya, I am so overwhelmed by the news. Despite the many sons that I must have sired, I never expected to know any of them, lost as they must be among the hundreds of Prospecti. I can describe the feeling as nothing short of joy, a joy that we will have a son together. I will see to it that he will rule Cathay and Teleri. Sharing our blood, he will be a strong emperor, ensuring the peace and order I have worked so hard to establish."

The man was delusional. Kaiya forced back a tear. How ironic. Her brothers' wives had both gone years of trying without success to conceive an heir to Hua. She'd spent a week out of every month consoling them as their disappointment dragged on.

Now, she might carry the product of rape, who might very well become a pawn in the occupation and subjugation of her nation. Her countrywomen would share her fate, forced to endure violation, only to bear more tools of Teleri conquest.

Heavens, let it be Tian's.

Tian spent the day alone in a tree, mentally walking through his rescue plan. It wasn't really much of a plan, with too many uncertainties and variables. Had the memories of the previous night not haunted him, he'd never even consider it. Some Architect he was.

Late in the afternoon, he came down from the tree to discuss his strategy with Ma Jun and the twins. They all hovered around as he sketched a layout of the fortress grounds.

Tian pointed at the bridge. "I'm going to attempt the rescue tonight. Through here. Before the Blue Moon rises. With the new White Moon, it will be dark."

Kosa clapped his hands in excitement. "Did you scout out the interior of the main keep last night?"

Tian shook his head. "No, but I know exactly where she's held. There's an access point on the roof."

Ma Jun's jaw dropped. "How do you plan on getting the princess down from the rooftop,

assuming you can actually get her out of her room?"

"Not from the roof. I'll take her out through the entrance."

Ma Jun's eyes and mouth widened. "You haven't even been inside the fort. Even if you get her out unseen, she can't climb under the bridge like you."

So much for the man's infectious optimism. Tian leveled his gaze at him. "That's where I'll need your help. You and the twins will create a diversion here at the eastern gate. It'll hopefully draw the garrison's attention to you. I'll take her out the back."

Ma Jun glared at him. "Hopefully? There are too many uncertainties. When the *Tianzi* ordered us to accept the *Moquan* as adjunct protection for his family, he assured us you were meticulous. This doesn't give me confidence." He had slipped into the Hua tongue, but even Kosa and Kona looked at Tian with creased foreheads.

Tian jabbed a finger at Ma Jun. "We can't wait for word from Hua. They're two weeks away. Every day Kaiya is imprisoned, a part of her is dying."

Ma Jun shook his head. "I don't want you to risk yourself, but it *is* your life to throw away. However, I can't let you risk the princess."

Had their roles been reversed, Tian would've agreed. Nonetheless, he couldn't let Kaiya suffer another day at the emperor's hands. He turned to Kona and Kosa. They idolized him and would accede to his requests regardless of what they thought of the plan. "I want you to—"

"Ma Jun is right," a female voice said. A familiar voice.

Tian spun around, looking left and right to find the source, one which could not possibly be there.

Jie.

Jie launched herself into Tian's chest, wrapping her arms around him as they tumbled to the ground.

She'd followed the Kanin tribeswoman, her heart racing at the imminent reunion with Tian. She admired how Lana could speak some of the Hua language. Even more impressive was the shaman's ability to pick her way through the forest, barely making a sound.

Meanwhile, Jie had constantly stepped on a hidden twig or dry leaf. Maybe the enemy would think it was a rabbit.

Lana had dropped into a crouch, and Jie froze. When the shaman beckoned, Jie crept up to her side. There, in a small clearing, squatted Tian, Ma Jun, and two Kanin boys.

Her heart had nearly leaped out of her chest. She started toward the clearing—

Tian and Ma Jun were bickering. And with just cause. Tian's plan was idiotic, something she would've expected of...well, nobody was *that* careless.

Now, she lifted her head and looked into his eyes, trying to read his blank expression. Feeling the weight of the stares around her, she picked herself up and helped Tian to his feet. When she spoke, her voice sounded too husky in her ears. "Zheng Tian, I thought you'd died."

He flashed a grin, but it seemed forced. "I'm glad to see you are alive and well, too. My plan can't fail with the two of us."

What? Someone deserved a painful reminder—

Tian opened his mouth to continue, but knowing what he'd ask and wanting him to *see* the answer, Jie cut him off. "Were you hit on your head so hard that you can't see the holes in that ridiculous plan? I never thought an imperial guard would have more sense than a *Moquan*."

Tian shrugged. "It'll have twice as much a chance of succeeding now that you are here."

Something was wrong about his demeanor. Her stomach hollowed. This was not how their reunion was supposed to be, even with a princess to rescue.

Ma Jun disentangled himself from Lana's embrace and pulled Tian aside. He leaned in and whispered, though Jie's elf ears heard it all.

"Neither Weiyong nor Lana told anyone in Hua the whole story. That is between the two of you. But you can't let your emotions get in the way of objectivity. It's one thing to risk your own life, it is something entirely different to risk all ours."

What was that all about? Jie sucked on her lower lip.

Tian looked up. His distraught, almost guilty expression settled into a *Moquan* blankness as his eyes met Jie's. "I think the two of us can do it."

"We have more assets a few *li* away, and I have a better plan. Follow me." She nodded towards Lana. "Or rather, follow her."

Tian trailed behind Jie in silence for a half-phase, remembering all the things that were left unsaid in the haste of the escape from Iksuvius half a year before. Had their mutual feelings been clarified, perhaps things would have turned out differently. But now, Jie's magnetism no longer pulled on him. That attraction, no matter how brief, now transformed into guilt.

He started to confess, but other words spilled out instead. "How did you escape Iksuvius?"

Jie glanced over her shoulder, her expression speaking of a silent hurt. "The Teleri destroyed the embassy, killed most of the staff and imperial guard." She cast Ma Jun a sympathetic eye. "They rounded up all the Hua residents and imprisoned them."

All those comrades, killed. And Tian had left Jie there.

"Then," she continued, "the *Tianzi* sent a dozen ships to blockade the coast. I took the fastest ship back to Hua with word of the princess' escape into the Wilds. Search parties embarked on futile forays into the plateau, but heavy snow forced the *Tianzi* to call the search off for the winter."

Tian nodded. "They would've stumbled on Teleri fortresses before they found us."

Jie shrugged. "They would've resumed their search tomorrow, but the embassy doctor and his guide delivered the news of the princess' capture two days ago. In the meantime, your brother Zheng Ming mobilized three thousand soldiers. They're heading this way."

Of course. Dashing Eldest Brother would volunteer to swoop in and save the princess. From the East Gate of Hua, they were two weeks away. Still too far, given Tian's urgency. But if they were two weeks away, "How did you—"

They stepped out into a meadow. Tian's unasked question was answered as he gaped at the five enormous birds resting there. The Hua called them *Difeng*, with some foreign cultures erroneously naming them phoenixes. With a wingspan of thirty feet, they were a fourth the size of the even rarer true phoenixes, known as *Tianfeng*.

They had heads that resembled pheasants, but a peacock tail. Their legs were long and taloned like cranes, while their wings were much like swallows. Their brightly colored gold-and-silver feathers sparkled in the sunlight.

Tian sucked in a breath. Eight lived in the imperial aviary, and came out for the New Year's processions. Besides female members of the royal family, only a handful of female imperial guards were trained to ride them. They hadn't been used in times of war since the *Tianzi*'s ancestor reunified Hua nearly three hundred years before.

Five women in the regalia of the imperial guard tended to the birds, pausing to greet Ma Jun with a right first in their left palm. Two other women wearing *Moquan* utility suits took stock of weapons and equipment. A similarly-dressed boy of no more than twelve years worked among them.

Jie went over to a saddle on the ground. "I brought you presents." She withdrew his curved *dao* sword, a black utility suit, and a bandolier of small throwing weapons. "You left these in Iksuvius, and I couldn't bear to imagine Bovyan paws on them."

Hefting the sword, Tian gazed at the phoenixes with a curious eye.

As always, Jie seemed to read his thoughts. "The *Tianzi* wanted his sister rescued as soon as possible. We knew you wanted a team of twelve brothers, but only five of the eight phoenixes were deemed fit to fly under the conditions. Weight also affects their range, so I picked three of the lightest *Moquan* to join in. We can send the imperial riders back and have another five of us within four days. Zheng Ming's troops are two weeks away, but there is also a fortress under construction halfway between here and Dongmen which may slow them down."

Tian shook his head. "We can't wait that long."

Jie narrowed her eyes at him. "Can five of us do it?"

Ma Jun also glared at him, his expression answering, *no.*

"We have to try." Tian sighed. Ma Jun's silent objection was right. Tian lacked objectivity and needed someone with fresh eyes.

He motioned for Jie to follow him back into the woods, dreading what he had to tell her. Ma Jun and Lana both offered him sympathetic smiles.

Out of sight and earshot of the others, he turned around to face his long-time friend and almost-lover, afraid she'd throw herself into his arms before he could open his mouth.

He didn't have to worry.

She stood at an angle, her eyes at the ground. "I concede our chess match. Your queen was in too strong a position. It's written in the expressions of your friends, and even your expression speaks louder than words."

The hurt in her voice yanked at Tian's heart. He'd betrayed his duty, betrayed his best friend. He hung his head, contrite. "Then you know why I need you now. The First Consul is doing horrible things to her. I heard it myself. All I can do is think about how much I need to free her." And kill him.

Jie didn't answer, and he looked up to meet her scathing glance. It hurt worse than any sword cut. He wouldn't blame her if she refused to help.

The half-elf let out a sigh. "I would like to believe the princess is my friend, and it's my duty to protect her where you couldn't. Come back and share what you know about their defenses with the rest of the team. Know that I will not risk the lives or virtue of the women in my charge unless there is a good chance of success."

Among the others, Tian was meticulous in his details: the position of buildings, the timing of the guard changing, their posts, when Kanin tribesmen were coming and going. The *Moquan* and imperial guards asked questions and provided input; Lana volunteered her tie to the spirits.

Jie's solution was simple.

CHAPTER 55:

Confrontations

With no indication of any weather besides clear skies, Jie gawked at Lana's invocation of the spirits. Clouds rolled in and blotted out the stars, and even the soft light of the Iridescent Moon. Thick fog billowed at ground level, to a height of a dozen feet. None of that affected her elf vision's ability to see either the sixteen soldiers circling the fortress roof, or the two guards in the crow's nest.

She looked behind her. Tian's phoenix lagged behind, burdened by his weight. Yet one more reason he was worthless.

Jie shook the bitterness out of her head. There were more important things to take care of. Like capturing the crow's nest.

The large guards there leaned against the tree, neither taking their duties seriously. Her superior hearing allowed her to discern the two men's conversation over the rushing wind.

"The emperor has been here a long time," the first said in a low whisper.

"Yes, he's too preoccupied with the Cathayi princess."

"Amazing to think the distinguished Emperor Geros, the greatest leader in our history, has lost his focus because of a woman."

"He spends so much time with her. What if the prophecy comes to pass?"

Jie signaled her rider with a tap on her shoulder, and the woman withdrew a bow from the saddle and nocked an arrow.

"Bah! Prophecies are fairy tales, meant to keep us in line."

"But—"

Jie opened the shutter of a light bauble lamp for a split second, spotlighting the guards. The man never had a chance to finish his sentence, as an arrow lodged in his throat. Several other arrows followed from different angles, felling the second before he could react.

Jie patted the rider's back, admiring her ability to shoot from a flying mount. Even more amazing was how she guided the phoenix into a smooth landing on the rail of the crow's nest. In short order, the others joined them, with Tian coming last.

The five *Moquan* dropped soundlessly to the platform, followed by the five lithe riders. As planned, Jie motioned for the latter to stay, while the rest darted down the stairs wrapping around the tree trunk.

She gauged the distance from the rooftop entrance to the sixteen soldiers circling the perimeter—too many to take out before they could raise an alarm. She passed the message with a series of pats on the sister behind her.

Quiet as death, they bypassed those guards altogether, instead continuing downwards into the fortress and onto the landing of the third floor.

The landing opened into a hallway, and Jie peered out. The interior light globes were shuttered at this late hour, leaving the corridor barely lit by a window at the end of the hall.

Her elf sight barely made out a blurry shape about sixty feet away to her right. His breathing capacity implied a large man, almost certainly Bovyan given the circumstances.

She extended a leg into the hall and placed her foot gingerly on the floor. Hardwood. She gradually shifted her weight onto it to test the sound. Firm, no squeaks.

She reached back and tapped Tian. The series of signals would let him know about the guard. If his brain wasn't too addled by love, he'd pass the order for the others to continue with their plan: the two women were to continue down to guard the stairwell on the second-floor landing, while the boy would hold his position on the third floor.

Jie crept towards her victim. He showed no signs of noticing her presence, and when she was close enough, she covered his mouth and slashed his throat with a curved dagger. The man crumpled to the floor.

She waited until the body went limp before removing her hand.

On her tactile signal, Tian moved to the door and ran skilled hands over it. He reached back and tapped her arm. *Locked. Can't see.*

She produced her magical light, cupping it carefully in her hands so that only a small sliver shone on the door handle's plate. They worked so well together, like the gears of a dwarf clock.

Tian removed his lockpick pouch and withdrew a tool. His hands trembled, causing the pick to scrape with a light sound.

Jie rolled her eyes. Taking the deceptively heavy pouch from him, she felt for the correct tool. With an expert twist, the lock yielded in her hands, and she gently pressed the door to test the hinges. The tremor on the door suggested they were well-oiled. She silently pushed the door open.

Tian slid in without a sound, while Jie stood guard at the doorway, wondering what to do with the body.

The room was almost pitch black, but Tian heard someone breathing. He knew the pattern. Kaiya. Heart racing with excitement and joy, he glided over and knelt by her bed. He put one hand over her mouth and another over her wrist.

Kaiya gasped in surprise and started to struggle.

"Shhhhhh. It's me," he whispered.

She sucked in a breath and sobbed. Sitting up, she wrapped her arms around him, her slim shoulders shaking against his body, her hot tears warm on his chest. Her hand rose to his face, which was covered by his mask.

He pulled down the mask and pressed his cheek into her forehead. Her suffering, the result of his decisions. He leaned in and whispered in her ear, "I'm so sorry. I'm so sorry to have put you through this."

She only shuddered. He stroked her hair, trying to calm and reassure her.

When she quieted, she whispered, "Tian, I'd given up hope."

Jie quietly dragged the dead guard into the room. "Tian, we must get out soon." From her tone, she must've been wearing the most sarcastic expression.

Tian stood and helped Kaiya to her feet. "We need to escape before anyone knows we're here."

He took her hand and guided her back through the dark hall towards the stairwell. Tian winced. Kaiya, though light on her feet, still made too much noise. If anyone heard...

The rest of the team waited at the stairwell. One grasped Tian's hand and tapped.

Emperor. Asleep. Second floor.

Tian's free hand clenched into a fist tight enough to crush rocks. The bastard! The night before...he would pay. For that, and what he must have done for the last two weeks.

Tian placed Kaiya's hand in Jie's and started toward the steps.

Kaiya grasped his sleeve. She tugged, even as he drew away. "Tian."

She'd broken the silence! Tian tensed, listening for telltale signs of guards. The rustling sounds suggested she and Jie were engaged in a minor tussle of wills.

One which Kaiya won. "Tian, don't leave me..." Her pleading voice chipped at his resolve. She needed his protection. He thirsted for revenge.

He whispered, "The emperor will pursue you. As long he lives. I'm going to punish him. For what he did to you, my beloved."

Around him, the *Moquan* drew sharp breaths, tensed up.

Jie hissed in a barely audible voice, "Tian, remember the mission. Remember objectivity. And if you cannot do that, remember your duty to your *beloved*."

"Tian, please." Kaiya drew him close, taking his hand and placed it over her belly. She leaned in and whispered in his ear. "I need you more than ever. To protect my unborn child."

Unborn child? Heavens. Tian's heart thudded in his chest. His child? With her?

All the keen-eared *Moquan* must've heard her. The collective gasp confirmed his worry. He stood dumbstruck.

Jie poked him. "If you don't want Geros raising your child, you need to come *now*."

Yes. Protecting the child and Kaiya took first priority. He took her hand and guided her up the steps. All they had to do now was gain the roof and slip quietly up to the tower without the perimeter guards seeing them.

The heavy thud of booted feet came from above. A glimmer of light danced near the exit to the roof.

"Hide," Jie whispered.

The *Moquan* women slipped inaudibly down the stairs, while the boy vaulted upwards into a ceiling corner and suspended himself there. Jie glided into the hallway. Tian and Kaiya, however...they were already halfway up the stairs.

Two Bovyans froze there with light bauble lamps in hand, eyes wide, mouths agape.

In the blink of an eye, Tian reached into his bandolier and threw three spikes. With the narrow stairwell, the lead Bovyan took the brunt of the attack and tumbled down with a pin in his throat.

The last spike grazed the other Teleri along the temple. He fell back. "Intruders!"

"Intruders!" The message relayed above them, shouts ringing out and horns blaring.

Tian groaned. Now they had to get past fifteen guards on the roof.

Bright lights flooded the top of the stairs. Heavy boots thudded and crossbows cocked. The fortress would soon be on full alert.

"To the tower. Eliminate all threats," Jie ordered.

Tian pulled Kaiya down to the third-floor landing. "They're gathering at the top. Armed with crossbows."

"They are mobilizing on the lower levels," announced one of the *Moquan* from below.

Outnumbered above and below! Tian's stomach clenched.

A chorus of pained grunts came from above. A Teleri voice yelled, "Archers in the tower!"

Jie growled. "That's our escape. The imperial riders don't stand a chance against the Bovyans in hand-to-hand combat."

The Teleri footsteps below were nearly upon them.

The *Moquan*'s voice from below shook with disbelief. "They have...muskets."

Muskets. When and where had the Teleri acquired them? Their range threatened a phoenix, though their accuracy was suspect. Tian tapped his chin. They couldn't take a chance with Kaiya's safety.

"We are trapped between a hammer and an anvil." The boy's tone sounded like he'd already accepted his fate.

Accept fate.

The words from Tian's vision echoed back to him now. Ever since he'd locked Kaiya in an armor cabinet a decade ago, it'd been his fate to selflessly toil as a cog in Hua's spy network. He found acceptance and belonging there. Work became his passion. In falling in love with Kaiya, and worse, acting on those emotions, he'd shirked fate, abandoned his duty.

It was time to correct that mistake now. *Accept fate.*

Tian gazed at Kaiya, memorizing every line of her angelic face. "I'll hold the stairwell. The rest of you make sure the princess escapes."

Kaiya's eyes widened in the dim, wavering light. "No, Tian, you must come with me. I beg it."

"I am sorry, my love. It's my fate to die here. So that you...and our child...might live."

Kaiya squeezed tight at his arms. "Come, Zheng Tian, I command it."

Tian ran his hand through her hair and down her cheek, brushing the tears away. "The penalty for disobeying your order is death. That is my fate."

She pressed herself against him, burying her face in his shoulder, clutching at him. His resolve faltered.

Accept fate.

He met Jie's eyes. The bitter expression she'd worn since their most recent reunion melted away, her face softening as she haltingly shook her head and blinked away tears. She could always read his mind. She understood the message, even if she denied its necessity. Her voice caught in her throat, but he made out the words, *I'm sorry.*

"Do it," he said. "The *Tiger's Eye.*"

Jie had grown tired of the lovers' quarrel almost before it had started. Tian had been more derelict in his duty than she imagined, had crossed lines that might very well lead to his execution if he returned to Hua.

That didn't matter if he planned to die this night.

She felt petty for harboring a grudge at a betrayal of unspoken feelings, made possible by time and distance.

And history. She'd wanted him to feel as awful as she felt, though knowing that they'd eventually resolve their differences. As they always had. Now, this would be the last time she saw him.

Flustered, her words tangled on her tongue.

Yet, Tian's slight nod indicated he understood her unspoken apology.

The *Tiger's Eye.* It'd buy them time. She locked eyes on him and made a simple gesture with her hand. "Your mission is to ensure the princess escapes."

Tian's expression transformed, the sad uncertainty replaced by an inhuman resolve. He returned her secret gesture with the subconscious hand sign that indicated he was locked in the *Tiger's Eye.*

He held the princess in his cold gaze, likely calculating the impact of his actions. Tears streamed in rivulets along her cheek. With obviously contrived gentleness, he slipped out of her grasp and disappeared down the stairwell. Sounds of metal crashing against metal rang out.

The princess started to lurch after him, but Jie blocked the way with her body. Her words came out surprisingly smooth. "*Dian-xia*, Tian is buying your escape with his life. Do not waste his gift."

The princess wiped her tears and straightened. While not exactly regal, she put on a brave face.

Jie pointed at the others. "Feng, you stay with the princess. Chang and Jian, come with me. Attack after they shoot their first volley." With that, she turned onto the landing, into the Teleri line of fire, and hurled several *biao* throwing stars and spikes in their direction.

In the split second before she ducked away, she counted ten defenders in a formation that maximized their volley. One tumbled down the steps, cut down by her weapons. A barrage of crossbow bolts lodged into the floor and walls where she had just stood a second ago.

No sooner had the bolts cracked against the walls than three *Moquan* surged up the stairs, drawing their swords while the Teleri reloaded. Covering ten feet of height and fifteen feet of distance in the flash of an eye, they were now among the enemy.

The Bovyans dropped their crossbows and drew swords. Too late. *Moquan* lacquered swords danced like shadows. Some of the men cried out in pain, while others simply fell silent.

There was still a chance.

Kaiya's pulse thumped in her ears, though not loud enough to drown out the sound of swishing blades and screams. Her stomach twisted in a knot. Tian...

Lights and shadows danced in the third-floor hall behind them, from where rasps of weapons being drawn rang out. The rapid pattering of booted feet coming up the steps grew louder, echoing the pounding in her chest.

They were trapped. She'd be recaptured. With Tian gone, it didn't matter. Nothing mattered. Better to die here and now than to go back to Geros' bed.

"*Dian-xia*, follow Jie up." The female *Moquan* urged her forward with a push. "I'll hold the third-floor landing."

With a last wistful glance at the stairs where Tian had disappeared, Kaiya hurried up the steps towards the sound of fierce fighting. Reaching the roof, she skidded to a halt. The boy *Moquan* had fallen, while the young woman drew off four Teleri with her sword. Jie dashed up the steps to the crow's nest, pursuing several more soldiers trying to retake the tower.

And above, four phoenixes! They circled the roof, their riders loosing arrows at enemy soldiers. Maybe there was a chance. At least for her. But Tian...

Kaiya bent over and picked up a dagger from a fallen Bovyan. Splinters bit at her bare feet as she climbed the winding stair.

A body dropped past her. From above, Jie's voice called out. "All clear."

Kaiya looked down. One of the *Moquan* women hobbled towards the stairs as well. Back towards the opening to the rooftop, there was no sign of Tian or the other female *Moquan*. Nonetheless, no Teleri burst through the entrance to the rooftop.

The phoenixes were landing as Kaiya gained the crow's nest. Chest squeezing, she scanned the rooftop again. Still no sign of Tian. She looked askance at Jie.

The half-elf shook her head, her eyes sympathetic. "Please mount up, *Dian-xia*. I'll go back down to investigate."

Kaiya nodded and climbed up behind one of the riders. The last *Moquan* also reached the top of the platform and eased her way over to the next phoenix.

Below, several Teleri soldiers surged out onto the roof. If they had made it that far...it must mean Tian... No.

A sob wracked Kaiya's shoulders. In years past, she might have put on a brave face for her people, but for all that had happened to her, all that had been taken from her, the tears trickled down her cheeks.

Jie reappeared on the platform and mounted up behind another rider. Her eyes, too, glistened. She met Kaiya's stare, her expression quickly turning stoic. "*Dian-xia*, we must go. Please give the order."

"Wait..." Kaiya choked on her tears. "There might still be a chance." A slim chance. Maybe no chance.

The soldiers filed up the steps, their collective weight sending vibrations through the crow's nest.

"We must go now, *Dian-xia*." Jie motioned for the riders to take off.

One at a time, the phoenixes spread their great wings and lifted gracefully into the air. From the higher vantage point, Kaiya continued to look down at the rooftop, hoping beyond hope that Tian would somehow emerge.

"Look!" Jie pointed down towards the southern side of the fortress, now bathed in the light of raging fires.

Kaiya followed the half-elf's gesture. A single figure fought viciously through waves of enemies.

Tian.

She looked back at the path of carnage he had taken, and to her horror, even at this distance she could pick out Emperor Geros pursuing her beloved at a deliberate pace.

"Fly in closer," she ordered the rider.

"What?" Voice shocked, the rider turned her head.

"Do as I command!" Kaiya snarled, unslinging the woman's bow from the saddle and fitting an arrow from the side quiver.

Around her, the phoenixes veered with their leader. Riders shot into the Teleri ranks. Many fell. Others looked up.

Now closer, Kaiya could see Tian clearly. Her stomach twisted in knots. He'd suffered numerous cuts, and his shirt was ripped to shreds. Yet he still fought on.

With a Teleri longsword in one hand and a dagger in the other, he hacked and slashed through the sea of Bovyans. Her heart surged with hope as he cleared the last enemy in front of him and broke into a run towards the palisade.

Geros had watched in admiration as the Cathayi man tore through his soldiers like Tivar's Archangel of Death. The Eye of Solaris painted it all as he littered the steps with dead and dying Bovyans, and now somehow gained the yard.

In the bright firelight, Geros remembered having seen the man at the banquet in Iksuvius. At the time, he was just another weakling. He was now proving Geros wrong. He worked his way towards the palisade, and if he managed to get away, Geros would not begrudge him a temporary victory.

One of his officers pointed up. "Cathayi phoenixes!"

Geros followed the gesture. Five huge birds circling downward. The fools! They were descending into crossbow range.

Several ranks raised their crossbows, and Geros lifted a hand, ready to give the signal.

"First Consul!" A male voice called from near the edge of the fortress.

Who dared address him by his former title? Geros looked. It was the Cathayi man, now ignored by his men after their attention turned to the phoenixes. Their eyes met.

Geros feared no one, let alone a lesser human. Nonetheless, a chill flared up his spine at the sight of the man's singularly focused glare.

Geros took a crossbow from a soldier by his side and leveled it at the Cathayi, who now limped back towards him.

He squeezed the trigger.

The bolt tore across the Cathayi's arm and ricocheted off the fence.

Unbidden, his own soldiers lowered their weapons and leveled them at the man.

Geros snatched a loaded crossbow and took aim again. The Eye of Solaris painted a yellow circle on the man's chest.

Just as Geros shot, yellow flashed high in his visual field, the Eye warning of an incoming attack from that direction. An arrow grazed his own thigh, throwing his aim off. The bolt would have sped past the man's head had he not plucked it out of the air with a quick swipe of his hand.

Ignoring the pain in his leg, Geros took another loaded crossbow, while looking up to see one of the phoenixes veering. The princess rode astride, a bow leveled at him. Her shot would be ludicrous from that range, launched from a moving platform. He turned his focus back to the man, who now broke into a hobbled run towards him.

A few men took shots at him, but he sidestepped the bolts with remarkable agility.

Yellow flashed in Geros' vision again. An arrow from above grazed his arm, just as he pulled the crossbow trigger. Gritting his teeth at the pain, he watched as his own bolt flew.

It slammed into the man's right upper shoulder with a dull thud, knocking him onto his back. He tried to crawl to his feet before collapsing into a sitting position.

Above, the princess screamed.

Flashing a taunting grin at her, Geros limped over with another loaded crossbow. Maybe the princess would be stupid enough to come closer. He turned and locked gazes with the man, who stared back with deadly resolve.

Geros almost faltered.

Then, the man's look faded into a peaceful tranquility, revealing neither fear nor defeat. His eyes rolled back into his head and he went limp, sagging forward.

Geros drove his heel into the man's chest. When he simply flopped to the ground, Geros knelt down to take the pulse at his neck. Nothing. His own shot should not have been a killing blow, but perhaps all of the other wounds had taken their toll.

Looking up at the princess, his mouth curled into a smile. They now hovered on the outer limits of crossbow range. "Bring those birds down! Take aim!"

His soldiers raised their crossbows in unison.

The phoenixes flapped their wings, gaining height.

"Shoot!"

Clicks of triggers and the twang of bows sounded in unison, sending a deadly barrage into the air.

Fighting through her tears, desperately wanting to recover Tian's body, Kaiya loosed arrow after arrow in reckless abandon until the quiver was spent.

"Down, down!" she ordered, pounding on the rider's back with her fists. Even still, the phoenix continued gaining altitude.

The rider would continue their escape regardless of what she said or threatened. It was useless. She looked down.

Oh, Heavens, no. Tian's body lay unmoving. Geros stood above him, shrinking as the phoenix flew. Oh, Heavens, no. Her chest squeezed so tight, it was impossible to take a breath. Jump.

She could reunite with Tian in death. It would take all the pain away.

But no. She carried his child. It had to be his. For his child, for his sacrifice, she had to live. Kaiya closed her eyes and sank into the saddle. The rush of cool night air was comforting, but how could she enjoy her freedom? Too much had been taken away from her.

CHAPTER 56:

Farewell

Jie's logical *Moquan* mind clashed with her emotions, the conflict between duty and friendship, love and betrayal, tearing her apart more than her elf and human halves ever had. She wiped the tears from her eyes as the phoenixes settled down in the meadow.

Beside her, the princess tumbled from her phoenix and collapsed onto her knees. She wrung her hands, shamelessly crying.

Hollowness seized Jie's chest. She'd treated Tian so curtly. He'd always survived. He wasn't supposed to die. She stumbled over and placed a shaking hand on the princess' shoulder. Wracking sobs reverberated into Jie's body, and her own tears flowed freely.

The imperial riders and the surviving *Moquan* sister slid off their saddles. Ma Jun joined them, and all dropped to one knee, fist to the ground.

The princess looked up at her. "We must recover his...their remains. Before the Teleri desecrate them."

Jie shivered, imagining the Bovyans hacking up Tian's body. As much as she agreed with the princess, it was an impossible task. And of course, protecting the princess was top priority. She shook her head. "*Dian-xia*, I am sorry."

The princess ripped at the collar around her neck, jerking her head from side to side as if it would loosen it. When the collar didn't so much as budge, she collapsed again, sobbing.

Lana sidled up to the princess, wrapping her up in an embrace. She held the princess' head to her chest, brushing her hair and whispering words in her own language. Such an open display of sympathy!

The princess nodded a few times before breaking away. She rose to her feet and raked a red-rimmed gaze over all assembled. She then bowed her head. "Thank you all for...for your hard work."

All of the Hua bowed their heads at the ceremonial words.

The leader of the imperial riders looked up. "*Dian-xia*, the phoenixes will be too tired after their long flight from Hua. If it is your order, we will rest for night and leave before dawn tomorrow."

The princess nodded.

Without any bedding, the riders all offered their cloaks for the princess to sleep on. After they settled the birds down, everyone found a place on the ground. Jie stood first watch, but was barely able to take her eyes from the trembling mass of cloaks that was Princess Kaiya.

Kaiya lay awake, curled on herself like a newborn, trying to will away the memories of all the awful things that had been done to her. With Tian gone, she was alone and abandoned, not unlike the feelings that she had suffered as a slave to a depraved man's sick fantasies.

Her thoughts strayed to her unborn child. Would Hua recognize her marriage to Tian, legitimizing the baby as the scion of the *Tianzi* and a *Tai-Ming* family? What if it was the first Bovyan member of the Imperial Family? She balled herself tighter.

It was in this position that Kaiya found herself when she awoke with a start before dawn. It had been the most restful sleep since her capture, the brutal emperor unable to haunt her dreams at least for that night. Warm arms cradled her.

Tian's? Her heart leaped. Maybe the last month had been nothing more than a horrible nightmare. But no. The arms were too small, the body pressed against hers slight compared to Tian's. She turned her head to find Lana asleep by her side.

Around her, the camp already stirred, with the imperial riders saddling the phoenixes.

Kaiya lay still, unwilling to rise. She'd once been confident and strong, beloved by her people. Hua's allies and enemies alike admired her for her poise and ability to manipulate affairs of state. Now, with her dignity stolen from her, she was a dried-out husk of her former self. To make matters worse, the man who'd sworn to love her forever, and with whom she'd shared her most intimate soul, was gone.

She untangled herself from Lana's embrace and pushed herself into a seated position.

Jie sat cross-legged nearby, watching her, and then transitioned to one knee, fist to the ground. "*Dian-xia*. I have something for you." Her voice was hoarse, her eyes red. Walking over, she withdrew a small pouch from her own and placed it in Kaiya's hands. "These belonged to Zheng Tian. His lockpicks. You should have them."

Kaiya turned the pouch over in her hands, feeling the weight of it. She opened it to find the rings of the imperial guards. The pouch flap itself was deceptively heavy, with Tian's haphazard stitching near the edges.

Her shoulders shuddered as sobs threatened to wrack her body again. She so wanted to be strong in front of her people. How had Tian been so focused in their escape?

Her gaze locked on the half-elf. "Jie, what did you do to Tian in the stairwell? How did he bring his anger under control so quickly?"

Jie frowned. "Our clan uses a technique called the *Tiger's Eye*. We use it on suicide missions, or on those who have been grievously injured and would not be able to otherwise complete their assignments. It helps him achieve a singular focus and objectivity, feeling no pain or emotion."

How convenient; a tool to keep someone from crumbling under the weight of their grief. "Can you perform it to someone else? Someone not from your clan?"

Jie's eyes narrowed. "I am not sure. Someone who has not undergone our mental training might not be affected at all. Or, the effect could be permanent."

"Then do it to me. I do not want to feel anymore. It is the only way I can survive right now."

Jie sucked on her lower lip. "*Dian-xia*... If I do that, then you will cease to be everything that the people love in you...that *he* loved in you."

"I am no longer that person anyway. I don't care. It takes all of my strength and willpower just to draw a breath. I don't want to feel anymore."

Jie sighed. "I have told you the risk. Is that your command, my liege?"

"It is."

Jie dropped to a knee, fist to the ground. "Then I obey." She took a deep breath and locked her gaze on Kaiya's eyes. She made a gesture with her hand.

A cool wave washed over Kaiya, all of her racing thoughts and emotions coalescing into a singular focus. The tightness in her neck and shoulders relaxed, and the vice-grip on her chest eased.

For maybe the first time in her life, she achieved absolute mental clarity. Perhaps if she were a *Moquan* warrior, who served the state unquestioningly, she might have lost herself to obedience to serve her country's interests—even if those interests conflicted with her own values. Instead, those values of life and dignity became her compass—an unambiguous beacon that would serve as a guide through this difficult time.

She straightened her carriage. "People of Hua, to me."

The riders, the *Moquan*, and Ma Jun all dropped to one knee, fist to the ground. "As the princess commands," they shouted in unison.

"My first command is silence. Even if the *Tianzi* himself asks you about my relationship with Young Lord Zheng, or the product of our union, you will beg for death before betraying my secret."

"As the princess commands."

She turned to Ma Jun. "Imperial guard Ma Jun. You are released from active service to the realm." Ignoring his shocked look, she held out the rings of the imperial guards who had sacrificed themselves for her. "For now, your duty is to pray for the repose of your fallen comrades in arms: Xu Zhan, Li Wei, Zhao Yue, and Chen Xin. Know that in the future, you may be called upon again. When you have settled in your final destination, send word to Hua of your whereabouts."

Head bowed, Ma Jun received the rings. "*Dian-xia*. Your humble servant accepts your command."

She took his hands in her own. "Jun, although you have always been my loyal guard, you are also my Maki brother. Please take care of Lana and the village."

She then turned to Lana and clasped her hands. "Sister, thank you for making me a part of your family, and then coming for me in my most desperate hour. Please take care of Jun for us."

Lana simply smiled. "Go with the spirits, Sister. Remember that you always have a home here, with us, among the trees."

After bidding the twins farewell, Kaiya mounted up behind the lead imperial rider. The phoenixes spread their great wings, taking flight. A spring headwind whipped through her hair as the meadow disappeared into the distance, along with the carefree life she'd always wanted.

Late in the day, Kaiya spotted the Great Wall, snaking its way above the forests through Hua's mountainous border. Stone watchtowers placed every dozen *li* along the wall sent smoke signals, relaying word of her return.

They landed near the Great East Gate of Hua. Here, the Kanin Plateau ended, and the North Kanin River spilled into the Hua basin as a six-hundred-foot-wide, fifty-foot-high waterfall not far from Tian's hometown of Dongmen.

Swollen by spring melt, the falls roared above all other sounds. The mist formed a rainbow that danced in the sunlight, providing a spectacular backdrop for the delicate pink plum blossoms that now reached peak bloom. Over the centuries, hundreds of poets had written thousands of verses about the stunning scene.

Kaiya's reaction was completely different. In years past, she would visit the falls in spring, allowing the breathtaking vista to fill her spirit with inspiration. Today, she did not feel her heart stirring; her mind simply analyzed the composition and mechanics of the scene.

On her command, the imperial riders set the phoenixes down in the central square of a town bordering the waterfall lake.

Dismounting, she turned to Jie. "I am going to Dongmen Castle. Spread rumors that I have sequestered myself there to recover from my trek through the Wilds. Send word to Doctor Wu in the capital to meet me there. I do not wish to see the *Tianzi* until after I have had time to consult with my doctor."

Jie's eyes wavered. "*Dian-xia*, your father is dead. Your second brother Kai-Wu is now *Tianzi*."

Had her emotions not been locked away by the *Tiger's Eye*, Kaiya imagined she would be reeling in shock. Not only was Father gone, but her second brother, the less capable of the two, now ruled. "Why did Kai-Guo not inherit?"

"He, too, is dead." Jie bowed her head.

Kaiya considered the implications with complete impartiality. It could not be coincidence that both her father and healthy brother had died in such a short time. After Kai-Wu, the next in line to the Jade Throne was...her cousin, the traitor Kai-Long. Or perhaps her unborn son?

EPILOGUE

In his fury at Princess Kaiya's escape, Geros executed many of the slaves who rose up that night. Their severed heads adorned the palisade walls as a warning to any others who dared defy him. Their mutilated bodies were left out for carrion birds to feast on.

However, Bovyan culture glorified valiant death, with enemy soldiers afforded the same respect as their own. The bodies of the three Cathayi, a woman among them, were cleaned and set on a crude raft with the Teleri dead. Their cold hands clasped weapons. Geros himself set the broken *dao* in the dead man's hands.

With a light bauble at the head of the raft to guide their souls into the netherworld, they were sent downstream in a solemn ceremony.

Geros watched the raft as it disappeared downriver in the direction of Cathay, where his operative worked to weaken the country from within. Civil war would tear the nation apart within two years—coinciding with Teleri pacification of the Wilds, and making it ripe for the picking. The Directori would again hail his genius.

With the Curse of Tivar, he would not be alive to witness it.

Or would he? The words of Princess Kaiya's ancestor came unbidden to his mind: *The best-laid plans rarely survive the first encounter.*

Geros had not expected to battle the Cathayi this early. Even though he had ostensibly won the first engagement, he left himself with an unenviable decision. He would not stand for his unborn son to be raised by a nation of artists and merchants.

He turned to a general. "Send word to Captain Miris in Fortress Ten. We will begin amassing soldiers for the invasion of Cathay immediately."

Soon, Cathay would be his, two years ahead of schedule...along with Princess Kaiya and their son.

For four days, Kaiya sat by a window in the private wing of Dongmen Castle, waiting for her doctor to arrive. If anyone could tell her something about her unborn child, it would be the ancient and mysterious Doctor Wu, who could look at a tongue and discern how long her patient slept on a specific night three years prior.

Kaiya's next move hinged on her baby. If it were Tian's, she would wed his brother Zheng Ming immediately. If it was Geros'...well, there was a Bovyan prophecy to consider.

"*Dian-xia.*" One of the castle servants came to the open door and dropped to a knee. "Doctor Wu has arrived from the capital."

By habit, Kaiya's hand lifted to the collar that marked her as Geros' slave—since removed by

Jie's lockpicking skills. Her heart beat in her ears, slow and steady. "Show her in."

With Fang Weiyong in her shadow, Doctor Wu entered and dropped down to her knees with the grace of a woman a quarter of her age. How old that really was, no one was really sure; though some speculated that as Master of the *Dao*, she had achieved immortality.

Pulled up into an austere coil, her long silver hair had a faint bluish sheen. Her eyes were unique among the Hua: a luminous pale blue, reminiscent of the moon Guanyin's Eye. Hair-thin lines of wisdom fanned out from the edges of those startling eyes, yet left her cheeks unmarred.

"*Dian-xia*, I have come at your summons. What is your bidding?"

"Thank you, Doctor. Please, take my pulse and tell me what you feel."

Doctor Wu motioned towards Fang Weiyong and smiled. "A master is as only good as her student."

"*Dian-xia*, forgive me for my impertinence." Weiyong bowed and placed three fingers on both of her wrists. After a minute, he looked up, his eyes sparkling as if a secret were passed between them. "You are pregnant. I would guess it is a boy."

Kaiya shrugged, and turned to Doctor Wu. The old woman brushed Fang aside as if he were a cherry blossom in a spring wind, and took up Kaiya's wrists in the same manner as Weiyong had.

She held Kaiya in her gaze. "Not *a* boy. Two."

Coming out of a coma on a funeral barge next to a dozen cold bodies was not as unsettling as knowing he had somehow intentionally put himself into that coma...the *Viper's Rest*? Though he didn't remember how he'd gotten on the log raft, or even who he was, he knew he'd awoken too early, before his injuries had stabilized.

His raft had come ashore, lodging in the rich-smelling earth. The river, swollen by spring melt, tumbled past, while the wind rustled in budding tree branches. A cool breeze brushed across his bare chest, causing his skin to erupt in goosebumps.

He groaned and pushed himself up into a sitting position. A warm sensation trickled down his back, emanating from the spot where pain seared in his shoulder. That stab wound, unlike the numerous cuts all over his body, would bleed him out. Each heartbeat brought him closer to death.

Two lithe figures dressed in doeskin clothing stared at him with wide, almond-shaped eyes. With the streaks of red and white paint across their face and feathers in their hair, they looked as rustic as the untamed forest around them. They were...elves. Though how he knew it, he couldn't tell.

The silence lasted only a few seconds. One—a brown-haired male with sharp features and a sharper dagger—put his hands on his hips and pointed at his feet. When he spoke, the threat in his voice belied the flowery language. "*Amane esaya na!*"

THE DRAGON SONGS SERIES · BOOK 4

SYMPHONY OF FATES

A LEGENDS OF TIVARA STORY

JC KANG

SYMPHONY OF FATES

PROLOGUE:

Of Gems and Dragons

Celastya had never seen a dragon transform into human form against its will before. From Avarax's shocked look as he swept his gaze over his now-tiny arms and legs, neither had he.

For millennia, he had forcibly mated with her and ate the resulting eggs to keep her energy low and enhance his own. Though she enjoyed a seven-hundred year reprieve as he dreamed through magically-induced slumber, Avarax had awoken on this night, when the heavens rained fire.

Thanks to her elf friend Xu transforming him into a human, she finally had an advantage. Her serpentine form now dwarfed Avarax.

The former dragon had little time to lament his frail new body. Xu thrust a thin sword at his chest.

The enchanted blade didn't even nick Avarax's soft skin. All three stared, wide-eyed.

Then Avarax looked up, bewildered expression transforming into a malevolent grin. He spoke a single word of power, sending the elf reeling to the sandy beach.

With Avarax's attention on Xu, Celastya dove at him. He was so tiny now, she'd rip him limb from limb with her talons. He met her first swipe with a punch to the claw. The pain rippled through her foreleg and into her core. The Pearl housed there shuddered. Undaunted, she swung her other claw.

She found only air. Avarax was gone.

Celastya snaked her head around. Neither elf nor dragon was anywhere to be found on the island beach. Before she could piece together what might have happened, Xu materialized out of thin air and collapsed into the sand.

"What happened, Xu?"

"We were lucky to take him by surprise. I froze time and transported him to the other side of Tivaralan. Though forced into human form, he still has all the vitality of a dragon. It took all of my energy to move him."

Celastya scratched her whiskers. She'd never imagined a mortal could be so powerful. "He will return."

The elf staggered to his feet. "Yes, but he will have to walk. It will take him years, unless he finds a way to regain his own form."

"And when he does?"

Xu sighed. "Let us hope I have time to teach someone with the right voice to sing him back to sleep."

Celastya's spine stiffened. The slave girl Yanyan, who had first accomplished the feat, died seven centuries ago. No one since had such a unique voice. It seemed hopeless. "Avarax will always find a way. He wants my Pearl, especially since he has not drained its energy for seven hundred years."

The elf searched her expression, and then pointed into space. "Tomorrow night, Ayara's Eye will be at its widest aspect this year. It will meet with the full white moon and full iridescent moon in the God's Eye Conjunction. *Istrium* energies will wax to their strongest in three hundred years. With the power of this island and your Pearl combined, I can open up a rift in time and space. Pick a time and place, and I will send you there. You can escape and never have to worry about Avarax again. Consider it and we can speak again tomorrow."

Celastya coiled herself around the rune-engraved arch that spanned the mouth of the atoll, allowing the vibrations of the island to resonate through her. She pondered the suggestion through the night.

How she longed to return to the last place where she had truly been happy. When she walked in human form. When she loved a human man; a man who died in a petty human struggle for mortal power.

The night brightened to dawn, and day darkened to night. Heavy clouds of ash from the previous night's devastation choked the atmosphere, blotting out the heavens. Though unseen, the celestial bodies rose to their inevitable meeting, low in the southern sky. The energy of the world resonated louder and louder to all who could feel it.

Toward dusk, Xu approached the arch. A young human woman accompanied him, dressed in tight-fitting black pants and a long black shirt, whose material and fashion looked out of place in this era. Her black hair and honey-toned skin marked her as Cathayi. She held a fist-sized globe of *istrium*, shedding a pale blue light. She gawked as her gaze swept across Celastya's serpentine form.

Xu bowed low. "Have you decided?"

Celastya drew a deep breath and coughed out her Pearl. The size of the elf's head, it swirled in colors like the iridescent moon.

Xu studied it, eyes curious. "When and where do you wish to go?"

Celastya recalled the moment she had fled the battlefield on her lover's orders, and held the image in her memories. She willed it into his mind.

With a nod, he chanted in the musical language of Deep Magic. Her Pearl's colors whirled faster, and the ground vibrated. The *istrium* sphere glowed brighter in the woman's hands as the island's energy coursed through Celastya and into the elf. The space under the arch wavered and flashed, and a wormhole opened.

Through the portal, the graceful eaves and wooden columns appeared familiar, as did the armor of the fighting men. A middle-aged warlord, ambushed and outnumbered, held a curved sword aloft. Yet it was not her lover, the one who had died two thousand years ago. When she saw silent flashes of musket fire, she knew it was the wrong era.

The human woman at her side gasped, nearly dropping the sphere, and looked from the portal to the elf and back.

Celastya shook her head. "This is the right place, but almost four hundred years too late."

The elf held the Pearl aloft. "I am sorry, this is the best I can do. Space is easy to traverse, but time is very hard to pinpoint."

Celastya's sigh sent waves across the atoll. It would be meaningless to go there; yet it would be a safe place to hide her Pearl against Avarax's return. She could remain here and, to some degree, even draw on her gemstone's energy across the vast distances.

The scene in the arch shifted, tracking the warlord as he retreated into a central building. Fires blazed around him. A wooden sign with *Original Mastery Temple* engraved in Cathayi script crashed to the ground. Celastya had lived through that era, as wife to one of the warlord's most trusted vassals. The building would burn to the ground, killing the warlord. Her husband would usher in a new age in that nation's history. "I will take the Pearl and hide it there."

Xu raised a halting hand. "Without our combined energies to hold the rift open, the portal will collapse. You will be trapped in that time and place."

The Cathayi woman raised her hand. She spoke in a strange language, foreign to this world, but not to the one beyond the arch. "I will take the Pearl there."

As a dragon, Celastya could understand her words.

Xu apparently could as well. He shook his head at her. "Miss Wang, though you come from that world, it is a different time than you know. It is a dangerous task."

Wang patted a weapon at her side. "I am up to the task. Both that era in history, and that man there, have always fascinated me."

Xu and Celastya exchanged glances. If Xu trusted the woman, Celastya could see no reason to doubt her. In any case, the Pearl would be safe. Celastya nodded.

Xu's ageless brow furrowed. "I will see if I can move the portal over to a safer place."

The scene shifted, pushing through burning temple halls. Flaming beams cracked and fell. At last, they settled on an interior courtyard, where some roof tiles had collapsed. The rubble partially obscured a well.

"There." Celastya pointed a talon toward the well.

The elf placed the Pearl into the woman's hands. She waded into the water and crossed through the threshold with a pop.

"Are you sure this is the right thing to do?" Xu regarded Celastya through half-lidded eyes.

"No. But when are we ever sure of decisions like these?"

Both turned and watched as Wang picked her way through burning debris. Reaching the well, she peered down. Then she dropped the Pearl into its depths.

Wang looked back through the portal for several seconds. However, instead of coming back through, she dashed through the halls.

"Turn around! Come back!" Xu yelled, though Wang would not hear him.

"She will alter the timeline of that world," Celaysta said, wondering about the consequences. Wang's weapon could turn the tide of the ambush, if she chose to interfere, and change the history of a nation. Maybe the world's.

Growling, Xu focused on the arch again. The image followed Wang as she ducked and weaved through fallen debris. At last, they saw the doomed warlord kneeling, broken katana in hand, preparing to disembowel himself. Behind him, a young warrior raised his sword, ready to behead the man.

Of course. Their culture glorified honorable deaths. Celastya remembered it well, how her lover had charged into his enemies. She could have saved him, but it would have meant revealing her true identity as a dragon. He would have reviled her, and cursed her for denying him a glorious death. Celastya turned back to the portal.

In the land beyond, Wang drew her weapon. A light flashed, and the younger man collapsed.

The warlord looked up. He pointed his blade at Wang.

She gestured toward the portal. The man's gaze followed, and his mouth gaped.

The warlord picked up a musket that lay beside him as she helped him to his feet. They then spilled back through the temporal threshold, just as the room behind them burst into flames. The opening snapped shut with a hollow popping sound.

Celastya's energy wavered as her connection to the Pearl stretched over time and space.

Xu jabbed an accusing finger at Wang. "What have you done? You cannot just change your history!"

Shrugging, Wang pointed at the man. "In our history, he died. His body was never recovered. They won't miss him."

The man spun around, wonderment written on his face. When he spoke, it was in yet another foreign tongue, one Celastya hadn't spoken in two millennia. "What is this place?"

Wang switched to a halting version of his language. "Far away, both in time and space."

Short of breath and limbs languid, Celastya's body shuddered. The pull of her Pearl was tentative, unable to support her mass. With the force of her will, she compressed her size, shrinking down and taking a human's frail form. She took a deep breath, and oxygen filled her newly-transformed lungs. Even at a distance, the power of her gemstone surged through her smaller body, awakening her with a renewed vitality.

Yet, faced with the prospect of living an eternity among mortals, regret overwhelmed her. Had she made the right decision? Whether or not she had the Pearl, Avarax would seek her out, if only for revenge.

Xu appraised her naked body, a wry smile forming on his lips. "Interesting choice. At least you will be able to walk among the Cathayi without drawing too much attention. Once you put on clothes." He turned to the real humans. "And what am I to do with you two?"

Wang stared into the elf's eyes. "Last night, you told me that this world is devolving into chaos." She gestured to the warlord. "Here is a military genius with the model for a superior weapon." She nodded toward Celastya. "Here is a *dragon*. We can restore order."

Xu rubbed his chin as he looked east toward the mainland. "We must protect this island at all costs. If not from Avarax, then from the Altivorc King. Very well, Wang Yuxiang. Tell me your ideas."

CHAPTER 1:

Deceptions

The setting sun outside the castle window taunted Kaiya, its descent marking one more day of concealing her pregnancy. Though Doctor Wu's unparalleled acupuncture skills detected the twin boys in her womb, she couldn't discern their father. Was it the exiled spy she'd to love during her escape from the frigid Northwest? Or the foreign tyrant who murdered him?

Neither was an appropriate match for a nineteen-year-old princess. Not when her unborn sons stood next in line to inherit the Dragon Throne.

"My choice is clear." Kaiya turned to her half-elf bodyguard, who was also her sworn sister and one-time rival in love.

Yan Jie sat on the wood floors of the guest suite's anteroom, sharpening a wicked knife that didn't match the softness of her plain, pink dress. She looked up, even as she continued to draw the knife across a whetstone in rhythmic swishes. Jie's childlike features had never appeared so forlorn.

Kaiya should've also been wallowing in grief. She'd ransomed her body and dignity to spare hostages from a brutal death, yet couldn't save Father, Eldest Brother, or her beloved Tian. The experience would have broken her, if not for the mental block of Jie's *Tiger Eye* technique.

It gave Kaiya emotionless clarity. "Ming is Tian's brother and heir to a province. He's the best match."

Jie shrugged. Her usually perky voice droned. "You already rejected him once. No, twice."

"I doubt he'll need much convincing," Kaiya said. Ming would likely jump at the opportunity for social mobility, but she'd use the magic of her voice if necessary.

Now if he would only return home from his deployment before her flat belly started to swell.

The double doors slid open, revealing the castle steward. His green court robes rustled as he sank to his knees and pressed his forehead to the floor. "*Dian-xia*, Lord Zheng has returned and is on his way to greet you."

Well, that was serendipitous. At last, after five days of waiting in his family's castle at the border to the Wilds. A week since missing her period.

After conveying her permission with a nod, Kaiya turned toward Jie. "This is it. Try not to kill him."

Staring at the wall, Jie nodded absently. A sudden jerk of her hand revealed a trickle of blood on her finger.

"Are you all right?" Kaiya took a step toward her. For the meticulous *Moquan* to nick herself sharpening a knife...

With a bob of her head, Jie thrust the bleeding hand behind her. "It is nothing, *Dian-xia*."

Kaiya peered at the girl. Despite the command to speak freely, Jie's tone and diction had reverted back to distant formality.

Someone cleared their throat at the door. Kaiya looked up, prepared to declare her intentions to Zheng Ming.

Lord Zheng *Han*, father of Tian and Ming, knelt on one knee, fist to the ground. His dark green travelling cloak, draped over his plain robes, smelled of a humid early spring. He must've come directly to meet with her. If only Ming travelled so fast.

"*Dian-xia*," he said. "Welcome to Dongmen Castle. I trust that my wife and steward have made your stay comfortable thus far?"

"They have, thank you." Kaiya motioned for him to enter.

Head bowed, Lord Zheng shuffled in and sank to a cross-legged position before her. "*Dian-xia*, I have just arrived from the capital. The *Tianzi* requests you return to Huajing."

Request. An emperor didn't make requests, he gave commands. Second Brother had yet to understand his new role. Nonetheless, his wording gave her the leeway to remain at the border, ready to receive Ming when his army returned from the now-moot assignment of finding her in an enemy-infested wilderness. Surely her message would've reached him by now.

Kaiya would broach the issue of marriage in due time; first came the news she couldn't have delivered without the *Tiger's Eye* walling off her heart. She pressed her forehead to the floor and then looked up to meet Lord Zheng's wide eyes. An imperial princess would only bow so low to the *Tianzi* himself. "I regret to inform you that your fourth son, Zheng Tian, perished in his attempt to convey me through enemy lines."

Lord Zheng's lips quivered before he arranged his expression into stoicism. "Did he die bravely?"

More out of habit than sentiment, her hand strayed to Tian's lockpick pouch under her sash. Her only memento of him. Revealing their secret marriage and pregnancy would've allowed her to console Lord Zheng as a daughter, let him know she understood his loss, even if the *Tiger's Eye* kept her from feeling it. No—Tian had been banished from the capital in disgrace, and his sons would be considered low-born bastards, if they were even allowed to live.

Kaiya straightened. "Zheng Tian performed admirably. I will never forget his service." Or his affection. If only she could remember what their passion *felt* like. The memories were detached, as if she had watched their love bloom from afar. Kaiya placed a hand over her womb, again wondering if her twins were Tian's sons, Lord Zheng's grandsons.

"Then it is my family's honor." Lord Zheng bowed again.

"I have one more request of your family. I would ask permission to marry your first son, Zheng Ming, at the earliest auspicious date. After the death of my father and brother, the realm needs both closure and hope."

Lord Zheng's eyes narrowed for a split second before his face blanked again. Did he suspect she was no longer a virgin bride? "While these are welcome tidings, it is sudden. Of course, we would first need the *Tianzi's* approval."

Drawing on the magic of her voice, which she'd once used to defeat Tivaralan's last dragon, Kaiya sang her next words of command. "Approve it."

Her voice came out melodic, but devoid of power. Her connection to the energy of the world sputtered in her chest. Instead of capitulating, Lord Zheng raised an eyebrow.

"Please," she added, as if it would change his mind. She must've looked like a fool, singing words like an opera diva. Why had she failed at such an easy invocation of power?

Lord Zheng's face betrayed nothing. "I appreciate your consideration, *Dian-xia*. I will convey to the *Tianzi* my desire to bind our families in the most auspicious of ties. With your leave, I must greet my wife and then make preparations for your departure."

Her departure. He sat there, perhaps hoping she'd obey Second Brother's request, to rid himself of the responsibility. Or perhaps he suspected something. Why else would he hesitate at the great honor of marrying a son to an imperial princess?

Kaiya dismissed him with a slight dip of her chin, and considered the implications of her voice's impotence. The loss of emotions was a necessary compromise to make it through the most trying time in her life. The loss of her magic, on the other hand—

Jie let out a long breath as Lord Zheng's footsteps faded down the hall.

Kaiya turned toward the half-elf. "I've lost the power of my voice. It has always been tied to emotion. I think the *Tiger's Eye* is blocking both. You must unlock it."

"Are you sure that is wise?" Sucking her lower lip, the sprite-like girl hardly inspired the image of wisdom. Her elf blood made her appear no older than a thirteen-year old despite her thirty-two years. "After all, before you learned to use your voice, you relied on charm and intelligence. Please reconsider."

In the past, Kaiya's feelings might have prompted an impulsive answer, without considering the repercussions. "Yes, but that girl was manipulated by treacherous Cousin Peng and deceived by a dragon." And forced into bed with a dictator she could've slain before he even had a chance to capture her.

Six months made quite a difference.

She played with her hair. Magic came with the burden of coping with immeasurable loss. No magic meant relying on wits alone. "I see no other way. If I can't consummate a marriage to Zheng Ming soon, I'll have a hard time convincing him—and the empire—my sons are legitimate."

And while a prince's bastard could inherit the throne, her babies might be murdered or thrown out on the streets, and she'd be branded a harlot.

Heavens, she might as well be one. She harrumphed. Less than three months ago, she was still a virgin; if she slept with Ming, he'd be the third man in as many weeks.

There was no real choice. For her sons. For the realm.

The half-elf sucked her lower lip again, her silence speaking louder than words.

Kaiya forced a chuckle she didn't feel. There was no love lost between Jie and Ming: she'd just as soon cut his manhood off and feed it to the carp; and since he knew it, he avoided her altogether.

In any case, it wasn't Jie who'd share the vain man's bed. Despite his weakness for women, Ming was the logical choice: a leader of men from a noble lineage, and uncle by blood to her sons—if they were indeed Tian's. "Do it. Unlock the *Tiger's Eye*."

Jie pursed her lips for a few seconds before nodding. "As the princess commands." She locked her gaze and formed a signal with her hands.

Kaiya stared at the shape of Jie's fingers. Soon, very soon, she'd have to cope with grief, but at least she'd have her magic. Then, influencing Zheng Han would be easy. The problem, quickly resolved.

"It is done," Jie said.

Nothing changed. No flood of emotion washing over to her. Kaiya's memories of Tian seemed just as detached and distant as before. She shook her head.

Jie sighed. "I feared this would happen. The effect on a *Moquan* is unpredictable, since the *Tiger's Eye* is usually reserved for missions from which there is no return. You are not trained in our ways and the effect is even less predictable." She'd said as much, when Kaiya first submitted to the technique.

"Will it wear off on its own, then?" A torrent of repressed emotions flooding back at an inopportune moment could be disastrous. When would she be able to draw on her magic again? Time was running out to legitimize her unborn sons.

"I cannot say." Jie shrugged.

So she'd have to live with the *Tiger's Eye* for now. Instead of the power of command, she had only wits and a pretty face. In all objectivity, formidable weapons. "Follow Lord Zheng. I need to know if he suspects anything, and if he will use the *Tianzi's* letter to force me to return to Huajing."

Jie dropped to her knee, fist to the ground. "As the princess commands."

Kaiya looked down at her belly. Even if she were his guest, she was still an imperial princess. Lord Zheng wouldn't dare force her to leave. She turned toward Jie, only to find the half-elf's dress crumpled on the floor.

Clad in a black utility suit, Jie made plenty of noise as she trailed Lord Zheng's retinue through the castle halls. The glossy wood floors, specifically designed to counter spies, chirped like a nightingale with each of her steps.

Which was why Jie stepped in concert with the entourage.

One foot in front of the other. Each pace, masked by the huge guard in front of her. Though her feet were as light as ever, a heavy heart weighed her down. As if the shock of the affair between the princess and Tian weren't enough, she'd then lost her best friend. The man who almost became her lover until a war came between them. If only she could put *herself* into the *Tiger's Eye*.

Now was not the time for self-pity.

"*Jue-ye*," the steward said, using the formal address for a *Tai-Ming* lord. "Your wife awaits you in your chambers."

Zheng Han didn't break stride, facing forward as he spoke. "Yes, I will go there presently. Does she know of Tian's death?"

The steward hurried to keep up. "Yes, *Jue-ye*. The princess told her when she arrived five days ago. She is very distraught."

Like everyone else, except maybe the princess with her mental block.

Lord Zheng sighed. "I imagine so. Tian was always her favorite, her baby boy. She never smiled the same after his banishment."

"And she always hated the princess for her role in that," the steward whispered. "The hate has only grown, because the Lady blames the princess for his death."

"Indeed." Zheng nodded. If only his face was visible from here. Not like the lord had shown much up to now. He might as well have been a statue carved by the most inept sculptor in the world. "Now tell me, what has the princess been doing these last five days?"

"She has stayed in the guest wing the entire time. Her only visitors were her doctors."

"Her doctors?" Zheng Han stopped in his tracks and turned.

Jie ducked behind the guard. She peeked around to catch Zheng Han's expression. Still blank.

The steward nodded. "Yes, Doctor Wu and her disciple, Fang Weiyong."

"Why would she see doctors?" Zheng Han stroked his narrow beard. If he knew, there'd be no marriage, and the princess would be shipped back to the capital in disgrace.

Jie altered her voice to mimic one of the counselors and threw it with a *Ghost Echo*. "After the princess' trek through the wilderness, they wanted to check on her health."

A few of the men in the back looked around in confusion, but those in the front murmured and nodded.

Lord Zheng resumed his walk. "Maybe there is more. The princess travelled in the woods, with a group of men. Where are the doctors now?"

"I believe Fang Weiyong is in town," the steward said. "Doctor Wu left for Huajing already."

Zheng Han turned to one of his guards. "Find Doctor Fang and bring him to me. I do not want to make any decisions about Ming's future until I know more."

Jie had to delay the guard. Fang Weiyong had accompanied the princess on her escape and knew *everything*. He'd been the one to consecrate Tian and the princess' vows.

Before she could follow the guard, Lord Zheng motioned toward the steward. "Send word to Huajing. If Chief Minister Hong wants her back in the capital so badly, the *Tianzi* should order her to return. She has no choice but to acquiesce. It would buy us more time to make a decision on the marriage proposal. I will not have Ming raising some other man's whelp."

The steward bowed as they walked. "As you command, *Jue-ye*. I will draft a letter right now and stamp it with your seal."

"Very good." Lord Zheng turned to his military aide. "The situation in the capital is tenuous. The *Tianzi* has requested ten thousand of our troops to help in the pacification of Nanling Province."

"Why us?" the aide asked. "We are far away from Nanling, and if the reports are true, a Teleri army approaches, just on the other side of the Great Wall."

Lord Zheng threw his hands up. "The *Tianzi* has made nothing but irrational decisions. Chief Minister Hong has his ear, and neither have a mind for military strategy."

Jie had warned the princess about Chief Minister Hong's reliability in the past. He might be conniving and self-serving, but foolish? Moving an army away from a potential threat bordered on recklessness.

With more urgent matters than troop movements, Jie pressed herself against a shadowed wall.

Too bad *Moquan* skills didn't teach one to be in two places at once. She'd have to choose between warning Fang Weiyong, or making sure a letter of her own got sent to the capital with Lord Zheng's seal. Leaving either problem unresolved meant the difference between Tian's children standing next in line to the throne; or being abandoned as a slut's bastards, just like Jie, herself.

CHAPTER 2:

All Warfare is Based on Deception

Zheng Ming rearranged himself on the hard cot, moving his head out of the blue ray from Guanyin's Eye. It peeked in through the poorly-thatched roof, returning his gaze wherever he moved. Yet it was neither the light nor the bedding which kept him awake.

He clutched Princess Kaiya's letter to his chest, rereading the contents in his mind. She'd made it through Teleri lines and now waited in Father's castle for him to return. Not only that, she wanted to marry at once, to heal a nation which worshipped the Imperial Family, after the death of the *Tianzi* and the Crown Prince.

At first light, he would torch this enemy fort he'd captured—it was little more than a half-completed palisade with a few ramshackle barracks and a bridge over a wide river—and return home with his victorious army. Then, into the arms of the realm's most beautiful, witty woman, who happened to be a princess.

A rap on the crude wooden door shook him out of his daydream. His jumpy second brother Shu must need guidance. Again. Ming had appointed him aide-de-camp, though the twenty-four-year-old had never seen battle until the day before.

Ming yawned. "What is it?"

Shu poked his face through the door. "Eldest Brother, our scouts report two hundred Bovyan heavy infantry, spears and swords, ten *li* to the east."

Two hundred? Ming had just routed over twice as many the day before, with his army of three thousand imperial musketmen. The enemy never even got close enough for his own province's two thousand spearmen to engage. "Any crossbows? Cavalry?"

Shu shook his head. "According to the scouts, no."

With the benefit of the fortress, shoddily built as it was, the Teleri didn't stand a chance. Though the palisade didn't reach the eastern side, the enemy would have to cross a shallow moat and charge up a steep embankment into his waiting guns. Not only that, it would take them at least three hours to arrive, even at a forced march.

Ming sighed at the decided lack of urgency. "Let the men rest another hour. After they have eaten, deploy them along the eastern embankment."

Shu bowed. "Forgive my ignorance, Eldest Brother, but with the princess safe, should we not make haste back to Hua?"

"No. Let them come to us, tire themselves out. We will use their own fort to minimize our losses. Then we won't have to concern ourselves with pursuit. Send the scouts back to keep an eye on them."

"As you command, Eldest Brother." Shu bowed again.

By the time Ming emerged from the barracks an hour and a half later, the imperial musketmen stood in a line that wrapped from the north to east sides of the fort, three ranks deep. His provincial spearmen, led by his third brother Lun, stood halfway up the embankment. They all turned and saluted, pressing their right fists into their left palms at chest level.

A chill of excitement ran up Ming's spine. *His* army. As a captain, he'd led a regiment of horse archers in defense of Wailian County. Now he was the *Dajiang*, Expeditionary Commander, ready to lead five thousand men to a second decisive victory. What had the Founder's Treatise on War said about morale?

Ming unsheathed his *dao* and cleared his throat. "Soldiers of Hua! Yesterday, we showed the Teleri what men of Hua are made of. We faced the stronger side of their fort and prevailed without losing a man. Today, we hold the higher ground with greater numbers and superior firepower. I do not want a single Bovyan to make it across the moat!" He pointed the tip of his sword at the tree line on the other side of the moat. "If any makes it to this side, make sure it is because they are walking over their own men."

The men roared in approval. An immoral warrior race had betrayed their princess and sought to invade their homeland. Now the Bovyans would pay.

By dawn the next morning, their enthusiasm wavered. Not from a blistering onslaught, but from boredom and a lack of sleep. Tired eyes all fixed on the spot where a road through the forest opened up into the clearing around the fort. Sweat gathered on brows as humidity clung to armored bodies. Not even the thick clouds and cool breeze did much to alleviate the heat.

Ming turned to Shu. "You said ten *li*?"

"Yes, Eldest Brother." Shu nodded.

"No word from the scouts?"

Shu shook his head.

The enemy should have arrived at this hour *yesterday*, and the ancient road they restored was the only way to move a large number of troops. The main river along the fort's south would be impossible for men to swim across— if historical records of the region were accurate; and the spring melt swelled the tributary river just to the west, leaving the fort's bridge as the only way to cross.

Ming looked back at the west side's palisade, now riddled with musket balls from two days before. "Shu, send more scouts out over the west side and turn north along the tributary to see if there is any place to ford. I want—"

A lieutenant pointed toward the opening in the forest. "Flags of parley!"

Ming followed the gesture.

Three light-haired Bovyan men, each standing a head-and-a-half taller than the tallest of the Hua, strode into the clearing. Their chain tunics jingled beneath black surcoats emblazoned with the gold, nine-pointed sun of the Teleri Empire. One held a white flag aloft. Behind them, black cloth flashed between the tree trunks.

Along the Hua lines, hands gripped musket barrels and spear hafts.

Ming motioned for Shu and another officer to accompany him. He grinned. "They want to negotiate terms for surrender."

Shu's jaw dropped. "Eldest Brother, we cannot trust them. They betrayed the princess in their negotiations."

Ming motioned for an imperial marksman who had distinguished himself two days before. "Xiao, I want you to target the big man in the center. If I give the signal or he shows any sign of treachery, shoot him."

Xiao pressed his fist into his palm. "As the *Dajiang* commands."

Ming edged his way down the embankment to meet the Teleri. They were even more intimidating up close. Two men with cropped brown hair flanked a man who radiated an air of importance and power.

His black mane, streaked with grey, hung loosely to the center of his broad shoulders and a scar on his right cheek marred his olive complexion. Eyes, one steel-grey, and the other disconcertingly blue, met Ming's as he spoke in perfect Arkothi, the common language of the North. "I am the First Emperor Geros of the Teleri Empire. You look familiar."

Geros, the turtle egg who betrayed Princess Kaiya and tried to capture her. Ming clenched his fists. He'd never seen a Bovyan leader so close before, let alone met one. He responded in his own halting Arkothi. "I am Ming Zheng, heir to the East Gate Province of Cathay."

Geros nodded, his expression registering recognition. "You must be closely related to the man I killed. I did not take him to be of noble blood, though he fought admirably and killed three dozen of my men. We sent his body downriver as is our custom for the honored dead."

The barbarism. Ming stifled a cringe and smirked instead. "Are you here to collect your dead from two days ago? Or to be added to the pile?"

Geros puffed his chest out. "I am here to make an offer. Surrender the fort as it is, then turn around and go back behind your Great Wall. On my honor, we will let you return unharmed."

Ming jabbed a finger at the Emperor. "I don't trust the honor of a man who reneges on his negotiations and tries to kidnap a defenseless woman."

"Renege? No, your princess attacked me by surprise, and we took her into custody to pay for her crimes against the Empire."

Ming clenched his fists. "You lie."

"I assure you, everything I said is true." Geros' grin widened.

Struggling to reach into his armor, Ming withdrew the princess' letter. He whipped it open and held it up for the emperor to see. "You never captured her. She made it past your blockade and is safe in my castle. She informed me, with her own words."

Geros' brow furrowed as his mismatched eyes flicked over the letter. "She forgot to mention she is now First Empress of the Teleri Empire, through marriage to me, and carries my heir in her womb. I only seek to reclaim what is mine."

Heat rushed to Ming's head, Geros' last words barely making it through the pounding in his ears. "Lie!"

Geros laughed. "So she did not admit to it in her letter? I wouldn't know, since I don't read your language."

The bastard was mocking him! Ming's fists clenched so tight, he might have been able to squeeze a lump of coal into a diamond.

The Bovyan's smug expression gave way to narrowed eyes. "You are taking the news quite personally. I restate my offer. Turn around and go in peace. When you arrive home, ask Empress Kaiya yourself."

"There are five thousand reasons for me to refuse your generous offer." Ming waved to the Hua lines atop the embankment. "Sources tell me I have a twenty-five-to-one advantage in numbers, and an insurmountable superiority in weapons and position."

Geros tugged gloves off his hands and began counting his fingers. "I am just a simple soldier, and mathematics has never been my strong suit, but..." He raised a hand.

With a resounding thud, thousands of black uniforms stepped out from the tree line surrounding the north and east sides of the moat, heavy crossbows in hand. Behind them, ruddy-skinned natives whooped with bows raised in the air.

"... I think my odds are better than you think," Geros finished.

Ming smirked. He'd gotten Geros to reveal his numbers. Despite the poor scouting, he still had superior range. Once the Teleri emerged from the trees, they would already be within musket range. If only he could wipe the patronizing smirk off Geros' face right here, right now. He drew his bow and nonchalantly tested the pull. "Consider yourself fortunate you are protected by the flag of parley. Once you cross back to your lines, my arrows will look for you."

"I give you until nightfall to reconsider my offer," Geros said. "A wise leader would not refuse it out of hand."

Ming did not care to hear lessons on leadership from a dictator who sacrificed his soldiers on a whim. Plans formulated in his mind.

"If any of your men so much as step into the clearing, we will fire upon them."

Geros grinned. "I would respect you less if you did not." He spun on his heel and strode back toward the trees.

Ming turned and climbed the embankment. At the top, he summoned his command team. "How many days of food rations do we have?"

"Eight, twelve if you include what we captured here, Young Lord," the quartermaster answered.

Shu's voice trembled. "Are we going to fight?"

"No." Ming pointed back toward the west. "We did not establish supply lines. All they have to do is wait us out. However, we cannot leave the bridge or extra supplies for them. It will take us five days to return to Hua at forced march. Dump excess food rations and the weapons we captured into the river. Set three kegs of firepowder on the bridge. Devise a plan to disguise our withdrawal."

And when they returned home, the princess would confirm Emperor Geros' words were all lies.

Geros studied the line of Cathayi soldiers glaring from the top of the embankment, muskets trained on the clearing's edge. If not for Princess Kaiya beguiling him, he would have visited the fort two weeks before and ensured the palisade surrounded the entire fort. How ironic that his own dereliction of duty made the fort easier to take back.

"Why did you give him until nightfall, Your Eminence?" Captain Mirin, who oversaw construction of the fort, kept his head bowed.

Geros locked his gaze on the man. "Because the savages tell me it will rain at dusk."

"Rain, Your Eminence?" Captain Mirin had a good mind for designing forts; less so for military tactics.

"Why do you think I slowed our march?"

Lines formed on Mirin's brow. "So that our vanguard could rest while more of our troops caught up?"

"And?"

Mirin's face blanked.

"Every move has multiple purposes. We sent the vanguard ahead to make their scouts believe they outnumbered us. They roused their troops early, and they have not slept for a full day. Also, by slowing our march, we will not sit idle waiting an extra day for rain. Rain will render their muskets useless and give our crossbows the advantage. Hand-to-hand, even with their superior position, a Bovyan is worth three of them. Despite what Zheng believes, the odds are very much in our favor once their guns are removed from the equation."

Mirin nodded enthusiastically. "Brilliant, Your Eminence."

"The brilliance," Geros said, "is in the strategies of the founder of Cathay's Wang Dynasty."

"Though what if Zheng accepts your offer?"

"Then we get your fort back intact. But he won't. He is a prideful man and I goaded him. Also, he is our key to breaching the Great Wall."

"What if he escapes?" The captain's eyebrows clashed together.

"He won't. Three thousand of our men are crossing the fords to the north as we speak, and will be behind them by dusk."

CHAPTER 3:
Loyal Men

Though spring sang its evening song outside her window, Kaiya didn't look up from her book until she heard Jie's quiet breathing by the door.

The half-elf dropped to one knee, fist to the ground. "*Dian-xia*, Lord Zheng suspects you are hiding a pregnancy. He sent his men to find Doctor Fang."

"I assume you warned Weiyong?"

Jie shook her head. "The legends of the *Moquan* being able to be in two places at once are mildly exaggerated. I was forging letters. Lord Zheng wanted to ask the *Tianzi* to order you home. I swapped the letter out for one of my own."

"What did you say?"

Jie shrugged. "I expressed your heartfelt desire to marry Zheng Ming. Lord Zheng approves and asks for the *Tianzi's* blessing."

Heartfelt indeed. As if she could *feel* anything. Even grief over Tian's loss couldn't blunt Jie's sense of irony. Or perhaps her distaste for Ming stoked it. Kaiya snorted.

Regardless of the wording, the fake letter solidified her position. Second Brother Kai-Wu had always looked out for her. *Tianzi* or not, he would approve the marriage. Hopefully. Because if push came to shove, she wouldn't undermine his authority. His position in the eyes of the hereditary lords was already tenuous enough without a rebellious sister. "Then we can stay with the plan," Kaiya said.

Jie's expression, the sucking on her lower lip, said otherwise.

"What's the matter?"

"You are relying on Lord Zheng's loyalty to the Dragon Throne." Jie traced a circle in the air. "Realistically speaking, here in *his* castle, surrounded by *his* men, we are at his mercy. The local imperial soldiers will obey you, but they are garrisoned in other parts of the city."

Kaiya frowned. "So realistically speaking, it is just you and me."

"Do you wonder why the *Tianzi* did not send a complement of imperial guards? I think—"

Chirping footsteps sounded in the hall, seeming almost an affront to the pleasant birdsong outside. Kaiya quieted Jie with a wave of her hand.

One of the castle pages stopped outside the door and dropped to his knee. "*Dian-xia*, Lord Zheng wishes to see you."

Had he made a decision on the marriage proposal? Or had they found Fang Weiyong? The doctor would never betray her secret...would he?

The Founder extolled the virtue of preparedness. Only a fool would walk into a meeting uninformed. Kaiya raised an eyebrow toward Jie, who tilted her head at the tacit order.

In the meantime, Kaiya would stall for time. She nodded toward the page. "I will call on him once I have made myself presentable."

The page bowed. "*Dian-xia*, the lord will pay his respects here. He would never presume—"

"It is all right. I have been sequestered in the guest wing for so long. Go, apologize to Lord Zheng on my behalf for the delay."

"As the princess commands." The man rose, shuffled back several steps, and then headed back down the halls.

She turned back to Jie, who was already gone. No need for an order, just like the first time. Thank the Heavens for reliable retainers and friends.

Left alone, Kaiya rose to her feet and glided over the plush red carpet to the bloodwood make-up table.

Upon Kaiya's arrival at the castle, Lady Zheng had offered lip rouge, eyeliner, and other cosmetics, which now sat on the mother-of-pearl inlaid table, untouched. It wasn't for fear of contact poison in the cosmetics—though Lady Zheng had little love for her—but rather because there was no need for impractical vanities.

Until now.

In the mirror, a gaunt young woman with sunken cheeks and red-rimmed eyes frowned back at her. Where was the once-in-three-generations beauty, who'd bedazzled kings and generals? Or even the naïve and pimply girl who'd been duped by a dragon in disguise?

Kaiya blinked away a tear.

A tear. Had she just experienced an emotion? Longing? She tried to grasp at it, to hold on to it, but the feeling slipped through her fingers. She gazed back at the mirror. The perfect lines of her image were frayed by sleepless nights of plotting and calculating. That woman, while beautiful, couldn't coax a man to her bidding without the magic of her voice.

It was time to conjure a different type of magic. She reached for the eyeliner.

After half an hour, her transformation was complete. Kaiya experimented with a few facial expressions, which looked as artificial as the layers of cosmetics hiding the ravages of worry and fatigue.

Jie's reflection appeared behind her, eyebrows scrunched together. The Insolent Retainer's childlike beauty spoke of an innocence which had probably never existed in the half-elf. "*Dian-xia*, Lord Zheng is in his audience chamber with his wife. It pains me to say Lady Zheng does not hold you in high opinion."

Unsurprised, Kaiya nodded. "Go on."

"They questioned Fang Weiyong, who claimed you wished your health to be evaluated after your long journey in the wilderness."

Fang knew her story well, yet chose to protect her. His lie made her deception easier. Kaiya rose to her feet. "Come, let us see what Lord Zheng wants."

With Jie in tow, Kaiya walked through the halls. Unlike the lumbering men, she deliberately stepped to make the dark floorboards chirp in harmony with the symphony of spring. It was almost like the perfect melody of songbirds in the Kanin Wilds, on the frigid day when she'd fallen into a freezing tidal pool and tricked Tian into jumping in after her. She stifled a scoff at the coy girl and gullible spy.

She turned into the main audience room. A dozen provincial guards and a handful of silk-robed advisors sank into salutes on the forest-green carpeted floor. Several three-panel screens, lacquered and inlaid with shells and stones, lined the plastered walls. Behind one of the screens, someone breathed rapidly.

From where he sat on an embroidered silk cushion at the front of the room, Lord Zheng pressed his forehead to the ground. His dark green formal robes rustled, and his jade bead necklace clattered. At his side, his wife pursed her lips before bowing as well. Her blue gown, with its pink cherry blossom motif, was more suited for a younger woman.

"You may rise," Kaiya said.

Both looked up, and while remaining bowed, Zhang Han stood and surrendered his place to her. He then took several steps back and sat cross-legged facing the mat. "Thank you for seeing me, *Dian-xia*."

She glided up and knelt on the mat, placing her hands in her lap while Jie came and stood behind her. As protocol demanded, Kaiya tilted her head a fraction to show appreciation for his etiquette. "To what do I owe the pleasure of this meeting?"

From his seated position, Lord Zheng bowed low. "Forgive my insolence, but I have heard rumors."

Rumors. Unless Fang Weiyong revealed it, nobody within Zheng Han's earshot would know of her secret; and Jie had said Weiyong lied for her. Lord Zheng was baiting her.

"As I once told your son, Zheng Ming, rumors proliferate like weeds after spring rains."

Lord Zheng nodded. "Yes. But for every dozen weeds, there is an occasional flower."

Zheng Ming had once responded with almost the same line, what seemed to be a lifetime ago. Their conversation had been lighthearted in nature, a dance between man and woman. Kaiya had little interest in games right now. "What kind of flowers do we speak of?"

Zheng Han stared at the floor. "Hopefully, those that have not yet been despoiled."

If not for the *Tiger's Eye*, Kaiya would've bristled at the audacity, despite the truth behind it. She feigned outrage nonetheless, scowling and lowering her voice. "Lord Zheng, given your many years of faithful service to my father and now my brother—"

He raised a hand. "One is dead. The other not only invites rebellion with weakness, but is also far away from here."

There it was, the first hint of mutiny. A stalwart supporter during Father's rule, even through the last unstable years, Zheng Han had never showed any signs of treason before.

And now, she was his virtual prisoner.

Jie fidgeted, eyes darting around the room and a hand inching into a sleeve. Yet even with her formidable martial skills, she wouldn't stand a chance against the entire castle garrison, let alone all of the provincial soldiers in the surrounding city.

It was time to persevere. Kaiya said, "So, what do you suggest?"

Lord Zheng pressed his forehead to the ground in a symbolic gesture that rang hollow, given his words. "My personal physician would like to confirm that the...uh...flower...is still...blooming."

Her younger self might have fainted from the suggestion. Instead, Kaiya pressed her hand to her mouth and widened her eyes for show, even as she weighed the alternatives. If she refused outright, Zheng Han would not dare force her; at the same time, he might hold her hostage.

On the other hand, the truth could give her leverage...*if* she could trust a hereditary lord who now questioned the authority of the *Tianzi*.

As Wang Xinchang, the founder of the dynasty, once said, *Ambitious men are easier to manipulate than loyal ones*. Maintaining a withering stare on the lord, she spoke. "Fang Weiyong, come out."

Lord Zheng straightened, and nodded toward the screen.

A guard emerged, leading a tall man whose head was covered by a black hood. The soldier lifted the cowl, revealing a gagged Fang Weiyong.

Zheng Han gestured toward his prisoner with an open hand. "Here is the source of the rumor: your doctor. I took him into custody for speaking ill of the Imperial Family. By the *Tianzi's* own law, I will have him publically lashed. Unless he spoke the truth."

Eyes round, Weiyong tried to shake his head through the guard's grip on his hair. Knowing him, he must've been horrified not so much by the threat of a whipping, but by the notion he might have betrayed her.

He ceased his struggle when she flashed a smile at him.

Kaiya leveled her gaze at the lord. "Doctor Fang is not just my doctor, but my friend. One who would not and did not betray my trust. The question is, can I trust you, Lord Zheng?"

Zheng Han bowed again. "Of course, *Dianxia*."

Indeed. "Then send everyone but your wife, my handmaiden, and Doctor Fang out, so we might confer."

"Your handmaiden must go, too."

"I see trust only goes so far. You have nothing to fear from a girl."

Lord Zheng's eyes narrowed. "It would not surprise me if the girl had more weapons concealed on her than all of my guards here combined."

It wouldn't surprise Kaiya, either. Though how Zheng Han knew... "Very well." She nodded toward Jie.

Smirking, the Insolent Retainer bowed and padded toward the door.

"All of you, withdraw." Lord Zheng waved his hand. His men bowed and shuffled back out of the room, though one ungagged Fang Weiyong first. The double sliding doors closed behind them.

Satisfied, Kaiya bowed her head. When she raised it, she pressed her hand to her belly. "As you suspect, I am already pregnant."

Lord Zheng's lips twitched, his look one of vindication. He opened his mouth to speak.

She raised her hand, silencing him. "Doctor Wu confirmed they are twin boys. Your first grandsons."

Zheng Han's satisfied smirk slipped, replaced by a raised eyebrow. "How?"

"Your fourth son, Zheng Tian."

His jaw slackened, even as Lady Zheng sucked in a sharp breath.

Kaiya nodded away their shock. "Unless the *Tianzi* and his wife conceive, your unborn grandchildren are next in line to the Dragon Throne."

With a cough, Lord Zheng shook his head. "They may be my grandsons by blood, but they are illegitimate. They will—"

Kaiya raised a hand to quiet him again. "They are not." She tilted her chin to Weiyong. "As a priest of Yang-Di, Doctor Fang consecrated my marriage to Tian. Were the rites and rituals carried out correctly?"

Fang Weiyong nodded. "Yes, *Dian-xia*. Your actions and corresponding vows followed ancient conventions, and are thus all legitimate."

Kaiya turned back toward Lord and Lady Zheng. "As you see, I am your son's widow. Yet his banishment would raise questions as to the validity of your grandsons' claim. That does not have to be the case, in the eyes of the realm. This is why I wished to marry your firstborn."

Lord and Lady Zheng exchanged glances, their expressions beyond Kaiya's skill at deciphering. If only Jie were in the room to gauge their reactions. Lord Zheng looked back at her, his face as blank as when he asked if Tian had died bravely.

"Timing is critical," Kaiya added. "Tian's seed has grown in my womb for three weeks now. If I do not consummate a marriage to Ming soon—"

He opened his mouth to interject, only to be interrupted by Lady Zheng. She rose to her feet, waddled forward, and pressed her forehead to the floor in front of Kaiya. When she rose, she extended a tentative hand toward Kaiya's abdomen. "Forgive me, *Dian-xia*, but may I?"

It was an audacious request, to be sure, but how could Kaiya deny it? The legacy of Lady Zheng's beloved, dead son grew inside of her. Kaiya took Lady Zheng's hand in hers and placed it against her abdomen.

Lady Zheng's tearful eyes met hers. Her voice cracked. "Are they really Tian's?"

Were they? Kaiya couldn't be sure, given the unfortunate circumstances. She contrived her most compassionate smile and nodded.

It was wrong to lie, not just on moral grounds, but also because the chance of exposure. The other potential father was just two weeks away, on the other side of the Great Wall. Emperor Geros didn't know she carried twins; he only believed the son she would bear was his.

He would spare no resource in the vast Teleri Empire to retrieve her. Fortunately, the Great Wall and a hundred thousand muskets stood between them.

CHAPTER 4:
Perfect Storms

From his place near the bloodwood dais, Chief Minister Hong Jianbin scanned the hundred-some men gathered in the Hall of Supreme Harmony. Whether it was his old eyes or the dozens of golden columns obstructing his view, he counted surprisingly few provincial lords kneeling among the blue-robed officials.

A messenger in dark green robes strode between the ordered rows of men, his boots clacking on the polished white marble floors. He dropped to a knee in front of the dais and bowed as he proffered a letter wrapped in rice paper.

Sitting on the jade Dragon Throne, the recently-anointed *Tianzi* gazed toward the tile ceiling mosaic of circling twin dragons high above. He probably would not have noticed if the messenger transformed into Hua's guardian dragon spirit.

Hong expected no less from his puppet.

From where she sat on the smaller gold Phoenix Throne, the Empress Wu Yanli coughed. The *Tianzi's* head shifted from right to left, the dangling pearls on his hat clicking. His lazy comportment clashed with the regal yellow robes, which he rearranged more than once. At last, he looked down at the messenger and waved a hand.

A minister shuffled forward and received the letter in two hands. He unwrapped it and snapped open the note inside. In a high-pitched voice, he read, "A missive from *Tai-Ming* Lord Zheng of Dongmen Province. To the *Tianzi*, Son of Heaven and Enlightened Ruler of Hua. Your sister,

Princess Wang Kaiya, wishes to wed my son Zheng Ming. I approve, and ask for your blessing."

Hong's heart lurched into his throat. Despite his attempts to smear Young Lord Zheng in the princess' eyes, despite the two being separated for half a year, she still had feelings for the philandering lordling. How could he secure his own—

"It is an appropriate match." The *Tianzi* grinned and turned to the Empress. "I introduced them myself."

The Empress nodded, her own lips curving up into a radiant, if measured, smile. One of the realm's foremost beauties, she appeared much too young for the imperial yellow robes. Still, she wore the trappings of state with more dignity than her husband, and stayed disengaged from state affairs as a woman should.

Hong did not plan for her to remain Empress for long. However, if he could not stop the marriage of Princess Kaiya, the *Tianzi* would have to stay alive so Hong could still influence policy. Hopefully, the *Tianzi* would remember their private conversation from just a few days earlier.

"*Huang-Shang,*" Hong said, using the formal address for the *Tianzi*, "while Young Lord Zheng would make an excellent husband for the princess, the Zheng family is old and unquestioningly loyal. Perhaps you should use her marriage to reward an up-and-coming lord." Like him, after another promotion.

General Shan, bedecked in ceremonial dragon armor, stood and bowed his helmeted head. Doubt hung in his voice. "*Huang-Shang*, did Lord Zheng agree to send the ten thousand troops you ordered for the pacification of Nanling Province?"

The *Tianzi* raised his eyebrow at the minister. So unsightly for an emperor!

The official scanned the letter again. "No, General."

"Thank the Heavens," General Shan muttered.

The shortsighted man apparently did not see the danger of insurgency from those still loyal to Nanling's former ruler, the fugitive Peng Kai-Long. Hong pursed his lips. He knew all too well the threat.

A snake like Peng could wreak havoc, even from across the border in Rotuvi, where he enjoyed asylum after Princess Kaiya had failed to secure his extradition. It was time for Hong to share his brilliant idea, inspired by his lover's silly notions of chess strategy. In their last several games, the girl had kept her knight in reserve, saying that, like the imperial garrison in Wailian County, it could be deployed at any time.

As ridiculous as it sounded, she had won those games, just like all the others. "*Huang-Shang*," Hong said, "As the Founder emphasized, only the sword can bring order to a province in rebellion. Perhaps we should redeploy your most battle-hardened troops in Wailian to help contain the insurgency."

General Shan coughed. "*Huang-Shang*, such a move is not only unnecessary, but foolish as well. There is no insurgency. The lords of Nanling have already forsaken the rebel Peng and sworn fealty to you. Furthermore, Wailian County is outside of the Great Wall, protected from Rotuvi only by a shallow river and your armies. It is our main source of firepowder ingredients."

Hong shook his head. "*Huang-Shang*, until you finish replacing the lords of Nanling, the old guard will always be faithful to Peng and remain a threat. As for Rotuvi, they are embroiled in a war with their northern neighbors and cannot possibly divert attention toward Wailian."

The *Tianzi* looked from Hong to the general and back again. At last, he waved toward the crowd of officials. "What is the disposition of Rotuvi, Minister Yan?"

The aged man, who rarely came to court, bowed. "*Huang-Shang*, Chief Minister Hong is correct. Rotuvi is not a threat to Wailian. However, I agree with General Shan. I do not think we should leave it defenseless."

Hong laughed. "You are here to report, not to think, Minster Yan. Thank you for reporting." He turned from the minister and locked his gaze on the *Tianzi*. He had not worked his way into the Emperor's good graces for so long, just to have a few upstarts reject his brilliant ideas.

The *Tianzi* sighed. "General Shan, draw up the orders to redeploy the imperial garrison in Wailian. Ensuring stability in Nanling is our utmost priority. Even in exile, Cousin Peng may still try to interfere in matters there."

Peng Kai-Long, ruler of Nanling Province before his plot to seize the Dragon Throne failed, counted his men in the low light of dusk. Only thirty. It was still twice the number of imperial army troops stationed at the Great Wall's southernmost gatehouse.

A light flashed in quick succession from the top of the Wall, clearly visible from the mill where his men gathered. The signal meant his twenty loyalists on the inside of the gatehouse had taken control. If they suffered no casualties, he would command nearly fifty men. Just enough to hold off a counter-attack by imperial forces until his reinforcements arrived.

If Kai-Long's other assets in the countryside did their job, that counter-attack would never come, because the main imperial garrison, based out of *his* castle, wouldn't know about their loss of this strategic point until it was too late.

With a silent gesture, Kai-Long motioned his men toward the gate. It took three excruciatingly long minutes to cross the meadow. The doors to the gatehouse opened, allowing a column of light to escape the hushed crack.

Fools. They were supposed to keep the interior dark until he and his other men slipped in. If he weren't so shorthanded, the imbecile in charge might face punishment.

Inside, the provincial soldiers each dropped to one knee, fist to the floor. A dozen bodies lay against the walls, while three bound imperial soldiers gawked at him.

Kai-Long motioned to the doors. "Close them."

While one man jumped up to obey, his loyal shift captain looked up. "*Jue-ye*, we suspected the imperial army was testing our loyalty to the Throne when we received your secret orders. I am heartened to see that you are truly here in Nanling and not a refugee in Rotuvi."

Peng nodded at him. "Yes, rumors of my flight were greatly exaggerated. Or contrived, as the case may be."

The imperial officer spat. "You'll never succeed. You don't have enough men to hold the gatehouse."

Kai-Long knelt over him. "Word of my return spreads through the province as we chat. Despite their vows of fealty to the *Tianzi*, my loyal retainers and soldiers will side with me. We outnumber the imperial army garrison."

The officer laughed. "Maybe you could defeat us, but not without sustaining crippling losses. The *Tianzi* will quell your rebellion. With the nation's vast wealth and power at his command, he will send another army, and another, and another, until you are battered into submission."

Kai-Long turned his back on the man and motioned for his lieutenant. "Flash the signals on the other side of the Wall, to let the Madurans know we hold the gatehouse. They must arrive by daybreak, before the changing of the guard."

The provincial captain raised an eyebrow. "The Madurans?"

Kai-Long gestured him into silence, even as he looked back toward the imperial officer. "Tell me, what did the Founder write about facing an opponent who cannot be overwhelmed with force?"

His question was met with a gawk.

Kai-Long shook his head, laughing. "This is why the loyalist governor sits idly in *my* castle, unaware that I am about to take it back. Even the imperial officers have grown complacent with the nation's wealth, and have forgotten military lessons." He motioned toward the provincial captain. "What did the Founder write?"

"Avoid confrontations which lead to unacceptable losses..." The captain's eyes widened. "...have others fight for you."

Kai-Long grinned. Over the past several months, he had corresponded with Madura's Prince Dhananad. With the prince's unhealthy obsession over Princess Kaiya since she'd danced for him a year ago, he'd jumped at the invitation to invade.

However, instead of helping a foreign invader crush the imperial army, Kai-Long planned to keep his own provincial troops in reserve. Once he deemed both sufficiently weakened, he would close off the South Gate and cut Madura's supply lines. The Madurans would be caught between a hammer and an anvil, and he would do everything to ensure his enemies thinned each other out before crushing them both.

In the meantime, he had a dilemma. Cousin Kaiya was within reach of his agent in Dongmen Castle. He would like nothing more than to exact vengeance for her role in foiling his previous coup.

The only question would be how to keep Prince Dhananad motivated once she was finally dead.

Before Madura invaded and occupied her homeland, Leina had once been a dancer. Now she spent her days—and mostly nights—choreographing Cathay's unraveling from a small house in the capital's entertainment district.

A spring breeze wafted in through her window, brushing aside satin curtains and carrying in afternoon sun and the flitting laughter of coy Night Blossoms. In this high-end section of the Floating World, the ladies unwittingly heard secrets—either as they served rice wine to lounging officials or lay beside clients muttering in their sleep.

It was again time to harvest those secrets.

Leina knocked three times on the back wall of the pantry. When no response came, she pressed the dwarf-made trigger, and the wall opened outward, revealing the rear corridor of the adjacent Jade Teahouse. The sliding doors to private rooms stood ajar. All empty, as was to be expected at this early hour.

She brushed aside the dangling curtain of jade beads and pearls and walked out into the main room. There, a handful of Night Blossoms congregated among the bloodwood chairs and tables, sharing tea and gossip before dusk. Perhaps even the legendary *Moquan* spies would never collect as much information as the girls in the Floating World.

Jasmine covered her mouth and laughed. Her sheer gown revealed the outline of the bloodwood chair she sat on, as well as her ample curves. Orchid lounged in a seat across the table, her eyes conspiratorially narrow.

Who came up with such names? Perhaps they took the term *blossoms* too literally. Or maybe feeding into the stereotypes excited the high officials and lords who sought them out.

Jasmine looked up and beckoned her over. "Lotus, Lotus, come!"

Leina chuckled. With a working name like Lotus, given for her half-Ayuri blood, she had no leeway to criticize floral names. She glided over and took a seat.

Orchid brushed a hand across Leina's sapphire-colored silk robe. "By the Heavens! This color brings out the walnut in your skin tone!"

Leina covered her mouth and giggled, imitating the irritating feminine conventions of Cathay. "Your gown, too. It emphasizes your dark eyes!"

Orchid batted her eyelashes. "That's what Minister Geng said, that lecherous old man. You know, he's looting the imperial treasury from beneath the *Tianzi's* nose."

Amazing to think how quickly the government fell into inefficiency, just with the death of the previous *Tianzi*. It almost made Leina's job too easy.

Jasmine sighed. "I wish some of the imperial treasury would find its way *here*. Many of my clients are tightening their belts instead of loosening them! Almost all of the officials and soldiers from Linshan Province went home."

A perky voice called from the entrance. "That's because Linshan's Lord Lin didn't want to be drawn into the Nanling expedition."

Purple Autumn. *Ziqiu*, in the local tongue. Now *that* was a clever name. Rumors swirled about the pretty young woman, like the lilac and silver gown she wore tonight. Supposedly only sixteen, she disappeared during the day, and only appeared some nights. Her clients were utterly secret, even to the other working girls' omniscient network of whispers. Perhaps like Leina, she had a powerful patron.

She sauntered over, swaying her thin hips, and took a seat at their table. With a lift of her chin, she tossed her rippling hair over her shoulder and then leaned in close. "Lord Lin has quite an independent streak. I wonder how long the realm will be able to rely on Linshan Province."

How could she know that? Could Lord Lin be her patron? Leina flashed a coy smile and threw out some bait. "I hear Lord Lin is quite virile."

Purple Autumn's pretty face contorted for a split second. Then her eyes flicked toward the entrance. When they returned Leina's gaze, her expression was unreadable. "As much as I would love to join you ladies for tea, I have an appointment to keep." She rose to her feet and strolled through the bead curtain and into the back rooms.

Orchid jerked her head toward the entrance and cringed. "Lotus..."

Leina looked in the long mirror behind the tea bar.

Her patron, Chief Minister Hong, hobbled in, shoulders slumped in a telltale show of defeat. Her stomach twisted.

"Until next time, my friends." Leina rose and nodded at the Night Blossoms. Of course they knew of her secret liaison with one of the most powerful men in Cathay. Nonetheless, what happened in the Floating World stayed in the Floating World.

Leina hastened to the secret door and back into her house, the one that Old Hong had bought just for their clandestine meetings. Little did he know of the other meetings she held there, with insurgents bent on toppling the Wang Dynasty.

Opposition to the *Tianzi* was the only thing certain about her visitor earlier in the day. She had kept Golden Fu at arm's length, feeding him a healthy mix of information and misinformation. The middle-aged spice merchant was likely much more than he appeared, but what he said rang true: the insurgency, while well-armed, would be too scared to act until the number of imperial troops in the capital declined. Maybe Purple Autumn's insights on Lord Lin could compel them.

Now, she had to clear the evidence of her meeting with Golden Fu before Hong limped in. A flash of gold in the parlor's red Ayuri carpet drew her eye. She snatched it up. A pin. It belonged to Young Lord Liu Dezhen, the heir to Jiangzhou Province. Married to the *Tianzi's* cousin, Wang Kai-Hua, his baby boy had crept up the line to the Jade Throne. Or at least, that's what she told Young Lord Liu.

By the time Hong made it into her sitting room, she had cleared Golden Fu's wine cup from the carved rosewood table. She slid out the matching chair and invited him to sit.

He plopped down, and before she could kneel beside him, he took her arm in his worn, leathery hand and pulled her into his lap.

"A letter from Lord Zheng arrived earlier today," Hong said. "The princess wants to marry Zheng Ming."

Mention of the handsome young lord stirred memories of when she had slept with him, in a failed attempt to frame him for sedition. Her heart fluttered at the reminiscence of their passionate lovemaking, but in this moment, Leina had other priorities. She had heard defeat in Hong's voice too often not to recognize it now. Without her subtle persuasion, he would have never become Chief Minister in the first place.

She reached out to stroke his leathery old skin, trying to avoid a shudder. "Dear Hong, you have the *Tianzi's* ear. All he has to do is order her to return before she has a chance to marry. She would never disobey her brother's direct command, especially with all of the hereditary lords questioning his fitness to rule."

Hong shook his head, his thin white hair ruffling the silken pillow cover. "But he won't force her to do anything. He is so fond of her."

Leina wondered if that were the case. After all, the *Tianzi* was actually considering allowing old Hong to marry Princess Kaiya. If only Hong knew that the princess was pregnant with—

Hong sighed. "I think the princess is lost to me."

If only he knew the whole story. Better that he didn't, because coveting the princess had kept him motivated for what, three years now?

To have the princess return to the capital would temporarily put her out of Zheng Ming's reach, thereby keeping Hong inspired. Yet it might also loosen Leina's hold on Hong, and therefore her indirect influence on the *Tianzi*.

Leina could not allow the latter to happen, at least not yet. Certainly not when the princess had demonstrated an ability to sniff out a conspiracy. Furthermore, from what Leina knew from the *other* letter she received earlier in the day, the princess' sudden desire to marry Zheng Ming showed she had a mind for conspiracy as well.

It was a gamble. Up to now, Leina had beaten the odds, using Hong as a game piece to outsmart and outmaneuver all of the other lords and ministers jockeying for power. Whether she decided to lure the princess to within reach of Hong's paws or her assassin's knife, the first step was the same: getting a message to her.

Now, she had to convince Hong the idea was his, something she did on a regular basis. She patted him on the chest. "It is a shame she does not want to come back yet. I am sure her brother's widow would like to see her."

Hong turned to her, his bright eyes gleaming in stark contrast to his wrinkled face. "Brilliant! Where would I be without your woman's intuition?"

Woman's intuition, indeed. Her plotting was masterful, worthy of the statesmen from the First Age of Empires. Nonetheless, she feigned delight with a girlish smile.

It was a look Leina had mastered in the three years since she arrived in Cathay in search of the Cathayi father who had left her behind in occupied Ankira. Using her mother as a hostage, Emperor Geros had given her a decade to undermine Cathay from the inside. His latest messenger bird came with a demand for immediate results, so he could claim Princess Kaiya and their unborn son.

Once Hong left tonight, Leina would contact her agent. Princess Kaiya would need to be harmed just enough to keep her convalescing at the border for when Geros arrived.

CHAPTER 5:

Luck Favors the Well-Prepared

Sitting on a bloodwood chair by her anteroom window, Kaiya strummed at a *pipa*. The pear-shaped, fretted instrument resonated in harmony with the birds outside, each note intertwining in the orchestra of spring sounds. Yet even if her music was technically perfect, it lacked the passion she'd evoked in the past.

Kaiya had held crowds enthralled as emotions rippled through her music. Today, her only audience was Jie, and the half-elf seemed more interested in sharpening her knives. Kaiya continued strumming, despite the futility of trying to charm the Insolent Retainer. At the very least, her sons could appreciate it as they grew in her womb.

The *pipa's* melody shifted as it bent around a newcomer by the open door. Even if her music couldn't influence others, at least she could still sense how others' positions and motion influenced sound.

Kaiya's hands froze as she looked up.

A page dressed in dark green livery knelt near the door. When her gaze met his, he shifted his eyes down as protocol demanded. He proffered a letter in two hands. "D-Dian-x-xia, y-you have a message from the capital."

Without waiting for acknowledgement, Jie padded over to the young man and plucked the paper out of his fingers. She ordered him out with a perfunctory jerk of her head, and then delivered it into Kaiya's hands.

Her name was written on the front of the cover paper in a distinct script. Though she didn't have to, Kaiya flipped it over to confirm it was Sister-in-Law Zhao Xiulan's name on the back. The former Crown Princess before the death of Kaiya's eldest brother, Xiulan was like an older sister.

Kaiya opened the cover, unfolded the message within and read:

Kaiya, I was overjoyed to hear you were safe after your months stranded in the enemy-infested Kanin Wilds. The news has helped at least a little in numbing my devastation at the loss of the crown prince. I hope to see you soon.

Her eyes glided over the enchanted script, its Artistic Magic imbued by Xiulan's hand. The uncertain sweeps and melancholy whorls tugged at Kaiya's heart for a split-second. The sensation quickly disappeared, replaced only by an appreciation of Xiulan's technical mastery, as displayed in the perfect balance of characters.

Even so, Sister-in-Law's misery screamed out in her handwriting. Xiulan had suffered through five fruitless years of trying to conceive an heir. The late *Tianzi's* poor health had made the pressure all the more oppressive. Now, she'd lost her beloved husband, and her position as mother of the future *Tianzi*.

Kaiya scanned the letter once more. A return to Huajing would put another three days between her and Ming, further delaying a marriage. Yet a sense of duty prodded, urging her to comfort the one who had always given her encouragement. Maybe even confide in the sister who always supported her.

Yet without emotions, how could Kaiya possibly empathize with Xiulan's loss? And if she shared her secret pregnancy, wouldn't it just crush someone who'd tried so hard and so long without success?

Kaiya glanced over her shoulder.

Jie stood above her, her mouth drawn into a pout. A trickle slid down her cheek.

A tear?

Jie's eyes had not so much as glassed over at the death of Tian, her best friend and the man she loved. Now, she looked miserable for Xiulan, whom she was not especially fond of.

"What is it, Jie?"

The half-elf's voice choked. "I...I... The misery in the words. It's crushing."

Even if Kaiya didn't feel it herself, the power of Xiulan's script made Jie cry. Jie never cried. Not only that, she'd proven immune to Artistic Magic ever since Kaiya started learning to focus it.

Kaiya rose and strode toward the door.

Whereas the letter's unhappy lines brought Jie to tears, it brought the princess to her feet. What did she plan to do now?

Whether the princess was charming dragons or enchanting dictators, Jie had learned that if anything was predictable about Princess Kaiya, it was impulsiveness. That meant constant vigilance.

Granted, under the *Tiger's Eye*, she'd been completely reasonable and logical. At least up to now. Jie wiped her eyes and trailed down the hall after her ward.

Yet the magic embedded in the miserable twists and turns of the former Crown Princess' handwriting continued to tangle through Jie's heart, yanking out bittersweet memories. Her near-kiss with Tian, forestalled by duty. Then she'd lost him. First to distance, then to the princess, and finally to death.

Persevere. It'd been her mantra for the last week. She wore her discipline like armor, and took pride in her ability to focus. Then again, she had yet to be truly tested with anything beyond trailing Lord Zheng, forging a letter, and snooping on a meeting.

Now, even the thought of the letter's words hacked away at years of training, leaving her a quivering ball of pathetic emotion. Just like any other girl. Just like the princess, before the *Tiger's Eye* transformed her into an efficient and practical dwarf clock.

Jie looked up. She'd been staring at her feet, lulled by the floor's rhythmic chirping.

Princess Kaiya was gliding down the halls a good seven paces ahead of her.

Just in front of the princess, the messenger from before dropped to his knee, left fist to the ground, the other hand—

The messenger. When he'd delivered the Crown Princess' letter, beads of sweat had gathered on his forehead. His eyes had darted back and forth while he clasped and unclasped his hands.

"*Dian-xia*! Danger!" Hand on a *biao* throwing star, Jie surged forward, her short legs covering half the distance in just a second.

A second too late.

The princess stopped where she stood. She looked back. Her eyes widened like a startled doe's.

A short blade flashed in the messenger's hand. He sprang at her.

Even as the princess' turn opened a window for Jie to attack, the assassin's lunge on the other side of the princess rapidly closed it. Where was his knife?

Jie flung the *biao*.

It whistled within a hairbreadth of the princess' ear, shaving off wisps of her hair and catching the man in the right breast.

He let out a shriek.

So did Princess Kaiya.

In a split second, Jie spun the princess out of the way and reached the messenger.

She spiraled out of his slow thrust and wrapped up his hand. With a quick twist of her wrist and jerk of her hips, she dislocated his elbow and shoulder.

He screamed again and the bloody dagger slipped from his fingers.

Jie silenced him with an elbow to the temple.

Even as unconsciousness quieted the would-be assassin, the rest of the castle roared to life. Provincial guards raced toward them with bared weapons, their feet kicking up a chorus of discordant chirps on the nightingale floors.

Heavens, that'd been close. Jie looked back toward the princess. "*Dian-xia*, are you unharmed?"

Though standing, Princess Kaiya's face paled and her eyebrows knitted together. She held her left hand to her right flank as she spoke through gritted teeth. "He...he grazed me. It hurts, but does not seem serious."

"Summon Doctor Fang," Jie called out. They'd gotten lucky. Perhaps Princess Kaiya's inadvertent spin had turned her out of the path of a more dangerous blow. Jie beckoned the guards.

She glared at the shift captain, who now knelt before them. "Why was the messenger not checked?" Unless in the hands of an imperial guard or a secret agent like Jie, no weapon was allowed near a member of the Imperial Family.

The captain bowed. "We *did* check him, at the entrance to the guest wing. He only carried the message, no weapons."

Bending over, Jie retrieved the curved knife. The imprint at the base of the blade showed it came from a provincial weaponsmith.

A weapon issued to a provincial soldier.

Her gaze raked over the assembled men as she held it up. "Is anyone missing their dagger?"

Two dozen hands checked their sides. A soldier rose, took a tentative step forward and dropped to his knees. He proffered a scabbard. "D-Dian-xia, it was m-my dagger. I s-swear, I didn't give it to him. I didn't even realize it was gone."

"You will submit to questioning." Jie snatched the sheath out of his hand and upended it. Fine white sand cascaded out. An old pickpocket trick; one used by her clan. Could the assailant be

one of her temple brothers? Until a year ago, she'd only heard of one renegade, the one she had been tasked with tracking down in the Eldaeri Kingdoms. Since joining Princess Kaiya's guard detail, she'd met two. She rolled the unconscious man over.

Probably no older than thirty, he didn't look like anyone she'd ever seen before, and she knew every *Moquan* to pass through the Black Lotus Temple over the last three decades. He was too small for a Teleri Nightblade. Perhaps he belonged to one of the small, less reputable clans than pawned their skills to provincial lords. "Do any of you recognize him?"

Heads shook.

"Very well, bind him and let me know when he wakes."

The man was skilled enough to find a way through a cordon of guards, steal a knife, and attack the princess. He'd hesitated, and they'd gotten lucky.

For the Imperial Family, luck was not enough. Jie would have normally sniffed out such an attacker in her sleep, but in her current state, she wasn't fit to serve.

Though an imperial guard's response to failure would be to offer his own life, the *Moquan* didn't live by such codes. She knelt. "*Dian-xia*, my skills are compromised. I must be released from your service."

"Jie, I—" Princess Kaiya tumbled to the ground. Her hand slipped, revealing a splotch of red, blooming out from the wound on her right flank.

CHAPTER 6:

Up In Smoke

With his brother Shu at his side, Ming peered through the darkness. Luckily, the dense clouds obscured the white and blue moons. The black of night, combined with the rustling of the river, covered his men's retreat. As he suspected, the Teleri would not launch a night attack, despite the expiration of their ultimatum.

A drop of cold rain plopped on his cheek, followed by another. He brought his hand up, feeling the wetness between his fingers.

A chorus of crossbows clicked and twanged, barely audible over the patter of rain in the moat.

"Take cover!" Ming threw himself into the dirt, dragging Shu down with him.

A few grunts and screams emanated from the embankment where the rear guard remained.

"Fire!" yelled an overzealous imperial officer.

"Hold your fire!" Ming barely heard his own voice over the disjointed roar of muskets. The sound would give away their dwindling numbers.

The second volley of muskets rang out, and then a third, each answered by shouts of pain in the moat.

Beside him, Shu struggled to his feet, pulling his *dao* from its sheath. All signs of his earlier nervousness disappeared.

Ming grabbed him. "Wait. Wait for the fourth volley."

That fourth volley, to be fired by the first line once they reloaded, never came. Only the clicks of triggers and hammers.

Ming strained his eyes through the darkness and rain to get his best view of the embankment. Nothing but dark shapes. Imperial musketmen shouted in frustration. Metal clashed on metal where his provincial spearmen stood.

He turned to Shu. "Fall back to the rendezvous point. At the first sign of Teleri on the bridge, blow it." Shu might not be much of an archer, but surely he could hit the firepowder kegs.

From among the spearmen, his other brother Lun yelled, "Fall back, fall—" A choke interrupted his command.

Ming strode forward, unslung his bow, and fit an arrow. Squinting, he tried to locate Lun in the fray. It was so hard to differentiate the dark shapes, even if the Bovyans were that much larger. Instead, he took aim at the figures slogging through the moat and loosed arrow after arrow into the Teleri surge.

The imperial gunnery officer nearly backed into Ming. "*Dajiang*, we can't hold the embankment much longer. We must sound the general retreat."

Ming clenched his jaw. This was becoming into a disaster. With a nod, he yelled, "Fall back to the bridge!"

A horn blared out, sounding the retreat.

As his own men ran past him, Ming worked his way backward, shooting arrows at Bovyan soldiers as they appeared at the top of the embankment. When he could no longer make out any of his own men in front of him, he spun and ran.

At the bridge, he withdrew a light bauble and dropped it among the kegs of firepowder to illuminate the area. Would a flaming arrow ignite the powder in the rain? If only he had been able to complete the evacuation on his own terms.

A cordon of his own spearmen at the other end of the bridge parted and let him through, then followed him in retreat. He raced to the opposite tree line, where Shu waited next to a burning brazier. He proffered an arrow coated with pitch and wrapped in cloth.

Ming dipped it in the brazier and it caught fire. He nocked the arrow, took aim at the bridge, and loosed.

His men all fell silent as the arrow arced through the clearing and landed in the middle of the bridge.

Nothing happened.

Ming loosed another half-dozen in quick succession, all with the same result.

Shu squeezed Ming's arm, his fingers trembling. "We must blow the bridge, take away their means to cross. Otherwise, the Teleri will be able to march right up to the Great East Gate."

"I know," Ming snarled. He looked among the officers and soldiers gathered around the brazier. The only alternative would lead to death or capture. "I need a dozen volunteers to follow me back, each bearing a torch and a spear. We'll fight our way back to the bridge and light the firepowder up close."

Several men stepped forward.

Shu's face paled in the flickering firelight. "But... Eldest Brother, that'll mean your death."

Ming frowned as his stomach tightened. As if he didn't know. He had much to live for: Marriage to the princess. Inheriting the province. Yet the last time he was faced with dying in glory or living with cowardice, he had chosen the latter. Not this time. "You are now heir to Dongmen Province, Shu. Give Father my regards."

With a deep breath, Ming drew his sword with one hand and took a torch with the other. "Charge!"

He and his men had sprinted three-quarters of the way through the clearing when the first Bovyan appeared on the bridge.

The soldier's head raked back and forth before he spun on his heel and yelled back into the fort, "The Cathayi plan to destroy the bridge!"

They needed to reach the bridge before the Teleri reinforced it. Ming pushed faster, blinking rain out of his eyes.

He reached the western end of the span just as five Bovyans joined the first on the east side. Forming a line, they marched with lowered spears, their heavy steps sending reverberations through the wood.

Ming's hands trembled as he thrust the torch at the several lines of firepowder leading back to the kegs. He prepared to jump back, in case he could escape the blast. From his sides, his men surged forward, swords held high.

None of the firepowder lit.

It should have! The rain couldn't have possibly made it so wet so soon. Or maybe they had scattered it as they ran through it?

There was only one way. He abandoned his desperate game and started toward the kegs.

The Teleri vanguard crashed into his men.

He was almost to the first keg, just ahead of the enemy.

A spear shaft slapped into the torch. The reverberation wrung his hands. The torch jerked from his grasp, flew over the side of the bridge, and sizzled and sputtered in the river. Another spear drove into his left shoulder, punching through his studded leather breastplate like paper.

Pain exploded in his shoulder before all went black.

The low murmurs grew louder, nudging Ming into consciousness. The throbbing in his temples intensified, screaming above the pain in his shoulder. It almost distracted him from the hard cot under his back. He lifted his head and blinked away his fuzzy vision. It was the same roughshod officers' room as before. This time, he had guests.

Surrounded by four imposing officers, Emperor Geros stood above the wood table, pointing at what appeared to be a map.

Ming struggled to sit up, though his left shoulder, now in a sling, protested.

A Teleri captain cleared his throat. "Your Eminence, Lord Zheng has awoken."

Geros looked up from the table and grinned like a wolf. "Don't be rude, Captain Mirin, help the lord up."

The captain strode over and assisted Ming as he rose into a sitting position. Even an enemy deserved courtesy, and Ming nodded in thanks.

In two steps, Geros loped over and knelt, meeting Ming's bleary eyes. "I commend your efforts, Lord Zheng. Your ploy to escape on your own terms almost worked. However, you really should have accepted my offer."

Ming blinked several more times, then glared. "You were lucky it rained."

"Luck favors the well-prepared and the better-informed." After quoting the Wang Dynasty founder, Geros' smirk reeked of self-satisfaction.

A wry smile tugged on Ming's lips, unbidden. "I—"

Geros raised a hand. "I hope you have learned from your experience, because I am going to make you one more offer."

Another offer? What could the Teleri Emperor want that Ming could provide? He cocked his head. "I don't have much to give you, except maybe a tour of your own fort."

Geros laughed. "What did the Wang founder say about knowing your enemy? You do not seem to know what I want. But I know what *you* want."

Ming remembered the last time someone spoke to him in riddles: when Golden Fu had virtually mugged him. Just like then, this time would undoubtedly be some kind of set-up. He started to throw his arm up, only to be greeted by a stabbing pain. "You have it all figured out, then. What do you need with me?"

"I want you to open the East Gate of Cathay for my armies."

He wanted *what*? Not that Ming would do it, even if it were within his power to do so. He closed his gaping mouth. "Why would I betray my people?

Geros snickered. "Because I will offer you governorship over all of Cathay. You will be the link between the Teleri occupation and the Cathayi people. Oh, the first few months will be difficult, but we will engineer some way to make you look heroic."

"I am no collaborator." He had decided in his charge toward the bridge not to be remembered as a coward. He certainly had no intention of being denounced as a traitor.

"You can also marry Princess Kaiya." Geros stared up at the thatching.

Ming's eyes must have stretched to the size of tea cups before pinching again. "You want her for yourself."

"Yes—but alas, due to the Bovyan Curse, my preordained death is a year away. After I am gone, she is yours."

From what Ming had heard, the curse limited a Bovyan's lifespan to thirty-three years. The balance was forfeited to sustain the Orc King. Nonetheless... "I do not want from you what I could claim on my own."

Geros laughed. "You are in no position to claim anything. Except a grave plot."

Ming shrugged. Better to die a hero than live in infamy. "Nonetheless, I won't help you."

"Maybe not willingly. Your father might have a different opinion."

So he would be served up as a hostage. But Ming's father was too loyal to open the floodgates, even. Even if it meant the death of his firstborn. Ming still had three brothers. Though that assumed Lun survived the battle. Nonetheless, he forced a confident tone. "My father will never be labeled a traitor for the sake of a single son."

A Teleri officer appeared at the door. "Your Eminence, we have cut off the retreating Cathayi. They are hunkered down three hours east of here. I request reinforcements to chase them down."

Shit. Ming's stomach clenched.

Geros flashed a toothy grin, which reached the kinks of his mismatched eyes.

CHAPTER 7:
Doubts

The stream rustled nearby, setting the rhythm for the chirping birds. Kaiya opened her eyes to the warmth of the midday sun. The orange blur of her eyelids gave way to a perfect blue sky. New spring grass caressed and cooled her back; her propped-up head felt warm. Something dug into her right side.

Kaiya started to dislodge whatever it was, when a round shadow encroached into her field of vision. She squinted, the image coming into focus.

Tian.

Upside-down. Her head was cradled in his lap, the cross of his legs a comfortable pillow. His intelligent eyes held her entranced.

He brushed an errant lock from her face. "Good afternoon, my love."

Kaiya's heart leaped so high, it might have joined the clouds outside. She pushed herself up, and tried to straighten out the wrinkles in her robe and untangle her hair. It would not do for her beloved to see her so disheveled. She looked up through her lashes.

He leaned in and took her cheeks in his hands.

She closed her eyes and parted her lips, inviting him closer.

Tian accepted the summons, pressing his lips to the divot between her collarbones. The heat of his breath sent a tingle down her spine, which intensified as he lavished kisses up her neck. Longing to feel his mouth on hers, she tilted her head forward to meet his.

But instead of meeting her lips, he leaned back. Kaiya opened her eyes. He grinned at her, the crooked smile emphasizing the defined curve of his jaw. "Not now."

She pouted. "Where are we? Did I join you in the world between death and rebirth?"

He shook his head. "I would be disappointed. I sacrificed myself so you might live. And our children."

Kaiya sucked in a breath and looked down at her belly. "They are yours?"

Tian's gaze followed hers. He placed his hand over her womb before lifting her chin. "It is not yet your time. You have much to do. He has much to do."

He? Not they?

She opened her mouth to protest, only to find Tian's lips against hers, his arms enveloping her. The energy drained from her body and she melted into him, all complaints forgotten.

Then his hand slipped to her right side. Pain seared in her flank.

Kaiya sat up straight on a bedroll, a kiss of warm spring air brushing across her face. Joy melted through her fingers like water, leaving only the ice of despair. Emotion, raw and uncontrollable, seized her breath.

Then pain tore at her right side. As quickly as they had come, her feelings disappeared. She blinked away the tears and brought her left hand to the wound.

"*Dian-xia*, rest easy," Fang Weiyong's voice called.

Rubbing her eyes, she found him in a chair by the window of her sunlit room. He slid down into a kneel.

She pulled her white sleeping robe tighter. Modesty seemed appropriate.

"*Dian-xia*." Jie sat cross-legged by the closed door. She rose onto her knees, head bowed.

Weiyong stood and shuffled toward her. "Please, rest. You lost a lot of blood, and were unconscious for two days."

Was that all she lost? Kaiya placed a hand on her belly. With all the doubts surrounding the pregnancy, perhaps it was for the better. No worries about who would inherit the Dragon Throne, no urgency to get married. At the same time, if they had been Tian's... Oh, no. Her chest squeezed, a long-forgotten sensation.

A smile danced across Weiyong's face. "Do not worry, *Dian-xia*, your unborn sons were safe last time I checked. May I?" He gestured toward her wrists.

The sadness that came with the prospect of losing Tian's children slipped away as if it had never peeked out from under the *Tiger's Eye*. She offered her wrists to him, and he knelt over and felt her pulses.

Brow furrowed, he nodded several times. "Yes, you still feel very pregnant to me. Unfortunately, my pulse diagnosis does not compare with Doctor Wu's, so I cannot tell you much more than that."

Her dilemma remained.

"May I see the wound?" Weiyong averted his eyes, not that it mattered.

With a nod, Kaiya laid her arms at her side. "Please."

Jie crowded in behind him as he opened the right lapel of her robe and untied the dressing. "*Dian-xia*, please lift your breast." His voice sounded professionally sterile.

The breast felt full and sore in her hand, the nipple sensitive, no different from the day she found out she was pregnant. Surely her twins were fine.

Kaiya craned her neck to get a good look at the wound. Delicate stitches melded the thumb-length cut together, barely noticeable from her vantage point. "I can tell you did the sewing, Weiyong. I have seen Jie's handiwork. She is much better at cutting flesh than sewing it back up."

The Insolent Retainer's cheeks flushed, perhaps at the verbal jab, or maybe in memory of the same words the half-elf had once used to describe Tian's skill with needle and thread.

Weiyong smiled again. "I am honored by your praise, *Dian-xia*. Fortunately, the blade entered obliquely and glanced off your rib. It nicked your liver. I disinfected the cut with an herb wine wash. I have been treating it with a balm that should hopefully compensate for my poor stitches. I do not think it will leave much of a scar."

At least not a physical scar. If and when she ever broke free of the *Tiger's Eye*, this incident would be yet another memory that might keep her up at night. And why? "Jie, did you coax some answers out of the assassin?"

Jie sighed. "Yes, *Dian-xia*. However, the answers were inconsistent. At first he insisted that Lord Zheng ordered him; later, it was the bidding of the *Tianzi* himself. Another remote possibility is Peng Kai-Long, meddling from beyond the Empire's reach."

Unless Lord Zheng had suddenly decided to wipe his hands clean of her, he would have no motive. Her brother, even less. As for Cousin Peng...a hired knife taking her unawares reeked of his underhanded methods. To think she had trusted him for so long. "Did you find out anything else?" she asked.

"My *biao* punctured his lung, and he did not last long enough for more subtle interrogation." Jie dropped to both knees and hung her head. "*Dian-xia*, I was careless. I should never have let him get too close to you. I—"

"You were thinking of Tian, weren't you?" It was the only way to explain the Insolent Retainer's mistake.

Jie stared at the floor, the tips of her ears flushing deep scarlet. "It doesn't matter. I am of no use to you right now. We must arrange for a replacement."

A year and a half ago, Kaiya hadn't wanted Jie as a bodyguard. Now, she was indispensable. Not just for her skills, but also for her willingness to speak her mind. However, there was something she was not saying. Kaiya propped an elbow underneath her. "Help me up."

If Weiyong shook his head any more, it might very well come off. "*Dian-xia*, you must rest more. The stitches will tear if you move too much. If that happens, if you lose much more blood, you might very well miscarry."

Energy flagging just from that small effort, Kaiya collapsed back down on to the bed. "Weiyong, please leave us."

He knelt there, eyes darting from her to Jie and back again. At last, he rose. Holding a low bow, he shuffled backward out of the room.

Kaiya reached over and took Jie's hand in her own. She gave it an affection squeeze, or at least the closest approximation of how affection would feel. "You are my sworn sister and I trust you more than you can know. I order you to hold your post."

Jie's lips pursed, her focus on the floor. "As the princess commands."

It wasn't convincing. Kaiya squeezed her hand tighter. Jie would not openly oppose her order, but would find some way to skirt around it. There had to be some way to coax her out of her sadness. "I order—"

"No." Jie pulled her hand back. "A sworn sister doesn't give orders. A sworn sister doesn't steal the man her sister loves."

At last, the unspoken truth, finally verbalized. Yes, Kaiya had surmised Jie's love for Tian long ago. She'd even asked directly, only to receive evasive answers that confirmed her suspicions. In her heart, Kaiya had known, and she had wronged Jie. That much was clear now.

"We were caught up in emotion. I can see that now, with the *Tiger's Eye*—"

"Which I used on you, so you could cope with *your* grief. How do I cope with *my* grief?" Tears welled in Jie's eyes as she glared. "Because of you, I don't even know what I am mourning. The death of my best friend? Loss of a love that never blossomed?"

Kaiya closed her eyes, the accusations weighing her down more than the blood loss. "I am sorry."

"Being your support is in direct conflict with what I need myself."

"What do you need?" Kaiya opened her eyes and looked at a truly insolent retainer.

Jie's lips twisted into an ugly frown. "Distance. From you."

From her spot near the door, Jie cast a glance at the princess sleeping on her bedroll. Once the princess' mind was made up, there was little anyone could do to change it. Her sense of right and wrong, combined with stubbornness, had put her in more than one unenviable position. Including the one she faced now.

Princess Kaiya was a worthy liege, and Jie now regretted her outburst.

Nonetheless, she could not perform her duties effectively until she had time to sort out her feelings. Letting an amateur assassin so close was proof of that.

She moved out into the hall, away from the princess' prying ears. She then wrote a letter encoded in the secret language of her clan. Her adopted father, the master of the Black Lotus Temple, would consider her request, even if the princess did not.

To Master Yan:

A rival clan sent an assassin to kill Princess Kaiya. Although they did not succeed, she was injured. I made several careless mistakes and failed in my mandate to protect her. I wish to be replaced by another adept.

Yan Jie

She folded the letter, using a six-crease pattern which only one of her clan could open without ripping. When a castle valet came by to check on the princess, she slipped it into his hand along with the princess' messages. "When the next rider goes to the capital, have him deliver this one to the Cold Sun Bell Foundry."

The horse-relay messengers would reach the capital in four hours. A mute worker at the foundry, hired anonymously by the Black Lotus Temple decades before, would drop the message into a funerary urn at a specialty shop. A *Moquan* trainee would pick up all the items left there and deliver it to Master Yan. A replacement might be able to relieve her within three days.

The chirping of floorboards interrupted her self-pity. At the door, the castle steward himself knelt. "Please wake Princess Kaiya. We have news of Young Lord Zheng Ming."

CHAPTER 8:

Viper Awakened

Coming out of a coma on a funeral barge next to a dozen cold bodies wasn't as unsettling as knowing he'd somehow intentionally put himself into that coma. Though he didn't remember how he'd gotten on the log raft, or even who he was, he knew he'd awoken too early, before his injuries had stabilized.

The barge had come ashore, lodging in the rich-smelling earth. The river, swollen by spring melt, tumbled past, while the wind rustled in budding tree branches. A cool breeze brushed across his bare chest, causing his skin to erupt in goosebumps.

He groaned and pushed himself up into a sitting position. A warm sensation trickled down his back, emanating from the place where pain seared in his shoulder. That stab wound, unlike the numerous cuts all over his body, would bleed him out. Each heartbeat brought him closer to death.

Two lithe figures dressed in doeskin clothes stared at him with wide, almond-shaped eyes. With streaks of red-and-white paint across their faces and feathers in their hair, they looked as wild as the untamed forest around them. They were...elves. How he knew that, he wasn't sure.

The silence lasted only a few seconds. The brown-haired male, with sharp features and a sharper dagger put his hands on his hips. When he spoke, the flowery language belied the threat in his voice. "*Amane esaya na!*"

How to respond to such gibberish? He cocked his head and shrugged, sending a surge of pain through his shoulder.

The girl with chestnut-colored tresses had rounded features that spoke of human blood. Her high-cut doeskin skirt revealed toned thigh and calf muscles. Appearing to be about twelve human years, she evoked an unsettling sense of familiarity. Had he met her before?

She poked her companion in the back, thankfully not with the steel dagger at her side. "*Esala iyani na.*" Even if the language remained unintelligible to him, her tone dripped with sarcasm. She then turned to him. "Bow before the messengers of the gods."

Messengers of the gods? He had to suppress a laugh; not just because the two carried daggers and all he had was the broken sword in his lap, but also because it hurt too much. At least he understood her words, though they were not his mother tongue.

He fumbled with a response in the language the girl spoke. "You are not messengers of the gods. You are just..." He frowned, trying to dig the word out of the cobwebs entangling his mind. The term translated to *spirit*. Perhaps the native speakers of this language considered elves to be angels? He switched to his own native tongue: "...elves."

The two elves exchanged glances and spoke animatedly in hushed voices.

He took the opportunity to survey the surroundings. Large men lay dead around him on the beached raft, their hands folded across their chests. All had suffered wounds delivered with surgical accuracy from swords, knives, and *biao* throwing stars. Two smaller bodies with black hair and honey-toned skin seemed familiar. Flies buzzed over the stinking, bloated corpses. Hopefully, he didn't smell as ripe.

He looked back up at the arguing elves. "I'm bleeding to death."

They both turned and stared at him. At last, the male extended an open hand, hopefully to help him to his feet and off the raft, and not to pull him into a gut stab.

His wounds complained as he took the elf's hand. Though small in his own, its callouses spoke of years of use, likely with a weapon.

When he lurched onto shore, the female pressed on his shoulder wound, sending flares of pain up and down his back. She started wrapping strips of cloth around his chest. "Hold still. We need to slow this bleeding until we can get you to a healer."

"I am Dior," the male said, the sound rolling of his lips like cherry blossoms dancing on the wind. "What is your name?"

His name. His brow furrowed as he tried to remember. "I don't know."

The female harrumphed. "We have to call you something."

"Munikai." Dior grinned.

She rolled her eyes. "In our language, that means *Sleeps With Dead.*"

Not-Munikai cringed and shook his head. "Maybe something else?"

Her eyes brightened as a cute smile blossomed. "*Feneyas.* The Awakened."

Feneyas nodded. "Better than *Sleeps with Dead.* What is your name?"

"Krztsh." It was more a grunt than a name, and could not have possibly belonged to the beautiful language they sang. She studied her feet.

Feneyas tried to repeat her, but his mouth couldn't imitate the sounds. He shrugged, sending another jolt into his shoulder and evoking an involuntary wince. "I am sorry, but your language—"

With a violent shake of his head, Dior clucked. "It's not *our* language. We call her Kiri."

Kiri. Now that was more manageable. Feneyas bowed, right fist in his left palm. "I am honored to meet you. Dior and Kiri."

Both stared at his salute until Dior met his eyes. "Kiri, do you think Feneyas can move without returning to sleep with the dead?"

She nodded. "I have slowed the blood loss, but he'll need to see Nayori if he stands a chance of living."

"Then let's get moving. Blindfold him."

"Blindfold?" Feneyas stepped back, raising his hands defensively—as if he could defend himself in his weakened state. Pain erupted in his shoulder again, forcing a wince.

Kiri grunted. "Hold still, or you'll start gushing again."

"Yes." Dior nodded. "You're a stranger, and while you don't look like one of the Metal Men, we need to ensure the safety of our village."

The large warriors must've been the Metal Men. Feneyas sighed and bent over to allow Kiri to cover his eyes.

"Don't worry," she said. "I'll point out any obstacles along the way."

A bumped head and a dozen near-stumbles later, they came to a stop. Yet despite their attempts to conceal the path to their village, the sounds and smells and the number of paces and turns told him they were just two *li* north-northeast of where they found him, high in the trees. At least seventy-three distinct voices whispered around him.

Dior's hands pressed on his shoulders, easing him down to sit on gnarled wood. Kiri's slender fingers worked the knot of the blindfold. It slipped off, the soft light of dusk blurring his vision.

Feneyas blinked, allowing everything to come into focus. Greywood tree limbs meshed together to create a broad platform towering high above the forest floor. Several male and female elves trained arrows on him from where they stood on branch bridges to other trees. Not like he posed much of a threat, with his energy flagging.

Kiri and Dior bowed as an older elfwoman alighted on the platform, from the ramp of branches that wound around the tree. She appeared to be forty. Her face paint formed circles and dots along her cheeks and forehead. Dark hair scattered down bare shoulders. A doeskin dress with tassels and shells hung down to her bare feet. She regarded Feneyas with large, dark eyes that spoke of both beauty and wisdom.

Dior raised his head. "Nayori, this is Feneyas." He continued in their own language, with the Metal Men mentioned twice.

Feneyas bowed, placing his right fist in his left palm, again attracting snorts and stares.

Nayori's nod wasn't reassuring. "Your salute is not of the Metal Men, nor of the Kanin humans who worship us as messengers of the gods. You look a little different, too." She pointed at him. "The eyes, the skin tone. You belong to the People Beyond the Wall. Your kind has not ventured here for centuries. How did you come to our lands?"

Memories drifted in the distance, beyond Feneyas'reach. He shook his head. "I don't remember."

Nayori's studied him. "Were you fighting with or against the Metal Men?"

His aversion to the large men and recognition of the other two bodies suggested they were foes, yet why would he have been lain with his enemy's honored dead? "Against. I think."

She flashed a smile. "Dior, bring blankets and lay him down. We shall see if Ayara favors him enough to allow me to channel her divine healing. Feneyas, do you submit to will of the gods?"

Feneyas nodded. "I don't have a choice. I will die. Without your help."

"Very well. After hearing my prayer, you will sleep. You will dream. You will share dreams with those who care about you. When you awake, it will either be before the throne of Koralas to receive judgment, or back among us. "

When Dior returned with blankets, Feneyas lay down. He closed his eyes, perhaps for the last time.

Above him, Nayori's voice lifted in song. Though he couldn't understand the words, the sounds were beautiful, like angels singing. Maybe that was why the Kanin humans thought the elves were messengers of gods. For him, it stirred fleeting memories of an onyx-haired beauty, which disappeared before he could grasp them. If this was the last sound he ever heard, he would die happy.

"Now sleep, Feneyas. You will dream. Of the past. Of the future. They may very well remind you of your life before you slept among the dead."

CHAPTER 9:
Unsavory Options

The low buzz of murmuring soldiers addled Kaiya's mind even more than the loss of blood. At Fang Weiyong's insistence, she'd been carried on a litter to the audience room. It now took all her energy to remain upright and seated on the cushion at the head of the chamber.

Her face must've been quite pale, given the gawking of the provincial ministers and officers when they saw her. Lady Zheng, in particular, wrung her hands and hyperventilated. She'd fussed and ordered Kaiya to return to her room and rest, though Lord Zheng had insisted on her presence.

He sat perpendicular to Kaiya, his expression stoic as a carved stone. Unlike the other men, who fidgeted and shared whispers, he remained absolutely quiet.

Sitting motionless across from him, Jie shared his silent stoicism. Beside her, Weiyong's eyes raked back and forth among the people present, occasionally meeting her gaze with a compassionate look. Thank the Heavens for reliable friends.

Two soldiers marched in, both with dirt-streaked faces framed by disheveled hair. Their torn uniforms rustled as they approached. One was an imperial army officer in royal blue, the other a Dongmen provincial solider in dark green. Both dropped to their knees, fists to the ground.

The imperial officer spoke first. "*Dian-xia*, I bring regrettable news. Almost our entire army of five thousand was killed or captured by the Teleri."

All five thousand! Lost because of her.

Lady Zheng sucked in a sharp breath. "What about my sons?"

The provincial soldier raised his head. "My Lady, I regret to inform you that Young Lord Lun was gravely injured while leading our spearmen. He might not survive. Young Lord Shu was captured. We are unsure of Young Lord Ming."

Lady Zheng wobbled in her place. Her husband placed a supportive arm around her, although his expression didn't change.

Kaiya made her best attempt at a sympathetic gaze. Nonetheless, all she could think about was Ming going missing. If she couldn't marry him, what was the next best option for legitimizing her sons? "Tell us what happened."

"*Dian-xia*." The imperial soldier bowed again. "After we captured the Teleri's westernmost fort, our scouts reported a small army rapidly approaching by forced march. *Dajiang* Zheng Ming ordered us to deploy immediately. However, the enemy did not appear until a day later, with significantly larger numbers than originally reported. *Dajiang* ordered a general retreat under the cover of darkness, while he stayed back to destroy the fort's bridge. He never rejoined us."

Lady Zheng's shoulders heaved as she raised a hand to cover her mouth. Her eyes glossed over.

Lord Zheng patted her shoulder, but nodded toward the solider. "Did he succeed in destroying the bridge?"

The man bowed. "No. The Teleri main army was able to cross."

"Continue." Lord Zheng's voice remained steady.

The imperial officer looked up. "The enemy cut off our retreat, and though we fought valiantly, we did not have much firepowder. Young Lord Zheng Shu surrendered. They sent the two of us back with a message: Emperor Geros will arrive by dusk today to negotiate terms for our prisoners' release."

Dusk! Despite Kaiya's mental haze, two things were clear. First, the chance of an expedient marriage to Ming had dwindled, along with the chance of legitimizing her sons. Second, Geros was close by. Oh, to get back to her room, close her eyes and think.

Lady Zheng jabbed an accusing finger at her. "You. It is *your* fault. My sons went to rescue *you*. Now one might have already joined his youngest brother in the grave, while another is a prisoner of war, and the eldest is missing. You are a curse on our family."

There was no denying the accusation. Kaiya was the cause of the Zheng family misfortune. If only she could *feel* the remorse as she bowed her head, contrite, as if it would make her any less a monster.

Yet it was the least of her concerns at the moment. In a castle whose lord contemplated rebellion, her standing had just become more tenuous. If she weren't pregnant with Tian's sons, Lord Zheng might just as soon use her as a bargaining chip. If he knew just how valuable she was to Emperor Geros...

Still holding her bow, she found Lord Zheng in the corner of her eye.

He stared at her, expression empty. If only it was easier to read him, to know what he was thinking. Beside him, Lady Zheng glared, lips pursed and brows furrowed. At this point, Kaiya's only worth to Lady Zheng was as a womb for her grandchildren.

If they were her grandchildren at all.

Lord Zheng waved a hand toward his guards and councilors. "Everyone, out."

The men exchanged glances, but rose all the same. They bowed and filed out of the room in a rustling flash of court robes.

"You too." Lord Zheng nodded at his wife, whose eyes widened. He then jerked his head at Jie and Weiyong. "Them as well. Princess Kaiya and I have matters to discuss in private."

Lady Zheng rose, hesitantly, keeping her eyes on her husband. Kaiya nodded to Jie and Weiyong. Once they were gone and the doors to the audience chamber shut, Lord Zheng shifted to stand directly in front of Kaiya.

He bowed low, then rose and made direct eye contact. "I am afraid my wife is too emotional. All she can focus on now is her sons. As lord of this province, I must look beyond that."

With a nod, Kaiya quoted the Founder's consort: "'At times, the ruler must make personal sacrifices for the good of his people.'"

He sighed. "Yes. I have been thinking your situation over. It might very well be that in order to protect all of Hua, I will lose my sons. You realize what this means for your sons, my grandsons?"

Kaiya nodded again. "I—"

"I have a solution." He bowed low. "If I take you as my wife, the realm would think the boys were mine."

What? He couldn't be serious. That solution was even more unpalatable than marrying Ming. Thank the Heavens for the *Tiger's Eye*, allowing her to stay objective.

Lady Zheng had no such objectivity. Her gasp could be heard from outside the room. The doors flew open, and she stomped in with several guards on her heels.

Jie, face flushed scarlet, slipped in behind them.

"Don't you dare." Lady Zheng pointed an impertinent finger at Kaiya. "Conniving whore! You will spread your imperial legs for anyone to get your son on the Dragon Throne."

It had been Lord Zheng's suggestion, and she was getting blamed! Even with the objectivity of the *Tiger's Eye*, her moral compass could never allow her to do such a thing to another woman. She shook her head. "I did not agree. I do not care about the throne, only that Hua survives."

Lady Zheng spat. "Hua will survive whether or not a Wang sits on the throne."

Kaiya shifted and bowed low to Zheng Han. "I must decline. The Edict of Marriage, as promulgated by Queen Regent Wang Yuxiang, ended polygamy in the Empire three hundred years ago. I would not have you discard your wife of three decades. There must be another solution."

Lord Zheng eyed her, his expression blank again. "At least consider it. We must have a contingency plan if Emperor Geros demands more than we can offer in return for my sons. Now return your room and rest. You will need all your energy when we meet with him this afternoon."

That was the worst possible scenario. Up to now, only a handful of people knew she'd been Geros' prisoner, pressured into his bed to guarantee the safety of hostages. If he saw her, he'd demand she be turned over as part of any prisoner exchange. If he told others that she carried his child, then Lord Zheng would trade her for his sons without a second thought. Lady Zheng might push her out the gates herself.

No; whatever else one could say about Geros, he was a smart man. He would downplay Kaiya's value so that he could demand more for the Zheng brothers. Though a new problem occurred to her.

Would the emotional armor of the *Tiger's Eye* hold strong if she faced her rapist?

Jie had figured out many ways to get around without sending the nightingale floors into a chorus of chirps. Stepping in the right spot, pop-vaulting at corners and other acrobatic tricks made the castle a virtual playground.

Of course, going through windows and climbing along the outside walls bypassed the chirpy corridors altogether. She now hid just outside of Lord Zheng's bedroom antechamber, eavesdropping.

He wouldn't find comfort in Lady Zheng's arms tonight.

"You Turtle's Egg! How could you even consider abandoning me?" If Lady Zheng's voice were any sharper, Jie's knives would be jealous.

"Calm down, my love," Lord Zheng said. "It would be in name only."

"Liar! You just want a young princess in your bed."

His silence was damning. Well, that would explain Ming. The shit didn't fall far from the bull's ass. At last, he spoke. "It was your idea to gain power for myself, to declare Dongmen independent. This is our chance—"

"Not at the expense of my sons. You have already given up on them, too. That little harlot is wrapping her tentacles around you."

Lord Zheng sighed. "Our sons are lost anyway. What they will ask—passage through the Wall—will mean the end of our province, the end of Hua."

His footsteps approached the window, and Jie crouched lower. He pushed open the shutters. When he spoke again, she heard the smile in his voice. "What I propose will make us rulers of all of Hua. Tian's son, legitimized by my name, will sit on the Dragon Throne with the Mandate of Heaven, and we will rule as regent."

"And this has nothing to do with your desire to bed the princess?"

"Of course not!" His answer was much too quick, much too defensive. Would Lady Zheng see through it?

A bell tolled, indicating the fifteenth hour of the day. When Lord Zheng left the window, Jie crept back along the walls toward the princess' chambers. With the Teleri arriving in two hours, the princess would have to make some difficult choices about her future.

And also, perhaps, the future of Hua.

CHAPTER 10:
The Doe-Eyed Girl

Sitting cross-legged in the cool grass, Feneyas leaned back and lifted his head to the warm rays of the spring sun. They danced in orange hues over his eyelids. Silky tresses brushed warmth across his lap. He opened his eyes and looked down.

A stream of black rippled across his legs, pillowing an ethereal face. The perfect lines of a delicate jaw accentuated high cheekbones and the slim nose of the young human woman as she slept.

The beauty opened her eyes.

Those eyes! Large and liquid like a doe's, they met his. Unbidden, his heart pounded.

"Heavens!" Her voice could have been an angel's, and she spoke in a language whose familiarity could only be his mother tongue.

A cool breeze blew a tendril of hair across her cheek, and he brushed it out of the way. Who was this girl, and why did she seem so familiar?

She sat up with the grace of a willow branch in the breeze. She swept delicate hands over her robe and through her hair before turning back to him. Chin down in a pout, she looked up at him through her lashes.

All the racing thoughts jolted to a stop. When he bent forward and cupped her face in his hands, she closed her eyes and parted her lips.

Thus invited, he brought his lips to the hollow between her collarbones. He pressed several kisses up the smooth skin of her neck.

She tilted forward to meet his lips...

Feneyas sat straight up on a soft fur blanket. The Doe-Eyed Girl was gone. His chest ached as if someone had torn his heart out.

He looked around, and paused where a little elf girl sat, staring at him. Just like Kiri, her rounded features spoke of familiarity and human blood. On closer inspection, she might have been his rescuer's younger sister, or perhaps even a younger version of the half-elf.

"You awake," the girl squeaked in the foreign language he understood.

He shook out the sleep and his strange dream, blinking his eyes. Sun filtered in through the tree canopy, dappling the platform in light. The elf woman who'd prayed for him was gone; though, as he rotated his shoulder, so was the pain. A male stood on a branch nearby, bow in hand.

The little girl scrunched up her nose and pointed at him. "Come. You stink. Bath."

Feneyas eased himself up, his joints complaining from lack of use.

She beckoned him, then skipped down the stair of branches.

At the bottom of the tree, she turned south. The rustling sounds of the river grew louder. Nobody else was around, yet eyes followed him from up in the trees. Even when he gazed directly back, there were only treetops with sun peeking through leaves and branches.

"Come, Feneyas." The girl tugged at his bare arm and they slipped through a gap in boulders.

On the other side, a small waterfall tumbled into a circular pool, about three times as long as a man's height. Above, the canopy of trees opened to allow sunlight to filter in.

Standing in waist-high water near the waterfall with her back to him, Kiri looked over her shoulder to acknowledge his arrival. Long, thin scars crisscrossed her toned back. A large blotch marred the vertebra at the base of her neck. She beckoned him. "Come in."

Something felt wrong about a grown man bathing with a—

"What's wrong?" Kiri turned all the way around, exposing smooth, unscarred skin. Feneyas averted his eyes.

"*Ish oklerk krazt sho, grztck.*" Kiri's ear-splitting words sounded nothing like the flowery language she spoke among the other elves. Nonetheless, they had a familiar ring to them.

The younger girl nodded. The tilt of her head revealed a similar scar at the base of her neck. She slipped through the gap in the rocks, leaving Feneyas and Kiri alone.

"Get in. You stink so bad, I can smell you from here." She took a step back, closer to the waterfall. "I am not going to hurt you. If I had ill intentions, I would have left you to bleed out among the Metal Men."

Wherever he was from, they must have different conventions. Keeping his eye on the water, Feneyas eased half a toe in the pool.

Kiri giggled. "Aren't you going to take off your pants? They need washing, for sure, but..."

Heat rose to his cheeks. He spun around, loosened his pants' drawstrings, and stepped out. Covering himself, he turned back around. He focused on her forehead.

Her expression stiffened and she placed a hand on her chest. "I'm sorry. I didn't realize you were injured *there*. Did *they* hold you prisoner, too? Was it punishment?"

Injured? Punishment? Why did she emphasize *they* and shudder? Feneyas shook his head. "I am *not* injured or punished. At least, I don't think so. It's just that...well, where I'm from...men and women don't bathe together."

Her face brightened and her mouth opened in a contagious smile. "What? So silly." She took a step to the side, which elevated her. The water now came up to the middle of her thighs. "To think I was concerned about you. Now get in and wash off your stench."

Feneyas looked back down. Maybe the heat in his cheeks would cause the pool to boil. Still concealing himself, he waded in. Through the cold, clear water, his feet squished into the bluish sand of the pool's floor. Several smooth rocks rose out of the sand. Only when he was submerged to the waist did he lift his hands and hug himself to counter the chill. He faced away from her.

"You *are* funny." Behind him, Kiri's hand plunged into the pool with a splash and came out with a rush of water. Something swished through the air toward him.

Without conscious thought, Feneyas shifted to the side and caught a wet cloth as it passed above his shoulder. He turned and glared.

"Wow..." Kiri's eyes rounded like river pebbles for a split second. "Use that to scour the dried blood off." Her surprise transformed into an ear-to-ear grin, reminiscent of a temple guard dog.

The memory of a knee-high, white-furred dog flashed through his mind. If only he could step back and see the sign by the temple door, maybe it would spark more recollections.

"Hey, you there?" Kiri asked.

He looked up and nodded.

She chuckled. "What did you dream about in the realm between life and death?"

"A beautiful girl with doe eyes." He scrubbed vigorously, turning his honey skin pink.

Kiri cocked her head. "Did you know her?"

"She seemed familiar."

"Maybe someone important to you. A sister, perhaps."

He shrugged. Kissing a sister felt as wrong as bathing with a girl. "Maybe."

"Here, let me help you with your back." She waded over.

Feneyas flinched, and then froze up when her warm hand pressed on his back.

With her other hand, she reached around and pried the washcloth from his fingers. "Wow, you have quite a few scars."

"So do you. Where did you get them from?" Perhaps having something to talk about would keep his mind off the awkwardness of having the girl wash him.

She froze in place, and he turned around. Tight lips and a faraway gaze replaced her usually mischievous expression and flippant demeanor. Apparently, he was breeching taboo territory.

"No need to—"

Without looking at him, Kiri dropped the washcloth in his hand and sloshed to the edge of the pool. After brushing the water off with her hands, she snatched up a towel on the bank and dried herself off.

Feneyas waded toward his own clothes, still shy about covering himself. By the time he got one foot through the pants legs, Kiri had already thrown on her clothes and was disappearing through the crack in the rocks.

"Kiri!" Feneyas hurried after her, nearly tripping on the second pant leg.

When he made it through the gap, Kiri was crouched by the opening, looking outward. She held an open palm behind her in the universal sign to stop.

Feneyas slid forward and knelt, craning his neck just above Kiri's shoulder.

A human woman in a deerskin dress ran on the path below, her feet crunching in the dry underbrush as she clutched a bundle of cloth to her chest. Her long dark hair, braided back in a single queue, indicated she was married. How did he know that?

Heavier footsteps cracked and thumped after her. Not far behind, two large men gained ground with loping strides. A golden nine-pointed sun blazed on the left breast of their black surcoats. Longswords and daggers thudded against their hips and thighs.

Feneyas started to rise, but Kiri pulled him down. She glared at him with eyebrows ferociously knitted together. He stopped in place and evaluated the scene unfolding below.

One of the soldiers dashed past the woman and stopped to cut her off. She skidded to a halt, just as the other came up from behind and seized her shoulder. He whipped her around with a sneer.

"Come back quietly, and your punishment will be lenient." His words were in yet another foreign language, one Feneyas also understood.

Apparently, the woman didn't. She tried to twist out of his grasp, screaming in a language similar to the one Feneyas used to communicate with the elves. "Let go, stop!"

The first man snatched one of her arms and yanked. The swaddled package she held started to wail.

Every instinct screamed to observe. It wasn't his fight.

A small voice tugged at him, reminiscent of the Doe-Eyed Girl's, from his dream. *You must help.*

But with what? He looked down at his hand to find Kiri's knife, though it was barely large enough to skin a rabbit. Nonetheless, it felt right in his hand, and the voice prodded him out into the open.

"You!" Feneyas emerged from the gap, speaking the same language as the men, though it came out haltingly. "Let her go."

Soldiers and woman all stopped and gawped, the baby's crying and Kiri's hiss cutting through the sudden silence.

"The ghost of the Warrior From Beyond the Wall," the woman whispered in awed tones.

The solider on the right smirked as he slid his sword out and pointed it. "This doesn't concern you. Go back where you came from and we will let you live."

"I have a dozen archers. Their arrows are trained on you." Feneyas pointed behind them. "Go back where you came from. We will let *you* live." Would they believe his bluff?

"Then shoot." The second man spread his arms wide, inviting an attack. When nothing happened, he jerked his head back up the path. "Come on, let's take her back."

Kiri whispered through her teeth, "What are you telling them?"

One man seized the crook of the woman's arm, spun, and started to walk away. The other kept his sword pointed at Feneyas and backed up. When he turned his head toward his comrade, Feneyas hefted a stone and flung it.

The rock smacked into the soldier's temple, sending him tumbling to the ground.

Feneyas picked up another and hurled it. The other man released the woman and covered his face. The stone slammed into his arm.

Staggering back, the soldier rubbed the wound.

Feneyas landed on the ground in a crouch, not even remembering his jump. What was he thinking? Armed only with a small knife, he didn't stand a chance against the angry soldier who now brandished a longsword.

Hack, chop, thrust—Feneyas turned out of the line of each attack as he closed in. Up close, he yanked his opponent's dagger out of its sheath with his left hand, joining his own knife in a crossing arc. The blades sliced through the flexor tendons of the man's sword arm, causing his fingers to go limp.

Sweeping out with the knife in his right hand, he slashed the enemy's left wrist, while cutting through the tendons in his right knee. The man's weight buckled and he collapsed to his knees.

"Look out!" Kiri yelled from her spot on the boulders.

Feneyas twisted to the side, just avoiding the other warrior's downward chop. The blow clove through his comrade's shoulder, shattering the clavicle and at least two ribs.

Finishing his spin, Feneyas set the edge of the dagger flush against the soldier's radius, halfway up his forearm. As his opponent yanked his sword free of his companion, the dagger sliced through flesh and nerves, severing the thumb tendons.

The man's bellow carried through the forest, cut short when Feneyas drove the knife into his neck.

The native woman huddled over and covered her mouth, her shoulders heaving. The baby continued wailing.

Kiri jumped down, appearing not the least bit fazed as she surveyed his handiwork. "Wow."

Feneyas stared at the dead men and then at his own hands. Killing felt wrong, even if these soldiers might've deserved it. Everything had happened so fast, and he'd acted so instinctively. Somewhere in his lost memories was combat training. He brushed his hands on his pants and paced over to the woman. "Are you okay?"

Her ruddy complexion faded green, hand still over her mouth. She looked first at him, then at Kiri. After a few deep breaths, she spoke. "You must be the Warrior Beyond the Wall. Brought back by a Messenger of the Gods." She nodded toward Kiri.

Straightening, Kiri cleared her throat and took on an authoritative tone. "Yes. Now go back home and tell your people of the gods' glory."

"Wait." Feneyas held a hand up to Kiri while he held the woman's gaze. "You said the Warrior Beyond the Wall. I don't remember him."

The woman shook her head, her eyes sad. "It *must* be you. Poor man; it is said that the reborn forget who they are."

Kiri nodded vigorously. "Yes. The spirits have said as much. Now, hurry home before more of the Metal Men return."

Feneyas glared back at her. "Wait. Tell me more."

"Our shamans," the woman said, "have told stories that you came from beyond the Wall and dwelled among the Maki tribespeople. Taught them how to fight. But then you were killed rescuing the Willow Beauty from the Castle of Trees. So the stories say."

Kiri looked him up and down. Apparently, she didn't believe the story any more than he.

"Where is the Castle of Trees?" Perhaps he could learn more about his identity by backtracking. Maybe find out who the Willow Beauty was.

Forehead crinkled, Kiri shrugged. "Never heard of it."

The woman, however, pointed back down the trail. "Maybe five days' walk, that way. The Metal Men defiled the forest and built the Castle of Trees by the Great River's north bank."

Feneyas followed her finger. "Is your home in that direction? May I accompany you?"

The woman's eyes widened. "The village would be honored—"

"No." Kiri rose up to her full height, admittedly only up to Feneyas' chest, yet she projected an air of authority. "First, your shaman must perform the correct rituals, and the spirits will determine whether or not he will go."

Feneyas met her gaze and she winked. He rolled his eyes with a sigh.

The woman placed a hand on her chest and headed up the trail. Somewhere, in that direction, he would find out more about his life.

CHAPTER 11:

Victory Without Fighting

The sweet evergreen forest below the Great Wall's East Gate obscured the invading army. Still, the low rumble of drums told Kaiya exactly where they were. The beat carried above even the roar of the spring-swollen waterfall half a *li* away. Soon, too soon, she would see Emperor Geros again.

She only hoped the stifling lamellar armor hid her identity as well as the *Tiger's Eye* buried her emotions. The steel helmet would've weighed her head down if she'd been in perfect health; still recovering from her wound, it might as well have been a dwarf anvil. It was the price she paid for the T-slit which exposed only her eyes.

The drums stopped. Black flags emblazoned with the Teleri's gold sun emerged from the tree line, almost a sixty feet below, borne by a dozen soldiers. A single white flag of parley fluttered alone among the swaths of black. A man, larger than all the rest, marched at the head of the procession.

Even though his features remained obscured by distance, his confident gait and sheer size announced the arrival of Geros.

Memories of his muscled mass pinning her down, taking, sent a chill down her spine. He'd violated her body and crushed her soul. The recollection was too close, too personal compared to her other memories. She faltered back a step.

A hand, Jie's, pressed between her shoulder blades. The small gesture served as a reminder that Kaiya was not alone. Around her, provincial musketmen trained their weapons on the unwelcome visitors. Lord Zheng Han stood by her side, accompanied by officers and lords, and fortunately not his emotional wife. Imperial soldiers from the local garrison were also conspicuously absent.

Geros wouldn't be able to pick her out from all of the men, not from this distance. The fear disappeared just as quickly as it had appeared. Kaiya straightened, squaring her shoulders as well as her energy allowed.

The enemy formation came to a halt. A single officer stepped forward and yelled, "I present Emperor Geros of the Teleri Empire."

If only she had the power of her voice. Conventions and rules of parley be damned, she would command the musketmen to fire on him.

Geros strode to the fore. "Great Zheng Han, Lord of East Gate Province, open the gates and swear loyalty to me."

Lord Zheng burst out laughing. "We Cathayi believe a man can only have one master. I already owe allegiance to the Son of Heaven, *Tianzi* Kai-Wu Wang. He happens to be on this side of the Wall."

Though truth be told, Lord Zheng had not acted as such over the last couple of days.

Geros' voice boomed loud in Kaiya's ears despite the distance and elevation between them. "And what has that allegiance gained you? New lands? Rewards of gold and silver? Auspicious marriages?"

"The Teleri Empire cannot offer me lands," Lord Zheng said. "Nor does the Bovyan race believe in marriages. Only a traitor, who would be reviled until history ends, would take treasure to betray his lord."

Geros shook his head. "I offer you all of Cathay. You will be governor, to administer the will of the Teleri Directori. You will rule your own province as an allied independent state. All you have to do is give me control of the East Gate."

Murmurs erupted among the gathered lords. Kaiya was among those who turned to gauge Lord Zheng's reaction. After his indecent proposal and Jie's report, she'd expected him to reject any offer—at the cost of his sons—and then take her to his bed, by force if she refused. This new proposal might be too sweet to decline.

He remained silent, face blank.

Emperor Geros, on the other hand, grinned. "Consider this, Lord Zheng. Cathay rots from the inside, with corrupt ministers and greedy lords undermining the nation for their own gain. Multiple enemies wait on the outside, ready to invade. We will restore order and prosperity, and defend your borders."

The weasel! Kaiya bit her lip. Hua's belligerent neighbors acted only on Geros' bidding. It would not be surprising if he had somehow meddled in Hua's internal affairs as well.

Lord Zheng echoed her suspicions. "I imagine our neighbors would behave differently if you ordered them to. I—"

"I have offered them generous rewards, as I will to you. Your title as Governor shall pass to your sons and grandsons."

Kaiya shuddered, knowing what would happen next.

The Teleri ranks parted and two soldiers pushed forth their gagged prisoners.

A shaky young man, his steps faltering.

A man almost entirely wrapped in bandages, dangling between two large Bovyans.

And Ming. Now accounted for.

He kept his chin high and walked tall. Despite his proximity, their marriage seemed farther away than ever. It was past time to consider a new course of action. For now, however, it remained to be seen how the events would play out.

With their resemblance to Ming and Tian, the other two prisoners were undoubtedly Shu and Lun. Lord Zheng's stoic expression wavered for a split second.

Remaining motionless to avoid drawing Geros' attention to herself, she spoke. "Lord Zheng, if you open the gates to the Great Wall—"

"Silence," he hissed through gritted teeth. When he spoke out loud, it must have been for her benefit. "My family has defended the East Gate for three hundred years. This is not a decision I can make without the counsel of my vassals and advisors."

"Do not deliberate too long." Geros reached over and yanked Shu's arm, eliciting a yelp from the young man. "I will remove one of your son's fingers each hour that I do not hear a satisfactory response. You have ten hours before I remove his head."

Lord Zheng's shoulders slumped. "You will have my answer within an hour." When the flags of parley retreated back into the forest, he turned around and strode toward the stairs. His advisors followed close behind.

Kaiya tore off the helm and stumbled to keep up with him. The armor might have well been a ship's anchor. "Lord Zheng, I never took you to be a collaborator. If you do this—"

Her jerked around and planted a finger in her chest. "If I do this, then my sons will live and pray for our ancestors and my own repose."

Since when had the great lords of mighty Hua given up so easily? They must have grown complacent after three hundred years of peace. With the armor of the Great Wall and a hundred thousand rifles pointed out, the nation's soul had rotted within.

She took Lord Zheng's sleeve in her feeble grip, not believing what she was about to say. Despair crept in through her emotional armor, nearly breaking her resolve. "Please, wait. Marry me, take my sons as yours so that they might one day rule. Just keep the Teleri out of Hua."

He wiped her hand away and turned. "I already have sons. I will rule, and so will they."

"Only as slaves to the Bovyan scourge. I—"

"Guards, take her to my family temple."

She reached for him again, using all her energy to lift her arms, to no avail. Her voice failed her, coming out no louder than a whisper. "Offer me. Offer me for your sons, but don't let them in."

He didn't acknowledge her. Perhaps he hadn't even heard her plea over the jangle of armor. Then he snorted. His stride lengthened and he disappeared behind a wall of trailing soldiers.

The truth. It was time to admit the truth. Surely Geros would trade Zheng's sons for her. Kaiya's lips moved, but no words came out.

She couldn't even speak, let alone channel the power of her voice. Unable to keep up with Lord Zheng's brisk pace without losing her breath, Kaiya had no hope of changing his mind. She hunched over and gasped for air as two guards came to either side of her.

The fleeting emotions rippled and eased enough for her to focus. There was another way to keep the Teleri out. Kaiya straightened and lifted her chin. Even if her voice held no magic, it still carried the tone of imperial authority. "Wait. Withdraw and give me a moment with my handmaiden."

Both soldiers took several respectful steps back and bowed their heads.

She beckoned to the Insolent Retainer. "Jie, scout out the Teleri army's numbers and weapons."

"What should I do if I find the Young Lords and cannot expedite their escape?" Jie stared at her feet.

The underlying question spoke more loudly than if Jie had yelled it out at the top of her lungs. The only leverage Geros had was Zheng Han's sons. Remove the sons from the trading block...

The dilemma gnawed at Kaiya's conscience. Could she trade the lives of three men for the livelihood of millions? The *Tiger's Eye* might have stifled her emotions, but her moral compass remained.

Yet she was forced to admit the real reason behind her order to scout out the enemy. The half-elf would not have the same compunctions toward taking away Geros' bargaining leverage, and Kaiya could wash her hands of the decision.

Until Jie asked.

The *Tiger's Eye*, battered by hopelessness, crumbled around her. Despair and guilt threatened to keep her from verbalizing what she must. Tears blurred her vision.

"Take away Geros' leverage."

As much as Jie disliked Young Lord Zheng Ming, the thought of murdering him didn't sit well in her stomach. It was the logical decision, one which the princess had forced through the crumbling wall of the *Tiger's Eye*.

It had reformed almost as soon as she choked the words out, standing as strong and steadfast as the Great Wall, which Jie climbed down before sneaking up on the Teleri camp.

With a skillset geared toward urban operations, each step on the uneven forest floor made her cringe. A twig here, dried pine needles there, all ready to crackle and reveal her location. Not that she would have to worry, since the Bovyans made plenty of noise themselves.

The sentries, placed every thirty feet along the perimeter of their camp, jingled in their chainmail. Other soldiers sat and sharpened weapons, the metal on whetstone whispering loud enough to mask her steps. Most soldiers leaned against trees and slept.

Jie skirted the edges, taking count. About six thousand heavy infantry in the vanguard. In the field, they might overwhelm Dongmen's provincial armies if they were able to close to melee range without taking devastating losses from musket fire. They would never stand a chance trying to breach the Great Wall.

Using trees and marching soldiers as cover, she then made her way into the heart of the army. Sixteen officers gathered around a fallen tree, discussing options in the event the cowardly gate lord refused their passage.

Ming and Lun were nowhere to be found. Zheng Shu however, sat at the end of the log, hands bound with rope. Sweat trickled down his brow, despite the cool afternoon breeze. A guard stood cross-armed beside him.

While Tian had always worshipped his eldest brother Ming, and admired his second brother Lun, Shu was more of a peer. Like Tian, Shu preferred painting over swordplay. From the way his eyes flicked nervously about now, he didn't seem suited as a warrior. The poor man didn't deserve death.

Jie could kill the guard, but not without drawing the attention of the officers just a few feet away. The camp would rouse, limiting her options. She needed to find Lun and Ming and reevaluate.

Creeping back through the enemy's encampment, she happened upon the supply van. With the last leg of the ancient highway yet to be restored, the Teleri had relied on porters: a thousand Hua prisoners of war, connected to each other with rope around their necks. It must have been a nightmare trying to traipse through underbrush at a quick pace while carrying packs of supplies.

A hundred enemy soldiers stood watch over her countrymen as they rested against trees. There was little she could do for them by herself. Lun lay flat, breathing heavily. Still no sign of Ming among them. Smart, keeping the most important hostages separated. The minute she rescued or killed one, the Teleri would secure the others. The mission was hopeless.

Jie leaned against a tree and stifled a sigh. When had she ever been so defeatist? Just over a week ago, she'd stormed an impregnable fortress against overwhelming odds to rescue the princess. Before that, she would've never dismissed a task as impossible out of hand.

Ming's grating voice hissed from beyond the camp. "Do three of you really need to watch a man squat and empty his bowels?"

Jie shook the image out of her mind, even as everyone else within earshot snickered. She then worked her way toward the source of his voice.

On the outskirts of the camp, three bareheaded Bovyans surrounded him. Their sheer size obscured Ming's bent-over form, much to Jie's relief. Imagining him in the act was bad enough; she would've never been able to banish the actual sight from her memory.

Plans formed: Draw the guards away and ambush them one at a time. Use the prisoners as a diversion. There wasn't enough time for either, unless Ming suffered from constipation. Besides killing Ming, that left only one option — a direct attack.

A single armored Bovyan would have little trouble beating her in a fair fight. Three would be suicide. Which was why she did not fight fair.

She crept from tree to tree until she was just a few feet from the back of the closest guard.

Modulating her voice to imitate Geros', she used a *Ghost Echo* technique to throw her voice behind the other two guards. "Men, over here!"

As soon as their heads started to jerk toward the source of her trick, Jie leaped onto the closest man's back and lodged a knife into his throat. His legs wobbled, and she dragged him down to his knees. When the farthest guard glanced down at his fallen comrade, she sent a *biao* throwing star whirling into his face.

Even before the second skidded into a convulsing pile, Jie slipped behind the kneeling man as he clutched his throat and choked up blood.

Turning back and forth, the remaining guard yanked his longsword from his sheath. Ming, pants down around his ankles, swept his gaze left and right, his mouth gaping. His right shoulder hung in a sling.

Jie threw her voice again, behind the remaining enemy. "Intruders, over here!"

He looked over his shoulder.

She darted across the spot, careful not to step in Ming's business, and lunged into a scissor-kick.

He toppled onto his knees and fell back in a jingling heap, while she used her momentum to spring up. She landed mounted on his chest and drove her knife into his eye socket.

Too much noise, so sloppy on her part. She turned to Ming and immediately averted her eyes. "Come on, come on, pants up, on your feet! You can wipe later!"

Ming wiggled his pants up with his free hand. "Jie! You came for me."

For him, indeed. "Princess Kaiya sent me." To kill you. "Now come on." Jie broke into a run, pulling Ming deeper into the forest. She took care to pull his sleeve, not his hand.

Behind them, the Teleri camp roused to life.

CHAPTER 12:

In Search of Self

Ming shuddered at the prospect of being stuck with the impertinent half-elf for the rest of his life. Their last journey together had involved a pyramid, two magic gemstones, and a hundred belligerent charlatans; and it hadn't been the charlatans who came closest to killing him.

A certain half-elf had.

He stepped on a branch, sending a loud crack echoing through the woods.

She pulled him down into the brush, then poked her head up and looked around. The last jerk of her head put those evil eyes directly on him. She hissed at him in a low whisper, "If you're going to make so much noise, then stop clinging to me like a wet leaf. Go home."

Go home. If only he could; but that choice evaporated days ago. It wasn't like he could have waltzed through the Bovyan horde to the gatehouse, or scaled the Wall like she suggested. Especially not with his shoulder still hurting. He brushed himself off with his good arm, avoiding eye contact with his tormentor.

And provider. She opened up that magic pouch of hers, the one with infinite space that the elf hag Ayana had given her, and pulled out some jerky.

His stomach rumbled at the aroma. He flashed his most smoldering gaze, the one which had charmed many a woman into his bed.

Jie rolled her eyes and thrust the dried meat into his face. Ah, the smell of home, the special spice mix that the castle chef made. All the food she pulled out of that pouch undoubtedly came from Dongmen Castle, so technically it was his, anyway.

She had left prepared. They had followed the Kanin River upstream for what, six days now? But why? He mumbled out his words as he chewed. "So where are we going?"

"I've told you." She threw her hands up. "We—I mean, *I* am looking to sabotage the Teleri supply lines."

She *had* told him. Each of the dozen times he had asked. However, he knew women, and Jie's focus and determination went beyond duty. There was more, and eventually she would relent and tell him.

Jie stared at Ming's sleeping form, curled up on dried leaves, and sighed. Why hadn't she followed Princess Kaiya's orders and just put him out of his misery?

Because he was Tian's brother. Tian didn't even like to kill enemies, and would be even less pleased if she'd murdered the brother he'd adored so much. Of course, no matter how many times she threatened Ming over the last year, she'd never really intended to follow through.

Which didn't explain why she hadn't just left him behind after the improbable rescue. She pulled the blanket up over him. The last thing she needed was for him to catch cold and slow her down.

He'd already slowed her down enough. At least on their quest in Selastya, he could swing a sword and shoot a bow. Well. *Really* well, if she had to grudgingly admit it. He had dropped fake Akolytes, Bovyan shock troops, and an altivorc who nearly killed her.

She pried back the dressing on his shoulder to inspect the wound. Whatever else she could say about the Bovyans, they knew battlefield medicine. Even so, Ming might never pull a bowstring again, and they didn't have a sword for him to swing with his good arm. Even with the knife she loaned him—well, gave him, because she sure didn't want it back after he put his paws on it—he didn't stand a chance against a ten-year-old version of herself in a knife fight.

And the incessant questions.

Question.

Where are we going? The one which she answered with the same half-truth. Out. There. Away from princesses and responsibilities and intrigue and wars. Pick a direction and walk, until the food and supplies she'd appropriated from the castle halved. Which was much faster with Ming's appetite.

Jie stared out into the forest, her elf vision picking out the hues of green.

Somewhere out there, she would find herself again. Ming would provide the semi-intelligent human interaction she needed to remain sane, or at least be a practice dummy to keep her tongue sharp. And if he got them both killed first, so be it.

Though the wild elves didn't forbid Feneyas from leaving, he didn't know the first thing about surviving in the wilderness. When a search for his identity meant a slow death by exposure and starvation, the treetop village became

a prison. If he wasn't their prisoner, he was their virtual pet, performing tricks in return for their generosity.

At least the tricks kept him occupied. He sidestepped a sword thrust and dumped the young elf man to the ground with a clip of his arms. Another elf stepped into the ring of warriors, spinning a quarterstaff in rapid circles. As the weapon swept in a broad arc toward his knees, Feneyas leapt over it with a butterfly twist and landed up close. He seized his opponent's hand in one of his, and the end of the staff in the other, and rotated it so that it put his opponent into a wrist lock.

How could he do all this? No matter how, he was living up to his reputation as the Warrior Beyond the Wall.

Whatever that meant. From what his new friend Dior had said, an enormous Wall rose up along the western edge of the Wilds. Humans who looked like Feneyas lived on the other side. Perhaps the mysterious Doe-Eyed Girl walked among them.

He could go east to the Wall, or west to the human village, and find out more about himself; yet here he was, trapped in a village in the trees. Spending each day sparring with elves who wanted to see if he was as good as Kiri said. At times, he'd accompany Kiri and her little sister Kala when they gathered spring shoots and searched for mushrooms. Perhaps eventually, he would know enough about safe food to set off on his own, but in the meantime...

Wait, his hosts said.

Wait for what? Feneyas swiped an arrow out of the air and tracked it back to its origin.

Dior grinned. "I was aiming to miss, anyway!"

Perhaps. No matter what good hosts the elves were, they still made him wait, all to maintain a charade.

Proper channels, Kiri had said. The elves fed the native humans' superstitions, tricking them into believing they were spirits. It seemed like a dishonest means of control, but Kiri claimed it was for everyone's protection. The elves stayed out of sight, while the local humans, who called themselves Kanin, made regular requests to the messengers of the gods.

Over the last several days, the requests had multiplied. Small forest animals came by, visiting Nayori, the older woman who had healed him. Powerful in magic, the elf was the closest thing to the wild elves' leader, at least as far as he could tell. The birds and squirrels apparently delivered requests from Kanin tribal shamans.

Feneyas snorted. As if animals could talk.

He used the arrow he'd caught to barely brush aside another sword thrust. A woman this time, who moved faster than any of the men thus far. He punched and thrust and tried to grab her, but Layani avoided all of his attacks with effortless grace. Her blade swirled in elegant twists and arcs, all of which missed.

On purpose. He raised his hands in surrender and bowed.

She was better. Maybe not in overall technique, but her speed and reflexes were like...memories of a brown-skinned man with a curved, guardless sword flashed in his head.

There was a name to the handsome face with its pointed beard. It taunted Feneyas' conscious mind, just out of reach.

He looked up at Layani, her expression as mirthless as always. "How do you move so fast?"

She shrugged. "You are just slow."

The spectators all burst out laughing, though none of them had even presented a credible challenge.

Kiri shook her head, even as the sides of her eyes crinkled. "No, Feneyas, it's her gift."

"Gift?"

"Martial magic," Dior said. "Some of us have it, some don't. Unlike our supposedly *civilized* brethren, we can't use all forms of magic."

Layani glared at Dior, then offered Feneyas a rare smile. "We are among the tribes which didn't believe Aralas was an angel sent by Koralas. Our ancestors didn't answer his call before the War of Ancient Gods. Nor did we leave our forest homes when his son became king of Aramysta and his daughter queen of Aerilysta. Unlike our kin, who have idle time to pursue a vast array of skills, we spend many of our waking hours providing for the village."

The fairy tale, or perhaps history, sounded familiar. A half-sized man with scruffy hair and mischievous eyes dashed through Feneyas' memory before he could catch it.

Nayori's voice danced in the tree tops. "Feneyas, come."

Yes, he was a pet. The fluffy white temple dog barked in his memories, but still gave him no sense of who he was or why a temple was important to him.

On instinct, he looked up to the voice. Just as each time before, there was nothing but the sun peeking in from the budding branches of countless trees. Magic, Kiri had said. Bending limbs to the elves' fancy and creating an illusion for the rare passerby who glanced up.

She took him by the hand, as was her wont. Hers was warm and moist, her grin perky. She was always jovial, with a tongue as sharp as a *dao*, at least if he didn't try to bring up her past. She seemed so familiar; just being with her invoked a sense of comfort and contentment. The Warrior From Beyond the Wall must've had a younger sister in his former life.

Kiri pulled him toward the tree, the one with invisible stairs encircling it. He could only climb it with his eyes closed, lest he trip and fall.

Seventeen steps above the ground, the tree branch steps materialized around him. No matter how many times he climbed the stairs, the transition from nothingness to solidity was disconcerting.

At the top, on the village gathering platform, Nayori sat on a gnarled knot, holding a haughty chipmunk in her palm. As it chattered away, she nodded.

Feneyas exchanged glances with Kiri, who just added a shrug to her mischievous smile.

Nayori's gaze then lifted to meet his. "Feneyas, the eyes and ears of the forest have told us the Metal Men are marching in greater numbers than ever before, heading west. The village shamans have all requested the gods to send the Warrior Beyond the Wall to teach them to fight."

Feneyas nodded. "I want to go west. I want to meet other humans. Maybe they can tell me who I am."

Her eyes, seas of liquid brown, searched his. She hefted the chipmunk, who afforded Feneyas a smug look. "My little friend here comes from the Maki tribal lands. He tells me there is a shaman who claims he can tell you who you are."

CHAPTER 13:

Resolve

The roaring falls of the North Kanin River poured into the Hua basin, drowning out all other sounds as Kaiya climbed from the palanquin. Along with Fang Weiyong and six provincial soldiers as *escort*, she made her way up the cliff path toward the Zheng family temple. The late afternoon sun danced in the falls' mist, forming a shimmering rainbow above the rocks.

Even with Fang Weiyong's support, her chest heaved as she fought for each breath. Pregnant, anemic, she struggled to climb the trail. If this short trip drained her, how could she hope to escape and make the three-day journey to the capital?

Weiyong apparently shared the same doubts. "*Dian-xia*, perhaps you should continue in the palanquin."

It was a sound suggestion, but Lady Zheng apparently wanted to make her trip as difficult as possible. The palanquin bearers waited at the bottom of the cliff. She shook her head and continued toward the flat bluffs halfway up.

Like the road, Zhengguang Temple was carved into the cliff face. Grateful to reach the waterfall pool overlook, Kaiya paused under the sloping tile eaves, which sparkled with condensation and sunlight. Heads turned and lips moved among the couple dozen common folk, and like a wave, they all sank to their knees.

It would not do to let them see her so haggard. Kaiya straightened her back and lifted her chin. She turned to the provincial soldiers. "Wait here. Weiyong, come with me."

The soldiers all bowed and held back.

Summoning all her grace, she glided through the red columns and into the temple. Trickles of smoke wafted from burning incense, cloying the air with a sweet fragrance. Light bauble braziers stood partially shuttered, casting the central chamber in a warm golden glow.

Several priests knelt and chanted before the Zheng family altar. Kaiya approached them, passing between two enormous statues holding silent vigil at the sides of the broad chamber. On the left stood Lord Guan, patron saint of warriors and guardian of the East Gate Province. Chest jutted out, he held a halberd whose haft touched the tiled ground and whose blade tip reached the vaulting ceiling. Wu-Long, the Dragon Protector of Hua, faced him, coiling up from floor to roof.

One of the priests met her gaze. Word of her arrival passed among them, and they all turned in place and pressed their foreheads to the ground.

Kaiya's voice caught in her throat, and she had to clear it. "Rise." Her own voice sounded weak in her ears.

They all came out of their bows. The abbot rose to his feet and approached with his eyes politely averted. "*Dian-xia*, thank you for gracing us with your presence in this trying time. Did you come to pray for our soldiers?"

Kaiya nodded. "Yes. And while I pray, bring me the tablet of Zheng Tian, fourth son of Lord Zheng Han."

The abbot looked at her, his eyes searching hers in a display of impudence.

In the past, she might have feigned anger. Instead, she kept her voice level. "That is my command."

The abbot bowed and disappeared down a passageway behind the altar, hustling into the temple's depths.

She took several steps forward and bowed before the altar. All this time, she'd played games, planning and plotting ways to legitimize her children. She was no better than the ambitious lords and ministers who jockeyed for power back at court. Perhaps the gods were punishing her.

It was time to make things right. After praying for the Hua soldiers' safety, she silently asked for forgiveness of the gods, and also of her true husband, Tian.

Outside the temple, at the edge of her hearing, a commotion broke out over the din of chanting monks and the raging waterfall. Before she could turn to see the source, the abbot returned with a hand-sized tablet.

Kaiya received it in two hands with her head bowed. All it took was a cursory scan to see Tian's birth name engraved. Was that a clenching of her stomach as she ran a finger across his birth and death dates?

In the only twelve days since he'd sacrificed himself so she could escape Geros, she'd abandoned his memory. She looked up and met the abbot's gaze. "You are not to tell anyone I have this."

"As the princess commands." He pressed his palms together and bowed.

Soft footsteps behind her drew her attention. She turned around to find Lady Zheng, dressed in silken riding robes, kneeling on the tile floor. Weiyong bowed low in apology.

"Lady Zheng," Kaiya said, "please rise."

The woman's eyes focused on Kaiya's hands. "You have Tian's tablet."

Kaiya bowed. "Yes, Mother."

The hard lines of Lady Zheng's face softened. "I have arranged for a regiment of imperial soldiers to escort you back to the capital."

That couldn't be right. How quickly an attitude could change. Kaiya raised an eyebrow. "You would betray your husband?"

"I have faith you will not betray yours." Lady Zheng offered a sad smile. "I cannot allow Teleri hands to sully the mother of my grandchildren and raise more questions about their legitimacy."

"Thank you, Mother." Kaiya kept her expression warm and grateful, despite the irony of Lady Zheng's words. As Father once said, sometimes half-truths and misdirection accomplished more good than the truth.

"You do not have long before my lord surrenders the gate. Make haste."

Kaiya bowed, then glided out of the temple, running her hand over the cool surface of the tablet as she did. Tian, her husband, jettisoned in the last few days for the sake of convenience. Her love, even though she couldn't feel it. She'd take the tablet back to her family temple in Huajing, and have Fang Weiyong vest it with hers to formalize Tian's marriage into her family. She tucked the tablet into an inner pocket of her robe.

Outside, dozens of imperial soldiers dropped to one knee. "*Dian-xia!*" they proclaimed in unison. Around them, commoners pressed their foreheads to the ground.

Her energy flagging, Kaiya straightened. "Rise."

The soldiers rose and stepped to the side, revealing the palanquin and kneeling porters. She stumbled with her first step toward it, but Weiyong caught her by the arm. Both he and a captain helped her in.

Once the doors slid shut, she slumped into the padded chair, grateful for the chance to sit.

"Where to, *Dian-xia?*" Weiyong asked from outside.

"To the capital."

"If Emperor Geros finds out you are near, there is no way we can stay ahead of them."

Especially in her condition. The objectivity of her thoughts suggested the *Tiger's Eye* still held her emotions firmly in check. "Lord Zheng may betray Hua, but I do not think he will betray the mother of his grandchildren."

"In any case," Fang Weiyong said, "enough people have seen you here. We cannot just leave by the highway."

"A diversion, then. Send the palanquin down the main highway with my guards, while you, Jie, and I will take a riverboat."

Weiyong's silence outside perhaps echoed Kaiya's own misgivings. Strategic diversions like this had failed her at least three times in the past. What would make it work this time?

"Weiyong," she said. "I don't think we have any other choice."

"Yes, *Dian-xia*." His voice wavered.

"Captain, send a runner to Count Du, telling him to expect us soon."

"As the princess commands," the captain said.

On her command, the palanquin set off toward the town bordering the waterfall's lake. The narrow confines, which in the past gripped her with terror, now provided a screen to hide her exhaustion.

After catching her breath, she slid the window open to see the ancient buildings, shrouded in mists. Even from a few *li* away, the commotion of worried townsfolk carried over the waters.

The noise grew as they made their way into the town. Commoners cleared the road for the palanquin. Perhaps the imperial soldiers drew the many points and murmurs.

"Fang Weiyong," she called through the window. "Make sure they know it is me."

He bowed in acquiescence, and then moved out of her line of site to the front of the palanquin. His usually timid voice rose, though its shyness remained. "Make way for Princess Kaiya."

A hush fell over the crowd. Like a wave, they sank to their knees, foreheads to the ground, rising with excited whispers as the palanquin passed. In a land where the Imperial Family was revered, hopefully her very presence gave them a sense of calm against the impending invasion.

Before long, they arrived at the villa of Count Du, the local *Yu-Ming* lord. She'd rejected his first son two years before, but he'd always been faithful to Father in the past. Then again, so had Lord Zheng.

As they approached the gates and passed through, Count Du's soldiers all dropped to a knee, fist to the ground.

The palanquin doors slid open, and Kaiya climbed out. The imperial soldiers serving as her escort and the villa guards all dropped into a salute.

Head bobbing, Count Du shuffled out to meet her. "*Dian-xia*, welcome. Had I known sooner, I would have made sure the entire town was out to greet you with waving banners of the Empire, and prepared a meal fit for the *Tianzi*."

Kaiya nodded. "I appreciate the sentiment all the same. Now, I ask that you allow me to stay here for an hour."

Count Du bowed. "It would be my honor."

Kaiya beckoned the captain of the imperial soldiers. "Leave eight of your best men to protect me. The rest of you, escort the palanquin down the highway toward Huajing."

Fang Weiyong startled from a dream and sat up straight on the thick blanket. Sweat clung to his neck and head, making the chill air of the guest room seem colder. Yes, he was near the great waterfall of Hua, not back in his recurring nightmare.

He rubbed his neck, where then-First Consul Geros had held him aloft in Iksuvius Heights. To think the giant Bovyan and his cohorts gathered outside the walls, just half a day away. The more distance between them, the better.

Weiyong clambered out from beneath his covers and padded over to the carved wooden bed where Princess Kaiya slept. Her chest gently rose and fell, even as her brow furrowed and she hugged herself.

He pulled the covers over her, and her body relaxed. At least the stubborn young woman had listened to his suggestion, to rest at Count Du's pavilion until early morning. Much to the count's and his own chagrin, she insisted he stay in the room with her.

Now if only she would stop calling him by name. Weiyong might be a priest, her doctor, her Maki tribe brother, and her friend, but he was still a man. A man who had no business wondering what it might be like to feel her lips against his.

Such a fool! He shook his head and stalked off to the window. Throwing open the shutters, he pushed his face out into the night air.

"Weiyong, is it already time to go?"

He turned around to find the princess sitting up on the bed. He dropped to his knees and bowed. "No, *Dian-xia*. We still have another hour before we set off for the docks. Please go back to sleep."

"You, too." She flashed a demure smile and eased herself back down.

His heart pounded in his chest, and he stared out the window. Once they returned to the capital, he could put more distance between her, too. But where to?

"That is my command."

He turned back and bowed, then shuffled back to his bedroll. Sleep did not come easily, and he spent the rest of the time staring at the ceiling tiles, trying not to think about beautiful princesses.

Hurried footsteps across wood floors jolted Kaiya out of sleep. Even so, she stayed buried beneath the covers, protected from the dark and cold.

"*Dian-xia*," an imperial soldier called from outside of the door. "We must reach the docks in an hour. Please get ready."

Groaning, she kicked off her blanket and sat up. Surprisingly, rest had done her good. Weiyong's herbal medicine probably helped, too. She tightened her gown around her shoulders. "Any news of the Teleri?"

"No, *Dian-xia*."

"Very well. I will be ready in ten minutes." Kaiya dangled her feet over the edge of the bed and set a foot down. The wood was cold. Poor Weiyong. He must've been freezing.

She pushed her feet into slippers and glided over. Kneeling by his side, she placed a hand on his shoulder. "Wake—"

He bolted upright, nearly crashing his forehead into hers. His gaze met hers before staring at the floor.

Kaiya giggled. It seemed appropriate for his faux-pas. "We leave in ten minutes."

"Yes, *Dian-xia*." He pushed himself to his feet, avoiding eye contact. Was he *that* embarrassed?

Kaiya returned to the bed and picked up the hooded travelling cloak hanging over the footboard. Draping it over her shoulders and pulling up the hood, she walked to the door. "Come, Weiyong."

Though he responded immediately, hesitancy weighed down his words. "As you command, *Dian-xia*."

Why was he so tentative? A walk to the quay should be nothing compared to their harrowing escape from Iksuvius. She flashed him a reassuring smile. "We will be all right."

He simply nodded, still avoiding eye contact.

In the courtyard, her eight new guards waited with Count Du. They all knelt as she emerged.

She nodded to her host. "Count Du, I thank you for your hospitality. My handmaiden Yan Jie will come here searching for me. When she does, tell her that I have taken a river boat to the Huajing. Do not tell anyone else."

He bowed. "As the princess commands. I wish you safe travels."

They set off. The waxing gibbous of the white moon Renyue and the almost-open blue moon Guanyin's Eye shone bright, providing little cover. They both hung close to the iridescent moon, also nearly full. Before long, all three would join in the Godseye Conjunction, a rare omen of great change. At this moment, that change didn't look good.

The windows of homes were all shuttered, and they encountered no one in the streets. Only the roaring of the waterfall and the owl calls accompanied them. If Count Du planned on betraying them, he had yet to make a move.

They arrived at the lakeside docks in short time, where sailors worked at preparing a riverboat for departure. A fresh-faced young man with broad shoulders approached and bowed. "I am Captain Su. I understand we are to take you to take your unit back to the capital?"

"Yes." The highest-ranking solider dropped a purse in the captain's hands.

Captain Su hefted the bag and then stepped aside. "We are almost ready to embark. Go ahead and board."

Not wanting to reveal her identity, Kaiya prodded Weiyong with a poke in his arm.

He flinched at her touch. "Captain Su, is there any news about the Teleri army?"

Captain Su sighed. "Yes. Lord Zheng will surrender the East Gate to them today, at first light."

CHAPTER 14:
Misinformation

Liang Yu looked past his tea cup at Chief Minister Hong Jianbin's cinnamon-skinned lover, Leina. The light blue gown emphasized her striking blend of Hua and Ayuri blood, and every movement spoke of grace—like the Beauty from his Black Lotus team, three decades before.

The pleasantly nostalgic feeling floating in his chest disappeared. To think the hideous old man had this exotic beauty warming his bed. Or rather, *her* bed, since he always met with her in this house he'd bought in the Floating World.

Ah, the perks of wealth and influence. Though if Hong knew Leina also entertained Young Lord Liu of Jiangzhou from time to time...

Smiling, Liang Yu set the cup down and placed his white *weiqi* piece on the board. Since helping Hong become Chief Minister, the old man had avoided him. Not as if it would be that hard to pay an unannounced visit; but sometimes a predator let his prey believe he had given up.

Especially if there was another way to get information. If Hong knew how loose Leina's lips were, he might not share state secrets with her. Secrets that Liang Yu could coax out. "The Night Blossoms tell me that fewer officers are coming to the high end of the Floating World."

"Oh, Golden Fu, I can't tell you how hard it is on everyone." Her accent flitted. With a dainty motion and tilt of her head, she played her black piece, setting a subtle trap. Clever; but with his eye for conspiracy, easy to see. "So many provincial and imperial troops went south to put down that rebel Peng. Many of the Night Blossoms are spending their nights alone."

So he'd heard. Now, only the most untested armies defended the North. Luckily their northern neighbor was preoccupied with a regional conflict and couldn't pose a threat. If only he'd succeeded in tracking down Peng, Liang Yu's knife could have prevented the civil war. Thirty years ago, his team wouldn't have failed. His own planning, the Beauty's wiles, and the Surgeon's scalpel would've vivisected the insurgency before it could spread.

What had she said? Something about Night Blossoms? He pretended not to see her trap, and placed his piece to make it seem he was attacking. "Well, there are still the ministers and officials."

"Fewer of them, too." She lowered her voice. "The new *Tianzi* does not inspire confidence. Many of the hereditary lords are concerned about their own domains and have gone home. Almost the entire Linshan provincial legation is gone."

This last piece of information he knew. His pupil, Lin Ziqiu, was the daughter of Linshan's *Tai-Ming* lord and had told him as much. He swirled the tea around in his cup. "Once the imperial armies crush Peng, things will come back to normal. Hopefully, it won't be too long."

The wistfulness of her sigh could have inspired poets. "Tonight wouldn't be soon enough. Maybe all the revelry when Princess Kaiya returns will help—"

Liang Yu almost spit his tea out, but choked it down. "Princess Kaiya?"

She placed a hand on her chest and sucked a breath in. With a conspiratorial look in her eyes, she leaned in and whispered, "Yes, she left Dongmen by river barge two days ago, in secret, with only a light guard."

That couldn't be true. Princess Kaiya's half-elf bodyguard would have sent word to her *Moquan* superiors, and Liang Yu had been intercepting their correspondence. There was no way Hong could find out about the princess' imminent arrival before the *Moquan*. If he did, however, Leina's slip was a good lead. He shifted in his seat. "Yes, the citizenry will be happy to have their princess back."

He, on the other hand, needed her to stay away from the palace. If her past gave any clues, the princess would likely try to find a peaceful resolution to the South's rebellion. She might even beg for clemency for Peng, despite his many attempts to manipulate and kill her.

It was time to pay a visit to the funerary shop to confirm this rumor.

Leina held a low bow as Golden Fu departed, his gold-threaded robes swishing out her side door. As much money as the avaricious spice merchant lavished in the Floating World on prostitutes, he probably spent even more funding the anti-imperial insurgency.

To what end, she could only surmise. He was just one of a dozen horrible men she had to deal with. Conflict and uncertainty increased demand for his other import: weapons. Like so many of the rich and powerful in Cathay, he profited on suffering and broken dreams.

Collecting up the tea set, she gave herself a mental pat on the back. The information she'd fed him would embolden the insurgents, and hopefully wreak havoc in the capital.

She lifted one of her cups to the light bauble lamp. A barely perceptible crack stretched across the surface. It would split it in two if mishandled. Cathay's cracks and fissures were far more evident, and deservingly so. Yutou Province had aligned itself with Peng's Nanling Province in rebellion. Linshan Province stood at the side, waiting to see where the pieces would fall.

With a cursory glance at the *weiqi* board, their game unfinished, she sighed. Golden Fu was good, much better than Old Hong at strategy games. Still, he was too concerned with surrounding her pieces; he didn't notice the weakness in his inside lines. In Cathay, that weakness was the semblance of unity among the Royalists. Jiangzhou Province's soldiers marched with the imperial army, but nobody else knew their *Tai-ming* lord had plans of his own.

Golden Fu would learn that, and the other information she'd withheld, soon enough. The armies of evil Madura, at Lord Peng's behest, already trampled on Cathay's soil. Lord Zheng in Dongmen Province had surrendered to the Teleri. Soon, Rotuvi would attack Cathay's source of firepowder in Wailian, and from there, maybe even storm the now lightly defended North Gate of the Great Wall. With armies in motion across three fronts, there was nothing keeping the capital from falling.

Except Princess Kaiya. That woman had proved resourceful, and if anyone could rally Cathay, it would be her. Hopefully, Golden Fu's insurgents would act on the information of her imminent—and more importantly, unprotected—arrival.

The plans of ambitious men were coming together in a perfect symphony of chaos. Now it was time for the climax to the opera she'd written. Leina opened a drawer in her altar table and withdrew a silk brocade box. The silver brooch inside, engraved by a master craftsman to evoke magic, ostensibly protected her against hooligans. To think a piece of Cathay's unique Artistic Magic would be used against its own people.

Even if Old Hong had outlived his use in sowing seeds of havoc and pushing the imperial court into disarray, he still served one last purpose. He had the *Tianzi's* trust, and she had his.

She sighed. Poor man. He wasn't that bad, really. Kind, even. But she was so close to getting her mother freed. Geros would surely keep his word, as Bovyans did, and it was going to happen years earlier than she could've ever hoped.

The secret entrance from the Jade Teahouse into her house whispered open. Old Hong had arrived.

Peng Kai-Long stood on the hill, flanked by his secret Water Snake bodyguard and several officers. In the stretch of farmland below, the Maduran invaders, thirty-thousand strong, braced against the onslaught of the imperial army.

No doubt the Maduran Prince Dhananad would be infuriated. The original plan had called for Kai-Long's own army of ten thousand musketmen to draw in the imperial vanguard of fifty thousand, and then for the Madurans to fall on their right flank.

Kai-Long grinned. He had sent one of his men, disguised as an imperial scout, to feed misinformation. Now, the Madurans would bear the brunt of the imperial army attack, while his own men, held in reserve, would attack the imperials' left flank. Well, once both sides had weakened each other.

Muskets roared in staccato, and firepowder smoke drifted across the plain. An hour in, and the *Tianzi's* troops seemed satisfied to keep out of range of Maduran archers. At this rate the Madurans would be too sapped to face the bulk of the imperial army, now marching through Hua's central valley.

He turned to his aide-de-camp. "Form up the musketmen on this hill in ranks of three."

"But *Jue-Ye*," the aide said, "that would reveal our position."

If only there were another way. In the corner of his eye, a young officer edged forward.

Peng snapped his fan shut and pointed with it. "The Madurans are pinned down. At this rate—"

"Look!" The officer pointed.

Kai-Long followed the gesture. Below, a dozen Madurans broke from their entrenched positions and zigzagged through the barrage of musket balls.

Not a single one fell.

Kai-Long tried not to gape. These were undoubtedly the vaunted Maduran Scorpions. Real ones. Not the boogiemen from the stories he'd manufactured over the last few years to instigate war. In seconds, they crashed into the imperial army's orderly ranks, breaking the long line in at least ten places. A couple of the Scorpions fell as hundreds of imperial spearmen surged in to relieve the musketmen.

"Hurry! Deploy!" Peng waved his fan emphatically. They had to make a show of attacking, lest even the dimwitted Dhananad suspected—

"*Jue-ye!*" The aide yelled.

Kai-Long turned, just in time to see a man chopping at him with a broadsword.

"A message from Prince Dhananad!" the assassin shouted. No time—

The weapon clashed against another sword, wielded by Kai-Long's bodyguard. The instrument of his death stopped just a finger-length from his neck.

"Take him alive!" Kai-Long fell back as his other men swept in to surround the would-be assassin. Blades flashed in the sun.

A few more swords clashed against the assassin's. With a quick jerk, the man raked the blade over his own throat. Blood sprayed out as he collapsed.

Dhananad had sent him? Kai-Long rubbed his neck. Perhaps the prince wasn't so stupid after all.

His bodyguard, from the Water Snake Clan, dropped to a knee. "*Jue-Ye*, the assassin was Black Lotus *Moquan*. You can tell by his technique."

To everyone else, *Moquan* were only rumors, tools for mothers to keep unruly children in line. No more real than the Guardian Dragon of

Hua. Still, Kai-Long had to keep up pretenses in front of his officers. He favored the man with a raised eyebrow. "There is no such thing."

The bodyguard bowed. "Of course, *Jue-ye*."

Kai-Long nodded. The slip could be forgiven, especially now that the Water Snake Clan had saved him from one of Cousin Kai-Wu's agents. "You will be rewarded."

The man bowed again. "Protecting my lord is my honor."

His honor, as long as Kai-Long kept paying the clan. They'd turned on Lord Tong during his rebellion three years ago, only recently resurfacing. Perhaps even after he gained the Jade Throne, he would keep them around.

He looked back at the battle, which his own men now joined, firing at the imperials' flank. The Madurans had suffered significant casualties and would need reinforcements if they were to face the brunt of the punitive expedition.

He motioned to his bodyguard. "Inform your superiors to keep the South Gate open. We can't blow it yet. Not until the Madurans weaken the imperial army more."

Soon. If the battles all worked out like today, the Madurans and Imperials would devastate each other, leaving the road back to the capital open and the North relatively undefended.

Hong Jianbin waited at the arching stone bridge between the castle and the rest of the palace grounds, clasping the jewelry box Leina had given him. A present for the *Tianzi*, one which would ensure Hong stayed in good graces despite the failed policies he suggested. The girl had exquisite taste, and undoubtedly it was a work of art. His hands tingled in excitement.

The rhythmic beat of a dozen footsteps approached. He looked up to see a contingent of imperial guards, surrounding the *Tianzi's* golden palanquin. Sunlight reflected off its dragon and phoenix carvings.

When the first guards reached him, Hong sank to his knees and pressed his forehead to the ground. "*Huang-Shang*, might I have a word?"

"Halt," the *Tianzi's* voice called from within.

The porters came to a precise stop and set the palanquin down. One slid the door open. Inside, the *Tianzi* leaned back on the cushions, his eyes soft and friendly.

He waved an open hand. "Chief Minister Hong, rise. Are we not finished with official duties for the day?"

"Yes, *Huang-Shang*." Hong looked up and presented the box. "I would like to present a token of my appreciation for your benevolent rule."

The *Tianzi* raised an eyebrow. In retrospect, it was strange for a minister to give something to the ruler, who had all. What had he been thinking? He started to return the box to the fold of his cloak.

"Well?" The *Tianzi's* eyebrows now scrunched together.

He wanted to see it! Hong bowed and rose again. His heart pattered like summer raindrops as he opened the—

The silver dragon pendant within glared at him with ruby eyes. It uncoiled in clouds of black smoke, clogging Hong's lungs. The flesh of his wrinkled hands withered to grey. What was left of his hair thinned and fell out. His manhood shriveled, and all energy seeped from his limbs.

His worst nightmare! Debilitating age and dotage.

"Ghosts!" yelled a man.

"Centipedes, crawling all over me!" screamed another.

Around him, the vaunted imperial guard fell into disarray. *Dao* rasped out of sheaths. The porters fled in all directions. A female servant looked about, bewildered.

"Retreat, retreat!" the *Tianzi* yelled. "Fall back to the castle and seal the gates. All the hereditary lords are rebelling! Hong, find the empress and make sure she makes it back to the castle."

"Yes, *Huang-Shang*!" Despite using all his energy to speak, Hong's voice came out a whisper.

He wobbled to his feet, even as his shriveled arms and legs weighed him down like ship anchors. One foot in front of the other, he staggered back toward the palace grounds. After a few steps, he hazarded a glance at the demonic pin in his hand.

It was just a silver brooch, formed in the shape of a dragon. Exquisite, really. What had happened?

He looked back. The *Tianzi* had disappeared into the winding alleys of the castle, leaving his own palanquin behind. Imperial guards watched over the bridge. Horns blared.

Those horns...the ones that indicated an enemy had breached the palace walls. Once the castle gatehouse closed, the *Tianzi* would be sealed off from the rest of the world.

Who would lead now?

Liang Yu huddled by a tree, just outside the pottery shop where the *Moquan* leadership received secret reports. If the old adage about information winning wars was true, the Black Lotus Clan might rival the Floating World in strategic value.

He unfolded the first missive from the agent in the South and deciphered the coded language. Peng had let the Madurans through the Wall. The fool! At least an assassination attempt on Lord Peng was in the works, and the *Moquan* were particularly adept at such operations. Thoughts of the Beauty and Surgeon, long banished to fond memories, surfaced yet again. Liang Yu was growing soft and nostalgic in his old age.

He refolded the message and sighed. With dumb luck, all the idiotic army deployments Chief Minister Hong had been whispering into the *Tianzi's* ears would avert disaster. The combined imperial and auxiliary provincial forces should have little problem repelling the Madurans, and that would send a warning to the independence-minded Lord Lin in Linshan.

The nation was on the brink, and he had put them there. His plans to unite the hereditary lords in the call for war against foreign neighbors had instead weakened Hua. Some Architect he was. He sighed again and unfolded another note.

Liang Yu's eyes widened. A missive from the *Moquan* guarding the palace. The *Tianzi* had barricaded himself inside the castle, insistent that the *Tai-ming* had risen up against the Jade Throne. The confused hereditary lords had declared the *Tianzi's* second cousin, a babe of just four-months, as acting *Tianzi*. His grandfather, *Tai-Ming* Lord Liu of Jiangzhou, would be his regent.

What had happened? The *Tianzi* was weak-willed and incompetent, to be sure, but insane? If anyone were more weak-willed and incompetent than the current *Tianzi*, it was Lord Liu. It couldn't all be a coincidental perfect storm. At the same time, anyone who could orchestrate so many parts was more of an Architect than he.

Harrumphing, Liang Yu almost tore the last message while trying to unravel it. A message from Princess Kaiya's *Moquan* bodyguard. The princess had been injured in an assassination attempt, and the half-elf requested a replacement.

Standing, he stashed the note into his robe. With a quick glance to make sure no one was watching, he returned to the funerary pot and dropped in the other two messages. The *Moquan* leadership needed to know about the unholy alliance between Peng and the Madurans, as well as the chaos inside the palace.

As for the half-elf's... That one, he would keep. If Hong's mistress was right, Princess Kaiya would be arriving at the river docks sometime tomorrow, expecting a new *Moquan* bodyguard.

Liang Yu could play that role. She would need it, since even though Regent Liu was incompetent, he would still see her as a threat to his grandson's claim to the Jade Throne.

By protecting her, Liang Yu could control someone with a legitimate claim to the Mandate of Heaven. Or make demands of the Royalists who supported the Wang family.

He just needed to get to her before the imperial guard. That might not be hard, since they apparently had their hands full in the palace.

Geros shifted in the bloodwood chair, not trusting the spindly struts to support his weight. He must look ridiculous, but better that than sitting on the floor like these uncivilized Cathayi. His own officers and soldiers stood at attention behind him, likely dubious of the other seats brought to the Lord Zheng's audience chamber.

If his sour face was any indication, the castle chamberlain had been none too pleased to bring one chair, let alone scrounge up a dozen. All the other assembled Cathayi councilors and officers appeared equally bewildered and angry.

Lord Zheng, on the other hand, revealed nothing in his expression. He sat cross-legged across from Geros, a sheathed Cathayi broadsword in front of him. "Where is my eldest son? Or have you gone back on your word?"

Geros snorted. "Viceroy Zheng, I only said that if you did not open the gate, I would start removing your sons' body parts. I have been generous and given two of them back." Of course, he would have returned Ming, if only for good will, had the slippery lordling not escaped.

"Where is he, then?" Neither Lord Zheng's face nor tone had changed. The most dangerous man was one who could not be read.

It was time to find out just how much his newest vassal knew. Geros laughed. "Let's stop playing games. You know, of course. Princess Kaiya's half-elf rescued him."

Now Zheng's expression did twitch, if only for a split second. He knew nothing of the escape, apparently, which meant...

In Geros' fury at the escape, he had missed the logical connection. His heart leapt as he leaned forward in his chair. "If the half-elf was here, where is Princess Kaiya?" If she had not yet fled to Huajing, he could delay the assault until Leina could thoroughly undermine the government.

"She returned to the capital." Lord Zheng's mask and glib tone had returned.

"When?" Geros kept the urgency out of his voice. Yet if had been recent, he could send some officers on horseback to chase her down.

"Three days ago, as soon as she was well enough to travel after the assassination attempt."

Geros sucked in a breath. She must have reached Huajing by now, into the nest of snakes vying for power. One of those had likely sent the assassin in the first place. Geros had to protect his love. Unless Lord Zheng lied. "So why was the half-elf still here?"

"I don't know," Lord Zheng said. "It was not my place to question the princess. However, she had expressed interest in marrying my son, so perhaps she had left her bodyguard here to greet him. Or facilitate his escape."

Geros scratched his chin. As soon as Princess Kaiya reached the capital, Leina would surely send a messenger bird to let him know. The intelligent Eldaeri-bred birds gave the Teleri a significant communication advantage over the horse-relay systems which most other nations used. "Make sure all imperial horse relays are cut off, Viceroy Zheng. You are dismissed."

Bowing, Lord Zheng collected his sword. He stood and backed out of the room, followed by his own men.

Geros motioned toward a shadow near the wall. "Was Lord Zheng telling the truth?"

Master Feiying stepped into view and bowed. "He is hard to read, Your Eminence, but I suspect he did not lie."

"Follow him and make sure he executes my commands faithfully." Geros beckoned the officer in charge of communications, a Bovyan of Kanin stock. "Lieutenant Espios, prepare a messenger bird bound for Leina in Huajing. Tell her that Princess Kaiya may be walking into a trap, and to arrange protection."

A familiar, annoying laugh erupted from the entrance. A sinking feeling settling into his stomach, Geros looked up.

The Altivorc King, with none of his usual retinue of vile guards, leaned against the door frame, twirling that wand of his. "Geros, Geros, since when did you care about a woman so much, you would forget all about military strategy?”

Heat rushed to Geros’ face. How dare the king mock him in front of his men? “The princess has important strategic value. The people adore her, and our son will legitimize Teleri rule over Cathay.”

Yawning, the altivorc strolled down the middle of the room. “As you say. It doesn’t matter to me, as long as you hold up your end of our deal.”

Geros waved him off. “Yes, yes, the Cathayi pyramid is yours.”

“There are two more things I want.” With a flourishing twirl, the King sheathed his wand. “Inside the Temple of Heaven in Huajing, there is a chunk of a fallen star. A token, really.”

Right. Geros grinned. Anything the lizard wanted had to carry some importance. “This was never part of our deal.”

“Of course not,” the Altivorc King said. “Which is why if you bring it to me, I will start ending the Bovyan Curse, beginning with you.”

An end to the curse. Geros gawked in spite of himself. He had promised Ming Zheng the hand of Princess Kaiya once he died, but now it seemed his death would not come so soon. All of the plans and timetables to secure his legacy, now less relevant. No; hope must not replace resolve. Even still… “And the second thing you want?”

“Information. I overheard something about the princess’ half-elf. Where did you see her last?”

CHAPTER 15:
Many Unhappy Returns

The sloshing waves changed in frequency and mingled with the nearly inaudible buzz of the Fallen Star in the Temple of Heaven, letting Kaiya know that she had reached the Songyuan river docks in Huajing.

She afforded herself a silent scoff. If the *Tiger's Eye* allowed her any sense of nostalgia, her inner voice might've waxed poetic about that naïve girl who had set off from these quays just over a year before.

Tested by conspiracies, dictators, and a dragon, she was no longer that girl. At what cost, though? Four of the five imperial guards who'd accompanied her that morning had died in her defense. Her beloved, also as dead as her emotions. Her beloved's brother, perhaps needlessly sacrificed.

She scanned the dockside. Dockworkers and sailors bustled about, seeming no different from the last time she'd been here. Did the imperial court know of the impending invasion? It didn't appear so. It had taken them three days by boat, but the horse relays should've brought news of the Teleri breaching the Wall within just a few hours.

Unless Lord Zheng had managed to silence every loyal imperial soldier... Impossible.

If that *were* the case, the imperial armies would have three less days to mobilize. She had to warn Brother Kai-Wu.

Though herbal medicine and rest had helped her regain some energy, her legs wobbled as she rose. Weiyong came to her side and helped her disembark with a firm hand.

She offered him a grateful nod, then turned to the captain of her escort. "We must make haste to the palace."

"*Dian-xia*," Fang Weiyong said, "For your safety, we should not travel through the city without a contingent of imperial guards."

He was right. She pursed her lips. Plenty of people in the capital would recognize her. If just one spotted her, news of her arrival would spread faster than she could walk. Who knew if the insurgents had been completely pacified?

Still, Brother Kai-Wu needed to know about the imminent Teleri attack. Withdrawing the pouch containing Tian's tablet, she proffered it in two hands to Fang Weiyong. With Lord Zheng's and Tian's names inscribed, it could only come from Dongmen. "Weiyong, take this to Sun-Moon Palace. It is proof. Tell them—"

"Wait, *Dian-xia*," a weathered male voice called.

Her guards all placed hands on their broadswords, their eyes shifting left to the source of the voice. She followed their gazes.

A middle-aged man knelt, one fist to the ground, the other hand clasping a walking staff. He bowed, exposing streaks of silver in his long hair.

Who was he? She lifted her chin. "Rise."

He raised his head, revealing an average-looking face with no defining features. Had she seen him before? If a foreign artist were to sketch a Hua male, this would be him—one who could melt in with the faceless crowds.

"*Dian-xia*," he repeated. He shuffled forward and held up a creased sheet of paper. The gibberish was likely *Moquan* code, written in Jie's unmistakable scrawl. "Your black lotus asked for a replacement."

Black Lotus? Unless he was describing Jie's dark heart and pretty looks, only a *Moquan* would know the clan name for the *Tianzi's* spies and assassins. Most of the select few people who'd even heard of the name would assume it referred to an order of cloistered monks who kept historical accounts. The half-elf must've disobeyed the order to hold her post, and asked for a replacement. If not for the *Tiger's Eye*, Kaiya might have taken it personally. Instead, she nodded. "What is your name?"

"Fu, *Dian-xia*." He bowed. "My cover name is Golden Fu."

Where had she heard that name before? Perhaps someone Zheng Ming had mentioned when the *Moquan* rooted out the former Chief Minister Tan as a conspirator. She stared at him. "You knew of my arrival."

He straightened and grinned. "Of course. It is our business to know things."

Definitely *Moquan*. No telling what kind of weapon the walking staff was. But… "If you knew, why did the *Tianzi* not send a contingent of imperial guards to greet me?"

Fu's gaze darted to her guards, then settled on hers. He edged closer, cupped his mouth, and whispered in her ear. "*Dian-xia*, we are not going to the palace. It is not safe right now."

Not safe? She leaned back and narrowed her eyes. "There is no place in Hua more defensible than Sun-Moon Castle."

He whispered again, his words barely audible. "The danger I speak of is inside the palace itself. Your brother never fully recovered from Peng's poisoning. He went mad and sequestered himself in the main keep. There has been no contact with him."

Could it be true? Gentle Second Brother, driven insane? "Who rules?"

"Lord Liu of Jiangzhou rules as regent, and plans to ship you off to a nunnery. On his command, the imperial guard will apprehend you the instant you step into Sun-Moon palace."

Never. Lord Liu's absolute loyalty came from an utter lack of ambition. The imperial guard would side with her, anyway. Keeping suspicion out of her voice, she summoned her most incredulous tone: "How did Lord Liu become regent? Why would he capture me?"

"His son is married to your cousin, Wang Kai-Hua. Her son, now four months old, was next in line to the Jade Throne. You are a threat to his grandson."

Kai-Hua, a mother. To an unwitting usurper, no less. She'd never willingly be part of such a plot. Had Lord Liu hidden his ambitions like Cousin Peng? "If you are loyal to the *Tianzi*, why are you helping me?"

"The imperial guard is loyal to the Jade Throne. Our clan is loyal to the Wang family. There are several of us here to protect you." He pointed a subtle thumb behind him to his right, then to his left.

A mirror flashed from a warehouse, then another from a tea shop. Both in the directions he had indicated. Six black-garbed faces bobbed up from a third rooftop.

Even if he wasn't who he claimed, they were surrounded. Perhaps by dozens of soldiers. But he'd flashed Jie's letter, so perhaps she could trust him. Though that would also mean Brother Kai-Wu was mad, and yet another cousin had betrayed her. "Where are we going, then?"

"One of our clan's safehouses." Fu handed her a travelling cloak. "Please cover your head." He turned to her guards and spoke up. "Soldiers of Hua. You are now the imperial guard. Your first duty is to the princess."

Kaiya pursed her lips. These men, while serviceable, were not imperial guards. It seemed like an insult to Chen Xin, Zhao Yue, Li Wei, and Xu Zhan.

The soldiers all snapped to attention. Golden Fu beckoned them to follow.

Never had Liang Yu been so close to the supposed once-in-three-generations beauty, and for the first time his old eyes could appreciate her gorgeousness. He guided the princess and her small entourage into an alley, grateful he'd been able to convince her to follow. Her suspicious questioning, hidden behind a decent semblance of shock, suggested she was no longer the gullible girl he remembered stalking a year ago. Even then-Household Minister Hong had manipulated her.

Liang Yu glanced around to make sure they weren't being followed. For the time being, he held a potential claimant to regent. The sooner he took care of her eight guards, none who appeared formidable—

"Fu," she said. "Everyone seems so calm. Life goes on as usual. Are the imperial armies ready to repel the invasion?"

Fu nodded. "Yes, *Dian-xia*. A combined force of imperial and provincial soldiers, three hundred thousand strong."

"Which provinces march with the imperial army?"

So idealistic. She was undoubtedly trying to think of a peaceful resolution to the rebellion. Her leadership would make Hua stronger...but only after they crushed Peng and his Maduran allies. "Zhenjing, Ximen, and Fengu Provinces all obeyed the Mandate of Heaven."

"And the others?" Her authoritative tone showed the slightest hint of worry.

He only had to keep her trust a little longer. He tilted his head toward a passerby. "We are almost to the safehouse. Let us speak more of this in private."

"Very well." Her passive expression would make a *Moquan* envious.

After a few more minutes, he brought them to a warehouse and opened the door for her. "In here. Imperial guards, the princess is safe for now. Wait here and one of my men will come and take you to a nearby inn."

Or rather, to a temporary prison, but they didn't need to know it.

The captain stepped forward. "Our duty is to the princess. We must accompany her."

The man took the title a little too seriously. Well, soldiers would be soldiers. Nothing he hadn't planned for. Liang Yu raised an eyebrow at the princess.

She nodded. "They will enter as well."

No matter. He had prepared for this contingency, even if he had hoped to prevent any bloodshed. Had the Surgeon been here, he'd already be killing. Liang Yu cast a quick glance around to make sure they'd not picked up a tail. "Come along, then. This is not our final destination."

He guided them through some twists and turns until they appeared thoroughly bewildered. At last, he came to his trading company's warehouse. He held the door open for the princess.

She nodded and stepped in. The doctor and the eight guards followed close behind. Inside, the light baubles illuminated the middle of the spacious empty room, but not the sides, just as planned. The guards and doctor looked around, taking in the new surroundings.

The princess' head swept from one side of the room to the other, before her gaze settled on Liang Yu. Her nose scrunched up. "This was not exactly what I expected..."

She wouldn't expect what happened next, either. He closed the door and edged forward, ready to separate his walking stick into a knife and spear. "Now."

Shrouded in the darkness of the mezzanine above, dozens of repeating crossbows cocked.

Taking advantage of the imperial soldiers' initial shock, Liang Yu slipped between them. They backed into a circle around the princess, but he was already close. He pushed the doctor to the side and hooked his knife around her throat. The doctor took a step toward him, but Liang Yu placed the tip of his spear at his chest.

"Don't try to sing any commands," Liang Yu said. No, after falling victim to the power of her voice a year before, he'd taken precautions. "Some of my men's ears are covered, and they await signals."

She raised her hands. "What is the meaning of this?"

How could she show no signs of fear? Liang Yu pressed the blade obliquely into her neck. "You are in no position to ask questions. You are all trapped. There is no need for anyone to die. Tell your men to stand down."

"We..." the captain said, "we are willing to...die for you, *Dian-xia*."

The lack of enthusiasm in his voice was depressing. Liang Yu snorted. Perhaps these men weren't worth keeping around.

Lowering her hand, the princess spoke in a steady voice, "Captain, order your men to surrender."

The captain's words trembled out of his mouth. "Men, drop your weapons. Hands on your heads."

The imperial soldiers wasted no time in obeying. There would be no need for bloodshed, at least not yet.

Liang Yu beckoned his own men with his spear. "Bind them. You, *Dian-xia*, come with me."

"Fu, if only three provinces stand with the throne, I must go to the palace to convince the others to join. Hua's survival depends on it."

Perhaps he misread her, if she wanted to unite the nation against the rebel. Still, her military acumen left a lot to be desired. He chuckled. "Only Yutou Province stands with Peng. They hardly constitute a threat. Even with the Madurans—"

"Madurans?" The shock in her wide eyes had to be genuine.

He cocked his head. "Who did you think was invading us?"

The princess pointed north. "The Teleri army, led by Emperor Geros himself, occupies Dongmen."

Dongmen? His men erupted in murmurs. She was pointing in the wrong direction, but still. It must be a trick, to throw him off-guard. The bonfires on the Great Wall and fire towers would have brought news within an hour. Even if no one

heeded the signal, they would listen to the daily couriers out of Dongmen.

Still, if she were telling the truth, nothing stood between Dongmen and Huayuan. The entire North was virtually undefended, while an incompetent ruled as regent. A perfect storm, caused in part by his own past actions. The Beauty would've been laughing at him right about now. She'd always predicted he would make a huge mistake. "Are you certain? There has been no such news."

The princess glared at him. "Of course I am certain. Lord Zheng was about to let the Bovyans in when I left."

A collaborator! That would explain it. Lord Zheng must have waylaid the imperial couriers and made sure the fire signals remained unlit. "Very well, *Dian-xia*. I will have one of my men send a warning to the palace now."

"You must let me go to the palace myself. I will take the risk. I will make them listen."

"Not so fast." First, he needed to confirm it. "We must talk first. Come along."

"Allow Fang Weiyong to accompany me."

Liang Yu evaluated him with a quick glance. The doctor had shown no signs of fighting skill, and probably wouldn't pose a significant threat. He also had the imperial plaque. "Very well. Your men are my hostages. Any sign of disobedience, and I will kill one of them, starting with your doctor." Snapping his spear and knife back together into a walking stick, he held an open hand toward the warehouse office. "Please."

She cast him a scathing glare. "Who are you?"

No sign of worry. He blanked his own expression. "I will answer your question, but in the privacy of that room. Please walk. The doctor first."

The doctor looked at the princess, and she nodded. He turned and led her to the office. Liang Yu followed one step behind. At the door, he darted to the side and opened it for them.

Kidnapping her had made so much sense before. However, if what she said was true about the Teleri invasion of the undefended North, maybe she was the only one who could bring the country together.

Without the least amount of fear, she walked into his office. It was time to ascertain if she was telling the truth.

Kaiya took a deep breath. She'd walked blindly into a trap, duped as if she were Avarax's fool again. Her hand strayed to Tian's lockpick pouch. For now, at least, her escort was safe. If she could only figure out who these people were and what they wanted. She stepped into a small room, with a single window that bathed the room in afternoon light.

A silhouetted figure stood on the other side of a bloodwood desk. He cradled what appeared to be a repeating crossbow in his arms. At least he didn't point it at them.

Fu gestured her toward the two bloodwood chairs in front of the desk. She glided over and settled on the edge of one, while Weiyong stood on her left.

Seemingly unconcerned about the Teleri invasion, Fu walked by them and took a seat behind the desk, next to the other man. With the sun at his back, she couldn't read his expression; not that she was good at it in the first place.

"Now, to answer your question," Fu said. "I am a spice merchant with the nation's best interests at heart."

And a *Moquan*. Perhaps the renegade who had perpetrated all the attacks a year before. She pursed her lips. If he really had the nation's best interests at heart, he had a strange way of showing it. "Then send a message to the palace. At least let them know of the Bovyan invasion."

"Of course." He bowed, and then gestured toward the doctor. "You gave him an imperial plaque earlier. Give it to me."

The imperial plaque? What was he talking...

The doctor cocked his head. "I—"

She held up an open hand, silencing him. Fu must have mistaken Tian's tablet for the imperial plaque. Now it was bargaining leverage. Blasphemous, all the same. "Weiyong, give me the plaque."

"But *Dian-xia*—"

He was sweet, but he could be so dense sometime. Of course, she didn't know where the real plaque was any more than Weiyong. In her frightened younger self's haste to escape Iksuvius, she'd forgotten it. Maybe Emperor Geros had recovered it. She suppressed a shudder as a twinge of fear sparked, only to be smothered by the *Tiger's Eye*. Keeping her focus locked forward, she extended her hand to the doctor. "You won't be taking it to the palace now."

Understanding bloomed in Weiyong's eyes. He bowed and proffered the pouch. Kaiya turned and received it in two hands. Fu's henchman took a step forward with an outstretched arm.

Fu barred his way with the walking staff. "*Dian-xia*, Little Song here needs the plaque to prove he is your messenger."

She glared at him. "I will not have an insurgent—"

"Patriot," Fu said. "Little Song cares about Hua. He is the son of the former Foreign Minister Song Henglin.

At Song's new angle, she could see his face clearly. Yes, it was Song Xingyuan, the son of Minister Song, who'd held the Chief Minister title for a single day...before it was revealed his son was an insurgent. She'd strongarmed the young man into giving her the Dragon Scale Lute, three years ago. Perhaps that disgrace had pushed him into rebellion. Maybe he held a grudge against her.

Song dropped to one knee, head bowed. Fu, too, nodded in respect to the supposed plaque. Apparently, he still recognized the symbol of the *Tianzi* and the Mandate of Heaven.

Summoning her tone of imperial authority, though not as effective as the power of her voice, she said, "For now, I will keep the plaque."

Fu smirked. "What keeps me from taking it from you?"

"Mutual benefit. I could have sung the order for your men to kill each other." She tucked the pouch into the fold of her robe. He believed she still had her power; would he believe her bluff now? If her frightened younger self could trick a dragon, her older self, armed with the *Tiger's Eye*, could deceive a man. "However, if you are a patriot and the information about Lord Liu is true, then I will need you."

She kept her expression impassive as his eyes searched hers.

At last, he leaned back in his chair. "I will bring a friend of yours here, one who can get into the palace with no proof of identity."

Kaiya pursed her lips. Who was he speaking of? "I do not want any more people kidnapped."

Fu grinned. "She will come of her own free will. Little Song, go to the Linshan legation and tell Lin Ziqiu I have a mission for her."

Apparently the *Tiger's Eye* couldn't suppress surprise, because Kaiya's mouth must have been gaping. Had Ziqiu been spying on her in the past, using flightiness as a disguise?

CHAPTER 16:
Cherry Pairs

Thirty-three days. Feneyas estimated more than a cycle of the white moon would pass before he ever learned his identity, just because the wild elves insisted on maintaining pretenses with the humans. He could've gone straight to the Maki village himself; instead, the woodland messengers would go and deliver instructions for the shaman to come visit the sacred pool.

Sacred, indeed.

As if blue sand and exfoliated elf skin made the pool magic. It was almost a joke among the elves. Dior laughed, recounting how he had tricked a shaman and his two young children when they had visited a half a year before, by whispering in the wind and tossing rocks into the pool.

In the meantime, life went on. More weapons practice, more hunting and foraging. Though restless, Feneyas at least had a chance to learn a little about woodcraft from Kiri and the others. Dior taught him the finer points of archery, though it did little more than earn the laughter of the elves when they watched.

Well before dawn on the eighth day, Feneyas jerked out of sleep and nearly tumbled from his hammock.

Kiri stood just ten paces away, frozen in her approach. She flashed him a mischievous grin. "No one can sneak up on you, even in your sleep. Now come, there's a dawn-blooming everblossom I want to harvest."

Feneyas shook the fog out of his mind and lumbered to his feet. Following Kiri through the other hammocks of sleeping elves, he made his way down the tree steps to the ground.

Little Kala beamed at him from the bottom, while Dior yawned. The bow and quiver strapped across his back did not seem suited for the task at hand.

Feneyas poked Kiri in the back. "Do we really need four of us to pick flowers?"

She batted her eyelashes. "No, but eight baskets carry more than four."

They set off down a path, with the three others barely making a sound. It helped that *they* could see in the dark. Then again, that was no excuse. He made plenty of noise traipsing across the forest paths in broad daylight.

"What are the everblossoms for?" Feneyas asked in a low whisper.

Kiri chuckled, but didn't answer.

Dior leaned in. "Women's issues."

Before long, they arrived on a low ridge overlooking a clearing in the trees. Broadleaf plants covered the ground. Kiri motioned for them to stop, and pointed at the shrubbery. Kala crouched and stared at the closed sepals.

The sky began to fade from black to dark blue, and the forest erupted with birdsong. Pink formed on the horizon, heralding the arrival of the sun. The groundcover burst forth in an explosion of yellow and white blooms.

Kiri squeezed Feneyas' hand, looking up to meet his gaze. Her smile was refreshing and happy.

His stomach fluttered. Perhaps who he was didn't matter, just that he belonged somewhere. All sounds of the forest quieted in that moment.

In the distance, metal jingled.

Feneyas spun in that direction, then back to meet Dior's eyes. The elf's ears twitched. His bow was already in hand.

As the sounds grew louder, Dior motioned them off the ridge and into some bushes. Huddled by Kiri's side, Feneyas lifted his head and ventured a glance out.

A squad of Metal Men, all wearing black surcoats over chainmail hauberks, pushed through some brush and paused on the path Feneyas and the elves had taken. They stood just fifteen feet away.

At point, a Kanin tribesman took a step and squatted, pressing his hand to the ground. The soldiers, eleven in all, gathered up behind him. Some passed a flask around and took swigs.

One, with spiked shoulder guards and a steel breastplate, pushed forward toward the front of the column. He stood only as tall as his companions' chests, but might have been just as broad and muscular. Shaggy black hair jutted out from beneath his half-helm, setting him apart from the others' close-cropped coifs. Unlike his comrades' longswords, this one had a wicked broadsword hanging at his side.

He turned in Feneyas' direction, revealing turquoise-colored skin in the early morning light. His squat, blocky face was so ugly, Feneyas probably would've remembered had he seen a more hideous person in his past life.

Kiri dug her fingers into Feneyas' arm as she shrank behind him.

The guide bobbed his head over and over again. "Sorry, sorry," he said in the Metal Men's language. "I lost the half-elf's trail."

Half-elf...they were searching for Kiri. Feneyas shifted over, as if it would protect his friend.

Turquoise Man turned back and smacked the guide across the cheek, sending a loud crack echoing through the woods. He let out a series of foul syllables that could only be a curse.

One of the Metal Men shoved the guide in the back. "If you don't pick up the trail, we'll chop your children to pieces. See if your legendary tracking skills can find them all."

The tribesman's voice trembled. "Only two, not easy. And dark. Too dark to see."

"But fresh." Turquoise Man seized the guide by the shoulder and yanked him to his feet. So strong.

Kiri tugged at Feneyas. He looked at her.

Let's go, she mouthed. Her eyes glistened with tears. Her other hand clutched Kala's hand. Kala's free hand covered her mouth, and her eyes were squeezed shut. Dior... Dior was nowhere to be found. Kiri let go of him and started to stand.

Feneyas grabbed Kiri's wrist and shook his head. Fleeing would give away their position. She squeezed his wrist back.

The guide pointed toward the forest floor. "A track. Smaller human. Went that way." He now pointed past Feneyas and the others, toward the ridge.

The Metal Man shoved him in the back. "Then lead us."

Kiri's grip tightened as the column jingled and clanged single-file past their hiding place.

Feneyas held his breath.

Kala burst into tears. She jumped up and bolted in the other direction. Kiri scrambled to her feet and ran after her.

"Look! The half-elf!" More armor clinked as bodies turned this way and that, swords sweeping out of their scabbards.

Turquoise Man jerked his head in Kiri's direction, then lumbered through the underbrush after her. Despite his short legs, he moved fast. Two Metal Men followed.

A bowstring twanged somewhere to the left. An arrow thwipped through air and lodged into a nearby Metal Man's throat. Another brute collapsed into a heap nearby with an arrow through his eye. The fletching marked it as Dior's.

"Trap! Take cover!" the first Metal Man blurted.

His comrades had already broken toward the cover of the trees, heads twisting every which way to find the source of the arrow. One poked his head out, only to take an arrow through the mouth.

Three enemies fallen, the others pinned down by Dior's marksmanship.

And three in pursuit of Kiri and Kala.

Feneyas leaped up and took off after his half-elf friends. Turning a corner on the path, he nearly tripped over one of the Metal Men, throat slashed with blood gushing out.

Kiri's scream tore through the forest from down the path. Oddly calm despite the chaos, Feneyas broke into a run.

After several seconds, a trail of black blood appeared. The sounds of metal on metal clashed louder. Then, there they were.

With his right arm hanging at his side, Turquoise Man leaned against a tree. He swung his broadsword in vicious arcs, keeping Kiri at bay.

How had Kiri gotten the upper hand against an armored warrior?

Not only that, she had changed her clothes? Gone was the doeskin dress, replaced by tight black clothes. At least, they might've been black if not for all the mud splattered on them. She'd apparently found time not only to change her clothes—and where had she stashed the new ones?—but to roll around in the dirt as well.

"You can drop your weapon and answer some questions," Kiri said, "or you can die." She could speak the Metal Man's language! And speak it *well*, even better than her proficiency with Kanin. Had she been keeping that a secret the whole time?

Still brandishing his sword, Turquoise Man burst out laughing. "Come on, Orc Slayer, see if you can get close enough to make good on your empty threats."

"Okay, have it your way." Kiri reached into the fold of her shirt and whipped out three *biao*. *Biao?* The name came to him unbidden, foreign and familiar at once. They whistled through the air and lodged into Turquoise Man's face, neck, and gut. With a squelch, he collapsed to the ground.

Feneyas coughed. Where'd Kiri gotten the clothes and the foreign weapons?

Kiri met his gaze. Her eyes widened as large as greywood tree leaves, and she stumbled back two steps. "*H-Heavens!*"

She could speak *his* native tongue.

From Feneyas' right, another man crashed through the bushes, longsword raised. Feneyas spun to his attacker's right, and would have broken the man's arm had the assailant not skidded short, mouth hanging slack.

"*Heavens!*" His would-be attacker's voice sputtered in shock and awe. Gawking, he lowered his sword. Apparently, the People Beyond the Wall enjoyed invoking the Heavens.

The man had also spoken in Feneyas' native language, and at cursory glance, he had the same honey skin, black hair, and almond-shaped eyes. He held a Metal Man's sword.

"Heavens..." Warrior Kiri took a tentative step toward him, hand trembling.

The second Metal Man burst out behind Yellow Man and hacked down with his longsword.

Feneyas reached out and raised Yellow Man's arm, angling his sword so that the Metal Man's clanged into it. The weapon jarred from Yellow Man's grasp.

Feneyas caught it underhanded by the hilt, and swept it up into the arc of the Metal Man's back stroke. Its edge smashed into the flat of Feneyas' sword with a clank. The reverberation wrung his hand, but he kept hold of the weapon. He butted Yellow Man to the side with his hip and drew his knife with his left hand.

The Metal Man transitioned to a strong thrust.

Brushing it to the side with his own sword, Feneyas spun in and slashed down with the knife, across his enemy's throat and to the inside of his left wrist. On the upstroke, he cut the inside of the Metal Man's right wrist.

Yellow Man lunged and tackled the Metal Man from behind. He pushed himself up, favoring his right arm, climbed on the Metal Man's back, and ripped off his helm. He then repeatedly bashed the hapless soldier's head into the ground.

Apparently satisfied with his handiwork, Yellow Man looked up, his mouth agape. "Heavens! You are alive!"

Yellow Man must have known him. On closer inspection, they had similar features. Unlike the diversity of elf faces, maybe the People Beyond the Wall all looked the same? Feneyas found his tongue, his native language stumbling out of his mouth after an eternity of non-use. "Who are you? Where did you come from?"

Yellow Man rolled his eyes. "*Heavens*! Stop being silly. I am bright—"

Dior appeared on the path, prodding the Kanin tribesman along.

Then, *another* Kiri peeked through the bushes. She took a tentative step out, pulling Kala along with her. She wore the same doeskin dress as before.

Warrior Kiri spun and held her knife aloft. Then her gaze met the real Kiri's.

The two looked exactly alike, even more similar than Yellow Man and Feneyas. Like the fruit dangling in a cherry tree, always in pairs, they mirrored each other.

Heads shifted from person to person, eyes widening and brows furrowing.

Both Yellow Man and Dior pointed back and forth at real Kiri and fake Kiri.

Warrior Kiri's stare fell on Feneyas', and then shifted to her twin. The knife slipped from her fingers, and she stumbled back several steps. "This can't be happening. This can't be real."

With mouth half-open, the real Kiri appeared surprised, but not nearly as dumfounded as Warrior Kiri. Clearing her throat, she gestured toward Dior. "Shoot, shoot!"

"Wait!" Feneyas took a step to interpose himself between Dior and Warrior Kiri.

Too late.

Dior had unslung his bow, nocked an arrow and loosed it at Warrior Kiri.

CHAPTER 17:
Limited Information

With Weiyong at her side, Kaiya sat serenely in Golden Fu's office. Footsteps and clanking weapons out in the warehouse indicated at least twenty rebels, while the cloying scent of a myriad spices roiled her stomach. Perhaps Fu was indeed a spice merchant.

An evasive one at that, whose questions begot more questions, and whose answers answered nothing. Apparently, the *Tiger's Eye* could do nothing to control impatience, even if she hid it. Every hour they waited meant Geros and the Teleri army approached unopposed.

Though if what Fu said was true, there was little the imperial court could do. Only a skeleton army remained in the capital, as a precaution against Lord Lin in Linshan attacking with his provincial soldiers.

Out in the warehouse, a set of lighter footsteps approached. Fu's attention flicked to the entrance, then returned to her. As the door opened behind her, Kaiya kept looking past Fu, at the window. Its muted reflection revealed a young woman in a grey commoner's dress, whose eyes met hers. Her supposed friend, Lin Ziqiu.

Fang Weiyong lacked any discretion, and turned to see who it was.

The woman padded in and stopped a few steps behind. "Master, I had a hard time sneaking out of my home. I came as quickly as I could."

The voice belonged to Ziqiu, yet the tone lacked its past capriciousness.

Fu motioned toward Kaiya with an open hand. "An old friend of yours, Little Ziqiu."

The girl shuffled a few steps over and leaned in.

Shifting in her seat, Kaiya met her gaze.

Ziqiu looked so different after just a year. Gone were the carefree smile and eyes dancing with mirth, replaced by serious intent. Then her expression settled into the flightiness Kaiya remembered. "Kaiya! *Dian-xia.* I thought you were in Dongmen. When did you get back? And what are you doing *here*?" She cast a sidelong glance at Fu.

Kaiya pursed her lips. "I would ask the same of you."

"Fu teaches me about information gathering." Ziqiu bowed to Fu. "He is my master."

Kaiya shook her head. "*I am his prisoner.* Or hostage, perhaps." As for information gathering...Ziqiu had only ever seemed interested in trivial gossip. The girl might've been spying on her all this time.

Ziqiu turned and slapped a hand down on the desk. "Master, how could you kidnap Princess Kaiya? I thought you cared about Hua."

Fu leaned back in his chair. "I do. The princess would have walked into a trap at the palace. Surely you know of the coup."

"Coup?" The incredulity in Ziqiu's voice sounded convincing enough. "I haven't been to the palace since my father returned to Linshan. Our villa is surrounded by imperial troops."

Fu scratched his chin. "There is another threat. A Teleri invasion through Dongmen."

Ziqiu faced Kaiya, her face pale. "Is it true?"

Kaiya nodded. They didn't need to know Geros was coming for her, to claim the twins she carried.

"True or not—" Fu said, "and I am not convinced the princess speaks truthfully—a foreign invasion will force the hereditary lords to reunite." He nodded toward Ziqiu. "Go to the palace and inform them."

That would do little to improve Kaiya's situation, and it also put Ziqiu in danger. Kaiya stood. "No. With doubts of Linshan's loyalty, they will take her hostage. We cannot endanger her. Let me go instead."

Weiyong shuffled his feet. Placing her hands on her hips, Ziqiu opened her mouth.

Fu held up a hand and chuckled. "You are just as much at risk as Little Ziqiu, unless you can absolutely convince Regent Liu of the invasion."

"And," Kaiya said, "you would just as soon keep me here."

Ziqiu's eyes flicked back to Fu's. "Forgive me, Master, but she is the princess. You can't do this."

"I can." Fu stared Ziqiu down, and then shifted his glare to Kaiya.

She held his gaze. He wasn't exactly wrong. Still... "The palace must be warned."

"How do you propose to do that?" Fu steepled his hands together.

How, indeed?

The door opened, and Song entered. "Master, the imperial couriers bring bad news from the South."

And how did these misguided rebels have access to the imperial couriers?

Fu motioned for Song to continue.

Song sighed. "Still no news out of Dongmen Province. Also, the Madurans have pushed into the central valley. When Ximen Province sent the bulk of its soldiers east to flank Peng's army, traitorous Lord Liang in Nantou attacked them from behind and occupied Ximen."

"The stupidity!" Fu slapped his hand on the desk. "If not for incompetent commanders, the imperial armies and their provincial allies should have crushed the rebellion and the Madurans in two weeks."

Summoning a map in her mind, Kaiya closed her eyes. Even with her poor sense of geography, she saw Hua faced imminent collapse. Traitors gobbled up the South. Foreign enemies trampled over the North, unchallenged. Three hundred years of peace and prosperity, over in two months. Jobless scholars who knew the secret of firepowder would find new employers, ushering in a new age of warfare. If only they could find a way to just let Regent Liu know—

Opening her eyes, she found everyone staring at her. She composed her expression into regal aloofness. "Fu, how are you intercepting the imperial couriers? And how did you get my half-elf's letter?"

"I have my ways."

If not for the *Tiger's Eye*, his roundabout non-answers might've been infuriating. "Then use those ways. Drop a message into the courier bags, if that is how you do it. However you got Jie's message, send another on. And..." why hadn't she thought of this before? "...what would it take to capture a message tower?"

Fu's face blanked.

Lin Ziqiu clapped her hands together. "Three *li* outside the north city walls, there is a horse relay station and a message tower."

"Yes." Fu turned to Kaiya. "Do you know the light tower codes?"

How would she? Even the *Tianzi* himself probably never concerned himself with such minutia. Well, that went without saying in her brother Kai-Wu's case, but certainly Father had too much to worry about to learn flashing light signals he might never see with his own eyes. Then again, Fu didn't need to know that. "I am surprised the *Moquan* don't know them."

Ziqiu's ears quirked. "*Moquan?*"

Fu laughed. "Imperial soldiers, not boogeymen, control the light towers. Those towers have not been used since the last time an enemy breached the Great Wall."

As in, never. Kaiya snorted. Still, this was a chance to escape from her captors. "Then you will need me to go with you."

"Or you can tell us." Fu's eyes narrowed again.

"And if I refuse?"

Fu laughed. "*You* were the one who wanted to warn the regent."

Kaiya looked out the office window. The iridescent moon waxed to its mid-crescent. Already late afternoon. Less than three hours of daylight. So much wasted time! "If you are truly a patriot, then you would see the need as well."

Fu stroked his chin, a gesture reminiscent of Tian. "I also see the need to keep an eye on you."

His motives, clearly stated. Kaiya frowned.

Lin Ziqiu sighed. "Master, you can't keep a Scion of Heaven prisoner."

Fu held a finger up. "We do not know if her brother still lives or not. If the grandson of Lord Liu sits as *Tianzi*, then Miss Wang Kaiya is no longer a Scion of Heaven."

It was true. How easy it would be not to carry the burden of responsibility. But no. The Teleri Empire would relegate Hua men to second-class citizens, and do much worse to the women. Someone had to do something. She opened her mouth to speak.

Fu opened his hand, stopping her. "Which is not to say she can't be Scion of Heaven. We must time her *return* carefully. Now, we must plan the capture of the light tower."

Which would mean unnecessary killing. There had to be another way. "Wait."

Fu looked up at Song, apparently ignoring her. "Inform our asset that we need to insert a message into the imperial courier network."

Song shook his head. "He'll share information, but I don't think he would pass fake messages."

"Even in an emergency?" Fu scowled.

Kaiya stood. "There is an easier way, one that can avoid any casualties. Allow me to go with you, and I will command the couriers and light tower to pass the messages on."

"With your voice, or imperial authority?"

She might not have either, but Fu didn't need to know. "Whichever it takes."

"And how do I know you will continue to accept my protection?"

Kaiya flashed a disarming smile. If he could mince meat as well as words, he might actually be useful. It was a matter of convincing him of her own worth. On her own terms, of course. With two hands, she raised the pouch containing Tian's tablet and bowed her head to it. "I swear on this."

The tablet might not have been what Fu thought, but it was just as important to her. She wouldn't break a promise. As she had learned from the Bovyans, an oath without specifics could be twisted. How long she would *accept* Fu's protection depended on how long he remained useful.

Fu bowed to the tablet. "Very well. Now, we have another problem. The thirty men out there are all anti-imperial insurgents, originally funded by your cousin Peng Kai-Long, before I took over. They aren't about to let you leave."

Liang Yu knew a thing or two about playing two sides, and had already planned a means for getting the princess out. Still, as long as she believed she needed him, he could control her.

Though she might no longer be so naïve, the princess would have a difficult time winning over hardened soldiers who wanted to oust her family from the Jade Throne. Surely her voice could not affect them all.

He just had to redirect their anger once she failed. No telling what they would do to her otherwise. He held the door to let her out of the office.

Back straight and chin lifted high, she stepped out into the warehouse. That wouldn't endear them to her! Her head immediately turned to her bound guards and the men guarding them. Murmurs broke out in the darkened mezzanine.

"Soldiers of Hua," she said, voice mellifluous. "I understand your grievances."

Or so she thought. Liang Yu grinned. He had told her just enough that she would still need him.

She placed a hand on her chest. "My father always had the nation's best interests at heart, even though you might not have agreed with his decisions."

"Hua stagnated!" a voice from the mezzanine called, followed by a chorus of agreeing murmurs.

"The lords got rich," another said, "while we soldiers were forgotten when we got older."

"We never got the rewards we were promised."

"There were no wars to fight."

Amid the barrage of complaints, the princess looked at Liang Yu, an eyebrow raised. She was already at a loss. She needed him, just as he planned.

He came to her side and opened his mouth. "Fellow patriots—"

"Soldiers of Hua." With dexterity rivaling the Surgeon, she slid in front of him and bowed low at the waist. It was unheard of for a member of the Imperial Family to bow to a solider, let alone an insurgent. "We now suffer the consequences of our complacency. Foreign invaders trample on Hua's soil."

"Madurans." One of the soldiers next to her guards spat on the ground. "They have no chance."

"No." The princess straightened. "The Teleri Empire has captured the East Gate and marches unopposed on the capital."

"A lie!" A crossbow cocked above. Liang Yu tightened his grip on the staff, just in case he had to knock a bolt out of the air. If his old eyes could see it in time. Alas, if only he were as good as the Beauty at it! Surely they wouldn't shoot at the princess. Would they?

"We would have heard."

"They can't just march an army down the highway in secret."

Liang Yu hid his grin. He had trained some of these men to think for themselves, and it showed now.

The princess raised a hand. "Lord Zheng has betrayed the realm and silenced all news coming out of his province. Once the Teleri Army reaches his borders, it will be too late to mobilize and save everyone between here and there."

The same story she'd told him. Plausible, but not likely. Liang Yu gauged his men's reactions, at least the ones he could see. Most looked to him for approval. He shook his head. Truth or not, she needed to know he was her only way out of the warehouse.

The princess swept a hand toward the mezzanine. "Duty to your nation calls. Only with your help can we save the North. I am conscripting you all as my personal guard, under the command of Golden Fu."

The mezzanine lit up. Robes rustled as several men dropped to a knee, fist to the ground. Others followed, more tentatively.

Liang Yu stared at her. *That* was unexpected, like the Beauty going off-script with his plans. The princess hadn't even used the power of her voice.

Well, let her play her games, because when it came down to it, honor and promises didn't feed hungry mouths. He was the one paying these men, and she had no access to the dwindling imperial coffers, anyway.

She turned to him. "General Fu, prepare for our march on the way station."

He bowed. "As the princess commands."

Now, how could they make it through the city without alerting the general populace of her arrival?

CHAPTER 18:
Existential Crises

The two arrows speeding toward Jie's face effectively delayed her existential crisis.

The first she caught as she spun out of the way of the second. A third, just loosed, she knocked out of the air with the first in her hand.

"Stop!" Tian, or Tian's doppelganger, stood between her and the elf, arms splayed out.

The girl who looked exactly like her, save for the doeskin dress, spewed out several unintelligible syllables. The male elf fitted another arrow and pulled the string back again.

Jie palmed a throwing spike. As soon as Tian, or whoever he was, got out of the way...

The elf circled, but Tian moved to stay between them. He repeated the same word over and over again. At last, the elf lowered his bow.

Tian turned around and stared at her. "Who are you?"

This couldn't be right. They must be in some bizarre land of dread sorcery, inhabited by mirror images of people she knew. Would the princess' facsimile burst onto the path next?

Her own doppelganger sidled up to Tian, stood on her tiptoes and whispered something in his ear. Not breaking his gaze, Tian leaned into her.

Think, think. There was no such magical place. They were still in the Kanin Wilds, harassing Teleri supply lines. She'd just killed a Bovyan and an altivorc, and then avoided a swift death by elf archery.

Which meant, if this was reality...

That man *really* was Tian. He had used a *Moquan* knife technique to defeat the Bovyan. Now, he tapped his chin, just like always. He whispered something back at her twin.

This couldn't be right. Tian had died—she'd watched with her own eyes as Emperor Geros shot him with a crossbow, then kicked him into the dirt.

Unless. Unless.

Jie sucked her lower lip, dredging up painful memories. Just before the Emperor struck, Tian's expression had melted into one of calm acceptance. It looked nothing like the confusion written on his face now.

Her mouth gaped. He'd lost the *Tiger's Eye*, and then must have put himself into the *Viper's Rest*, which would have slowed his heartbeat and breathing to imperceptible levels.

Which also meant he might not have any idea who he was. *Moquan* masters practiced the technique with utmost care, to prevent memory loss. Only the legendary Architect had mastered the *Viper's Rest* to the point that he would not lose his sense of self, and some stories suggested he bordered on insane. Jie shuddered to remember her own experiences with the technique.

So that probably explained Tian, whose eyes now moved from her to the half-elf girl. Who apparently wanted her dead. Who was she? An identical twin, separated at birth? The princess had mentioned something about twins, and a berry that grew in the Wilds. But then her lazy dastard of a father would've abandoned both of them at the temple, right?

Was the arrow-happy elf their father? Like a weed, perhaps he had scattered his seeds farther than imagined. That could possibly explain the little girl, who was sucking on her lower lip. Except Hua people never came out here, and she *did* look a whole lot like the ten-year-old version of herself who could've beaten Ming in a knife fight.

Apparently, just thinking about Ming prompted him to break the shocked silence. "Tian, I am glad to see you alive. Jie told me that Emperor Geros killed you."

The floodgates opened, with questions erupting from all over the place. Everyone spoke at once. Fingers pointed. The elf. Her twin. The little girl. Tian, trying to silence them with frantic gesticulations. Only the Kanin savage hung back, not saying a word.

Ming took a few steps toward Tian, arms outstretched. Everyone quieted.

Tian backed off. Awkward.

"Uh..." Ming stopped in his tracks. His attention fell on Jie's twin. "...interesting company you keep, I—"

The half-elf silenced him with a glare. If anything good came out of this, it would be that Ming could now be terrorized by *two* half-elves.

Though Tian's eyes flicked in Ming's direction, they instantly returned to meet hers. Dark and intelligent as always. Jie's heart hammered in her chest.

Ming's brow furrowed. "Tian!"

Tian's eyes again flashed to Ming before settling on her. He must not even know his own name. Certainly a possible side effect of the *Viper's Rest*.

"Ming, he has lost his memories." Jie wobbled forward a few steps.

With a frown, Ming said, "Apparently. And filled them with swordsmanship. Last time I saw Tian with a sword in his hand, Princess Kaiya beat him with ease."

Her again. Jie's stomach knotted. There was no escaping the princess.

Yet Tian didn't react to the name. He looked from Jie to Ming and back again. "How do you know me?"

Ming spoke loudly enough to scare away the forest animals, enunciating each word with deliberate slowness, as if Tian had lost his hearing and not his memories. "Because. I. Am. Your. Brother."

Tian's nod could only be described as tentative. "You bear a resemblance to me. I agree. But I don't know either of you. I don't even know my own name."

"Tian," Ming said. "Tian. Fourth son of Zheng Han, *Tai-Ming* Lord of Dongmen Province."

Jie drew the character for his name in the air. "Tian, as in sky; Tian as in heavens."

Tian's expression brightened. Did he remember? "That's what the Doe-Eyed Girl called me. In my dream."

Doe-Eyed Girl. That could only be...

"And you." Tian lifted his chin at Ming. "You called me that, too. I thought you were invoking the Heavens."

Ming snorted. The elf archer in deerskin clothes blurted out a few halting syllables.

Tian nodded at the elf. "Tian," he said.

"Tian," her twin repeated. She then jabbed a finger at Jie and unleashed a tirade of foreign words.

He turned back to Jie. "Kiri wants you to show the back of your neck."

Kiri, eh? So she had a name, and an elf-sounding name at that. In order to get answers to her growing number of questions, Jie dropped to a knee. It was safe; the elf had lowered his bow and stowed the arrow. Even if he could nock it pretty fast, Tian wouldn't let the elf shoot her. Hopefully. And she would hear Kiri approaching in time to defend herself. Unclasping the frog ties at the front of her blouse, she shrugged her shirt down to her shoulders and bent her head forward.

Kiri let out a long breath and said a few more words.

"So who are you?" Tian asked.

Who was she? Best friend. Jilted lover. Maybe a twin sister, all of a sudden. Some things were better left unsaid. Jie stood and turned around. Maybe everything was better left unsaid. She flashed their clan hand signals at him. *You Moquan.*

Brow furrowed, he returned a sign. *What Moquan?* His ability to respond left absolutely no doubt it was Tian.

The others' heads jerked back and forth, following the exchange. Kiri threw her hands up and blurted out a string of unintelligible words. Tian shrugged.

Jie pointed a finger at her nose. "My name is Jie. You and I belong to the same clan of warrior-spies."

"What?" Ming's mouth slackened.

Kiri tugged at Tian's sleeve, while he shook his head, slowly, and eased back.

Jie stepped toward him and shot her hand out. He lifted his in defense, and their wrists met. The elf's bow was in his hand, an arrow nocked, while Kiri stumbled back a few steps.

Ignoring them, Jie lowered into a broad stance and pressed her wrist against his. His body melted into the same stance as he turned at the waist and redirected her force to the side. He twisted his hips back and pushed into her. Sinking deeper into her stance, Jie unleashed a flurry of preset patterns. Tian reacted with prearranged responses, the pressure at the point of contact between their hands remaining constant.

She disengaged, pirouetting back in a flourishing end to the form. She settled into the final pose, a single arm outstretched, wrist bent and palm upturned, her other hand arced above her head.

A few steps away, Tian mirrored her. His Yang to her Yin, they were meant for each other.

Maybe the *Pushing Hands* game of *Supreme Ultimate Fist* had jolted his memory.

Moquan. The word meant nothing to Feneyas, beyond Jie's explanation of warrior-spies.

However, there was no doubting the veracity of her claims after their martial dance. His every technique harmonized with hers, an orchestra of offensive and defensive energies. Now, there she stood just six feet away, her pose mirroring his exactly.

He looked up and stared at his arms. At least 'Moquan' explained where the fighting skills came from. No telling what those hands had done in the past.

If he and Jie belonged to the same clan, it might explain the sense of familiarity Kiri stirred in him. Though how did Kiri and Jie look exactly alike? Identical twins?

He turned to Kiri. "Why did you want to see the scar on her neck?"

Her brows scrunched together and shook her head. "She doesn't have one."

"She has a few marks, like yours." Though in truth, unlike Kiri's ugly long scars, Jie's had been masterfully stitched. Except one on her right shoulder, whose jagged lines looked like a sailor had knotted them together with rope.

"Not like mine. And not one here." Kiri turned and tapped the blotch on her back, at the base of her neck. "She's not one of us."

"One of you?"

"Vrztchkrn."

Feneyas cringed at the strange sound. "I don't know what it is."

Kiri pointed at Turquoise Man's body. "*Their* language. I don't know how to translate in Kanin or Elvish. Maybe *sisters.* Exact sisters."

"Twins," Feneyas used the word from the Kanin dialect. Though the term, at least as he understood it, didn't exactly mean the same as *identical twins* in his native language.

Dior pointed at Ming. "And what about you and the other Man From Beyond the Wall? Is he your twin?"

"A brother, at least," Feneyas said, shrugging. One he didn't remember, and who seemed more like Jie's comic sidekick.

Jie cleared her throat. "What's Kiri saying about the altivorc?"

Altivorc. The race of non-human mercenaries, Feneyas remembered now. Kiri didn't even understand the language spoken among the Metal Men, yet the very sight of the altivorc sent her into a panic. She could also speak the altivorc language. He shook his head and locked his gaze on Jie. "Nothing really, just told me a word in their tongue. *Identical twins.*"

Ming nodded. "They look exactly alike, like two cherries from the same tree." His smile then melted and he muttered something inaudibly under his breath.

Jie shot him a glare, and he stared down at his feet. Harrumphing, she shifted her gaze to Kiri. "That must be it: we are identical twins." She took a hesitant step toward her twin and stretched out her hand. "May I?"

Kiri stared at the hand, then looked up. "I'm sorry I had Dior attack you. I thought you were someone else."

The two just talked past each other, neither understanding their counterpart's language. How strange that a man without memories would most likely end up as translator between long-lost sisters. Jie's hand touched Kiri's shoulder, making the girl flinch.

Jie looked up at him. "I never knew I had a real sister. An identical twin, no less." Her eyes bent toward Dior. "Is the elf our father?"

Feneyas almost choked. "Dior? No. Just a friend."

"What did she say?" Dior stroked an arrow's fletching.

"She asked what your relationship was to Kiri."

Dior chuckled. "Guardian. Conscience."

"And what about her?" Jie tilted her chin at Kala.

Feneyas scratched his chin. Their relationship had never been explained, since Kiri refused to talk about her past, and Kala barely spoke Kanin. He had always assumed that from the way Kiri cared for Kala, and their similar appearance, they must be sisters. "Sisters, maybe?"

Ming nodded. "Just like us, brothers."

"Can you ask?" Jie's stare bored into him.

Tian nodded, then turned back to Kiri. "Are you and Kala sisters?"

"Vrztchkrn."

That word again, which sounded like a pack of angry dogs fighting over table scraps. Tian looked back at Jie, nodding. "Sisters."

Jie and Kiri peered at one another, sizing each other up.

He would have to mediate. But first, he had a lot of questions, one which pricked at him more than the others. "I want to ask you something. I have dreamed about a beautiful Doe-Eyed Girl. She seems to be an important part of my past, but I don't recall how. What can you tell me about her?"

CHAPTER 19:

Smoke Signals

The last time Kaiya marched at the head of an army, it'd been a contingent of Paladins and her imperial guard, to face down Avarax.

Today, she led a ragtag militia of forty-two insurgents and eight green imperial soldiers, commanded by a middle-aged spy. Who walked with a staff.

Not to mention he held Weiyong hostage back at the warehouse, to ensure her good behavior. Apparently, trust only went so far.

At Fu's insistence, she kept her hood up as they travelled in small clusters through the capital, where the crowds went about their daily lives. Little by little, they wasted precious time regrouping on the road by the way station, three *li* outside the city walls as Ziqiu had said.

Kaiya found the iridescent moon, now waxing to half. Not long until dusk. Soon, the light signals would be visible for several *li*. She turned her attention to the tower.

Cut from blocks of stone, it rose some sixty feet into the air. Beside it, several imperial soldiers lounged outside the stables and barracks. Some gambled over dice, while one read. More than a few afforded her army a cursory glance, yet made no move to approach or warn the rest of the garrison. The martial discipline Father had once inspired was gone.

Kaiya looked to Fu. "We do not want to make them nervous with so many armed men. You

and Song accompany me. There will be no need for violence." She hoped.

Fu smirked. "And if you do take command of the tower without drawing a sword, what is to keep you from ordering the imperial soldiers to arrest us?"

"I swore on this." She held up Tian's tablet, still hidden its pouch. No need to mention that Weiyong's safety depended on it, since they both knew it.

"Very well, *Dian-xia*." He bowed and stretched a hand toward the tower.

Tired and wearing commoners' travelling clothes, she hardly looked the part of a princess. Without the power of her voice, convincing the imperial soldiers of her identity might prove to be difficult. Perhaps she should ask Fu to come up with a backup plan, just in case...

No; he probably had a plan ready anyway, most likely involving the killing of loyal men. With a deep breath, she took several steps toward the tower. Fu and Song followed just behind.

The imperial soldiers watched their approach with disinterest, most turning back to whatever they were doing.

Unacceptable. With such poor discipline, they didn't stand a chance against the Teleri. Lifting her chin and straightening her carriage, Kaiya lowered her hood and shifted her hesitant gait into a delicate glide. The soldiers now murmured and pointed, and many squared their backs and shoulders.

She stopped by the tower. The two sentries' roving eyes served as a reminder that her beauty alone was formidable weapon against gullible men. Infused with magic or not, her tone carried imperial authority. "Summon your commander."

The soldiers glanced among themselves, their confusion clear in their expressions.

Fu slammed the butt end of his staff into the ground. His voice flared with anger. "Princess Kaiya gave you a command!"

The men dropped to a knee, fist to the ground. "Yes, *Dian-xia*," the shouted in unison.

"Rise." She lifted a hand. Thank the Heavens for Fu's impeccable timing.

The sentries stood and held rigid stances. One ran into the tower. Hopefully, the commander would be just as compliant.

Presently, a middle-aged man with oil-coifed hair and an impeccable uniform emerged. His insignias marked him as a captain. His eyes fell on her and widened. He dropped to a knee. "*Dian-xia*."

"Rise, Captain," she said, "and tell me the latest news out of Dongmen Province."

Standing, the captain's attention shifted from her to her companions and back. "The last message out of Dongmen was four days ago. The palace has not sent any couriers in this direction in days."

Four days ago. Right before her escape. Lord Zheng must have cut communications soon after. She cast a sidelong glance at Fu. Hopefully he'd be placated. She turned to the commander, who returned her gaze instead of averting his eyes as protocol demanded. "A Teleri army marches on the capital from Dongmen. Send a rider through the relay stations to confirm that."

He shook his head. "*Dian-xia*, this is highly irregular. I must have official authorization."

"I am the sister of the *Tianzi*. Do it." She drew herself up to her full height and glared at him, sending his eyes downward.

He, along with his fellow guards, dropped to a knee, fist to the ground. "Yes, *Dian-xia*."

"Send another courier to the palace to inform them of the invasion."

The captain looked up, his mouth agape. "Before we confirm it?"

"Time is of the essence. Do you not believe a Scion of Heaven?" She squared her shoulders.

"Of course I believe you." He bowed again. "However, this is just a relay station. I don't have the official correspondence seals."

Kaiya placed a hand on her chest. "Have your scribe write it, and I will sign." Would the relay stations believe it? While the nations of the Arkothi North used signatures and wax imprints, Cathay only used such means for personal correspondence. Probably no one outside her circle of friends and the rebel Lord Peng had even seen her handwriting before.

"Yes, *Dian-xia*." The captain beckoned one of his men. "Prepare for a dispatch, both inbound and outbound."

As the soldier ran off to the stables, she peered west, where the hazy red sun peeked just above the horizon. With an open hand, she waved toward the tower. "Now captain, let us alight the tower and prepare a message."

If the captain's mouth could open any wider, he probably still wouldn't be able to fit his equally large eyes in it. "The light tower hasn't been used in...in..."

"Never." Kaiya composed her most grave expression. "My ancestor erected the towers, and since then, Hua has never suffered an invasion. She does now."

"Yes, *Dian-xia*. Please follow me." Holding a bow, the captain beckoned them into the tower.

Kaiya placed a hand over her belly, where her twins grew. It was a long climb up those steps.

With Little Song flanking him, Liang Yu eyed the princess, who sat at the captain's wooden desk, panting. Surely, a short trip up two flights of spiraling stone stairs should be easy for such a young woman, a dancer no less. Nonetheless, her brow furrowed with unmistakable fatigue. She had not so much as whiffed the tea and egg custard pastry the lieutenant had offered.

Still, tired or not, her poise and authority had captured the tower with only words, and prevented needless bloodshed. Perhaps she was worth much more than any of the nearsighted hereditary lords had thought.

The captain reappeared at the office door and bowed. "*Dian-xia*, I have sent couriers toward Dongmen."

Eyes narrowing, she stood and walked around the desk, interposing herself between Liang Yu and the captain. "What about the capital?"

"Yes, that too." He scratched his nose, a telltale sign of a lie.

The princess pointed up. "Then let us alight the tower to send the signals."

"Forgive my impertinence, *Dian-xia*." His eyes darted from her to Fu and Song and back. "I will wait until a courier returns before I send the message."

Such a waste of time. The relay couriers would take at least two hours to reach the border of Dongmen. Not to mention, they weren't scouts, looking out for enemies. Even if they didn't get caught, the message to the capital would be delayed for four hours. The princess had already gotten them inside, past the bulk of the garrison. The rest was easy. It was time to channel his inner Surgeon. Shuffling forward a step, Liang Yu grasped both ends of his staff, ready to expose the spear and sword. They didn't need this capt—

The princess shot her hand back, barring the path to his intended victim. "Captain, I understand your concern. However, every hour we wait gives the imperial armies one less hour to mobilize."

Chewing on his lip, the captain's attention shifted from Song to Liang Yu and back to the princess.

Her head tilted, and she ran a hand behind her ear. When she spoke, a breathy, sultry tone replaced her imperial voice. A trick the Beauty had

used time and time again. "Please. I will accept full responsibility."

"I....uh, as the princess commands." Pupils dilated, the captain sucked on a lip and bowed. What had the nation and its soldiers come to? Apparently, a beautiful woman's charms could work better than imperial authority these days. The man straightened and strode to a bookshelf. He pulled out thread-bound book and dusted it off.

Liang Yu frowned. If only his old eyes could make out the title on the cover before the captain opened it. "This is no time to read."

The captain held it up. "These are the codes for the light signals."

Incompetence! They should know these codes by memory. "I am sure it is not every day that royalty strolls into a watchtower, but—"

The princess shot him an angry glance, one that demanded silence. Why? She could just tell him the sequence of signals.

Unless she had lied about knowing the codes. Not only that, if she were in such a hurry, why did she waste time making requests instead of just using the magic of her voice?

Kaiya fought to stay upright, hands on her knees as she huffed for air. The climb to the top of the tower had proved even more daunting than it initially appeared. It didn't help that the pungent pastries had sent waves of nausea roiling through her stomach. Hopefully, Fu hadn't noticed.

She looked up. His narrowed eyes relaxed and his expression blanked. Flashing a smile, she straightened and gazed through dusk's cloak over the surrounding farmland. A courier horse clopped in the distance, heading toward Dongmen.

Of course, the light signal would arrive sooner, if only the captain could get the shutters to work. He fiddled with the metal slats. "*Dian-xia*, the hinges have rusted."

Rusted! Perhaps the Expansionist faction had been right all along. The realm had fallen into complacency, too secure with a hundred thousand guns pointed out from behind the Wall. The great lords, Father included, never considered the possibility of fighting an invading army on open ground. She frowned. "Hurry."

He bowed. "Sorry, *Dian-Xia*."

Fu sidled up to the captain, who in turn nudged Fu to the side. With a graceful twist which belied Fu's age but lent credence to his claims of a *Moquan* background, he spun around to the other side of the captain, right next to the shutter mechanism.

He snorted. "*Dian-xia*, the hinges are fine." He pulled on a lever, and the dozen slats whispered open. Bright light flared from the crystal globe within.

Blinking away the orange glare in her visual field, Kaiya gasped. Had the crystal carried a magical enchantment all this time, for three hundred years? Glowing unknown in perpetuity, until this very moment? Maybe the elf lord Xu had enchanted them himself.

"Look!" Song pointed into the countryside.

In the indeterminate distance, small orbs lit up in slow succession, forming a dotted line to the north. Kaiya turned in the other direction. A light glowed on the main gatehouse of the north capital walls. A couple dozen seconds later, another one flashed from a tower inside the city, followed not long after by one on Sun-Moon Lake.

The palace knew! What must they be thinking? What about the general populace? The lights had never been seen before, after all. Kaiya's heart fluttered with excitement before the *Tiger's Eye* stifled that emotion. "Captain, hurry. Send an encoded message."

The captain licked his lips, and shifted on his feet.

Something wasn't right. She exchanged glances with Fu, who jerked his head toward the light with a look of askance. Of course, he believed she knew the codes. She'd implied as much. She glowered at the captain. "I order you to send the message."

"As the princess commands." He bowed and placed his hands on the lever. With several pushes and pulls of varying lengths, the light blinked and flashed.

She squinted back toward the palace, some thirty *li* away. As far as she could tell, the dots of light blinked the same sequence.... Followed by a new one?

Fu apparently noticed, too. "What was the response?"

The captain's face contorted. "That they received the message, and for the towers to await further orders."

With a rasp, Fu separated his spear and sword. One he placed across the captain's throat.

Song's hand took her wrist in a strong grip and wrenched her arm behind her back.

"Now, captain," Fu said, "what did the response *really* say?"

"Just what the princess commanded. That a Teleri army has breached the Walls at Dongmen."

Fu snorted. "And why did you only send a horse toward Dongmen, but not to the capital?"

Kaiya listened again. Yes, a horse clopped north, but none headed south.

The captain shouted, "Men, surround the tower. Don't let anyone in or out."

CHAPTER 20:
Old and New Scars

Though she'd spent a year blindfolded during her training, Jie had never excelled at blind techniques like her human *Moquan* clan members. With elf vision, she rarely needed them. Now, however, she tripped and stumbled on numerous occasions as they traipsed through the forest, each time bruising her ego as much as her body.

All Tian's fault. If he hadn't decided to be alive, maybe she wouldn't be so bewildered. The simultaneous discovery of a missing twin, now holding on to her arm and doing an awful job of guiding her through obstacles, didn't help matters.

What was her twin's story? Did she know their father? She could apparently speak the altivorc language and was scared of Jie. There was an unbelievable story somewhere in there, even beyond the improbable reunion with an amnesiac Tian.

Meanwhile, the Teleri moved supplies through the Wilds unhindered, to support their invasion of Hua.

Crack! She stepped on a dry branch, and would've fallen on her face if Kiri hadn't supported her.

Brushing off her hands, and also what was left of her dignity, Jie sighed. "Is the blindfold necessary? I'm lost."

"It's not that bad," Ming chirped from somewhere behind her.

How humiliating. Shown up by Ming, of all people. However, it seemed like Tian was doing a better job at leading him through the forest compared to her own guide.

"We're almost there." Tian's voice bore into her back, his unanswered question undoubtedly still weighing on him. Amnesiac or not, his need to know, and know *now*, remained.

A wife and unborn children, possibly his, were more than he needed to learn about in his state. Right? Yes. There'd be a better time and place for that.

Heavy boots clomped on pavestones in the distance. A hand pressed on her shoulder and pushed her down. The underbrush rustled as Tian, Kiri, Kala, and Dior sunk to the forest floor.

"Ouch!" Ming hissed as he clumsily fell into a shrub. "The shoulder!"

"Shhhh," Tian said.

The blindfold came off, and Jie's eyes adjusted. She peered through the trees in the direction of clopping boots and jingling chainmail. Light glinted off metal, with the occasional flash of red feathers. At least thirty Bovyan soldiers guarded over a hundred natives and ten horse-drawn provision carts. They headed west to supply the Teleri invasion of Hua.

She and Ming—or rather, *she*—had been harassing these convoys for over a week now, first on the overgrown paths near Hua, and later on the restored roads. With an elf archer and Tian, it would be even easier. She started forward to get a better view, only to be restrained by Tian's hand.

He shook his head and flashed the Moquan signals, *Stay down, keep quiet.*

Why?

Too dangerous. He grinned for the first time, the crooked smile that sent her heart pounding.

She glanced back at the others. The elf watched their hands dance with a look that could only be described as bored. Ming gawked, while little Kala huddled low, oblivious. Kiri, on the other hand, scowled, her lips tight enough to crush a walnut.

Jie knew that expression. Her own, when jealous. Used with alarming frequency while in service to the princess. Perhaps her twin shared expressions *and* an attraction to a not-so-dead man.

The sound of marching boots and creaking wheels faded in the distance, and with it, the opportunity to wreak havoc on the Teleri supply lines. Dior motioned them up.

"We could've slowed them down." Jie put her hands on her hips. "I've been doing it for over a week now. I—"

"*We,*" Ming inserted.

Jie raised her voice. "*I* have sabotaged their supplies, and made their lives miserable. We need to get back to that."

Ming snorted. "You couldn't have done much without my help." If *help* meant distracting the Teleri with incompetence...

The elf faced Tian and spoke in a string of syllables that sounded not much different from the secret Hua imperial language. Tian pointed in the direction of the men, then Jie, all the while fumbling through the same language. Kiri apparently added her opinion as well, leaving Ming and Jie to exchange glances.

With a shake of his head, Tian turned to her. "Their village is close by. The elves don't want the Metal Men to even know they exist. It's the best way to protect their home."

Jie sucked on her lower lip. "What about *your* home? The Teleri march on Hua, and your own father let them in."

He stared back at her, expression empty. Ming studied his feet, sharing Tian's guilt.

No, she wouldn't let their guilty feelings cow her into silence. Not when the realm and all its women relied on their help. She continued, relentless, "Think of what they did to the natives here. They will do the same, if not worse, to your *own* people. What Emperor Geros himself did to—" no, better not to bring *her* into the conversation, for Tian's own good, "—so many women."

Dior poked Tian in the back and they exchanged more words. Kiri joined in, her frown and tone evidently conveying her opinion in no uncertain terms.

Tian turned back. "That's not the elves' concern." Apparently, he'd gone native.

"It will be." Ming kept his voice low. "The Wilds lie between Hua and them, and they will eventually connect it all. No one on the plateau will be safe, not even these elves."

Jie studied Ming. Someone had swapped out the bumbling buffoon for a *Tai-Ming* heir. She nodded at Tian. "Translate."

His gaze shifted from Ming and settled on her. He then spoke again to the elves.

After a brief exchange, Tian nodded. "Dior says your argument has merit. He will present your case—"

"*Our* case." She glared at him.

"—our case back at the village for the people to discuss."

Great. More elves, and from the look of it, more blindfolds, too.

Tian. His name was Tian, even if the revelation didn't jar any memories.

Now he couldn't get back to the treetop village soon enough. Whoever this Jie was, whatever his relationship to her, she remained tight-lipped about the Doe-Eyed Girl from his dreams. So many questions about his past, and yet, Jie cared more about the future. Namely, the threat of the Metal Men to a homeland he didn't remember.

"Were you looking for me?" He pulled Ming to the side, just avoiding a limb that would've smacked his supposed brother in the face.

"Ow! The shoulder!" Ming winced. "No, I thought you were dead."

"Then how'd you come to be here?"

"The insane half-elf." Ming pointed in the wrong direction. "We were stuck on the wrong side of the Wall, and instead of trying to find a way back in, she took us deeper into the Wilds."

'Insane' didn't quite seem to do Jie justice. But Ming was leaving something out. Tian frowned. "Why?"

"Ask her. I'm still trying to figure it out." Ming threw his hands up, but then immediately grimaced and grabbed his left shoulder. "Though I am pleased we found you."

"What happened to your shoulder?"

Expression souring, Ming rubbed it. "A Teleri soldier stabbed me. It will be a miracle if I ever draw a bow again."

Miracles apparently happened around here. Tian removed his brother's blindfold and pointed up the tree. "Here we are. Perhaps the elves' shaman can help you."

Ming looked up the circling branches. "It's just a tree canopy."

The others gathered around the base of the tree, except for Kala, who pranced up the branches. Jie tracked the girl, then met Tian's gaze. She raised her eyebrow and quirked her lips in the cutest manner.

Her question was clear. Tian nodded. "Yes, the village. You'll be surprised."

With a shrug, she followed Kala up. Kiri's glare was sharp enough to shear cured leather, yet she said nothing as she joined her unexpected twin. The rest of the group followed.

At the top, dozens of elves gathered, many gazing with curiosity at Jie. Ming's eyes rounded as wide as walnuts. Jie's expression blanked, but her irises drifted across the platforms and bridges, pausing on any elf with a weapon. Just like Tian himself had done the first time.

Dior called out, "More strangers, and even more mysteries." He pointed to Ming. "Feneyas'

brother, coming to search for him." As attention drifted to Ming, Dior shifted an open palm toward Jie. "And her."

The elves murmured among themselves in a low hum of musical voices. Though their language escaped him, Tian could guess the general sentiment from their nods and gestures: she and Kiri looked exactly alike. Jie stared back at them, her brow wrinkling.

Layani, the elves' best warrior, spoke with Kiri, their voices getting louder with each exchange. Kiri shook her head vehemently before snapping her lips shut and staring out into the forest. Oh, to be able to speak their language.

Tian sighed. What was it with these half-elves withholding information? Kiri apparently knew more about her relationship to Jie, yet refused to explain. Jie would not speak of the Doe-Eyed Girl.

Sidling over as the elves' debate reached a crescendo, Ming whispered in Tian's ear, "What are they saying?"

"I'd surmise they have the same question. As you and I." Tian jutted his chin first at Kiri, then at Jie.

"And me." Jie crossed her arms. "I hate that they're talking about me and I have no idea what they're saying."

"Enough." Using the Kanin dialect, the shaman Nayori's voice cut through the animated discussion, bringing the treetops to silence. She sang several words, and a wind whistled through the village. When she spoke again, her elf words echoed back in the Hua tongue. "Feneyas, you wished to learn who you are. You have been reunited with those who know you."

The unspoken message left no doubt: he should go. To the elves, he must be like a wolf that scavenged on the edge of a Kanin village. Tolerated, amusing to watch, yet not loved like the tribe's dogs. They would not miss him if he left.

Yet how could he, with so many questions left unresolved? Only Kiri could answer some of those, if they could coax her to talk about something so obviously painful.

"Wait," Tian said. "The Metal Men come in greater numbers."

Nayori nodded. "Headed west, to your home beyond the Wall."

Jie raised an open hand. "Not if we sabotage them here. Their army needs supplies, transported across the plateau."

At least until they established a foothold in Hua and ravished the lands there. Tian's eyed edged toward the shaman.

Nayori regarded Jie with a frown. "You would turn *our* home into a battleground."

Muttering under his breath, Ming said, "The elf's got a point."

Jie's glare immediately cowed him into silence. "If the Teleri occupy Cathay, they will engulf this area from two sides."

"Just like the stories." Dior sounded strange speaking in the language from beyond the Wall. "Our grandparents lived through the first human empires, who cut down the sacred trees and carved up our homeland."

Kiri chimed in, her voice's similarities to Jie's more than a little disconcerting. "Until the Heavens rained fire."

The elves murmured, their voices swirling around them like ghosts of the people from beyond the Wall. A shiver crawled up Tian's spine.

"Allow us to stay just a little longer," he said. "Until the shaman who knows me arrives." It would not be much longer, maybe only four or five days.

Nayori's gaze met each of the elves'. Some nodded, others shook their heads. None seemed completely convinced. "We will consider it," she said. "Eat and rest. I will inform you of our decision tomorrow."

Perhaps that would be enough time to get Kiri to reveal what she knew of the half-elves' shared past—and in turn, get Jie to shed some light on the Doe-Eyed Girl.

Ming jerked straight up in his hammock, the bizarre dream yanking him from much-needed sleep. Princess Kaiya. His father. An unenviable choice. All slipped from his memory before he could process the meaning.

Bright light filtered in through the tree canopy, the dappling falling right across his face and waking him for good. Apparently, everything in this forest taunted him. He blinked the gunk from his eyes, and the little half-elf girl came into focus next to him.

Pointing down, Kala babbled something in a melodious language and beckoned for him to follow.

What was her rush, so early? Ming stretched his arms out...and his shoulder *didn't* hurt. His eyes must be round as gold *yuans*. He stood and followed the girl down the trees. At the bottom, he looked up. Like before, there was no sign of the treetop village.

A tug on his sleeve brought his gaze back down. Kala held out some dried berries and lifted her chin to him. An offer. Ming extended his hand and she dumped them into his palm.

Chewing on the sweetish-sour berries, he followed the half-elf through twists and turns between the trees. Birds chirped and animals scuttled through the branches above, yet there was no other sign of intelligent life.

He tapped Kala on the shoulder. "Where are we going?"

She turned and cocked her head, but then pointed. "Friend. There."

Ming scratched his chin. Apparently, the girl could speak a few words of the Hua tongue. After a few minutes they emerged into a clearing.

A dozen elves were gathered, practicing archery. Ming skidded to a halt, even as Kala continued walking. His shoulder felt great; maybe he could draw a bow. With all the women so beautiful, he sauntered over to the most scantily-clad. The brunette's top, made of finely-stitched animal skin, exposed her midriff and revealed more than a Hua bust binder.

"May I?" He extended a hand toward her weapon.

She stared at him with liquid brown eyes that sent a tingle up his spine. Speaking a few words in what didn't sound like Elvish, she patted the shoulder of a boy and proffered her bow and a quiver of arrows.

Kala appeared at his side. "She challenge."

Challenge? A woman? All Ming wanted to do was test the draw. He pointed to the maiden and raised an eyebrow.

Kala shook her head, then tilted her chin toward the youth. He couldn't be much older than the equivalent of twelve human years, and his bow looked like a toy. "Son."

The insult! Ming fit an arrow and pointed at the rotting stump at thirty paces.

Shaking her head, the mother pointed in the distance.

Ming squinted. Apparently, she'd chosen a cone hanging from a sweet evergreen twice as far away as the stump. A difficult shot with his own weapon, and the weight and tension of the elf bow felt all wrong. At least his shoulder didn't hurt at all. Just a little stiff. The shaman's magic was nothing short of miraculous, despite the bizarre dreams that accompanied the healing.

He took aim at the cone. A little left. Up a little...and loosed.

The arrow flew between the gaps in the trees and lodged deep into a trunk just a few hands from the target. So much power! And close. Still, a sinking feeling settled in his gut. Could this kid hit such a small target, so far away? If he did... Oh, the embarrassment.

At his side, the boy drew the bow and shot in a quick, smooth motion. The arrow sailed true, dislodging the cone from the branch. He met Ming's gaze, eyes curious, with no hint of maliciousness or gloating. Many of the elves afforded Ming a sympathetic, if patronizing nod. He looked back down.

The boy was gone.

He glanced around the clearing to find himself alone. The birds had stopped chirping. A chorus of chainmail jangled somewhere not far away.

CHAPTER 21:

Homecoming

Sword still held at the captain's throat, Liang Yu stared at the princess. After claiming her allegiance, it looked like she had betrayed him. If that were the case, she'd join a long list of betrayals, which started with his own master and comrades thirty-three years before.

Unlike the others, she'd earn her comeuppance now. He pointed the spear tip at her. "What did the light signals say?"

For good measure, Little Song twisted her arm.

The princess yelped. Gritting through her teeth, she said, "I don't know. I swear." Her gaze shifted to the captain. Pleading?

"Your oaths aren't worth much." He used the spear to lift the pouch containing the imperial plaque from the fold of her robe. "You swore on this."

She nodded. "To accept your protection."

"You lied."

Eyes narrowing, she shook her head. "I did not lie. I never said I knew the codes, just that I was surprised the *Moquan* didn't."

True enough. Or at least, a half-truth. Liang Yu pursed his lips. "Then why?"

"So you would bring me here. So I could get my message sent to the capital, and you wouldn't kill anyone."

Her voice sounded sincere, and there were no signs of lies in her expression. Then again, leaders regularly manipulated their underlings with pretty words. If she truly cared about the lives of anonymous soldiers...there was a way to test that.

"I will kill someone now." He pressed his sword into Captain Zhou's neck.

Zhou went rigid.

"No!" She reached out with her free hand and struggled forward. Little Song wrenched her arm up, sending her to her knees with a squeak. "No, please. You don't have to kill him. Captain Zhou, please tell us what your message was." Her hand strayed to her belly, even though she had fallen to her knees.

The captain let out a long breath. "That this tower was commandeered by insurgents, led by someone claiming to be Princess Kaiya." His pulse remained rapid beneath Liang Yu's grip, no other physiological sign of a lie.

"And?" the princess said. "What was the response?"

"The palace commanded me to detain you until they arrive."

Of course. The unprecedented use of a tower light. If Regent Liu believed it was the princess, he'd see her as a threat to his grandson. A cavalry unit could mobilize and reach the tower in less than an hour. Liang Yu pulled the captain to the edge and looked down. Below, the way station garrison formed up in defensive positions, maybe thirty men in all.

He could get out of this trap, but not with the princess, maybe not with Little Song. Not unless he let his men fight against imperial soldiers. Toe-to-toe, his partisans wouldn't stand a chance against regular soldiers. Better to live and fight another day. If only he'd thought that way in his youth, maybe the Surgeon and Beauty would still be alive.

The princess, still on her knees, bowed low. "Let the captain go. We gain nothing by killing him."

Liang Yu shoved the captain toward the others and snapped his weapons back into staff form. "Little Song, surrender. Do your best to protect the princess." With one last glance at her, he swept out of the door and into the stairwell.

Shocked murmurs erupted among the armored cavalrymen as Kaiya emerged from the tower. Hands folded in front of her, she straightened her carriage and swept her gaze over the hundreds of people. Light bauble lamps illuminated their faces and cast shadows over wide eyes and gaping mouths. Sent from the palace, they were here to take her into custody. Nonetheless, their expressions suggested they recognized her. Many looked down, as protocol demanded.

"Here are the insurgents we captured. The rest retreated back toward the city." Captain Zhou prodded Song forward, hands bound in front of him. He then placed a hand at the small of her back and pressed her forward. "This one claimed to be Princess Kaiya."

The cavalry commander dismounted from a black imperial stallion. Reaching back, he received a lamp from a lieutenant and held it up to her face.

Kaiya squared her shoulders and locked gazes with him.

He sank to his knee, fist to the ground, and bowed. "*Dian-xia*."

Captain Zhou gasped. Then he shuffled back two steps and dropped to his knees. He pressed his forehead to the ground. "Forgive me, *Dian-xia*."

"Rise," she said. "There is nothing to forgive. You made the correct choice, but now we must warn the regent of the impending Teleri invasion. Release my aide." She gestured toward Little Song.

"No." The cavalry commander rose in a jingle of armor. "I am sorry, *Dian-xia*, but Regent Liu has ordered us to take you into custody."

Taken into custody! Then what Fu had said was correct, Liu Yong saw her as a threat to his grandchild. And where was Fu? He'd disappeared down into the tower. With just one exit, he was certainly trapped inside...or was he? Jie had escaped from worse situations.

Was it for the better, or worse? Though an invaluable resource, Fu was a tenuous ally at best. A dangerous bedfellow. By the glint in his eyes, he'd been about to kill the captain. Her plea must have persuaded him. Hopefully, he wouldn't do anything to Fang Weiyong.

"Hurry, then. We must return to the capital to warn the regent of the pending invasion." She presented her hands, palm up, for the commander to bind.

He shook his head. "That is not necessary. You upheld the honor of our captain Xie Shimin, and for that we are grateful."

Kaiya's heart stirred from beneath the *Tiger's Eye*. It was just over a year since Xie Shimin had tried to assassinate Tarkoth's Prince Aelward. Such a short time, yet she was no longer the naïve girl who'd convinced Xie to reveal clues to the conspiracy.

"Are you well enough to ride?" The commander motioned to the horses.

Kaiya nodded.

The commander beckoned to an underling. "Bring the princess a mount."

A soldier rode his horse forward and swung out of the saddle in front of her. He dropped to all fours and bowed. "Please, *Dian-xia*."

Grabbing the pommel, she stepped onto the man's back and pulled herself into the saddle. The smell of horse sent her stomach into rebellion. She covered her mouth. Curse this morning sickness. Would it be safe to ride? If only she'd paid more attention to Doctor Wu's physiology lessons. She beckoned toward Song. "Allow my guard to accompany me."

The commander nodded and waved for another horse. Even with his hands tied, Song swung into the saddle with nonchalant grace. Mounting up, the commander gazed out over his men and then gave a signal. With expert precision, the horsemen peeled off in ranks of four and trotted back toward the capital with rhythmic clops.

The ride jostled Kaiya in the saddle. She kept a hand over her belly. Hopefully, her babies would be all right despite the knocks and bumps. And what would happen when she faced Regent Liu? Would he believe her news of the impending Teleri invasion?

She'd find out soon enough. In ten minutes, they reached the city's open north gate. Soldiers pounded on drums, the combination of low beats signaling the arrival of an Imperial Family member. In the distance, the same pattern repeated.

Even at this late hour, windows and doors opened as they rode by. Excited commoners whispered and pointed. Most bowed low. Several shouted out.

"Princess Kaiya has returned!"

"The princess!"

"*Dian-xia.*"

Before long, her return after half a year would be on everyone's lips.

Had her emotions guided her, the sights and smells of the city might pique nostalgia. Now, the blooming plum blossoms did little to bring back memories of an innocent youth.

"What do the tower lights mean?" one woman yelled.

The crowds nodded and repeated the question over and over again, each time with more urgency. What had she done? Instigated mass panic? Of course, no one had ever seen the tower lights actually in use, and nobody knew what the signals meant.

The cavalrymen formed up around her, insulating her from the amassing cityfolk. Kaiya glanced over her shoulder. Where had Song disappeared to? She looked from side to side. Nowhere to be seen. Pointing and waving, some of the cavalry discussed his disappearance.

Another drumbeat echoed, its deep bass marking it as a palace drum. She gazed up to see the gates of Sun-Moon Palace up ahead.

They dismounted at the first moat. Flanked by a commander and several of his men, they crossed over the arching marble bridge. In the plaza on the other side, twenty imperial guards in blue robes and burnished breastplates dropped to a knee.

"*Dian-xia,*" they all shouted in unison.

The cavalrymen stepped back and sank down as well, leaving her halfway between the lines of soldiers, in the moons-cast shadows of the palace walls.

An unfamiliar imperial guard—the commander, by his insignia—rose and stepped forward. "Welcome back, *Dian-xia.* I am General Jin. Please accept my apologies that I must present you to the regent as a prisoner."

A prisoner, in her own home. Her supposed bodyguard Song had also disappeared. When? Kaiya suppressed a wry smile. Another wave of nausea threatened, but she squared her shoulders. Eschewing feminine grace, she purposefully strode toward the open main gates. The imperial guards formed up behind her.

Keeping her attention forward, she asked the general, "Is there any news of my brother, the *Tianzi?*"

"No, *Dian-xia.* He has sequestered himself in the main keep, with no communication in or out. For all intents and purposes, he has abdicated. Liu Zhu is acting *Tianzi* until we can confirm the previous *Tianzi's* fate."

Kaiya stifled a sigh. Despite the well-organized ministries and official bureaucracy, the nation was paralyzed unless someone at the top gave those first orders. Now, that person was a baby boy.

She looked up, to where the nearly-full white moon, near-open blue moon, and waxing iridescent moon floated inexorably toward their conjunction.

A crier yelled out. "Princess Kaiya has returned."

On the other side of the main gate, the moonlight bathed the central courtyard. Boasting their spring blooms, hundreds of espaliered fruit trees formed a path to the Hall of Supreme Harmony. Up a hundred and sixty-eight steps, tiring enough when she was *not* pregnant *and* wounded.

General Jin abruptly turned off the central path.

"Where are we going?" Kaiya stopped in her tracks, sending the imperial guards behind her into a rustling halt. There was no time to waste; Regent Liu had to hear the news of the Teleri invasion immediately.

The general faced her, though he kept his eyes averted. "The Hall of Bountiful Harvests, *Dian-xia.*"

"Not an audience with Regent Liu?" She gestured toward the Hall of Supreme Harmony.

The general shook his head. "No, *Dian-xia.* The regent has already retired for the night."

Gone to bed! Rebels in the South, an invasion to the North, and the regent was more concerned about his beauty sleep. "Where is the regent staying?" Her eyes strayed toward the residential section of the palace grounds. If the castle itself was barricaded, there would be no other place for him to stay.

General Jin extended his hand. "Please, *Dian-xia.* To the Hall of Bountiful Harvests."

"I command you to take me to the regent."

The general bowed. "I am sorry, *Dian-xia.* You may be an honored prisoner, but you are still a prisoner."

Fire flared in her face before fizzling out under the *Tiger's Eye.* Liu Yong considered her an adversary. Though why did they bother to bring her to the palace? Kaiya glared at General Jin, whose attention remained fixed on the ground. Even with a weapon, she was no match for him. Without the power of her voice, there was little she could do about her situation.

"Very well," she said. "Please take me to the Hall of Bountiful Harvests."

The general let out a long sigh and raised his head. His wrinkled brows looked nothing like the imperial guards' ubiquitous stoicism. "Again, I am sorry, *Dian-xia.*" He extended his hand toward the hall.

With a nod, Kaiya resumed her stride. Apparently, Fu had told her the truth about one thing: the imperial guard were loyal to the Jade Throne, no matter who sat on it. She tilted her head and assessed General Jin out of the corner of her eye. Tentative, nothing like his predecessor. Tian's grizzled cousin, General Zheng, would certainly have sided with her in this matter. Unfortunate that he, along with a hundred of the finest imperial guards, had perished in her escape from Iksuvius.

After three turns and a flight of marble steps to a veranda, they arrived at the Hall of Bountiful Harvests. Its blue-tiled eaves glistened in the light of the moons, reminiscent of so many nights spent here as a starstruck sixteen-year-old. This was where it all started, where she had met a dragon in man's clothing. That magically-induced infatuation had been a prison of a different sort.

Servants opened the doors and dropped into kneels. Inside, light bauble lamps revealed other servants preparing cushions and blankets for a makeshift bed on the marble floor. A sleeping robe lay folded at the side. They all stopped their frenetic activity, sank to their knees, and pressed foreheads to the floor.

"Rise." Kaiya lifted her chin.

The servants returned to their duties, though more than one flashed an apologetic nod. An older man, dressed as a chamberlain, shuffled forward, bowing. "I am sorry for the poor accommodations."

Kaiya nodded. It wasn't his fault. Liu Yong was sending a message: she didn't even warrant a guest room.

General Jin cleared his throat. "We will leave the princess to rest."

"Wait." She bowed at the waist.

All the guards and servants dropped to their knees in a rhythmic swoosh of armor and robes.

"Please wake the regent. Let him know the Teleri army, led by Emperor Geros himself, is headed this way."

"As the princess commands," the general said. Holding bows, the servants all shuffled backward out of the room, taking all the light bauble lamps. The doors closed behind them.

The lack of conviction in the general's voice didn't inspire confidence. She closed her eyes and listened. Outside, at least six imperial guards stood at the door. She might be light on her feet, but she was no *Moquan*. There would be no secret forays into the palace, like that night three years ago when she sought out Prince Hardeep in the Nine Court. For now, with the Teleri marching on the capital unopposed, she was stuck here, alone.

And tired. Her arms and legs weighed her down as she slipped out of the travelling robe. At least the nausea had subsided. Bust binder untied, her breasts felt swollen, the nipples sensitive. Still, her belly remained flat. With a sigh, she slipped into the robe and wrapped the sash around her waist.

Kaiya settled into the cushions and pulled a cover over to protect herself from the dank chill. How long would they keep her here? Would she be able to present her case to the regent?

The sounds of guards shuffling outside settled. A nearly-imperceptible breathing hid in the voice of the night. Kaiya bolted upright, heart in her throat. Apparently, the *Tiger's Eye* did little to prevent surprise.

From behind, a hand clamped down over her mouth, and warm steel pressed into her neck.

Kaiya froze in place. Perhaps the regent wanted to be done with her altogether. Though if that were the case, this interloper could've already killed her.

"*Dian-xia*," a girl's voice whispered in the dark. "I am letting go. Please keep quiet."

Jie? Had she made her way back? No. The voice was wrong. Kaiya nodded.

The hand and blade withdrew. Kaiya turned and squinted through the darkness.

A wisp of a shadow knelt there, her expression unreadable in the dark. "I—"

"—rescued me from the Teleri Fortress. Your name is Feng."

The *Moquan* girl nodded. "Yes, Feng Mi."

Likely a code-name, since it sounded like the word for *honey*. A moniker suited for spies in the Floating World. Yet Feng had come to rescue her. "Have you heard from Jie?"

"She is not with you?"

Apparently, the *Moquan* didn't know *everything*. "I sent her on a mission, and then we were separated by the Teleri invasion."

Feng's scowl, while not visible, was clear in her tone. "Young Master Yan was responsible for you."

Kaiya nodded. Just leave it at that. There was no need to revisit that drama. "It looks like you are my new bodyguard. Can I rely on you, even if Regent Liu rules?"

"The Black Lotus is loyal to the Wang Family." Feng bowed and placed a fist on the ground.

"Good." It seemed Fu was correct about the *Moquan*, or at least the Black Lotus Clan. "Now, how do we get out of here?"

"*We* don't. I can't get you past six imperial guards, and I can't fight them. Their breastplates' aura is too strong."

Kaiya stared at the doors, picturing the palace layout in her mind. "Are there other clan members around?"

"No. All the others nearby are in the castle proper with the *Tianzi*."

"Can you contact them?"

Feng's lips pursed. "Our clan designed the castle defenses to prevent one of our own from being able to penetrate it."

Kaiya sighed. Even with a *Moquan*, she was still a prisoner in her own home.

"There is another way." The coldness in Feng's tone might have sent a shiver down Kaiya's spine if not for the *Tiger's Eye*. "The regent's power comes from his grandson. Kill—"

"No." Kaiya shook her head emphatically. There had to be another way than slaying her cousin's infant son. Though, if it might save more people...

A commotion erupted outside. The doors swung open.

Hong Jianbin's heart rattled in his chest as he stepped through the doors. At long last, after over half a year, he would see Princess Kaiya again. Though perhaps his chest ached from his precarious situation. For now, he was in the regent's good graces; but if the real *Tianzi* emerged from the castle, Hong might very well lose his head for his role in accidently deposing him.

Unless he convinced the princess to marry him. Though if the regent retained power, he would find a way to remove her from the picture.

Ah, that petty little tyrant, having power drop into his lap by virtue of noble birth and a freak accident. Not like Liu Yong had the brains to harbor any traitorous thoughts beyond which rice-wine merchant to stiff.

Hong raised the light bauble lamp, which filled the room with a gentle white glow.

The princess sat, one hand clasping a sheet to her body, the other shading her eyes. Was she naked underneath?

If Hong's heart beat any faster, he would faint. Leina might be exotic and charming, but none could rival Princess Kaiya's beauty. Hands trembling, he lowered the lamp and creaked into a kneel. "*Dian-xia*, I am relieved to see you are home safe."

"Chief Minister Hong." She ran a hand through her hair and lowered the cover. The top of her cleavage peeked out from beneath the sleeping robe. Had her breasts grown since he last saw her? To think in this very room, three years ago, when they had greeted Avarax in human form, she had been a plain bean pole. Now, she was the most desirable woman in the realm.

"I am sorry to disturb your sleep, *Dian-xia*." He raised his head and met her smile. Had she lost weight? Her face seemed thinner than several months before. No doubt her winter in the wilderness had taken its toll on her health. He lingered a few more seconds on her plump breasts.

"I am happy to see a friend," she said. "What brings you here?"

Hong looked back to the doors. Closed, safe from prying eyes and ears. "*Dian-xia*, I have come to warn you. Even at this late hour, Regent Liu is meeting with the hereditary lords. He plans to brand you as a traitor." The news would crush her. He leaned forward, ready to provide support after the shocking revelation.

"I see." Her expression remained…impassive? Too shocked, maybe. Still, she didn't back away, despite the inappropriate distance. Maybe…

Hong edged even closer. "There is a way to protect you." Something he could do.

"How?" Her tone wasn't desperate, more…disinterested.

Hong took a deep breath. "Avoid a political marriage to a provincial lord. Marry a commoner, ideally in Regent Liu's good graces."

"There is no time before my audience with the regent." The stoicism in her face could rival that of an imperial guard. She did not even seem to be considering his reasoning. All of that shock—betrayed by a tyrant, forced to wander in the wilderness, coming home to be branded a traitor. Poor Kaiya. The Dragon Charmer had faded, replaced by the naïve girl from years before.

He reached forth with a trembling hand and placed it on her shoulder. So soft and warm. A tingle jolted up his arm and settled in his chest. His other hand extended of its own volition, coming to rest on her other shoulder. He opened his mouth to speak, but only a croak came out. Clearing his throat, he said, "*Dian-xia*, I will marry you. I have always had a wonderful relationship with Lord Liu."

Her eyes studied his. Her plight must finally be dawning on her.

This was his chance, at long last. It might never come again. So much for timidity. Heart pattering like a rabbit's, he drew her forward and leaned in. If she returned his kiss—

The princess turned and cast her gaze down. Not an outright refusal. Shy, just like an appropriate maiden should act.

He pecked her on her cheek. So smooth and soft, it sent heat coursing through him. Waves roared in his ears. At long last, after three years of planning and maneuvering, the princess was his.

CHAPTER 22:

Black Fists and Stone Arrows

Exhausted from his harrying trip back from the light tower, Liang Yu stumbled to his warehouse just as a predawn line of black-blue appeared on the eastern horizon. Even at this hour, the capital buzzed with rumors of Princess Kaiya's return and a possible invasion.

He rapped out a code on the door, which whispered open a crack. It was Little Song. He had done what a Black Lotus *Moquan*, trained from youth, could not: escaped with the princess from a heavily armed escort.

No, impossible. Keeping his expression blank, Liang Yu slipped past Song and into the warehouse. "How did you get back here?"

"The imperial cavalry allowed us to ride horses. When we arrived in the city, I used the citizenry's confusion to escape."

Impressive, but, "Where is the princess?"

Little Song slouched over. "I am sorry, Master. We were separated, and she was too heavily guarded."

"Unacceptable." Liang Yu slammed his staff into the wood floor. "My order was to stay close to her."

Song hung his head. "Forgive me, Master."

Liang Yu snorted. A warrior might atone for such a transgression by taking his own life. In the bureaucracy, from which Song's family came, failure was met with demotion or forced retirement. His talented father had failed only once—raising a son who became an insurgent,

exposed by Liang Yu himself—at the cost of his short tenure as Chief Minister.

A Black Lotus *Moquan*'s failure, however, was met with greater challenges. Liang Yu pointed out the door. "Intercept the imperial couriers, find out what they know."

Song raised a hand. "First, there is other news. I sent a scout out on horseback to verify the princess' claims. She was telling the truth." He unfurled a map. "A Teleri army, fifty-thousand strong, marches along the main highway, a day away by forced march."

Fifty thousand! A day away. With the bulk of the imperial armies engaged with Peng and the Madurans, there couldn't be much more than ten thousand soldiers in the capital. The only other army nearby...he looked up at Song. "Seek out Lin Ziqiu. Inform her of the situation. Ask her to return to Linshan Province and ask her father to mobilize his armies."

Watching Song dart out the door with youthful exuberance, Liang Yu headed back to his office. The princess' doctor slept in a chair, right where Liang Yu had left him, hands bound to the armrests. Liang Yu started unravelling the knots.

Doctor Fang's eyes shot opened. "Where is the princess?"

"The palace, I believe." Unless the regent had locked her away in a secret dungeon somewhere.

The doctor rubbed his wrists. "The regent will treat her as a traitor." His voice spoke of adoration, like the Surgeon's unrequited love for the Beauty.

Liang Yu laughed. "Maybe. Don't worry. The princess is hardly a damsel in distress. She is quite resourceful, actually."

"What are you doing with me?" Doctor Fang stood.

Liang Yu blindfolded him. "Go to her. One of my men will guide you out of the warehouse district. If she has need of me, she can tie her command to the second branch of the third tree on the path to Jianguo Shrine."

Once the doctor departed, Liang Yu leaned back in his chair. Resourceful indeed, that princess. His hand found the imperial plaque inside his robes and he withdrew it from its pouch.

He sat up straight. It was no imperial plaque, but a jade funerary tablet. The princess had tricked him yet again, swearing on the name of Zheng Tian, fourth son of Zheng Han: *Tai-Ming* lord and now Teleri collaborator. If his sources were correct, Zheng Tian had been banished from the capital, then eight years later appeared at the Hua embassy in the Northwest as a clerk for a trade official.

Liang Yu snorted. Not likely. Zheng Tian's resume, or lack thereof, screamed of Black Lotus *Moquan*. Now dead, like so many of his former clansmen, his spirit roaming the afterlife.

Tian threw his hands up in exasperation, barely avoiding a low-hanging branch. Playing translator for two twins who didn't understand each other was hard enough. Kiri refusing to speak of her life before joining the wild elves made the task even more frustrating, since that was all Jie asked about.

"It's not important," Kiri said. "I'm here now."

Jie prodded him in the ribs. If she were really a *sister* in their clan, she was a mean one. "What did she say?"

Tian shook his head. Kiri had repeated the words so often, Jie must certainly know what they meant by now. "She doesn't want to talk about it."

Sighing, Jie drew circles on the forest floor with her foot. "All my life, I wanted to at least know who my parents were."

It was a different, less open-ended question. Perhaps Kiri would answer. Tian asked, "Do you remember your parents?"

Kiri sucked on her lower lip. "No parents."

Tian turned to Jie and shook his head again. "She doesn't want to talk about—"

The wildlife quieted. Both Kiri's and Jie's pointed ears twitched like a temple dog's, and they turned to the north. Tian followed their stares.

The river rustled in the distance, but other than that—chainmail and boots, marching down the main path, not far away.

Jie pulled him down, almost on top of her. The closeness and heat at once felt comforting and *right*.

Dropping into a crouch, Kiri put hands to her mouth and called out like a wild bird. At other points in the forest, birdcalls responded at quick intervals. The idea seemed familiar, even if the specific calls did not.

Kiri met their gazes and twirled her finger in a big circle. Then she held up two fingers, closed her hand, one finger, then six. Tian exchanged glances with Jie, who quirked an eyebrow up. She wanted a translation.

How should *he* know what Kiri meant? Even if he knew what Jie's expression did. He flashed his best guess back in hand signals. *Two altivorcs, sixteen Teleri.*

Jie nodded, then started to crawl forward. Kiri placed a hand on her shoulder. With wide eyes, she shook her head. She held both hands up, thumbs and fingers forming crescents, then brought them together into a small circle. Were the Teleri surrounding them, drawing the noose tight? Sixteen wouldn't stand a chance against the elf village, unless....

A voice boomed out from a distance, speaking in the Kanin dialect. "We know the messengers of the gods are here, around the sacred pool. We have the area surrounded. Surrender now and you will be spared.”

Kiri paled. With her eyes, Jie prodded him to translate.

Surrounded, he signed. The elves, with their forest dexterity, could likely get into the trees and their hidden village two *li* away before the Metal Men could entrap them. He and Jie, on the other hand...and Ming, wherever he was, with his bad arm.

Hunching low, Kiri beckoned for them to follow. Elbows in the dirt, Tian crawled after her, with Jie close behind. Shouts and curses in the Metal Men’s language erupted nearby, but there was no sound of clashing swords or men felled by elf archery.

Ming’s voice rang out from closer to the village. “Help!”

Stranger or not, Ming was a brother. Tian rose next to a tree and peered around the corner. Nothing.

“Down,” Kiri hissed through her teeth.

Tian glanced at her. Shaking his head, he darted from tree to tree.

Jie was on her feet just behind him, crackling just as many leaves and twigs despite her smaller size. Not like the enemy would hear; they were making even more noise with their boots and armor.

He skidded to a stop at the edge of a clearing where the elves sometimes practiced archery, close to the sacred pool. Seven Metal Men lay dead or dying with arrows through impossibly small openings. Arrow nocked and bow drawn, Ming took aim...at the edge of the clearing, where a Metal Man hid behind a tree, hand clamped over an elf boy’s mouth. At least thirteen other Metal Men ducked in the cover of the trees. So much for there only being sixteen of them... Had Ming killed those seven? With an injured shoulder, no less?

One at Ming’s back jumped out, sword raised. Ming spun and loosed his arrow into the attacker’s throat. At the same time, two more arrows struck the man. Ming turned back to the kidnapper. Apparently, Nayori’s divine magic had healed him.

“Ming. You protected. Watch first man.” The words were in the language from Beyond the Wall, and the speaker...was little Kala.

Ming nodded, then spoke in the language of the Metal Men. “Let the boy go, and we will allow you to leave here alive.” It wasn’t likely the elves would let that happen, even if they understood Ming’s words.

“Attack!” one of the Metal Men yelled.

Eight—eleven—no, fifteen of them charged into the clearing from different angles, longswords raised. Arrows zipped in from all directions. Three men fell. Ming took deliberate steps toward the hostage-taker, seemingly oblivious to the enemies closing around him.

Tian surged in. Swiping a dagger from one of the fallen soldiers, he ran up behind another. Heavens, they were huge. A leap put him on the Metal Man’s back. A yank on the helm’s T-slot jerked his head up. Tian thrust his weapon into his victim’s eye. As he crumpled to the ground, Tian landed on his feet.

Two more steps toward the Metal Man with the boy, and Ming loosed his arrow. He cursed.

It struck the man right in the chest. His hands clawed at the shaft as he stumbled back. The boy bolted deeper into the woods.

A heavy boot crunched on pine needles behind Tian. A sword swooped down. He twirled and sidestepped out of its arc, then ducked under the follow-up. A backward handspring took him out of range, but the Metal Man pressed his attack. An arrow zipped in from the side, skewering the man from flank to flank.

Tian stared at the stone arrowhead protruding from the collapsing soldier, then looked up to reassess. There...

Jie danced through five enemies, her moves familiar yet blurred at impossible speeds. Like the elf woman Layani. And the brown-skinned man that plucked at Tian’s memories. Slipping thrusts, ducking hacks, and lodging knives into impossibly small spots. If combat were poetry, Jie would be a master poet; her enemies, rice paper anchored by a weight stone for her to write on with impunity.

Pain exploded in the back of Tian's head, and everything went black.

In the heat of battle, Jie had seen Tian's attacker.

Ever since training with the Master Paladin on the Shallowsea skiff, combat automatically slowed in her perception, whether she wanted it to or not. Her opponents might as well have been slogging through honey. Even so, she could do nothing to save Tian from his own inattention. With all her energy channeled into fighting, words died on her lips.

He should've been able to sense the hulking brute. Even a *Moquan* trainee could detect someone sneaking up from behind. Yet a Teleri soldier had lumbered up and slammed him over the head with his sword pommel.

"No!" Kiri yelled from the trees, using the only word Jie recognized in the Kanin language. Her twin raced to Tian's side.

More Bovyans poured into the clearing, streaming past Tian's inert form. Arrows flew in from the sides, but not nearly enough to stem the tide. No! Jie couldn't let them capture him. Not after she just found him.

Butterfly-twisting between two enemy slashes, she landed on her feet and ran toward him. Disorientation jolted her as time returned to normal for six steps before slowing down again. Exposed targets, which once blinked open and closed in a split second, now remained gaping wide holes in the warriors' armor. Duck under one sword, stab to the unprotected knee tendons. Dodge right and slash another's wrist. Leap over a spear thrust and drive a knife into a third's eye slot.

Stop short of an elf arrow. Lean back under the sweep of another sword. It was almost too easy. Behind a wall of three men, Kiri shielded Tian's body with her own, clinging to him while another Teleri tried to pull her off.

Jie spun around the wall of men, leaving them swinging at air. On the other side, a short, thick soldier chopped his broadsword down at Tian, with no apparent regard for Kiri being in the way. They were no longer interested in taking prisoners.

She leapt into the arc of the attack her knife extended. If she caught it just right, maybe her weapon could alter the broadsword's path.

The force of impact sent a jolt up her arm. She had misjudged the angle, and the broadsword ricocheted up instead of down. It travelled slowly, so slowly, heading right to her collarbone...and there was nothing she could do to get inside of the attack, no leverage to change her direction and get out of the way. The blade caught her in the collarbone. Pain blossomed from the site. She looked up through her tunneling vision to see...

An altivorc, mouth locked in a snarl.

The sword was yanked out. He raised the blade with two hands and chopped. She started to lift her knife, but her arm barely rose.

Ming had missed! He knew as soon as he loosed the arrow that it would miss the T-slit of the Teleri's helm, and instead bounce harmlessly off his chainmail. Somehow, the stone arrowhead not only penetrated the metal, but went all the way through to the other side.

He stared at his next arrow, its head glittering in a ray of sun. Other than the sparkles, it seemed like ordinary stone. Though perfectly smooth and razor sharp, it still shouldn't have been able to penetrate metal.

Several Teleri shouted, Kiri yelled, Jie screamed.

Ming turned to see yet another altivorc ready to decapitate Jie, whose arm hung limply at her side. He nocked and loosed two arrows in quick succession. Both found their mark, knocking the brute on his back. The half-elf owed him her life one more time, for saving her from the orcs *yet* again.

He raked his gaze across the clearing. Tian lay on his back, breathing but unconscious. Kiri was sprawled on top of him, and Jie over her. A virtual threesome with identical twins! One of Ming's daydreams—albeit with statuesque beauties in place of a homicidal smart-mouth and her taciturn sister.

Several more able-bodied Teleri looked up from the half-elf heap and met his eyes.

He only had two arrows left. He nocked and loosed both, dropping the closest and slowing the next. Behind them, an amorphous gaggle of enemies charged. In the back, the elves ventured into the clearing and pulled Tian and the half-elves into the trees.

Someone tugged at his arm. He looked down to find little Kala, her gaze intense.

"Run!" she said.

Not daring a glance back, he took off down some random path. There was no way they could outrun the long-legged Bovyans, especially not his diminutive guide. Who'd just spoken in the Hua tongue.

Twigs and needles crunched under Teleri boots behind them, yet the sound grew distant. They burst out into another clearing, where tall boulders rose out of the forest floor. Somewhere, water tumbled over stones. Kala pulled him along the edge of the rocks, then turned sharply back into a crevice.

Where had that come from? Rounded steps rolled up the rock formation, blending in seamlessly with the surroundings. Another cleft opened into a small basin with a pool, whose waters glowed a luminous blue. Just like Guanyin's Teardrop in Fenggu Province, which he'd visited several times as a youth. Its waters supposedly had healing powers.

Kala covered Ming's gasp before it escaped. She pointed down, where the Teleri soldiers jogged by. Nine in all.

One stopped right near the crevice. He looked left, looked right... But never up. Another voice called from the distance. "We've lost them!"

"Go find one of the native trackers," another voice said. "Bring them here."

The man at the base of the boulders turned around and jogged back the way he came.

Ming let out a long sigh and faced Kala. Something was wrong here; things didn't quite add up on a broken abacus. "How do you speak our language?"

Kala's eyes rounded, but then she cocked her head and raised an eyebrow. Unintelligible syllables spilled out of her mouth, replacing her broken Hua.

CHAPTER 23:
Indecent Proposals

Thank the Heavens for the *Tiger's Eye*. Without it, none of Kaiya's discipline could've kept her from recoiling from Chief Minister Hong's attempted kiss. He was old enough to be her father, maybe even grandfather.

Still, his literal proposal might be a viable option if no others presented themselves. She maintained the shy girl façade, drawing back before he kissed her neck, and pulling her sleeping robe tighter to completely cover her breasts. "I...I appreciate your willingness to make such a sacrifice. Please, it has been a long day. Let me consider it over sleep." She bowed low, like a potential bride at the matchmaker's.

Still kneeling, Hong waddled back and bowed. "*Dian-xia*, no matter what you choose, I will do everything I can to protect you."

"Thank you, Chief Minister." She bowed again. Undoubtedly, he was squinting at her cleavage again. Jie had said something about him obsessing over her. Perhaps there was quite a bit of truth to that.

His knees and spine creaked as he rose to his feet. Retrieving a lantern, he held a bow as he tottered backward to the entrance. He knocked on the doors, which opened, and backed out.

When the door closed, plunging the room in darkness, Kaiya snorted. Hong was old, and marriage to him would likely not last long. It couldn't be any worse than what Geros had done to her, and as long as the *Tiger's Eye* pent up her emotions, it wouldn't matter anyway. Though if

Hong couldn't perform in *that* ministry, then her babies would still not find legitimacy. Unless he died before their births.

None of it would matter if Geros captured her, and as of yet, nothing stood between the enemy army and the capital.

Feng Mi, forgotten in the drama, cleared her throat from up in the eaves. "You should rest, *Dian-xia*. There is a lot to think about." Her voice couldn't be much more disdainful.

Kaiya smiled at her, even if she probably couldn't see it. "I always insisted Jie speak freely. Tell me, what do you think?"

"The Chief Minister keeps a half-Ayuri concubine in the Floating World. He is unfailingly careless whenever he visits." That explained the disdain, though her tone now hinted at something more.

"There is something else you want to say."

"That would not be appropriate." Feng's voice sounded like a raging torrent behind a dam. It wouldn't take much to get her to speak.

"I command you to speak your mind."

Feng harrumphed. "I cannot believe you are actually considering marrying Hong. Especially after you ruined things between Young Master Yan and Zheng Tian."

Kaiya sighed. It couldn't be safe to have so many *Moquan* resentful of her. Yet how could she explain it? She remembered what love felt like, but her logical mind still wondered what she ever saw in Tian. Handsome and sweet, to be sure, but still a banished fourth son.

It didn't matter. Tian was dead, only rarely visiting in her dreams.

Kaiya stood at the edge of Huajing's largest market, usually noisy and vibrant during the daylight hours. Not today. Flags and paper lanterns hung lifelessly over deserted city streets.

She was utterly alone. Where was everyone?

A distant chorus of yells and shouts broke out behind her. She turned around to find herself on an abandoned river dock, looking out over the angry waters tumbling by. Dark clouds gathered above, sending streaks of lightning across the sky. Sunlight bathed the opposite bank, where crowds of her people beckoned. Some pointed at her.

Or maybe behind her, where war drums pounded and boots clomped on Huajing's paved city streets.

She whirled back around. A sea of Teleri heavy infantry, with Geros at the fore, marched in perfect ranks through the marketplace. His eyes locked with hers, and a grin formed on his lips.

That cruel smirk, the one he wore each time he... Kaiya's heart seized. Her chest constricted, denying her even a single breath. She had to flee—right, left, back, anywhere—but her legs seemed made out of lead, her feet fused to the ground.

Several of the advancing soldiers fell, breaking the Teleri's perfect formation. They collapsed, driving an approaching crevice through their ordered lines, each time punctuated by grunts and groans. The gap opened up in the front phalanx, and a lithe figure spilled out.

Jie! The half-elf spy, bloodied *dao* held in two hands, studied Geros for a split second, then turned and ran toward Kaiya. A rescue! If anyone could help her, it would be Jie. Their gazes met. Or did it? Jie looked past her, at...

Kaiya twisted around, as best as her heavy legs would allow.

Tian. He stood just a few feet away, looking...past her.

Kaiya turned back around to find Jie closing. Behind her, the Teleri marched at double time, the holes in their ranks now closed. Geros sheathed a sword and loped over. Kaiya watched as Jie sprinted by and into Tian's outstretched arms.

Tears blurred Kaiya's sight. He should be embracing *her*. Protecting *her*. She raised a hand to wipe her eyes.

A huge gauntleted hand seized her wrist. Geros.

Not again. Kaiya screamed.

Kaiya jerked up in her bed, her body wracking with sobs. Tian had abandoned her, in favor of Jie. Her sleeping robe was soaked.

The *Tiger's Eye* took hold, scattering all the unpleasant thoughts. It was only a dream. Tian was dead.

Kaiya wiped away her tears just as the doors swished open. Squinting through the light of dawn, she brushed out the creases in her robe. Shadows at the door began to take shape.

The weight and length of the footsteps sounded familiar. Her sister-in-law, Zhao Xiulan, knelt beside her. Her beautiful hair, gone. Extravagant gowns exchanged for the robes of a Praise Spring Temple nun. No longer was she the paragon of beauty and grace whom Kaiya's younger self had idolized. More concerning was how thin her face looked.

"Eldest Sister." Kaiya bowed.

Xiulan shook her head, expression serene. "I have taken the temple name An-Guo to represent my hopes while I pray for Kai-Guo's repose."

An, for peace; *Guo* for nation, the same character as Kai-Guo's. A beautiful double entendre, but nonetheless, the kind and thoughtful sister-in-law would always be Xiulan, *Extraordinary Orchid*, in Kaiya's heart.

If she could ever find her heart under the blanket of the *Tiger's Eye*. Kaiya leaned forward and wrapped her arms around Xiulan. "I am so sorry for your loss. I so wanted to come back as soon as I got your letter."

Xiulan nodded. "Chief Minister Hong asked that I write it."

Hong again. Apparently, this unlikely suitor had been thinking of her for a while. "Thank you for visiting me, though it might not be wise to call on a potential traitor."

Xiulan beamed and shook her head. "I asked to be your attendant."

Again, the *Tiger's Eye* didn't block Kaiya's surprise, even if it prevented her from feeling mortified by the proposition. She waved her hand. "I could never face Kai-Guo in the afterlife if I allowed you to do that."

"I could never face him if I didn't." Xiulan squeezed Kaiya's hand, then turned and waved toward the door. "And you will never live down the embarrassment of presenting yourself to the regent dressed in a sleeping robe or travelling rags."

A servant shuffled in, holding a low bow. She extended a blue court gown in two hands.

"Leave us," Xiulan said, receiving the dress.

The servant backed out and closed the door, leaving the room illuminated with a light bauble lamp.

Clambering to her feet, Kaiya straightened the covers on the makeshift bed.

Xiulan sucked in a sudden breath. "Since when do you make your own bed?"

"The testy half-elf handmaiden never helped in my travels."

Xiulan nodded. "She was poorly trained."

At least as a handmaiden and in court etiquette. In other ways... Kaiya smiled. "Hopefully, I will come back to a bed and not to the executioner's block."

"I will pray for your exoneration." Xiulan bowed. Apparently, Liu's intentions were no secret, at least in the court. "If Heaven fails you, I will slit my own throat." She reached for the sash's knot at Kaiya's waist.

Fighting off her hands, Kaiya undid the binding herself and shrugged out of the robe. Exposing herself might be out of character, or at least from what Xiulan knew from their past, but it wasn't like they hadn't soaked in hot springs together before.

Nonetheless, Xiulan coughed. "You have lost weight, except..." She shook her head and presented the inner gown.

Kaiya received it in two hands. She slipped it on and wrapped a white sash around her waist. It squeezed around her pregnancy-swollen bust.

"I thought I knew your size." Eyes narrowed, Xiulan cocked her head. "Perhaps I was wrong, and unfortunately, your wardrobe is in the sealed-off castle."

Those dresses likely wouldn't fit, either. Kaiya stretched an arm into the hanging sleeve of the outer gown. Perhaps it'd been a bad idea to undress in front of Xiulan. She'd tried to conceive for so long. If she deduced—

A wave of morning sickness rolled through her. Covering her mouth, she heaved, but luckily, nothing came up. She glanced up.

Xiulan's eyebrow rose, though her lips squeezed tight. "Come, the regent awaits."

Kaiya nodded and followed Xiulan out of the hall. Outside by the steps knelt a dozen imperial guards, and several familiar faces. Among them, Chief Minister Hong's gaze met hers, perhaps searching for an answer to his question. Doctor Wu, as well, looked at her through her unique blue eyes. Or maybe not so unique; the luminous color seemed familiar somehow. Where—

"*Dian-xia.*" One voice out of the chorus stood out. Fang Weiyong's. How had he gotten here? The bright robes of Yang-Di and meticulously coifed hair felt strange after all these months of seeing him dress like a Kanin tribesman.

"Fang Weiyong," Kaiya said. "I am glad to see you safe. Your hair."

He bowed. "Yes, *Dian-xia*. I came straight away from...but yes, there was no time to shave my head."

It might have been faster to shave it than to put the effort into coiffing it. In fact, Weiyong never appeared so gentlemanly. And he was somehow here, out of Fu's clutches.

"You did not find time to keep it cut during your time in the wilderness?" Eyes slitted, Xiulan looked from Kaiya to Weiyong and back.

He bowed. "Unfortunately, my razor dulled, and we also tried to blend in with the natives."

"*Dian-xia*." Doctor Wu's voice silenced everyone. "I came to the palace as soon as I heard you had arrived. Everyone in the streets is talking about it. Luckily, I was able to get Weiyong in. Now come along, we mustn't try the regent's patience." Without waiting, she turned and walked down the steps with the speed and grace of someone a quarter her age. However old that was.

Kaiya followed her and the rest of the entourage fell in behind. Despite the hour, when the palace grounds would normally be awash with ministers and servants, the walkways and courtyards were nearly deserted.

At the foot of the one hundred and sixty-eight steps to the Hall of Supreme Harmony, Kaiya looked up. Sleep had done little to refresh her. After the climb, she'd be exhausted again.

Weiyong's eyes followed the steps up as well. "Allow me to help you, *Dian-xia*."

Minister Hong bowed. "I will assist you, as well."

Kaiya nodded, and they proceeded up the marble steps. Weiyong kept his firm hand in hers, pulling her with encouragement when she slowed. Minister Hong offered a tentative hand on her elbow as well. Behind them, imperial guards and other officials muttered at the breach of decorum.

At last, they arrived at the top. Her legs protested as she stepped over the ghost-tripping threshold, but with Weiyong's help, she made it across without an embarrassing tumble to the ground. The room quieted as soon as she stepped in.

How could there be so few people? Whereas the ministers, officials, and hereditary lords used to cover almost every *chi* of the floor, today there couldn't be more than sixty. The Jade Throne at the front of the hall stood empty, though Regent Liu sat at its right hand. Beside him knelt an old man...Treasury Minister Geng.

Kaiya took a deep breath and straightened her carriage. Murmurs surfaced again as she glided down the central row between the thin ranks of men. Just before the throne, she stopped, stretched out her arms to straighten her sleeves, and knelt. How low to bow? Maybe if her baby nephew sat on the throne, recognized as *Tianzi*, it would warrant her forehead to the floor. A regent...no one had held that position since the Founder's consort, over two centuries ago; and in any case, an imperial princess' rank stood only a rung lower than a prince.

Whether Liu Yong considered her an imperial princess or not was another story. Either way, playing the role of demure woman would more likely win him over. Waiting until Chief Minister Hong took his place on the dais, she set her hands in front of her knees and bowed low. Whispers rumbled through the assembled men.

"Rise." The regent waved a dismissive hand. Behind him, Minister Geng whispered something in his ear.

She raised her head. "*Jie-xia*, I—"

"—are trying to incite a revolt against my grandson's rule, I hear." He scowled.

At least Chief Minister Hong had warned her, so it didn't come as a surprise. "No, *Jie-xia*. I have come with dire news of a Teleri invasion."

The lords and ministers broke out in a low murmur of confusion. Minister Geng leaned in and whispered something to Liu again. Chief Minister Hong tried to approach the regent, only to have Minster Geng box him out. Perhaps Hong had less influence than he thought.

The regent slapped his hand down on the armrest. "A distraction, making use of the light towers to scare the populace and rally the troops to you. You cannot fool me. No army can breach the Great Wall."

Kaiya shook her head. "I assure you—"

"What you say does not agree with what you did." Minister Geng wagged his finger at her.

"The way station claimed you approached with a ragtag militia of insurgents and imperial soldiers. I think you were raising an army of your own."

It was clear who was in charge. A baby might act as *Tianzi*, a fool might be regent, but ultimately, it was an ambitious minister who pulled more than purse strings. Kaiya placed a hand on her chest and faced Liu Yong, whose bewildered expression did not bode well for Hua. "*Jie-xia*, I only wanted to warn the capital as quickly as possible."

Brows furrowed, the regent looked at Minister Geng, who in turn stared at her as if she were a commoner.

Chief Minister Hong cleared his throat. "Princess Kaiya has always had the realm's best interests at heart."

Minister Geng counted on his fingers. "Misappropriation of imperial resources. Fomenting rebellion. *Jie-xia*, you must ascertain her loyalty to your grandson, the *Tianzi*. Allow me some time with her, alone, for questioning." A lurid smile formed. No surprise, given his lecherous reputation.

Hong's complexion blanched. "*Jie-xia*, I have always been loyal to you. I will retire. Please allow me to marry Princess Kaiya, and I will ensure she does not meddle in your affairs."

The assembled ministers and minor lords all broke out into animated discussion.

Kaiya suppressed a scoff. No one believed the Teleri were invading. The nation was on the brink of collapse, and two old men were fighting to bed her.

A smirk formed on Regent Liu's face, his eyes narrowing. That was an idea forming, and if the current proceedings were any indication, that idea would have nothing to do with bolstering the capital's defenses.

He raised his hand, and the room ebbed into quiet. He turned and grinned at Chief Minister Hong. "I seem to remember a promise you made me a year ago, when you were Imperial Household Minister. It was at Lord Peng's pavilion, the night he tried to assassinate our beautiful young princess and frame the Madurans."

Apparently, Lord Liu was much more aware of things than he let on, or at least he remembered this particular detail. Minister Geng leaned in to the regent's ear, only to be rebuffed with a wave of the hand. On the other side, Hong's leathery face flushed an interesting shade of crimson as his eyes met Kaiya's. He opened his mouth, but no words came out.

Lord Liu's stare fell on her as well. "Imagine how differently things might have been if Peng had succeeded. You would be dead, and it would be him sitting here," he nodded toward the Jade Throne, "instead of leading some insignificant rebellion."

Kaiya looked from the regent to Hong and back. Where this was headed was anyone's guess, though it likely had little to do with mobilizing the army.

Liu beckoned Chief Minister Hong off the dais with a jerk of his hand. "I accept your resignation, since I had to fulfill your promise on my own. You," Liu said, pointing an obtuse finger at her, "will marry my second son, Liu Deying, who will serve as Chief Minister."

CHAPTER 24:
That Which The Spirits Brought Together

Jie hid behind a vacant street vendor stall as Teleri soldiers marched through Huajing's busiest marketplace. Storm clouds hung high above, while wind blew through flags and paper lanterns in the deserted city streets. Crushed squashes and fall greens lay scattered about, strange to see during the spring.

Time to sit and wait. Once the Teleri column passed, she'd resume her search for...Tian? No, she'd found him. She was searching for...her parents? What a strange notion.

Somewhere down a side street, a woman spoke with frantic urgency, in the feeble voice of a dying person. "The elves won't protect her. My father will."

That voice! Familiar. It plucked at the primordial chords of Jie's very existence. Teleri army be damned, she had to find the speaker. She rose and picked the most likely side street. Her shoulder hurt as if Yanluo, God of Death, was yanking on her arm from down in Hell, while leaving the rest of her in the world of the living.

At least the Bovyans didn't seem too interested in her. They kept their eyes forward, marching inexorably toward the river docks. The woman had spoken somewhere nearby, but Jie scanned several side streets to no avail.

A male voice rose in song, each note perfect, rising and falling like the hymn the gods sang to create the world. Its beauty rivaled Princess Kaiya's singing.

Ears perking, Jie froze in place. That song! A lullaby. A wave of calm washed over her. In a daze, she ambled forward, one foot in front of the other, heading toward the music like a moth toward a flame.

There! By an abandoned shop, near stacked crates, the singing man knelt, cradling the dying woman. His golden hair tumbled behind a pointed ear. Even though distance and shadows obscured their faces, their love resonated in the man's music and the woman's dying breaths.

Jie took several more steps, moving to within a *biao's* throw away. The man looked up and met her gaze with large violet eyes. He had to be one of the most handsome men she'd ever seen, and yet, even thinking that felt wrong. With a smile, he proffered an arrow. Silvery impurities veined in regular patterns through its transparent crystal point.

A gift? From an elf? Jie stopped mid-stride. To receive it seemed like accepting that part of herself, the one she denied. No. She faltered back.

A regiment of snarling altivorcs streamed out from between two buildings, blocking her view of the elf man and his arrow. Glaring at her, they parted to make way for a leader who stood a head taller than the rest. Dressed in a dapper military uniform, he was handsome, even more so than the altivorc prince she'd killed in Iksuvius. He spun a magic wand around his finger.

Jie drew her *dao*. Refusing the gift from the elf was one thing; being denied by some pretty altivorc prince and his henchmen was another. She took a long stride forward.

With a grin that exposed his fangs, the prince thrust the wand into a sheath on his belt. He stepped aside and yanked on a chain. A little half-elf girl...Kala...stumbled forward. A short, cloaked figure emerged on the other side of her.

An unknown variable. Jie paused. A prince and foot soldiers already posed a challenge. How could she rescue Kala—

The cloaked figure lowered its hood.

Jie gasped. She might have been looking in a mirror. Kiri? Her twin gazed back with a killer's eyes, so unlike her usual sadness. Drawing a shorter version of an altivorc broadsword, Kiri charged.

Metal clashed against metal, the reverberation sending vibrations through Jie's hand. The pain in her shoulder flared. Combat, instead of slowing, seemed to speed up. Kiri moved blindingly fast, like the Golden Scorpion Jie had faced in Vyara City. That encounter hadn't ended well.

Jie fell back under the onslaught of slashes and hacks. There was no way to win this, not with her shoulder. Heart hammering in her chest, she turned and ran.

In seconds, she caught up with the crowd of Teleri heavy infantry. With their huge size, they offered a perfect place to hide from Kiri. She picked her way through the ranks, slaying Bovyans who blocked her. One, three, six—they fell before her, opening a path of escape. She had to get away.

One collapsed, and a ray of light sprayed in the opening he left in the orderly lines. In her blind fear, she'd reached the front! Maybe it would be safer to keep running.

Jie burst out of the line of soldiers, not far from the river docks. Only one man stood ahead of her: Emperor Geros. If she killed him, the invasion of Hua would surely falter. An uneasy feeling settled in the pit of her stomach. No, that felt wrong. Killing Geros felt like killing Tian.

Yet another strange notion, in a day of strange notions. She ran around him instead. On the other side, Tian stood, beckoning her. Jie raced

into his embrace. Warm, protective, comforting. They could stay like this forever...

Jie's eyes fluttered open. Fluffy and cool, the bed beneath her back might've been made of clouds, while a puffy fur blanket covered her to the chin. A warm hand clasped hers outside the blanket. She craned her neck to see.

Tian. Sitting on the treetop floor, he leaned against her bed. His head rested in the cradle of one elbow while his other hand held hers. Eyes closed, his back rose and fell.

An elf with gifts, altivorcs, murderous twins, and Teleri emperors. It must've all been a dream. A very real dream. Yet, just like at the dream's end, here she was, with Tian.

Pulse racing, she squeezed his hand.

His eyes popped open and he sat up straight. "Jie! I'm so glad you are okay. You were unconscious for several hours."

"No thanks to you." She pouted at him.

He grinned sheepishly. "Yes, so Ming told me. I owe you my life."

"Again. So, are you all right?" With her free hand, she beckoned for him to lower his head. "The Bovyan hit you pretty hard."

"Yes, just a lump." He rubbed a spot on his scalp.

She giggled. "Apparently, amnesia claimed your sense of awareness." To sit up, she brought her elbows up under her... Her right shoulder moved, pain-free, but inordinately stiff. Like it wasn't her own arm. She freed her hand from Tian's grasp and tried to stretch it out.

Tian lifted a quizzical eyebrow. "What's wrong?"

"My arm." Though it didn't hurt, everything felt bound up around the wound. Her heart stuttered. If she couldn't use her arm, what use was she as a *Moquan*? "My arm," she repeated, panic rising in her voice.

"Let me see." Tian started to pull back the fur blanket.

No, he would see her boyish figure, so flat compared to Princess Kaiya's curves. Jie pressed the blanket down, only exposing her shoulder. She twisted to get a look herself, but the wound was too close to her neck.

He shook his head. "Nayori bandaged the cut. Let me get her."

"No." She pulled his hand as he started to rise. "Stay with me, please."

Tian searched her eyes, and with a nod, settled onto the floor beside her.

Jie tested her arm again, yielding the same result. Though painless, her shoulder seized and her arm refused to move. Her very identity laid in her *Moquan* skills. If she couldn't use her arm, she would be...normal. Tears threatened to overcome her, but she blinked them away and buried her face in her left arm.

The elf shaman Nayori's voice rode on the wind, in the language of Hua. "You have woken from your dreams."

Jie wiped her eyes and peered up.

Nayori flashed a grim smile. "Sit up."

Clasping the blanket at her neck, Jie sat up. Cool air brushed across her shoulders, but her back seemed covered. She pulled the covers forward and peeked... and let out a sigh of relief. A long dress of animal skins passed under her arms and wrapped around her chest.

"Kiri's," the shaman said.

It would make sense that her twin's clothes would fit. Still...memories of Kiri from the dream sent a shudder through her.

Nayori leaned in and pulled away the bandage, which stank of pungent herbs. She smiled. "It is completely healed."

Crowding in, Tian nodded. "There's no sign of an injury at all."

No injury at all? Jie tried to move her arm again, and again, the shoulder locked up. "Then why can't I move my arm?"

Nayori sighed. "The grace of Ayara has healed your body. Your spirit, on the other hand...perhaps only Aralas himself could channel the energy to repair that."

Tian tapped his chin. "You said you didn't believe Aralas was the Angel of Koralas."

"We don't. It doesn't mean he wasn't powerful in magic."

Now was not the time for a history lesson. Jie's voice cracked. "How do I heal my spirit?"

Nayori searched her eyes. "What did your dreams tell you?"

The dreams didn't make sense, and certain parts remained better untold. Jie shrugged, but even then, her shoulder refused to obey her brain's command. "I was chased by Kiri."

"Then maybe you will find answers with Kiri." Nayori's gaze swept along the other trees before returning to Jie. "With those answers, you might regain use of your shoulder."

It wasn't like she hadn't tried to get Kiri to talk. It was hopeless. Tears again welled in Jie's eyes.

Tian leaned in and enveloped her in his embrace, pulling her close. It was so soothing, and Jie buried her head into his shoulder. He stroked her hair and pressed his chin into the crest of her head. It felt so right, the way things had been meant to be before the princess had come back into Tian's life.

She looked up and pressed her face into his neck. She had found him, alive. Perhaps spying and killing didn't define who she was any more than the elf blood she never wanted. Maybe as long as she had him, they could reinvent themselves and she wouldn't need her arm.

Nayori cleared her throat. "Tian, the human shaman you lived with awaits you at the pool."

Tian held Jie's hand as they headed to the sacred pool, the memory of her lips on his neck sending shivers through him. It felt so right. She felt so right. No wonder he'd felt so close to Kiri, her identical twin, in such a short amount of time. Maybe the Doe-Eyed Girl was just a figment of his imagination, some fantasy, while Jie was here and now. Had they been more than just clan brother and sister? It might explain the way she looked at him. Yet she was holding back, not telling him everything.

Her palm felt cold and clammy in his. Each of her steps was tentative. Maybe she felt as excited as him about meeting this shaman. Maybe it would spark memories where his reunion with Ming and Jie had not.

Heart racing, he turned to glance at Ming, just a few steps behind. His brother stared at Tian and Jie's clasped hands, his expression alternating between bewilderment and relief. No doubt, whatever history lay between Ming and Jie would make for an interesting tale.

They climbed up the rocks to the gap between the boulders. On the other side, voices spoke in the Kanin language. What would the shaman say? Tian's legs wobbled beneath him. With a deep breath, he entered.

Two men stood by the pool, gawking at him. One wore the feathers and shells of a Kanin shaman; the other dressed like a tribesman, though his face was from Beyond the Wall. Neither sparked a rushing back of repressed memories. On the other hand, beyond the expected disbelief in their expression, there was something else...anger, perhaps? Such a strange response.

"Brother," the shaman said in the Kanin language. "The spirits did not deceive us with their most unbelievable news, that your own spirit had returned to the land of the living."

The man from Beyond the Wall nodded. "Several people saw you die."

"A skill from our clan." Tian squeezed Jie's hand, drawing stares. "However, it has cost me my memories. I'm sorry, I do not even remember you or your names."

The shaman's mouth formed a circle. Then he placed a hand over his chest and spread it out in an arc. "I am Yuha, shaman of Swiftrun Village."

"Ma Jun, imperial guard of Hua." The other put his right fist in his left hand, and also exchanged nods with Ming. "Young Lord Zheng."

Ming grinned. "It has been a long time since we all assaulted the Levanthi pyramid." He cast Jie a sideward glance.

"Evidently, you've forgotten more than our names." Lips pursed, Yuha pointed at their joined hands. "You do not belong to this woman."

Jie's palm clasped his tightly, sending his stomach fluttering like a dragonfly's wings. No, it couldn't be. Certainly they were meant for each other.

Nodding vigorously, Ma Jun said in the language from Beyond the Wall, "Jie, you know Tian's choice."

His choice? Jie turned to Tian, her glassy eyes searching his. "Tian is reborn. The choices of his past were forgotten, by Heaven's will."

She was being evasive again, avoiding talk of whatever his choice had been. As much as he wanted to know, he couldn't bear to hurt someone who already wore such a pained look. Ma Jun leaned in and whispered into the shaman's ear. Jie's own ears twitched, and a scowl formed on her face.

Yuha spread out his arms. "You cannot simply undo what the spirits have brought together. You swore by the rituals of our people and your own."

Tian shook his head. How could he live by an oath he didn't even remember? "Who do I belong to?"

"Kaiya!" Ma Jun and Yuha said it together, and Jie recoiled as if slapped across her face.

"Kaiya!" Ming's jaw slackened, and then his eyebrows clashed together.

Kaiya. The name meant nothing to him, even if the three men spoke it as if invoking the gods. He shook his head again.

"We called her the Willow Beauty," Yuha said.

Tian slowly nodded. The Kanin woman he'd saved from the Metal Men had mentioned something about the Warrior From Beyond the Wall rescuing the Willow Beauty. Still, the moniker meant nothing more now than it had at the time.

Yuha made two circles with his fingers. "With eyes like a doe."

The Doe-Eyed Girl. Tian's heart jolted.

Sniffing, Jie stared at the ground. Ming coughed. Ma Jun nodded emphatically.

Tian lifted Jie's chin. "It was another life; it doesn't matter." The words felt like a lie, even as he spoke them. An urge deep inside fueled his need to know who he once was, even if it meant that Jie was not *that* part of it. Still, after she'd sacrificed her arm for him...

"The spirits' wrath will come down on you," Yuha said. "If you are to break your commitment to Kaiya, then you must do so with the correct rituals."

Jie met his gaze. Her lips trembled. "You must make your decision based on all information. That is who you are, who you have always been. What I loved in you from the time we first met."

"It obviously wasn't his good looks," Ming muttered under his breath.

"Emperor Geros wants to occupy Hua." Jie pointed west. "However, he is even more focused on capturing the princess. He thinks she carries his child."

Ming choked. Tian's head spun. If the Doe-Eyed Girl was his, and yet might carry the child of the Metal Men's leader....

"When I left her," Jie said, "your father was holding her prisoner."

"You didn't tell me that!" Ming's eyes widened.

Jie shrugged. "He was also about to surrender the East Gate of the Great Wall."

Ming threw his hands up. "And you sent us deeper into the woods?"

"Go to her," Yuha placed his hand on Tian's shoulder. "I will come with you to undo your vows if that is your final choice."

Shouldering his pack, Ming kicked the dirt. A day which had started with him winning the well-deserved respect of the elves now ended in despair. His father, a traitor. The woman he was supposed to marry, already married to his kid brother. In addition, it appeared Emperor Geros' claims were true, that he'd indeed despoiled her.

Ming sighed. Now their ragtag group was heading back to Hua, something he would've welcomed the day before. What was Jie thinking? It would be so much better if she and Tian just stayed here and made quarter-elves, and left the princess for...no, did he really want to be third in line?

Several of the elves gathered to bid them farewell, or rather to see *Tian* off. Dior grinned and gesticulated, each motion graceful like a lady. The elf shaman gave him trinkets. Kiri clung to him like a burr to horsehair, while Jie pursed her lips at the contact. What was it with him and half-elf girls?

Wait, one half-elf was missing. Ming scanned the crowd a couple of times. "Where's little Kala?"

Heads turned every which way, and Dior disappeared up into the trees. That would take some time getting used to, the idea that entire village was up there, hidden.

A tug at his sleeve drew Ming's attention down. The little boy he'd rescued grinned. Beside him, his beautiful mother bowed and spoke in mellifluous tones. A well-deserved thanks, no doubt. She handed him a quiver of arrows, each head ground from stone.

"Made by their master craftsman," Tian chimed in. How had he snuck up like that?

The stone heads that could penetrate metal. Ming bowed to the woman. "Thank you."

She nodded again, flashing an alluring smile. If only there were more time...

"There's Kala." Jie pointed with her left hand, the one she could still move.

The young half-elf looked at Jie, and then cast her eyes down.

Ming frowned. "You spoke our language. How?"

Kala raised her head. "*They* taught me."

They? Ming's brow furrowed. Tian, Jie, and Ma Jun all stared at Kala.

"*They* trained me in many things. Once I grew up, I was supposed to hunt down my sisters. But Kiri rescued me and we fled."

"Sisters?" Jie gawked at the younger half-elf.

Kala exchanged nods and words with Kiri before facing Jie. "Kiri says you aren't what she expected. She hopes you succeed."

"Succeed?" Jie shook her head in slow turns. "At what?"

"Killing *him*."

CHAPTER 25:

I, Regent

Surprised conversations filled Kaiya's ears as she stared at the floor, feigning acquiescence to Regent Liu's order. Perhaps it would work for the better. Marriage to Liu Deying would legitimize her babies and keep her close to the throne.

Hong, former Chief Minister, plodded by her. His defeated gait suggested his head must be hanging quite low. The other supplicant for her bed, Minister Geng, hissed in Liu's ear. "*Jie-xia*, only someone who has passed the civil service exams may serve as a minister, let alone Chief Minister. Your son—"

"—will preside over your execution for insolence," Liu said, "if you do not quiet down."

Minister Geng's immediate silence set the tone for all other conversations coming to a sudden halt. Kaiya looked up to see the old lecher's gawk.

The regent beckoned the imperial guards. "As of today, Mister Geng is stepping down from his position as Minister of the Treasury. He will be reassigned to Nanling Province, as stablemaster. Remove him from the palace."

Nanling Province! Currently in rebellion under Cousin Peng. If this was the way Liu would rule over Hua, the nation was doomed. No matter how corrupt former Minister Geng was, someone had to remonstrate the regent.

As the imperial guards strode forward, Kaiya rose to her feet. "*Jie-xia*, if you remove everyone who disagrees with you, sooner or later there will be no one left."

The regent's eyes narrowed. He'd started to lift his hand, when someone cleared their throat and stood in a rustle of robes.

Kaiya glanced back.

There stood Young Lord Chen Qing, *Yu-Ming* heir to a county in Jiangzhou Province. "The classics assert that a wise leader listens to diverse opinions and builds consensus, lest the nation fall into disorder."

Several of the hereditary lords voiced their agreement; unlike the ministers, their positions didn't depend on the *Tianzi*. Kaiya settled back into her kneel. Young Lord Chen had been one of her early suitors, one whom she had dismissed as dumb as a rock. Perhaps clouded by the dragon Avarax's enchantment, she'd failed to see Chen's potential.

Regent Liu jumped to his feet and pointed at Lord Chen. "Insolence. I order you to cut your throat."

Tiger's Eye or not, Kaiya gasped. Though it was certainly the regent's prerogative, Father had never given such an order. Wouldn't have, even if a hereditary lord had spat in his face. She rose again, the sudden motion sending her stomach into rebellion. She swallowed the words on her lips along with the rising nausea.

And now, she stood before everyone in silence, looking like a fool.

Fool or not, even without the power of music, she'd apparently struck a chord. Behind her, court clothes shuffled and armor jingled. She turned her head. Several hereditary lords marched to her side, many with hands on their shortswords. She glanced to the dais, where imperial guards now drew their *dao*.

Young Lord Chen dropped to one knee at her side. "I stand with Princess Kaiya."

"I stand with Princess Kaiya." Lords crowded in around her and knelt, reminiscent of their salute to Father when he recovered from Peng's first poisoning attempt. Perhaps if she could feel emotions, it would be moving.

Lord Liu's shoulders huddled, and he took several steps back. Then he straightened and wagged a finger at all of them. "Then you will all die, traitors to the Dragon Throne! Guards!"

Weapons rasped from sheaths, for perhaps the first time ever in the Hall of Supreme Harmony. Imperial guards formed up in front and back, while ministers cowered on the floor.

Even with *dao*, the lords wouldn't have stood a chance against imperial guards. It'd be a slaughter, at a time when the realm needed to come together. There could be no more internal fighting if the nation hoped to withstand a rebellion in the South and an invasion from the North. Submitting to the regent would buy them a temporary reprieve, though it had to be on her terms. She lifted her chin. "Stand down."

Even without the power of her voice, she could still imitate Father's imperial tone. The guards halted their advance, though their swords remain drawn.

Kaiya stretched out her arms to smooth out her sleeves, and then folded her hands in front of her as she bowed. It was time to expose her secret, portraying herself as a mourning widow. Prevented by convention to marry for a year, she was still available to be *protected* by the all-powerful, yet easily manipulated regent. He'd protect her sons, believing them to be his. She'd influence policy by making the regent believe the ideas were his own.

It wasn't much different from sacrificing her dignity to Geros to protect seven hundred prisoners—save for the higher stakes and the *Tiger's Eye* which made the decision all the more logical. Straightening, she tilted her head to expose

her bare neck and pressed her arms inward to flaunt her cleavage.

As expected, Regent Liu's stare dipped. Minister Geng, pressed between two imperial guards, craned his neck as well. If she'd been less naïve years before, and knew how to use her blossoming tools, perhaps she could've prevented Cousin Peng's conspiracy and the ensuing upheaval.

"*Jie-xia*, I am afraid I cannot marry your son." She paused to let it sink in, ready to deliver her veiled offer at the right moment.

The room fell into silence again, the collective surprise mirrored in Lord Liu's expression. Still, his gaze remained firmly focused on her chest.

"Instead," she said, "I—"

Booted footsteps stomped across the tile floors. Robes swished and heads turned. This inopportune interruption was ruining the precise timing of her offer.

Kaiya cast a sideward glance toward the entrance. An imperial messenger dropped to his knee just a few steps behind her. "*Jie-xia*, the messengers sent by Princess Kaiya to scout the countryside have returned with urgent news. A Teleri army, at least fifty thousand strong, now march down the highway. They are a day away."

Gasps echoed in the hall. Eyes turned to the regent, whose faced blanched. His hands trembled like a maiden's on her wedding night.

Like hers, on *her* wedding night. Kaiya studied his panicked look. The poor man, he was playing mahjong without money to back his losses. When accepting the position, he probably thought the imperial army would vanquish Cousin Peng in short order, and he would win all the glory. He would reap the rewards of future peace and prosperity. Now, confronted with an actual crisis...

Around the room, ministers, guards, and lords muttered in bewilderment. If there was a time to unify them all, it was now.

She cleared her throat. "Men of Hua. I am Daughter of the Dragon Throne. Hear me."

Young Lord Chen dropped to his knee before her. "What do you command, *Dian-xia*?"

Eyes shifted from the regent to her. Most importantly, the imperial guards sheathed their swords, and their commander, General Jin, looked at her with an expectant gaze.

What should she say? Warning the regent of impending invasion was one thing; taking command, something completely different. Somewhere, Jie was laughing at her expense. No, leave strategies to the military leaders, provisioning to the experts.

Tilting her head, Kaiya extended an open hand to the messenger. No, too feminine. She squared her shoulders and tightened the hand into a fist. "Send messengers to all imperial barracks in and near the capital, ordering them to mobilize. Summon all our generals to the palace at once."

She took four steps and alighted the dais, then turned to face the assembled officials and lords. Someone among them had to know something about provisions and administration. Chief Minister Hong was nowhere to be seen. "Who is the senior-most official present?"

The ministers looked among themselves, and several inched back. Not a single one stood. All these officials had passed civil service examinations, yet apparently none had ever endured true adversity.

In matters of hardship, she had much more experience. She nodded to a page. "Summon former Chief Minister Song to the palace to resume his post." A post he'd only held for a few days, but he'd proven his administrative skills during his tenure as Foreign Minister.

The hall burst into quiet whispers. Minister Geng, still staring at her chest, said, "Minister Song's son was an insurgent."

She shook her head. "It doesn't matter. In these desperate times, a man's capabilities overshadow the sins of his family."

"But the classics say—"

She scowled at him. "The classics teach a ruler wisdom, but they do little to repel invaders."

Young Lord Chen cleared his throat. "I nominate Princess Kaiya to replace Lord Liu as regent."

Kaiya stared at him. Was that even possible? Removal of a sitting regent? And how was a regent appointed? There was no precedent: in the three hundred years of the Wang Dynasty, only the Founder's consort had ruled as regent before Lord Liu, and she'd pretty much assumed the position.

She looked at Lord Liu's cushioned chair. Whoever sat there in these trying times had to contend with bickering lords, corrupt officials, and perhaps an assassin's knife. Only a fool would want the position.

Yet right now, the realm needed her. "I proclaim myself Regent of Hua."

The hereditary lords followed Lord Chen's lead, dropping to their knees and bowing. "*Jie-xia!*" they shouted in unison.

Officials pressed their foreheads to the floor, repeating the chorus.

The imperial guards all faced her and dropped to a knee, fist to the ground. As the only ones with the swords, perhaps their acquiescence mattered the most.

"*Jie-xia*," General Jin said.

Eyes glazed over, Lord Liu staggered back into his chair. "I resign as regent. *Jie-xia*, please take care of my grandson until he comes of age."

Kaiya swept her gaze over the bowing men. The trust of the lords and ministers might very well be misplaced. If the imperial armies couldn't mobilize in time, her reign as regent might be short-lived.

Reduced to riding a rickshaw. Hong Jianbin bounced in the seat, each joint between the pavestones sending a flare of pain through his old spine. Now forced into retirement, he had lost the perk of riding in a palanquin, protected from the masses by a wall of guards.

Instead, the rickshaw offered him a front-row view of the panicked citizenry, all rushing to the markets to hoard supplies. The buzz of hushed whispers all repeated the same thing: the Teleri Empire had breached the Great Wall and now marched on the capital.

The driver stopped in front of the Jade Teahouse. Unlike the rest of the city, the Floating World seemed calm as always. If one thing remained constant, regardless of whether the *Tianzi* or a foreign conqueror sat on the Jade Throne, it was a man's need for entertainment.

Tripping over his robes, Hong stumbled out of the rickshaw. He straightened himself and offered a silver ring to the wide-eyed driver, though it was worth much more than the cost of the trip. Hong carried no money. He never had to in the palace. Without looking back, he trudged into the teahouse.

The proprietress bowed as he walked through the common area and into the back hallway. He pushed open the secret entrance to Leina's house. His house. Now stripped of his title, he would probably never see his official villa ever again.

Inside the parlor, Leina sat, studying a *weiqi* board. A white stone danced between her delicate fingers, but the other seat across the table was empty. Hong creaked into the vacant chair, and Leina looked up. Sucking in her breath, she stood and bowed. "My lord, I did not hear you come in. Let me get you some tea." She turned toward the kitchen.

"Wait." He cast her a bitter smile.

"My lord, why so glum?" She placed a hand on his shoulder.

Why, indeed. Because his dreams were dead. He would not become a hereditary lord, not marry Princess Kaiya, nor become regent. Years of planning, all for naught. They were Leina's dreams, too, and he had failed her as well. A tear threatened to cloud his vision, but he blinked it away. "I was forced to resign."

Her hand pulled back and she stared at him, mouth almost agape. "What happened?"

"Regent Liu no longer had need of my services. I am sorry, you will not become the second most powerful woman in Hua, as I promised."

"My lord." She sighed. "It doesn't matter. You have already given me so much. We still have each other. Come, have some tea. Tea makes everything better." She glided across the room with a grace of a dancer and disappeared into the kitchen.

Did she really not care about their forfeited dreams? If so, perhaps it was not a total loss. He was a fishmonger's son, yet had once risen to the most powerful office in Hua. An exotic young woman loved him. He still had her, this house, and plenty of money in a bank.

He studied the *weiqi* board. A game of simple rules, yet so complex in strategy. Who had she been playing with? Black stones controlled the board, with her remaining white pieces all in precarious positions. Whoever it was appeared to be thoroughly beating her, something beyond belief in itself. Though Leina might be naïve, without a mind for real strategy or politicking, she excelled at these kinds of games.

Leina reappeared and placed a tea cup in front of him. She flashed a demure smile.

Beaming back at her, he drew in the sweet scent and took a sip. A comforting warmth trickled down his throat. "Who were you playing against?"

She cocked her head. "Myself."

"You did not give yourself much of a challenge."

Leina grinned at him. "Much earlier in the game, the white side had a seemingly insurmountable advantage. Unfortunately, it left insignificant gaps in its lines. Black was able to exploit what appeared to be white's strengths, but were ultimately weaknesses."

So confusing! How could she see all of it? Hong took another sip of the tea. "Does white stand a chance now?"

"There is always a chance, no matter how improbable." She giggled. "I guess if we bent the rules so white could play four pieces at once... just like when I swapped some white pieces for black earlier."

Hong laughed. "But that's cheating."

"Nobody said life was fair." She shrugged. "As it stands, a fool leads white and black is relentless."

He took a deep swig of tea as his brows furrowed. The silly girl, rambling again. "What *are* you talking about?"

She stared at him, her cheerful demeanor darkening. "You really never saw it, did you?"

"What?" Perhaps his unemployment had driven her mad, despite her earlier claims otherwise.

Pointing at the board, Leina said, "Hua is white. It rotted from the inside while its enemies gathered strength."

He shook his head. "Impossible. How could that happen?"

"You. *You* made it happen. The troop movements *you* recommended left strategic areas undefended. *You* alienated loyal hereditary lords so that they turned their back on the Jade Throne." She blew out a long breath. "And then *you* used magic engraved in art to depose the *Tianzi*."

Thoughts bouncing in his skull, Hong squinted at her. All these things, ideas she had inadvertently given him. Or maybe it hadn't been inadvertent. Maybe... "You...*you* planned all of this!"

Her smile appeared more sad than triumphant. She nodded.

All this time, he had looked down on her. Now... "Why?"

"In its greed, Hua sold muskets and firepowder to Madura, which allowed Madura to conquer my homeland." Tears trickled down her cheeks. "Then, the Madurans let the Bovyans in. Sharing your bed was nowhere near as bad as being used by a dozen of them a day. When First Consul Geros released me and gave me a chance to free my mother, I took it."

All her hate and bitterness! Never was it so evident. Hong's head spun. "Why did he do that?"

"Because my father was a trade official from Hua, and I could use that as a connection to meet a benefactor like you. Someone who could weaken Hua from the inside with the right manipulation."

He was a fool, tricked by a woman. Still, she had made a mistake in revealing it to him. Once

he told Regent Liu, he might be reinstated and she would be executed. He rose to his feet.

Then collapsed back in the chair.

His vision began to darken, and each breath took more effort.

She faded out of focus, and her words cracked beneath her sobs. "You won't be telling anyone. The poison in your tea will give you a merciful death."

Poison! Death! Murdered by his own concubine. The one who had engineered Hua's downfall with him as a pawn. He could have prevented it at any time, if only he had seen it coming.

"Goodbye, Old Hong."

Leina wrung her hands. She had wished for Old Hong's death time and time again, and yet, now that it had come to pass, her heart ached.

He sprawled in the chair, lifeless eyes seemingly locked on the *weiqi* game, the one they had played in real life for the last three years. He wasn't a bad man, just a misguided one. He had cared for her, which was more than she could say about the father who abandoned her or any other man in her life. Most of the time, he had been sweet, albeit patronizing.

Out in the city, sonorous bells tolled a foreboding chorus. Not for Hong's death, but as a warning of impending danger.

Leaning over, she closed Old Hong's eyes with a gentle sweep of her hand. She kissed his forehead, and with one last look at him, turned and left.

It was time to initiate her final plan, the one which would leave the city defenseless.

CHAPTER 26:

Reunions

From the clearing's edge, Ming stared at the site of both his greatest success and greatest failure as a leader. Still incomplete, the Teleri peninsular fort he'd captured and lost bustled with activity. Natives and Bovyans alike worked at packing and moving weapons and supplies, their activity visible across the moat through the unfinished palisade.

Ming leaned in to Jie and whispered, "We must be lost. We didn't pass this on the way."

The half-elf harrumphed. "Can't you picture a map?" The shoulder wound made her even testier than before. Now she knew how he felt when he couldn't draw a bow. He would take the high ground and not rub it in. Plus, even with one good arm, she could still slash his throat in the night. She pointed east, along the moat which spilled into the Great Kanin River. "We forded the tributary several *li* to the north."

Right, north. Probably where the Teleri had cut off his army's retreat, as well. Still, they were stuck. "We can't wade through the shallows, because the Teleri would see us." He pointed at the wide river, which flowed past the fort. "And it's too wide to swim." For Jie, at least, with her arm, but some things didn't need to be said.

"Can we go the way you came?" Tian's gaze shifted from the fortress back to the group.

Ming cringed. It was a wet, bug-infested walk through swamp to the fords. Not all that much easier than just wading across the moat, walking through the fort, and over the Teleri-made bridge.

"Wait," Ma Jun said. "If we can sabotage their supplies here, it might slow their invasion of Hua." The erstwhile imperial guard turned and spoke in the jumbled native language to the shaman Yuha. Tian nodded and pointed, while Yuha shrugged.

Ming had some good ideas about sabotage, but they were leaving him out of the conversation. He grunted at Jie. "I wonder what they are saying."

The irritable half-elf snorted. "Probably that four and a half of us don't stand a chance."

Half? Even after saving her miserable life, *again*, she still insulted him. He jabbed a finger at her. "I am not a half. I would bet—"

"*I* am the half." She studied the ground.

Such pessimism. Ming sighed. It had to be more than the arm stifling Jie's irrepressible nature. He opened his mouth—

"Shhhh, get down." Jie crouched, ears twitching.

Though alert, her expression still looked forlorn. His snappy comment about her worth as a watchdog died on his lips.

She exchanged a few hand signals with Tian, who nodded and whispered something in Yuha and Ma Jun's ears. Yuha sunk low to the brush and crawled northward. Ma Jun crept east.

Ming rolled his eyes. All the secrecy, and he was left out, again. To think there'd been a time when he, Jie, Ma Jun, and his imperial guard comrades had helped those Southerners assault a pyramid. They—

"Don't move, you are surrounded," a shrill voice called from deeper in the forest.

Ma Jun and Yuha froze in place on the ground. Tian pressed his back to a tree, a Teleri longsword in hand. Jie jerked her head and peered somewhere to the west. Even with a bad arm, she still had amazing senses. Ming drew his bow, nocked an arrow and aimed in that direction.

A mop of shaggy brown hair ventured out from behind a tree, and Ming loosed and nocked another arrow. Whoever it was ducked back out of the first arrow's trajectory, and peeked out again. "Hey, I come in peace. You aren't really surrounded."

Tian gaped at the half-sized man who skipped out from behind a tree, Ming's arrow in hand. Too mature-looking to be a child, too short to be a human. The word for the newcomer's race flitted at the edges of his addled recollections. Even more disconcerting was that this same little man appeared in his memories when he watched Layani and Jie fight. Him, and the brown-skinned warrior with the pointed beard.

"Fleet!" Mouth agape, Ma Jun rose and dusted himself off.

"Fleet..." Jie droned in monotone, as if she'd just seen a spirit.

Fleet. The name sounded no more familiar than Kaiya.

"My, my, Ma Jun and Tian." Fleet eyed the rest of them, nodding in turn. "A Maki shaman and Princess Kaiya's bodyguard. And you—" he pointed at Ming, "—the princess' former beau."

The princess' former beau? Tian's eyes bulged. He looked to Ming, who cast his gaze downward. How much more awkward could this get? A woman who he had apparently loved but couldn't remember, stolen from a brother.

"Halfling," Ming said haltingly in the Metal Men's language, "who are you, and how do you know me?"

The madaeri—that was the term—sauntered over and grinned at Ming, twirling the arrow between his stubby fingers. "Your notoriety precedes you. You shouldn't waste an elf-sharpened arrowhead."

Cheeks flushed, Ming snatched the arrow away and shoved it back into his quiver. Jie's lips twitched upward, the first sign of a smile since they'd set off from the wild elf village.

Fleet bent over, revealing a scar on the back of his neck, and rummaged through Ma Jun's pack. He withdrew some dried berries and tossed them into his mouth. "So. My friends in the local tribes speak of a Warrior From Beyond the Wall. I assume it is one of you?"

All eyes turned to Tian. More awkwardness. The locals revered the Warrior From Beyond the Wall, but his exploits were tales Tian had heard but didn't remember experiencing. He shook his head. "I don't remember anything."

"That explains the blank look, despite all the good times we had together." Fleet pulled on his ear. "Then again, you weren't the sharpest sword in the armory to begin with. Maybe some familiar faces will help jolt your memories. Follow me."

Familiar faces? Tian started to speak, but the madaeri disappeared into the woods without a sound. The others exchanged glances and shrugs. "Who's that?" Tian said.

Jie's voice rang with awe. "He helped me track the Water Snake *Moquan* clan in the Eldaeri Kingdoms."

"He guided us through the hills of Iksuvi," Ma Jun said, "during Princess Kaiya's escape from Iksuvius."

Yuha beckoned them to follow. "The Traveler brings good luck. He's visited our village in the past, and always the spirits bless us afterwards."

Probably coincidence, but Yuha hurried after Fleet, so unlike all the caution he'd exhibited over the last several days of travel. With a sigh,

Tian followed, and the rest trailed after him. The madaeri moved quickly, oftentimes stopping to wait for them.

The tumbling of water over rocks grew louder, and a *li* to the east, they arrived at the river bank. A canoe lay partially hidden by shrubs, and the underbrush had clearly been disturbed. Fleet whistled.

Three faces of varying brown shades popped out from behind different trees. The darkest, a pretty woman with a chocolate complexion and coarse hair, smiled broadly. Dirt streaked her white dress, and its band of colored patterns across her chest was faded. One of the men bowed his shaved pate, and a gold disk hanging from his neck spilled out of his ascetic robes. The third...was the other man from Tian's memories. Flowing black hair and a pointed beard, a curved sword in hand.

Ming and Ma Jun hurried forward, exchanging excited greetings with the newcomers, though Jie hung back.

Yuha sidled up to Tian. "It looks like a reunion of old friends."

Tian nodded. "I'd wager there is a story behind this."

"Involving a pyramid," Jie said. "And charlatan priests and magic gemstones."

Pointed Beard strode over. "Well met, Tian," he said in the Metal Men's language, though with a thick accent. "I didn't expect to meet you here."

Tian didn't expect to be here either. He stared at the newcomer. "You look familiar."

"He lost his memories," Jie said, her tone acerbic. "He doesn't know who you are, Sameer."

The man's lips formed a ring. He pressed his hands together and bowed. "I am Sameer. You have saved my life, and I have saved yours." He pointed his chin toward the others. "I, and my comrades Cyrus and Brehane, owe your brother, Ma Jun, and Jie a favor we can never repay. Come."

Frowning, Tian followed Sameer. All this interpersonal history, lost to him. Only Sameer's fighting skill made any kind of impression, and that was through dreams. Up close, the other two looked no more familiar than almost everyone else he'd met since waking from the *Viper's Rest*. Brehane held both of Ma Jun's hands.

"...going to Cathay," the bald man, apparently Cyrus, was saying.

Ming cocked his head. "Whatever for?"

Sameer chuckled. "Princess Kaiya offered to take us to your pyramid."

The image of a four-sided pyramid, by a large lake with blue waters, flashed in Tian's memory.

"Princess Kaiya is in no position to offer anything," Jie said. "And you would have to get through the Teleri army to reach her."

Ming snorted. "Just like us."

Fleet whistled. "I'd warned the princess that the Teleri were heading that way. I didn't expect it to be so soon."

"So what's your plan?" Tian asked Sameer. Maybe they had a better idea.

"We still need to visit the pyramid," Cyrus said.

Sameer pointed at the dugout canoe. "We were waiting until dark to row past the fortress."

A boat. Tian smiled to himself. Why hadn't *he* thought of that when they left the wild elf village? Too bad this canoe wasn't big enough for an extra five people. At least— "Could you ferry us, too?"

"Wait." Ming held up a hand. "The Teleri invasion is supplied from this fort. I know firsthand. We need to destroy the bridge on the other side of the fort."

Fleet stroked his chin. "Sameer and his friends must make haste and can't risk capture by the Teleri."

"However," Brehane chirped in, accent thick, "We can take care of the bridge."

As they drifted by the fort under the cover of darkness, Jie peered at the soldiers on the bridge with her elf vision. Earlier in the day, her heart had raced as she approached the napping Akolyte Cyrus. If he felt the same as Sameer about returning her a favor, surely he would invoke the healing powers of his One God.

She had shaken him awake, and his eyes fluttered open.

"Can't you let a man sleep?" He groaned and turned back over again.

"I need your help." The pleading in her voice sounded pathetic, but maybe this was her only hope. "You *owe* me."

"All right." Grumbling, Cyrus sat up. Sleepy eyes wandered to her injury. "It's about your arm, right?"

She nodded. He had always been perceptive.

"You never believed Athran was the One God," he said.

In fact, she'd mocked Cyrus at the pyramid in Levastya when he had lost his power, but... "I will convert to your faith."

"Right." Cyrus snorted. He withdrew the golden disk hanging from his neck. Clasping it, he placed a hand on her shoulder and chanted in his language.

Warmth flooded through her shoulder, and her pulse skipped a beat. Perhaps she had better invest in a gold disk.

When Cyrus finished his prayer, he opened his eyes and looked expectantly at her.

She reached for her dagger and...nothing. Her shoulder remained just as frozen as before.

"I am sorry," Cyrus said, his voice sincere.

Despite her best efforts to control them, tears had filled her eyes then.

They did again now, blurring the shades of grey and olive of her elf sight as Fleet poled the boat to shore. She wiped her eyes with her good arm and cleared the lump in her throat. To think the only things making her useful were the exceptional senses from the elf blood she hated. Still, she couldn't let Tian see her cry.

Ming, Yuha, Ma Jun, and the Southerners waited on the banks. Ma Jun took her hand and helped her disembark, while Tian and Fleet jumped off with ease after her. She ripped her hand from

Ma Jun's. Her arm might not work, but she was no invalid.

Ming pointed at the bridge over the great river's tributary, some hundred feet away. "Logs lashed together with rope. We tried to use gunpowder to destroy it, but it wouldn't light in the rain."

Or Ming had been incompetent. Jie snorted. She'd imploded Wailian Castle and obliterated a quarter of the Hua embassy in Iksuvius with firepowder.

"We could slash the ropes now," Tian whispered. "From underneath."

Jie shook her head. "It would take too long by yourself. I can't help you, and you are the only one who stands a chance at succeeding without them seeing."

"I'm standing right here," Fleet muttered.

Brehane raised a silencing hand. "We need to get closer. I will use magic, but it will tire me out. I will need you to help me back to the boat."

Jie stared at her. The most impressive magic Brehane had mustered a year ago was putting a bunch of fake Akolytes to sleep, and even that had left her on the verge of collapse from the fatigue.

Yet Sameer and Cyrus nodded at her confidence now.

Fleet pointed a chin at Ming. "You provide cover with your bow. Tian, Sameer, and Ma Jun, come with me just in case we run into some baddies when we approach."

"What about me?" Jie would've thrown her arms up if both had worked.

Fleet grinned. "You guard the boat with Yuha. Cyrus, wait in the boat so we can make a quick getaway."

Guard the boat, indeed. More like, *don't get in the way.* Jie sighed as the others shuffled off toward the fort, making plenty of noise as they did. She tracked their progress as they stepped on pine needles, fallen branches, and dried leaves. It'd be a miracle if they didn't rouse the entire garrison.

Brehane stopped them with an open hand, just thirty-some feet from the bridge. She barked out several guttural syllables. The men in the fort turned and pointed—

An explosion blossomed out from the center of the bridge, erupting in brilliant streaks of sparks and flames. Jie shielded her eyes against the sudden brightness as the ground trembled beneath her. Men screamed, and the fortress descended into chaotic cacophony. The bridge lay in charred ruins. Burning logs sizzled in the water.

Since when had Brehane grown so powerful? Jie met the Aksumi's eyes as she staggered back, panting, supported by Tian and Ma Jun. Sameer followed them, backing away from the fortress with sword in hand.

"Hurry!" Fleet zipped past her toward the shore. "There might be patrols on this bank."

They gathered on the shore, and Sameer helped Brehane into the boat.

Fleet waved. "We part again. Perhaps we will meet again, in Hua."

Jie stared at the madaeri. How would the three Southerners get past the East Gate? How would *they* get past the East Gate?

CHAPTER 27:
Loose Threads

Stomping boots, swishing robes, and garbled conversations in the palace grounds below interrupted Kaiya's fleeting moments of quiet and peace. With just a couple of hours before the generals and Chief Minister Song arrived, she had cleared the Hall of Supreme Harmony in hopes of collecting her thoughts.

It was not to be.

The double doors opened, revealing Cousin Kai-Hua. With husband Liu Dezhen and a pair of imperial guards in tow, she cradled the new *Tianzi* in her arms. Asleep and innocent, beautiful as only a baby could be, he was an unwitting pawn in a power struggle which promised to continue despite all the oaths of loyalty and pledges of support.

Kaiya relinquished the central dais and knelt on the floor before it. Her cousin stepped up and, bowing deferentially to the Jade Throne, took a seat. With the dizzying shifts of fortune, Kai-Hua must have been bewildered. Nonetheless, she had always been a close confidante. If not for the awkward circumstances, the two would likely have hugged.

"Cousin... Queen Mother," Kaiya said. "It is good to see you again."

Kai-Hua nodded. "Yes, Kaiya... *Jie-xia*."

"*Jie-xia*." From his place next to his wife, Liu Dezhen bowed low. "Forgive me for my outburst earlier. I am grateful for your patience and confidence."

Kaiya waved a hand. "There is nothing to forgive. As far as I am concerned, until we ascertain the fate of my brother Kai-Wu behind the castle walls, your son is *Tianzi*." She pressed her forehead to the cool marble floors. "I swear to defend him and faithfully administer affairs of state in his stead until he comes of age." Perhaps her maternal ancestor had prostrated herself and spoken the same words to her adolescent son three hundred years before. Unlike the Founder's consort, Kaiya would relinquish her position. She raised her head.

Liu Dezhen and Wang Kai-Hua bowed. She smiled when she straightened, but the glint in *his* eye didn't inspire confidence. Kaiya's spine pricked. Perhaps a knife in the back awaited her later. Queen Regent Wang Yuxiang had faced several challenges to her rule, all underhanded and life-threatening.

Kaiya held a low bow as they left the hall.

"*Dian-xia*," a female voice called from the entrance.

Rising, Kaiya returned to the bloodwood chair beside the Jade Throne and squinted at the doors.

With Doctor Wu and Weiyong at her side, handmaiden and body-double Han Meiling bowed as much as her enlarged belly would allow. Sacrificed so that Kaiya could escape a doomed city, Meiling was yet another one of Emperor Geros' rape victims. Kaiya's own womb twinged. Memories of his calloused hands sent a chill up her spine and squeezed her chest. The fear disappeared as quickly as it appeared, the emotional armor of the *Tiger's Eye* forming up.

Hands supporting her stomach, Meiling tottered to the front of the room and started to kneel.

Kaiya held up a commanding hand. "As you are, Meiling." She stood and bowed at the waist. "I am so sorry for what you endured in my defense."

Meiling shook her head. "It is my honor."

More like a dishonor, at least in the eyes of a man looking for a virgin bride. Meiling had probably hoped to improve her marriage prospects by serving as an imperial princess' handmaiden. Kaiya forced a regal smile. "If you wish it, after you give birth, I will adopt your son and arrange a suitable husband for you."

Meiling blew out a sigh and bowed. "As you command, *Dian… Jie-xia*."

"Please take care of yourself in the meantime." Kaiya gestured toward Weiyong and Doctor Wu. "My doctors are at your disposal."

Weiyong's face flushed. It was cute in its own way. He supported Meiling as she shuffled backward toward the exit.

As if Kaiya's own twins weren't enough responsibility, she was volunteering to take on a third child. She watched as Meiling departed and passed by three new petitioners. Behind the palace chamberlain stood a short human male with a rough, sun-drenched complexion and long brown hair. He supported a woman with a lighter bronze skin tone and unruly red hair. A free hand cradled the swell of her belly.

The chamberlain stepped over the threshold and bowed low. "I present—"

Kaiya bowed. "Prince Aelward of Tarkoth and Princess Alaena of Serikoth. I owe you both a great debt of gratitude."

"That you do, lass." Prince Aelward chuckled. "Little did I expect to see you in the big chair."

Kaiya bowed to the Jade Throne and shook her head. "No, my baby cousin sits here. Until he comes of age, I will act as regent."

"Then perhaps you can repay those debts of gratitude." Princess Alaena gritted her teeth. There had been no sign of a pregnancy four months before, when her rangers and Tian had rescued Kaiya from ogres, but now she looked even more pregnant than Meiling. Which meant Tian was not the father. Maybe the elf Thielas. The two had seemed close.

Prince Aelward nodded. "Princess Alaena's baby is due in a month, and I had hoped to have her resting in Vyara City by then. However—"

"He is coming sooner," Alaena said. "I am sure of it. I want a good midwife."

Always so blunt. Kaiya nodded toward Doctor Wu. "My personal doctor will see to your needs. However, Cathay might not be the safest place. A Teleri Army with Emperor Geros at the head is just a day away."

Aelward and Alaena exchanged glances as Doctor Wu approached and placed her wizened fingers over the princess' wrist.

The doctor looked up and nodded. "Yes, your boy will come in three days."

Kaiya gestured toward the doors. "I suggest that you return to the Invincible in Jiangkou so that you might make a quick escape if need be. Doctor Wu will accompany you."

"Thank you," Prince Aelward said. "I also have bad news. Ayana Strongbow died peacefully in her sleep."

"My condolences." Kaiya bowed her head. The old elf wizard had guided her in magic and helped during the confrontation with Avarax. A loss, to be sure, even if the *Tiger's Eye* prevented Kaiya from feeling it.

The Eldaeri prince and princess turned and departed with Doctor Wu, passing yet more familiar faces waiting outside.

Iskuvi's refugee Queen Ausra stepped over the ghost-tripping threshold, with her husband's two teenage sisters at her side. A wet nurse bounced a toddler on her hip—the queen's nephew and heir to Iksuvi, except…the queen herself cradled yet another baby. Which meant, if he were hers, she had been pregnant when they fled Iksuvius; and she now held the new heir in her arms. He appeared especially robust, even for a baby of Nothori stock.

All of the newborns and babies and pregnant women. A fluttering erupted in Kaiya's heart. To think she would be joining these women in motherhood before long, glowing...no, the supposed radiance was no more than an illusion conjured by poets to assuage fatigued, sleep-deprived mothers.

"Princess Kaiya, I was surprised to hear of your sudden return." Queen Ausra curtseyed in the fashion of the North, at least as well as she could while holding her treasure. "We heard only rumors of your escape from my homeland. I did not know what became of you until I received your summons just now."

Kaiya nodded. "The last time we met, I sent you into exile on a Hua ship. I am afraid I must do the same now. A Teleri Army of fifty thousand, with Emperor Geros at its head, is only a day away."

The queen sucked in a breath. "So the rumors are true. Fifty thousand. No one is safe."

"No. Least of all your son, the heir to an occupied nation, a symbol of its hope."

Queen Ausra nodded. "Born in safety because of your assistance."

So the child was King Evydas' son. Kaiya pointed to a captain at the doors. "His men will escort you to Jiangkou, where you will board a trade ship bound for Ayudra Island. I will make arrangements for you to stay at our embassy in Vyara City."

"Vyara City." The queen sighed. "When we spoke of Vyara City at the banquet, it had been about nostalgic memories." She rocked the baby. "To think Iskuvi's heir will be nothing more than a pauper there."

A pauper, like the Ankirans whom Kaiya had met, forced into exile by the same Madurans who now invaded Hua from the South. In selling muskets and gunpowder to Madura, Hua had invited a future enemy to its doorstep. As regent, she would have to consider recent history in order to formulate future policy. If the realm survived the current crisis...

Boots clopping across the Hall of Supreme Harmony drew Kaiya's gaze up from the queen. Minister Song shuffled behind three generals, who strode down the center of the room. Helmets were tucked under their arms, and capes flowed behind them.

All three dropped to a knee, fist to the ground. Minister Song bowed low. "*Jie-xia*," they all shouted.

The title of regent still sounded strange in her ears. She nodded at them. "Generals, I would hear your plans for the defense of the capital."

"As you command, *Jie-xia*." General Tang unfurled a huge map, the length and width of two men, with the help of the others. "Fifty thousand Teleri heavy infantry march on the highway, a day away from the city. We have eight thousand imperial infantrymen and a thousand cavalry, as well as a smaller number of provincial soldiers, at our disposal."

Kaiya kept her face impassive, just as her father would have. Still, even with her lack of military acumen, the odds did not sound promising. "How about the bulk of our soldiers in the South? They must have seen the light towers' signals. They could help bolster the city's defenses."

"No, *Jie-xia*." General Shan shook his head. "Our armies in the South are holding off an onslaught from the rebel Peng and his Maduran allies."

Kaiya buried a snort. Somehow, a treacherous cousin who wanted her dead had managed to ally with a lecherous prince who wanted her in bed. "What if they retreated to the city?"

General Shan pointed to the map. "We would cede control of the central valley and the food supplies it provides to Peng."

Looking at the map, it made sense, but— "If the capital falls, there will be no need for those supplies. We are overwhelmingly outnumbered."

General Tang cleared his throat. "If I may, *Jie-xia*. The Jade River and city walls negate the Teleri's numerical advantage. If they assault the north gate over the bridge, our guns would decimate them."

The bridge was wide enough for thirty men to walk abreast. Kaiya frowned. The stakes were too high.

"Before they could even form up on the other side of the river," General Shan added, "they would be in range of our cannon."

"Are there any places where they could ford?" Kaiya pointed and traced a line along the Jade River and Sun-Moon Lake.

"No, *Jie-xia*," the third general said. "The heavy winter snows have led to higher water levels. The only place any army could cross would be east in Dongmen Province. Even then, they would have to conquer Linshan Province to reach the capital."

For whatever reason, the *Tiger's Eye* faltered. Her chest tightened. Heavy winter snows had stranded her in the Wilds, yet now helped defend her against Geros. It would be welcome news if the Teleri fell back to Dongmen Province, where she had sequestered herself for two weeks waiting for Zheng Ming.

Still, that left all the people in the towns and villages north of the river undefended, with no way of escaping. The women, falling prey to the depravations of the Bovyan scourge...her stomach clenched.

Again, the emotions disappeared just as quickly as they had surfaced. They *were* safe. Unless... "Are there any towns where they could commandeer boats?"

General Shan shook his head. "Not enough to ferry over a credible threat before we discovered them. I will assign the cavalry to patrol the river to ensure that."

She turned to Minister Song. "Minister, you will manage the non-military aspects of the crisis. Generals, I entrust the defense of the city to you."

A river and city walls stood between them and the invaders. It should have been reassuring. Still, Emperor Geros had proven resourceful and unpredictable.

Astride his horse, Emperor Geros led his army through a village on the highway. Cathayi peasants lined the road, holding low bows. An industrious yet docile folk. No wonder Cathay's founder had unified the lands with so little effort, and then prospered. The grains in the North and rice in the South would all feed the Teleri's righteous cause in the future.

A runner pounded a fist on his chest. "Your Eminence, a message from your spy inside the capital." He proffered a tightly wound piece of paper.

Rice paper, from Leina. Geros unrolled it and read.

City in upheaval. Only 10,000 defenders. Camp outside the city. Approach under flag of parley. Await my signal.

It would be some signal. Geros grinned. Whereas the Teleri used Eldaeri messenger birds, stolen from Tarkoth a century before, Cathayi news travelled at the speed of ships and horse relays. It only took the right bribe at the right time and place to paralyze their communications systems. How surprised Princess Kaiya would be to find fifty thousand Bovyans at the city walls.

Geros looked south. They could be no more than a day away at their pace. If he took off on his horse, he could be at the city and closer to his love by early afternoon.

He snorted. A fool's errand, obviously, one which only a besotted rube like Prince Dhananad would take up. That proved the Altivorc King wrong about Geros eschewing strategy. He turned and beckoned the only non-Bovyan in his army forward.

Feiying jogged up and pounded his fist to his chest. "Yes, Your Eminence?"

"Take a horse and set off for Huajing. You will find Leina in the Floating World, at the Jade Teahouse. You are to assist her in weakening the city's defenses, but your first priority is to steal the imperial regalia from the Temple of Heaven."

Master Feiying gawked for a split second before his expression blanked. "Yes, Your Eminence."

CHAPTER 28:

Home is Where the Heart Is

The last time Ming had looked at the Great East Gate, Emperor Geros had paraded him as a prisoner of war. Now, with Guanyin's Eye almost completely open, and Renyue less than a half-crescent to new, he stared through the darkness at the gatehouse parapet. A single Teleri soldier paced, torch in hand. Just enough to illuminate himself, leaving Ma Jun and Jie shrouded in darkness on the ground just outside the gate.

Unable to accompany his cuckold of a little brother up the Wall, the irritable half-elf grew even more sour. Maybe a fight would be good for her, or at least put her out of her misery.

Yuha tapped him on the shoulder and pantomimed something. It was either a buxom maiden or torrential rain. With the only female around being a flat-chested spy, and not a cloud in the sky, Ming grumbled to himself. If only the shaman could speak Hua. Though it wasn't like they could even hear each over the roar of the waterfall in the distance.

Yuha jerked a finger three times at the gate.

Rising, Jie and Ma Jun rushed toward it.

Drawing his bowstring, Ming aimed and shot. The arrow arced and lodged in the sentry's face. The torch floated off the Wall and extinguished halfway down.

Now, Yuha scampered across the yard between the tree line and the gate. Arrow nocked, Ming ran after him.

Back against a wall, Jie held position just inside the gate. Light bauble lamps stood mostly shuttered, allowing for only a dim light. Ma Jun and Tian were nowhere to be seen. Ming met her gaze and raised an eyebrow. Her pointed ears twitched. She pointed toward the other side of the gatehouse, then up.

A muffled grunt emanated from somewhere nearby, and Ming raised his bow. Footsteps approached, followed by a sword-wielding silhouette.

"Hold, Ming," Jie said. "It's Ma Jun." How she could tell, he could only guess. He certainly wasn't going to ask and let it go to her head.

Ma Jun neared and sheathed his weapon. "I took care of two soldiers, but there don't seem to be any others on this level."

With a nod, Ming pointed up. "Only one on top of the gate." With one of his elf arrows stuck in his skull. He'd have to retrieve it, even if it was the one the little halfling had put his grimy paws on.

"Only three others on the second level," said Tian from somewhere in the dark, "as well as our own winch operators."

It was still hard to believe his little brother was such a skilled killer. Ming scanned the darkness. "Why would the Teleri leave such a small garrison?"

Tian's voice spoke again, this time just a few feet away. "In their minds, they control everything. Between their heartland and here. They need only hold strategic points."

"Once your father swore fealty to the emperor," Jie said, "the Dongmen provincial army became the Teleri rear guard. The soldiers serve the

Tai-Ming lord without question, and now he serves the Bovyans."

Ming gritted his teeth at memories of Geros' condescending attitude. It made Father's capitulation, after having sworn fealty to the *Tianzi*, all the more unbelievable. Where was the sense of loyalty he'd always instilled?

"What about the imperial garrison?" Ma Jun counted on his fingers. "There must be at least five thousand national soldiers here. They would have resisted the invasion."

Ming shook his head. "Against fifty thousand Teleri and ten thousand provincial soldiers, they would've been slaughtered. I don't blame them if they surrendered."

"There must be someone loyal to the Jade Throne here," Ma Jun said.

"Count Du in Pujin." Ming pointed south toward the great falls.

Jie waved in another direction. "That way."

"Watchdog *and* compass," Ming muttered under his breath.

"It doesn't matter," Ma Jun said. "We got past the Wall; now we can go to the capital and find the princess."

Ming shook his head. "No, from here we have a chance to attack the Teleri rear."

"But we've already cut off their supplies." Jie drew a hand across her throat.

"The invaders will just live off the land," Tian said, "and as long as our father serves the emperor, the province will provision them."

Ma Jun held up a hand. "You will need an army."

Ming grinned.

Tian's city of birth seemed just as foreign as the wild elf village and every other place he'd visited since coming out of the *Viper's Rest*. Yet one thing felt out of place as he walked at Ming's side: the people who ventured out of tidy wooden stores and into the stone-paved streets looked downtrodden.

There were very few, as well. In the six and a half *li* from the city gates to the castle walls, only forty-two citizens had passed by. Not enough to make just one of the three market squares he passed seem busy. If Tian didn't know any better, he'd think a plague had settled over the town.

He turned to Ming. "How many people live here?"

Ming kept his focus on the castle, as he had the entire walk. "Seventy thousand, maybe?"

Too round a number, but it would suffice. With the lack of patrols, without even the Metal Men around, it was a wonder the populace wasn't rioting. "It's too quiet."

"Huh?" Ming tore his gaze away from the castle. "Oh. Right. Yes. That's the sound of a subjugated people. *Our* people."

Tian met a lone commoner's eyes, and the man immediately stared down. Perhaps all of the lands Beyond the Wall would end up like this if the Metal Men succeeded.

A woman's scream rang out from down a side street they had passed twenty-six feet back. Ming froze in place and whirled around. Tian followed his line of sight.

Sounds of struggle arose. Men laughed. One of the four said, "Come on now, the fun is just starting."

Tian hesitated. They had to get to the castle...but they couldn't just let four men take advantage of a woman. He looked at Ming.

His brother's face flushed red. He unslung his bow and marched back toward the unseen commotion. Loosening the heavy Metal Man sword from its sheath, Tian hurried to keep pace. They turned the corner, and Ming already had an arrow nocked and ready to fly.

He lowered the bow and gawked.

Tian too, hesitated. It wasn't Metal Men pinning a young woman's hands to the wall. Soldiers from Beyond the Wall, wearing light green tunics with a twin mountain symbol stitched into the left breast, touched her in inappropriate places.

"Stand down." Ming's voice carried a tone of authority, though certainly his raised weapon punctuated the command.

The men backed away, hands raised. The young woman gathered her tattered clothes around her and scampered away. Poor girl. Tian started to follow.

Ming raised a hand. "Soldiers of Dongmen are supposed to uphold propriety and honor, shining above mountains like the symbol emblazoned over your heart. Has becoming vassals of the Teleri wolves turned us into rapists? No, even the Teleri don't rampage in the streets, taking lone girls at will. You aren't even wolves, you are pigs."

One of the men opened his mouth, then closed it as his eyes widened. He dropped to his knee and bowed his head. "Young Lord Zheng! Please forgive us."

Gawking, the other men followed his lead. Tian tightened the grip on his sword. Unless they did something to silence these rogues, news of their arrival would be on every mouth.

Shutters from second-floor windows opened and faced peeked out.

"It's Young Lord Zheng!"

"He is alive!"

"He's returned!"

Voices rose not just in loudness, but in hope. They *adored* Ming. How could they not? In the forest, he looked lost and childish; now, his aura commanded respect. Even in ragged clothes.

Bowing, the lead soldier pulled a sheathed broadsword from his sash and held it up in two hands. "My Lord, I have dishonored Dongmen with my actions. You may take my head if that will allow me atone for my men's actions."

Ming received the weapon and unsheathed it. He was really going to execute the soldier. Without hesitation, the man brushed his hair to the side and exposed his neck. His comrades rushed up to his side and bowed.

One of them sank to both knees. "Please, Young Lord—"

"Silence." Ming's tone carried a lethal authority in it. "The condemned will announce his name and rank."

"Ku Wenshen, Lieutenant of Dongmen's Third Infantry Division."

Ming raised the sword. "Ku Wenshen, I presume the Wen in your name means cultured. You have tarnished not only your province and unit, but your own name." The blade swooped down.

Tian turned. Certainly not because of gore, when he'd seen so much. So why? Despite the heinous crime, public beheading was too cruel a punishment. He looked back.

Ming's blade rested a hair's width from Ku's neck. "Soldier of Dongmen," he said, "I have come to cut away the blight left by the Teleri. Rise now. Your honor will be restored when you find the girl and give her family three months of your pay."

Hair stood on the back of Tian's neck. His brother had such indomitable strength of spirit. A tear gathered in his eyes.

Likewise, tears plopped from Ku's face onto the pavestones. "Thank you, Young Lord. I will commit to becoming a better man."

"Good," Ming said. "Now, tell me where the imperial soldiers are."

"Disarmed and confined to barracks, Young Lord." Where they couldn't pose a threat to their father.

Ming patted him on the shoulder. "Take your patrol and go to the barracks and tell the guards to release the imperials into my custody. Have them brought to the castle."

"That is treason against the lord!" One of the soldiers whipped out his broadsword and swung.

Tian had a dagger in hand, but Ming was in the way. Yet Ming held his own, deflecting the swing with a loud clang before reversing the cut and hacking across the dissenter's arm. Blood sprayed, and he man staggered back several steps, holding the wound. The sword slipped from his fingers and clattered to the ground.

Ming pointed the tip of the weapon at him. "The lord committed treason against the *Tianzi*, who holds the Mandate of Heaven. Drop to your knee and swear allegiance to the Jade Throne."

The soldier looked to his comrades, who forcefully nodded. Still holding his arm, he submitted as commanded. "I swear my life to the *Tianzi*."

Ming turned to Lieutenant Ku. "If he shows any sign of violating his oath, execute him. I *will* see that all of Dongmen recognizes the *Tianzi's* authority. "

Ku bowed. "As you command, Young Lord."

"And so begins our army." Ming grinned at Tian.

Only if these soldiers succeeded in convincing their superiors. Tian forced a smile.

Ming could never imagine his province's soldiers behaving so barbarically. Father had always chosen quality men, those of martial skill and high caliber. Now, he had let them become roving bandits, shirking the rule of law in favor of the rule of might.

He glared past the bridge over the moat, to the castle gate, and growled. No. Not in his province. Not in his hometown.

The double doors swung open, revealing the gasping chamberlain. "Young Lord Zheng! I did not believe that you had survived in the wilderness, and... Young Lord Tian." The man paled, looking as if he would faint. "I...I...will summon the lord and lady. Come in, come in."

Holding a low bow, a page shuffled forward and extended his arms to receive their cloaks and weapons. Ming placed his cloak and sword in the boy's hands, but kept his bow strapped to his back. Tian just stared while the page waited. With Ming's prodding, Tian proffered his blade.

Advisors and servants bowed as they passed. Ming afforded them nonchalant nods, yet kept gazing at the walls. So many memories in these halls, of Father teaching them the virtue of

service to the *Tianzi*. The responsibilities of ruling a province. How could he have made a deal with the Teleri?

In the corner of his eye, Tian might have been dancing, the way he startled at the nightingale floor's chirp. An efficient killer or not, heart thief or not, he was still a little brother.

The double doors to the audience chamber slid open. Soldiers dressed in light green Dongmen livery lined the walls. Directly ahead, his father, the *Tai-Ming* lord, sat cross-legged on the central dais. From where she knelt to the left, Mother stumbled to her feet. Among several officers on the floor to either side of the dais slouched his second brother Lun, arm in a sling. He had survived the gruesome wounds, but looked too pale. Ming's own fault for his defeat at Emperor Geros' hands.

His third brother Shu was nowhere to be seen. His gentlest of brothers—now that Tian had turned out to be as deadly as the half-elf demoness—hadn't been injured at all, so where was he now?

Almost as disconcerting as Shu's absence was the Teleri presence. A Bovyan of Kanin stock, dressed in a high-collared uniform, sat on a chair behind and to the right. Several fair-skinned Bovyans formed a semicircle around his parents on the dais.

"Ming! Tian!" Mother staggered forward off the dais, her eyes glistening. "You're alive." She wrapped Tian in a tight embrace, though his expression betrayed no emotion. He tentatively hugged her back. Of course he wouldn't remember that she loved him most of all. "Is it true, that you married the princess?"

Tian cast him a sidelong glance at Ming before turning back to their mother. "I think...yes."

She squeezed him tighter. "So the children are yours." She released him, and turned to clasp Ming's hands. Warmth radiated between them. "Oh Ming, I was so worried those ghastly Bovyans had killed you. I didn't believe what their lying brute of an emperor said was true, that you had escaped."

"Yes, Mother. We are home now. I am happy to see you." Ming guided her toward the dais. While she returned to her kneel at their father's side, Ming sank to his knees and placed the elf bow on the floor in front of him.

Tian knelt as well, though the look on his face bordered between confusion and scheming. Was he assessing the threats? Devising an escape?

Father cast a rare smile, perhaps the first one in years. "Welcome home, Ming, Tian. I am overjoyed to see you alive. And safe."

"We cannot be but so safe." Ming pointed his chin at the Bovyan leader, who listened to another whispering in his ear. A translator, perhaps. It didn't matter if they understood or not. "Father, I had hoped rumors of your collaboration with the Teleri were just that."

His father looked at the leader before turning back. "Son, I had no choice. The realm is falling into chaos. The *Tianzi* has lost the Mandate of Heaven. Emperor Geros appointed me Viceroy of Cathay."

Ming harrumphed. "So he gave you the highest seat in Hua. As long as the Bovyans rule, that will be no better than a chamber pot. Besides the honor of becoming a puppet, what else did they offer you?"

"You." His father might have shown no emotion, but his tenor cut through the air like an arrow. A magical elf arrow, maybe. He gestured at Lun. "And your brothers."

Ming pointed at his father. Impudent, to be sure, but warranted given the severity of treason. "We all swore allegiance to the *Tianzi*. We are all ready to sacrifice ourselves to keep the realm free and prosperous. All you had to do was hold the gate. Our lives, your new positon, aren't worth tarnishing your name in history."

His father scowled. *Actually* scowled, sending a chill down Ming's spine. "Do not take that tone with me, boy. History is written by the victors."

The Bovyan smirked and cleared his throat. "Now that have you exchanged pleasantries, you must speak in Arkothi, the official language of the Teleri Empire."

The gall. Whatever the puppet master thought, this was still Hua. Ming continued in his native tongue. "Father, will you not reconsider?"

Father shook his head. "Never. The Emperor has kept Shu to ensure our loyalty."

"My father taught me that the only thing more important than family was honor."

Father snorted. "He also taught you to be practical. Hua's imperial armies are busy fighting Lord Peng's rebellion in the South, and the Teleri will overwhelm whoever is left. Our province will remain de facto independent, and you will inherit the title of Viceroy."

As if a pretty title meant anything. "The Teleri Directori will rule over Hua and harness our resources toward their war machine."

"An oath is an oath."

"Yes, it is." Ming grabbed his bow, nocked an arrow, and shot.

The arrow drove through Father's right breast. He sucked in a labored breath and coughed up blood. Around them, everyone stared for a full second of absolute silence. Ming's heart fluttered. Had he done the right thing?

Tian jumped to his feet, dagger in hand, and lunged toward their mother. The Hua soldiers all took several steps forward, though Ming now realized they were unarmed. The Teleri all drew swords. One stabbed at Mother, but Tian pulled her out of the way.

Ming shot again and downed the attacker, then nocked and loosed, felling the leader. Nine remained. He leveled the bow at the closest. "Surrender."

The Teleri formed up into a tight square, weapons facing out. Hua soldiers approached, but stayed out of range of the blades.

Ming loosed another arrow. It lodged into another Teleri, who dropped with a choke and a clatter of a sword. "I have more than enough arrows to kill the rest of you twice over."

The Bovyans grunted and mumbled among themselves until their highest-ranking officer ordered a surrender. Some Hua soldiers collected weapons and herded the prisoners into a corner. Other soldiers surrounded Ming, giving no indication who they sided with. Tears filled Mother's face.

"Eldest Brother," Lun said, voice weak. "What have you done?"

Tian cast him a scathing glance. "That wasn't part of the plan. At least you could've given me some warning that you were about to commit patricide."

Stomach clenching, Ming sighed. It hadn't been his initial intention. Father, if anything, was steadfast once he made a decision. Now the one who had instilled in his children a sense of leadership and honor was dying, because he had forsaken those lessons himself.

Father gasped another breath, his shaking hand beckoning. Still alive.

Mother stumbled to his side and propped his head on her lap. Lun, too, huddled in. A lump formed in Ming's throat. He leaned over.

A trembling hand clawed at Ming's tunic. Barely audible, Father's voice rasped. "Fool. Your future was...secure. Now...you must...make your own...name. Make me...proud." His hand slipped away. His eyes stared blankly at the ceiling.

Tears blurred Ming's vision. Maybe he'd made the wrong choice. Maybe with enough convincing, Father would've changed his mind.

No. If Father was anything, it was decisive. No argument in the world would have changed his mind once it was made.

Standing, Ming made eye contact with each of his fellow countrymen before locking on Lun's. "When our children's children read the histories of these trying times, they will learn how we took decisive action in defense of the nation. All of you here today, swear to me that when asked, you will say that Lord Zheng Han of Dongmen Province realized the error of his ways and took his own life as atonement."

The soldiers dropped to a knee. "Yes, *Jue-ye*."

Jue-ye. Now he was *Tai-Ming* Lord of Dongmen. How would history judge him? Ming turned to Father's military advisor. "Mobilize our provincial soldiers and have the commander of the imperial garrison present himself before me." He then nodded at the chamberlain. "Prepare a message for Emperor Geros."

CHAPTER 29:
Explosive

Peng Kai-Long squinted through a spyglass at the imperial army defending the mountain pass between his province and Fenggu. Smoke rose after each volley into the Maduran lines, now whittled down to fifteen thousand as they tried to slam through the bottleneck.

He snapped the glass closed. Prince Dhananad was a fool, convinced by Madura's past victories over pathetic neighbors that a sledgehammer could pick a lock. The Madurans hadn't weakened the imperials as much as he'd hoped, though they had spared Kai-Long's own men from the brunt of the hostilities.

Passing the spyglass to one of his advisors, he grinned to himself. Not only had he minimized losses, his numbers had doubled. Local *Yu-Ming* lords, ostensibly loyal to the *Tianzi*, had come crawling back to him, bolstering the Nanling provincial army to twenty thousand. The ten thousand men under minor lords in occupied Ximen also flocked to his banner, while his ally in Yutou kept the Ximen loyalists pinned down on the coastal road. His chest puffed. Everything worked as he planned.

Kai-Long turned and gazed at his well-rested armies. Only he was fit to rule, the sole descendant of the Wang Dynasty Founder with enough political and military acumen to bring greater prosperity to Hua. Once he left no doubt who held the Mandate of Heaven, the provincial and imperial holdouts would surely choose him over a baby too small to sit on the Jade Throne.

A soldier raced up to the command post and dropped to a knee. "*Jue-ye*, we have intercepted a message bound to Madura from Prince Dhananad."

"Report," Kai-Long said.

"He has asked his father for an additional ten thousand men."

Kai-Long laughed. The Maduran fool had already received ten thousand reinforcements and lost them in several ill-advised charges into the imperial center. In the future, after losing forty thousand of their men in a foreign land, Madura's own capital would be too weak to repel an attack. For now, however, Kai-Long's campaign to liberate the Madurans would have to wait until he consolidated his hold over Hua. "The Madurans have outlived their use. We don't want them depleting our supplies."

"*Jue-ye*, we cannot possibly take the pass without help," General Zhang said. Others nodded in assent.

Kai-Long favored them with a mirthless smile. He had not shared all his plans: the Aksumi Mystic he'd hired to summon the Guardian Dragon of Hua, nor the Black Fist spies who carried correspondence with the former empress Wu Yanli's father in Zhenjing Province. The first would remain secret. "*Tai-Ming* Lord Wu's army holds the western pass into Fenggu, behind the imperial lines. He is amenable to switching sides. When he does, we will attack."

Or rather, once everyone saw the Guardian Dragon of Hua answer Kai-Long's call, perhaps not a single musket need be fired.

In the meantime, he needed to cut off the Madurans. He turned to the messenger. "Send word back home. Detonate the firepowder at the South Gate to seal it off."

A clap of thunder followed a flash of light at the open doors to the Hall of Supreme Harmony. The roar rumbled in from the north, rattling Kaiya in the regent's chair beside the Jade Throne. The military advisors and ministers all looked up, their murmurs mingling with the sound.

"What was that?" she asked.

Chief Minister Song bowed. "I would guess lighting struck somewhere to the east."

It certainly didn't sound like thunder to her trained ears. She gestured with an open hand toward the main entrance, which opened up onto the cityscape. The thunderstorm from the night before had given way to morning sun. It now burned off the fog, leaving the sky a pale blue. "There are no storm clouds."

More chatter among the assembled men.

She sighed. If there *were* a lightning strike, then fires would follow. Alarm bells would be ringing any moment now. "General Shan, send a messenger to find out—"

A low drone bellowed out from a bell in the east. Several others followed. Fires? Certainly the Teleri, entrenched beyond cannon range outside the north gate for three days, had no way of striking inside the city, certainly not in the east.

Could they? Kaiya scanned her advisors, searching for any sign of treachery. Geros had sent a demand to parley. Her sharpshooters had used warning shots to rebuff him. In the ensuing three days of tortuous waiting, the remaining handful of Black Lotus *Moquan* hadn't reported any incursions across the river.

A page raced through the door and down the center of the hall between the rows of men. He dropped to a knee, fist to the ground. "*Jie-xia*, our firepowder magazine in the east exploded."

Kaiya's brow furrowed. That magazine wasn't far from the walls, but it couldn't be coincidental, not with a Teleri army at their doorstep. Though why the east? She turned to Chief Minister Song. "Find out about fires and damage to the walls. I entrust all civilian response to you."

She then faced the military officers. "How would the enemy strike within the city? And why in the east?"

"Perhaps the insurgents are in league with the Teleri," a general said. "Sowing chaos before they strike."

"The magazine is well guarded." General Shan pointed to a map of the city. "We have eliminated most of Peng's rebels inside the city."

Kaiya wondered. She found Weiyong in the crowd, and he looked down. Unbeknownst to her other advisors, Golden Fu manipulated the remaining insurgents, who wouldn't help the Teleri. From what Weiyong had said, Fu was willing to support her, and even take on covert tasks. Then again, despite his proclaimed patriotism, he had an unpredictable streak. "General Shan," she said, "where are the firepowder stores?"

He pointed to eight locations on the map— one in each cardinal directions. His eyes rounded. "They might be trying to neutralize the advantage our guns provide."

Kaiya sighed. With so few troops, the capital's defense relied on their ability to concentrate musket and cannon barrage on the last remaining bridge over the river. It, too, was laden with enough firepowder kegs to destroy it. "Move some of our firepowder reserves to different locations."

Another flash flared at the entrance. Kaiya gripped her chair's armrests, just as another rumble erupted from the northwest. Significantly louder than the previous explosion, the aftershock shook the hall.

She looked to General Shan. "Another magazine?"

"I will find out." The general stood and marched to the doors with several aides in tow.

Kaiya frowned. The northwest magazine was very close to the north gate. If the blast had damaged the walls, they would have to blow the bridge, cutting the northern fifth of the country off from the rest.

Deep horns blared in the distance. A series of poofs burst somewhere to the northwest. Cannons.

Another page appeared at the entrance and bowed low. "The northwest firepowder magazine exploded."

Kaiya rose. "Did it damage the walls?"

"Not that we know of yet, *Jie-xia*."

She pointed. "Those are our cannons firing."

As if to contradict her, the deep bursts stopped, followed by the staccato of a thousand rasping pops. Musket fire? Another series answered, and then another. Twice as fast as the typical Hua volleys. That couldn't be humanly possible. She rose to her feet.

A panting soldier arrived next, dropping to his knee at the threshold. "*Jie-xia*, General Shan sent me to report. The Teleri are attacking."

She held a finger up. "Listen." The volleys prattled on in the distance, the initial frequency falling into perpetual shooting. "We do not fire so fast, do we?"

The soldier met her gaze and shook his head.

Kaiya gritted her teeth. "Then they have guns." But how? Likely taken from the embassy in Iksuvius, and Ming's defeated soldiers. "*Our* guns."

The military men set their jaws and exchanged glances. Many of the ministers moaned and wailed. So pathetic. Even without the *Tiger's Eye*, she wouldn't have devolved into such blubbering. She'd survived assassination attempts, stared down a dragon, been chased by orcs and ogres. No matter how afraid or hopeless, she'd always put on a brave face.

Except when Geros had raped her. Kaiya's heart pounded in her chest. Images of him marching into the capital roiled her stomach. Or

perhaps that was just the morning sickness. The *Tiger's Eye* certainly found inopportune times to weaken. She bit her lip and composed her expression into regal aloofness. "Send word to the gate. They must blow the bridge *now*."

"Yes, *Jie-xia*." Bowing, the soldier stood and ran off.

She sighed. Rebellion and invasion whittled away at the realm. Now, her own decision would cut away the North from the rest.

Geros watched as his men in the trenches fumbled with the Cathayi muskets. They had gotten better with practice, especially after his ingenious idea of specialization. Unlike the locals, who loaded, fired, and backed off to reload, he had several men reload and pass the guns to shooters. Thanks to the Eye of Geros, their shots traced yellow lines across his vision.

Once they conquered Cathay and learned the secret of firepowder, the musket might be worth integrating into their own armies.

For now, he just needed the enemy to waste their own firepowder as they shot blindly into the fog. A cannonball pounded harmlessly into the earthworks not far away, sending dirt flying. The three days of preparation and the wait for the right weather had been worth it.

The first explosion in the east had been the signal to deploy, the second in the north to start shooting. Now, a third explosion roared from the gatehouse, followed by screams and shouts. Enemy cannon and musket fire stuttered to a trickle. Feiying had worked hard in the rain and dark, cutting the barrels of firepowder from the bottom of the bridge so that his men could collect them downstream. He also jury-rigged some explosive device connected to the Cathayi's fuses. They apparently assumed the Teleri didn't know much about firepowder, since as expected, they had just destroyed their own gates instead of the bridge.

"The gates are open!" one of his men yelled.

Geros straightened out his uniform and turned to his signaler. "Order the assault."

The man blew the sequence on his horn. His riflemen continued shooting as they cleared a space for his heavy infantry to pass through. With shields angled up at the walls, the staggered column marched quadruple-time in perfect precision, as only trained Bovyans could.

A runner approached and thumped a fist on his chest. "Your Eminence, a message from Viceroy Zheng in Dongmen Province."

Geros hazarded a glance at the bridge. The enemy had resumed its volley fire, albeit at a slower pace. Lines of yellow streaked across his visual field. He needed to join his men *now*. "Report."

"An army of two thousand soldiers from Linshan Province have crossed the Jade River and plan to sabotage our supply lines." He pointed to a map on the table. "The Viceroy has mobilized ten thousand of his provincial soldiers to combat this threat."

Geros frowned. With that blank expression, Viceroy Zheng Han could bluff Fortuna herself in a game of mahjong. All reports spoke of his staunch sense of honor and loyalty; but then again, he had betrayed the *Tianzi*. Geros motioned for one of his aides. "Leave five hundred men at the north gate once we take it. Make sure that the Viceroy's son *leads* them." Ready to take the first arrow.

"Yes, Your Eminence." The aide thumped his chest.

Geros' heart soared. Grabbing a Teleri flag, he jogged toward the bridge. The head of his column had already entered. "To me, men. The capital of Cathay is ours!"

Soon, very soon, he would be reunited with Kaiya, who according to his spies now ruled as regent of her crumbling homeland. This time, he would prove his love by bringing peace and stability to her nation.

After the third explosion, Kaiya shuffled in the regent's chair. The sound of cannon fire trailed off to intermittent bursts, though musket volleys continued in diminishing numbers and frequency. Perhaps Geros had withdrawn out of range.

The military officers all met her eyes, many smiling and nodding. Of course, with the bridge destroyed, the threat on the capital had ended for now. The Teleri would have to build bridges, and they were no engineers. Their only other choice was to head far upstream and wait for the spring melt to end, before fording the Jade River and fighting through forested Linshan Province. A victory, for now.

At what cost? The great bridge, a marvel designed by the Founder's consort herself, perhaps irreparably damaged. Her people in the north, now under Geros' boot. Her stomach roiled again, the pent-up emotions pushing up against the *Tiger's Eye* dam. It might burst any time now, reducing her into a quivering sack of feelings and doubts.

She leaned back in her chair. No, she had made the logical decision. Leave the bridge in place, and the Teleri would soon occupy the North *and* the capital. "General Tang," she said, "send someone to check on our firepowder stores. We must maintain vigilant watch along the banks to make sure the Teleri do not find some other way to cross."

"Yes, *Jie-xia*." General Tang bowed and started to stand.

A pale, sweating foot soldier rushed into the hall and dropped to a knee. "*Jie-xia*, the enemy has breached the gates. General Shan—"

Kaiya leaped to her feet and raised a hand. "The bridge?"

"Intact. When we went to blow it, the gates exploded instead. General Shan holds the gate tower, while General Sun defends the northwest quadrant."

Chest tightening, Kaiya sunk into the chair and gripped the armrests with sweaty palms. Because the Founder mandated that nothing above one story could be built north of the palace, much of that area was parks and temples. Very little defensible terrain. Outnumbered and apparently outgunned, they didn't stand a chance. Emperor Geros would be there soon, ready to take her again.

Several times a day, for the rest of his curse-shortened life. Those hands, the anger...

Kaiya took a deep breath. Hold it together, she had to hold it together. This wasn't about her, but the nation. Twenty million young women alive today, and untold girls yet to be born, would share her fate. Reduced to playthings and breeders for a depraved race of rapists.

She loosened her fists and stood. "General Tang, what is our contingency plan now that the Teleri have gained a foothold in the city?"

From where he knelt, General Tang bowed. "We will fall back and defend the palace. We have enough munitions and food stores here to last a year."

Kaiya clenched her jaw again. Such a strategy would mean leaving a million souls in the city to predation by the Bovyans. After a year, the Teleri would be thoroughly ensconced, with more and more reinforcements streaming through the Wilds.

With a shaking voice, the chamberlain announced a visitor at the door. How strange that anyone would come at such a desperate time. "Lady Lin Ziqiu brings a message from her father, *Tai-Ming* Lord Lin of Linshan."

Kaiya lifted her gaze from the generals to the seventeen-year-old who had deceived her for so long. She walked with a purposeful stride between the rows of men, her serious expression so different from the carefree flightiness that had defined her for years.

"*Jie-xia.*" Brushing her brown travelling skirts to her knees in typical court fashion, she pressed her forehead to the ground. She looked up and grinned, her capricious mask showing for a split second before returning to dignified serenity. "My father sends his greetings. He is mobilizing twenty thousand of his men to help repel the invaders."

"Thank you for coming," Kaiya said, though Linshan was five days away. By the time they arrived, Geros would occupy the city and could repel them at the east gate. In front of her, the military officers' dire expressions confirmed her worries. There had to be some way to spare the capital from the ravages of Bovyan indiscretion.

What would Father have done? Nothing, perhaps—he had never gone to war. No *Tianzi* from her bloodline had, except the Founder himself. What would *he* have done? She had no way knowing, but... She turned to the military advisors. "What did the Founder say about facing more powerful enemies?"

An officer bowed. "Create the illusion of weakness where you are strong, enticing the enemy to attack."

Kaiya nodded. But still, with nothing save for weakness, there was little need to create any illusion of it. She beckoned another general to speak.

"If the enemy is on the march, dangle out bait and keep him moving. He will tire."

Not likely for Bovyans, but it gave her a thought. Kaiya rose. The imperial armies remained strong in the central valley. There was one piece of bait which Geros had thrown caution to the wind in order to pursue, but it would mean the regent fleeing the capital. "Emperor Geros will pursue me to the Eldaeri Isles and back. I would be the bait to lure him into Fenggu, where our main army can crush him."

A soldier cleared his throat. "Or be crushed by him. Our army would be caught between the Teleri and the traitor, Peng."

Kaiya sighed. Chief Minister Hong's machinations had drawn so many men away from the capital. It was so clear. Maybe even now, he was responsible for the sabotage of the armories. He would need to be tracked down and—

"And, forgive me, *Jie-xia.*" Chief Minister Song pressed his forehead to the floor. "The regent should not abandon the capital."

"Shed your skin like a cicada," General Tang said, "and while the enemy is distracted, you can escape in secret."

Kaiya shook her head. "The point is to make him chase me. There can be no secrecy."

"If I may, *Jie-xia*." General Tang bowed. "It works the other way, too. You have a double."

A very pregnant double who would have difficulty travelling. However, it appeared they had exhausted all other options, and even this plan carried significant risks. Kaiya nodded to the assembled ministers. "Chief Minister Song, inform Meiling of this task. General Tang, prepare an escort. What else needs to be done to create the illusion?"

"Spread disinformation among the populace," an officer said, "that the regent has fled Huajing to join up with the remnants of the imperial army in Fenggu. Enough men to get the Teleri to commit the bulk of their own solders to pursuit."

Lin Ziqiu cleared her throat. "Blow holes in the city's eastern walls so that my father's army can reinforce your men here when they arrive."

Kaiya nodded. It was the logical choice to protect as many people as possible. Even if it meant putting Meiling through more hardship, and risked the utter obliteration of the imperial armies caught between Cousin Peng and the Teleri. Maybe even Peng would put his ambitions aside to save Hua from a foreign invader.

"*Jie-xia*," a voice called from the entrance.

Kaiya looked.

Doctor Wu held up a familiar mirror. "Lord Xu wishes to speak."

Lord Xu! Kaiya's heart leaped through the *Tiger's Eye*. With his formidable magic, perhaps he could find a solution to this problem. She searched the room. "Where is the councilor?"

His image materialized above the mirror, much larger than life, perhaps as large as his ego. He didn't bother to bow. "*Jie-xia*, it is you who must personally go to Fenggu and rally the imperial armies. Only you can do it."

Kaiya snapped her gawking mouth shut. "The regent cannot—"

"—do anything of consequence hiding behind the palace walls." Xu flashed that annoying smirk, the one she hadn't seen in a year.

"Can't you do something to destroy the Teleri?"

He shook his head. "My magic has faded. It is your time. In twenty days, a rare conjunction of the three moons and the energy of Teardrop Lake will allow you to draw on far more power than when you confronted Avarax. Enough to defeat the Teleri yourself."

The famed Godseye Conjunction. It had heralded the start of the Founder's dynasty. Still...Kaiya stared at the floor. "I have lost my magic."

"You will find it again. I have foreseen it."

Her heart pounded in her chest. She would regain her power. More importantly, the realm would be safe. She nodded. "Very well."

"I will meet you there," the elf said. "Bring the fallen star from the Temple of Heaven."

Kaiya looked down at the city map. The Temple of Heaven would soon be behind enemy lines, and even if the Teleri didn't know its significance, she had no way of getting there. In any case, an attempt to remove the artifact, even on order of the *Tianzi* himself, would be met with firm resistance from the priests and monks. She met Lin Ziqiu's gaze. "Find your master. I have a mission that only he can do."

CHAPTER 30:

I Spy

Jie flexed her fingers, but try as she might, her arm wouldn't budge. Sighing, she looked up from her horse, to where Ming rode at the head of six thousand men under fluttering green banners. Tian and Ma Jun rode beside him, with Yuha clutching Tian tightly enough to make her jealous. They discussed what could only be described as a monumental logistical risk.

Ming had sent horse couriers out to the *Yu-Ming* lords, announcing his ascension as *Tai-Ming* and ordering them to join the main provincial army as it marched down the highway. Supply lines would come later. In all, they hoped to muster fifteen thousand men. Still, they would be lucky to acquire a thousand muskets, since the Teleri had plundered the provincial capital's armory. The firearms Ming's army had salvaged were left in the hands of a castle garrison, to fend off any minor lord whose loyalty went only as far as the range of the weapons pointed at him.

Horse hooves rapidly clopped in the distance, making Jie's ears twitch. She spurred her own mount to meet up with the brothers. "A horse approaches." She pointed down the highway.

Unslinging his bow, Ming nocked an arrow. How gallant he looked in his armor and green surcoat, like a member of the Founder's cavalry. Despite his many shortcomings, he would make a fine lord.

If he survived.

She squinted at the cloud of dust up ahead. A green pennant fluttered above the rider. "One of ours," she said.

Once he got closer, the rider leaped from his saddle and sank to a knee. "*Jue-ye*, news from the capital."

"Speak." Ming beckoned the man up.

"Emperor Geros received your message and welcomes your arrival. Also, there were explosions inside the city, and the Teleri breached the walls."

Explosions. Potentially from lightning strikes, but more likely an act of sabotage, given the timing. Jie sucked on her lower lip. As much as they hated the Jade Throne, the insurgents wouldn't work for a foreign invader. Perhaps Teleri Nightblades had infiltrated.

Surely the Black Lotus would be able to root them out. The Nightblades were such amateurs by comparison. Unless the *Moquan* were otherwise indisposed. She turned to Tian. "There are enemy spies inside Huajing, I'm sure of it. Our own army is still seven days away at this marching pace. You and I must go ahead."

And hasten their reunion with the princess.

As distasteful as that would be, the fate of the nation relied on them. How much easier life would be if she hadn't been left at the Black Lotus Temple as a baby. If her good-for-nothing elf father had never abandoned her. She would've never ended up a spy, never met Tian or the princess. Never had to feel as empty as she did now. She ran a hand through her hair.

The hand attached to her bad arm.

Heart pounding, eyes wide, she stared at the arm and willed it to move again. Nothing.

From his hiding place in the abandoned streets, Liang Yu gazed at the eight-tiered stupa. Sparkling in the midday sun, its blue gables stood high above the white marble walls surrounding it. As always, a complement of twenty-four honor guards dressed in ceremonial robes circled the walls. Thirty-two priests now defended the steel gates.

Perhaps Princess Kaiya was sending him into a trap. It certainly wouldn't be the first time she'd tricked him, and all these leader types sacrificed their loyal servants on a whim. The extra protection around the temple might not faze armored Bovyans, but it posed more of a challenge for a middle-aged man.

Maybe not for a pretty young woman.

Challenge accepted. Per his command, Lin Ziqiu intercepted the guard approaching the insertion point close to the rear of the complex. She leaned against the wall, feigning exhaustion. His usual fifteen steps a minute sped up to meet her.

She looked up. "Sir, the Bovyans are rounding up women. Please, help me hide."

The guard's eyes shifted left and right, passing right over Liang Yu's hiding position before settling back on Lin Ziqiu. He beckoned her back in the other direction, toward the main gate, and turned around.

With speed enough to impress a man half his age, Liang Yu darted across the street. Jabbing the walking staff into the ground, he flipped over and drove the climbing claws on his feet into the mortar between the marble blocks, about three-quarters of the way up near the top of the wall. From this inverted position, he curled up, dug the hand claws into the mortar, and pushed himself to the top.

Now at the height of two men above the ground, he crouched and peered down the streets. All empty. Sporadic gunfire popped in the distance. He turned to survey the elliptical temple grounds,

which no commoner had seen since its completion three hundred years before.

The stupa stood at one end, on a circular, three-tiered marble base. Just like the hand-drawn diagram Regent Kaiya had sent with Lin Ziqiu. Or maybe she knew more, but just hadn't told him. No guards prowled the grounds, just a single priest sweeping the marble dais across from the stupa. Still, that priest held the broom like a weapon, and seemed unperturbed by the Teleri invasion.

In fact, he moved with an unsettling familiarity as he looked up and south toward the iridescent moon.

Liang Yu followed his gaze. The moon waned to new, disappearing for a few seconds at noon. Below, eight honor guards entered the compound from the gates, one carrying Lin Ziqiu in his arms. She must have put on a convincing show for them to let her in. He was taking her toward a long rectangular building close to the entrance—the priests' quarters, according to the princess' sketch. The temple administrators would probably have something to say about that. The priest—

The monk had worked himself closer to the stupa, not far from where eight more honor guards emerged.

Too many unknowns! Intentional or not, the princess had given him so little information about the temple: Whether the stupa was one large room or several. How many men defended it. Even the size of the fallen star.

Liang Yu snorted. He was a planner, not an operative. In his day, this would be just the sort of mission The Surgeon Feiying and The Beauty Meiyun would have savored. Always rushing in, trusting their abilities and instincts over the proven benefits of methodical planning. It had gotten Meiyun impregnated by an elf, and Feiying killed.

With so little time before the regent retreated south, there was no choice but to improvise now. Liang Yu slunk along the top of the wall toward the rear of the stupa. Sliding down, he landed like a cat on the marble ground and ran to the base. After a quick glance to assess the position of the approaching honor guards, he ducked under the railing of the first tier and made it to the second, and then to the curved stupa wall. Inching around, he slipped into each of the towering doorways along the way toward the front. Not a single door; all just façades. He continued, stopping where he could just see the approaching guards. A dozen more steps in their agonizingly slow march and they would pass through the doors.

The sweeper...where had that priest disappeared to? Already inside, perhaps. Yet another unknown element, especially with the familiarity of the gait. Who was he? With an ability to make connections equal to his own, and an uncanny memory, Meiyun would have figured out this conundrum already. Yes, with their complementing skillsets, the three of them had made an unparalleled team. With her observational skills, perhaps Lin Ziqiu could be the new Beauty. If he recruited a new, more pliable Surgeon, he could establish a *Moquan* clan to rival the Black Lotus, to serve the most worthy leaders.

One day. For now, there was an unenviable task at hand. The arriving honor guard passed through the entrance, and Liang Yu darted after them. Inside, shuttered light baubles cast the gallery in a dim light. He pressed himself in a column's shadow when the guards came to a halt. One by one, they turned left, marching down a single corridor that appeared to wrap around the stupa's interior. The space between each man allowed the next to always maintain line-of-sight around the bend of the hall.

Unless he went to the left, counterclockwise.

A clear shortsightedness on the part of whoever came up with the pattern. Or perhaps part of the princess' trap. Liang Yu dashed as quickly and quietly as his age-inhibited body allowed. Not six paces later, he ran into a priest. The man's eyes widened as he opened his mouth. Forsaking all stealth, Liang Yu reached him in three long strides and jabbed his walking staff in the priest's solar plexus. His shout died with the blow, and Liang Yu spun around to his rear and seized him in an unremitting chokehold.

One second, two seconds. Only about half a minute remained before the first guard made it around to their position. Three seconds, four seconds. The priest crumpled, his struggles ceased. He would come to a few minutes later with an awful headache.

So much for quiet. Liang Yu raced down the hall, smashing another priest on the side of the head. The princess either knew nothing of the security protocols, or had deliberately set a trap. A little farther, and at last he came to a set of double doors, flanked by two more priests. Before they could unsheathe their swords, Liang Yu knocked them out with two quick thrusts of his staff. None so far, at least to his age-weathered vision, looked to be the sweeper.

The heavy eldarwood doors creaked open with a hard push. A quiet rhythmic whirr pulsed outward, along with a musty smell. Liang Yu stepped into the central hall, scuffing through a year of accumulated dust. Of course, the *Tianzi* had missed New Year's prayers this year, the only time when anyone ever entered the inner sanctum.

Sunlight poured in through eight windows on each of the eight levels. Eight red columns with golden scrollwork reached to a green-and-blue tiled dome. In a niche above, the shard from a fallen star pulsed with a light blue glow. It was all stunningly beautiful, a view only several *Tianzi* and High Priests had beheld for the last three centuries.

Liang Yu squinted. At the height of eighty-eight feet, the chunk's spherical shape blurred in his old eyes. How could he possibly reach it, let alone escape?

A disembodied voice echoed around him. "Surely the Architect has come up with a flawless plan to reach the fallen star."

That voice. So familiar. Liang Yu spun around. A shape dropped down directly in front of him, just outside the entrance. He must have been hiding on the ceiling outside the doors.

The sweeper pointed at the two unconscious priests. "You always had others do most of the dirty work. I was surprised."

No. It couldn't be. The face was too gaunt, yet the thinness almost emphasized Feiying's hard features. Liang Yu's eyes must be opened wide enough to fall out. "You...you are dead."

Feiying grinned. "I thought the same about you. I saw the elf knock you into Vyara City's harbor with a blow that would kill the stoutest warrior. Meiyun and I never found your body."

Liang Yu shrugged. "The *Viper's Rest*. And a peasant girl."

"I never considered it," Feiying said, nodding slowly. Of course, the Surgeon was not so much a thinker as a near-infallible tool for executing complex plans. "To think we are reunited after thirty years in engineering the downfall of the motherland that forgot us."

Engineering the downfall? Liang Yu nodded, but wondered. Betrayal had only strengthened his own resolve to root out corruption and favoritism in the realm. Apparently, it had pushed Feiying to treason.

It must've been him working for the Teleri, which could account for his disappearance long ago. He was likely the one behind the Bovyans with *Moquan* skills, the one the Black Lotus Clan had sent Princess Kaiya's half-elf to Arkothi lands to root out so many years before. Now, his reemergence could explain how the enemy had struck within the city. Though with Feiying's particular skillset, he must have a contact working on the inside to guide him.

Time to find out who. Liang Yu said, "I was never told about you. I thought I was the only asset inside the city."

"I've only been here for a week, and then it took time for me to contact her. The Floating World is infested by the Black Lotus."

So the contact worked out of the Floating World. Female. Liang Yu looked back up at the shard. "What could the Teleri possibly want with it? She never told me."

Feiying followed his gaze. "Me, either. Legitimacy perhaps. A symbol of imperial rule."

Muffled shouts broke out in the outer hall. The honor guards would've seen the unconscious priests by now. Liang Yu pointed at the doors. "Close them."

"So here we are, together again," Feiying said, starting to shut the doors. "What's your plan?"

"Wait, Master!" Lin Ziqiu slipped through the closing crack, breathless.

Feiying sheathed the sword he'd pointed at her. "Master?"

"Feiying, this is my disciple, Ziqiu." Liang Yu chuckled. "It looks like we have a new Beauty."

Ziqiu cocked her head, but Feiying pursed his lips. Of course. She had no idea who the Beauty was, and he'd always been smitten by Meiyun.

Bad idea to bring up those old scars. Liang Yu looked back up. "I didn't have time to plan. Maybe you could just improvise, like always."

A smirk replaced Feiying's sour expression. He placed a hand on one of the columns. "Spider-climb up between this and the walls?"

"We're old men." Liang Yu nodded to Lin Ziqiu. It would be better for the relic to be in *her* hands instead of the Teleri's.

Eyes scanning the columns, she shook her head. "It is narrow enough on this level with the hallway wall, but it flares out from the second level."

Curse his poor eyesight. He squinted at the upper levels, which tapered toward the dome. He nodded to Feiying. "Can you do it?"

"With help." He laughed. "I'm old, but I have kept my body prepared for tasks like this. Ziqiu, meet me on the second level."

Both spider-climbed between the column and the wall to the second-level ledge. Twiddling his index and middle fingers, he described an old *Moquan* trick. She pressed her back against the outer wall while he set his against the column. Foot to foot, they ascended. Easy work for *Moquan* in their prime, but Feiying was no longer young, and Ziqiu was a mere trainee. Outside, the guards pounded on the barred doors. Luckily they didn't have a battering ram, nor the space to use one if they had.

At the top, Ziqiu reached over and grasped Feiying's ankles, and both lunged upward toward the lip beneath the dome. Feiying caught it, and then swung her up on the other side. They worked so well together, like he had with Meiyun before. They'd been a great match, really, and it was a shame she never loved Feiying like he did her.

Maybe their Vyara City mission would've ended differently.

Feiying examined the dome's interior, then donned his cat-claws. The scraping of the spikes into the mortar between the tiles sent dust dropping. It was excruciatingly slow. The pounding at the door got louder, and the bar buckled.

At last, he made it to the niche. With one hand, he scooped the fallen star out and tossed it to Meiyun...Ziqiu. How uncanny, the way these two worked together, just like the Surgeon and the Beauty.

"Now how do we get down?" she asked.

"Watch." Feiying swung again and landed on the ledge. He scooted over to a column, and then lowered himself down. Wrapping his arms around the column, he made it look easy as he slid down.

Ziqiu stalled on the ledge. "My arms aren't long enough to do that!"

Liang Yu sighed. Now she was stuck, with the imperial regalia.

Another hard smash into the door. They were running out of time.

"Don't worry about me," she said. "You divert the guards, and I'll find a way to escape and get this to Princess Kaiya."

"What?" Looking first to Ziqiu and then to Liang Yu, Feiying drew his curved sword. "Who are you working for?"

Heart racing, Liang Yu separated his staff into a sword and spear. He sank into a defensive position and angled himself away from Feiying's strong right.

"You still work for *them*, even after they left you for dead." Feiying snorted. "Join the winning side. We'll hunt down the Black Lotus, and establish our own clan."

Liang Yu shook his head. "Hua comes first."

"Still a slave. I'd hate to kill you. You know I've always been the better fighter."

It was too true. Liang Yu shifted his stance. The only way he would survive this encounter is if the honor guard broke through the doors and created a distraction.

Unless he came up with a good plan.

Like showing weakness where there was strength. Simultaneously attacking and defending. Liang Yu turned to expose his ribs.

Feiying lunged forward, blade sweeping. Liang Yu lifted his sword to defend while thrusting with his spear.

An elementary move, one which Feiying easily avoided. Liang Yu followed up with a sword chop and another spear stab.

After an initial parry of the sword, Feiying followed with a downward slash, cutting into the spear haft. He might as well have yawned. "Come now, Liang Yu, I know all your moves. You follow such a predictable script."

Liang Yu disengaged and flipped the spear back. The precise cut went at least halfway through the shaft, two handlengths from the blade, rendering it useless.

As a spear, at least.

Smashing the ruined weapon across his knee, he finished the break and transformed the spear into a knife.

"Not bad," Feiying said. "You've finally learned to improvise. Though now you've lost your reach advantage." He surged in with several quick moves, one which cut across Liang Yu's bicep and another that sliced across his abdomen.

All intentional distractions, surgical strikes meant to weaken first. The pain burned. He staggered back.

Feiying leaped forward again, but yelped and disengaged. A throwing pin lodged high in his right breast.

Liang Yu looked up, from where the pin had flown. "Ziqiu, I will not survive this. You must escape and warn the regent: the Teleri's agent is a woman in the Floating World."

"Fool." Blood flecked Feiying's lips. The pin must've penetrated his lung. Maybe there was a chance.

The doors burst open with a crack of the bar. Soldiers rushed in.

Feiying swung his sword, the first blow knocking the knife from Liang Yu's hand and the second cutting deep into his right flank.

Such a perfect attack. Pain flared and only grew worse. A ruptured liver, with a precise insertion as only the Surgeon could perform. There was no surviving the wound, but the right plan could eliminate the threat to the regent. He just had to get close enough. Liang Yu thrust with a feeble stab to the right, one which would invite a counter-attack to the left.

Feiying twisted toward the left, as planned. Liang Yu dropped the sword and tackled Feiying, using a hand to drive Ziqiu's pin deeper.

With a moan, Feiying staggered back and fell. The honor guards surrounded them, not that it mattered. Neither of them would live through the wounds. Liang Yu rolled off of him.

Feiying let out a labored chuckle. "I wonder what the Black Lotus will make of this. The Surgeon and the Architect came out of hiding to kill each other. Master Yan will be shaking his head."

"Goodbye, old friend," Liang Yu said. "Even though it ended this way, I'm glad to have met you again."

Feiying nodded. "Now, the Three Young Masters are truly dead, with only a half-elf to show for it."

Half-elf... Princess Kaiya's half-elf, raised by the Black Lotus, was Meiyun's. Liang Yu laughed, even though each chuckle sent pain surging through his body. So obvious, and yet even he had missed it. "She doesn't even know, does she?

Feiying's voice was barely audible. "I told her, but only while she was drugged with *Yinghua* flowers."

Maybe she remembered, maybe she didn't. Liang Yu's vision dimmed. High above, Ziqiu slipped out of the closest window. How had the Architect not thought of such a simple solution?

CHAPTER 31:
City Under Siege

The carriage wheels purred over the city's pavestones. It was a mere whisper in Kaiya's ears compared to the clopping of the three hundred imperial cavalry and the sporadic musket fire. Outside, frightened citizens ran by clutching possessions, oftentimes stopping to bow toward her carriage. An occasional patrol of soldiers passed, the men affording her quick nods before continuing on their way.

In the distance, several crooked columns of smoke filled the air with the smell of burning wood. Thank the Heavens for the *Tiger's Eye*. Her hometown under siege conjured memories of her escape from Iksuvius, the start of the mad flight from Geros. Then, Iksuvi's King Evydas had fought and died in the futile defense of his city. Now, she, the regent, was fleeing hers.

The carriage slowed to a stop, and she looked out the window. They'd reached the southern market square, now abandoned. Vendor stalls sprawled across the flagstones, their remaining valuables strewn about. It was all similar to her dream with Jie, Tian, and the Teleri army; though they were now far from the river docks and not a cloud blotted the blue sky. A stream *did*, however, rustle nearby. Once upon a time, before an earthquake changed its path, it emptied into nearby Qingjinghu Amphitheater, where she'd witnessed an attack on Tarkoth's Prince Aelward over a year ago. Now, White Duck Stream drained into Sun-Moon Lake.

The cavalry commander, Zhuang, rode up. "*Jie-xia*, we do not have much time. The Teleri already control the northwest quadrant. Our scouts say they are marching toward the palace. When they find out you are not there..."

Yes, they needed to have enough of a lead to avoid capture, but not so much that Geros would give up the chase. Which wasn't likely anyway.

"Wait," she said. Liang Yu was supposed to meet her here after he completed his mission. The minutes raced by as she repeatedly checked the iridescent moon. They had to stay ahead of Teleri pursuit, and needed to reach Fenggu in two weeks.

Maybe Liang Yu had failed. Maybe he'd betrayed her. *Tiger's Eye* or not, her heart began to skip.

"Easy, *Jie-xia*." Sitting across from her, up to now forgotten, Doctor Wu placed a cool hand on her knee. Since Princess Alaena had given birth to her baby boy and the elf Thielas had returned to protect the Tarkothi ship, Doctor Wu had not left Kaiya's side. "Xu's predictions are rarely wrong."

From her side, Fang Weiyong, his head still unshaved, nodded. Not that he would know much about the enigmatic elf.

Kaiya lowered her hand from where she'd been fiddling with her hair. A girlish habit she'd abandoned...right about the time Tian shaved her bald. She pressed Tian's lockpick pouch, always concealed in her sash as a memento, even if the *Tiger's Eye* blocked any feeling toward it. "But Lord Xu *has* been wrong, hasn't he?"

The doctor pursed her lips. So much for reassurance. Perhaps abandoning the capital was a mistake. Maybe it would be better to stay and give the people hope.

Kaiya harrumphed to herself. What hope could one woman hiding safe behind palace walls give to a beleaguered citizenry? No, serving as bait, drawing Geros' army out of Huajing, was the most effective way to serve her people.

Light feet pattered across the market. Kaiya looked out.

Dressed in loose-fitting clothes, not too unlike Jie's, Lin Ziqiu stopped several feet away as guards interposed themselves.

"Allow her through." Her voice came out weary. As much as the *Tiger's Eye* stifled her emotions, it did nothing to ease physical fatigue.

Ziqiu appeared at the window and bowed. She reached into the fold of her shirt and withdrew a glowing blue sphere the size of a cannonball. A perfect sphere, like all the other stars still dancing in the night sky. Up close, it was so bright it almost shone through Ziqiu's outstretched fingers.

Kaiya took the fallen star in two hands. And nearly dropped it. It was deceptively heavy, dense like gold or lead. Cool and perfectly smooth and round, the globe reflected in the doctor's eyes. A low pulse emanated from within, sending a shiver through her spine.

The tone! It was always present in Huajing, a barely audible throb every few minutes, magnified by the geomantic perfection of the Temple of Heaven. It was the power she'd drawn on when she healed her brother and father. It resonated so closely now, yet the energy seemed so distant, beyond her reach.

She looked up and met Doctor Wu's smile.

"Soon," the doctor said.

Soon? Would she regain her power soon? Kaiya turned back to Ziqiu. "Where is Liang Yu?"

A tear formed in the girl's eye. "Dead. Killed by an old comrade in our attempt to secure the star."

With a sigh, Kaiya nodded. Though misguided, Liang Yu had the nation's best interests at heart. In the end, he proved his worth. "If we make it through this crisis, I will ensure his name is enshrined in the *Jianguo* shrine with the realm's other patriots and martyrs."

"Just before he died," Ziqiu said, "he mentioned that a Teleri agent worked in the Floating World."

The Floating World. Kaiya nodded again. Ming had spent some time there, and supposedly Hong owned a house... She jerked her head toward Ziqiu. "Chief Minister Hong. Many of his policies led to the realm's state of disarray."

Ziqiu's eyes widened. "No, the agent is a woman. But Hong keeps a half-Ayuri concubine there."

A woman, working for the enemy, to manipulate an old man who just three years ago was a minor official. Kaiya shook her head. What kind of person could engineer so many improbabilities to fruition, and deceive even the paranoid Liang Yu the whole time? Not even Tian, with his ability to see connections, could rival this adversary.

"We must set off now if we are to stay ahead of Emperor Geros." She pointed in the direction of the Floating World, which might as well have been its own city. "I want you to find out as much as you can about this concubine."

Riding at the head of his army through the conquered city, Geros scoffed at Cathayi wastefulness. So much stone used to pave city streets. Garish banners of red and bright yellow hanging from storefronts. Ostentatious ceramics and furniture. No wonder they were such a weak people. He would teach them the value of frugality.

He'd put Cathay's abundant resources, and its industrious but docile tradesmen, to good use. The First Geros' Last Testament bade the Bovyans to bring peace and order to the lands of the old Arkothi Empire. Why not all of Tivaralan?

An aide rode up and thumped his chest with a fist. "Your Eminence. Most of the enemy has withdrawn to the palace. All other resistance is disorganized."

All too easy. "Our casualties?"

"Sixty-four men killed, eight hundred seventy-seven with varying degrees of injury."

Leaving more than enough able-bodied Bovyans to maintain peace. Still, a visit to the wounded would raise morale. "Where are the injured soldiers?"

The aide pointed. "We have set up two field hospitals, one in the central square and one in the northwest park."

A park. An entire stretch of land, wasted by the vanity of the Founder's consort. "Is there any word from Master Feiying?"

"No, Your Eminence."

Geros clenched his jaw. He should have returned from the Temple of Heaven by now. Exchanging the fallen star with the Orc King would ensure a longer life, one where he could see the results of all the plans he'd set in motion.

Soon enough. Though not a Bovyan, Feiying was unfailingly reliable. "Find him at the national temple. What about the firepowder stores?"

"I am waiting to hear from the field commanders."

Geros nodded. "Under a flag of parley, demand an audience with the regent." And in the city's southeast... "Find Leina in the prostitute's district and command her to meet me at the palace." Rewards were due.

The aide pounded his chest again and rode off to convey the orders to underlings. The army marched in perfect unison behind him. Smoke plumes rose in the distance, yet the city remained otherwise quiet. No panic. Citizens lined the streets and held low bows. How easily they submitted. The Nothori and Arkothi peoples were far less compliant at first. Perhaps a sizeable garrison wasn't needed.

With a white flag of parley in hand, one of his officers waited by the moat around the palace. On the other side of the bridge stretched a broad courtyard with no cover. A high wall of white marble rose above, lined with Cathayi musketmen.

Geros dismounted. Squaring his shoulders and drawing himself to his full height, he crossed the bridge with two generals three paces behind him. Muskets followed his every step. Scanning the officials atop the gatehouse, he came to a halt halfway into the courtyard. She wasn't there. "Where is my wife, the regent?"

An official in blue robes stepped forward from the crowd. "She has fled the city."

Fled! Geros jerked a head toward his aide. "You said she was here."

Brows furrowed, the aide nodded.

Geros snorted. Kaiya was smarter than that. She could hole up behind the palace walls indefinitely, but instead risked being caught in the open. He looked back at the minister. "Open the gates and surrender."

The minister laughed. "The palace is a city in itself, provisioned for ten years."

Geros snorted. The gall. "I can wait." Turning on his heel, he headed back over the bridge. He leaned toward the aide. "Deploy five thousand men to maintain order, crush whatever resistance remains, and blockade the palace. "

On the other side of the moat, Leina pressed her palms together in the Ayuri manner. She had certainly aged in the last five years, but still maintained a unique beauty. And a sharp mind. Both were formidable weapons when some men were foolish enough to abandon all sense of logic and reason for a pretty face and charm. She met his eyes. "Your Eminence."

"Leina," he said. "You have done well. I have already sent orders to our garrison in Ankira to have your mother brought here, to be released into your custody."

Leina's lip quivered. Tears welled into her eyes. She sank to her knees and pressed her forehead to the ground. Cathay's weak customs were rubbing off on her. Still, she proved to be a valuable asset. Motivated by dislike of the Cathayi, she might prove an unparalleled advisor in the new regime.

A soldier ran up and thumped his chest. "Your Eminence, Master Feiying is unaccounted for."

Geros stiffened. He needed that artifact. He turned to Leina. "Did he bring anything to you?"

"No, Your Eminence." Leina shook her head. "After he helped sabotage the firepowder stores, he disappeared."

"Return to your home and await further orders. In the meantime, see if you can find out anything about him. You will coordinate our Nightblades."

Leina nodded. "Yes, Your Eminence. But I fear that a man of his particular abilities will not be found if he chooses to remain hidden."

Only too true. However, the straightforward Feiying did not play games. Nor did he have any reason to betray the Teleri. Geros' jaw clenched.

Another soldier approached and pounded a fist to his chest. "Your Eminence, we have news of the regent. She fled south four hours ago in a carriage, escorted by Cathayi cavalry."

Geros slammed his fist into his hand. Without horses, they had little chance of catching her. The stunning victory meant nothing without her or the fallen star. Still, she had nowhere to flee with the Madurans blocking her way out of Hua's central valley. "General, prepare the army for a march. I will chase her across Cathay if need be, and crush whatever army she summons in her defense."

CHAPTER 32:
Occupied Lands

Tian crouched among the shrubs, high on a hill overlooking farmland. The capital's north walls rose through the light morning fog, barely visible. In front of them, a river flowed out of the enormous Sun-Moon Lake.

At his side, Jie pointed at the bridge and the gatehouse, its doors gaping open at strange angles. Black banners emblazoned with the nine-pointed Teleri gold sun declared new ownership. "Does it look familiar?"

Apparently, before his banishment by the *Tianzi* himself, he had passed through these gates dozens of times in his youth on the journeys between Dongmen and Huajing. Still, they felt just as foreign as his hometown. He shrugged.

On his other side, Yuha peered through Jie's spyglass. The poor man had probably never thought he'd see the Great Wall in his lifetime, let alone go a couple of hundred *li* into the strange land beyond. He passed the scope over. "So many Metal Men, but a Man from Beyond the Wall leads them."

Tian stared through it. Twenty-seven dark shapes prowled the battlements, though one stood a head shorter and much thinner than the others. Another collaborator. Yet more disconcerting was the heavily-guarded bottleneck. "We could pose as farmers or merchants."

Jie rolled her eyes. "Because Kanin Shaman come to the city so often, and it's not like every last Bovyan knows about the princess' half-elf. In any case, I doubt any citizens will approach the city while it's occupied."

Such a sharp tongue. He chuckled. "There has to be another way in."

"*You* can make it in." Jie pulled out hand straps with metal spikes...*cat-claws.* "All you have to do is climb along the underside of the bridge, creep along the waterline, and then scale the walls in a less guarded section. Then come around and kill them all."

Tian gawked at the bridge, which looked a *li* long. It would take extraordinary stamina to accomplish such a feat, and then to climb the walls, and then fight. Even though his body had already done amazing things, "This task is impossible."

Jie searched his gaze. "At the very least, you have to go in alone. Along the northeast wall, you will find a locked grate where White Duck Stream feeds into the lake." She pointed back toward the lake, past the castle where the blue flag of Hua still flew, to a spot on the walls. "Yuha and I will commandeer a boat in one of the villages we passed and meet you there."

Tian snorted. They'd followed the highway along the lake's edge for dozens of *li*, not finding a single undamaged boat in the several towns they'd ridden through. Then, there was the locked grate. "Do you have a key?"

Sucking on her lip, Jie squinted at him. Then, she sighed. She reached into a pouch and gave him a smaller bag. "Take my lockpicks."

Tian hefted the tool bag. There was a comforting familiarity to it. "Are these mine?"

"No, yours are..." She frowned. "No. But everyone in our clan has a similar set."

He withdrew one of the long metal wires. It felt right in his hand, just like the weapons had before.

"It will come back to you." Jie grinned. She offered the cat-claws again.

He took them and stared through the thinning fog.

Yuha prodded him. "What's our plan?"

"You and Jie will find a boat and meet me across the lake." Tian pointed toward the spot Jie had indicated. Hopefully, Yuha's limited Arkothi would be enough for the two of them to communicate. He patted the shaman on the shoulder.

"Remember," Jie said. "We have to hurry. The princess will be at the palace, along with whoever is left to defend it. Enemy agents will be trying to penetrate it."

Tian squeezed her hand, regardless of Yuha's reproachful glare. With a nod, he scrambled down the hill. He covered himself in yellow brush and crept among the low rows of greening winter wheat, well to the east of the bridge. The fertile smell of spring piqued memories of a little girl with doe eyes, which merged with a half-elf girl with larger eyes.

After a *li*, the fields ended at a stretch of rocky flatland about twenty paces wide. Beyond that, a stone retaining wall ran along the river bank. All designed so that a defender on the walls could see an approaching enemy. In his forest-green long coat and black pants, he'd stand out to anyone whose gaze happened to pass over him.

He scanned the battlements. Though the Metal Men paced the gatehouse in the distance, none actually ventured onto the walls. Perhaps swimming across here would be safer than trying to climb under the bridge. Then again, the *li*-wide river coursed with spring melt. He'd never make it across without either getting washed away or freezing to death.

Working his way through the wheat toward the bridge, he came to hastily constructed earthworks near the highway. From the scars in the ramparts and the sprayed clumps of dirt, the position must've faced a light bombardment from the city.

The piquant scent of burnt firepowder lingered in the air. Paper cartridge remains littered the trenches. The attackers must've fired back, despite the impossibly long range from here to the walls. A lot of firepowder and musket balls must've been wasted by both sides. A deliberate strategy, no doubt. This Emperor Geros must be a formidable adversary. Images of a hulking man with a scar on his cheek blinked in and out of Tian's memory.

He peeked up from a trench. Covering the distance from here to the bridge would take ten seconds. A risk, unless there were some distraction. Wait for someone to approach the city? Unlikely, since as Jie had said, no one in their right mind would walk into an occupied city.

Or would they? Wagon wheels creaked and horse hooves clopped to the east. Up the highway, which continued to northwest, a caravan approached with a Metal Man on horseback at the head. Sixty-four more flanked the sides as commoners pulled twenty-seven carts of foodstuffs and firepowder. Counting, always counting; numbers brought order to his thoughts.

Heart pumping, Tian edged toward the end of the trench closest to the highway. Little chance he could blend in with the porters with his uniform, but he could use them as cover. He took a deep breath, and his pulse settled. Toward the back of the line, he waited for the second-to-last Metal Man to pass. Tian tossed a rock onto the highway behind him.

The soldier turned.

Tian zipped under the nearest wagon and clung to the bottom. He held his breath. Maybe he hadn't gone fast enough. He didn't stand a chance against so many enemies.

The Metal Man's booted feet jogged up to just beside the wagon...and resumed their march. The wagon continued, the wheels thumping into the edges between the pavestones. The porters whispered among themselves, lamenting the death of the old *Tianzi*. The head of the bridge came closer. With a little speed and luck, he could slip out without being seen and then duck under the bridge.

And hold on to what? Maybe Jie knew something about the underside of the bridge, or assumed he did. Too much of a risk. In any case, as long as the Metal Men didn't check underneath the wagon, this was an easy ride into city.

The bridge rose up in a gentle arch before descending again. The gate guards didn't even stop the caravan as it rolled through the darkness of the gatehouse and into the city. It continued straight down a tree-lined road. Tian's hands, arms, abdomen, and legs all ached from the effort. All the feet visible from his spot wore heavy boots, which clopped on the white stones.

If his muscles gave out, the enemy would see him. Maybe climbing under the bridge would've worked better; at least he could have worked at his own pace. No. No point in regrets. He drew in a slow breath and contemplated the sound of one hand clapping, distracting his mind from the burn.

The caravan turned onto a winding path of packed gravel. The white canvas and poles of tents were pitched among the grass and trees. A campsite, or rather an urban park used as such. Men groaned all around. At last, the wagon came to a stop. The straw-sandaled feet of Hua porters pattered away, followed by the Metal Men's boots.

Tian's limbs protested as he lowered himself to the ground and blew out a long breath. The new angle provided a slightly better view. Bandaged and splinted Metal Men, some on crutches, queued outside of several tents. This was more than a campsite; it was a field hospital. Sabotaging the medical supplies, poisoning the food, and assassinating the doctors would slow the enemy down.

His stomach clenched. What kind of man thought of such things? He rolled out on the side of the wagon away from the tents and stood. Manicured trees with budding limbs stood at regular intervals. Each could provide cover as he worked his way into the city and found clothes that would make him look more like a citizen, less like a military officer.

"You!" a voice called from the tents. "Stop!"

With his back to a tree, Tian cast a glance at the supply wagon and the medical tents beyond. A boy, not yet a teen, froze with his hand on a loaf of bread. Dozens of the Metal Men started toward him, pointing.

Tian suppressed a sigh of relief. They hadn't seen him, but... Two able-bodied Teleri loped toward the would-be thief.

The porters—the only other Hua people around besides the boy—stepped to the side. Tucking the bread into his shirt, the thief dashed off, running right by Tian. The two Metal Men gave chase, also passing him without any sign they'd seen him. No telling what they would do if they caught the boy.

Tian bolted after them, darting from tree to tree, occasionally checking back to see if any other Bovyans followed him. Reaching the edge of the park, where it bordered a paved avenue, he stopped. Buildings of wood and stone stood in a row across the street, many with colorful signs he could read. Shoes. Tanner. Butcher. Vegetables. Still, the shutters on the sixteen storefronts remained closed, as were the residences above. No one so much as poked a head out of the windows.

The boy sprinted across the street, then ran down the deserted road, the pursuers only a dozen paces behind. That they hadn't caught up with their longer legs was a testament to the boy's speed and guile. He'd be fine on his own.

Maybe he wouldn't. Gritting his teeth, Tian followed.

The boy turned down a side street. When Tian reached the corner, he looked around just in time to see the Metal Men turn into an alley. Tian made a quick scan of the surrounding area. In the windows above stores, people now peeked out from cracked shutters. He took a deep breath and ran to the alley, stopping at the edge of a building for cover. He craned around the corner.

In the morning shadows, the boy stood with his back to a dead end, his hands pressed against the wall.

One of the Metal Men put his hands on his hips. "Return the bread now, cretin, and your punishment will be light."

Tian eased the grip on his dagger. If the punishment was light, then he didn't need to risk exposing himself.

Dark shapes dropped down from the balconies overhead, enveloping the two Metal Men. They collapsed to their knees with muffled grunts.

Tian started to back away from the ambush. A hand clamped down on his shoulder. He raised his hand and stopped a knife from pressing into his throat. Securing his assailant's hand on his shoulder with his own, he spun and swept his leg out. A twist of the wrist, and the knife clattered to the ground. He straddled his attacker…

A teenaged girl.

Her eyes widened. "Zheng Tian! You're supposed to be dead."

Moquan. The ambush was so elementary, only a child would fall for it. Or a Metal Man. And him, apparently. This girl must've been the rear lookout. Not only that, she knew his name. He raised an eyebrow. "Who are you?"

She pouted. "Feng Mi. We attacked Wailian Castle together. Don't you remember?"

Had she? *Honey?* She was cute enough. Yet with his memory, she could've been the once-in-three-generations Doe-Eyed Girl and he wouldn't recognize her. Composing his best apologetic expression, he shook his head.

Behind him, a male said, "Who…"

Tian turned and met a young teen's eyes, which widened. Beside him the first boy stared as well.

"Zheng Tian," he droned. "I'd never believe it was *you* following me. I thought it was a Teleri Nightblade. Come on, back into the shadows." He beckoned them back into the alley.

Tian helped Feng Mi to her feet. She gazed at him with adoring eyes. Heat rose to his cheeks, and he quickly turned into the alley.

Two other young male *Moquan* worked at stripping the Metal Men of their armor. They all looked up from their work and gawked. He might

as well have been the village shaman, given the attention.

Feng Mi skipped over. "You really don't remember me? You taught me the *Ghost Echo* at the temple."

"I lost my memories to the *Viper's Rest*."

Her mouth formed a circle and the others nodded. Such bright faces, so young. The Black Lotus Clan must have been severely depleted to depend on youth.

"Who is leading?" he asked.

Feng Mi stared at the ground for a few seconds before meeting his gaze. "Me."

Her? He sized her up with a discerning eye. "If I taught you a technique at the temple, you can't be that old."

One of the boys nodded. "Most of the clan is defending the inner castle. Feng Mi was the most senior on the outside."

Tian looked from him back to girl. Princess Kaiya must've been in the inner castle. "How many adepts do you have? Who's giving you orders?"

"There are seven of us. We take turns going to Cold Sun Bell Foundry, getting orders from Master Yan."

"What's your mission?"

"For now, harass the occupying army."

"Two at a time." Tian snorted.

The first boy crossed his arms. "We were sabotaging their supplies. I was just a diversion so our last two could do the sabotaging."

The others nodded.

It was almost cute. Though it made sense: as long as the senior clan members defended the princess in the castle, the younger ones could operate on the outside. Tian scratched his chin. "How many enemy soldiers are there?"

"About five thousand," Feng Mi said.

Only five thousand, out of an expeditionary force of fifty thousand. They must've sustained significant casualties breaching the north gate. Still, five thousand was more than seven—now eight—*Moquan* could defeat. Tian scratched his chin. "Where are they concentrated?"

Feng Mi used a finger to sketch the city in the air. "Mostly in the northwest quadrant and around the palace. Smaller units stationed at the north and west gates, and around the holes left in the east walls."

Leaving the south gate undefended. A trap perhaps, to entice an attack there, or maybe allow an escape route. If only he could remember the city layout. "What does that tell us about their objectives?"

The youngsters glanced among themselves.

The first boy said, "They're keeping our soldiers bottled up in the palace."

Tian cocked his head. That wasn't what he would've thought. More like preparing an assault. "How many soldiers are in the palace?"

"Eight thousand."

Tian scratched his chin again. None of it made sense. Outnumbered, cut off from their homeland, the Teleri had still managed to control the entire city and its resources. "Why hasn't the regent ordered a counteroffensive?"

Feng Mi shook her head. "The regent fled the city to draw the main Teleri army away."

Fled? Main Teleri army? Tian looked from spy to spy. "How many soldiers?"

"Forty-five thousand," one of the older boys said.

They'd hardly suffered any casualties, then. "Who's protecting the regent?"

"Three hundred of the Huayuan provincial cavalry," said another boy.

Tian glared at them. This was the woman that he supposedly loved. "What about a Black Lotus *Moquan* adept? Aren't we supposed to protect the Imperial Family?"

Feng Mi popped her lips. "I was guarding her, but she ordered me to stay in the city."

"And you obeyed?"

She shrugged. "Our orders to guard her were given by the late *Tianzi*. As regent, she is head of the Wang Family. I could not disobey."

Tian snorted. If anyone was more stubborn than the *Moquan*, it had to be this Doe-Eyed Girl. With Yuha or not, he had to go after his *wife*. Even if he didn't love her. She needed his protection. "I'm going after the regent."

The others gaped. As he turned to leave, Feng Mi grabbed his sleeves. "How can you leave at a time like this?"

Tian met her gaze. It wasn't as though he had much to contribute. "This evening, Yan Jie will come in through the sluice gate where the White Duck Stream empties into the lake."

Glancing around the square, Jie didn't think the town looked occupied. They were about six *li* from where they'd parted with Tian, whose lack of confidence in his own abilities had proved troublesome. Here, people went about their everyday lives, though most stared at Yuha as they passed. Not a single Teleri prowled the streets. They must've just marched through without leaving a garrison.

They'd apparently procured supplies, though. People crowded around carts and stalls, bidding outrageous prices for common vegetables. Spring greens, carrots, radishes, and winter squashes—usually in abundance this time of year—barely filled one farmer's cart. No meat hung in the butcher's stall, and indeed, from the smells, there were too few pigs and cattle around. A decent amount of fresh crustaceans sold for high prices, but there were hardly any salted fish.

Down toward the docks, men, and children cast lines. No boats bobbed in the lake beyond. Jie beckoned Yuha to follow. Many of the fishermen gawked as they approached. Give a shaman and a half-elf a fish...there had to be a good punchline for the oddity of it.

She bowed to a middle-aged man with a weathered complexion. "Where might I find a boat?"

"If we knew, do you think we we'd all be fishing from the banks and docks?" He swept a hand across the riverfront, at all the other fishers. "You won't find a boat anywhere on the north shore of the river or lake. If you want one, go ask the regent in Huajing."

Another man, carrying a rod, walked up. "First, the regent impounds the boats across the lake, for *fair* compensation. Then the Teleri come and force us to sell over half our food stores. What good is the money if a turnip costs five times the regular price, and neighbors turn on neighbors in the struggle to feed themselves?"

The first man spat into the water. "And then, the Teleri captured the city anyway. Incompetence, I tell you."

"Would've never happened under the late *Tianzi*." The second harrumphed.

Jie nodded, but had her doubts. The *Tianzi* might've had a good mind for trade and economics, but Hua was ill-prepared to defend itself on this side of the Wall. Meanwhile, invasion might as well have been the Teleri's national religion. She turned to Yuha, cupped her hands to pantomime a boat, and shook her head. "No boat."

He pointed upshore, where dozens of eldarwood trunks bobbed in a holding pen on their trip to the shipyards. He wound his hands around in a circle, while the fishermen gaped at him. He grabbed her hand and pulled her toward the logs. Several of the fishermen followed.

Yuha repeated the motion. Lashing the logs together? Was he suggesting building a bridge? They had neither the carpentry skills, nor the time. Not to mention Sun-Moon Lake was several *li* wide. He threw his arms up and dragged her to a vegetable garden just twenty paces from the riverbank.

He looked up and down the rows before locking on some vines. He marched to the thatched hut and called inside, using heavily accented Hua. "Hellllloooo?"

A young woman poked her head out, her eyes widening before shifting to the small crowd that gathered.

Beaming, Yuha placed a hand on his chest, then swept it outwards. He then pointed at the garden. "Want."

The woman's gaze shifted to Jie. "What does he want?"

Jie flashed a sheepish grin. As if she knew.

Yuha beckoned them to the garden, and the woman followed, revealing a baby swaddled in her arms. Yuha smiled and nodded at the child, then came to the vines. "Want."

The mother cocked her head. "Whatever for? There aren't enough tender leaves for even one meal."

"I give you." Still smiling, Yuha removed a necklace with feathers and polished river stones and proffered it. A trade? Around them, the fishermen chuckled.

"A pretty necklace won't feed my family."

Whatever Yuha wanted, it seemed urgent. Jie produced a silver *jiao*.

She held up a finger. "One plant."

"One?" Jie threw up her hands. "That's enough to buy a field of vines."

"We can't eat silver."

Yuha put a hand on Jie's shoulder and nodded. He held up one finger.

Just one? He must be insane.

The look the young mother afforded them left no doubt she felt the same, but she nodded nonetheless.

Yuha took the woman's free arm and clasped her wrist. He closed her hand around his own wrist and nodded again. Freeing his hands, he enunciated a few melodic words.

The ground trembled. Before everyone's rounded eyes, the vines lengthened and fattened. Side tendrils unfolded, and small white flowers opened.

"Heavens," the woman gasped.

Some of the men ran among the vines, now crawling over the land and toward the riverbank and logs, and dabbed their fingers from flower to flower. Snow peas grew out from where they touched. Other men ran back into the town.

Yuha, and Jie behind him, followed the snow peas. He wound his hands in circles again, and the vines wrapped around several of the logs. He busied himself with snapping off the side tendrils.

Jie stared. He was making a raft.

Around them, the excited townsfolk harvested peas and pea leaves. Within an hour,

Yuha had bartered his services for oars and a long pole, with yet more people begging to trade. By the time they set off, his shoulders hunched and he walked with a trudge.

Nonetheless, he pushed off with the pole and guided the raft across the lake to the city walls. Once they reached a deep point, he knelt and paddled. Slow going, for sure, and Jie was useless because of her arm. All she could do was point toward their destination.

When they reached the city wall, Yuha poled again. Past the palace, past the castle and the *Tianzi's* personal residence. At last they floated to the grate where White Duck Stream emptied into the lake. She looked up to the iridescent moon, now waxing to half-crescent in the fading sunlight.

Jie pressed up to the grate. With a rattle, it opened. "Tian?"

No answer. It'd been thirteen hours since they'd parted. He should've arrived long before. Had he unlocked it and left? No, he wouldn't be dumb enough to do that, not even in his amnesiac state. So who'd unlocked it?

CHAPTER 33:
Threshold of Greatness

Standing alone outside his tent, Peng Kai-Long stared at the imperial army's flickering torches in the mountain pass above. They lit the night like fireflies, stretching out in orderly lines as the night progressed. Without a doubt, the imperials were preparing for the total annihilation of the dwindling Maduran army camped out below.

His plans could not be working any better. *Tai-Ming* Lord Wu, in exchange for Kai-Long's marriage to his pretty second daughter, now marched on the imperial army's rear. Just two weeks away, Zhenjing's provincial armies would swell Kai-Long's numbers to three-quarters the size of the imperials.

"*Jue-ye*, urgent news," a voice called from inside his tent.

Inside his tent! Only the Water Snake Clan operative, who had saved him before, could've crept behind his back and through the guards. Kai-Long slipped past the flap.

In the darkness, a voice spoke in a low whisper. "The imperial army is retreating north to Fenggu."

Retreating? Kai-Long opened the flap and pointed at the sea of torches winking in the distance. "They are fanning out. I would wager they will launch an attack on the Madurans at first light."

"You'd lose that wager." The *Moquan's* words held a hint of laughter. "They are setting out torches to cover their march."

Clever. General Lu, the imperials' commander and self-proclaimed *Guardian Dragon of Hua*, had learned the Founder's rules of warfare well. "The imperials must have heard of Lord Wu's betrayal." Their rear guard could hold this pass while the rest overwhelmed Wu. Kai-Long's stomach clenched.

"No, *Jue-ye*," the spy said. "A Teleri legion has captured Huajing and now heads this way."

The Teleri? Kai-Long's jaw clenched. They couldn't have possibly breached the Wall...unless Lord Zheng in Dongmen and perhaps Lord Lin in Linshan had joined them. This situation had devolved into an unmitigated disaster, thanks to the accursed court sycophants and ambitious lords. "Why are we just now learning about the Teleri invasion?"

"The Water Snake network is weaker in the South. A situation that will be remedied once you rule and root out the Black Lotus. We should attack the imperial rear."

Kai-Long snorted. These spy clans were just as backstabbing and ruthless as the ambitious lords. "I might not rule if the Teleri occupy the capital."

"If I may, *Jue-ye*, find opportunity in disaster," the man said. "If *you* are the one to defeat the Teleri, you solidify your claim to the Dragon Throne."

"I need to know how many men the Teleri have."

"Initial estimates are thirty thousand, with Emperor Geros in command."

So few. A fifth of the imperial army; a fourth of his own. Kai-Long cocked his head.

Emperor Geros was no fool, and yet his army did not stand a chance against either the imperials or Kai-Long, let alone their combined forces.

Unless the Bovyan didn't plan to engage in battle.

Kai-Long stepped back out into the night. "Deploy the troops," he yelled. "Be prepared to attack the Madurans at dawn." If anyone was to defeat foreign invaders, even those he had invited himself, he would be the one.

"Wouldn't it be wiser to ally with the Madurans and attack the imperial army?"

Kai-Long shook his head. "No. We will take care of the Madurans first."

Timing was everything, according to the Founder. Kai-Long cast a quick glance to the south, where the iridescent moon, Guanyin's Eye, and the white moon came closer together. In a few days, they would meet in the Godseye Conjunction, an omen of great change.

As the camp roused to life, Kai-Long made his way to a private tent not far from his own. The grunts and moans of wanton sex emanated from within. It was a wonder the camp wasn't already awake from the noise. The guard outside stepped aside, and Kai-Long pushed open the tent flap and entered.

A Hua soldier, a specimen of masculinity with chiseled features and square shoulders, looked up from where he mounted a panting girl. Unlike the Night Blossoms of the Floating World, she was a homely prostitute, her tanned complexion suggesting she had followed the army up from the south.

The man grinned. "It couldn't wait?" Despite his decidedly Hua features, his accent stank of the Aksumi South.

Kai-Long snorted. "Get out, girl."

Wrapping a blanket around her—though most of the men had probably seen her naked anyway—she collected her clothes and ducked out of the tent.

Kai-Long watched her leave and turned back. He spoke in Ayuri. "We will attack the Madurans in the morning. I will be in need of your services earlier than planned."

"So your interruption *could* wait." The soldier stretched his arms and yawned. His form shimmered, the honey tone darkening to chocolate, his long black hair shortening into coarse, white-flecked curls. Gone was the handsome face, replaced by middle-aged, blunt features. An amazing illusion, indicative of Master Melas' power. He had been the one to infuse glass baubles with the image of young Kaiya, which had been used to sneak a Black Lotus operative into Wailian Castle three years before.

"I leave nothing to chance," Kai-Long said. "It has to be perfect. Show me."

"I have to conserve my energy." Melas laughed. "Fear not, I understand how to find and summon your Guardian Dragon."

Such confidence, especially since Kai-Long didn't even believe in such tales. Still, the rest of Hua did, and history claimed the Guardian Dragon had appeared after the Hellstorm to anoint the Founder. "Surely someone of such great power can show me what is possible without depleting himself."

The Mystic harrumphed. He uttered several foul words and opened his hand. In his palm danced a flaming pearl. A dragon pearl, just like all in all the paintings.

The air shook and shimmered. A black space opened in midair, as if someone had torn a gash there.

Kai-Long stared at it, mouth agape. "Beautiful. Will the Guardian Dragon come for it?"

Melas closed his hand, snuffing the illusion out. The gash in the air closed. "Of course. I've summoned him more than once with the pearl. Had I not dispelled the pearl image now, he would've emerged from the rift."

"Rest well. I need the dragon to appear for at least a few minutes once we engage the Madurans, and again on the night of the Godseye Conjunction." Kai-Long grinned. General Lu fancied himself as the Guardian Dragon of Hua. Wait until the vain man saw the real one.

Gazing at the mirror, Prince Dhananad fiddled with the sole remaining gold button of his high-collared uniform. The other six had long since snapped free, and his tailor had tucked tail and ran over a month before. The once-magnificent fabric had faded, with threadbare patches on his knees and shoulders.

At least his handsome looks made up for it.

His assistant stepped back with the foundation brush, and Dhananad patted his smooth complexion. It covered that horrid scar on his neck, while the eyeliner brought out the mysteriousness in his gaze.

The tent flap opened. In the mirror, his last surviving Golden Scorpion pressed her hands together. Her voice betrayed about as much emotion as her featureless metal mask. "Your Highness, you must hurry."

He snorted. What was the rush? If today was the day he'd die, he would look good doing it. Curse Princess Kaiya for leading him on. Curse Lord Peng for tricking him. Curse Father for his abandonment. Would that Yama would drag them all down to Hell with his infinite arms.

With deliberate grace, he lifted his chin and sauntered out of the tent. Around him, men screamed and ran like rats from a disturbed nest. Cowards. More musket shots rang out.

"Order the surrender!" The Scorpion pulled him to the side. A musket ball buzzed by his ear.

Wait. The attack, which had started half an hour before, had come not from the Cathayi imperials, but from Peng's ragtag rebels. Dhananad stared back to see the lines of Peng's musketmen, shooting even the soldiers who'd thrown down their arms. Butchers!

His stomach twisted into knots. He cast a glance toward the imperial army, whose flags had not moved from the mountain pass. That bastard Peng. It had gone past dereliction and abandonment and had escalated into downright betrayal. Well, if the imperials weren't attacking, the Madurans could at least punish that traitor. He grabbed a Maduran banner and waved it. "Soldiers of Madura, to me! Show the Cathayi we will not die like pigs!"

A smattering of cheers rose up among his men, gradually at first, then building to crescendo. It sounded nothing like their half-hearted chants in previous battles, when he'd motivated them with the threat of punishment back home. The archers and spearmen formed up, even as their comrades fell around them.

He drew his *talwar* and raised it high. "Let history remember our brave expedition by this last glorious fight, when we punished the betrayer who had begged us for help. Charge!"

His men roared in approval and surged toward the musket volleys.

A firework exploded above. High in the dawn skies, a snaking form of golden scales materialized. Eyes glowed red, boring into his heart. Guns stuttered to a stop. The besieged camp fell silent, all gazes transfixed on the dreadful sight. A dragon.

A real dragon.

The bastard Peng's voice rose up above the eerie quiet, speaking words in the hideous Cathayi tongue. His men cheered. In the mountains, horns blared.

The Scorpion tugged at him. "Your Highness, the imperials are descending. We will be crushed between them."

Peng spoke again from behind his lines, his diction reminiscent of a peasant Ayuri with a horrid accent. Hard to believe he was related to Princess Kaiya. "Prince Dhananad, surrender and you will be spared."

Spared. Dhananad rubbed the scar on his neck, a souvenir from previous Cathayi treachery. No, he was just a child then, and the nick had been an accident. He was more valuable alive. He started to sheath his *talwar*.

The Scorpion's hand stayed his arm. "No, Your Highness. They will use you to conquer Madura. It would be more honorable to die."

Die? No—while there was life, there was hope. If his men held out a little longer... He shook his head. "No, we shall retreat and surrender to the imperials instead of that snake Peng." Princess Kaiya would certainly spare him.

"Peng will catch you first." The featureless mask mocked him.

"No!" He grabbed the damned Scorpion's neck.

Pain seared through his neck, and the dark blue sky filled his vision for a split second before spinning to the mountains and then trees. His ear smashed into the ground. He started to turn his head...it wouldn't move. He tried to move his arm...where was his arm? It hurt, his entire body hurt. Such excruciating pain was unimaginable.

His vision dimmed into an ever-narrowing tunnel, focused on a headless body in a threadbare uniform. Above it, his Scorpion sheathed her glowing sting and started removing the corpse's jacket.

All faded to black, and the pain subsided.

Kai-Long walked among the tattered remains of the Maduran campsite. Bodies lay strewn at awkward angles, many unarmored, ungroomed. Moans and screams echoed in the early morning sky, several abruptly silenced by the slash of a sword. It had been more a slaughter than a battle.

Meeting the gaze of the few Maduran survivors, Kai-Long pursed his lips. "Has Prince Dhananad been accounted for?" The coward had likely fled into the nearby woods at first sign of the attack. No matter. Trapped by the mountain's roots, it would not be long before they caught him. "He should be easy to spot in that flamboyant uniform of his."

"No, *Jue-Ye*," an aide said. "We are searching among the Madurans, both dead and alive."

Alive, right—some of rodents had survived the order to kill them all in battle. The remnants were likely the most cowardly, the ones who had surrendered before the first shots were fired. Now they were mouths to feed, chained feet to slow him down. Kai-Long scanned the vermin. "Kill them all."

The aide's eyes widened. "*Jue-ye*, they surrendered."

"They were foreign invaders who sought to rape and pillage our glorious nation." At his invitation. When he sat on the Jade Throne, future histories would write otherwise. Kai-Long glared back.

The man bowed. "Yes, *Jue-Ye*. What about the servants and whores?" He pointed to a gaunt older woman, not worth the air she breathed. She scowled at Kai-Long with unbridled disdain.

A pair of prostitutes, dressed in faded *sari*, passed by with heads bowed. One cast a fearful glance at him as she trudged. Without make-up, her skin looked rough and blemished, though still pretty by Ayuri standards. The other, however, had a wondrous complexion when she met his eyes. How this woman, who might have been a noble, fallen in with this lot?

Lest anyone think him as cruel as the Founder, Kai-Long smiled. Hardness must be tempered by softness, severe punishment must sometimes be moderated by lenience. "Spare any servant who is willing and able to work for us. If they wish to stay, the prostitutes can join our own as an exotic treat for the men."

An imperial soldier bearing a flag of parley ran up and dropped to a knee. "Lord Peng, General Lu believes you have won the Mandate of Heaven. He wishes to declare his loyalty to you."

Kai-Long hid a grin. The famous, self-styled Guardian Dragon would lend legitimacy to his cause once they confronted the bulk of the imperial army. "Where is he?"

"Our army awaits your orders in the pass." The messenger pointed back toward the pass.

"There is a town on the other side of the pass," Kai-Long said. "The Valley View Pavilion there serves a unique tea. Extend my invitation for lunch to the general."

Bowing, the man rose and hurried off. Soon, they would confront the main imperial army. With the Guardian Dragon of Hua on his side, he'd win them over without a shot fired.

The Water Snake agent, dressed as a soldier, watched the messenger leave, then leaned in and whispered, "Regent Kaiya is on her way south in a carriage with an escort of imperial cavalry. They are half a day out of the capital."

Kai-Long turned to the *Moquan*. "I thought she would hunker down in the palace. But no, it seems she comes to rally the troops." Against him, or… "To fight the Teleri. They are not coming to engage the army, but to capture her."

A possible snag in the plan. If she got to the imperial army first, she might vanquish the Guardian Dragon as she had Avarax. Kai-Long had to reach the army before her. He beckoned another aide over and whispered, "Send word to General Lu to move up our meeting by two hours, and in the meantime, have him prepare his troops to march. And bring me a brush and paper."

He'd write a message to his secret allies, *Yu-Ming* Lords Fen and Mu in Jiangzhou Province. They might not risk open rebellion by detaining his meddlesome cousin, but they could certainly slow her down with hospitality.

Or sabotage.

The rattle of the imperial carriage's wheels over pavestones pounded in Kaiya's ears. It mingled with the clopping of the imperial cavalry and set the rhythm for the melodies in her mind. The fallen star played a steady refrain, pulsing to the beat of her heart.

Or perhaps her heart answered the star. She cradled Lord Xu's magic mirror for the first time since her confrontation with Avarax a year ago, studying songs of power. Chants to stir troops into a frenzy. An aria designed to curb aggression.

And music to make the bravest armies cower. That would be the one to force the Teleri to surrender.

The acoustic theories made sense, and she'd used them in the past on a smaller scale. But even if…no, *when* she regained the power of her voice, Heaven knew if it would work. She sighed.

"Sighing is a sign of shallow breaths," Doctor Wu said from the seat across from her. "Your liver energies congest and lock your *Qi*

inside. Perhaps the regent should call for a break and take some time to get out and breathe deeply."

Kaiya met the doctor's gaze and smiled. Six days out of the capital, hitching new horses at the courier stations along the way, they approached the border of Jiangzhou and Fenggu Provinces. At this rate they'd make it to the pyramid in a day, a good week before the conjunction. If time were the only constraint, they could afford to take a break. She waved a hand outside the carriage window.

Zhuang, the cavalry commander who had taken her into custody at the way station, rode up. "Yes, *Jie-xia*?"

"What is the news on the Teleri army?"

He pointed back the way they'd come. "The courier system reports that the Teleri have fallen well behind."

"How far to the next way station?"

His forehead furrowed. "I would guess eighty *li*."

A ways away, though it made sense: they had departed the previous relay point not long before. "Inform the troops that we will rest there."

"As the regent commands." He bowed, and then spurred his horse forward.

Outside the windows, eldarwood trunks ambled by. What had Tian said? That the Mandate of Heaven was just an illusion, that Hua's greatest asset was its eldarwood ships? That as long as the ships brought luxuries from abroad, the people would be content and the nation would be stable?

Kaiya sighed again. Hua had reached the pinnacle of its prosperity under Father's rule, and the realm now teetered on the edge of fragmentation and occupation.

A loud crack burst from below. The carriage lurched, the rear rising and slamming back down again. The jolt threw Kaiya into Doctor Wu's lap. The doctor helped her back into her seat, and she slid over to the window. Outside, the orderly ranks of mounted soldiers staggered to a halt.

Commander Zhuang rode up and opened the door. "*Jie-xia*, are you all right?"

Kaiya composed her expression and stepped out of the carriage. "Yes, Commander. What happened?"

Soldiers milled around the carriage, several forming up a defensive line around her. Face pallid, rubbing his arm, the driver bent over and looked under the chassis. "The front axle snapped near the right wheel. Had we been travelling at normal speed, the carriage might have flipped."

Kaiya pursed her lips. "Can it be repaired?"

The driver bowed. "I cannot say. Only a wheelwright could tell."

Commander Zhuang pointed. "The maps indicate the town of Hualian not seven li away. Shall I send a patrol ahead?"

Kaiya nodded. "If you cannot find a wheelwright, then go to the castle and ask Lord Fen to provide a palanquin." She'd met the *Yu-ming*'s son years before, under the pretense of visiting the scenic gorge nearby. Hopefully, the young man didn't hold a grudge.

Commander Zhuang bowed. "We will never make it to Fenggu in time if you ride a palanquin."

"Then bring me a horse. We will all ride to Hualian. If it turns out the carriage is beyond a quick repair, then we will be seven *li* closer to our destination."

Doctor Wu placed a weathered hand on her shoulder. "No, *Dian-xia*. Not in your condition."

Kaiya suppressed a scowl. Only a handful of people knew of her pregnancy. "Doctor, we have no choice."

The doctor's severe gaze almost cowed Kaiya into acquiescence, but the *Tiger's Eye* held strong. A soldier swung down from his horse and knelt on all fours beside the saddle.

Using him as footstool, Kaiya mounted. She turned to the doctor. "Don't worry, we won't be riding at a full gallop."

Doctor Wu shook her head, but then beckoned a horse over. Without a word, the soldier dismounted.

With a spryness of a woman a quarter of her age, the doctor swung into the saddle. "I am coming with you, stubborn girl."

They set off at a trot. By the time they reached the castle in Hualian, Kaiya wished she had listened. Cramps gripped her womb, and a wet hotness pooled between her legs. A few weeks into the pregnancy, this shouldn't be happening! Her chest squeezed.

The visit to Lord Fen's castle looked to be a request for a bed instead of a palanquin.

CHAPTER 34:

You, Spy

In his dark green and black uniform, Tian might as well have had a target on his back. All the Metal Men lurking the streets would see him as an enemy soldier. They made plenty of noise, affording him time to duck into alleys before they spotted him, but still, it made for a slow traipse through the enormous city. At this rate, the Teleri might very well catch up to Princess Kaiya before he even made it to the city's south gate.

Waiting in an alley for a patrol to pass, he caught sight of a laundry line on a second floor balcony. He pop-vaulted up and took a closer look. Plain beige robes and pants hung among socks, shirts, and undergarments. He swapped out his tunic for simple but loose-fitting clothes that would make it easier to dissemble if a Metal Man stopped him. He folded his own garments and left them on the balcony with a silver *jiao*.

Tian jumped down and landed lightly in a crouch. Not letting his guard down despite the disguise, he continued on his trek to the south gate. A handful of people ventured out—twenty-seven males, no females for the first *li*. Those that stopped and talked all repeated the same thing: the *Tianzi* had been murdered by his sister, the regent, who now refused to repel the occupying army.

Impossible. According to his Black Lotus brothers and sister's earlier report, Princess Kaiya had fled the city.

Others huddled near street vendors, chatting. Apparently, collaborators had started going door-to-door, taking a census for the Teleri and issuing identity papers.

One citizen held up his own, a sheet of rice paper with a wax seal. "They say that as long as you carry one, they won't bother you in the streets."

Nodding, his larger companion showed off his own. "It'll be safe again, like before the insurgents started attacking the nobles."

Tian wondered. If the Metal Men treated the people from Beyond the Wall like they had the Kanin peoples, safety would be purchased at the cost of dignity. Men forced to work. Women forced to procreate. In any case, if he could procure such an identity paper, he could make it through the city unmolested. He skidded to a halt at a pile of charred stone and splinters. Soot covered the pavestones, blackened nearby buildings. A fire had struck here.

No, more than a fire. A blast, from the way the debris field spread out. Curious, Tian worked his way toward the epicenter. The scorched frame of stone and wood was all that remained of what must've been a fairly large building. The stench of spent firepowder hung in the air. A significant amount of it had been stored here. Perhaps an armory.

Princess Kaiya had probably had it destroyed to prevent weapons from falling into enemy hands. Or perhaps the enemy had ignited it later. He continued on his way, avoiding patrols until he could borrow identity papers.

Up the street, a queue of chatting young men looped around a corner building. A promising place to glean information. Tian approached and cleared his throat. "What is this for?"

Several in line turned around. An exceptionally burly man, almost large enough to be Bovyan, said, "The Teleri are offering work."

Tian craned around to see the line entering the stone building. The sign above the door indicated a stonemason's workshop. He turned back. "What kind of work?"

"Repairing the east walls."

"What happened?"

"Where have *you* been?" Another fellow cocked his head. "The regent left two gaping holes."

Tian offered him a sheepish smile.

"Right," the big man said. "The regent is busy destroying things, and at least the Teleri are trying to fix it."

"Is that what happened to the armory?" Tian pointed northeast.

"Two of them." Another man waved toward the east. "Before the Teleri even breached the north gate."

Before. Why would Princess Kaiya do such a thing? Unless it hadn't been her. Jie had mentioned something about Teleri *Moquan* operatives in the city. If they'd destroyed two armories, they must've been well-informed and well-organized.

The larger man's eyes locked on Tian's. Insistent. Not unlike the earlier man showing off his identification papers. Could they be Metal Men? Though big, neither was as enormous as the brutes he'd fought in the Wilds. Also, all of those had been fair-skinned, except for one who looked Kanin, in Father's castle.

Tian pointed at the man's identification, clutched in his hands. "Where do I get my papers?"

"The scribes didn't come to your home?" The man raised an eyebrow. "What part of town do you live in?"

Where, indeed? More people had been out north of here, so they had likely already registered with the city's new owners. Tian jutted his chin in that direction.

The man nodded, but his gaze shifted past Tian, up, and then back. "Perhaps they haven't come to your neighborhood yet. You are brave to come out without them."

Tian shrugged. "It seems safe enough."

"Well, you'd better get your papers." The man pointed toward the front of the line. "They won't let you work without it."

"Right." Tian backed up and bowed, then walked east. Once the stonemason's and the line fell out of sight, he picked up his pace. That large man, and likely the first one with identification papers, were both smaller Metal Men of Hua stock.

Of course. With only five thousand soldiers to maintain order, the Teleri were now engaging in an organized campaign of disinformation. Seeding rumors and subjugating the city with propaganda alone.

Hair prickled on the back of his neck. Something wasn't right. Somewhere out there, eyes watched. He glanced at the windows in the buildings around him. Nothing. No shutters closed, no faces withdrew. Beyond the distant marching boots, there was no indication of anyone else around.

Except for that unsettling feeling.

Another look around. Nothing. Still, the last man must've sent a signal to his friends. Now, they followed him. It would only take time to expose them. Tian continued on his way.

In the city's vast central square, fourteen merchants stood by their carts while seventy-three citizens shopped. A patrol of twelve Bovyans prowled from cart to cart, but didn't interfere with trade.

Ducking low, Tian worked his way through the people. Very few dared make eye contact with each other, let alone the Metal Men. Then, a large Hua man's gaze fell on Tian for a split second. A bodyguard, maybe? He might not compare to a Bovyan in size, but he was easily the largest Hua around. Like the other two. No weapons to speak of. The weight of his stare...

Tian stopped at a vendor selling pork buns. He held up a polished silver coin and found the large man's reflection. Definitely watching him. Likely the source of his disconcertion.

Chewing on the pork bun as he continued his walk, Tian kept track of the man in reflective surfaces. He continued south along the nearly-deserted main boulevard. For the first two *li*, he encountered only two citizens heading north, and no Metal Men at all. Only this one shadow, pretending to mind his own business, walking just far enough away to stay in sight.

Capture him, and chances were he wouldn't talk. Lose him, and he would stick around to cause more trouble for the young Black Lotus Clan members.

A quick glance around revealed no sign of anyone watching from alleys or windows. It was time to act.

Jie listened at the sluice gate for a few minutes, differentiating the various sounds above the lazy flow of the stream. Fish swam, plopping in and out of the water. Crustaceans clawed their way over the paved streambed, undoubtedly enjoying the feast of garbage. No signs of humans, besides the missing lock on the grate.

She motioned Yuha to help her open it. With her good arm, she pulled herself into the rectangular tunnel. Though wide enough for eight men to march abreast, the passage was just tall enough for her to stand upright. The water came up to her waist.

Meanwhile, a hunched-over Yuha grimaced. He stared at the refuse with unbridled disdain. White Duck Stream must've looked and smelled nothing like the pristine streams and rivers meandering through his homeland. His doeskin pants would stink for days.

With a snort, Jie waded toward the other end of the tunnel, where the stream passed under the city walls. Like all the waterways in Huajing, the streambed was paved. At the mouth of the channel, she paused and peeked out.

Noble's villas and pavilions, along with the occasional temple, formed a dark silhouette against the dusk sky. A stone bridge arched over the stream not far away. In the aristocrats' section of the city, on such a beautiful evening, there would usually be poetry parties and receptions. Yet tonight, only birds chattered. No sign of any human activity—

A person moved, ever so slightly, in the shadows of a pagoda.

Jie ducked back into the tunnel and palmed a *biao*. Whoever was out there didn't want to be seen. If not for her elf vision, she might've missed him.

"Master Jie," a voice called. A male voice. Familiar. But not coming from the movement near the pagoda.

A Ghost Echo, perhaps? But why? She glanced out again, zeroing in on the source of the voice. A person, not quite grown, crouched by a stone lion. He must've been expecting her. The person by the pagoda, however—

Something whizzed through the air at her.

Jie stepped back and nearly bumped into Yuha. A dart. Coming from the pagoda. She sprung out and whipped her *biao* at the large man as he dashed toward the cover of manicured bushes.

The *biao* zipped past him. Curse the bad arm, throwing her balance off!

The boy at the stone lion came out from his hiding place and hurled his own *biao*. The bushes quivered, and the man, still hunching low, yanked the throwing star from his calf and hobbled toward a nearby wall.

With deliberate aim, taking into account her new throwing mechanics, Jie flung another spike at him. It flew true, lodging into his right upper back. He tumbled and crashed face-first against the wall. Both she and the boy raced forward, converging on the Teleri at the same time. He turned and reached for a shortsword.

The *Moquan* boy slashed with a knife, severing the man's wrist tendons before he could draw his own weapon. A dagger in hand, Jie hooked his ankle with her foot and swept it up, then kicked out the other knee.

The Nightblade collapsed onto his back. His chest heaved with labored breaths, while blood pooled around his lips.

"Roll him over," Jie said. "He's less of a threat."

The boy met her gaze, revealing a teenager with thin lips and narrow eyes. Huang Zhen, if memory and age progression skills served. They'd served in the same cell in Jiangkou during Lord Tong's rebellion. He bowed and pushed the Bovyan over.

The Teleri flopped like a sea cucumber. Her throwing spike was now buried deep into him, undoubtedly puncturing a lung. Even if he could talk, he wouldn't last long.

Huang rifled through his possessions. "Master Tian told us to be on the lookout for the Nightblades and to triangulate the source of their orders. This one started trailing me at the *Jianguo* Temple on my way over to meet you."

Jie snorted. "You could've found a way to warn me. He almost hit me with his dart."

"Hit *you*?" Huang's eyes widened.

She used her good hand to hold the other arm up. "I'm not what I used to be." She beckoned Yuha over.

Gawking, his head turned left and right, and then down at the stone road, which he stamped on a few times. He mumbled several foreign words which nonetheless conveyed the universal message of awe. The poor man had probably never seen a grand city before.

"Where's Tian?" she asked.

Huang's lip quivered. "He went after Princess Kaiya."

Jie sighed. Yet again, he chose the princess first. "Where is she now? The palace?"

"No, she fled south to Fenggu Province just yesterday."

Jie shook her head in disbelief. The *Tiger's Eye* must've worn off in order for the princess to do something so emotional and stupid. She'd be safer behind the castle walls, where they could hold out for years. Tian, too, had gone. Had the princess not fled, perhaps they'd be reunited by now. Jie's stomach knotted. "She has put herself in danger, for no reason."

"No, no." Huang held up a hand as he tried to pry the *biao* out of the Nightblade. "The regent wanted to draw the Teleri army south, away from the capital."

"And?"

"It worked. Only five thousand enemy soldiers remain in the city, mostly surrounding the palace."

Jie sucked on her lower lip. "How many men do we have?"

"Maybe eight thousand? But they're holed up in the palace."

Choking breaths coming to a stop, the Nightblade stilled.

Jie tapped him with her foot. No response. Even if he *were* playing dead, they would likely not get any information out of him.

Kneeling over him, Yuha placed fingers along the man's carotid pulse. "Dead," he said in Arkothi. He bowed and chanted several words.

She sniffed. "He has a faint flowery smell."

"I didn't notice." Huang gaped at her. Of course, her elf senses surpassed a human's.

She pointed at the shoulder of the man's black stealth suit. "Gold and silver cosmetic dust."

Huang's brows furrowed, his eyes shifting back and forth. "The Floating World."

Jie nodded. Perhaps this operative had already partaken of the Floating World's pleasures. Or he'd been there for other reasons. "Are there any adepts who gathered information there?"

"Feng Mi. During Minister Hong's entrapment of Chief Minister Tan, she was the one who choked him out."

Jie sucked on her lower lip. In retrospect, Minister Hong never showed any knack for conspiracy, yet had somehow cornered a master conspirator. "Where's Chief Minister Hong now?"

"The regent dismissed him and he's now unaccounted for."

A man's muffled yell trickled through the air, so quiet Huang Zhen didn't notice.

With her elf ears, Jie tracked the source. A villa, not far upstream. She gestured in *Moquan* code. *Over there. A sound.* It might have come out unintelligible with only one hand, but Huang nodded and padded lightly in the direction she'd indicated.

"Dump it," Jie whispered to Yuha, pointing at the corpse before running after Huang.

"Spirits not approve," Yuha grumbled.

Kneeling by a wall, Huang motioned for Jie to halt. He pointed.

With barely a sound, a dark human shape in the shadows of a nearby villa wall dragged a body toward an evergreen hedge. Undetectable without elf vision.

Investigate, Jie signaled.

Huang nodded, and then crept up on the interloper. He reached in.

The stranger let go of the body and grabbed Huang's arm. With a graceful spin, he dumped Huang on his back, mounted him, and placed a short blade to his throat. He was good. Nightblade good.

Jie whipped a throwing star at the Nightblade's back, but he twisted out of its path.

"Stop." He stood and held his hands up. "It's me. Tian."

Jie's heart skipped a beat. It was Tian's voice, though perhaps the Nightblade had learned the *Mockingbird's Deception*. Still, whoever it was helped Huang to his feet. She dashed over.

Up close, it was clearly Tian. She careened into him, wrapping her good arm around his back. "I thought you'd run after the princess again."

"I'd planned to. But something puzzled me." He pointed at the body. "This Teleri tried to trail me. I evaded him. And stalked him instead. He came here. He started making notes. About the mansions in this district."

"The nobles' quarter," Huang said.

Jie shuddered. "Standard operating procedure for the Teleri as they subjugate a land. They will kill all male royalty and take all women of childbearing age to breed the new ruling class. No doubt they'll be sending troops here once they've accomplished more pressing objectives."

"They already know so much," Tian said. "About the city and its defenses. They were able to capture a well-defended city. While taking minimal losses. They must have had someone in the city. For quite a while."

Leina stared at the *Weiqi* board, continuing the game with her only worthy opponent. She placed a black piece down right next to where she had set the white, closing off an escape route. Cathay was doomed, and if they saw the board as she did, they would just surrender and spare their soldiers brutal deaths.

A tear formed in her eye. News out of the far south had come to a sudden halt once Emperor Geros had captured Huajing and proceeded on his mad pursuit of Princess Kaiya. He had promised the release of Leina's mother from the Madurans, but... Practically speaking, an old woman with a small escort would have little means of making it first through Peng's rebellion and then Cathay's imperial army.

If her mother made it to the capital, at least, she would find it pacified. Leina was seeing to that, even with her limited resources. Five thousand heavy infantry, with nearly six hundred injured and unable to fight. Thirteen Nightblades, though their leader Feiying had disappeared and two had not reported back. The enemy might outnumber them two to one, they might have a handful of the mysterious *Moquan* at their disposal—but she kept them plugged up in Sun-Moon Palace and tricked the populace with rumors.

Leina stood and stretched out her tired legs. The stress of strategizing weighed heavily in her neck and shoulders. How ironic that a nation of rapists, who saw women as a vagina and womb, now relied on a female to spearhead their occupation. How ironic that she did so. Cathay might be a hateful nation of greedy, immoral merchants, but they probably didn't deserve absorption into the Teleri Empire. Regardless, as long as there was hope for her mother, she would do Geros' bidding. Her home would serve as the brain center for the occupation, with the Nightblades coming and going in secret, relaying her orders to the Teleri officers.

She walked through the sitting room, avoiding the spot where Old Hong had died. Even though the Nightblades had disposed of the body, it seemed like his spirit still lingered there, gazing at her through those sad eyes. Shuddering, she came to the pantry and released the dwarf-made trigger to the secret door into the Jade Teahouse.

The common room was empty, save for pretty little Purple Autumn sipping tea at a bloodwood table with the proprietress. The silence felt so different from the Floating World's heyday, when Night Blossoms entertained rich patrons at this late hour. The teahouse's high-class clientele had fled the city, and the Bovyans were not allowed to partake of women until they set up the mating compounds. Leina shuddered again at her own experiences in a rape camp in Madura.

With a sway in her hips, she sauntered over to the table. "May I?"

"Please." Purple Autumn nodded and extended her hand to an open seat. The poor girl had spent so many days here, wearing a simple dress instead of one of her extravagant gowns.

The proprietress stood. "I'll get another tea cup."

Leina settled into the bloodwood chair. "I've seen you here a lot recently."

"The Teleri prowl the streets, and I have nowhere else to go." Purple Autumn dabbed her eyes.

With a pat on the girl's arm, Leina cast a sympathetic smile. Always women suffered the most in war, through loss of children or their dignity. The poor girl's mysterious patron must've been one of those who had fled, deserting her. Leina's own surviving patron, Liu Dezhen, hid behind the palace walls with his infant son, the *Tianzi*. He had probably forgotten all about her in an attempt to save himself.

"Where are you staying now?"

"Here, until my money runs out." Tears gathered in Purple Autumn's lashes.

If not for the Nightblades' constant coming and going, Leina would offer Purple Autumn a place to stay. Maybe she still could. The girl was just a sixteen-year-old pampered prostitute who wouldn't notice the frequent backdoor visitors. Even if she did, she had always proven smart and witty. Perhaps given the chance to avoid gang rape at the hands of the Bovyans, she might make a capable lieutenant.

CHAPTER 35:
Allies

A *guzheng* twanged somewhere nearby, each note strummed to the beat of Kaiya's heart. Cool silken sheets caressed her body while the residual shiver of lovemaking receded in her core. Limbs languid, she shifted to her side.

Tian. He lay there beside her, the smooth tone of his bare body sending her pulse pounding again. He flashed his crooked smile, and her belly erupted into a swarm of butterflies.

He rolled onto her, pressing his chiseled abdomen and chest against hers. Heat flared inside of her. He propped himself on his elbows and met her gaze. His dark eyes saw past the regal princess, saw *her*. "Don't tell her. The babies are safe for now, but she couldn't handle the news."

News? Her? Who did he mean? And why was he speaking in Levanthi-accented Ayuri?

She blinked and looked again.

Tian was gone.

Replaced by Geros.

Pressed against her, he grinned. When he spoke, it was in Ayuri as well. "We'll keep it to ourselves."

Jolted from sleep, heart racing, Kaiya jerked up to find herself on a soft bed, covered by a cool silk sheet. Neither Tian nor Geros were to be found. The *Tiger's Eye* rose up around her, squelching the conflicting tidal wave of emotions.

Where was she? The Paladin Citadel in Vyara City? That would explain the sing-song intonation of Ayuri spoken among the dark, human-shaped forms around her. Somewhere

nearby, a *guzheng* played. She blinked, clearing her vision.

The elegant bloodwood furniture, fine porcelain vases, and hanging scrolls could only belong in a Hua noble's villa.

"She's awake!" a deep voice said in Arkothi.

Kaiya tracked the voice to its source, a man with a curly mop of brown hair. He stood beside Doctor Wu, but only came up to her chest. Fleet! And next to him, the chocolate-skinned Mystic Brehane.

"Athran smiles upon you," said someone on the other side of the bed, in halting Arkothi.

She turned to see Cyrus Estazadeh, one of the few remaining true Akolytes, bowing his head.

By his religion's moral standards, her sleeping robe exposed too much of her bust. Kaiya pulled the sheets up to her chest, and Fleet's lower lip jutted out.

At Cyrus' side, Sameer pressed his palms together in Ayuri greeting. "Princess Kaiya, I am glad to see you awake."

"How long have I been asleep? Where are we?"

"Foolish girl," Doctor Wu said. "We are in Lord Fen's castle in Hualian. It has been three days since you fainted from blood loss. You are fortunate the Akolyte's divine magic could heal you."

Three days. Only five days to reach the pyramid. Kaiya looked from her to Cyrus and placed her fingers and thumb in a circle over her heart, in the fashion of the Levasti. "Thank you, Cyrus. How did you find us?"

Cyrus started to speak when Fleet cut in front of him with a wide smile. "We were paddling up river when we saw your men on the highway, just outside the city. We thought they were going to join up with the Cathayi army until we saw you with them, hunched over your horse."

Doctor Wu wagged a finger at her. "If not for the Akolyte thrashing through the water to get to us, you might have bled out."

Cyrus bowed. "Your baby is safe."

Kaiya met each of their gazes. Their expressions said it all; they knew. No point in hiding it, anyway. "Babies."

Fleet leaned in. "Whose—ow!"

Sameer let go of the madaeri's ear and pressed his hands together. Brehane sidled over and clasped her hand. The warmth was as reassuring as it had been during their escape from Iksuvius, when the altivorcs were chasing them.

Kaiya turned to Doctor Wu. "How far away are the Teleri?"

"They have gained ground on us. The latest scouting report puts them in Long-An."

Closing her eyes, Kaiya summoned a map in her mind. Now if only she had a better sense of geography. Long-An lay north, but the distance...well, they had passed through the town the day the carriage axle snapped. Which meant... She opened her eyes. "Summon Commander Zhuang."

Doctor Wu frowned. "You are in no condition to ride a horse."

"What about the carriage?"

The doctor shook her head. "Lord Fen's men say it could take them several days to repair."

Several days seemed too long to repair an axle. With the Teleri in pursuit and the conjunction just four days away, they didn't have several days to wait. She sighed. "How can I travel while keeping my unborn children safe?"

"A palanquin," Doctor Wu said.

Kaiya shook her head. "The palanquin won't outrun the Teleri, nor will it make it to the pyramid in time."

"Pyramid?" Fleet stood on his tiptoes. "There *is* another way. On the other end of Hualian's famous gorge lies a town on Teardrop Lake. Yanhu. You can take a boat to the pyramid."

Kaiya gawked at the madaeri. How did he know so much more about *her* country? "Will there be enough time?"

Nodding, Fleet pointed out the window. "That's the way we planned to go."

"You are going to the pyramid, too?"

Sameer chuckled. "In Iksuvius, you offered us a tour of the Cathayi pyramid."

She had. Though not under such unforeseen circumstances.

"How serendipitous." Doctor Wu pursed her lips.

With a glance around the room, Kaiya found clean travelling clothes on a bloodwood chair. "I will dress now. Have Commander Zhuang meet me here in ten minutes."

When everyone had filed out, Kaiya threw off the covers. Her bare feet found the hardwood floors, though her legs wobbled as she stood. Stuttering over to the chair, she shrugged off the robe and slipped on the dress. Tian's lockpick pouch tumbled out of her folded sash as she picked it up. After winding the sash around her waist, she retrieved the pouch.

As always, it felt heavy in her hand, like her heart whenever the *Tiger's Eye* faltered. Always at the most inopportune times, and a now with increasing frequency. If—no, *when*—it finally gave way for good, she might be left a quivering tangle of emotions, unable to mother her fatherless twins, let alone rule a crumbling nation.

A knock at the door startled her. "*Jie-xia*," Commander Zhuang called.

Kaiya straightened. "Enter."

The doors slid open and Commander Zhuang marched in with two aides. They all dropped to a knee.

"*Jie-xia*," the commander said, "messengers report that Lord Wu leads the Zhenjing provincial army through the western pass into Fenggu. The main imperial army is also marching north."

Both converging near the pyramid. Kaiya nodded. As long as they stayed just ahead of the Teleri, Emperor Geros would be walking into the imperial army's waiting guns. There would be no need to rely on magic that she might not be able to conjure. "Send word to Lord Wu to hold his position and fall upon the Teleri rear when they pass him on the central highway."

With his officers nodding in agreement, Commander Zhuang's lips twitched before finally smiling. "Very good, *Jie-xia*. I will send one of our men immediately. We are ready to ride on your order."

She shook her head. "I cannot ride a horse in my condition. I will have to ride in a palanquin."

His eyes widened. "The Teleri will overtake us before we meet with the imperial army."

"Which is why you will continue on the highway with a decoy while I go through the gorge." Similar plans had ostensibly worked twice before, first in the escape from Iksuvius and again when fleeing from Dongmen.

Commander Zhuang rose to his feet. "*Jie-xia*, we cannot leave you unprotected."

"I have travelled with far less protection." She beckoned to the door, where her friends waited. "They will be with me, and while I do not doubt your men's abilities, you serve the realm better with my plan."

He exchanged looks with the two officers, who shook their heads. He opened his mouth in protest.

"That is my command."

"Yes, *Jie-xia*." He bowed. "I will have Lord Fen prepare palanquins for you. We will procure some of his uniforms and banners to disguise thirty of us as his soldiers, to make it appear as if it is his family fleeing ahead of the Teleri invasion."

A sound idea. Kaiya nodded. The Southerners and thirty imperial cavalry would be more than enough protection against enemy patrols.

Peng Kai-Long rode at the head of one hundred thousand soldiers, the imperial and provincial banners mingled amongst them. In every town they passed, the people all kowtowed to him. One day, soon, they would be rewarded. The nation would prosper again, growing as other civilizations bowed before Hua's superior culture.

From his place right behind, General Lu spurred his horse forward and bowed. "*Huang-Shang.*"

Kai-Long lifted his chin. The formal address for *Tianzi* might be a little premature. There was still the rest of the imperial army to convince, and then coronation rites to be held. "Speak."

"The rest of the imperial army is encamped near the Luzhou, about five days away at our current march. If it is your will, I shall send word to have the commanders meet us first, to ensure their loyalty."

"You did not think the Guardian Dragon answering my call on the battlefield was reassuring enough?" Kai-Long straightened on his horse and stared back.

The general cast his gaze down. "Of course not, *Huang-Shang*. The Mandate of Heaven is clearly with you."

As long as the Aksumi Mystic stayed pleased. Kai-Long snorted. The illusionist's sexual appetite was becoming quite the tale around camp. He had already partaken of several of the new Maduran prostitutes they'd rescued from Prince Dhananad's defeated army.

Except the noble-looking one. If rumors were to be believed, she had yet to take any clients. How she fended off drunken soldiers, or even fed herself...

The Water Snake spy, disguised as a messenger, ran up. He dropped to his knee and held up a missive. "*Huang-Shang*, the latest dispatch from the North."

"Rise."

With his head still bowed, the man stood and proffered the message. Taking it with a hand, Kai-Long snapped it open and glanced over the news. Nothing they didn't know already. The Teleri army and Lord Wu's men were all five days away from the Luzhou. He squinted, trying to decipher the coded language embedded within.

From Fen. Regent left. In gorge.

Kai-Long gritted his teeth. Lord Fen was supposed to have kept the princess until the Teleri arrived. Through the gorge would take her to Yanhu, on the lake, off-course from Luzhou…unless she found a boat. Damn her!

The spy cleared his throat. "We have several friends who can solve this problem."

Friends, as in Water Snake *Moquan,* most likely. Kai-Long nodded. "Yes, take care of her."

Water bubbled over rocks outside of the palanquin, setting a soothing rhythm for Kaiya to practice a magical song in her mind. If not for the urgency and secrecy, it might've been worth walking through the gorge, where smooth white rocks towered high above a stream. The path, carved in the cliff face some thirty feet above the brook, was just wide enough for the porters to carry her palanquin. Interspersed rock columns supported an overhanging path. To think that, if not for the *Tiger's Eye,* she would be frozen in fear from the tight confines *and* the thought of the height.

The procession came to a halt, and the porters lowered the palanquin to the ground. Kaiya slid open the window and looked out. "Why are we stopping?" With the narrowness of the path, they had to exit the gorge by sundown.

"*Jie-xia,*" Doctor Wu said, "The porters need rest. You should stretch your legs, as well."

Kaiya squirmed around, readjusting her seat. Yes, her legs would benefit from a walk. "Very well."

The door slid open, allowing in the afternoon sun. She climbed out and found herself on a broad ledge that jutted out from the path, uncovered by the overhang. Her feet tingled as she

shook them out. Around her, guards dismounted. The three Southerners sat. They had abandoned their own palanquins at the mouth of the gorge in favor of walking.

Fleet balanced on the lip of rocks that lined the ledge. "Kind of reminds me of when we fled through that ravine in Iksuvi, escaping the altivorcs."

Kaiya sighed. That misadventure had taken days and claimed her loyal imperial guards Zhao Yue and Li Wei. Tian had been so sure Fleet was leading them into a trap, and yet, the madaeri saved them time and time again.

Now, he froze in place, ears perked. Just like when the altivorcs ambushed them.

Kaiya closed her eyes and listened. From above, something clicked and twanged. Air displaced, coming toward her. She dropped to the ground. A bolt thwacked into the palanquin. She dared a glance up. It would've hit her in the head.

A cocking clack betrayed the weapon as a repeating crossbow. The trigger clicked. The string twanged. Another bolt whizzed at her. She rolled to the side, and a cramp gripped her womb. The bolt struck the ground right where she'd been.

Then Sameer was there. His *naga* swirled so fast it seemed like a parasol of glowing blue. *Clack. Click. Twang. Woosh. Thunk,* the *naga* cut through another incoming bolt, this time from another direction.

"Protect the regent!" Commander Zhuang mounted up, withdrew his bow and loosed. Around him, other cavalrymen jumped into their saddles. Yet with the limited space, the horses lost the advantage of mobility. Instead, they formed a protective ring. Several horses reared as bolts struck them.

"Get back," Cyrus said. "Back onto the covered path."

Fleet zigzagged between falling bolts and came to her side. Helping her to her feet, he pulled her back behind a column of rock. Sameer backed up with them, swinging his *naga.* Brehane already waited behind cover.

"Thirty men on the other side of the gorge," Fleet said, pointing. "Armed with repeating crossbows."

It was too similar to the altivorc ambush from before. Another cramp squeezed her belly. Kaiya grimaced, and then peeked around the column.

Hand on the golden circlet of Athran around his neck, Cyrus braved the storm of bolts, helping wounded men back. Blood stained his robes—whether his or one of the guards, it was impossible tell.

Someone, or a few someones, shuffled around the rock columns, too far away to be one of imperial soldiers. Fleet's eyes darted in that direction even before Kaiya pointed.

A dark shape leaped at her, the flash of the sun reflecting off his sword blinding her. A blade whistled through the air and cut into flesh. A man screamed.

"Black Fists," Fleet yelled. "They're cornering us on the path while the crossbowmen keep us pinned down."

No wonder. They were certainly too well coordinated to be random bandits. Vision brightening and coming into focus, Kaiya took stock of the situation. The guards fought and loosed arrows while enemy *Moquan* darted back and forth, engaging and disengaging. Men clutched wounds and yelled; others just fell to the ground, silent. Bolts continued to fly in from a sharp angle above.

"Protect me," Brehane shouted. She turned out from behind the cover of a column and started chanting in the guttural language of Shallow Magic. Sameer stood beside her, nonchalantly knocking away incoming bolts. At the end of her spell, a fireball exploded across the gorge, louder and brighter than any firework. Brehane collapsed into Sameer's arms.

Kaiya blinked. Brehane had become so powerful.

The barrage of bolts dwindled, and the imperial soldiers now renewed their own shots with increased speed. Soon, incoming attacks trickled to a halt.

Commander Zhuang dropped to a knee in front of her. "*Jie-xia*, we have repelled the insurgents."

At what cost? Kaiya looked around again. Several black-clad *Moquan* lay on the ground, their blood painted across the stone path. Her men, too, had taken significant casualties. It also meant that the *Moquan* had turned against her, and that they knew she was coming through the gorge.

Fleet appeared around a column, clasping a torn swath of cloth with a *wen* emblem. A link of wisteria blossoms, the symbol of the Lord of Yanhu.

Right where they were heading. Now that the wounded needed tending, there was no way they could exit the gorge by nightfall.

CHAPTER 36:

Spider in the Web

Jie paused outside the doors of *Tiantai* Shrine's main building, confirming that she hadn't been followed in the predawn hours. Even with a useless arm, stealth still came naturally, and elf senses prevented anyone from sneaking up on her.

It was deserted and dark, the surrounding derelict compound and overgrown gardens lit only by the iridescent moon as it waned to its fifth gibbous. Satisfied, she pushed the door open just wide enough for her to slip through. The interior hadn't changed from a year before: just a plain stone floor and a large chest on a raised dais.

Everyone in Huajing believed the chest had once housed some jade relic from the previous dynasty. However, she had learned its true purpose during the princess' clandestine departure for Vyara City a year before. She depressed a button on a rear hinge, which led to a whispering swish inside the chest. Opening the lid now revealed a set of steps leading down into the secret passages beneath the palace and castle. Maybe her *Moquan* brethren could surreptitiously scale the palace walls in designated areas, but now her handicap relegated her to easier ways.

The musty stone corridors appeared completely undisturbed. Only the senior-most imperial guards knew of the passages, and from the layer of dust on the pavestones, none had come through here since the princess' journey. The tunnel leading into the inner castle had been walled off as if it had never existed, suggesting that the castle defenders had come at least this far. However, the steps leading up to the outer palace

grounds remained unblocked. At the top, she released the dwarf-made trigger and the wall slid open without a sound.

The manicured garden from a year ago now looked like a supply depot. Crates crushed new spring grass while kegs of firepowder crowded shrubs under the eaves of adjacent buildings. With a sigh, Jie made her way toward the Hall of Supreme Harmony, where her clansmen said the leadership gathered.

Walking among the many buildings, she stumbled upon a city of tents in the vast central courtyard. Some armed men moved about, but for the most part, everyone seemed asleep. Unwilling and possibly unable to castrate any belligerent soldier who might decide to take advantage of a palace maid, she avoided contact and instead crept up the steps to the hall.

She passed through open doors and into the vast, dark chamber. With no one inside, the light baubles remained mostly shuttered, filling the room with a dim illumination. Two maps lay on the floor, with black and white pebbles on them like a *weiqi* game. One map depicted the nation, with the white stones representing the imperial forces and their provincial allies, and the black stones a mess of Peng's rebellion, Madurans, and Teleri.

The other map was the capital. The position of black stones showed just how little the army crowded into the palace knew of the occupation. *Moquan* secrecy likely accounted for much of the ignorance. The lack of communication that checked and balanced loyalties in times of peace now proved a weakness in times of war.

Jie began rearranging the enemy positions. Several thousand outside the palace gates. A central command center in the northern marketplace, not far away. Four hundred, mostly wounded, in the northwest quadrant. Two hundred at the north gate, five hundred at the west gate, and eight hundred along the holes in the east walls. Patrols fanning out and back.

With the eight thousand Hua soldiers on hand, a surprise attack coordinated from the rear and flank could defeat the Teleri. Though, as Tian said, they had to first root out and eliminate the brains behind the occupation. If the foolhardy commanders here behind the palace walls knew about the secret tunnels, they'd rush out at the first opportunity.

Servants opened the double doors and filtered in, opening the shutters as they went. Many paused when their gazes fell on her. One rushed out, yelling, "Intruder!"

Jie harrumphed. Certainly someone would recognize her as Princess Kaiya's handmaiden.

Soon enough, imperial guards burst in with flashing *dao*. Not that she could fight them all even if she had the use of both her arms. She ignored them, continuing with her work of organizing the stones on the city map. Though they kept their weapons bared, they didn't try to stop her.

Presently, Minister Song and two generals stepped over the threshold.

The minister jabbed a finger at her. "Who are you? How did you get in here?"

"And why are you rearranging our maps?" General Tang, whom she recognized from the past, glared at her. The soldiers would be better served if General Shan were in command.

Jie stopped and bowed. "I was Princess Kaiya's bodyguard, though I masqueraded as her handmaiden. The acting *Tianzi's* mother Wang Kai-Hua can vouch for the handmaiden part. You have heard of the *Tianzi's* agents—that is my clan."

Minister Song gawked, and then nodded.

"And the maps?" General Tang pointed.

She waved a hand across the rearranged stones. "Our clan has observed enemy positions and I have made changes based on what we know now. We have harassed their supply lines. You have enough men to defeat them."

The other general—Sun?— furrowed his brows. "We knew that. However, we are stuck behind the walls while they concentrate *our* muskets and *our* firepowder on the only way out."

"There is another route. The same way I came in."

General Tang harrumphed. "The soldiers can't climb walls like the *Tianzi's* agents."

"Neither can I." As much as she hated her handicap, Jie used her good arm to hold up her useless one.

"The escape tunnels." The imperial guard commander's voice sounded awestruck.

She nodded.

"Only the senior-most imperial guards know how to get in," he said. "And they are all behind the inner castle walls. How do *you* know?"

"I watched the late Chen Xin engage the trigger."

The imperial guard general bowed.

General Sun stomped on the floor. "Then we will mount a counter-attack."

"No," Jie said. "Not yet. We don't know if there are any spies among us, and there is a mastermind behind the occupation. Once my clansmen find him, I will let you know how to get out. In the meantime, plan that counter-attack."

Tian stared at the lines of thread weaving across the abandoned Floating World theater stage, each sagging with clues and evidence. With the Bovyans' lack of high culture and their mating habits highly regulated, the entertainment district would be a safe place for his attempts to uncover the brains behind the Teleri occupation.

The threads came up organically as he categorized the Nightblade sightings, Teleri patrol patterns, and citizen arrests. The origins and impact of the myriad rumors regarding the *Tianzi* held a particular interest. He had gone mad. He had died. He had fled the city. The Metal Men were clearly working hard to undermine the people's confidence.

With the rest of his gang of young *Moquan* out on missions, Feng Mi and Huang Zhen watched him from the audience seating. Despite what they thought, the Teleri didn't have any interest in the palace and castle, except to make it seem like they did. His people had already countered half-hearted insertions by Nightblades, and they'd proven adept at avoiding capture and tailing. No, those attempts were merely a distraction, to prevent organized resistance to a small occupying army.

"Up to your old habits." Jie said from the entrance. All heads turned her way. "How you see anything in these cobwebs you construct…"

Old habits, ones he didn't remember. Using the strings made perfect sense, and there was an order to it, one which only he seemed to see. He pointed to three pieces of evidence, one at a time. "The timing between these events suggests at least seven Nightblades and no more than twelve. If we know their number, I can triangulate the source of their orders. A spider lurks somewhere in this web."

Jie laughed. A cute laugh which stirred a sense of nostalgia, even if no concrete memories surfaced. "In *that* web, *you* are the only spider I am seeing."

The two younger ones chuckled. With a snort, he contorted between several strands…and paused. "What do you mean?"

She tilted her head. "Just that you look like a spider in your web."

He turned around, a full rotation in place, as he scanned his notes. A Nightblade sighting at the palace. Another in the noble's district. One by the east wall. No activity in the far west of the city. Now, he had an excellent vantage point to see it. "Here. In the Floating World."

"What?" Jie worked her way down the aisles.

Tian tapped a foot on the stage's hardboards. "The spider is here. In the Floating World."

Jie came to the edge of the stage and pointed with her good arm at the note about the Nightblade she and Huang Zhen had killed in the noble's quarter. "That one had a smudge of prostitute's make-up on his suit."

Huang Zhen nodded emphatically. "And smelled of perfume."

"Right." Tian traced a line connecting Chief Minister Hong to the center of the web. "You also believe our proverbial spider might be hiding out here?"

"Hong is connected to the insurgency through Chief Minister Tan, and then the decisions to move soldiers away from the capital." Jie pointed at the same thread, then another branching off of it. "He had access to couriers and could've ordered the assassination on the princess at your father's castle. He was present when the *Tianzi* sealed off the inner castle, yet somehow ended up on the outside, in the palace grounds."

Feng Mi stood. "I've turned the Floating World upside-down, inside-out, and there's no sign of him."

Tian tapped his chin. Stubble prickled his fingers. "I'm certain the mastermind is here. What did Hong have to gain? What did he want?"

Jie sucked on her lower lip. "From my observations, he was obsessed with the princess. Maybe for power, maybe just because she was unattainable to someone of his station."

She shouldn't have been attainable to Tian, either. He pointed to the thread which included the assassination attempt on her. "Then he wouldn't want her killed. He was either very skilled at manipulating all these improbabilities into reality…"

"Or he is an unwitting puppet," Jie said.

"If that is the case, who pulls his strings?" Tian scratched his chin again. Having been posted abroad during the insurgency, he didn't know all of the minister's associations firsthand.

"Peng Kai-Long," Jie said. "I saw them together several times."

The one behind the rebellion in the South. Tian closed his eyes and tried to conjure a memory of what this Peng looked like. "Why would he want the nation invaded?"

"To divert the imperial armies?" Feng Mi said.

Huang Zhen nodded. "To defeat the Teleri and win the admiration of the people."

"He would need to take command of the imperial army first." Tian snorted. Not very likely. "And he would have no means of communicating with Hong now. His past actions make him appear very hands-on. Even if he lets others get their hands dirty."

Jie sucked on her lower lip. "Emperor Geros delegates efficiently."

"But the clan would be aware of Hong communicating with someone out of the country."

"What if Geros used an intermediary?" Jie pointed back at the web. "You believe the occupation is coordinated from here, in the Floating World, and Hong is not here."

Feng Mi jumped up and down, expression bright. "Hong's concubine."

A concubine. Tian swept his gaze over his notes. Nowhere was there any mention of a concubine. "What do we know of her?"

"Half-Ayuri from Ankira," Feng Mi said. "She arrived in Hua about three years ago, searching for her father."

Tian furiously scribbled notes and clipped them to a new thread intersecting Hong's. "What was Hong doing three years ago?"

Jie sucked on her lower lip again. "That was during Lord Tong's insurgency. He was promoted to Minister of the Imperial Household after serving as a palace valet."

"...And would've arranged many of the matchmaking meetings," Tian said. "For Princess Kaiya." Not that it mattered to the Teleri's spider. Still, it showed a pattern of ambition, making Hong attractive to someone looking for influence inside the court. "He made sure she didn't marry. All so he could one day claim her for his own." His stomach twisted. Jealousy? Over a woman he didn't remember?

"He visited his concubine often," Feng Mi said, "especially after he became Chief Minister and bought a house. We deemed it typical male behavior."

Or plotting? Tian maneuvered the concubine's thread over several others. "We are going to pay a visit to Hong's house. If she is still there and coordinating the Teleri occupation, we will eliminate her and launch Jie's counter-attack." He turned to Jie. "Go back to the palace to help them prepare, and await my message."

Back to the palace. Jie snorted to herself as she crept through the darkened streets. Tian might not have run after the princess, but it wasn't as if the time they had together now brought them any closer. In fact, with her handicap, they seemed to be growing further apart. At least before, he had respected her as a comrade. Now she was nothing more than a messenger girl.

A messenger girl with superb senses. She froze in place. Somewhere, someone watched her. How far she'd fallen. Her skills must have deteriorated for even a Nightblade to best her in routine stealth techniques.

Well, her stalker probably hadn't counted on her elf vision. She scanned the surroundings, focusing on the shadows cast by the moons. Two-story row houses lined the road. Trees stood every—there, behind one of the trunks. A stout man. Too short for a Bovyan, though with her bad arm, he could probably overpower her.

Now who would be out so late? Certainly not a rapist in an occupied city. No women came out, and Teleri patrols roamed the streets. Better not to find out. Jie darted to the closest tree and prepared to evade.

"Wait," the man called out in heavily accented Arkothi. He stepped out from behind the tree and raised his hands. His cloak flared open, revealing a broadsword at his waist. "I have a proposition for you, half-elf."

The dark olives of his complexion in her night vision suggested someone from the South, yet his accent didn't sound familiar. The features— heavy, with fangs. An altivorc, and a prince, no less, given his good looks. Her experiences with altivorcs over the years had never been friendly.

She reached for a *biao*. "What do you want?"

He scanned up and down the street, then up into the windows. He lowered his voice. "I have been searching for you. My king has a proposition. And as a reward, he will heal your arm."

CHAPTER 37:
Lights and Magic

A light breeze whistled through the boughs of flowering plum trees, sending their petals tumbling down like fragrant snow around Kaiya. Her younger self would've fought the urge to spin in a circle at the beauty, but the *Tiger's Eye* made maintaining imperial propriety easy.

Just as well, since Doctor Wu would undoubtedly reprimand any spring frolicking as dangerous to the babies. At her insistence, they now rode horses slow enough for a tortoise to keep pace. The trail through the gorge descended, while the stream widened. Soon, the gulch would open up to the quaint town of Yanhu, where the *Yu-Ming* lord had aligned himself with either Peng's rebellion or the Teleri invasion.

Fleet walked ahead, at point. A small, dark silhouette as dusk approached, he would occasionally pause and signal for the rest of her entourage to stop. Her honor guard had dwindled, with those too wounded to travel left behind with her palanquin and porters. It had been hard to convince Commander Zhuang to comply. The one thing she missed most about the power of her voice was not having to waste time with logical arguments.

They reached the mouth of the gorge as the iridescent moon waxed to its first gibbous. The white moon Renyue waxed to half, while Guanyin's Eye neared full-open. Only four days until the conjunction of the three. Their light now mixed together, casting the lake town of Yanhu in a curious hue. Yet it was Teardrop Lake itself, glowing a faint blue, which lit up the sloped roofs, winding paths, docks and boats. It'd been years since she visited.

Fleet pointed. "Soldiers. At least sixty of them, two kilometers...three *li*...away."

Kaiya squinted along the stream, now about six or seven paces wide, but saw only indistinct shadows. Her ears couldn't pick out the men breathing from such a far distance. Still, they had twenty of the best cavalry soldiers with them. "Commander?"

"They won't dare stop imperial cavalry." Commander Zhuang rested a hand on his sword hilt.

Fleet chuckled. "Sometimes a surgeon's knife works better than a hacksaw."

The soldier glared at the madaeri, then turned to Kaiya with pleading eyes.

Kaiya stared out into gorge. "What do you suggest?"

Commander Zhuang bowed. "Wait until dawn. Then we ride in a defensive position around the regent. Even if that traitor of a lord wishes her ill, the general populace will bow down before her."

"If they are on their knees, the traitors will have a better shot with their crossbows." Fleet rolled his eyes. "Let me go first and borrow a boat."

"Borrow?" Kaiya raised an eyebrow.

He grinned. "Procure. Commandeer. I am sure commandeering a boat in an emergency is well within the regent's purview. I will row it as far as it will go upstream, flash a signal with my light bauble, and you sneak down in small groups to meet me.”

Kaiya turned to the commander. “I appreciate your fervor and dedication. However, in this situation, perhaps something more subtle would be prudent.”

Lips drawn in a tight line, Commander Zhuang shuffled in place before bowing. “As the regent commands.”

Kaiya pointed back the way they’d come. “Whoever cannot fit in the boat shall return to the wounded and the porters in the gorge. As soon as you are able to travel, return to this town and await my command.”

“Yes, *Jie-xia*.” The commander bowed again, though his lips quivered.

Fleet skipped down the road without any obvious concern for his safety. Kaiya tracked him until he disappeared into the background.

“Sit and rest, *Jie-xia*.” Doctor Wu appeared at her side. Though the old woman’s hand on her shoulder felt light as silk, Kaiya sank to the ground. The imperial cavalry clopped forward, their hooves’ rhythmic beat lulling. Her leaden eyelids weighed down on her brow.

“*Jie-xia*,” Commander Zhuang’s voice called. Someone shook her shoulder.

Kaiya’s eyes flew open. She was lying on her side, a pack beneath her head and a cloak covering her from the night’s chill. Sitting up, she looked around.

“The halfling has returned,” Commander Zhuang said.

Returned...several hours must’ve passed, even if it seemed only a few minutes. Down near the town, perhaps a *li* away, a tiny light flashed three times. She stretched out her arms. “How long have I been asleep?”

Sameer strolled up and extended his hand. “Less than two hours.”

Kaiya took the Paladin’s hand. Around her, the imperial cavalry murmured, but bowed as she flashed an imperious glance.

“May I escort you to the boat?” Sameer pressed his hands together and bowed.

The commander gritted his teeth. “That is my responsibility.”

Sameer bowed. “On horseback, you must be a formidable archer. However, I am accustomed to fighting on my feet. Please give me the honor of walking with the princess, while you follow behind with your deadly bow in hand.”

As diplomatic as ever. Kaiya suppressed a smile that the *Tiger’s Eye* couldn’t contain.

Commander Zhuang grunted. Beckoning two of his men, he mounted up and drew his bow. “We will follow fifty paces behind you, *Jie-xia*.”

“Thank you, Commander.” Kaiya took Sameer’s hand, and he helped her down the slope to the stream. Her feet squished into the rich soil. Just like the time Tian had helped her along a river bank in the Wilds. He’d been so sweet, for the first time since they were children. Now, she pressed his set of lockpicks in her sash. Her heart fluttered, and a tear formed in her eye. Heavens, the *Tiger’s Eye* crumbled with disturbing frequency. It had to hold out, just a little longer.

Each footstep strengthened her resolve. On the other side of the stream, the first shoots of spring poked out of the farmland. After several dozen paces, they came to a broad weir. Beyond it churned a farm’s waterwheel, silhouetted by the moons’ light. The breaths of several men hid among the splashing water.

“Look out.” Kaiya gripped Sameer’s arm and pointed toward the waterwheel.

Hoe in hand, a man stepped out on the other side of the stream. “No trespassing on my farm!”

Kaiya squinted. He didn’t seem to have any weapons other than the hoe, and he wore a simple robe. Sameer’s body relaxed beneath her grip. “Forgive us,” she said. “My friend has never visited this area and wanted to see your waterwheel. We will be going on our way.” She waved up toward the road, where three of her horsemen trotted.

“Too authoritative a tone,” Sameer hissed. “I don’t even understand your language and I can tell. Plus, your posture is too regal.”

He was right. Slumping her shoulders, Kaiya cast her gaze down. Perhaps a commoner wouldn't notice.

"Princess Kaiya?" The farmer lowered the hoe and bowed.

So she looked and acted like an aristocrat. Still, a farmer had identified her by name despite the darkness. He also happened to be out at a late hour. She met his gaze. "How did you know?"

He started to kneel, then glanced back toward the town and stopped. He leaned in as far as the stream would allow and whispered, "Lord Zhi ordered us to keep an eye out for you. He has offered a reward of ten golden yuan for anyone who reports you."

"Why?"

The farmer shook his head. "These are uncertain times. Lord Peng marches this way, and rumor has it that a foreign army does as well. Talk in the village says our lord is trying to align himself with the one he thinks will win."

Apparently, Lord Zhi gave the imperial army even less of a chance than she did.

The man pointed back toward the town. "Many of our lord's men are watching the roads for you. Please be careful, *Dian-xia*. The people support the *Tianzi*."

Even if the *Tianzi* was an infant. Kaiya bowed her head. "Thank you. I have nothing to give you now, but when the imperial armies prove who has the Mandate of Heaven, I will make sure you are rewarded." She turned to Sameer and gestured toward the town. "Potential enemies are watching the roads. We need to stay by the stream."

Sameer nodded and pulled her along. Not far behind, small footsteps squelched in the mud. Kaiya looked back. Two small shapes, likely Brehane and Doctor Wu. Well behind them slunk two more people. Up ahead, maybe a quarter-*li* away where the stream again widened to about ten paces, a boat waited. Not much farther now.

"Halt!" A voice called from a road running above the other side of the stream. Between her and the boat, six men leveled repeating crossbows at them while another ran back toward the town. "Identify yourself," the first man called.

Sameer drew his *naga*, glowing a brighter blue than she'd ever seen. So much for peaceful negotiation.

Crossbow triggers clicked. Bolts zipped through the air. Sameer interposed himself between her and the attackers. His *naga* danced, deflecting the incoming barrage with superhuman speed. Wooden shafts snapped with staccato cracks.

From upstream, Brehane and the others' footsteps quickened.

"Loose!" Commander Zhuang yelled from the road above. Bowstrings twanged and horse hooves clopped. Several more horses charged from the mouth of the gorge. Arrows found their targets, and the local soldiers fell back. The commander had gotten his wish, and it was apparently the better plan after all.

"Hurry," Sameer said, pulling her into a trot. He swung his sword on occasion, clipping errant bolts.

Kaiya's feet squished between mud and water. She nearly tripped a couple of times, but they made it unscathed to the boat.

Boat? It didn't look that much wider than the canoes the Maki used during her winter sojourn in the Wilds. It might hold six, maybe seven with the madaeri and the smaller women. Despite the arrows and bolts, Fleet relaxed near the rear, his feet kicked back. He waved as they approached.

Sameer helped her in and pushed the boat with the current. Brehane and Doctor Wu tumbled in, and Cyrus joined Sameer, sloshing through stream as they splashed through knee-high water. The barrage of bolts dwindled to a stop, and the imperial cavalry kept pace on the road above.

"I don't know much about boats," Cyrus said, climbing in, "but how is this going to get us across the lake to the pyramid in four days?"

Fleet threw his hands up. "Not enough room for you to lie back, Your Majesty?"

"It *is* a little narrow." Sameer chuckled as he boarded, nearly capsizing the boat.

"Now you see the benefit of being small." Fleet grinned and pointed to the oars.

Kaiya gave the canoe a once-over. The Paladin was right; it would be a tight for four days, over open water, and... "Wait. We won't be near the shore, and we can't possibly paddle the whole time."

Fleet laughed. "We are going to steal—I mean, appropriate—the local lord's pleasure boat. I just used the canoe to get upstream."

"And where is this boat?" Brehane glared at the madaeri.

He pointed downstream. "Docked not far from the mouth."

Sameer sighed. "Guards?"

"Nothing we can't handle."

Kaiya stared at Fleet. He hadn't been so flippant in their escape from Iksuvius. "How about a crew?"

He puffed out his chest. "I'm quite the sailor." He then turned and scanned the banks. Where the madaeri found time to get good at everything was a mystery.

The waterway skirted away from Yanhu, and they reached the lake without further incident. The imperial cavalry had only kept up as far as a bridge that led into the town.

The lake's light blue waters reflected in Doctor Wu's eyes, bringing out their luminescence. Without the stream's current pushing them along, the men strained as they rowed along the lake's edge toward the town.

Lights shined in windows. Shouts carried across the water. Kaiya squirmed in her seat. It sounded like the imperial cavalry had drawn Lord Zhi's men away. She looked toward the closest dock, where an elegant skiff was moored. The name *Wind Dancer* was emblazoned in red on the hull.

"See?" Fleet pointed at the dock. "Completely unprotected."

They rowed up and climbed aboard the larger vessel. Large enough for the lord to entertain eight guests while he showed off his sailing skills, it would be comfortable enough for the six of them. Fleet worked the rigging while Sameer and Cyrus untied it from the mooring.

The sail billowed out and the skiff lurched forward. Kaiya's stomach rebelled, either from morning sickness or seasickness. She fought it

down. The waters shined brighter the further they sailed from the shore.

Brehane's expression danced with wonderment. "Why do the waters glow?"

Kaiya gestured toward Shenyue. "The blue moon is the Eye of Guanyin, Goddess of Mercy and Healing. When the Lord of the Sun, Yang-Di, created Tivara as a gift to her, she shed a tear. It landed here, giving birth to the Cathayi."

"Listen." Doctor Wu held up a finger. "Do you hear it? The energy of the world."

Closing her eyes, Kaiya listened. The vibration pulsed in her ears, slow but powerful. She opened her eyes.

At her side, Brehane nodded. "Yes, I feel it."

"Like around all the other pyramids we visited," Sameer said.

"Yes, yes." Fleet yawned. "Where the elves first built their cities. Where the Tivari erected the pyramids. Places in the world where energy is the strongest. I can't even count how many times I've repeated this story to you."

With a snort, Doctor Wu broke her glare from the madaeri. "Keep listening. It will only get louder."

It did. Over the next several days, the vibration resonated in Kaiya's core. At times, memories stirred her emotions, poking through the *Tiger's Eye*. Lord Xu's vision must be true. For better or worse, she would regain her emotions and her power at the pyramid.

Kai-Long looked up at the sky, where the white moon neared the blue moon. Tonight was the night, when the three moons would conjoin, just like they had three hundred years before to herald in the start of the Wang Dynasty.

A constellation of seven twinkling stars hovered above the moons, like a crown. Legends claimed the Golden Flock was frequently visible during the Age of Orcs, only to vanish after the War of Ancient Gods. It had appeared once since, during the Hellstorm, making it an omen of great change.

Tonight, it would herald his ascension to the Dragon Throne.

He shifted his gaze down from the hilltop to the imperial army camped not far from the pyramid. Soon, General Lu would return from his parley on Kai-Long's behalf. Lord Wu's provincial army held the mountain slopes on the imperials' flank. At Kai-Long's signal, they would switch banners to declare their loyalty to him. The final touch would be the reappearance of the Guardian Dragon.

When they yielded to him, his army would number three hundred thousand. Cousin Kaiya might have escaped his trap in the gorge and Yanhu, but there was nothing she could do to prevent his victory now.

On the evening of the fourth day, the song of the world's energy sang loud in Kaiya's ears. Guanyin's Eye rose low as always on the eastern horizon, silhouetting the pyramid beyond the shore. Gigantic trees lined the side of a road to the pyramid. Light filtered through the buds, forming veins of webbed light that branched toward the heavens.

Kaiya gazed at the grove for the first time in years. The elf angel Aralas had planted the Trees of Light over a millennium before, prior to the War of Ancient Gods. One still stood near Wild Turkey Island, where Geros had first raped her. Her most recent dream resurfaced, and the *Tiger's Eye* faltered, sending a shudder down her spine.

Much farther up the shore, thousands of other lights flickered. Campfires and torches. Kaiya pointed at them. "Fleet, can you make out the sigils on the banners?"

Fleet craned forward. "A golden dragon on a blue field."

The imperial banners. The imperial army must be camped here, stretching from the shore to a nearby mountainside. No, that couldn't be right; the imperial army numbered close to a hundred and fifty thousand, and it looked like far more men than that. She gestured toward the mountain. "How about them? Can you see the banners?"

Fleet whipped out a spyglass and stared through. "A black wolf on a red field." He proffered the scope.

Peng's army, so close, and busy. Kaiya took the glass and scanned from mountain to plain. Men marched in orderly ranks. Preparing to engage? At dusk, no less. "We must hurry to the pyramid. How much farther?"

"Just a few minutes." Fleet pointed toward the Trees of Light, looming large above them. Beneath their canopies, two humanoid shapes moved. Scouts, perhaps, though one was quite smaller than the other, and they were far from the two armies.

The skiff ran aground. Kaiya pitched forward in her seat. Clambering over the bulwarks, she splashed into the knee-high water and slogged to shore. Her companions followed, except for Fleet who sounded like he was fiddling with the rigging.

Doctor Wu waded after her. "Don't get too cold. It's bad for the babies."

Kaiya suppressed a laugh. The doctor was so persistent, but that wasn't important. Not now, when they were so close. So close to regaining her magic. So close to preventing the Hua armies from fighting each other instead of the invading Teleri.

Her feet found solid ground and she strode into the grove. Light from the trees illuminated the path in gentle white. The omnipresent energy pulse went silent.

Up ahead, the two shapes from before came into focus. A black cape flowed behind the taller, merging in color with his long dark hair. Certainly not a scout, looking so conspicuous. The other wore tight black clothes, but stood no taller than a child. He paused, then whirled around and met her gaze.

Pointed ears poked out from beneath short brown hair. Large, almond eyes.

Jie.

The other turned around, revealing a stout, handsome man with a turquoise complexion and a

thin crown on his head. He resembled the altivorc
prince she'd seen in Iksuvius, but even more
handsome.

The two exchanged words in a guttural
language. Apparently, Jie spoke it. Maybe, like
Avarax pretending to be Hardeep, she'd deceived
Kaiya all this time.

At Kaiya's side, Sameer and Cyrus both
drew their weapons.

"I had a feeling I would find you here." The
altivorc prince withdrew a magic wand and leveled
it at them.

CHAPTER 38:

We All Spy

From his hiding place on the ground level of a recently abandoned brothel, Tian peered through the shutters at the small home connected to the Jade Teahouse. Though no one had used the front door since he'd arrived three hours earlier, his team flashed mirrors anytime someone came or left through the secret door in the roof. Three times so far.

This had to be the place. Right now at noon, at least four Nightblades congregated inside. No telling how many were there in total, so it was too risky to launch an attack with just him and four young *Moquan*. They could ambush individual Nightblades as they left, but the concubine would likely grow suspicious if her eyes and ears began disappearing.

He was about to give the signal for his comrades to regroup at the theatre when the front door of the house opened. Tian reached into the fold of is robes for a throwing star.

A pretty Hua girl walked out. Probably no older than fifteen or sixteen, she wore a plain grey dress. Not the concubine, whom Feng Mi said was in her late twenties, and had mixed Ayuri blood. Nor a Teleri Nightblade, since they were all male. Maybe a collaborator.

Tian abandoned his post and slipped out the front. The girl had reached the teahouse and now opened the door. A servant or prostitute, perhaps, though she might still be an enemy asset. No matter which, she'd recently been inside the concubine's house, which meant she knew more than him.

He flashed hand signals to inform the team of his decision. *I go in. All clear?* Mirrors flashed twice, indicating a safe window of time. Tian made a quick check of the empty streets, dashed across the street, and opened the green door to the Jade Teahouse. Bells jingled as he entered.

Light bauble lamps with thin jade screens shed a dim light over the bloodwood tables and chairs in the common room. A curtain of stone beads dangled over a back corridor, likely where the Night Blossoms provided private entertainment.

Hovering over a chair in the far corner, the girl paused as her eyes met his. They flashed downward as she sat.

A door at the back slid open, revealing a middle-aged woman kneeling in a green silk gown. "Ziqiu, welcome back. What would you like?"

"Jasmine green tea," the girl answered with a bow. "I am expecting a client."

The proprietress covered her giggle. "The same one, I would wager."

"You would win that wager." The girl, Ziqiu, smiled and nodded.

"Maybe it is a sign that bees will return to the blossoms." The proprietress turned toward the kitchens, but paused when her eyes swept across Tian. She looked to Ziqiu, who shook her head ever so slightly, then back to him. Eyes wide, she bowed.

"Welcome, my lord. The flowers do not bloom these days, but might I offer you some tea?"

Flowers not blossoming. A reference to the sex trade. "I will have the same as her." He lifted his chin to Ziqiu, who studied the hardwood floors.

The older woman gestured with an open hand toward a table far from Ziqiu. "Please, make yourself comfortable and I will be back with the tea."

"Thank you." Ignoring the seat she indicated, Tian strode toward Ziqiu. The girl kept her head down, but her eyes still watched him. He placed a hand on the back of a chair at her table. "May I?"

Ziqiu bowed. "I am sorry, my lord. I am expecting company."

Tian sat anyway. "I have not seen another soul in days. At least share your ear until she joins you."

"He," she said, at last looking up at him.

A male. Another information relay, perhaps. Tian grinned. "Will I make him jealous?"

She studied his face, then shifted a hand from the table to her lap. "Have we met before?"

"I don't believe so. I haven't visited the capital in a while." For ten years, thanks to his banishment.

Her brow wrinkled. "Your accent...you are from the North."

Observant, this girl. No use in denying it. Tian nodded. "You, too. Linshan Province?"

She shyly tilted her head and covered a hand over her cheek. "Yes. Better opportunities here."

Tian searched her eyes, at least as best he could from the angle she presented. Something in her tone...she was telling half-truths and using body language to misdirect. Trying to present herself as a country girl who came to the big city as a prostitute. She was hiding something.

The front door opened, and the girl's expression lightened up. Relieved. She beckoned whoever it was, and then settled her gaze on Tian. "My...friend."

The innuendo sounded too forced. The stranger at the door was no buyer, at least not of

flesh. The footsteps clunked across the floors, the sound and length of the stride suggesting an average-sized man in boots, certainly too small for even the Metal Man spies.

Bowing, Tian rose. "Thank you for the company."

Her eyes shifted from him to the stranger and back. Tian turned to evaluate him. A thin man with soft features, smooth hands, and a light complexion. He was someone who had grown up in affluence, perhaps the son of a high official, from his body language. His plain cotton robe concealed a dagger. Tian offered him a smile.

Eyebrow raised, the man looked from Ziqiu to Tian.

In the corner of Tian's eye, Ziqiu shook her head, imperceptible to the untrained. These two were up to something, and if he gave them space, they'd likely reveal what it was. Either that, or he would be listening in on the primal screams of purchased sex. He walked over to the table where the proprietress had already set a white-and-blue porcelain tea set.

Sitting, he sipped the tea and stared into the cup. The pair stood and retreated behind the curtain of jade beads. That side of the teahouse shared a wall with the concubine's house. Perhaps they were once part of the same building until partitioned.

Tian stole a quick glance toward the kitchens, where the proprietress' shadow moved about. He went to the front door, counting his steps along the way. Eleven. From here to the back corridor would take three seconds at a fast but quiet pace. The proprietress' shadow disappeared.

Pushing the door open, he yelled, "Thank you," then dashed to the back and slid under the jade beads and into the private hall. One foot in front of the other, he tip-toed to each of the sliding doors and listened. Low whispers emanated from the third. Tian slipped into the second, crept across the firm reed mat floor and pressed an ear horn to the thin wall.

"Teleri spies are relaying Leina's orders," the girl said.

The man harrumphed. "I can't imagine the Teleri relying on a woman."

"She is very intelligent. And there is always at least one spy around. They are skilled, so you won't be able to get in."

"Then it's up to you," the man said. "Catch her off-guard." Something clunked on the floor.

The thud's sound indicated the dagger. These two must have some sort of training to have uncovered the spider in the web before the *Moquan*. Whoever they worked for, friend or foe, they had the same goal at this point.

Ziqiu gasped. "Song, I can't. I've never killed anyone."

Tian had and could. If they worked together—

A soft click emanated from the hallway, followed by the very soft padding of three people trained in stealth. The door to the next room slid open with a woosh and the thump of wood on wood. Ziqiu screamed. Metal clanged on metal.

Drawing his knife, Tian swept through the door and turned into the adjacent room. Three Nightblades held swords in an offensive formation. The man from the common room, Song, held the dagger in one hand, his other pressed against a bleeding slash across his abdomen. Ziqiu huddled behind him.

One of the Nightblades growled. "If you are going to plot against us, then at least be smart enough to do it somewhere we can't hear." Apparently, neither the walls between the private rooms, nor the partition to the concubine's house, were particularly thick. He leaped toward Song with a downward slash.

Song lifted the dagger. It stopped the sword cut, but jarred from his hands. The Nightblade kicked it out of Song's reach and took a step back. "Now, come with us."

Tian jumped toward the closest enemy. He drove his knife into the back of the Bovyan's neck and plucked his sword from his hands. The two others turned. Song tackled one and fought for the weapon.

Holding his sword two-handed, the third Nightblade edged toward the door.

Tian interposed himself between him and Ziqiu. "Go into the street. Yell *Tian Attack*."

Staring at him with wide eyes, the girl nodded and dashed out. The Nightblade flung a star *biao* at her, but Tian knocked it out of the air. He swung the sword and stabbed with the knife. Dodging, the Nightblade countered with a horizontal chop. Tian ducked under the blow and thrust his sword into his enemy's exposed armpit. As the Metal Man recoiled, Tian followed through with a stab and lodged the knife in his solar plexus. Yanking both weapons free, Tian turned to the struggle on the ground.

The Nightblade straddled Song and pressed the sword down. Song pushed back, while the blade bit into his hands. Tian yanked the Nightblade's head back and slashed his throat, sending blood spraying across the mats.

Song coughed, flecking his lips with blood. "Who *are* you?"

Tian helped him into a seated position. "A friend, for now. Wait here." He peeked into the hall, where a secret door opened into the adjacent house. The concubine's house. He ran over and paused at the entrance to listen. Inside, furniture crashed, doors opened and slammed shut, metal clanked against metal.

"Fall back, fall back," yelled an unfamiliar male voice.

"Protect Leina," another screamed.

The light footsteps of an untrained woman shuffled toward the secret door. Tian turned the corner.

An exotic beauty stopped in her tracks, large eyes rounded, shoulders hunched. Her blue gown accentuated cinnamon-toned skin. Here cowered the mastermind behind the Teleri occupation, perhaps the entire splintering of Hua. The Spider in the Web.

Tian raised his sword. Behead the demon, and the body would surely fall.

Leina knelt and closed her eyes, too afraid to watch the implement of her impending doom. It didn't matter, really. If the latest reports were true, Peng Kai-Long had slaughtered the Maduran army. He would have little use for an aging woman, not knowing her significance. All these years in Hua, sacrificing her body to Old Hong, all for naught. A country, brought down by her in the slim hope of being reunited with her mother. The greedy men deserved their fate; but now, countless women would endure gang rape because of her choices.

She deserved death. She bowed her head and brushed her hair to the side to expose her neck. If this swordsman could defeat three Nightblades, hopefully he was skilled enough to kill her mercifully. If only she could have seen her mother one last time.

"No!" Purple Autumn screamed, sending a jolt through Leina's heart.

She had consigned herself to death already. She opened her eyes and straightened. Purple Autumn's hand rested on the handsome young man's shoulder. He looked familiar, with large, intelligent eyes and a high-bridged nose. Leina tilted her head. "You are one of Zheng Ming's brothers." Like the one the Teleri were holding at the north gate.

Lowering the sword, the man nodded.

Face flushing, Purple Autumn gasped. "That's why I thought I recognized you."

Leina let out a wistful sigh. Making love to Zheng Ming had been the best experience in her three years in Cathay, even if the passion and ecstasy had lasted just one afternoon. Apparently, Purple Autumn knew him, too. How foolish Leina had been, letting the girl into her home.

"All clear," a young male's voice said from somewhere in her house.

"All clear," repeated a woman. Honey's voice. She was another one of the Night Blossoms who sometimes came to the Jade Teahouse, and apparently a Cathayi Black Fist spy.

"Your operatives are dead," Zheng said. "You are next. First, tell me. Why did you help the Teleri?"

"Emperor Geros held my mother hostage in Ankira."

His tone betrayed no emotion. "And now?"

"I don't know. Murdered by Lord Peng. Or lost on the road."

His expression softened. "Your life is forfeit. But tell me what you know. I will do everything in my power to ensure your mother's safety."

Leina bowed and motioned toward her parlor. "Come. Perhaps you can undo what I have done."

Zheng nodded again and followed her. Inside the parlor, three of the Nightblades lay dead. Five young spies, four boys, and Honey gathered around, watching her. Evaluating. Chairs lay strewn in splinters, the rug ruffled up. Only her *weiqi* game sat undisturbed.

Zheng gazed at the game board. "How many Nightblades do you have in the field?"

She held up five fingers. "Plus the three sent after you in the teahouse."

He shook his head. "Dead. When will the others report back?"

"In three hours."

With a nod toward one of the boys, he pointed to the front door. "Go to the palace. Tell Jie she can commence the attack. In three hours."

Leina's stomach knotted. They were revealing names, which meant she would not survive this afternoon. She pointed at the board. "The Teleri Empire has been targeting Cathay for some time, using Madura and the Nothori nations to keep your armies distracted while they connected the roads through the Kanin Wilds. I was sent here three years ago, while they were establishing the Water Snake Clan."

Purple Autumn's lips formed an O. "During Prince Kai-Wu's wedding ceremony. I remember that. It was the first assassination attempt on Princess Kaiya."

Leina shook her head. "The timing is right, but that was purely coincidental. The Water Snake had nothing to do with it. I suspect Lord Peng was behind that."

The man's lips pursed, his knuckles white around the sword hilt. "How do you communicate with the Directori?"

"Through messenger birds. The birds are in the attic rookery. The codes are in my bedside table drawer." Leina pointed toward her room. "Then-First Consul Geros had estimated seven years to finish the roads and pacify the surrounding area. I had that much time to undermine Cathay. But when Princess Kaiya escaped home, carrying his son in her womb, he moved his timetable up."

Zheng's face betrayed nothing, but Purple Autumn gawked. Perhaps revealing the princess' secret would end up hurting yet another woman. Leina sighed.

"What about Hong?" Zheng's tone held monotone. "Did he have anything to do with the plot? Where is he now?"

Old Hong. Leina's chest constricted as she looked at the spot where he'd died. If her dalliance with Ming had been her only joy in her three years in Cathay, Hong's kind gestures had at least blunted the horror of the rest.

And she'd poisoned him. "He was an unwitting fool I manipulated. Him, and Young Lord Liu Dezhen. They undermined Cathay—Hong, because he didn't foresee the results of his actions. Young Lord Liu, because he wanted his son to become *Tianzi*." She set her jaw rigidly, hoping to sound disinterested. "Hong is dead, by my hand."

Zheng nodded. "And you sabotaged the firepowder?"

She shook her head. "The leader of the Nightblades did that. A non-Bovyan, one of your own. He arrived just ahead of the invading army."

"Oh...." Honey nodded. "He must be the one Master Jie hunted in Eldaeri lands."

Leina shrugged. "I did not even know the Black Fists were real until several days ago when I met him."

"Where is he now?" Zheng asked.

"I don't know. He disappeared the day of the invasion."

Purple Autumn gasped. "He was the one who tried to take the fallen star from the Temple of Heaven. He and my master killed each other."

The young Black Fists exchanged glances, while Zheng regarded Purple Autumn through narrow eyes. He then turned to Leina. "I am sure the local authorities will have you tortured and executed. But I understand. You wanted to save your mother. I give you the option of fleeing Cathay forever."

The Black Fists all murmured among themselves, but he silenced them with a glare. Tears gathered in her eyes, blurring her vision. He was letting her go.

But where? With nobody left, she had nowhere to go and no reason to live. Even if her mother had somehow survived, they would never find each other wandering a strange land. No, this was her house. Only now did she see that, only after she killed the man who had made it her home. She shook her head and pointed to her room. "I have a fatal poison. Allow me to take it."

Zheng gestured with an open hand, and followed as she went in and withdrew the crushed leaves and the messenger bird codes from her bedside table. She went back into the parlor and sprinkled it into her still-warm tea. Sipping it to savor the sweet taste, she said, "I am sorry for what I did."

Zheng nodded. "If your mother lives, I will make sure she is protected." He then pointed at the *weiqi* board and pointed. "White has lost. Because Black controls this one interior intersection. If a white piece held that instead of black, your plan would fail."

Mind spinning, Leina offered him a wry smile that took most of her energy. Each breath seemed harder to draw in. "So much rode on chance, especially after Emperor Geros pressed the attack three years ahead of schedule. In a game of *weiqi*, your idea would be cheating."

"In life, it can still be done." His handsome face blurred.

She started to speak, but her breath seized and she coughed. Hand trembling, she reached to the board and removed the piece. She mouthed, *Princess,* but the only sound was the rasp of her last exhale.

CHAPTER 39:
Choices

The silence made Kaiya wonder if she'd lost her hearing. The pulse of the world, so strong and steadfast just moments before, was gone. Only the fallen star in her pack vibrated and hummed, ever so slightly, and the sound vented upward into the tree canopy.

Sameer's *naga* looked grey and lifeless. Cyrus frowned, in a rare show of emotion.

At her side, Brehane's hands quivered as she chanted several guttural words. The air around them cracked and shimmered.

"Interesting, Mystic," the altivorc said. "You are drawing power from somewhere. Still, your shield never stopped me before. They say trying the same thing over and over again and expecting the same result is madness." A bolt of red buzzed out from his wand. The light fizzled and cracked in a hemisphere around them, and faded.

Brehane coughed and wobbled. "The shield can't take another hit. Scatter!"

Taking Kaiya's hand, Sameer pulled her off the path to a tree. "I can't feel the energy of the world!"

"Nor can I." Cyrus huddled behind another tree with Brehane.

The altivorc nodded at Jie. "Go. I will handle them."

With a bow, the traitorous half-elf raced toward the pyramid. He turned back and grinned, baring fangs. Wand spinning around his finger, he strode toward Cyrus' tree. "Give me all your pyramid gemstones, and I will let you go."

Coming out from cover, Brehane barked several foul syllables and pointed her fingers at the altivorc. Nothing happened.

"You are powerless." The altivorc laughed. With his back to Kaiya, he made for a vulnerable target. If only she had a weapon. He spun and pointed the wand at her. "Which means you must have a power source." A flash of red streaked at her.

Doctor Wu stepped in front of the pulse and settled into a low horse stance. Energy fizzled through her and into the ground. Webbed wisps of red streaked through the soil, then up the tree trunks and into the buds. The doctor staggered to one knee, her beautiful luminescent eyes fading to a light blue.

Kaiya blinked. What had just happened? It should've been her, not beloved Doctor Wu.

"Run! To the pyramid." Pressing a hand on tree roots, Doctor Wu looked up. Her eyes glimmered, feebly at first, then building. "The Altivorc King can't get past the tree canopy while the Tear of Guanyin sits at the pinnacle."

"Something that my half-elf will take care of soon enough." The Altivorc King— King?— laughed.

Kaiya gaped. She'd heard of him, of course. On the rare occasions he appeared among humans, a dozen elite altivorcs protected him. From what she'd heard, the altivorcs had a personal vendetta against Jie. Yet here she was, working for him.

"Run, fool!" Doctor Wu staggered to her feet.

Shaking the confusion from her mind, Kaiya bolted down the path. Toward Jie, who even asleep could probably kill her. She hazarded a glance back.

The Altivorc King pointed his wand at her. Then a rock popped him in the side of the head, which jerked like the lash of a whip.

"Run, Princess!" Fleet yelled from somewhere.

A hand clamped around hers. Sameer's. He pulled her along the path. Behind them, Cyrus and Brehane gave chase. The King's wand flashed again in repeated staccato buzzes, which flashed red on the tree trunks.

The edge of the grove lay close ahead. Kaiya's belly cramped. Just a few more steps. She stumbled to her knees as she reached the clearing. Her ears roared from blood coursing through her...no, from the low, primal drone of the pyramid itself. Like the Ayudra pyramid.

At her side, her friends stared up at the Tear of Guanyin. Like the Lotus Crystal she'd returned to the Temple of the Moon, it sparkled atop the pyramid in myriad rays of light blue. Just a few degrees behind it, the nearly-full iridescent moon swirled in soap-bubble colors, not far from the full white moon, with the fully-open blue moon forming a backdrop. The Golden Flock constellation, an omen of great change, hovered above them.

Together, the moons resembled a light blue face with two mismatched eyes, crowned with a halo. It was so beautiful that Kaiya's heart stirred from beneath the *Tiger's Eye*, and she let out a gasp.

Jie turned from where her gaze had been locked on the Tear and glared at them. Her form-fitting clothes shined dark grey, like lightning flaring along the underside of a storm cloud. She pulled a hood over her head, leaving only a slot which revealed the bridge of her nose and the cruel glint in her eyes. The rest of her body disappeared like haze on a hot day.

"How did she get here so fast?" Cyrus exchanged glances with Brehane and Sameer. "She

was just with—" He coughed as Brehane elbowed him.

Sameer stepped forward, his *naga* now glowing bright blue. "I don't want to hurt you."

"Don't you feel it?" Brehane's voice tittered in excitement. "The resonance of the world has never coursed through me like this."

"Nor me." Jie's chameleon form darted forward, her blade whirling in a blur.

Sameer engaged, their weapons never touching as they circled and stabbed and chopped in a dance of swords. It looked nothing like Jie's vicious and efficient style.

Kaiya clasped Brehane's dress. "Do something!"

The Mystic threw up her hands. "I can't. They're too fast, too close."

"How do you know the *Bahaduur* arts?" Sameer disengaged.

In that split second, Brehane chortled out several syllables and waved a hand at Jie.

Webbing shot out and entangled the half-elf. Growling, she slashed it away, but at least now she was visible. She pulled the hood down. Her clothing returned to the same storm-cloud grey and she surged forward. Her broadsword caught Sameer in the shoulder, cutting deep. The *naga* slipped from his fingers. She drove her boot into his chest, sending him sprawling to the ground.

Brehane choked out several guttural words in the language of Shallow Magic. Glowing darts appeared and streaked toward Jie.

The half-elf spun out of the way. "You might as well surrender now," Jie cackled. She'd always had a disrespectful streak, but never had she sounded so malicious. "I will make your deaths quick."

Hand on his golden circle, Cyrus chanted a prayer in his language, calling on Athran to do something.

Anything. Kaiya couldn't tell. Tears, real tears, blurred her vision. "Why, Jie? Why are you doing this?"

Jie ignored her, instead striding toward Cyrus with her sword raised.

A shadow darted between the two. Jie's weapon clinked, stopping before it decapitated Cyrus.

Fleet. The little madaeri brandished two shortswords, twirling them like a hummingbird's wings. He snaked toward Jie with quick stabs. Sameer might be fast, but Fleet made him look almost normal. Jie backed away, losing ground.

His eyes tracking the combatants, Cyrus circled around toward Sameer. Brehane grunted out more Shallow Magic.

And here Kaiya was, useless. Pulse racing, she fought for each breath. The taste of panic sat in her mouth, she could barely contain the emotion now bubbling up from under the *Tiger's Eye*.

Yet, even with the song of the pyramid coursing through her with energy, the power of her voice still felt pent up. "Please Jie, stop." Traitor or not, if the Insolent Retainer was seriously injured...

A warm hand rested on her shoulder. Her heart must've jumped out of her chest. She turned. Lord Xu stood there, his ever-mischievous smile replaced by a grave expression.

"You said I would get my magic back." Her voice sounded petulant, like the sixteen-year-old lovestruck child she'd once been.

"You will." His stare bore into her. "You brought the fallen star. Give it to me."

Kaiya cast a glance at Jie, whose weapon went spinning to the ground. Maybe now she'd just surrender. Fleet apparently had other ideas. His swords dragged across her body like shears, slashing through the remnants of web, yet never cutting open her clothes. Jie punched and kicked, unrelenting.

"Jie, stop." Kaiya clenched and unclenched her fists. Surely, Jie would hear reason.

Moving in a blur, Fleet jumped and drove his blade toward her face.

Kaiya's stomach leaped into her neck.

The madaeri's blade smashed through flesh and bone. Jie crumpled to the ground, motionless.

"No!" Kaiya choked on the lump in her throat. It couldn't be.

Her sworn sister was dead.

Tears welled in Kaiya's eyes. No. She'd lost both her doctor and her friend in the span of a few minutes. She started to run over.

Xu's grasp on her wrist restrained her. "The fallen star."

A friend had just died, and all he could think of was an artifact? Hands trembling, she unshouldered her pack and threw it to the ground. The flap popped open. The smooth sphere of the star shined from within.

Jie was dead. Her closest confidante, perhaps her best friend. Kaiya's chest tightened as she tried to pull out of Xu's grip.

Without releasing her, his gaze shifted up to the Tear. Xu withdrew the star and looked down at her friends. "Such a coincidence to find you all here." He turned back to her, even as she tried to pull free of his grip. "But where is Doctor Wu?"

"Here. And I have company."

Kaiya turned around to see Doctor Wu sprinting out of the trees. For someone so ancient, she ran fast. The Altivorc King loped up behind her. The doctor cleared the tree line, and the King skidded short.

Pointing his wand, he snarled. "I might not be able to get close, but I can still use this!" Energy beams zipped toward them in quick succession.

Without looking back, Xu waved a hand toward the King. The bolts crackled against an invisible barrier.

"What?" The King stared with wide eyes.

Xu turned to the King.

"Aralas!"

Aralas? Kaiya gaped. Certainly the Altivorc King must be mistaken. One too many rocks to the head, maybe. The elf angel had returned to the Heavens a thousand years before.

Xu laughed. "Of course I knew you would attempt something on the Godseye Conjunction." He held the fallen star aloft. "With all of this energy, the pyramid is very well protected, and now your minion is dead." He gestured toward Jie's body and shook his head.

The Altivorc King snarled and stomped off in the other direction.

"The other pyramids are also protected," Xu yelled at the King's back.

Kaiya's stomach clenched. This felt like another deception on top of all the others, this time perpetrated by Xu himself. "Having me bring the fallen star here had nothing to do with saving Hua, did it?"

Xu favored her for a moment with an unreadable gaze. "What did Aralas tell your people before she returned to the Heavens?"

She looked to Fleet, who nodded emphatically. He'd asked her the same question during the escape from Iksuvius.

Kaiya closed her eyes. "Keep well the pyramids, reminders though they may be of your enslavement."

"Right," Fleet said. "If the King of the Orcs ever controls all the pyramids again, the Orc Gods will return on their flaming chariots."

"So you see, this is larger than Hua." Xu patted her on the shoulder.

Kaiya shook her head. "The Teleri Empire and the altivorcs are allies. If they conquer Hua, they will give the altivorcs the pyramid."

Xu pointed down into the valley below. Peng's rebellion and the imperial army faced off against each other, with Lord Wu's contingent ready to fall on Peng's flank. "The winner of this battle will have more than enough resources to defeat the Teleri."

"Not if they annihilate each other," Kaiya said. "And if Lord Peng wins, he might very well entreat with the altivorcs." Not likely, but there had to be *some* way to convince Xu to help.

"Behold!" Cousin Peng's voice carried through the night.

The dark sky above the battlefield shimmered. An undulating form of sparkling golden scales materialized. A real dragon, though far more graceful than Avarax's gargantuan form. Its eyes glowed red. Each claw had five talons, a symbol of the *Tianzi* and the Mandate of Heaven.

Kaiya gawped at it. The Guardian Dragon of Hua, resembling all the paintings she'd ever seen. He'd only appeared a few times in history, during times of great change to anoint a new dynasty. The three hundred thousand soldiers below all sank to their knees in a ripple of kowtows. Perhaps Lord Peng did hold the Mandate of Heaven. All of the strategizing and power struggles of the previous years had all led to this. She let out a long sigh.

Mumbling what amounted to a curse of sorts, Doctor Wu scoffed.

"Do you feel it?" Brehane pointed. "It feels like Shallow Magic. The pearl is an illusion."

Shallow Magic...a trick! Anger welled up in Kaiya's chest, heat flaring in her face and burning off the *Tiger's Eye*. This was nothing short of sacrilege. That traitor Peng was trying to steal the Mandate of Heaven, and the sacred Guardian Dragon had fallen for his deception. "How dare he!"

"It is Lord Peng, after all." Doctor Wu snorted again, then muttered in a barely audible voice, "At least he could do the decency of getting the color right."

Gazing into the distance, Xu tapped his chin, looking a little like Tian with the gesture. He exchanged glances with Doctor Wu, then searched Kaiya's eyes. "Are you willing to sacrifice yourself for Hua?"

She placed her hand over her belly. She bore the shame of possibly carrying Geros' twins, not to mention all the other things she'd done over the last month to ensure Hua's safety. She nodded.

"Very well, *Dian-xia*." He turned to the Southerners. "Do you have a pyramid Greystone?"

"Whatever for?" Sameer's eyes must've been wider than tea cup saucers as they darted to Cyrus.

Cyrus clutched a pouch to his chest.

Xu's gaze lifted from the pouch. "So you do. I could take it from you, but I give you the choice. With it lies the opportunity for the princess to save her country."

The three exchanged glances. Cyrus shook his head, but then relented under Brehane's glare. He opened the pouch and withdrew a fist-sized gem, which resembled solid smoke.

"Madaeri," Xu said. "Take it and swap it with Guanyin's Tear at the pyramid's font."

Fleet's mouth gaped open. "That's what the Altivorc King wants!"

"And what about our magic?" Cyrus kept shaking his head. "We will lose it, too."

"Technically, the King might be able to approach the pyramid." Xu looked back toward where the orc had disappeared. "However, I don't sense him, and with the Fallen Star and Doctor Wu, we can all have a tie to magic and can block his path." He pointed toward the moons. "At the conjunction, swap them out. Follow me, *Dian-xia*."

Kaiya trailed Xu up the steps to the pyramid's sealed entrance. She looked at it, then at Fleet, who scrambled up the structure's side with effortless grace. She turned back to Xu. "Nobody has been in here since the War of Ancient Gods."

Xu nodded. "Aralas took this pyramid's Greystone on the day the Dwarves sacked the Temple of Tivar, and then placed a magical ward on the entrance." He pointed near the middle of the pyramid, where large gashes ripped into the smooth stone. "Do you know what that is from?"

"Damage from the Hellstorm."

"No." Xu shook his head. "You might as well know the truth. Avarax awoke during the Hellstorm. That night, he clashed with Hua's Guardian Dragon. He left those scars in the pyramid."

Kaiya's thoughts spun. The legends and histories never spoke of such things. Avarax had awoken thirty-three years before...unless he hadn't replaced Rumiya, but had *been* Rumiya the whole time. "Why?"

"He wanted the Guardian Dragon's Flaming Pearl."

Her legs wobbled. She shot a hand out and clasped him for support. "When he took the form of the Dragon's Envoy, he told me something about the Flaming Pearl."

"I helped your ancestor hide the Pearl where Avarax could never reach it."

One shock after the other. Muscles she did not even know she had cramped her face. "The Founder?"

"No, his consort."

She took several deep breaths. Either Xu lied, or the histories she knew so well were false.

"Easy, *Dian-xia*." He placed a reassuring hand on the small of her back.

"Why are you telling me this?"

"I am going to open a portal to the Flaming Pearl." He grinned. "If you bring it back, perhaps you can win the Guardian Dragon's approval."

"Where is it?"

"So many questions." He looked up at the moons and yawned. "Great Peace Island."

Great Peace Island...where her ancestor had come from. Still, it didn't make sense. Thielas Starsong and Ayana Strongbow had whisked her all around the world with just a few words, and Xu needed a rare conjunction to pull it off? And from what Brehane had said, the Greystone had created a magical deadspot around the pyramid in Selastyas. "How will you use magic if a Greystone blocks the pyramid's font?"

"Silly girl; you may have learned a lot about Artistic Magic, but it is still just a drop in the ocean." He pointed up. "The Godseye is upon us. You will not live to see the next time it comes."

Kaiya followed his finger. The three moons lined up, the larger blue moon forming the backdrop for the white, and inside the white, the smallest iridescent moon. The pulse of the world sounded louder and more jubilant than ever.

Xu lifted his voice in song. The world hummed around her, and the door into the pyramid swirled in a rainbow of lights. A gaping hole opened, and bright white light poured out.

It looked nothing like the inside of a pyramid.

Wind danced through the green leaves of a single cherry tree, in front of a dark stone road. And the light spilling from the pyramid entrance...was sunlight in the land beyond.

"You will be on your own in a strange land," Xu said. "Use the lessons you have learned. Listen for the Flaming Pearl's call."

"I still don't have the power of my voice."

"That could be a problem." He tapped his chin again. He then spoke a single word, and a shiny metal tuning fork appeared in his hand.

"Wang Yuxiang left the Dragon Pearl in the well of a burning temple. When you are near it, strike this on something hard."

So many things to remember. Kaiya's mind swirled; her knees felt like jelly. She took the tuning fork.

He studied her face. "Hurry. The portal will close behind you. I will open it again when the conjunction ends, in about a half-hour's time. If you are not back by then, you will be trapped there forever."

For Hua, she would have to succeed. With a deep breath, she stepped through the portal.

CHAPTER 40:
Stranger

The low whir of cicadas droned in Kaiya's ears, and oppressive, humid heat hung in her lungs. She shielded her eyes from the bright sun, which seemed larger than usual. The iridescent moon...nowhere to be seen. Gauging the half-hour time limit would require plenty of guesswork. She looked around, taking in the bizarre surroundings of her ancestor's homeland. If Xu was to be believed, this was indeed Great Peace Island.

It was like nothing she'd ever seen before. The smooth black road warmed her feet through her shoes' thin soles. Perfectly square pavestones, all white with some bright flecks, lined either side. The buildings were blocky and unsightly, made of metal and stone, with windows of actual glass. Not like the beautiful stained glass the Estomari craftsmen made, but plain and clear.

A loud horn blared behind her, making her heart leap into her throat. She turned around. A cart moving of its own accord glided toward her. A handsome man, whose fine features and skin tone suggested Eldaeri blood, leaned out from the front and yelled at her, in a language which made no sense. Then he gaped. With arms covered in sleek blue sleeves, he gestured her to the stone-paved roadside.

Bowing, she moved to the side while the cart floated past her, its bottom not even touching the road. Magic, perhaps. Supposedly, as the gods' haven in this world, Great Peace Island was full of

it. She stared at the man as it passed, and he stared back.

She turned around and gawked again.

A brown wooden gate with pitched tiled eaves rose before her. Though the architecture might have belonged in her own homeland, it looked ridiculously out of place with everything else around her. The plaque above, in white lettering, read *Original Mastery Temple.*

Kaiya's mouth hung open wider. This was the gate which the Founder himself had passed through, at least according to all the Imperial Family histories. A stone obelisk at the side of the gate had some sort of inscription, a bizarre mix of the Hua language and some other unintelligible scribble—like Xiulan's handwriting, only much uglier.

She read what she could. It mentioned her ancestor, Xinchang, though it used the symbols Zhitian, *Woven Field,* for his surname. Something about death and fire and ruins.

"Ahr yuu oukei mihss?" a man called from behind her.

She spun around to find the cart driver. Tight blue clothes, smooth as a sharkskin she'd once seen, covered his entire body. She took several steps back.

"Ihtz oukei. Ai wount hahrt yuu." He held up both hands.

She shook her head. "I don't understand."

The man cocked his head.

Perhaps it was a waste of time. She searched for the iridescent moon, still not there. "I don't understand," she repeated in Arkothi, Ayuri, and finally, on a desperate whim, the secret imperial language.

His eyes and mouth widened. "How you talk sun origin speech?"

"How do you speak the imperial language?"

His brow furrowed. "Im-Pe-Ri-Al language?"

She nodded.

"I learned in big study. Long ago, everyone speak it here." He opened his arms wide.

Wherever the big study was. Perhaps Great Peace Island had been conquered in the three hundred years since the Founder left, so much so that his language had fallen into obscurity. She forced a smile.

"So you okay?" He reached for her sleeve and rubbed the fabric between his fingers.

Such poor manners. She pulled away. "Yes, just a little lost. I am looking for a well."

His head cocked again. "A we–ll?"

She pantomimed drawing water out of a well and drinking.

"You thirsty?"

Kaiya started to shake her head. But no, her mouth *was* dry. She nodded.

He flashed a naughty grin. "Would you like do tea?"

"I am in a hurry." She frowned. He was asking her to perform a tea ceremony, for a stranger no less.

His lower lip jutted out and he cast his eyes at the ground. "Okay. I get water." He turned back to his cart and reached inside. He withdrew the strangest clear water skin, with water visibly sloshing inside, and gave it to her. "Please."

She bowed her head in thanks and lifted the water skin to her lips. Nothing came out.

The man laughed. He extended his hand to the water skin. "May I?"

Confused, she returned it to him. With a twist of his fingers, a clear peel came off the top. He handed it back to her.

Bowing again, she took a sip. Cool and delicious.

"What is your name?" He smiled back.

"Kaia." At least, that's what it was in the imperial language.

"Well, enjoy visit Kaia. This place is kept from old times." He pointed past the gate.

"Thank you." Searching for the iridescent moon, still not there of course, she turned around and passed through. She glanced back to see the man staring at her, while talking to his...wrist.

He lifted his chin and waved. She turned back and looked straight ahead.

The gate opened up into a courtyard, framed by a building with thin metal columns and glass. The metal sign above was inscribed in large black letters, *Original Mastery Temple Little Study*. It might as well have been gibberish, for all *Little Study* meant to her. Whatever the building was, it easily dwarfed the Hall of Supreme Harmony, though it did not match the architecture of all the other, even more gargantuan, structures beyond. Whoever built these enormous edifices must have had both incredible skill and a sick imagination. If not for the *Tiger's Eye* forming up, she might have vomited from the strangeness of it all.

At least the courtyard itself felt like home. The ground was paved in uneven stones, and up ahead were what appeared to be funerary tablets. In a row. A wooden signpost had a long list of strange names, all faded with time. She came closer to the row. One of the stones was marked with the name of her ancestor, though with the same incorrect characters for his family name.

As if he had died here, and not in Hua. This outlandish place was just too disconcerting. Better to focus on finding the Dragon Pearl before the portal opened again, lest she spend the rest of her life among strangely-dressed Eldaeri who spoke broken Imperial. She closed her eyes and listened.

There. Somewhere beyond the courtyard, a low, steadfast pulse called to her, its reassuring beat reminiscent of her mother's heartbeat. No, maybe Doctor Wu's heartbeat. She walked around the side of the building as the sound got louder, pausing only to look at another obelisk tucked into a small concave wall. *Original Mastery Temple Track* was inscribed in the single column, the symbols worn with time like the various ruins from the War of Ancient Gods.

Windows in the building slid open. Boys in high-collared black uniforms pointed at her and chattered, while girls in white blouses with red kerchiefs covered their giggles. All Eldaeri. They'd been bloodthirsty conquerors when they arrived on the shores of Tivaralan three centuries before; maybe they'd conquered and occupied Great Peace Island since then, and wiped out all vestiges of its original culture. Though if they could build such colossal buildings, certainly they could sail across the seas and overwhelm the Teleri, Levastyans, and everyone else who stood in their way.

She shook the idea out of her mind and continued toward the source of the pulsation. On the other side of the building lay a broad field of orange-brown dirt. Boys in tight white uniforms ran back and forth. More than one paused to stare at her.

Up ahead, on the other side of the field, another concave wall surrounded a stone well. The throbbing sound came from there. Picking her way through the boys, she approached. Like the other ancient-looking places in the area, a stone obelisk bore identifying marks. *Original Mastery Temple Well.*

So this was it. Prominently displayed in such a conspicuous spot, surely the man from before knew of the well, but was too busy requesting tea ceremonies to guide her. She peered down into its depths, from whence the pulse came. Withdrawing the tuning fork Xu had given her, she tapped it against the side of the well.

A clear tone rung out. Down in the well, something flared a gentle blue. Now how would reach it?

Several boys came up beside her. One looked down the well. "Wuht ahr yuu duuween?"

She pointed down the well and pantomimed dropping something. "I lost a ball."

He squinted at her, then waved someone over. She turned.

A young woman, perhaps only a little older than her, approached. She wore a sharp black uniform like the boys in the windows, albeit with a pleated skirt instead of pants. "Mei ai herup yuu?"

"I lost a ball." Kaiya pointed back down into the well.

The woman's eyes widened. "You speak sun origin speech, but not hero speech?"

Kaiya snorted. These people thought their language belonged to heroes. Just like most of the other Eldaeri she had met. If only Prince Aelward or Princess Alaena were here to translate for her. *Mei ai herup yuu.* If, no, *when* she saw them again, she would see if they understood the words. "Sorry, yes," she said.

The woman nodded, then turned around and yelled. A wiry young man jogged over and the two exchanged words. He smiled at her. "I will check."

"Dangerous," Kaiya said.

He laughed. "No, it dry for thousand years. I down many times—" he gestured to the gathered boys. "—them, too. There are only rocks."

She snorted. The man bragged about violating the sanctity of a holy spot. "Look." She pointed into the well and struck Xu's metal again. The sound rung out and the blue light flashed again.

Everyone stared down the well, murmuring.

The man looked from the well to her and back again. He climbed up and over the edge, then shimmied down. "Dark! Hit again!"

Kaiya struck the clip against the well's lip. The sound rang out, clear and jubilant. Pale blue light flared up, flickering as the sound of rocks and stones shuffling and rubbing against each other echoed down below.

"Got it!"

Kaiya peered down the well. Some thirty feet down, a glowing blue ball the size of a human head cast the man's figure in blue sheen. He tucked it into his tight shirt and spider-climbed up. Time had to be running out. She searched for the iridescent moon—again, not there.

He emerged looking much like a pregnant woman. How she might look in several months. If she survived this war. He pulled the globe from his shirt. The blue light had faded, leaving a sphere caked with dirt and limestone sediment. It hummed deep in her ears, though it did not seem to bother anyone else.

The man offered it to her. "How you know it here?"

She smiled. "Mine."

"Never saw it down there before." The man took out a make-up case from his pocket. He held it up to her. Everyone else reached and held up make-up cases, bracelets, rings... Kaiya took several steps back. They had been so helpful before, but now...perhaps they wanted to subdue her and take back the Pearl, this treasure that could possibly save Hua.

The man held up a hand. "No. Good. Look." He presented his make-up case. In it flashed the image of her holding the Dragon Pearl. Dirt marred her complexion, and her hair looked as if birds had nested in it. And...wait, his make-up case. It was like Xu's magic mirror. Indeed, the gathered children shouted and jostled to show her an image of herself, some projected from rings, others in the flat surfaces of their bracelets.

Whoever said the Eldaeri had no connection to magic was wrong. She pushed her way through the growing crowd of excited, shouting kids, shuffling back the way she had come. On occasion, she pulled her arm away from a child who grabbed her dress skirts. There couldn't be much more time left.

Despite the time constraint, she stopped in the courtyard, where her ancestor's grave marker stood. It couldn't be a grave marker. No. He'd died in Hua. It was a memorial of sort, perhaps commemorating the gods dispatching the Founder to unify Hua. If only the entire sign made sense. She scanned her throng of followers for the woman, or either of the two men who could speak a halting version of the imperial tongue.

There. The woman waved. Kaiya beckoned her over, and she threaded a path between the kids.

"What does this say?" Kaiya gestured toward the sign.

The woman peered at it, then back at Kaiya. "Dead speech. I not learn."

"This place has history." The man who'd retrieved the Pearl sidled up to them. "A great lord cheat his boss. Burn down old...shrine. Boss die. Many die."

Kaiya's brow furrowed. Had her ancestor been the traitor? He certainly wasn't the boss who'd died. She bowed. "Thank you. I must be going." She turned back toward the main gate.

Outside the courtyard, the streets erupted in excited chatter as she exited. Lights swirled on top of another floating cart. Eldaeri men and women in the most colorful, outlandish clothes surrounded other floating wagons. Several of the people held up shiny tubes to her. Two men in sleek, tight-fitting red and silver clothes looked at her and exchanged words. They strode with purposeful steps toward her.

"Furiz!" one yelled.

Kaiya skidded to a stop. The crowd charged toward her, past the two men, all yelling and shouting excitedly in the foreign tongue as they surrounded her. More than one shoved a tube toward her.

"Huu ahr yuu?"

"Wayrr yuu furam?"

"Wuutz za rahk?"

Kaiya's mind spun. "I don't understand. Does anyone speak the imperial language?" She looked for the moon. The portal should open soon.

"I speak!" A middle-aged man pushed his way to the front. Perhaps he could answer her questions.

Kaiya pointed back at the grave stones. "What does the sign say?"

"First, everyone wants to know who you are." He took her sleeve in his hands and rubbed his fingers back and forth. "No one has worn this material since ancient times."

These people had even worse sense of personal space than Ayuri folk. Kaiya pulled her arm back. "How do you speak the imperial language?"

"Im-pe-ri-al?" He squinted at her. "It's Sun Origin Speech. It used to be the language here. I am a teacher at the big study." He pointed off in the distance, then nodded at her. "Where are you from?"

She bowed. A teacher, even from an unknown Big Study, deserved respect. "Tivaralan."

"Where?" He shook his head.

Where indeed. Though the Tivaralan Eldaeri wouldn't admit it, rumor had it their ancestors had been criminals and exiles. Perhaps those who remained in their original homeland had never sailed west to Tivaralan.

The first man, the one who'd nearly run into her with his cart, spoke and gesticulated wildly. He pointed to the street, then up. People followed his gaze upward.

The teacher looked from the heavens to her. "They think you come from the stars."

Kaiya choked down her shocked laugh. As if she were a human angel! She shook her head. "No. Magic."

The man's jaw slackened. "What?"

The throng burst into excited chatter, everyone gesturing and turning to the street. The air shimmered, and black space opened. The portal! People pointed and gasped.

Kaiya shouldered her way through the crowds. The portal had only stayed open for a moment when she arrived, and she had to get there now, if only to prevent any children from slipping through the ethers into a dangerous, war-torn land. The sea of people parted to make way for her.

She peered in. Xu stood there, his intense gaze locked on her. At her side, everyone gasped.

"Elestrae!" one yelled, mistaking Xu for an elf angel. It was the only word in their language she had picked out so far, and surely given the Eldaeri's mixing with elves in the past, they knew what one looked like. Others jostled to get a better glimpse.

With a frown, Xu beckoned her. She stepped toward the portal, then turned and found the individuals who had been so helpful. With a bow at the waist, she stepped backward through the portal.

The sound of cicadas and excited shouts ceased, immediately replaced by the ponderous thrum of the world's energy. The circle snapped shut, the sunlight blinking out. The sealed entrance to the pyramid stood where the door to Great Peace Island had been.

Kaiya turned to Xu. "That was Great Peace Island?"

"Yes." Xu grinned.

"In the three hundred years since my ancestor's departure, the Eldaeri conquered it."

He cocked his head. "Not exactly. I wouldn't know where to begin and explain. Now, did you retrieve the Dragon Pearl?"

Kaiya lifted it.

"Good. None worse for the wear after so many centuries." He pointed to the valley, where the fake Guardian Dragon of Hua undulated in a circle above Cousin Peng's central banner. "The *Tianzi's* armies pay obeisance to Lord Peng as we speak. Go and present yourself before him."

Kaiya bowed low. "Thank you for your help. I will see you are well rewarded."

"Your ancestor said the same thing. Do you really think riches or power interest me?" Xu smirked. "Now go. If the Heavens smile on you, perhaps the true Guardian Dragon will reveal herself."

Herself? Xu must have misspoken, since everyone knew the Guardian Dragon was male.

Kaiya took the steps down from the pyramid entrance in twos, to where Cyrus and Doctor Wu tended to Sameer's wound. The doctor raised her head and locked her gaze on her. Kaiya smiled, but then looked past the three to where a cloak covered Jie's body. Brehane laid the broadsword over it.

Poor Jie. A lump formed in Kaiya's throat. Surely after travelling to the ends of the world and back, the *Tiger's Eye* must have finally faded, along with the life of the person who had put it on her in the first place.

She closed her eyes, pushing out a few tears. The energy of the world pulsed in her ears...yet still did not resonate in her heart. She came to Brehane's side and pulled the cloak back.

Fleet's sword had shattered the half-elf's pretty face from the nose up. Beyond recognition. Everything else remained unscathed, from her mouth down to her shoulder. Chest clenching, Kaiya looked up at her friends. "Where is her armor? Where's Fleet?" The scoundrel must have taken it.

Cyrus pointed up. Kaiya followed his finger's path to the pyramid. Guanyin's Tear sparkled at its top again, and Fleet now glided down the side, Greystone in hand. If not Fleet, then—

Brehane placed a hand on her chest. "I wanted to study the armor. I have never seen or felt magic like it before."

It made logical sense, but it still seemed inappropriate to leave her Insolent Retainer's body naked. She should be angry, and yet, only the logic of the choice resonated in her. The *Tiger's Eye* still held in check her emotions. She pulled the cloak back over her sworn sister's head.

Cyrus bowed. "I will ensure her remains are prepared for their final journey. She will leave this world the way she came, soul bared to Athran."

Kaiya nodded. Better that than to leave her to the carrion birds.

"Ten Thousand Years!" rang a chorus from the valley below.

With one arm in a makeshift sling, Sameer pointed down to where a sea of soldiers bowed in a ripple. "Come. You have an empire to save."

CHAPTER 41:

Brotherly Love

All the towns and villages Zheng Ming marched through had been devoid of enemy garrisons, or even small squads of light infantry enforcing Teleri rule. Now, he rode his horse up to the abandoned earthworks outside of Huajing, Ma Jun at his side and an army behind him. Up ahead, the north gate stood agape. Only a small complement of Teleri soldiers defended it. Just as his scouts had reported.

Shouts, screams, and gunfire pierced the clear afternoon sky.

He pulled his horse up out of musket range and withdrew a looking glass. The Bovyans atop the gate...faced inwards. Toward the city. He passed the scope to Ma Jun. "What do you think?"

Ma Jun squinted through scope and lowered it. "If the Teleri aren't looking at us, they must be fighting someone on the inside."

Ming's thought as well. He turned to an aide. "Have the musketmen line up in ranks of three on the river bank. I will lead spearmen though the gates. If the enemy sees us, lay down volley fire."

The aide bowed and turned to relay the commands. In short order, the provincial army had deployed along the river.

Ming drew his *dao* and pointed at the gate.

His infantry surged across the bridge. Ming followed, watching. When Bovyans turned to see the commotion, his musketmen began volley fire. The enemy remained huddled low behind the wall's crenellations. Any who rose to shoot a crossbow met a barrage of muskets from both sides.

It was almost boring. By the time Ming passed through the gates, the gunfire had fallen silent, replaced by groans. Hua soldiers crowded the square near the gates, cheering. Ming searched for a commander.

"Lord Zheng!" A young man in a uniform too big for him bowed at his waist. "Young Lord Zheng Tian told us to keep an eye out for you. He is nearby with your brother Shu. Come with me."

Ming dismounted and left his horse with an aide. "I would like to present myself before the *Tianzi*."

The messenger held his head at an angle which made it hard to see his face. "The *Tianzi* has sequestered himself in Sun-Moon Castle. No one has heard from him in weeks."

Weeks? Ming tugged his gloves off as he followed, Ma Jun in tow. "Then who is in charge?"

"Chief Minister Song is administering civilian affairs while General Tang leads the counteroffensive to retake the city."

No hereditary lords? With no one at the top, it was a wonder anything could get done. Ming cocked his head. "Who came up with such a strange idea?"

"The regent."

So a regent had been appointed, for the first time in nearly three centuries. Ming exchanged glances with Ma Jun. If the regent had left a minister and general in charge, he couldn't be all that competent. "Who is the regent?"

"Princess Kaiya."

Ma Jun's lip twitched into a grin.

If Ming's jaw hung any lower, he could probably lick the ground. "Where is she?"

"She drew the main Teleri army out of the city by fleeing south."

Ming's head spun.

Ma Jun asked, "How many Teleri occupy the city?"

"Four thousand. They control the southeast quadrant, along the White Duck Stream from the south gate to Qingjingtian Amphitheater."

So many memories. Qingjingtian was where he'd shot his friend Xie Shimin and saved several dignitaries. White Duck Stream had been where the insurgency began, with an attack on him. Ming pictured a map of the city in his mind. An assault across the stream would be difficult for either side, depending on their numbers. "How many men do we have at our disposal?"

"Nine thousand imperial troops hold positions along the stream. Sixteen thousand Linshan provincial soldiers control the northern front to the east gate."

And fifteen thousand of his own men. Ming gritted his teeth. With a ten-to-one advantage—

"Lord Zheng!" a sultry voice called.

He turned.

A pretty girl, maybe sixteen or seventeen, batted long eyelashes at him. Wearing a plain pink dress, she looked familiar. She exposed the curve of her neck in a flirty tilt of her neck.

Now if only he could remember where he'd seen her. She was certainly too young for him to have slept with, though give it a year or so... He flashed his most charming smile. "It's been so long. My day is brighter now that you have come into it."

She pouted. "You don't remember me, do you?"

Ming tried to keep his smile enthralling, but undoubtedly looked sheepish despite his best efforts.

Her pout curved into an alluring smile. "Lin Ziqiu."

Lord Lin's daughter. No wonder. "Last time we met, you were just a little girl."

She swatted him on the shoulder in the most playful way. "No, last time was a year ago. You were about to give Princess Kaiya an archery lesson. I guess you only had eyes for her."

Ming hid a grin. If only the girl knew. The princess apparently had eyes for others, anyway.

"Well, come along now." She pointed toward a restaurant. "Your brothers are waiting for you."

Brothers? As in more than one? Ming followed her, watching the sway of her hips. She knelt at the door and bowed as she pulled it open. Ming flung his hair over his shoulder and winked as he passed through.

"Eldest Brother!" Panting, Shu rose from a chair.

At Shu's side, Tian bowed. "Eldest Brother."

The Kanin shaman and Fang Weiyong rose from a seat and embraced Ma Jun in a bizarre greeting. What was it with the natives? Not to mention Ma Jun and Fang Weiyong.

Ma Jun, in turn, wrapped his arms around Tian. "Do you have your memories back yet?"

Tian shook his head.

"I see." Ming glanced around the room. A handful of other teenagers, all dressed in plain clothes, turned their heads at angles when his gaze fell on them. Whoever they were, they didn't seem to be part of any army. He turned back to Tian. "I had expected to meet with our generals to discuss a strategy for finishing off the Teleri."

Tian gestured to the others. "My friends and I help the army. However, we don't have any say, except for the north gate."

The door closed and Ziqiu sashayed in. "Young Lord Tian urged General Tang to delay an assault on the north gate until we rescued Young Lord Shu." She tilted her chin in the cutest way toward his brother.

Ming looked around again. Someone was missing. The discourse was too normal, without a hint of sarcasm or insult. "Where's Jie?"

The silent response was awkward. The youngsters all stared at the ground. Yuha shook his head. The only sound came from outside as boots marched across the paved streets.

Tian scratched his chin. "Jie is unaccounted for. After she showed the imperial troops the secret path out of the palace, we've heard no word from her."

"How many days now?" Ma Jun asked.

Ziqiu held up four fingers.

Ming sighed. If anyone were to throttle the half-elf, it should be him. "I am sure she is all right. She is like a cockroach. It would take a lot to kill her."

Several sets of eyes glared daggers at him, including all the young people who'd avoided his gaze.

Ming sucked in a breath. "Well, I had better go meet with—"

The door slid open and a young woman slipped in. She bowed and dropped a rolled sheet of paper into Tian's hands. "An Eldaeri messenger bird arrived at Leina's house," she said.

Leina... Ming conjured an image of the exotic beauty he'd slept with on New Year's Day, just over a year ago. Now why would a messenger bird go *there*? Tian unrolled the sheet, revealing a hypnotic combination of foreign symbols. His lips tightened as his eyes darted back and forth over the words.

"You can read that?" Ming asked.

Tian nodded. "Leina gave us the codes."

Which meant— "Leina was a spy?"

Ziqiu nodded.

Ming's heart felt like lead. It must've been her who planted the false evidence connecting him to the insurgency a year before. How gullible he'd been. "Where is she now?"

"Dead." Tian studied Ming's expression.

Ming shuffled on his feet. "So what does the message say?"

Tian looked back. "It appears the Teleri embedded a Nightblade in Peng's rebellion. He has won Peng's confidence. Peng has convinced Lord Wu to turn on the imperial army. Peng also has a secret he won't share with anyone."

Yet another betrayal. If the princess had met up with the imperial army, she'd be in danger. Ming sighed. "We need to warn her."

"Her?" Ma Jun raised an eyebrow.

"How?" Ziqiu gazed at him with adoring eyes. "The Teleri army stands between us and the princess."

Ming looked at Tian. Surely his little brother had an idea.

"We can't reach the regent," Tian said, "but we can send the emperor false information with the messenger birds."

Ma Jun grinned. "Something that will scare the Teleri into retreating."

"Or something that will get him to fight Peng first," Ming said.

CHAPTER 42:
Illusion of Power

Peng Kai-Long watched as the last group of imperial commanders swore their loyalty with three kowtows. Their soldiers, lined in orderly square ranks, followed suit.

"Ten Thousand Years to the *Tianzi!*" yelled General Lu.

"Ten Thousand Years!" repeated the imperial and provincial generals.

"Ten Thousand years!" droned the rank and file as they bowed in a wave from front to back. They knelt, pressed their foreheads to the ground, and stood again. Three times, each time repeating *Ten Thousand Years*. The Guardian Dragon circled above them, his red eyes and five claws gleaming as the Godseye Conjunction ended.

Kai-Long's heartbeat roared in his ears. His stomach somersaulted. The Mandate of Heaven was his. All without a shot fired, not a single Hua casualty. His genius! Years of planning, all culminating in a provincial lord's second son rising to the Jade Throne. Guns, firepowder, and a fleet of trade ships at his beck and call. Hua would be wealthy and powerful again.

With all eyes on him, he puffed out his chest. "Men of Hua! On this auspicious night, when the Godseye looks down on us, the Heavens have spoken. I humbly accept their mandate to bring order and prosperity to Hua!"

The men broke out into resounding cheers.

Kai-Long raised a war fan, and the soldiers fell silent. "These are uncertain times. The Bovyan scourge tramples upon our sacred land as we speak.

The infant *Tianzi* and the regents failed to stop them, and indeed let them in, either with incompetence or maybe even treason."

Jeers directed at Lord Liu Yong and Princess Kaiya erupted among the men. More than one used words reserved for prostitutes to curse her.

Kai-Long raised his fan to silence them again. Rival or not, it would not do to have the Wang royal blood—his own blood—deprecated in such vulgar terms. "I have annihilated one foreign invader; now it is time to crush another. Rest well, for at dawn we march." He chopped the fan northward, snapping it shut.

The armies roared in bloodlust. Kai-Long closed his eyes to revel in their applause. Convince a people their precious homes were under attack, and a clever man could bend them to his will. Just like his ancestor, the Founder. Once Kai-Long defeated the Teleri and consolidated his rule over Hua, he would liberate Ankira from the Madurans and civilize the Wilds.

A hush settled over the ranks of men, their clamor falling from its crescendo. That wasn't supposed to happen, not unless he silenced them himself. Kai-Long opened his eyes. At the far end, the sea of soldiers began to part. He squinted. Several figures approached.

Cousin Kaiya among them.

Whore. Slut. Harlot. Kaiya flinched at the barely audible murmurs. Geros had whispered those insults in her ear, and now her own countrymen dared utter them. Hurt as the words might, none stung as much as *traitor*. Not when she had sacrificed so much for the nation.

Kaiya's lip trembled as she fought back tears. Curse the *Tiger's Eye*, coming and going at the most inopportune moments! Now, when she needed to be resolute, it failed her, stripping her of her wits. The power of her voice, gone. Her dignity, torn away. All she had was some rock cradled in her arm and no idea how to use it.

Cousin Peng had won the soldiers over with some flowery words, and an illusion of a flaming pearl. The Guardian Dragon of Hua fluttered in circles above, his ruby red eyes sparkling in the moonlight. Certainly a great, magical being should be able to see through the deception. Hopefully Brehane would be able disperse the magic.

A reassuring hand pressed between her shoulder blades. Jie had always been the one to do that, but now, the deep pulse vibrating into her heart could only come from Doctor Wu's steadfastness. Brehane and Sameer followed several steps behind, their breaths short and shallow. Yes, they were as nervous as her.

"Don't worry," Brehane said. "I feel the magic. I can dispel the pearl illusion."

The Mystic's wobbling voice did little to inspire confidence, but Kaiya nodded. With one hand, she reached over and grasped the pole of an imperial banner. The soldier holding it bowed and released it. If at least some men recognized her legitimacy, perhaps not all was lost.

She held the banner aloft. "I—" Her voice choked until she cleared out the lump. "I, the regent for *Tianzi* Liu Yiping, demand an audience with *Lord* Peng Kai-Long."

Around her, several of the imperial troops sank to a knee, fist to the ground. Still others remained standing, their raised heads not concealing their scowls. At least in the eyes of some, Cousin Peng had succeeded in painting her as both conspiratorial and incompetent, if the combination was possible.

His voice now rose above the silence, from his place far ahead. "I thank you for your service, but as an adult *Tianzi*, I do not require a regent. Men, please escort the princess to a tent of honor."

An assassin's knife would doubtless find her throat in that tent. Kaiya straightened her back and squared her soldiers. Even without the power of her voice, she still knew how to project the image of imperial prestige. "*Jue-Ye*," she said, using the address for a *Tai-Ming* lord, "You have not made your oaths in the Temple of Heaven. You do not even hold the imperial seal. Until then, your claim might be considered...treasonous."

Though his smirk was indiscernible from the distance, it carried in his voice. "Look above, Kaiya. The Guardian Dragon of Hua has already appeared twice to anoint me, to celebrate the defeat of a foreign invader and the unifying of our brothers in arms. Both tasks *you* failed to accomplish."

Over half the soldiers pounded the ground with their spear hafts, cheering, "Peng, Peng, Peng."

Behind her, Brehane barked several syllables in the language of Shallow Magic, setting her considerable power against whoever conjured the flaming pearl illusion. Her spell stopped on a hard grunt. Weapons rasped out of sheathes. Someone crumpled to the ground.

Kaiya spun around. Brehane sprawled in the trampled grass, her eyes staring up into her skull. A soldier raised the butt of his spear. Had she completed her spell, or had the strike to her head cut her words short? Other warriors surrounded Sameer with naked blades as he brandished his *naga*, left-handed.

And up above, the Guardian Dragon still danced in circles over Cousin Peng, still held in thrall by the fake pearl.

No, there could be no bloodshed. Kaiya lifted the banner. "Men of Hua, stand down. Sameer, sheathe your weapon. Fleet..." She looked around. The madaeri was nowhere to be seen. However, several of the Hua soldiers backed off. Sameer lowered his weapon. Doctor Wu pushed through the men like a breeze through flower petals, and kneeled by Brehane. Silence fell over the armies again.

"Bring the traitor and her friends to me." Peng's snarl echoed in the valley.

Hands seized her elbows, though she cradled the Pearl as if her life depended on it. It probably did. Another soldier shoved her forward. She caught her balance and straightened again. Other men pushed forward, either to her aid or to restrain her.

"At ease." She kept her voice level and authoritative, just as her father would have. The soldiers back off, giving her space. Lifting her chin, she strode forward. The ranks of men cleared a path, though their expressions varied from anger to sympathy, lust to admiration.

Each step drew her closer to Cousin Peng, while the sounds of Sameer's and Brehane's breathing disappeared into the thousands of breaths around her. Nobody was there to protect her if Peng decided to behead her on the spot. At least when she'd faced down Avarax, she'd had Sameer, Jie, and an army of Paladins and priestesses there to support her. Now, with Jie dead and her friends all held at the back, she only had herself to rely on.

Then again, Peng was no dragon, despite what he might think of himself. She had thwarted his plans several times. Her steps matched the beating of her heart. Firm. Resolute.

Then something pushed into the back of her legs.

She fell to her knees, prostrate before the outcrop where Peng stood gloating. Someone pulled her sash from behind, yanking her robe flaps open to her shoulders and sending Tian's pouch clattering to the ground.

With one hand holding her dress together, Kaiya dropped the Pearl and reached for the pouch. A soldier's boot stomped down and barely missed crushing her hand. The motion inadvertently kicked Xu's tuning fork, which skittered closer, just within reach.

The tuning fork, the Pearl, the dragon. Kaiya swiped it up and tapped it to a rock. A clear sound rang out. The Pearl hummed out and glowed a faint blue through its dirt and limestone crust. Certainly that would get the Guardian Dragon's attention! She looked up.

No, the dragon still swirled in lazy circles above Peng, its glowing red eyes locked on the fake pearl. Stupid dragon! Kaiya struggled to stand, but a hand restrained her shoulder. Another wrenched the tuning fork from her hand. She glared back at the man, then at Peng. "How dare you? I am a princess of Hua—"

The soldier tossed the tuning fork up to Peng, who caught it. With a furrowed brow, he turned it over in his hands. Then he looked up and jabbed an imperious finger at her. "This woman is no princess. She is nothing but a whore who slept with an enemy in order to undermine Hua from the inside."

The gall! She tried to rise again, but her captor held on to the lapels of her gown. To stand would likely rip her dress away, baring her to three hundred thousand men.

Peng waved dismissively toward the back. "She cavorts with Southerners who do not have Hua's best interest at heart. I offered her a place of honor, and instead, she calls my legitimacy into question." He lifted his chin to a man beside her. "General Lu, go put her with the Maduran prostitutes where she belongs."

Kaiya turned. There stood the proud general she had spurned years before, in favor of Prince Hardeep…Avarax. His stare burned with hatred. Like Geros' the first time he'd… Her chest constricted. He marched toward her and grabbed her wrist. *Tiger's Eye* or not, anger welled inside, replacing the fear.

And with it, something sparked inside her. Power. A long-forgotten friend. She scowled at General Lu and sung her command: "Kneel."

The resonance of the world, so strong in this place near the pyramid, amplified by the closeness of the moons, flowed through her.

Stronger than when she faced Avarax. General Lu dropped to his knees. Soldiers behind him followed suit, rippling out in a wave of obeisance.

Peng gaped at his hand, where Xu's tuning fork now vibrated of its own accord.

Lying ignored near a bush, the Dragon Pearl hummed louder in answer. Rays of blue flared between the cracks in the covering sediment, pulsing at the same frequency as the tuning fork, the same frequency as her command. Similar, yet different, from Avarax's gemstone. Replicating the tone, she lifted her voice in song.

The Dragon Pearl lifted off the ground, growing larger and floating higher up into the air. Everyone's gaze followed it, including hers.

But still not the Guardian's!

Peng raised both arms to the dragon. "The Guardian Dragon still recognizes me!" With a cackle, he stared down at her. "You are no Dragon Charmer." He pulled a *dao* from his sash and pointed at her. "Kill her!"

Many of the soldiers rose and drew swords or levelled spears. General Lu seized her wrist and pulled her to him. With his free hand, he covered her mouth. Kaiya struggled in his grasp.

"Drop your weapons and kneel." A loud, yet flowery female voice echoed from the army's rear. Spears, daggers, crossbows, muskets, and swords clattered to the ground. Every last man sank to his knees. General Lu's grip went slack as he knelt. The sound washed over Kaiya like a tidal wave, compelling her to her knees as well.

An enormous chain of silvery white scales snaked through the banners and flags, whipping them with a gust of wind. Kaiya shielded her eyes and turned as the brightness surged closer. Squinting, she snuck a glance just as the dragonhead turned, revealing silvery whiskers and luminous blue eyes. Beautiful eyes, like...

The dragon swallowed up the Pearl and vaulted skyward, growing larger as he ascended. Larger and more magnificent than Peng's dragon. It wasn't possible. Unless two dragons served as messengers of the gods.

Though still smaller than Avarax, the silver dragon now dwarfed the golden one, and was far more beautiful. Long and elegant, each silver scale glistening in bright white. Spindly claws, like a willow's branches. And the hum.

Kaiya listened, trying to decipher the unique resonance of the two powerful beings. The familiar buzz of the Dragon Pearl combined with...no, it was just one sound. Come to think of it, the golden dragon had been silent this whole time, not emitting the energy pulses like Rumiya said all dragons did.

The pearl wasn't the only illusion.

The silver dragon coiled around the imposter, to three hundred thousand collective gasps. When the silver dragon pulled straight, the golden one blinked out of existence, pearl and all. The remaining dragon could only be the one true Guardian of Hua.

While everyone else repeatedly looked up and bowed, Kaiya tore her gaze away from the spectacle and sought out Cousin Peng. Sword hanging loosely in his hand, eyes fixed upward, he staggered to his feet and backed away from the edge of the outcropping.

The Guardian Dragon pointed a talon at him. "Usurper," she—she?—said, voice echoing into the night.

A sea of heads turned to face her shamed cousin. Peng shrunk back.

The Guardian Dragon pointed a talon down at Kaiya. "The gods decree that only Wang Kaiya, daughter of the late *Tianzi*, is fit to be regent. Let her wisdom guide her in choosing the next *Tianzi*."

Kaiya's heart swelled. Still...wisdom? Not yet twenty, she wasn't even considered an adult. Her eyes found Tian's lockpick pouch in the grass, and she picked it up. She looked up.

The Guardian Dragon swooped in graceful circles three more times, then flashed out in a majestic bloom of light more magnificent than New Year's fireworks.

"Ten Thousand Years to the regent," someone called out.

"Ten Thousand Years!" the chorus repeated. The imperial and provincial armies bowed before her, even those from Cousin Peng's own province.

Peng. Kaiya looked to the outcropping above, where her cousin had just groveled. Now it was abandoned. He must've fled. No, they couldn't let the traitor escape, to stir up more trouble. Not again. He couldn't have gotten far. She cleared her throat...and the magic was gone again. The *Tiger's Eye* must have locked away her emotions once more. No matter, the legitimacy conferred by the Guardian Dragon of Hua was magic enough.

"Soldiers of Hua," she called, bringing the men to silence. "The rebel Peng Kai-Long is hiding among us. I will reward a silver *jiao* to whoever brings me his head. Ten thousand gold *yuan* if you bring him to me alive."

Peng Kai-Long picked his way among the forest of his provincial army tents as quickly and quietly as he could. How rapidly fortunes changed. He had been just one step from the Dragon Throne, and now he huddled like a scared rat. All because of a meddling, impossibly lucky girl, who had escaped three, no four...actually, *five* of his attempts on her life. If only he had snuffed her out years ago.

He would, if it was the last thing he ever did. Clenching his dagger, he paused by the right tent and peeked in.

The Aksumi Mystic, still maintaining his illusion as a handsome young Nanling provincial officer, was filling a pack.

Kai-Long slipped in. "You. I need your help. I can still reward you."

"With what?" The Mystic turned around with a smirk.

"I have jade and gold stashed away."

"Do you now?" The Aksumi's eyes glinted. "What do you need?"

"A disguise. One that can be maintained, like the baubles you made for me in the past." The ones he'd used to sneak Kaiya out of Sun-Moon Palace, only to have her survive the assassination he'd planned.

"I can do that." The Mystic studied him from head to toe. "What did you have in mind?"

A plan within a plan, and a contingency—just like the way he had risen from second son of a provincial lord to almost-*Tianzi*, by hijacking Chief Minister Tan's and old Hong's schemes. He grinned. "Make me look like an old Maduran woman. Not too old." Knowing his cousin, she'd personally check on the wellbeing of the servants and prostitutes, which would put her closer to his knife.

The Mystic nodded. He produced a light bauble from his pocket and spoke a single word. The light winked out, and he dropped it to the floor. He barked out a long string of foul-sounding grunts worthy of feral dogs fighting for scraps, and the bauble flashed.

"Take it," he said.

Kai-Long snatched it up.

The man withdrew a hand mirror from his pack and held it up.

Looking into the mirror, Kai-Long suppressed a gasp. Fine lines crinkled his now-bronze skin. Coarse black hair framed a middle-aged face. Not particularly pretty, but that would prevent the soldiers from trying to take advantage of him.

"Keep the bauble with you at all times." The Mystic yawned. "Now, how about my payment?"

Kai-Long gestured toward the tent flap. "Let's go get it."

Nodding, the Mystic turned to the doorway.

Dagger in hand, Kai-Long covered the fool's mouth and slashed his throat. The Mystic clawed at his neck and choked on his words.

"Your payment," Kai-Long said. "For lying to me about summoning the Guardian Dragon."

The man's fingers went limp first, then his entire body. His illusion remained the same, which must mean he held a bauble as well. Kai-Long patted the corpse down and was rewarded with a hard lump beneath his sash. When Kai-Long dug it out from next to the man's still-warm flesh, the body's form shimmered back to a middle-aged Aksumi male.

Kai-Long peeked out the tent. With no one around, he dragged the remains and dumped them in the closest tent. Then he went back to the Mystic's pack and looked at the mirror. With just one of the baubles touching his bare skin, he appeared as either the young Hua male or the middle-aged Ayuri female. With one in each hand, he appeared as an androgynous, half-Hua, half-Ayuri mix. Perhaps a homelier version of Hong's concubine—yet another person who deserved retribution for her role in his downfall.

All the easier to accomplish now that he had three different disguise combinations. Now, he just needed appropriate clothes. He fished an extra uniform from the Mystic's clothes and then tucked the Hua bauble next to his skin.

It was time to seek out the Water Snake agent to help him with an assassination.

CHAPTER 43:
Race to Vengeance

Peng Kai-Long looked to where the real Guardian Dragon had just anointed his hateful cousin; a woman, no less. Gone. Of course, in the histories, the Guardian Dragon had only made brief appearances. It didn't feed hungry mouths or reward men with treasure and women. When it came down to it, legitimacy only went as far as happy men with swords took it.

For now, it meant a level of discretion. He crept out into the night, hoping to avoid all the men searching for him. He'd taken three steps when a hand clamped down on his shoulder, sending a jolt up his spine. He turned around to meet the gazes of several Nanling provincial soldiers.

"Oh, Commander." The one who had grabbed him stepped back and bowed. The others followed suit.

Right. With the magical disguise, Kai-Long could rove with impunity among all the men searching for him. Find out who he could trust and who deserved a knife in the back. He nodded, allowing the men out of their bows.

"Lord Peng was last seen somewhere around here," one said. "Have you seen him?"

Kai-Long shook his head and pointed toward the supply tents. "Lord Peng is smart. If I were him, I would be collecting provisions."

One of the men snickered. "Lord Peng would never survive without a comfortable bed to sleep in."

Kai-Long memorized the man's face. "He is more resourceful than that. Remember, he masterfully deceived the imperials when he fled the capital and returned home to take back his province. If you do not respect your enemy, you can never defeat him. Now go check the supply tents!"

Wide-eyed, the men bowed and jogged off. With a snort, Kai-Long stalked off toward another tent. No wonder things had turned against him, saddled by such stupid men. Just outside the flap, he paused.

"May I help you, Commander?" a male voice said from behind.

Kai-Long spun around. There stood the Water Snake agent, still disguised as a messenger. Kai-Long beckoned him in.

Folding his arms over his chest, the spy narrowed his eyes. No, one of his hands went into the folds of his robe.

Kai-Long pinched the bauble under his sash and pulled it from his skin.

The agent's eyes widened. "Lord Peng."

"Yes, now come in." Kai-Long pushed through the flap.

The spy padded in after him. "What use are you to us now? I should just capture you and collect the reward the regent is offering."

"A dead woman can't fulfil a reward."

The agent shook his head. "What did you have in mind?"

Kai-Long shrugged. "You are a messenger, after all. You can get close to her. Kill her."

"Why would my clan want that?"

"Because once she is out of the way, the nation will look for leadership. I will be there to step in. When I do, your clan will be rewarded."

The spy chuckled. "I do believe a Guardian Dragon labelled you a usurper."

"It could've been yet more magic. She had a Mystic with her."

"Unconscious."

Kai-Long harrumphed. Nobody would remember all those details. "What do you have to lose? As long as the princess is regent, the Black Lotus will serve the *Tianzi*. At least with me, you have a chance."

The spy's eyes searched Kai-Long's. "Very well." He turned and slipped out of the tent.

Kai-Long followed. Now time to find General Lu. The imperial soldiers looked up to him, and he had no love for the princess. Then again, he had laid a hand on her, so he must be with the Maduran prisoners by now.

As the agent crept off in one direction, Kai-Long headed toward the Madurans, the ones he had been forced to spare as a demonstration of his leniency. Groups of soldiers still dashed about, his name on their lips. He searched the faces in the makeshift stockade. All Ayuri males. The single Hua guard paced outside the fencing, his gaze following his rushing comrades.

Just beyond stood the large tent for the servants and whores, unguarded. For the most part, they had been casually supervised to prevent acts of sabotage, but all had been docile and compliant. Except the pretty noblewoman who refused to let a man touch her.

"*Jie-xia*, the prisoners are this way." General Lu's voice carried from not far in the distance. That turtle's egg must have submitted to her, and she, in a show of magnanimity, must have forgiven his transgressions. So predictable, down to her visit to the servants and prisoners. The sound of jingling armor and heavy boots approached.

Ducking into a tent, Kai-Long swapped the magical baubles. To confirm the transformation, he withdrew the mirror. The plain, middle-aged Ayuri woman stared back at him. The voices got closer. Kai-Long dashed from the tent. To his right, the princess walked with General Lu, the halfling, and the Ayuri Paladin with his sword arm in a sling. The Mystic and doctor were nowhere to be seen.

He pushed the flap aside and slipped in. Several women gawked at him. It didn't make sense, since he should look just like one of them.

"Who are *you*?" the pretty noble said.

Of course, they wouldn't recognize a newcomer. Thank the Heavens he spoke perfect Ayuri from his years as a diplomat in Vyara City. He opened his mouth...and then shut it. Even if he *looked* like an Ayuri crone, he would still *sound* like himself. Or would he? Not worth the risk. He pointed to his mouth and shook his head. Let them think he was mute.

An older woman—likely the one who had glared at him with such anger when he defeated the Maduran army—appraised him. "Why are you wearing *their* uniform?"

Curse the Heavens! He'd been in too much of a rush. He now pointed out of the tent and mouthed, *I lost my clothes and a soldier loaned me his.* He gestured toward a pile of clothes as he worked his arm out the uniform sleeve. *Let me borrow one.*

With a raised eyebrow, the noblewoman offered him a *sari.* Outside, General Lu's voice grew louder. They couldn't be more than twenty feet from the tent. Curses! He struggled out of the robe, revealing sagging breasts and rolls of flesh on his stomach.

How horrendous! And amazing. The magic was so...complete. Who would have ima—the bauble slipped off his skin before he caught it. His own honey tone and smooth muscle flared for that split second before returning to the Ayuri illusion. The noblewoman narrowed her eyes at him. The tent flap opened.

Kai-Long turned to see who it was.

General Lu froze in place, staring at Kai-Long's exposed chest. Kai-Long crossed his arms, one hand squeezing the bauble, the other reaching for his dagger caught in the folds of cloth.

"General, please wait outside. Fleet, out." The princess guided him out with just a wave of her hand. Now, it was just her. She looked to Kai-Long.

"I am sorry for the intrusion." She averted her gaze to the others. "Has everyone been well cared-for?"

With the bitch's back turned and nobody guarding her, she didn't stand a chance.

The low murmurs of Ayuri in the spacious tent reminded Kaiya of the journey to Vyara City. Meeting with dignitaries. Dancing for that buffoon Prince Dhananad. Learning Hardeep's true identity. And of course, singing to Avarax.

Perhaps the Guardian Dragon had been right: perhaps she did have wisdom, garnered from so many experiences. Among those experiences was meeting this beautiful young Ayuri woman somewhere...but where? A musician or dancer, perhaps. Or maybe one of Dhananad's wives. Whoever she was, she now glared at the half-naked, middle-aged woman with such hatred. There must have been some dynamic that had developed over the weeks on the march.

One which no amount of wisdom would diffuse. It wasn't her place, either; not among foreigners who had to be somehow repatriated. Kaiya offered a nervous smile. Then behind her, the middle-aged woman moved in a rapid ruffling of clothes. The young woman surged forward in a blur, faster than anyone Kaiya had ever seen, besides...Paladins.

Women screamed. Kaiya's sleeve sheared with a rasp. Pain bit into her arm. She turned to see the middle-aged woman on her back, dagger in hand. The young woman stomped on the other hand with blinding speed, sending bones crunching. It sounded like glass shattered in her hand.

The woman's face disappeared, replaced by—Cousin Peng. His expression filled with a hatred that made Kaiya shiver. Wincing at his hand, which curled at a strange angle, he staggered to his feet. The tent flap opened, and Sameer, Fleet, and General Lu rushed in.

They were too far away. Peng lunged forward with a stab.

The woman wrapped a sash around his wrist and pulled his arm to the side. With a deft twist, she plucked the dagger out of his hand.

Peng's eyes darted over the tent, his gaze pausing for split seconds over weapons, drawn and sheathed. With a sigh, he raised his hands above his head. "Curse you, Kaiya." He spat her name.

Kaiya sighed, too. The Hua civil war was finally over, Peng Kai-Long finally in custody—

The young woman zipped in toward him. Faster than the eye could see, the blade whispered across his body eight times in a split-second before she jumped out again. He stared as blood spurted from several surgical slashes over major arteries. He collapsed to his knees.

The woman curled her lip. "That was for every Maduran you lured into Cathay. For every prisoner you butchered in cold blood." She darted in again and yanked Peng's head back by his hair.

Kaiya held a hand up. Deserved as it might be, this was nothing short of murder. Paladins did not dispense justice this way. They needed to drag Peng before the rest of the hereditary lords for proper punishment.

"Sohini!" Sameer gaped. "What are you doing here?"

The woman looked back at him and her scowl softened. Her knife lowered. She looked...embarrassed.

That face, that expression. Kaiya sucked in a breath. The woman—Sohini—was no Paladin. She was a Golden Scorpion, *the* Scorpion who'd tried to poison her and defeated Jie.

Sohini's mouth curled into a sneer. "This is for betraying my prince." She plunged the dagger deep into Peng's throat with a sickening squish. He fell over into a twisted heap of *sari* and uniform, his lifeblood soaking into the tent floor.

The Golden Scorpion Sohini pushed Sameer to the side by his bad arm and flashed out of the tent. Sameer whirled around and gave chase.

Kaiya's mind spun. So much had just happened. The woman who had tried to ambush her had reappeared into her life. Then disappeared just as fast, taking Sameer with her. Cousin Peng now lay on the ground, probably dead from the brutal attack.

Fleet rolled the body over and shrugged. "Can't say he didn't deserve it."

Maybe so, but what would the army say? All of it had happened in the close confines of a tent, with only a handful of witnesses. She had promised justice, not revenge. No one would collect the reward for Peng's capture. And the Guardian Dragon and her Pearl were no longer around to reaffirm the Mandate of Heaven.

"*Jue-ye*," a voice called from the entrance to the tent.

Kaiya turned to see a large messenger kneeling there, fist to the ground. "Speak," she said.

"The Teleri have launched an attack on Lord Wu's rear."

CHAPTER 44:

Dance of Heavens

Geros scanned the valley, trying to decipher the positions of the Cathayi imperial and provincial armies. The messenger birds between him and the Nightblade embedded with Peng's rebellion had ceased three days prior, and now he acted on what he had known at the time: Peng's armies faced off against the imperials, with Lord Wu's provincial army about to fall on the imperial flank.

Once Lord Wu descended, Geros had planned to lead his men to occupy that position. It would've not only provided a commanding view of the battle, but also a superior position from which to engage whichever army emerged victorious...and depleted.

Yet Lord Wu had left long before the Teleri army had arrived, and from this vantage point, it was impossible to tell if they planned to engage the Cathayi imperial troops or *join* them. He looked back at his own orderly ranks, the Bovyans showing no signs of wear after they had stolen a march on his enemies.

Past First Consuls had noted in their memoirs that he Eye of Geros allowed them to see details more clearly, and see in the dark, but he'd yet to experience it. He held his hand back to an aide. "My looking glass."

The aide thumped his fist to his chest and withdrew the scope.

Geros swiped it and took in the scene. Peng's troops seemed to be in disarray, even though there were no signs of a battle having taken place. Strange, since Peng had proven a capable leader. Geros shifted to Lord Wu's men. They looked to be...resting?

If only he knew more. Tivar take the Nightblade for failing to maintain communication! Or perhaps they had ferreted him out. Geros examined the imperial troops. They were breaking camp, when they should be annihilating Peng's disorganized army. On a hillside outcrop, at the close end of the imperial armies on Lord Wu's left...

Princess Kaiya.

He snapped the looking glass shut and turned back to his aide. "How many Cathayi soldiers did we count?"

The aide pointed at the groups in turn. "Lord Peng has a hundred and twenty thousand. The imperials, a hundred and fifty thousand. Lord Wu, thirty thousand."

In total, a nearly six-to-one advantage over his own forty-five thousand men. Yet none of the enemy were Bovyans, and in a pitched hand-to-hand battle, the enemy's muskets would be useless. If Peng saw the tide turn in his favor, ambition might get the better of him. Might.

For Kaiya, Geros would take that gamble.

He turned to his command team. "The Cathayi outnumber us, but their closest group is resting and the rest are not prepared. If we stretch out in thin ranks, we will be too close for them to use guns once we engage. General Tanos will attack their left-center, while General Baros falls on their left rear flank. General Kros will hold our own left flank. I will personally slide behind Baros and attack their central command." Which was Kaiya.

General Baros gawked at him. "Your Eminence, if they see you coming, Lord Peng will be able to fall on your right and isolate you."

"Lord Peng's men are too disorganized, and he might very well turn on her...I mean, them." Another risk he would take, since this might now be his only chance to seize the princess and his unborn son. He glared at the men, who bowed their heads. "Now attack! Quickly and quietly, before they can organize."

The men all thumped their chests and hurried to their divisions.

Geros looked back at the valley, where his prize waited unawares. Soon, very soon, she would be his again. Or he would be dead.

The energy of the world hummed in Kaiya's ears, providing a backdrop for the sounds of war. Metal clashed on metal as the Teleri smashed into Lord Wu's rear. Boots stomped, men screamed, all in a symphony of slaughter. If only she could connect to the energy, harness it into her voice, she could turn this battle into a rout. There had to be a way.

Emotions. Enough emotions would topple the *Tiger's Eye*, hopefully for good. Kaiya conjured up memories, seeing if they would stir her feelings. Hardeep's enchantment and Avarax's deception. Zheng Ming's charm. Tian treating her like dirt in their escape from Iksuvius, followed by his affection in the Wilds. The love only she evoked in him. The joy and rapture of making love to him. Geros taking her. Her father's death. Tian's death. Jie's death.

She was now all alone in this world. Yet, all the images and memories felt like she was reading a sterile, historical account of her life. The energy of the world remained close and torrential, but walled off, just like when Geros had collared her with the grey metal neck ring.

Hand to her throat, Kaiya looked down at the battle from the outcropping. Lord Wu's men were fleeing from the onslaught. The Teleri snaked along the provincial army's edges in the most bizarre fashion to her untrained eyes. It seemed inconceivable that such a small force could even stand a chance against a much larger one. Beneath her, Hua officers scurried about, mobilizing their men to arms.

And then she saw it: the Teleri reserve slipped behind the wall formed by their forward troops. Headed where? She followed the curve of the battle lines, meandering down the mountain, along the road...to her.

A lump formed in her throat. The reserve troop, marching double-time or perhaps faster, came for *her*. Like the Founder's victory at Narrow Barrel Valley on Great Peace Island. Facing an army twenty-five thousand with under two thousand of his own men, he had killed the enemy lord, and the opposition crumbled.

This time, they didn't plan to kill the leader. Geros undoubtedly had other plans for her.

And no one to protect her. Her generals and senior officers raced among the men in a vain attempt to organize them. Sameer had run off after the Scorpion. Brehane—she would be using her magic by now if she were able. Perhaps Doctor Wu was still tending her wounds. And Fleet... Fleet had disappeared yet again, after waylaying a messenger to who knows where.

As her gaze swept across the valley, something glinted in the corner of her eye. Right by her side, where she had somehow missed it. Xu's magic mirror, the one she'd carried to Vyara City and back, rested on a folded pile of fine silk. Instead of a reflection on its face, several black words burned on a parchment background. The title of another book, perhaps. She read.

When a regent looks the part, her people will listen.

Never a straight answer from that elf, even in his letters. She knelt down and ran her fingers across the gold embroidered blue silk. She lifted it, revealing an outer robe with five-clawed dragon patterns stitched into it. It was beautiful. A silver-threaded sash tumbled out.

She appraised her plain travelling dress, light brown and soiled with mud, dirt, and blood. Her own sash, hastily wound back after General Lu tore it off, was creased and ratty. In whole, certainly not the bearing of a princess, let alone a regent. She looked back at the Teleri reserve, jogging unopposed toward her position, with Geros' unmistakable gait at the head of their column. Only a few minutes away.

It left scant time to rally her army. Cold ran up her spine. Nothing kept Geros from capturing her again. Her heart pounded in the constricted confines of her chest. Where was the cursed *Tiger's Eye* when she actually needed it?

Put on the sash and robe, Xu's voice spoke in her mind, exasperated.

Kaiya's stomach leapt into her throat. There was no sign of the elf lord. If he could see what was going on, why didn't he help?

Because if I saved the day, your people would look to me for leadership. Xu's words blew out like a long sigh. *Success or failure is on your shoulders. Now put on the clothes I made especially for you!*

What was that supposed to do? Make her appear regal in defeat? Create an extra layer for Geros to strip away?

Just do it! his voice snarled.

The elf should've just said something instead of leaving a cryptic message about fashion sense in his magic mirror. Hands trembling, fingers stiff, she unwound her sash. Tian's pouch again tumbled out, this time hitting the rocks with a dull thud. A strange sound, really. She shook her head, trying to focus as she tore the old sash away and started wrapping the other.

She froze mid-wind. The energy of the world buzzed in her feet, resonating to her heart. Could it be? Tentatively, she sang a single note. The power surged through her, echoing into the night. Soldiers from both sides froze on the battlefield and looked up at her. Geros stopped mid-stride and stared at her through his mismatched eyes.

Perhaps her fear had battered down the *Tiger's Eye*, even if she didn't feel that fright now.

Still, the energy of the world coursed through her. The magic mirror's surface flashed at her feet. A Hua marching song flickered into view, one which the slave girl Yanyan had sung during the War of Ancient Gods to mobilize Hua slaves against their altivorc masters.

Holding the memory of Tian facing three Teleri with only a stone-headed spear, Kaiya sang. The world's pulse vibrated through her. From where she stood, radiating out, Hua soldiers formed up. Their unified chant and the pounding of their spear hafts on the ground followed the cadence of her voice.

Still, the Teleri lines held. Their expeditionary force scrambled up the hillside. Geros himself had closed enough for her to make out his ravenous smirk. Her song did not affect them either way, nor did she know any Arkothi songs that could evoke fear in them.

Geros was just ten paces away. There had to be something she could do. A word of power. It had been so long—well, besides ordering Peng's men to kneel—since she'd used one. It had to be simple, one syllable at most, and in the Arkothi language. Even with the energy of the world welling in this spot, it might not be enough to affect so many.

Kaiya gripped the ground with her toes and straightened her spine. She sucked in a deep breath. Guanyin's Tear atop the pyramid darkened, and the Trees of Light dimmed, shrouding the battlefield in the light of the three moons alone.

"Flee." The Arkothi word rolled off her tongue and boomed. It echoed throughout the valley. The pyramid and trees lit up again. All the energy drained out of her. Her wobbly legs unable to support her, Kaiya buckled to the ground. Tian's pouch lay near her hand, and she picked it up. Though her head and shoulders felt like a dwarf anvil, she pushed herself into a sitting position and looked to the battlefield.

The Teleri lines broke. The Bovyans threw down their arms and fled in an all-out retreat. A rout. Just three steps away from her, Geros took tentative backward steps before turning into a full sprint. He tripped over his feet and stumbled the rest of the way down the hillside.

Her words struggled to break free of her throat and came out only as a hoarse whisper. "Cap—capture. Capture him..."

Lord Xu materialized out of thin air. "Kaiya, come with me." He placed a hand on her shoulder, and the battlefield winked out.

Kaiya blinked. They now stood near an enormous arch, which spanned the mouth of an atoll. Her feet sunk into fine white sand. At last, after her armies had already turned the tide of the battle, he appeared.

"Sit," he said, indicating a worn boulder behind her.

She nodded and settled on the edge, letting her legs dangle over the side. Just like she had often done at Sun-Moon Palace, looking out over the lake. Those days had been filled with uncertainty, as plotting and insurgency roiled the realm. Though Peng, the source of all the turmoil, was dead, the road ahead still felt daunting. The North lay pillaged by the Bovyans. Bridges destroyed. Ambitious lords who might not necessarily believe in or care about Guardian Dragons.

He sat down beside her and pointed to the moons, now going their separate ways. It would be three centuries before they met again in the high halls of heaven. He patted her on the head. "The annals of history tell you the Godseye Conjunction and the appearance of the Guardian Dragon heralded in the Wang Dynasty. Let me tell you another story."

Tiger's Eye or not, Kaiya's spine tingled.

"Three hundred years ago, I sat with your ancestors under this same sky. It was not for the celebration of victory, but to mark the beginning of a new road. The next years were not easy. Warlords had undermined Yu Dynasty imperial authority for a decade before the Hellstorm, and the Long Winter would leave the people starving. Yet Wang Xinchang and Wang Yuxiang overcame the hardships and reunited Hua."

Kaiya nodded. The histories often glossed over the process in favor of the grand story of the Guardian Dragon and the Mandate of Heaven. Still, there were more complicated stories left untold.

Xu turned her chin to meet his gaze. "Your ancestors were strangers to this land, and I daresay, not as resourceful as you. Have faith in yourself. I have faith in you. You have far surpassed my expectations."

"Expectations?"

"Remember that I once said you were born to face Avarax?"

She nodded.

"The late Queen Regent's bloodline does not easily beget scions. Your father asked for my power to help conceive his children. I gave you Yanyan's voice so you could vanquish Avarax once her ward on his power failed."

Kaiya's mind spun. How was it even possible?

"You defeated him when I could not." He grinned. "Now, you are reuniting Hua."

Kaiya stared back at him. "Why? Why did you help my ancestors? Why do you help me? Why do you care about Hua?"

He gazed back up at the stars. "Did you see it before? A constellation appeared above the moons just before the Godseye Conjunction. It is gone now."

"The Golden Flock." Kaiya looked. Indeed, the new stars she had seen at the pyramid had disappeared.

He pointed toward the red star, Yanluo the Conqueror. "If you watched the heavens from there, you would see a very different picture. In the elaborate dance of the stars, Tivara is just one of the performers. Yet, it is one of the most important. Sometimes a stagehand must work with a diva."

A diva. Kaiya pouted like a child. Was he referring to Tivara, or her?

He laughed. "The Hellstorm, elf angels, the Altivorc King: they are all part of an intricate choreography, the push and pull of good and evil. What you do here, in undermining the altivorcs and their allies, ensures that the universe unfolds as planned."

As always, Lord Xu talked in riddles. Kaiya let out a long sigh. As if the realm wasn't enough responsibility.

Plucking the mirror from her hands, he held open the regent's robe he had made for her, the one she never managed to slip into. Indeed, her new sash still dangled from her hastily tied knot.

She threaded her arms into the sleeves. "Is it magic?"

He grinned. "You should have learned from these last few weeks that you do not always have to rely on magic."

Evasive answers yet again. She sighed. "Now what?"

Ignoring her, Xu fiddled with the mirror, and different images flashed across its face. One painting appeared. Was that the Dragon Pearl, in someone's hands? Her hands? Or was it just a reflection? It disappeared with a sweep of his hand. He pressed the mirror to his chest and looked up. "If *I* were regent, I would worry about the remnants of the Teleri army and their capable leader."

She kept her eyes locked on the mirror. "If you were their capable leader, where would you go?"

He lowered the mirror, which now showed only a reflection. "I would hunker down in a defensible location, perhaps behind walls."

Which likely meant Huajing. Kaiya's heart sank.

CHAPTER 45:
Mad Dashes

Geros crumpled the messenger bird's missive. Leina insisted he bring the remnants of his army through Huajing's east gate instead of the more convenient south gate, yet left no reason why. The city's south walls rose in the distance, so close.

He looked back at the remnants of his once-proud army. Just ten thousand remained. So many had fallen on that fateful night of battle. The rear guard of ten thousand was unaccounted for, though even faced with overwhelming numbers and superior weapons, they had stalled Cathayi pursuit for a couple of days. His current ragtag band was all that had survived eight days of forced marching with little food and constant skirmishes. The wounded had to be left behind.

He growled deep in his throat. Now, Leina wanted them to leave the highway and traipse through farmland and marsh. She should've sent supplies instead. Still, she'd proven reliable in the past. With a sigh, he beckoned his men onto the farmland.

Outside of Kaiya's carriage, long since repaired, birds screeched at each other as they competed for mates. Horses clopped, and boots marched through along the highway. She had rode at the head of an army too many times for her nineteen years. Hopefully, this would be the last.

She cradled the chunk of fallen star, whose steadfast throb felt comforting, even if its power seemed distant and walled-off again.

Across from her sat Brehane, now recovered from the spear butt to her head. She pulled and stretched Jie's mysterious armor while Cyrus stared out the window. Perhaps he thought about Sameer, who'd chased after the Golden Scorpion Sohini, and Fleet with him. Also missing was Doctor Wu. Kaiya had searched and searched the battlefield herself, to no avail.

In the far distance, the staccato cracks of musketfire made her heart jump. Even so, the other two showed no signs of hearing it.

Commander Zhuang rode up to the window. "*Jie-xia*, the capital is within sight."

At last. It had taken nine days, their pursuit of Geros slowed by the Teleri rear guard's defense of the central valley's final gap. "Any sign of the Teleri?

"No, *Jie-xia*." The cavalry commander shook his head. "They had a significant lead on us because of their rear guard action."

Kaiya sighed. If Geros reunited with the garrison he'd left there, they might have enough men and supplies to hold the walls and gates. "Tell General Lu to start making preparations for a siege." Despite his earlier betrayal, the general had volunteered to lead all the assaults. He had more than proven his worth, and his soldiers adored him. Still, she'd keep a wary eye open.

Commander Zhuang said, "Our scouts reported trampled fields and bootprints up ahead."

Perhaps Geros had sent men into the fields to forage for food. Still, nothing besides radishes and leafy greens were in season. They must surely be hungry.

More musketfire pattered up ahead, though again, her companions did not appear to have heard it. She looked out the window. Far beyond, Sun-Moon Castle and the Hall of Supreme Harmony stood out above the south walls. Had her brother survived the siege? And even if he still lived, the Guardian Dragon had entrusted her with choosing a capable *Tianzi*. As much as she adored Kai-Wu, he made a more suitable poet or teacher than ruler. Could she depose her own brother? And would the people accept that decision?

She sighed again. The *Tiger's Eye* must be weakening if she considered choosing fraternal feelings over a logical choice. In any case, the decision would need to wait until they controlled the capital.

In the distance, horse hooves pounded the pavestones.

Commander Zhuang appeared at the window again. "A messenger, *Jie-xia*, riding with the flag of the *Tianzi*."

"Send one of your men to meet with him," she said. They'd met too many spies and imposters for her to take a risk of getting to close to this messenger.

Just north of Cherry Blossom Boulevard, Ming sat astride his horse, with Tian, Shu, and Ma Jun at his side. Waiting. He turned his dagger over in his hands. The wait was going to kill him.

Unless Tian killed him first. His brother's hands clamped down on his. "Stop it. You are driving *us* insane."

Ma Jun nodded.

A messenger ran up and dropped to a knee. "*Jue-Ye*, the Teleri have passed through the east walls. Maybe ten thousand."

So the fake message had worked. Ming grinned at Tian. The combined forces of Linshan Province, the imperials, and his own Dongmen Province had attacked the remnants of the Teleri occupation over the last several days. Though they had captured key positions, the Bovyans still held out near the south gate. The last thing they needed was the emperor to join up with that group.

He then addressed his generals. "Wait until they are at least six blocks from the east gate before the ordering the cavalry to cut off their escape. Sound the horn when they are in position, and we will attack their flank."

"As you command, *Jue-ye*!" the soldiers all said in unison.

Ming turned to Tian. "You know what to do."

Tian crept along the rooftops as he approached the Teleri column. They marched twenty abreast along Cherry Blossom Boulevard, weapons at the ready as if they were launching an attack themselves. Ten thousand, two hundred and seven in all.

At their head, predictably, rode Emperor Geros. He was taller than the rest, with a scar on his cheek, just as Ming had said. His eyes swept back and forth, and like most people he didn't bother to look up. He pursed his lips, his stiff shoulders and jerky motions suggesting he knew something was out of place. Even still, he rode high above everyone else, an obvious and inviting target.

Taking aim, Tian fitted one of Ming's elf arrows and pulled the bowstring taut. He loosed.

A horn blared.

The Teleri kept their orderly ranks, but froze in place with their shields facing out. Geros pulled his horse up. The arrow cut right through the mount's head. As it tumbled, Geros leaped from the saddle and into the mass of Bovyans.

Tian cursed to himself. Not that he would've hit Geros anyway. It should've been Ming, the master archer, taking this shot, only he refused to climb a rooftop and get his uniform messy. At least the poor beast didn't suffer.

Provincial soldiers flooded the side streets on the northern edge of the boulevard. They stopped at point-blank range and fired into the Teleri column. Enemy officers barked out orders, and Bovyans on the interior loaded crossbows. Those on the edges bulged out into squares to charge the side streets. One more command, and the front rows knelt and the crossbowmen shot. The last row of Hua musketmen fired a volley, and spearmen surged forward.

They crashed into the Teleri with spears and swords. Still, the Bovyans held their line. Tian nocked another arrow, searching for Geros in the fray. In close-range pitched battle, the Metal Men might have the advantage, despite being outnumbered two-to-one. If only musketmen could fire from rooftops!

Another horn pealed from the Teleri rear. Ming's cavalry.

And there was the emperor, taking command of his exhausted troops. Tian took aim.

"Hold the line!" Geros yelled, his heart thumping at a steady beat. "Do not let the histories say we lost to merchants, no matter how many bodies they throw against our spears!"

They sure were throwing a lot. How many in total was impossible to know without accurate intelligence, and apparently, that traitor Leina had lured them into a trap. Once they reoccupied the capital, he would be paying a visit to her home.

A high-pitched horn screeched from somewhere near the rear of his column. The feminine squeal certainly wasn't a Teleri horn, though it carried above the clanking of metal and screams of men.

Yellow flashed in his vision a the Eye of Geros warned him of danger. He involuntarily leaned his head back. An arrow zipped by his face and lodged into one of his men's arms. Geros turned to see where it had come from.

Up on the rooftop of a two-story building stood a Cathayi man, now nocking another arrow. *The* Cathayi man. The Angel of Death, whom Geros had killed once before. Now back to claim him. Geros cackled and snatched a loaded crossbow from a nearby soldier. How similar it was to the faceoff at the fortress in the Wilds. He took aim, just as the Angel of Death loosed another arrow. Yellow flashed in his vision.

Dao flashing, Ming smashed into the Teleri rear with the rest of his cavalry. They lumbered through the enemy's interior lines almost unopposed, hacking and slashing through crossbowmen. While his plan hadn't worked exactly as he hoped, they were dealing a significant blow to the exhausted Teleri troops. As long as they kept this returning army from linking up with the former occupiers, they could slowly strangle and starve them out.

From astride his horse, Ming saw Emperor Geros toward the front, crossbow in hand, barking orders. Ming's free hand strayed to his bow. It would be quite a shot from this distance, but not beyond his superior archery skills, and certainly faster than wading through the Bovyans.

Not far ahead, Bovyans dropped crossbows and drew swords and spears. One Teleri at his side tried to drag him off the horse, but Ming kicked him in the face.

One of his officers sidled over. "*Jue-ye*, if we go much deeper, we will be trapped."

Ming looked to the fore, where a forest of blades awaited, and then behind him, where the Teleri swarmed around the horses. His man was right. In these close quarters, they would eventually get dragged down. It would be better to veer onto a side street. Hua spearmen clogged up the streets to the north of the boulevard, so he waved his sword southward. "Linshan cavalry, to me!"

They chopped a path through the Bovyans. When Ming reached the side street, he paused and glanced further up the Teleri lines. Somewhere in the mess, Emperor Geros shouted out orders.

There he was. An arrow flew down and lodged into his shoulder, just as he took a shot into the rooftops. The bolt zipped upward. Ming whipped his head to follow its path. Tian snatched it out of the air.

Ming could only gawk at his little brother's skill.

"Protect the emperor!" a Teleri yelled. Others repeated the call until thousands of voices chanted it like a mantra. Their rectangular shields came together and their spears jutted out like a centipede's carapace. The entire column wheeled and lumbered southward down a side street.

Ming wiped sweat from his brow. Hopefully, Linshan Province's troops had succeeded in overwhelming enemy-controlled points along White Duck Stream, and could cut the Teleri off from the rest of their army.

Cheers erupted to the north and west. Hua cheers. They must've surrounded the emperor.

An aide rode up. "*Jue-ye*, news from the south gate. The princess has returned, bringing two hundred thousand men."

Ming stifled his grin. The Teleri numbers must have dwindled to around ten thousand in total by now, paltry compared to the imperial reinforcements. Still, it was a lot of Hua soldiers to bring through the gate, and they might not get enough to keep the two pockets of Teleri resistance from joining the main army.

Tian ran along a street parallel to the Teleri retreat. At every intersection, he looked over to see how quickly the column of Metal Men moved.

Somewhere, behind the marching wall of shields and spears, the Teleri Emperor must be laboring with an arrow in his shoulder.

Hua musketmen, both provincial and imperial, stood in three-rank lines in the side streets, shooting at will. The closest rank knelt, the second stood, and the third reloaded muskets. The Metal Men took casualties at each intersection, though any man falling on the outside was immediately replaced by another.

Perhaps the emperor had already bled out, since it seemed more logical for the column to turn down a side street, crash into the thin lines of musketmen, and break out from the path where they took constant fire.

Tian looked up ahead to see a large battalion of Hua troops marching toward him, their banners a white ship on a black field. At their head rode a helmeted man in a black-and-white uniform and a steel breastplate. Those color, that sigil... Zhenjing Province? Why were they here?

Hurrying over, Tian bowed. "Sir—"

Two men thrust him to his knees. "Address Lord Wu of Zhenjing with proper manners."

Appropriate terms... "*Jue-ye*, The Teleri could break out of any of these streets."

Lord Wu waved him off the street. "Out of the way. Go back to your home."

Tian brushed his hands over his clothes. Of course, he wore civilian garb. Still— "If you attack them now, you can break them in two."

With a wave at his men, the commander said, "We are to cut off possible escape routes to the west, under orders from the regent herself."

The regent was in the city... He had come so far looking for her, to satisfy Yuha and his spirits. The column had come up from the south, so she must be there.

Kaiya entered the city at the head of the army, astride a horse, keeping her chin up as musket shots rang out in the distance. Beyond the nearby rows of two-story buildings, several plumes of smoke rose above the southeastern part of the city. Teleri casualties lay strewn around the gatehouse and walls. The stench of sulphur and burning charcoal hung in the air. Though her nausea had subsided in the last couple of weeks, it threatened to rise again now.

General Tang, at the head of an imperial guard contingent, rode up and dismounted. He dropped to a knee, fist to the ground. "*Jie-xia*, thank you for coming in our relief."

She searched among his command staff. "Where is General Shan?"

"Killed at the north gate in the initial assault, before you left."

Kaiya heart sank, even through the *Tiger's Eye*. "I am sorry to hear that. General Shan had been a wise and courageous leader." She sighed, resolve firming again. "What is the Teleri army's status now?"

"Lord Zheng Ming tricked Emperor Geros into entering the city from the east, to prevent him from joining with their garrison here." He gestured to the south gate. "We recaptured the gate not long ago and have pushed them east. I have word that Lord Zheng is driving Geros south, while the rest of our armies hold White Duck Stream to prevent him from going west."

Zheng Ming...had survived Teleri capture, and the orders she'd given Jie. Kaiya nodded, even though she only had a vague idea of the map. Better to leave strategy to the professional military. In the meantime, there was something only she could do. "General, how dangerous are the roads to the Temple of Heaven?"

General Tang looked to the east. "The Bovyans are nowhere near there right now. I will personally escort you."

Kaiya patted her saddlebag, where the fallen star hummed its unfaltering tune. One of her ancestors' first acts was to erect the temple in an auspicious location, and then place the star there. She would return the relic to its rightful place.

She turned to General Tang. "Send Emperor Geros my terms for his surrender..."

The wound on Geros' right shoulder had stopped bleeding, but it still seared with pain. Especially after the healer had applied a balm. Each time the man tied another stitch, Geros had to hide his wince. He scanned the grassy basin and stone seating around him. It looked similar to an Estomari coliseum, except that the stands only lined one side.

Low ground to be sure, but defensible enough from the stands and also the barricades his men had erected along the side streets feeding into the plaza. The garrison had managed to meet up with them, not only bolstering their defenses but also bringing much-needed food and supplies. If they rationed everything, they could hold out a week or more until reinforcements arrived from the North.

Wishful thinking. He laughed out loud, drawing the stares of his men, who immediately averted their eyes. No, it had been Dongmen provincial soldiers who had attacked. Either Lord Zheng had turned on him, or the son must've grown some balls and learned a little military strategy. There would be no reinforcements.

Geros pushed the healer off and stood. All his men snapped to attention.

"My friends, this is our last stand. No help is coming. But we will make them remember the day they fought the Teleri Empire. Their descendants will quiver at our name."

The men broke into cheers. Every last one of them would die for honor. Him, too. In any case, without the fallen star to give to the Altivorc King, he only had a few months before his thirty-third birthday and inevitable death soon after. It had been a good life. His only regret was not to have conquered Cathay for Kaiya and left a stable and peaceful realm for their son to rule.

General Baros called from the top of the stone seats. "The regent has sent a request to parley. She demands our immediate surrender and

Emperor Geros to turn himself in to her. The rest of us will be allowed to return home."

Geros snorted. Undoubtedly an attempt to turn the men against him, and in any other army, the terms of surrender would not be shouted out for everyone to hear. But they were Bovyans, and their response was predictable.

His men pounded on their chests. "We will fight!"

Geros grinned and strode toward the stands. It was an answer he planned to deliver himself.

Ming watched from horseback as a group of Hua imperial officers approached the amphitheater under the flags of parley. Teleri soldiers appeared at the top of the stone amphitheater seats. Though out of earshot, he could guess what message they delivered.

Alas, the poor communication between the provincial lords and the imperial army had allowed the enemy to reach Qingjingtian Amphitheater and meet up with the garrison they had left. If they refused to surrender, they would lose, but not without inflicting devastating losses first. He turned to his aide. "Where is the regent now?"

"Word has it she is heading to the Temple of Heaven."

"What?" Regent or not, now was not the time to pray. The Heavens rewarded those with the most guns and a better field position. Ming gestured back at his provincial soldiers, who now stood in orderly ranks along the northern end of the enemy's hastily erected wall of carts, house doors, furniture, and Heavens knew what else.

"Look." His aide pointed to the top of the amphitheater seats.

The sun gleaming off his breastplate, Geros stood tall and imposing at the top of the amphitheater's stone seats.

Ming's heart skipped into his throat. The last time he had met the Teleri to discuss terms, he had lost a battle and fallen into the emperor's hands. His hand tightened on his *dao* hilt.

"Deliver this message to the girl." Geros' voice echoed through the streets. "I will surrender only if she spreads her legs for me."

Beyond the barricades in the basins, Bovyans erupted into laughter.

Emperor Geros raised a hand, silencing them. "Otherwise we will set your precious city ablaze."

CHAPTER 46:

Wash Out

Kaiya listened to birds chirping in the eaves of the Temple of Heaven as she approached the compound's front gates on horseback. The birds' part in spring's song echoed off the compound's elliptical walls, carrying the sound over her own horse's clopping and the sporadic musket shots in the distance.

It had been over a year since she'd last visited, the day Zheng Ming failed to accompany her to the temple as he'd promised. She'd been a naïve, infatuated girl, who rode off into a city on edge in hopes of nursing handsome Zheng Ming back to health.

Now, she scoffed at her younger self. If anything need be taken from that day, it was Father's prayers and the way the temple grounds magnified his voice. With the magic here, maybe she could finally break the *Tiger's Eye* for good and do something impactful in this war.

The bald, yellow-robed temple abbot shuffled forward, head bowed. "*Jie-xia*, welcome to the Temple of Heaven. I regret to inform you that the Fallen Star was stolen and—"

Kaiya withdrew the relic from her saddlebags. It pulsed in her hands as she presented it. "See it returned to its rightful spot."

The abbot gaped and bowed as he received it reverently in two hands. "Yes, *Jie-xia*. However, there is another security concern inside the temple grounds. I do not think it wise to—"

Several sets of horse hooves cantered toward her. Her honor guard clattered into defensive positions. Her own cavalry formed into a circle. Behind her, Brehane and Cyrus shuffled as they prepared their own magic. She turned.

Three cavalrymen approached, their green flags with the sun rising over twin mountains marking them as Dongmen provincial soldiers. The one in the lead rode his horse with such ease, it seemed horse and rider were one entity.

He swung out of the saddle before his mount came to a stop and dropped to knee, fist to the ground. Glossy black hair spilled out as he removed his helmet and looked up, revealing Zheng Ming. "*Jie-xia*, welcome back to the city."

Flamboyant as ever. Kaiya suppressed a smile. "Lord Zheng. I was just thinking about you."

"Oh?" With his eyebrow raised, his grin was all the more charming.

She gestured toward the Temple. "I was thinking of the last time I was here, and how you broke your promise to me."

Her men exchanged glances, and Zheng Ming's face flushed.

Brehane pushed past the men and came to Zheng Ming's side, placing a hand on his shoulder. She winked at Kaiya. "Your Majesty, if it is your wish, I will make this predatory dandy disappear."

"Perhaps later." Kaiya chuckled. "He might still prove useful."

Zheng Ming bowed. "*Jie-xia*, I have come ahead of your messengers. The Teleri refuse to surrender. In fact, Emperor Geros..." His gaze shifted to the assembled soldiers. "Emperor Geros made uh, inappropriate counter-demands."

It didn't take much imagination to guess what those were. It might be worth it, to save the city without more losses, if she wouldn't lose face among all the soldiers whose loyalty she'd gained. Alas, the fact that she didn't bristle or blush at the suggestion showed the *Tiger's Eye* must still be in place, no matter how tenuously. She gestured to a runner. "Go to the palace and tell Chief Minister Song to come up with a plan for fighting potential fires." She looked to Brehane and gestured to the Temple of Heaven's gates. "Now, perhaps you would like to see one of the marvels of our capital."

"I can already feel it," the Mystic said.

Kaiya nodded toward Zheng Ming. "You will accompany me into the temple this time." An honor, for his loyalty. Not to mention that eventually she would have to marry, and he was certainly pleasant on the eyes.

He gawked, then bowed. "I do not think that would be appropriate, *Jie-xia*."

"Why not?" She raised an eyebrow. It wasn't as though he ever stood on propriety.

His eyes darted back and forth, taking in all of the assembled soldiers. "Some matters can only be discussed in confidence."

She studied his expression. He must know about Tian' death, then. Of course, Ming had already confronted his father, and surely those details would have come out. "In any case, I am setting up the army headquarters here, since it is close to the invading army. Fall in line with General Tang and the other hereditary lords." She pointed her chin toward the commanders and aides behind her.

Zheng Ming's mouth hung agape, but then he bowed. "Yes, *Jie-xia*."

As he joined the other commanders, Kaiya gestured toward the temple guards. The abbot opened his mouth in protest, but she silenced him with a pursing of her lips. Bowing, the guards opened the double gates into the temple grounds. She dismounted, squared her shoulders, and strode through.

She stopped mid-stride. Sitting atop the three-tiered marble base, in the center of the near focus, was...

Jie? At her side stood Fang Weiyong, fiddling with acupuncture needles in Jie's shoulder while a familiar yet unfamiliar young woman stood over his shoulder.

The stranger looked up with blue eyes. Beautiful, luminous eyes, like...Doctor Wu's. The resemblance was uncanny. Perhaps this woman was a granddaughter—though, since no one knew how old Doctor Wu really was, this could be her great-great-granddaughter. She beckoned. "*Jie-xia*, come."

The voice. It was Doctor Wu's.

Kaiya's mind spun. The last she'd seen the Taoist Master was before the confrontation with Cousin Peng. There was no way the aged doctor could possibly make it back to the capital first, let alone *un-age*. Kaiya took tentative steps forward, unsure if her legs could hold her. The *Tiger's Eye* must've all but faded.

A firm hand took her elbow. She turned and blinked through her misty eyes to find Zheng Ming there, as well as other soldiers trying to peel him off of her. She raised a hand and feebly gestured them off. Zheng Ming's support felt so reassuring, so...right. Even if it was wrong.

With his help, she climbed to the raised marble base where Jie sat. No, this must be one of those bizarre dreams again. Jie was dead. Killed by Fleet. Still, up close, the half-elf sitting there was unmistakably the Insolent Retainer, eyes closed. And beside her, a younger version of Doctor Wu.

"How?" was the only word she could manage to choke out.

Young Doctor Wu smiled. "*Jie-xia*, you know I was always looking for the secret to immortality. You helped me find it when you retrieved the Dragon Pearl." She winked.

Kaiya couldn't find words at the moment.

Doctor Wu rolled her eyes. She took Kaiya's head and pressed it to her bosom. Her heart thumped, setting the rhythm to a resolute, powerful song. The same song as...the Guardian Dragon.

Kaiya's jaw slackened. Her mouth moved, but no words came out. Doctor Wu, her physician for so many years, was the mythical Guardian Dragon. Who wasn't *supposed* to be a dragon in the sense that Avarax was, as much as a messenger from the Heavens.

Doctor Wu nodded. "You know the secret. Keep it that way."

With a slow nod, Kaiya turned from Doctor Wu— the Guardian Dragon—to Jie, then back to Doctor Wu. All she could do was point.

"She has lost the use of her arm, and neither my best student—" she gestured toward Fang Weiyong—"nor I can figure out why. There is nothing physically wrong, and even in this spot, where the energy of the world is strongest in the capital, we cannot heal her."

That much would make sense, except the fact Jie was dead. Words stumbled out of Kaiya's mouth. "How is she alive?"

Jie's eyes flew open. She and the two others stared at her with curious expressions.

"Fleet killed you."

Jie cocked her head and patted herself with her good arm. "I don't think so." Her tone sounded just as bitter as when they had last parted, in Dongmen. When she'd given the order to kill Zheng Ming.

"I think I know what is going on," Zheng Ming said. "Jie has an identical twin."

Two? Kaiya shuddered at the thought of two insolent half-elves. Ming's sour look suggested he felt the same.

Cyrus appeared at their side. "That would explain it. I was wondering how you had made it to the pyramid so fast, after we had seen you in the Wilds."

"And you fought so differently," Kaiya said.

Jie nodded and sighed. "It's a shame. Kiri wasn't bad. I don't know why the madaeri would kill her."

"So where have you been all this time?" Ming demanded. "Tian said you've been missing for days."

Tian? Tian was dead; unless he too had a magical twin. Kaiya's gaze swept from Jie to Ming. Surely he had misspoken, or this was one of those realistic dreams. She pinched herself, sending a flare of pain through her arm. No, quite awake.

Jie's gaze met hers. "*Jie-xia*, your city has a rampant altivorc infestation I have been trying to eradicate."

Pulling Brehane forward, Cyrus said, "Since you can't figure out the armor, perhaps you should give it to someone it fits."

Brehane clutched her pack to her chest.

A messenger presented himself at the bottom of the dais. "*Jie-xia*, the Bovyans have set fire to the area surrounding Qingjingtian Amphitheatre."

Kaiya looked up. Beyond the Temple walls to the east, thick plumes of black wafted to the heavens. Winds typically swirled off of Sun-Moon Lake, which would carry sparks from wood building to wood building. It wouldn't be long before the entire southeast quadrant turned into a hellish conflagration. She turned to Doctor Wu. "Legends say the Guardian Dragon controls weather and water."

"Would that the Guardian Dragon were to make an appearance," Doctor Wu said. "However, legends also say she only comes during the time of greatest need, to anoint a leader with the Mandate of Heaven."

It couldn't be. Doctor Wu, who revered life so much, would let tens of thousands perish in a fire. Kaiya plead with her eyes.

"Have you learned nothing?" Doctor Wu shooed Jie off the foci. "Stand here. Feel Mother Earth course through you. You read Xu's book on how Yanyan brought a rainstorm."

Kaiya swept her gaze around all the assembled people. Mouths agape, all the generals and officers looked from the doctor to her and back again. They probably couldn't believe a mere doctor was ordering a regent around on matters unrelated to health.

With a sigh, she strode to the focus. Sinking into a high horse stance, she gripped the marble through her shoes with her toes. The song of the world resonated in her soles and vibrated up through her legs.

Still, it stopped at her waist. The scent of burning wood drifted on the air, and she looked east. An orange gleam gathered on the horizon, like a sunrise in Hell. Pulse racing, she turned to the doctor. "The energy is there, but I can't connect to it."

"Link to it. Lower." Doctor Wu pressed her hand into Kaiya's shoulder, pushing her into a deeper stance. She then turned to the temple and yelled, "Hurry up with the fallen star."

The energy welled beneath her feet, calling to her from so close. Tears collected in her lashes. If she couldn't do this, so many people would die. Geros would win, would probably gloat at her from beyond the grave. Just like the world's resonance, taunting her.

She glanced around at all the expectant faces. Cyrus nodded at her, while Brehane smiled. Doctor Wu and Fang Weiyong, too. All of the soldiers knelt, fists to the ground. The Heavens must have a sick sense of humor to place the fate of so many people on a nineteen-year-old's shoulders.

A low pulse throbbed out of the Temple of Heaven, washing over her from all directions. The fallen star, that was it! The energy she could borrow if that of Mother Earth refused to answer her call. On the next pulse, she sang Yanyan's rain song. Letting the frequency of Doctor Wu's heartbeat guide her, Kaiya enunciated each word.

Doctor Wu's eyes brightened ever so slightly, still pathetic compared to Avarax's eyes glowing to her song in the past. "Connect," the doctor said. "Let the song of the fallen star link with the hum of Mother Earth."

Another messenger ran up to the base and dropped to a knee. "The Teleri are pouring out of the amphitheater. They are slaughtering citizens."

The star's and earth's melodies were there, in her chest and in her lower abdomen, and yet they didn't merge. Yells and screams mingled with intermittent musket shots in the distance. The story of her failure would be written in blood. Her shoulders shuddered, rattling at the speed of her racing heart. The *Tiger's Eye* had to be gone for her to have such reactions, yet the energy of the world remained walled-off, rising no higher than the *dantian* point beneath her navel.

"You can do it," the doctor said.

A tear rolled down Kaiya's cheek. The Guardian Dragon could do it, too, but refused. Voice cracking, she sang again, elocuting each note of the song once more. Clouds formed overhead, and a drop of rain splattered on her nose. Unless it was just another tear.

A commotion erupted near the entrance to the temple grounds. Had the Teleri gotten here so fast? Kaiya hazarded a glance. It looked like Zheng Ming in the corner of her eye, deftly avoiding the imperial guards.

"Focus!" Doctor Wu's stern reprimand drew her back to the task at hand.

The power in her was gone. She gripped her toes to the ground again and listened for the pulse. The energies were all there, but beyond her ability to use. The forces in her chest and belly struggled to meet, even though they had merged so easily and automatically in the past. Screams grew louder. As regent, she was quickly becoming a failure, at the cost of so many lives. Her hands trembled as tears filled her eyes again.

"Let him through," Zheng Ming said from somewhere.

Cyrus and Brehane both evoked magic around her, through his uplifting prayers and her grunts and snarls. None of them helped her. Jie's forlorn sigh sounded miserable.

She was failing, and nothing in this world could save the city's southeast, and maybe more, from burning.

Arms enveloped her, warm and heartening. They lifted her out of her stance, breaking her connection with the ground, and turned her around. Her cheek pressed against coarse fabric, and the toned chest beneath. The heartbeat...so familiar. She looked up.

Intelligent dark eyes gazed back at her. The high-bridged nose and strong chin resembled Zheng Ming, but—no.

No, it was impossible.

If this was a dream, would that she never woke. If she were awake, she never wanted to sleep again.

"It's all right. You can do it." He spoke with concise economy as always, yet his words could have been an epic novel for all the affection in their warm tone.

Pulse racing, she dried her tears in his high collar. His hand ran through her hair. Her stomach flipped in twists and turns worthy of a zigzagging dragonfly. "I can't. It's stuck. Here." She placed her hand over her belly.

His hand covered hers, then slid down over her womb. "They need your strength." Their babies. His hand rose up toward her waist, pausing at her sash, right over his lockpick pouch.

She pushed back, just enough to reach into her sash. She pulled it out, her only memento of him. With the *Tiger's Eye*, she had kept it not for any type of emotional connection, but rather as a reminder that she had once known love. With him here, she didn't need it anymore. She looked up into his eyes and pressed the pouch into his palm.

As his fingers closed around it, a surge flowed through her body. Rising from the ground, sinking with her breath, mingling in her core. Power, like that around the Wild Turkey Island and the Temple of Shakti in Palimur, coursed from toes to fingertips. It built up, ready to explode unless...

She started to sing.

Tian looked up as a raindrop splattered onto his cheek, hopefully hiding his own tears. Several more followed, pattering in a light drizzle, then building to a downpour.

Like all the memories flooding back. Kaiya, the Doe-Eyed Girl. His childhood friend, separated from him by Peng Kai-Long's cruel joke. Reunited in Iksuvi to learn that she had changed. But then they had found each other, the spirit of who they had been as children not lost in adulthood, despite the responsibilities that suppressed them. Here

they were again, reunited after his death and rebirth.

His heart pounded in his chest. This was where he was supposed to be, who he was supposed to be with. He turned the lockpick pouch over in his hands, pausing each time at the flap and the awkward stitching. It weighed too much for just a set of picks.

Of course. Withdrawing his knife, he cut away the stitches on the flap and opened the secret pouch he had sewn in during their sojourn in the Wilds. Inside hid the dull grey metal of the Teleri imperial crest.

Somewhere behind him, Jie stifled a cry.

Jie could only watch the reunion she'd tried to sabotage several times over. But now, they looked so right together, the Big Brother she adored and the Sworn Sister she hated.

Oh, what could've been, with Tian. They'd come so close, not once, but twice. Still, their love had never been allowed to blossom, thwarted by circumstance and bad timing. Now, he was with *her*. Against all odds, their hearts came together in a way his would never beat for Jie.

It was meant to be. Her life would continue forward, without Tian in it. She wiped a tear away.

With her bad hand.

She stared at it in awe, but when she went to move it again, nothing happened. She searched the heavens through the driving rain, wondering why the gods played such evil tricks on her. With a sigh, she turned back to the fires in the east. To duty, like she always did.

There, the flames persisted despite the downpour. The rain might've cleared some of the smoke from the air, yet still the city burned. Thousands of yells and screams erupted in a disjointed cacophony.

Jie turned back toward the hated princess at the focus. "*Jie-xia*, harder! The fires are still burning."

The princess' voice rose, angelic yet powerful.

The temple well bubbled over, spilling onto the ground.

"Wells are rising everywhere," Ming yelled from the front gate. "The stream and canals, as well."

Fang Weiyong shook his head. "Impossible. It's rained a lot, but not so much that it could raise the water level."

"The music," Doctor Wu said. "Sun-Moon Lake itself rises to salute the gods. Backflowing into the canals and streams."

Ming chuckled at the couple. Apparently, only his kid brother could melt the heart of the Ice Princess. Still, as sappy and charming as it might be, their love alone couldn't save the city. Though perhaps a different type of magic would help.

"Come with me." He grabbed Brehane's hand and tugged her toward the entrance and the horses.

She fought back, a scowl crossing her face. "Didn't we go through this before? It's a beautiful moment, but no means no."

"No, not that." There were too many negatives to keep track of. "No, I need your help. The city needs your help. Can you ride a horse?"

Her pursed lips answered the question. Of course, they had ridden in Selastyas.

"Come on, then."

She followed him out. Ming gestured his aide off a horse, then Brehane onto it. He mounted up and spurred his mount into a gallop. Rumor had it the princess had taken off from the Temple of Heaven on a New Year's Day, in a mad dash through the city to come visit him. Now, he might very well have been retracing her path.

Except now he had a different destination in mind. Her song reverberated in his ears, no matter how far away he galloped. Everyone else's ears, too, as soldiers, commoners, and even the

occasional Bovyan wandered aimlessly, staring in the direction of the Temple of Heaven. He looked back to see if Brehane was keeping up.

They arrived at White Duck Stream, now rising nearly to street level. He followed it until they reached a famous pile of rocks—debris from an earthquake a century ago that had transformed Qingjingtian from a reservoir to a grassy basin. Water gurgled over the levee, feeding into the old streambed which the locals had since filled halfway with dirt to grow vegetables. It might take work crew days to clear the rocks, but Brehane...

He pointed at it. "Can you do something about the levee?"

Her eyes tracked from the pile of rocks to the streambed, now green with vegetable seedlings, then back to White Duck Stream. "It will wash all of the crops away."

"And the Bovyans with it."

Brehane shook her head. "The people will go hungry."

Ming threw his hands up. "Dead people won't eat at all. Plus, it's not like this one stretch feeds even a fraction of the populace."

She glared at him for a few seconds before closing her eyes and starting her chant.

Geros listened to Princess Kaiya's song, so loud she might've been standing right next to him. But she wasn't. She never would. If only she'd come, he would've found a way to prove his love for her.

And in his anger at her refusal, he had set the city ablaze. His men almost refused, grumbling that it went against the tenets of the Last Testament of the First Geros. The Bovyan race was to bring order and build prosperity, not to wantonly destroy cities out of vengeance.

Returning from their forays into the nearby city blocks, the soldiers now gathered stoically around him, only their eyes indicating that they waited for some word of encouragement. Or maybe even absolution.

He had failed them all. He might reach his preordained death in just a few months, but many of these men still had years to serve the Teleri Empire. He'd let his passions turn a sure future victory into a premature invasion and defeat.

Let history remember him as a fighter. He cleared his throat so they could hear him over the pounding rain. "Bovyans! The enemy is marching on us, though the rain renders their guns useless. Defend the barricades. Let no Cathayi set foot in this basin until the last of us is dead. They shall rue the day they invited us in. Our people will celebrate our last stand. Now go, up to the barricades!"

The men broke out in cheers. They chanted his name as they sloshed in the mud toward the barriers.

Let the Cathayi come fall on Teleri spears. Let *her* know her people had died because she refused him.

Outside the amphitheater, the crackling flames fizzled. The orange-and-red glow dulled. Gurgling at the western end of the basin led to a gush of water from a gully. Filling in from the west to east, and then spilling from the rim of the basin and down the slopes, the water level rose.

His men cursed and yelled as the makeshift barricades toppled under the torrent and tumbled into the growing lake. Water rose to his knees already. Geros looked toward the stone seat tiers. Even when the water completely flooded the basin, at least those would still be dry. Better to die fighting than to drown like a rat.

He slogged through the waist-high water toward the seats. By the time he reached the slope, the water came up to his chest. Dropping to all fours, he dug his hands into the grass and mud, yet still couldn't find purchase on the stones through the storm surge. A wood rafter tumbled down the banks and slammed into him, knocking him back.

It was all he could do to hold on to it as the water level rose. Many of his men floundered in their heavy armor, and very few held on to weapons. Those on the stone seats shouted,

beckoned, and men who had managed to climb onto floating wood paddled with their hands.

Then the princess' song ceased. The rain slowed as the clouds thinned. Sunlight lanced in ever-widening blades across the new lake. Thousands upon thousands of Cathayi musketmen lined the edge of the basin, weapons covering every angle.

"Throw down your arms," called a male voice in accented Arkothi.

Geros searched the ranks of men and found Zheng Ming astride a horse. The lordling had come of age, it appeared. Geros growled. "Men, attack!"

The soldiers on the seats yelled out a war cry and charged, only to be cut down by volleys of musketfire. In a matter of moments, his men were either dead or incapacitated in the stands, or floating.

Ignominious defeat. The only thing that could make it worse—

"Emperor Geros," Kaiya called from where she sat on horseback at Zheng Ming's side. "You have lost."

The water's tumble sounded like applause as it receded back into the streams, sewers, and canals. Kaiya watched as Teleri gratefully accepted the ropes thrown to rescue them. Oftentimes, it took three or four of her men to subdue just one unarmed Bovyan as he came ashore.

She sighed. Behind them, the rain and rising water had doused the flames, but they would undoubtedly leave both a physical and emotional scar on the neighborhood and its residents. The victory, in what was hopefully the last battle, had come at great cost.

Kaiya turned back to the remnants of the once-proud Teleri army. There might be only a few hundred survivors at this point, out of the fifty thousand who had joined the invasion. Among them, Emperor Geros. Without the *Tiger's Eye* protecting her, even the sight of him sent a chill up her spine.

Still, she forced herself to look at the emperor. Though one arm hung limp, he fought against all the ropes pulling his wooden beam toward land. If only he would just let go and let the waters swallow him up. If he came ashore alive, it meant facing him.

Tian's hand found hers, from where he sat awkwardly in his saddle. It was warm, comforting, and she would lean into him now if it wouldn't send the both of them tumbling into ankle-deep water. His gaze fell on her. "When he reaches the bank. I will kill him. For what he did to you."

Her shoulders trembled as horrifying memories of Geros' calloused hands on her surfaced. Now, here he was, coming closer to land. Closer to her. Her free hand balled into a fist so tight it might draw blood. He clawed his way to the far end of the beam.

A rope dart whizzed in and wrapped around his limp arm. Another caught around his neck. Two young men in plain clothes held the other ends of the cords. Soldiers grabbed the ropes and pulled. Geros lurched onto land, flopping like a fish out of water. Men crowded around him, seizing his arms and forcing him to his knees. Others cleared a path between him and her.

So similar to what he had done to her, in the Wilds, humiliating her before all his men. Another shudder wracked her. Tian... where was Tian? His hand had been there just a second before. She looked around, from his horse, to the crowd of her soldiers, and finally to Geros.

Tian rose up behind the emperor, yanking his hair back. A knife flashed in Tian's other hand. Just like when the Golden Scorpion had killed Cousin Peng.

Her lips moved, but no sound came out. This was nothing short of murder. "Stop," she finally croaked, though not loud enough for her to hear her own voice. She cleared her throat. "Stop."

Tian's blade halted against Geros' neck. He looked up at her, eyes questioning. Geros' stare fell on her as well, his mismatched eyes twisting her stomach into knots.

Straightening her back and squaring her shoulders as she had done so many times in the past, she raked her gaze over the expectant faces before settling somewhere between Tian's chest and the top of Geros' head. "We will act with justice, not vengeance. Enemy generals must be accorded every respect. Confine him to the Hall of Water Spirits in Sun-Moon Palace."

Geros shook his head. "Kill me now. Better yet, allow me to kill myself."

It would be so much easier if he did. Kaiya sighed. "I have a mind to let you live what remains of your god-cursed life as a warning to others who might try to attack us."

Tian withdrew the knife from Geros' neck, stepped back and bowed. "As you command, *Jie-xia*."

What was that expression? Disappointment? Relief? Kaiya sighed. Whatever it was, they now had time to sort it out. The war was over.

CHAPTER 47:

Just Rewards

Kaiya fanned herself as she listened to the buzz of cicadas whirring outside the Hall of Supreme Harmony. Her belly now pushed out, with the occasional kick as a reminder of the two lives growing inside of her.

In front of her knelt a crowd of ministers and hereditary lords, lined in orderly ranks throughout the cavernous hall, and spilling out into the courtyard one hundred and sixty-eight steps below. In the three months that had passed since the defeat of the Teleri army, she'd worked behind the scenes, helping Chief Minister Song and General Tang administer the government and military as they labored to restore stability and imperial authority throughout the realm. Today, she would hold court as regent for the first time, where many expected her to announce her choice of a new *Tianzi*.

Beside her, the Jade Throne remained empty, which allowed her to relax in a cushioned chair at its side. The inner castle had opened months before, but her brother had never emerged, at least not publically. Having never wanted to be *Tianzi* anyway, he had been grateful for the Guardian Dragon's anointing Kaiya the decision-maker, and he let the rumor spread that he had died in the attempted coup. Today, he was enjoying a life of anonymity in Peng's province with his wife Wu Yanli. He said he wanted to be a teacher, and without a doubt, his gentle nature would serve him well in that endeavor.

Despite Lord Liu Yong's ambitions, his heir Liu Dezhen had relinquished his son's claim, probably at the urging of Cousin Kai-Hua. For the first time in seven centuries, there was no *Tianzi*.

"Take your time, make a wise choice," Doctor Wu had said a month before, with a wink. "The Guardian Dragon might very well reappear if need be." Since the victory, she had stopped by often. Why such a powerful being had an interest in her pregnancy remained a mystery. Now, she stood toward the back with Fang Weiyong.

Kaiya pushed herself up from the chair. In front of her, the assembled lords, ministers, and generals pressed their foreheads to the ground. Many of them had served admirably throughout these trying times. Future historians might try to hail her singlehanded quelling of the rebellion and defeat of the Teleri army; for now, she'd make sure everyone got their just recognition.

"Rise," she said.

The men straightened. A thousand pairs of eyes met hers, in what would be considered impertinence if not for the awe and admiration written in their expressions. Admiration for a girl, now officially an adult at twenty years old.

She took a deep breath. "Today, because of your contributions, Hua is once again secure. Safe from insurrection and invasion. I command you all to strive to keep it that way, through your work in the ministries, in the administration of your provinces, and in the training of your troops."

"As the regent commands." The chorus rang out, from inside the hall to out in the courtyard. Heads bowed again in a wave.

She nodded toward Chief Minister Song, who bowed. He cleared his throat and started the lengthy process of calling important ministers, generals, and lords to present themselves before her, to swear loyalty and receive their rewards.

Lord Lin's reward was generous; certainly not for his attempted declaration of independence and late help against the Teleri invasion, but rather for his daughter's role. Lin Ziqiu would serve in secret as a spy until she married the man of her choice. Kaiya suspected that man might be Zheng Ming, the only one she could not allow.

Ma Jun, with Lana and Yuha at his side, was assigned an ambassadorship to the Kanin Tribal Council, though he retained his status as imperial guard. She committed to consecrating a shrine in the Wilds, where he might pray for the repose of his comrades who died in her defense during the escape from Iksuvius. Fang Weiyong had wanted to join him, but she appointed him Chief Imperial Physician.

General Altos Di Bovyan, who had tried to protect her from Geros in the Wilds, had come at the behest of the Teleri Directori to demand that the emperor, now stripped of his title and reassigned his original name Haros Bovyanthas, be repatriated, along with the Teleri imperial crest and the Eye of Geros. She would have liked nothing more than to give them back, since Tian suspected the crest, not the *Tiger's Eye*, had constrained her power. She offered it in return for the Teleri relinquishing their gains in the Nothori Northwest and the Wilds, and ending their breeding program in Madura—knowing well the Directori would refuse. In any case, she would ensure Hua worked to free those countries, and Geros—Haros—would die from the curse sometime soon anyway. Before then, they would try to get as much information out of him as possible.

Cousin Peng's province in Nanling was gifted to her late imperial guard Chen Xin's cousin Lord Chen, who had nominated her as regent in the first place. Chief Minister Song's son was forgiven

and assigned to the Ministry of Foreign Affairs, where his planning and spying skills could be put to good use.

Princess Alaena and Prince Aelward presented their baby girl, born in Jiangkou just before the Teleri's breaching of Huajing's wall. Kaiya gave her the Hua name *Jin-Feng* for *Golden Phoenix*. Cyrus had set off in search of Sameer, though Brehane had stayed behind to meet Lord Xu, as Kaiya had promised in Iksuvi. Leina's mother, whom Tian had sought out and found wandering north alone, was allowed to live in Leina's Floating World house until the end of her days.

Throughout the proceedings, Zheng Ming remained handsome and dignified, bowing as each person received their reward. He undoubtedly wondered why he had been left out when all the other *Tai-Ming* lords had been recognized. Let him guess. She judiciously avoided his gaze the whole time.

At long last, Chief Minister Song looked up from his list of names and turned to her. "That is all. Shall we adjourn, *Jie-xia*?"

The chamber broke out into low murmurs.

She stood. "I have an announcement to make."

A hush fell over all the assembled men.

"For now, the Jade Throne shall remain empty." She cradled her belly. "By laws of succession, my unborn son shall inherit." Which meant she would continue to rule as regent until he came of age, and which son...well, the lords didn't need to know about twins.

She'd expected grumbling, but the hall remained silent save for the shuffle of robes as the men pressed their foreheads to the floor. She continued, "For his valor and exploits, I will take *Tai-Ming* Lord Zheng Ming as my husband in name, and as their uncle by blood, he shall be the adopted father of my sons. He shall retain his hereditary rule over Dongmen Province and be allowed to choose his heir from what I imagine will be a long list of sons from concubines."

Cheeks pink, Zheng Ming rose from his bow and cleared his throat. "I am honored, *Jie-xia*, but if I might be so rude. Do you not plan on marrying someone?"

And by someone, he meant Tian.

She shook her head. "Let there be no question that I rule as regent, and that no one man shall influence my decisions on affairs of state."

Affairs of the heart, however, were another story. Tian had shuddered at the thought of being the regent's husband, and the social duties that came with it. She looked toward the column where his breathing betrayed his presence to her ears alone.

The old proverb asserted that those who didn't have *yuan*, destiny, could pass each other each day and never meet; while those who had *yuan* would cross oceans and mountains to be with each other. Certainly, when neither banishment, war, nor even death could keep Tian and Kaiya apart, they were destined to be with each other.

EPILOGUE:

Parents and Prophecies

Cradling her two-day-old secondborn, Kaiya shuddered as she listened to the frantic brush strokes across rice paper inside the Hall of Water Spirits. It wasn't that she wanted to face Geros again—the memory of what he did to her was still fresh, even after nearly a year—but, as General Altos had reminded her after his audience several months prior, there were prophecies to uphold.

A Bovyan who knew his true mother and father would end the Teleri Empire and restore the Bovyans' honor.

Her loins still ached after laboring for countless hours, and despite Doctor Fang's insistence that she stay bedridden for a month to recover, the curse could claim Geros any time now. At least she'd rested for a day.

Behind her, Tian held the smaller, weaker twin. So frail and blue he'd been, his energy sucked by a dominant twin. Doctor Fang had thought the newborn wouldn't make it to his first hour. Yet the little one was a warrior. He'd survived. On his name day, she would call him *Yi*, for perseverance. The one of Geros' seed, she would name *Xi*, for hope. Her hope that one day, the Teleri Empire might fall. Not because of the threat they posed to Hua, which they no longer did, but because of the misery of the peoples they had conquered.

With a deep breath, she peered past the steel-barred door they'd installed to hold their prisoner.

Mismatched eyes wild, Geros scribbled frantically, his script growing as messy as his disheveled hair and unruly beard. A ghost of his former self, flesh hung from his bones.

A pang knotted her stomach. Despite what he'd done to her, the suffering carved into what remained of his body filled her with sympathy. Was this the curse, coming to claim him?

Some of what he wrote, in fluid Arkothi, made sense—memoirs of past glory, regrets of his last mistakes. Gibberish of the Arkothi alphabet filled other pages, reminiscent of the words she'd seen on Great Peace Island.

She cleared her throat. "Geros, come meet your son."

His brush paused, his body stilled. Slowly, he turned around, meeting her gaze. "Kaiya, you are so pale."

Behind her, Tian's hand tightened around his *dao*.

She reached back and placed her free arm on his, lest he drop his own son. "You are looking...well." A lie, certainly, but what else could she say? "Come, meet our child."

Papers clenched to his breast, Geros scuttled across the floor on one hand and two knees. He crouched by the bars, his eyes bright as he smiled.

Her stomach flipped again. The powerful, domineering man had been reduced to a dog, waiting for a treat. Deserved? No, maybe she should've let Tian kill him seven months prior. Heavens, the curse should've claimed him by now. She held up Wang Xi and cooed. "Your father, little one."

The baby let out an adorable squeak, which made her heart race and stomach flutter. To think something so perfect could have come from *him*.

Geros reached through the bars, but Kaiya took a step back. No—even with that gentle expression, he would not be allowed to touch their son. She lifted her chin to the papers at his chest, the ones with the nonsensical alphabet combinations. "What is that, Geros?"

Blinking, he scratched his head. "My last will. Or maybe the last will of the first Geros. I'm not sure."

Ramblings of a madman. Kaiya forced a smile. "Goodbye, Geros. We will not meet again. If you need anything to keep you comfortable in your last days, be sure to let the guards know."

She turned and hobbled away, ignoring whatever the former emperor babbled. From the threshold of the building, she caught sight of the Hall of Bountiful Harvests; where, four years before, a naïve, gangly princess' journey started when she met a dragon in man's clothing.

She leaned into Tian, and he wrapped his free arm around her. It was comforting, just like when he consoled her as a child, just like his affection in the Wilds. With him providing a reminder of who she really was, despite the image of princess and regent she projected, she would rule fairly and justly.

Jie climbed the steps to Black Lotus Temple, her first visit back in several years. The meeting with her adopted father, Master Yan, might prove interesting after what she'd learned a few months before.

The day of the regent's first audience, she'd accompanied Brehane to a meeting with Lord Xu in the Hall of Bountiful Harvests.

"There is no reason why your arm shouldn't work," the elf had said. Even his powerful magic had no effect.

She sighed. "It has moved on three occasions, when I wasn't even trying."

Staring at her, he pressed a finger to the center of her chest. "You must resolve something in your heart."

Tian, perhaps? She'd already given up on that. What else could there be?

"Jie!" a female voice called from the door. Princess Alaena stood there in a frilly Arkothi dress that didn't suit her, cradling her baby. "They said we might find you here."

"Aye lass," Prince Aelward said. He, too, looked handsome in his formal sailor's uniform. "We 'ad to say goodbye before we sailed home."

A handsome male elf peered around them. His eyes widened when he met her gaze. He looked at the royal couple. "This is the half-elf you were telling me about?" He turned back to her. He felt familiar.

The elf from her dream.

He had bowed, his focus never leaving her. "It seems our paths have come close, but never crossed until now. I am Thielas Starsong. And you are?"

Hair prickled on the back of her neck. No words came out of her mouth for a few seconds, probably a first. When she finally spoke, it was a squeak. "Yan Jie."

"Yan," he repeated, voice hollow. "Adopted daughter of Master Yan?"

Jie's mind had spun. Hardly anyone knew Master Yan even existed. "Who are you?"

He moved closer, arms wide. "I think you know."

"No." She had taken a step back. "You can't just appear thirty-three years after you abandoned me and my twin."

"Abandoned? Twin?" He shook his head, so violently his ears might've caught the wind and made him take flight. "No, there was only you. I had to protect you...your mother...the prophecy."

Jie's own elf ears twitched. "Prophecy?" And no twin?

Thielas' voice was almost a whisper. "A half-human girl of Aralas' blood shall slay the Orc King."

Lord Xu had choked. "Such silly tales. The elf angel was something of a philanderer, with a fetish for human women. It wouldn't surprise me if he made that up."

Everyone gawked at the blasphemy. It was hard to believe that Xu, no matter how powerful he might be, could so easily dismiss an elf angel.

"That *fetish*," Brehane had said, voice acerbic, "the nine loves of Aralas, helped win the War of Ancient Gods."

Xu scratched his chin. "Were there only nine?"

Jie had ignored the elf lord, turning instead to the other one, her supposed father. "If anything sounds made up, it's your pathetic excuse for giving me up."

Hands raised, Thielas had shaken his head. "I had to hide you, somewhere the Altivorc King would never find. Where better than your mother's people? I begged Master Yan to give you your birthright."

Jie had frowned. "He said I was left abandoned at the temple gate with a note attached to my swaddling blanket."

"And how would I find the temple gates without your clan knowing? What did the note say?"

"Master Yan lost it." That's what he'd always said.

"Since when does one of your clan lose *anything*?"

Which was how Jie now found herself outside the temple's gravesite, behind her unknowing stepfather.

"Father," she said.

He spun around with amazing speed for his age, the clan's Black Lotus Blade in his hand. He lowered it when his gaze fell on her. "Jie. I don't think anyone has ever succeeded in sneaking up on me."

Fitting her like a second skin, Kiri's magic armor made her stealth even better, even hid her scent from the temple guard dogs. It kept her cool in the stifling summer heat, as well. Despite her frustration at his hiding the truth of her birth, his kindly eyes melted her heart. Her angry tone slipped. "Where is my birthright?"

Master Yan sighed. "You met him, then. Your father."

She nodded.

He pointed to two new grave markers. "Here lie the Architect and the Surgeon, their bodies recently returned to us. Their lives were indelibly tied to yours. Your mother was the Beauty, my daughter. You are my granddaughter by blood, though I could never tell you. Come with me."

She followed him in silence back to his study, where he opened a secret compartment built into the wall and withdrew an object bound in black cloth. He unwound it, revealing an arrow. Silver impurities veined in regular patterns through its transparent crystal point.

"Here is your birthright."

She reached...with her bad arm...and took it.

***

Jie picked her way through the wild forests of Kanin, again in search of self. She'd always taken pride in not letting destiny dictate her life, that she molded her own future; the magic arrow wrapped and hidden in her magic pouch proved otherwise. Never good at archery, she knew where to seek out a good teacher... as well as more answers.

She looked around. With her poor woodcraft skills, the forest looked more or less the same. However, the rock formation rising before her in this clearing could only be the magical pool in wild elf lands. She lowered the hood to Kiri's... no, her stealth armor.

"Kala!" she yelled, removing a sealed funerary urn from the pouch. "I have Kiri's ashes."

Birds chirped and cawed. Bowstrings pulled back from all around.

Jie sucked on her lower lip. She'd never fulfill her destiny to kill the Orc King if elf arrows killed her first.

Kala's voice, familiar only in that it was a younger version of Jie's own, called out. "On your knees. Show your neck."

Kneeling, Jie bent forward and pulled the hood down further, to expose her nape.

Elf voices tittered from all around.

"Hand's up," Kala said. "Why you wear *her* armor?"

Setting the urn down, Jie raised her hands. "My friends killed her and took it. I am sorry."

"Why sorry?"

Jie's brow furrowed. "Kiri was your friend, right?"

"Still is." Kala stepped out from between two trees.

Kiri emerged, the same haunted look in her eyes, rambling in the wild elf language.

With a gasp, Jie looked down at the urn, then at the sisters. If the ashes didn't belong to Kiri... "How many sisters do you have?"

"*Vrztchkrn*. When we escape, eight." Kala held up eight little fingers, then pointed at the urn. "*She* first. *His*... weapon. Hunt you."

Grabbing Kala's shoulder, Kiri broke out into a tirade.

Jie shuddered. The *him* must refer to the Orc King, and the idea that her identical septuplets were out to kill her wasn't reassuring. Still, something did make sense: people who'd claimed to have seen her all over the world, in before she'd even visited. "What about the rest?"

"Slaves. Like Kiri." Kala motioned to Kiri. "*He* do bad things. Hurt them. Make sick. *He* afraid you."

Jie gave a slow nod. The prophecy. No wonder Altivorcs always attacked her on sight. Still, something didn't add up. Thielas had said she was the only baby, that he'd held her in his arms. And, Kiri was clearly much younger. "*Vrztchkrn.* What are we?"

"You not *Vrztchkrn*. We *Vrztchkrn*" Kiri pointed at herself and Kiri, then stared straight at Jie. "You... you... I don't know word..."

Jie's soul might be squirming, given the weight of Kiri's stare.

"You..." Kiri cocked her head like one of the Temple dogs when they tried to understand human language. "You... mother."

THE END

Please turn the page for a short story about what happened thirty years before Songs of Insurrection.

BIRTHRIGHT:

An Origins Short Story

Thielas Starsong held the bowstring taut, the green fletching of the arrow prickling his pointed ear. One well-placed shot would be the latest momentum change in the six-thousand-year war between elves and orcs.

Concealed behind a tree at the top of a wooded ridge, he watched as the column of two dozen tivorcs shambled along the path below. They were infamous for a lack of discipline, and their unsynchronized steps could hardly be considered marching. Their plated shoulder and chest guards clanged in nerve-wracking cacophony, scaring wildlife deeper into the forest. Sweat on their turquoise skin glistened in blinking patches through the dappled noon sun.

A horse the size of a house, armored from head to tail-less rump, walked at the rear of the formation. It moved quietly compared to the Tivorcs. Astride it rode an altivorc, a more intelligent cousin of the Tivorcs. A prince, no less—a begotten son of the Altivorc King himself.

Straight, meticulously groomed black locks cascaded out of his crowned helmet, contrasting with the tangled hair of his minions. While the T-slotted helm protected his head, he wore only a dark tunic—an inviting target for the misinformed.

However, Thielas was well-informed: neither his magic nor his razor-sharp steel arrowhead would penetrate the cloth. Even though the orcs had lost their ability to channel magic after losing the War of Ancient Gods a millennium before, the King and his princes hoarded a handful of artifacts from before that time. Like this tunic.

The prince snarled something which Thielas, despite his century of battling the brutes, barely understood: "By the Second Sun!"

Thielas stifled a laugh, imagining the obsessive and stodgy altivorc to be appalled by his underlings' poor excuse for marching.

Don't worry, he thought, *I will end your frustration just as soon as you present me a good target.*

As if obeying a subliminal suggestion, the altivorc turned his head, exposing an eye in the helm's slit. A near-impossible shot for a human, but routine for Thielas.

Just as he was about to loose his arrow, a frail voice whispered on the winds.

It's a girl...

The urgency in the voice threw off his concentration. The arrow flew errant, jolting the Prince's head back as it plinked off the side of his helmet.

The tivorcs sank into defensive stances with growls, heads jerking this way and that to find the source of the attack. The prince himself looked straight in Thielas' direction.

He would not see Thielas.

Thielas had uttered one guttural syllable worthy of a tivorc profanity and disappeared into the ethers.

He rematerialized at the mouth of a cave, his limbs heavy and languid from the draining effect of his invocation of Shallow Magic.

Disoriented, he looked around to find the area surrounded by the straight trunks of vaulting eldarwood trees. The low-lying sun cast the wispy clouds above in a swath of red hues. He scanned the sky for the iridescent moon, Riyalas, which never moved from its spot in the heavens. It was high and to the south-southwest, waning to half.

Dawn.   Somewhere in the mountains between Cathay and the Elven Kingdom of Aramysta.

Thielas felt his energy increase by the second, and he patted the pouch that hung over his chest. It held a rare Starburst jewel, a relic from the First Orc-Elf Wars that helped offset the fatigue of Shallow Magic.

His keen eyes were drawn to the fresh black and red blood smeared across the ground.

His heart lurched into his throat. Just a step into the cave laid a dead altivorc, a flat metal pin lodged in his eye.   A young elf woman lay sprawling beside him, gutted by a horrendous slash across her abdomen.   A clear orange jewel—his own beacon—sparkled just out of the reach of her lifeless fingers. Sadness yanked his racing heart back into his constricted chest, even as he buried his emotions to stay focused.

He slung his bow and drew his longsword, knowing that it would be difficult to shoot through the dense forest.   Then he froze in place and listened.

Not far down a rocky path, Thielas heard the distinct cries of a newborn, high-pitched and full of vitality, almost drowning out the rhythmic jingling of metal. Looking down, he saw a trail of fresh blood heading in that direction.

As he raced through the trees, the sounds got louder. He jumped over the hacked-up body of an elf lady, lamenting that he could do nothing for her.   He swerved around a pair of altivorcs, crumpled dead over a fallen tree trunk.

And then he saw them, blurs of color dancing through the trees: four altivorcs in chainmail, wielding bloodied broadswords, and a silver-haired elf maiden in a gown of starlight. Despite being a head shorter than her attackers, she held them at bay with elegant thrusts of a thin longsword.   Behind her, a human woman staggered, clutching a screaming bundle close to her chest. In the other hand, she gripped a curved, black-lacquered sword, which now served more as a crutch than a weapon.

He needed to reach her side, to save her and the elf woman.

The elf maid twisted out of the slash of one of her assailants, while simultaneously stabbing another in the neck through the narrow gap between his helmet and armor. A third altivorc met her as she finished her spin, plunging his sword into her belly.

Enraged, Thielas grunted a throaty word and the altivorc exploded in a fiery blast. Ignoring the instant fatigue creeping into his limbs, he charged into the fray as one of the attackers turned to face him.   Time automatically slowed in his perception as he engaged, his enemy seemingly moving through molasses. With this advantage, he sidestepped to his opponent's blind side, just out of the sluggish downward arc of the broadsword, and slashed across his midsection. The altivorc's armor held, and the elf had to raise his own weapon to block a slow horizontal hack. As his enemy cocked back to swing again, Thielas flipped his sword and cut through the eye slot of his helm.   A black shower sprayed from the wound as time resumed its normal pace.

Not waiting to see if the altivorc was dead, Thielas turned toward the human. She was on her knees, bent over. Beside her, her own foe lay motionless in a puddle of black, her sword lodged in its chest. The baby's cries echoed through the valley.

He looked back at the elf woman, torn between who to help first, then bounded over to the human and eased her into a sitting position. Black hair was matted against her pale, sweat-streaked face, and she afforded him a smile through wan lips. Fresh blood began to soak into the ground under her. Cooing through shallow breaths, she opened her dirty robe and brought the child to her breast.

It was then that Thielas saw the baby for the first time, her face wrinkled and flushed red. A thick shock of black hair crowned her head. Her cries stopped as soon as she latched on to the breast and suckled. *A girl...*

Behind them, the elf maid crawled forward, and Thielas tore himself away from mother and child to attend to her.

"My Lord," she whispered. "They fell upon us so fast—they came out of nowhere. We did our best to defend Meiyun. Her own male companion disappeared, probably killed first. There are still more out there."

Thielas brushed the hair out of her face and smiled kindly. He knew she would not last long, for he was far too depleted to use divine magic to heal such a horrendous wound. "Meiyun lives. You did well. I am sorry I did not get here earlier."

"It is my honor. I believe the prophecy." The woman's voice trailed off, and her eyes closed for the last time.

Thielas fought back tears as he gently laid her head down. "May Ayara take you to her bosom."

Not far in the distance, armor jangled and heavy boots crunched through the fallen eldarwood needles. He turned back to Meiyun, gauging his own strength and weighing his options. Grief overwhelmed him when he realized a cruel fact: he lacked the energy reserves to heal her, and he did not have the dozen minutes needed to draw on the less-depleting, ritualistic Deep Magic to teleport mother and babe to safety.

Meiyun looked into his eyes. Her voice was weak, no louder than a whisper. "I am dying, Thielas. Take her. Take her to safety. My sword remembers its home. Use it. My father will ensure that she stays safe."

"I will take her to my home in Aerilysta. My sister, the queen, will watch over her."

Meiyun scowled. "Now that the handmaidens are dead, the only ones who believe the prophecy are you and the altivorcs. The elves won't protect her. My father will."

Before Thielas could rebut her, several altivorcs stormed toward them, broadswords drawn. Behind them, an altivorc who stood a head above the rest stepped forward. He was handsome, as beautiful as an elf. In his hand he held not a sword, but a wand. It was the Altivorc King himself, clothed in the dapper uniform of a military officer going to a banquet, his head covered only by a crown. None of it would protect him from Thielas' deadly archery.

Thielas unslung his bow, and in a blink of an eye nocked an arrow. The Arrow. Silvery impurities veined in regular patterns through its transparent crystal point. There were only a dozen such arrowheads, passed down through generations of royal elves from the Elf Angel Aralas—The Hero of the War of Ancient Gods. He had said that this arrowhead could kill the Altivorc King with a single shot.

"Thielas, Thielas." The King was almost laughing. He stretched out his arms, inviting the elf to shoot. "You may have killed many of my sons, but it is not you who will slay me. Not even your esteemed grandfather could do that. You know the prophecy."

The prophecy. It wasn't worth risking such a rare relic. Thielas lowered the bow, and his eyes darted to the babe, wrapped in her mother's arms.

The Altivorc King followed his glance. A cruel smirk formed on his lips. He made a sharp motion with one hand and pointed the wand at Thielas with his other. "Kill the woman and bring the whelp to me. The elf is mine."

The King's cohorts surged forward, broadswords raised. The Great Orc uttered a harsh snarl, and a bolt of red energy exploded from the wand.

Time seemed to slow again, unbidden.

Thielas spun back, out of the line of fire, dropping his bow and taking up Meiyun's blade as he finished his turn. Another blast just barely missed him, as the horde of altivorcs closed in on the new mother and her child.

He had to get there first.

In three bounding steps, he reached Meiyun's side. He held her desperate gaze as she thrust forth the bawling babe in outstretched hands. In a decision that would haunt him forever, Thielas took the child into his free arm and uttered the single syllable that spirited them away through the corridors of magic, leaving Meiyun to face her fate alone. The vision of her last wistful smile burned in his mind's eye.

He popped back into existence in utter darkness that not even his night vision could penetrate. The cloying scent of incense assaulted him. Exhausted to the core by his repeated use of Shallow Magic, he did not have the power for the simplest of spells, a magical light. He collapsed to the ground, taking care not to harm the whimpering child in his arms.

Tears burned his eyes as reality set in. Meiyun. Dead.

As he tried to draw breath into his grief-tightened chest, his sensitive hearing picked up the almost inaudible shuffling of a dozen footsteps. He wobbled to his feet, rocking the child in one arm while drawing his sword in another.

His blade had barely slid free of its sheath when someone twisted his wrist and knocked the weapon away. He found himself sprawled on the ground, cradling the now crying babe. Cold steel crossed his neck in two directions, while his leg was pinned, knee twisted at a painful angle. Completely helpless, he relaxed, using what little energy he had for patting the baby.

Blinding light flooded the room, and he squinted as his eyes adjusted. Blurry, dark shapes coalesced into a dozen human male and female forms, all with black hair and honey-toned skin. They wore tight black clothes, and held weapons.

A few cleared a path to allow a man of middling years to step forward. "Starsong." He almost spat his name. "How did you find us?"

Thielas made a slow, unthreatening gesture toward Meiyun's sword.

The man made a horizontal gesture, and all of the warriors backed away. "The Black Lotus Sword. Where is Meiyun? And Feiying?"

"Young Master Yan," Thielas addressed the man, tentatively climbing to his feet. "Feiying was nowhere to be found. I assume he was killed by the altivorcs, who fell upon them unawares. Meiyun... she bid me to save her baby, to bring the girl here to be put under your protection..."

The man's face contorted, eyes narrow and jaw tight. "Her blood is on your hands. My daughter was born to rule our sect. Feiying was to be her husband. They cared for one another until you came along. I rue the day she met you. You never loved her; you just wanted to fulfill your outrageous prophecy. How did it go? A half-

human girl of Aralas' Blood? Who believes such fairy tales? And now..."

The elf flinched, the ranting accusations hitting him like physical blows. Still, his heart hurt even more. "I *did* love her. It was never about the prophecy. I am sorry."

"You are sorry? Get out of my sight."

"Just give me a few moments to regain my energy and I will leave you forever."

"You will leave *her* forever, too." Young Master Yan motioned toward the babe in Thielas' arms. "She is my granddaughter, and the heir to the Black-Fist Sect now that Meiyun is dead. I will raise her as my own, and she will be protected here, for nobody—not even the King of the Altivorcs himself—will find our Temple unless we allow it."

Thielas bowed his head, contrite. In that moment, he met the girl's curious gaze. She had brown eyes, large as an elf's, and even more almond-shaped from her Cathayi heritage.

His daughter.

For a few seconds, he considered keeping her, escaping through the ethers back to his homeland. Would he even survive a third Shallow Magic teleportation in such a short time? Maybe. However, the Young Master Yan was right. She would be better cared for here. The elves back home would always look down on the half-human, even if she were of his royal blood. And certainly, the altivorcs would look for her there. He extended his arms, his daughter in his hands. She was screaming again, even as a young woman stepped forward to receive her.

His daughter. A half-human girl of Aralas' Blood. Destined to slay the Altivorc King.

Thielas withdrew the Arrow. "Whether or not you recognize me as her father, whether or not you believe in the prophecy, this is her birthright. I beg you to give it to her one day, when she is ready to receive it."

With one last longing look at his daughter, he sang a half-minute lullaby in the musical language of Deep Magic. Her crying ceased, and her gently pointed ears perked up at the sound of his glorious voice.   With the last syllable, he disappeared.

The End

*Jie's adventures, past and present,
continue with more stories in 2018*

Thank you for reading the **Dragon Songs Saga**. I am humbled and honored that you have spent time in Kaiya's world. More stories in Tivara are planned for 2018 and beyond.

I would love to hear from you. You can email me at jc.kang.author@gmail.com.

Sign-up for a free copy of A Dragon's Guide to Hatching a Rebellion, a story about Avarax from before The War of Ancient Gods.

A SNEAK PEAK AT MASTERS OF DECEPTION

Standing by the aft bulwark on the *Indomitable*, Yan Jie was about to let personal affection get in the way of a mission for the first time in her life. With effort, she tore her gaze away from the handsome foreign prince giving orders from the quarterdeck, and looked across the stone quay to the black-hulled, five-masted behemoth she was supposed to infiltrate.

The *Intimidator* might've been the *Indomitable's* twin. Its crew had already withdrawn the gangplank, and were busy casting off the moorings. Meanwhile, she fidgeted on the *Indomitable* as it finished docking procedures. There was no time to cross the wharf, and board the other ship, which she suspected harbored the assassin who'd murdered two lords back home.

But if anyone could do it, it would be her, an orphan half-elf raised in the Black Lotus Clan.

She looked at Aryn one last time, his refined features a vestige of his people's traces of elf blood. He was so handsome, and charming, and amazing between the sheets. And above the sheets, or with the sheets twisted into bindings. He'd been a fun diversion, to keep her mind off a certain clan brother back home, who never saw her as anything more than a little sister.

He turned, a smile blooming on his face. Oh, that handsome face! There was no time for a long, passionate farewell kiss— their relationship had been a secret to his crew, anyway.

Fixing her expression to vapid girl in love with a prince, she waved back, all the while gauging the distance from deck to dock. At about forty feet, it was much too far to jump without leaving a bloody splatter of half-elf on the grey stone. However, the dockworkers had already moored the ship, and the calm harbor kept the lines taut. Even in the cute pink dress, she'd be able to tightrope-walk down one of them, while giving the sailors and dockworker's a view of the lacey undergarments Aryn had given her. Then again, a display of acrobatics would compromise her identity as a simple translator sent from Cathay.

She sighed. Her time with the Tarkothi prince was over, so there was no need to continue hiding her skills.

Or maybe she could hedge her bets. Just in case there really wasn't enough time to get down, grab a pole, dash up the dock, and pole vault to the Serikothi ship's stern gallery.

Aryn turned his head to one of the deck officers. No one was looking.

Gathering her skirts in the crook of her elbow, she turned and dove over the gunwhale. She hooked her elbow over the line. The dress' smooth satin slipped down the rope.

A little too easily.

The dock rushed up to meet her. Her billowing skirts must've put her flat body on display for the likely undiscriminating sailors and dockworkers who might happen to look up. In seconds, she'd become the aforementioned bloody splatter of half-elf.

She pulled herself up and wrapped her legs around the line. The fibers, while fine, first warmed, then seared into her thighs and calves. Nevertheless, rope burn was far preferable to death, and her descent slowed to a manageable speed. At the last second, she tucked and rolled several times over the dock's seamless stone, bowling over a couple of laborers along the way.

Despite preventing a concussion, her head swam from the spins. The dock was cold beneath her back... and smooth. Dwarf-carved, perhaps? Seagulls cawed above, either mocking her, or in disappointment of being denied half-elf splatter for dinner.

Shouts erupted. Burly dockworkers in baggy pantaloons and white shirts joined other men with black armbands in rushing over and crowding around her. The stench of man sweat and stagnant salt air did little to clear her head.

"Are you all right?"

"Anything broken?"

"Stay still."

She'd saved time by sliding instead of tightrope walking down, but no, hands held her down. Feigning disorientation—or perhaps not feigning it—she peeked out from the throng at the Serikothi ship. It was free of its moorings, and a tug was pulling it clear of the dock. There was still a chance, when the *Intimidator* set oars to guide it out of the harbor and into open seas. Maybe she could swim out, climb up an oar, and squeeze through the oarlock before the sails took over.

Right. Getting off one ship had required the skills of an actor and an acrobat—maybe a career change to opera singer would be safer—but getting onto the other ship with that harebrained scheme would need talents beyond even her wide-reaching abilities. In retrospect, not even the clan's three legendary-but-long-dead young masters could've accomplished the feat, given the exceedingly slim window of opportunity.

With a sigh, she brought her focus back to the center of the commotion and splayed out on the dock. Another opportunity to get aboard the Serikothi ship would present itself at the next port. Perhaps that would be her last chance to root out the conspirators. In the meantime, she could spend a little more time with—

Prince Aryn and his marines pushed the gawking bystanders aside. He waved his hands back, then knelt beside her. "Stand back. Give her space."

Men grumbled, but otherwise complied.

His eyes roved over her in a more professional way than she was accustomed. When he spoke, his Arkothi accent mangled her name in the most sensual way. "Jyeh, are you all right?"

Her insides twisted in delightful ways. She propped herself up on one elbow while covering her forehead with the back of the other wrist. "I...I think I'm okay. I tripped over the gunwale. Only my butt hurts. And I seem to have some rope burns."

Aryn blew out a breath. "You are so clumsy. That could've been a nasty fall onto concrete. You're lucky you managed to catch the dock line."

If only he knew. At least for now, she hadn't betrayed her cover. "Concrete?"

"Yes. Quite ingenious." He stamped on the ground. "It's used throughout the North."

She gingerly staggered to her feet. Aryn shot out an arm to support her.

Lightning jolted up and down her spine, perhaps from an unseen injury, but more likely from his touch. "Thank you, Your Highness."

"Are you sure you're all right? Come along now, let us see if we can find you a doctor." He gestured toward his marines. "Men, go find a healer."

Behind him, his aide-de-camp, the enormous Peris, snorted. "She looks fine to me."

"She fell over twelve meters!" With a growl, Aryn pointed back to the *Indomitable*.

She looked from one to the other. Driving a wedge between the lifelong friends had been as inadvertent as ending up in Aryn's bed, but only the pesky emotions attached to the latter had sparked a modicum of guilt.

"I'm all right. Nothing seems broken. Let's just walk." She waved toward the storefronts, but she stopped as the pyramid of Tokahia came into view. When they'd been well out to sea, six kilometers according to the Tarkothi standard of distance, the crystal at the pyramid's pinnacle twinkled like a night star.

Up close, with the sun behind it, the massive structure cast a shadow over the one and two-story daub and wattle buildings along the waterfront. The shade didn't dim the garish storefronts, nor the equally flamboyant clothes of people gesticulating in large enough motions to kick up the wind. Hawkers pawned all kinds of colorful wares of varying practical use. So far, the Estomari were living up to their reputation as artists and merchants.

"I'm fine," she repeated. "Let's just go for a stroll." Why not, when they had one, maybe two days while the *Indomitable* re-provisioned? She pointed to where the stone-paved street curved along the harbor. Elegant white plaster buildings with actual glass windows and brown and red tile rooves lined the streets. They stood in stark contrast to the gaudy stores at the other end. Neither architectural styles resembled the wooden structures back home.

Aryn shook his head. "Not that way, Miss Jyeh. That's mafia territory." He pointed in the opposite direction. "It's safer this way."

Following his finger, Jie took in the cityscape. It looked no different from the supposed *mafia territory*—in itself, a novel idea, since in her homeland, the emperor held absolute power. "How do the Signores tolerate a challenge to their authority?"

Peris scoffed, looking at her as if she were an imbecile. "In the Estomar, authority only reaches as far as the tips of the Signores' swords."

Aryn chuckled. "There's an unspoken understanding: as long as the crime families don't meddle with the Signores' affairs, the Signores won't move against them."

Jie nodded. It wasn't that much different from the entertainment district in her homeland's capital. As long as they paid taxes, they were free to govern their territory with their own conventions, and the emperor left well enough alone.

"The status quo might be changing," Peris said in a low voice. "Our informants say the crime families are organizing and plan on making a move to seize the city."

"In any case, everything we could possibly need is this way." Without any sign of concern about political upheaval, Aryn gestured in the opposite direction and gave her a tug.

Jie followed along, but wondered. If she were in Aryn's boots, instead of his pants, she'd be more concerned about the implications. Still, control of a faraway city had little to do with her own mission. She looked back to Peris.

Instead of chastising Aryn for his lack of interest, Peris kept flicking his eyes to a large man, with a jagged scar on his forehead, who stood in the doorway of an antique shop at the far end of the docks. A man who seemed to be looking at them.

"Oh, look!" Aryn pointed, jerking Jie's attention away. In the direction he indicated, a crowd gathered around a street vendor of some sorts. "A fortune teller."

Seriously? Jie looked back to the large man, only to find him gone. She met Aryn's gaze and raised an eyebrow. "Do you really believe this?" After all, fortune tellers back home tended to find fortunes in the pockets of the gullible.

"Don't you know? Estomari can predict the future, with magic. Come on!" Aryn's face lit up like Black Lotus clan children when they received their first throwing star. With the marines clearing the way, he tugged her along through the masses of bodies to the vendor.

While everyone on Tivaralan knew the tales of Tatiana, the first Diviner, it took a special kind of naiveté to believe her predictions helped humans overthrow their orc masters a millennium ago. Rolling her eyes, Jie followed. No prophecies hung over her; she made her own destiny.

Still, with the mission on hold until they could catch up with the Serikothi ship, she might as well humor the prince.

At the front of the crowds, a brown-haired young man shuffled cards in his hands, flipping them in and out of his fingers with mesmerizing dexterity. The brilliantly painted cards matched his flashy orange long coat, puffy red shirt, and purple hosiery. "Come, learn your future from me, Roberto Romero, the best diviner in Tokahia! No, the best in all the Estomar! I predicted the rise of the Pirate Queen and the election of Haros Bovyanthas to First Consul of the Teleri Empire. My results are guaranteed!"

Aryn flicked a gold draka into the air. "A reading for this pretty young woman."

Roberto swiped the coin out of the air. The smile which started to materialize on his face slipped as his eyes met Jie's and widened. Blanching, he shook his head. "I'm sure your future hasn't changed since the last time you came. No refunds."

Jie cocked her head. "What?"

The fortune teller tucked away his cards and started folding up his table. He scowled at her. "If you haven't succeeded in killing your father, that's not my fault."

Aryn gawked at her, while somewhere behind them, Peris chuckled.

Heat flared to the tips of her ears. The crowd gasped and stared as she shook her head incredulously. As satisfying as it would be to find the dastard who abandoned her as a baby, and stick a knife between his ribs, no one had ever told her her future. At least, not beyond the occasional, no alarmingly frequent, *Prepare to die.* Those fortunes had yet to come true.

"Come on, let's forget about this." Jie turned to Aryn, when a ghost from her past strode by.

Her jaw dropped. Princess Kaiya, the daughter of Cathay's emperor, took uncharacteristically long steps and swung her arms in the most unladylike fashion. White silken robes with bright embroidery on the hems fluttered behind her. It looked nothing like a court gown; and instead of imperial guards, she was accompanied by a tall, middle-aged man and an attractive young woman, both with dark skin, coarse black hair, and similar but cheaper robes that marked them as Aksumi Mystics. Both the princess and the woman gesticulated with broad motions, while dismissing the man whenever he tried to speak.

No, it was impossible. Even though the Emperor gave the princess more leeway after she put down a rebellion with the budding magic of her music, he'd never let her come this far away from home. Certainly not without an army of Imperial Guards. Not to mention, she'd been in Cathay's capital when Jie had departed. There was no way she could reach Tokahia first. Jie took a longer, more careful look.

While the young woman resembled Princess Kaiya, she was too pretty, too filled out, too— Jie sucked on her lower lip. The face and curvy figure was less like the actual princess, and more similar to the illusion from the magic bauble which the aforementioned rebel leader had used in plotting an assassination of the imperial family. Which meant, these mystics might be tied to the conspirator aboard the Serikothi ship, and the clan traitor she was tracking. In town, just as mafia might try to take over the city.

Heedless of Aryn's protests, Jie slipped between the dispersing crowds and trailed the trio. How ironic it was, that the pretty pink dress that would make her stand out back home was actually quite muted compared to the flashy clothes the locals wore.

The fake princess tossed a glass bead over to the man, her image instantaneously shifting to a young, dark-skinned woman who looked so similar to the other, they had to be related. The second the man caught the bauble, he shrunk and transformed into the likeness of Princess Kaiya, only in the clothes he was already wearing. His form returned to normal when he slipped the bead into his pocket. Passersby gawked and pointed.

The magic couldn't be a coincidence. This was a clue tied to her mission. It would be child's play to pick his pockets once they got back into a crowd. After winding through the wide, stone-cobbled streets, the group came to what looked like a market square, with dozens of fortunetellers set up around the edges.

None of the dozens of people paid these charlatans any heed. Instead, they gathered around several huge, rectangular stones jutting out from the ground, forming what looked to be a circle. The three Aksumi jostled their way through the crowd.

Jie edged up to the closest spectator. "Why are there so many people here?"

The man looked down through his nose at her, his expression one of disbelief. "This is the Cassius Larusso. He's a confirmed descendant of Tatiana, herself. The best Diviner in the Estomar. Protector of the pyramid."

If she had a draka for every claim she'd heard in the crowds today, she could buy a ship and hire the crew to serve her for a year. Still, these Aksumi Mystics—the most powerful sorcerers in the world—had come straight to this Cassius Larusso. Maybe there was something to him.

She looked back the way she'd come. Aryn and his crew were nowhere to be seen. No matter, he'd said something about staying at the posh *Regent*. Surely it would be easy to find. She slipped through the people toward the front, to the edge of the megalith circle, right beside the Aksumi Mystics. Some exotic flower scented the females' hair.

Inside the middle of the circle stood a short column that served as an altar. Beside it, a handsome Estomari man with dark curls twisted and turned the rings of a strange metal device. With a green embroidered long coat over a black shirt and brown pants, it was clear his taste in clothes was much more subdued than his compatriots. His eyes—one brown, one blue—roved over a chart of some sort.

He looked up and gestured to three dark-haired, bronze-skinned warriors who wore high-collared long shirts. The heavy, curved swords at their sides marked them as Ayuri Paladins, the defenders of the South. This was the first time she'd actually seen one, up close no less, and they certainly didn't look like the mythical warriors of legend.

They had ordinary builds, nothing remarkable. The eldest was a woman, whose wrinkled skin, grey hair, and thin arms brought into question if she could possibly lift that heavy, primitive-looking blade, let alone wield it. The other two were men, one middle-aged and the other young. How strange it was for both Aksumi Mystics and Ayuri Paladins—not to mention a Cathayi half-elf—to be in the same, otherwise ethnically homogenous city. This was either a strange coincidence, or the start of a bad joke with an equally awful punchline.

The magic bauble was in the male's left pocket. Simple enough to retrieve. Sidling up to him, she started to tug the lacey gloves off for better tactile sense, but then thought the better of it. If it changed her image on contact, like the one she'd used back home, it would draw undue attention. She reached—

The female mystic in the cotton robes clasped a jewel about her neck. Her head turned and her gaze locked on Jie. "Why have you been following us?"

APPENDIX

MAPS

Cathay (Hua)

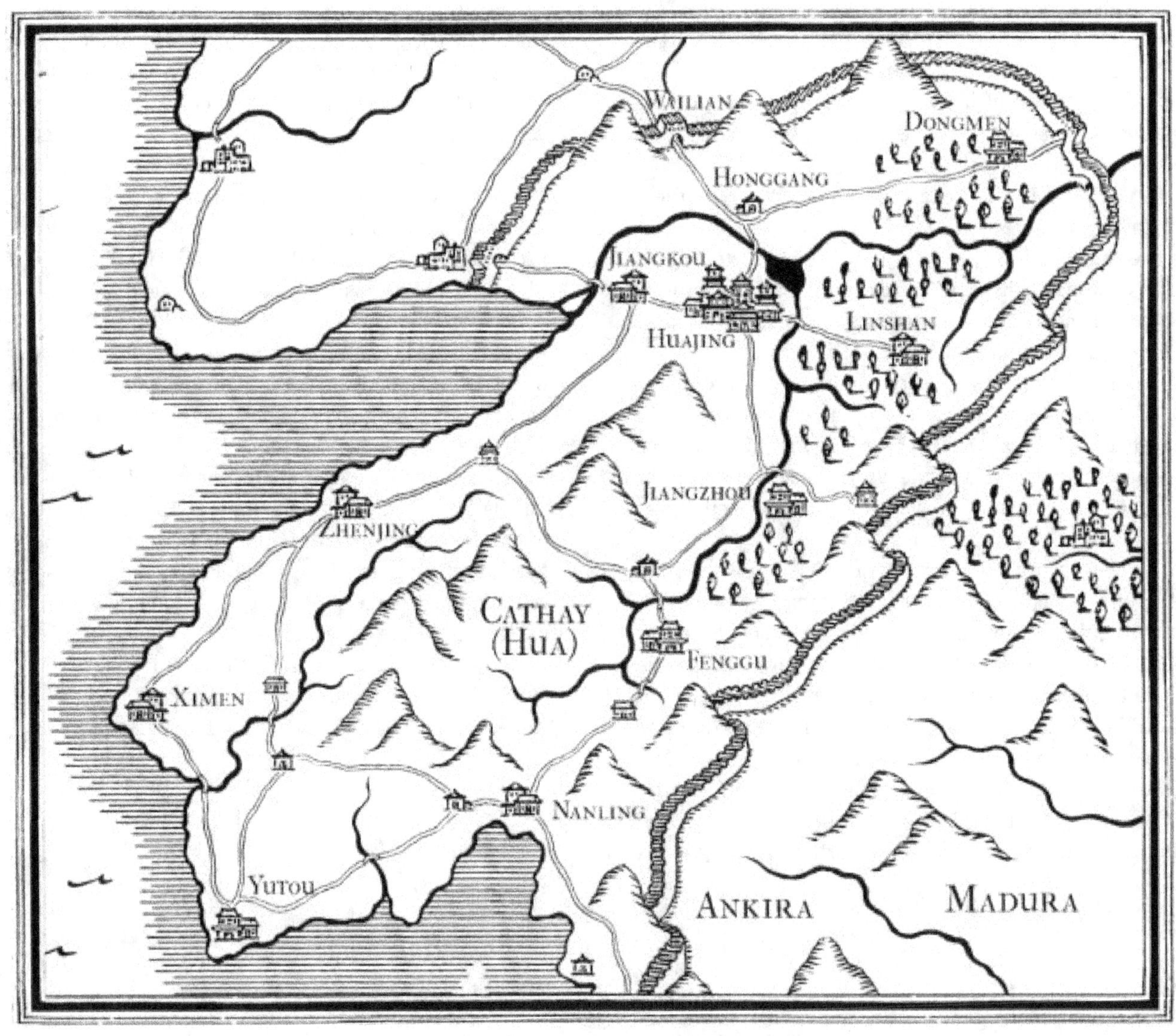

Ayuri Lands

Ankiras
ANKIRA
DRAGON
LANDS
KANIN
Birapur
Vadapur
Palimur
MADURA
BIJURA
Ushwar
Curinar
VADARA
SELASTYA
Maduras
Dohar
Vadaras
Bijuras
Vyara
Topur
Daburas
Pul
DABURA
AVASTYA
Lakhar
Sanuras
Peshwar
SANURA
Ayudra
Island
Eburas
Pelastyas
EBURA
MENDIL

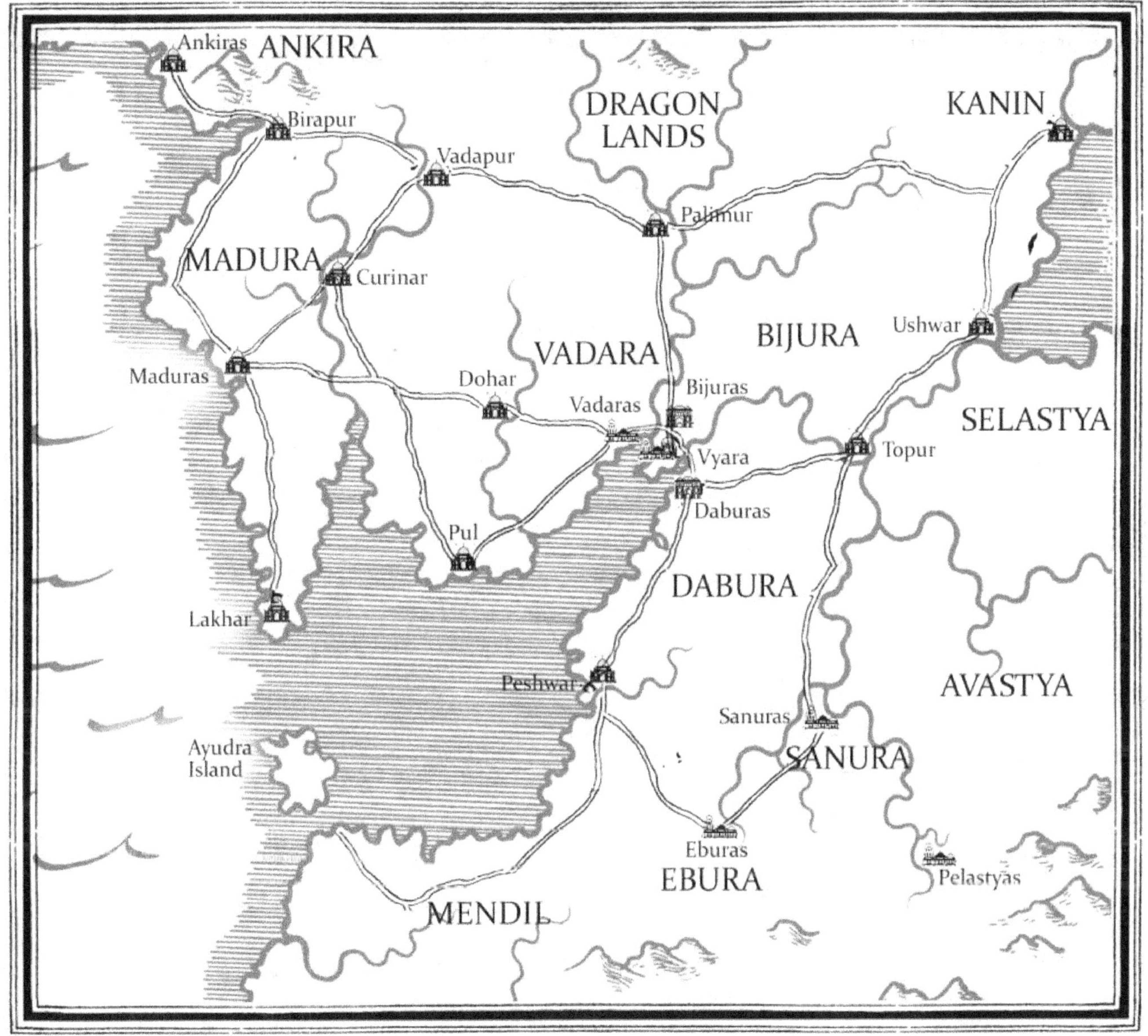

NOTHORI LANDS
ALTOGRINA
IKSUVIUS
IKSUVI
KALMIES
LARAMIES
KALENAI
LIETUVIUS
LIETUVI
THE WILDS
ROTUVIUS
ROTUVI

Who's Who in Songs of Insurrection

Imperial Family:

Wang, Zhishen:	*Tianzi* (Emperor)
Wang, Kai-Guo:	Crown Prince
Zhao, Xiulan:	Crown Princess, of Ximen Province
Wang, Kai-Wu:	Second Prince
Wu, Yanli:	Second Prince's fiancée, Zhenjing Province
Wang, Kaiya:	Princess

Hereditary Lords and Families

Chen, Qing:	*Yu-Ming* heir to a Jiangzhou county
Lord Liang:	*Tai-Ming* heir to Yutou Province
Lord Liu:	*Tai-Ming* heir to Jiangzhou Province
Lin, Ziqiu:	Kaiya's cousin, daughter of the Lord of Linshan
Peng, Kai-Long:	Second son of *Tai-Ming* Lord of Nanling Province
Peng, Kai-Zhi:	*Tai-Ming* heir to Nanling Province
Peng, Xian:	*Tai-Ming* Lord of Nanling Province
Tong, Baxian:	*Yu-Ming* Lord of Wailian County
Wang, Kai-Hua:	Kaiya's cousin, daughter of the Lord of Jiangzhou
Lord Wu:	*Tai-Ming* Lord of Zhenjing Province, father of Yanli
Lord Zhao:	*Tai-Ming* Lord of Ximen Province, father of Xiulan
Xu:	Elf counselor
Zheng, Han:	*Tai-Ming* Lord of Dongmen Province, father of Tian

Ministers, Secretaries and other Officials

Geng:	Minster of the Treasury
Hu:	Minister of Appointments
Hong, Jianbin:	Secretary of Appointments
General Shan:	Minister of War
Song:	Foreign Minister
Tan:	Chief Minister
Yan:	Deputy of Information, Black Lotus Clan Master
Chu:	Harbormaster official

Military:

General Lu:	Commander, Army of the North
General Shan:	Minister of War
General Tang:	Commander of the Huajing Division
General Zheng:	Commander of the Imperial Guard
Chen, Xin:	Imperial Guard Captain
Zhao, Yue:	Imperial guard
Xu, Zhan:	Imperial guard
Ma, Jun:	Imperial guard
Li, Wei:	Imperial guard

Spies

Yan, Jie:	Half-elf *Moquan* adept, adopted daughter of Master Yan
Zheng, Tian:	Planner, fourth son of the Lord of Dongmen Province
Master Yan:	Master of the Clan
Feng, Mi:	Moquan initiate
Huang, Zhen:	Moquan initiate
Chong, Xiang:	Moquan adept
Wen:	Female Moquan adept
Bu:	Moquan adept
Li:	Moquan adept
Qu:	Moquan adept

Others

Ding, Meihui:	Princess Kaiya's *pipa* teacher
Fang,	Imperial Physician

Weiyong:

Fu, Jinxian:	Owner of Golden Fu Trading
Gu:	Agent for unknown conspirator
Han, Mei-Ling:	Handmaiden to Princess Kaiya
Jiang:	Victorious Trading Company manager
Little Ju:	Tian's messenger
Song, Xingyuan:	Son of Minister Song
Doctor Wu:	Head Imperial Physician, master of the *Dao*
Yong, Shu:	Princess Kaiya's *erhu* teacher

Foreigners:

Aryn Corivar:	Second Prince of Tarkoth
Captain Damaryn:	Koryn's aide
Peris:	Aryn's aide
Koryn Vardamcar:	Crown Prince of Serikoth
Hardeep Vaswani:	Prince of Ankira

Legendary Figures:

Aralas:	The elf-angel
Avarax:	The Last Dragon
Yanyan:	Slave, founder of musical magic

Who's Who in Orchestra of Treacheries

Imperial Family
Wang Zhishen, the Tianzi (Emperor)
Wang Kai-Guo, the Crown Prince
Wang Kai-Wu, the Second Prince
Wang Kaiya, princess
Wu Yanli, wife of Kai-Wu, from Zhenjing Province
Zhao Xiulan, wife of Kai-Guo, from Ximen Province

Kaiya's Friends
Lin Ziqiu, Kaiya's cousin, from Dongshan Province
Wang Kai-Hua, Kaiya's cousin, married to the heir of Jiangzhou Province
Han Mei-Ling, Kaiya's Handmaiden

Kaiya's Mentors
Lord Xu, Elf Lord of Haikou Island
Doctor Wu, Taoist from Haikou Island

Expansionist Lords
Jiang, Lord of Nantou Province
Lin, Lord of Dongshan Province
Peng Kai-Long, nephew of the *Tianzi*, Lord of Nanling Province

Royalist Lords
Han, Lord of Fengu Province
Liu Yong, Lord of Jiangzhou Province
Wu, Lord of Zhenjing Province
Zhao, Lord of Ximen Province
Zheng Han, Lord of Dongmen Province
Zheng Ming, Kaiya's main suitor
Zheng Tian, Kaiya's childhood friend

Ministers
Fen, Council Minister
Geng, Treasury Minister

Hong Jianbin, Minister of Household Relations
Song Henglin, Minister of Foreign Affairs
Tan, Chief Minister

Conspirators
Leina, half-Ayuri from Ankira
Liang Yu, former Moquan
Song Xingyuan, Liang Yu's apprentice

Soldiers
Chen Xin, captain of Kaiya's imperial guard detail
Li Wei, Kaiya's imperial guard
Ma Jun, Kaiya's imperial guard
Xie Shimin, mounted archer from Huayuan Province
Xu Zhan, Kaiya's imperial guard
Yan Jie, Moquan spy, Kaiya's bodyguard
Zhao Yue, Kaiya's imperial guard
Zheng Jiawei, General of the Imperial Guard

Foreigners
Aelward Corivar, Prince of Tarkoth
Ayana Strongbow, Prince Aelward's bodyguard
Benham, Levastyan Empire ambassador
Devak, Paladin elder
Dhananad, Prince of Madura
Gayan, the Oracle's apprentice
Hardeep Vaswani, Prince of Ankira
Mehal, Paladin elder
Piros, Teleri ambassador to the Ayuri Confederation
Sameer Vikram, Paladin apprentice
Sabal, Paladin master
Thielas Starsong, elf prince

Legendary Figures
Aralas, elf angel
Avarax, Last Dragon
Celastya, Guardian Dragon of Hua

Yanyan, founder of musical magic

Who's Who in Dances of Deception

Kaiya's Retainers:

Chen Xin	Captain of Kaiya's imperial guard detail
Han Meiling	Kaiya's handmaiden and decoy
Li Wei	Imperial guard
Ma Jun	Imperial guard
Xu Zhan	Imperial guard
Zhao Yue	Imperial guard
Zheng Jiawei	General of the imperial guard

Black Lotus *Moquan*

Cheng	Newest member of the Iksuvius cell
Shun	Moquan
Old Tong	Eldest member of the Iksuvius cell
Yan Jie	Kaiya's half-elf bodyguard
Zheng Tian	Head of the Iksuvius cell
Zu	Moquan

Hua Embassy Staff in Iksuvius

Wu Liming	Ambassador
Zhu	Trade officer

Teleri

Geros Bovyan	First Consul
Marius di Bovyan	General
Thieros Bovyanthas	Ambassador
Feiying	Black Lotus defector, head of the Nightblades

Dignitaries in Iksuvius

Arvydas	King of Lietuvi
Ausra	Queen of Iksuvi
Evydas	King of Iksuvi
Gunvydas	King of Rotuvi
Manuwaya	Ambassador from Kanin

Pyramid Quest

Cyrus Estazadeh	Akolyte from Selastya
Brehane	Aksumi Mystic
Sameer Vikram	Paladin knight
Fleet	madaeri guide

Eldaeri Nations

Aelward Corivar	Prince of Tarkoth
Ciro	Marine
Thielas Starsong	Elf ranger
Alaena Vardamcar	Princess of Serikoth
Keril	Ranger
Markel	Ranger
Rami	Ranger

Maki Tribe

Hati	Chief's son
Kona	Young warrior
Kosa	Young warrior
Lahi	Village beauty, Yuha's sister
Lana	Yuha's sister, shaman
Nadi	Yuha's daughter
Noki	Refugee
Nuwa	Chief
Yuha	Shaman
Waka	Yuha's son

Who's Who in Symphony of Fates

Imperial Family

Wang Kai-Wu, the *Tianzi*
Wang Kaiya, princess
Wu Yanli, wife of Kai-Wu, from Zhenjing Province
Zhao Xiulan, wife of Kai-Guo, from Ximen Province

Kaiya's Friends

Ma Jun, Kaiya's imperial guard
Han Mei-Ling, Kaiya's handmaiden
Lin Ziqiu, Kaiya's cousin, from Dongshan Province

Wang Kai-Hua, Kaiya's cousin, married to the heir of Jiangzhou Province
Yan Jie, Moquan spy, Kaiya's bodyguard

Kaiya's Mentors
Lord Xu, Elf Lord of Haikou Island
Doctor Wu, Taoist from Haikou Island

Royalists Lords
Du, Yu-Ming lord
Chen Qing, Yu-Ming heir
Han, Lord of Fenggu Province
Liu Yong, Lord of Jiangzhou Province
Liu Deying, Heir of Jiangzhou Province
Wu, Lord of Zhenjing Province
Zhao, Lord of Ximen Province
Zheng Han, Lord of Dongmen Province
Zheng Ming, Kaiya's main suitor, Heir to Dongmen
Zheng Lun, Third son of Zheng Han
Zheng Shu, Second son of Zheng Han
Zheng Tian, Fourth son of Zheng Han

Rebel Lords
Jiang, Lord of Yutou Province
Lin, Lord of Dongshan Province
Peng Kai-Long, cousin of the *Tianzi*, Lord of Nanling Province

Ministers
Fen, Council Minister
Geng, Treasury Minister
Hong Jianbin, Minister of Household Relations
Song Henglin, Minister of Foreign Affairs
Tan, Chief Minister

Insurgents
Liang Yu, former *Moquan*
Song Xingyuan, Liang Yu's apprentice

Black Lotus Clan
Master Yan, Master of the clan
Huang Zhen, Clan initiate
Feng Mi, Clan initiate

Teleri Empire

Geros Bovyan, Emperor of the Teleri
Altos Di Bovyan, Teleri General
Leina, half-Ayuri from Ankira
Feiying, Master of the Nightblades

Wild Elves
Kiri, half-elf
Kala, half-elf
Nayori, Shaman
Dior, archer
Layani, warrior

Foreigners
Aelward Corivar, Prince of Tarkoth
Brehane, Mystic
Cyrus Estazadeh, Akolyte
Fleet, Madaeri Guide
Sameer Vikram, Paladin apprentice
Thielas Starsong, elf prince
Yuha, Maki Shaman

Legendary Figures
Aralas, elf angel
Avarax, Last Dragon
Celastya, Guardian Dragon of Hua
Yanyan, founder of musical magic

Celestial Bodies

White Moon: Known as Renyue in Cathay, and represents the God of the Seas. Its orbital period is thirty days

.

Iridescent Moon: Known in Cathay as Caiyue, it is the manifestation the God of Magic. It appeared at the end of the war between elves and orcs. It never moves from its spot in the sky. Its orbital period is one day, and can be used to keep time.

Blue Moon: Known in Cathay as Guanyin's Eye, it is the manifestation of the Goddess of Fertility. It sits low on the horizon. Its phases go from wide open to winking.

Tivar's Star: A red star, a manifestation of the God of Conquest. During the Year of the Second Sun, it approached the world, causing the Blue Moon to go dim.

Golden Flock: A constellation which appeared frequently when the Orcs controlled the world. It has only appeared once since the War of Ancient Gods.

Time

As measured by the phases of the iridescent moon:

Full = Midnight
1st Waning Gibbous = 1:00 AM
2nd Waning Gibbous =2:00 AM
Mid-Waning Gibbous = 3:00 AM
4th Waning Gibbous = 4:00 AM
5th Waning Gibbous = 5:00 AM
Waning Half = 6:00 AM
1st Waning Crescent = 7:00 AM
2nd Waning Crescent = 8:00 AM
Mid-Waning Crescent = 9:00 AM
4th Waning Crescent = 10:00 AM
5th Waning Crescent = 11: 00 AM
New = Noon
1st Waxing Crescent = 1:00 PM
2nd Waxing Crescent = 2:00 PM
Mid-Waxing Crescent = 3:00 PM
4th Waxing Crescent = 4:00 PM
5th Waxing Crescent = 5:00 PM
Waxing Half = 6:00 PM
1st Waxing Gibbous = 7:00 PM
2nd Waxing Gibbous =8:00 PM
Mid-Waxing Gibbous = 9:00 PM
4th Waxing Gibbous = 10:00 PM
5th Waxing Gibbous = 11:00 PM

Provinces of Cathay

Province	Ruling Family	Resources
Dongmen	Zheng	Grain, stone, guns
Fenggu	Han	Timber, rice, grain
Huayuan	Wang	Livestock, rice, wheat, lumber, firepowder, guns
Jiangzhou	Liu	Timber, wheat, silk
Linshan	Lin	Wheat, millet, timber, porcelain
Nanling	Peng	Livestock, steel, stone, gems, crossbows
Ximen	Zhao	Fishing, rice
Yutou	Liang	Fishing, rice, iron, copper, fish paste
Zhenjing	Wu	Ships, rice, fish

Human Ethnicities

Aksumi: Dark-skinned with dark eyes and coarse hair. On Earth, they would be considered North Africans. They can use Sorcery.

Ayuri: Bronze-toned skin with dark hair and eyes. On Earth, they would be considered South Asians. They can use Martial Magic.

Arkothi: Olive-skinned with blond to dark hair and light-colored eyes. On Earth, they would be considered Eastern Mediterraneans. They can use weak Mental Magic.

Bovyan: The descendants of the Sun God's begotten son, they are cursed to be all male and live only to thirty-three years of age. They are much taller and larger than the average human. Their other physical characteristics are determined by their mother's race. They have no magical ability.

Cathayi (Hua): Honey-toned skin with dark hair and eyes. High-set cheekbones and almond-shaped eyes. On Earth, they would be considered East Asians. They can use Artistic Magic.

Eldaeri: Olive-skinned with brown hair. Fine features and small frames, they are shorter in stature than the average human. In a previous age, they fled the orc domination of the continent and mingled with elves. They have no magical ability.

Estomari: Olive-skinned with varying eye and hair color. They are famous for their fine arts. On Earth, they would be considered Western Mediterraneans. They can use Divining Magic.

Kanin: Ruddy-skinned with dark hair. On Earth, they would be considered Native Americans. They can use Shamanic Magic.

Levanthi: Dark-bronze skin and dark hair. On Earth, they would be considered Persians. They can use Divine Magic.

Nothori: Fair-skinned and fair-haired. On Earth, they would be considered Northern Europeans. They can use Empathic Magic.

Acknowledgements

First, I would like to thank my wife and family for the patience they have afforded me as I pursued my childhood dream of fiction writing.

A shout-out goes to my old Dungeons and Dragons crew: Jon, Chris, Chris, Paul, Conrad, and Julian, for helping to shape the first iteration of Tivara twenty-five years ago. Huge thanks to Brent, who contributed so much backstory to the new literary version.

A huge thanks to my sister Laura for her spectacular job with the maps and cover treatments

Thanks to the readers and writers on Wattpad for their encouragement and feedback.

Thanks to Anne Loshuk, Hannah West, Jen Strand, Jay Philippi, Tabitha Ormiston-Smith, Krystal Xu, and all the other super fans.

And finally, to writers over at critiquecircle.com who motivated and helped me along the way. Jason, for patiently providing countless ideas. Victoria, for showing me how to layer scenes. Leanne for story development and amazing suggestions. Ernie, for teaching me the fundamentals of fiction writing. Lindy and Kathryn for your sharp eyes. Rick and Traci for the numerous suggestions, and all the others who critiqued.